World Music

Volume 1: Africa, Europe and the Middle East

THE ROUGH GUIDE

Edited by

Simon Broughton, Mark Ellingham
and Richard Trillo

with
Orla Duane and Vanessa Dowell

THE ROUGH GUIDES

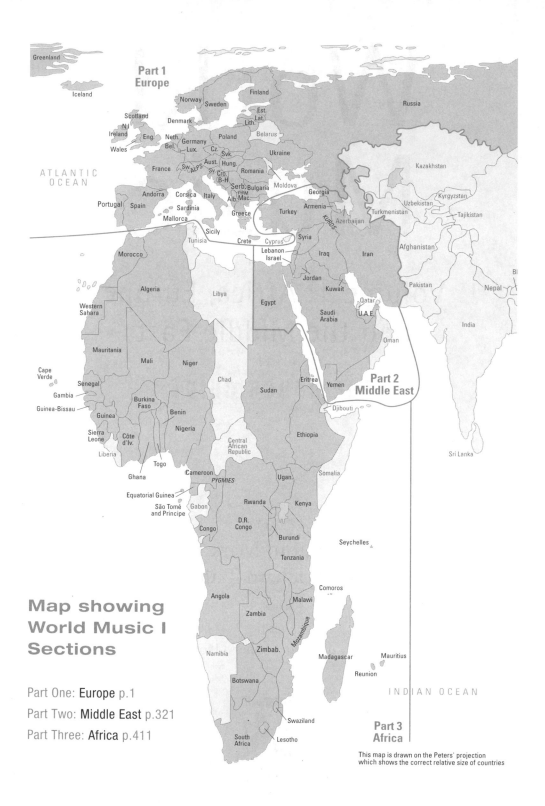

Greenland

Iceland

**Part 1
Europe**

ATLANTIC
OCEAN

Norway
Sweden
Finland
Scotland
N.I.
Denmark
Eng.
Wales
Neth.
Bel.
Germany
Lux.
Poland
Cz.
Svk.
Aust.
Hung.
Sw.
ALPS
Sv.
Cro.
B-H
Romania
France
Serb.
Alb.
FYRM
Mac.
Bulgaria
Andorra
Corsica
Italy
Portugal
Spain
Sardinia
Mallorca
Greece
Sicily
Tunisia
Crete
Cyprus
Morocco

Est.
Lat.
Lith.
Belarus
Ukraine
Moldova
Georgia
Turkey
Armenia
Azerbaijan
Syria
Lebanon
Israel
Jordan
Iraq
Iran
Kuwait

Russia

Kazakhstan

Kyrgyzstan
Uzbekistan
Turkmenistan
Tajikistan
Afghanistan
Pakistan
Nepal
Bl

Algeria
Libya
Egypt
Saudi
Arabia
Qatar
U.A.E.
Oman

Western
Sahara

Mauritania
Mali
Niger
Chad
Sudan
Eritrea
Yemen

Cape
Verde
Senegal
Gambia
Guinea-Bissau
Guinea
Sierra
Leone
Liberia
Côte
d'Iv.
Burkina
Faso
Benin
Nigeria
Togo
Ghana
Central
African
Republic
Ethiopia

**Part 2
Middle East**

Djibouti

India

Sri Lanka

Cameroon
PYGMIES
Equatorial Guinea
São Tomé
and Principe
Gabon
Congo
D.R.
Congo
Rwanda
Burundi
Ugan.
Kenya
Somalia

Tanzania

Seychelles

**Map showing
World Music I
Sections**

Angola
Zambia
Malawi
Comoros
Mozambique
Madagascar
Mauritius
Reunion

Namibia
Zimbab.
Botswana
Swaziland
South
Africa
Lesotho

INDIAN OCEAN

**Part 3
Africa**

This map is drawn on the Peters' projection
which shows the correct relative size of countries

World Music

Volume 1: Africa, Europe and the Middle East

THE ROUGH GUIDE

Other Rough Guides music reference titles:

Music Reference Series

Classical Music • Country
Jazz • Music USA • Opera • Reggae • Rock
World Music 2 (Americas, Asia, Pacific)

Mini Guides

Drum'n'bass • House • Techno

100 Essential CDs

Classical Music • Opera • Reggae • Rock

www.roughguides.com

Cover photos

Front cover: Main image: Ismael Lô (Senegal). Tinted images (from left): Oumou Sangaré (Mali), De Danaan (Ireland), Carmen Linares (Spain), Khaled (Algeria).
Back cover (from top): Les Amazones de Guinée (Guinea), Bisserov Sisters (Bulgaria), Les Musiciens du Nil (Egypt), Shooglenifty (Scotland).

Rough Guide Credits

Editors: Mark Ellingham, Orla Duane, Vanessa Dowell
Proofreading: Elaine Pollard
Photo research: Vanessa Kelly
Design and image scanning: Henry Iles and Justin Bailey
Typesetting: Justin Bailey, Helen Ostick, Judy Pang, Link Hall
Production: Susanne Hillen, Julia Bovis and Michelle Draycott

Editors' acknowledgements

The **editors** would like to thank: all of the contributors for their hard work over a prolonged period, in particular Kim Burton and Andrew Cronshaw for careful attentions above and beyond the call of duty; Jak Kilby for delivering large boxes of exactly the right photos; Ian Anderson, editor of *Folk Roots*, for making available the magazine's extraordinary archive; Andy Morgan for preparing the appendix on record stores; Thomas Brooman and WOMAD for their inspiration over the years; all of the many record labels and distributors who responded to strings of requests; Orla and all those on the project at Rough Guides; and Henry and Justin at the masterful Henry Iles studio.
Simon thanks Kate, **Mark** thanks Nat (and Miles), and **Richard** thanks his long-suffering family, for their forebearance over the processing of a million-odd words.

Publishing details

Published November 1999 by Rough Guides Ltd, 62-70 Shorts Gardens, London WC2H 9AB.
Reprinted October 2000.
Distributed by the Penguin Group:
Penguin Books Ltd, 27 Wrights Lane, London W8 5TZ
Penguin Books USA Inc., 375 Hudson Street, New York 10014, USA
Penguin Books Australia Ltd, 487 Maroondah Highway, PO Box 257, Ringwood,
    Victoria 3134, Australia
Penguin Books Canada Ltd, 10 Alcorn Avenue, Toronto, Ontario, Canada M4V 1E4
Penguin Books (NZ) Ltd, 182–190 Wairau Road, Auckland 10, New Zealand

Typeset in Bembo and Helvetica to an original design by Henry Iles.
Printed in Spain by Graphy Cems.

Text © Rough Guides, 1999
All photographs copyright of credited photographers, agencies and record labels.
784pp.

A catalogue record for this book is available from the British Library.
ISBN 1-85828-635-2

Contents

Part Two • Middle East

Part Three • Africa

Part Four • Directories

Introduction

It's fitting that this new edition of the **Rough Guide to World Music** coincides with the start of a new millennium, for it deals with the oldest and newest music in the world – from centuries-old traditions to contemporary fusions. It includes the most sacred and profound music and the most frivolous and risqué, music of healing, music of protest, the loudest music you'll ever hear, the softest and most intimate, and maybe also the most moving and enjoyable.

The Guide sets itself a clearly impossible task: to document and explain the popular, folk and (excluding the Western canon) classical music traditions around the globe. However, since the first edition appeared in 1994 it has been the chief handbook for enthusiasts and become a resource for those working in and around the World Music business itself. In producing a new edition we were aware of omissions and shortcomings in the first edition and we have added many new pieces on countries that weren't covered before – France, Germany, Italy, Iran, Israel, Angola, Mozambique, Burundi and Uganda, to name a handful in this volume. Other articles were expanded, revised and rewritten;

Scandinavia, for example, turned from one piece into five, as did the former Yugoslavia.

In addition, the new edition reflects the huge expansion of the whole World Music market over the past five years. There are more concerts and festivals than ever before – and many would say that there is actually a surfeit of CDs. In preparing this edition, we surveyed the lot, completely overhauling our discographies, adding biographical entries for artists, and reviewing and highlighting the best discs available.

That's the main reason why this new edition of the *Rough Guide* is not one book, but two: this volume covers Africa, Europe and the Middle East, while *Volume Two* has the Americas, Asia and the Pacific. Even with two books, each volume has turned out longer than the entire first edition.

The articles – from more than eighty contributors – are designed to provide the background to each country's music styles, explaining how they relate to history, social customs, politics and identity, as well as highlighting the lives and sounds of the singers and musicians. We hope you'll find this enriches the whole experience of listening to World Music.

How this book works

This volume is divided into three geographical sections: **Europe**, the **Middle East** and **Africa**. Within each section the entries are arranged alphabetically by country or by ethnic group (for instance the entries on Gypsy, Jewish Sephardic, Kurdish and Pygmy music). There are running heads and an index to help you find your way.

Our **discographies** follow the arrangment of each article and when it makes things clearer by style (for example, Nigeria has sections for Traditional, Juju, Fuji, Highlife, and Afro-beat). Compilations are listed first and artists follow (listed A–Z), with a brief biography and reviews of their key discs.

Each section has one or two **'star discs'** which are indicated by a larger than usual CD symbol (⊙). These are the ones to buy first. All other selections are preceded by a CD (⊙), cassette (▭) or vinyl (●) symbol: those specified as cassette or vinyl are not available on CD but worth checking out all the same. To avoid any conflict of interest, as some of our contributors are professionally involved with bands or record labels, the selections are the responsibility of the editors.

In the **directories** at the end of the book we've included addresses and websites of the most important **record labels** releasing the music featured in this volume, as well as the best specialist **shops** to track down CDs.

ONE

Europe

This map is drawn on the Peters' projection
which shows the correct relative size of countries

Greenland

Iceland

Faroe
Islands

Norway

Sweden

Finland

Estonia

Russia

Scotland

Latvia

Denmark

Lithuania

Russia

N.I
Ireland

Belarus

England

Neth.

Poland

Wales

Belg.

Germany

Ukraine

ATLANTIC
OCEAN

Luxembourg

Czech Rep.

Slovakia

Austria

Hungary

France

Switzer.

ALPS

Slov.

Romania

Croatia

Moldova

Andorra

B-H

Serbia

Bulgaria

Corsica

Italy

FYRM
Mac.

Spain

Alb.

Portugal

Sardinia

Greece

Turkey

Mallorca

Sicily

Albania

the eagle has landed

Albania is called by its inhabitants Shqipëri (often translated as 'the land of the eagles' although there's an alternative interpretation, 'the land of clear speech') and the country still retains many elements of its patriarchal and tribal past, with concepts of honour, hospitality and family ties to the fore. Isolated from the outside world for many years by geography and politics, the country has, through the 1990s, suffered the realities of contemporary Balkan life – hitting the headlines when Albanians tried to escape economic breakdown and political anarchy on boats to Italy, and as Albanian refugees fled from the Kosovo conflict in neighbouring Serbia in 1999. Its music, however, claims **Kim Burton**, is as startling and beautiful as any in eastern Europe.

The Albanians in the Balkans are divided between the Republic of Albania (3.2 million) on the Adriatic Sea and the republics of former Yugoslavia (about 2 million). The Albanians of Kosovo in Serbia, where they make up around 90 per cent of the population, together with their cousins in western Macedonia, became separated from those in Albania itself at the end of the nineteenth century when the final collapse of Ottoman imperial power in the Balkans led to the creation of new states and the drawing up of new maps. In the jostling for land and influence that accompanied the formation of these new states, independent Albania ended up as a small strip on the sea, bordered for the most part by forbidding mountains. During the years following the Second World War, its natural isolation became still more pronounced, as the hardline Stalinist regime of Enver Hoxha drew in upon itself, resisting influence from abroad and attempting to enforce unquestioning obedience upon its citizens. With the fall of the communist government in 1991, the Albanians found themselves at last able to travel (within immigration constraints), to follow the Western media and to make contact with foreign individuals and ideas without fear of imprisonment, forced labour or internal exile. Yet at the same time, waves of economic and political disasters added to their burdens.

In a sense, the deepest, most secret soul of a people lies in their music, and Albanian music, still little known to outsiders, is as rich, complex and beautiful as any. It falls into three major and very different stylistic groups; there is an important contrast between the two cultures of the northern **Ghegs** and the southern **Tosks** and **Labs** which is reflected in their music, while the style of the capital **Tirana** and its surrounding area shows the strong **Turkish influence** common to urban music throughout the Balkan region. In a small and separate category, the songs of the northern city of **Shkodër**, which is generally regarded as the most cosmopolitan and sophisticated community in the country, express a romantic and inward character all of their own.

What unites all these styles is the intensity that both performers and listeners give to their music as a medium for patriotic expression and as a vehicle carrying the narrative of **oral history**. Although everybody puts the purely musical content first, composers and performers are always aware of the extra-musical meaning that their music carries. In the days of Hoxha this aspect was forced into service to build support for the Party – even lullabies contained the wish that the infant would grow up to be a strong worker for Enver and the Party.

The outbreak of new freedoms after Communism's collapse led to a surge of songs dealing either whole-heartedly, or slyly, with the new circumstances: support for political parties, the revival of the custom of *gurbet* (seeking seasonal work abroad) or other changes in everyday life. At concerts, no matter how formal, audiences are given to breaking into applause and furious whistles of support at a line in a song that reflects their feelings, and if their approval is strong enough they will rush onto the stage to force small gifts on the singer.

It is not simply music with a traditional basis that fufils this role. Even out-and-out **pop** – usually based on an Italian model, and a relatively new development in a country where in the 1970s singer Sherif Merdani was given a twenty-year jail sentence for performing The Beatles' song "Let it Be" – deals directly with everyday life and its problems.

The most important popular singer to emerge so far is **Ardit Gjebrea**, who sprang to fame in 1993 with a rather sentimental song called "Jon" dealing with the desperate and risky attempts that many made to cross the Ionian sea to Italy, and the family break-ups it caused. It was a constant presence on radio and TV for a couple of years, often inciting an overtly emotional and personal response from its hearers. Gjebrea's recent attempts to fuse pop song with the polyphonic vocal music of the Gjirokastër district has met with great popular acclaim if perhaps not yet complete artistic success.

Epics of the North

Albania itself can be divided roughly into two cultural areas, with the river Shkumbin dividing the two. The **Ghegs** of the north also make up the population of Kosovo and the vast majority of the ethnic Albanian population of Macedonia, and much of their music shares a rugged and heroic quality.

The most serious and uncompromising musical form of north Albania is the **sung epic poem**. The oldest type, known as *Rapsodi Kreshnikë* (Poems of Heroes) and accompanied by the singer on the one-stringed fiddle, the *lahuta*, sounds very similar to the music of the Montenegrin and Serbian guslars (see Serbia – p.275), with a set of melodic cells that produce a structure on which poems of immense length can be sung. This music is the province of old men, and when Albanians talk about it they will sweep their fingers across their upper lip with a flourish to express the luxuriant growth of moustache thought necessary for the singer.

Only rarely heard these days, this tradition is particularly identified with the inhabitants of the remote northern highlands, but another, more accessible ballad tradition is found throughout the Gheg area, with particularly important schools in Dibër (Debar) and Kerçovë (Kičevo) in Macedonia, as well as districts of northern Albania. Here the singer is accompanied by the *çifteli*, a deceptively simple two-stringed instrument related to the Turkish saz, of which one string carries the melody while the other is used mainly as a drone.

The tales tell of heroes such as the fifteenth-century warrior Skanderbeg, leader of the struggle against the Turks, and their semi-historical, semi-mythical events are bound up with the constant Albanian themes of honour, hospitality, treachery and revenge. The performances can be highly emotional with compelling shifts of rhythm and tempo quite unlike the epics of their Slav neighbours. Up until recently the performers were always men, but there has been a new development as women have started to make inroads into the field of epic balladry in their own right. In the past the only women performing a traditionally male repertoire were the **Vajze të betuar**, genetic women who lived as men either for reasons of conviction, or to ensure that family inheritances were not alienated from the line of descent.

Both epic traditions serve as a medium for oral history in what was until quite recently a pre-literate society (there was not even a generally agreed alphabet until the early 1900s) and also preserve and inculcate moral codes and social values. In a culture that retained the blood-feud as its primary means of law enforcement until well into this century such codes were literally matters of life and death. Song was one of the most efficient ways of making sure that each member of the tribe was aware of what obligations he or she was bound to.

The historical dimension remains important. On the Topic recording mentioned in the discography, there's an excerpt from a song about the ill-fated, American-backed uprising in the 1940s, and singers such as **Sali Mani** continue to treat such contemporary themes as the events in Kosovo as subjects for their songs. Among the many singers living and dead that are famed for their interpretations in the traditional style Tropoja's **Fatime Sokoli Shaqir**, **Cervadiku** and **Muça-Mustafa** stand out.

The çifteli is also used, together with its big brother, the *sharki*, the violin and the tambourine-like *def*, to accompany dances and lyric songs, whose imagery is generally drawn from country life. ("You are the flower of the mountain . . . the

Sharki player Altush Bytyci from northern Albania

KIM BURTON

morning dew"). Since the Second World War bands of massed **çiftelie and sharki** have become popular with Albanians both inside and outside Albania. The same repertoire of songs, given an ad hoc harmonisation, is performed by small bands based round clarinet and accordion at weddings and feasts.

In the countryside it's also possible to meet with **shepherds** who play for their own amusement using various homemade wind instruments of the type common to shepherds and cowherds throughout the Balkan area. More unusual is the *zumarë*, a double "clarinet" made from two tubes of cane or the hollow bones of a bird tied side-by-side and provided with a simple reed at one end, and with a flaring bell of cow or goat horn at the other. The tone is piercing and rousing, yet most of the tunes

sophisticated, with oriental-sounding scales and a constant interplay of major and minor, they bear an affinity with the *sevdalinke* of Bosnia (see Bosnia – p.33) and the neighbouring Sandžak, but differ from them in their extreme and typically Albanian restraint and the exceptional fluidity of rhythm and tempo. Early descriptions of such groups, which date from the end of the nineteenth century, suggest a remarkable sound: violin, clarinet, saz, def, sometimes an Indian-style harmonium and percussion provided by rattling a stick between two bottles. These days the accordion and guitar have replaced the more exotic instruments, but the intimate approach of the singers remains the same. Among the most important players are **Bik Ndoja**, **Luçija Miloti**, **Xhevdet Hafizi** and the handsome **Bujar Qamili**.

are melancholic and contemplative. The player uses circular breathing, taking air in through the nose while blowing out through the mouth using the cheeks as a kind of reservoir without needing to stop for breath. Children learn the technique by blowing through a straw into a glass of water, keeping a continuous stream of bubbles.

The songs of the northern city of **Shkodër** – always the most cosmopolitan of Albanian towns and the centre of intellectual life – are very different to the rural music. Lyrical, romantic and

Alb-pop

In the capital, **Tirana**, and central Albania in general, much of the popular music has a noticeable Gypsy flavour, exemplified in the hot clarinet-led band of the gravel-voiced **Myslim Leli**, whose tapes are sold on every street corner. Mixed with influences from the eastern Mediterranean (Turkish music, particularly the oriental and sentimental type known as Arabesk, is very popular in Albania), this forms the basis for the nearest approach to an indigenous pop music that Albania has so far developed, to be heard in the work of **Merita Halili** and glamour queen **Parashqvili Simaku**, both of whom are presently living outside Albania and performing for the large emigrant audience in the United States and western Europe.

Roses of the South

The music of the southern Albanians – Tosk and Lab alike – is profoundly different. Lacking the determined heroic ethos of the north, this music, both vocal and instrumental, is relaxed, gentle, and exceptionally beautiful. It has a highly developed

Famille Lela de Përmet

polyphonic structure of up to four independent parts, depending on the area from which it comes. The **Labs** have a saying that "one traveller is alone, two will quarrel, but three will sing."

The most complex and strangest of the **vocal styles** − some fine examples of which are to be heard on the Chant du Monde recording *Albanie: Polyphonies Vocales et Instrumentales* − stems from around the port of **Vlorë** in the southwest. Each singer has his or her own title − taker, thrower, turner or drone − and a separate part to play in the web of independent lines and sustained notes which create a rich and moving sonic world decorated with falsetto and vibrato, sometimes interrupted by wild and mournful cries. Much of the power of this music stems from the tension between the immense emotional weight it carries, rooted in centuries of pride, poverty and oppression, and the strictly formal, almost ritualistic nature of its structure. The force of these songs is extraordinary and unparalleled in any other Balkan music, and the tradition remains vibrantly alive. It's heard and sung with great pleasure.

Tosk music, although it also has a complex polyphonic structure, is even gentler, and in small towns the predominant ensemble is one which mixes instruments − violin, clarinet, *llautë* (lute), def, and often these days accordion and guitar − with two or three singers. The most important centres are the city of **Korçë**, home of **Eli Fara**, now yet another emigrant but still one of south-

ern Albania's most loved female singers, and the remote mountain town of **Përmet**, one of the great musical centres of Albania and birthplace of two of the country's most important musicians, clarinettists **Laver Bariu**, who still lives there, and the late **Remzi Lela**, founder of an important musical dynasty whose members are now represented in every aspect of musical life in Tirana from wedding band to symphony orchestra. The group he led has been one of the few to have toured and recorded in the West under the title of **La Famille Lela de Përmet**. Albanians say that the most beautiful of Përmet's songs are those sung for the bride at weddings. "The bride stands in the middle of the room, arrayed like the Morning Star", they sing. "The many-petalled rose passes down the lane, the boys and girls follow after her."

Instrumental music in the south obeys more or less the same rules as the vocal music. Southern Albanians use many string instruments of the lute family related to the Turkish saz and Greek bouzouki to perform dance melodies and rhapsodic meditations on slow airs, but the glory of their instrumental music is the **kaba**. A kaba (the word is Turkish meaning 'low' or 'deep') is a half-improvised melancholy form led by a clarinet or violin supported by a drone from accordion or llautë and usually followed by a dance tune to release the tension. The melodies, ornamented with swoops, glides and growls of an almost vocal quality, sound both fresh and ancient at the same time, and exemplify the combination of passion with restraint that is the hallmark of Albanian culture.

The district of **Dropuli**, south of Gjirokastër, has a sizeable ethnic Greek population, and their music is related to the music of Epirus, south of the border. Using the same scales and rhythmic patterns as their Albanian neighbours, but without the same polyphonic complexity and with a rougher and more aggressive tone, their music is well worth seeking out.

Live on Stage . . .

Unless you are lucky enough to happen across a wedding celebration or other festivity, or to make the acquaintance of a musician, amateur or professional, it can be difficult to hear live music in Albania. In previous years the Communist government maintained control over musical life just as it did every other aspect of life in Albania. As well as organising large orchestras of traditional instruments "in the spirit of collective labour", they used to support local amateur groups in a network of festivals which culminated in the huge quinquennial **festival at Gjirokastër**, on the understanding that every group included a song in praise of Enver Hoxha and the Party.

Now there is no money for such activities. The only organisation actively involved in the promotion of music is **Albanian Radio-Television (RTSh)**, which is hoping to reorganise the festival network in collaboration with private sponsors. In 1995 there was a national festival in **Berat** that RTSh helped to organise along with the Ministry of Culture, which met with considerable success, and there were hopes that it would become a permanent fixture.

However, since the collapse of the pyramid schemes in which many people lost what savings they had, and the resulting widespread social unrest, any event in Albania is hard to predict. There are still sporadic concerts at the Opera (the one-time Palace of Culture in central Tirana) but otherwise few opportunities. The poverty of the country means that those usual Balkan venues for bands – cafés and restaurants – either can't afford to employ musicians, or if they can, cater for well-to-do foreigners, the occasional ambitious tourist, or the temporary visitor on business. The bands in these restaurants rarely play local music.

Meanwhile many of the best-known singers are now living abroad, performing for the exile community, and they provide the best opportunity to hear the hard-driving, popular style of Tirana and other large towns. Germany, Switzerland and Aus-

tria, in particular, have a wide network of venues where visiting stars play, but they can be difficult to locate.

The more ancient layers of folk music may sometimes be heard at World Music festivals abroad, but the best place to hear them is in situ, at a wedding or around the family table. With luck, time, and a little persistence, the traveller should be able to make the acquaintance of one of Europe's most startling and beautiful musical traditions.

Kosovo and Macedonia

Most of the ethnic Albanians that live outside the country are Ghegs, although there is a small Tosk population clustered around the shores of lakes Presp and Ohrid in the south of Macedonia. The most significant communities, however, are those of **Kosovo** a population long suppressed by Serbia-Yugoslavia, and then brutally displaced during the war and 'ethnic cleansing' of 1999.

Music might seem a minor element in the war and tragedy of Kosovo, but it was not ignored. The political repression in Kosovo had for years before the war meant that Albanian songs with nationalistic connotation could not be sung in public without risking arrest or ill-treatment. This lent the music a significant role in articulating historic background and current aspirations.

In Macedonia (and in pre-war Kosovo), an extensive recording industry, bankrolled by successful members of the diaspora, churned out popular music of all types, ranging from ballads to lyrical love songs.

In Macedonia, Skopje's **Vëllezërit Aliu** (the Ali brothers) exemplified the popular style, backing their vocal duets in deeply traditional style with clarinet or saxophone, synthesiser, drum box and electric bass to create a highly successful and energetic music.

Kosovo's capital **Prishtina** (Priština) was – before the war – home to similar singers and musicians, among whom Gypsies were prominent. Among the stars of this form were **Mazllum Shaqiri** ('Lumi') who led the search for a contemporary way of singing old songs. The inhabitants of Kosovo's second city, **Gjakovë** (Djakovica), were known for a sweeter sound, with romantic harmonies and expansive vocal flourishes. The best-loved singer in this style was undoubtedly **Qamil i Vogël** (Little Qamil). At time of writing, in mid-1999, the whereabouts of these musicians is unknown.

discography

Compilations

○ Albania: Canti i Danze Tradizionale
(I Suoni Cetra, Italy).

Produced in collaboration with the Academy of Sciences in Tirana, and drawing on their massive archives which cover the traditional styles of the whole country, this series of dics is well worth the trouble it takes to track down. The three LPs still represent the best collection of Albanian traditional music.

Albania: Vocal and Instrumental Polyphony
(Le Chant du Monde, France).

Music from the southern half of Albania, starting with an astonishing song from Vlorë and ending with a very lovely one from Përmet. Most of this is a cappella, with a couple of instrumental kaba laments on clarinets, violin, flute, lutes and def. Very well recorded.

Albanian Village Music (Heritage, UK).

An interesting collection of archive recordings made in Tirana and Shkodër by HMV in 1930, this CD features music from all over the country, although the extensive notes focus on the recording history and the recording engineer A.D. Lawrence more than the music.

Folk Music of Albania (Topic, UK).

The first commercial Western recording of music from Albania, this dates from 1966 but is a good introduction to the musics of Albania. Unusually, A. L. Lloyd, the compiler, seems to have been able to make some original field recordings instead of relying on 'approved' material, and the rough and ready nature of some of the performances is very appealing.

Greatings from Macedonia
(Toska Radio FM, Macedonia).

Creative spelling and all, this is actually one of the best overviews of the various strands of Albanian music available on CD, tailored for an Albanian audience looking for a good time rather than a respectful foreign folklorist. The performers all hail from the Republic of Macedonia.

Music from Albania
(Rounder, US).

A recent release of recordings made in the more optimistic days of 1993 including epic music from the north, beautiful polyphonic music from the south including an instrumental kaba plus hard-edged and passionate urban music from the Roma Gypsies. The finest available introduction to music from Albania with excellent booklet notes.

Vocal Traditions of Albania (Saydisc, UK).

Don't be put off by the rather academic title – this might as easily be called 29 All-time Albanian Greats. Recorded in front of an obviously enthusiastic audience at the 1995 festival in Berat, the music – including a couple of examples of the type of urban wedding songs tremendously popular inside Albania but rarely recorded for Western audiences – comes from all over the country. Informative notes are a plus, though the sometimes idiosyncratic approach of the Albanian Radio sound engineers can be a little irritating.

Yugoslavie 2: Sous Les Peupliers de Bilisht
Yugoslavie 3: Bessa ou la Parole Donnée
(Ocora, France).

These very fine, well-recorded examples of music from the Tosk (Vol 2) and Gheg (Vol 3) Albanian minorities in what is now Macedonia, include both instrumental and vocal performances – the latter the more important.

Artists

Laver Bariu

Përmet's great clarinettist Laver Bariu has been a bandleader for over forty years, and has exerted a tremendous influence over younger generations by passing on the tradition that he learned as a child while making his own individual contribution felt.

Songs from the City of Roses (GlobeStyle, UK).

Recorded in Përmet itself, this collection of favourite songs (including a couple of classics by Laver's father) and instrumentals by a group spanning three generations is a great introduction to the southern repertoire. As a bonus it includes a couple of songs and dances learned from musicians in Tirana and points north.

Famille Lela de Përmet

The extensive Lela family are an important Albanian musical dynasty, who moved en masse from the southern town Përmet to the capital Tirana in the years following the war. Members of the family have colonised both the capital's wedding scene and symphony orchestra.

 Polyphonies Vocales et Instrumentales d'Albanie (Label Bleu/Indigo, France).

A very beautiful and very approachable collection of songs from the Përmet and Korçë regions of southern Albania, and one with an enchantingly mournful sound with clarinet, lute, accordion and violin.

Alpine Music

the alpunk phenomenon

Behind the stereotypical image of Alpine music – lederhosen, cowbells and red-faced farmers puffing away on tubas – lurk more subversive talents. Punk yodelling, hardcore thigh-slapping, alphorn-didjeridoo hybrids and beery jazz fusions. There are strange goings on in the Alpine regions of Germany, Austria and Switzerland. Strange, because this is a bastion of conservatism, where the mountain fastness has long made a virtue of experience and tradition. **Christoph Wagner** reveals all.

Alpine traditionals of course, remain in place. There are authentic, old-style Alpine musics, sometimes differing from one valley to the next – and a variety packaged into a predictable thump by commercial bands who play in the hotels and restaurants. But of late, beneath the snowline, things are moving as young musicians reshape the traditional folk music. It's this music that most demands your attention.

Bavaria

Munich, the capital of Bavaria, is the home of **BavaRio**. As the name suggests, this group presents a combination of Bavarian melodies with samba rhythms from Rio – and this isn't just another World Music fusion dreamed up by the

BavaRio hanging out in their Alpine hothouse

A&R boys. The sound was born from a real historical migration. On an extended visit to Brazil, Wolfgang Netzer, the leader of the band, came across a style that sounded strangely familiar to him and touched childhood memories of when he used to be a member of a schuhplattler (thigh and leg-slapping dance) group complete with lederhosen. The music had been taken to Brazil at the turn of the century by a wave of Bavarian immigrants: ländlers, polkas and waltzes mingled with the sounds of the Brazilian south, where there is a Bavarian community to this day.

Back in Munich, Netzer developed the music by adding Brazilian instruments like *cavaquinho*, viola caipira and samba drums and percussion to the traditional Bavarian stubenmusik string band sound of hammered dulcimer, harp, zither and guitar and made a real link between the two cultures.

Munich is also the home of **Die Interpreten** who do a similar tightrope act with variations on Bavarian folk music but add a sharper edge to it. They bring their jazz background plus a range of saxophones to traditional melodies. Once they've got hold of the mainly sedate dance tunes and subjected them to lively intonation and overblowing techniques it sounds as though jazz saxophonist Albert Ayler were lost in a Bavarian beer tent. This is eccentric music that is surprising and refreshing, although it sometimes borders on parody.

The best-known alternative Bavarian group and the pioneers of the whole genre is **Biermosl Blosn**, founded in 1976 by three brothers from the Well family who play trumpet, horn and accordion and irritate local right-wing politicians by writing satirical lyrics to traditional tunes and producing records with titles like *The Yodeling Horror Monster Show*. Their most notorious performance was on Bavarian TV in 1980, just before Bavarian president Franz Josef Strauss made his

Biermösl Blosn

During the 1990s the revival of alpine folk became a fashionable trend under the banner of "Neue Volksmusik". New faces were brought into the public eye. **Hundsbuam**, formerly known as Hundsbuam Miserablige, is an all-Bavarian band founded in 1994. With noisy guitars, heavy drums and wild on-stage antics, they try hard to fill the gap which was left when Hubert von Goisern, the most popular star of the Alpine New Wave, left show business.

These attempts to develop alpine folk music by opening it up to other styles should be seen against the background of a growing interest in traditional music by amateur players. In Munich alone there are hundreds of *stubenmusik* ensembles playing just for the fun of it. Many of these are disciples of **Sepp Eibl**, one of the most influential figures of the old school. His group favours tunes from the richest period of Bavarian folk music, the mid-nineteenth century, reconstructed from musicians' notebooks. The

New Year speech, when they played the Bavarian anthem with new words which directly attacked his politics, resulting in a long-term ban from Bavarian radio and TV. They still do political cabarets, often with satirist Gerhart Polt. Leaving politics aside, they exist in another incarnation called **Well–Buam** (Well Boys), specialising in stomping dance music on clarinets and brass.

In a gentler mood are the sounds of **Fraunhofer Saitenmusik** who play traditional music from Bavaria and related countries using only string instruments such as the harp and a variety of zithers – an instrument which was introduced to the south of Germany by vagrant musicians in the eighteenth century. The **hammered dulcimer** was an even earlier arrival. Today the best-known virtuoso of this instrument is **Rudi Zapf**, who plays a huge range of styles from classical music to jazz and avant-garde. In a family band with his wife Ingrid on double bass and her sister Evelyn Huber on harp, he takes us on a musical world trip from Bavaria to Greece, China and Venezuela and back again. With the addition of guitarist Wolfgang Neumann the group becomes **Zapf'nstreich**, moving more boldly into new territory with a mix of acoustic textures and electric sounds of the guitar.

music of this authentic movement is a far cry from the commercial dilutions of 'Volksmusik' which, surprising as it may seem, sweep across prime-time television nearly every day.

Many young musicians hold traditionalists like Eibl in high esteem, but most seem sceptical as to whether purity of tradition alone will ensure the survival of the old music. Wolfgang Netzer speaks for most of the young generation when he says: "Genuine folk music means vitality. Life goes on and you can't keep re-hashing what was made a hundred years ago. It won't improve. When it was made a century ago it was very powerful stuff, but when played today, it loses that intensity."

The series of early recordings reissued by Trikont (the leading label for Alpine music) show this to be true. Often the old 78s sound rougher and tougher than the "authentic" recreations of today. Brass bands like the **Original Dachauer Bauernkapelle**, founded in 1906 and first recorded two years later, played with such a drive and passion that most modern bands sound limp by comparison. But on the other hand, these traditions are vulnerable and easily disappear if nobody protects them.

Swiss in Space

The desire for a new approach is shared by **Appenzeller Space Schöttl**, one of the most prolific bands in Switzerland's folk music revival. The name plays on the absurdity of a technologically advanced space shuttle coming from rural Appenzell – an area known for its cheese and for giving women the right to vote only fifteen years ago.

Töbi Tobler plays a special local hammer dulcimer, which is the core of any traditional streichmusig ensemble in Appenzell, and Ficht Tanner plucks the bass. Their music reflects the Appenzeller world, where clocks move a little bit slower than elsewhere. Starting with free improvisation and psychedelic rock more than twenty years ago, Tobler and Tanner brought the spirit of these styles to their acoustic music and now mix it together in their schöttl (meaning shake). Recordings of Appenzeller Space Schöttl are a rarity, as they believe "there's enough plastic in the world!" (CDs presumably haven't made it to Appenzell yet).

Newcomers on the scene, **Stimmhorn** from Basel, have achieved a high profile in just a few years. The band is a partnership between Balthasar Streiff on trumpet, alphorn and *alperidu* (an Alpine horn played like a *didjeridu*) and the amazing vocalist Christian Zahnder who combines Mongolian overtone singing with archaic yodelling as well as playing self-invented instruments such as the 'rockordion' – transformed from an accordion and a "milking-machine organ" (organ pipes operated by a milking machine). Their general approach is minimalistic and meditative at the same time. They paint colourful musical landscapes of jagged sounds like the Alps around them and enrich their performances with theatrical effects.

Austria

In Austria the scene was dominated for years by **Attwenger**, who triggered the whole new musical avalanche. Starting as alpine punks (some called them the Austrian Pogues) Markus Binder and Hans-Peter Falkner developed musically with each succeeding record. With the distorted sound of a

CH. BÜHTER

Stimmhorn

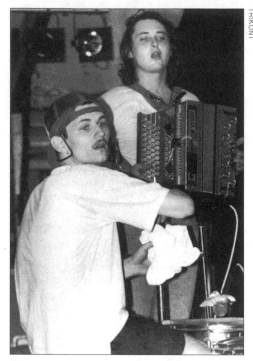

Attwenger

button accordion from the Steiermark mountain region played through a wah-wah pedal, gunshot drum tracks and electronic hip-hop rhythms, they tried "to find the meeting point between folk music and punk". Markus Binder, drummer and lyric writer, explained: "We take particular elements from the old traditions and try to amplify them. Old and new styles are contrasted, fresh and strong, by using reduced instrumentation arranged in a dense, expressionistic manner."

Attwenger regard both alternative pop culture and traditional tunes as an expression of rebellion in everyday life. Despite their underground gloss, however, Binder and Falkner's starting point is the music of their home region where a number of unique dance-tunes have survived. In their hands *Schleiniger*, *Innviertler Ländler* and *Aberseer Ländler* become wild songs with aggressive beats. Although they enjoyed tremendous critical acclaim and were twice voted best band, they folded in 1995 due to musical exhaustion and a refusal to be part of the Alpine New Wave hype. Refreshed, they reunited two years later and took the public by surprise with an even more radical reductionist attitude. The folk elements were so diluted that they only surfaced occasionally over repetitive trip-hop and jungle beats.

A totally different approach is used by two highly sophisticated ensembles, which mix Alpine sounds with either jazz or new classical music. **Die Knödel** (The Dumplings), formerly known as Die Verkochten Tirolerknödel (The Overcooked Tyrolean Dumplings) are an intellectual underground band founded in the early 1990s. Their instrumentation – using violins, viola, clarinet, bassoon, trumpet and fluegelhorn – is closer to a classical music ensemble than a ländler band. The four male and four female members of the octet are highly educated musicians who earn their living in the symphony orchestras of Austria and Germany. Though classically trained, they are not ashamed of their traditional roots or of pushing folk music into new areas. Their music rarely suffers from their instrumental virtuosity – it's clear and balanced.

Until the summer of 1995 the Dumplings' leader, Christof Dienz wrote all their material, mixing Michael Nyman-style minimalism with impressionistic atmospheres to create a contemporary chamber folk music. To keep fresh they have recently commissioned pieces from composers based in their home region of Tyrol, who come from contemporary classical, jazz, rock and experimental backgrounds. The result is an exciting patchwork of alpine polkas, waltzes and instrumental yodels, each viewed from a different angle.

While Die Knödel use classical music, **Broadlahn** uses jazz. Founded in 1982 by three school friends playing guitar, mandolin and accordion, they became a sextet in 1990 adding three experienced jazz players to their line up, on saxophone, bass and drums. Searching for the other kind of groove in traditional music patterns, they have stretched the framework to the limits and occasionally beyond them. Trying to dance to their complex rhythms and complicated riffs could be disastrous!

Although these are all highly individual bands, what they have in common is a vision of Alpine folk music which is rooted in tradition, but modern at the same time. It's a successful mix, often leavened with humour and imagination.

discography

Compilations

 The Alps: Music From The Old World
(World Network, Germany).

Both the old and new school of alpine folk music – although more old than new. Includes alphorn duets, exuberant yodeling

THE ALPS: MUSIC FROM THE OLD WORLD

WORLD NETWORK

THE ALPS
MUSIC FROM THE OLD WORLD

from Austria's Citoller Tanzgeiger and even three rare tracks by the legendary Appenzeller Space Schöttl who haven't made any recordings before or since.

**Bayern – Volksmusik.
Rare Schellacks 1006 1041** (Trikont, Germany).

Driving brass and string bands from the suburbs and countryside of Bavaria on this unique collection of rare 78rpm recordings. Not the bland oompah you might expect.

**Oberösterreich-Salzburg – Volksmusik.
Rare Schellacks 1910–1949** (Trikont, Germany).

Proving there's more to the region of Salzburg and Upper Austria than Mozart – polyphonic yodels, heavy brass and driving string music make this collection a gem.

Österreich: Musik der Regionen (Vol 1–10)
(Österreichisches Volksliedwerk, Austria).

This comprehensive survey of traditional Austrian music styles is like a sound atlas. Archive and contemporary recordings from different areas. From Upper Austria around Linz and Salzburg to Lower Austria south of Vienna, you can hear the best performers play music ranging from wild yodelling and Alpine horn playing to three- and four-part singing. Or take to the dance floor for traditional waltzes, marches and ländlers played on accordion and fiddle or by small brass bands. There's an accompanying booklet with introductions to the regional styles (in German and English), song lyrics (in German), but hardly any information about the musicians. **Distributed** by Daniela Schwarz, 1230 Wien, Anton Baumgartnerstr. 44/A2/213 ☎ (43) 1 6673169.

Urmusig (CSR Records, Switzerland).

Wonderful field recordings from the Swiss Alps. This double CD was originally taken from a film sound track including some of the living legends of traditional music in Switzerland, like eighty-two-year-old Rees Gwerder pumping out some driving dance tunes on his Schwyzer Örgeli, a special melodeon only found in Switzerland.

Artists

Attwenger

Since their arrival in the early 1990s, Attwenger, comprising Markus Binder (drummer and lyrics) and Hans Peter Falkner (accordion), have taken the scene by storm becoming the most influential band and kick-starting a whole new genre.

 Most
(Trikont, Germany).

Their first and best album, from 1991, features liberal radical humour and traditional dance tunes played with hip-hop drum rhythms and a head-banging ländler-beat from the wildest of the Alpine groups.

Song (Trikont, Germany).

Attwenger's clubby 1997 release blends jungle and trip-hop hypnotics with a light flavour of traditional accordion.

BavaRio

BavaRio, led by guitarist Wolfgang Netzer, comprises four Bavarians and one Brazilian from Munich. It was the first band of the revival movement to gain a record deal with a major label.

Hoi (Meilton, Germany).

As ever BavaRio mixes the best of both worlds: ländlers and samba, cavaquinho and zithers. Mainly their own compositions, but also a 'forro' number and music by composer Anibal Augusto Sardinha, a contemporary of Villa Lobos. With their latest album they have returned to a small record label.

Broadlahn

Founded in 1982 and led by singer, composer and guitarist Ernst Huber. It was eight years before they made their first record and went on to win high acclaim and the prestigious Deutschen Schallplattenkritik award.

Leib & Seel (BMG, Austria).

In this 1993 album, jazz improvisations emerge from folk tunes, and ländlers get a new look with original arrangments using everything from hand clapping to marimba.

Fraunhofer Saitenmusik

The ensemble got its name from the famous Fraunhofer restaurant in Munich where they played as a house band for years. For a long time Richard Kurländer (harp and hammer dulcimer), Heidi Zink (hammer dulcimer and zither) and Gerhard Zink (acoustic bass) played as a trio. With fourth member Michael Klein they added the sounds of guitar and forest zither.

Zwischenklänge (Trikont, Germany).

The title means 'Sounds in between' which might be described as Bavarian 'chamber music' folk with a New Age touch. Pleasant or bland depending on taste.

Hundsbuam

Bandleader Streitbichi Michi's inspiration came when he visited an Attwenger concert and was converted to Alpunk. In 1994 he formed Hundsbuam Miserablige, now known as Hundsbaum.

Hui (BMG,Germany).

With funky tuba lines, heavy metal guitar chords and accordion staccato, these Bavarians show how to rock the beer tent. Released in 1997.

Die Interpreten

The trio of Erwin Rahling (drums), Andreas Koll (baritone saxophone) and Thomas Binegger (tenor saxophone) are one of the pioneer ensembles and are still going strong with the same line up after fifteen years.

⊚ **Stollen 4** (Trikont, Germany).

Hard-edged drum beats with rough saxophone roars mining the roots and blowing dust from traditional tunes.

Die Knödel

Die Knödel are an octet from Austria founded in 1992. Since then they have released three CDs and played hundreds of gigs around the world in classical concert halls, folk festivals and jazz clubs.

⊚ **Panorama** (RecRec, Austria).

Panorama is Die Knödel's best record to date: a collection of pieces from different composers with a wonderful blend of timbres and textures. It is a welcome change from their own often somewhat overcomplicated material.

Stimmhorn

Stimmhorn, from Switzerland, are Christian Zehnder (voice and bandoneon) and Balthasar Streiff (Alpine horn and trumpet). They began collaborating in 1995 and were soon noticed for successfully bridging the gap between the old and the new.

⊚ **Schnee** (Röhrender Hirsch, Switzerland).

This 1997 release is their second album, recorded in the wonderful acoustic of Olsberg abbey. "Snow" features spectacular vocal effects – yodel related and overtone singing – and moving and fascinating contributions from accordion, bandoneon and alphorns.

Well-Buam

An off-spring of Biermösl Blosn, this eight or nine-piece band is led by the powerful trumpet tones of Christoph Well. Famous for their lively and eccentric versions of Bavarian dance classics with clarinets, brass, accordion and bass.

 Sautanz
(Trikont, Germany).

A live album complete with chatter and foot stomping. Great fun and highly recommended, whether you have your own lederhosen or not.

⊚ **Boarischer Tanzbodn** (Trikont, Germany).

An equally good second volume, including Ravel's Bolero as "Flaschlwischabolero" (Wipe-the-bottle bolero).

Bavarian Dancefloor
Boarischer Tanzbodn
Live mit den Well-Buam

Zapf'nstreich

Hammer dulcimer virtuoso Rudi Zapf has been a key player in the Bavarian revival movement for many years. He is not only an excellent musician but also the organiser of the International Hammer Dulcimer Festival, which takes place every two years in Munich featuring music from all around the world. The 'string' ingredient in his new band Zapf'nstreich is guitarist Wolfgang Neumann.

⊚ **MCMXCVI** (Pantaleon Records, Germany).

This is the first record by Zapf's latest band. The 'hammer dulcimer king' focuses mainly on new adaptions of alpine string music played on harp, hammered dulcimer and electric guitar, but also includes pieces from other parts of the world.

Trikont Records are distributed in Britain by Klang, Clonan House, Midgehole Road, Hebden Bridge HX7 7AA; ☎/fax: 44 (0)1422 842212.

Austria

soul music of old Vienna

Viennese music is not all Strauss waltzes, Mozart arias and Beethoven symphonies. The Austrian capital on the Danube, once one of the world's greatest political and cultural powerhouses, is the home of a particular brand of urban folk music which developed in the nineteenth century and continues today. Schrammelmusik, as **Christoph Wagner** explains, is still just about alive and kicking.

Once a week in a charmless modern restaurant in a suburb of Vienna, the atmosphere is transformed as **Kurt Girk** croons the traditional Viennese songs – *Wienalied*. Girk, looking like an Austrian Yves Montand, is one of the few singers left who celebrate the city's folk music heritage. The audience gathers round the tables, washing down *wiener-schnitzel* and dumplings with large glasses of local wine, and as the evening draws on, Kurt Girk carefully removes his jacket and tie, and rolls up his sleeves, before signalling to his accordion player – "When you're ready, bandmaster." A heartbreaking song follows, and he underlines the pathos with dramatic gestures. "To sing a Viennese song you don't need a voice, you need a soul!" he says and asks the small audience to join in. **Schrammelmusik** is the proof of Vienna's wistful and melancholy heart. These half-forgotten songs from the past are still in high demand, and for 70 schillings Girk will sing any one of them. He has known them all by heart since he was a boy.

Elsewhere, in a busy suburban wine bar, where people are eating at long wooden tables, two different musicians are also keeping the tradition alive. The duet of **Karl Hodina** and **Edi Reiser** play their way from table to table throughout the evening. Hodina, in his early sixties, is one of the old masters of the accordion – which was invented in Vienna in 1829 – while Reiser plays a special kind of Viennese guitar with a double neck. They play instrumental dances and waltzes in the old fashioned way, slowing down in particular passages to change the dynamics, before dramatically speeding up again, to accompany their perfect harmony singing.

Occasionally a long-haired, bearded man in a hat can be seen here listening. **Roland Neuwirth** is from a younger generation but is respected as a unique figure on the traditional music scene of Vienna. His acoustic quintet, **Die Extremschrammeln**, with a traditional line-up of accordion, two violins, contra guitar and vocals, stretches the tradition to its limits, adding blues chords and soul grooves.

CHRISTIAN POTZMANN

Roland Neuwirth

Schrammel Band, early twentieth century

Schrammel Roots

Although purists protest, Neuwirth is true to the tradition of Viennese folk music, which has evolved from a clash of musical styles. It emerged as a result of the industrial age, when tens of thousands of people from rural Austria, the Alps, Hungary, Bohemia, Moravia and Slovenia poured into the slums of the fast-growing capital of the Austrian-Hungarian empire, transforming it within a few decades into a multicultural metropolis. It soon developed its own musical language. Polkas, Gypsy melodies, tunes from the Balkans, rural Alpine yodels and dances mingled with Viennese waltzes, ländlers and string quartets to create an exciting new style.

The key event in the city's folk music tradition was in 1878 when **Johann** (1850-93) and **Josef Schrammel** (1852–1895) formed a trio with bass guitarist Anton Strohmayer. They called it D'Nussdorfer after the Viennese wine suburb where they performed. The two brothers became so famous that their name was given to the whole genre. Schrammelmusik was born

Before long, the style settled into a regular quartet form, with the addition of a small G-clarinet (played by folk-clarinetist Georg Dänzer in the Schrammels' original band), sometimes replaced by an accordion. In the 1880s and 90s, Schrammel quartets emerged all over Austria and over the border in the Alpine regions of southern Germany.

Neuwirth and the New Wave

As a young man Roland Neuwirth was not interested in Schrammelmusik at all. He wanted to be a blues singer, and it was only when he realised that the Danube could never be the Mississippi, that he discovered the "Viennese Blues" on his own doorstep. As he searched for his city's musical roots, he discovered similarities with the history of the blues. Schrammelmusik has strong links with the red light district of Old Vienna, where love songs and murder ballads were sung in taverns and brothels.

Neuwirth first mixed the Mississippi and Danube blues together but later started more radical experiments, adding electric guitars and drums to create the **Danube New Wave**. It was only in the 1980s that he returned to the acoustic format, aiming to sound as authentic as possible, only adding new ingredients which seemed to fit naturally.

He rehearsed with two violin players for many weeks to achieve the classic Viennese timbre of slow vibrato. His accordion player Walter Soyka, who plays one of the famous squeeze boxes built in the workshop of Fritz Budowitz more than a century ago, knows the secret of achieving the right sound. To soften the tone of the instrument the old players used to put a page of newspaper inside it, but not any page would do the job. It had to be page seven of the tabloid *Die Kronenzeitung* – with the pin-up girl – as only something round and soft would guarantee the velvet tone. For Neuwirth, the lyrics are as important as the music. He is a poet in his own right, exploring in words the cracks in modern day life and showing the grin of death behind the charming face of Vienna.

When Neuwirth and his musicians want to get away from the present day, they perform under the name of **Herzton-Schrammeln**, playing instrumentals from the repertoire of legendary ensembles such as the Original Lammer Quartett, the Butschetty Quartett and the Strohmayer Quartett playing before the First World War. Herzton-Schrammeln found their pieces on old 78s and transcribed them onto sheet music, but that's the easy part. The real challenge is to perform them as well as the old masters did. "Simply to play music the way the Schrammel Brothers did is a lifelong job", Neuwirth reflects. "The Schrammel Brothers lived at a time when the tradition of popular Viennese music had reached its peak and they even counted the famous Johann Strauss among their friends and patrons. The line up of two violins, clarinet or accordion and bass guitar existed before, but the Schrammel Brothers turned it into a small orchestra", explains Alfred Pfleger, and as he slides into one of the melodies on his violin, the Viennese sound of the last century is alive again.

discography

❯ See also the features on Alpine music (p.7) and German folk (p.114).

Compilations

⊚ Wien: Volksmusik: Rare Schellacks 1906–1937 (Trikont, Germany).

A superb historical collection featuring the main singers and ensembles of Vienna some 70 years ago. Performing the characteristic repertoire from the heurigen (wine bars) which has almost disappeared. Soulful songs with passion – Danube blues!

⊚ Die besten Schrammeln Instrumental (Trikont, Germany).

Compiled by Roland Neuwirth, this is a superb collection of rare instrumentals by the great masters of the genre. In a recording from early this century you can even hear Anton Strohmayer who was guitarist in the original Schrammel Brothers trio. Real star dust!

Artists

Roland Neuwirth

The 'Schrammel King' of contemporary Viennese folk music works with his four-piece progressive Die Extremschrammeln and its offshoot Herzton-Schrammeln. The aim with the latter was to recreate Schrammelmusik as authentically as possible.

HERZTON-SCHRAMMELN

⊙ Herzton-Schrammeln (Ariola, Austria).

After years of research and practice Neuwirth's group have achieved the same elegance and sensitivity as the originals – a couple of tracks feature the same numbers as the Trikont compilation opposite for comparison. More than a dozen standards (including Josef Schrammel's "Weana Gmüath" and Anton Strohmayer's "Slibowitz Tanz") played here faultlessly. Musicians include Alfred Pfleger (violin), Manfred Kammerhofer (violin), Walther Soyka (nineteenth-century chromatic accordion) and Roland Neuwirth on contra guitar.

DIE EXTREMSCHRAMMELN

⊙ Essig & Öl (WEA/Warners, Austria).

Die Extremschrammeln at the height of their art on this recording from 1994. Songs with the expressive harmony singing of Neuwirth himself and Mizzi Moravec alternate with fine instrumental dances where the schmalz of the twin violins mingles perfectly with the colours of the accordion. Not as extreme as the name of the band suggests! Just extremely good!

Thalia-Schrammeln

Harald Hümer and Reinhold Rung (violins), Gerald Grünbacher (G-clarinet) and Heinz Hromada (Bass guitar) are graduates from the Vienna MusikHochschule and are dedicated to the original, unsentimentalised sound of the original Schrammel line-up with G-clarinet instead of accordion.

⊙ Music from Old Vienna (Naxos, Hong Kong).

Stylishly played music by the Schrammel brothers and several other composers in the genre. The piercing G-clarinet sound lends it a special character.

The Baltic States

singing revolutions

The characteristic Baltic singing festivals – hugely popular events – played a major role in expressing the national identities of Estonia, Latvia and Lithuania during their move to independence. Now there are increasing signs of interest in their other musical traditions, many of which draw on ancient ways of making and hearing music. **Andrew Cronshaw** assesses the state of play.

At the beginning of the 1920s, after much suffering in the First World War succeeded by independence struggles, all three Baltic states – **Estonia, Latvia** and **Lithuania** – escaped the imperial clutches of Russia and Germany. Freedom and peace didn't last long, however. In 1940 (1939 in Lithuania) Soviet troops broke the 1920 treaties and invaded, followed a year later by the German army, which was ousted in 1944 by the returning Soviets. In the process, hundreds of thousands of Baltic people were deported to Siberia or killed. Many more fled to the West, depleting the population of these three small countries by up to a third and swelling Baltic exile communities, particularly in North America. Repression continued after the war. On a single day in 1949 almost 43,000 Latvians were deported to the Gulags. As part of the Soviet Empire, the Baltic states were 'colonised' by large numbers of Russians.

On September 6, 1991, after another traumatic series of events which were variously bizarre, tragic, heroic and musical, the three countries regained independence. For each of them, the **mass singing festivals**, which had taken place since the nineteenth century and regularly involved tens of thousands, were a focus for national consciousness. In 1988, the year when the '**singing revolution**' began, 300,000 singers gathered at the *Eestimaa Laul* (Estonian Song) rally in Tallinn, at which Trivimi Velliste, the head of Eesti Muinsuskaitse Selts (the Estonian Heritage Society), voiced the demand for independence.

Ironically, it was Stalinist policy that had decreed Baltic folk music dead and ordered its replacement by mass song. Even in Soviet days, however, paeans to the merits of collectivisation were by no means the only form of song. As Latvian folk musician and ethnomusicologist Valdis Muktupāvels, who was regularly summoned by the KGB to explain his dubious activities with the patently not deceased folk tradition, puts it: "The Russians didn't speak Latvian, so we sang the songs they told us we had to sing and added a whole lot more that we wanted to sing!"

The language issue was crucial for Baltic culture. All three **Baltic languages** use Roman characters, rather than the Russian Cyrillic alphabet. Estonian is closely related to Finnish in the Finno-Ugrian linguistic group while Latvian and Lithuanian languages are related to each other and form a Baltic subgroup of the widespread Indo-European linguistic group.

There are considerable national and regional differences between (and within) the three countries. But they share in the continuity of culture around the Baltic (including Finland and the Russian Baltic areas) which reaches back thousands of years. All have folk song-poetry of the **runo-song** type and they have in common several traditional instruments, notably **Baltic psalteries** variously called *kantele*, *kannel*, *kokles* or *kanklės*. As a result of historical domination, however, the Baltic states manifest Germanic and Slavic cultural traits not found in Finland.

Though the inevitable changes in village life have meant that the context of much song and dance has disappeared, there's still a great deal to be found in living memory. In the 1960s folklore movements sprang up which encouraged field trips to the villages and performances by urban enthusiasts which attempted to reflect still-living musical traditions rather than than the idealised, classically-harmonised, folk-costumed approach of the soviet-style ensembles.

Now there is the freedom for individual expression, but though the economies are growing, incomes are small and there's little money available for CD recording or high-powered staging. Baltic roots music remains relatively low-profile and uncommercial.

ANDREW CRONSHAW

Setu singers

Estonia

Estonia's traditional culture, while distinct, has strong links with that of the linguistically and geographically close Finland, with **runo-songs** and its own variants of **Baltic zither**.

Runo-song

Estonian runo-song has the same basic form as the Finnish variety to which it is related: the line has eight beats, the melody rarely spans more than the first five notes of a diatonic scale and its short phrases tend to use descending patterns.

A large number of runo-song texts have been collected, largely from women, and thus offering a female point of view. They cover most aspects of life, including work, rituals, spells, ballads and mythical stories, and tend to a stoic sadness, or wry observation of life's realities, rather than extreme expressions of joy or love. The more ornamented **swing-songs** were sung while sitting on the big communal village swing whose movement made its own rhythmic demands.

Estonia's national epic **Kalevipoeg**, by folklorist **F. Reinhold Kreutzwald** (1803–1882), was published in the 1860s, paralleling folklorist Elias Lonnröt's creation from runo-song sources of Finland's *Kalevala*, first published in 1835. **Armas Launis'** collection of melodies of the runo-songs from which Kalevipoeg had been constructed was published in 1930.

By the early twentieth century runo-song was largely overtaken by more European forms of rhyming folksong with wider-spanning tunes and sometimes instrumental accompaniment. Nevertheless it survived in a few areas – notably in Setumaa, which straddles Estonia's Russian border, and also on the island of Kihnu and among Estonian-resident members of Ingria's repeatedly displaced population.

Setu Song

The songs of the **Setu people** have considerably influenced contemporary roots singers, both in Estonia and in Finland. There's been a recent revival in Setu culture and the speaking of its dialect. Several villages, such as Värska, Kosselka, Helbi, Obinitsa and Uusvada have established women's vocal groups that perform songs traditionally sung and danced while working or at social events, particularly the three-day wedding celebration. The eight-syllable runo pattern of these songs is often interrupted by extra syllables and refrains, and unlike other Estonian vocal traditions, they are sung polyphonically, the other singers taking the leader's line (the *torrõ*) and adding a lower part (the second torrõ), and a higher, penetrating single voice (the *killõ*) which often uses just two or three notes.

Kannels and Zithers

The old pastoral wind instruments such as animal horns, wooden birchbark-bound trumpet, willow overtone whistle and bagpipe have lost their traditional herding context but are used to some extent by present-day folk-rooted musicians. The fiddle, the ever-popular accordion and the long-bellowed concertina are used in the playing of couple-dance tunes, the most prevalent form of which is the **polka**.

Polkas also feature, together with older music, in the repertoire of the **kannel**, the Estonian version of the Baltic psaltery, which, though it tends to have six strings rather than five, is of the same basic design as Finland's *kantele* – a carved, wedge-shaped box, with strings passing direct from pegs to a single attaching bar. Players died out during the twentieth century but the instrument itself survived (if only to hang on the wall) amongst the many exiles in North America – where the small kannel has had something of a revival. In Estonia itself, the formation of Soviet-style folkloric ensembles involved the creation of an 'orchestral series' of bigger chromatic box-kannels. However, visits from contemporary Finnish kantele-players such as Hannu Saha and Antti Kettunen have helped to stimulate new interest in small kannels.

Setumaa has its own form of kannel, usually with a soundboard extended wing-like beyond the box rather like those found in eastern Latvia and parts of western Russia. This form is increasingly used, for example by Finnish kantele virtuoso Timo Väänänen. Leading Estonian kannel players include **Tuule Kann** and multi-instrumental ethnomusicologist **Igor Tõnurist**.

In Estonia, as in Latvia and Lithuania, folk players of a wide and ingenious range of **board-zither** or **chord zither** can be found. These aren't true kannels/kanteles but are closer in design to the factory-made zithers, autoharps and other domestic multi-stringed instruments made largely in German factories and sold across northern Europe and North America. The bowed lyre, **hiiu-kannel** (called a **jouhikko** in Finnish) was played until the twentieth century in the Swedish enclaves of Estonian islands (relics of Sweden's fifty-year rule over Estonia from 1660 until 1710), particularly Runö, and is finding a role again today in some of the modern folk bands.

Ensembles and Festivals

During the 1960s instructions were sent by Moscow to cultural organisers throughout the Soviet Union that supervised manifestations of genuine, living folk culture were to be encouraged, to demonstrate the government's support for the needs and expressions of the masses. In the Baltics, reluctant members of these "masses" were

researching these same living cultures, not in response to Moscow's wishes but in order to explore the distinctiveness of their own culture.

Performing ensembles fell into two groups: 'ethnographic' – which came from a particular area and specialised in local forms – and 'folkloric' – which drew on the whole country's traditions. The first of the 'ethnographic' type to appear in the more liberal climate of the 1960s was the Setu choir **Leiko** from Värska, formed in 1964. Of the 'folkloric' type, **Leigarid** (formed in 1969 to entertain tourists at Tallinn open-air museum) soon turned away from the colourful folkloric spectacle approach towards a more authentic style rooted in village traditions. Regional ethnographic performance groups were formed, too, as were young city-based ensembles such as **Leegajus** (led by **Igor Tõnurist**) and **Hellero**.

In 1985 the conference of CIOFF (Conseil International des Organisations de Festivals de Folklore et d'Arts Traditionelles) was held in Estonia, and in 1986 the **Viru säru** folk festival took place in Palmse. The **Baltica** festival, which moves each year to a different Baltic state, began in 1987, and Tallinn first hosted it in 1989. These growing performance opportunities stimulated more groups and further cultural developments including the opening of a folk music department at the Cultural College in **Viljandi** in 1990.

More fuel for revival, or for continuation of the traditional music in different 'post-traditional' circumstances, had been provided by the publication between 1956 and 1965 of the five volumes of **Eesti Rahvalaule Viisidega** (Estonian Folk Songs with Notations) edited by **Herbert Tampere**, who had been working on and publishing folk music since the 1930s and who at the end of the 60s also began a radio folklore programme. In 1969 appeared the first book of the eight-volume anthology of Estonian folk song texts *Eesti Rahvalaulud*. The first anthology of recordings on LP, **Eesti Rahvalaule ja Pillilugusid** (Estonian Folk Songs and Instrumental Music), was released in 1967 and a second followed in 1970.

Contemporary composers and musicians have gone to work on traditional sources. The choral folk and runo-song arrangements of composer **Veljo Tormis** became popular, having influence as far away as the Estonian community in Australia where the choir **Kiri-uu** added avant-gardist synths and samples to their own choral performances using many of Tormis' arrangements. Kiri-uu nowadays is no longer a choir but a vocal and technology duo comprising **Olev Muska** and **Coralie Joyce**.

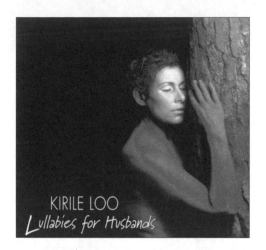

KIRILE LOO
Lullabies for Husbands

Singer **Kirile Loo** combines traditional runo-song influences and modern sensibilities. After two albums (on a German label - there are virtually no roots music CDs on Estonian labels) she has recently begun to take these approaches into live performance with a band fusing samples and traditional instruments.

Finally, and although not rooted in traditional music, a major Estonian contribution to modern music is the instrumental and choral work of one of the twentieth century's major composers and musical innovators, **Arvo Pärt**.

It is still a little early for Estonian roots performers to be making an impression on the world music touring and festival circuit, but at home the scene is growing. The annual **Viljandi** folk festival at the end of July attracts a young audience to see a variety of roots bands, and whether it's in Estonia, Latvia or Lithuania there's a substantial list of Estonian performers on the bill of **Baltica**.

Latvia

The land of amber has more Baltic zithers, drone-based singing, and a large body of traditional song-poetry – **dainas** – with strong pre-Christian symbolism and a lack of heroes.

The Daina

The Latvian **daina** is a short song of just one or two stanzas, one or two lines long, without rhyme, and largely in the same four-footed trochaic metre as runo-songs. Dainas feature mythological subjects and most aspects of village life, but the stories and heroic exploits described in many countries' folksongs are notably absent.

The sun is a dominant image, often personified as **Saule**, and her daily course across the sky and through the year is linked metaphorically with human life. While the sun is female, **Mēness**, the moon, is male, and a frequent song theme is courtship between them or other celestial figures such as the twin sons of Dievs (God) and the daughter of the sun. The solstices were traditional occasions for celebration – in particular **Jāni** (midsummer) – whose central figure was Janis, the archetypal vigorous, potent male with strong phallic associations. As the *ligotne* (midsummer song) "Jana Daudzinajums" describes him:

> Oh Janis, the son of Dievs,
>   what an erect steed you have
> The spurs are glittering through forests,
>   the hat above trees
> Janis was riding all the year
>   and has arrived on the Jani eve;
> Sister, go and open the gate, and let Janis in

(Translation by Valdis Muktupāvels)

The major collection of dainas was made by **Krišjānis Barons** (1835-1923); the six volumes of his *Latvju Dainas* were published between 1894 and 1915, and contain about 300,000 texts.

In keeping with other regions of the Baltics, newer song-forms spread during the nineteenth century, when chordal, fixed-scale instruments – such as the accordion – arrived. Thus **zinge** is a singing style with a strong German influence. The older forms remained, however: **dziesma** means a song having a definite melody, while **balss** means 'voice' or 'speech' and has no clearly defined melody, changing with the rhythm of the words. Balss was the style used in calendar celebrations as well as during work. It usually follows a three-voice form: the leader sings a couple of stanzas of a daina, then the others repeat them. In some regions these repetitions are sung over a vocal drone – a distinctive feature not found elsewhere in the Baltics but still a living tradition in some parts of Latvia.

Kokles and Citara

For village dance music and song tunes (*sadzīves* music), the traditional Latvian instruments include bagpipe, goat horn, whistles and rattle-stick, and more recently fiddle and various accordions. But as elsewhere in the Baltic, it is the zither that is dominant.

The Latvian Baltic zither is called the **kokle** or **kokles**, and in its traditional form it has between five and twelve strings. It is seen as a national symbol, and as elsewhere in the Baltics larger, box-built instruments were developed for use in Soviet-style folkloric ensembles. These, fitted with screw-in legs and often ornamented with a central jewel of the locally abundant amber, are attractive in appearance and ensemble sound, but not very responsive as instruments, with musicians displaying a rather stiff playing style based on a Western classical approach.

Renewed interest in the traditional smaller carved kokles began during the folklore movement of the 1970s. The instrument survived in the living tradition of only a few areas: the Catholic enclaves of Kurzeme in western Latvia and Latgale in the east. The strongest influence in this revival was **Jānis Porikis**, who made a couple of hundred kokles and organised workshops and performances. **Valdis Muktupāvels**, Latvia's leading player, learned the style of the Suiti region from Porikis, and has gone on to champion the instrument.

Muktupāvels normally plays a nine-string kokles of the type found in eastern Latvia – with a 'wing' extension of the soundboard beyond the soundbox and pegs. Drones occur in Latvian singing, and it's usual to tune the lowest string of a kokles to a drone a fourth below the key note. There are several regional playing styles involving plucking or strumming and damping, including – as in some Estonian styles – that of resting the fingers of the left hand on the soundboard between the strings and moving them from side to side, damping sets of strings alternately to leave the rest ringing as chords while strumming with the other hand.

In North America the small kokle has become the main instrument of Latvian-American cultural groups. While in Latvia there's no dominant design - the instruments were home-made and each maker-player put in individual features - most of these American kokles are of a single pattern, wingless and with almost identical soundboard decoration, probably because buyers from the handful of North American makers want an instrument identical to the one they've seen played at Latvian-American gatherings.

A wide variety of interesting designs of **citara** (chord-zither) are still in use in Latvia. Most have large numbers of strings, some or all of which are tuned as ready-made chords. These are not principally related to Baltic psalteries but rather to the mostly German factory-made chord-zithers and autoharps sold since the nineteenth century across Europe and North America. Individual Baltic makers have made ingenious modifications, some resulting in very big instruments and a few that are cylinder-shaped. There are also hybrid forms between citara and kokles, known as **citarkokles**.

In the eastern province of Latgale, **hammered dulcimers** have been played since the early nineteenth century, a borrowing from nearby Belarus.

Performers

The leading groups performing traditional music in Latvia are **Iļģi** (formed in 1981), **Grodi** and **Rasa** (both formed in the late 1980s as Soviet rule was crumbling), and **Auri** (formed in 1991 and led by Māris Jansons). Rasa's **Valdis Muktupāvels** also performs solo as a vocalist and kokles and bagpipe player. Popular Latvian rock band **Jauns Mēness** (New Moon) has a distinct folk music component, featuring Iļģi members Maris Muktupāvels (Valdis' brother) and Ilga Reizniece, and Jauns Mēness leader Ainars Mielavs and his UPE record label are taking a leading role in the evolution and popularisation of new Latvian rooted music.

The Baltica Festival

The **Baltica International Folklore Festival** is held each July in rotation by Estonia, Latvia or Lithuania. It sponsors Baltic folk music, dance and customs and customarily attracts over 100 groups from the host nation, and a dozen or so from Estonia, Lithuania, Scandinavia, Austria, Russia and Belarus.

Baltica was first held in 1987 in Vilnius, Lithuania. On 5th April 1989 the official 'Folklore Association Baltica' was founded and the Latvians used the occasion to raise their national flag for the first time in forty years. The festival gathered momentum during the 'national awakening' which led to the independence of the Baltic states.

When the Festival last took place in Riga (in 1997), music was played in a variety of venues, from outdoor concerts in stadiums to intimate acoustic sessions in galleries and museums. A procession through the old town heralded the start of the event and the streets were suddenly flooded with people wearing crowns of oak leaves and flowers. The Riga group Grodi, often at the centre of such events, led the way playing bagpipes (dudas) and drums (bungas). Watched by the crowds, they passed specially erected 'gates of fire' and 'gates of stone' (representing different stages of human life) before stopping to silently place flowers at the foot of the Freedom Monument.

"Grodi' & 'Vilki'

The festival continued in Riga all week, and on some days musicians would make excursions to small towns and villages in the Latvian countryside to give non-city dwellers an opportunity to sample the 'Baltica experience'. In one particularly beautiful valley, a ceremonial bonfire was lit and hundreds of people joined together to sing songs of the summer solstice (ligotnes). The PA system was unobtrusive and the audience only too happy to join in with the singing, not to mention the seemingly compulsory consumption of rye bread, cheese and beer.

If you visit a Baltica festival, try to catch the ethnographic ensembles, such as the famous Latvian groups Suitu Šievas or Gudenieku Suiti, comprised mostly of the older generations. While their folk costumes and heavy bronze and amber jewelry may only be worn for special occasions like these, their music is probably the most true and unaffected you will find. These people, some now in their eighties, are the direct inheritors of Latvian folk song and have known the repertoire since childhood. They are said to be able to select the perfect song for any occasion. Some songs, particularly those associated with weddings, are competitive and improvised, with two women taking turns to outwit the other, while others provide an accompanying vocal drone. For those unfamiliar with the language, the jokes might be lost, but the roars of laughter indicate that these women have a wicked sense of humour.

In contrast to the ethnographic ensembles, the Riga festival also included music from modern Riga-based folk groups – a younger generation exploring the song and dance of their ancestors and bringing new life to the music through their own creativity. This has become known as 'post-folklore' in Latvia – a term invented by the group Iļģi when they felt they could no longer describe their music as 'folk'. Nonetheless, it was this group who, long after their concert had officially finished, kept everyone dancing and singing into the early hours.

Andris Kapusts, Artistic Director of the Latvian branch of the festival, believes that the aim of the event is to present and preserve the national heritage. *Baltica* certainly does that, although no one is pretending that people wander around in elaborate costumes performing ancient rituals all year round. It is a display of what the Baltic states are rightly proud of, and an opportunity for others to discover more about Baltic folklore and tradition. As the leader of one group pointed out: "If only rock'n'roll is danced around the world, we will soon disappear as a nation."

Baltica returns to Riga in 2000.

Leah Zakss

Lithuania

The largest Baltic state has a notably rich variety of folk forms, including layered **polyphonic music**, sung or played on reed instruments, flutes and – in common with its neighbours to the north – Baltic zithers.

Song

Thousands of Lithuanian traditional songs – **dainos** – have been collected. They deal with every aspect of life, and wedding and love songs feature particularly prominently. Some would be passed on as well-known songs, but others, such as lullabies, would be varied or improvised to suit the occasion. In the early twentieth century many women who were predominantly the creators and carriers of songs had repertoires of a hundred or more songs.

Singing can be solo or in a group, in unison or in parallel chords of thirds, fourths or fifths. Aukštaitija, Lithuania's northeastern region, has a distinctive and well-known tradition of polyphonic songs, **sutartinės**, whose melody and form are also transferred to instrumental music. They are duophonic – two voices, or groups of voices in harmony. In the case of **dvejinės** (by twos) and **keturinės** (by fours) two harmonising lines are sung together, then they stop and are replaced by a second group of singers and two different harmonisations, while in **trejinės** three parts overlap, two at a time, as in a canon. The word stresses create a syncopating internal rhythm.

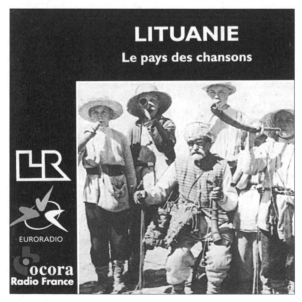

Instruments

There is a relatively large range of Lithuanian traditional instruments. The basic form of the Lithuanian version of Baltic zither, the **kanklės**, differs regionally in playing style and in the number of strings which can be anywhere between five and twelve. The repertoire of the traditional kankles consisted of old style material such as sutartines and more modern dance tunes such as polkas, waltzes and quadrilles. A 'concert series' of large many-stringed box kankles was devised for the Soviet-style ensembles.

Whereas previously the old round dances (*rateliai*) were traditionally accompanied by singing only, during the nineteenth and twentieth centuries instrumental ensembles commonly played the newer dance forms. Instrumental groups playing kankles and *lamzdeliai* (wooden or bark whistles) existed as far back as the sixteenth century. Later the fiddle and three-stringed bass *basetle* joined them, and in the nineteenth and early twentieth century accordions, bandoneons, concertinas, Petersburg accordions and harmonicas, mandolins, balalaikas, guitars, modern clarinets and cornets. During the Soviet era, dressed-up ensembles emerged using box kankles and *birbynės* (folk clarinets – they used the developed form which is a mellow-sounding thick tube with a cowhorn bell). These groups actually made quite a pleasant sound, not so different from a disciplined village band, but they were often used, to the annoyance of those searching out the 'real thing', in classically influenced arrangements to accompany choral singing of harmonised and denatured so–called sutartinės with all their dissonances smoothed out.

In the northeast, tunes of the sutartinó type were played on *skudučiai* – rather like dismantled pan-pipes, played by a group of men. The same type of tune was played by five-piece sets of birchbark-bound wooden trumpets (*ragai*), or alternatively, by pairs of the straighter, longer *daudytės*; each of the latter could produce up to five natural harmonics, so only two daudytės were needed for a set.

Other wind instruments include *švilpas* (overtone whistle), goat-horns, and *sekminiu ragelis* (a single–drone bagpipe). Percussion instruments include tabalas (a flat piece of wood hung and hit like a gong) and drums. An unusual stringed instrument is the *pūslinė* – a musical bow with an inflated pig's bladder resonator containing a rattling handful of dried peas.

Performers

As the social structure changed, and Sovietization altered Lithuanian society from the outside, the old ways of music lost much of their role. Tradition moved to post-traditional, or 'secondary folklore', with material collected from those who remembered the old ways converted to a form considered suitable for performance to an audience.

The first Lithuanian folklore ensembles were formed around the beginning of the twentieth century. One of them, formed in 1906 and still existing, is the **Skriaudžiai kanklės ensemble**. Subsequently ethnographic plays such as **The Kupiskenai Wedding** were staged. While these tried to reflect genuine village life, concert ensembles worked on the premise that the rough old folk songs needed sprucing up.

A choral movement gathered momentum, resulting in the huge song festivals, **Dainu Sventes**. The first of these was held in 1924, and then every five years during the Soviet period. As well as choirs, professional concert folk ensembles such as **Lietuva**, formed in 1940, appeared at such events. 'Modernised' folk instruments were created, and traditional dress was formalised into national costume.

While this was an acceptable form of national expression within the Soviet regime, a back-to-the-villages folklore movement began during the 1960s, spurred on later in the decade by the Prague Spring events in Czechoslovakia. Rasa (the summer solstice) and other Baltic pagan events were publicly celebrated despite persecution by the KGB. **Folklore ensembles** sprang up in towns and cities, and the village musicians from whom they collected formed performing units themselves, usually known as 'ethnographic ensembles'. There were folklore camps and competitions. The first republic-wide ensemble competition *Ant marių krantelio* (On the Sea Shore) occured in the 1980s at Rumsiskes attracting a thousand contestants. The annual *Skamba skamba kankliai* in Vilnius' old town began in 1975, and Kaunas hosted *Atataria trimitai*. The first **Baltica** International Folklore Festival, which moves between the Baltic states each year, took place in 1987 in Vilnius.

discography

Compilations

◉ **Voix des pays Baltes – Chants traditionnels de Lettonie, Lituanie, Estonie** (Inedit, France).

Ethnographic vocal recordings of (mainly) older women and ensembles singing the traditional repertoire. Work songs, calendar and family celebrations, some recorded back in the 1930s, including Lithuanian sutartinės, etc. The recordings come from Latvian and Lithuanian Radio, plus a recording of the Leiko Ensemble from a Paris performance in 1992.

Estonia

Compilations

◉ **The Folk Music of Estonia** (Melodiya, USSR).

Double LP released in 1986 of recordings from the Kreutzwald Literary Museum of the Estonian Academy of Sciences. 44 tracks of recordings of traditional instruments, including horn, pipe, shepherds' trumpet, fiddle, Jew's harp, hiiu kannel, concertina and song from around Estonia including Setu-land.

◉ **Setu Songs** (Mipu, Finland).

Setu women's singing groups from villages of Helbi, Kosselka, Obinitsa, Uusvada, Meremäe and the Leiko group from Värska, recorded in situ and in Helsinki.

Artists

Kirile Loo

Born in the northern Estonian village of Varinurme, singer Kirile Loo studied at Tallinn school of music. Promoted in CD blurbs as some sort of Baltic witch-spirit, she's nevertheless strong and interesting, moving recently and promisingly into live performance with a band combining sound modules and traditional instruments.

◉ **Saatus (Fate)** (Erdenklang, Germany; Alula, US).

Runo-song based material in sparse, atmospheric settings with traditional instruments (kannel, bagpipe, reed-pipe, straw whistle, Jew's harp) plus keyboards and guitar, arranged by Peeter Vähi.

🔘 **Lullabies for Husbands** (Erdenklang, Germany).

Loo's excellent 1999 album, with more developments of traditional lyrics and melodic forms, in collaboration with Tiit Kikas, who plays all the instruments, acoustic and electronic.

Veljo Tormis

Influential composer of choral arrangements of Estonian folk songs.

◉ **Forgotten Peoples** (ECM, Germany).

Critically acclaimed double CD of six Tormis compositions based on the music of Livonian, Votic, Izhorian and Karelian Finno-Ugrian peoples, sung by the Estonian Philharmonic Chamber Choir.

Ummamuudu

Ummamuudu are an electric folk-rock band performing original and traditional material.

◉ **Ummaleelo** (Ummamuudu, Estonia).

This five-track EP is the band's most recent (1997) release. It features traditional tunes arranged for the band together with Setu choir Leelonaase.

Latvia

Compilations

 Beyond the River: Seasonal Songs of Latvia (EMI Hemisphere, UK).

A credible and widely available introduction to the leading contemporary Latvian roots groups. 17 tracks of Auri, Iļģi, Grodi and Rasa.

Artists

Iļģi

This leading Latvian band explore traditional repertoire and create new material using largely traditional instrumentation – recently in electrified form. Their fiddler Ilga Reizniece and kokles, stabule and bagpipe player Māris Muktupāvels also form the folk-music component of Jauns Mēness (see below).

◎ **Riti** (Labvakar, Latvia).

An acoustic album featuring songs about the symbolic myths of sun and moon, and marriage.

◎ **Saules Meita** (UPE, Latvia).

This 1998 album saw a move to a more electrified approach, and some lineup changes, but still with strong attachment to traditional styles and instruments.

Jauns Mēness

This very popular pop-rock band are a Latvian equivalent of Scotland's Runrig. They are led by singer Ainars Mielavs, a dynamic figure both on stage and as head of UPE records, fast emerging as the focus of Latvian roots music recordings. The band are often accompanied live by a large dance troupe.

◎ **Dzivotajs** (UPE, Latvia).

The group's most recent (1998) album has a mainstream rock approach, spiced by Aigars Voitiskis' mandolin and the traditional instruments of Iļģi's Ilga Reizniece and Maris Muktupāvels.

Ugis Praulins

Programmer, producer, singer, keyboard, kokles and flute player Praulins combines traditional music with current studio technology.

 Paganu Gadagramata (UPE, Latvia).

Material from the folk song collections of Emilis Melngailis, in very sympathetic atmospheric settings featuring Jauns Mēness guitarist Gints Sola and the voices and traditional instruments of Ilga Reizniece and Maris Muktupāvels. Released in 1999, it's an impressive start to the 'Latvian Folk Music Collection' from Ainars Mielavs' UPE label.

Rasa Ensemble

A group led by Valdis Muktupāvels, singing and playing Latvian traditional music exclusively on traditional instruments – kokles, bagpipes, violin, flutes, reeds, drums, rattles – while incorporating interpretative ideas from other traditions.

◎ **Latvia: Music of Solar Rites** (Inedit, France).

Traditional songs, both polyphonic (with vocal drones) and monophonic, for summer and winter solstices, weddings, funerals, working and drinking, plus instrumentals including a kokles solo and dance music.

Lithuania

Compilations

◎ **Lithuanian Folk Music** (33 Records, Lithuania).

46 recordings from 1930s to 1980s of work, ritual, wedding, nature, children's, historical and war songs, and instrumental music – with extensive English notes.

◎ **Lituanie: Le Pays Des Chansons** (Ocora, France).

Excellent, varied collection of 35 traditional songs and instrumentals, including horn, kanklés and sutartinés, recorded for Lithuanian Radio between 1958 and 1990. Notes in French and English.

Artists

Ethnomusic Ensemble Ula

Folk music group using violin, bandoneon, whistles, flute, harp, wooden trumpets and stringed instruments.

◎ **Ula** (Ula, Lithuania).

34 tracks of instrumentals and songs.

Sutarus

This five-strong group was formed in 1988 by musicians from the Lithuanian Folklore Theatre. They specialise in reviving ancient instruments and repertoire.

 Call of the Ancestors (Lituanus, Lithuania).

A fascinating survey of ancient and modern Lithuanian folk music. 38 tracks including the extraordinary sound of vocal and instrumental sutartinés, several kankles tracks, horns, flutes, pipes, the pūslinė musical bow and polkas and other dance tunes for fiddle, accordion, harmonica and basetle.

Belgium

flemish, walloon and global fusion

Belgium lies at the point in Europe where Latin and Germanic cultures converge: the north is Flemish and its 5.5 million inhabitants speak Dutch while in the south 4.5 million Walloons speak French. The capital, Brussels, is bilingual but predominantly French-speaking, and in the east a minority speak German. Strange then, that Belgium's most famous world music group, Zap Mama, is African – or to be more precise, draws on the band's dual Belgian and Congolese heritage. But as everywhere in western Europe, the twentieth century has seen local cultures undervalued. Broadcaster and folk singer, **Paul Rans** tells the story.

Flanders

As flautist and researcher **Wim Bosmans**, of the folk group **Jan Smed**, demonstrated on the group's latest CD *Airekes* (Tunes), many traditional Belgian tunes have migrated from one part of the country to another and are now shared not only by Flanders and Wallonia but by various European countries, their real origins unknown. Some are even in the Classical mainstream, having been adopted by nineteenth-century opera composers. The repertoire, which also has distinct Flemish and Walloon traditions, began to decline early in the twentieth century but much survives due to the efforts of folk-song and dance-tune collectors of the 1900s.

the most outstanding singer in Flanders – and **Hubert Boone**, who besides his fieldwork – collecting, for example, from village brass bands or the old guilds' instrumental ensembles – also led the traditional music group **De Vlier** and is now leader of the **Brabants Volksorkest**. During the early 1970s **Herman Dewit** with his group **'t Kliekske** (Little Clique/Small Band), went on a legendary trip around Flanders with horse and cart, performing in villages and towns, and at the same time collecting songs and tunes from older people.

At the end of the 1960s and during the early 70s there was also a movement to modernise traditional music, with Wannes Van de Velde singing his own urban songs in his native Antwerp dialect, as well as traditional ones. Van de Velde's songs are some of the best ever written in Flanders. They are musically and lyrically innovative, yet rooted in tradition, drawing on traditional elements from Flanders but also on those of other European countries, especially Greece and Spain, and even on contemporary classical music. Wannes also works in theatre and is an excellent guitarist who regularly accompanies the imaginative flamenco singer **Amparo Cortés**, born in Seville but now living in Brussels.

MARC MASSCHELEIN / SOFAM

Wannes Van de Velde

Interest in folk music was rekindled in the 1960s by people such as **Wannes Van de Velde** – still

Ghent-born sculptor and singer **Walter de Buck** revived many of the old Ghent broadside ballads and added his own, meanwhile initiating the *Gentse Feesten* – street parties which have since evolved into a two-week summer festival.

Rum was a group which first took Flemish folk (in a blend of ballads and dance-songs, exciting instrumentals and humorous presentation) across the language border into Wallonia and then around Europe from 1969 to 1978 when the group finally split up. Singer/guitsrist Dirk Van Esbroeck and guitarist Juan Masondo continued Rum in a different format for a number of years. Fiddler and tenor-guitarist Wiet Van de Leest then started the contemporary folk group **Madou** with singer Vera Coomans.

Hubert Boone's **Brabants Volksorkest** has also travelled widely and has taken its mainly nineteenth-century traditional repertoire from Flanders to Siberia, and from Cuba to Africa. The orchestra specialises in dance and serenade music of the Brabant and the Campine region: structured melodies, harmonised in a style which flourished in the nineteenth and early twentieth centuries. The repertoire is partly based on written sources and partly on Boone's own fieldwork. This is no longer limited to Flanders, and in recent years he has released several CDs (on Auvidis) with field recordings from the Ukraine, Russia, Belarus and Armenia.

The 1980s were not very propitious for folk music. Although Wannes Van de Velde, 't Kliekske and the Brabants Volksorkest kept the flame burning, and the folk-rock band **Kadril** continued to widen its own audience, folk music of any kind was considered unfashionable. Herman Dewit didn't worry too much about fashion and continued to perform, making bagpipes, fifes and hurdy-gurdies and organising annual summer courses in Gooik, West of Brussels. The latter were, and still are, very successful events which began to bear fruit in the mid-1990s with young groups emerging such as **Marc Hauman & De Moeite**, **Ambrozijn**, **Fluxus** and **Laïs**.

The quality of these groups' playing and singing bodes well for the future. The three girl singers of Laïs, for example, give impressive renderings of traditional as well as new songs in fine unaccompanied harmonies, and from time to time join forces with the folk-rock group **Kadril**, their vocals taking on a rawer edge in the company of electric guitars, drums and acoustic bagpipes. Unaccompanied harmony singing is also **Water & Wijn**'s trademark, a dozen singers – including Wannes Van de Velde and Marc Hauman – who love experimenting with style and technique.

Wallonia

In Wallonia the folk music revival has not been as strong, but old traditions such as fife and drum bands, fanfares (brass bands) and hunting-horn ensembles are still very much alive. Groups such as **Rue du Village** (Village Street) play lots of dance music for popular *bals* (barn dances) in a traditional vein, but not oblivious to what's happening elsewhere in the world.

MUSIQUE POPULAIRE DE LA BELGIQUE
VOLKSMUZIEK UIT BELGIË
Folk Music from Belgium

The latest Walloon band is **Coïncidence** which offers its own creations in a Gallic folk-rock idiom. Bagpipe maker **Remy Dubois** is also a fine performer who plays regularly with **Olle Geris** – a Flemish maker and player who was his apprentice and who has a particular gift for improvisation. Together they show that it's still possible for Flemings and Walloons to get on and enjoy playing each other's music. **Jean-Pierre Van Hees** is another fine bagpipe and musette player who was in the final incarnation of Rum and who can be heard in a variety of traditional music projects.

The adventurous and virtuoso fiddler, **Luc Pilartz**, (once in the successful, but now defunct, **Verviers Central**) is now part of the Belgian 'supergroup' **Panta Rhei**. This band combines folk, jazz and classical musicians to play music from all over Europe: feisty playing which always manages to reach the heart of the music. **Claude Flagel** is a French singer and hurdy-gurdy player whose repertoire spans many centuries of French and Walloon balladry. He has lived in Brussels for several decades and has worked with both Flemish and Walloon musicians. He also runs the **Fonti Musicali** label specialising in ethnic music from Wallonia to Congo-Kinshasa, Rwanda and Burundi.

Festivals

Dranouter Folk Festival

The **Dranouter Folk Festival** (usually the first week-end of August) has grown from its modest and intimate first outing (some 300 people) in 1975 to a gigantic three-day event attracting over 60,000 festival goers. The atmosphere is easygoing despite the huge numbers and many people go for that alone. Musically, the biggest stars don't always remember their roots, but the organisers do their utmost to cater for all tastes, from classic folk and ethnic to post-modern world music.

The Dranouter Festival also sponsors the traditional music *Feestival 2002* in Gooik (between Brussels and Ghent); an annual Jewish festival in Antwerp; and co-operates with a number of other musical events, including the CD label MAP.

The festival advertises widely, and has a site on the Internet: *www.folkdranouter.be*

e-mail: *mdeswarte@unicall.be*

☎ (32) 57 446 424; fax: 57 446 243

Sfinks Festival

For more than twenty years the **Sfinks Festival** (end of July beginning of August) has been looking at music from around the world. Each year it attracts some 45,000 people and offers traditional as well as contemporary music, ritual and trance music, acoustic and electronic sounds, hip hop, ethno-house – anything goes on the four different stages. Many top musicians also give workshops during the festival and are happy to just meet people informally to chat and talk about their culture and their music. Besides the concert stages *Sfinks* also has a Virtual Village with video and multimedia productions. As in Dranouter, a colourful market adds to the international atmosphere.

The *Sfinks* organisation's offices are also the seat of the European Forum of Worldwide Music Festivals (EFWMF) which represents 35 festivals in 15 countries and is possibly the biggest promoter of world music. Sfinks (*www.sfinks.be* ☎ (32) 3 455 6944).

Other Beligan festivals

Antilliaanse Feesten, Antwerp: music from the West-Indies: second weekend of August. ☎ (32) 3 314 3732.

Brosella, Brussels: second weekend of July. ☎ (32) 2 270 9856.

Brugges Festival, Bruges: second weekend of February. ☎ (32) 50 348 747.

Couleur Café, Brussels: last weekend of June. ☎ (32) 2 672 4912.

Gentse Feesten, Ghent: ten days during the second half of July. ☎(32) 9 225 3676.

International Jewish Music Festival, Antwerp: end November. ☎ (32) 57 446 923.

Open Tropen, Turnhout: music from the tropics: first weekend in July. ☎ (32) 14 420 961.

Zap Fusion

Belgium's main link with Africa lies in what is now again called the **Congo**, formerly Zaire and before that the Belgian Congo (1884–1960).

During the colonial era – and indeed, up until the 1980s – not much attention was paid to Congolese music, outside ethnomusic circles. However, immigrants, students and temporary visitors from Congo, Rwanda and Burundi have always performed their music in Brussels for themselves. The recent interest in World Music has ensured that some of those excellent musicians and singers have been able to reach wider audiences, and in **Zap Mama** (see box overleaf), Belgium has one of the most dynamic bands on the World Music scene.

The old Afro-Belgian links first bore fruit in the early 1980s with **Bula Sangoma**, a group where Flemish percussionist **Chris Joris** was joined by some brilliant Central-African musicians, such as singer/composer **Dieudonné Kabongo** (who finds inspiration in his Luba tradition), Rwandan singer **Cécile Kayirebwa** (who sings both traditional songs and her own compositions), and Congolese singer **Princesse Mansia M'Bila**, as well as by jazz musicians such as American sax player **John Ruocco**. Besides being a percussionist, Chris Joris also plays tenor sax and piano and is a jazz composer at ease with different music forms. He continues his explorations with African and other musicians today in ever-changing combinations.

Among the various immigrant communities of Belgium there have been some genuinely interesting fusions: **Dirk Van Esbroeck** grew up in Argentina and joined Rum soon after his return to Belgium. He later met bandoneon player **Alfredo Marcucci** and guitarist **Juan Masondo** and went on to form **Tango al Sur**. The group's repertoire includes original tangos, Argentinean music and their own compositions with lyrics in Dutch as well as Spanish.

Brussels-based Moroccan oud-player **Abid El Bahri** has joined forces with Flemish lutenist **Philippe Malfeyt** and Chinese pipa player **Hua**

Zap Mama: The Pygmy Connection

"I feel I can be a bridge between two cultures," says Zap Mama's leader **Marie Daulne**. True enough. Her group has proved to be a vibrant bridge between many cultures, stunning audiences all round the world.

Daulne's story is extraordinary. She was born in 1964 in what was then the Democratic Republic of the Congo (1960–71), but three weeks after her birth her Belgian father was killed in a rebellion and her mother took her children into the forest for eight months where they were protected by Pygmies. The Belgian Army airlifted the family to Belgium and she grew up in Brussels. There she teamed up with other Belgian-Africans and two white singers with a genuine feel for multi-culturalism. Drawing on Pygmy polyphony and yodel techniques, as well as other African and European vocal styles, they thrust their virtuoso five-strong female a cappella group on an unsuspecting world in 1989.

In their first eponymous 1991 album (called *Adventures in Afropea* in its incarnation on the Luaka Bop label) they explored all sorts of vocal sounds – squeals, grunts, pants, laughs, giggles, vocal percussion as well as warm velvety tones and harmonies. What's more they put together one hell of an energetic, inventive and polished stage show.

While the first album grew out of Daulne's experience with the Pygmies (although its musical influences were pretty wide), the second, *Sabsylma* (1994) took a more global viewpoint. "Before I spoke about the Pygmies and the people around them. Now I want to talk about the people around me. Some of the most rewarding travel I've done was just ringing my neighbours' doors. My Moroccan neighbour shared her Moroccan world. The Pakistani man at the grocery showed me Pakistan. That's what *Sabsylma* is about. I suggest that people dream and travel in their own cities by talking to their neighbours."

Zap Mama's latest album, *Seven*, brings their a cappella music into closer contact with modern Western life. There's a band and electronics, but Daulne still sees herself as a sort of global griotte bringing a power from an ancestral world: "A man in Mali told me that there are seven senses. Everyone has five, some can use their sixth, but not everyone has the seventh. It is the power to heal with music, calm with colour, to sooth the sick soul with harmony. He told me that I have this gift, and I know what I have to do with it."

Simon Broughton

Zap Mama

Xia to form **Luthomania**, a global trio of lute maniacs, strong on improvisation and offering an excellent roots salad.

Planet Flanders is the name of a CD which brings together a cross-section of musicians settled in Flanders during the past few decades. These include **Largo**: two Belgians and a Moroccan who produce a very contemporary sound; **Tam 'Echo 'Tam** comprising a French, a Moroccan, a Belgian-Guyanese and a Congolese voice in unaccompanied singing, carefully avoiding the Zap Mama sound; **Tezerdi**, a Turkish-Italian-Flemish combination with virtuoso saz, guitar and keyboards; **Zahava Seewald**, born from a Moroccan mother and a Polish father in the Jewish part of Antwerp and many more. All of these musicians are part of the increasingly multi-cultural landscape of Flanders and a second edition of *Planet Flanders*, stressing the relevance of these musicians in today's society, is on its way.

Despite the fact that officialdom does not make it easy for musicians to survive, the future looks fairly bright. An increasing number of concert organisers and festivals are interested in World Music and public radio is generally supportive. Besides the home-grown groups there is a constant flow of touring bands – from the most commercial type of world pop to the most authentically ethnic – performing to steadily increasing numbers of World Music converts.

discography

Flanders and Wallonia

Compilations

Belgique: Ballades, danses et chansons de Flandre et de Wallonie (Ocora, France).

Reissue of older BRTN/VRT Radio 3 recordings from 1952 to 1980 but still a fine selection of traditional performers representative of both Flanders and Wallonia, juxtaposing old field recordings and revival versions.

Flemish Folk Music 1997 (MAP, Belgium).

A double CD of the good, bad and the ugly ... with an emphasis on the good, including all the best-known groups in Flanders. Produced by the Dranouter Folk Festival and the Flemish Folk Music Guild who have provided an extensive booklet with a mine of information (in English!) on the bands, clubs, societies, festivals, concert organisers, instrument makers, museums, cafés et al. You name it, it's there.

Folk Music from Belgium (Auvidis Ethnic, France).

Good mix of authentic traditions and revival groups, all recently recorded by Hubert Boone, leader of the Brabants Volksorkest, field worker and curator of folk instruments at the Brussels Museum of Musical Instruments. Old traditional forms on this double CD include fife and tabor bands, hunting-horns in the Ardennes, accordion players, drummer bands in Antwerp and the famous carnival drums of the 'Gilles de Binche'. The revival groups include some of the best such as the Brabants Volksorkest, 't Kliekske, Polka Galop, Rue du Village and Kadril 'unplugged'.

Gentle Men (Irregular Records, UK).

The latest of the Passchendaele Peace Concerts, a double CD looking back on the Great War in Flanders' fields. This suite of folksongs about WW1 is an Anglo-Flemish co-operation centred around Robb Johnson's grandfathers during and after World War I. Excellent singing by Vera Coomans, Roy Bailey and Johnson himself, with effective instrumental support from Koen de Cauter's Golden Serenaders. The previous concerts, available on the No Masters and Map labels, are equally moving.

Artists

Brabants Volksorkest

The Brabant Folk Orchestra was founded in 1978 by Hubert Boone to revive the music from his own and others' field recordings and collections, as well as to make his contemporaries dance (and listen).

Crispijn (Auvidis Ethnic, France).

Dance music and instrumental traditions from the Flemish Brabant: waltzes, scottisches, polkas, quadrilles and contradanses played on flutes, clarinet, dulcimers, fiddles, double bass, bagpipes, accordion and percussion. Flemish but also European.

Laïs

'Laïs' means voice in Flemish – and also refers to medieval erotic minstrel songs: a good choice for this trio of fine Flemish women singers, Jorunn Bauweraerts, Nathalie Delcroix and Annelies Brosens.

Laïs (Wild Boar Music, Belgium).

The group's 1998 debut – a treat of Celtic-sounding vocal harmonies, with unintrusive backing from the band Kadril. The songs are mainly arrangements of traditional Flemish material, along with the odd number from Sinead O'Connor and Jacques Brel.

Panta Rhei

Fiddler and piper Luc Pilartz and flute/sax player Steve Houben and friends playing fiddle, cello, melodeon, guitar, bass and percussion. They found their roots in an old Heraclitus' saying "Panta rhei ..." (All things flow, nothing lasts forever).

European Music Today (Biz-Arts, Belgium).

Roots music from all over Europe brought together in short suites, linking East and West, North and South with great skill and ardour. Heartfelt music-making.

Wannes Van de Velde

The best-known voice of Flemish folk. Born in 1937 he has an encyclopaedic knowledge of tradition but has also written some of the best songs in Flanders.

De kleuren van de steden (Granota, Belgium).

'The colours of the cities' offers a selection of Wannes's own songs, inspired by urban life and life in general – often poetic, sometimes bitterly critical, sometimes funny. Modern arrangements by the late Walter Heynen for voice, flute, violin, double bass and guitar.

Fusion

Compilations

Planet Flanders (PAN Records, Netherlands).

An excellent collection including Largo, Princesse Mansia M'Bila (sings Congolese songs and plays the balafon), kora player N'Faly Kouyaté, Tam 'Echo 'Tam, Tezerdi, Zahava Seewald and music from north African and Arab roots.

Marockin' Stories (Music & Words, Netherlands).

Marakbar, Al-Harmoniah and the Blindman Quartet share this disc and show three different approaches to immigrant roots music in Antwerp, each one involving mastermind Luk Mishalle: Moroccan roots-pop with Marakbar, two dozen sax players with some twenty percussionists in Al-Harmoniah – "a deliciously rich cocktail", as Folk Roots put it – and the more intellectual approach of the four saxophones of the Blindman Quartet.

Artists

Pierre Van Dormael, Soriba Kouyaté, Otti Van der Werf

This group has jazz guitarist Pierre Van Dormael exchanging musical cards with Senegalese kora player Soriba Kouyaté, reinforced by Otti Van der Werf's bass guitar.

Djigui (Igloo, Belgium).

The fruit of several years' teaching as well as learning in Dakar, sharing the music and a way of life. Listening to others is what these musicians find essential and this meeting between European jazz and African roots certainly makes you listen to them.

Zap Mama

The most famous group from Belgium: five women of mixed ethnic background whose original a cappella singing and strong stage presence have taken them around the world. They mix every influence going.

Zap Mama/Adventures in Afropea (CramWorld, Belgium; Luaka Bop/Warners, US).

Zap Mama's first 1991 album is still a World Music classic with its imaginative and virtuoso vocal arrangements. Draws on sounds from Central African Pygmies, Zaire, Rwanda, Syria and Cuba plus wonderful yodelling, compelling harmonies and rhythms. The Global Village at its best.

Seven (Luaka Bop/Warners, US).

Marie Daulne dominates this 1997 album, assisted by several new Zap Mama sisters and brothers. Not digging for further roots but exploring a more urban musical world beyond unaccompanied vocals with more of a techno tinge.

Bosnia-Herzegovina

sad songs of sarajevo

When you think of Bosnia, unfortunately it's not music that comes to mind. The irony is that the ethnic diversity that tore the country apart made it musically very rich. **Kim Burton** picks over the pieces of the current roots music scene in this quarter of former Yugoslavia and outlines the unique specialities of Bosnian music.

With the break-up of **Yugoslavia** an ideal died. Overnight, it seems, the country changed from being a cheap holiday destination for those with a taste for mild exoticism, to being associated with brutality and internecine slaughter on a level not seen in Europe since the days of World War II. The countries of southeastern Europe, as a whole, have a reputation as a flashpoint for conflict which stems not only from their historical role as a human chessboard upon which great power politics played out their rivalries, but also from their complex and interwoven mixture of races and religions. What was Yugoslavia had probably the most diverse ethnic and cultural mix of any of these countries, and one that, despite the best efforts of those of its citizens who were committed to a multi-ethnic ideal, proved to be the most fragile of all.

Before Yugoslavia became a single country in 1918 it had a complex and often bloody history of invasion and foreign control, resulting in what is now the major cultural divide within the country and one of the primary contributors to the ferocity of the conflict. From the fourteenth century onwards the east and south were part of the Ottoman Empire, while Croatia and Slovenia in the west were part of the Holy Roman Empire and later Austro-Hungary.

As a result, what was Yugoslavia and is now a collection of independent states consists of not only Catholic Slovenes and Croats, Orthodox Serbs and Macedonians, Muslim Albanians and Bosnians, but also Turks, Hungarians, Gypsies, Vlachs and many other small communities. Each of these groups has its own music – distinctive, and yet a part of the ethnic mix. And while traditional music in its pure form is inevitably dying out, throughout the new nations it's being brought up to date in *novokomponovana narodna muzika* (new-composed folk music), heard everywhere in cafés, bars and taxis, and forming a lucrative industry even in the chaotic, economically shattered and fragile societies that are rebuilding themselves amid the ashes.

In the days of the Yugoslav state, the rather different task of deliberately preserving old songs, dances and crafts was undertaken by the amateur ensembles known as **Kulturno Umetnička Društva** (Cultural-Artistic Societies) or KUDs, which received state support in the form of finance, or artistic direction from well-known performers or academics. These still survive – one even has an Internet presence – and these days they hope for business sponsorship as well. At one time practically every small town, or even factory, would boast a KUD, and those that remain perform at folklore festivals at home or abroad, sometimes recording for the radio and occasionally making tapes or records for small local labels. These are often well worth hearing as they give an idea of the contemporary village or small-town sound, whereas the professional and officially sponsored folklore groups are impressively drilled but rarely as soulful.

Meantime, between the traditional and contemporary styles are various professional and semi-professional groups working outside the recording industry who play for money at social occasions like weddings, Saturday-night dances and village feasts.

The Bosnian Mix

Bosnia-Herzegovina, in the centre of former Yugoslavia, is the area where Turkish influence was the most developed and perhaps lingered the longest, and where the ethnic diversity and interpenetration contributed to the most bitter fighting in the struggle for territorial control. It has a population of about five million, three million of whom are Muslims (many of whom prefer to use the less religiously loaded term Bosniac to refer to themselves), most of the remainder being either Catholic Croats or Orthodox Serbs.

In its ethnic mix, the area was a microcosm of the entire country, and was ironically held up as the place where, more than anywhere else, people had conquered the distrust of their neighbours and lived harmoniously. When the Croatian conflict was beginning, Bosnians frequently denied that the war could ever move to their republic, as the bonds between its inhabitants were too strong to break. But they were no match for the sinister manipulations and ambitions of the political leadership of the surrounding republics and their cohorts. And although many of the inhabitants of the capital, **Sarajevo** – an extraordinary melting pot of Catholic and Orthodox Christians, Muslims and Jews until it was pounded by Serbian shelling in the spring of 1992 – strove to uphold their inheritance of tolerance and traditional companionship, they too succumbed and Sarajevo became a divided city.

At present, Bosnia is divided into two parts which are intended to cooperate in the building of one nation; a troubled **Federation of Croat and Bosniac Entities**, and the **Serb Republic**, which has its own internal stresses and strains. The principle on which the war was fought – the forced displacement of ethnic communities in order to create ethnically pure areas – has led to a refugee crisis of enormous proportions. Hundreds of thousands of people fled the country, and their return is slow and painful, with local authorities often putting obstructions in their way, or standing aside while returning refugees are harassed and attacked.

Even before the process of ethnic cleansing changed the map of Bosnia, perhaps forever, many of the areas of the country could be seen as predominantly Croat, Muslim or Serb. Everywhere, though, there were minorities within the majority group, so that the mainly Muslim area of eastern Bosnia held a sizeable Serb minority, and Herzegovina in the west, mainly Croat, held many Muslims.

This interpenetration of communities meant that styles of music tended to be geographically based rather than linked to ethnic identity, for instance, in the northeast both Serbs and Muslims played the energetic and compelling violin and *Šargija* (SA2) music referred to as *izvorna* (original), and in the hills above the southern reaches of the river Neretva both Croat and Muslim villagers sang the ancient and dissonant vocal *gange* of the Dinaric mountains.

As is often the case, the most important general divison – in a wider cultural sense and more specifically in the field of music – lay between the village and the town; the village with its rough and ready sounding antique harmonies and powerful rhythms, and the town with a more sophisticated, supple and sinuous melody supported by harmonies with a clear Western component.

JESÚS MORENO/VDE

Nešidu-I-Huda – ˙Sufis of Sarajevo

Sevdalinke

The most typical form of **urban music** in Bosnia is the **sevdalinka** or love-song. (The name is derived from the Turkish word *sevda* – love – but in the Bosnian sense it has come to mean a yearning, hopeless, and painful love, doomed, never to be consummated). The broad, ornamented melodies often use oriental scales and chromatic inflections, with a free and flexible rhythm and sweeping arches of melody. The lyrics speak of star-crossed lovers, faith or betrayal and breathe an atmosphere of regret and resignation. There are tales, possibly somewhat exaggerated, of listeners who were so moved by a particularly impassioned performance that they left the room and shot themselves out of grief.

The origins of sevdalinke lie in the interaction of the musical forms that the Turkish invaders brought with them with the ballads and lyric songs of the Slavs that they found there. Many of the Bosnians accepted Islam much more readily than did the other inhabitants of southeastern Europe, possibly because they had been Bogomils, a Christian sect proclaimed as heretical and attacked by both Eastern and Western churches. As a result, the towns of Bosnia became centres of Islamic culture, and it is believed that some oriental religious melodies known as *ilahije* were adopted by the townspeople and fitted with new lyrics to become sevdalinke. This does not mean that all sevdalinke were introduced from the East. Many sevdalinke show typically Slav melodic formulae and cadential patterns, and the melody of the celebrated "Kad ja podjoh na Benbašu", which has been proclaimed the unofficial anthem of Sarajevo, has had a Jewish origin claimed for it.

Each of the towns of Bosnia or Herzegovina has its own sevdalinka tradition, and their subjects relate to their home-town's particular quirks of history or geography. Zvornik, for example, on the River Drina between Bosnia and Serbia, was known as the Gate of Bosnia and was, in the time of Turkish rule, the point from which armies were despatched to put down revolts and uprisings in Serbia. Consequently, many of the sevdalinke from Zvornik deal with loss and with lovers who are never to meet again. One famous song says: "The Drina flows from hill to hill, not with rain or white snow, but with the tears of the maidens from Zvornik."

In contrast, Sarajevo, the capital of the province, was the home of rich landowners and merchants who carefully guarded the honour and marriage prospects of their daughters by keeping them hidden away from undesirable suitors. So many Sarajevske sevdalinke speak of thwarted love. The story goes that young women, forbidden to meet or even see their lovers, would sing of their love through the barred windows of their walled gardens to the young men strolling in the dusk through the narrow lanes of the city. The following is a typical lyric:

> *A red rose has blossomed*
> *In the lane, there is but one left.*
> *Through that lane my sweetheart passes*
> *And with his horse he tramples the flowers.*
> *Let him, O let him trample them*
> *If he but pass this way more often.*

Traditionally sevdalinke were performed to the accompaniment of the **saz**, a stringed instrument of Turkish origin with a pear-shaped body and long neck. Ideally the singer would also be his own accompanist (women rarely if ever were acquainted with instrumental technique, save for the tambourine-like *daire*, although they were and are frequently valued as singers). The sound of the saz is quiet and contemplative and fits the mood of sevdalinke perfectly, but it is a dying art and in Bosnia before the war there were perhaps only thirty *sazlije*, mostly of the older generation. Among the most notable of the singers were **Hasim Muhamerović**, **Kadir Kurtagić**, **Emina Ahmedhodzić** and **Muhamed Mesanović-Hamić**, some of whom were also sazlije.

Far more common these days is the performance of the same songs to the backing of a typical folk orchestra of accordion, violin, clarinet and guitar, with harmonies influenced by (but not identical to) Western models, and less rhythmic subtlety, but retaining the supple and mournful beauty typical of these songs. The older sazlije looked on this style as adulterated and less capable of expressing subtle emotions, but there is no doubt that performers such as **Safet Isović**, **Hanka Paldum**, **Zaim Imamović**, the late **Himzo Polovina** and others are part of the long and sophisticated tradition.

Bosnian Roots

Although there are many other types of music in Bosnia, including a Muslim tradition of heroic ballads similar to those of the Serbs and Montenegrins, but often accompanied by the strummed tambura (lute) and celebrating the feats, naturally enough, of Muslim rather than Christian warriors, the most widespread is a style known to the locals as *Izvorna Bosanska muzika*, which means roughly 'roots music'. This is a relatively recent development of the village music from the Drina valley and the surrounding area in the eastern part of the country, with the small market town of Kalesija its one-time centre; the savage fighting and subsequent maneouvrings in the area have not been conducive to sustaining musical life.

At one time performed at village celebrations known as *sijela* (sittings), marking the end of harvest time, ploughing, sowing, or on feast days, and more recently at the Saturday-night dance in the local house of culture or bar, this kind of music is usually performed by a small group of a couple of singers, two violinists and a player of a *šargija* (the village equivalent of a saz), sometimes accordion or even, on occasion, a rough and ready assault on a drum kit.

The sound of this roots music is quite startling to Westerners, as its ideas of harmony and consonance draw on a tradition totally different to that of western Europe or its descendants in American popular song. Essentially it involves two voices singing together in very close harmony – so close, indeed, that the Western ear perceives a grinding

GlobeStyle's great but tragically titled album

dissonance where the Bosnian hears a charming consonance. It's an ancient way of singing and widespread in southeastern Europe, from Istria on the Slovenian and Croatian coast to eastern Bulgaria, but the Bosnian bands have developed it in a very interesting way, being remote enough to preserve it but close enough to trade routes and small towns to acquire modern instruments and adapt them to the old music.

It was around the time of the First World War that such string bands of this type made their first appearance, but in the 1960s and later, as the music's local audience began to travel abroad as *gastarbeiter* (guest workers) to Germany and other relatively wealthy European countries, they increased their economic power, both in their own lives and by sending money back home to their families. This provided the impetus for many local record companies to record the music, giving it an unusually wide distribution for what had been a rather obscure form of village music.

Consequently, you can find discs and cassettes of practically pure folkloric performers like the **Jelić sisters**, the very lyrical group of **Mohamed Beganović** and the almost punkish energy of **Zvuci Zavičaja** (Sounds of Tradition) next to **Kalesijski Zvuci** (Sounds of Kalesija). The latter's excellent *Bosnian Breakdown* album, released on the UK GlobeStyle label, is an astonishing mixture of local singing and fiddling styles with a hot village-dance rhythm section.

The problems created by the massive displacement of population and the vast numbers of refugees mean that the largest audience for Bosnian music of the traditional sort is probably to be found abroad. However, at home there are still concerts of sevdalinke and newly composed folk

Aljo the Bully Blocked the Road

Aljo the bully blocked the roads
And demanded tribute from the girls.

Aj, he didn't only demand tribute
from beautiful Hajrija
But Aljo spoke to her:
"Aj, you will not pass before I kiss you."

Aj, beautiful Hajrija started to say:
"Don't, Aljo my mother will notice."
Aj, Aljo screamed like an angry snake.

And he kissed beautiful Hajrija.
Aj, how much he kissed her.
He left four marks [on her face].

Aj, the first mark was on the eyebrows.
The second mark was
in the middle of her white cheek.
Aj, the third mark was
at the middle of her white neck.
Aj, the fourth was where the rain doesn't fall.

Traditional sevdalinka sung by Kadir Kurtagig on Smithsonian Folkways *Bosnia: Echoes from an Endangered World.*

music, and there are also groups that concentrate on representing the whole field of Bosnian music. One such is the Sarajevo-based **Bosansko Kolo**, while most of the communities in their temporary exile have amateur or semi-professional groups of varying capabilities.

Sarajevo's one-time position as the centre of former Yugoslavia's music industry was, understandably enough, damaged by the war, and the unabated tendency to take political affiliation into account when choosing those who occupy positions of power in the media and in cultural life has naturally influenced the way in which music is presented and mediated, but both the city and the country are still noteworthy as the source of rich musical talent.

discography

> See the article on Serbia (p.273) for discs that cover the whole of former Yugoslavia.

Compilations

Bez Sevdaha Nema Milovanja (Diskoton, Bosnia).

This outstanding two-cassette collection of sevdalinke by various well-known singers, accompanied by a small band from Radio Sarajevo. The best possible introduction to a wonderful style, if you can find it.

 Bosnia: Echoes From An Endangered World (Smithsonian Folkways, US).

Covering more or less the whole spectrum, with a focus on Muslim performers, the music chosen covers sevdalinke with outstanding performance by Himzo Polovina accompanied by saz and a beautiful "Kad ja podjoh na Benbašu" with the radio orchestra – as well as dance music, a fiercely dissonant ganga, Sufi music and a muezzin's call to prayer. Good sleeve notes, too.

 Sevdah u Becu (Sevdah in Vienna) (RST Records, Austria).

This CD of refugee musicians is of variable quality, understandably, given the random selection of performers thrown together by an appalling fate, but is worth getting hold of for the beautiful and sensitive saz playing of Himzo Tulić alone.

Artists

Kalesijski Zvuci

This is a great rustic six-piece band from northeastern Bosnia with vocals, violin, cargija, accordion, bass and drums. They come from the village of Donji Rainci, a short distance from the market town of Kalesija from which they take their name 'Sounds of Kalesija'.

Bosnian Breakdown (GlobeStyle, UK).

The title of this CD, recorded in 1991 shortly before the outbreak of the war, has gained a terrible irony, but the music is as powerful as ever. Two of the tunes are performed in traditional style with two violins and šargija, the rest are beefed up with electric guitar, bass and drums.

Nešidu-l-Huda

The name of this ensemble, focussed on the Tabaćki Mosque in Sarajevo, means 'Divine Instruction'. Founded in 1985 they were semi-underground during the communist period and then lost several members during the Bosnian war.

Bosnia: Sufi Chanting of Sarajevo (VDE/AIMP-Gallo, Switzerland).

Excellent collection of Sufi music (ilahija and kasida) in Bosnian, Arabic, Turkish and Persian. Male vocals with accompanying frame drum or tambourine recorded in Geneva on a concert tour in 1995. Excellent notes.

Bulgaria

the mystery voice

After wine and footballers, music has become Bulgaria's best-known export. The distinctive women's singing style of Le Mystère des voix Bulgares has been a World Music hit, popping up in commercials and film soundtracks while their concerts and discs still sell strongly. On the instrumental front, wedding-band clarinetist Ivo Papasov is internationally known, while at home the traditions are very much alive, whether at social occasions or at the great quintennial festival in Koprivshtitsa. **Kim Burton** checks in.

The sound of Bulgarian music, direct, soulful and unashamed, is unmistakable. Although it undeniably forms part of a continuum that stretches from the western Balkans to Turkey and beyond, both its matter and manner are powerfully individual. The first thing to strike the unaccustomed ear is the characteristic vocal timbre of such singers as **Nadka Karadzhova, Yanka Rupkina** and **Konya Stojanova** – the soloists on the popular *Le Mystère des Voix Bulgares* album recorded by Bulgarian Radio's women's choir. Their rich, direct and stirring sound has rather oddly become referred to in the West as 'open-throated'. In fact, the throat in this style of singing is extremely constricted and the sound is forced out, which accounts for its focus and its strength, and which allows the articulation of the complex yet clean ornaments that are such a striking feature of these singers' performances.

Another common misconception about the *Mystère* album was to put it in the category of 'folk music', when the compositions, for the most part, were highly sophisticated modern choral compositions or arrangements of village song, notably the slow, heavily ornamented solo numbers. These are traditional women's songs which used to be sung at the social events called *sedyanki*, evenings when the unmarried girls would gather together to sew and embroider, gossip and compare fiancés, or sung to guests on the occasion of various festivities. Their

ROGUE RECORDS

Mystery voice Nadka Karadzhova

ornaments, although subtly varied with each performance, are percieved as a vital part of the tune, and the only time you will ever hear a song without them is when the singer is too old to cope.

Much Bulgarian music, both sung and played, was traditionally performed without harmony, or with, at most, a simple drone like that of the bagpipe. Nonetheless, in some districts a most extraordinary system of polyphonic performance grew up. In the Shop district near Sofia, women in the villages sing in two- and three-part harmony – though not a harmony that western ears readily recognise, as it is characterised by dissonance and tone clusters and decorated with whoops, vibrato and slides. The singers themselves say that they try to sing "as bells sound". In the Pirin mountains of the southwest, the villagers sometimes sing two different two-voiced songs with two different texts simultaneously, resulting in a four-part texture. In general, this polyphonic style of performance is the particular domain of women, and was associated with women's gatherings. In the Pirin district men also sing in harmony, albeit with a different repertoire and in a simpler, more robust style.

The rhythmic complexity and speed of Bulgarian music is also striking. Most of the countries of southeast Europe use a rhythmic system based on beats of irregular length so that such times as 7/8 or 11/8 are commonplace, but the Bulgarians have developed this, and the fleet dance steps associated with such patterns, to an unrivalled peak of intricacy. The most widespread of these irregular patterns is probably the *râchenitsa* dance, with its three beats of irregular length arranged as 2–2–3, closely followed by the *kopanitsa* (2–2–3–2–2). More complex patterns are by no means uncommon. These rhythms, so foreign to Western ears, are ingrained in Bulgarians, who snap their fingers in such patterns while queueing for a bus or hanging around on the corner of the street. On the other hand, ordinary two-beat patterns of the sort found in the simple 6/8 Shopsko *horo* are probably the commonest of all.

Ritual Music

Even though Bulgaria is a relatively small country – the population is just nine million – there are several clearly defined regional styles. The earthy, almost plodding dances from Dobrudzha, in the northeast, are quite different in character to the lightning-fast dances of the Shop people who live around Sofia, the capital city, and the long, heart-rending songs from the Thracian plain contrast with the sweet and pure melodies from the northwest and the Danube shore. In the remote mountains of the Rodopi, in the south, you can still hear the distant sound of a shepherd playing the bagpipes (*gaida*) to his flock of a summer evening, and in the villages or small towns of the valleys groups of people sing slow, broad songs to the accompaniment of the deep *kaba gaida*.

The yearly round of peasant life was defined by the rhythm of the seasons – sowing and harvest and the winter lull – and many of the ancient rituals, intended to ensure fertility and luck, survive, though the belief that they will have a magical and supernatural effect is more or less superseded by force of habit. These customs include the Christmas-time *Koleduvane*, when groups of young men process around the village asking for gifts from the householders; *Laduvane* at the New Year; and the springtime *Lazaruvane* (songs of St Lazarus Day), the most important holiday for young women, who take their turn to sing and dance through the streets. All have particular songs and dances connected with them – usually simple and repetitive and almost certainly stemming from ancient times.

Once performed in the villages of Bulgari, Kondolovo and Rezovo in the Strandzha area, the most startling of these rites, **Nestinarstvo** – when the chosen fell into a trance and danced on hot coals to the sound of bagpipe and drum to mark the climax of the feast of saints Konstantin and Elena –

has vanished as a living tradition, but is sometimes presented at festivals and folklore shows where the wild and stirring music remains the same.

The two most important rites of passage in contemporary Bulgarian life, whether in the country or in the town, are getting married and leaving home for military service – the latter affecting both the recruit himself and the family he leaves behind. Both these occasions are marked by music. Every moment of a **wedding** – the arrival of the groom's wedding party, the leading out of the bride to meet it, the procession to the church, and so on – has a particular melody or song associated with it. Traditionally, the songs sung at the bride's house the night before the wedding are the saddest in the whole body of Bulgarian music because the bride is leaving home, never to live again in her parents' house.

Parties to see the young men **off to the army** are more cheerful affairs. In towns, the family of the recruit hires a restaurant and a band – normally some combination of accordion, violin, electric guitar, clarinet/saxophone and drum kit which plays a promiscuous mix of folk, pop and other melodies – and the guests eat, drink and dance. In the country the feast is often held in the evening, and out of doors.

Typical of such occasions was one I saw in Mirkovo, a village in west central Bulgaria. The main street was jammed with trestle tables and the guests were entertained by a little band of two clarinets, trumpet and accordion, who played the slow melodies called *na trapeza* (at the table) while the guests ate. Later the young soon-to-be soldier – glazed of eye and rather unsteady on his feet – was led round and presented with gifts of money, flowers or shirts. (Shirts play a great role in Bulgarian folk life. At weddings each member of the party wears a handkerchief pinned to their breast, but the more important relatives sport an entire shirt, sometimes still in its cellophane wrapping.)

After all the food had gone, the band struck up a set of local dance tunes, and everyone rushed to join in a *horo* (a ring dance) whose leader capered and leapt, all the while flourishing an enormous flag on a long pole. Bulgarians, especially villagers, love dancing, and at the end of a festival or similar event, once the official part of the programme is over and the band starts to play for pleasure, you can see people – from grannies to young children – literally racing across the grass to join the circle. Even the trendiest of young things needs no persuasion to take their grandmother's hand and be swept into the ring.

Traditional Bulgarian Song

A big sedyanka was gathered
In the dancing-place of the village.
Two young girls began to sing
Began to sing and didn't stop.
A monk heard them
from Sveta Gora monastery
And that monk cursed them bitterly:
"God damn you, two young girls
Why didn't you start to sing a little sooner,
Before I became a monk?
I would have married one of you,
Either the younger or the elder."

Bands and Instruments

Most Bulgarian **bands** that play at weddings and other events use modern, factory-made instruments, often amplified with more enthusiasm than subtlety. Around the town of Yambol in the Strandzha area, in the east, however, people prefer the old folk instruments, and if they can afford it hire a specialist band of professionals to travel from Sofia for the occasion. Such a band will almost invariably consist of gaida (bagpipes), *kaval* (end-blown flute), *gadulka* (a bowed, stringed instrument) and *tambura* (a strummed, stringed instrument), sometimes with the addition of the large drum, the *tapan*.

These instruments were always common throughout the country and after World War II, when the state founded its ensembles for folk songs and dances, they were the ones chosen to make up the new 'orchestras'. As a result they have undergone certain technical developments and refinements to aid tuning and tone, while the invention of a paid class of professionals allowed their players to reach unprecedented heights of virtuosity.

The **gaida** is the best-known of all these instruments. Although of simple construction – a chanter for the melody, a drone, mouth-tube, and a small goatskin bag which acts as a reservoir for air – it's capable of a partly chromatic scale of just over an octave and, in the hands of masters such as **Kostadin Varimezov** or **Nikola Atanasov**, its wild sound has an astonishing turn of speed and rhythmic force. These players also have the ability to use the potential of the gaida's rich ornamentation to perform beautiful versions of slow songs

and other na trapeza melodies. In the Rodopi mountains in the most southern part of the country the musicians use a much larger instrument, the deep-voiced kaba gaida, to accompany singing or dancing, sometimes alone and sometimes in groups of two, three, four or even more. One enormous ensemble goes by the title of **Sto Kaba Gaidi** (One hundred bagpipes), a precise indication of its size, and both the sight and the sound of one hundred bagpipes playing in unison is undeniably impressive and indeed overwhelming.

Like the gaida, the **kaval** was originally a shepherds' instrument, and some of its melodies – or rather freely extemporised meditations on certain specific motifs – go by such names as "Taking the herd to water", "At noon", and "The lost lamb". The modern kaval is made of three wooden tubes fitted together, the topmost of which has a bevelled edge that the player blows against on the slant to produce a note. The middle tube has eight finger holes and the last has four more holes which affect the tone and the tuning. They are sometimes called *Djavolski dupki* (the Devil's holes), and the tale goes that they were made by the Devil, driven to such jealousy by a young shepherd's playing that he stole his kaval while he was sleeping and bored the extra holes to ruin it. When the shepherd awoke he discovered that his instrument sounded still sweeter than before, and the Devil's plans were, as is usual in folktales, sent wildly awry.

The school of kaval playing that has grown up since the war, led by **Nikola Ganchev** and **Stoyan Velichkov**, is extremely refined and capable of all manner of nuances of sound. The tone is sweet and clear (the folk say 'honeyed'), the low (kaba) register is rich and buzzing, and in the last fifteen or so years some of the performers have developed a new technique called *kato klarinet* (clar-

Sto Kaba Gaidi (One Hundred Bagpipes Ensemble)

Le Mystère des Voix Bulgares

Dora Hristova, who has led Le Mystère des Voix Bulgares for over a dozen years reveals some of the mysteries:

What's the secret of the singing style?
"It is impossible to train somebody to sing like this. These women are born with this ability. We have worked with a group of American women who love Bulgarian music and have formed a choir specially to sing it. Of course they are good, but it is an imitation. Secondly, this technique is very harmful to the vocal chords. If you are not born with the right physiology you can easily damage your vocal chords because the tension of the air passing through them is so great to make the sound piercing and strong.

"The vocal technique was once widespread in Europe, but the historical circumstances meant that it was only preserved in Bulgaria. With five hundred years of Ottoman oppression we had no real contact with European vocal culture while they developed a *bel canto* vocal style. In European bel canto resonance is in the head and chest while in Bulgarian singing the resonance is always in the chest, never in the head. That's why the vocal range is restricted – only an octave."

Where do you get your repertoire?
"Our singers come from villages all over Bulgaria and they bring their own repertoire. These are usually solo songs, or diaphonic if they come from the Shop region of western Bulgaria. When they come to us I record the song and give it to one of our arrangers (Nikolai Kaufmann and Kosta Kolev, amongst others). Then the singer who brought the song is the soloist in our arrangement so that its original character is preserved. "A singer from another region is not able to reproduce the style, they might be able to imitate it, but not give it the genuine character. The choir is like a bunch of flowers. Everyone is individual, and as a director I try to tread a fine line between keeping people's individuality and unifying the voices into a choir."

When not performing internationally, what is the choir's role in Bulgaria?
"We are employees of Bulgarian television. First of all we record vocal music for radio and TV programmes and then we're invited to give concerts for official festivals and celebrations. Most of the local ensembles no longer exist because they couldn't survive these difficult years. We are lucky because we are still employed."
Simon Broughton

inet style) – the instrument is played as though it were a trumpet producing a sound indeed very like the low register of the clarinet.

The **gadulka** is a relative of the medieval *rebec*, with a pear-shaped body held upright on the knee, tucked into the belt, or cradled in a strap hung round the player's neck. It has three, sometimes four bowed strings and as many as nine sympathetic strings which resonate when the instrument is played to produce an unearthly shimmering resonance behind the melody. The gadulka is exceptionally tricky to play, there are no frets, not even a fingerboard. The top string is stopped with the fingernails instead of the fingertips, and the technical ability of some of its players is astonishing. **Mihail Marinov** and **Atanas Vulchev** are notable among older players, and **Nikolai Petrov** is an important member of the younger generation.

The **tambura** is a member of the lute family, with a flat-backed pear-shaped body and a long fretted neck. Its original form, found in Pirin and in the central Rodopi, had two courses of strings, one of which usually just provided a drone while the melody was played on the other. These days the common form of the instrument has four

SIMON BROUGHTON

Gadulka player

courses tuned like the top four strings of a guitar, and in groups it both strums chords and runs counter melodies. It has thus changed its form and its role in Bulgarian music more than any other instrument, as chordal harmony is not typical of village music and was only introduced by academically trained composers in the course of this century.

Around the end of the nineteenth century factory-made instruments like the accordion, clarinet and violin began to arrive and were soon used to play dance music and to accompany songs. Modern **accordion** style was pretty much defined by Boris Karloff who played very elegantly and wrote a number of tunes, notably "Krivo Horo", which have become standards. More modern accordionists worthy of note include the Gypsy **Ibro Lolov**, **Traicho Sinapov** and **Kosta Kolev** – the latter, also well known as a composer, arranger and conductor, plays in a unique style which contrasts in its restraint and care with the high-speed acrobatics of some of the younger players. By far the most brilliant of these is **Petar Ralchev**, a Thracian who, unlike some of the speed-merchants, combines new ideas with a great deal of taste and, more importantly, soul. Another Thracian accordionist with an invigorating approach is **Boris Khristev**.

More recently, the accordion has been replaced as the keyboard instrument of choice by the **synthesiser**, easier to amplify and with a greater range of sounds, although many of the players who have moved to it from the acoustic instrument play it with the keyboard held vertically on the thigh, as though an instrument laid parallel to the ground were an offence against nature.

State Ensembles

The familiar sound of Bulgarian **musical ensembles** was developed in the late 1940s and 50s, when various local and national State Ensembles were set up by the new government as part of a cultural drive on the Soviet model.

The most important of these was based in the capital Sofia, and drew on talent from all around the country. This was the **State Ensemble for Folk Songs and Dances** under the leadership of **Philip Koutev** (1903–1982), an extraordinarily talented composer and arranger whose style of writing and arranging became the model for a whole network of professional and amateur groups across the country. His great gift was the ability to take the sounds of village singers – drone-based and full of close dissonances, but essentially harmonically static – and from this forge a musical

language which answered the aesthetic demands of western European concepts of form and harmony, without losing touch with the atmosphere of the original tunes. If you compare his work with the attempts of earlier arrangers to force the tunes into a harmonic system which they really didn't fit, his success is as obvious as their failure.

HANNIBAL

Trio Bulgarka with singing pal Kate Bush

It is Koutev's heritage that is heard on the popular Bulgarian recordings: the *Mystère des voix Bulgares* CDs, and those of the **Trio Bulgarka** and the instrumental group **Balkana** (a slightly expanded Trahiiskita Troika trading under another name) which had some success abroad in the early 1990s.

It is impossible to overestimate the tight grip that the Communist state had on every aspect of Bulgarian life, and this is as true of music as of anything else. What began as a praiseworthy attempt to preserve and enrich folklore became a straitjacket to which all musicians had to conform or else stop working as musicians. It reached such ridiculous extremes as prescribing a certain percentage of Russian songs to be played in the course of an evening's entertainment in a restaurant to demonstrate the eternal friendship of the Bulgarian and Soviet peoples, while the presence of watchful figures with their notebooks ensured that the musicians complied.

One musician told me how he had had to audition all his new songs and dances to 'The Committee of Pensioners' before he was permitted to perform them on the radio. If they were 'not Bulgarian enough' then permission was refused. Even if it was granted, the style of performance had to be acceptable. "Once they told me that I was playing too fast, and that Bulgarian music is not played so fast. This was a tune that I myself had written, it was I that was playing it, and I am a Bulgarian musician. How could they tell me the way to play my own song? But they could. I tell you, Bulgarian music used to be behind closed shutters – but now the shutters have been opened."

Koprivshtitsa: Bulgaria's Main Event

Imagine a cross between a pop festival and a medieval fair: 18,000 people singing and playing music in the mountains of central Bulgaria surrounded by traders exploiting the new free-market potential, the smell of grilling kebabs, beer tents, plastic-trinket sellers, stalls with the latest in Bulgarian CDs, and Gypsies weaving through the crowds with performing monkeys and dancing bears. This is the festival that takes place every five years on the hillside above the picturesque village of Koprivshtitsa.

It began in 1965 as a showcase for Bulgarian folklore financed by the Ministry of Culture. The Bulgarian Communists were generous in supporting their own idea of folk music: state song and dance troupes presenting a 'rich national heritage' abroad and professional dance ensembles going into villages to show the locals how Bulgarian dances should be performed. But Koprivshtitsa was one of the better ideas. Here the music is performed in something like its raw style by ordinary villagers.

Its supporters say the Koprivshtitsa Festival shows Bulgarian music at its most authentic. I don't see that performing a mid-winter dance on a concrete platform in August, with men dressed in woolly bear-suits in a temperature of 30°C, is remotely authentic, but the

Villagers strut their stuff

FOLKROOTS ARCHIVE

music, if not the event, is genuine. The performers may have been assisted by 'consultants' but this is village music as performed by the villagers, not arranged and cleaned up by professional ensembles. Still, I suspect that nowadays most mid-winter rituals in Bulgaria are performed at Koprivshtitsa in August rather than at their proper time. Beware too the endless 'folk plays' full of butter churns and spinning wheels that pop up between the musical numbers. It's clear that the social changes since the war have changed the nature of village life for ever.

Unlike Romania, where folk music has kept its original function in spite of the regime, in Bulgaria it has rather lost its true meaning, thanks to sponsorship by the state. Now it needs to find a natural life again, but I wonder if it can do so when the link between the music and everyday life is broken. It may have become permanently festivalised!

The best music at Koprivshtitsa happens offstage away from the dreaded PA systems. You can find little groups just singing to themselves, or solitary bagpipe and fiddle players on the hillside. This is where the music belongs and where it sounds at its best. Going off in search of a kebab, I stumbled across a clutch of Bulgarian Turkish musicians at the centre of a ring of dancers playing zurna and tupan drum. For a few leva, you could have the dubious thrill of the zurna blown directly into your ear – 'ear fucking' as they call it. With the rhythms insistently pumping out, the dancers were in fact in a sort of sexual frenzy. Some of the men had beer bottles tucked into their wide waistbands and, thrusting their groins, they carefully controlled their movements until the climax of the dance, when the beer frothed over and sprayed the crowd.

What Koprivshtitsa demonstrates above all is that there is incredible musicality amongst ordinary people. Could you find 18,000 performers like this in a population of nine million anywhere else? And what the festival contributes is an impetus for non-professional people to preserve their traditions and a focus where professional musicians can go to keep in touch with music at the roots.

Simon Broughton

This is not to say that the people working in the field of folklore during the Communist years were all apparatchiks, nor that they failed to produce immensely beautiful music. The network of regional professional ensembles, fed by a stream of talent trained in schools set up to teach folk music, meant that there was time, money and opportunity available for people to develop the approved language in their own way, and many composers created

their own individual style. Amongst arrangers and composers, **Kosta Kolev** is one unmistakable voice, and the work of **Stefan Mutafchiev** and **Nikolai Stoikov** with the **Trakiya Ensemble** in Plovdiv was very inventive.

The series of regional competition-festivals held around the country and culminating once every five years at the vast gathering of amateur music groups at **Koprivshtitsa** (see box), the mass-production of folk instruments, and the encouragement shown to amateurs, has managed to keep music alive in the villages. The lack of state funding and the resulting commercial pressures have led to a plethora of cloned women's choirs capitalising on the success of *Mystère*, and a consequent struggle for scarce resources on the part of other groups performing a less high-profile music. However, in recent years fledgling private companies are beginning to play a part in developing a new folk-based popular music. At the moment much of this is in a fairly underdeveloped state, with a simple juxtaposition of a folksong with a beatbox, but the conditions for the development of a truly Bulgarian pop music (as opposed to the usual cabaret-style Eurodisco imitations) are beginning to bear fruit.

The festival at Koprivshtitsa is particularly important, not merely because of its size (there are literally thousands of performers bused in from all over the country) but because it is the only one devoted to amateur performers. Practically the only recordings of genuine village music that the state record company Balkanton has ever released are from this festival, and they are among the most beautiful and valuable commercial recordings of Bulgarian songs and dances ever made.

Wedding Bands

The **wedding bands** are a fascinating example of the formerly 'underground' folk music that is currently an extremely important part of Bulgarian musical life, and is likely to develop still further. Unlike the musicians mentioned above, who were approved and employed by the state (though none the worse for that), they existed outside the framework of official music making, being hired to play at weddings, the seeing-off of recruits and various village festivities. Because they did not have to pay much attention to the Communist ideal of workers and peasants marching into a glorious dawn in order to record or get on the radio (as semiprofessionals the air-waves were not open to them in any case), they were free to experiment with instrumentation, mixtures of folk instruments like gaida and kaval with electric guitar, synthesiser and kit drums, rock and jazz rhythms, and foreign tunes.

As the state-monopolised recording industry in Bulgaria didn't allow the formation of a commercial style, some of the musicians simply learned songs from Serbian and other radio broadcasts or from pirated cassette tapes and performed them to a public that responded to their directness and energy. Others, particularly in Thrace, went further

and began a far-reaching reinvention of their local music. It was only in the mid-1980s that officialdom picked up on the existence of this music, and through the efforts of some far-seeing musicologists was persuaded to recognise it as worthy of public support. A triennial festival was set up in the town of **Stambolovo** (hence the wedding bands' alternative name of *Stambolovski orkestri*) and the results issued on the Balkanton record label and more recently Marko's Music. The festival presented the new music in maybe a slightly bowdlerised form – bands were subjected to the 'assistance' of approved musical directors – but the performances and the resulting recordings were a revelation nonetheless.

Clarinettist **Ivo Papasov** (see box) became the best known abroad of these musicians. He started out with the Plovdiv jazz-folk ensemble, and in his own later work has flirted with jazz and produced some startling transformations of traditional Thracian and Turkish music. His family is of Turkish origin, and even in the period just prior to the fall of the Zhivkov regime, when the very existence of a Turkish minority in Bulgaria was denied (the Balkans suffered greatly under the Turkish Empire for over five hundred years and the attempt to whip up anti-Turkish feelings was part of an ultimately unsuccessful attempt by the communists to retain power by playing the nationalist card), you could get homemade recordings of Papasov playing Turkish melodies with a small band of the type common today in Istanbul.

When the ethnic basis of music became less highly charged and releases of Turkish music began to surface both on Balkanton and private labels, it looked as though some interesting innovations could be expected from him – his second release, *Balkanology,* on UK-based Hannibal records, kicked off with a Turkish dance and also included Macedonian and Greek material – but in recent years he has had a lower profile, occasionally making an appearance on more of the folk-jazz projects of which Bulgarian musicians seem so fond.

There are many other wedding bands of this type in which Rom musicians are often prominent whose approach is still more eclectic and adventurous. The orchestras **Sever**, **Juzhni Vetar**, **Shoumen** and **Trakiîski Solisti** all have fresh and intriguing ways of interpreting their traditional music. Some have now made commercial recordings; others are still only to be heard live or on homemade tapes sold in the markets of the small towns where they live, but all have a freshness and excitement that overcomes all but the most hidebound ideas.

HANNIBAL

Ivo Papasov – the Wedding King

With a huge gut and unwieldy frame, **Ivo Papasov** seems an unlikely source for some of the most nimble and virtuoso music you'll encounter anywhere in the world. After seeing him in concert, though, you'll be left in little doubt that he's one of the most interesting clarinettists around. He and his band race through numbers based on the complex rhythms of Bulgarian folk dances, grafting on jazzy improvisations for clarinet, saxophone, accordion and keyboard.

He is also one of the few jazz musicians to have been in prison for propaganda. "It was in 1982 when there was a campaign to make Bulgarian Turks change their names. I was often playing at Turkish weddings and the police came, arrested us, beat us and took us to prison. I was in prison twenty days and then was to be sent to a labour camp. They wanted to make an example of me, but a friend of mine, a prosecutor, managed to get the judgement changed and I was released."

Ivo Papasov is a Bulgarian Turk from Kardzali close to the Greek and Turkish borders. "I am from Thrace where Orpheus was born. It is an area very rich in music." He has an immense following in Bulgaria, not just among Turks and Gypsies but amongst young people as well. It's now easier than it was for him to give concerts, but he's most famous for playing weddings for those who can afford it.

"They are big weddings – maybe 1000 or 1500 people with lots of eating, drinking and dancing. They last more than twenty-four hours, starting in the morning at the bride's house. There's eating and drinking and money is bestowed or maybe a car or a house. In the late afternoon when it's cooler there's a dance outside and then more eating and drinking till morning."

Ivo cites some of the greatest jazz clarinettists and saxophonists as influences – Benny Goodman, Charlie Parker, David Sandborn – but alongside them is Petko Radev, a great Bulgarian clarinettist, also from Thrace. Always keeping his background in mind, Ivo Papasov is one of the many musicians in Bulgaria who is brilliantly forging contemporary music out of traditional forms.

Simon Broughton

New Sounds

It is not only the wedding bands that have been pushing back the boundaries of late. Some of the bands that play purely traditional instruments have been experimenting. Sofia's **Loznitsa**, which features both the old master of the gaida Nikola Atanasov and the incredible young kaval player **Georgi Zhelyaskov** are good representatives of the new trend. Particularly worth investigating too is the work of the kaval player **Theodosii Spassov**, who has not only recorded a very beautiful and practically avant-garde folk album, *Dulug Put,* in collaboration with composer Mutafchiev, but has also played to great acclaim with the well-known Bulgarian jazz pianist Milcho Leviev at his first concert in Sofia after twenty years of exile. He has become renowned as a composer of film scores, and at the time of writing has pretty much abandoned pure folk music and its arrangements in favour of experimenting with timbre and form in a loosely jazz like way.

Bulgaria shares the problems of many post-Communist societies in its economic underdevelopment and social instability, exacerbated by the chaos and lawlessness that have flowed from the recent conflicts in former Yugoslavaia. Great efforts have been made to sustain the network of festivals of music, dance and folk art despite the lack of people to support them. The biggest of all, at Koprivshtitsa, has survived, and looks set to do so for the future, while the local festivals continue as a result of local efforts and the eagerness of the amateur musicians to retain a platform for their performances. A lack of money is also problematic for the wedding bands, whose place is nowadays often taken by smaller groups relying on sequenced keyboards and drum machines.

Over the past couple of years several small private labels have emerged which are playing a part in the development of a new folk-pop – or rather, several types of folk-pop in which Gypsy musicians and singers are often prominent. Some of it is heavily influenced by Serb *novokomponovana narodna muzika* (see p.273) – orchestras **Kristal** and **Eros** are good examples – while other bands like **Palantiri** and **Rodopi** show a clear debt to Papasov, though usually without his hair-raising virtuosity and with, some might say, better taste.

From the Black Sea coast **Orkestar Slunchev Bryag** delivers a sort of Gypsy-influenced Bulgarian pop-soul with gaida, kaval and gadulka instead of a horn section. Other musicians – singer **Daniel Spasov** stands out – are gently updating the Koutev sound; the Subdibula label specialises in this area.

All in all, it seems that Bulgarian music will continue to be as thrilling and inventive in years to come as it ever has been.

discography

Compilations

⊚ **Anthologie de la Musique Bulgare**
(Le Chant du Monde, France).

Between 1977 and 1983, Belgian folklorist Herman Vuylsteke made a series of trips to Bulgaria, where he collected a vast amount of material from village musicians all over the country. Vuylsteke can be a bit sniffy about the state ensembles and their 'perversion' of folklore, but given the riches that he uncovered, he can certainly be forgiven. So far five volumes have been issued, with Vol 5, from north central Bulgaria the most varied.

⊚ **Bulgaria** (Auvidis/Unesco, France).

A good cross-section of styles from the various regions of Bulgaria which includes both amateur and professional musicians, like Yanka Rupkina of the Trio Bulgarka with excellent solos on the kaval, gaida, tambura and gadulka.

❂ **Koprivshtitsa '76 and Koprivshtitsa '86**
(Balkanton, Bulgaria).

The quinquennial Koprivshtitsa festival is the most important in the country, drawing together literally thousands of amateur performers from all over Bulgaria. These two recordings contain performances of some of the finest of these, recorded during the heats when the line-up of the festival was being chosen. With some astonishing performances on gaida and gadulka as well as remarkable solo and group singing, they rank as some of the most valuable and beautiful recordings of Bulgarian songs and dances ever made.

❂ **Popular Clarinettists from Thrace**
(Balkanton, Bulgaria).

Thracian musicians took to the clarinet like basil thirsty for water, as the Bulgarians say, and this is a cracking collection, with superb playing from six of Bulgaria's best clarinettists, including Petko Radev and Ivo Papazov. Perhaps it's a bit old-fashioned by now, and it might be hard to get hold of, but if you can find it, grab it!

⊚ **Song of the Crooked Dance:**
Early Bulgarian Traditional Music 1927-42
(Yazoo/Shanachie, US).

A well-researched pre-war collection of Bulgarian music excellently remastered from 78rpm recordings. It is fascinating to hear the lively and rhythmic kaval playing of Tsvyatko Blagoev, so different from today's legato, meditative style. Other highlights include a song about an earthquake in 1928, the striking heroic song "Kapitan" and some catchy precursors of Ivo Papasov. The notes by Lauren Brody are both scholarly and accessible.

⊚ **Stambolovo '88** (Balkanton, Bulgaria).

When the wild and wonderful experiments of the wedding bands became too popular for the authorities to ignore, they responded in the only way they knew how – by organising a festival and selecting a panel of judges. This is a selection of live performances by some of the wedding bands who took part in the 1988 Stambolovo festival. They came from all across the country, and gaily shovelled all manner of traditional and electric instruments together to get the crowd on their feet and roaring approval.

⊚ **Two Girls Started to Sing . . .** (Rounder, US).

These real field recordings focus on vocal music made in 1978–88 in village locations round Bulgaria and provide a fine example of the sort of music that you might be lucky enough to hear sung spontaneously in the field (or in the pub), including work, sedenka, table, wedding and dance songs sung by non-professional musicians. Good notes.

 Village Music of Bulgaria (Nonesuch Explorer, US).

An excellent selection of material (first released in the 1970s), mostly by professionals but with their village roots showing unabashed. It includes a stunning performance of the Rodopi song "Izlel e Delyo Haidutin" by Valya Balkanska, the first Bulgarian song to escape the bonds of gravity when it traveled on the spacecraft Voyager as one of its examples of Earth culture.

Artists

The Bisserov Sisters (Sestri Biserovi)

A trio of chunky looking villagers from the highlands of southwestern Bulgaria, the Bisserov Sisters are one of the more authentically traditional of that country's musical exports. Performing both the dissonant sounding unaccompanied polyphonies of the mountain villages and the rather less challenging songs of the muslim Pomak community to tambura and tarabuka accompaniment.

 Music from the Pirin Mountains
(Pan Records, Holland).

Simple and direct, this makes a wonderful introduction to the music of the Pirin district. The backing by the Trio Karadzhovska on kaval, gadulka and tambura is a little more elaborate than usual for this group, who normally accompany themselves, but none the worse for that.

The Bulgarian All Stars Orchestra

The Bulgarian All Stars Orchestra is a relatively new collection of younger musicians, virtuosos on both folk and factory made instruments and skilled in all manner of regional styles, brought together under the aegis of Frankfurt's Network Medien.

⊚ **Dusha: The Soul of Bulgaria**
(World Network, Germany).

This startling mixture of musics, unlike many of the other discs around, bears some resemblance to what Bulgarian musicians play for their own pleasure. Traditional, modern, Turkish and Romanian melodies are all included, and instead of the usual three-minute arrangements, long medleys result as the musicians slip from one tune to another seemingly spontaneously. The disc is also notable for the presence of Bulgaria's first (and so far only) female professional gaida player, Maria Stoyanova, and some beautiful gadulka playing. The singing is rather disappointing, unfortunately.

Bulgarian Voices "Angelite"

This choir, conducted by Valentin Velkov, has toured widely and favours more contemporary arrangements and an experimental approach. From Bulgaria with Love – 'the Pop album' – in 1992 with rap and hip-hop fusions being a horrible example.

Ⓓ **Mountain Tale** (Jaro, Germany).

This is a successful 1998 example of Bulgarian fusion including the Tuvan throat-singers Huun Huur Tu and the Moscow Art Trio. A great opening track with two female voices singing the repetitive, narrow phrases of a Bulgarian song over which Sergei Starostin (one of Russia's leading folklorists) sings a Russian song with a broader voice and wider range, followed by plenty more inspired collaborations and only a couple of miscalculations. An ambitious and successful global fusion.

Krâchno Horo

Amongst Bulgarians Gabrovo has the reputation of being the home of the stupidest people in the entire country – a reputation that is belied by the playing of Krâchno Horo, a four-piece wedding band from the town.

Ⓓ **Musiques Populaires de Bulgarie** (Auvidis/Silex, France).

A showcase for the quartet's breathtakingly skilful and precise performances for the dance-crazy; all displaying an attractive sense of enormously good-natured enjoyment. Clarinet, sax, accordion, electric bass and percussion.

Le Mystère des Voix Bulgares

This name was dreamed up by French mining engineer (and musicologist) Marcel Cellier for his initial compilation of tracks from the archives of Bulgarian Radio and TV. The four volumes of *Le Mystère* on Philips/Disque Cellier are compilations of various choirs from the archives. Since the huge success of the first compilation, the name has been applied to the Bulgarian State Radio and Television Female Choir, currently led by Dora Hristova, who have subsequently recorded using the name Le Mystère de Voix Bulgares.

 Le Mystère des Voix Bulgares Vol 1 (Philips/Disque Cellier, France).

This was the disc that introduced so many people to Bulgarian music, and although it doesn't claim to represent the entire field, its echo-drenched ambience, classic melodies and stunning choral arrangements given a hauntingly beautiful performance make this an indispensable disc. There are three further volumes.

Ⓓ **Ritual** (Nonesuch, US).

This disc of Dvora Hristova's choir draws on music for Christmas and St. Lazar's Day, and includes some good instrumental tracks. Reflective and powerful.

Orkestar Sever

Orkestar Sever are one of Bulgaria's very hottest Gypsy-led bands, who don't even pretend to pay attention to the concerns of the traditionalists.

▭ **Albaniya '93** (Payner, Bulgaria).

With its rather fetching English language introduction (a bid for the international market?), this is a treasure. A cassette-only recording unfortunately, but worth getting just for Miladin Asenov's extraordinary synthesiser playing.

Ivo Papasov

Irrepressible clarinet virtuoso Ivo Papasov has been experimenting with fusions of jazz and traditional Thracian music since the early 1970s, and is the best-known exponent of the wedding band movement.

 Balkanology (Hannibal, UK).

Audiences love it, musicologists despair. Ivo rips his way through those thrilling rhythms in the manner born. His first Hannibal album Ⓓ *Orpheus Ascending* is equally recommendable, but this includes more ethnically diverse material with a tip of the hat to neighbouring countries, his Turkish roots and, with the allusion to Charlie Parker, perhaps a touch more jazz.

The Philip Koutev National Folk Ensemble

This ensemble, founded by folklorist and composer Philip Koutev in 1951 remains perhaps the most important of all Bulgaria's many professional and amateur ensembles. Its repertoire is drawn from the cream of the country's composers and arrangers.

Ⓓ **Bulgarian Polyphony I** (JVC, Japan).

This and Vol II of the JVC series contains some of the best-known works written for the ensemble, given experienced and committed performances by a thirty-four-strong women's choir plus a small group of folk instrumentalists. Although some of the instrumental performances are a little lacklustre this is more than made up for by the chance to hear a recording of this music that isn't drenched in digital reverb in a spurious effort to increase the atmosphere of mystery.

Theodosii Spassov

Kaval player Theodosii Spassov is one of the most interesting of Bulgaria's younger musicians, with breathtaking control over tone and phrasing, and an adventurous attitude that although sometimes leading him down free-jazz paths that were tramped to death in the 1970s, usually comes up with some fascinating ideas.

Ⓓ **Dulug Pât (The Long Road)** (Balkanton, Bulgaria).

A collaboration with some of Bulgaria's finest arrangers, with echoes of Bartók and Hindemith mixed in with folk sources. Stunning playing from all involved, on brass instruments, folk instruments and the drum-kit, quartal and quartal harmony, mainly brief enharmonic excursions.

Ⓓ **Welkya** (Gega New, Bulgaria).

This develops Spassov's ideas further, and is more varied in approach although sparser in sound.

The Trio Bulgarka

Singers Yanka Rupkina, Stoyanka Boneva and Eva Georgieva are the members of the Trio Bulgarka, without question Bulgaria's most prestigious vocal trio. Respectively hailing from Strandzha, Pirin and Dobrudzha districts and each one famed in her own right as a soloist, they combine to perform arrangements and original compositions by some of Bulgaria's finest composers.

Ⓓ **The Forest is Crying** (Hannibal, UK).

The three singers peform some of their favourite repertoire, re-recorded for a Western audience. Most tracks are a cappella, but some are accompanied by the Trakiiskata Troika (Thracian Trio) instrumental ensemble. A pity that some of the tracks are spoiled by less than top-class playing, but nonetheless well worth having.

Croatia

toe tapping tamburicas

While the Croats and Serbs largely share a language (which used to be called Serbo-Croat), they write it in different alphabets: the Croats use Latin letters while the Serbs use Cyrillic reflecting their respective Western/Catholic and Eastern/Orthodox tendencies. The way Croatia tries to define itself musically is similar. **Kim Burton** tiptoes through the *tamburicas*.

For the most part the character of Croatian music is attractive and cheery, easy on the ear and with few of the intricate structures found further east. Amateur groups abound, playing their local music either in the village bar or on the square, and there are some high-quality professional groups that perform arrangements of folk material somewhat after the Bulgarian model. Zagreb's **Lado** is probably the best and most versatile of these, and you're unlikely to come across the sort of folkloric music that they perform in any other context than the concert hall or the festival.

Of course, individual singers and musicians do preserve the older types of music but it is difficult to hear anything spontaneous unless you're invited to some rite of passage or informal gatherings of friends and neighbours. The peasant musicians themselves, particularly the women, tend to hide their abilities from the crowd, as if it were faintly shameful to be caught singing.

There is a wealth of festivals, however, in which amateur groups, some highly skilled, perform, and the fairly efficient, reviving tourist industry can point the vistor towards these. The most important is Zagreb's **Medjunarodna Smotra Folklora** (International Folklore Review), a week-long event which, as its name suggests, presents groups from abroad as well as all over the country. It usually takes place in the second half of July.

Tamburica

Tamburica Bands

Although Croatian music uses a wide variety of instruments, including violin, zither, accordion, clarinet and various folk wind instruments, the typical ensemble, found all over, but most highly developed in the area of the Slavonian plain to the north and east of Zagreb, is a **tamburica band**. The tamburica is a plucked and strummed string instrument that comes in various shapes and sizes, from the tiny mandolin-like *prim* to the large *berde*, the size of a double-bass. The tamburica is actually a small tambura – the Balkan version of the Turkish saz, one of the many musical legacies of Ottoman occupation and a clear demonstration that Croatia's musical links reach East as well as West.

Ensembles range from the huge, like the Tamburica Orchestra of Croatian Radio-Television, to smaller ensembles of five or six people, and sometimes the instrument is played alone as an accompaniment to singing, when it is usually referred to by the name of *samica*. The lively dances (principally the *kolo*, round dance) and dance songs are often accompanied by encouraging whistling from the men and a high-pitched squealing from the women. Slower songs are sentimental and betray the sticky-sweet influence of Vienna, while the fast ones are extremely lively with scurrying inner parts and counterpoints.

As well as the usual amateur societies there are many professional ensembles. The first of these, formed in the 1970s, was the Zagreb-based group **Ex Pannonia**, who are still active. They have since been joined by many more, notable among them **Zlatni Dukati**, **Zdenac**, and the **Berde Band**, playing some traditional songs, but concentrating on writing new material. The most contemporary-sounding of them is **Gazde** (The Bosses), whose shows owe more to leather-clad rock'n'roll than the village green.

Krunoslav ('Kico') Slabinac and Vera Svoboda are probably the best-known individual singers. Kico's collaboration with tamburica player Antun Nikolic in the group Slavonski Becari (Slavonian Bachelors), founded in the early 1970s, preserved a good deal of traditional material which was in danger of being lost.

The tamburica orchestra bears an added weight as a symbol of Croatian national identity, and during the period of conflict there was an upsurge of new songs in response to the fighting and the expulsion of people from areas under the control of the Serb separatist forces. These new songs were accompanied by a revival of songs from World War II, some tainted by their association with the ill-famed Ustase, the Croatian Fascist movement. When in the summer of 1995 rockets launched from the Krajina, south of Zagreb (then held by ethnic Serb separatists), fell on the capital, within a few minutes of the first blast nothing but patriotic and sentimental songs, each one accompanied by tamburice, were broadcast on the radio.

Pozega, in central Slavonia, hosts an annual festival, *Zlatne zice Slavonije* (Slavonia's Golden Strings) which is dedicated to the performance of newly composed songs. Most of these are on the soupy side, but some of the faster examples have startling echoes of bluegrass – the influence of Croatia's best-known Bluegrass band Plava Trava Zaborava has spread wide. Practically every singer or notable group appears at the festival, which is also broadcast on television.

Contemporary Developments

Alongside the tamburica bands, the last decade has seen an increasing hybridisation of Croatian roots music with a string of performers attempting to breathe new life into traditional forms with studio technology or new musical styles. Most of them have drawn inspiration from the fringe areas of Croatian folk (notably Medjimurje and Istria), thereby offering an alternative to the nationalistic folk-schlager-pop on the airwaves.

First off the mark were Vjestice, a group formed in 1988, who gained a wide audience by blending Medjimurje folk songs with 1990s' rock attitude. This interest in the archaic styles of northeastern Croatia was picked up in the early 1990s' by the group Legen and singers Dunja Knebl and Lidija Bajuk, all of whom mined collections of folk melodies. They collaborated on the 1995 album *Ethno-Ambient Live*, an outstanding recording of acoustic performances in a Zagreb nightclub.

Since then Knebl and Bajuk have gone on to record albums of their own; while Legen have dabbled in techno-folk crossover, souping up traditional songs with synthesisers, samples and breakbeats in the manner of Transglobal Underground or Loop Guru. A second *Ethno-Ambient* album featuring Legen, Bajuk and Istrian folk/jazz singerTamara Obrovac was released in spring 1999.

Other Regional Traditions

Towards the end of the 1980s the songs from the area of Medjimurje, in the north of the country, bordering Hungary, became very popular. Mostly lyrical, with a few more energetic examples, some of the songs have melodic and structural qualities in common with the music of Hungary, so much so that some have the air of being 'Croatianised' by the simple expedient of adding a tamburica orchestra. Others feel strongly Croatian, while yet others are neither one nor the other, but contain recognisable elements of both. There is also a strong tradition of unaccompanied narrative song which is largely the domain of women.

A little further south, in the hills of the Zagorje around Zagreb the music is almost indistinguishable from the polkas and waltzes of Slovenia and Austria, with forceful harmonised singing accompanied by accordion and guitar. Although locally it is highly popular – with many small amateur and semi-professional groups in and around the areas playing and recording – it has not made many inroads outside the Zagreb area.

All along the Dalmatian coast and on the islands, small male voice choirs called klape, with up to ten members, perform smoothly harmonised and sentimental songs, with chromatic inflections and 'barbershop' harmonies. There is a good-sized Italian minority in the area, and the influence of the Italian vocal tradition is explicit. Further south, towards Dubrovnik, the small bowed *lirica* with its three strings still survives and is used for accompanying dance.

Utterly different and quite startling is the music from the coastal area of Istria, where they not only sing and play using a distinctive local scale with very small intervals, but also harmonise it in parallel seconds. It is probable that this is a very ancient tradition, and the singing style has given rise to an entire body of instruments dedicated to reproducing such harmonies. The *rozenica* or *sopila* is a type of large oboe and is always played in pairs, one large and one small. The much smaller *curla*, two pipes played with a single mouthpiece, allows one player to play two parts at once. After a period of acclimatisation it can be quite attractive.

The **Istrian bagpipe**, the **diple**, works on the same principle – it has no drone, but a double chanter, and is still to be found along the Dalmatian coast and inland into Herzegovina (now part of Bosnia-Herzegovina, with a large and militant Croatian population). For hardened discord lovers there's a Folkways album of songs and religious music made on the Istrian island of Krk in the early 1960s (only available on cassette from Smithsonian Folkways), while within Croatia, revivalist groups are active in performing and recording the music.

discography

Compilations

Croatian Folksongs and Dances
(Harmonia Mundi/Quintana, France).

Music from the Croatian communities in mainly south Hungary (many Slavs fled north to escape the Ottoman invasion) in archive recordings mostly from the 1950s and 1960s, but as recent as 1985. Some really archaic songs are included, and bagpipe playing and excellent fiddle playing from Stipan Pavkovics, a renowned virtuoso. Lots of virtuoso tambura bands, notably the Pavo Šimora 'Baraban' orchestra from Felsöszentmárton, still a centre of tambura music today. Most of the bands have a vital raw sound, rather than showy glitz. Those who know the music of the Hungarian band Vuycsics will recognise a couple of tunes here. Strongly recommended.

Croatie: Musiques d'autrefois (Ocora, France).

A survey of traditional songs and instrumental music in the best Ocora tradition, taken from Croatian Radio Archives from 1958–1993. Divided into regional areas, it begins with some Medjimurje songs and includes plenty of good tamburica bands, Istrian and klapa singing and instruments such as the diple, sopila and licera.

Croatie: Musiques Traditionelles d'Aujourd'hui (Auvidis/Unesco, France).

This excellent record documents practically the whole range of Croatian music, from obscurities that you would be lucky to hear, to the sort of commercial and sentimental songs given so much radio play that you would be lucky to avoid. Music from Istria, Medjimurje, Slavonija and Dalmatia and more. This is undoubtedly the best place to start, and the highly informative notes will point those interested in discovering more in the right direction.

Da si od Srebra, Da si od Zlata
(Croatia Records, Croatia).

This classic record restricts itself to the more traditional side of Croatian music, but has some splendid examples.

Ethno-Ambient Live (Crno Bijeli Svijet, Croatia).

Not the exercise in folk electronica the title might suggest; rather a sparkling collection of traditional songs acoustically rendered. Legen, Lidija Bajuk and Dunja Knebl all figure prominently. Most of the material is from Medjimurje and Slavonia, although the odd Dalmatian and Istrian pieces squeeze in.

Pozega '94 (Croatia Records, Croatia).

This is a record of the performances from the 1994 Golden Strings festival, re-recorded in the studio, and features both the biggest stars, Krunoslav Slabinac, Zlatne Dukati and Gazde, and some less-known but still delightful bands. The subjects of the songs range from love to patriotism via the experience of being stopped by the police for speeding. This has been succeeded by more recent Pozegas, but it's a great collection.

Village Music from Yugoslavia
(Elektra-Nonesuch, US).

Despite the misleading subtitle 'Songs and Dances from Bosnia-Herzegovina, Croatia & Macedonia', this is all Croatian music, except for one Macedonian zurle and tapan track. Excellent songs from village performers and dance music from typical tamburica bands.

Artists

Berde Band

The eight-strong Berde Band was formed in 1992 from tamburasi who had already made their names playing in various groups, and has become one of the most popular of the contemporary groups. Their repertoire includes folk tunes, newly composed music in a folk-pop style and religious songs.

Poletit ce Sokol Moj (Croatia Records, Croatia).

Probably this band's best recording so far, it is both typical of the contemporary tambura scene and a good example of the band's individual strengths.

Dunja Knebl

Singer and guitarist Knebl from Zagreb discovered indigenous folk traditions relatively late in life and began singing professionally aged 47. Nevertheless, she's one of the more authentic figures of the Croatian folk revival, bringing a fresh, untutored singing style to the narrative songs of northern and eastern Croatia which had all but disappeared from the mainstream folk repertoire.

Iz globine srca (Dancing Bear, Croatia).

Predominantly wistful Croatian folksongs from Medimurje, the district of northern Croatia along the Hungarian border. Soft, sometimes haunting, contemporary arrangements with acoustic guitar and instrumental contributions from Mladen Škalec. Lyrics in Croatian with short English translations.

Czech & Slovak Republics

east meets west

Since 1993, the three lands of Czechoslovakia have been divided into two states: the Czech Republic (comprising Bohemia and Moravia) in the west, and Slovakia to the east. In spite of the political division, there are strong historical and cultural links. Musically the territory charts a transition from Bohemia's regular, symmetrical structures of west European folk to the spicy and idiosyncratic melodies and tunings of Slovakia in the east, sharing features with Ukraine and Hungary. **Jiří Plocek** reports from Moravia.

Collections of **folk songs** have been a vital source of traditional music for village ensembles in western Bohemia, south-eastern Moravia and Slovakia. Tens of thousands of songs were written down around the turn of the twentieth century, allied with the national movement. The region was also fortunate to have the composer **Leoš Janáček** (1854–1928), who helped to lay the foundations for modern ethnomusicology in the Czech lands. Like his fellow Hungarian composer Béla Bartók, Janáček made important cylinder recordings in the field and this familiarity with his country's folk music was crucial in forming his own composing style – amongst the most distinctive of the twentieth century. Of course Janáček and the other great Czech composer of the twentieth century, **Bohuslav Martinů** (1890–1959) were themselves following the illustrious nineteenth-century tradition of **Bedřich Smetana** (1824–1884) and **Antonín Dvořák** (1841–1904) in drawing on national music.

Folk to Folklorism

By the time Janáček was recording folk music, in the 1880s, traditional music was declining in everyday life and migrating to concert and festival performance. Folk music was giving way to 'folklorism'. Nonetheless, the music was adopted with enthusiasm. At the 1895 National Czecho-Slavonic Ethnographical Exhibition in Prague Janáček prepared a musical programme from Moravia featuring his beloved string band from Velká nad Veličkou. It became apparent that folk music expressed not only an inner need, but also a national identity. The exhibition ushered in an era of folk music gatherings, celebrations and festivals, bolstered by the creation of the Czechoslovak Republic in 1918. Similar feelings of joy at

the liberation after World War II, gave rise to the foundation of the biggest folklore festival in the country in Strážnice, Moravia in 1946. There are several other similar festivals in Moravia today.

The **Communists**, who ruled the country from 1948, co-opted the folklore movement and used it for ideological presentations of socialist culture. In the 1950s and 60s they started to support ensembles financially and influence them politically and also created new professional ensembles. The idea was to create a new sort of popular music removed from the influence of decadent Western pop and jazz. The musical style of these ensembles tended to be conformist, artificial and sanitised – what Milan Kundera described as 'fakelore'.

However, the pan-European strains of the folk revival blew in the sounds of jazz and rock together with an interest in the genuine forms of traditional music. An important impulse to the folk movement was the two-week visit of **Pete Seeger** during his world tour in 1964. He left in his wake a burgeoning movement of Czech singer-songwriters.

Two streams of traditional folk music existed in the 1970s and 80s. One was officially supported, and stressed a professional attitude in composing and arranging. The **National Radio Folk Orchestras** in Brno and Bratislava are good examples. The second stream returned to genuine folk music while encouraging new and individual interpretations. **New and electric folk music** carried an exciting 'non-conformist' caché in a totalitarian state, and the **Porta Festival** (established in 1966) attracted over 30,000 young people in its peak in the late 1980s and was nicknamed the 'Czech Woodstock'.

Since the Velvet Revolution of 1989, musicians have been able to experiment more freely with the different sorts of music, including traditional and modern folk music, rock and jazz, both local and world. For example, the **Českomoravská hudební společnost** group fuses rock, Moravian and Celtic music.

Bohemia

The most famous Czech dance must be the **polka**, a lively Bohemian couple dance in duple time, which became one of the most popular society dances of the nineteenth century – and has had vast influence on music throughout Europe and even Latin America. It's thought that its name may come from the Czech *půlka* (half) referring to the half-steps in the dance; or from *polska* (a Polish girl) pointing to a link to the *krakowiak* dance-songs of southern Poland. Like many Czech songs and dances, it begins with a heavily accented first note. The sort of upbeat common in Anglo-German music, for instance, is virtually unknown as Czech words are stressed on their first syllable.

In Bohemia today, the main living traditional folk music is in the Chodsko region in the southwest. This hilly district in the Czech-German borderlands has its own distinctive identity and is famous for its **bagpipes**. The annual **Chodsky Festival** in Domažlice presents local virtuoso bagpipers such as Zdeněk Bláha, Antonín Konrády and Vladimír Baier. An **International Bagpipers Festival** also takes place in **Strakonice** every other year. Outstanding local names are Josef Režný and his Prácheňský Ensemble (founded 1949), and the Pošumavská dudácká muzika. The Chodsko musical bands are typical for a rich repertoire of songs, a remarkable polyphonic style of instrumental playing by small peasant bands of bagpipes, clarinet and fiddle and some distinctive local dances with variable rhythms.

The bagpipe tradition has survived thanks to the appearance of revival players in the 1910s and 20s – school teachers such as Stanislav Svačina from Domažlice and Karel Michalíček from Košíře, Prague. Preceding them were the first cylinder

Famous old Czech bagpiper Jan Kobes from Domažlice

L. RUTTE

recordings of Chodsko bagpipers (1909) and collections of songs in the nineteenth century. The fear that the button accordion, which appeared in the 1860s, and string and brass band music would push traditional bagpipe music out never materialised. In fact, today's revival groups are so strong, they've helped resurrect the vanished tradition of bagpipe music just over the border in Germany and Austria.

Another type of genuine Bohemian folk music (dating from the early nineteenth century) can be found farther east, in the Czech-Moravian Highlands. **Skřipácká** music employs a rough, home-made rectangular violin, viola and double bass. It was a virtually vanished exotic tradition, but has had something of a revival with good bands in Jihlava and Telč.

The folk boom of the 1960s gave birth to a group called **Minnesengři** whose sweet harmony vocals gathered around singer-songwriter **Pavel Žalman Lohonka**. The band discovered many lost folk songs from the south Bohemian lake area in the archives and revived them. During the 1980s and 90s **Dagmar Andrtová** evolved from a ballad singer into a remarkable guitar-player and composer, while the folk singer, guitar and lute player, **Vladimír Merta** moved from songs directed against the totalitarian regime to music inspired by Jewish, and especially Sephardic, roots. A professional approach to old Czech music – medieval to nineteenth century – has been taken by pioneering outfits like **Skiffle Kontra**, **Musica Bohemica** and **Spirituál kvintet**. Many imitators make a living performing to foreign visitors on Prague's tourist highway, Charles Bridge.

From the mid-nineteenth century, **brass band music**, originating in the military bands of the Hapsburg Empire, spread rapidly through Bohemia. It was one of the things that destroyed the traditional folk music and nearly did the same in Moravia in the first half of this century. Until the arrival of modern bands and taped music, brass bands were used for weddings, dances and even funerals (and still are, to some extent). The repertoire was arranged folk songs and marches and dances by brass band composers like František Kmoch (1850–1913).

Pub Songs and Tramps

Prague's celebrated *pivnice* (bars) are home to **staro-pražske písniéky** (old Prague songs), performed most notably by **Šlapeto**, a band whose traditions stretch back more than a century. The name roughly translates as "It's going well" and they play these old pub songs and love songs, accompanied by accordion, fiddle, guitar and double bass. The style owes something to Viennese schrammel music (see p.13) thanks to its historical connections with Vienna and mixed Czecho-German culture.

Another sort of urban folk, called **trampská hudba** (Tramp Music), is a favourite amongst Czechs who hit the road to form emmigrant communities all over the world. The music of the *trampové* grew out of the migrations of young workers to industrial areas in the early decades of this century and it reflects the popular music of the era with guitars and mandolins. It's a specifically Czech phenomenon with no equivalent in any other European country. Current groups include the **Červánek Duo**, who have been around for at least thirty years, and **Kamelot** (formed in 1982). Tramp music also had its swinging '60s and poppy '80s manifestations. The sentimental lyrics typically express the desire for freedom and love.

Czech tramp music is probably responsible for the fraternal welcome that greeted American **blue grass and country music** in the early 1960s. The **Annual Banjo Jamboree** first held in 1972 in Kopidlno, (east Bohemia) is the oldest European bluegrass festival. There are many bands trying to imitate traditional American bluegrass music. However, the national favourites, **Robert Křest'an** and **Druhá tráva** (Second Grass), which evolved from the pioneering band **Poutníci**, enrich bluegrass and newgrass music with Czech lyrics – deeper and more emotional than your average bluegrass song – and a few traditional Czech tunes.

Moravia

Dozens of festivals a year and hundreds of musicians present traditional **Moravian music**. The most vital tradition can be found in southeast Moravia where the lowlands meet the rolling hills. Bands still play for weddings, dances, fairs and at Shrovetide when musicians go from house to house. While Bohemia is beer country, in south Moravia it's wine or *slivovice* (distilled from plums). In the fields, near the villages, there are wine cellars where, in the summer or autumn there's music and singing coming from the open doors.

The music is provided by **cimbalom bands**, the best known of which is **Hradišt'an**, led by violinist Jiří Pavlica, who have toured Europe, America and Asia. Hradišt'an (formed in 1950) is known for its performances of traditional music, original compositions, and also for its fusions of Moravian roots with rock and World Music – for example in a recent album with Japanese instrumentalist and composer Yas-Kaz.

FRANTIŠEK OKĚNKA ARCHIVE

Martin Hrbáč and his band with guest cimbalom player Zuzana Lapčiková

A cimbalom band like Hradišt'an represents the most widespread type of instrumental group in Moravian folk music, with the cimbalom, several violins, clarinet and double bass. The original small portable cimbalom has been replaced by the large Hungarian-type of concert cimbalom with a pedal. Besides the *primáš* (leader – usually the first violin) and other instrumentalists, there are male and female vocalists and sometimes choirs.

While some people disapprove of Hradišt'an's contemporary leanings, primás and singer **Martin Hrbáč** and his Horňácká cimbalom band appeal to the most traditional tastes. Hrbáč is a disciple of the legendary primás Jožka Kubík (1907–1978). His music comes from the Horňácko region in the Moravian Highlands, where Janáček did some of the best field collections. Today there's a good festival in **Velká nad Veličkou**. Violin players Jaroslav Staněk, the founder of Hradišt'an, Slávek Volavý and Jura Petrů were other important band leaders of the post-war era in other Moravian regions.

Other small, but distinctive, folk regions in the north are **Valašsko (Valachia)** and **Lašsko (Lachia)** where Janáček was born in Hukvaldy. Valachia is famous for its pastoral, shepherd culture and the name comes from a historical or legendary migration of Romanian shepherds (Wallachs) in the Middle Ages, while Lachia has strong Polish influences. Many cultures have met and intermingled in Moravia.

The most typical Moravian dance is the **sedlácká** (peasant dance, from *sedlák* – peasant). This is a fast couple dance, often with disconcerting rhythmic flexibility. There is also the Hungarian style male dance, **verbuňk** (with its distinctive dotted rhythms) and **táhlá**, a slow song without a regular rhythm sung or played by the primáš with the accompanying musicians following his solo.

There are two other types of traditional band in Moravia: **gajdošská muzika**, bagpipes sometimes accompanied by a fiddle; and **hudecká muzika**, string band music with one or twin fiddles, viola, double bass and sometimes a clarinet. The early twentieth century influence of popular dance music also left its legacy in the **brass bands** of Moravia.

Based on Moravian traditions there's a lively contemporary roots scene. **Vlasta Redl** is a charismatic composer, singer and guitarist. He has worked with the rock groups **Fleret** and **AG Flek** though all of them exist independently now. Then there is the singer and fiddler **Iva Bittová**, who has done many international tours. Her Moravian and Gypsy roots plus her composing talent make her a star of alternative music wherever she appears. Her sister **Ida Kelarová** also brings an ethnic approach to her singing projects.

The foremost Czech jazz pianist, **Emil Viklicky**, together with violin player **Jiří Pavlica** (Hradišt'an) and cimbalom player and singer **Zuzana Lapčíková** have fused jazz with Moravian traditional music in the trio **Ad Libitum Moravia**. Brother and sister **Petr** and **Hana Ulrychovi** are vocalists who brought Moravian melodies into the popular music of the 1970s and who now compose their own music accompanied by the Javory cimbalom band. The excellent cimbalom player **Dalibor Štrunc** has combined traditional and contemporary folk music in his Cimbal Classic band, and **Teagrass**, with a mandolin instead of a fiddle in the hands of the primáš, mixes Moravian, Balkan, Klezmer and American bluegrass music into a compelling global sound.

Slovakia

The beautiful, mountainous landscape of northern and central **Slovakia** is the home of various **shepherds' flutes**: from a small-size whistle to a *fujara* two meters long made from one piece of wood. They can be played solo – as in the hands of **Pavel Bielčik** – or combined with small bagpipes (*gajdy* in Slovak). Other instruments in the mountain music bands include fiddles, a half-size double bass and a small button accordion.

Slovakia's mountain regions are where the best **folklore festivals** take place, highlighting bands and singers like the **Mucha Brothers** from Terchová, **Ján Ámbroz** from Telgárt, **Ďatelinka** from Detva, and **Šarišan** from Prešov. The instrumental music of the Tatra mountains – with string bands of several violins and a cello – is similar to the *górale* music of Podhale in Poland across the border. As in southern Poland, the popular subject of song texts here is **Jánošík**, the local Robin Hood. In Slovakia he occurs in songs and fairy tales and for poor people he was, and still is, the embodiment of justice – even if in reality these brigands were often common criminals.

The southern lowlands have absorbed Hungarian and Gypsy influences into their cimbalom bands and the result is the swinging, virtuoso style that is usually associated with Slovak music. The most popular dance is the fiery **čardáš**. Bandleader and fiddler **Miroslav Dudík**, grandson of the legendary Slovak fiddler **Samko Dudík** (1880–1967) and much admired by Janáček, is an heir to the Slovak cimbalom band tradition, although his recordings favour ensembles that are too big and folkloristic.

Eastern Slovakia is a world apart. It is isolated and culturally very rich with Slovak, Polish, Ruthenian (Ukranian), Hungarian and Gypsy influences combining in the music of some wild cimbalom bands and a living folk culture. The traditional music is still strongly connected with folk customs and village celebrations and therefore has not really been transformed into contemporary folk music. Singer-songwriter **Zuzana Homolová** works with old Slovak ballads and performs them in their most powerful form – a cappella. The group **Ghymes** comes from the Hungarian minority in the south of the country and, as many tancház groups in Hungary

have done, they've drawn on local traditions combined with their own eclectic tastes and imagination to produce some excellent recordings and great gigs.

The village of Dolná Krupá (near Trnava northeast of Bratislava) has an intriguing place in musical history. It was the home of the **Dopyera family** before their emmigration to the US in 1908. The Dopyera Brothers invented the famous **Dobro guitar**, with its circular resonating plate, in 1926 and Trnava has hosted an annual Dobrofest since 1992.

Festivals

Czech Republic

Chodské slavnosti (Domažlice, Bohemia). Festival of Czech bagpipe music in August.

Horňácké slavnosti (Velká nad Veličkou, northern Moravia). Very traditional festival of the Horňácko region, second half of July.

Strážnice. The biggest festival in the Czech and Slovak republics with local and international artists. In the small town of Strážnice, southern Moravia, the last weekend in June.

Západoslovenské folklórne slavnosti (Myjava, Slovakia). Traditional festival of west Slovakia, in June.

Slovakia

Prázdniny v Telči (Holidays in Telč, south Moravia). One of the most popular non-traditional festivals, located in the beautiful medieval town of Telč. Main performances held in the courtyard of the castle, with bands like Hradišťan, Teagrass, Cimbal Classic and Vlasta Redl. It lasts two weeks at the turn of July and August.

Detva. The traditional folklore festival of central Slovakia, in July.

Východná. Traditional festival that presents folklore of northern and eastern Slovakia, the last weekend in June.

Gnosis Brno (see discography on p.55 for address) can provide information about festivals and other musical events, traditional and non-traditional, in the Czech Republic.

Roma – Gypsies

Gypsies have been living in Bohemia, Moravia and Slovakia for centuries – although all but six hundred Czech and Moravian Gypsies were killed in Nazi concentration camps during World War II. The communities revived somewhat in the post-war years but relations today are not easy, and in Slovakia, in particular, Gypsies have been subject to violent harassment from their settled neighbours in the post-Independent nation.

As in many of the countries of eastern Europe, Gypsies figure prominently in the Moravian and Slovak cimbalom bands. Their music is highly

Věra Bílá – Rom Pop Queen

"I am neither Gypsy nor gadje (white). I see myself as a facade which looks respectable and well-maintained from the outside, but inside there is the heart, blood and nerves of an old Gypsy woman and she has quite another story to tell." So speaks **Věra Bílá** – the most successful Romani musician to emerge from former Czechoslovakia.

In appearance and style Bílá is reminiscent of American blues singers of the 1950s, but her music combines Romani lyrics, a Latin beat and a passionate intensity to produce a distinctively modern sound. Her voice is deep and very strong, almost masculine. She writes most of her songs, but also sings traditional material. Her career illustrates the difficulties of presenting Gypsy music to a largely white public.

Born into a musical family in one of the squalid townships of eastern Slovakia in 1954, Bílá's early interest in traditional *cimbalová muzika* was opposed by her parents. They knew what little chance there was of escaping a life of poverty through cimbalom tunes. Nevertheless, whilst working in restaurants, bakeries and even digging roads, she pursued her musical career. Singing at weddings, funerals and local dances she teamed up with guitarists Jan Dužda, Dezider Lučka and bassist Emil Pupa Miko who were to become the nucleus of her band **Kale**. Bílá means 'white' in Czech and kale means 'black' in Romani.

The group were saved from obscurity by a chance encounter with **Zuzana Navarová**, a member of a mainstream Czech popgroup. In 1994 she invited Kale to support them at a concert in Prague's prestigious Lucerna Hall. Their rapturous reception earned them a regular contract at the *Koruna* bar under Charles Bridge. *Koruna* was (and remains) an unusual meeting place for fashionable Czechs, bewildered tourists and enthusiastic South American students. Playing there was probably responsible for the Latin flavour Bělá and Kale bring to Romani songs. In 1995 record producers overruled sceptical reports from their local Czech managers and *Rom Pop* was produced to general acclaim in France.

International success has brought some local recognition for Bílá and Kale. After living in the western Bohemian town of Rokycany for fifteen years, the mayor invited them to perform at the municipal hall, and Czech television has made a documentary about her. But it has also brought cultural dilemmas. Racial difficulties between Czechs and Gypsies in certain areas have escalated since 1989 and some of Bílá's Romani friends have been attacked by skinheads. She suffered racist taunts at a concert in Brno, but returned to perform there with huge success in May 1998. Bílá also finds that when she now visits relatives back in Slovakia, there is jealousy at her success and also resentment at what she has done to traditional Gypsy music. But, despite enormous pressure for her to produce a more commercial sound, her latest CD is much closer to her Gypsy roots.

"I am just myself and I am alone. I have my music which gives meaning to my life. It liberates and restores me."

David Charap

NIKOLA TAČEVSKI

Věra Bílá

emotional and band leaders, such as Evžen Horváth, Josef Griňa and Ňudovít Kováč, show great virtuosity and showmanship on violin or cimbalom. One vocalist to watch out for is **Věra Bílá** and her band **Kale** (see box). They have become popular in the Czech Republic and have toured Europe. A festival of Gypsy music (Romfest) was established in 1991, but lasted only a few years.

See Gypsy Music article (p.146) for more on the wider context of Gypsy Music in Europe.

With thanks to Jan Sobotka and Irena Přibylová

discography

Sadly, few of the discs below have any international distribution. The **Lotos** label Is at Plzeňská 113, 150 00 Praha 5, Czech Republic ☎/fax (420) 2 5721 1478 while some of the other small labels below can be obtained through **Gnosis Brno**, Rezkova 30, 602 00 Brno; Fax: (420) 5 4321 5463; email: *plocek@iach.cz* website: *www.mujweb.cz/www/gnosis_brno*

Bohemia

Compilations

ⓔ **Bohemian Folk Songs from Chodsko**
(Supraphon, Czech Republic).

A good selection of the best singers and musicians of the Chodsko region from 1970–1985. Includes the 70-year-old folk singer Markéta Volfíková; leading figures in the bagpipe revival, the Svačina Brothers, and many others.

ⓔ **Cikánský pláč/Gypsy Lament**
(Supraphon, Czech Republic).

An excellent anthology of Gypsy songs and cimbalom music in Czechoslovakia, full of emotions and deep feeling.

ⓔ **Hrály Dudy: The Hidden Spell of the Czech Bagpipe** (Bonton, Czech Republic)

Field recordings (1974–1992) from the collection of Josef Režný, veteran Czech expert on bagpipe music. Includes bagpipes with fiddles and remarkable historical bagpipes.

ⓔ **Strážnice Folk Festival 1946–95** (Supraphon, Czech Republic)

This includes many rare and precious recordings of Bohemian, Moravian, Slovak and Gypsy folk music with an emphasis on the authentic village style. Compiled by producer Jaromír Nečas who has made recordings in Strážnice since the beginning in 1946.

Artists

Pošumavská Dudácká Muzika

This is a pretty traditional bagpipe band from the region at the foot of the Šumava mountains, with some 1960s folk revival influences.

ⓔ **Poslyšte mládenci: Wedding Songs from Čestice and Pošumaví region** (Musicvars, Czech Republic).

Traditional music with some unusual repertoire and instruments. A good example of development within the tradition.

Moravia

Compilations

ⓔ **The Oldest Recordings of Folk-singing from Moravia and Slovakia 1909–1912**
(Gnosis Brno, Czech Republic).

A selection from the wax cylinders originally recorded by Leoš Janáček and his collaborators. Obviously of specialist interest, but the CD comes complete with English translations and descriptions of Janáček's ethnomusicological activities.

Artists

Cimbal Classic & Polajka

Cimbal Classic is one of Moravia's top non-traditional folk bands, while Polajka, a female choir from Rožnov (a town in northern Moravia where there's a beautiful village museum) is an authentic folk choir.

ⓔ **Vánoce v Rožnově/Christmas in Rožnov**
(Valašské muzeum v přírodě, Czech Republic).

A great collection of Valachian carols. Authentic female folk-singing with a contemporary cimbalom band that leans towards classical music. CD available through Gnosis Brno.

Martin Hrbáč

The charismatic singer and fiddler Martin Hrbáč (born 1939), and his cimbalom band, is one of the legends of Moravian folk music.

ⓒ **Horňácký hudec Martin Hrbáč**
(Gnosis Brno, Czech Republic).

The traditional music of the distinctive Horňácko region of northern Moravia. Examples of string band, cimbalom band and bagpipe music idiomatically played. Slow songs and wild dances.

František Okénka

Born in 1921 in the Horňácko region, Okénka is a singer, teacher and member of the legendary Jožka Kubík band. He now works as a guide at the windmill which is part of the museum of Horňácko life in Kuželov.

ⓔ **František Okénka** (Gnosis Brno, Czech Republic).

Archive tracks and new recordings from 1996 when Okénka was 75, this is some of the most authentic Moravian rural music recently recorded. Okénka is accompanied on most tracks by a four-piece string band lead by Martin Hrbáč – considered the purest Horňácko folk sound.

Varmužova Cimbálová Muzika

Probably the best band of singers in Moravia and a real family band. There's the father, Josef Varmuža (bass), his brother Pavel (cimbalom), Josef's four sons – Pavel (lead violin), Petr (second violin), Josef (viola) and Jiří (viola) plus the gentle voices of the mother Hedvika and daughter Kateřina contrasting with the men's strong sound.

Na Kyjovsku (Gnosis Brno, Czech Republic).

Music from the region of Kyjov in southern Moravia. Often wild and spirited, although some numbers sound more formal.

Slovakia

Compilations

 Prekrásne Slovensko/Beautiful Slovakia (Musica, Slovakia).

Despite the kitsch title and cover, this is a great selection of traditional Slovak music. Shepherds' flutes, mountain string bands, great mountain singing and cimbalom music performed by some of the best Slovak folk musicians – the Mucha Brothers, Anna Hulejová, Darina Laščiaková, the Štefan Molota band and others.

 Slovak Csardas: Dance Tunes from the Pennsylvania Coal Mines (Heritage/Interstate, UK).

Slovaks emigrated to the US to work in the coalmines and refineries of Pennsylvania and these recordings were made for the Victor and Columbia labels from 1928–30. There are four bands and (apart from the Michael Stiber tracks which are badly distorted) the recordings sound good for their age. The repertoire is Gypsy-style csardas and polkas, but what's remarkable is their raw, unsanitised style evoking the rowdy village bands of Slovakia in the first decades of this century.

Artists

Samko Dudík

Dudík (1880–1967) was a legendary fiddler and bandleader who was championed by Janáček and influenced many Slovak and Moravian folk musicians. Jožka Kubík was the great Moravian fiddler and Samko Dudík was the Slovak equivalent.

O Samko Dudík (Opus, Slovakia).

Rare recordings made by Brno Radio in the late 1950s of the Dudík family band – an eight-piece ensemble of strings and cimbalom. Wonderful old-style Slovak music which should be reissued on CD.

Mucha Brothers

The four Mucha Brothers are an excellent string band from Terchová, a village in the mountains of northern Slovakia. This is the highland music also heard across the border in Poland. They sometimes also use shepherds' flutes and a button accordion (*heligonka*) played by Rudolf Patrnčiak.

 Do hory, do lesa Valaši (A.L.I. Records, Slovakia).

Some of the best Slovak traditional music played with incredible energy. This disc is actually a collection of folk carols. Any of their other CDs are equally good.

Šarišan

The Šarišan cimbalom band based in Prešov is among the most famous and representative bands of eastern Slovakia.

 Do nas, chlapci (A.L.I. Records, Slovakia).

Beautiful, vital music of the eastern Slovaks from the Šariš region. In the singing you can detect slight Polish or Ukranian accents, likewise in the instrumental music with strong

Hungarian flavour in the cimbalom band. Bright and vigorous, not sentimental or cloying.

New Folk

Artists

Ad Libitum Moravia

An unusual band featuring one of the best Czech jazz piano players, Emil Viklicky, together with well-known folk violin player Jiří Pavlica and singing cimbalom player Zuzana Lapčíková.

 Prší déšť/Fast Falls the Rain (Lotos, Czech Republic).

This interesting project connects Moravian folk songs with a modern jazzy approach and feeling. Sweet singing and cimbalom playing is followed by jazz improvisations backed by drums and upright bass.

Věra Bílá

Small, but packing quite a punch, Bílá is the most successful Romany performer to emerge from former Czechoslovakia. She was born in 1954 into a musical family in eastern Slovakia, but with her band Kale has broadened her musical sound to embrace Latin sounds performed in an unmistakably Romani manner.

 Queen of Romany (BMG/GIGA, Austria).

A 1999 'best of' disc drawing together tracks from her two albums. Some fizzing up-tempo numbers with Kale's guitars and vocal harmonies and the tragic 'When I'm getting drunk', one of the greatest Romani vocals on disc.

 Rom-Pop (BMG/Ariola, Czech Republic; Last Call Records, France; RCA Victor, US).

Her debut 1995 album is infectiously catchy with its Latin-influenced rhythms and occasional sax and piano in the mix.

Iva Bittová

Iva Bittová, folk singer and violin player of Moravian and Gypsy origin. She started as an actress, but since the mid-1980s has made a name with her one-woman performances with vocals and violin. She has also collaborated

A B **CZECH & SLOVAK REPUBLICS**

with drummer Pavel Fajt, rock band Dunaj and has recently composed a piece to perform with the excellent Škampa Quartet as part of a survey of her work on Supraphon.

⊚ Bílé Inferno/White Inferno
(Indies Records, Czech Republic).

Bittová and guitar and bass player Vladimír Václavek make beautiful expressive music, minimalist in style, drawing on classical music, Gypsy, Moravian, Slovak, and other east European styles.

Českomoravská Hudební Společnost

The bizarrely-named Czecho-Moravian Musical Society founded by composer and arranger Jiří Břenek. He died tragically young a couple of years ago, but the group remains the most promising 1990s folk-rock band in Bohemia.

⊚ Mezi Horami/Amidst the Mountains
(Polygram/Venkow, Czech Republic).

This 1996 album blends together Bohemian and Moravian songs in a way that satisfies both innovators and purists. There's also a touch of Celtic inspiration.

Zuzana Homolová

Zuzana Homolová is one of Slovakia's strongest and most interesting folk singers.

⊚ Slovenské Balady/Slovak Ballads
(Pavian Records, Slovakia).

1995 album in which sad and dramatic Slovak ballads are accompanied by multi-instrumentalist Vlasta Redl, who brings great sensitivity to his arrangements and performance.

Hradišt'an

Hradišt'an is probably the most innovative cimbalom band in Moravia. The band started in the 1950s as a traditional outfit led by Jaroslav Staněk, but since 1978 under the leadership of Jiří Pavlica it has become far more eclectic.

⊚ Ozvěny Duše/Moravian Echoes
(Lotos, Czech Republic).

1994 album that takes a journey through the history of Moravian music from Old Church Slavonic music to regional and pan-Moravian styles.

Ida Kelarová

Ida Kelarová is known for her experiments with the human voice and various forms of ethnic music.

⊚ Ida Kelarová a hosté (Lotos, Czech Republic).

On this 1997 album Kelarová brings in a unique roster of female guest artists – her sister Iva Bittová, Gypsy singer Věra Bílá and others from Bulgaria, Zimbabwe and Spain.

Vlasta Redl and Jiří Pavlica

Folk singer and rock musician Vlasta Redl is one of Moravia's favourite contemporary performers and Jiří Pavlica, primáš of the Hradišt'an ensemble, is an outstanding personality in traditional music.

⊚ Vlasta Redl, AG Flek & Jiží Pavlica – Hradišt'an
(BMG/Ariola, Czech Republic).

This 1994 album is a tasteful combination of rock and pop with Moravian cimbalom band music. On top there's the deeply emotional voice of Alice Holubová, one of the best young Moravian folk singers.

Teagrass

Teagrass blends together Western music styles (swing, bluegrass) with the Moravian and other Eastern European traditional music to create its own synthesis full of improvisations. Brings together instruments like mandolin, taragot, cimbalom, panpipes, dobro, etc.

⊚ Cestou na východ/Eastbound
(Gnosis Brno, Czech Republic).

A non-traditional journey from Moravia to Bulgaria.

Denmark & the Faroe Islands

a new pulse for the pols

Throughout Europe's folk revivals, ever since the 1960s, Denmark has proved a good host to external music at its venues and festivals. Now, though, it's time for the host to come in from the kitchen and do a turn. Musicians and bands are emerging in Denmark who draw on regional dance music traditions, ballads and the country's present-day mix of cultures. And they're working together to make things happen, as **Andrew Cronshaw** discovered. The distant Faroe Islands, who have a remarkable culture quite distinct from Denmark's, get a solo spot at the end of his article.

A Nordic country with a Nordic language, Denmark controlled the whole of Scandinavia in the Middle Ages. But it differs from its neighbours in two factors: a relatively compact size and lack of isolation. It's a densely populated and low-lying country with no place more than about forty miles from sea, and none of Norway or Sweden's distant valleys where traditions remained sheltered against the breezes of innovation. Nevertheless, individual areas and islands once had distinctive traditions, and some, such as that on the island of Fanø, have continued to the present day, and are being drawn on by musicians and bands in the present renaissance.

Past and present, most Danish folk comes from that universally popular dance duo – the **fiddle** and **accordion**. Most fiddlers tend to play with groups and there's no expressive solo fiddle style as there is in Norway and Sweden. In Danish roots music the guitar is also more visible than elsewhere in the Nordic countries. It has a leading exponent in **Morten Alfred Høirup**, well-known for his swing playing, particularly in the Danish/American/Finnish **American Café Orchestra**, and now eschewing that for modal and drone styles in new roots and traditional ballads.

Dance Music – and Fanø

The overall feel of Danish folk dance music is rhythmically fairly straightforward, closer to that of English folk dance bands than to the complexity of Swedish and Norwegian dance music. Its leading instruments have been, since the 17th and 19th century respectively, the **fiddle** and **accordion**. Other folk instruments used in the past in Denmark and now being to some extent revived

are the *humle* (a long fretted zither) and, depicted in Danish church murals as long ago as the 15th century, the *nyckelharpa*.

The oldest folk-dance surviving in Denmark is the **pols**, which was common in the seventeenth century. Its strongest survival has been on the isle of Fanø, off west Jutland just south of Esbjerg. The local form there, the **sønderhoning** (named after the Fanø town of Sønderho) is unusual because the dance alternates between a duple-time march and a triple-time swing while the music stays in duple time. The main tradition-bearers in Sønderho into the twentieth century were the Brinch family, of which the last musicians were fiddlers **Søren Lassen Brinch** (d.1988) and **Frits Attermann Brinch** (d.1993), and piano-player **Erling Brinch** (d.1994). Erling was a member of the trio **Jæ' Sweevers**, and since his death fiddler **Peter Uhrbrand** and accordionist **Ole Mouritzen** have continued the Fanø music as a duo.

Fanø has another distinctive dance, the **fanik**. This, the pols, and other dances in the Danish folk-dance repertoire such as polka, *vals* (waltz), *hopsa*, *rheinlænder*, *schottisch*, *trekanter* and the set dances *firtur* and *tretur* are variants of the dances which became popular across Europe from the seventeenth to the nineteenth century. They also survive in places such as Thy, Læsø and Himmerland.

Song

The current roots revival is only slowly moving towards exploring them, but Denmark has its share of Europe's **medieval ballads** – some of which survived in the oral tradition into the twentieth century – and other songs related to spheres and ceremonies of life.

A strong force in the circulation of new songs and old ballads from the sixteenth century until the beginning of the twentieth were the **skillingstryk** or **skillingsviser**, printed ballad sheets sold by street vendors, named after the smallest coin, the skilling. From the mid-nineteenth century a regular theme of these sheets was emigration – over 300,000 Danes emigrated, mostly to America, between 1850 and 1914.

The songs covered such subjects as the gold rush, ship disasters, going to Utah with the recruiting Mormons, and nostalgia for the homeland. The fact that many broadsheet copies of a song were sold, however, didn't necessarily mean that it entered the folk culture, any more than a number one hit record does today.

The Folk Scene and Revival

While in the 1970s there was a turn towards indigenous traditional musics in other Nordic countries, Denmark's folk festival and concert promoters played host – particularly to Irish, Scottish and American performers – and young Danish musicians tended to take up their instruments in those styles. A few, though, moved on to look at Danish music, and for some of these a mentor was Himmerland fiddler **Evald Thomsen** (1913-1993), who was recorded by pioneering folklorist **Thorkild Knudsen** and employed in the 1970s by the state as a folk music consultant. Thomsen was a lively player who stressed lift and drive above a missed note.

The late 1970s and '80s saw a dip in popularity of the whole folk scene except festivals. Seeds had been sown, though, and in the 1990s there has been an accelerating growth in tradition-rooted activity and bands, as well as in Danish-language singer-songwriters and multi-ethnic bands. An important factor in focusing and publicising this music has been the coming together of Denmark's music organisations, in particular the formation of The Danish Folk Council, which publishes a magazine and releases an annual showcase compilation CD.

There are clusters of revival groups around regions where traditions survive. Fanø has **Jæ' Sweevers**, for example. East Jutland has quite a concentration, including the fiddle bands **Rasmus** (named after a 1760 tunebook from which much of its material derives) and **Mølposen**, and the fiddles-accordion band **Jydsk På Næsen**.

It's not unusual for a musician to be in several bands, often moving between acoustic and rockier approaches. Fiddler **Michael Sommer** plays in all three Jutland groups, while button accordionist and singer **Carl Erik Lundgaard** pops up in many Danish groups. He runs a folk music record label, and is a member of the trio **Lang Linken**, which has been playing traditional music on fiddle, melodeon, bagpipe, hurdy-gurdy and humle since the 1970s. He was also a central player in roots-rock band **Danish Dia Delight**, which made an impression on the festival circuit until it broke up in 1997. Its energetic blend of traditional roots and rock pulled in a fun-seeking following and filled their heads with the shapes of traditional music. Another of the band's members was guitarist **Morten Alfred Høirup**, a fine swing player in such bands as the Café Orchestra, who has recently been exploring a more modal style and Danish traditional ballads, leading a band, **Vingården**, that includes members of Lang Linken and fiddler **Harald Haugaard Christensen**.

Haugaard is a busy musician. Not only is he, with Lundgaard, in the acoustic quartet **Puls**, which creates new dance tunes in traditional forms, he's also the driving fiddler in folk-rock band **Dug**, and plays with **Sorten Muld**, whose **techno-folk** centring on Danish ballads and the breathy vocals of Ulla Bendixen is showing considerable crossover success.

Festivals & the FFS

Denmark's largest folk music festivals are **Tønder** (four days at the end of August) and **Skagen** (the last weekend in June). Both of these feature Danish and world music acts.

Leading events dedicated to Danish roots music include **Roskilde Spillemandsstævne** (the last weekend of the school summer holidays, usually in early August) and **Spillemandsstævne i Århus** (the penultimate weekend in August).

The central information access point for Danish roots music is **Folkemusikkens Fælles Sekretariat** (**FFS**) (The Danish Folk Council), Karetmagergården, Graven 25 A, DK-8000 Århus C, ☎(45) 86 76 11 41; fax: 86 76 11 47; email: ffs@folkemusik.dk

The FFS publishes the bi-monthly magazine *Folk & Musik* and a directory *Folkemusik Scenen*, both of which give details of events and venues.

Other evolving bands include the clarinets, accordion and fiddle of **Phønix**, the swingy dance music with rhythm section of **Baltinget**, and **Kætter Kvartet**, which makes new music that fits the steps of Danish folk dance, drawing grooves from African and other musics.

Lars Lilholt Band

Not all Danish **singer-songwriters** are American-oriented guitar players; there is a Danish song tradition of literary ballads and setting poems to music, exemplified by such as the successful songwriter-poet team of **Povl Dissing** and **Benny Andersen**. The similarly named, less famous but nonetheless interesting **Benny E. Andersen** with his group **Blå Baller** writes songs moving between folk, avant-garde and Brecht-Weill styles. Others include **Erik Grip** and **Niels Hausgaard**, who sings in the dialect of his native Vendsyssel in North Denmark.

Singer-songwriter, guitarist, fiddler and bagpiper **Lars Lilholt** leads his own rocky band which first had pop chart success in the late 1980s and is a major concert attraction. He maintains, and indeed has intensified, contact with the folk tradition, as a member of Rasmus and with the **Next Stop Svabonius** project which draws together his band and many of the leading traditional players to revitalise eighteenth-century dance music.

The Faroe Islands

The beautiful, wild **Faroes** – eighteen islands in the North Atlantic with a total population of 47,000 – are a largely self-governing part of Denmark, roughly equidistant from Norway, Iceland and Shetland, and a two-hour flight northwest from distant Copenhagen. Their everyday language is Faroese, but everyone can speak Danish, and many also English.

There have long been fishing contacts, but the Faroes aren't on a major sea-route, and from 1709 until 1856, a time of great change in Europe, the presence of a monopoly trading station meant that the only official commercial contact was with Denmark. Culturally, the Faroes have remained very distinct.

Circle-dancing

The old Faroese traditional music was vocal. The fiddle arrived in the seventeenth century, and by the eighteenth the Faroes had the pan-European dances such as minuet, polka, and English and Scottish dances, but such innovations were largely restricted to the Danish smart set in the capital, Tórshavn, and among the wider population they didn't displace the old custom of **circle-dancing ballads**.

Throughout northern Europe it was common for groups of people to sing ballads while dancing in a circle. Only in the Faroes has this tradition persisted (unrevived) to the present day. The group holds hands, facing inwards, and the circle moves clockwise. Normally the singing has a leader and chorus. The song rhythm, particularly in the oldest heroic ballads, is frequently a different number of beats from the unchanging rhythm of the footstamp, giving a polyrhythmic, overlapping feel.

There are three main types of ballads danced. The majority, and still the most sung, are of the heroic type, called **kvæði** – members of the family of medieval ballads shared with other Nordic and Germanic peoples, with stories of the

Nibelung, Charlemagne and others, or of Nordic history and myth, featuring heroes battling trolls and giants. The second type, called **vísur**, are often not clearly distinguishable from kvæði, but they include Danish ballads converted to Faroese form. The third are satirical ballads, **tættir**, mocking individuals or politics, with tunes which are more regular rhythmically and structurally than those sung to the old ballads. Some broadsheet and biblical ballads from Norway and Denmark also found their way into the round-dance repertoire.

There was a time after World War II when it appeared ballad-dancing would die out, so **dance societies** were formed. Nowadays there's a small but determined number of young Faroese who dance the ballads. They're essentially an entertainment for the people in the circle not a performance for an audience – the dancers face inwards, not outwards. There is also a sense of the dance as a Faroese statement.

In the nineteenth century people began to write down the ballads, and many were later published as *Corpus Carminum Færoensium* – a volume which contained 44,000 stanzas – a huge number considering they were collected from a population which then only numbered about 5000. That suggests that they must have been sung very frequently.

No wonder – they're sung to winding, rhythmic tunes with long interesting melodic lines and are packed with rich imagery and strong stories carried through the centuries: Charlemagne killing an army with the dead Roland's sword at Roncevaux; Signhild murdered by the dwarf father of her fifteen children; Nornagestur who was 300 years old and couldn't die until a candle inside his harp burnt down; a young man who makes silver wings to fly to his beloved.

Another Faroese song tradition is that of **skjaldur** – songs of magic and fairytale sung by adults for children, with irregular beats following the rhythm of the words – has continued, though nowadays the songs are often sung by the children themselves. And then there are **hymns** – used not only in church but also often before or after a fishing or egg-collecting trip. Unlike in Iceland, the nineteenth-century installation of church organs didn't completely oust the old rhythmically free, pitch-sliding microtonal way of singing hymns. This was known as **kingosálmar** or **kingosangur** after the *Kirke-Psalme-Bog* – a hymn-book published in 1699 by Thomas Kingo. The kingosangur tradition disappeared from normal church use during the twentieth century, but recordings were made of singers who remembered the old way as late as the 1970s.

Faroese Music now

The most prevalent live music in the Faroes is rock or pop – that's what you'll get in a sports hall dance. However, **folk-rooted bands** do exist, and play in smaller clubs, and in one place in an old boat. Radio on the Faroes has had a positive attitude to folk music, and so, to some extent, has TV. There is also a folk festival (mid-July), which takes place in schools and other local venues around the islands.

Present-day Faroese roots music is characterised by musical seafaring – a creative linking of traditional forms with ideas and musicians from other cultures. Its major exponent is keyboard player, composer, promoter and head of Tutl records **Kristian Blak**. Blak is a communicator between diverse musical worlds, from his role as piano-player in the twin-fiddle led dance-music band **Spælimenninir**, through his Nordic jazz inflected arrangements of Faroese traditional song and hymn tunes, to his own compositions (both jazz and classical orchestral) and his series of albums and projects featuring musicians from the Faroes and abroad, including Finnish-resident kora player Malang Cissokho and Jan Garbarek percussionist Marilyn Mazur. In his 1995 *Loaned Finery* CD, Blak and a frequent collaborator, guitarist-singer **Lennart Kullgren**, created a new jazz sound based on Native American musical themes and vocalising, paralleling in feel some of the Sámi joik fusion projects of mainland Nordic countries.

Others working from Faroese roots include the progressive and ever-evolving **Enekk**, a group which brought in Bulgarian musicians for a recent project, and Copenhagen-resident **Annika Hoydal** who writes songs often based on the lyrics of her brother **Gunnar Hoydal**, and who has travelled to Scotland to work with its musicians on her recent recordings.

FØROYA SKÚLABÓKAGRUNNUR

Ballad dancing, early 20th century

discography

A specialist supplier who should have in stock most of the Danish and Faroese CDs below is GO' Danish Folk Music, Ribe Landesvej 190, DK 7100 Vejle, Denmark; ☎/fax (45) 75 72 24 86; website; www.homel.inet.tele.dk/eswo/

Denmark

Compilations

🔘 **Danemark: Chanteurs et Ménétriers**
(Ocora, France).

Recordings from the 30s to the 80s of traditional musicians and singers from various regions, including Ingeborg Munch, Evald Thomsen, Frits and Søren Lassen Brinch, from the collections of the Danish Folklore Archives, Danmarks Radio and the Folk Music House in Hogager.

🔘 **Folk Music from Denmark '99** (MXP, Denmark).

Each year the Danish Folk Council releases a compilation of tracks from new folk releases. Initially it's a promo-only, but later it usually goes on commercial release.

Artists

Danish Dia Delight

This seminal Danish roots band featured Morton Alfred Høirup, Lang Linken melodeon player Carl Erik Lundgaard, and saxist Henrik Bredholt, along with bass and drums.

🔘 **Live** (CE Musik, Denmark).

Traditional and new tunes and songs thrown around with accessible energy, charm and wit, a lot of skill and no educationalism or pompousness.

Dug

Dug are a young, energetic folk-rock band featuring fiddle, bass clarinet, sax, accordion and vocals.

🔘 **Beware of Fafner** (Nix, Denmark).

Not just folk-rock here: there's a good deal of subtle playing linking with the band's acoustic-trio origins.

Morten Alfred Høirup

A leading voice in the new Danish music, Høirup is a journalist, broadcaster, singer and guitarist from a circus-music family background. He is best known for jazzy-swing playing in his backing of fiddle tunes, but is also exploring a more specifically Danish-rooted style.

🔘 **Vingården** (Between Your Ears, Denmark).

A bold move into a more modal guitar style, combining with the American Café Orchestra and the traditional instruments of Lang Linken in Danish ballads and new tunes.

Kætter Kvartet

With voice, fiddle, mandolin, guitar and keyboards, plus drums, Kætter combines the structures of Danish and other Nordic dance tunes in new material with the lift and backbeat of other, hotter parts of the world.

🔘 **Kætter Kvartet** (Olga, Denmark).

Fun, excellent musicianship and bright ideas.

Lars Lilholt

Singer-songwriter, guitarist, fiddler and bagpiper Lilholt has had pop hits with his band, but also maintains contact with Danish traditional roots.

🔘 **Next Stop Svabonius**
(Danish Folk Council, Denmark).

Per and Lars Lilholt and their band of leading roots players here use approaches from string quartet to screaming rock to explore the dance music of the 1700s.

Lang Linken

Long-experienced trio, playing fiddles, melodeon, piano, plus hurdy-gurdy, bagpipe, humle, etc.

💿 **Lyst**
(CE Musik, Denmark).

Danish traditional dance-music at its best, with some new tunes and danceable songs, expertly played with a chugging, swinging lift.

Sorten Muld

Fast-rising, techno-based band featuring Ulla Bendixen's breathy vocal, making impressive atmospheric grooves around material mostly from Danish folksong collections.

🔘 **Mark II** (Sony/Pladecompagniet, Denmark).

The raw material is largely Danish traditional ballads, the sound is well-varied techno with blended-in instruments, including Søren Bendixen's guitar and Thomas Holm's bagpipe.

Faroe Islands

The main Faroese record company is Tutl (Reynagøta 12, FR-100 Tórshavn, Faroe Islands; ☎ (298) 314 825, founded in 1977, and boasting a catalogue of more than 80 jazz, rock, classical and Faroese roots releases, virtually all featuring new material played by Faroese musicians.

Compilations

 Flúgvandi Biðil (Tutl, Faroes).

Twenty songs and ballads, mostly from the Faroese University archive, from the first recordings in 1902 up to 1997. Fine voices singing rich old stories to remarkable winding, tripping rhythmic tunes. A revelation, showing the Faroes' importance among north European song traditions.

⊙ **Alfagurt Ljóðar Mín Tunga (Tutl, Faroes).**

Kvæði, visur, tættir, kingosálmar and skjaldur, recordings made between 1959 (a fine kingosálmar example) and 1990, accompanying the excellent paperback *Traditional Music in the Faroe Islands* (Føroya Skúlabókagrunnur) which was a major source in the writing of this chapter.

Kristian Blak

The key musical mover in the Faroes, Blak is involved in a multitiude of projects and recordings, moving between traditional music, jazz and classical compositions.

⊙ **Kingoløg** (Tutl, Faroes).

A suite based on 15 kingosálmar, led on piano with harmonium, flute, recorder, cor anglais, bassoon, mandolin and bass.

⊙ **Klæmint** (Tutl, Faroes).

When weather permits, Blak organises for musicians and audience to be taken by boat into a sea-cave, and has written pieces especially for these grotto-concerts. This, featuring guitar, keyboards, trumpet, voice, naverlur, bass and percussion, is the second such suite, recorded on the waters in the cave Klæmintsgjogv.

Enekk

This progressive roots band – vocals, bass, guitars, piano – plays arrangements of traditional Faroese and original material, and increasingly draws on outside influences.

⊙ **Fýra Nætur Fyri Jól** (Tutl, Faroes).

Their most recent album, featuring Bulgarian folk musicians Valeri Dimchev and Dragomir Dimov.

Spælimenninir

Six musicians, including Kristian Blak, from Faroes, Sweden, Denmark and USA playing Nordic music on two fiddles, guitar, recorder, piano, bass, with occasional vocals.

⊙ **Flóð og Fjøra (Tutl, Faroes).**

Lively, strongly-played dance music akin in feel to a Scottish ceilidh band and reflective instrumental interpretations of Faroese traditional songs.

England | Folk/Roots

england's changing roots

A decade or so ago it was impossible to imagine England's own folk music heritage playing anything but a cartoonesque bit part, ridiculed and kicked around by a mainstream popular culture seemingly sympathetic to every hybrid known to music-kind except its own traditions. Old clichéd images of beards, fingers in ears, nasal voices and overweight morris dancers die hard, but the emergence of a World Music constituency has opened ears to some esoteric riches at home – and slowly chipped away at the deeply ingrained disdain for all notions of Englishness. **Colin Irwin** takes a closer look at the image of English folk past and present.

England's multi-cultural status has, in the 1990s, at last begun to express itself in music through the emergence of second generation immigrants developing a whole new genre of styles involving a cross-fertilisation of everything from banghra and reggae to hip-hop, Celtic and Baltic. The blurring of the edges regarding what is to be regarded as English music has, paradoxically, encouraged a disparate range of musicians to re-assess the roots and discover a dramatic song form that goes way beyond the usual misinformation about incest ballads and fey ditties concerning jolly ploughboys.

A status akin to folk royalty has also been granted surviving veterans from the original heady days of the 1960s/'70s revival, as evinced by a newly respectful media treatment of anything involving the Waterson/Carthy clan in the wake of a brace of Mercury Music prize nominations for Norma Waterson's self-titled solo album and her daughter Eliza Carthy's *Red Rice*, a prestigious celebratory London Royal Albert Hall concert for Roy Bailey in 1998, and relentless reissues of classic early material. Even relatively overlooked figures such as Anne Briggs and Robin and Barry Dransfield have had their work re-issued and acclaimed with an enthusiasm that must have amazed artists so acclimatised to scornful indifference.

The great Nic Jones, tragically forced into retirement following an horrific road crash in 1982, has been re-discovered; and England's leading folk label, Topic, has embarked on an imaginative re-issue programme, including the launch of the 20-CD *Voice of the People* series documenting the history of the great traditional singers like Harry Cox, Sam Larner and Walter Pardon, alongside Ewan MacColl's legendary *Radio Ballads* series originally issued on Argo.

Birth and Rebirth

The heyday of the **English folk club movement** was in the 1960s and '70s when, fuelled by the protest era, the clubs acquired social relevance and an unlikely scent of alternative trendiness. There were interesting developments in contemporary songwriting - from **Ralph McTell**, **Roy Harper** and **Al Stewart** onwards; there was a veritable gold-mine of guitar stylists from **Davy Graham** to **Bert Jansch** and **John Renbourn**; there were the great folk-rock experiments led by the **Fairports** and **Steeleye Span**; there was a formidable array of artists of varying styles providing a formidable backbone for the scene, including **Robin** and **Barry Dransfield**, **Shirley Collins**, **Nic Jones**, **June Tabor**, **John Kirkpatrick** and **Sue Harris**, **Bill Caddick**, **Dave Burland** and **Vin Garbutt** – all providing exciting daily bread for a scene whose heartbeat still lay in the great traditional music of English history.

But if you stand still you go backwards, and other styles and movements queued up to kick sand in the face of English folk music. Folk clubs have never regained fashionable status – and probably never will do – but the music has slowly re-affirmed its dignity, albeit in a dissipated fashion, ironically establishing its respect through patronage from other territories.

The re-birth had its beginnings during the mid 1980s when the likes of **Billy Bragg**, **The Pogues** and **The Men They Couldn't Hang** – too brash and unselfconscious to to be tarnished by the dictates of cultural fashion and old hang-ups involved in puritan values – set about English/Irish folk song with an almost manic energy that was as shocking as it was exciting. Outraged letters to the folk mags from diehard folkies appalled by the primitive irreverence worn like a

Pub session at Sidmouth - England's most enjoyable gathering of folkies

badge by these new wave bands confirmed the necessity of such radicalism. English folk music had carefully constructed and protected its own elitist ghetto in the folk clubs for too long, a blindly independent strand paying not even lip service to the rest of the music industry, and unbeknowingly stagnating, crumbling and turning into a ridiculed museum relic as a result.

The sudden outburst of **punk-folkery** swiftly lost its appeal as a movement as it became obvious the artists involved had little in common beyond attitude and a genuine respect for the giants of the preceding generations – the MacColls, Carthys, etc – but the long-term ramifications were huge and they remain inspirational. After being divorced for a while The Men They Couldn't Hang returned at the end of the 1990s to pitch the social history mini-dramas of main songwriter Paul Simmonds back into the mainstream. **Billy Bragg** bodyswerved his own reputation as political-commentator-in-chief to re-invent himself as Woody Guthrie's voice on earth with his *Mermaid Avenue* album of newly discovered Guthrie material, and a whole range of electric bands like **The Levellers**, **Blyth Power**, **Blue Horses**, **The Rattlers**, **Daily Planet** and **Waulk Electrik** have continued to join longstanding giants **Oyster Band** rampaging noisily along the perimeters of English rootism. The times indeed have been-a-changing.

A mesmerising array of exotic talents have subsequently taken – with varying degrees of effectiveness – ever more daring liberties with the music, forging an English sensibility to various

World Music rhythms and contexts. Some of these attempts have been appalling, but at best they've breathed new life into a moribund form. The likes of **Blowzabella** and **3 Mustaphas 3**, for example, did much exciting work mixing the music with Eastern European styles, working wonders for both forms. Perhaps more astonishingly, it has even found a voice of sorts within club culture, with the purity of folk expression absorbed into mixing desks in intriguing styles. It's a radical departure eagerly advocated by some of the more visionary musicians, emboldened by pioneering experiments with dance music by people like Sharon Shannon, Martyn Bennett and Afro-Celt Sound System. **Eliza Carthy** embraced hip-hop on her *Red Rice* album, experimenting further in live shows, while even before they'd got a record deal rising stars **Tarras** were getting their demos remixed by M People.

The pleasing paradox of all this is that far from flushing out the baby with the bathwater, it has also had the effect of focusing attention on the real traditional music of England – a tradition that continues to survive the ravages of fashion and cultural abuse and, against all the odds, is as rich, potent, relevant and better represented than it has been for a very long time. Gifted young musicians, from the wonderful Yorkshire singer **Kate Rusby** to the amazing 'duelling flute' band **Flook!** abound; **Eliza Carthy**, **Nancy Kerr**, **Tanteeka**, **The Fraser Sisters**, **Equation**, **Tarras**, **Epona**, **Acaysha**, **Carleen Anglim** and **The Poozies**, to name just a few.

Lords of the Dance

Morris dancing is at the very heart of clichéd English imagery and hasn't yet been rescued from ridicule by roots music. Who knows, perhaps it never will be. But for all its apparent absurdity, the dance is amazingly popular, and there is, after all, something spectacular and heart-warming in the sight of the dancers in their whites waving bells and hankies, re-enacting some obscure fertility ritual. Isn't there?

The history of morris is ancient and cloudy. Nobody's quite sure how it evolved, or indeed if it's a specifically English tradition. Nonetheless, with its related off-shoots, it has evolved as an eccentric culture entirely its own. Long-held customs that women are not allowed to dance the morris have been the subject of fierce debate, with female dance teams emerging at a frantic pace with variations of morris, rapper and clog. The 'serious' teams, meanwhile, preserve their own territorial traditions with a protective discipline that seems positively archaic, but is rigorously encouraged by the Morris Ring, the movement's unofficial governing body.

Mention morris dancing and everyone thinks of the stereotypical whites, bells and floating hankies of Cotswold Morris, hailing from Oxfordshire; but at any festival or morris gathering, you'll also see the fast stomping clogs of Northwest Morris dancers – a quite different tradition hailing from the industrial towns of Lancashire. The outstanding singer and melodeon player John Kirkpatrick is also an ace dancer and one of the leading lights of the Border Morris side in Shropshire – yet another traditional morris style identifiable by the colourful tatter jackets, blackened faces, and a raucous, whooping dance style. You may laugh but it's serious stuff!

And there are any number of other strange traditions lurking where you least expect to find them. Most exhilarating of all, perhaps, is the annual May Day **Obby Oss** celebration at Padstow in Cornwall – a song and dance ritual of mindboggling colour and alcohol intake. **Rapper** and **long sword** dancing still abound, notably in Yorkshire and the north east; and you'll find lots of clog dancing. Chance upon the Staffordshire village of Abbots Bromley in September and you might encounter the strange **Horn Dance** ritual that has been a feature of the area since the mid-seventeenth century at least. Yet more bizarre still is the tradition of the **Britannia Coconut Dancers**, who dance with garlands, frocks, clogs and blackened faces through the streets of Bacup in the Calder Valley of Lancashire on Easter Saturday. They also wear coconuts strapped to their hands and knees which they clap together – providing them with the not altogether inappropriate nickname of 'nutters'!

JAK KILBY

The art of Morris

And yet English roots remains the Cinderella music of the British Isles. While its Celtic cousin has risen remorselessly through the 1990s to enjoy the patronage of mass audiences, the very thought of an English *Riverdance* would be laughed out of sight by a media seemingly intent on burying the beast alive. Only *Folk Roots* and – to a lesser degree the Scottish-based *Living Tradition* – offer press coverage of any depth and national radio coverage lies solely in the hands of the BBC's *Folk On Two*, presented by Lancashire singer/comedian Mike Harding (who had a hit in the 1970s with "Rochdale Cowboy") following the retirement in 1998 of veteran presenter Jim Lloyd.

Yet a quick glance across the hundred or so **folk festivals** regularly held all over England throughout the year certainly doesn't suggest that here is a music without a future. You need to get in early to ensure a ticket for **Cambridge**, the biggest binge of the lot held in the grounds of Cherry Hinton during the last weekend of July. And the oldest – **Sidmouth** – triumphantly approaches its half century with outstanding showcases of English (and other world) music and dance which it scatters around the Devon seaside town during the first week in August in a glorious pageant of colour and celebration. Odd still, then, that however inventive, exciting and heartfelt the music gets, it still seems forever destined to remain in the shadows of national consciousness.

Northumbrian Roots

Nowhere is the English living tradition more in evidence than in the border lands of **Northumbria**, the one part of England to rival the counties of the west of Ireland for a rich unbroken tradition. It is a tradition sustained uniquely by the rich splendour of a countryside that has constantly been interwoven with its indigenous music.

The changing times may have dissipated that music's importance to the local communities, but it has never come close to eradicating it. Whether it be sheep-farming in the moorlands or raucous nights in the pubs in the mining communities, the old music still survives as a backdrop even while the mining industry itself has grimly declined – a process documented in the 1997 Richard and Danny Thompson album *Factory*.

The work of **Tommy Armstrong**, a unique Tyneside balladeer of the late nineteenth/early twentieth century, remains in popular circulation and his "Trimdon Grange Explosion" – momentously recorded by Martin Carthy – is still one of the most heartbreaking songs you'll ever hear.

Modern artists like **Ed Pickford** and **Jez Lowe** are to a certain extent maintaining that tradition.

Sometimes bleak, sometimes tragic, often wildly happy, Northumbrian music has remained an integral part of the local character, and names like Jack Armstrong, **Joe Hutton**, **Billy Atkinson**, **Jimmy Pallister**, **Tommy Edmondson**, **Willy Taylor**, **Tom Clough**, **Billy Conroy**, **George Hepple** and **Billy Pigg** are revered locally for their role in perpetuating that tradition.

Much of this proud tradition is due to the proximity of Scotland and its history of country dance bands, and to the influence of Irish migrants. As a result, outstanding accordion players, fiddlers and even mouth organists have consistently abounded, though the instrument that really gives the area its unique role in English music is the **Northumbrian pipes**. One of the smallest and least intimidating members of the bagpipe family, these pipes are also more versatile than most of their Celtic relatives and as a result blend in more easily with other instruments. **Billy Pigg**, who died in 1968, is still regarded as the king of the Northumbrian pipes for the vibrant orginality of his playing, his prolific writing of tunes and the high profile he gave the instrument in particular and Northumbrian music in general.

His influence remains strong and there's a clear line between him and the still youthful **Kathryn Tickell** (see box overleaf) who at times has appeared to be on a one-woman crusade for the instrument and has done so much to break down musical barriers and take the music to new audiences. Tickell's current influence in the perpetuation of the legend of Northumbrian music is incalculable and she may even have redefined Northumbrian music with her superb 1999 album Debateable Lands, revolving around a suite inspired by the disputed area between England and Scotland that was long a target of border raiders. But it would be wrong to ignore the role of many others, both musicians and enthusiasts, who have promoted the music of the area with fanatical zeal.

Bob Davenport and **Louis Killen** were key figures in the early days of the British folk revival. Davenport did much to align Northumbrian traditional songs with a more modern folk tradition – he'd think nothing of merging an old Geordie favourite like "Cushy Butterfield" with Bob Marley's "Get Up Stand Up"; and Killen was both a superb traditional singer and concertina player, who did much to popularise the music in America. **The High Level Ranters** flew the local flag internationally for many years. Northumbrian culture was served magnificently by their devotion to colourful dialect songs like "The Lambton Worm", "Blaydon Races", "Keep Your Feet Still Geordie Hinnie" and "Dance To Yer Daddie", as well as grittier stories of strife in the collieries.

The Ranters' **Colin Ross** acted as an ambassador for the Northumbrian pipes at a time when most people looked at the instrument and fled, and his work was admirably continued by **Alistair Anderson**, originally noted as a vigorous concertina player, and subsequently also noted as a piper and composer of a new Northumbrian tradition. His *Steel Skies* suite, directly inspired by the Northumbrian countryside and its genetic traditions, remains one of the most important original works of recent years. "It was written to be played by musicians steeped in traditional music and its development from the tradition was evolutionary rather than revolutionary" Anderson said of the work. "I hope it retained the spirit of the music it has grown from, while opening up some new musical ideas on the way."

The **Northumbrian Pipers Society** has also worked wonders to keep interest in the instrument alive, to the extent of helping to open a pipes museum in Newcastle. A number of border festivals have doggedly and successfully concentrated on local music, even including (somewhat controversially) competitions for various instruments in the manner of the Irish fleadhs.

It's a tradition that has even seeped into the rockier side of the story. Great Geordie folk-rock bands **Lindisfarne**, **Jack The Lad** and **Hedgehog Pie** dug into their own local heritage for inspiration in a way that bands from other areas never did. **Alan Price** had a Top 10 hit in 1974 with "Jarrow Song", glorifying the 1936 mass march of the unemployed to London. It was an event further commemorated by the area's best-loved band Lindisfarne's "Marshall Riley's Army". The band, who took their name from the famous Holy Island off the northeast coast, created something of a Northumbrian anthem in "Fog On The Tyne",

The K Factor

DAVE PEABODY

If there's one musician who has personified the upward trend of English roots music in the last decade, it has to be **Kathryn Tickell** (and a sharp blow to the ear to anyone who pronounces it 'tickle'). More than anyone else, she has reformed the stuffy old image of folk music, inspiring a legion of others in her wake.

Her very youth and attractive personality made heads turn from the time, as a confident and supremely gifted teenager, she first started wielding her pipes in earnest around a roots circuit of then profoundly ageing

Kathryn Tickell

personalities and dated values. But without any of the shock tactics usually employed for maximum impact, Tickell has swiftly risen to a position of unrivalled eminence, blending technical expertise with progressive ideas and youthful vitality. After all, she spent some vital formative years playing with Asian and reggae musicians and feels there is no incongruity in applying some of their ideas and values to her own heritage of Northumbrian

music. She's also a fan of classical, bluegrass and jazz music and her outstanding recordings have included commendable experiments with Greek, Cajun and Irish music.

Yet much of the esteem in which she's held is due to an implacable commitment to her roots. She will talk, at any opportunity, of her debt to the great Northumbrian musicians of old – people like Joe Hutton, Willie Taylor and Billy Pigg – and makes that past real and accessible to her audiences with consummate playing and easy introductions, whether in Newcastle or Nova Scotia. Her 1993 album *Signs* was an adventurous sally into other cultures, contrasting neatly with her 1998 'back to the roots' statement, *The Northumberland Collection* and its superb 1999 successor, *The Debateable Lands*. Galled by the removal of music from the education curriculum in Britain, she's even launched a charity to provide financial support for children to study the instrument of their choice.

The Coppers: First Family of English Folk Song

The great patriarch of English traditional song is, without doubt, one **Bob Copper** of Rottingdean, Sussex. The **Copper Family** are synonymous with the folk tradition, and they have songbooks dating back two centuries to prove it. Their songs of rural country life were handed through many generations of the family and became a staple of the British folk revival of the 1960s.

The revival, rightly, saw the Coppers as perhaps the last living link with the English tradition, and they were in in great demand on the burgeoning festival circuit. And quite a sight they were, too: Bob in a suit and tie flanked by his long-haired son John and blonde-haired daughter Jill, each of them using a tuning fork to pitch their voices, and using the ancient family songbook as a crib sheet. Their appearances provided the inspiration for many upcoming young revival singers, notably the flamboyant Young Tradition.

Bob Copper's importance to the folk tradition was confirmed by regular radio apearances and two highly readable autobiographical books, *A Song For Every Season* and *Songs And Southern Breezes* (published by Heinemann in the early 1970s) colourfully describing life in a small Sussex farming community and placing the musical history in its proper context. The Coppers' magnificent four-album boxed set, *A Song For Every Season*, complete with lavish booklet and interviews telling how their songs were used either for specific social occasions or simply as family entertainment, was probably the most important traditional folksong recording of the 1970s.

The advance of age and pressure of family commitments limited the Coppers' visibility through much of the 1980s, but they maintained their presence with their own monthly club at Peacehaven. In the 1990s they started appearing again more regularly, their ranks swelled by Jill's husband John. They had lost none of the informal warmth and natural feel for harmonies which was always such a feature of their live performances. And the family songbook and tuning fork are never far away.

The Copper family retain a very special place in the hearts of all English roots fans.

BARRY SHUEL

The Copper Family (1970), from left: Bob, Heather, PB, Ron, Royston W and John

and although their primary songwriter **Alan Hull** died during the 1990s, they continue to operate. Even **Sting** examines his Geordie roots from time to time, and has occasionally worked with the Northumbrian piper Kathryn Tickell.

All of which has all provided a healthy incentive to young musicians in the area, as proven by the emergence of outstanding musicians like the pipers **Becky Taylor** and **Pauline Cato**, ubiquitous piano–accordionist **Lynn Tocker**, and fiddle player **Nancy Kerr** – Eliza Carthy's early partner who has further blossomed in the excellent young band **Epona** (with a promising first album *Shine Again*) and in partnership with **James Fagan** (heard to good effect on the *Starry Gazy Pie* album). The upcoming Borders band **Tarras** maintain strong roots in Northumbrian/Cumbrian history, with a family lineage involving Hedgehog Pie, Jack The Lad and the Doonan Family, and an excellent debut album, *Rising*.

Young musicians thrive in Northumbria unlike anywhere else in England, with a character also unlike anywhere else in England. You'll catch some of it at the better folk festivals, though to hear it at its best there's no beating local events like the **Rothbury Traditional Music Festival**. Alternatively, ask around in the pubs and clubs of Alnwick and Morpeth and over the border in Hawick and Jedburgh. And even if you don't find any music the local hospitality is renowned.

The Rural Tradition

Not that Northumbria is the only area where the tradition has survived unbroken. Indigenous music flourishes in East Anglia, Sussex, Cornwall and Humberside – although you may need to hunt it down.

East Anglia might seem an unlikely setting for a roots scene but scratch around and you will find some surprising riches. Informal pub sessions still abound both in Suffolk and Norfolk. Two of the greatest traditional singers in the entire folk tradition were from this area: farm labourer **Harry Cox** from Yarmouth and **Sam Larner**, a fisherman from Winterton. Larner was seventy-nine when he made his first record but his subsequent output, and that of Cox, gave the 1960s folk revival a huge source of material

and inspiration. It was given further impetus by Norfolk revivalist **Peter Bellamy**'s mid-1970s discovery of the great traditional singer **Walter Pardon**, who had lived all his life in the same cottage at Knapton, Norfolk without realising that the fund of long-neglected songs he'd learned as a child could form such a vital ingredient of England's folk tradition. Pardon went on to make a couple of important albums for Topic and sang locally and nationally for several years until he died in 1996.

Sussex also has a proud folk music tradition. Much of the local traditional repertoire came through the hands of the late great **Scan Tester**, who played dance music in local pubs with his Imperial Band from before World War I right up until his death in 1972. Tester's music is still a delight and can be heard to good effect on the Topic compilation album *I Never Played Too Many Posh Dances*. Sussex is also the base of the **Copper Family** of Rottingdean (see p.69).

There's plenty of music to be found, too, in Yorkshire, home of another famous roots family, the **Watersons**, still going strong, albeit in different guises (again, see box opposite). And in Shropshire, another area where you'll find the music intact if you look hard enough, you might still come across **Fred Jordan**, a rugged farmworker and one of the last surviving source

IAN ANDERSON/FOLK ROOTS

Billy Bragg tries the old finger-in-the-ear trick with the Watersons

Watersons/Carthy – Roots Royals!

Initial amazement was followed by unbridled joy when the Queen's 1998 Birthday Honours List included an MBE for a certain **Martin Dominic Forbes Carthy**. No musician from this neck of the woods ever got remotely near a gong before and it seemed almost unreal that it had actually gone to the single most influential, popular and enduring artist of our times.

As the supreme guitar stylist and classic singer, Carthy has been ominipresent since the early days of the 1960s folk revival, playing a major role in its genesis. There was his profound influence on visiting American singer-songwriters (ask Paul Simon where he got "Scarborough Fair"); his memorable duo work with Dave Swarbrick; significant contributions to the early Steeleye Span and Albion Bands; a significant role in the groundbreaking 1980s band Brass Monkey – his CV goes on and on. And running through it all, a brilliant solo career in which he established that highly individual and much copied guitar style, a proud body of important solo albums, and a reputation for unimpeachable integrity built on three decades of absolute, uncompromising commitment to English music and the folk clubs which has been its natural habitat through that time.

Somewhere along the way he became a Waterson, too. His marriage to **Norma Waterson**, surely England's greatest living female singer, firmly established folk's first royals. The **Waterson Family** defined harmony singing in the most distinctive manner possible, igniting the burgeoning revival scene of the 1960s with their passionate Yorkshire voices and charismatic unaccompanied performances. Norma, **Mike** and **Lal** should be canonised for their work during that period alone and albums like *A Yorkshire Garland* still sound terrific today. But after several years away from music they reunited in the early 1970s to make the bold contemporary electric album *Bright Phoebus*. Despite revealing both Mike and Lal as outstanding writers, it was not a practical direction to pursue and they resumed their career as Britain's foremost harmony vocal group, with one M. Carthy slotted into the ranks in what was now traditional music's dream team.

Further magnificent albums like *Green Fields* and *For Pence And Spicey Ale* confirmed their status as the ultimate English harmony singers, tracing their own inspiration from the source singers of old. And when Lal and Mike decided it was time to take a step back from the fray, a new generation was ready to step in. Lal Waterson's son **Oliver Knight** is a fast-rising guitarist and producer, and other members of the family are also making their mark. All were outshone by Norma Waterson in 1996, however, when her very first solo album, *Norma Waterson*, was runner-up (to Pulp!) in the prestigious Mercury Music Prize.

But it's Norma and Martin Carthy's daughter **Eliza** who looks set to be the unrivalled star of the family in the next century. Eliza initially earned her spurs singing with The Watersons and has played a prominent role in two excellent Waterson/Carthy albums with her parents. Yet the inventive, wilful fiddler had too much energy and imagination to be contained within one vocal group. "I never saw the point of doing exactly the same that others had done before me", said Eliza as she embarked on a dazzling career of her own. Apart from her Waterson/Carthy work, she's recorded with Nancy Kerr and the innovative Kings Of Calicutt, in which young bass player Barnaby Stradling has notably proved himself one of the scene's most enlightened arrangers.

Most tellingly, Eliza Carthy's solo work has attracted the greatest attention. The double album *Red Rice* (1998) not only saw her experimenting excitingly with modern dance styles, it enabled her to emulate her mother's achievement the previous year in winning a Mercury Music Prize nomination – as well as providing her with more national publicity than any folk artist in living memory. It was scarcely any surprise when she was snapped up by the corporate might of Warner Brothers to be marketed as a serious crossover artist. She is, she admits proudly, on a mission to restore English music to the nation's consciousness and as an individual every bit as single-minded, dedicated, determined and opinionated as her celebrated dad, few would argue she can't achieve it.

Martin Carthy, meantime, emerged with a defining new album *Signs Of Life* (1998) which reflected his long, enriching musical journey through the songs that shaped him, even to the point of featuring sensational re-workings of old hits by Elvis ("Heartbreak Hotel") and the Bee Gees ("New York Mining Disaster"). Not to be outdone, Norma Waterson followed it with her own musical history lesson, *The Very Thought Of You* (1999) on which she reflects on her own musical education through songs about Josef Locke, Al Bowlly, Fred Astaire and Judy Garland by writers as disparate as Nick Drake, Richard Thompson and Freddie Mercury.

Sadly, the dynasty suffered a massive loss in late 1998 with the sudden death from cancer of **Lal Waterson**, whose own highly individual songwriting talent had blossomed dramatically on one of the decade's most original albums, *Once In A Blue Moon* (1996), recorded with her son Oliver Knight. It made the posthumous release of her equally stark follow-up *A Bed Of Roses* (1999) almost unbearably poignant.

singers. He sings like an angel and still makes occasional public appearances.

The **vocal tradition** was a key area in the great British folk revival of the 1960s and '70s. The Coppers' harmonic style was adopted and adapted with fine results by the flamboyant **Young Tradition**, who were immensely influential in the 1970s, and The Watersons have kept the vocal torch burning to wondrous effect in various guises through the last three decades. But there have been many others along the way. Fronted by the ebullient Dave Brady, **Swan Arcade** picked up on Young Tradition's bullish harmonic unaccompanied style and raised it several decibels. And while modern groups like **Coope, Boyes & Simpson** capably continue this proud vocal tradition, the great solo performers like **Martin Carthy**, **June Tabor** and **Shirley Collins** are followed by fast emerging talents **Kate Rusby**, **Kathryn Roberts** and **Eliza Carthy**.

The one record that is still cited as the biggest influence in traditional music circles is *English Country Music*. Put together in 1965 by **Reg Hall and Bob Davenport**, it was issued in a limited edition of ninety-nine copies and sold out within a fortnight. Among the primarily Norfolk musicians featured were the fiddler Walter Bulwer, Billy Cooper on dulcimer, Reg Hall on melodeon and fiddle, Daisy Bulwer on piano, Mervyn Plunkett on drums, and Russell Wortley on pipe and tabor. It was, astonishingly, the first ever recording of English traditional instrumental music and it fired in a variety of young musicians a feel for their own tradition that has led to all manner of development and experimentation.

For serious students of the English tradition, a trip to the **English Folk Dance and Song Society** headquarters in Regents Park Rd, Camden, North London, may be essential. The EFDSS has long been criticised for its failure to move with the times and its perception of being greatly more interested in dance than song – and many of the events staged there can be unbearably starchy. But it does house a magnificent library and is a goldmine of history and information. It also marked its 100th anniversary in the summer of 1998 with an important 25-track CD including many of the source singers who sustained the revival through the last century.

Electric Avenue

It all sounds unbelievably mundane now, but back in 1971 English folkies thought the world had stopped when **Martin Carthy** plugged in his electric guitar on stage. Dylan thought he'd been given a hard time with all that 'Judas' baiting when he went electric at Newport Folk Festival a few years earlier, but at least he was pillaging his own songs. Martin Carthy, the doyen of English folk musicians, was doing it with a national treasure.

The idea of a band playing traditional English music with all the trappings of a rock band had initially been discussed by **Ashley Hutchings** and **Bob Pegg** at Keele Folk Festival at the end of the 1960s. Having coaxed the folk singer Sandy Denny into their ranks, Hutchings propelled **Fairport Convention**, then perceived as a Muswell Hill interpretation of Californian soft-rock, full-tilt into an English folk direction. The move was to invest their guitarist **Richard Thompson** with a unique songwriting style of his own that has served him brilliantly for over two decades, and it turned their *Liege And Lief* album into a momentous bit of musical history.

But Fairport were seen mainly as a rock band playing with folk music, and Hutchings wanted to pursue the idea of an electric folk band to the limits. He quit Fairport Convention specifically to form that beast, engaging the most respected musicians on the folk club circuit to see it through. The result was **Steeleye Span**, initially involving **Maddy Prior** and **Tim Hart** and the Irish duo **Gay and Terry Woods**, whose presence instantly scuppered any purist notions of Englishness. They made one album, *Hark The Village Wait*, before the Irish contingent quit to form their own band (Terry later re-emerging with The Pogues) and Steeleye really got underway with the induction of **Martin Carthy** and fiddler **Peter Knight** on the seminal *Please To See The King* album.

Steeleye went on to a glorious career, exerting a positive influence on the whole genre which had spawned them, even if some of their ideals became blurred in the process, and the hit singles "All Around My Hat" and "Gaudete" are probably better forgotten. They still tour intermittently (though Maddy Prior finally called it a day in 1997 to be replaced by her original foil in the band, Gay Woods). Carthy was a relatively early casualty (though he did return briefly in company with John Kirkpatrick for what was generally conceived as their last throw of the dice) and Hutchings himself abandoned ship to launch another new vehicle for his vision, the **Albion Country Band**, when he saw the pressures of success diluting intent. None of Steeleye had ever envisaged that worldwide tours and hit singles would ever become part of the equation for traditional music.

DARREN ANDREWS

Sid Kipper (on the pint) with The Albion Band

The Albion Country Band were something of a folk supergroup, featuring various ex-Fairports, Richard Thompson and Martin Carthy amid its ever-evolving incarnations. In the early 1980s, Hutchings changed the group's name to the **Albion Dance Band**, and shifted the music accordingly, deciding that the future lay with 'English Country Dance', a music rooted in history yet which didn't have to be rigidly structured – and indeed provided scope for development.

Many other folk-rock bands emerged in the wake of the Steeleye success. Most of them were awful, though the other half of that original Keele thought-tank, **Bob Pegg**, achieved great critical acclaim if little commercial success alongside his fiddle-touting, singing wife, **Carole Pegg**, in the volatile **Mr Fox**. One of their offshoots, **Five Hand Reel**, later took the notion of electric folk to new areas of authenticity with the Scottish traditional singer Dick Gaughan; and there was a brief flurry of folk-rock excitement during the 1980s when two respected folk figures, **Bill Caddick** and **John Tams**, combined to create **Home Service** from the remains of one of Hutchings' Albion enterprises, merging Steeleyesque ideas with a full-blooded brass section.

But bands like the Home Service were impossibly expensive to sustain and with the record industry moving on to new toys, the folk-rock movement collapsed amid grumbling about insensitive drummers and going up one-way streets backwards. The one really enduring group were the **Oyster Band** (see box overleaf), a wonderful outfit who dipped liberally into folk and pop traditions, and hit on a more rock sound in collaboration with **June Tabor**.

Folk-rock effectively died as a trailblazing force once the initial energy, excitement and commercial impact of the form had faded in a haze of rigid drum rhythms and mechanical adaptations of traditional styles. Its legacy remains, however, and not merely through the work of the Oyster Band or the occasional nostalgic Fairport and Steeleye tours. Bands like the **Blue Horses**, **Daily Planet** and **Pressgang** have gamely found fresh ways of rejuvenating old styles. Maverick fiddle king **Dave Swarbrick** proved there was life after Fairport by making further progress with **Whippersnapper** and various partners, including a nostalgic reunion with Martin Carthy which culminated in a couple of albums. Serious illness curtailed his work in 1999 but he recovered to laugh at his own obituary printed in one national newspaper.

The ideas and instrumentation ventured by those original folk-rock pioneers are these days scattered routinely across a wide selection of musicians of differing backgrounds and inspirations borrowing from the English tradition much as others might borrow from reggae or hip-hop. Such an environment creates disastrous possibilities – and beware of the inevitable opportunist imposters intent on leaping on to the next bandwagon before it has even begun. But ultimately the presence of an inordinate proportion of dross should not blind us to the exciting possibilities available to the genuine visionaries.

The Oyster Bandits

The **Oyster Band** have dominated English roots music to such an extent across the last fifteen years it's easy to imagine they've been keeping the flame alive entirely on their own. That's maybe unfair on others who've made valuable contributions along the way, but the Oysters have nevertheless pioneered a highly individual style of specifically English music and unflinchingly defied the fickle dictates of fashion and business pressure, developing their art within the parameters of a hostile rock world. More than that, they've become a major international name, establishing a clear root to the English oral tradition while evolving an often ferocious instrumental sound coupled with biting, political lyrics.

The group started out purely as an informal dance band of flexible personnel and erratic style after meeting at Canterbury University in the 1970s, with some initial adventures under the guise of Fiddlers Dram. Interested in exploring the relatively uncharted territory of roots dance music, the Oysters achieved a settled line-up with **Ian Telfer** (actually a Scotsman!) on fiddle, **Alan Prosser** (guitar), **John Jones** (melodeon/vocals) joined by **Ian Kearey** on bass. After several well-received folk albums, things really exploded in the mid-1980s when they added drummer **Russell Lax** and, raising the roots in a dynamic rock setting, they dramatically upped the decibel count and the fan base. An explosive version of the old traditional standard "Hal-An-Tow" was their unmistakeable statement of intent and their 1986 album *Step Outside* was a notable landmark for roots music.

"Being English can be the kiss of death", commented John Jones. "You've got to overcome so many things to actually make it feel radical and different and genuinely alternative." They took a huge credibility risk by plunging into fullblooded electric status, but they were rewarded by taking their own unique brand of roots music to an entirely new audience, while staying friends with the old.

Their next two albums, *Wide Blue Yonder* and *Ride* saw them progress into savage songwriters railing against the complacency of 1980s music and the iniquities of the Thatcher government. The arrival of bass/cello/kitchen sink player Chopper in place of Ian Keary – and later still Lee (new members aren't allowed surnames) taking over the drumsticks – seemed to drive them on to even greater fury and innovation and they've continued to startle, amaze and delight ever since. Their intriguing collaborative *Freedom And Rain* album and subsequent tour with June Tabor was hugely successful and they've continued to grow through spectacular albums like *Holy Bandits* and *The Shouting End Of Life*.

Here's a band who've included traditional English standards and New Order covers on the same album. In 1998 they even twisted the folk tradition on its head, embarking on an 'unplugged' tour, and ended the millennium with another huge leap, forming their own label Running Man to release the Alaric Neville-produced 'look back in anger' album *Here I Stand*, complete with guest appearances by musicians as diverse as Canadian folk-rockers Great Big Sea and erstwhile anarchic chart-toppers Chumbawumba. Long may there be pearls in those Oysters...

The Oyster Band

JAK KILBY

Tiger Moth

Wild in the Country

If the 1960s were dominated by protest music and the singer-songwriters, and the '70s by Steeleye/Fairport folk-rock, then the '80s were the domain of **roots dance music**. Working from a new and wonderful fusion of influences, these new roots bands might, a few years ago, have been labelled folk-rockers, but most of them wouldn't understand the significance of the term were it to bite them in the upper groin region.

The moving spirit behind this new roots scene was one **Rod Stradling**, a long-time iconoclast on the folk scene who'd been involved since the early 1970s in a series of hugely influential bands. The first of these, **Oak**, concentrated on English country music, inspired by that seminal 1965 album, and they were followed by the **Old Swan Band**, who affected defiant attitudes as an antidote to the Celtic music that obsessed the English folk scene of the time. Then came the **English Country Blues Band**, with bottleneck and slide-guitarist Ian A. Anderson, who laced their dance music with blues, and slowly transmuted into **Tiger Moth** – a raucous electric band who themselves splintered into **Orchestre Super Moth**, mixing in all manner of World Music influences.

In the late 1980s, however, Stradling concentrated his considerable energies on yet another new band, **Edward II & The Red Hot Polkas**. This was his most ambitious and defiant idea to date, forging English country dance music, sublimely, with reggae. You can't take such liberties without getting up somebody's nose and Edward II certainly did that, but their work with reggae dubmaster the **Mad Professor** at the mixing desk is possibly the single most significant leap for English country music. You have to like reggae in the first place, of course, but the idea of merging the music of last century rural England with the sound of the modern cities was a masterstroke, and for all its audacity a logical one. The band's first album, *Let's Polkasteady* in 1987, was a veritable earthquake in roots circles, and in the ensuing decade, most of it sans Stradling, Edward II moved on to develop an arresting Caribbean-English fusion, which influenced other free-thinkers from the folk idiom like Irish accordion superstar Sharon Shannon and, even more tellingly, one or two reggae/dance groups too.

Stradling had originally seen Edward II as a dance band, albeit somewhat more visionary than the Ashley Hutchings' Albion incarnations. Subsequently people with ever wilder hair and stranger instruments took up the baton. **Blowzabella**, erratic but never dull, carved out a starring role, introducing English country dance to rhythms from the Balkans and beyond, with Nigel Eaton cranking things out on hurdy gurdy.

JAK KILBY

Blowzabella

3 Mustaphas 3: The Szegerely Connection

As the 1990s draw to a close, it seems that just about every major city in Europe and North America has a band of (mostly) local musicians playing some hybrid of global beats: Balkan, Klezmer, African, Cajun, Salsa. It wasn't always thus: in fact, until the early 1980s there was scarcely any band of this kind, indeed, there was scarcely any kind of awareness of 'World Music' itself.

It was in these unpromising waters, in North London, that the 3 Mustaphas 3 appeared: a worldly crew of musicians who had played in various punk, African, Latin, jazz and rock outfits, though the group's official line was that they had all been working for years in the *Crazy Loquat Club* in Szegerely, and that, as they modestly explained, was why they were so skilled, and so ineffably Balkan.

3 Mustaphas 3

The band had a floating cast, all bearing the Mustapha family name. The guiding spirits were **Uncle Patrel** (on saz, of course) and **Hijaz** (bouzouki/violin/Hawaiian guitar), while other founding Mustaphas included Houzam (drums), Isfa'ani (percussion), Oussak (cello) and Niaveti Mustapha III (accordion/flute/vocals). They made their live debut in London in August 1982, and in 1985 released a mini-album, *Bam! Mustaphas Play Stereo*, on their own branch – Fez-o-phone – of the newly established GlobeStyle world music label.

Bam! promulgated a Balkan bad boy image and unleashed an eclectic mix of Greek songs alongside a version of the Kenyan classic 'Singe Tema' (sung, like all their adapted material, in its original language). It was recorded in an (empty) North London swimming pool – the first singing-in-the-baths album, Hijaz claims.

By the time of their first LP proper, *Shopping* (1987), the Mustaphas had lost Oussak, but gained an electric bassist and singer, **Sabah Habas** – whose voice, oddly enough, resembled Bryan Ferry's – along with the prodigiously talented **Kemo** (accordion/keyboards). The band's Balkan beat remained intact but the musical range was extended to African and Indian styles.

The Mustaphas were a very flexible (promiscuous, in their own words) unit and were occasionally joined by **Expensive Mustapha** (trumpet) and vocalist Lavra Tima Daviz Mustapha, who seemed equally at ease singing in Arabic, French, Greek, Hindi, Macedonian, Spanish and Swahili. The Mustapha projects ranged across cultures with superlative ease, with musicians confident in Latin and African, as well as Balkan, rhythms. In 1985 they surfaced in Berlin as **Orchestra BAM De Grand Mustapha International And Party**, a fifteen-piece ensemble, while in Britain, their musical eclecticism led to work backing visiting stars of the world music circuit, such as Israeli singer Ofra Haza, and West African kora players Dembo Konte and Kausu Kouyateh.

In their 'regular' incarnation, the Mustaphas recorded two further albums. *Heart Of Uncle* (1989) was a wild array of songs which may once have been Hindi filmi (film music) and Nigerian Hi-Life, but were transmuted into idiosyncratic Mustapha fare. *Soup Of The Century* (1990) took the mix-and-match approach even further, with prominent woodwinds from new member **Daoudi Mustapha**, and material extending to the Japanese "Soba Song". Both discs showed the Mustaphas at the peak of their powers, the latter deservedly being voted #1 in that year's *Billboard* world music charts.

Unfortunately, the financial pressures of maintaining a big band, and one whose members worked in all kinds of other projects, and lived as far apart as Berlin and Jakarta, led to an extended sabbatical for the Mustaphas – back in Szegerely, of course.

They were, in retrospect, extraordinary, trailblazing pioneers, on a par with the German group Dissidenten (see p.120), and arguably more influential on world roots music-making than better known popularisers like Ry Cooder, Paul Simon and David Byrne.

Mark Ellingham

Other notables included **Flowers & Frolics**, who played more traditional dance material - jigs, polkas, hornpipes, and the like – in a somewhat Oyster Band mode, and the **Cock & Bull Band**, from the unlikely roots home of Milton Keynes, lacing an exotic range of instruments with the inspiration of French piper, Jean-Pierre Rasle.

From Brighton came the anarchic **Levellers**, playing a defiant roots music to predominantly rock audiences, asserting that "being called a folk group makes us very angry". Originally rooted in the New Age traveller world of alternative 1990s England, and deeply committed to radical/green issues, they've recently mellowed, flirting with the big, bad commercial world, mainstream radio airplay and pop chart status.

The Barely Works – an unfeasibly big-band jazz-folk oufit – took on the gauntlet of musical anarchy and invested it with a colourful conglomerate of melodies and styles, offering a richly joyous resumé of everything from bluegrass to eastern European Gypsy music. Barriers and prejudices were decimated in the full-blooded wake of a series of fascinatingly oddball albums. They split in 1993, but splintered into the equally enthralling **BigJig** while their accordion player Sarah Allen is also to be found alongside Brian Finnegan, Michael McGoldrick and Ed Boyd in the innovative flurry of flutes that is **Flook!**

This revival of roots music was a significant bonus to the rebirth of traditional music among young musicians at the all-important ground level during the early 1990s, leading to the emergence of the impressive **Eliza Carthy**, **Nancy Kerr**, **Chris Wood**, and **Andy Cutting**, who first made his name as a precocious teenage melodeon player with Blowzabella.

The onset of the Young Tradition Award – replaced in 1998 by the Young Folk Award – actively encouraged this trend, with outstanding musicians like **Simon Thoumire**, **Catriona MacDonald**, **Carlene Anglim** (check out her outstanding debut album *Mellow Frenzy* with Allister Gittens) and piano-accordion player **Luke Daniels** emerging as genuine forces in its wake. And, of course, talent is self-perpetuating. For each glamorous young star who comes on the scene to pick up a bit of publicity and sell a few records, another few hundred may be tempted to pick up a fiddle or an accordion or an acoustic guitar or whatever to see if they can give it a go.

English roots music's increasingly cosmopolitan nature also bodes well for the future. Edward II's experiments with reggae were but a drop in the ocean of musical cultures now second nature to most urban areas of the country. Already the Asian bhangra and ghazal traditions (see following article) have got a grip on English music, a path beaten by the likes of ghazal singer **Najma Akhtar** with her fusion album, *Qareeb*, and **Sheila Chandra**'s melting pot albums *Weaving My Ancestors* and *The Zen Kiss*. Even **Cornershop** – *Brimful Of Asha* chart-toppers and all – might be considered a veritable archetype of the English roots band of the future. Their *Born For The Seventh Time* album embodies many of the colourful colliding cultures encompassing England in the twenty-first century, from Tjinder Singh's own Punjabi roots to almost whimsical expressions of English pop and modern techno. **Talvin Singh**, who first hit the scene backing Najma Akhtar, has gained crossover acclaim as a genuine British roots musician, techno wizard and would-be world music superstar, while **Transglobal Underground** show the ultimate face of techno clubbers as roots wannabes. They are moving the corner flag, the grandstand and the centre circle as well as the goalposts, and that's no bad thing.

Fifty years on from the arrival of Windrush and the first West Indian emigrées, the colour and patterns of England's roots have changed dramatically. In musical terms this offers the thrilling potential of mixing new cultures with the old. A few have experimented with encouraging results but the surface of this potential has scarcely been scratched. The upsurge of younger musicians with minds that are open and free from old preconceptions and a misguided loyalty to traditional purity at the exclusion of all else suggests that English music could be on the verge of a brave new world.

discography

Compilations

 A Century Of Song (EFDSS, UK).

Sub-titled *A Celebration Of English Traditional Singers Since 1898*, the traditional treasures on this 25-track CD include cylinder recordings made by the renowned folk song collector Cecil Sharp dating back to 1907. Among the legendary, but rarely heard, source singers featured are Harry Cox, the Copper Family, Fred Jordan, Walter Pardon, Phil Tanner and Mary Ann Haynes. A must for all serious students of the English traditional folk song.

The Rough Guide to English Roots Music (World Music Network, UK).

This pitches together some of the greatest influences in English music (The Watersons, Albion Band) with source singers and musicians (Louise Fuller, Harry Cox, Billy Pigg) and modern strands of the revival (Oyster Band, Edward II,

Rory McLeod, Billy Bragg, Hank Dogs). The result is a well-balanced overview that entertains as much as it educates and somehow manages to keep most bases covered.

◉ New Electric Muse Vols 1 & 2 (Essential, UK).

Good value mid-price release in two volumes updating a celebrated album release of the 1970s telling the 'story of folk into rock'. Includes most of the usual suspects, using its own sub-title as the vaguest excuse to include everything from the Copper Family and Davey Graham to Richard Thompson, June Tabor and Energy Orchard.

◉ Troubadors Of British Folk (Rykodisc, US).

Momentous three-volume series depicting the story of English folk music across three decades, including imaginative selections from most of the big names who've had lasting influence in that time. The three volumes – each depicting a different era – are available separately and have the additional advantage of superb packaging and a detailed booklet, mostly with personal recollections about each track from the artists involved.

◉ The Voice Of The People (Topic, UK).

This is a definitive 20-volume anthology compiled by Tony Engle and Reg Hall of the primarily unaccompanied source singers, fiddlers, accordion players and the like who provided the bulk of the material and inspiration for modern folksong. Virtually every traditional singer of note (bar the Copper Family) is featured somewhere on the anthology and placed in the context of their character and lifestyle in Reg Hall's superb notes. Each of the 20 volumes (which are available individually) is distinguished by subject matter – ranging from drinking songs to dance music to tragedy ballads to songs of travellers. A hugely important series.

Traditional and Revival

Artists

Anne Briggs

Nottinghamshire's Anne Briggs was blessed with a beautiful voice, an instinctive feeling for the oral folk tradition and terminal wanderlust. She was young, sexy, talented, wild and mysterious . . . and seemed to disappear off the face of the earth after a frustrating spell with folk-rock band Ragged Robin in the early 1970s. A re-discovery article about her in *Mojo* magazine in 1998 tracked her down to a remote Scottish island and inspired a flurry of re-issues and media attention.

◉ Anne Briggs: A Collection (Topic, UK).

A 22-track compilation of early Briggs dating from 1962 and issued by Topic in 1999. It's a good showcase of a singer who seemed to know no fear, tackling hugely demanding ballads like "Willie O'Winsbury" and "Polly Vaughan" without stylisation or ornamentation. Earthy and dangerous, the album clearly shows that she was indeed the modern embodiment of the source traditional singers who kept the music alive for so many years without thought to anything else but the love of the songs. And on the opening cut "The Recruited Collier" she sounds remarkably like Kate Rusby sounds now.

Robin & Barry Dransfield

The Dransfields were a Yorkshire duo who lit up the scene in the 1970s and '80s with their imaginative and compelling interpretations of traditional songs. Barry's earthy fiddle playing and rich vocal style contrasted attractively with elder brother Robin's smoother approach, and their regional Yorkshire accents and charismatic stage presence gave them a strong identity. When they also developed into intelligent songwriters they were signed to a major record company, but turned their back on fame and money in a perhaps misguided loyalty to the roots scene. Both have subsequently recorded as solo artists but haven't appeared together for many years.

◉ Up To Now (Free Reed, UK).

Definitive 2-CD compilation, including material from all their albums as a duo and solo artists, including several previously unreleased tracks. A 32-page booklet accompanies the package.

Nic Jones

Nic Jones was one of the great revival performers and a massive influence both as singer and guitar stylist until an horrific road crash effectively ended his working career in 1982. The intricacy and contemporary feel of his arrangements of traditional songs made the albums he recorded in the 1970s landmarks for revival music. He also enjoyed a spell with the 'supergroup' Bandoggs and there was every sign that he was about to blossom as a songwriter when the accident occurred. In 1998 a compilation of amateur live recordings made in the early 1980s, *In Search Of Nic Jones*, was released on his own Mollie Music label, but Jones now only plays within the privacy of his own home in York.

ⓒⓓ Penguin Eggs (Topic, UK).

A seminal album for the English revival, marking Jones' sudden transformation from accomplished but more or less straightforward interpreter of folk song, to innovative arranger and intricate performer. It remains a classic.

John Kirkpatrick

A seminal figure through the last 25 years, Kirkpatrick is a fine accordion and melodeon player, singer, writer and morris dancer so absorbed in the tradition he was one of the prime forces in the upsurge of interest in roots dance music in the 1970s/80s. He and his wife, the singer and oboe player Sue Harris, were for many years one of the folk scene's most popular attractions, recording several outstanding albums together, and he went on to play a significant part in the Albion Band and Steeleye Span. He's still an influential figure, developing as a songwriter through a succession of solo albums.

◉ Plain Capers (Free Reed, UK).

Originally released in 1976 (reissued by Topic in 1992) this was a landmark collection of 27 morris dance tunes from a wide range of Cotswold traditions. But, far from an academic exercise designed purely for the morris fraternity, it focused on the tunes as an exciting end to themselves, couching them in vibrant folk-rock arrangements with John K's lively accordion style imaginatively backed by Sue Harris on oboe and hammered dulcimer, Fi Fraser on fiddle, Martin Brinsford on mouth organ and old sparring partner Martin Carthy keeping rhythm on guitar. Ultimately a much more credible collection than the more famous Morris On.

◉ One Man and his Box (H&W, Netherlands).

This 1999 release is a splendid solo recital album. Mostly traditional dance tunes magnificently performed on accordion, melodeon and concertinas plus a few songs. A fine record.

Kate Rusby

A terrific young singer from Yorkshire, Rusby has been submerged in traditional music since she was a child and is deeply committed to the cause of English roots music. Her beautiful voice first came to prominence in a celebrated duo with Kathryn Roberts. With Roberts she joined the three young Lakeman brothers from Devon in the 'brat folk' band Equation, but split when she realised they were intent on moving away from her beloved traditional songs. Merging her magnificent singing with sensitive material and great stage presence, her solo career took off in a big way in 1997, but she managed to juggle it with regular appearances with the excellent all-female group The Poozies until mid-1999 when pressure of work forced her departure from the band, following the acclaim heaped on her second solo album, *Sleepless*.

 Hourglass (Pure, UK).

Rusby's beautifully unassuming debut solo album is delicate and sparsely produced, allowing the purity of her voice to read the primarily traditional ballads in her broad Yorkshire accent. She also reveals appetising promise as a songwriter within the traditional idiom, emphasising that folk song is not a stopping point but a destination for her. *Hourglass* stands as a compelling milestone in the resurgence of English folk song, reclaiming credibility and commercial clout for pure English folk song.

Sleepless (Pure, UK)

Rusby's 1999 outing is another stunner. It was shortlisted for the Mercury Music Prize – an amazing acheivement for a release on her family's cottage industry label.

June Tabor

The charismatic Tabor has been dividing opinion for twenty-five years with the stark stylisation and suppressed passion of her singing. She has recorded and toured with The Oyster Band, Maddy Prior, Martin Simpson and Huw Warren, and she's dabbled in jazz, standards and Brecht. Yet her main forté remains the traditional ballad which she invariably delivers with a uniquely telling tension.

Aqaba (Topic, UK).

Dark, sullen and mysterious, this is an uncompromising, demanding but nevertheless wholly fulfilling work, merging traditional song with a shrewd selection of more modern material. The title track is one of the greatest songs by the criminally underrated Bill Caddick.

Kathryn Tickell

Leading Northumbrian piper and fiddle player, Tickell draws direct lineage from great northeastern musicians like Billy Pigg and Joe Hutton and has inspired a whole new wave of dedicated young traditional musicians.

 The Northumberland Collection (Park, UK).

After various excursions into other territories, Tickell showcases her Northumbrian heritage in blissfully pure form, with a supporting cast including famous fiddle player Willie Taylor and – for the first time on a Tickell album – vocal tracks from Carolyn Robson and Terry Conway.

Waterson/Carthy

The Watersons are a legendary Yorkshire vocal harmony group, hugely important to English Roots music for the past thirty-odd years. In their current incarnation, they feature the British folk revival's crown prince Martin Carthy with his wife Norma Waterson and their daughter Eliza Carthy, displaying passionate homage to the past with an eye on the future.

Waterson:Carthy (Topic, UK).

The 1994 album that effectively transported the Waterson legend into a new era and a new audience. Immaculate performance throughout, some terrific material, and extraordinary vitality given that two of the leading performers are approaching veteran status. The third, Eliza, was barely twenty when the album was recorded – and it played no small role in elevating her to major artist status.

waterson:carthy

Young Tradition

This young unaccompanied harmony trio of the 1960s took their cue from the songs of the Copper Family and ignited the folk scene with their passionate harmonies and flamboyant stage performances. They were relatively shortlived but their influence was profound and their re-issued albums remain stirring. Peter Bellamy went on to a celebrated solo career, doing important work setting Kipling poems to music and creating the first folk opera (*The Transports*) but like fellow member Royston Wood, Bellamy was destined to a tragic early death. The third member Heather Wood now lives – and occasionally performs – in America.

The Young Tradition/So Cheerfully Round (Transatlantic, UK).

Two seminal albums reissued in 1996 in one bargain-priced package. For a group who sang primarily unaccompanied they generated a startling energy and sense of drama which was often aped but rarely matched. This was Young Traditon at the height of their considerable powers.

Electric and Contemporary

Albion Band

After Fairport Convention and after Steeleye Span, bass player and English music visionary Ashley Hutchings turned his formidable attention to an electronic band incorporating even wider aspects of the English tradition, such as country dance rituals. Through the last fifteen years it has variously involved too many star turns of English music to fully document here (notables have included Martin Carthy, John Kirkpatrick, Shirley Collins and Cathy LeSurf) and at one point had its own morris side. The band changes personnel every couple of years or so, and is sometimes acoustic, sometimes electric, but Hutchings remains the lynchpin of the band and, many would say, of English music too.

◉ **The BBC Sessions** (Strange Fruit, UK).

Superb collection of recordings made at the BBC between 1972–78, taking in several incarnations of the band. The paradox of Shirley Collins' mumsy voice against the band's full-blown folk-rockery still works stirringly, while Graeme Taylor's exuberant guitar and Ric Sanders' jazz-inflected fiddling sound equally impressive.

Billy Bragg

The bard of Barking arrived ranting and howling in the mid-1980s to apply a punk offence to the genteel inaction of the English roots scene of the time. He came with roaring electric guitar and brashness and applied a well-deserved boot to the backside of the Roots scene. And once it got over its initial shock English Roots music realised that Bragg's sharply drawn social observations like "Between The Wars" and "New England" were indeed modern folk songs. In 1998 he even broke his most solemn vow and, at London's Royal Albert Hall, played an acoustic guitar on stage for the first time.

◉ **Mermaid Avenue** (EastWest, UK).

For an artist indelibly associated with East London, it's perhaps strange to be recommending an album dripping in Americana. This pits Bragg with US band Wilco and an important project setting newly discovered Woody Guthrie lyrics to music and it's easily the best thing he's ever done. The idea of primitive Essex boy representing the modern spirit of the old reprobate Guthrie is somehow oddly fitting.

Eliza Carthy

The daughter of Martin Carthy and Norma Waterson may have been bred in the tradition but she has accepted the baton and scampered off with it at an astonishing pace. After a few appearances singing with the Watersons she made an impressive duet album with fellow fiddle player/singer Nancy Kerr, but it was her involvement with a likeminded group of 'folk brats' in Kings Of Calicutt where she really made her mark, experimenting with daring arrangements and demanding material. Since then she's become the perfect figurehead for the brave new young world of English folk song, acknowledging the importance of promotion and marketing and cheerfully going along with all the 'folk babe' publicity. Her long-term future, however, may be in her own elusive songwriting style, rarely exhibited yet as darkly mysterious as her aunt Lal, and thought to be one of the reasons major label Warners saw such commercial potential in her.

◉ **Red Rice** (Topic, UK).

Eliza broke all the rules with *Red Rice*. An unfashionable double-CD album, it flirts with drum'n'bass, hip-hop and other elements of club culture, while striving to maintain the purity of folk song in its more traditional material. Against all odds it worked because there's a magical energy about her that conveys itself to the musicians she surrounds herself with. The disc won a Mercury Music Prize nomination, was *Folk Roots*' album of 1998, won unprecedented airplay and took folk music halfway to the masses.

Martin Carthy

Born in Hertfordshire in 1941, guitar stylist, singer and song researcher Martin Carthy is the single most influential and celebrated living figure on the English roots music scene. A young pioneer of the early post-skiffle folk club movement he was a resident at London's famous Troubadour Club in the 1960s folk boom and a role model for such emergent American folk singers as Bob Dylan (who based "Bob Dylan's Dream" on Carthy's version of "Lord Franklin") and Paul Simon (who adopted his arrangement of "Scarborough Fair"). Carthy had a brilliant partnership with Dave Swarbrick, was a pivotal figure in the folk-rock movement of the 1970s during spells with the Albion Band and Steeleye Span, and later helped lead the introduction of brass into folk song with the excellent band Brass Monkey. His marriage to Norma Waterson completed a kind of folk dream team as he leant his considerable voice to the Watersons' stirring vocal harmonies. In the 1990s he has played and recorded with Waterson:Carthy – which incorporated a new generation of the family and attracted a new audience as a result, while maintaining his solo folk club career.

◉ **Signs of Life** (Topic, UK).

Carthy sets out his musical signposts of a thirty-year career, including radical interpretations of material as varied as "New York Mining Disaster 1941", "Heartbreak Hotel" and "The Lonesome Death Of Hattie Carroll", performed inimitably with stark arrangements. From Trad. Arr to Hoagy Carmichael, the master does it his way.

Sandy Denny

A wonderful singer and impressive songwriter whose unmistakeable, husky voice always seemed to be in the frame whenever anything significant was going down in the halcyon folk revival days. After early acclaim with The Strawbs, she provided the catalyst for Fairport Convention's conversion to English roots, subsequently forming her own band Fotheringay before embarking on a solo career. English music lost something extraordinarily precious when she died after falling down a flight of stairs in 1978. A modern cult following and several posthumous releases rightly keep her name alive.

◉ **Who Knows Where The Time Goes** (Island, UK).

Ambitious, but worthy four-album boxed set, displaying the frequent frailties as well as the soaring glories of her work. It mixes her own poppier material with traditional songs and various demos and unreleased tracks, complete with handsome booklet, and through it all runs the almost unbearable sense of pain and melancholy that were to be her epitaph.

Fairport Convention

The first of the onrush of late 1960s/early '70s bands who changed the face and dusty image of traditional English song by playing it with electric instruments and the intensive power of a rock band. In durability and versatility they were also the best, repeatedly overcoming adversity (the death of original drummer Martin Lamble, departures of key members at vital moments) to create a distinctive and greatly loved folk-rock style built variously around the glittering talents of Sandy Denny, Richard Thompson, Ashley Hutchings, Dave Swarbrick, Simon Nicol, Dave Mattacks, Dave Pegg and Ric Sanders. They still tour regularly and their annual reunion festival in the Oxfordshire village of Cropredy is a real highlight.

Liege And Lief
(Hannibal, UK).

The 1969 album commonly cited as the launching pad of the folk-rock revolution. Sandy Denny and Richard Thompson majestically conspiring to create an explosively dramatic vision previously alien to such a purely English music. Fairport's body of work includes other exceptional albums (*Unhalfbricking*, *Full House*, *Babbacombe Lee*) but this is the one that made it all possible.

Davy Graham

Graham is the acoustic guitarist most other guitarists point to as the guv'nor from those halcyon 1960s days of the British singer-songwriter boom. Before you qualified for anything you had to be able to master "Anji" by Davy Graham. It was a tall order. Graham, who worshipped blues gods like Big Bill Broonzy and Leadbelly and modern jazz icons Thelonius Monk and Charlie Mingus, fell into the English folk movement by accident. He was equally intrigued by Far Eastern music and indeed any other strange styles he chanced upon, and was constantly off on different tangents, inventing new fusion styles that no-one else could get near. The big rewards eluded him, but for many, Davy Graham was – still is – the man.

WITH SHIRLEY COLLINS

▣ **Folk Roots, New Routes** (Topic, UK).

It still sounds bizarre: the idea of Shirley Collins, princess of English traditional folk song, linking up with the most eclectic guitarist in the country. But producer Austin John Marshall's idea of linking Anglo-Appalachian ballads as interpreted by Collins' rustic voice with 'World Music' arrangements (about 30 years before the term was invented) seemed natural enough to a visionary like Graham. Released in 1964, it was Graham's first album and shocked the folk scene of the day who didn't quite know whether to be horrified or thrilled. But it certainly opened doors and many believe the folk-rock revolution of five years later couldn't have happened without *Folk Roots, New Routes*. Reissued in1999, it still sounds good.

Home Service

A wonderfully strong, inventive band built around a front line of John Tams, Bill Caddick and ace guitarist Graeme Taylor, Home Service were unlucky to arrive at the tail end of the folk-rock boom and they struggled to capture either public imagination or the major record deal necessary to keep them afloat. Yet their bold use of a brass section was another major innovation enhanced immeasurably by Tams' richly evocative songwriting. They drifted into the sunset in the mid-1980s – the great folk-rock band that got away.

▣ **Alright Jack** (Fledgling, UK).

An album released in 1986 (but still available) which merged savage political comment with enlightened revamps of traditional material and truly uplifting use of brass arrangements. Confusingly it's an album that is both celebratory and provocatively dark.

Oyster Band

The most enduring and distinctively English band of the modern era, the Oysters flew in the face of fashion to create a unique form of folk-rock, blending John Jones' very traditional style of singing with dance tunes, subtle social commentaries and violent tirades which serve as telling condemnations of Thatcher's Britain. They'e still going strong and they're still special.

 Trawler
(Cooking Vinyl, UK).

A Greatest Hits compilation with a difference. The album serves as a decent resumé of a decade of Oysterism, with the added interest of several of the older tracks being re-recorded to allow the newer members, drummer Lee and bass player Chopper to put their own proud stamp on the proceedings. It worked too and if you are new to the band, this is as good an introduction as any.

Steeleye Span

The most commercially successful English electric folk band of them all, Steeleye, in one glittering spell in the mid-1970s enjoyed a succession of chart hits. Their greatest attraction was always the twirling front lady Maddy Prior, although their ranks also variously included Gay & Terry Woods, Ashley Hutchings, Martin Carthy, John Kirkpatrick, Peter Knight, Tim Hart, Bob Johnson and Nigel Pegrum. They still tour occasionally, though Prior finally quit to concentrate on her solo career in 1997.

▣ **Please To See The King** (Mooncrest, UK).

The crucial 1971 album which gave profound impetus and credibility to the great folk-rock monster. Martin Carthy strapped on electric guitar for the first time, Maddy Prior's voice soared gloriously and Peter Knight was full of guile and daring on the fiddle. It has aged well.

DAVE PEABODY

The ubiquitous Ashley Hutchings

Richard Thompson

Arguably the most complete and consistent English performer thrown up in the 1970s folk-rock explosion, Thompson would be worthy of special mention for his blitzkrieg guitar playing alone – a key ingredient of Fairport Convention's early impact – but the immense quality and originality of his songwriting mark him out in a class of his own. After Fairport he formed a wonderful partnership with his wife Linda until their marriage split, when he reverted to a solo career that has survived all the vagaries of fashion and age. His songs now play a front-line role in the entire pantheon of English roots music.

ENGLAND

Watching The Dark
(Hannibal, UK; Ryko, US).

Triple CD compilation charting most aspects of Thompson's celebrated career, ranging from his most traditional excursions to occasional outbursts of pure rock'n'roll. Includes material from his days with Fairport, Linda and various backing bands (notable luminaries include Christine Collister, John Kirkpatrick and Clive Gregson) as well as a healthy proportion of otherwise unreleased cuts.

3 Mustaphas 3

The Mustaphas unleashed upon the world a whole panoply of imitators, combining their local roots music with explorations of Balkan, African and Indian beats. There's room for apology there, perhaps. But in the original hands of this floating group of legendary Szegerely musicians, the music was (nearly) always a revelation, the time signatures bafflingly complex, and the wit upfront.

Heart Of Uncle (GlobeStyle, UK).

This 1989 album is the best possible introduction to the Mustapha sound. Indeed, it's the best thing they ever did.

Lal Waterson

The folk fraternity was deeply shocked when Lal suddenly died of cancer towards the end of 1998. She had been at the very heartbeat of English music for three decades as a member of The Watersons, although most people were entirely unaware of her stunning songwriting ability until her brilliant 1996 album *Once In A Blue Moon*, recorded with her son, Oliver Knight In fact, some of the songs she'd written for the Watersons' controversial album *Bright Phoebus* (1971) were still in circulation courtesy of singers like June Tabor, but her writing had effectively been buried for 20 years amid the outcry over the very idea of the Watersons singing contemporary songs with a band behind them. Lal herself, self-effacing and publicity shy, hated touring and the whole process of being in a serious group and was quite happy to hide her light under a bushel, communing with nature in Yorkshire. It may have been one of the reasons she was such an incredible songwriter and singer.

WITH OLIVER KNIGHT

Once In A Blue Moon
(Topic, UK).

You can listen to this intently for months on end and still not come anywhere to getting to grips with the subtle nuances and stark truths of Lal's lyricism and spellbinding voice, steeped in a tradition too rich and intense for light listening. This is a really GREAT album. The posthumously released follow-up, **A Bed Of Roses** (Topic, UK) is equally stark, brooding and magnificent.

England/UK | Bhangra/Asian Beat

one-way ticket to British Asia

It's a fairly simple story. Immigrants arrive in a stiff-upper-lip land. They bring with them their own culture, traditions, food, languages and music. Over a generation, the music is merged with the omnipotent influences of the host country, and then – voila! – new sounds are born. **DJ Ritu**, BBC radio presenter and co-founder of the Outcaste label, takes a journey through the new music of Asian Britain, from Bhangra through to Asian drum'n'bass.

Post-war Britain invited subjects from its former colonies to rebuild the depleted labour force. The Caribbean and the Indian sub-continent responded eagerly, mindful of the colonial adage 'Britain is best', and seized the opportunity of a new life for their families – better education, housing, food and employment. The 1950s, as a result, saw Indians and Pakistanis settling predominantly in industrial cities such as London, Birmingham, Leicester, Manchester, and Bradford. More south Asian settlers were then added to these communities in 1972 following the expulsion of 30,000 Asians from Amin's Uganda, as well as a large Bangladeshi community which had started to arrive in east and north London. Gradually, the new settlers found employment – as bus-drivers, labourers, airport-cleaners, or as hired help in sweatshops and factories. By night, however, some of them found the time and energy to follow their creative pursuits – as writers, artists and, above all, musicians.

The communities up and down the UK, whether delighted by the Rolling Stones, baffled by Ravi Shankar and George Harrison, or bemused by T-Rex and Mud, still longed to hear some familiar sounds from back home. Cassettes – and in particular Hindi film soundtracks – were imported into the UK, but there was a growing demand for 'live' bands to perform at weddings, cultural functions and in temples. And so by the mid-1970s a number of Asian dance bands, notably **Bhujungy** and **Alaap**, were in circulation.

Already evident at this stage was the variety of popular music styles from different parts of the sub-continent. The Pakistani communities favoured *quwali* and *ghazal*; Bangladeshis listened to Bengali folk music; Gujeratis had *bhajans* and *gharbar*, while Hindi film music transcended most regional or religious bias. But the most high-profile music style to emerge in a British Asian context was undoubtedly Bhangra, imported from the Punjab.

Bhangra Roots

Bhangra began life as a folk dance, celebrating the harvest and New Year *mela* (festival) in the fertile Punjab region of northwest India. It moved into the towns and cities around 200 years ago, and became established as the Punjab's most popular dance – a position it still holds. It kept its rural past in the dance steps which mimic agricultural activites – sowing, reaping, and so on – and in its name, which came from the word *bhang* – hemp, which is grown across the Punjab.

ALAAP

Alaap lead singer, Channi

Bhangra's strong dance sensibility, led by the *dhol* – a loud and playful wooden barrel-drum – calling people to the harvest celebration dance, and its light, romantic and often humorous lyrics, lent itself to crossing over into a 'street style' pop music. As it developed in Britain in the 1970s, western instruments – electric guitar, bass, keyboards – were added to cut through the hubbub of weddings and parties. The loping beat of the dhol, meantime, with its complex cross-rhythms, was just a groove away from the drum machine.

The story of its transition belongs to the mid-1970s, a decade when the BBC TV Asian programme *Naya Zindagi, Naya Jeevan* – a beacon of light to a community rendered invisible by the British media – brought a weekly fix of the big Bollywood stars of the day, and (unique in the British media) turned its attention to British Asian artists. One group, who had an early break on the programme, was **Alaap**, formed in Southall, West London, in 1977.

Alaap's new take on Asian music was that they concentrated on traditional Punjabi folk – bhangra – but brought to it the energy and brazen trappings of disco. In 1978 they were discovered by the Polygram talent-scout **Pran Gohill**, the first individual to realise the huge potential of the bhangra sound. He had just set up the UK-based **Multitone label** to import music from the subcontinent and having initiated an Indo-disco wave in the UK with artists like **Salma Agha** and **Mussarrat Nazir**, was on the lookout for new artists and new Asian genres.

Alaap's guitarist **Deepak Kazanchi** worked with Gohill to put together *Tere Chunni De Sitare* – an album of traditional dhol and *tumbi* merged with synth sounds and electro beats, and singer Channi Singh's powerful vocals on top. Bhangra with a British twist had arrived and the 'Southall sound' was born. It appealed right across Britain's Asian communities.

The Pioneers

Alaap had entered the recording business in style. What followed was nothing short of a landslide. Inspired and reassured that it was actually possible to release a record, new Asian bands sprung up in their droves. Deepak Kazanchi himself set up a new band, **Heera**, and went into production with his own label, **Arishma Records**.

The new wave of bands varied a great deal in terms of musical emphasis. Whereas **Apna Sangeet** chose a very traditional bhangra style with their dhol player given pride of place centrestage,

groups like **DCS** didn't feature a dhol player at all and concentrated instead on Westernising their sound as much as possible using keyboards, electric guitar, and conventional drum kit. The same differences were apparent in stage costume, with the former band adopting smart, colourful silk *lunghis* from the Punjab, while the latter chose English suits or white jeans. What they all had in common were Punjabi lyrics, largely centred on themes of drinking, dancing, chasing girls, or nationalistic pride, driven by pulsating, heavy rhythm percussion.

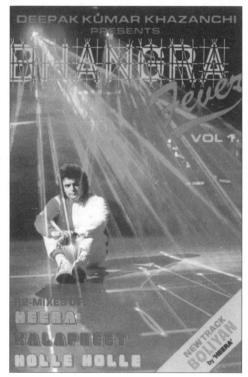

Electro-bhangra: it started here . . .

Other forefathers started to emerge. **Amarjit Sidhu** sang with bhangra pioneers **Chirag Pehchan** and went on to set up the annual Asian Pop Awards and the Kamlee record label. **Kuljit Bhamra**, a musician and composer, produced the first ever bhangra album by a female artist – his mother, **Mohinder Kaur Bhamra**. Through his label Keda, Kuljit went on to unleash **Sangeeta**, the biggest female Asian artist ever known in the UK. She caused a sensation not only because of her gender, but also because she sang in Hindi; her gentle love songs were wrapped in unforgettable melodies – yet percussively the flavour was firmly bhangra, with dhol, *dholki*, and "hoi hoi"

Sangeeta

the **X-tra Hot** series of best-selling remix LPs through Multitone, cutting and splicing existing bhangra tracks and adding **house** or **hip-hop** beats plus extra voice samples to make them more dancefloor-friendly. Well-known bhangra and Western tracks wove in and out together, simply synchronised for a wider, younger audience.

A hugely successful album, *Wham Bam*, appeared in 1990. This was a collection of remixed material from **Bally Sagoo**: a highly sophisticated production that caused a stir, merging classic bhangra tracks with a wide range of dance beats exclusively for the disco floor. The **Sahotas**, born and bred in the UK, started merging reggae rhythms with their bhangra sound whilst the 'great Punjabi hope' **Malkit Singh** kept his music pure, unadulterated and strictly traditional. **Achanak** meanwhile, a Birmingham band set up by tabla player Ninder Johal, with a state-of-the-art synth sound, initiated a revolution in dress code by declaring medallions and flares out – Armani suits in!

calls in the chorus. The BBC's *Network East* TV show and LBC Radio's *Geetmala* programme, meantime, continued to propel things forward.

By 1982 **DJs** playing at Asian events increasingly put aside Boney M and Michael Jackson in favour of such songs as Alaap's classic "Bhabiye Ni Bhabiye". More DJs came on board, giving wider exposure to the music, creating new audiences, new bands, and widespread interest. Bhangra was roots. Bhangra reaffirmed cultural identity – positively. Mother-tongue sounds and instruments merged with those of the West. Here was music made in British Asia, and by 1986, the British press wanted a piece of it.

By the early 1990s extensive touring abroad by bands and prominent DJs rocketed British Asian sounds into the previously untapped Asian diaspora – Vancouver and Toronto in Canada, New York and L.A. in the US, the Arabic markets, and, of course, the selling ground with the biggest potential – the subcontinent itself.

An underground infrastructure of pirate radio stations, magazines and distribution companies began to take shape. But a lack of knowledge on how to play the system soon became apparent. CDs were rarely barcoded. Tapes were cheap in local Asian stores, bypassing the chart return shops

Bhangra Goes Disco

In the mid-1980s **Bhangra raves** were commonplace in London and the Midlands – taking place mostly in daytime, as evening slots could not be secured. Groups of Asian youngsters would miss school to go and dance at these events where they felt safe, in a familiar all-Asian environment. They could indulge in checking-out the most promising DJs like **X-Executive Sounds** and **Hustlers Convention** who served up the latest bhangra beats mixed with soul, disco and hip-hop tracks.

The scene quickly gained momentum. More events. More punters. More DJs. More Western influences. DJs like X-Executive Sounds produced

Moody beat masters Achanak

so that Bhangra never made it to the mainstream pop charts. And there was ignorance and racism, too: the major labels were about as bad as Britain's football clubs in looking for stars amid the Asian scene, and the media was little better. Artists were thus deprived of exposure and royalty payments despite regular UK-alone sales in excess of 50,000 units for releases by leading bhangra bands.

Clubs and Remixes

In 1990, however, despite the odds, the UK's first Asian pop star arrived. **Apache Indian** was not (and did not claim to be) a bhangra artist, instead creating a 'Bhangramuffin' fusion – slipping between Punjabi lyrics and patois, while laying tabla beats over reggae rhythms. Signed to a major mainstream label, Island, his song "Boom-Shak-a-lak" reached an unprecedented No. 5 in the British singles charts.

IAN ANDERSON/FOLK ROOTS

Najma Akhtar, with a young Talvin Singh on tablas

Over on the dance floor, UK Asian music was entering yet another era, as its 'underground' embraced club culture. A number of **London clubs** became unofficial Asian hangouts; at *Jaclyns*, DJ Taz Jay catered for those with Asian and soul cravings, and the gay scene spawned Asian nights at *Asia* and *Shakti*. Then in Autumn 1993 *Bombay Jungle* opened at the Wag Club in London: a two-floor venue offered swing, soul and hip-hop downstairs, while upstairs DJs moved the crowds with bhangra, ragga and swing mixes. More weekly clubs opened in prime venues across the UK and one-off events happened at 5000-capacity venues in Bradford, Birmingham and London.

Also in 1993, **Bally Sagoo** became the second Asian artist to sign to a major label, Sony Columbia. Bally's superb *Bollywood Flashback* album spawned a **'Hindi-remix'** fever which swiftly took hold. He had chosen to mix up a collection of songs by the great Hindi film composer, RD Burman, adding scratch sounds, swing or house backdrops and generally 'phattening' up the beats and bass-lines in 'blow your speakers' street-style.

Once more the mainstream press became interested, this time on a global level. International film crews arrived at *Bombay Jungle* with alarming regularity. Local BBC radio started to develop a growing network of Asian music shows across its stations up and down the UK. The 24-hour Asian Sunrise Radio in London gained its license to broadcast legally. By 1994, Apache Indian had become the first Asian radio presenter on BBC Radio One, sending out ragga/bhangra to his listeners, and DJ Ritu repeated this coup on London's KISS 100 and with the *Bhangrabeat* series on BBC World Service. On TV, the arrival of ZEE TV (24-hour Asian programming) encouraged more exposure.

New Asian Beats

The bhangra spirit of a new Asian music was being reincarnated into other 'alternative' Asian forms through the 1980s. In 1982 **Sheila Chandra** appeared on BBC TV chart show *Top of the Pops* singing "Ever So Lonely" with her band **Monsoon**, while Deepak Kazanchi could be spotted playing guitar next to percussionist Pandit Dinesh in pop band **Blancmange**. In 1987, **Najma Akhtar** released *Qareeb* – a ghazal and jazz album, with saxophone and *santoor* working harmoniously to capture the musical essence of Urdu love poetry, that became a major hit on the World Music scene.

Similar to other groups of second-generation migrants, Asian youth in Britain acquired a taste for contemporary black music styles. Amongst the middle-class young, soul heroes like George Benson and Stevie Wonder were hugely popular. In working class communities an identification with rap, hip-hop and reggae developed. By the mid-1980s, a sizeable underground **Asian rap** scene was alive and kicking. In London's East End, a number of soundsystems – **Osmani Sounds**, **The State of Bengal**, and **Joi Bangla** (later renamed Joi) firmly introduced conscious rap – centring on East End racism and poverty, mixed with traditional Bengali folk lyrics and break beats – into the music agenda.

In Bradford, **Aki Nawaz** was inspired by the punk movement and pretty much everything else

– dub, techno, bhangra – shouting a "no compromise in the fight against racism" message through his band **Fun<Da>Mental**. He founded Nation Records in 1989, signing unknown artists for the label's first releases. The compilation album *Fuse* included contributions from Mahatma T. (real name Talvin Singh) and Pulse 8 (Jah Wobble and On-U-Sound's David Harrow). Nation went on to sign other conscious bands, including Aki's **Transglobal Underground**, **Hustlers Convention** (the original DJ outfit now expanded into the world's first Sikh hip-hop crew), **Natacha Atlas**, **Asian Dub Foundation** (ADF) and **TJ Rehmi**. A 'world-fusion' sound evolved: tabla loops, African chants, and electro beats breaking in with powerful, defiant lyrics.

Outside the Nation label, other 'alternative' groups appeared: **New Conscious Caliphz** (later renamed Kaleef); all-girl band **The Voodoo Queens**; the **KKKings** who baffled everybody musically but charmed the media into dubbing everything that was going on as 'New Asian Kool'; and Tejinder Singh's **Cornershop** who stuck two fingers up at the Indie scene, and at the end of the 1990s have gone on to phenomenal success, as an Asian band on the rock circuit.

The Underground Surfaces

Within this flurry of activity the bubbling 'Asian underground' was ready to spill overground. In 1994 **Outcaste Records** arrived to nurture Asian artists not producing bhangra, but able to create an even balance of Eastern-ness and Western-ness in their music. It released **Nitin Sawhney**'s critically acclaimed album *Migration*, melting tabla, jazz piano, flamenco, and classical Indian and Asian vocals into a perfect East/West blend. *Outcaste* – the monthly club – promoted this underground fusion and received rave reviews.

The following year young tabla prodigy **Talvin Singh** set up his **OMNI** label, and in 1996 he launched the *Anokha* club at London's *Blue Note*. His 1997 *Anokha: Soundz of the Asian Underground* compilation CD cemented 1997 as the year of British Asian Underground. Nation had placed the fuse, Outcaste lit it, Talvin Singh was the climactic explosion! His 1998 debut album, *OK*, was greeted as almost visionary by the mainstream UK music press. Here was a melting-pot of Indian classical instrumentation with Western underground dance styles – drum'n'bass, techno and trip-hop.

The Asian Underground success story should maybe come as no surprise, being immediately accessible for non-Asian audiences and journalists unable to cope with bhangra's overwhelming Indian-ess. Its familiar dance music references have crossed easily into the wider non-Asian club scene, and, as 2000 beckons, some forty years on and two or three gener-

ALEXANDER BRATTELL

Talvin Singh applies polish

ations down the line, the picture looks promising. There's an established infrastructure of Asian labels, PR companies, journalists, magazines, labels, promoters, pluggers, and so on, all in place to support the continued development of a multi-faceted industry, as colourful and vibrant as the subcontinent itself.

The mainstream labels have finally caught the British Asian music bug, too. Talvin Singh records for Island; Warners signed Apache Indian, **Amar**, **Spellbound**, **Black Star Liner** and **Deepika** all within the space of one year (1997); London Records adopted ADF; and **The State of Bengal** joined Bjork's One Little Indian label. *Top of the Pops* appearances are no longer the novelty they were in Sheila Chandra's day. **Jas Mann**'s "Babylon Zoo" reached No. 1 in the UK singles chart; it was followed by **Jyoti Misra**'s "Whitetown"; and then Cornershop's "Brimful of Asha" mixed by Norman (Fatboy Slim) Cook. Meantime there is much excitement about Fatboy Slim's new stablemate at Skint Records, young Sanjay Sen, aka **Indian Ropeman**.

Asian bands are certainly now an established feature of the rock and World Music festival and tour scenes. Anokha has hit New York and WOMAD; The Asian Equation landed at Tribal Gathering; Bally Sagoo supported Michael Jackson in India; Cornershop went on tour with Oasis. Meantime, Talvin Sing won the UK's prestigious Mercury Music Prize in 1999.

Back on the bhangra circuit, too, new stars continue to revitalise things. Musicians like **Jazzy B.**, **Daler Mehndi**, **Surjit Bindrakhia**, **AS Kang**, and **Surinder Shinda** hold onto traditional roots, with strong Punjabi emphasis in their music, while a new generation of superstar producers have emerged – the likes of **Bally Jagpal** and his phenomenally successful group **B21**, Balwinder Safri's **Safri Boys**, **Harjinder Boparai** and **Ravi Bal**.

A postcard from British Asia reading "we've landed" is being sent to all corners of the globe.

Thanks to Rita Hirani

discography

Bhangra

Compilations

◎ **Bhabi Nach Le** (Multitone, UK).

One of many compilations released by Southall-based record company set up by Pran Gohill in the late 1970s. Features some classic tracks by early bhangra pioneers like Premi and Mahendra Kapoor.

◎ **Purely Nachural Vols 1–6** (Nachural, UK).

Nachural Records was set up in Birmingham by Ninder Johal in 1989 and has spawned a range of excellent, largely bhangra bands such as Achanak, Saqi and Panjabi MC. Six albums have been released so far allowing listeners to sample some of the best Nachural label artists.

◎ **The Rough Guide to Bhangra** (World Music Network, UK).

A much needed disc that provides a mainstream distribution, historic trawl through the music. It's forthcoming in July 2000.

Artists

Alaap

Formed in Southall, West London in 1977 by Channi Singh to cater for Punjabi functions, Alaap became the pioneers of modern bhangra.

 Dance with Alaap (Multitone, UK).

Probably their most successful and accessible album, featuring their huge tune "Bhabiye Ni Bhabiye."

B21

Brothers Bally and Bhota Jagpal formed B21 with teenager Jassi Sidhu, after he was dared to sing at Bhota's wedding. They shot to fame in 1996 and are currently the UK's most popular Bhangra group.

 The Sound of B21 (Movie Box, UK).

The group's massive debut album, including their first and greatest hit, "Put Sardaran Dey".

Bally Jagpal

Bally Jagpal is a young Birmingham-born musician, a stockbroker by day and producer by night. He also performs with the groups B21 and Safri Boys.

◎ **Dark and Dangerous** (Movie Box, UK).

A 1999 'solo' album from Jagpal, featuring the huge club hit "Aaja Sohniya" sung by Pakistan's Shazia Mansoor.

Panjabi MC

Panjabi MC is a much loved Birmingham producer and artist.

◎ **Legalised** (Nachural, UK).

This 1998 album is Panjabi MC's finest: beats, B-lines, bass and completely authentic Punjabi vocals.

Partners In Rhyme

Coventry-based Prem and Hardip set up their duo in 1993.

◎ **Distant Voices** (OSA, UK).

Remix and production outfit PIR display a wide variety in tempo and style across the album, but keeping bhangra and Hindi intact.

Safri Boys

Balwinder Safri's Birmingham-based band formed in 1990 after Balwinder himself had won numerous 'best vocalist' awards as a solo artist.

Get Real (Multitone, UK).

Brilliant bhangra created by one of the most popular bands ever seen in the UK.

The Sahotas

The Wolverhampton Sahota brothers who released their debut LP Gidda Pao while still at school in 1987.

 Decade (Kamlee, UK).

The boys celebrate ten years in the business with some magical reggae–flavoured bhangra on this superb 1997 release.

Sangeeta

The Midlands-based premier lady of UK bhangra who began her singing career in 1987.

 Flower in the Wind (Keda, UK).

Her timeless second album, including the brilliant composition by Kuljit Bhamra, "Pyaar Ka Hai Bari".

Malkit Singh

Trained in the Punjab, Malkit began his star-spangled British career in Birmingham in 1986.

 Midas Touch (OSA, UK).

An excellent album which caught on big time in bhangra nightclubs, though perhaps Malkit's least 'traditional'.

Asian Overground

Compilations

 Anokha. Soundz of the Asian Underground (OMNI, UK).

Talvin Singh's essential selection. It includes, among other riches, one of the biggest British Asian dancefloor tunes ever, "Flight IC 408" by The State of Bengal.

 ...And Still No Hits: Nation Records – The Story So Far (Nation, UK).

Two-CD compilation of Nation artists, including TransGlobal, Joi, Asian Dub Foundation, Fun<Da>Mental and TJ Rehmi. A

dynamic record of Aki Nawaz and Kath Cannoville's pioneering west London label.

 Untouchable Outcaste Beats – Volume 1 (Outcaste Records, UK).

A must-have compilation for anyone excited by the Asian 'overground', this features classic tracks from forefathers of the genre – the late Amanda Shankar, Dave Pike Set – and showcases upcoming acts on the Outcaste label such as Badmarsh & Shri and Niraj Chag. Volume 2, **Outcaste Too Untouchable**, is pretty essential too, including Massive Attack's remix of Nusrat Fateh Ali Khan's "Mustt Mustt", along with tracks from Cornershop, Badmarsh & Shri, Nitin Sawhney, and Ananda Shankari's rendering of "Jumping Jack Flash".

Artists

Najma Akhtar

After winning the Asian Song Contest in 1984, Najma recorded a groundbreaking album of *ghazals* (Urdu love poetry) with jazz-inflected backing, for the Triple Earth label. She had major success with the record in the World Music market, but seems to have drifted from the scene.

 Qareeb (Triple Earth, UK).

Years ahead of its time, this is a beautiful mix of ghazal, sweet vocals and jazz, fearuing an illustrious cast of musicians – among them Kiran Pal Singh (santoor) and Nawazish Ali Khan (violin) – still prominent on the UK circuit.

Asian Dub Foundation (ADF)

"Massive not passive" was an early motto for this band of radical dub-rap-trip-hop-influenced London and Birmingham musicians. Their sound is unmistakable, stemming in part from guitarist Steve Chandrasonic's habit of tuning all his strings to one note, like a sitar, and from speed rapper Master D. They are a committed band, delivering a conscious message in their music, and educational work with the community.

 Rafi's Revenge (Slash, UK).

Asian instrumentation meets Jungle rhythms on this Mercury Prize nominated release, with drum'n'bass, sitars, tablas and a ton of attitude backed by heavy breakbeats.

Sheila Chandra

Sheila Chandra has been a fixture on the Asian scene for twenty years, beginning with the mainstream pop of Monsoon in the early 1980s, dabbling in Indi-pop, and moving on to experiments with solo voice and drone.

 Moonsung (RealWorld, UK).

A fine retrospective of 'The First Lady of British Asian Music', with emphasis on her more experimental voice creations.

Cornershop

Cornershop grew out of the Mancunian guitar and Indie band scene, and was the brainchild of Tejinder Singh and Ben Ayers. They're basically a pop/rock band but their whole sound is underpinned by India.

 When I was born for the 7th time (Wiija, UK/Luaka Bop, US).

Asian references to the minimum, but a sparkling album nonetheless, with their No.1 hit, "Brimful of Asha" and a nicely

ironic Bengali-language version of The Beatles' "Norwegian Wood."

Joi

Joi – the brothers Farook and Haroon Shamsher – emerged as the Joi Bangla Sound in East London's Bangladeshi youth movement of the 1980s, and went on to record EPs for Rhythm King and Nation before finally landing an album deal with Real World. Tragically, just as mainstream success beckoned, Haroon died suddenly, at the age of 34, in July 1999.

 One and One is One
(RealWorld, UK).

This excellent debut album from the Shamsher brothers mixed trance, breakbeats and electro with powerful Asian melodies and chants.

T.J. Rehmi

T.J. Rehmi is a leading Fusionsit (the title of his 1996 debut album), with trip-hop/ambient tendencies.

Mindfiller (Nation, UK).

Rehmi's mesmerising 1998 outing, with his sitarguitar to the fore.

Bally Sagoo

Birmingham-based DJ who turned producer/remixer in 1990.

On The Mix (Mango, UK).

"Wham Bam!" mixmaster's finest moments, wedding superb vocals from the likes of Nusrat Fateh Ali Khan to dense, imaginative dub.

Bollywood Flashback (Sony, UK).

RD Burman's finest songs reincarnated for the younger generation.

Nitin Sawhney

A name to watch, Nitin Sawhney mixes Asian vocals and tabla with jazz piano and flamenco guitar – brilliantly.

 Migration
(Outcaste, UK).

Sawhney's critically acclaimed debut.

Talvin Singh

Classically trained tabla-player Singh has forged an amazing reputation, working with Björk and Massive Attack, as well as running his own club and label. He is a key figure in British music at the end of the 1990s, and picked up the 1999 Mercury Music Prize.

 OK
(Island, UK).

Singh's award winning debut solo album proclaims "Music without boundaries" and proceeds through ambient and drum'n'bass by way of synths, flutes and sitars.

Finland

new runes

Finnish music has burgeoned in the 1980s and 90s, with names like Värttinä, JPP and Maria Kalaniemi becoming well known both at home and on the World Music scene. There are more likely candidates waiting in the wings, too, though it's hard to transfer much of what's special in Finnish music to the world stage. It is at heart a subtle creature of quiet places or small gatherings, and is best understood in situ. An easy and outgoing stage manner doesn't come easily to Finnish musicians. Still, when performers do break through the reserve there's often bold experimentation and powerful performance, aided by a national ability to keep a straight face while doing the strangest of things. **Andrew Cronshaw** takes a closer look.

inland is a big, quiet place of lakes and forests, its flattish terrain only rising to mountains well north of the Arctic Circle. It's divided from all but the extreme north of the Scandinavian peninsula by the Gulf of Bothnia.

Politically and economically the country faces west, but its cultural ties tend to go east and south, towards the Balto-Finnic peoples within Russia and the Baltic states, particularly those in former parts of Finland and in Estonia, which is the only other country whose language is close enough in the Finno-Ugrian group to be mutually comprehensible with Finnish.

Finland hasn't existed as a state for long. It was ruled by Sweden until 1809, then by Russia until the Bolshevik revolution, when it painfully emerged after a war of independence and civil war. Part of the region of Karelia, a heartland of traditional culture, remained in the Soviet Union then, and more was lost to Russia between 1939 and 1944. Then the northern third of Finland was completely devastated by retreating German troops, who had been allowed in to fight Russia.

Peace with the USSR entailed the payment by Finland of huge reparations, but it has emerged as a highly technologised country – currently riding the export-economy changes associated with EU membership and the collapse of the Soviet Union – which has a standard of living contrasting sharply with the Russian poverty just across its forested eastern border.

Song: Runolaulu and Kalevala

In all **Finnish song** (*laulu*) a good deal of the rhythmic character is the effect of two particular aspects of the language – the stress is virtually always on the first syllable, and the length of a sound can radically affect the meaning of a word.

Until the seventeenth century, and in some areas much later, virtually all Finnish singing was of the **runolaulu** (runo-song) form, of which close relatives are found throughout the Balto-Finnic area. The rhythm of the words – typically something like 'dum-di dum-di dum-di daa daa' – is virtually always four-footed trochaic (four syllables per

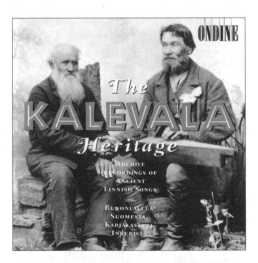

line are stressed). The tunes have a narrow range, usually using just the first five notes of a scale (major, minor or somewhere between). Time signatures are nearly always 4/4 or 5/4 and much of the melodic interest stems from variation of the melodic line. The line-ends don't rhyme, but there's strong alliteration, as there is in other ancient European poetry such as the Icelandic sagas, or Beowulf.

Among runo-songs there's a large body of epic poetry – tales of heroes such as Kullervo, Lemminkäinen and, centrally, Väinämöinen, who could control the forces of nature, sometimes holding all in thrall with his kantele-playing. It was these epics that doctor and folklorist **Elias Lönnrot** linked and organised to make **Kalevala** (sometimes called in English *The Kalevala*, but there's no definite or indefinite article in Finnish). Its first publication in 1835 didn't make much impression, but twenty years after the revised second edition appeared in 1849 it became the focal point for an awakening of Finnishness in a country dominated by Tsarist Russia, whose intellectuals were more likely to speak Swedish or Russian than the language in which it was written. Kalevala, and Lönnrot's second volume of runo song, *Kanteletar*, were the inspiration for further research and a great deal of monumental and romantic art, and became iconic in the emerging national identity. Karelia, where Lönnrot and others collected many of the Kalevala stories, came to represent the artistic soul of Finland.

It isn't all tales of epic deeds, however. There are runo-songs of everyday life, love and misery, many of them made and sung by women, as were the extraordinary sobbing *itku* (crying) songs, and lullabies sometimes even wishing for the merciful death of the infant. There were many songs, both happy and warning of sadness, associated with the biggest ritual occasion – the wedding. The other important ritual – death – was accompanied by singing as well, although laments tended to be more freeform than normal runolaulu.

In common with much of the old layer of song-poem throughout the Nordic countries, runo-songs were often danced, and in Ingria (an area of constantly displaced population at the south of the Karelian Isthmus, north of St. Petersburg) a more recent layer of **dance-song** is still performed, notably by the Röntyskä group from the village of Rappula.

Runo-songs are increasingly performed in the present-day folk revival, one of the most spectacular uses being by **Heikki Laitinen**, **Kimmo Pohjonen** and modern dancer **Reijo Kela** in their stunning performance-art piece *Kelavala*. There are signs, too, of a new era of composition. **Tellu Virkkala**'s *Suden Aika* (Time of the Wolf) is a song-cycle in which she combines and modifies traditional runo-songs and melodies to tell a timeless, image-rich story. Runolaulu's melodic, rhythmic and lyrical forms are also dominant in the material written by **Sanna Kurki-Suonio**, who is an increasingly important force in Finnish roots

music with her own projects, as a member of Hedningarna, and in collaborations with modern dancer Petri Kauppinen, rock singer **Ismo Alanko**, and the Norwegian/Sámi band **Transjoik**. **Värttinä** also shows ever more clearly its runolaulu roots – as leader Kari Reiman says: "five notes have always been enough for me!"

Rekilaulu

During the seventeenth century rhyming in songs began to take over from alliteration; runolaulu evolved into **rekilaulu** (sleigh-song), which has a very regular pattern, with four lines per stanza, the second and fourth lines rhyming.

In some areas, notably Karelia, the change was slower, partly because the dominant Christian religion was Orthodox. The Orthodox priests were often not Finnish-speakers and showed little disapproval of their flocks' songs, whereas the Lutherans of the western regions shared their parishioners' background and tended to disapprove of 'pagan' customs and songs; furthermore their worship involved rhyming hymns in stanzas. Although this worked against runo-song, another tradition evolved of distinctive Finnish hymns, neither runo nor rekilaulu, which still exists and whose melodies have as yet been little heard in the folk music revival except in the work of Sinikka Järvinen-Kontio.

Right up to the present day reki-song is common in popular Finnish songs, a form on which to hang new stories or improvise humour, with ready audience participation because of the tune's familiar structure. It's a prevalent pattern in the old-fashioned, but still appreciated, rural-comic

Kantele – the Baltic Zither

Instruments of the **kantele** type are played in Finland and the Baltic States and northwest Russia. They are basically forms of zither, whose root design is a tapering box with strings, usually now of steel, but sometimes made of gut or horsehair in the past, attached at the wider end to wooden pegs and at the other to a metal bar. Unusually among stringed instruments, a kantele has no bridges or direct contact between string and soundboard, and though this makes it comparatively inefficient in terms of volume, it means that a high proportion of the sound reaches the ear direct from the strings, producing a distinctive silvery ring.

Old-time kantele players

In Finland the basic form has five strings which are usually tuned to the first five notes of a diatonic scale, the same note range as most runo-song. The instrument's role in the past was one of self-expression rather than performance; a player would get immersed in the rhythmic and melodic possibilities of those five notes. Three fingers of one hand and two of the other would have a string each or, in a style more common in the east and across the Baltic, one hand would damp while the other strummed.

There are also new designs with more strings. On those with more than fifteen or so strings the box is made not by carving, but by gluing boards together; metal tuning pegs are used and the single horizontal bar holding all the strings replaced by a pin for each string. These larger instruments called for changes in playing technique: the hands moved apart, and one took an accompaniment role to the other's melody. Around the beginning of the twentieth century players began to turn the whole instrument around so that the longer strings were nearest to them.

Turning it around never caught on in Central Ostrobothnia, one of the strongest areas of kantele tradition, where there is a vigorous style of playing dance music on big kantele, particularly in the area around Kaustinen. Notable players in the Perho tradition include **Eino Tulikari** (1905–1977) and the three **Alaspää brothers**, of whom one, Toivo, now teaches at Sibelius Academy and leads an ensemble of many of the nation's leading young players.

In central Finland, particularly **Saarijärvi**, a different style – both of kantele design and playing – has evolved, in which strings are plucked with a pick (traditionally a matchstick) held in the right hand, while the left damps unwanted strings.

During the nineteenth century big kanteles began to be used as instruments for solo performance to an audience. **Kreeta Haapasalo** (1815–1893) from Kaustinen earned her living, and national fame, as a performer. Kantele makers, teachers and tuition books appeared, and soon aspirations arose to kantele music in the Western Classical tradition – for which a chromatic instrument was considered necessary. In the 1920s Paul Salminen developed a lever mechanism for raising and lowering the tension on the existing strings, and the 'concert kantele' was born.

Meanwhile, folk players continued regardless. One of them was **Martti Pokela** from Haapavesi in North Ostrobothnia. From the 1950s he attracted a lot of attention as a player of small and large kanteles, and the new music he made bridged the gap between classical and folk approaches. In 1975 he became the first teacher of kantele at the Sibelius Academy, and he was a crucial influence in the creation of a folk music department there in 1983. He has virtually given up performing now, but works with players such as Loituma's Timo Väänänen and Sari Kauranen in evolving more of his open-minded, innovative compositions.

There's a breath of fresh air blowing through the kantele world at present, but as an instrument for public performance rather than personal exploration the kantele has problems. The big kanteles are usually played flat on a table, which means that when a player is on stage, strings and hands are almost invisible to the audience. There's also the problem of audibility; quietness is an aspect of the instrument and its music, and it's hard to amplify without brutalising the sound.

The national Folk Music Institute, and director Hannu Saha in particular, have played a strong role in researching, recording and stimulating kantele playing to reestablish it as a musical instrument rather than simply a national icon. Saha's appearance at *Kaustinen Festival* in the 1980s with an ostentatiously electrified five-string kantele was a mischievous challenge to the instrument's iconic status – a 'banish stuffiness, back to the people' gauntlet.

FINLAND

songs of such singers as **Erkki Rankaviita** and a style updated by a new-generation duo **Pinnin Pojat** (Arto Järvelä and Kimmo Pohjonen) which also renews connections with the Finnish-American comic song of 1920s stars such as Arthur Kylander. And rekilaulu is there strongly in many of the new songs performed by the new wave of young bands from Kaustinen and Rääkylä.

The Old Instruments

The old instruments of Finnish music include various wind instruments, among them horns, whistles and folk clarinets made out of wood bound with birch-bark. An important carrier into the modern age of the playing and making of such whistles and trumpets was Ingrian-born **Teppo Repo** (Feodor Safronoff 1886–1962). They maintain a place in current music – for example, **Virpi Forsberg** specialises in playing animal horns, **Leena Joutsenlahti** in whistles, and **Etnopojat/The World Mänkeri Orchestra** make new music using the old instruments whose construction they explore in their workshop in Nakkila.

The old instruments, sometimes combined with modern sounds, have been a feature of a number of bands in the past twenty years, including early pathfinders **Karelia** and **Primo** ('Primitiivisen Musiikin Orkesteri') and later **Tuulenkantajat**. All of these bands have also used the two principal early Finnish stringed instruments, *kantele* and *jouhikko*.

The **kantele** – a form of zither – is Finland's national instrument (see box on previous page). It was raised to iconic status by the success of Kalevala, with its story of Väinämöinen making the first kantele out of the jawbone of a giant pike, stringing it with hair from the Devil's gelding and, when the prototype was lost at sea, making the second from birch and a maiden's hair.

For me the moment when kantele, and much of Finnish music, made sense was watching Hannu Saha and Anna-Maija Karjalainen playing an interlocking, silvery, chiming duet in the quiet morning as the sun streamed dustily through the low window of Kaustinen's wooden Pelimannitalo – the same light as illuminated the lined faces of the flowing-locked, white-bearded players in the old photos.

The **jouhikko**, like the kantele, goes far back into Baltic history. In Finland its tradition survived into the early twentieth century in Savo and Karelia. It's a bowed lyre with three or four horsehair strings and is held upright in the lap, the notes changed by touching the strings with the back of the fingers. Played with a briskly driven small

arched bow, it has a whispery tone, the melody against a chugging drone, and is increasingly finding a place in the new Finnish-rooted music.

Ethnomusicologist **A.O.Väisänen** did much of the collecting, recording and photography of old-style Finnish music and musicians in the early twentieth century; and the jouhikko music played to him in 1916 by **Feodor Pratsu** of Impilahti on the Karelian isthmus has proved particularly influential on such modern players as **Outi Pulkkinen**, **Tytti Metsä** and **Mari Järvinen**.

Pelimanni Music

Pelimanni (from the Swedish *spelman*) means 'folk musician', and in particular the term is applied to players of folk dance music. **Pelimanni music** and its dances are a much more recent development than the runo-song layer of Finnish music. The first couple dances to become popular were the minuet and polska; by 1800 the waltz had arrived, followed by polka, mazurka and schottische. All of these developed Finnish character – on the whole rather restrained. The Finnish polska, for example, has none of the rhythmic complexity of the Swedish version. Later developments and imports included *humppa* and *jenkka*.

Weddings were always the major and most relished social occasions, and presented the biggest opportunity for dance. Special music was associated with the almost theatrical sequence of events in the traditional wedding celebration – both songs and instrumental music, including marches for processions, happy dance tunes and sad ones for the bride's leaving. The **fiddle** (*viulu*), which arrived in the mid-seventeenth century, became the main instrument for dance music. When the **accordion** (*haitari*) – first one or two-row diatonic (*hanuri*), then the larger chromatic versions (*haitari* or *harmonikka*) – spread throughout Europe in the nineteenth century the fiddle was to some extent drowned out. In some areas, however, the fiddle remained strong, sometimes joined by clarinet and kantele (as for example in the Aarnio family band of Humppila in southwest Finland), as mixed ensembles developed toward the end of the nineteenth century.

This was the point at which the **harmonium** (*harmoni*), the pedal-powered reed organ, first took its place as a characteristic feature of Finnish pelimanni music. Pumped energetically, its keys are often hit in a manner so lively that the playing style of young star **Eero Grundström** incorporates a deft action to replace those which jump from their row on his rickety blue-painted folding harmoni-

Maria Kalaniemi

Kaustinen

Inevitably, in talking about pelimanni music, indeed in any discussion of current Finnish roots music, the name of a group of small townships on the Perho river in Keski-Pohjanmaa (Central Ostrobothnia) comes up regularly – **Kaustinen**.

Early in the twentieth century, Santeri Isokangas' coffee-shop in Kaustinen was a place where music was encouraged; there was a harmonium, and a fiddle hung on the wall ready for use. The fiddlers of Kaustinen, Veteli and Halsua such as **Friiti Ojala** and **Antti Järvelä** would gather. **Konsta Jylhä**'s mother worked there, his family played music; it was natural he would too. In 1946 the church organist Eero Polas assembled a ten-piece band for weddings, including Konsta, where they played the suites of seven to twelve linked dances known as *purppuri* (pot-pourri). So the band was called **Purppuripelimannit**. By the 1950s the line-up had resolved to the typical Ostrobothnian wedding band line-up of two fiddles, harmonium and double bass, and it made recordings and radio appearances. In 1961 Konsta, who worked as a lorry-driver, had a road accident which stopped him playing the fiddle for a while, so he began writing songs and tunes. His first effort, "Konstan parempi valssi" (Konsta's better waltz) became popular, and many others followed up until his death in 1984.

The 1960s was a boom time for roots-discovery and in 1968 Kaustinen staged its first **International Folk Music Festival**. It strongly featured local music and dance, particularly the now famous Purppuripelimannit, and also brought in guests from abroad. It was clear the Finnish folk revival had begun: 20,000 people came, and the number doubled a year later. (The Woodstock character in the *Peanuts* cartoon strip in Finland is called Kaustinen). In a country whose population has moved relatively recently from the country to the towns, and whose old family homes have become its summer cottages, *Kaustinen Festival* gave a focus for celebration of the old ways and the old fun. Striped-waistcoated *pelimannit* showed up from all over Finland, joined by both the older generation and the newly interested youth.

um. A regular sight at *Kaustinen Festival* is piano-sized harmoniums being wheeled between venues, and an impressive spectacle is the large harmonium line-up of **Kaisu Försti**'s pupils, who include Grundström and another very watchable player (and singer) **Meri Tiitola**.

Despite the great popularity of accordions in the mid-twentieth century, and their ongoing widespread use, the fiddle has re-emerged as the main lead instrument in pelimanni music. Meanwhile, the big chromatic accordion is gaining new, more subtle aspects, notably in the widely admired, sensitive and articulate music of **Maria Kalaniemi**, which draws on Finnish tradition, tango and other influences. Amongst a variety of projects Kalaniemi also plays in a five-strong, two-row accordion group, the flowery-frocked **Helsingin Kaksrivisnaiset** (Helsinki Melodeon Ladies). The one-man performance art show by the other leading folk-skilled, genre-crossing player, **Kimmo Pohjonen**, is a tour de force of huge rolling live-sampling waves and dramatic lights in which the accordion stars as musical instrument, wrestling opponent and sacrificial object.

FINLAND

JPP hit the road with their customised tour bus

At that time, if city youth joined in it was more likely to be on guitar than fiddle or kantele. Nowadays though, no one is to be found thrashing out three chords to a Dylan song – an energy has been found much closer to home. The festival has become a showplace for new projects in Finnish music, spiced by top musicians and dance groups from abroad, but still very much centred on local music and dance.

In 1974 a fine old wooden log house was bought and reconstructed atop a rise on the festival site to become Pelimannitalo, the headquarters of **Kansanmusiikki-instituutti (KMI)**, the national Folk Music Institute, which has a leading role not only in research but also in encouragement and propagation of roots music, publishing many recordings and books. Instead of being an ivory-tower institution in the capital city, the Institute, built literally in the field, was right from the start a part of local everyday culture, with Pelimanni-talo used for fiddle lessons, weddings and other social functions.

In 1997 a high-tech **Kansantaiteenkeskus** (Folk Arts Centre) was opened to accommodate KMI and its library plus a 400-seat concert hall, recording studio, rehearsal rooms, the Folk Music Festival's offices, the state-salaried folk group **Tallari**, a folk instrument museum with computerised audio-visual presentations, a shop, café, bar and, of course, a sauna.

Folk music courses are run in Kaustinen by the Ala-Könni Opisto (named after the late folk music researcher and first president of the Festival, pro-

fessor Erkki Ala-Könni), and a Chamber Music Festival has become an annual event. Music has become Kaustinen's major industry. The stamp of individual musical personalities remains strong; indeed quite a few of them can be found amongst the players in the local bar-restaurant, which has a fiddle on the harmonium for customers' use and is called, naturally, Pelimanni.

JPP and other Kaustinen Bands

A very obvious aspect of the Finnish revival has been the ever-decreasing age of impressive fiddlers, and the increasing complexity of the tunes they play. A strong influence in both these phenomena has been the band that in the 1980s took the flag of the Ostrobothnian pelimanni tradition and gave it a twirl – **JPP**.

Järvelän Pelimannit, based in Järvelä (one of the Kaustinen cluster of villages), comprised members of the Järvelä and Varila families. Their offspring formed Järvelän Pikkupelimannit (Young Järvelä Musicians) – JPP for short. Seeing the Swedish band Forsmark Tre playing at Kaustinen in 1982 gave JPP ideas which led to a new approach to arranging and harmonising and a gradual metamorphosis into a swingy string orchestra with twisting key changes, using an increasing number of new tunes largely written by the main arranger, harmonium player **Timo Alakotila** from Helsinki, and by **Arto Järvelä** and his uncle **Mauno Järvelä**. The style spread, and now one can hear teenagers like Suolahti sibling trio Jälkisytytys – pupils of Tallari's Ritva Talvitie – playing with ease material that would have been astonishing for players three times their age a generation ago.

Mauno Järvelä, feeling more could be accomplished back in Kaustinen, had come home from playing with orchestras in Helsinki. He played in **Kankaan Pelimannit** with another local classical musician who had returned to his roots, **Juha Kangas**, now conductor of the Ostrobothnian Chamber Orchestra. Mauno teaches fiddle to local children, and his approach is so successful that a band of two hundred current and ex-members of Näppärit (nippers) can be amassed; some of them have already moved on into other bands and music colleges, and a contingent has toured the USA.

Some involvement with live music, from childhood to adulthood, is central to Kaustinen's social life. Active local groups include **Purppuripelimannit** (still featuring Jylhä's co-fiddler Hannu Rauma), the wedding choir **Hääkuoro**, the women singers and fiddlers of **Akkapelimannit** (several returning home for the festival from classical studies elsewhere), a brass septet of mostly **KMI** staff, the youth dance group **Ottoset** (which has grown from folk-dance into ever-developing choreography and new music from its own bands), a string of brashly energetic poppish bands with a distinct Kaustinen identity and humour – **Folkkarit, Prusikoukku Soundmachine** (a tongue-in-cheek name referring to a small bend in the Perho river), and the unpredictable duo of Ville Kangas and Turo Myllykangas, **Viitalan Pelimannit.**

Another strong take on the newly-expanded pelimanni tradition is provided by **Troka**, featuring JPP fiddler Matti Mäkelä, accordionist Minna Luoma, Timo Alakotila, JPP/Folkkarit bassist Timo Myllykangas, and Folkkarit's Ville Ojanen (who is proving not only a fine fiddler but a fast-developing composer and arranger). The very promising **Luna Nova** features Tellu Virkkala's vocals and fiddle, plus fiddlers Mika Virkkala and Ville Kangas, and bassist Timo Myllykangas, and there again is the composition, arranging and keyboard work of one of the quiet architects of modern Finnish roots music, **Timo Alakotila**.

Rääkylä and Värrtinä

Kaustinen is still Finland's largest folk festival, but there's increasing choice. The festival at **Haapavesi**, about 130km northeast of Kaustinen has a growing reputation, as does the *Kihaus* festival at the Finnish Karelian village of **Rääkylä**, centre of the **Värttinä** sound.

Värttinä (spindle) began as a large number of national-dressed children delivering energetic up-tempo songs to accordion-led accompaniment. It reduced in number, acquired new skills and a tight backing band, and drew a strong influence from the music of the Setu people, who live in the border area where southeast Estonia meets Russia. With its exuberant female vocal line-up, and traditional songs which surprised people in Finland with their feminine outspokenness, the band became extremely popular at home and the best-known Finnish roots band abroad. It continues to develop, with fiddler **Kari Reiman** and other

BMG / WICKLOW

Värttinä

band members taking a stronger compositional role since the departure in 1997 of leader Sari Kaasinen. Rääkylä continues to spawn new young musicians and bands, including Sirmakka and singer and accordionist Pauliina Luukkanen.

"Study familiar culture as if it was exotic" – Heikki Laitinen

A strong contributing factor to the new wave in Finland is the dynamic involvement of research institutions, particularly the Kaustinen-based KMI. There is an ongoing opening up of music colleges to folk music, the most important of which is the **Sibelius Academy**, the national music university in Helsinki, offering in-depth, performance-oriented degree courses of usually six or seven years in length.

Martti Pokela's presence at the Academy as a teacher was instrumental in the setting up of a folk music department in 1983, and his influence and the charismatic, free-thinking directorship of **Heikki Laitinen** (now succeeded by kantele player **Sinikka Kontio**) make it a non-stuffy, creative place, full of technology, in which to carry through Laitinen's aims: "To learn the old styles of playing and singing and to break through all perceived limits to create the folk music of the future." Many of the leading names in roots music are to be found there, either as students or teachers.

Facilitating Finland's impressive folk music research and education programmes has been finance from a government which, although it fluctuates, recognises that traditional music is a major part of its national culture.

Swedish Finland and Finnish Sweden

Parts of west-coast Finland, and the islands of Ahvenanmaa/Åland and the Turku/Åbo archipelago, are mainly Swedish in language and culture; indeed well into the twentieth century they harboured aspects of old song and culture that had become rare on the mainland. There are a number of Swedish-style **spelman groups** and, in Vaasa, a folk music research institute – Finland's **Svenska Folkmusikinstitutet**. A large collection of music, song, dance and custom in many volumes, *Finlands-Svenska Folkdiktning*, has been published by Svenska Litteratursällskapet i Finland, and archive recordings are released on CD by Swedish labels MNW and Caprice. Rising young Vaasa-based

band **Gjallarhorn** (see also Sweden – p.303) focuses on this Finnish-Swedish material and is likely to become an international name.

Conversely, in the north of Sweden are many Finnish-speakers, and recognisably Finnish music. Particularly notable in this respect are the Swedish bands **Norrlåtar** and **JP Nyströms**; the latter has a distinctly Kaustinen-like fiddle ensemble sound.

The Sámi

A highly significant group, both culturally and musically, are the **Sámi**. Their territory runs across the northern parts of Norway, Sweden, Finland and on into northwest Russia. The section on Sámi music in all these countries is to be found elsewhere in this book (see p.255). Suffice it here to say that Sámi musicians with Finnish connections include **Wimme Saari**, **Annel Nieiddat/ Angelin Tytöt**, **Nils-Aslak Valkeapää** and **Ulla Pirttijärvi**.

Finnish Gypsies

Particularly striking on a Finnish city street are Gypsy women in wide-hipped black velvet long skirts and bright, waisted blouses – an unexpected flash of exoticism. In so much of Europe aspects of traditional music which have all but disappeared in the country as a whole have been preserved among Gypsy musicians, and that's particularly true in Finland, where Gypsy singing has been an important influence on many of the emerging generation of Finnish revival singers.

The older Gypsy songs, and many of the new, are in a minor mode with a characteristic Eastern-sounding dip of a semitone or tone onto the last note of the melody. The prevailing singing style is lyrical, slightly swooping; remarkably similar to that of the great Scottish traveller-singers such as Belle Stewart. Horsemanship, prison, love and remembrance of lost friends are frequent themes in the lyrics, which are mostly in Finnish but occasionally in Romany. The warm, but sad-sounding delivery sometimes comes close to that of the older Finnish tango singers, amongst whom Gypsies have often figured.

Tango

Tango – which reached Finland in the 1920s – has made its way into Finnish tradition to become part of the standard repertoire of pelimanni bands. It took strong root in Finland particularly during World War II – a welcome touch of warmth,

Where to hear Finnish music

Folk-rooted music isn't lurking round every corner in Finland. There are few consistent roots venues around the country, and very few of the Finnish roots musicians make their entire living from performing; many combine it with teaching or studying.

The best (and most enjoyable) course is to go to a summer festival. The three main ones are all in July – **Haapavesi** in northern Pohjanmaa (Ostrobothnia) is three days at the beginning of the month, **Rääkylä Kihaus** in Karelia is four days around the second weekend, and **Kaustinen** in central Pohjanmaa runs for nine days at the end of the month.

If visiting Finland at other times of year, it's worth scanning the entertainment ads of the national daily *Helsingin Sanomat* for any of the names in this chapter, for Helsinki area gigs at least. Sibelius-Akatemian Kansanmusiikin Osasto runs a couple of club-nights, 'Susiraja' and 'Taiga', on Wednesdays in central venues, and there are other concerts and sometimes a small bar-session.

Alternatively, contact **Kansantaiteenkeskus** – the national Folk Arts Centre – which has a Website (*www.folk.art.kaustinen.inet.fi*) and is responsible for *Kansanmusiikki ja Tanssitieto* (a biennial directory of all things roots-musical), and the bi-monthly magazine *Uusi Kansanmusiikki* (New Folk Music).

exoticism and physical contact. Today it doesn't figure in the pop charts but it remains familiar to most Finns, a part of their culture, or that of their parents. By Argentinian standards the style of dance isn't very passionate, it's more of a sedate shuffle, but in the Finnish lyrics sentiments are expressed which might be hard for a tough male to utter otherwise.

Musically, Argentinian tango evolved with the complex New Tango of Astor Piazzolla, and though he is a strong influence on some Finnish musicians – notably accordionist **Maria Kalaniemi** – he and even Carlos Gardel are unknown to most Finns. Most popular Finnish tango music is fairly simple in form and characteristically in a minor key. The button-keyed bandoneon used in Argentina is replaced by an accordion, and it takes a subsidiary role to the principal stars of the genre – the singers. The most famous of these was **Olavi Virta** (1915–1972), who was at the peak of his career in the 1950s, before his lifestyle caught up with him. Later a rock'n'roll approach manifested itself also to some extent in the music, with the likes of **Topi Sorsakoski**, but today things are generally pretty MOR. Of the older generation still performing, **Eino Grön** remains a big name, while among rising stars is the female singer **Arja Koriseva**.

Many of the new names first reach a substantial public at summer outdoor tango events, particularly the big **Tangomarkkinat festival** at Seinäjoki in early July.

Incomers and Fusions

Piirpauke, the folk–world–jazz fusion band led by **Sakari Kukko**, has been a pioneer in crossing world influences with Finnish traditional music since its formation in 1977. It's now a trio with a Spanish singer and Senegalese percussionist. And music from other cultures is starting to make a wider impression. The Helsinki *mbalax* band **Galaxy** includes among its Senegalese members one of the world's most skilled tama players, **Yamar Thiam**.

There are also all-Finnish bands playing music inspired by another culture – for example the exuberant, rocky Balkan sound of **Slobo Horo**. Since there are still relatively few immigrant musicians making their home in Finland they often find Finnish musicians to collaborate with – Senegalese kora player **Malang Cissokho** has made connections with kantele players and there are mixed-origin bands playing soukous, highlife, or Irish music; there's even a Helsinki Scottish pipe band.

discography

All of the CDs below are normally available from Digelius Music, Laivurinrinne 2, 00120 Helsinki; ☎ (358) 9 666 375; *http://www.digelius.com*

Compilations

🄬 **Arctic Paradise** (Arctic, Finland).

An overview of the new developments – 18 tracks from latest albums by many of the new-roots performers. Put out by the Finnish Music Information Centre, it's a not-for-sale promo CD but well worth tracking down.

🄬 **Finnischer Tango – Tule Tanssimaan** (Trikont, Germany).

The definitive album to illustrate the strange history of Finnish tango. The choice of its twenty-four tracks from a range of labels and sources from 1915 to 1998 is spot on, and the booklet is rich with human stories.

◉ **The Kalevala Heritage** (Ondine, Finland).

No amount of text will convey the distinctiveness of runo-singing. These field recordings made between 1905 (the oldest recordings of Finnish folklore) and 1967 in Finland, Karelia and Ingria, drawn from the archive of SKS, reveal a great deal more. Lonnröt made Kalevala from songs such as these, telling of Väinämöinen, Lemminkäinen, the first kantele, the birth of fire, and everyday life in another world which to us is drifting away but these singers still inhabited.

◉ **Könni ja Kaaleet: Könni and the Gypsies**
(KMI, Finland).

The fine and distinctive singing of Finnish Gypsies, from the collection made by the late Erkki Ala-Könni in the 1970s plus three 1990 tracks. Includes Viljo Salojensaari and particularly impressive rendition by thirteen-year-old Marus Baltzar.

◉ **Soundscape of Finland** (KMI, Finland).

Excellently programmed 33-track sampler, a cross-section of the music in this chapter, from the label of the national Folk Music Institute (Kansanmusiikki-instituutti), a rich source of archive, current traditional and progressive Finnish roots recordings and publisher of many books on folk instruments and music.

 Tulikulkku
(KMI, Finland).

A surprise fiftieth birthday present from many of Finnish new roots' finest to the man who has carried through a vision of the folk music of the future, Heikki Laitinen. In prime form are Me Naiset, Hedningarna, Arja Kastinen, Martti Pokela with Pirnales, Niekku, Virpi Forsberg, Etnopojat, Tuulenkantajat, Väinönputki, Wimme Saari, Hannu Saha ironically setting fire to a kantele (literally) with Primo, and the unsuspecting birthday boy, howling in the street with Suomussalmi-ryhmä.

Artists

Nikolai Blad

Songwriter, guitarist and player of a snakelike long-bellowed concertina. Quirky, dryly humorous manner, ingenious original music, unusual and compelling singing of vivid, often surrealist, lyrics. One day Blad will be recognised as a national treasure.

◉ **Nikolai Blad** (EiNo, Finland).

Full of ideas, which transmit even to non-Finns. Intuitive support from regulars mandolinist Jarmo Romppanen and Tapani Varis (double bass and overtone flute) plus percussionist Kristiina Ilmonen, Maria Kalaniemi, Me Naiset's Pia Rask and Maari Kallberg, Minna Raskinen, Kurt Lindblad and fiddler Piia Kleemola.

Gjallarhorn

A young band destined for wide popularity featuring singer/fiddler Jenny Wilhelms, fiddle and viola player Christopher Öhman, with rippling, barking didjeridoo drones and deep drums well fitting the ringing dance tunes and epic ballads from the tradition of Finland's Swedish-speaking minority.

◉ **Ranarop: Call of the Sea Witch**
(Warner Finlandia Innovator, Finland).

A hugely impressive, excellently produced debut album. Strong melodies, fine microtonal singing, interweaving fiddle and viola, an exquisite balance between beauty and guts.

Hedningarna

At core a Swedish trio (see Sweden, p.300) but with much influence from Finnish singers Sanna Kurki-Suonio (recently replaced by Liisa Matveinen) and Tellu Virkkala (now replaced by Anita Lehtola) so the hugely powerful band is highly relevant in Finland too.

◉ **Karelia Visa** (Silence, Sweden; NorthSide, US).

For this 1999 album the band took a trip to Karelia for inspiration and the result was its most Finnish and runolaulu-slanted album yet. It is more acoustic than its predecessors, with Kurki-Suonio's voice prominent.

Sinikka Järvinen & Matti Kontio

Two key figures in contemporary kantele. Sinikka is Director of Sibelius Academy folk music department, Matti was a member of the band Karelia, and is a pioneer in the technology of recording and amplifying kantele.

◉ **Kantele Duo: Finnish Folk and Favourites**
(Ondine Octopus, Finland).

Ignore its dull title – this is extremely skilful playing of duets on chromatic concert kanteles. The duo use a range of techniques (including train impersonations) largely on their own compositions.

JPP

JPP are the central band of contemporary pelimanni music. The line-up's liable to expand at home in Kaustinen, and on disc, but nowadays for touring it's Arto Järvelä, Mauno Järvelä, Matti Mäkelä, Tommi Pyykönen (fiddles), Timo Alakotila (harmonium) and Timo Myllykangas (bass).

 String Tease
(RockAdillo, Finland).

This 1998 release comprises largely new compositions – it's a living tradition – by Alakotila and Arto Järvelä.

◉ **Devil's Polska/Pirun Polska**
(Olarin, Finland; Xenophile, US).

JPP's 1992 'greatest hits' album is also recommended for a sense of the evolution of their distinctive twist to Kaustinen tunes. Polkkas, polskas, waltzes and more, including of course a tango.

Maria Kalaniemi

Finland's subtlest accordionist, drawing together threads from runo-song to Astor Piazzolla on five-row button accordion, using both chordal and free-bass techniques. Her fluid playing, extremely skilled but never showy, is far from the brashness often associated with accordions; she radiates a focused intensity.

 Iho
(Olarin, Finland; Hannibal/Rykodisc, UK/US).

Kalaniemi with her band Aldargaz plus brass and string sections in rich, melodic original and traditional material, arranged by her, guitarist Olli Varis and producer/keyboardist Timo Alakotila.

Arja Kastinen

Meditative kantele: Kastinen sits hunched on the floor, the fifteen-string kantele propped on one foot, building a web between the shifting flecks of light on the walls, the single candle burning steadily down through time until it flickers out and the silvery ringing dies away.

◎ Kantele Meditation (Finlandia Innovator, Finland).

Touching the soul of the old way of kantele music, this consists of a single improvisation. (Previously issued as *Iro*).

Kiperä

A dance and music group, formed in 1993, making contemporary dance with Finnish tradition-rooted dance music with occasional appealing singing. Most of the original musicians moved on to other projects in 1997, leaving a lively CD as a reminder of phase one.

◎ Nousu ja Uho (KMI, Finland).

Button-accordionist and singer Maija Karhinen, fiddlers Minna Ilmonen and Mika Virkkala, guitarists Matti Laitinen and Topi Korhonen, bassist Timo Myllykangas and percussionist Kari Kääriäinen in light, tight arrangements.

Sanna Kurki-Suonio

A singer of rivetting live presence and subtlety, who has brought a new strength to the vocal aspect of the new Finnish roots music, working in various bands and ensembles and now emerging with her own projects.

 Musta
(Zengaroen, Finland; Northside, US).

Her long-awaited solo album (1998), remarkable singing from silky to ululating, full of intense energy, in new songs shaped by the scale-forms, lyrics and inexorable rhythms of the runosong tradition and moving freely among techno tools.

Anna-Kaisa Liedes

After working with the group Niekku (see below), Anna-Kaisa Liedes has turned to solo work with her own band as well as performing in Me Naiset and Tellu.

◎ Kuuttaren Korut/ Oi Miksi
(Olarin, Finland/Riverboat, UK).

Liedes' serene voice goes from tranquil to ecstatic in songs from Ostrobothnian, Ingrian, runolaulu and Gypsy traditions, with backing vocals from the rest of Me Naiset and accompaniment by members of Niekku and Aldargaz.

Me Naiset

"Us women", the first a cappella vocal group (apart from formal choirs) in the Finnish revival, originally put together from singers in Sibelius Academy's folk music department by Sanna Kurki-Suonio for a Kaustinen show; she left before it recorded. Powerful – a group of individuals.

◎ Me Naiset (KMI, Finland).

Old, strong songs newly understood from the traditions of Ingria, Setumaa, Mordva and Finland.

Niekku

Exploring new ideas and forming bands are key aspects of Sibelius Academy's folk music course. Niekku, formed by the first intake, comprised Anna-Kaisa Liedes, Maria Kalaniemi, Liisa Matveinen, Anu Itäpelto, Leena Joutsenlahti, and sometimes Arto Järvelä.

◎ Niekku 3 (Olarin, Finland).

The final album, ahead of the new roots developments at the time and still relevant. Chiming kanteles, ingenious accordion, silky vocal arrangements twisting to hardness.

Pirnales

An excellent, under-exposed instrumental band with two incarnations, one centred on atmospheric kantele explorations, the other on robust dance music.

◎ Aquas (KMI, Finland).

The kantele incarnation: Sinikka Järvinen, Marianne Maans, Markku Lepistö, Pekka Pentikäinen, kanteles, jouhikko, fiddle, accordion, bass. Developments of music from tradition and by band and guests Martti Pokela and Hannu Saha.

◎ Paraste Ennen/Bäst Före/Best Before
(Olarin, Finland).

Expanded to a seven-piece, including the driving harmonica and harmonium of a name to watch in the new music, Jouko Kyhälä; lively, big-sounding, in Ostrobothnian and Swedish polka, polska, hambo, brudmarsch.

Pinnin Pojat

The skilful, droll duo of Arto Järvelä (vocals, fiddle, mandolins, nyckelharpa) and Kimmo Pohjonen (vocals, harmonica, two and five-row accordions, gogo marimba).

◎ Gogo 4 (Amigo Finland).

Original material and hands across the Atlantic to Finland USA, including "Vuoma Pertti and Eastwoodin Clintti" and Minnesotan Kip Peltoniemi material.

Martti Pokela

The most influential figure, as player, composer and motivator, in modern kantele.

◎ Snow Kantele: Sámi Suite
(Warner Finlandia Innovator, Finland).

This is Pokela's most recent CD (1997), in which he, Sari Kauranen, Timo Väänänen and Sinikka Kontio play his new compositions as well as others evolved between them. Instrumentation is mainly the big silky-sounding concert kanteles, with a touch of the small five-string plus *jouhikko* (bowed lyre), musical saw and occasional wordless vocals from Anna-Kaisa Liedes and Maija Karhinen.

Progmatics

Progmatics are a dance-music band with attitude and haircuts: multi-instrumentalists Jouko Kyhälä, Markku Lepistö and Janne Lappalainen (harmonicas, keyboards, accordion, sax, cittern, banjo), with fiddler Perttu Paappanen.

Vaarallinen Lehmänkello: Lethal Cowbell (Olarin, Finland).

The album is not perhaps as wackily innovative as it could be, but it's enjoyable enough, with lots of tight, energetic playing of Finnish and Swedish trad and new tunes, a swingy reel and a folk-rocky song.

Minna Raskinen

Raskinen, like many of the Pokela-inspired new generation of players, uses most of the Finnish kantele types in performance. She draws on both the tradition and her own compositions, some of which show Japanese and celtic influences.

 Paljastuksia/Revelations (Olarin, Finland).

Her own pieces for the concert kantele. A fine, melodic exposition of the instrument and its possibilities – harmonics are vibratoed koto-like, bent notes played while the levers are moving sing through the deep-chiming resonance of strings plucked, hit or brushed.

Tallari

State-salaried Kaustinen-based group formed in 1986 to display the styles and instruments of Finnish folk music. Leading singers and musicians pass through it, joining core members Antti Hosioja, Ritva Talvitie, Timo Valo and Risto Hotakainen.

 Komiammasti (KMI, Finland).

The tenth anniversary album; old and new material, with kantele player Anna-Maija Karjalainen and the rich vocals of Pia Rask, and also the infrequent, but heart-touching singing of fiddler Hotakainen.

 Lunastettava Neito (KMI, Finland).

1990 album illustrating the range of Finno-Ugrian musics, and featuring one of Wimme Saari's most magnificent recorded moments, his soaring joik accompanied by a magical arrangement of bowed strings over shifting harmonium and bass drones.

Tellu

Four-member unaccompanied female vocal group formed by Tellu Virkkala, ex-Hedningarna, to perform Suden Aika

and new works. The live group's line-up has changed from that on the CD.

 Suden Aika (KMI, Finland).

The story, in resonant runo-song images, of a woman's birth, entrapment and quest for her own life. Stark and magnificent; the intertwining voices, moving between silky and hard-edged, of Tellu, Sanna Kurki-Suonio, Liisa Matveinen and Pia Rask, with Outi Pulkkinen, Anita Lehtola and Swedish percussionist Tina Johansson.

Troka

Another new twist in the Kaustinen dance combo tradition, with a lively spring from top young players: fiddlers Ville Ojanen and Matti Mäkelä, accordionist Minna Luoma, bassist Timo Myllykangas, with the new-pelimanni eminence grise, Timo Alakotila, on harmonium.

 Troka (Olarin, Finland; NorthSide, US).

Traditional material as well as some written by members, interesting winding, fresh melodies with a Balkanish whizz in places.

Vimpelin Väinämöinen

The remarkable Eeli Kivinen (1900–1990) from Vimpeli; a man with a unique, eccentric personal tradition using the kantele to accompany his extraordinary, graphic singing.

 Vimpelin Väinämöinen (Love, Finland).

Sadly hard to find, on a legendary but defunct Finnish label, and no CD re-release as yet.

Värttinä

Finland's best-known roots band, Värttinä produce a high-energy runo-song-based sound. They comprise energetic women singers plus a skilful band.

Vihma (BMG/Wicklow, US).

In this 1998 release, the Värttinä approach comes together triumphantly – much-developed vocals, including touches of throat-singing and pygmy hocketing, with strong technologised and acoustic instrumental backings which pick up ingeniously on the rhythmic shifts and interplays within the narrow-range runolaulu which remains central to the band's music.

France

music of the regions

"How can you govern a country with two hundred and forty six varieties of cheese?" asked President de Gaulle. Equally, how do you sum up the music of a country that boasts almost as many varieties of bagpipe? The two may even be connected – what better use for a goat when the creature is finished for making cheese? Yet, unlike the wines and cheeses, French traditional – or, more accurately, regional – musics are not well known. World Music fans tend to see no further than Paris, with its hotbed of rai (see p.413), zouk and other immigrant sounds but as **Philippe Krümm** and **Jean-Pierre Rasle** contend, it's possible to take a Tour de France around the renaissance of traditional music.

Western Europe in the 1960s and 70s saw a strong folk revival movement which, in France, was spearheaded by musicians like Breton harpist **Alan Stivell**. But French music stretched a long way beyond Brittany, and right now it is in active revival, as scores of artists, groups and festivals rework the regional traditions of the country into contemporary forms.

The strongest of these traditions have survived either in the more remote or mountainous areas like the Auvergne and Corsica, or in those with a strong regional identity like Brittany, the Basque country or (again) Corsica. The music of these regions acts as a reinforcement of identity and, for years, it has also served to break the monotony of daily toil (street fairs from the Roussillon to the Artois), or as an expression of religious fervour (Christmas and Easter processions in the central provinces, and songs nearly everywhere).

These elements often overlap and the original reason for their existence is often blurred: many outside events have survived or been revived to attract tourists, sometimes creating in turn their own versions of the original traditions. Many of the summer *groupes folkloriques* performances, in particular, tend to have an emphasis on

turn-of-the-century melodies and a bland overuse of the piano accordion. But the musicians involved are often part of a non-tourist scene, too, and might be found playing a completely different set for a regional function or on stage at a major festival.

Brittany

Like Galicia in Spain, France's westernmost province – **Brittany (Bretagne)** – is a Celtic outpost. Breton music draws, in its themes, style and instrumentation, on the common Celtic heritage of the Atlantic seabord and it has been for centuries a unifying and inspiring part of the culture of the province. The clearest expression of this is at the pan-Celtic extravaganza of **Lorient**, France's best-known music festival.

Traditions

Literature in the Breton language survives from the fifteenth century, but the historical record of Breton music really begins with the publication of **Barzaz-Breizh**, a major collection of traditional songs and poems in 1839. It was compiled by a nobleman, **Hersart de la Villemarqué**, from his conversa-

COLLECTION CHRISTOPH WAGNER

Breton pipers, around 1910

tions with fishermen, farmers and oyster-and-pancake women, and in view of the scarcity of other literature in the native language it is seen as a treasure of Breton folk culture.

One of the oldest forms of Breton music is that of the **bagad**, the Breton **pipe band**. It comprises quintessential Breton instruments: the loud and raucous *bombarde* (shawm) and *biniou* (small Breton bagpipe), plus marching drums. Such bands were an essential component of any procession or festival, and they still appear, though usually with the larger *biniou braz* (essentially a copy of Scottish pipes). The older form of bagad has been recreated by **Roland Becker** and his trio **L'Orchestre National Breton** who've also elaborated the music into theatrical shows with nineteenth century costumes and masks. There are also more modern bagad incarnations of which the **Bagad Kemper** (with jazz musicians) and **Kevrenn Alre Bagad** (with forty musicians and ranks of dancers) are amongst the best known.

The most rewarding setting to witness traditional Breton music is undoubtedly a **festoù-noz** (night feast) – a night of serious eating, drinking and dancing, similar to an Irish *ceilidh*. During the summer months, such events are common, attracting hoards of revellers from miles around. Though they are often held in barns and halls in the more isolated parts of the region, discovering their whereabouts shouldn't present any problem, as an avalanche of posters advertising them appears everywhere. Once the evening gets underway, the dancers, often in their hundreds, whirl around in vast dizzying circles, hour after hour, sometimes frenzied and leaping, sometimes slow and graceful with their little fingers intertwined. The oldest dances, the *an-dro*, *hanter-dro*, *rond* and *gavotte* are all **line or circle dances**. It can be a bizarre and exhilarating spectacle – and a very affordable one too, with modest admission fees.

The traditional **festoù-noz music** is a **couple de sonneurs** – a pair of musicians playing bombarde and biniou. They play the same melody line, with a drone from the biniou, and keep up a fast tempo – one player covering for the other when he or she pauses for breath. This is defiantly dance music, with no vocals and no titles for the tunes, although there are countless varieties of rhythms, often localised and generally known by the name of the dance.

There is a purely vocal, and probably older, counterpart to this, known as **kan ha diskan**. This is again dance music, but is performed by a pair of unaccompanied 'call and response' singers. In its basic form the two singers – *kader* and *diskader* –

alternate verses, joining each other at the end of each phrase. As dances were in the past unamplified, the parts were often doubled up (or more), creating a startling rhythmic sound. The best singers might also give the dancers the odd break with a **gwerz**, or ballad, again sung unaccompanied.

Over the past couple of decades, these festoù-noz accompaniments have been supplanted by **four- or five-piece bands** who add fiddle and accordion, and sometimes electric bass and drums, to the bombarde and (less often) the biniou. The tunes have been updated to give a more rock sound, while the ballads have given way to more folk-style singer-songwriters, with guitar backing. Purists might regret the changes, but they have probably ensured the survival of festoù-noz. They have also nurtured successive generations of Breton musicians who move on to the festival and concert circuit.

Stivell and folk-rock

It was **Alan Stivell** who started the ball rolling for the modern Breton music scene with one of the first **folk-rock** bands in Europe. He was born Alan Cochevelou and adopted the name Stivell (Breton for 'spring' or ' source') in the 1960s. The playing of the *telenn* or Breton harp had effectively died out until Stivell's father decided to revive it and his son put it decisively back on the map. His internationally successful album, *Renaissance of the Celtic Harp* (1971) helped introduce Breton – as well as Irish, Welsh and Scottish – traditional music to a worldwide audience, and subsequently stimulated interest in less accessible material.

The album that followed, *Chemins de Terre*, went further, combining – in a similar fashion to that of Fairport Convention or Steeleye Span in Britain – a rock rhythm section with folk instruments. Stivell played harp, bagpipes and Irish flute alongside **Dan Ar Bras** on electric and acoustic guitar.

Both Stivell and Ar Bras are still performing and recording individually. Stivell remains at his best accompanying himself in traditional ballads, with the combination of Breton words and rhythmically plucked metal strings evoking the heart of Brittany. His more recent Stivell projects have been more esoteric, and not always successful. **Ar Bras**, who played with Fairport Convention in 1976, now produces mellow acoustic solo albums. The other key figure from Stivell's band was (non-Breton) **Gabriel Yacoub**, who went on to lead the non-Celtic folk-rock band **Malicorne**, the best-known French band of the 1970s and 80s.

Alan Stivell

Current singers and bands

Folk rock has been just one direction for Breton music in recent decades. On the concert circuit the biggest names tend to be the **singers**, amongst whom the most famous is **Andrea Ar Gouilh**. Her output includes a return to Breton roots with a recording of old songs taken from the Barzaz-Breizh. **Yann-Fanch Kemener** is celebrated amongst Bretons for his powerful voice and unbelievably long performances of traditional gwerz. **Youenn Gwernig** and **Kristen Nikolas** are both idiosyncratic balladeers, while the duo **Bastard Hag e Vab** (Bastard and Son) have been stalwarts of the live circuit for years.

Festoù-noz singers are sometimes accompanied by **harpists**, among whom the best contemporary players are **Anne-Marie Jan**, **Anne Auffret**, **Job Fulup**, **Ar Breudeur Keffelean** (who are virtuoso twin brothers), and the mystically bearded Merlin lookalike, **Myrdhin**.

It's the instrumental groups, though, who are likely to be more immediately appealing for newcomers. A fine festoù-noz act to look out for is **Strobinell**, who have a line-up of bombarde, biniou, violin, flute and guitar and make occasional forays into a looser, jazzier groove. The trio **Tud** (a Breton word meaning 'the people') are a compact ensemble of bombarde or biniou with guitar and accordion, who play the festivals

in western Brittany. For the electric festoù-noz sound, complete with full rock drum-kit, the best exponents are **Bleizi Ruz** (Red Wolves) and **Sonerien Du** (Black Musicians), both active since the 1970s.

Musically the most adventurous band has been **Gwerz** who made several records of traditional songs and ethereal instrumentals, using bombarde, biniou, uilleann pipes and guitars. Their singer **Erik Marchand** is one of France's leading figures in musical fusion, frequently working with Gypsy musician **Thierry Robin** (see Gypsy Music article – p.146) as well as Indian and Romanian performers. Marchand is also a fine clarinetist, one of five in the group **Quintet Clarinettes** who give a classically oriented but punchy new take on traditional material with inventive arrangements and outlandish key shifts.

New on the scene are **Manau and Denez Prigent** – Breton **folk-rappers** who, after a notable solo album, have been mixing techno and dance music with traditional and contemporary words over a base of traditional dance airs and ballads remixed by DJs.

Dastum

An important resource for those involved in Breton music is the Rennes-based **Dastum** organisation, founded in the early 1970s. *Dastum* is a Breton word meaning 'to collect' and it has an archive of over 30,000 recordings, 30,000 manuscripts and printed materials, as well as postcards and photographs. However Dastun stresses that its purpose is to use its materials to keep the Breton language and culture a part of the modern world. It has a good computerised library for research and has become a source of material for many of the contemporary bands. (Dastun, 16 rue de la Santé, 35000 Rennes. ☎(33) 2 9930 9100).

Central France

The provinces of central France – **Berry**, **Bourbonnais**, **Nivernais**, **Morvan** and the **Auvergne** – form one of the strongholds of traditional music. This is the heartland of the **bagpipe** and **hurdy-gurdy** and of a dance called the **bourrée**, which comes in two rhythms, 2/4 and 3/8, the first heard more in the north, lending itself to virtuosity and the second, in the south, to rhythmic improvisations on both instruments.

Bagpipes and Hurdy-gurdys

France claims a greater variety of **bagpipes** (*cornemuses*) than any other country, and the stars among them are the *grande cornemuse* and *chabrette* from the old provinces of **Berry and Bourbonnais**; these date back to the seventeenth century and are often works of art in their own right. It's in this central region that most modern bagpipe players are found, many of them within stringing distance of the 'Stradivarius of the bagpipe', Bernard Blanc.

The region is also a stronghold of the **hurdy-gurdy** or *vielle-à-roue*; indeed it once had a whole town (Jenzat in the Auvergne) involved in hurdy-gurdy manufacture. Although also found in Spain, Hungary and Russia, it was in France that this instrument reached its most elaborate design with a curved oval body decorated with mother-of-pearl, a row of black and white keys and a distinctive curved handle. It is placed on the player's knee and the handle turns a revolving wheel which bows the strings, which are stopped with the keys – a cross between a violin and piano accordion. The sound is coloured by a number of drones and hidden sympathetic strings and there's also a moveable bridge controlling an extra string to give it its characteristic 'buzzing' sound.

Among the region's notable musicians are hurdy-gurdy players **Gilles Chabenat** (original-

ly with the Berry group Les Ecoliers de St. Genest) and **Patrick Bouffard**, and masters of the *grande bourbonnaise* bagpipes such as **Philippe Prieur** (also a wine-maker in Sancerre, following in the time-honoured tradition of part-time musician and tradesman), **Eric Montbel** (see Limousin below), **Jean Blanchard** (with his bagpipe big bands, **Quintette de Cornemuses** and **La Grande Bande de Cornemuses**), musicians of the ensemble **La Chavannée**, and especially bagpipe and clarinet player **Frédéric Paris**, who can also be found in the **Duo Chabenat-Paris**. These players explore new melodies based on the old 2/4 bourrée and also develop mixed polyphonic ensembles – like the **Trio Sautivet** and the **Trio Patrick Bouffard**.

Several of the names above – Bernard Blanc, Jean Blanchard and Eric Montbel – were involved in two of the best folk revival groups of the 1970s, **La Bamboche** and **Le Grand Rouge**, whose excellent eponymous albums of Auvergnat and Limousin music were groundbreaking in combining ensemble and solo playing.

Berry is home to the annual festival at **St. Chartier** (near Chateauroux), where players and makers of bagpipes and hurdy-gurdies gather for concerts, workshops and networking. The festival – perhaps the most enjoyable of all French music festivals – has a strong regional focus, but also includes international groups. It's become a place of pilgrimage for bagpipe (and roots music) aficionados the world over.

In the Morvan, a wooded area east of the centre, the group **Faubourg de Boignard** with its piper **Raphaël Thiery** has revived old melodies and taken them on a more muscular path with the addition of a rhythm section and occasional stream-of-consciousness poetry.

Some of the most thorough collecting of songs was completed here and in the next province, the Nivernais, in the early part of this century by **Achille Millien**, and this repertoire is being revived by the groups **Les Ménétriers du Morvan** and **Achille**.

The Auvergne: Cabrettes

The Auvergne, further south and dominated by the Massif Central, is largely mountainous and remote, especially the **Parc des Volcans** national park, dotted with the plugs of extinct volcanoes. The volcanic ash has made some of the lower-lying areas rich and fertile; on the mountains though the land is poor, fit only for grazing sheep

The Bal-Musette

The Eiffel Tower, whisps of smoke from a Gitane and the sound of an accordion wafting through the night air. Black and white pictures and rather scratchy sound, but classic Paris. That accordion sound – evoked in the *chansons* of Edith Piaf and the cliché of travel films today – belongs to the **bal-musette**.

The music arrived in Paris from the Auvergne, a poor, mountainous region where life was tough. And ironically it was the poverty of this mainly agricultural area that led to the creation of the Auvergne's greatest cultural export – at least to the rest of France, the *Bal-musette*, literally, the smallpipes dance. These events started up as migrant workers from the Auvergne met up in bars of the Paris suburbs at the end of the nineteenth century. By 1880 there were some 150 dance halls in and around Paris specialising in Auvergnat music. The Auvergnat publicans cum coal-merchants – the famous **"Café-Charbons"** – were also often the pipers, leading the dance, like the most famous of them all, **Antoine Bouscatel**. He was the man who allegedly invented the pairing of Auvergne smallpipes and Italian accordion, in which the latter originally acted as accompaniment, before fashion reversed the relationship, and

Martin Cayla

the *cabrette* was eventually relegated to the role of second fiddle, so to speak, and eventually was only remembered by the title of the dance-halls.

The earliest bal-musette recordings date from the early years of the twentieth century and document the 'masters' of the cabrette – **Léon Chanal** (1864-1912), **Antoine Bouscatel** (1867-1945) and **Martin Cayla** (1889-1951). Cayla also built and played accordions, but the man who is credited with creating the bal-musette sound is accordionist **Emile Vacher** (1883-1969). Playing small diatonic accordions, his light rhythmic style with a characteristic tremelo defines the genre. Alongside the accordion the dance bands often included piano, banjo, double-bass, clarinet or sax and the old style dances endured until World War II after which larger accordion-led orchestras evolved.

Today, there's something of a revival in the bal-musette tradition, although the preferred location is the more rural guinguette, with a dancefloor, tables outside and wine and music liberally flowing. On a sunny Sunday afternoon the popular **Guinguette de l'Ile du Martin-Pêcheur** on an island in the Seine close to Paris takes you back to another era.

and goats. And those goats are a vital part of the story of the music of the Auvergne. The *cabrette* – 'little goat' in Auvergnat dialect – is a droneless bagpipe made of goatskin, 'blown' by a small pair of bellows pumped by the elbow, like the Northumbrian pipes or Irish uillean pipes. The sound is bright and shrill: one of its original players, **Joseph Ruols**, would tell his students: "Make sure that the little goat sings; that's what makes the sound beautiful."

Today, many players are following in Ruols' footsteps, notably **Michel Esbelin**, **Jean Bona** and **Dominique Paris**, all experts in the typical 3/8 dance music of the area, which also has some

beautiful, slow ritual airs (*regrets*) full of melancholy. The *cabrette* was also the humble origin of France's famous bal-musette tradition (see box).

Limousin

To the west, the Limousin repertoire is being explored by the Lyon-based **Eric Montbel**. With his group **Ulysse** (and before them, **Lo Jai**), Montbel has tried out combinations of local instruments, including the *chabrette* (Limousin bagpipe), the *pifre* (the very short old army fife) and the melodeon. He has been particularly instrumental in the rediscovery and revival of the chabrette, uncovering older musicians with unusual playing techniques (like the use of the chanter as a sort of 'wah wah' effect).

Limousin, and particularly the Corrèze plateau, is also known for its **violin music**, in particular the **Trio Violon** and **Françoise Etay**. In the region a great deal of work has gone into carrying the traditions on to a new generations of fiddle players such as **Jean-François Vrod**, **Olivier Durif**, **Jean Pierre Champeval** and **François Breugnot**.

On the **hurdy-gurdy**, there are some radical musicians like **Valentin Clastrier** who has an electroacoustic instrument fitted with nearly 30 strings and makes surprising musical journeys between traditional, jazz and contemporary music. **Dominique Regef** and **Pascal Lefeuvre** are two other hurdy-gurdy players forging new sounds in contemporary music and don't confine themselves to music from the central region.

The South

In the foothills of the Pyrenees in southwest France, there are strong regional traditions and languages – Occitan and its dialects, Gascon and Béarnais, and of course Basque and Catalan. Singers like **Rosina de Peira** and **Jean-Luc Madier** have revived the old songs in the **Occitan** language, derived from the Provençal of the twelfth-century troubadours.

Gascony

Perlinpinpin Folc was a leading group of the traditional revival in the 1970s and their seminal album *Musique Traditionnelle de Gascogne* was important in cultivating the cultural identity of Gascony. They have since evolved into an extraordinary band called **Ténarèze**, named after the region famed for Armagnac. Led by **Christian Lanau**, the group features clarinet, violin and a variety of traditional and 'created' instruments, made from plastic tubes, vacuum cleaners and assorted bits of plumbing. They are great at festivals and, whatever instruments they're playing, the musicianship shines through.

Gascony also has some pretty arresting small pipes in the form of the **boha** or *bouhe*, with a unique rectangular chanter and drone combination. The sheepskin bag with the fleece showing gives it an eerie animal-like appearance and old photographs show shepherds living in the swamps of the area, playing them on stilts!

Languedoc

Languedoc too has some strange local instruments: traditional **oboes** like the *graille* and the *aboès,* often played alongside the **bodega**, the local bagpipe. The latter is a very striking instrument with a huge bag made of an entire goatskin (the process involves decapitating the animal and breaking its bones so that the flesh and bones can be removed through the neck), and a single large shoulder drone. Carvings and murals show it was already in use in the fourteenth century. It has a bright low sound.

The bodega and oboes are used in the regional ensembles **Calabrun**, **Trencavel** and **Trioc**. Oboe player **Laurent Audemard** was the inspirational figure behind the group **Une Anche Passe** (a punning title involving involving a reed, an angel and a pregnant pause), which has combined a love of Languedoc-style oboes with related instruments from elsewhere. Besides the Languedoc oboes, their line-up might include a Catalan *gralla*, Basque *gaïta*, Italian *pifferos* plus saxophones and brass.

Rousillon

Southwest French definitely has a reedy tendency and it extends to the **Catalan** region of France, centred on the city of Perpignan and the region of **Rousillon**. As in Spanish Catalonia, the national dance is the **sardana**, most commonly played by brass and wind bands or *cobles*. The instrumentation is predominantly reedy with three sorts of oboe in the bands – the *tible*, the *tarota* and the *tenora* ranging from top to bottom. The little flabiol flute tends to preface each of the dances with an introductory melody. Several French bands, however, have revived the older timbres with shawms and bagpipes. Amongst the traditional ensembles, look out for **La Cobla de Joglars**, **La Cobla els Montgrins**, **Els Ministrels del Rossellano** and the **Cobla Mil-Lenaria**.

This area, and the Camargue at the Rhone estuary, are where most of the **French Gypsies** are based. They have a strong musical tradition of their own (see Gypsy Music article – p.146).

Béarn

In the Béarn region of the Pyrenees, the star voice is **Marilis Orionaa**, and one that is making waves internationally. Orionaa's debut album *Ça-i!* (named after a local cow-call) hangs on her agile voice, with minimal accompaniment on guitar, percussion and bass. One of the most memorable

Marilis Orionaa on the road

songs, sung in the Béarnais dialect describes the south wind which comes and leaves women pregnant, like a thief in the night. Another song "Etnocide" is about the encroachment of mainstream France, but her work is rarely political: "I'm more interested in Béarnais the language than Béarn the place," she says. "The language is my country!"

Pays Basques

The most famous figure in the French Basque music scene is singer **Benat Achiary** – though it must be said that his overwrought performances and arrangements with operatic stylings make the Basque music in Spain (see p.292) an altogether more attractive proposition. The same might be said of the forty-strong choir **Oldarra**, based in Biarritz.

Provence

The typical Provençal sound is that of a duo with **fifre** (the fife, a small transverse flute) and drum, or from ensembles of **galoubets-tambourins**, three-holed pipes. Both are played with drums and used for street processions. But since the folk revival, virtuosos like **André Gabriel**, **Patrice Comte** and **Yves Rousguisto** have enlarged the instrumentation and repertoire.

In the Alpes Maritimes area there is a choral tradition that spills over into the Piedmont and Ligurian regions of Italy, with the group **Corou de Berra** and **La Compagnie Vocale** being the best examples. Further North, **Patrick Mazellier** and the groups **Drailles** and **Rigodon Sauvage** have revived the violin tradition and its local dance, the *rigaudon* of the Dauphiné province.

The old province of **Savoie** has strong links with the Italian valleys of Aoste and Piedmont, harking back to the times when these regions were a single political unit straddling and communicating via the high mountain passes of the Alps. Here a specific repertoire explored by **La Kinkerne** reminds us that the hurdy-gurdy was the instrumental emblem of this area for centuries.

Corsica

One of the great rediscoveries of traditional music in France has definitely been **Corsican polyphonic singing**. Polyphonic song has survived in other French mountainous areas – the Basque Pyrenees and the Alps – but the tradition is nowhere as strong as on Corsica (or the neighbouring Italian island of Sardinia where there is a related tradition).

Polyphonic Song

The **Corsican songs** are usually sung by men in three parts. The *siconda*, the middle voice, carries the tune while the *bassu* holds the bass and the *terza* (the highest voice) completes the harmonic structure with ornamentations over the top. The slow moving harmonies and the clashing parts create a strong musical architecture and there's a gorgeous, sustained process of slowly passing through discords to a satisfying resolution at key moments throughout a piece. The songs may be secular (the *paghjella*), poetic (the *terzetti* or *madrigale*) or sacred. But with half a dozen men, usually grouped in a circle, hands cupped over ears, it's some of France's most beautiful music.

French Roots Festivals

For information on French traditional music, check out **the Association Française d'Action Artistique** (AFAA), which has a good Website (*www.afaa.asso.fr*) with information about regional festivals and organisations. The most important music festivals include:
Festival de Cornouaille, 41/43 rue de Douarnenez, BP 1315, 29103 Quimper. ☎ (33) 2 9855 5353. Regional Breton festival. End of July.
Festival Interceltique de Lorient, 2 rue Paul Bert, 56100 Lorient. ☎ (33) 2 9721 2429. Brittany's international Celtic festival. First fortnight of August.

Festival de la Sardane, Foment de la Sardane de Céret, Casa Catalana de la Cultura – Mairie, 66400 Ceret. ☎ 33 4 6887 4649. Sardana and Catalan culture. End of August.
Les Rencontres de St. Chartier, Comité Gerorge Sand, 5 place du Marché, 36400 La Châtre. ☎ 33 2 5406 0996. Great meeting of hurdy-gurdy and bagpipe maniacs. Mid July.
Les Rencontres du Sud, Suds, 17 rue Jouvène, 13200 Arles. ☎ 33 4 9096 0627. Music from the south. End of July.

The major traditional groups are **Canta u Populu Corsu** and **Chjami Aghjalesi**, and from these have sprung newer subgroups like **Tavagna**, **A Filetta**, **Voce di Corsica** and the media-aware **Nouvelles Polyphonies Corses**. One of the most successful groups, also breaking down the male hegemony, is the female quintet **Donnisulana**. Some new groups – including A Filetta and the very commercial **I Muvrini** – also mix singing and instrumentals.

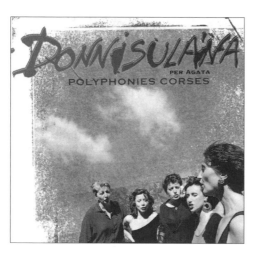

New France

As mentioned in the introduction to this tour, France also has a very active music scene among its communities of North African origin. French-based rai singers – including the superstar Khaled – are covered in the Algeria/Rai article (see p.413). But there are a number of new North African bands and artists coming through who employ a range of styles outside the confines of rai. Notable among them are the singer **Rachid Taha**, who has unleashed Arabic techno-trance on the nation, with huge success, and the **Orchestre National de Barbès**, who take their name from their home base – the North African Barbes quarter of Paris.

The Orchestre National is led by Algiers-born Youcef Boukella, who came to France in the mid-1980s to play with rai superstar Cheb Mami and *kabylia* group Takfarinas. Other members of the band have histories in other Maghrebi sounds – Algerian classical music, Moroccan *chaabi* (pop), and *gnawa* music. Like that of Taha, their music is a kind of voyage through the Maghreb taking in all these sounds and more, something that would never happen back home. The band is driven by the raucous sound of gnawa clappers and includes an extravagant line-up of keyboards, sax, guitars, bass, drums and many vocalists.

Amongst other eclectic fusion musicians, Gypsy guitarist and oud player **Thierry Robin** is a world class musician who's been making interesting collaborations with musicians and musical styles from round the world (see Gypsy Music article, p.146). And in a more rock/roots domain, the 1980s unleashed the great French-Spanish band **Mano Negra** (named after an Andalucian anarchist organisation). Influenced by The Clash and punk ethics as well as global sounds, including rock, rap, rai and flamenco, Mano Negra was led by Spanish vocalist **Manu Chao** and included other Spanish musicians, plus north Africans and Frenchmen recruited amongst buskers on the Paris metro. After four albums the band more or less dissolved, but Chao re-emerged in 1999 with a stonking new album, *Clandestino,* which ranges widely in its languages and musical styles and keeps his characteristic cool and subversive attitude.

JAK JILBY

Lo'Jo

Another group that's recently attracted a lot of attention is **Lo'Jo** – although they've actually been around for over a decade, living as a sort of multi-ethnic musical collective in Angers on the Loire. Led by the energetic and eccentric **Denis Péan**, Lo'Jo did a lot of work with street performers, circus artists and dancers, but suddenly achieved international success in 1998, the same year as France had a multi-ethnic football triumph in the World Cup. It was a fitting parallel: Lo'Jo music is warm, danceable and compelling and draws heavily on North African sounds, plus Gypsy and Caribbean ingredients, to create a fitting template for the future. "There's nothing more fascinating than Lo'Jo in France right now', said the paper *Liberation* in 1998.

discography

The two key French labels are Ocora, which has some excellent recordings of traditional material, and Auvidis/Silex, which has a very good catalogue of new traditional music. Breton music, new and old, is well served by **Keltia Musique**, 1, Place au Beurre, 29000 Quimper – Breizh, France; ☎33 2 9895 4582; email: *keltia@eurobretagne.fr*

Compilations

ⓓ Anthologie de la Chanson Française: La Chanson Traditionnelle (EPM, France)

A monumental set of recordings (14 CDs) covering every aspect of French song over 5 centuries. Mostly revival arrangements with a wide range of collaborators, including singer-songwriter Gabriel Yacoub of Malicorne fame, who supervised the project.

ⓓ L'Ame de l'Auvergne (Sony, France)

A recent compilation gathering a wealth of original recordings for piano-accordion, cabrette and hurdy-gurdy, with a strong 1920s flavour, containing some of the original sources for many revival groups.

ⓓ Blues De France (Auvidis/Silex, France)

As the leading label of new French traditional music, Silex has put together some good samplers. This is predominantly

melancholy and emotional, as the title suggests, and includes mainly vocal tracks from all areas of France with highlights from La Cobla el Montegrins, Trio Violon, Donnisulana and singer and trombonist Alain Gibert's quartet. Shame there's no information about performers or the music.

ⓓ Cabrette: L'Age d'Or de la Cornemuse d'Auvergne (Auvidis/Silex, France)

The most fascinating of the recent reissues of historic recordings, from a cylinder recording of 1895 to the 1976 track of the last of the great masters, Jean Bergheaud. The roots of the *Balmusette* are all here, with the fledgeling start of the piano-accordion as humble accompaniment to the cabrette. With Chanal, Bouscatel, Cayla etc the real sounds of the Auvergne in Paris.

ⓓ Cobles: Gammes en sang et or (Auvidis/Silex, France)

'Scales of Blood and Gold' is the title of this splendid load of cobles from French Catalonia. The four groups featured are La Cobla els Montgrins, La Cobla de Joglars, Grallers Montonec and La Cobla Principal de la Bisbal. Great tunes, played with a robust reedy swagger.

ⓓ Corsica/Sardinia: The Mystery of Polyphony (World Network, Germany).

A good disc for comparing and contrasting the vocal polyphony of neighbouring Corsica and Sardinia. The latter sounds a lot more rugged and rough hewn. Groups include Canta u Popolu Corsu, A Filetta and Donnisulana from Corsica and various groups including the Tenores di Bitti from Sardinia. Luigi Lai on launeddas is an added bonus.

ⓓ Musiques, Chants et Danses de Bretagne (Keltia, France)

A fine compilation album showing the range of contemporary Breton music from the leading Breton label.

ⓓ Musiques en France (Auvidis/Silex, France)

A more leisurely survey of French music than the single disc below. There are four discs (available separately) covering the four areas where the music survives strongest, Brittany, Central France, the South and Corsica. *The Mark of the Celts* (Brittany) includes vocal and experimental styles with Erik Marchand and Bagad Kemper; *Music from Central France* is mainly instrumental with strong offerings from Eric Montbel, Jean Blanchard, Patrick Bouffard and Jean François Vrod; *Couleurs Sud* is a mixed bag including Catalan Cobles, Une Anche Passe, Benat Achiary and Perlinpinpin Folc. *Music from Corsica* is of course principally vocal with a selection from the island's excellent polyphonic choral groups. Central France and Corsica are the strongest.

Musiques Traditionelles Aujord'hui
(Auvidis/Silex, France)

Sixteen tracks representing the best introduction to the new traditional music of France on the Silex label. Not all winners, but good offerings from Quintet Clarinettes, Trio Violon, La Chavannée, Tavagna, Donnisulana and the Catalan Cobla els Montgrins.

La Vielle en France (Auvidis/Silex, France)

A companion disc to the cabrette one featuring great players of the hurdy-gurdy from central France from 1930-1991. An acquired taste, though, with a strong 1920s flavour.

Artists

Une Anche Passe

A group formed in praise of the humble reed, led by Laurent Audemard on the piercing local Languedoc oboes. Other members of the ten-strong band play related reeds, sax, brass, accordion and percussion.

Entre tarentelle et sardane (Auvidis/Silex, France)

The title suggests some sort of meeting between Italy (and the tarantella) and Catalonia (and the sardana). Both those are there plus some great comic touches in Tempo Italiano, Tango Sense and many others. A very inventive album that really grows on you.

Jean Blanchard

Bagpipes Blanchard has been involved with several of the important folk revival groups in central France – La Bamboche, Beau Temps, and later La Grande Bande de Cornemuses and Le Quintette de Cornemuses. He now runs the Centre des Musiques Traditionnelles Rhône-Alpes with Eric Montbel with whom he has recorded two fine albums.

Musiques pour Cornemuses (Ocora, France)

Arguably the best of the 'New Tradition' solo recordings, showing a juxtaposition of superb new compositions with a selection of wonderful melodies from the central provinces. Uncompromising in its simple arrangements but played by a modern master of the instrument.

Ménagerie (Auvidis/Ethnic, France)

Jean Blanchard's Quintette de Cornemuses, which actually includes just four bagpipes – Blanchard, Robert Amyot, Eric Montbel and Raphael Thiery – plus Max Di Napoli on percussion. One of the most imposing bagpipes ensembles.

Les Brayauds

Through the organisation of the same name based in Saint Bonnet-près Riom, the various musicians of the group have released a number of records exploring the music of their area (Lower Auvergne) and new compositions. The members also appear in the groups Bardane (melodeon and hurdy-gurdy duo), Passe Aqui (violin trio), and Eau Forte, with other local musicians.

Eau Forte (Ocora, France)

A classic album from past masters at creating timeless arrangements of traditional themes with bagpipes, hurdy-gudies and melodeons.

Gilles Chabenat

One of the most adventurous of the new generation of hurdy-gurdy players, he now explores new ways to use the instrument. He also works with a number of groups including the Corsican outfit I Muvrini.

Musiques pour Vielle à Roue – Blue Nuit
(Ocora/AMTA, France)

A riveting voyage into the musical world of one of the best exponents of this extraordinary instrument. The juxtaposition of traditional and new melodies is inspired.

Manu Chao

Manu Chao is the Spanish-born singer who headed alternative band Mano Negra from 1986–94. Including his trumpeter brother Antoine Chao and other diverse musicians they played a high-energy post-punk fusion, captured at its joyful, crazy best on *Puta's Fever* (1989, Virgin). Manu now plays 'solo', weaving in all manner of global influences.

Clandestino
(Virgin, France/Palm Pictures, UK).

Moving freely between Spanish, English, French and Portuguese lyrics, the title track of this 1999 album refers back to Chao's earlier incarnation and more besides: Mano negra clandestina, Peruano clandestino, Africano clandestino, Marijuana ilegal. Inventive and compulsive.

La Chavannée

Folk group based in the Château du Plaix led by the bagpipes, melodeon and clarinet of Frédéric Paris. These well-respected musicians have released a dozen recordings over twenty years, mostly the fruits of their research within the old county of Bourbonnais. They also run a yearly folk festival as well as regular concerts, dances and workshops.

Cotillon (Silex Mosaïque, France)

One of many beautiful recordings by the most consistant of groups from Central France, essential for its tasteful arrangements using all the standard instruments of the area.

La Compagnie Vocale

Sixteen-strong mixed choral group (and social club!) based in Provence performing a cappella music from various regions of southern France in the local dialects and a good rootsy sound.

Piada Desliura – chants polyphoniques provençaux. (Iris, France).

Music from Provence, Piedmont, Béarn and Auvergne. The Provencal song of shepherd struggling across the mountains to bring cheese to the baby Jesus is charming.

Donnisulana

Quintet of five Corsican singers taking on a male preserve and writing their own material.

Per Agata – Polyphonies Corses
(Auvidis/Silex, France)

Beautifully recorded in a Corsican monastery, this disc features traditional and new material and Donnisulana bring arresting new timbres and harmonies to this music. The album is dedicated to a colleague who died tragically young and ends with a requiem prayer.

Lo'Jo

Led by singer Denis Péan, Lo'Jo began in the early 1980s, but has been through several manifestations – at one period working extensively with circus artists and acrobats. Currently the band has a strong line-up with two north Africans (including the striking Yamina Nid El Mourid on sax), violin/kora, accordion etc. Latest plans have involved working with musicians in Mali.

◉ **Mojo Radio** (Emma Productions/Night & Day, France).

One of the most talked about roots albums of 1998 which kicks off with the gravely voice of Péan and then the catchy title track. Slipping between several languages, this is a very contemporary-sounding album with diverse instrumental sounds that manage to keep a distinct sense of identity. Late-night chill out music.

Orchestre National de Barbès

This twelve-piece band, based in Paris, have taken the North African and French music scenes by storm in recent years with their powerful mix of rai, chaabi, Moroccan gnawa and European rock-funk. They are led by bass player and vocalist Youcef Boukella and include mainly north African musicians, plus French guests.

 En Concert (Virgin, France).

The ONB are very much a live band and so tight that it's hard to believe that this, their first recording, was made at a single concert (in a Paris theatre in 1996). Highlights include their trademark welcome "Salam", the chaabi-influenced "Ma Ychali" and Gnawa celebration "Labou". Raucous and not too slick, it seems to hit the mark.

Marilis Orionaa

The voice of the Béarn region, Orionaa makes rather a lot of her mysterious sylph-like mountain presence and strong, but breathy voice. A unique figure in French folk.

◉ **Ça-i'!** (La Voce, France)

Don't let the opening title track put you off with its reverberant multitrackings, the second song about the south wind is extraordinary and there's more where that came from. Subtle accompaniment on guitar, bass and percussion.

Jean-Pierre Rasle

Rasle is the UK's resident French bagpiper. He has run the Cock & Bull Band, specialising in Anglo-French dance music, for over 20 years and six albums. He also has a bagpipe ensemble, the Dancing Drones and is a full-time member of Jah Wobble's Invaders of the Heart.

◉ **Cornemusiques** (Celtic Music, UK)

Traditional music from the Berry and Auvergne plus French Renaissance and Baroque tunes on a cornemuse 20 pouces, musette Béchonnet, cabrette and musette de cour. Rasle also sings the vocals on this album.

Alan Stivell

Breton harpist who kicked off the French folk revival, no less. From his pioneering work for Breton music in the early 1970s and almost twenty albums, he's ventured more recently into some rather unappealing world fusion with Youssou N'Dour, Khaled and Paddy Moloney.

◉ **Renaissance of the Celtic Harp** (Philips, UK)

The 1971 album that began it all.

Rachid Taha

French-Algerian Rachid Taha is a top star, up there in the pantheon with Paris-based Algerian rai singers like Khaled. He sings rai himself, but only a couple of numbers a show or album, and, having started out as a rocker with the group Carte de Sejour, is now producing techno flavoured albums with producer Steve Hillage – one-time hippy guitarist with Gong before reincarnation in the 1990s with techno-ambient band, System 7.

◉ **Oyé Oyé** (Barclay, France).

With this album, Taha revealed the first fruits of his collaboration with Hillage and a brand new sound as contemporary and shocking (to North African Paris) as the peroxide cut he sports on the cover. Always the revolutionary, he sticks his neck out with a hitherto unheard mix of sampled and sequenced backing tracks peppered with Arabic flavours and his own rough and rasping vocals. Arabic techno trance was indisputably on the map.

 diwân (Barclay, France).

Again produced by Hillage, this is Taha's 1998 masterpiece – not only because the pairing of tradition and technology so boldly attempted on *Oyé Oyé* reaches maturity but because a myriad of styles from Morocco, Algeria, the Sahara and Egypt are unified by a single overriding approach – and keep their individual charms and flavours. The opening song, "Ya Rayah" was a huge hit in France and Lebanon.

Tud

Tud (the word is Breton for 'people') come from Cornouaille (or Kerne in Breton) in the west. Three musicians, Thierry Beuze (melodeon), Franck Le Rest (guitar and bouzouki) and Eric Ollu (bombarde, biniou) playing strong, rootsy acoustic Breton dance music.

◉ **Musique à danser de Bretagne** (Escaliber, France)

A good sample of the sort of small ensembles that ply the Breton festival circuit. Includes local gavottes des montagnes, dans plinn, hanter-dro etc.

Emile Vacher

Once the accordion took over from the cabrette in the bals-musette, Vacher (1883-1969) was the star of the new style. He didn't write music, but kept hundreds of tunes in his head and played with a light and rhythmic agility.

◉ **Créateur du genre Musette** (Auvidis/Silex, France)

Recordings of popular dances – javas, polkas, valses – from 1927-39. A piece of history and a wonderful interview with Vacher, full of personality, in the notes.

Christian Vesvre and Serge Desaunay

Duo of bagpipes and melodeon/accordion from Central France. Vesvre also works with Patrick Bouffard (hurdy-gurdy) in the Duo Bouffard-Vesvre playing music from the Bourbonnais area, and the three of them with François Breugnot (violin) in the group Carré Croisé playing traditional music from Central France

◉ **Musiques Pour Cornemuses et Accordéons – Matins Gris** (Ocora/AMTA, France)

A new twist on an age-old combination: Vesvre and Desaunay create delicate atmospheres with new compositions showing unexpected uses of the instruments.

Germany

kraut kaunterblast

Germany's roots music scene is scarcely known abroad, yet it is actually quite a success story, ranging from the traditional to the radical, with innumerable detours en route. **Ken Hunt** is so enthused he's dreamed up a festival of the top acts playing just for him.

O kay – the big surprise first. German roots music is a lot of fun. It is not serious nurturing of dusty folk traditions but vibrant, danceable and unruly. There are few wilder roots excursions in Europe than, say, musical subversives like **Hundsbuam Miserablige** doing their "Hoizhakka Pogo" (Woodchopper's Pogo), hollering out their Bavarian attitude to a backdrop of screaming electric guitar, trombone and accordion frills. They would top my bill in a dream German roots festival. And playing on the same program would be a real feast

PROFOLK

JAMS

of the regions. There would have to be **JAMS** – whose "Fischshanty" is improbably sung as Low German hip-hop; and **Wacholder**, playing "Alte Berliner Moritat" – a potboiler of political intrigue and star-crossed lovers reminiscent of Brecht/Weill; and **Thomas Felder**, moaning "So Beni" a lapsed Catholic word-jazz catechism whipped on by piano and hurdy-gurdy; and multi-kulti fusionists **Dissidenten** slipping a hip in time to "Lobster Song" wailed in English by their Curaçao-born singer Izaline Calister and in Tamil by Manick Yogeswaran.

Make no mistake, **Volksmusik** (folk music) is

experiencing a Blütezeit – a heyday, a folk flowering. Its days of slow death on TV and in tourist-trap as oompah cliches and lederhosened thigh-slapping are history.

Reunification and Renaissance

Until October 1990 when the two Germanys reunited, Germany supported two folk congregations. One of the least fanfared fall-outs of the political process was the formulation of the **Deutsch-Deutsche Folkszene** – as the amalgamated folk scene was dubbed. Unifying the *Ossi* (East German) and *Wessi* (West German) scenes coincided with folk song and dance acquiring a new 'sexiness'. Folk's denominations of lapsed church-goers began returning to the fold, mingling with a new host of celebrants.

Today's renaissance is multi-faceted. It embraces diverse linguistic voices, such as **Swabian** (Thomas Felder), **Bavarian** (Hundsbuam Miserablige) and **Mecklenburger Low German** (JAMS), **folk dance bands** such as Die Hayner and Horch, **New Wave** outfits such as Hoelderlin Express and the Merlons and **Old Guard** survivors Fraunhofer Saitenmusik, Liederjan and Wacholder. Borrowings from other cultures have also led to a truly world-class **World Music** scene, in the form of the Jewish and Yiddish music-makers Aufwind, the Godfathers of World Beat Dissidenten, or the Kurdish-German alliance Nûrê.

Representing bygone traditions is Thuringia's Mandolinenorchester Wanderlust which has kept the flame of the **mandolin orchestra** alight since 1919 and the **bandoneon** preservation league Bandonionfreunde Essen. Borrowings from the *Liedermacher* (songmaker) and *Kabarett* traditions have also added intellectual substance and barbed wit.

Critical to folk's regeneration has been the emer-

Kabarett and Liedermacher

Shadowing the German folk scene are two separate but related movements, the urbane roots of which are tangled up in Europe's cross-bred cabaret, literary and bohemian movements. Intertwined at some points, they have cross-pollinated and influenced. The first is world famous. Talk of **Kabarett** and conversation instantly turns to the interwar Berlin of Christopher Isherwood and his kind with images provided by Bob Fosse's film *Cabaret* (1972).

Kabarett, in the Weimar Republic, inhabited a murky world of late-night clubs in which sexuality was opaque, petit bourgeois conservatism denounced and political-satirical cabaret thrived. Foremost composers and lyricists were **Mischa Spoliansky**, **Friedrich Hollaender**, **Kurt Tucholsky** and **Marcellus Schiffer** while performers such as **Marlene Dietrich**, **Margo Lion** and **Karl Valentin** were household names. The satire was insightful, but the most popular subject was sex, often of a surprisingly liberal hue. Schiffer's "Wenn die beste Freundin" (When the Special Girlfriend), first performed by Margo Lion and Marlene Dietrich in 1928, became the unofficial anthem of the German lesbian movement. Commenting years later, **Lotte Lenya** (the Austrian singer, wife of Bertolt Brecht's librettist Kurt Weill and Dr. No actress) clarified, "People often think it was all left wing, but of course much of it was non-party and purely satirical."

More than a century on from Brecht's birth in 1898, and as Germany slouches towards what the right-wing perceives as multicultural bedlam, Kabarett still retains its reputation as 'the Muse with the sharp tongue'. The former East German scene produced work of great political subtlety wielding irony and ambiguity to get past censor and Stasi (secret police). Equally importantly, Ossi acts such as **Barbara Thalheim** and **Duo Sonnenschirm** produced work after the Wall came down which packed the punch of Brecht or Tucholsky. Inequalities between the two-in-one state, environmental and sexual issues and politics' perennial absurdity provide enough ammunition for today's satire boom and Berlin still toasts a thriving Kabarett club scene.

There is a somewhat blurred line between Kabarett and the **Liedermacher movement** (literally, songmakers), which, since its craft lies in the words, has received inevitably curt treatment outside the German-speaking countries. Its finest writers were able to take the French cult of the song and infuse it with a German sensibility. Although they were as far from folk as Dylan's *Highway 61 Revisited* was from folk protest, **Wolf Biermann** and **Franz-Josef Degenhardt** remain spectral godfathers to the German folk scene. Their candid, crafted material both set standards for others to aspire to and suggested alternatives to the Anglo-American mire into which the German folk scene looked like sinking. Instead of looking to America for inspiration, they looked to the French-language chanson tradition of Brassens and Brel.

Liedermacher singer, **Joana Emetz**, for example, had her first hit in 1964 with a cover of Piaf's "Non, Je Ne Regrette Rien" while Degenhardt himself produced an entire album of Georges Brassens' material in 1986 called *Junge Paare Auf Den Bänken* (Young Couples On Benches). Biermann remains especially important. He really suffered for his art, being stripped of his East German citizenship in 1976 – an act at the time seen as the GDR's equivalent of excommunication.

As their notable contemporary Christof Stählin admits: "Back then, in the 1960s, we thought we'd discovered a new profession. In the 1970s this movement was worldwide. There was a great expression of support from the public. We all believed, whether prominent or not, that it was all for us." The Liedermacher movement has gradually declined in popularity compared to the mid- to late-1960s when Degenhardt's *Spiel Nicht Mit Den Schmuddelkindern* (Don't Play With The Grubby Children) was essential listening, but its key figures are still making music and performing their intellectually stimulating songs.

gence of a considerable festival scene. Chief among these is the **Tanz&FolkFest Rudolstadt**, whose origins go back to 1955 when it had only been able to offer acts from comrade states for foreign colour beside East German proletarian Kultur. Since 1991 Rudolstadt has blossomed, attracting droves of festival-goers with the lure of its many stages in castle, park, town, theatre, church and on cobbles. Now it is *the* press and media showcase for international acts wishing to break into the German market. At the other end of the scale, the **Kaltenberg festival** is newer, more intimate, and – as reflected in its tantalizing *Folkfestival Kaltenberg: Highlights 1982–1997* retrospective – is adept at selecting a range of German and European acts (see box on p.118).

Folk Manipulation

By 1984 Florian Steinbiss's book made it official: *German-Folk: In search of the lost Tradition*. And if ever a folk culture had been impaled on its own past, it was Germany's. Since the 1950s, Anglo–American folk music had had much more currency than its

Bavarian group c 1920s

lukewarm domestic variant, an image that was really only thrown off in the 1990s.

For much of the twentieth century German folk-music served as a gambit in the politicians' propaganda *Kriegspiele* – decoy culture deployed in the name of national identity or party political purposes when preaching the cultural high ground. Furthermore, asserting the cultural primacy of High German had enforced central state supremacy and deliberately enfeebled dialect culture. The German experience boomed the dangers of misappropriating 'National Music' for nationalistic purposes.

'Get them young' has long been a folkie rallying cry. In Germany between the wars, this had more sinister overtones. The so-called *Jugendbewegung* (youth movement) dated back to 1900 and was built on pioneering youth organisations such as the **Wandervögel** (birds of passage), which championed the great outdoors and the concept of healthy minds in healthy bodies. After rambling, they would end the perfect day with campfire singsongs to *zupfgeige* (guitar) accompaniment and dance folk dances. Soon after attaining power in 1933, the **Nazi party** began tapping the potential of Germany's youth organisations, and by 1940 **Hitler Jugend** (Hitler Youth) membership was compulsory. Volkslieder and *Volkstänze* (folk dances) made for innocent indoctrination to state ideology. Going as it were from the rosy-cheeked good life and the headiness of rose blossom of "In

der schönen Rosenzeit" to "The Horst Wessel Song" (the classic Nazi marching song) took a few easy lessons and before long jolly campfire singalongs chorused party lines.

The legacy of the Nazi era was twofold. A haemorrhaging of the tradition had occurred. The slaughter of German menfolk, the postwar displacement of German communities and minorities with the knock-on effect of diluting local tradition, the memory of Volksmusik as a propaganda tool – all of these elements rent holes in the folk fabric.

Folksong as ideological weapon did not cease with the toppling of the Nazis, however. The **Communist East German regime** trumpeted Volksmusik as the cultural expression of the proletariat. It became the state-approved voice of the worker, in an attempt to reclaim it from its recent Nazi manipulation. Festivals reinforced this. Stadtfeste up and down East Germany rammed home how folk music was people's culture. West Germany was only different in the detail. Right-wing parties appropriated Volksmusik during campaigns and party faithful get-togethers. The common purpose, as ever, was to bolster political credibility and legitimacy and to reinforce a cultural identity. It similarly allowed Bavarian right-wingers to tap a sense of regional identity. Cultural paralysis followed cultural manipulation. Folk's credibility was shot to ribbons. Or so it seemed.

Resuscitation

The European and American folk movements of the 1950s and 60s were in part a distancing from the commerciality and banality of pop music. Many Germans, who could find no way back to their own folk roots, embraced Anglo-American folk and folk-blues idioms instead. But there were German initiatives, both East and West.

In the West, a low-key wave of **new folk acts** emerged. **Ougenweide** embraced early music traditions. **Lilienthal** explored a German branch of folk-rock which, in Britain, Fairport Convention, Steeleye Span and the Albion Band pioneered. **Liederjan** became early champions of singing in German with their witty, punningly comic songs – a tradition they continue. Acts such as **Fiedel Michel**, **Werner Lämmerhirt**, **Hannes Wader** and **Zupfgei-genhansel** were also part of this movement.

Interestingly, a different music culture continued around the industrial heart of West Germany. In the Ruhr, **bandonion orchestras** have survived to the present, as exemplified by the **Bandonionfreunde Essen** – a formidable army of massed accordions from Essen. Heinrich Band's invention defined working-class German culture along with pigeon lofts, allotments and the Schalke 04 football team just as bandoneon defined Argentine culture, whorehouse entertainment and tango music.

Bandonion Freunde Essen

On the other side of the border, folklorists laboured away – Wolfgang Steinitz being the prime figurehead – and their work would illuminate Germany's folk revival. But by the 1970s, there was a really thriving independent **Ossi folk scene**, based around clubs, folk-workshops, a circuit of *Tanz-Häuser* (dance houses comparable to Hungary's *tánchaz* scene) and the inevitable Stadtfeste. Such was the level of interest, organisation and infrastructure that **JAMS** – one of the country's finest roots bands, formed around 1980 – could comfortably play 150–180 gigs a year.

After the Wall came tumbling down, JAMS were the first East German band to play both Britain and the United States. Their music was compellingly danceable and in no sense dependent on language – and it stood up brilliantly on disc.

They were not alone. East German acts such as **Bierfiedler**, **Folkländer** and **Wacholder**, given to jamming like everyone else, developed fearsome levels of professionalism. Iron Curtain seclusion made them not only musically hungrier, it also forced them to rely on alternative sources of repertoire. West German archives and libraries were largely denied them because of travel and currency restrictions. As a result, folkies looked to Gesellenlieder – songs of the 1848 Revolution – and alternative sources including Steinitz's research. Wacholder, a word-orientated band, fashioned a particularly interesting repertoire using texts from Heinrich Heine. The Nazis had denounced (the Jewish) Heine's work as unpatriotic (and when they had to publish it, published it as 'author unknown'). It was not lost on Wacholder that, even though Heine was reinstated politically, his work still glinted with wicked barbs with descriptions of Germany as a "land of oaks and stunted minds".

Performing live was the key to Ossi success. Unlike their Wessi counterparts, they had few opportunities to record and any repertoire had to be approved before going into the studio. Wacholder, for example, started auspiciously, receiving their radio debut in May 1978, a month after forming. It took until 1983 to release their debut album, *Herr Wirt, so lösche unsre Brände* (Landlord, that's how we put out our fires) and until 1989 to release the follow-up. Consequently, very few Wessis had vinyl experience of the Ossi scene until the first bands began to cross the border.

Regional Voices

In common with English and Spanish, German pays little deference to a 'standard tongue' as its regional voices confirm – whether dialects from

Stadtfeste and Folk festivals

Germany is a country rich in the tradition of **Stadtfeste** (town festivals). These may be an outgrowth of some earlier country fair or merely a good excuse for frivolity, barbecued meat, beer and a chance to inspect the local fire engine. But even the tiddliest *Nestfest* (hamlet festival) may field a folkloristic troupe hoofing it in regional costume (*Tracht*) like some throw-back to when each rural community dressed differently and Tracht distinguished them. Indeed it still does in Bavaria.

Alongside, **commercial folk festivals** are increasing in popularity with *Kaltenberg* and *Tanz&FolkFest Rudolstadt* leading the way. **Kaltenberg**, some 30 minutes west of Munich by car, was first held in 1982. Taking place on the last weekend of June, the festival, originally dedicated to Southern German folk and art music, is intimate and low-key, but musically compelling. Its booking policy features North and East German, Italian, Austrian, Swedish, Czech and other European acts.

Rudolstadt, about 30 minutes south of Weimar in Thuringia, is an old town with cultural associations aplenty – including Goethe, Schiller and Wagner. It held its first *Fest des deutschen Volktanzes* (Festival of German Folk Dance) in 1955, an event extolling the German Democratic Republic's ideological stance on people's culture. The festival, not always annual, was still lurching on when the Wall came down. In July 1991 a mixture of Ossis and Wessis put together the first **Tanz&FolkFest Rudolstadt** and Germany was on the way to getting its showcase festival. While it has presented acts as different as Fun<Da>Mental (UK), the Bisserov Sisters (Bulgaria) and U. Srinivas (India), gloriously it retains much of its East German flavour (including a sprinkling of acts from the former socialist states). Each year the festival picks an instrumental and a regional theme to sit beside the remainder of the billing. In 1995 it was mandolin and South African music, in 1997 saxophone and the Indian subconti-

nent, in 1998 banjo and Portugal. And in contrast to *Kaltenberg*'s intimacy, Germany's largest world music festival takes over Rudolstadt, with give-or-take fourteen stages set up in the Heidecksburg (the castle towering over the town), the marketplace, the baroque church, in side streets, boulevards, squares and park.

Kaltenberg Festival, Schulstrasse 2, D-86949 Windach. ☎: +49 8193 95 00 34
Tanz&FolkFest Rudolstadt, Stadt Rudolstadt, Kulturdezernat, Markt 7, D-07407 Rudolstadt. ☎: (49) 3672 486401; email *TFFRudolstadt @saale-net.de* Website *www.rudolstadt.de*
PROFOLK (Germany's umbrella organisation for folk and World Music), Rathausstr. 9, D-10178 Berlin; ☎ (49) 30 2472 2145 Website *www.PROFOLK.de*

Bavaria, Saxony or the Saarland. Furthermore, along the Baltic and North Sea coasts and further south another language is spoken. **Plattdütsch** (Low German or *Plattdeutsch* in High German) is a salty, earthy, predominantly working-class tongue, rich

in folklore. Acts such as **Hannes Wader** and **Piatkowski & Rieck** tapped into Plattdütsch's oral and written culture while JAMS' "Fisch" project breathed new life into the often vilified shanty form, affirming its vigour and relevance.

In the Nazi and East German regimes, dialect artists and *Mundarten* (dialects) were deemed abjectly uncultivated or questionable and often fell foul of officialdom. The songstress-poet **Lene Voigt** from Saxony, for example, was in effect silenced by the Nazis. Yet what was once banned is now being fêted, and in a nation where received pronunciation has long prevailed, the rediscovery of people singing in their natural voices works like mental floss. Hearing the likes of Swabian songwriter **Thomas Felder**'s captivating language or **Saure Gummern**'s blues drolleries delivered direct from the Hesse delta has generated political debate. Some voice the concern that here art might be hymning the break-up of the Federal Republic. But it hymns different, not separatist.

Born in 1953, **Thomas Felder** grew up being taught that High German was the proper way to talk, but in 1975 experienced a personal epiphany in London. Thumbing through the records at the Goethe-Institut, he happened upon an Austrian dialect singer. It connected him with dialect artforms and soon afterwards he began writing in dialect tongue. Felder's *Schwaebische Vesper* remains a pinnacle of dialect composition and eerie transcendence. One minute he is delivering a mass on a theme of flux, egged on by sublimely simple hurdy-gurdy, the next he is yelping along in "So Beni".

In a similar way to Thomas Felder, it was Austria that inspired the Alpine band **Hundsbuam Miserablige** to work in their native Bavarian. Their model was the punkish-roots Austrian-Alpine group, Attwenger. The Hundsbuam take on Alpine music is pure Bavarian and unmistakably their own. Their debut album, *Hundsbuam Miserablige*, begins with quacking ducks on the pond. All of a sudden searing guitar and choppy rhythms shatter the bucolic idyll. (See Alps article, p.7, for more on Hundsbaum, Attwenger and Alpine bands).

Alternative Postcards

Talk to even university-educated Germans and the likelihood is that the name of one of Germany's longest-established minorities will still turn up a blank. The **Sorbs** are a Slav minority around Bautzen in the southwest, long pressured to relinquish their culture, but at last, perhaps experiencing an artistic resurgence. It's not before time for the likes of the **Serbski Ludowy Ansambl Budysin** (the Sorb National Ensemble of Bautzen), which celebrated its forty-fifth anniversary in 1997. But growing numbers of young Sorbs are living

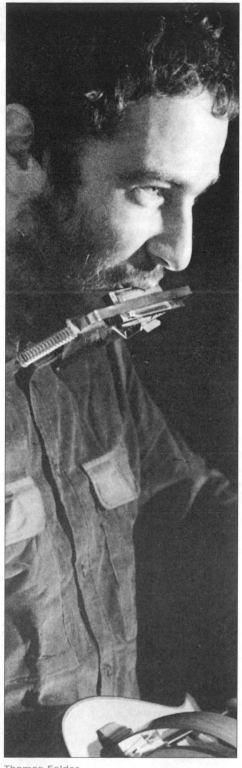

PROFOLK

GERMANY

Thomas Felder

Dissidenten and the Art of WeldBeat

Travelling around the world, gathering sound-bites on DAT, jamming and recording with local musicians and releasing CDs to preserve the experience for posterity has become something of a standard road to travel for the globally oriented, turn-of-the-millennium music maker, but **Dissidenten** are a group who've been at it longer – and into it deeper – than most. Their co-founders, **Uve Müllrich** and **Friedo Josch**, had made one of the earliest 'world fusion' albums with the prog-rock band Embryo, and in 1980, together with ex-Piri Piri drummer **Marlon Klein**, they spent a charmed year in the palace of the Maharaja Bhalkrishna Bharti of Gondagaon recording material with the Karnataka College of Percussion. The results were unleashed in 1982 as the first Dissidenten album, *Germanistan*.

This German trio of musicians, with their love of travel and the oriental world view, became the nucleus of a moving musical adventure which they kept in a constant state of mutation, recording in different corners of the globe, with different collaborators, exploring different roots and approaches. Their sojourn in Tangier and Spain – from 1983 to 1989 – resulted in the classic album *Sahara Elektrik*, on which they shared the billing with Moroccan group **Lem Chaheb**. Released in 1985, during the salad days of the 'world beat' explosion, it made a huge impact, setting the standard for future fusionistic endeavours.

A single, "Fata Morgana", taken from *Sahara Elektrik*, climbed to the top of the charts in Spain and sold by the container load in Brazil, Europe and Canada. The band went on to tour the world, and to produce two further Arabic flavoured albums, the second of which, *Out of This World* (1990), featured members of the three major Moroccan supergroups of the era – Lemchaheb, Jil Jilala and Nass El Ghiwane – as well as the string section of the Royal National Orchestra of Morocco.

In 1992 the Dissidenten caravan moved from Berlin, home-base since late 1989, back to India where *The Jungle Book* album was recorded with input from percussion guru Trilok Gurtu and many others. In 1994 the tapes of the album were handed over to the Kaiser of German trance techno, Sven Vöth who produced a single called "Jungle Book Part II" and introduced Dissidenten to European ravers. An album's worth of *Jungle Book* remixes appeared on Dissidenten's own label, Exil Musik, in 1996.

Hitherto Dissidenten's album projects have tended to focus on one distinct corner of the globe but their latest opus, *Instinctive Traveller* (1997), is a truly worldwide affair with its tendrils in Native American, North and South Indian, Hawaiian and blues music. The album introduced the voice of Uve Müllrich's daughter, Bajka,

who was born in The Maharajah of Gondagaon's palace, way back at the beginning of Dissidenten's amazing peripatetic adventure.

Dissidenten's story was very much a part of the late 1970s German rock scene, which was more experimental and far more global in outlook than that of Britain or the US. The krautrock band **Can** had been playing with global rhythms in the late 1970s and their electronics wizard Holger Czukay mixed a stunning fusion

track, "Persian Love Song", on his album *Movies* (1980), using a radio recording of an unknown Iranian singer. Such experiments presaged Brian Eno and David Byrne's seminal *My Life In The Bush of Ghosts* (1981), which used tapes from across the globe, and after that, the deluge.

Yet whereas many musicians have tinkered with the global experiment, Dissidenten have always plunged into it whole-heartedly, living for long periods at the heart of various musical cultures, listening, learning, fraternizing and recording ceaselessly. Their next chapter promises an aural safari to New Zealand and Micronesia. No visa necessary, just an open mind and healthy pair of ears.

Andy Morgan

in both cultures, which promotes the need to discover their Sorb identity.

In the former East Germany, opportunities for experiencing other cultures were limited. In practice this meant folkies had to look to the states on their own side of the Iron Curtain. For instance, **Aufwind**, who've explored and researched the post-Holocaust world of Jewish and Yiddish music, visiting Hungary, Poland and Romania. Klezmer (covered in *The Rough Guide to World Music: Volume 2*) naturally figures in their repertoire, but their's is distinct from the more familiar klezmer as transplanted and played on American soil.

One act which took a very different path is **Dissidenten** (see box opposite), who began as a spin-off from the Krautrock group **Embyro**, famed for a seminal album, *Embryo's Reise* (1980), recorded in Afghanistan, Pakistan and India. Dissidenten took the journey further, fusing traditions through immersing themselves in North African and Indian life, and taking location recording to new heights.

The Future

World Music is often criticised for being mere musical tourism. In musical terms Germany will probably remain well off the main tourist routes – which may well be its saving grace. What is happening in Germany is a counterblast. Acts are no longer trammelled by the past. The Folkszene has already illustrated that, proving that German folk has snapped out of its long nightmarish dream.

discography

Compilations

 It's only Kraut . . . but I like it
(Profolk, Germany).

An excellent general introduction to the German scene, compiled by PROFOLK, Germany's lobbying organisation for folk and World Music. It mixes commercially available and hitherto unreleased live recordings from Hundsbuam Miserablige, JAMS, Wacholder, Saure Gummern and others.

 Folkfestival Kaltenberg
(HeiDeck, Germany).

The Kaltenberg festival is held on the last weekend in June each year. This salute, subtitled *Highlights 1982–1997*, assembles a remarkable spread of artists, a high proportion of whom are from the German-speaking lands. Seventeen acts contribute including Switzerland's choicest Appenzeller Space Schöttl, Austria's Broadlahn, the festival organisers Fraunhofer Saitenmusik, the Czech Republic's unique Jablkoň, JAMS, Liederjan, the Schäl Sick Brass Band and an English performer long resident in Germany, Colin Wilkie. Another fine compilation.

München (Trikont, Germany);
Bayern (Trikont, Germany).

Compared to, say, *Topic's Voice of the People* series taking the music of England, Ireland, Scotland and Wales back to the people and Document's comprehensive programme for disinterring Austria's folk music, the paucity of historical German folk releases is glaringly apparent. Trikont's *München* (Munich) beacon volume draws on shellac releases from 1902–1948 from Volkssänger (folk singers) such as August Junker, Liesl Karlstadt and Karl Valentin. The *Bayern* (Bavaria) volume does the same for Volksmusik recorded between 1906–1941 by assorted ensembles and soloists.

Tanz&FolkFest Rudolstadt 1996
(HeiDeck, Germany).

In 1991 the Rudolstadt festival, first held in 1955, went international. From 1991 Rudolstadt inaugurated the cunning ruse of releasing an annual fund-raiser from each year's festival. One of the best Rudolstadt souvenirs with contributions from the Hundsbuam, Austria's Deishovida, Cathrin Pfeifer & Topo Gioia and the Euro-collective supreme Freyja.

Artists

Bandonionfreunde Essen

At the turn of the century the bandonion was extremely popular around the Ruhr, a region famed for heavy industry and mining. As Karl-Heinz Beckedal, the band's leader, puts it: "If one was a civil servant, one had to have a piano in order to demonstrate one's position – whether one could play it or not. For the little man it wasn't obligatory and a bandonion was affordable and one could accommodate it far more easily." Essen's Friends of the Bandonion preserve a playing style from a time when the bandonion was an ensemble instrument, not a soloist's ticket to fame.

Tango dei Gruga (Satiricon, Germany).

Imagine the impact of big band bandonion in the style of the old-time mandolin or balalaika orchestras in a 17-piece orchestra plus conductor. Literally like nothing on earth, the last of the Ruhr's famed bandonion orchestras.

Bierfiedler

Bierfiedler were one of East Germany's best-loved groups. Their history is complex even if only talking about personnel to-ings and fro-ings. An Ossi Who's Who.

Bierfiedler (RUM Records, Germany).

Folk-rock German-style circa 1997 from a pool of eleven musicians. They define the very texture of Ossi folk as many remember it and perceive it nowadays and nowhere better than on this album.

Folkländer

Folkländer grew out of rehearsal sessions in Leipzig in January 1976. The group went on to become one of the East's most important folk-rock bands although Folkländer and Bierfiedler were a classic example of Ossi intertwining. Band members came and went like bees at an orchard hive on a sunny day but with that entomological nightmare tendency to return to the wrong hive. Jürgen B Wolff, later of Duo Sonnenschirm fame, later graphic artist for Rudolstadt, conducted research that would greatly inform Folkländer's repertoire.

 Folkländers Bierfiedler (RUM Records, Germany).

An exemplary anthology gathering tracks from radio broadcasts originally released on *Frisch auf ins weite Feld* (1979) together with studio recordings from *Wenn man fragt wer hat's getan* (1981) and *FolksTanzHaus* (1985).

Die Hayner

Die Hayner have been together since 1978 surviving unscathed with unusually few personnel changes. They specialise in regional dance music played on hurdy-gurdy, melodeon, flute, fiddle, accordion, recorder and a dozen or so other instruments.

 Cimbria (Verlag der Spielleute, Germany).

This 1996 album captures the flavour of their act admirably. They concentrate on material from Hesse. An utterly central German dance experience.

Hoelderlin Express

Friedrich Hölderlin (1770–1843), the German poet who made his home in Tübingen, would unwittingly donate his name to the group who won the *Folk Newcomers Competition* at Rudolstadt in 1993. At the heart of the group's appeal is its front row – Elke Rogge's electric hurdy-gurdy and Olav Krauss's sonic cascades on violin. In 1994, at the time of their debut album, they were still spelling their name as the poet had. They became the lower case, less German-looking Hoelderlin Express.

 Hölderlin Express (Akku Disk, Germany).

An impressive debut marked by outstanding original compositions from what would become one of the consistently most exciting groups on the German folk scene. "Der Yeti", a major stepping-off point for live improvisation (comparable to Fairport Convention's "Sloth") is straight out of the folk avant-garde. Nobody does Himalayan howls and yeti wails better.

 Electric Flies (Akku Disk, Germany).

1996's Electric Flies ushered in a simplified name – simplified for foreigners, that is – and a new four-piece line-up after Johannes Mayr's departure. The group now consists of Ralf Gottschald (percussion/drums), Olav Krauss (violins), Jørgen W Lang (guitar/low whistle) and Elke Rogge (electro-acoustic hurdy-gurdy). Another strong collection of material synthesized from folk-rock's avant-garde tradition.

Hundsbuam Miserablige

The Hundsbuam have polarised opinion since bursting upon the scene in 1996. Assertively Bavarian, they sing in a dialect that would bamboozle people from Oberbayern (Upper Bavaria), let alone mere mortals in the other federal states. Even before a gist of what they are singing gets across, what communicates loud and clear is the band's raw energy and musical iconoclasm.

 Hundsbuam Miserablige (BMG/Lawine, Germany).

After a chorus of barnyard beasts, the Hundsbuam (Curs) blast in with one of the great, all-time album openers, "Hoizhakka Pogo" (Woodchopper's Pogo). This highly coloured 1996 debut slashes a dividing line between what had gone before and what is to come. Kow-towing to nobody and tattooed with black humour, they pull off the dangerous balancing act of mad dogs savaging Bavarian conformity while remaining vehemently Bavarian. A crash-course in the contemporary Bavarian aesthetic.

 Hui (BMG/Lawine 1997).

Humour got more savage still on *Hui*. "Mei Liab" (My Love) is fatal attraction terminated with extremest prejudice. Doffing its deathcap to Hitchcock and blood-and-cochineal murder ballad, its narrator knows a way to keep his obsession's love forever. "Heit" (Today) by contrast is tranquillity in the eye of the hurricane.

JAMS

Darlings of the GDR dance scene that they were, in 1997 JAMS – taking a lead from Hundsbuam Miserablige – unveiled Plattdütsch (Plattdeutsch or Low German) songs within its already strongly northern German-flavoured repertoire. Low German is, for many in Mecklenburg, their first language. East Germany's northernmost federal state happens to be their leader Jo Meyer's birthplace.

 Fisch (John Silver, Germany).

Too busy to record because of a full diary, after a personnel revamp, the discovery of their own voices and the realisation that the Low German contingent was now a quorum, they changed tack. Shanty, polka, waltz and hip-hop ferry these fisherfolk across the briny. Truly innovative. One of the most outstanding folk albums of 1997 – in a global, not German sense.

Liederjan

It is nigh-impossible to over-estimate the way the north German group Liederjan shook up the scene. Along with Zupfgeigenhansel, pre-Reunification they were one of the few Wessi acts who caused Ossi ears to prick up. Simply too original to ignore, with a succession of unapologetically German repertoires they have no need to court foreign audiences. A catalogue of national traits as riddled with wordplay as Jörg Ermisch's "Brigitte" renders translation pointless. Either one speaks German or is damned to have no Liederjan in one's life.

Liederjan

Die Wirrtuosen (Stockfisch, Germany).

This album's title puns on virtuoso and *Wirr* (confusion). As shorthand for their mission statement of providing "Satire, Irony and Profound Meaning" it is perfect. Tracks include "Online Shanty" and the BSE-garnished lunchtime greeting "Mahlzeit" and a reworking of Colin Wilkie's "If I Knew How" ("Wüsste Ich Nur Wie").

Saure Gummern

The farcically named Saure Gummern (pickled cucumbers or gherkins) hail from the central German state that gave English the word and fabric hessian. They began singing the blues in the local Hesse dialect and met with a positive response. *Mir Speela De Blues* is an historic or anarchic overview of Hesse's little-known blues genre.

Nei Poor Schuh (Dickworz Bladda Verlag, Germany).

The songs on this album are witty and droll. The English-German "Albino Blues", a lament by a German blues fan called Mississippi Mojo Meier (although his mother calls him Karlheinz), includes a rallying cry for blues footwear fetishists everywhere from the hootchie gootchie man. "Awwer isch schwitz" is a manifesto proudly preaching the gospel of total underachievement.

Trio Grande

The original group began life in 1984 although there have been personnel changes over the years. Their sound is a blend of hurdy-gurdies, accordion, guitar and percussion.

Bagage (Verlag der Spielleute, Germany).

One of the scene's most accomplished and versatile instrumental groups. Tunefulness personified with especially memorable melodies geared to a dance audience and for listening pleasure both.

U.L.M.A.N.

The Leipzig-based U.L.M.A.N. stands for Un Limited Music And Noise. In 1994 Johannes (aged 18) and Andreas Uhlmann (aged 17) came first at the German Folk Newcomers Awards. The group that eventually coalesced draws on friends and family loyalties. They play a Central European-accented dance music with contemporary colourings from jazz and rock.

Acoustic Power (RUM/Löwenzahn, Germany).

A most assured debut deploying, amongst other instruments, hurdy-gurdy, accordion, brass, violin, bagpipes, trombone, whistles, fiddle, and percussion. The new blood of Germany's folk renaissance.

Wacholder

Wacholder (Juniper), founded in April 1978 in Cottbus, grew to become a Deutsch-Folk (East-German Folk) institution, epitomising the Ossi folk scene. They marshal Gesellenlieder (apprentice or traveller songs), 1848 Revolution songs, tongue-in-cheek barbs from Heinrich Heine and the Moritat tradition, and assorted folk, Kabarett and democratic songs. Wacholder's core line-up is Scarlett Seeboldt, Matthias Kiessling and Jörg Kokott.

In der Heimat ist es schön (Stockfisch, Germany).

The title of this 1994 album translates as 'It's Beautiful In The Homeland' (1994), social satire guying straight society's conformity. German is essential to get the point of their political laments, lampoons and lays since the music more often than not functions as messenger of their word-based repertoire.

Unterwegs (John Silver, Germany).

Celebrating twenty years into the game in 1998, *Unterwegs* (On the road) is an authoritative statement of their music. Seeboldt is confirmed as the most consistently seductive female vocalist of the German folk scene, whether singing unison vocals on the title track, working miracles on Heine's "Karl I" or the Berlin dialect-inflected "Ik hebbe se nich up de Scholen gebracht".

Liedermacher and Kabaret

Artists

Wolf Biermann

The rebel writer who made it uncomfortable for the East German regime. Tit for tat, they made it uncomfortable for Biermann. Far worse was to befall him before he settled in the West. An iconic figure on the German scene and one of Germany's finest ever Liedermacher.

Chausseestrasse 131 (Zweitausendeins, Germany).

The cover of the original release on Wagenbach's Quartplatten in 1969 showed a mustachioed Biermann staring impassively at the photographer/listener. Back then Chausseestrasse was a street in East Berlin but for the songs emanating from that apartment Biermann paid for their thorny, politically embarrassing content by having the East German authorities strip away his citizenship, his so-called *Ausbürgerung* in 1976.

Süsses Leben – saures Leben (Zweitausendeins, Germany).

A visionary flow streaming from his adopted town of Hamburg. Biermann's poetry deserves the respect and attention accorded another great German writer, the centenary of whose birth was celebrated in the year of its release (1998): Bertolt Brecht.

Franz-Josef Degenhardt

Degenhardt, born in 1931 in Schweim, Westfalia, ranks as one of the figureheads of the German Liedermacher movement with clarity of vision and a linguistic precision – he is a doctor of law. His complete output was released in 1981 on 12 CDs,

Spiel nicht mit den Schmuddelkindern (Polydor, Germany).

First released in 1965, time has given no cause to view this album as other than a masterpiece. It made him one of the most important voices in the German counter-culture.

Thomas Felder

Swabian dialect had a long tradition, but was the poor relation of High German. Felder: "I wanted to make serious poetry. There wasn't any model in Swabian." His music turns apprehension into appreciation. "It's the sound that gets across, that communicates," he explained in 1997. "If it depends on understanding the content then I don't need to sing a song: I can give a lecture."

Sinnflut (Musik & Wort, Germany).

Sinnflut puns on *Sintflut* – the Biblical flood – to translate as 'Sense Flood'. Vocally Felder bends notes till their eyes pop out. For fans of footnotes, this album also contains Buffy Sainte-Marie's little-known Swabian period protest song "Hald Ao Soldat" which she later translated into English for Donovan as "The Universal Soldier".

Fusion groups

Artists

Aufwind

The main focus for Aufwind (Up-current) is Eastern European Jewish and Yiddish music. Their repertoire reveals considerable originality, remarkable disquisition and inspiring musicianship. The current line-up comprises Jan Hermerschmidt (vocals/clarinet), Claudia Koch (vocals/violin/viola), Hardy Reich (vocals/mandolin/guitar), Andreas Rohde (vocals/bandoneon/guitar) – the last three of whom founded Aufwind in 1984 – and Heiko Rötzscher (bass).

◉ **Awek Di Junge Jorn** (Misrach, Germany).

As Ossis they accessed sources behind the Iron Curtain, talking to survivors of the Holocaust. "Jidisch Tango" exemplifies their highly distinctive, unorthodox vision. A world-class klezmer album, nothing less.

Dissidenten

Dissidenten grew out of the German progressive rock movement, starting life as a side shoot of Embryo. Light years removed from the World Music tourist experience, the intensity and authenticity of their music dazzles, the product of steeping themselves in various cultures – notably those of Morocco and India. The core line-up comprises Friedo Josch (flute/soprano sax/keyboards), Marlon Klein (drums/percussion/keyboards/vocals) and Uve Müllrich (bass/guitar/vocals). The latter was replaced in 1997 by Izaline Calister from Curaçao, unexpectedly taking the group's repertoire to still greater heights.

◉ **Sahara Elektrik** (Exil, Germany).

Partly recorded in the old Sultan's Palace in Tangiers, this 1984 collaboration with Moroccan musicians gave a new dimension to the word 'fusion' and demonstrated the huge potential of North African music to evolve in weird and unforeseen directions. Hugely influential, it put Dissidenten firmly on the map.

◉ **The Jungle Book** (Exil, Germany).

By 1993 Dissidenten were distilling many of the experiences and ideas they had picked up during their long globe-trotting career, with street sounds and other aural atmospherics woven in tightly funky grooves. The group employ German folk idioms alongside those of India, exploring what they call the 'Global Esperanto' – the common language of all indigenous music. The disc was given an inspirational dance remix as 1998's ◉ **Mixed Up Jungle** (Exil, Germany).

◉ **Instinctive Traveler**
(Exil, Germany).

This 1997 album found Dissidenten casting their cultural net the furthest yet. Arabic, Hawaiian, Native American, North Indian and Tamil influences ripple through the songs. The result is no stylistic Tower of Babel, rather a NASA-like time capsule of musical cultures and styles blasted into space. Bajka Müllrich, daughter of Dissidenten's bassist, turns "Lobster Song" and "Instinctive Traveler" into two of Weldbeat's catchiest ever tracks.

Embryo

Embryo, cult darlings of German prog rock, evolved into something with a still lower profile: even Germans are surprised to learn that they still exist! The collective includes

◉ **Schwaebische Vesper**
(Musik & Wort, Germany).

Co-conceived with Michael Samarajiwa, this suite was debuted in 1995 on the fiftieth anniversary of Dresden's obliteration by British bombers. Felder delivers a series of inspired performances ranging from what he calls the *Klangerlebnis* (sound experience) or "Pappmaschee" (Papier mâché) which begins with mimicked air-raid sirens before going surreal, to the tender "Deine Nähe" (The Nearness of You) and the uplifting "Dag" (Day). There is no need to work hard to like Felder's *Swabian Vespers*. His voice and hurdy-gurdy shatter the language barrier.

Ute Lemper

Lemper's career took off when Andrew Lloyd Webber selected her for the Viennese production of *Cats*. She then moved on to the Sally Bowles character in *Cabaret*. She's recorded many of the Brecht/Weill collaborations and recently starred in the London production of *Chicago*.

◉ **Berlin Cabaret Songs** (Decca, UK)

Part of Decca's *Entartete Musik* series of composers banned by the Nazis, this is an idiomatic selection of wonderful Berlin cabaret songs from the 1920s and 1930s performed with the Matrix Ensemble conducted by Robert Ziegler. Includes the best of Spoliansky, Hollaender, Tucholsky and Schiffer with English translations included.

Barbara Thalheim

Leipzig-born, Thalheim found her craft and metier in Berlin, the city she moved to when she was four. Her first album *Lebenslauf* appeared in 1978. Her work grew ever more confident, honed and pertinent. More than an essential voice of the East German literary revue scene, she is a coup de theatre motherlode.

◉ **Neue Reiche** (Deutsche Schallplatten, Germany).

This revue, recorded in March 1990 in the Landestheater Eisenach, is the stuff of history, capturing the anxieties and torn loyalties experienced by East Germans with Reunification looming. With a timeless topicality, it articulates a society in transition.

Dieter Serfas (percussion/drums), Christian Burchard and Edgar Hoffman (woodwinds), all of whom were together as far back as 1963 in the Contemporary Trio 'playing music from Bartók to nowhere'.

⊙ **Embryo's Reise** (Schneeball, Germany).

One of the earliest World Music albums, predating the term's adoption by a decade. In late 1978 Embryo set off for Afghanistan, Pakistan and India playing Goethe-Institut, maharajah's palace and impromptu settings, filming and being filmed, all the while gathering recordings. *Embryo's Reise* traces that musical pilgrimage. Local musicians throng.

⊙ **Ibn Battuta** (Schneeball, Germany).

Embryo's gypsy genes kept them moving musically. This album, named after an Arabic explorer whose journeying supposedly far exceeded Marco Polo's, blends World Music and jazz grooves and voicings. "Komet 41", for example, employs the un-Teutonic 41/8 time signature.

Nûrê

Berlin is home to Nûrê's Kurdish vocalist, Aynur Erdogan, and to an expatriate Kurdish community settled in Germany to flee Turkish persecution in Kurdistan. An eloquent mouthpiece for the Kurdish cause, Erdogan fronts the all-woman quintet, they mix saz, electric guitar, saxophone, clarinet, electric bass and percussion.

⊙ **Rasthatin/Begegnung** (Sacco & Vanzetti, Germany).

Kurdish music from Berlin, circa 1994, mixing Kurdish protest and dance tunes. Its four-piece line-up evolved into today's Marika Falk (percussion), Cindia Knoke (electric bass), Nûrê (vocals), Veronika Vogel (saz/ electric guitar) and Tina Wrasse (clarinet and saxophone).

Schäl Sick Brass Band

Rather different from your usual oompah band, this Cologne-based big band ranks as one of the most exciting World Music groups on the German scene. Brass figures to the fore, and in their Persian vocalist Maryam Akhondy they have someone who adds something extra to their sound.

⊙ **Majnoun** (Network, Germany).

Persian songs given the treatment. They begin traditional, with the love themes "Majnoun" and "Leyla" and then proceed to mutate.

Greece

songs of the near east

Greek music, like Greek food, has had a bad press for years – Nana Mouskhouri, muzak versions of "Zorba's Dance" and interminable 'Souvenir from Greece' bouzouki cassettes are largely to blame. But looking beyond the clichés, **Marc Dubin** and **George Pissalidhes** assert that Greek music, both historic rembétika and contemporary folk, is as rewarding as any in the world, with its unique mix of European and Middle Eastern influences.

Greek music, like most aspects of the country, is a fortuitous mix of east and west. The older songs of the folk (or *dhimotiká*) tradition are invariably in Eastern-flavoured minor scales, with antecedents both in Byzantine religious chant or secular song, and in Turkish and Iranian music through the centuries of Ottoman rule. The flavour of the Orient is even more immediately evident in the blues-like **rembétika** music, which had its heyday in the 1920s and '30s, and has been revived at various intervals since.

Western music had surprisingly little impact until well into the twentieth century. Almost all the native Greek **instruments** are also found throughout the Islamic world, though it's an open question as to whether Byzantines, Arabs or Persians first constructed them, or indeed how they spread; some Greek musicologists claim their original descent from now-lost melodies and dances of ancient Greece. To this broadly Middle Eastern base, **Slavs**, **Albanians** and **Italians** have added their share to various of the Greek regions or island groups. The result is an extraordinarily varied repertoire, with local and national traditions still very much alive in both music and dance.

Folk Music

The most promising opportunities for live **folk music** are at the numerous summer *paniyíria* (saints' day festivals) – or more tourist-oriented cultural programmes – when musicians based in Athens or city clubs during winter tour the islands and villages. These tend to be very public and community-based performances, often using town or village squares or monasteries.

Such music is essentially traditional, though as throughout the world, groups have steadily adopt-

ed electric and rock instruments since the 1970s. Purists argue that much of it is heavily vulgarised and it is perhaps true that, as the oral transmission of technique from older master players has broken down, musicianship has declined. Certainly, few shows appear to match the skill and spirit shown on CD re-releases of old archival 78s material. But there are some superb revival groups, attempting to recapture the musicianship of the old-timers.

Island Music

The arc of southern islands comprising **Crete**, **Kássos**, **Khálki** and **Kárpathos** is one of the most promising areas of Greece for hearing live folk music at any season of the year. On Crete, in particular, there is a network of music clubs (*kendrá*) in the main towns.

The dominant instrument on these islands is the **lýra**, a three-stringed fiddle directly related to the Turkish *kemençe*. It is played not on the shoulder but balanced on the thigh, often with tiny bells attached to the bow, which the musician can jiggle for rhythmical accent. The strings are metal, and since the centre one is just a drone, the player improvises only on the outer two. Crete's undisputed lýra master was the late **Kostas Moundakis**, who was widely recorded. One of the finest living lýra players is Andonis Xylouris, who performs under the name **Psarandonis**.

The lýra is often backed by one or more **laoúto**, similar to the Turkish/Arab *oud* but (especially on Crete where the Venetians ruled for several centuries) more closely resembling a mandolin. These are rarely used to lead or solo, but a virtuoso player will find the harmonics and overtones of a lýra piece, coaxing a pleasing, chime-like tone from the instrument. In several places in the southern Aegean, notably northern Kárpathos, you also find a simple, droneless **bag-**

pipe – the *askómandra* or *tsamboúna*. And if you recall Kazantzakis's classic Cretan novel, *Zorba*, his hero played a **sandoúri**, or hammer dulcimer – an instrument introduced to the islands by Greek refugees from Anatolia. Today, accomplished sandóuri players are few and the instrument tends to be used in a supporting role.

On most of the Aegean islands, particularly the **Cyclades**, you'll find the lýra replaced by a more familiar-looking **violí**, essentially a Western violin. Accompaniment was provided until recently by laoúto or sandoúri, though these days you're more likely to find a rhythm section of bass, guitar and drums. Amongst violí players, **Stathis Koukoularis**, born on Náxos, and two young fiddlers **Nikos Ikonomidhes** and **Nikos Hatzopoulos** stand out.

The island of **Lésvos** occupies a special place in terms of island music. Before the turbulent decade of 1912–1922, its 'mainland' was Asia Minor rather than Greece, its urban poles Smyrna and Constantinople rather than Athens. Accordingly, its music is far more varied and sophisticated than the Aegean norm, having absorbed melodies and instrumentation from the various groups who lived in neighbouring Anatolia. It is the only island with a vital tradition of brass bands, and virtually every Greek dance rhythm is represented in its local music.

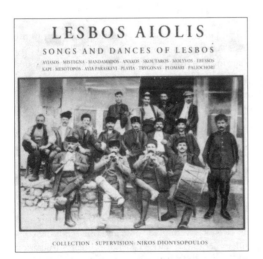

LESBOS AIOLIS
SONGS AND DANCES OF LESBOS
AYIASOS · MISTEGNA · MANDAMADOS · ANAKOS · SKOUTAROS · MOLYVOS · ERESSOS
KAPI · MESOTOPOS · AYIA PARASKEVI · PLAYIA · TRYGONAS · PLOMARI · PALIOCHORI

COLLECTION · SUPERVISION · NIKOS DIONYSOPOULOS

By way of contrast, the **Ionian islands** – alone of all modern Greek territory – never saw Turkish occupation and have a predominantly Western musical tradition. Their indigenous song-form is Italian both in name – **kantádhes** – and instrumentation (guitar and mandolin). It's most often heard these days on Lefkádha and Zákynthos.

Island folk songs – **nisiótika** – feature melodies that, like much folk music the world over, rely heavily on the pentatonic scale. Their lyrics, especially on the smaller islands, touch on the perils of the sea, exile and thwarted or forbidden love. Among its best known **singers** are the **Konitopoulos** clan from Náxos, while older stars like **Anna** and **Emilia Khatzidhaki**, **Effi Sarri** and **Anna Karabesini** – all from the Dodecanese archipelago – offer a warmer, more innocent delivery.

Mainland Folk Music

Many of the folk songs of mainland Greece – known as **dhimotiká tragoúdhia** – hark back to the years of Ottoman occupation and to the War of Independence; others, in a lighter tone, refer to aspects of pastoral life (sheep, elopements, fetching water from the well and so forth). Their essential instrumentation consists of the **klaríno** (clarinet), which reached Greece during the 1830s, introduced either by Gypsies or by members of the (imported Bavarian) King Otto's entourage. Accompaniment is traditionally provided by a group or *koumpanía* comprising *kithára* (guitar), *laoúto*, *laoutokithára* (a hybrid in stringing and tuning) and *violí*, with *toumberléki* (lap drum) or *défi* (tambourine) for rhythm.

Many mainland tunes are **dances**, divided by rhythm into such categories as *kalamatianó* (a line dance), *tsámiko*, *hasaposérviko* or *syrtó*, the quintessential circle dance of Greece. Melodies that aren't danced include the slow, stately *kléftiko*, which relates, baldly or in metaphor, incidents or attitudes from the years of the Ottomans and the rebellions for freedom.

Stalwart vocalists to look for on old recordings include **Yiorgos Papasidheris** and **Yiorgia Mittaki**, both of whom were Arvanites – descendants of medieval Albanian settlers. Among players, clarinettists **Vassilis Saleas**, **Yiannis Vassilopoulos** and **Yiorgos Yevyelis** are remarkable; all three of them are Gypsies, who dominate instrumental music on mainland Greece. Other noteworthy instrumentalists, not of Gypsy origin, include **Nikos Saragouda**s (oud) and **Yiorgos Koros** (fiddle).

The folk music of **Epirus** (*Ípiros*) exhibits strong connections with that of northern Epirus (now in Albania) and the Former Yugoslav Republic of Macedonia, particularly in the polyphonic pieces sung by both men and women. The repertoire tends to fall into three categories, which are also found further south: **mirolóyia** or laments (the instrumental counterpart is called *skáros*); drinking songs or **tis távlas**; and various danceable melodies as noted above, common to the entire mainland and many islands also. Most famous of the Epirot clarinettists are the late **Vassilis Soukas** and **Tassos Khalkias**, and the younger (unrelated) **Petros-Loukas Khalkias**.

In the northern Greek regions of **Thrace** and **Macedonia**, whose bewilderingly mixed population were under Ottoman rule until the beginning of this century, the music can sound more generically Balkan. Owing to the huge influx of Anatolian refugees after 1923, the region has been a rich treasure-trove for ethnomusicologists seeking to document the old music of Asia Minor. *Kálanda* (Christmas carols), Carnival dances, wedding processionals and drinking songs abound. Noteworthy singers include **Khronis Aídhonidhis** and **Xanthippi Karathanasi** – both still alive and active.

Among Thracian instruments, the **kaváli**, or end-blown flute, is identical to the Turkish and Bulgarian article, as is the drone bagpipe, or **gaïdha**. The **zournás**, a screechy, double-reed oboe similar to the Islamic world's *shenai*, is much in evidence at local festivals, in combinatiuon with the deep-toned **daoúli** drum, a typical Gypsy ensemble. The klaríno is present here as well, as are two types of lýras, but perhaps the most characteristic melodic instrument of Thrace is the **oúti** (oud), whose popularity received a boost after refugee players arrived.

An oddity in western Macedonia are the **brass bands**, introduced in the nineteenth century by Ottoman military musicians.

Rembétika

Rembétika began as the music of the Greek urban dispossessed – criminals, refugees, drug-users, defiers of social norms. It had existed in some form in Greece and Constantinople since at least the turn of the century, but it is as difficult to define or get to the origins of as jazz or blues – genres with which (tenuous) comparisons are often made, not so much for the music as for its inspirations, themes and tone. Rembétika songs tell of illicit or frustrated love, drug addiction, police oppression, death – and their delivery tends to be resignation to the singer's lot, coupled with defiance of authority.

Musically, rembétika is bound in with the **bouzoúki** – a long-necked, fretted lute derived, like the Turkish *saz*, from the Byzantine *tambourás*. It has become synonymous with Greek music but early in this century, prior to the popularisation of rembétika, it was used by only a few mainland musicians. As to the term 'rembétika', its derivaton is uncertain, the favoured candidate being the old Turkish word 'harabat,' whose meanings cover both 'shanty town', 'drunkard' and 'bohemian' – all definitely aspects of rembétika culture.

Origins: Café-Aman

At the beginning of the twentieth century, in the Asia Minor cities of Smyrna and Istanbul (Constantinople), music-cafés became popular. Owned and staffed by Greeks, Jews, Armenians and even a few Gypsies, they featured groups comprising a violinist, a sandoúri player and a (usually female) vocalist, who might also jingle castanets and dance. The songs were improvised and became known as **café-aman** or *amanédhes* for the frequent repetition of the exclamation 'aman aman' (Turkish for 'alas, alas'), used both for its sense and to fill time while the performers searched their imaginations for (often earthily explicit) lyrics.

Despite sparse instrumentation, café-aman was an elegant, riveting art song, and one requiring considerable skill. It harked back to similar vocalisation in the *Ghazals* of Persia and the East. Some of its greatest practitioners included **Andonis 'Dalgas' (Wave) Dhiamantidhis**, so nicknamed for the undulations in his voice; **Rosa Eskenazi**, a Greek Jew who grew up in Istanbul; her contemporary **Rita Abatzi** from Smyrna; **Marika Papagika** from the island of Kós, who emigrated to America where she made her career; **Agapios**

Rembetes at Piraeus, 1937

Tomboulis, a *tanbur* and oud player of Armenian background; and **Dhimitris 'Salonikiyeh' Semsis**, a master fiddler from Strumitsa in northern Macedonia. The spectrum of nationalities for these performers gives a good idea of the range of cosmopolitan influences in the years preceding the emergence of 'real' rembétika.

The 1919–1922 Greco-Turkish war and the resulting 1923 **exchange of populations** were key events in the history of rembétika, resulting in the influx to Greece of over a million Asia Minor Greeks, many of whom settled in shanty-towns around Athens, Pireás and Thessaloníki. The café-aman musicians, like most of the other refugees, were, in comparison to the Greeks of the host country, extremely sophisticated; many were highly educated, could read and compose music, and had even been unionised in the towns of Asia Minor. Such men included the Smyrniots **Vangelis Papazoglou**, a noted songwriter, and **Panayiotis Toundas**, a composer who headed the Greek divisions of first Odeon and then Columbia Records. But the less lucky lived on the periphery of the new society: most had lost all they had in the hasty evacuation, and many, from inland Anatolia, could speak only Turkish. In their misery they sought relief in another Ottoman institution, the *tekés* or hashish den.

Vamvakaris and the Tekédhes

In the *tekédhes* of Athens and its port, Piraeus, or the northern city of Thessaloníki, a few men would sit on the floor around a charcoal brazier, passing around a *nargilés* (hookah) filled with hashish. One of them might begin to improvise a tune on the baglamás or the bouzoúki and begin to sing. The words, either his own or those of the other *dervíses* (many rembetic terms were a burlesque of those of mystical Islamic tradition), would be heavily laced with insiders' argot. As the *taxími* (introduction) was completed, one of the smokers might rise and begin to dance a *zeïbékiko*, a slow, intense, introverted performance following an unusual metre (9/8), not for the benefit of others but for himself.

By the early 1930s, several key musicians had emerged from tekédhes culture. Foremost among them was a Piraeus-based quartet comprising **Markos Vamvakaris** and **Artemis** (Anestis Delias) – two great composers and bouzoúki-players – the beguiling-voiced **Stratos Payioumtzis**, and, on baglamás, Yiorgos Tsoros, better known as **Batis**. They were a remarkable group. Stratos, the lead singer, went on to perform with other great rembétika stars, like Tsitsanis and Papiannou. Artemis, the son of a sandoúri player from Smyrna, was a remarkable lyricist and composer, who lived a rembétika life of hard drugs, and died in the street (as his song "The Junkie's Lament" had predicted), aged 29, outside a *tekés* with his bouzouki in his hand.

Vamvakaris, however, was the linchpin of the group. Born on the Aegean island of Syros in 1905, he is often described as the 'grandfather of rembétika'. He had a tough childhood, leaving school at eight and, at fifteen, stowing away on a boat for Piraeus.

COLL. ILIAS PETROPOULOS/KEDROS

Markos Vamvakaris (right)

As time went on such lyrics got cleaned up. The most commonly heard version of this song, from the 1950s, for instance, substitutes "Play us a fine bit of bouzoúki" for "Fix us a fine nargilé", and so forth.

Tough Times

This **'Golden Age of Rembétika'** — as indeed it was, despite the unhappy lives of many performers — was short-lived. The association of the music with a drug-laced underworld would prove its undoing. After the imposition of the puritanical Metaxas dictatorship in 1936, *rembétes* with uncompromising lyrics and lifestyles were blackballed by the recording industry; anti-hashish laws were systematically enforced and police harassment of the tekédhes was stepped up. In Athens, even possession of a bouzoúki or baglamás became a criminal offence and several of the big names served time in jail. Others went to Thessaloníki, where the police chief Vassilis Mouskoundis was a big fan of the music and allowed its practitioners to smoke in private.

Within six months of arrival, he had taught himself bouzoúki as a way out of a particularly grim job in a slaughterhouse, and was writing songs and playing in the tekédhes with Stratos, Artemis and Batis.

At first, Vamvakaris did not consider himself a singer, leaving the lead vocals to Stratos, but when Columbia wanted to release a record by him they persuaded him to have a go, and were pleased with his metallic, hash-rasping sound. Subsequently, he went on to sing on nearly all his records and his gravelly style became an archetype for male rembétika singers. His bouzoúki playing also set a standard.

Lyrics about getting stoned, or *mastouriaká*, were a natural outgrowth of the tekédhes. One of the most famous, composed by Batis and first recorded in the mid-1930s by Vamvakaris, commemorated the exploits of the quartet:

On the sly I went out in a boat
And arrived at the Dhrakou Cave
Where I saw three men stoned on hash
Stretched out on the sand.
It was Batis, and Artemis,
And Stratos the Lazy.
Hey you, Strato! Yeah you, Strato!
Fix us a terrific nargilé,
So old Batis can have a smoke
A "dervish" for years he's been
And Artemis too,
Who brings us "stuff" from wherever he's been.
He sends us hash from Constantinople
And all of us get high;
And pressed tobacco from Persia
The mangas smokes in peace.

For a time, such persecution — and the official encouragement of tangos and frothy Italianate love songs (which had a much wider audience) — failed to dim the enthusiasm of the *mánges* (wide boys) who frequented the hash dens. Police beatings or prison terms were taken in stride; time behind bars could be used, as it always had been around the Aegean, to make *skaptó* (dug-out) instruments. A *baglamás* could easily be fashioned from a gourd cut in half or even a tortoise shell (the sound box), a piece of wood (the neck), catgut (frets), and wire for strings, and the result would be small enough to hide from the guards. Jail songs were composed and became popular in the underworld.

However, the rembétes suffered from all sides, incurring the disapproval of the puritanical Left as well as the Right. The growing Communist Party of the 1930s considered the music and its habitués hopelessly decadent and politically unevolved. When Vamvakaris was about to join the leftist resistance army ELAS in 1944, he was admonished not to sing his own material. The Left preferred *andártika* (Soviet-style revolutionary anthems).

Like most ideological debates, it was largely academic. World War II with its harsh Axis occupation of Greece, and the subsequent 1946–49 civil war, put everyone's careers on hold, and the turbulent decade erased any lingering fashion for hash songs. When Greece emerged in the 1950s, its public were eager to adopt a softer music and new heroes.

Tsitsanis and Cloudy Sunday

The major figure of post-war rembétika was undoubtedly **Vassilis Tsitsanis**. Born in Thessaly, the son of a silver craftsman, he was a very different personality to Vamvakaris, whose mantle he took on as both the most significant composer and bouzoúki master of his generation. A shy man, with sad-looking eyes, he made rembétika sound softer and more mellow, and its words more pleading than defiant.

Tsitsanis embarked on his career in Athens, just before the war, cutting his first record for Odeon, at that time directed by rembetic composer Spyros Peristeris, in 1936. After military service, he was released from the army in 1940 and sang through the 1940s in his own ouzo bar in Thessaloníki. The period gave rise to his most famous song, "Synefiazmeni Kyriaki" (Cloudy Sunday):

> Cloudy Sunday, you seem like my heart
> Which is always overcast, Christ and Holy Virgin!
> You're a day like the one I lost my joy.
> Cloudy Sunday, you make my heart bleed.
> When I see you rainy, I can't rest easy for a moment;
> You blacken my life and I sigh deeply.

Although it wasn't recorded until 1948, the song became widely known after its composition in 1943, and became a kind of anthem for the dispossessed, occupied Greeks.

After the war, Tsitsanis obliged a traumatised public with love songs and Neapolitan melodies. This new rembétika enjoyed, for the first time, something of a mass following, through top female singers such as **Sotiria Bellou**, **Marika Ninou** and **Ioanna Yiorgakopoulou**. Tsitsanis himself remained a much-loved figure in Greek music until his death in 1984; his funeral in Athens was attended by nearly a quarter of a million people.

If Tsitsanis's 'softening' of rembétika was a first key change to the music, a second, perhaps more dramatic, was the innovation in 1953 by Manolis Khiotis of a fourth pair of strings to the bouzoúki. This allowed it to be tuned tonally rather than modally. In its wake came **electrical amplification**, over-orchestration and maudlin lyrics as a crest of popularity led to the opening of *bouzoúkia*

– huge, barn-like clubs, where Athenians paid large sums to break specially provided plates and to dance flashy steps that were a travesty of the simple dignity and precise, synchronised footwork of the old-time zeíbékika. The music was largely debased: virtuoso bouzoúki players – **Khiotis**, **Yiorgos Mitsakis** and **Yiorgos Zambetas** – assisted by kewpie-doll-type female vocalists.

Vassilis Tsitsanis

Rembétika Revivals

Ironically, the original rembétika material was rescued from oblivion by the colonels' junta of 1967–1974. Along with dozens of other features of Greek culture, rembétika verses were banned. A generation of students growing up under the dictatorship took a closer look at the forbidden fruit and derived solace, and deeper meanings, from the nominally apolitical lyrics. When the junta fell in 1974 – and even a little before – there was an outpouring of re-issued recordings of the old masters.

Over the next decade live rembétika also enjoyed a revival, beginning with a clandestine 1979 club near the old Fix brewery in Athens, whose street credentials were validated when it was raided and closed by the police. These smoky attempts to recapture pre-war atmosphere – which led to dozens of rembétika clubs in the early 1980s – saw performances by revival groups such as **Ta Pedhia apo tin Patra**, **Rembetiki Kompania** and **Opisthodhromiki Kompania** (featuring Eleftheria Arvanataki), and the performers **Khondronakos** and **Mario**. In the northern capital of Thessaloníki, a leading figure was **Agathonas Iakovidhis** with his group **Rembétika Synkrotima Thessalonikis**.

A feature film by Kostas Ferris, *Rembétiko* (1983), attempted to trace the music from Asia Minor of the 1920s to Greece of the 1950s, and garnered wide acclaim in Greece and abroad. These days, however, the fashion has long since peaked, and only a handful of clubs and bands remain from the 1980s revival heyday.

New Waves

Alongside folk and rembétika, post-war Greece developed its own forms of 'art' (**éntekhno**) and pop (**laïkó**) music, while since the late 1970s the scene has broadened to include roots-minded **rock and fusion** experiments, and even new explorations of **Byzantine** forms.

The Éntekhno Revolution

The 'Westernisation' of rembétika that had begun with Tsitsanis and escalated with the electric bouzoúki craze paved the way for the **éntekhno music** of the late 1950s. Éntekhno (literally 'artistic') encompassed an orchestral genre where folk instruments, rhythms and melodies, where present, would be interwoven into a symphonic fabric, still recognisably Greek to a greater or lesser extent. Its first, and most famous, practitioners were **Manos Hatzidakis** and **Mikis Theodorakis**, both classically trained musicians and admirers of rembétika.

Already in 1948, Hatzidakis defended rembétika in a lecture, suggesting that Greek composers be inspired by it, rather than bow to the prevailing left-wing/middle-class prejudice against it. In a period when most Greek tunes imitated Western light popular music, he had transcribed rembétika for piano and orchestra, keeping only the

spirit and nostalgic mood of the original. Theodorakis, a disciple of Tsitsanis, included zeïbékika tunes on his earliest albums, with Grigoris Bithikotsis or Stelios Kazantzidhis on vocals and Manolis Khiotis as bouzoúki soloist.

The éntekhno of Theodorakis and Hatzidakis combined rembetic and Byzantine influences with Western ones, but – more memorably – fused Greek music with the country's rich poetic tradition. Among Theodarakis' early albums were *Epitafios* (1963), based on poems by Yiannis Ritsos, and *To Axion Esti* (1964), a folk-flavoured oratorio incorporating poetry by Odysseas Elytis. Hatzidakis countered in 1965 with a recording of *Matomenos Gamos*, a version of García Lorca's "Blood Wedding" translated into Greek by poet-lyricist Nikos Gatsos, and also tried his hand at rendering Elytis in song.

Together, these works changed Greek perceptions of bouzoúki-based music, popularised Greek poetry for a mass audience and elevated lyricists such as Gatsos and Manos Eleftheriou to the status of bards. The downside was that the sophistication and Western classical orchestral arrangements distanced the music from its indigenous roots, and in particular, the modal scale which had served Greece so well since antiquity. The genre suffered, too, from the demands of the film industry, who commissioned many éntekhno works as soundtracks. At its worst, it was muzak.

Theodorakis and Hatzidakis paved the way for successors who were generally less classicising and more pop-leaning, such as **Stavros Xarhakos**, most famous abroad for his soundtrack to the film *Rembetiko*; **Manos Loïzos**, who gave George Dalaras his start in 1968; the Cretan **Yiannis Markopoulos**, the most folk-based, and most accessible to foreign audiences; and **Stavros Kouyoumtzis** and **Dhimos Moutsis**, who collaborated with a galaxy of stellar vocalists during the early-to-mid-1970s – in retrospect, the Indian summer of éntekhno.

Laïkó: Son of Rembétika

Diametrically opposed to éntekhno was the authentic **laïkó** or 'popular' music of the 1950s and '60s, its gritty, tough style a direct heir to rembétika, undiluted by Western influences. Laïkó used not only zeïmbékika and hasápika time signatures but also the *tsiftetéli* – another age-old rhythm from Asia Minor mistakenly labelled as 'belly-dance' music abroad. Once again, 'debased' oriental influences dominated Greek pop, to the

COLLECTION GEORGE PISSALIDHES

Stelios Kazantzidis & Marinela c.1966

chagrin of the bourgeois classes and Greek Left, who also objected to the apolitical, decadent, escapist song content. This orientalising reached its high – or low – point during the brief mid-1960s craze for *indoyíftika*, Indian film music lifted straight from Bollywood and reset to Greek lyrics; chief culprit was the Gypsy singer **Manolis Angelopoulos**.

The most influential laïkó performer in the 1960s was **Stelios Kazantzidhis**, whose volcanic, mournful style was often imitated but never matched. His work, frequently in duets with Marinella (Kyriaki Papadhopoulou) and Yiota Lidhia, immortalised the joys and sorrows of the post-war Greek working class which faced a choice of life under the restrictive regimes of the time, or emigration. A trio of other rising stars in this period were (George) **Yiorgos Dalaras**, still the top-selling Greek pop singer, who had already attained gold sales status by 1971; and **Yiannis Parios** and **Haris Alexiou**, both of whom emerged on albums by the composer **Apostolos Kaldharas**.

Two other major laïkó composers, in recent decades, have been Khristos Nikolopoulou and Akis Panou. **Khristos Nikolopoulos**, a young bouzoúki virtuoso, worked with Kazantzidhes in the early 1970s, and went on to mega-selling co-efforts with Dalaras and Alexiou. **Akis Panou** has been less prolific and commercially success-

ful, but he too has made noteworthy albums with Dalaras, Bithikotsis and Stratos Dhionysiou as well as Kazantzidhes.

Although laïkó and éntekhno represented opposite poles of the Greek music world, the extremes sometimes met. Éntekhno composers such as Yiannis Markoulos hired laïkó singers for dates, or tried their hand at writing in laïkó style. A good example of the latter was Dhimos Moutsis' and Manos Eleftheriou's 1971 album *Ayios Fevrouarios*, which made singer **Dhimitris Mitropanos** a star overnight. But these syntheses were increasingly exceptional; after the success of *Epitafios* and *Axion Esti*, Greek record labels tried to marginalize laïkó, a trend accelerated under the military junta, when the greater portion of laïkó was banned from the radio as being too 'oriental' and 'defeatist'. In these conditions, the genre turned into **elafrolaïkó** (light popular), in which more honeyed voices were preferred. However, the stage was set for the emergence of singer-songwriters – many of them from Thessaloníki – and groups of folk-rockers, who together arrested the descent of Greek music into anodyne pap.

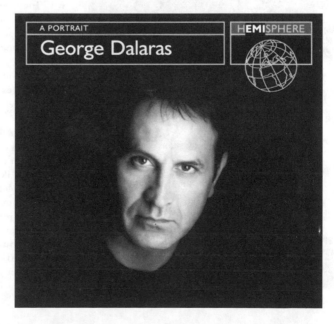

A PORTRAIT
George Dalaras
HEMISPHERE

Singer-Songwriters and Folk-Rock

The first significant musician to break out of the bouzoúki mould was Thessaloníki-based **Dhionysis Savvopoulos**, who burst on the scene in 1966 with a maniacal, rasping voice and elliptical, angst-ridden lyrics, his persona rounded out by shoulder-length hair and outsized glasses. Initially linked with the short-lived **néo kýma** (new wave) movement – a blend of watered-down éntekhno and French chanson performed in Athenian boites soon closed down by the colonels – Savvopoulos's work soon became impossible to piegeonhole: equal parts twisted Macedonian folk, Bob Dylan and Frank Zappa at his jazziest is a useful approximation. Though briefly detained and tortured, he was able to continue performing under the junta and was a symbol of opposition for many.

Out of Savvopoulos' 'Balkan rock' experiments sprung a short-lived movement whose artists alternated electric versions of traditional songs with original material. Few left much trace, except for the folk updater **Mariza Koch**, the Gypsy protest guitarist-singer **Kostas Hatzis**, and folk-éntekhno performer **Arletta**, all of whom are still active to various degrees. During the 1980s and '90s other singer-songwriters emerged under the influence of Savvopoulos, the most outstanding of whom is **Nikos Portokaloglou** who started his career with laïkó-rock group Fatmé.

As an independent producer and (briefly) head of Lyra records, Savvopoulos gave breaks to numerous younger artists, many of them also from northern Greece. The first of his protégés were **Nikos Xydhakis** and **Manolis Rasoulis**, whose landmark 1978 pressing, *Iy Ekdhikisis tis Yiftias* (The Revenge of Gypsydom), actually embodied the backlash of laïkó culture against the pretentiousness of 1960s and '70s éntekhno. Its spirited, defiant lyrics – with **Nikos Papazoglou** handling many of the vocals – and *tsiftetéli* rhythms were both homage to and send-up of the music beloved by Greek truck-drivers.

As with mainland folk instrumental music, Gypsies have been disproportionately important in laïkó, both as performers and composers, though some go to considerable lengths to conceal the fact. For every assimilated personality, however, there are others, such as Eleni Vitali, Makis Khristodhoulopoulos and Vassilis Païteris who make no bones about their identity.

New Laïkó

During the 1980s, **Xydhakis** went on to pursue a successful independent career, creating a style that hard-core laïkó fans dismiss as *koultouriárika* (high-brow stuff), for its orientalised instrumentation and melody. His most successful venture in this vein was the 1987 *Konda sti Dhoxa mia Stigmi* with **Eleftheria Arvanitaki** guesting on vocals. Arvanitaki, who is currently the leading Greek woman singer, went on to participate in a host of éntekhno and laïkó sessions.

Other performers to emerge from the Thessaloníki scene included the group **Khimerini Kolymvites**; laïkó composer **Yiorgos Zikas** and most recently Papazoglou disciple **Sokratis Malamas**.

Back in Athens éntekhno and other Westernising trends took longer to relax their grip, under the aegis of composers such as classically trained **Thanos Mikroutsikos**, briefly Minister of Culture after Melina Mercouri's death, who worked with Alexiou, Dalaras and top laïkó/éntekhno vocalist **Dhimitra Galani**. The composer **Stamatis Kraounakis**, lyricist and producer **Lina Nikolakopoulou** and female singer **Alkistis Protopsalti** made a splash with a number of hit albums stretching into the 1990s, exploring the boundaries between rock, jazz-cabaret and éntekhno.

ARGYROPOULOS

Nikos Papazoglou

Eleftheria Arvanitaki

There's no doubt about it, the hot name internationally on the Greek music scene is **Eleftheria Arvanitaki**. Her voice has a clarity and emotional depth that registers whether or not you understand the words, and the music she sings has a lyricism and instrumental sophistication that sets it apart. Her performances at WOMAD festivals in 1998 marked a transition from performing to Greek communities round the world to a new audience of World Music fans. They weren't disappointed.

Of course Eleftheria had long been a familiar figure in Greece. She was 'discovered' in 1979 by a couple of rembétika revivalists when she was singing for friends in a taverna, and joined the group **Opisthodhromiki Kompania**. Since then, she's followed a career embracing rembétika, many of the leading names in Greek music, and notably the New York/Armenian musician **Ara Dinkjian** who, with **Mihalis Ganas**, composed the songs for her most beautiful and successful album *The Bodies and the Knives (Ta Kormia keh ta Maheiria)*. It's a recording that thrillingly exemplifies one of her musical ambitions to create a real Mediterranean sound and Greece's crucial location between two worlds.

"Greece is one of the few countries in Europe that has kept its own traditional music," she says. "Perhaps because we have very deep roots in music and in history, of course. Because we are between the West and East we know very well the music of Europe and America, but we know the music of Asia as well. We are well-positioned to take the best from both worlds, but we keep doing our music in our own way."

That meeting of two worlds also lies behind rembétika, whose 1980s revival gave Eleftheria her break. "After the fall of the Colonels, this music came out through the students and people started to take notice

of it. Rembétika is an important part of our history. It describes how the people lived when they came from Asia Minor and what they had to face. It was a very important time in my life when I re-discovered our music. Like many Greeks, I was a big fan of Dylan and the Rolling Stones, but suddenly we found our own music."

Eleftheria is always keen to renew her contacts with her musical roots and her latest recording (*Ektos Programmatos*) returns to rembétika repertoire: "I play with my band some traditional songs and classic rembétika – not the big hits of rembétika, but great songs, by Vamvakaris, Tsitsanis and others, with something deeper behind them. Songs from the 1920s up to the '60s, plus traditional songs from the mountains. Through this music we can understand the history of our country."

Simon Broughton

On the more commitedly laïkó side, Khristos Nikolopoulos, Kostas Soukas and Takis Mousafiris ignited the 1980s, writing dozens of hits for a range of singers including **Eleni Vitali**, **Stratos Dionysiou**, **Dimitris Mitropanos** and **Pitsa Papadopoulou**. Younger promising laïkó names to watch out for include the vocalists **Eleni Tsaligopoulou**, **Melina Kana**, **Yerasimos Andhreatos**, **Manolis Lidhakis**, **Andhreas Louridhas** and the singer–songwriter **Orfeas Peridhes**.

Byzantine and Folk Revivals

An offshoot of éntekhno during the late 1970s and early 1980s involved combining **folk** and **Byzantine traditions**. Influential in this was the musicologist and arranger **Khristodhoulos Khalaris**, who produced a version of the Cretan epic *Erotokritos*, showcasing Nikos Xylouris and Tania Tsanaklidou, and followed it with the riveting *Dhrossoulites*, which featured Khrysanthos, a high-voiced male singer of Pontic descent, on alternate tracks with Dhimitra Galani. He has gone on to more speculative and less musically successful ventures in Byzantine song.

Ottoman rather than Byzantine Constantinople was the inspiration for **Vosporos**, a group co-ordinated in Istanbul from 1986 to 1992 by *psáltis* (church-chanter) and *kanonáki*-player **Nikiforos Metaxas** to explore Ottoman classical, devotional and popular music. In the late 1990s, the group reformed as **Fanari tis Anatolis**, with Greek and

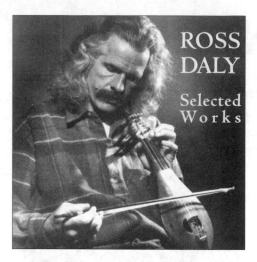

Turkish singers alternating Greek folk material with Anatolian songs or mystical Alevi ballads.

Ross Daly, whose interests and style overlap slightly with Vosporos, also merits catching on disc, live in Athens clubs or touring abroad. English-born but Irish by background, Daly has updated both Greek and Turkish folk material. He plays a dozen traditional instruments and has absorbed influences not only from Crete, where he was long resident, but from throughout the Near East; his groups have featured sitar and Egyptian ney. Other Cretans reworking folk material include mandolinist **Loudhovikos Ton Anoyion**, and the six-member group **Haïnidhes**, both of whom produce accessible and exciting music. A dryer, more scholarly approach is undertaken by **Domna Samiou**, who has collected and performed material from every corner of the Greek world.

Other, newer performers attempting to explore neighbouring influences on Greek music include **Notios Ikhos**, led by Ahilleas Persidhis; the innovative young clarinettist **Manos Akhhalinotopoulos**; Armenian oud player **Haig Yagdjian**; and the versatile vocalist **Savina Yiannatou**.

discography

The best selection of Greek discs is to be found at the London shop *Trehantiri*. For details of this, and shops in Athens and Thessaloníki, see the 'Shops' listings, at the end of this book. For ideas on current sounds, check out *Dhifono*, a music and arts monthly magazine, which usually comes packaged with a Greek CD.

Folk/Traditional Music

Compilations

⊚ Kritiki Mousiki Paradhosi, Iy Protomastores 1920–1953 – 10 CDs (Aerakis, Greece).

This is the definitive compilation of early Cretan recordings. The 10-CD set is a tad prohibitive for casual exploration, and some volumes are of specialist interest, but fortunately discs are available individually. Go for Vol 1 (Rodhinos and Baksevanis, lýra and small orchestra); Vol 4 (Stelios Foustalieris, the last master of the tambur-like voúlgari, knowledge of which died with him); Vol 5 (Yiannis Demirtzoyiannis, guitarist and epic singer) and Vol 6 (Yiorgis Koutsourelis, on melodic laoúto).

◐ Lesvos Aiolis: Tragoudhia keh Khori tis Lesvou/Songs & Dances of Lesvos (University Press of Crete, Greece).

Two decades' worth (1974–1996) of field recordings of the last traditional music extant on the island, a labour of love supervised by musicologist Nikos Dhionysopoulos. The quality and uniqueness of the instrumental pieces, and the lavishly illustrated booklet, merit the expense.

⊚ Seryiani sta Nisia Ma, Vol 1 (MBI, Greece).

An excellent retrospective of vintage nisiótika hits and artists, mostly from the 1950s. A highlight is Emilia Hatzidhaki's rendering of "Bratsera".

⊚ Songs of . . . (series) (Society for the Dissemination of National Music – SDNM, Greece).

A thirty-disc-plus series of field recordings from the 1950s through 1970s, each covering traditional music of one region or type. Quality can vary, but they're inexpensive, and all contain notes in English and are easily available in Athens in LP, cassette or CD form. Good choices include *Thrace 1*, *Epirus 1*, *Peloponnese*, *Mytilene and Chios*, *Mytilene and Asia Minor*, *Rhodes*, *Khalki and Symi*, and *Kassos and Karpathos*.

⊚ Takoutsia, Musiciens de Zagori (Auvidis/Inédit, France).

Drinking songs, dance tunes and dirges performed by one of the last working clans of itinerant Epirot Gypsy musicians. Lots of fine fiddle and clarinet, with an all-acoustic *kompanía* providing support.

Artists

Khronis Aídhonidhis

Born in the Évros valley of western Thrace, Aídhonidhis moved to Athens in 1950 where he fitted recording and live broadcasting sessions around a civil service career. He is unquestionably the greatest male singer of material from Thrace and western Asia Minor.

 T'Aídhoni tis Anatolis (Minos, Greece).

That rare thing – a folk collection of sterling material flawlessly produced, this 1990 session features Yiorgos Dalaras guesting on 4 tracks, and Ross Daly in charge of a traditional orchestra.

Banda tis Florinas

Brass bands are unique (in mainland Greece) to western Macedonia. This is probably the best of them all.

Banda tis Florinas
(Ano Kato-Rei, Thessaloníki, Greece).

Wonderfully twisted brass-band music, verging into ethnic-jazz territory with a nudge from guest saxophonist Floros Floridhis, one of the foremost personalities on Greece's avant-garde/improvisational scene.

Xanthippi Karathanasi

From Macedonia's Khalkidhikí Peninsula, Karathanasi is one of the foremost interpretators of northern Greek folk material.

Tragoudhia keh Skopi tis Makedhonias/
Songs and Tunes of Macedonia
(University Press of Crete, Greece).

High quality, like all UP Crete releases; the only possible quibble is that the sidemen are so good that they threaten to overshadow Xanthippi's vocals.

Petro-Loukas Khalkias (Chalkias)

Born in Epirus, near the Albanian border, in 1934, clarinettist Khalkias lived in America for twenty years before returning to Greece in 1979 to commence his recording career. Since the deaths of Vassilis Soukas and Tassos Khalkias, Petro-Loukas he has become the most sought-after session player in the country, injecting new life into the tradition in the best possible taste.

 Petro-Loukas Chalkias and Kompanía
(World Network, Germany).

Khalkias is at his best on this superbly recorded disc, as are his *kompanía* (group), the traditional backing of laoúto, violí, kithára and percussion. There are meaty oud solos by Khristos Zotos and fiddle licks by Petro-Loukas' brother Ahileas, which realise the true sense of the kompanía: tight co-ordination, but clearly articulated instrumental voices.

Konitopoulos Family

It's hard to keep track of all the siblings and generations of this musical family, originally from Náxos; basically, the late George played fiddle, Vangelis plays laoúto, while Angeliki and daughter Stella sing. The other sister, Irini Konitopoulou-Legaki, is a star in her own right.

Thalassa keh Paradhosi (Columbia, Greece).

Standard party and taverna aural fare across the islands – and a better-produced disc than the host of bootleg tapes beloved of Greek bus drivers.

Anefala Thalassina (Lyra, Greece).

This is Irini off the club stage: a riveting, intimate performance, with accompaniment by octogenarian Dhimitris Fyrogenis on tsambouna and backing vocals.

Yiorgos Koros

Considered Greece's foremost fiddler, Koros (born 1922) has been playing since childhood, and appeared at paniyíria at the age of 17. His discography spans three decades, unfortunately little of it on CD

To Magiko Violi (BMG, Greece).

This welcome re-release of an out-of-print 1982 disc features daughter Katerina and Yiannis Kondoyiannis, both of the Rembetiki Kompania, on vocals.

Yiorgos Papasidheris

Papasidheris (1902–1977) lived on Salamína, which though technically an island lies firmly in the mainland cultural sphere. Thus he was also known as an intepreter of rembétika.

Yiorgos Papasidheris Tragoudha Spania
Dhimotika Tragoudhia (FM, Greece).

An interesting, if rather scratchy, re-release of sides – some sung in Arvanítika, a dialect of medieval Albanian – from the 1930s.

Demotika Anthologia No. 1 (EMI Regal, Greece).

A more standard sampler, released in the early 1970s.

Nikos Xylouris

This Cretan singer (who died young in 1980) lent his golden voice to éntekhno endeavours as well as accompanying himself on the lýra on Cretan material.

O Arkhangelos tis Kritis, 1958–1968
(MBI, Greece).
Ta Khronia stin Kriti (MBI, Greece).

These are the best two retrospectives, with copious notes; the first covers his initial decade of recordings.

Rembétika

Compilations

The Greek Archives – multiple volumes
(FM Records, Greece).

Luxuriously packaged (though skeletal notes in English), this multi-disc series is uneven but generally worthwhile. Discs are arranged in two batches, each title devoted to a theme or particular artist. From the first, twelve-volume series, choose from among *1: Rembetico Song in America 1920-1940*; *6: Women of the Rembetico Song*; *7: Unknown Smyrna*; *8: Armenians, Jews, Turks & Gipsies*; and *9: Constantinople in Song*. From the second, unnumbered batch, *Anthology of Rembetiko Songs 1933–1940*, *Anthology of Smyrean Songs 1920–1938* and *Songs of the Sea* are wonderful.

 Greek-Oriental Rembética
(Arhoolie, US).

A superb rembétika collection spanning 1911–1937, featuring the singers Rosa Eskenazi; Rita Abatzi, Marika Papagika and Dhimitris Semsis. Good sleeve notes and lyric translations.

Historic Urban Folk Songs from Greece
(Rounder, US).

The above-cited artists, plus many more on terrific selections, mostly from the 1930s; complements the Arhoolie disc well, with no duplications.

Iy Megali tou Rembetikou – 10 volumes
(Margo, Greece).

This collection actually comprises over twenty albums, arranged by composer, though only the first ten are on CD (and worthwhile). Pick of the bunch are No. 1 *Early Performers*, No. 3 *Vassilis Tsitsanis*, No. 4 *Yiannis Papaïoannou*, No. 7 *Stratos Payioumtzis*, No. 8 *Kostas Roukounas* and No. 9 *Spyros Peristeris*, but showcasing Markos Vamvakaris on vocals.

Iy Rembetiki Istoria – 6 volumes
(EMI Regal, Minos, Greece).

This series was among the first rembétika material re-issued after the junta fell, and is still a good start to a collection. No.1 and 4 are mostly Smyrneic/Asia Minor songs; No.2 is mostly from the 1930s; while No.3 and 6 stress Tsitsanis and other 1950s material. No.5 is the runt of the litter.

 Lost Homelands: The Smyrnaic Song in Greece, 1928–1935 (Heritage, UK).

Like all the Heritage releases, this has excellent sound quality and editing, plus intelligent notes. It features lots of Dalgas, the two great peers Rosa Eskenazy and Rita Abatzi, and instrumental improvisations.

Artists

Rita Abatzi

Born in Smyrna in 1914, Rita Abatzi came to Greece as a child and began singing at sixteen. She had a huskier, more textured voice than her great rival Eskenazi, and seemed to gravitate toward meatier lyrics as well – though she often worked with the same sidemen: Semsis, Toumboulis, et al.

 Rita Abatzi 1933–1938 (Heritage, UK).
 Rita Abatzi (Minos-Arkheio, Greece).

The only two discs devoted exclusively to Abatzi; as usual, the Heritage release has the edge with its outstanding instrumentalists, sound quality and notes.

Sotiria Bellou

Born in Évvia in 1921, Bellou lived in Athens from 1940 until her death in 1997. Though her forthright lesbianism, left-wing political views and addiction to gambling sometimes drew more attention than her artistry, there's no denying that on a good night she could sing the socks off most contemporaries with her searching, no-nonsense voice.

 Sotiria Bellou 1946–1956 (Minos, Greece).

No. 5 in the series *Iy Megali tou Rembetikou*, this is virtually the only disc under her own name without the electric backing of later years; here she performs mostly with Tsitsanis. Includes the original of the classic "Ta Kavourakia".

Dalgas

Born in Constantinople in 1892, Dalgas had established himself as one of the premier amanés singers prior to arriving in Athens in 1922.

 Andonios Dhiamandidhis 1928–1933 (Heritage, UK).

The best disc devoted entirely to Dalgas.

Elleniki Apolavsi

Among the half-dozen or so rembétika revival groups of the early 1980s, this was perhaps the grittiest – and stands up well with the early masters, twenty years on.

 Apagorevmena Rembetika (BMG-Falirea, Greece).

A welcome re-release on CD, this is an atmospheric recording, with ample Asia-Minor material (and instrumentation, including tzourás, saz, oud and toumberléki).

Rosa Eskenazi

Though born in Istanbul around the turn of the century, Eskenazi moved to Greece before the 1922 disaster and then lived in Athens until her death in 1980. Her voice inimitably combined innocence with the come-hither sensuality that was supposed to be intrinsic to all the *hanumákia* (bar girls) from Asia Minor.

Rosa Eskenazi

 Roza Eskenazi 1933–1936 (Heritage, UK).

Superb renditions with her usual sidement Semsis, Tomboulis, plus Lambros on kanonáki; extremely varied selection of standards and rare gems make this the best of several collections available.

Marika Ninou

Born in 1918 in a Greek community of the Caucausus, Ninou came to Greece as a child and sung with Tsitsanis from 1948 until her premature death from cancer in 1956. She was more obviously feminine in demeanor and delivery than Bellou, but no less the artist for it.

Stou Tzimi tou Khondhrou/At Fat Jimmy's (Venus-Tzina, Greece).

Poor sound quality since it was a clandestine wire recording, but still a classic. Performing with Tsitsanis at their habitual club in 1955, Ninou gives it her all, including two cuts in Turkish. Well worth rooting out.

 Marika Ninou & Vassilis Tsitsanis (Philips, Greece).

Not as soulful as the Venus disc, but far better sound and more than adequate renditions of their favourites, including "Synnefiazmeni Kyriaki" and the gut-wrenching "Yennithika".

Marika Papagika

Born on Kós in 1890, Papagika emigrated to the US in 1913, where she performed with her husband Gus between 1918 and 1937, for the considerable and nostalgic Greek community in New York.

 Greek Popular and Rebetic Music in New York 1918–1929 (Alma Criolla, US).

Marika Papagika's best work, with Gus on sandoúri; includes an affecting, rare kantádha duet with Marika Kastrouni.

Vassilis Tsitsanis

One of the giants of rembétika, mellowing and popularising the style, Tsitsanis began his recording career in Athens but spent the critical war years running a small club in Thessaloníki, where he performed live and accumulated the material that was to make him a household name. A shy, nattily dressed man, he never quite lost the air of the law student he'd once briefly been.

 Vassilis Tsitsanis 1936–1946 (Rounder, US).

A fine first disc to begin exploring Tsitsanis. It features mostly male singers, but includes his reputed first recording, a mastouriaká with Yioryia Mittaki.

 Dhïskografia Tsitsani Vols 1–4 (HMV, Greece).

Four Cds – available separately – encompassing his best early work from the mid-1930s to 1955.

Markos Vamvakaris

The 'Grandfather of Rembétika', Vamvakaris was born on Siros into a poor Catholic family in 1905, stowed away on a freighter bound for Pireás at age 15, and worked odd jobs around the port before discovering bouzoúki and hash – more or less in that order. The rest is Greek musical history.

 Markos Vamvakaris, Bouzouki Pioneer (Rounder, US).

Excellent sound quality, good notes and unusual material – not a trace of his hackneyed and over-covered "Frangosyriani" – make this a top choice.

 Afthentika Rembétika tis Amerikis No.2 (Lyra, Greece).

Mostly Markos, and wonderful; title's a wild misnomer, as Vamvakaris never went to America, though some 78s may have been simultaneously issued there and in Greece.

 Rembetica in Piraeus 1933–1937, Vols 1 & 2 (Heritage, UK).

The gang that played – and smoked – together, in top form: Markos, Batis, Statos and Artemis, plus lesser-known figures.

Stavros Xarhakos

 Rembetiko (CBS, Greece).

Soundtrack to the namesake film, available as a double LP or, in somewhat edited form, on one CD. Virtually the only 'original' rembétika to be composed in the last 40 years, with lyrics by Nikos Gatsos.

New Waves

Compilations

 The Dance of Heaven's Ghosts (EMI Hemisphere, UK).

A well-balanced compilation of the most accessible (and slickly produced) laïkó, with tracks from Haris Alexiou, Yiannis Parios and Eleni Vitali, among others.

 Songs of Greece's Gypsies (FM Records, Greece).

A good introduction to self-identified gypsy laïkó performers, including Makis Khristodhoulopoulos, Eleni Vitali, Vassilis Paíteris, and Kostas Pavlidhis.

Artists

Haris Alexiou

Born in Thebes in 1950, Haris Alexiou reigned virtually unchallenged as the queen of Greek laïkó (pop) throughout the 1970s and 1980s, her unschooled but incredibly expressive voice gracing the albums of improbably varied composers.

 Dhodheka Laïka Tragoudhia (Minos, Greece).
 Ta Tragoudhia tis Haroulas (Minos, Greece).

These discs, the first mostly rembétika, the second with lyrics by Manolis Rassoulis and Manos Loizos, secured Alexiou's position.

Laïkó superstar Haris Alexiou

Eleftheria Arvanitaki

The wondrous Arvanitaki (see feature box on p.135) began her career as a rembétika revivalist, moved on to frequent, effective collaboration with Nikos Xydhakis, and is now considered the leading all-round female vocalist in the country.

 The Very Best of, 1989–98 (Mercury, Greece).

This draws largely on a trio of albums – **Meno Ektos** (1991), **Ta Kormia Keh ta Maheiria** (1994), **Tragoudhia yia tous Mines** (1996) – all of which went gold or platinum in Greece. They are discs that engage whether you understand the language or not. Refined instrumental arrangements exquisitely support Eleftheria's extraordinary voice, which is both gutsy and ethereal.

◎ **Ektos Programmatos** (Mercury, Greece).

Eleftheria revisits her roots, interpreting much-loved old laïkó and dhimotiká songs on this two-CD set of live, mainly accoustic sessions. Recorded in 1998, it is an irresitable gallop through Greek music of the past fifty years.

Yiorgos (George) Dalaras

Born in 1950, the son of a Piraeus rembétika player, Dalaras has appeared on nearly 80 recordings since his 1968 debut, spanning the range of Greek music from Anatolian, dhimotiká and éntekhno; in effect he has worked with everybody who's anybody on the Greek music scene. Virtually a national institution, Dalaras has always – even during the junta years – remained a staunch supporter of popular struggles, giving benefit concerts for various worthy causes. In his commitment to quality musicianship, he has scrupulously avoided the more banal extremes of the pop scene.

◎ **Peninda Khronia Rembetika Tragoudhi** (Minos, Greece).

The 1975 disc that helped kick-start the rembétika revival.

◎ **Seryiani sto Kosmo** (Minos,Greece).

Dalaris's appearance with Yiannis Markopoulos – plus the material's merit – guaranteed this disc's best-selling status.

◎ **A Portrait: George Dalaras** (EMI Hemisphere, UK).

'Best-of' sampler with both live and studio work spanning his entire career.

Ross Daly

Alone or with his floating workshop-group Lavyrinthos, Daly has recorded strikingly contemporary interpretations of traditional pieces, as well as original compositions.

◎ **Selected Works** (Oriente, Germany).

A representative compilation from several earlier, out-of-print albums (a chronic problem with his work).

◎ **Mitos** (World Network, Germany).

1991 concert recordings with Spyridhoula Toutoudhaki singing.

Glykeria

Born near Serres in 1953, Glykeria (Kotsoula) was one of the most popular and versatile laïkó singers and rembétika revivalists of the 1980s, and is equally accomplished when exploring dhimotiká and nisiótiká.

 Me ti Glykeria stin Omorfi Nhykhta (Lyra, Greece).

All the above styles get a look-in on this enduringly popular 1983 album.

Haïnidhes

Haïnídhes is an old Turko-Cretan word meaning bolshy layabouts; this all-acoustic group has turned the slur on its head, their rebellion if anything is against the ossification of Cretan lyrics and music.

◎ **Kosmos ki Oneiro ineh Ena** (MBI, Greece).
◎ **Haïnidhes** (MBI, Greece).

The group's first (and most would say best) discs. Unlike many other 'revival' groups, they feature mainly all-original lyrics and compositions on traditional instruments.

Manos Hatzidhakis

Even more than Theodhorakis, Hatzidhakis (1925–1994) suffers from being categorised as a composer of movie soundtracks and Greek elevator music. But there's much to enjoy, especially on his earlier discs.

◎ **Matomenos Gamos: Paramythi khoris Onoma** (Columbia, Greece).

Nikos Gatsos-translated lyrics, with Lakis Pappas singing.

◎ **O Megalos Erotikos** (Lyra, Greece).

A 1972 outing, with Dhimitris Psarianos on vocals, and lyrics based on Greek poetry from Sappho to Seferis.

Apostolos Kaldharas

Born in the central Greek town of Trikala in 1922, the late composer Kaldharas regularly tipped his hat to rembétika and éntekhno.

◎ **Mikra Asia** (Minos, Greece).

A disc which marked Haris Alexiou's 1972 debut and, with vocals from George Dalaras, helped spark the rembétika revival of the mid-1970s.

◎ **Vyzantinos Esperinos** (Minos, Greece).

From 1973, with more of Haris and less of Dalaras.

Stelios Kazantzidhis

A great bear of a man, born in 1931 of Asia Minor parentage, Kazantzidhis is an incredibly versatile performer, with a repertoire ranging from rembétika to mainland folk, and the ability to sing in Turkish if needed.

◎ **Kazantzidhis 3, 1959–1962** (EMI-Regal, Greece).

This is the quintessential early laïkó classic that made him a national institution.

◎ **Ena Glendi me fon Stellara** (MBI, Greece).

Stelios celebrates his birthday around a taverna table with acoustic sidemen. An earthy and intimate session.

Khimerini Kolymvites

Led by architect Arghyris Bakirtzis, this engaging northern

Greek group has pursued various directions in the 1980s and '90s.

◉ **Khimerini Kolymvites** (Lyra, Greece).

Their debut album quickly acquired cult status with its blend of rembétika, laïkó and a dash of island melodies on plucked and bowed strings.

◉ **Okhi Lathi Panda Lathi** (Lyra, Greece).

After disappointing subsequent efforts, a welcome return to form with this live 1997 album, shared with Banda tis Florinas.

Loudhovikos Ton Anoyion (Yiorgos Dhramoundanis)

Born in 1951 in Anóyia, Crete, as his pseudonym suggests, Loudhovikos was one of Manos Hatzidhakis' protégés at the Seirios label.

◉ **O Erotas stin Kriti ine Melangolikos** (Seirios, Greece).

His second album restored the mandolin – downgraded in Crete to the role of rhythm laoúto – to its rightful place.

◉ **Pyli tis Ammou** (Mylos, Greece).

A later evolution in a larger group, with guest appearances by Malamas, Papazoglou and Nena Venetsanou.

Yiannis Markopoulos

Born in 1939 in Iraklio, Crete, Markopoulos began recording in the mid-1960s and hit his peak a decade later. Certainly the rootsiest of the éntekhno composers, he has been fortunate in the range of quality artists who have sung for him: Yiorgos Dalaras, Nikos Xylouris, Lakis Khalkias, Tania Tsanaklidhou and Kharalambos Garganourakis among others.

◉ **Thiteia** (EMI, Greece).

With lyrics by Manos Eleftheriou, many consider this – with hits like "Malamatenia Logia" – Markopoulos's best effort.

◉ **Anexartita** (EMI, Greece).

This is also a strong contender, featuring an incredible range of talent, and the original live version of the bitter "Iy Ellada", recorded just after the junta fell.

Khristos Nikolopoulos

Born in northern Greece in 1947, Nikolopoulos is the most prolific and arguably most influential laïkó composer of the past three decades.

◉ **Yparkho** (Minos, Greece).

With Stelios Kazantzidhis singing, this represents both of them in peak form.

◉ **Iy Sythetes kai ta Tragoudhia tous No. 4** (Minos, Greece).

A definitive collection of his songs that changed the course of laïkó for the 1980s.

Akis Panou

Panou is a versatile composer, lyricist and bouzouki whiz.

◉ **Ta Megala Tragoudhia** (EMI, Greece).

The 1993 retrospective is one of the best possible starts to a laïkó collection.

Yiannis Parios

Born on Páros in 1946, Parios is George Dalaras's only serious rival for the title of Elafro-laïkó King.

◉ **Ta Nisiótika Vol 1** (Minos, Greece).

This 1981 release, with the Konitopoulos family accompanying, became Greece's most successful disc ever, with nearly a million copies sold to date. Though a curious chimaera – authentic folk instrumentation, laïkó-style vocals – it obviously tapped a vein.

Nikos Papazoglou

Born in Thessaloniki in 1948, Papazoglou was the first to successfully blend laïkó and Western-style rock, as opposed to the folk-rock endeavours of the early 1970s.

◉ **Haratsi** (Lyra, Greece).

Alternates introspective ballads with hard-driving electrics.

◉ **Synerga** (Lyra,Greece).

Gentler, even mystical, more in the mould of later Xydhakis.

Dhionysis Savvopoulos

Despite a modest discography – he took early 'retirement' in the late 1980s after his much publicised return to religious Orthodoxy – it's difficult to overestimate Savvopoulos' effect on subsequent guitar-based songwriters; the credit (or blame) for much Greek folk-rock and folk-jazz can be laid at his door.

◉ **To Fortigo** (Lyra, Greece).

His néo kýma-style 1966 debut, alone with his guitar.

◉ **Ballos** (Lyra, Greece).

The radical, electrified Balkan folk release that set off the brief folk-rock movement.

◉ **Trapezakia Exo** (Lyra, Greece).

The best of his later work, more digestibly folky, with a cameo by Eleftheria Arvanitaki.

Mikis Theodhorakis

After his overplayed, over-covered 1965 soundtrack for *Zorba the Greek*, Theodhorakis shunned Byzantine/folk/rembetic influences in favour of overtly political symphonic works and film soundtracks dictated by his then-Communist affiliation.

◉ **Epitafios** and **Epifania** (EMI Columbia, Greece).
◉ **Axion Esti** (EMI Columbia, Greece).

These are Theodhorakis's most influential, reputation-justifying works. Be sure to get the original versions only: second-rate instrumental covers abound.

Vosporos/Fanari Tis Anatolis

Vosporos was a pioneering group led by Nikiforos Metaxas, consisting largely of Istanbul musicians, and strictly orchestral. In 1992, Metaxas formed Fanari tis Anatolis, showcasing Greek singer Vassiliki Papyeoryiou and (often) Turkish artist Melda Kurt in untypical renditions of Greek and Anatolian folk songs, plus instrumental interludes.

VOSPOROS

◉ **Vosporos** (HMV, Greece).

The original group demonstrated their 1987 debut's pertinence to Grecophiles with the album subtitle *Greek Composers of The City* (ie Constantinople), highlighting the contribution of Greek and other non-Turkish musicians to the Ottoman courtly tradition.

FANARI TIS ANATOLIS

◉ **Ellenika keh Asikika** and **Balkania Oneira** (MBI, Greece).

Hard to choose between these two albums, the best of the group's recent output.

Nikos Xydhakis

Birth (1952) and early childhood in Egypt seems to have predisposed Xydhakis to oriental influence; critics say that since 1989 his albums all sound the same, but if you get hooked on the sound, you'll want them all.

◉ **Iy Ekdhikisi tis Yiftias** (Lyra, Greece).

A groundbreaking 1978 debut which effectively rehabilitated laïkó in Greece.

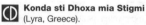 **Konda sti Dhoxa mia Stigmi** (Lyra, Greece).

This classic 1987 album with lyrics by Thodhoros Gonis, and guest appearances by Ross Daly and Eleftheria Arvanitaki,

offers a particularly beguiling blend of folk, Byzantine and Asia Minor styles.

Savina Yiannatou

It's hard to classify Athens-born Savina, whose two decades of versatile recordings have taken her from éntekhno to folk revival by way of children's lullabies and avant-garde classical suites. Her high, penetrating voice, like those of several other female vocalists currently the rage in Greece, can take some getting used to.

◉ **Anixi sti Saloniki** (Lyra, Greece).

Re-settings of Sephardic songs in Ladino, with Middle Eastern instrumental backing arranged by Kostas Vomvolos; the most recent of several such efforts by various artists.

◉ **Songs of the Mediterranean** (Lyra, Greece).

Encouraged by the critical and commercial success of *Anixi...*, and with the same musicians and arrangers, Savina broadened her scope to include not only songs from the Aegean but Italy, Sardinia, Albania and North Africa.

Greenland

sealskin hits

It was Erik the Red who gave Greenland its unlikely name after he 'discovered' it in 982 AD. It was a deliberate attempt to make the place sound appealing to settlers from Iceland – and it worked. According to the chronicles he "gulled twenty-five ship loads of men, women, serfs and animals and off they sailed." It must be one of the earliest PR successes on record and Greenland can boast many such surprises – including the world's most successful record label. **Etienne Bours** fills in the details.

The town of Sisimut, just north of the Arctic circle, boasts 5000 Eskimos, 3000 dogs and a twenty-four track recording studio. This is the home of **ULO**, who could be legitimately described as the world's most successful record label. Their least successful recordings sell the equivalent of four times platinum in Europe. Their biggest sellers move over 10,000 units to a population of 50,000. That equates to sales of twenty-five million in the States. The company was created by **Karsten Sommer**, a Dane, and **Malik Hoegh**, an Inuit musician from the group Sume in 1976. "ULO can only function," says Sommer, "because people in Greenland love to listen to their local music. Greenland is the biggest island in the world, stretching half the length of Africa. Fifty thousand Inuit live in towns or villages, far from each other, and the only connection between people is by ship or plane. The CD and the cassette, therefore, have become the link between people all over Greenland. And music is the medium for new poetry. Rock and pop present thoughts and feelings, tell stories and ideas to Greenlanders. They repay us by buying CDs in quantities that make the island one of the hottest music markets in the world – if you compare the sales figures with the number of inhabitants."

Drum Songs

Greenland now sustains a wide range of music from drum dances to hip-hop. ULO's biggest sellers are rock and pop groups like **Sume** and **Zikaza**, but they also make a great effort to record and release **traditional Inuit music**. This has survived best in the northeast (Thule) and east of the country (Ammassalik). The south and west were more

accessible to the outside world and developed more rapidly. Now Greenland, like the rest of the world, is a place of fast communication, and new music reaches every small community.

The ancestral Inuit **drum dances** are played by one or two people on a small oval drum with a wooden frame covered with a bear-bladder and struck with a stick on the frame rather than the skin. It is related to the Inuit drums of Canada and Siberia, although smaller in scale and played more intimately.

The Inuit used to sing and play the drum for many occasions: feasts and gatherings, to tell stories, to play games and to tease or charm partners. Personal songs or **pisiq** (the word comes from Canada) are bound up with daily life events – something like a Sami *joik*. The singer is the owner of the song and if somebody else sings it, the song is often named after its original author. A song can be passed on and be sung practically unchanged in 1909 and in 1984 – as

Greenland polka dance

DANISH POLAR CENTRE/ULO

TRADITIONAL
GREENLANDIC
MUSIC

Polka, Rock and Hip-Hop

The Inuit always liked to sing, play and dance. So when the new settlers arrived, they soon adapted the instruments brought by the Whites. Danes colonised the island over two hundred and fifty years ago and there were visiting whalers from other parts of the world, so the influences were diverse. From the missionaries the Inuit learned to sing hymns; from the whalers they learned to play accordion and fiddle; from the Danes they learned the polka.

This new music had a dramatic effect and the results were something new again – like the Inuit polka, the **kalattuut**. This Inuit music was danced at feasts and passed down from generation to generation like the drum dance before. The musician's relationship with their instrument is often very physical, joyful and passionate. People talk, for example, of the late accordion player **Louis Andreasen** who would talk and laugh to his instrument when playing.

A younger generation took to the guitar and sung about their life between two worlds. Their **folk songs, rock and blues** can sound like a pale imitation of Western music, but it's the words that are important. The young groups tend to avoid ancestral instruments like the drum, but with guitars, keyboards, bass and drumkit they've sung their own experience and dared to say that the forefathers knew the way and that even the sound of the drum should be heard again:

> Be aware of the power of nature
>   because it is the very source of life
> You yourself have to revitalise
>   the fading sound of the drum.
>   **The song "Inngerpalaaq" by the group Silamiut.**

Some modern musicians have in fact sampled Inuit drums, or used a traditional performer in their music.

Another singer, **Rasmus Lyberth**, one of the most powerful voices of the Arctic, sings about the experience of trying to eek out a living in Denmark as an economic migrant:

> One evening alone with my thoughts,
>   I think of my land, so far away.
> Memories of my childhood
>   make me want to go back,
> But here I am, homeless
>   with no work and no money.

But in Greenland itself it is cultural identity that is important and music is a major part of that, as ULO recognises: "We must supply Greenland with

you can hear on the *Traditional Greenlandic Music* CD. Some personal songs don't use words, just vocables – *ay-ay-a*. That's why some people call these chants *ayaya*.

The drum was also the instrument of the **shaman** (*angakkog*) who brought luck for hunting and made magic. It was even a kind of judicial weapon maintaining the social order. When somebody's behaviour was causing problems, instead of a sanction against him, the community sometimes organised a **song duel** between the offender and the victim. The problem was brought in front of the group. The spectators were the court, determining the winner by their shouts, exclamations and laughs. The one who made the audience laugh the most won. Here's an example:

> I long to answer him who stands before me
> I am married, I am not like you
> Maybe you would like to try them again
> Try those up in the tent
> I will tell who you have visited
> You have visited my wife
> You lay with her as I have lain with her
> But you got tired of that. Toruka got tired
> How strange that I should sing about that.
>   **(Recorded in 1961 on Traditional Greenlandic Music).**

Even if this system is now obsolete, some singers are keeping the tradition of drum songs alive, mainly in the northern and eastern parts of the country. They maintain a repertoire of old songs, extracts from contests, games and personal songs. Drum songs are performed on stage, too, and this is a way of keeping the tradition alive and attracting new interest.

recordings of the best music that exists there, and then try to urge the most gifted musicians to look deeper into their tradition."

One of the most successful of contemporary groups, the Greenland rappers, **Nuuk Posse** have sampled drum songs from ULO's own catalogue and have their own messages about Greenlandic identity:

The city is a jungle with hunters and prey
Pale riders passing by I'm trying to find my way
Sick and tired of street signs
Written in a language that's not mine
I want to write in Greenlandic
Be proud of who you are and open your mind.

"Oqariartuut" by Nuuk Posse.

discography

ULO Greenlandic Music can be contacted at PO Box 184, DK-3911 Sisimiut, Greenland ☎ (299) 1 865811; fax: 865812; *www.ulomusic@greennet.gl*

Compilations

 Traditional Greenlandic Music (ULO, Greenland).

A cross section of traditional styles from the different areas of Greenland. Shaman songs, drum songs, epic songs and singing games etc. Recordings from 1905 to 1987. Not an easy listen, but fascinating. Good notes.

 Kleemannikkut 4 (ULO, Greenland).

For accordion fans, Joergen Kleemann and his family playing kalattuut-polka music on various accordions, bass and drums – sounding rather like a Scottish ceilidh band. Also some songs accompanied by guitar. An important part of contemporary Inuit music.

Qavaat: Music from South Greenland (ULO, Greenland).

Old and new music from the south. Traditional drum songs, fiddle, accordion and mouth organ for polkas and square dances, plus contemporary pop songs. Features fifteen tunes from accordionist Louis Andreason.

Artists

Rasmus Lyberth

Greenland's most popular folk singer has been singing for over twenty years now. He is at his best accompanying himself on guitar or joined by a couple of fellow musicians.

 Erningaa (To my son) (ULO, Greenland).

Lyberth's debut CD. Simple, but effective, songs about life, work, love, his forefathers and snow.

Nuuk Posse

Literally 'The gang from Nuuk' the capital of Greenland. Six singers who combine hip-hop and rap with traditional drum dance and the sound of whales, etc.

 Nuuk Posse (ULO, Greenland).

This debut CD was a big success in Greenland – and in Japan. It is the voice of a new musical generation: "We're Greenlanders, Arctic rappers, Northern funkers, Greenland rap is here to stay." Move over, Compton.

Silamiut

This Inuit rock group was among Grenland's most popular in the 1980s.

 Inuugujoq (To my Friend) (ULO, Greenland).

This disc from 1987 features female singer Vivi Nielson backed by guitars, keyboard, bass and drums. A good example of Greenlandic rock – the lyrics are more important than the music. Songs about the Inuit, the traditional drum, life, liberty and identity.

Sume

Sume (Where?) were Greenland's first pop group releasing their first record, *Sumut* (Where To?) in 1973. It was bought by twenty percent of the population and kick started the Greenlandic pop industry. They re-united in 1994 for another hit album *Persersume* (Snowdrift). Their songs have always looked at the cultural confusion of Inuit life.

ULO

 Sume 1973–1976 (ULO, Greenland).

Some of their best songs from various line-ups around composers, singers and guitarists Malik Hoegh and Per Berthelsen. "It's time to live again as Inuit and not as Westerners" says the song "Nunaqarfiit" (Restoration).

Zikaza

Greenland's most popular group. Seven musicians with guitars, keyboards, sax, bass and percussion producing sophisticated rock.

Miki Goes To Nuussuaq (ULO, Greenland).

ULO's most successful album, which won the band a 'Sealskin disc'. Zikaza sing about generational conflicts in the Arctic where young and old don't necessarily live in the same world. It's time to be careful to stay masters of their own country or it's going to be the end of their culture.

Gypsy Music

kings and queens of the road

El Camarón, Django Reinhardt, the Taraf de Haidouks, The Gipsy Kings: the words Gypsy and music appear together with astonishing regularity throughout Europe and the Middle East, as exponents of popular styles from belly dance to flamenco. Gypsies – or *Roma*, as they call themselves in the *Romani* language – are important practitioners of the music in many of the articles in this book – notably in Spain, Hungary, Romania, Macedonia and Turkey – yet the Gypsy music of these regions is only a partial glimpse of a wider story of migration only scantily researched. *Simon Broughton* traces the Roma journey from India to Spain and listens out for unifying threads in the music.

The great flamenco singer **El Camarón de la Isla** sings a Lorca poem accompanied by a sitar, not the expected Spanish guitar, on the opening track of World Network's compilation of Gypsy music, *Road of the Gypsies*. It makes an impressive and appropriate connection between the beginning and end of the Gypsy trail, one that stretches from roots in Northern India to Andalusian flamenco. In a similar way **Hameed Khan** (not himself a Gypsy), who leads the group of Rajasthani Gypsies, **Musafir**, has brought his Indian ear to flamenco music and plans a collaboration with Andalusian musicians after feeling the musical affinities for himself: "I heard two guitarists playing in Cordoba. I took out my *tabla* – they'd never seen one before – and played along with them. I could feel their rhythms and a Gypsy girl got up to dance. There is definitely a shared musical language."

These examples are deliberate attempts to forge links between India and Spain as a statement of identity and common culture. It's difficult to pin down specific links between the various types of Gypsy music in Europe, the Middle East and India. Clearly, they share characteristics: an upfront, declamatory, raw singing style is evident in flamenco, Rajasthani Gypsy music and much of the Gypsy music of eastern Europe, and each of these musics share a tendency to make exaggerated slides between notes, wringing out the emotion. But perhaps more intersting and more important is the way the Gypsies in all these regions have become the leading folk musicians, practising music as a trade, just as they do other caste-professions as blacksmiths, horse-traders, peddlers, and bringing to it a distinctive showmanship and display.

Wherever they have ended up, it seems that Gypsy musicians have an unfailing ability to absorb local styles and make them their own. Among folk musicians they tend to be much more open to new sounds and influences than the 'indigenous' locals, retaining a kind of nomadism of musical taste. International tunes – the "Lambada" is a popular favourite in eastern Europe – get reworked as part of a local tradition, and as professionals, Gypsy musicians essentially play what is popular.

This drives folk music 'purists' to despair, as centuries-old traditions are 'corrupted' in the time it takes for The Gipsy Kings to record, say, Frank Sinatra's "My Way". Yet by the very voraciousness of their borrowing, Gypsy musicians have kept, and are keeping, living, traditional music alive into the twenty-first century.

Dom, Rom, and Rights

The word **Gypsy**, and its equivalent in other European languages – the German *Zigeuner*, French *Tzigane* and Spanish *Gitano* – is often thought to be pejorative. It derives from the word 'Egypt', where the Gypsies were assumed to have come from at one time, though they in fact originated in India. *Dom* – of which **Rom** is thought to be a corruption – refers to a lower caste group doing menial work in India today, but in the past it just meant 'man' which is also the meaning of 'Rom' in Romani, the Gypsy language.

It's probable that there were several migrations of Rom from India into the Middle East and Europe – today, there are an estimated 12 million Gypsies outside India with about eight million in Europe. Linguistic differences divide the Indian Gypsies into various subgroups, and once they'd arrived in Europe the dispersals got ever more complex as per-

Opré Roma (Rise up Roma)

I've travelled, travelled long roads
Meeting with happy Roma
Roma where have you come from
With tents on fortune's road?
Roma, o fellow Roma

Once I had a great family
The Black Legion* murdered them
Come with me, all the world's Roma
For the Romani roads have opened
Now's the time, rise up Roma,
We shall now rise high
Roma, o fellow Roma.

Romani anthem, written by Jarko Jovanovic;
(** Black Legion refers to the Nazi SS*)

secution forced movement one way and then anoth er. In virtually every European country there has been popular or state persecution against the Gypsies, culminating in the extermination by the Nazis of an estimated half a million during World War II. Since the fall of Communism in eastern Europe, there has been a resurgent and violent racism against Gypsies, with communities forced in fear from Slovakia, in particular, and, most recently, from Kosovo, following the Serbian war.

On a positive front, however, since the 1970s, there hs been a growing awareness of Gypsy identity and culture, and political moves to establish rights. The popular Balkan Gypsy song "Djelem, Djelem" (I've travelled) was chosen as the **Romani anthem** (see above), and in 1979 the UN recognised the Roma as a distinct ethnic group.

were given corn, oxen and donkeys so they could become farmers, but ate the oxen and corn and returned after a year starving, whereupon the angry Shah told them to fit their instruments with strings of silk, put their possessions on their donkeys and wander the world.

It's not known which tribe or tribes of nomads might have made the voyage to Persia, but the links between Romani and Indian languages such as Hindi, Punjabi and Sanskrit make it pretty certain that is where the Rom originated. It's probable that several migrations occurred at different times, given the Muslim invasions of northwestern India from the eighth century, but linguistic specialists think the Gypsies must have left India before 1000AD.

Northwest India, and **Rajasthan** in particular, still has a high concentration of nomadic tribes and Gypsies, many of whom have specific professions: the Gadia Lohar are blacksmiths (a profession associated with Gypsies everywhere), the Kamad are travelling jugglers, the Bhat are puppeteers, the Sapera are pipe-playing snake charmers and the Langa, Manganiyar, and Bhopa storytellers are all musician castes in Rajasthan (see article on 'Folk and Tribal music in India' in *Volume Two* of this book). Acrobats, fakirs, illusionists and magicians: all arts that seem to have informed the showmanship and manner of Gypsy music.

Of the many professional musicians of Rajasthan, the **Manganiyars**, who operate in the Thar desert around Jaisalmer, seem the closest to European Gypsy musicians; they have low social status and are always on call to provide a party. Typically they play the **kamayacha**, a bowed fiddle with four strings and a large skin-covered circular belly carved out of mango wood. Like most folk musicians from

Rajasthan Music Roots

Arab and Persian historians describe how **Shah Bahram Gur**, who ruled Persia from 420–438 AD, invited musicians and dancers from northwest India to entertain his people. One source says four thousand, another twelve, but they were spread throughout the kingdom and left dark descendants 'who are experts in playing the flute and lute'. A later Persian history, written by Firdausi in 1011, tells a story about how the Shah's musicians

+++ MUSAFIR | GYPSIES OF RAJASTHAN +++

the region they play and sing music which has the essential Gypsy qualities of declamation, emotion and ecstasy, but unusually, for percussion, they use pairs of **khartal** – hard *sal* wood clappers used just like flamenco castanets. Who knows if the Manganiyars, or their ancestors, are the proto-Gypsies? The castanets may be coincidence, but they are as strong a musical connection as you'll find on the Gypsy road.

The Baluchi Ostâ

Spread out over a vast territory of **Pakistan** and **Iran**, and a part of **Afghanistan**, are around ten million (traditionally nomadic) **Baluchi** people. Within Baluchi society, the **ostâ caste** are the music makers and share a fairly low status with other categories like blacksmiths and carpenters. They have been cited as possible descendants of the musicians cast out to wander by Bahram Gur, but they have absorbed so many different ethnic groups (who have adopted their language and customs) that it's hard to come up with hard evidence.

Like all the musician castes of the region the ostâ are fiery performers with declamatory voices and great instrumental virtuosity. The most important instrument is the bowed **sorud** (fiddle) carved into a complicated skull-like shape with four playing strings and a number of vibrating sympathetic strings. The instrument has a soft, but edgy tone with wonderful colours – often used to accompany songs and epic chants, but also as a solo instrument and for trance music. The **tanburag** lute often gives a rhythmic drone accompaniment.

The Road to Europe

Linguistic ingredients in the Romani language indicate prolonged periods in **Persia** and **Armenia**. There are still groups of Indian origin in Iran and the Middle East today, but it seems likely that the Gypsies that ended up in Europe left before or shortly after the Arab conquest of Persia in the seventh century. Persian absorbed many Arabic words but very few are to be found in Romani. There are, though, a large number of Armenian words which suggests that Armenia was the next stop after leaving Persia.

From the fringes of the medieval Byzantine Empire the Gypsies were attracted to the capital, **Constantinople** (now Istanbul), where from 1050 on there are references to fortune tellers, acrobats, snake charmers and bear trainers who are thought to have been Gypsies. In their wanderings, the Gypsies encountered Christianity and they called

the cross *trushul*, the same word they used for the trident carried by the Hindu god Shiva in India.

The migration of the Gypsies often seems to have been connected with Muslim invaders, for whom they often took on the role of playing music (as Muslim musicians were not encouraged by the religion), but by whom they were often persecuted for their lack of a monotheistic faith. Gypsies in **Turkey** have long been a part of the rich ethnic mix of Istanbul and are still an important part of Turkey's musical life today (see opposite).

From Constantinople the Gypsies crossed into **Europe** in advance of and after the Ottoman conquest of the city in 1453. From the fourteenth and fifteenth centuries there are records of Gypsies in the **Balkans** – **Bulgaria**, **Greece**, **Serbia**, **Romania** and **Hungary**, all countries where they have made a huge contribution to the music and still do so today.

In Turkey and the Balkans the pairing of **zurna** (wooden *shawm*) and **davul** (barrel drum) is frequently heard outdoors at weddings and festivities. The insistent wailing of the zurna, usually played with continuous 'circular breathing', and the driving rhythms of two furiously wielded sticks on the drum slung round the neck is strongly associated with Gypsy musicians and this **shawm and drum duo** is found stretching back along the Gypsy route through Iran and into Central Asia, India and China.

The names of the instruments remain virtually unchanged across this vast territory. The word 'zurna' originates from the Persian *shahnai* (from *shah*, king and *nai*, flute), which bears the same name in India, becomes *sornai* or *sorna* in Afghanistan, *suona* in China and *zurna* (in Turkey); the Persian *dohol* becomes *davul* in Turkey and Greece. Similarly the Persian **santur** (hammer dulcimer) was probably brought by the Gypsies to Greece (*sandoúri*) and Hungary (*cimbalom*), where it's long been a favourite in Gypsy bands.

While many Gypsies went west through Turkey and into Europe, others left Persia and went south into the Arab lands and then on to **Egypt**, reaching as far south as **Sudan** in the fifteenth century. Musicians from Gypsy families have played an important role in Arabic music, in both the folk and classical fields. The late **Matar Muhammad**, for example, was one of the great *buzuq* player of the Arab world. The **buzuq**, a long-necked lute, is a popular instrument amongst Gypsy families of the Middle East.

There are still Gypsies – called **Nawar** – in **Upper Egypt** and they are frequently entertainers, acrobats, dancers and musicians, playing *rebab* or *rebabah* (upright fiddle), tambourines and those tell-tale castanets. Egypt's best-known group of traditional players, **The Musicians of the Nile,** includes Gypsy or Gypsy-related musicians.

It's possible that, with a migration across north Africa, it may have been Egyptian Gypsies that arrived in Moorish Spain, but most evidence suggests they came from the north.

Turkey

In **Turkey** today, the vast majority of restaurant and *gazino* (nightclub) musicians are Gypsy (called *Roman* in Turkish). They are also widely employed in the radio orchestras and for pop and arabesk recordings. However, the style of music with which Roman are inextricably linked is **fasil** (light classical) and **belly dance**.

With the virtuosity and panache that characterise Gypsy bands everywhere, these **fasil musicians** are masters of the Turkish clarinet (*klarnet* – a metal instrument usually pitched in G), violin (*kaman* – typically played with yelping and screeching glissandos to attract attention), *kanun* (lap-top zither lending a lacy texture to the ensemble) and darbuka (goblet drum). The *ud* (lute) and *cümbüş* (a type of banjo) are also common. The fast fasil tunes are driven by the *darbuka* while clarinet and violin weave melodies on top with furious runs and impossibly long sustained notes. The slower melodies and songs are highly ornamented, with lyrics of love, betrayal, poverty and drink.

Gypsy musicians were already in Constantinople (Istanbul) before the arrival of Mehmed the Conqueror in 1453. Throughout Anatolia, they were folk musicians and they were also involved in the **Karagöz shadow theatre** – which is thought to have been brought from the east, and may even be about a Gypsy character as *karagöz* means 'black eye'. Turkish historians relate that Mehmed brought Gypsy musicians to Istanbul and into the **court orchestras**. Ottoman music was sustained by a multicultural range of musicians who were organised into guilds according to their ethnic group. There were guilds of Turkish, Armenian, Greek, Jewish and Gypsy musicians.

The **belly dance** grew out of the professional and courtly entertainments which included the **raks** dance in which female dancers, clicking finger cymbals, moved the belly, shoulders and other parts of the upper-body while dancing. During the twentieth century Egyptian influences were absorbed into the dance and the style became the staple entertainment in cabarets and nightclubs, more or less erotic depending on the venue. Less showy and professional versions of the dancing can still be seen at Gypsy weddings, particularly, in Thrace (the European part of Turkey towards Bulgaria) where many of the best Gypsy musicians come from.

Clarinettist **Mustafa Kandıralı**, the **Erköse** brothers and the **Istanbul Oriental Ensemble**, led by **Burhan Öçal**, are among the top Turkish Gypsy performers (see Turkey article – p.409 – for more on them).

Greece

As throughout Turkey and the Balkans, Gypsies in **Greece** – known as **Yiftoi** ('Egyptians') – have long been involved in music as well as other typical Gypsy professions – horse-traders, acrobats, bear-trainers and Karagöz shadow puppeteers. They are found almost exclusively on the mainland and especially the Peloponnese; they are not part of the musical scene on the islands (where the communities have perhaps been too small to sustain them) and played little role in *rembétika* music which was dominated by Greeks from Asia Minor.

Traditionally Greek Gypsies played instrumental music and rarely sang. There were two types of ensemble, the ubiquitous **zurna and davul duo** and the more refined **koumpaneia** music, the equivalent of Turkish fasil, frequently heard in the coffee house or *Café Amán*, and at weddings, parties, and funerals. The clarinet is the lead instrument along with violin, lute or accordion.

Koumpaneia music was frequently played by Jews until World War II, but with the devastation of the Greek Jewish communities it became the province of Gypsy musicians. The city of Ioannina in Epirus has long been an important centre of this style.

More recently, with the growth of the Greek popular music industry over the past thirty years, Gypsy singers like **Yiannis Saleas** and **Kostas Pavlidis** have become popular commercial artists.

Eastern Europe

It's estimated that 47 percent of Europe's Gypsies live in the **Balkans** which makes the region the densest concentration of Gypsies in the world. Throughout eastern Europe, Gypsy musicians have been primary carriers of the folk tradition since the nineteenth century; indeed, most of what we think of as east European folk music is almost exclusively played by Gypsies. But the forms and sound of the music vary from place to place as the Gypsies have adapted to local styles; even the same band will vary its repertoire and instrumentation depending on who it is playing for.

Albania and Macedonia

In **south Albania** it's essentially the Epirus-style of *koumpaneia* music that's played on the clarinet, violin and accordion or lute. The same sort of music is called *čalgia* in **Macedonia** where it also exists in a modernised electric form largely played by Gypsies. In **Macedonia** and **Serbia**, it's the brass band that is predominant.

Emir Kusturica's film *The Time of the Gypsies* was shot in the Macedonian Gypsy suburb of **Shuto Orizari** (or Shutka), the largest Gypsy town in the world. The music from the film (by Goran Bregovic), and particularly the hit song "Ederlezi", a traditional tune (reputedly of Albanian origin) catapulted to international popularity by the film, is now a staple for Gypsy brass bands of the region and other groups in the Balkans and Turkey (where it became a hit performed by Sezen Aksu). **Hindi film soundtracks** are also a popular source of music. The tunes are often reworked into čoček forms far from the original, but they reflect an important awareness of Gypsy ethnic origins.

Amongst the leading Macedonian Gypsy musicians are the brass **Kočani Orkestar**, the great saxophone and clarinet player **Ferus Mustafov,** and the singer (usually in Romani) **Esma Redžepova**. Her voice, often with the ensemble led by her late husband, clarinetist **Stevo Teodosievski**, is one that takes you back the thousands of miles to the Gypsies' origins with its raw power and declamatory emotion.

Many of the east European Gypsy **female vocalists** like Redžepova, Slovakia's **Věra Bílá** and Hungary's **Mitsou** have a paradoxical but winning combination of childlike innocence and long-suffering world-weariness. That could be almost a defining quality of the typical Gypsy voices in eastern Europe and beyond.

Bulgaria

Bulgaria's large Gypsy population was during the Communist period, like the country's Turkish population, pressurised into Bulgarianising their names. Nonetheless, they remain a distinct group, and Bulgarian Gypsy musicians are important in local wedding band music.

Romania

In **Romania** it's string bands that predominate and the **lăutari** (Gypsy musicians) are the principal players. In Wallachia, the south of the country, a typical ensemble, called a *taraf* (the word comes from Arabic through Turkey, has fiddles, accordions and/or cimbaloms and a double bass. There are long accompanied ballads and furious dances, the lead fiddle carrying the melody, accompanying violins and the rippling textures of the cimbalom filling out the middle parts, and a rhythmic plucked bass. Almost every village will have its taraf, but the best-known internationally is the **Taraf de Haidouks** who have recorded and toured extensively. Their strength is that they are a real village band, used to regular wedding gigs, and not some folkloric ensemble. They are a loose group of around a dozen musicians who also break

Kalotaszegi fiddler Sándor Fodor

HUNGAROTRON

down into smaller units of three or four players in the way they might for different sized weddings in their home village of Clejani, near Bucharest.

In **Transylvania**, northwest Romania, within the sweep of the Carpathian mountains, Gypsies are still the principal musical providers, but the instrumental line-up and musical style is slightly different. Here it's a trio or quartet of lead fiddle, over the strong rhythmic base of one or two accompanying violins playing off-beat chords and a strongly-bowed double bass. Accordions and cimbaloms are rather less common. Transylvanian music has a more central European harmonic structure

Changing Styles: Taraf de Haidouks

Right across eastern Europe the Gypsies have, by default, helped preserve the local musical cultures, by maintaining its function and life, particularly in places such as Greece and Romania. Ironically, though, Gypsy musicians are rarely purist in their approach – they will borrow tunes and instruments voraciously and they're frequently accused of diluting the traditions. But the fact is, they have an ear for what their clients want and this is what keeps their music in demand. In the recordings of the *Taraf de Haidouks*, the most recorded Gypsy band of them all, you can hear the way the music has altered over the course of twelve years from their first disc (Romanie: *Les Lautari de Clejani* on Ocora) recorded in 1986 through to their most recent (*Dumbala Dumba* on CramWorld) in 1998.

The first Haidouks disc, before the band had played much beyond their immediate region, includes a lot of long ballads and some furious dance numbers from the pure Wallachian tradition. The more recent discs bring in Bulgarian and Yugoslav-style tunes from further afield, played by younger musicians in the group. There's a more self-conscious showiness and celebration of virtuosity in the younger musicians' playing, as well as

complex walking bass lines and instrumental solos that show a growing familiarity with stage performance and jazz.

While the group's success may have brought a faster change into their music the process is nothing new and the Romanian musicologist Constantin Bra*iloiu noted in the 1930s how the Gypsies were grafting on new dance rhythms and introducing elements from popular urban culture. That is one of the defining features of Gypsy music, and it's a process that works two ways. The Taraf de Haidouks' veteran violinist *Nicolae Neaşcu* creates an extraordinary sound by tieing a horse-hair to the bottom string of the violin and playing it by rhythmically pulling it at it with his resin-coated finger and thumb. The sound is like a deep cry from the earth (you can hear it on "The Wife of the Innkeeper" on the Ocora recording and, most famously, the "Ballad of the Dictator" on their first disc for CramWorld). The group have recently been recording with the Kronos Quartet who've adopted the idea in their own music – a new technique entering the Kronos' high art Californian sound world.

and sound, which is strikingly beautiful. Of the countless village Gypsy musicians, the **Palatca band** is well-known and the Kalotaszeg fiddler **Sándor 'Neti' Fodor** is recognised as one of the last great masters of the old style. **Maramureş**, to the north, also has its share of great Gypsy fiddlers, but as the territory rises into the Carpathian mountains Gypsy musicians thin out and 'indigenous' musicians take over. (See Romania article – p.237 – for more on these styles).

Poland

Generally, Gypsies are found on the lowlands and in urban areas, rarely in the highlands. They are not active in the rich folk tradition of the Tatras, for example, the heartland of folk music in **Poland**, although the country has Gypsy communities.

Slovakia

Slovakia has large Gypsy communities, although there are few musicians or singers who've become widely known. The Slovak singer **Valerie Buchačová** appears on Network's *Road of the Gypsies* compilation, but the greatest voice of the Slovak Gypsies – indeed, one of Europe's most remarkable Gypsy voices – is the formidable **Věra**

Bílá, now resident in the Czech Republic (see p.54). Small in height, wide in girth, Bílá has a powerful almost male-sounding voice that can really swing with her band **Kale**, as she expresses (in Romani) the hardship and tragedy of Gypsy life. Her song about drinking herself to death because her lover's left her, "Te me Pijav Lačhes Rosnes" has extraordinary grief-stricken sliding between pitches.

Hungary

Hungary has been famous for its Gypsy music since the end of the eighteenth century, although Gypsy musicians were already mentioned in the sixteenth century playing 'in the Turkish manner' for the Pashas occupying Hungary and 'in the Hungarian manner' for the Hungarian princes in Transylvania standing out against the occupation. Again Gypsy musicians can be seen caught up in both sides of a Muslim invasion.

The first celebrated Gypsy band leader was **Czinka Panna** (1711-1772) – a woman, very unusually, then as now. The most famous, though, was **János Bihari** (1764-1827), who was known as the Napoleon of the fiddle. Bihari's band usually consisted of four strings plus a cimbalom, the hammer dulcimer the Gypsies probably brought with them from Persia.

Many of Bihari's pieces are still in the repertoire of Hungary's restaurant ensembles today. The most celebrated fiddlers now playing in this style come from the Lakatos family – notably **Sándor Lakatos** and his nephew, the young **Roby Lakatos** – said to be direct descendants of Bihari himself. Their repertoire is essentially the light classical music of Liszt, Brahms and Monti's Csárdás played with lots of exaggerated rubato and up-front virtuosity. More slick than soul, but technically impressive.

There's a completely different style of music that the **rural Gypsies** in Hungary (and Romania) play amongst themselves. Oddly, considering the skill of the Gypsy musicians, it hardly uses instruments at all. It comprises slow songs called, in Romani, *loki djili* and dance songs, *khelimaski djili*. Though there are no instruments, many of these songs are accompanied by rhythmic grunts, the tapping of sticks and cans and imitations of instruments in a 'doobie-doo-bie-doobie' sort of way called **oral-bassing**.

These 'rolled songs' and dance songs, which have a wild, improvised sound are hard to hear without a personal invitation to an event, though some of this music features on the *Dumbala Dumba* album of the Taraf de Haidouks and it has also provided raw material for some of Hungary's professional Gypsy groups, notably **Kalyi Jag** (Romani for Black Fire) and **Ando Drom** (On the Road). Both have added guitars and other instruments to the vocal and percussion line-up and both groups have strong dark-voiced vocalists singing in Romani – **Gusztáv Varga** and **József Balogh** in Kalyi Jag and the extraordinary female singer **Mitsou** in Ando Drom (see Hungary article – p.161 – for more on these groups).

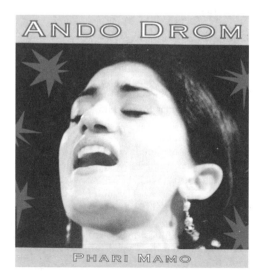

Russia

In **Russia** Gypsies became popular performers in the late eighteenth century, during the reign of Catherine the Great. It's said that Count Orlov heard Gypsy musicians in Moldavia and in St Petersburg assembled a Gypsy chorus from his Romani serfs. In 1807 he freed them to form the first professional chorus in Russia. They sang Russian folksongs, but enlivened with a romanticised Gypsy spirit. *Tsiganschina* (Gypsyness), meaning a wild, untamed quality, became a preoccupation and stereotype in Russian literature (for instance Pushkin's *The Gypsies*), however far from the truth it may have been.

During the course of the nineteenth century Gypsy choral singing gave way to romances and urban songs which were hugely popular at themed restaurants, like *Yar* on the outskirts of Moscow, to which it was customary to drive in a troika in winter. While the Gypsies propagated a romanticised view of Gypsy life, they probably also created the stereotyped image of the Russian soul with sad songs, fiery dances and devil-may-care drinking.

The 1917 revolution was a blow to the Russian Gypsies and most chose to leave. Their aristocratic patrons had gone, they were persecuted as entertainers of the bourgeoisie, and the Bolsheviks introduced bans on nomadism. Even so, the love of Gypsy music didn't go away. "Dark Eyes", one of the most popular Gypsy songs was taken up by 'folk' ensembles and Red Army choirs. **Romen**, a Gypsy theatre, was established in Moscow in 1931 and still survives today.

One of the most popular Russian émigré performers, from the 1930s through to the '50s, was **Pyotr Leschenko**, not himself a Gypsy, but a celebrated singer of Gypsy songs, romances and tangos. His recordings were smuggled into Soviet Russia and were avidly danced to and cried over round the gramophone. In Bucharest, he set up a themed restaurant with Tiffany lamps and a mural of a Russian troika harking back to the romantic days of *Yar*. In 1951 Leschenko was arrested on stage in his Gypsy dress and died three years later in a penal camp near Bucharest.

The Russian Gypsy violinist **Jean Goulesco** (who played for the Tsar for many years) left St Petersburg in 1917 with his newly born daughter **Lida Goulesco** and settled in Paris where she became another of the great Russian Gypsy voices in exile.

Currently the best-known Russian Gypsy group is **Loyko** – two classically trained Gypsy violinists with guitar accompaniment (based in Ireland). They

The Gipsy Kings

The sound of *The Gipsy Kings*, and their mega-hit song "Bamboleo", seem so redolent of tapas bar nights in the late 1980s that it's hard to imagine they might be the real thing. But they are Gypsies, from Arles and Montpelier in the south of France, and they are kings, from the *Reyes* (Kings) family who migrated from Spain to France during the Spanish Civil War. José Reyes, the father of lead singer *Nicholas Reyes*, was a celebrated flamenco singer and his children were brought up to follow in the tradition.

"There's a Gypsy legend," Nicholas Reyes recounts, "that says when an old Gypsy singer or guitarist is going to die, he will sing or play for a pregnant woman. Then the child that is born will inherit his gift." It's that easy. The Reyes children formed a group called *Los Reyes* and The Gipsy Kings were formed when the four brothers, who were essentially singers, joined with their cousins, the *Baliardos*, who were guitarists. The music they play is rooted in the popular, rhythmic Rumba Gitana style of southern France and northern Spain.

Legend has it that the band were busking in St Tropez when they were spotted by Brigitte Bardot who invited them to perform at a celebrity party. Their fans soon included Elton John, Peter Gabriel, Duran Duran, Francois Mitterand, Princess Diana and Eric Clapton. Now with eight albums to their credit – some of them broadening or diluting the music, depending on your point of view, with accordions, synthesisers, strings and a Latin horn section – The Kings are frequently to be found in the *Billboard* World Music Charts and their *Greatest Hits* album is said to be the biggest-selling World Music album of all time.

continue the prerequisites of the Russian Gypsy tradition – heightened emotion, impulsiveness, fire and breathtaking virtuosity.

Spain

The most celebrated Gypsy music is, of course, **flamenco**, born of the fusion of cultures in Andalucía, southern Spain. Flamenco isn't Gypsy (*Gitano*, in Spanish) in origin, but – as with most of the music in this survey – it's a style Gypsies have made their own.

Gypsies were first recorded in Spain in 1425 and following on from the Christian re-conquest of Spain in 1492 the first anti-Gypsy (and anti-Muslim and anti-Jewish) legislation was introduced. Nonetheless, Gypsy communities grew in Spain over the following century, particularly in Andalucía, where many migrated – from Europe, perhaps also from North Africa – to fill the gap left by the expelled Moors.

Over the years a tradition of leading flamenco families grew up in the main Andaluían cities – Granada, Cordoba, Seville – and in the nineteenth century, with the rise of flamenco cafes and *juergas* (private gatherings), Gypsies and flamenco became firmly linked in the popular imagination.

There have been flowerings and declines in the music since then, but districts like Triana in Seville still retain something of the traditional character.

One of the things that characterises flamenco is the dominance of emotion over text. Often the words are broken up and obscured by sighs and emotional outbursts; vowels are often extended into long oriental-sounding melismas which take flight as the emotion is conveyed through the performance – the singing of Pastora Pavón, known as **Niña de Los Peines** (1890-1969), is renowned for this. It is tempting to liken this declamatory style of singing with the other Gypsy styles in northwest India and eastern Europe – and indeed flamenco and the eastern European vocal styles share the expressive outbursts of "ai" and "yai" in the performance of the music.

There is an extended article on flamenco elsewhere in this book (see p.279).

France and Catalonia

Gypsies were first mentioned in **France**, near the Rhine, in the early fifteenth century, but these days the main areas of concentration are in the south – in the **Camargue** at the mouth of the Rhône and around **Perpignan** (Roussillon).

Bratsch

The Perpignan Gypsies have moved back and forth from Spanish **Catalonia** over the years and the music to be heard on both sides of the border – in Barcelona and Perpignan – is **Rumba Gitana** (Gypsy Rumba), made most famous by **The Gipsy Kings**. It grew from the Gypsy music of Catalonia, but with a melange of flamenco, north African music, Cuban and rock grafted on. Its essence, though, is virtuoso guitar players, some agile clapping and those formidable declamatory Gypsy vocals – in Catalan or Spanish.

In Spanish Catalonia, the big star is **Peret** who opened the Barcelona Olympics, while the late **Gato Perez** was one of the best-known stars of rock-rumba, and **Antonio Gonzalez** keeps to the rough and tumble rose in the teeth and glass in the hand style of this music's roots. In France, alongside **The Gipsy Kings**, who grew out of an earlier group called Los Reyes (see box on previous page), look out for the **Espinas** family and **Chico & the Gypsies**, led by former Gipsy King, **Chico Bouchikhi**.

An earlier French-based Gypsy star was the jazz musician **Django Reinhardt** (1910-1953); he was actually born in Belgium, but spent most of his life working in France. He was working as a guitarist, aged eighteen, when a fire broke out in the caravan where he was sleeping. His left leg and third and fourth fingers of his left hand were badly burnt, but guitar therapy led to him adopting his particular playing style and a hugely sucessful career in jazz swing. He formed the Quintet Hot Club de France in 1931 with violinist **Stephane Grappelli** and, after the war, embarked on hugely successful international tours. A dynasty of French Gypsy musicians, notably **Angelo Debarre**, has continued Reinhardt's style of Gypsy swing.

The most interesting Gypsy musician working in France today is guitarist and oud player **Thierry 'Titi' Robin**. He began playing in the Rumba Gitana style but his bands these days frequently draw in great flamenco artists or, harking back to Indian roots, such musicians as Rajasthani singer Gulabi Sapera and tabla player Hameed Khan. His recent recordings have also explored north African and Sub-Saharan music – always with sensitivity and musical depth.

Although not Gypsy at its core, the Paris-based group **Bratsch** should be an honourary Gypsy band. They can be a dream wedding band in any number of styles along the Gypsy road and are frequently joined by Gypsy guest artists.

There are two important French Gypsy festivals. In the Camargue there's a vast gathering at **Saintes Maries de la Mer** where Gypsies from France and Spain congregate to celebrate the feast day of their patron saint, Sara, on May 24th and 25th. Here the music is predominantly flamenco in style with a large number making the pilgrimage from Andalucía. A secular music festival, **Mosaïque Gitane** takes place each July in Arles.

Britain and Ireland

Gypsies reached the **British Isles** around 1500 and there are estimated to be approximately 100,000 in Britain today. The Irish 'Tinkers' are probably not of Rom origin, but indigenous folk who took to a travelling life.

The music of the British Gypsies is very much part of the common folk heritage, although there are some trad songs ("The Squire and the Gypsy", for example) about the Gypsy way of life, and a few that include elements of the Romani language. Popular instruments are those commonly found in traditional British music – the violin, mouth-organ, melodeon and spoons. Most contemporary British Gypsy songs seem to follow **Country and Western** styles.

discography

There is a mass of Roma information – including disc reviews – available at *www.geocities.com/~patrin/*

General compilations

 Gypsy Queens
(World Network, Germany).

A daughter of Network's *Road of the Gypsies* collection (see below), this 2-disc set focuses on six women singers – Esma Redžepova and Džansever (from Macedonia), Romica Puceanu and Gabi Lunca (from Romania), Mitsou of Ando Drom (from Hungary) and La Macanita (from Spain). It's passionate and emotional stuff and, as ever with Network, nicely packaged with a full-colour booklet.

 Latcho Drom (Caroline, France).

The soundtrack for Tony Gatlif's rather ramshackle film about Gypsy music features fine contributions from Rajasthan to Spain, with stops en route in Egypt, Turkey, Romania, Hungary, Slovakia and France. Aural connections are pretty self-evident.

The Rough Guide to Gypsy Music
(World Music Network, UK).

If you want a single disc on gypsy music, this compilation will do nicely. Alongside obvious choices such as Taraf de Haïdouks and Musafir, there are more surprising selections from Greece, Albania, Finland and the UK.

 Road of the Gypsies
(World Network, Germany).

This 2-CD set of Gypsy music, stretching from Rajasthan to Spain, is a superlative compilation. It could perhaps have included more from that western end but makes up for it with Camarón's excellent homage to the Gypsies' Indian roots and a fantastic range of tracks from eastern Europe including Goran Bregovic's film music, the wonderful Esma Redžepova (singing the Roma anthem, here titled "Szelem Szelem"), the Taraf de Haidouks, Hungary's Kályi Jag and Ando Drom, and

strong Greek and Turkish contributions. The notes are a little disappointing, but this is an essential first buy.

India/Middle East

Compilations

Inde – Rajasthan:
Musiciens professionnels populaires (Ocora, France).

The best introduction to the various caste-musicians of Rajasthan, including Langa and Manganiyar performers. There's more than a hint of Gypsy-style showmanship in many of these tracks. Good photos and notes.

The Mystic Fiddle of the Proto-Gypsies: Masters of Trance Music (Shanachie, US).

A haunting collection of instrumental numbers from veteran Baluchi sarod players who live in Pakistan. Playing of great intensity and power, whether they are Proto-Gypsies or not.

Sulukule: Rom Music of Istanbul
(Traditional Crossroads, US).

A splendid selection of instrumental numbers and songs that really evoke the earthy character of Turkish urban Gypsy music. The band is led by Kemani Cemal (named after his instrument, the violin – *keman*). There are good notes about the history of Turkish Gypsy music and translations of lyrics.

Artists

Istanbul Oriental Ensemble

This ensemble of Roma musicians, led by percussionist Burhan Öçal, are Turkey's best Gypsy recording artists. They feature a traditional line-up of clarinet, violin, oud, kanun and darbuka drums.

 Gypsy Rum
(World Network, Germany).

Fourteen tracks of tight instrumental playing. Emotional twists and lightning virtuosity will have your belly dancing – and listen out for the screaming shrieks from Fethi Tekaygil's violin. If you're hooked, there's a follow-up, **Sultan's Secret Door** (also World Network, Germany).

Mustafa Kandıralı

Born in Kandıralı in 1930, this Gypsy clarinet player toured the Middle East, Soviet Union and the US as a *fasil* band leader in the 1960s. In the US he had his formative encounter with jazz, which earned him the nickname of 'Turkey's Benny Goodman'. Charlie Parker would not be a bad comparison either. Kandıralı's performances have a quiet radicalism to them and the melodic invention of his improvisations blend seamlessly with the restless, dance tunes.

◎ **Caz Roman** (World Network, Germany).

This is the epitome of instrumental fasil, including some of the genre's best-known instrumentalists – Ahmet Meter (kanun), Metin Bükey (ud) and Ahmet Kulik (darbuka). The final section of dance tunes was recorded live at a 1984 concert.

Karşilama

A group of Istanbul Gypsy musicians led by Selim Sesler on clarinet, with Canadian vocalist Brenna MacCrimmon.

◎ **Karşilama** (Green Goat, Canada; Kalan, Turkey).

Rom music from western Turkey and the Balkans, played with real panache. It's especially good to hear some of the vocal repertoire – gleaned from archive recordings and manuscripts – so expertly sung.

Matar Muhammad

Matar Muhammad (1939-1995) was born into a Gypsy family in the Bekaa Valley of Lebanon. He took up the buzuq aged seven and made his professional debut in the early 1960s on the BBC's Arabic programmes. With performances at the *Baalbek Festival* he became celebrated throughout the Arab worlds, but sadly partial paralysis stopped him playing for the last twenty years of his life.

◎ **Hommage à un maître du buzuq** (Inédit, France).

Recordings of some of Muhammad's last performances live in the Beirut Theatre in 1972. What makes him a remarkable musician is the free-wheeling imaginative fantasy of his improvisations within the classical Arabic modes. There are four such here, and the exclamations and applause of an appreciative audience add to the extraordinary atmosphere.

Musafir

Musafir is a loose group of mainly Rajasthani Langa musicians put together by tabla player Hameed Khan. The group perform Gypsy and folk repertoire alongside spectacular circus and fakir displays.

◎ **Musafir: Gypsies of Rajasthan** (BMG/Blue Flame, Germany).

Good professional performances of folk music, Sapera snake charmers' music and devotional songs to Baba Ramdev. Instrumentation includes several flutes and pipes, sarangi and harmonium.

The Musicians of the Nile

A group of fine traditional musicians from Upper Egypt with links to Gypsy families, although these things are hard to ascertain in Egypt. They are led by singer and rababah (upright two-string fiddle) maestro Metqal Qenawi Metqal.

◎ **Luxor to Isna** (RealWorld, UK).

The ensemble play dry deserty music on the zumarin (the Egyptian version of the zurna), with drums and an unusual arghul (a double clarinet that can be extended to alter the pitch). There's also strong rootsy singing and playing on the rababah with lots of overtones.

Nedim Nalbantoğlu

Turkish violinist Nalbantoğlu was born into a musical family and plays classical, jazz and Turkish music. His playing has all those difficult-to-define elements of exaggeration, dynamism, kitsch and staggering virtuosity.

◎ **Müzik kimé aittir** (Al Sur, France).

The title translates as 'Who the music belongs to' – which could be hard to define as this is contemporary roots fusion, albeit with a strong Gypsy character. The line-up features Romanian accordionist Roberto de Brasov, plus guitar and percussion, and tracks include a great version of a Bulgarian tune made famous by Ivo Papasov, here reworked as "News from Constantinople".

Eastern Europe, the Balkans and Russia

Compilations

◎ **Greece: Epirus – Takoutsia, musicians of Zagori** (Inedit, France).

Lovely recordings of an old-style *koumpaneia* Gypsy band from Epirus in northwestern Greece. Various members of the Kapsalis family feature in an ensemble with clarinet, violin, lute and tambourine. The disc opens with a rare recording of elaborately ornamented funeral music, plus dance music and drinking songs.

◎ **Gypsy Music of Macedonia and Neighbouring Countries** (Topic, UK).

A good disc for those wanting to explore the characteristic Gypsy duo of zurna and drum in the Balkans and beyond. Its title is rather misleading as it features only one track from Macedonia, but plenty more from Kosovo, Romania, Greece and Turkey. Wild stuff recorded in the 1970s and '80s.

◎ **Music of Greece's Gypsies** (FM Records, Greece).

A great disc recorded live at a concert featuring some of Greece's top Gypsy performers. Very strong vocals from Eleni Vitali, Kostas Pavlidis, Yiannis Saleas and others plus masterly instrumental playing, notably on *zurna* and clarinet. Some songs are traditional in character, others more modern. Bregovic's "Ederlezi" inevitably appears.

◎ **Rom Sam Ame!** (Fonti Musicali, Belgium).

A specialised, but excellent survey of authentic Gypsy songs from six towns and villages in central and eastern Hungary – vocals, in Hungarian and Romani, with accompanying spoons and struck pots and tables. Gypsy music for Gypsies. Excellent photos and notes.

Artists

Ando Drom

Ando Drom are currently the most successful of Hungary's professional Romany ensembles. The band have been around since the early 1980s, led by Jenö Zsigó, and have transformed the rural Gypsy traditions into a dynamic concert music featuring the swarthy vocals of Mónika 'Mitsou' Juhász Miczura.

Phari Mamo (World Network, Germany).

This is, as the subtitle says, 'magnificent Gypsy music from Budapest' – and not the schmaltzy café variety. Ando Drom, with a vocal and percussion line-up, has real soul and a melancholy edge. They are backed on this recording by violin and accordion players from the French group Bratsch.

Věra Bílá/Kale

Bílá is an extraordinary Slovak Gypsy singer, now resident in the Czech Republic. With her band Kale – guitars, backing vocals and hand-claps, with occasional guest musicians on sax, piano, violin – she has recorded two albums in Romani on the Czech BMG subsidiary, Ariola.

 Kale Kaloré
(BMG/Ariola, Czech Republic).

This 1998 ablum, Bílá's second CD, is the more Gypsy in character, although her band have also picked up Latin and Rumba Gitana ingredients. Catchy tunes and some tragic-sounding tracks – "Te Me Pijav Laches Rosnes" (I Always Drink) – in which Bílá's dark voice reaches into the depths.

Sándor 'Neti' Fodor

Neti (born 1922) is the most respected Gypsy fiddler of the Kalotaszeg region of Transylvania.

**Hungarian Music from Transylvania:
Sándor Fodor** (Hungaroton, Hungary).

A compelling disc of both Hungarian and Romanian music from Transylvania, played with real energy and bite, by an old master.

Kočani Orkestar

This Macedonian Gypsy brass band is led by trumpet player Naat Veliov and comes, as you might expect, from the town of Kočani. The line-up features two trumpets, three tubas, sax, clarinet, zurla (shawm) and drums.

L'orient est rouge (CramWorld, Belgium).

The title comes from the Chinese Communist anthem – totally transformed into a Balkan dance – which opens the album. Other cuts include a radical arrangement of the popular "Ederlezi' tune, with an endless slow *taksim* (improvisation) on trumpet and zurla leading into a frenetic dance, and the Romani anthem "Djelem, Djelem". Full-bodied and brash.

Lida Goulesco

Born in Petrograd in 1917, Goulesco was taken by her violinist father when he fled Russia after the revolution to Paris where she grew up in an atmosphere of decadent Russian Gypsy parties in restaurants and cabarets.

Chants folkloriques tziganes
(Buda/Musique du Monde, France).

This is probably as close as you can get to the music played at decadent restaurants in Moscow and St Petersburg around the end of the nineteenth century. Goulesco's husky voice speaks volumes, guitars and fiddles provide the right accompaniment and lots of drunken-sounding guests make it into a party.

Nicolae Gutsa

Nicolae Gutsa was born near Petroşeni, Romania, in 1967 and now works in Timişoara in the Banat region. A very popular singer, he performs traditional music in a contemporary style.

The Greatest Living Gypsy Voice
(Auvidis/Silex, France).

Despite the absurd title, this is a great disc with excellent vocals and some wild instrumental playing, notably from Ion Trifoi on violin and Remus Kiroaci on sax in a band that also includes piano accordion, guitar and synth.

Roby Lakatos

Born in 1965, Roby is one of the younger members of the famous Lakatos dynasty of professional Hungarian Gypsy musicians. He learned in the family tradition as well as at the Budapest Music Academy. He has lived in Belgium since 1985 where he's expanded his style to include jazz and Stephane Grappelli-style violin. The Hungarian café-style is often sneered at, but Lakatos makes it work.

In Gypsy Style (M&W, Netherlands).

The violin swoops and sighs with the characteristic rippling of cimbalom and strings on these Hungarian, Russian and Django Reinhardt melodies, along with the inevitable Gypsy standard, "The Lark". Inventive arrangements, great virtuoso playing plus a strong personality.

Pyotr Leschenko

Leschenko was a hugely popular Russian exile singer from the 1930s through to the '50s, when he was arrested and imprisoned in Romania. He was not a Gypsy, but was famed for his Gypsy songs and tangos.

Gipsy Songs & Other Passions (Oriente, Germany).

Atmospheric performances recorded (in England) in 1931 and containing the best of Leschenko's Gypsy related material, plus the odd tango and waltz. Good remastered recordings. There are several other such reissues on Oriente.

Loyko

A band comprising Russian Gypsy fiddlers Sergei Erdenko and Oleg Ponomarev, the first more traditional, the second more experimental, with guitarist Vadim Kulitsky. All were classically trained in Moscow, though they are now based in Ireland.

Road of the Gypsies (World Network, Germany).

A mixture of newly composed and traditional material, catchy and virtuoso, with a sound that seems a whole lot bigger than an acoustic trio.

Ferus Mustafov

Clarinettist and sax player Mustafov is one of the top band leaders in Macedonia and has worked for the Romani language radio and TV in Skopje.

King Ferus (GlobeStyle, UK).

An excellent collection of dances and songs in catchy and seemingly unplayable rhythms. Good-time music for your Shuto Orizari style wedding.

Palatca Band

Palatca are one of the best Transylvanian Gypsy Bands, from the Mezőség region. They feature two violins, two accompanying violas playing chords, and a string bass.

Báré – Magyarpalatka (Fono, Hungary).

The third disc in Fono's *Új Pátria* series of traditional Transylvanian music. It's the real thing, with dodgy but idiomatic intonation. Powerful stuff with exquisite slow dances, songs and furious fast csárdás dances where the bows really lay into the battered instruments.

Taraf de Haidouks

A loose ensemble of Romanian Gypsy musicians from the village of Clejani near Bucharest. Some of the most genuine, inspiring and skilled Gypsy musicians in Europe.

 Dumbala Dumba
(CramWorld, Belgium).

The Taraf's 1998 outing, which includes the sort of music the Gypsies play for themselves with percussion and vocalisation as well as their spectacular mix of old- and new-style repertoire, performed with a brace of fiddles, cimbaloms, accordions and bass. For the purer style try their first disc – recorded in 1986 before they acquired the Haidouks name **Roumanie: Les Lautari de Clejani** (Ocora, France).

Western Europe

Compilations

 Early Cante Flamenco:
Classic Recordings from the 1930s (Arhoolie, US).

Great recordings from the seminal early flamenco artists, including Pastora Pavón "La Nina de los Peines"; her younger brother Tomas Pavón, one of the greatest Cante Gitano performers; the flamboyant voice of Manolo Caracol; and Manuel Vallejo, one of the first non-gypsy singers hailed as king.

 My Father's the King of the Gypsies: Music of English & Welsh Travellers & Gypsies (Topic, UK).

Volume 11 of the extraordinary *Voice of the People* anthology of British folk music, this comprises mainly unaccompanied songs, plus melodeon and stepdance tunes. Most of the repertoire is not specifically Gypsy. And it's not easy listening.

 ¡Vaya Rumba!
(Nascente, UK).

The subtitle proclaims 'fiery rhythms from the heart of Catalonia', which means the Rumba Gitana style popularised by The Gipsy Kings. This is a good, budget-priced compilation beginning with Antonio Gonzalez who sounds like a down-home, husky version of The Gipsy Kings, and moving through more commercial styles from Peret and Gato Perez to Los Lachos' seductive rumba version of Mory Kante's hit "Yeke Yeke" – a real World Music number.

El Camarón de la Isla

Spain's greatest flamenco singer of the second half of the twentieth century, El Camarón de la Isla (born José Monje Cruz) had a voice of unrivalled passion and flair, and was unsurpassed in his interpretation and tone. He died, aged 41, in 1992 and was mourned throughout Spain, with all the national newspapers devoting their front pages to his life (troubled by drink and heroin) and career.

 Soy Gitano
(Phillips, Spain).

A 1989 recording with the London Royal Philharmonic Orchestra and regular guitar accompaniist Tomatito, amongst others, this begins with the dramatic and confessional "Soy gitano" (I am a Gypsy) and ends with the song to Lorca lyrics "Nana del caballo grande" (Lullaby of the big horse). It is perhaps the most clearly 'Gypsy' of Camarón's many albums.

Bratsch

Bratsch are a new wave French roots, Paris-based, five-piece band featuring guitar, violin, accordion, clarinet, double-bass and vocals. They are not Gypsies but play post-modern Gypsy and Gypsy-style repertoire, often with Gypsy singers and musicians as guests.

 Rien dans les poches (World Network, Germany).

An entrancing 1998 album with guest Bulgarian, Iranian and Hungarian Gypsy (from Andro Drom) musicians. The opening track plays on slow moving improvisations and clashing harmonies which finally trip over into a Balkan style dance. A couple of klezmer-style tracks underline the connections between Gypsy and Jewish repertoire plus one of the best versions of the ubiquitous "Ederlezi" on record with searing vocals from Mitsou of Ando Drom.

Espinas Family

Three brothers, Jérémie, Moïse and Salomon Espinas, plus uncle Jérôme from a family of Perpignan Gypsies.

 Tekameli: Chants Religieux Gitans
(Long Distance, France).

Devout Catalan style rumba canticles for the evangelical Catholic church. Strong, passionate voices, guitars and clapping palmas. A rootsy Gipsy Kings sound in the pews.

The Gipsy Kings

Has anyone missed The Gipsy Kings? It seems unlikely, given their dominance at bars and cafés worldwide in the late 1980s/early '90s. They are basically a Catalan Rumba group, with lead singer Nicholas Reyes providing a nicely rough edged sound and harmonies, handclaps and guitar from other members of the Reyes and Balliardo families. They diluted their original sound somewhat on the early '90s albums *Este Mundo* and *Love & Liberté*, but returned to rootsier music with 1996's *Tierra Gitana*.

 Gipsy Kings
(A1, UK/Nonesuch, US).

World superstardom beckoned for the Gipsy Kings on this 1998 album, with its bouncy and unforgettable rendering of "Bamboleo" and the soaring vocals of "Djobi Djoba". It had fine guitar playing, infectious melodies and rhythms, and just the one questionable MOR track – "A mi Manera" (My Way). If you want to hear a slightly different selection, **Best of the Gypsy Kings** (Nonesuch, US) is a good alternative.

Thierry Robin

French Gypsy guitarist 'Titi' Robin was inspired initially by the singing of El Camarón and the oud playing of Mounir Bachir. He has been at the centre of several cross-cultural music events and recordings and is one of the most interesting musicians on the French World Music scene.

 Gitans
(Auvidis/Silex, France).

Of Robin's several recordings, this 1993 album is the one with the strongest Gypsy character, featuring guest musicians from India and Spain on top notch arrangements. **Kali Gadji** (1998) is another good outing, though less Gypsy in character, ranging into North African music with powerful sax playing from Renaud Pion.

Hungary

a musical mother tongue

Of all the countries in Eastern Europe, Hungary probably has the most accessible folk music scene. This is not because there are villages bursting with Gypsy music, but because as Hungary has transformed itself into a modern urbanised country it has created a lively movement of players, dancers and enthusiasts who are in touch with the music's roots and play it continuously in Budapest. And it's out of this scene that Hungary's best-known performers, Márta Sebestyén and Muzsikás, have developed. **Simon Broughton** tells the story.

"It's crucial for us Hungarians to play our music, dance our dances and know our musical mother tongue. Without these things we lose our identity." So a music researcher told me in Transylvania, and his sentiments are echoed by most people involved in Hungarian folk music. In Eastern Europe everybody's music stands as a national label, but it has an especially potent force for Hungarians.

The Magyars – like the Romanians to their east – are a cultural island with a distinctive language unrelated to the sea of Slavs around them. Like the people, the music is now thoroughly "Europeanised" but it remains highly distinctive. In very large part, this is down to the Hungarian language, which is invariably stressed on the first syllable, lending a strongly accented dactylic rhythm to the music. Its infectious sound has been surprisingly influential on neighbouring countries (thanks perhaps to the common Austro–Hungarian history) and it's not uncommon to hear Hungarian-sounding tunes in Romania, Slovakia and southern Poland.

In Transylvania (Romania) and southern Slovakia there are also large Hungarian minorities where village music is still a living tradition – far more so than in Hungary itself (see Romania article p.237). In these areas the music as well as the mother tongue are crucially important in maintaining that all-important sense of identity.

Bartók, Kodály and Roots East

Béla Vikár started collecting Hungarian folk music as early as 1895 with an Edison phonograph machine, so the composers **Béla Bartók** and **Zoltán Kodály** were not the first to systematically investigate the peasant music of Hungary. But

Bartók with his cylinder recorder in 1908

they were the most famous and influential. On their collecting trips with a phonograph at the turn of the century, they revealed the 'real' Hungarian folk music – as opposed to the popular salon tunes played by Gypsy orchestras that were taken to be folk music until then. Both men were fine ethnographers as well as composers and by using folk material in their own work they not only found their individual voices but brought the folk music to the attention of an international audience. They were also responsible for recognising the Asiatic roots of Hungarian music.

Kodály's interest was in Hungarian music and the creation of a truly national style. Bartók's concerns were more international, rooted in the peasant music of all the nationalities of Eastern Europe and beyond. By the time the First World War brought his expeditions in Eastern Europe to an end, he had collected over 3500 Romanian tunes, 3000 Slovak, 2721 Hungarian, plus Ruthenian, Serbian and Bulgarian pieces.

What Bartók and Kodály discovered on their expeditions to remote Hungarian villages was a music that was earthy, fresh and hitherto unknown. More than that, it was distinctly Hungarian and in its oldest layers stretched back to the **Magyars' roots** on the fringes of Europe or beyond. Exactly where the Hungarians originated is still debated; but they are not of Indo-European stock like most Europeans, but belong – with the Finns and Estonians – to the Finno-Ugrian linguistic group, whose ancestors lived over 4000 years ago in the Ural region and southwest Siberia.

Much research has been done to see if there are musical connections between the Hungarians and Finns but virtually none have been found; not surprising, perhaps, as the tribes are thought to have split around 4000 years ago. Kodály, however, found a link between the oldest Hungarian songs, with their pentatonic (five-note) tunes and descending pattern, and songs of the Mari people, a Finno-Ugrian group who still live close to the ancestral home around the Volga and Kama rivers in Russia. Kodály came up with a substantial number of Hungarian tunes that had direct equivalents in these eastern territories: musical fossils apparently dating back to a shared past 2500 years old. "Time may have wiped away the eastern features from the face of the Magyar community," he concluded "but in the depths of its soul, where the springs of music lie, there still lives an element of the original east, which links it with peoples whose language it has long ceased to understand, and who are today so different in mind and spirit."

For those seriously interested in the music of this little-known area of Russia and the links with Hungarian music, there's a CD of Finno-Ugrian and Turkic melodies from the Volga-Kama on the Hungarotron label.

'New Style' and Gypsy Bands

The Hungarians' musical history evolved as they settled in the Carpathian basin (around 895–902 AD), adopted Christianity (under the canonised King Stephen who ruled from 1000 to 1038) and began to come under the influence of European culture, before Suleyman the Magnificent put a stop to that in 1526 and Hungary endured one hundred and fifty years of Turkish rule. But most of the Hungarian music familiar today has its roots in the eighteenth century when the country rebuilt itself as part of the **Hapsburg Empire**. The close contact with central European culture brought 'new style' music with a regular metric structure for dancing and marching instead of the free speech rhythms of the old style.

Solo bagpipers used to play these tunes for village dances but they were gradually replaced by the new **Gypsy orchestras**, and the medieval-style drone accompaniment gave way to the central European harmony of the string bands. Just as bagpipes mean Scotland, so Gypsy bands mean Hungary in the popular imagination. When nationalist composers like Liszt composed their "Hungarian Dances" and "Rhapsodies" in the latter part of the nineteenth century they took as their models the music of the urban Gypsy orchestras much as you can hear it in Budapest restaurants today. Most of this repertoire, often showy and sickly sweet, was composed in the nineteenth century.

Following Bartók's lead, folklorists tend to dismiss this urban Gypsy style in favour of authentic "peasant music". Yet the music the Gypsies play is no less Hungarian, and it has more in common with peasant music than the folklorists like to admit. Hungarian folk song was often an influence on popular songs, and even in the remotest parts of the country urban songs have become part of the oral tradition and serve the function of folk songs. In the Transylvanian village of Szék you can still hear a *csárdás*, which pops up in Brahms' "Hungarian Dances", often cited as prime examples of Gypsy-style fakery.

Gypsies (or more correctly Roma) were first recorded in Hungary in the fourteenth century, and the country's Gypsy musicians became famous from the eighteenth century on. "The Hungarian has a musical score which can compete with that of any nation . . . This score lives and travels in the form of the Hungarian Gypsy," wrote one observer in 1858. Most of the early Gypsy bands seem to have been located in western Hungary and were often invited to perform at aristocratic celebrations.

In addition to society gigs, the Gypsies also performed at recruiting ceremonies where young lads were enticed into the army with **verbunkos** music (from *werbung* – the German word meaning 'recruit'). The Hapsburgs only introduced universal conscription in 1868, so before that the men were lured with dancing, music and the promise of a carefree life. Vebunkos music is strongly rhythmic, consisting of a slow dance followed by a fast one. The steps were developed from the showy men's dances of the village. Probably the most famous verbunkos tune is the Rákóczi Song, which later evolved into the Rákóczi March – featured in compositions by Berlioz and Liszt.

The Hungarians, always searching for a musical identity, found it in the verbunkos music and it typified the Hungarians abroad. A German officer saw the dance in 1792: "It expresses the character of the nation in an extraordinary way. The true

Hungarian dances have to begin really slowly and then continue faster. They are much more becoming to a serious moustached face than to a young lad no matter what forced capers they do. The whole art of the dancer is to be seen in the artistic movement of his legs and the rhythmic clicking of his spurs." The slow and fast dances of verbunkos music have been seen as the two contrasting aspects of the Hungarian character and in the nineteenth century, Liszt felt unequivocally that the Gypsies were Hungary's national musicians and verbunkos was the inspiration for his "Hungarian Rhapsodies" (including the Rákóczi March).

Amongst the most celebrated Gypsy performers of the "golden age" were the female *primás* (lead violinist) **Czinka Panna** (1711–1772) and Gypsy musicians from the town of Galánta – both celebrated in pieces by Kodály. The most famous Gypsy band leader was **János Bihari**, born in 1764 and known as the Napoleon of the fiddle! "Like drops of some fiery spirit essence, the notes of this magic violin came to our ears", wrote Liszt. Bihari's band usually consisted of four strings plus a *cimbalom*, the hammer dulcimer so common in Gypsy bands, derived, it's thought, from the Indian santur and brought with the Gypsies.

The most celebrated fiddlers now playing in this style come from the **Lakatos family** – notably Sándor Lakatos and his nephew, the young Roby Lakatos – said to be direct descendants of Bihari himself. Their repertoire is essentially the light classical music of Liszt, Brahms and Monti's Csárdás played with a showy verve and abandon. There is lots of exaggerated rubato and up-front virtuosity. More slickness than soul, but technically very impressive.

Sadly these days in Hungary it is very hard to find real **village music** in the way Bartók and Kodály did. The music was already disappearing in the early years of the century although it persisted up to the 1960s and beyond. Today, the best areas to try – at traditional weddings and so on – are **Szabolcs-Szatmár** county, out on a limb in the northeast, and **southwest Transdanubia** in the south of the country bordering Croatia.

A more fixed event, with a guarantee of music-making, is **Busójárás Carnival in Mohács** at the beginning of March. The music played in Mohács is basically Serbian and Croatian. The celebrated **Bogyiszló orchestra** was until recently the best in the region but is, alas, no longer active.

There's also a rich tradition of **Serbian music** from the communities in Szentendre and Pomaz north of Budapest where the excellent group **Vujicsics** is based.

Gypsy Folk

So if the music played by Hungary's ubiquitous Gypsy bands is Hungarian, what's the Gypsy music? Oddly enough, considering the number of Gypsy instrumentalists, the music of the Roma themselves hardly uses instruments at all. Most of the Gypsy musicians who play in the urban bands don't actually live amongst the (generally poorer) Gypsy communities, they play exclusively for a non-Gypsy audience and often they don't know the traditional Gypsy repertoire. There's a big difference between the urban and rural sounds.

Rural Gypsy music includes slow songs about the hardships of life and faster dance songs. The music is not intended for others, and is only performed at Roma gatherings. When a Roma dies, for example, his friends gather to sing his favourite songs and "draw the strength from his soul" as they say. Although there are no instruments, many of the songs are accompanied by rhythmic grunts, the tapping of sticks and cans and imitations of instruments in a 'doobie-doobie-doobie' sort of way called 'oral-bassing'.

These 'rolled songs' and dance songs have a wild, improvised sound and though they are hard to hear for real without personal access to Gypsy communities they have provided the raw material for some exciting professional Gypsy groups performing in Hungary and on tour. **Kalyi Jag** (Romany for Black Fire) and **Ando Drom** (On the Road) have added guitars and other instruments to the powerful vocal and percussion line-up. Both groups have some strong dark-voiced vocalists – Gusztáv Varga and József Balogh in Kalyi Jag and the extraordinary female singer Mitsou in Ando Drom. The Gypsy group **Rományi Rotá** (Gypsy Wheel) play in a similar style and have a regular tánchaz in Budapest.

The jazz guitarist **Gyula Babos** (from a long line of Gypsy musicians) has taken rural Gypsy music in a different direction in his **Project Romani** with a jazz and avant-garde twist.

(See Gypsy Music – p.146 – for the wider context of Roma music in eastern Europe).

The Tánchaz

The Hungarian capital Budapest is one of the best places in Europe to hear really good folk music, and the place to go is a **tánchaz** – literally a 'dance house', named after traditional village dancing places (see box on p.164). The atmosphere at a tánchaz is a cross between a barn dance and a folk club but without the self-conscious folksiness of

Márta Sebestyén

Márta Sebestyén (centre) with Muzsikás

I first met **Márta Sebestyén** in the late 1970s when she was already a rising star on the Budapest folk scene. She took me to a **wedding in Transylvania** – an overnight train journey, a morning mist around the eerie spires of Dracula's birthplace Sighişoara, a couple of bus journeys and finally a trudge up a track deep in mud to a village in the Carpathian Mountains. There was lots of mud, lots of plum brandy and wild music played on battered instruments which went on for a couple of days. Exhilarating stuff, particularly as we were staying illegally in peasant homes and were fearful of Ceauşescu's Securitate police. I became hooked on Transylvania and its music.

Since then Márta has gone on to become an international star at what she does best – singing Hungarian and particularly Transylvanian music. Her voice, other worldy, yet human and vulnerable, was used singing a simple, but evocative, Hungarian folksong for the Oscar-winning film, *The English Patient*. And there's a lot more besides. Her traditional repertoire includes several other traditions and languages, she's performed in a Hungarian rock musical and prominently featured on the Grammy Award-winning Deep Forest *Bohème* album. But if there's one thing that drives her, it is her love and faith in the traditional music she sings: "It's silly to lose something that has survived for so long. It's important to take care of nature and the environment and also to look after music. It's not simply nostalgic, but also contemporary. Now we have TV and video but the human soul still needs to sing and play. We still have emotions, thank God." The power this faith gives her is impressive. I once saw her silence a restive and rowdy crowd audience at a rock concert with a simple unaccompanied folk song.

Márta's mother, an energetic music teacher and pupil of **Kodály**, instilled in her daughter a passion for folk music and the urge to hear it first hand. "When she got pregnant with me, my mother was studying ethnomusicology at the Liszt Academy. In her stomach I heard those lessons and the words of Zoltan Kodály." Some of the first songs Márta learned came from her mother's transcriptions of field recordings, like the Hazafelé tune from southwest Hungary on her *Kismet* album. Márta, in turn, has done her own collecting in northern Hungary and, of course, Transylvania. "Even when I knew many of the songs from field recordings it was amazing to go there personally and hear the songs in different forms, with different ornaments. It's like a living river, you never put your legs in the same water. It's not simply the melodies, but everything around them – the customs, the personality of the singer, the life. Each song is a gem for me – it's part of somebody's life which is given to me."

"Szerelem, szerelem" (Love, love), the sad love song that she sings in *The English Patient*, she learned from the local cantor (priest) from the Transylvanian village of Magyarszovát. "I first recorded that song years ago, when I was going through a difficult period in my life and it had a real personal meaning for me. It's interesting that years later this song was used to reflect other peoples' problems (in the film). And people all over the world respond to it. I think that's what folk music is all about. It is about universal feelings. You can use it when you need it and you can pass it on."

Simon Broughton

its Western counterparts. The dress may be blue jeans and trainers with the odd Transylvanian jacket or skirt, but for the most part the clientele – teachers, doctors, lawyers – know the music and can dance it well. Once again this is a statement of identity. In a world where everybody wears the same blue jeans or Benetton clothes, this music and dance comes with a Hungarian designer label.

The tánchaz movement started in the 1970s as a reaction to the regimented folklore of the state ensembles. Following in the footsteps of Bartók and Kodály, musicians like **Ferenc Sebő** and **Béla Halmos** collected music from the villages, learned it and brought it back to Budapest. But whereas Bartók and Kodály had been interested mainly in songs, this new generation was interested in the instrumental music and traditional dances – György Martin and Sándor Tímár were the principal dance researchers. The idea was to bring the music back to the grassroots rather than present it on stage and, despite the urban setting, keep it closer to its original form.

Even though it had virtually no official support, the movement grew from strength to strength. For many years it also had a political dimension. The wellspring of Hungarian tánchaz music was in neighbouring Romania where the Hungarian minority of **Transylvania** has kept a living folk tradition to this day (see Romania article, p.237). Tánchaz musicians often travelled there in very difficult circumstances to collect music and dances. Since the fall of Communism there's been a regular flow of great Transylvanian village performers to the tánchaz of Budapest bringing a welcome rough-edged note of authenticity.

Tánchaz music falls into two types. One is music from Hungary proper which, with less of a living tradition, has usually been learned from archive recordings or written collections and arranged by the groups in the manner of folk bands all over Europe. But the most popular music comes directly from the village tradition and that means Transylvania (or occasionally the Hungarian communities in Slovakia). The basic **instrumental line-up** is a lead fiddle, an accompanying violin (*kontra*) playing chords and a bowed bass – there's often a cimbalom included as well. If at first the tunes all sound similar, keep listening. The better you know this music the more rich and varied it becomes. In the right hands it has a beauty unrivalled in Europe.

Tánchaz dances are played in sets, generally moving from slower tempos to fast – beginning perhaps with a verbunkos or Lad's Dance, giving the chance for the men to show off, and ending with a fast and furious csárdás. It's the *primás*, the first violinist of the band, who keeps an eye on the dancers and judges when to make the move and tempo change into the next dance. When it's done well it's thrilling.

The **csárdás** is the most famous Hungarian dance tune and you won't spend five minutes at a Budapest tánchaz (or a Transylvanian wedding) without hearing one. They can be fast or slow, 'whirling', 'quivering' or 'leaping' – and there are all sorts of regional variations. All of them are couple dances which can reach great virtuosity, but at their most basic it's two steps left, two steps right followed by a turn. The music has a regular four-square rhythm with a distinctive spring.

Internationally, the best-known names in Hungarian music emerged from the tánchaz scene: **Márta Sebestyén** (see box opposite), a truly remarkable singer (and not just of Hungarian music) and **Muzsikás**, the group she has often performed with. As a band they have succeeded in keeping the fine balance between a professionalised approach on stage and the raw gutsy sound of the village. Regularly playing the music as a functional thing in their tánchaz can only help that. They have recently explored the links between Bartók's music and the authentic village tradition.

Other top musicians to watch out for include fiddler **Csaba Ökrös** and his ensemble and the **Kalamajka**, **Téka** and **Jánosi** groups who specialise in the Hungarian and Transylvanian repertoire, and **Vujicsics**, who play fantastic tambura music from southern Hungary and the former Yugoslavia. Other notable singers are **Éva Fábián** and **András Berecz**.

The virtuoso Gypsy cimbalom player **Kálmán Balogh** is frequently collaborating with many of these musicians and has also drawn on wider influences from Balkan, Latin and American music. Clarinettist, saxophonist and cimbalom player **Mihály Dresch** pursues a much more experimental line in a jazz/folk quartet with violin, bass and percussion which probably doesn't do a lot for the dancers in the tánchaz, but appeals to another clientele. The young virtuoso violinist **Félix Lajkó** (a Hungarian from Subotica in Serbia) is classically trained, but with his group Zenekara plays a rhythmic and infectious concert music drawing on Hungarian, Balkan and Middle-Eastern traditions. Great playing and definitely a name to watch out for.

As Hungary modernised in the 1970s, the local folk music styles gradually lost their context to commercialised music. Today, as Romania makes up for lost time, and the older generation of village

Táncház in Budapest

A grimy bar in the basement of the Budapest Sport Hall (Népstadion) seems an unlikely Mecca for lovers of Hungarian fiddle, but every year on a Sunday in the middle of March this is the place to be. Here fiddlers from Transylvanian village bands mix it up – over watered beer and home-brewed plum brandy – with the young hotshots from the Hungarian táncház scene. Jam sessions like this aren't rare in the Hungarian folk music scene, but at the annual **Táncháztalálkozó** (Meeting of the Dance Houses or just plain National Folk Festival) it's the sheer numbers of fiddle virtuosi that get you. Village bands from all over the Carpathian basin come to Budapest for the festival, do a fifteen minute performance on the main stage, and then drift into the bar behind the stage for a drink or three and a tune or fifteen.

Over Friday, Saturday and climaxing on Sunday, some of the great Transylvanian Gypsy bands will be sawing away all afternoon and evening in the bar, interrupted only by their brief stage appearance. The **Codoba Family Band** from Palátka, the **Szászcsavás Band, Neti Sándor's Band** from Kalotaszeg, and others were all there in 1998, showering their young urban fiddle protégés with big sloppy Gypsy kisses after each tune. The lead fiddlers from the established Budapest bands crowd the tables and greet each other with the old time peasant courtesy that has long gone out of fashion in modern Budapest. A couple twirl in a csárdás near the stairs. The bar reeks with the signature aroma of Transylvanian music – sweat, plum brandy, and cheap cigarette smoke.

The Dance Houses are still a feature of Budapest social life, although attendance has shrunk in recent years. Back in the days when the Party Line dictated culture, the pursuit of folk music and dance was considered an affront to proletarian internationalism and the Dance Houses were meeting places for dissidents, samizdat editors, and daring college students. Even so, about a dozen **regular Dance Houses** operate weekly in the capital, sponsored by bands like Muzsikás, Téka, Méta, and others.

One new thread of Hungarian táncház music emerged in the 1990s: the music of the 30,000 **Csángó Hungarians** living in the Seret Valley of **Moldavia**. Under Ceauşescu the Csángós were subject to heavy assimilationist pressure and research among them was forbidden. Their Moldavian culture and archaic dialect strongly differentiate them from the Hungarians of Transylvania. Today young Csángós come to Budapest to find work, and many meet at the Tatros Group's dances on Wednesday night where it is hard to tell the Folk from the folkies. Csángó dance music makes even Transylvanian string band music seem tame, played on throaty flutes (one 'growls' into them while playing to increase the volume) fiddles, drums, with the Moldavian *koboz* lute providing the rhythm.

A DANCEHOUSE DIARY

Budapest has a great variety of Dance Houses including some for Greek, Balkan and Irish music. Below is a list of the principal clubs for Hungarian and other East European styles. The venues are usually 1970s style culture centres, although the Gyökér Club is a cut above the rest. There is always a bar and snacks are usually available. There is often dance instruction before the táncház really gets underway, usually from around 8pm to midnight. Entrance fees are minimal.

TUESDAY
Gypsy Music
Rományi Rota
Almássy téri Szabadidőközpont
1077 Budapest, Almássy tér 6. ☎ (36) 1 352 1572

WEDNESDAY
The *Final Hour* Club
Hosted alternately by the Ökrös or Tükrös band
Fonó Budai Zeneház
1117 Budapest, Sztregova u. 3. ☎ (36) 1 206 5300

Gyimes and Moldavian Music
Guzsalyas Tatros Dance House
Marczibányi téri Művelődési Központ
1022 Budapest, Marczibá nyi tér 5/a. ☎ (36) 1 212 0803

THURSDAY
Hungarian and Transylvanian Music
Muzsikás Club
Marczibányi téri Művelődési Központ
1022 Budapest, Marczibányi tér 5/a. ☎ (36) 1 212 5504

Hungarian Folk
Vasmalom Club (every second Thursday)
Gyökér Klub-Restaurant, 1067 Budapest, Eötvös u. 46.
☎ (36) 1 302 4059

FRIDAY
Hungarian and Transylvanian
Téka Dance House
I. Kerületi Művelődési Ház, 1011 Budapest,
Bem rakpart 6. ☎ (36) 1 201 0324

Hungarian and Transylvanian
Méta Evening
Gyökér Klub-Restaurant, 1067 Budapest, Eötvös u. 46.
☎ (36) 1 302 4059

SATURDAY
Hungarian and Transylvanian
Kalamajka Dance House
Belvárosi Ifjúsági Ház, 1056 Budapest, Molnár u. 9.
☎ (36) 1 117 5928

SUNDAY
Hungarian and Transylvanian
Méta Dance House
Józsefvárosi Klub
1085 Budapest, Somogyi B. u. 13. ☎ (36) 1 118 7930

Current information about Dance Houses is available at *www.datanet.hu/táncház/thmain.htm*

Bob Cohen

musicians pass away, the music of Transylvania faces the same danger in a world filled with music videos and disco lights. Growing out of the tánchaz movement, the ambitious *Utolsó Óra* **(Final Hour) project** aims to record the best of Transylvania's traditional bands before they inevitably disappear. The selected bands (who play not only Hungarian, but also Romanian, Gypsy, Saxon and Jewish repertoire) are invited to Budapest for a week where academic study of the music is done and recordings are made. This ancient music is made accessible to a modern audience at a weekly tánchaz in the Fonó club – and once the dancing begins the atmosphere is strictly traditional – sweat, pálinka, smoke.

The plan, supported by the Hungarian Academy of Sciences, the Ethnographic Museum and the Soros Foundation amongst others, is to produce 45 CDs. The series is called *Új Pátria* (New Patria) named after the important Patria recordings, mainly of vocal music, made by Bartók, Kodály and others in the 1930s. The first recordings have already been released on the Fonó label.

FONÓ RECORDS

Village dance in Kalotaszeg

discography

A lot of Hungarian recordings feature music from Transylvania (Romania) – played by tánchaz ensembles as well as real village bands. Some of the most important Hungarian tánchaz groups playing Transylvanian repertoire are included below, while the local village bands and 'New Patria' recordings will be found in the Romanian discography (p.245).

Traditional Compilations

 Elueszett Éden (Lost Eden) (Etnofon, Hungary).

A specialist, but important collection featuring archive recordings of Hungarian music mostly from 1970s–1990s although some are earlier. Singers, instrumentalists and bands. The first disc includes recordings from Hungary, the second from Transylvania, Moldavia and Carpathian Ukraine.

◉ **Hungarian Folk Music 3** (Hungaroton, Hungary).

Four-album boxed set devoted to the ancient layers, the new European style, instrumental music, and folk customs. The best overall introduction to the music, well presented with translations and transcriptions of the material plus some good photos. It hasn't yet made it to CD.

🄲🄳 **Hungarian Instrumental Folk Music** (Hungaroton, Hungary).

A fine 2-CD set covering the typical sounds of Hungarian folk music from cow bells and horns, through bagpipes, hurdy-gurdy and zithers to various sizes of Gypsy band.

◉ **Traditional Music from the Carpathians** (Harmonia Mundi/Quintana, France).

A variable selection of Hungarian, Gypsy and other music from communities over the border in Ukraine. Made before the political changes and the information and notes are scanty.

Gypsy Music and Gypsy Bands

Compilations

◉ **Hungarian Folk Music from Szatmár Region** (Hungaroton, Hungary).

A great CD of four traditional Gypsy bands from villages in the northeast of the country playing Hungarian dance music plus some Jewish repertoire. Terrific stuff.

◉ **Descendants of the Itinerant Gypsies: Melodies of Sorrow and Joy** (Multicultural Media, US).

Field recordings of variable quality made by Japanese researchers in the 1980s of rural Gypsy music in Hungary and village bands in Transylvania. Musicians and bands are not identified (although the Transylvanian band from Palátka appear on the cover and sound like they're featured on a couple of tracks). The rural Gypsy music, though, is the real thing and hard to find elsewhere.

◉ **Rom Sam Ame!** (Fonti Musicali, Belgium).

A specialised, but excellent survey of authentic Gypsy songs from six towns in central and eastern Hungary – vocals, in Hungarian and Rom, with accompanying spoons and struck pots and tables.

Artists

Ando Drom

Ando Drom are currently the most successful of Hungary's professional Romany ensembles. The band have been around since the early 1980s led by Jenö Zsigó and have transformed the rural Gypsy traditions into a dynamic concert music featuring the swarthy vocals of Mónika 'Mitsou' Juhász Miczura.

◉ Phari Mamo
(World Network, Germany).

The title track, in Romani, is the song of a son missing his mother and the family she has to look after. This is, as the subtitle says, 'magnificent Gypsy music from Budapest', but not the schmaltzy café variety. Ando Drom, with a vocal and percussion line-up, has real soul, a melancholy edge and on this recording idiomatic instrumental contributions on violin and accordion from the French Gypsy group Bratsch.

Kálmán Balogh

Balogh, from a family of Gypsy musicians, is one of Hungary's leading cimbalom players and is regularly pulled in to play along with most of the leading groups.

◉ Roma Vándor (M&W, Netherlands).

A really wild recording made live at a festival of Gypsy music in Amsterdam in 1994. You can feel the audience holding their breath as Balogh cranks up the pace and the hammers just skate at lightning speed across those strings. The band brings in Balkan, Spanish and rock 'n' roll sounds – with some cracking trumpet playing from Ferenc Kovács.

Csókolom

Small, three-part ensemble of violin, kontra and double bass led by violinist Anti von Klewitz. Born in Yugoslavia, she is now based in Berlin and Amsterdam. She has played classical and jazz music as well as this idiomatic Hungarian and Gypsy material. Csókolom (pronounced Chokolom) is an old Austro-Hungarian greeting.

◉ May I Kiss Your Hand: Hungarian and Gypsy Fiddle Music and Songs (Arhoolie, US).

Arhoolie's Chris Strachwitz was behind this recording when he heard Csókolom live in Memphis, Tennessee. Days later

the band were recording in the infamous (thanks to Elvis) Sun Studios for this excellent debut album. Wonderfully raw instrumental playing of Hungarian and Balkan dances, songs sung in Hungarian, Romanian and Romany, including a haunting example by Kalyi Jag's Jósef Balogh. Some very unusual repertoire, well played and strongly recommended.

Kalyi Jag

Another fine ensemble forging new music out of rural Gypsy sounds, led by singer and guitarist Gusztáv Varga.

◉ Gypsy Folk Songs from Hungary
(Hungaroton, Hungary).

This 1994 collection is catchy and representative – traditional songs given the 'Black Fire' treatment with the guitar and mandolin of József Balogh. Several of these have since become Roma 'standards'. Translations of the lyrics are included.

Roby Lakatos

Born in 1965, Roby is one of the younger members of the famous Lakatos dynasty of Gypsy musicians. He learned in the family tradition as well as at the Budapest Music Academy. He's lived in Belgium since 1985 where he's expanded his style to include jazz and Stephane Grappelli-style violin.

◉ In Gypsy Style (M&W, Netherlands).

The violin swoops and sighs with the characteristic rippling of cimbalom and strings. Hungarian, Russian and Django Reinhardt melodies in inventive arrangements, plus the inevitable Gypsy standard, "The Lark". Great virtuoso playing plus a strong personality.

Ferenc Sánta and his Gypsy Band

Sánta trained at the Music Academy in Budapest and has led a Budapest Gypsy Orchestra since the 1970s.

◉ Csárdás: Hungarian Gypsy Music
(Naxos, Hong Kong).

While Sánta isn't amongst the best-known of Gypsy bandleaders, this budget Naxos collection includes many of the favourites of the Budapest Gypsy orchestras like Monti's Csárdás and the popular encore, "The Lark". Typical of its type.

Tánchaz Groups

Every year the *Budapest Tánchaz Festival* releases a CD of selected groups from the Festival. This gives a good overview of what's happening on the Dance House scene.

Compilations

◉ Musiques de Transylvanie (Fonti Musicali, Belgium).

One of the best introductions to Transylvanian music featuring mostly Hungarian repertoire. Includes great music from Kalotaszeg, Mezőség, Gyimes, plus Romanian dances from Bihor and Moldavia. Performances by the best musicians of Budapest's tánchaz scene.

Artists

Ghymes

An excellent five-piece band led by Tamás Szarka and based in Slovakia. Growing out of the tánchaz movement the band occasionally add saxophone and drum kit to their line-up to create a more jazzy or contemporary sound.

⊚ **Üzenet (Message)** (Ghymes, Slovakia).

An impressive collection of some traditional and more experimental material – the title track includes some impressive bagpipe, cimbalom and percussion.

Béla Halmos

Singer and violinist Béla Halmos was one of the leading figures in the early days of the tánchaz movement and remains so today.

⊚ **Az a szép piros hajnal** (Hungaroton, Hungary).

A strong collection of Transylvanian music – mainly from the central region of Mezőség. Joining Halmos are some of the best names on the Hungarian music scene, singers Márta Sebestyén and András Berecz and flautist Zoltán Juhász.

Muzsikás

Now over a quarter of a century old, Muzsikás have established themselves as Hungary's leading tánchaz group, and often feature the singer Márta Sebestyén. The quartet of Mihály Sipos (lead violin), Péter Éri (contra, tambura etc), Dániel Hamar (bass) and Sándor Csoóri (bagpipe and contra) survived until the latter's recent departure. They have researched and performed Jewish tunes of Transylvania as well as music from western Hungary to the eastern outpost of Gyimes. They have recently been exploring the folk roots of Bartók's music in their excellent 1999 release, *The Bartók Album*.

 Morning Star (Hannibal/Ryko, UK).

All of Muzsikás's albums come highly recommended, but this 1997 disc more than any other has the freshness and rough-edged feel of the village. Great songs too from Márta Sebestyén.

⊚ **Blues For Transylvania** (Hannibal/Ryko, UK).

An earlier 1990 recording of mainly Transylvanian repertoire that stands up well including some wild dance music and beautiful slow songs.

Ökrös Ensemble

Csaba Ökrös is a tremendous fiddler and his traditional ensemble is one of the best – working regularly with some of Transylvania's best village musicians in concert and on record. They've recorded a number of excellent CDs of Transylvanian music on small labels.

 Transylvanian Portraits (Koch World, US).

With its international distribution, this is the most widely available of the Ökrös discs and contains a beautiful selection of traditional Hungarian music from different regions of Transylvania. Csaba Ökrös demonstrates his extraordinary violin technique in the traditional 'shepherd who's lost his sheep' piece and Márta Sebestyén sings.

Márta Sebestyén

Hungary's most celebrated female vocalist – bringing her distinctive qualities to the soundtrack of *The English Patient*, the popular concoctions of Deep Forest and a Hungarian rock musical amongst other things. A strong and searing voice at its best in traditional Hungarian and Transylvania repertoire.

⊚ **Márta Sebestyén** (Hannibal/Ryko, UK).

A 1988 album of Hungarian and Transylvanian music with Muzsikás – featuring a beautiful "morning song" from Kalotaszeg (Transylvania), one of her specialities.

⊚ **Kismet** (Hannibal/Ryko, UK).

A much more wide-ranging album including Bulgarian, Bosnian, Hindi and Irish songs. Not traditional in the pure sense, but beautifully produced by Nikola Parov.

Vujicsics

One of the best groups anywhere playing Serbian and Croatian music – a six-piece ensemble with guitars, tamburas and bass from the South Slav communities north of Budapest.

⊚ **Vujicsics** (Hannibal/Ryko, UK).

A great collection of fast and furious kolos and other dance tunes. Vocals from Márta Sebestyén and others.

Iceland

waiting for the thaw

While the other Nordic countries have experienced an upsurge in their roots music, Iceland has been the exception. Despite a strong sense of national and cultural identity, a language very close to old Norse, a rich musical tradition (not just of the famous sagas but also of songs and ballads) and a thriving performing and recording scene for classical, pop and other global forms, what would seem to an outsider to be obvious roots possibilities are largely ignored in contemporary Icelandic music. **Andrew Cronshaw** investigates.

Björk is probably the best known Icelander – and certainly the country's most popular musical export. Though she's clearly a rock musician, and for much of her working life has been based in Britain, her distinctive approach might be at least partly ascribed to her origins. She has made Icelandic-language versions of her songs, and on French keyboardist and producer Hector Zazou's album *Songs of the Cold Seas* (an impressive project in which he builds powerful soundscapes around leading singers from the world's northernmost countries) she sings a traditional song.

A few Icelandic musicians do draw on the tradition, but few specialise in it. The best-known folk group, and the only one whose recordings are distributed abroad, is **Islandica**. Its repertoire and rather staid approach cannot be described as 'the real thing' nor as a modern Icelandic tradition-rooted music, however. Most songs described as Icelandic folk songs are poetic works of the nineteenth and twentieth century set to tunes from other parts of Europe (including, for example, "Eldgamla Ísafold", set to the tune of the British national anthem). They're folk songs in the sense that the folk sing them, but they're very different from the old musics.

Religion and Decline

The decisive factor in breaking the traditional musical thread seems to have been the influence of the church. Iceland has been Christian for a millennium, and until the nineteenth century church singing – based on translated German protestant hymns, but later written by Icelanders such as Hallgrímur Pétursson (1614-1674) – had a strong Icelandic character, often in the lydian mode, with parallel fifths and augmented fourths. But in 1800 Magnús

Stephensen brought Iceland its first pipe organ, and in 1801 he published a new hymn-book. Reykjavik Cathedral led the way in using the new instrument and the new Danish-style hymns with their formal rhythms and harmonisations. By the end of the 1870s most churches had bought harmoniums and the old styles which were judged cacophonous and old-fashioned were relegated to the home. The arrival of radio in 1930 completed the 'enlightenment', affecting not only religious music but the whole musical taste of the population. The folk rejected their previous folk music.

A printed anthology of folk melodies collected by **Bjarni Þorsteinsson** was published between 1906 and 1909, but much of what was distinctive – the sound and style of the singing – is hard to convey on paper. At that time the first sound recordings were made of Icelandic folk song, and more have been made episodically throughout the twentieth century, but neither print nor recording can fully convey the context and musical world of those days. In addition, dancing displeased the island's nineteenth-century religious authorities, so the old **ballad–dancing** died out, to be replaced by more universal European fashions when people eventually started dancing again.

Used in the playing of hymns, but nevertheless falling into disuse in the nineteenth century, were two stringed instruments considered to have been distinctively Icelandic – the **fidla**, a soundbox with strings stretched from a perpendicular upright, and the **langspil**, a wedge-shaped fretted zither akin to a Norwegian langeleik or Swedish hummel.

Sagas and Ballads

Iceland is famous for its heroic ballad-poetry, the **sagas**. These were passed down orally for many centuries, but with Christianity came literacy, and

A. MAYER

Langspil player, 1835

they began to be written down as long as a thou-sand years ago, so becoming fixed and perceived as poetry rather than song.

A tradition of sung ballads, **rímur**, continued alongside, however. These are epic heroic songs whose lyrics use both alliteration and line-end rhyme. Performance is usually solo; the word for the singer - or perhaps more descriptively the chanter - of a *ríma* is 'kvæðanaður'. The melodic style falls somewhere between speech and song, and there's always a pitch dip on the last note of the phrase. The tradition has just about continued to the present day, mainly through the efforts of two societies dedicated to the preservation of rímur, who have made some archive recordings.

Very little of the quantity of recordings of Ice-landic traditional music in archives, however, has been made available in commercial form. Publi-cation and fieldwork related to rímur and other traditional music has virtually no financial back-ing; it's not seen as important by either govern-ment or media, whereas there's a great deal of research and published material about the sagas. It is, says Smári Ólason (who in 1990 released a cas-sette of field recordings), "a sad situation". Most of the handful of researchers, such as Ólason and the late Hreinn Steingrímsson, have worked at their own expense.

There may be signs of a new beginning. In 1998 a CD was released of vocal recordings from the

archive of the main institution for Icelandic culture, the **Árni Magnússon Institute**, part of the Uni-versity of Iceland. Though mainly dedicated to medieval manuscripts which have recently been transferred from Denmark (Iceland was under Dan-ish rule until 1944), the Institute houses a collection of about 2000 hours of recorded folklore material, including rímur and folk stories collected both in Iceland and among the Icelandic population in Cana-da. Its folklorist and librarian is Rósa Þorsteinsdót-tir ☎ (354) 525 4020/4010; *rosat@rhi.hi.is*

discography

Compilations

⦿ **Íslensk Alpydulog: Icelandic Folk Songs** (FD, Iceland).

Very little Icelandic roots material is released, but this is gen-erally reckoned the most interesting available on CD.

▦ **Íslensk Þjóðlög, Kvæði og Sálmar** (Skógar Folkmuseum, Iceland).

Field recordings of singers. Obtainable from Skógar Folkmuseum, Ytri-Skógar IS–861 Hvolsvöllur, or Smári Ólason, Hraunteig 24, IS–105 Reykjavik; *smari@rhi.hi.is*

⦿ **Voices** (Árni Magnússon Institute, Iceland).

Selections of singing and chanting from the Institute's archive, from the first-ever recordings, made back in 1903, up to 1973.

Ireland

dancing at the virtual crossroads

One of the great figures of Irish legend, Fionn MacCumhaill, asked to define great music, replied: "the most beautiful music is the music of what happens". Irish traditional music, through alternate cycles of rapid change and complete stagnation, has remained faithful to Fionn's dictum. And, as **Nuala O'Connor** reports, it is Europe's most commercially successful traditional music, dominating the global village and sustaining large communities of players – from the thousands of music sessions taking place every night in Irish pubs to the glitz of international shows like *Riverdance*.

A stunning aspect of traditional Irish music is its survival as a fully living form. It has had no shortage of folksong-academics, collectors and societies (from the 1850s onwards), but essentially it still belongs to the people, in both cities and countryside, at home and in communities abroad.

Because Ireland remained a largely agricultural country until the 1960s, and perversely because of three centuries of emigration, its traditional music managed to make a successful transition from rural to urban, feeding into whatever prevailing modes required. Thus Irish music can accommodate 'pure' sessions and players and singers in trad pubs or at dances, and any number of mutations, whether it is Van Morrison's reshaping R & B, Moving Hearts doing the same with rock, The Pogues fusing Irish airs and punk, or the Afro-Celt Sound System, at the end of the 1990s, bringing Irish traditional music into a worldly meeting with African and techno rhythms. The music of what happens: for sure . . .

Turning a Tune: Traditional Dance Music

Most instrumental Irish traditional music heard at sessions and concerts originated as **dance music**. It was the repertoire of the rural working people and was part of a communally expressed cultural life. Traditional music was played to accompany dancing at celebrations – usually performed in houses and barns or out of doors when weather permitted – including weddings, fairs, saint's day observances known as 'patterns', and wakes. For centuries it was the recreational and social expression of Irish people and it has not entirely died out in this form yet.

This traditional dance music was not in any real sense a 'performance'. There was rarely any payment, no expectation of a 'show', and music and dancing were two elements among a number of other activities that could include singing, story-telling, card-playing, game-playing, and so on. It was above all a participatory activity with all the informality and unevenness of skill that that implies. Little is known or recorded of traditional music and dance before the seventeenth century but it seems clear that the traditional repertoire current today is between two and three hundred years old.

Ornamentation, decoration and embellishments are the ways in which musicians continue to breathe life into traditional music. It's a kind of controlled extemporisation in which the player recreates the tune with each performance. Technical mastery is neccessary, of course, but the skill with which a musician **decorates a tune** is the measure of creative power, and often even accomplished players will play the settings of established master players, reproducing their particular phrasing, decorations and intonations.

Nearly all **Irish tunes** conform to the same basic structure: two eight-bar sections or strains, each of which is played twice to make a 32-bar whole, which is then repeated from the top. In a session one tune is followed without any appreciable break by another, and after a brief pause for refreshment the musicians might break into another selection of two or three tunes. The change or 'turn' in the tune is communicated through gesture – a nod or wink or movement of some kind.

The majority of these dance tunes are **reels** and **jigs**, but most musicians will also draw on hornpipes, polkas, slides, mazurkas, *scottiches* and highlands. At the last survey (in 1985) the number of jigs, reels and hornpipes in the national repertoire

From Crossroads Dancing to Lords of the Riverdance

Until well on into this century the **house dance** or **crossroads dance** was the most popular form of entertainment in rural Irish communities. The dances were either group dances, now known as 'sets', based on quadrilles where two sets of two couples danced facing each other, or solo dances performed by the best dancers in the locality. Rural depopulation, church interference, the commercial dance halls, the radio and the record-player nearly killed the custom off. Since the early 1980s, however, the country witnessed quite a phenomenal revival in **'set dancing'** – a revival that went global with the success of Riverdance (see below).

The crossroads dances did not themselves reappear but from the 1980s, increasing numbers of pubs and local centres made space available for dancers. The dance tunes they use are the **jigs**, **reels** and **hornpipes** known to every traditional player – though during a dance it is the dancer and not the piper who calls the tune. Playing for dancers requires special skills. The beat must be rock steady, the tunes are played at a slower tempo than is usual in a session, and the player is restrained from excessive improvisation and personal expression. Nonetheless, the popularity of set-dancing has involved more people than ever in an active relationship with traditional music. Anyone who knows the steps is welcome to join in step-dancing sessions, and if you're a beginner it's always possible to turn up at a class and learn from scratch.

The show that, of course, really fired interest in set dancing was **Riverdance**, which famously began life as an act for the interval of the 1994 Eurovision Song Contest in Dublin. Its alchemical mix of virtuoso Irish dancers from the electrifying stars **Michael Flately** and **Jean Butler**, and the integration of Flamenco and Eastern European dance influences with Irish traditions was an immediate phenomenon. Following

its debut, composer Bill Whelan, with choreographer Michael Flateley, developed and expanded *Riverdance* into a full show, with singers, instrumental solos, and an eighty-strong chorus-line of Irish dancers liberated from the constraining folk uniforms and rigid upper body posture of traditional dance.

The dance tradition on which the show is based is competitive **step dancing** as taught to generations of Irish children and the children of Irish emigrants. Performed by Flately and Butler – both competition champions – the themes explored through the dance are universal folk celebrations based on the seasons, emigration, exile and the Irish diaspora, and man's fundamental humanity expressed in the metaphor of the River. The expanded show first opened in Dublin in 1995, went on to London, and has now grown into three touring companies performing worldwide. Flately, meanwhile, who had a much publicised dispute with the show's producers, went on to devise **Lord of the Dance** – a broadly Celtic extravaganza with music written by the Irish composer Ronan Hardiman. As with Riverdance, the show features traditional musicians, but not traditional music as such.

Crossroads dance in Co. Wicklow

stood at over 6000. The tradition is largely an oral one, with tunes being handed on from player to player in performance, and the repertoire is constantly changing as new tunes are added and others shed. Although tunes and technique are formally taught, once a player is out on his or her own the arena in which this music takes place is known as the **session**.

Pub Sessions and Crack

In Ireland today the **pub** is widely regarded as the most authentic locale for the traditional **music session** and the purveyance of 'crack'. Indeed, the whole Irish pub session phenomenon has become a global commodity, to be found in almost any city you care to mention. The 'crack', of course, can't be produced to order, but when good music, good company and drink combine in the right proportions then a sort of critical mass is achieved and crack ensues. If it is really there, then not only will the music be memorable and the musicians on form but those present will have felt themselves to have been celebrants, not mere spectators or consumers.

Pubs actually came into the traditional music picture in Ireland as late as the 1960s. Before then traditional music was played in a domestic setting or at loosely organised community events. The first pub session, as we now know it, took place not in Ireland at all but in *The Devonshire Arms* in London's Camden Town in 1947. The players were Irishmen, all traditional musicians, all immigrants working in the building industry on the post-war reconstruction of London. Packed into lodging houses and living in a city for the first time, away from their families, the old ways of music-making were not available to them. Pubs offered the opportunity to meet and play with other musicians with the informality required by players and listeners alike. This development had long-term implications for traditional music. It took it out of the domestic or community environment and further separated it from dancing, which was not allowed in most pubs. It also brought drink, publicans and ultimately the drinks industry into an influential relationship with traditional music.

Within a decade the pub session idea had spread to Ireland and by the 1960s there were Irish pubs that were synonymous with traditional music – *O'Donoghues* of Merrion Row in Dublin being one of the best known (and still in business). At the **Fleadh Ceoil,** Ireland's annual festival of tra-

ditional music, pub sessions became a feature of the informal or fringe events around the organised concerts and competitions. As the Fleadh Ceoil moved from town to town each year the practice spread and very quickly publicans realised the opportunity presented by the session. These Fleadh Ceoil sessions were and still are 'the real thing'. They are spontaneous, unplanned, and depend only on the desire of the musicians to make music. Professionals, non-professionals and semi-professionals meet up and play and the atmosphere is one of kinship and deep respect for the music.

By contrast, little of what passes for traditional session-playing in Irish pubs nowadays corresponds to an authentic session. This is not to say that good traditional music cannot be heard in pubs: many excellent young and not so young traditional and more modern musicians earn their living in pubs, and in places like Donegal, especially, you can still find a great session erupting. But the pub session is essentially a business driven by tourism and the drinks industry. The music may be viewed as just another facility, like pool tables or slot machines, and may well have to compete with them. Pub musicians, in fact, have always had to compete with noise and clatter and the ringing of tills and have developed a kind of pub repertoire as a result – amplification, a preponderance of reels played fast and loud, almost no traditional singing, and no unaccompanied singing.

The real session is by definition something that cannot be scheduled, so the pub which guarantees a session is in fact offering a formal traditional music gig, where the musicians are paid and expected to turn up at a certain time, and finish at a certain time. In a real session, different conventions apply, usually none of the above. Where musicians frequent a pub because the owner is into the music they are not paid, but neither are they under any obligation to play or even to turn up. It's possible to arrive at a pub known for its sessions only to find that on this particular night no one is in a playing mood. The venues of sessions are as changeable as their personnel, and situations change constantly. A new landlord, a difference of opinion, or too many crowds can force the musicians out to other meeting places.

At first sight sessions may seem to be rambling, disorganised affairs, but they have an underlying order and etiquette. Musicians generally commandeer a corner of the pub which is then their sacred domain. They also reserve the right to invite

Johnny Doran: Last of the Travelling Pipers

Johnny Doran worked as a travelling piper throughout Ireland during the 1930s and '40s, until his untimely death, aged forty-two. He has had a huge influence over almost every subsequent Irish piper, including several modern players such as Davy Spillane, Finbar Furey and Paddy Keenan.

Doran was born into a piping family and grew up in the village of Rathnew, Co. Wicklow. He moved with his family to Dublin and in his early twenties embarked on the life of a travelling piper, setting out each spring in a horse-drawn caravan to play at crossroad dances, fairs, races and football matches. It was that caravan that caused his death, crushing him after a wall collapsed on its roof; Johnny was left crippled and died two years later, in 1950.

Doran was recognised as one of the greats in his lifetime, and his arrival in a village was treated as a considerable honour. As one writer of the time put it, he was "a man of tremendous personal charisma and capable of sending out a musical pulse which utterly captivated the listener". Although Doran never made a commercial recording, he played on a handful of 78s made by the Comhairle Bhéaloideas Éireann (Irish Folklore Commission) and re-issued by them on a cassette, *The Bunch of Keys*.

Johnny Doran (right), with Pat Cash and son

What's special about Doran's playing is the rhythmic backing that supports the melody. His rhythms are continually varied and masterfully accentuated and the two recorded versions he left of "Rakish Paddy" reveal the truth that traditional musicians never play the same thing twice. *The Bunch of Keys* also includes recordings of reels, jigs, hornpipes and airs, all played with astonishing virtuosity. As an outdoor player, he played in a legato or open-pipe style, although as the music historian Brendan Breathnach observed, his style was essentially personal: "It always strikes me he was playing for himself, in response to some innner urge or feeling, and he went over and over the tune until he got the whole thing out of his system."

Simon Broughton

selected non-playing friends to join them there. The session is not open to all comers, although it might look that way, and it's not done to join in without introduction; a newcomer will wait to be asked to play, and may well refuse if they consider the other musicians to be of a lower standard than themselves.

In the summer, during or around local **fleadhs** or festivals, you also find **all-inclusive sessions** when large numbers of musicians congregate in one place. These can be terrific occasions when it seems the music just couldn't get any better and no one is willing to put an end to it. During the Fleadh Ceoil or the Willie Clancy Summer School held in Miltown Malbay, Co. Clare every July, such sessions notably abound, with space in the pub at a premium. Sessions can feature group playing, solo playing, singing in Irish and English or

any combination of these: it all depends on who's in the company and where their musical bias lies. Singers may gang up and keep the musicians from playing or vice versa.

All of this traditional music was originally an unaccompanied form. Usually a single fiddler, piper, flute-, whistle- or accordion-player played for the dancers. The single decorated melody line was the norm in playing as in singing, and the music had no rhythmic or harmonic accompaniment. Nowadays there are few traditional musicians who play exclusively solo and unaccompanied, but all good players can and will **play solo** on occasion. However, Western ears are now attuned to playing and singing with a chordal backing, and over the past fifty years this has inevitably found its way into traditional playing and singing.

Instruments and Players

We've included mention of the best instrumentalists on the Irish music scene in this round-up of traditional instruments. If you get a chance to see any of them at the festivals, don't miss it.

The Harp

There are references to harp playing in Ireland as early as the eighth century. Irish legend has it that the harp is credited with magical powers and it has become symbolic of the country (as well as of Guinness!). The old Irish harpers were a musical elite, serving as court musicians to the Gaelic aristocracy, and had a close acquaintance with the court music of Baroque Europe. The hundred or so surviving tunes by the famed, blind eighteenth-century harpist **Turlough Ó Carolan** – which provide much of the repertoire for today's harpers, and is often heard in orchestral or chamber music settings – clearly reflect his regard for the Italian composer Corelli.

The harp these players used was metal-strung and played with the fingernails. Today's Irish harpers play (with their fingertips) a chromatic, gut-string version, which one of its best exponents, **Máire Ní Chathasaigh**, describes as 'neo-Irish'. Maire has been notably successful in adapting Irish dance music for the harp, drawing on her knowledge of and love for the piping tradition. Another outstanding player, who has brought the instrument into traditional session playing, is **Laoise Kelly**; she is also a member of the Bumblebees, an all woman traditional four-piece band.

Beware that there is also a bland, prissy irish harp tradition, associated with anodyne tourist versions of Ireland, often as accompaniment to ersatz medieval banquets. About as trad as green beer, it should be given a wide berth.

Uilleann Pipes

'Seven years learning, seven years practising, and seven years playing' is reputedly what it takes to master the uilleann (pronounced 'illun') pipes. Perhaps the world's most technically sophisticated bagpipe, it is highly temperamental and difficult to master. The melody is played on a nine-holed chanter with a two-octave range blown by the air from a bag squeezed under the left arm, itself fed by a bellows squeezed under the right elbow. As well as the usual set of drones, the uilleann pipes are marked by their possession of a set of regulators, which can be switched on and off to provide chords. In hands of a master they can provide a sensitive backing for slow airs and an excitingly rhythmic springboard for dance music.

The pipes arrived in Ireland in the early eighteenth century and reached their present form in the 1890s. Taken up by members of the gentry, who became known as 'gentlemen pipers', they were also beloved of the Irish tinkers or travellers, and two different styles evolved, the restrained and delicate **parlour style** exemplified by the late **Seamus Ennis**, and the **traveller style** which, designed as it was to coax money from the pockets of visitors to country fairs, is highly ornamented and even showy.

FOLK ROOT ARCHIVES

Seamus Ennis and Jean Ritchie, 1952

Some of the most acclaimed traditional musicians this century have been pipers: Seamus Ennis, **Willie Clancy**, and brothers **Johnny** and **Felix Doran**. Today **Liam O'Flynn** is regarded as one of the country's foremost practitioners and has pushed forward the possibilities for piping – initially as a member of the mother of all trad bands Planxty, and later through his association with classical composers Shaun Davey and Mícheál Ó Súilleabhain.

The Bodhrán

The bodhrán is an instrument much in evidence at traditional sessions, and a recent addition to the dance music line-up. It is not universally welcome, partly because it looks like an easy way into playing – and it isn't; the great piper Seamus Ennis, when asked how a bodhrán should be played, replied "with a penknife". The bodhrán is a frame drum usually made of goatskin and originally associated with 'wren boys' or mummers who went out revelling and playing music on Wrens Day (Dec 26). It looks like a large tambourine without jingles and can be played with a small wooden stick or with the back of the hand.

Since it was introduced into mainstream traditional music in the 1960s by the great innovator **Sean Ó Riada** there has been a huge surge of interest in the bodhrán and in percussion generally. Accomplished players like **Johnny 'Ringo' MacDonagh**, **Donal Lunny**, **Mel Mercier**, **Tommy Hayes**, **Jim Higgins** and **Frank Torpey** have brought Irish traditional percussion to a highly developed state of expertise. In their hands, and those of a skilled player, the bodhrán sounds wonderful, a sympathetic support to the running rhythms of traditional music. **Christy Moore** is a notable player, too, and was one of the first to use the instrument to accompany his own singing.

The Bodhrán (left) as played by De Dannan

Flutes and Whistles

It's the **wooden flute** of a simple type that is used in Irish music, played mostly in a fairly low register with a quiet and confidential tone which means that it's not heard at its best in pub sessions.

The master flute player of his generation is **Matt Molloy** from Roscommon. He is also well known as a member of **The Chieftains** and in the 1970s was the flute player with the never to be forgotten **Bothy Band**. He and his wife own a pub (*Molloys*) in Westport, Co Mayo, renowned for its music sessions. At the younger end of the spectrum, also from Mayo, is **Emer Mayock**, an accomplished traditional player and a gifted tune maker. **Desi Wilson** and **Paul McGrattan** are superb players in northern regional style and repertoire.

While anyone can get a note, though not necessarily the right one, out of its little cousin the **tin whistle**, it can take a long time to develop an embouchure capable of producing a flute tone, and so piper **Finbar Furey** has introduced the **low whistle**, which takes the place of the flute when there is no proper flute player around. In the right hands, those of **Packie Byrne** or **Mary Bergin**, or The Chieftains' **Paddy Moloney**, for example, the whistle itself is no mean instrument, but it's also suitable for the beginner. If you're interested, make sure you get a D-whistle, as most Irish music is in this key.

Fiddles

The **fiddle** is popular all over Ireland and many areas still retain particular regional characteristics in style and repertoire. Donegal fiddle style is melodic but with lively bowing techniques, whereas the Sligo style, exemplified in the playing of the great **Michael Coleman**, is more elaborate and flamboyant. The Donegal repertoire would incline towards reels, flings, highlands and tunes with a Scots influence while in Kerry the repertoire does not feature reels so much as polkas, jigs and slides. There are literally hundreds of fine fiddle players: **Tommy Peoples**, **Kevin Burke**, **Eileen Ivers**, **Liz Carroll**, **Frankie Gavin**, **Sean Keane**, **Paddy Glackin**, **Martin Hayes**, **Paul Shaughnessy** and **Matt Cranitch** are but the tip of the iceberg.

Bouzouki and Guitar

At first sight it might seem odd to include the **bouzouki** on a list of traditional Irish instruments. Nevertheless, its light but piercing tone makes it eminently suitable both for melodies and providing a restrained chordal backing within an ensemble, and since its introduction to the island by **Johnny Moynihan** in the late 1960s, and subsequent popularisation by **Donal Lunny**, it has taken firm root. In the process it has lost much of its original Greek form, and with its flat back the Irish bouzouki is really closer to a member of the mandolin family. Along with other string instruments like the guitar and banjo, which provide supporting harmonies in a 'folky' idiom, bouzoukis crop up at sessions all over the country, and some of the best accompanists are bouzouki players.

The **guitar** is still the most common accompaniment in traditional music and over the decades a traditional style has grown up around the instrument. A guitar player of genius is **Steve Cooney**, partner to the west Kerry box-player and singer Seamus Begley, whose individual style – a blend of rhythm and syncopation rooted in the dance tradition of that area – has influenced a whole generation of younger musicians. Other outstanding players include **Arty McGlynn**, **Alec Finn** of De Dannan, and **Donal Lunny**.

Accordions and Concertinas

The **box** or **accordion** is an important instrument in Irish traditional music. Despite being derided by Ó Riada as an ugly sounding import, it (or the smaller **melodeon**) features in most traditional ensembles. **Sharon Shannon** is the big name at present amid a cast that perhaps has more outstanding players than any other instrument except the fiddle. **Jackie Daly**, **Mairtin O'Connor**, **Dermot Byrne**, **Joe Bourke**, **Josephine Marsh**, **Tony MacMahon**, **Breandan** and **Seamus Begley**, **Paul Brock** and **Dave Hennessy** are just a few who spring to mind.

The **concertina** – also free reed – was a popular instrument in country houses in the last century, particularly in Clare, which produced some exemplary players like the renowned **Mrs Crotty**. **Mary MacNamara** and **Noel Hill** carry on the tradition of fine Clare concertina playing today while **Niall Vallely** from Armagh, the front man of Nomos, is one of the most innovative traditional players around on any instrument.

Sharon Shannon with a button accordion

Airs and Groups

The instrumental repertoire is, as already described, made up mainly of dance tunes. But there is also a group of instrumental pieces known as **Fonn Mall** (slow airs) played without accompaniment. Most of them are laments or the melodies of songs, some of such antiquity that the words have been lost. The **uilleann pipes** (see instruments box) are particularly well suited to the performance of airs, as their plaintive tone and ability to perform complex ornaments cleanly allows them to approach the style of *sean nós* (unaccompanied) singers, but most good players, regardless of their instrument, will have a repertoire of airs.

Playing airs offers the musician challenging expressive possibilities. Just listen to the great box (accordion) player **Tony MacMahon** on "Port na bPucai" (The Ghosts' Tune), a haunting and exquisite air supposedly taught to fishermen in the Blasket Sound by fairy musicians at the dead of night. Or listen to **Davy Spillane**, one of the top contemporary pipers, reworking the conventions of the slow air in his own composition "Equinox", which incorporates electric guitar and low whistle. To listen to a solo player, whatever their instrument, is to get close to something old and fundamental in the tradition.

Playing in **groups** or with accompaniment is a prominent feature of traditional music performance today. Most concerts that charge for entry feature at least two musicians playing together, and frequently more plus a singer or two. **Altan** (see box on p.180) is perhaps the exemplary group in this mode, a combination of 'pure' tradition and contemporary accompaniment. The band moves easily between the base traditional repertoire and modern arrangements and all the combinations in between.

Ireland's best-known traditional band, **The Chieftains**, carry on the virtuoso tradition, too. This group was the spearhead of the 1960s revival of Irish traditional music – indeed, the revival is largely down to the efforts of the group's founder, composer and arranger, **Seán Ó Riada**. Living in the *Gaeltacht* (Irish-speaking area) of Cúil Aodha,

JEFFREY CRAIG/CLADDAGH RECORDS

Seán Ó Riada:
the genius of Irish traditional music

in West Cork, renowned for its singers and passionate devotion to music, Ó Riada hit on the idea of ensemble music-making using traditional instruments like the pipes, fiddle and whistle. It was a brilliantly obvious innovation and, over the next three decades, The Chieftains developed the concept of ensemble playing to the point where it became universally accepted. In addition, Ó Riada brought his genius for interpretation to bear on choral, liturgical and orchestral music. The choir he founded in the 1960s is still in existence and can be heard every Sunday in the church in Cúil Aodha as well as at sessions and concerts.

The most prominent solo traditional player to go the ensemble route is **Sharon Shannon**. A precociously skilled accordion player with a dazzling technique and a unique and much-copied personal style she is also an accomplished fiddle and whistle player. Her home county of Clare remains a stronghold of traditional music and of a particular regional style, and has produced some of the greatest players of this century including **Willie Clancy**, **Bobby Casey**, **Micho Russell**, **Martin Rochford** and **Paddy Canny**, to name but a few.

After a spell playing with Mike Scott and the Waterboys, and with Arcady, Sharon went on to form her own band, while guesting occasionally with Donal Lunny's Coolfin. She mixes well-known Irish traditional tunes with Cajun, Swedish and North American material, even Reggae. More than any other traditional musician she has an uncanny feel for the apropropriate mix of styles in the right proportions. Her energetic, driving and highly melodic personal style hits the Irish zeitgeist head on making her probably the most popular traditional musician in the country.

A quieter but perhaps equally significant course has been charted over the past couple of decades by **Mícheál Ó Súilleabháin**, who has created a fusion of Irish traditional, Classical and jazz music, developing a unique piano style. Ó Súilleabháin is also a significant figure in Irish music through his work at the pioneering Limerick University music department, which offers courses in traditional Irish music and has an associated World Music Centre (for more on which, see *www.ul.ie/~iwmc/*).

Clancys and Dubliners

The guitar revolutionised not only the presentation of instrumental and folk/traditional material in Ireland, but also changed the singing tradition. The guitar was the instrument of the 1950s and made possible harmonic chordal accompaniment formerly provided by the unwieldy and immobile piano.

Singing folk songs to instrumental accompaniment became universally popular in Ireland in the 1960s with the triumphal return from America of **The Clancy Brothers and Tommy Maken**. The Clancys had taken New York's Carnegie Hall and the networked Ed Sullivan Show by storm and they were welcomed home to Ireland as conquering heroes. Their heady blend of rousing ballads accompanied by guitar, harmonica, and five-string banjo revitalised a genre of folk song that had been all but scrapped. Hundreds of sound-alike ballad groups decked out in a motley selection of ganseys – The Clancys' hallmark was the Arran sweater – sprang up.

The ballad group fashion eventually petered out, but it had laid the foundations for a revival of interest in popular folk singing that has remained solid. Another great group of this era, one still going strong, was **The Dubliners**. As well as fielding two unique singers, Luke Kelly (who died in 1984) and Ronnie Drew, they boasted two fine traditional players: banjoist Barney McKenna and fiddler John Sheehan. The Dubliners were resolutely urban and their repertoire and approach to performance was gritty, energetic and bawdy.

Songwriter Elvis Costello once remarked of north London Irish folk-punk band The Pogues that their music was "the promise of a good time", and this was ever the case with Dubliners. No surprise then to see the two bands coming together in 1987 to record "The Irish Rover" which stands as one of the most thoroughgoing deconstructions of a bowdlerised oirish ballad ever to be recorded.

BRIAN SHUEL

The Clancy Brothers with Tommy Makem, 1963

Sean Nós and the Vocal Tradition

Songs in the Irish language are at the heart of the Irish tradition, freighted with significance as one of the few fragile links to the culture of Gaelic Ireland. The most important of them belong to a repertoire known as **sean nós** (old style) – an unaccompanied singing form of great beauty and complexity. It is thought to derive from the bardic

tradition which died out in the seventeenth century with the demise of the old Gaelic order and may also have connections to the sacred music of the early Christian Church in Ireland. Sean nós makes heavy demands on both singer and listener. The former requires the skill to vary the interpretation of each verse by means of subtle changes in tempo, ornamentation, timbre and stress, while the latter needs to possess the knowledge and discrimination to fully appreciate the singer's efforts.

Different areas have slightly differing sean nós styles although there are songs common to all regional traditions. The songs of Connemara, for example, have elaborate melodies that lie within a small vocal range, whereas those from Munster are simpler but have a wider range. The sean nós repertoire is made up of long songs which have an allusive and delicate poetic style. There are also many less complex songs, ballads, love songs, lullabies, children's songs, comic songs, and local songs of all sorts. In addition, most sean nós singers have English language songs in their repertoire: ballads of great antiquity such as "Barbara Allen" or "False Knight On The Road", as well as Irish songs composed in English – love songs, carols, emigration songs, and rebel songs.

The tradition of **informal singing** is still a strong one in Ireland. The spectacle of four or five thousand Irish people singing along word perfect at, say, a Christy Moore gig is not unusual.

Visiting singers have often remarked on this side to Irish gigs and enjoy playing in Ireland because of it. Singers in pubs, however, have had to struggle to be heard in recent years as publicans have opted to refit with bigger rooms for amplified groups. To hear traditional singing, you need to look for sessions promoted by singers' clubs (which hire rooms), or to find a singers' session at one of the festivals.

One of the highpoints of the sean nós singers' year is at the **Oireachtas**, the great gathering of the Gaeltacht community to promote and encourage traditional culture, when the prestigious **Coirn Uí Riada** competition is held. The winners bring acclaim not only on themselves but also on their region, as most singers come from one or other of the Gaeltachts. In Dublin, there is also a singers' movement, **Sean Nós Cois Life**, who organise an annual festival in the city and run workshops and sessions.

Afro-Celt Sound System: Sean Nós Grooves

The **Afro-Celt Sound System** was conceived in 1996 at a RealWorld Recording Week – a week of concerted recording and musical collaboration at the label's Wiltshire studios that follows each summer's WOMAD festival at Reading. The idea sounded distinctly half-baked, nightmarish even: to combine Celtic and West African instruments and vocals with state of the art dance production. But, steered by producers **Simon Emmerson** and **Martin Russell**, and fired by a group of virtuoso talents, it worked surprisingly well on disc – *Volume One: Sound Magic* (1996) – and even better out on the road.

In 1999 the Afro-Celts returned with a new album, release, *Volume Two: Release*, and an enhanced line-up, featuring, on the Irish side, sean nós vocalist **Iarla Ó Lionáird**, uillean pipers **Michael McGoldrick** and **Ronan Browne**, and a certain **Sinead O'Connor**. West Africa contributed the griots (master musicians) **N'Faly Kouyate** (vocals, kora, balafon) and **Moussa Sissokho** (talking drum), while other Celts included the Breton harpist **Myrhdin**.

The group and its discs have been outstandingly popular and, amazingly, critically well received, for such fusions don't often come off. Yet the Afro-Celt approach has

shown that you can have a dance mix appealing to club culture that doesn't destroy its components. Indeed, among the highlights of the albums are the ways in which the bodhrán drives a groove with African percussion, and the way that O Lionáird's meditative vocals emerge from the ambient sounds of kora and sequencers. Live, meanwhile, they're something else, with a full-on sound that can make leaps from traditional Irish material to hard-core techno.

Afro-Celt sean nós vocalist Iarla Ó Lionáird

Moving Hearts

Less obvious, perhaps, is the influence of sean nós on Irish rock singers with the vocal confidence to take on unaccomapanied material, among them **Sinead O'Connor**, **Van Morrison**, **Dolores Ó Riordan** of The Cranberries, and – above all – **Liam Ó Maonlaí** of Hothouse Flowers (who is an accomplished sean nós singer in his own right). Their raw, stripped-down singing style and a developed range of vocalisations derives in part from exposure to folk or traditional material. The hugely popular Irish singer-keyboard player **Enya** also owes a large debt to sean nós in her Gaelic-New Age styled music. She actually began her career singing with the roots-oriented group, **Clannad**.

Most recently sean nós has had an unlikely implosion with African and dance rhythms through the **Afro-Celt Sound System**, a RealWorld fusion group which features the Donegal singer **Iarla Ó Lionáird** (see feature box opposite).

Shamrock'n'roll

Since the 1960s Ireland has had an indigenous rock scene which at times owes little or nothing to traditional music. However, even a band like U2 – who once rejected traditional music as part of the repressiveness of Irish culture – have incorporated its strands in recent years. And London-Irish iconoclasts **The Pogues** emerged in the early 1980s playing a chaotic set of 'Oirish' standards and rebel songs, bringing a punk energy to the Irish ballad. They were also blessed with one of the finest Irish songwriters of recent years, **Shane MacGowan**, who, in his subsequent solo career with The Popes continues to capture the state of Irish exile in a series of raw pain-filled ballads.

Moving back, however, to the 1960s and '70s, when rock was emerging as a force, a revival of interest in traditional music and singing was also taking place. Ireland is a small country so it was inevitable that a certain amount of crossover took place, although the traffic was mostly in one direction, as rock musicians raided the storehouse of Irishry to lend a Celtic air to their songs. The most influential figures in blending rock with traditional music, from the 1970s on, have been bouzouki and keyboard player **Donal Lunny** and singer **Christy Moore**, the founders, with **Andy Irvine**, of **Planxty**, a band which really changed the way young Irish people looked on the old folk repertoire. Their arrangements of old airs and tunes, and Liam O'Flynn's wonderful uillean piping, opened a lot of ears and inspired a lot of the new Celtic groups of the last two decades.

In 1981 Lunny and Moore made a more radical attempt to fuse traditional and rock music with the launching of **Moving Hearts**. Their objective was to bring traditional music up-to-date by drawing on all the apparatus of rock, yet without compromising the folk element. It was a tall order, but they came as close as any Irish band has ever done, using rock and jazz to rethink the harmonic and rhythmic foundations of Irish music. The line-up was led, remarkably, by pipes and saxophone, with backing from bass and lead guitars, electric bouzouki, drums and percussion. Their gigs were feasts of music that seemed both familiar and new at the same time, while the lyrics, unusually in (southern) Ireland took on politics head on, with a commitment to the rights of the dispossessed – in Ireland and beyond. They lost momentum when Christy Moore departed for a

Altan

In the 1990s, **Altan**, along with the Bothy Band and De Danaan, were the flagbearers for the Irish traditional band scene, taking the place of the old guard of The Chieftains and Clannad. A band who have always mixed group numbers with traditional solo playing, they were forged by fiddler and singer **Mairéad Ni Mhaonaigh** from Donegal and the late, much-missed flautist and whistle-player **Frankie Kennedy** from Belfast.

Kennedy, who was struck down in his thirties, was a huge talent, helping to shape the group's classic *Island Angel*, a landmark album for contemporary traditional music, reworking traditional songs and airs in a rock-infused format. On the traditional side, a strong infouence was the music of Donegal – a county strongly associated with the fiddle (Mairéad's father, Proinsias, is a well-known fiddler in the Donegal tradition). Since Kennedy's death, the band have consolidated this regional bias – and their traditional firepower – with the addition of virtuoso Donegal box player Dermot Byrne.

The group's sound, for all its crossover success, was and is resolutely traditional. They play within traditional structure, and although they play Scottish tunes (notably from Cape Breton Island), they don't try and incorporate blues or Cajun (of which they are fans). They don't plan their albums a lot either, taking songs and airs from the oral tradition in time-honoured fashion. And their roots are reinforced by the fact that Mairéad sings mainly in Gaelic – naturally enough, as it's her first language. Altan's albums, as a result, incorporate all the elements of contemporary arrangement and instrumentation while retaining regional and local coherence to a remarkable degree.

A winterschool and festival in the Gaeltacht region of Gaoth Dobhair in Co Donegal is held shortly after Christmas in Frankie Kennedy's memory. This has become a winter highlight of the traditional music year and regularly turns in memorable concerts, sessions and workshops.

STEVE GILLET

Atlan's Mairéad Ni Mhaonaigh

solo career in 1982, and folded in 1984, but they had created a space for future Irish groups to follow. Each of their chief players, too – **Christy Moore**, **Donal Lunny**, **Declan Sinnott**, **Davy Spillane** – have remained influential solo and group players through the 1980s and '90s.

Another hugely influential group, through the 1990s, have been **Altan** (see feature box above), who achieved the rare success of fusing a rock sensibility on traditional music without compromising the latter. Midway through the decade, they were joined by a new Donal Lunny supergroup, **Coolfin**, featuring Maighréad Ní Dhomhnaill on vocals, Nollaig Casey on fiddle, John McSherry on pipes, and Sharon Shannon on box: a stunning band, on disc and especially live.

Other groups working in the borderlands of rock in the 1990s included **Alias Ron Kavana** and **Déanta**, and the sadly extinct **Four Men and a Dog**, each of whom maintained a traditional core repertoire, using rock mainly for its image and sound. "Traditional music with balls" is how the Four Men classified their very danceable and likeably unclassifiable mix, forged by such players as Conor Keane on accordion and veteran guitarist Artie McGlynn, whose career takes in the Clancys, Planxty and a spell with top 1980s band **Patrick Street**. Ron Kavana, who is responsible for the series of trad re-issues on the GlobeStyle Irish label, has a somewhat different approach, combining Irish material and instruments (including pipes) with African and Latin rhythms, and an energetic delivery hailing back to his R&B days.

Newer groups include **Goats Don't Shave**, featuring singer Pat Gallagher; **Nomos**, a Cork-based four-piece ensemble, who present a mix of contemporary traditional music and Irish and English language material by singer-songwriter John Spillane; and the Dublin band **Kíla**, who offer an eclectic and beguiling and danceable melange of trad, rap and funk. And then there is the aforementioned **Afro-Celt Sound System** (see box on p.178), mixing Irish sounds with those of Africa and the techno dance scene.

discography

For ease of reference, reviews below are grouped first into general compilations (and series), followed by sections on singers, instrumentalists, and groups.

General compilations/series

**Claddagh's Choice:
An Anthology of Irish Traditional Music:
Vols 1 and 2** (Claddagh, Ireland).

The prestigious Irish label has been releasing the cream of traditional music since the late 1950s and this double album is both a marvellous trawl through its back catalogue and a fine introduction to the genre.

 GlobeStyle Irish Series: Treasure of My Heart (GlobeStyle, UK).

This is a fabulous sampler of GlobeStyle's Irish Series – a series of compilations of material taken from the extensive archives of the Topic record label by musician Ron Kavana. Each of the main series CDs has a thematic angle and there's not a duff track to be heard throughout. Available in the main series are:

- **Leaving Tipperary: Irish Music in America**
- **The Gentleman Pipers: Classic Irish Piping**
- **In the Smoke: Irish Music in '60s London**
- **The Rushy Mountain: Music from Sliabh Luachra**
- **The Wandering Minstrels: Irish Dance Music**
- **Hurry the Jug: Songs, Lilting and Storytelling**
- **A Living Thing: Contemporary Classics**
- **The Coolin: Irish Laments and Airs**
- **Happy to Meet: Traditional Irish Dance Music**

Sleeve notes on these are admirably copious, too, providing an excellent overview of the various strands of Irish music.

Beauty an Oileain: Music and Song of the Blasket Islands (Claddagh, Ireland).

The rich folk culture of The Blasket Islands – islands off the southwest coast of Ireland, abandoned in 1952 – has been well documented and this album reveals that it also produced a remarkable traditional music culture. Sourced from a variety of recordings, from the 1950s to the '90s, these songs, tunes and airs are moving evocations of island life. Accompanying notes are particularly informative.

Bringing It All Back Home (Hummingbird, Ireland).

Music from a TV series which documented the journey, development and influence of traditional music overseas. Songs in Irish and English, dance tunes, airs, laments, group and solo, country, contemporary, traditional and classical.

Dear Old Erin's Isle (Nimbus, UK).

Superb recording of a 1992 Cork festival which brought together some of America's best Irish musicians, including old-timers like piper Joe Shannon and melodeon player Tom Doherty, and young fiddlers like Eileen Ives and Liz Carroll.

Our Musical Heritage (Funduireacht an Riadaigh, Ireland).

With its accompanying book, this three-cassette anthology of singers and instrumentalists, compiled by Seán Ó Riada from 1960s radio programmes, is an indispensable guide to all aspects of Irish traditional music.

A River of Sound: The Changing Course of Irish Music (Virgin,UK).

With its genesis in another television series, the music on this CD has been (well) chosen to illustrate the diversity of traditional musical styles to be found in Irish music as well as some of the more experimental attempts at fusion with both Western classical and global traditions.

Singers

Artists

Begley and Cooney

The matchless partnership of West Kerry box player and singer Seamus Begley with Australian guitarist Steve Cooney has to date produced one classic album.

Meitheal (Hummingbird, Ireland).

A glorious life-affirming recording of Sliabh Luachra repertory: polkas, slides, jigs, reels, and three 'big' regional songs tenderly sung and beautifully accompanied.

Dominic Behan

Brendan Behan's younger brother, Dominic was a dramatist, too, and a successful satirist, balladeer and singer. His ancestors were Fenians and his uncle, Peadar Kearney, penned the Irish National Anthem. His voice was not the best, but there was a force to his singing which perfectly matched the rebel songs he recorded.

Easter Week and After (Topic, UK).

The ultimate rebel song album, on which Behan sings sixteen songs telling the tale of the IRA from the Easter Rising to the late 1950s – from Erin Go Brath (Ireland So Fine) by Peadar Kearney to Behan's own famous "The Patriot Game" inspired by an abortive IRA attack on the RUC's Brookesborough Barracks in 1957.

Mary Black

Ireland's most popular female singer, Mary Black has been performing and recording since the 1970s, including spells with her brothers and sister Frances (herself a star in Ireland) in The Black Family and also with De Dannan. Her solo career really took off when she teamed up with Moving Hearts' guitarist Declan Sinnott as her producer and arranger. Her 1993 album Holy Ground went platinum in Ireland on the day of its release.

Shine (Grapevine, UK).

Though this, Black's latest album, was produced by Larry Klein in California, it still bears all the hallmarks of her sound: a powerfully emotional voice backed by a mixture of rock and traditional instruments.

Luka Bloom

Christy Moore's younger brother Barry achieved greater success afrer he changed his name to Luka Bloom (after Suzanne Vega's song and Joyce's protagonist in Ulysses) and travelled to record in America. More rocking than Christy, but sharing the same percussive guitar style, he is also a lyricist of some poignancy.

Riverside (Reprise, US).

Bloom's debut and still his best album, this includes two of his most notable songs, the wistful "Dreams in America", and the more boisterous "You Couldn't Have Come at a Better Time", featuring Eileen Ivers on fiddle.

Paul Brady

Singer-guitarist Paul Brady was a member of folk group The Johnstons before replacing Christy Moore in Planxty in the mid-1970s. Subsequently, he changed tack and enjoyed a successful career in mainstream rock, his songs being covered by Tina Turner amongst others. However, Brady retains the respect of traditional musicians and pops up occasionally on their own albums.

 Hard Station (Rykodisc, UK/US).

Brady's first venture into the rock world, and arguably still his best, this includes his incisive account of the experiences of Irish émigrés to London – "Nothing But the Same Old Story".

 Molloy, Brady, Peoples (Mulligan, Ireland).

A largely successful 'supergroup' outing featuring Brady's voice and guitar, Matt Molloy's flute and the sadly underrecorded Donegal-style fiddle of Tommy Peoples on a grand selection of jigs, reels and songs.

Karan Casey

Casey is a fine young singer, originally from Waterford but long resident in the US, and was lead vocalist until summer 1999 with prominent American-Irish band Solas.

 Songlines (Shanachie, US).

This solo album features mainstream traditional English and Irish language material. Casey's singing displays a very finely tuned senstivity to the vocal tradition.

Maighread Ní Dhomhnaill

Maighread Ní Dhomhnaill is one of Ireland's most accomplished traditional singers. Her repertory is sourced in the Donegal tradition transmitted through her family, particularly her late aunt Nellie Ní Dhomhnaill. She started out in the 1970s with the highly-rated band Skara Brae and currently sings with Donal Lunny's band Coolfin and also with her sister Triona.

 No Dowry
(Gael Linn, Ireland).

Here is Ní Dhomhnaill in wonderful voice, singing in Irish and English, both unaccompanied, and accompanied with understated skill and sympathy by Donal Lunny.

Joe Heaney

From Carna in the Connemara Gaeltacht, the late Joe Heaney was one of the greatest singers of the pure traditional style called sean nós. His powerful voice led someone to say of him, "he opened his mouth and the voice came out like an iron bar".

 The Best of Joe Heaney – From My Tradition
(Shanachie, US).

This fine selection includes classics of the sean nós repertoire as well as Irish traditional material in English.

Dolores Keane

The possessor of perhaps the purest voice in Irish music, Dolores Keane sang with De Dannan before embarking on an increasingly successful solo career. In recent years her choice of material has drifted close to MOR and light Country, which many feel unsuited to such a fine interpreter of traditional songs.

 There Was a Maid
(Claddagh, Ireland).

"Seven Yellow Gypsies" is one of many highlights on Keane's best traditional album, recorded in the late 1970s, and exemplifying all the brio and ornamentation that are synonymous with her singing style.

Dolores Keane and Mary Black

Séan Keane

Dolores's brother Séan (no relation to the fiddler in The Chieftains) is also a superb singer.

 All Heart, No Roses (Cross Border Media, Ireland).

After building a formidable reputation, Sean Keane finally released this debut album in 1993 – a fine collection of songs recorded with able assistance from Jackie Daly on accordion.

Christy Moore

Kildare-born singer Christy Moore is an Irish institution, notable both for the strength of his political commitment and massive stage presence. He was a founding member of first Planxty then Moving Hearts before revitalising his own solo career in the 1980s. Long acclaimed for his sensitive yet highly personal interpretation of others' material, he finally recorded an album of his own songs, *Graffiti Tongue* (Columbia), in 1996. He has recently started performing again after a period of ill-health.

 Ride On (WEA, UK).

Moore's 1984 breakthrough album contains many of his most popular songs and remains a prime showcase for the breadth of his material which here ranges from the pensive romanticism of the title track to the jubilation of the Spanish Civil War song "Vive La Quinta Brigada", as well as his satirical take on the music scene in Lisdoonvarna.

 Christy Moore At The Point Live
(Grapevine, Ireland).

This great live album captures all the vitality and contrasting moods of a Moore concert, including his tremendous distaste for hecklers and his ability to have his audience (literally) rolling in the aisles with numbers like "Joxter Goes to Stuttgart".

Lillis Ó Laoire

Ó Laoire is one of the best young sean nós singers to emerge from the Donegal gaeltacht in recent years and twice a winner of the prestigious Corn Uí Riada.

 Bláth Gach Géag da dTig
(Cló lar Chonnachta, Ireland).

A showcase of Donegal regional song and style lovingly collected from old singers (particularly from the Tory islands).

Iarla Ó Lionáird

Iarla Ó Lionáird, another superb contemporary sean nós singer, has consistantly sought to push out the frontiers of his art, both in his solo work and with the Afro-Celt Sound System (see 'Groups', p.185).

The Seven Steps to Mercy
(RealWorld, UK).

Although sean nós has a a quite a reputation for being difficult and inaccessible, the ambient settings and relaxing sound of the arrangements on this album make accessible many of the great songs of the tradition.

Instrumentalists

Compilations

The Drones and the Chanters Vol 2
(Cladagh, Ireland).

A collection of well-known and less well-known tunes by a selection of mainly young pipers paying tribute to and re-interpreting the tradition, with especially good contributions by Gay Mc Keon and Ronan Browne. A good introduction to current developments in the field of Irish pipering.

Fiddlesticks (Nimbus, UK).

This CD, recorded at a festival of Donegal fiddlers in 1991, gives a more than decent view of recent developments in Irish fiddle playing. As well as forceful ensemble playing, it features solos from the legendary Tommy Peoples and Seamus and Kevin Glackin.

Artists

Mary Bergin

Mary Bergin is Ireland's most accomplished tin whistle and pipe player. An exemplary traditional player she is also a member of Dordán – the all woman Galway based group (harp/fiddle/whistles/vocals) – with whom she plays a beguiling mix of hiberno-baroque and trad.

Feadóga Stáin 1 and **Feadóga Stáin 2**
(Gael Linn, Ireland).

Bergin's two solo albums are classics. She is accompanied on both recordings by longtime collaborators Johnny 'Ringo' McDonagh on bodhrán and Alec Finn on bouzouki, and Dordán feature on one track on Volume 2.

Nollaig Casey and Arty McGlynn

Partners both in marriage and music, Casey and McGlynn are two of the most respected musicians on the traditional circuit and beyond. Cork-born Casey is a talented fiddler while guitarist McGlynn has played with Van Morrison and was a member of Four Men and a Dog. His talents as a producer are also heavily in demand.

Causeway (Tara, Ireland).

Inspired by The Giant's Causeway, this is a parson's egg of an album with some highly memorable moments, including Nollaig Casey's solos and Arty McGlynn's wonderful application of a jazz guitar style to a traditionally inspired backing, though it at times comes close to sinking in an ambient mire.

Máire Ní Chathasaigh and Chris Newman

Harpist Máire Ní Chathasaigh and guitarist Chris Newman are figures from the more classical and arranged side of Irish music.

The Carolan Albums (Old Bridge Music, Ireland).

Guitar and Irish harp join together on arrangements of harp music by the great Turlough Ó Carolan, the so-called 'last of the old Irish harpers'. Ó Carolan's music interfaces the old Irish harp repertoire with the Baroque music popular in Ireland in the seventeenth and eighteenth centuries. These superbly and precisely arranged tracks sparkle with life.

Michael Coleman

Sligo fiddler Michael Coleman has been probably the most influential Irish musician of the twentieth century. Although he moved to the US as a teenager, the recordings that he made there fed the imagination of generations of musicians back home.

 Viva Voce: Michael Coleman 1891–1945
(Viva Voce, Ireland).

Wonderful recordings of the great Sligo fiddler at his best, digitally remastered on a superb double CD.

Seamus Creagh

Seamus Creagh is one of the best-kept secrets in Irish fiddle playing. In the 1970s he was a partner of box virtuoso Jackie Daly.

Came The Dawn (Ossian, Ireland).

Creagh's long-awaited solo album is a gem; he displays in equal measure superb techinque, subtle, beautifully judged playing, and an expressiveness which defies attempts to describe it.

WITH JACKIE DALY

 Jackie Daly and Seamus Creagh
(Gael-Linn, Ireland).

This 1977 album of fiddle and box is, simply, one of the best Irish duo albums of all time.

WITH AIDAN COFFEY

Seamus Creagh/Aidan Coffey (Ossian, Ireland).

Creagh has been partnering young Co. Waterford and ex-De Dannan accordionist Aidan Coffey since 1992, and this stunning 1997 collection shows the partnership in full flow. There's an exuberance to their music that transports you to their weekly session in Cork City . . . and Coffey turns out to be a wizard at the polka.

Johnny Doran

Johnny Doran, one of the last of the travelling pipers, was feted for his wild, unique and compelling approach to his music. He only recorded once in his life, shortly before his death; these few precious fragments have an almost legendary status among connoisseurs.

📷 **The Bunch of Keys** (CBE-Gael Linn, Ireland).

The classic 1940s recordings of Doran on uillean pipes. A CD re-release is very long overdue.

Seamus Egan

Philadelphia-born Egan had by age 20 already won all-Ireland titles for four different instruments – an unprecedented achievement. At home on flute, whistles, banjo or mandolin, he is currently a leading light in the Irish-American band Solas.

📷 **A Week in January** (Shanachie, US).

Seamus Egan recorded this album at 20 and there's a characteristically youthful vigour in his interpretations of assorted jigs and reels, though he shows a delicate touch too, especially in his flute-playing on the air "Dark Slender Boy".

Seamus Ennis

Late great master-piper, and a major figure in performing, collecting and preserving traditional music, Seamus Ennis still influences traditional players of all instruments today with his quirkily joyous approach to dance, tempered by emotionally mature airs and laments.

📷 **Return to Fingal** (RTE, Ireland).

This magnificent survey of Ennis's life and work covers recordings made when he was barely in his twenties up to a couple of years before his death in the early 1980s. A bonus is the inclusion of some of his singing. Indispensible for anyone who wants to understand how a giant of Irish music developed his highly personal style.

Paddy Glackin

Paddy Glackin is a superb fiddle player, with a strong Donegal influence in his style and selection of tunes.

📷 **Rabharta Ceoil: In Full Spate** (Gael Linn, Ireland).

On this enjoyable CD Glackin is joined by brothers Kevin and Seamus on fiddle and Robbie Hannon on uillean pipes. The album also benefits from the arrangement and accompaniment skills of Donal Lunny.

Martin Hayes

Although his roots lie in the Clare style of fiddle playing learnt from his father and uncle, both famous musicians, Martin Hayes also draws on blues and jazz influences to create a personal style of playing, notable for its blend of energy and lyricism.

WITH DENNIS CAHILL

📷 **The Lonesome Touch**
(Gael-Linn, Ireland/Green Linnet, US).

Hayes found a true soul-mate in American guitarist Dennis Cahill, whose sensitive accompaniment provides a solid foundation for the fiddler's inspired extemporisation. This isn't quite up to their stupendous live shows, but it's not far off.

Noel Hill and Tony MacMahon

Concertina wizard Noel Hill owes much to the piping tradition while his collaborator accordionist Tony MacMahon is one of the finer exponents of his instrument.

 I gGnoc na Graoi'
(Gael Linn, Ireland).

Recorded one memorable night at a session in Dan Connell's

pub in Knocknagree, County Kerry. Hill and MacMahon play for a group of set-dancers, this session of wonderful music captures the party atmosphere to perfection.

Eileen Ivers

Eileen Ivers is a young Irish-American fiddler – and already among the best in the business, with a well-judged balance between tradition and innovation, despite a sustained spell with Riverdance.

📷 **Wild Blue** (Green Linnet, US).

Slow airs and electrifying performances of dance tunes abound on this remarkable 1997 album. The opening track, "On Horseback" is virtuoso fiddling at its very best.

📷 **So Far: The Eileen Ivers Collection, 1979–95**
(Green Linnet, US).

A sparkling anthology tracing Ivers' development from her days as a student at Martin Mulvilhill's celebrated fiddle school in West Limerick to the soulful interpreter of traditional airs. Her "Lament for Staker Wallace" should bring tears to anyone's eyes.

James Keane

Brother of Sean (of The Chieftains), accordionist James Keane played with many of the great figures of the 1960s traditional revival before settling in the US in 1968, where he became a major name in Irish-American music.

📷 **With Friends Like These** (Shanachie, US).

Keane returned to visit Ireland in the late-1990s and this is a glorious souvenir of his stay; fifteen tracks, including a couple by the accordionist himself, featuring the fiddles of Paddy Glackin and Tommy Peoples, the pipes and flute of Liam Ó Flynn, Matt Molloy, and the lilting voice of Kevin Conneff.

Paddy Keenan

Ex-Bothy Band piper Paddy Keenan is in the opinion of many the greatest living exponent of the uillean pipes.

📷 **Paddy Keenan** (Gael-Linn, Ireland).

On this, his first album, Keenan was accompanied by his brothers John (banjo) and Thomas (whistle), along with Paddy Glackin on violin. The resulting brew was an Irish classic where the piper's and fiddler's shared mastery of harmonics blended to memorable effect.

📷 **Ná Keen Affair** (Hot Conya, US).

This recent outing, Keenan's first solo recording for a decade, proved well worth the wait. It features contributions from great players young and old, including fiddlers Tommy Peoples and Seamus Creach, and Niall Vallely on concertina. Recording quality is a variable but the playing is magnificent throughout. Available by mail order only from *Hot Conya*, 226 Banks Street, Suite 6 Cambridge MA 02138, US.

Mary MacNamara

Concertina player Mary MacNamara comes from a family of musicians, and is a worthy member of the latest generation of musicians in her native East Clare.

📷 **Traditional Music from East Clare**
(Claddagh, Ireland).

This collection of solos, interspersed with duets with fiddler Martin Hayes, shows MacNamara's gift for the graceful interpretation of dance music.

Josephine Marsh

A wonderful young box player from Co. Clare, Josephine Marsh is also an acomplished maker of tunes – some of which feature on her sparkling debut album.

 Josephine Marsh (Claddagh, Ireland).

A fine first album. Well worth seeking out.

Matt Molloy

Matt Molloy, a flute player from the Roscommon/Sligo region, is a musician of consumate sensitivity. He plays and tours with The Chieftains, is the landlord of a well-known music pub in Westport, Co. Mayo, and commands great respect as a player from the critically demanding traditional hard core.

Shadows on Stone (Virgin, UK).

Molloy's first solo album for a number of years justified all the superlatives used to describe his playing. A must for any Irish music collection.

Liam O'Flynn

One of the most versatile musicians of his generation and a master piper of impeccable traditional credentials, O'Flynn excels both as a solo and ensemble player – the latter both with Planxty and accompanying a symphony orchestra in "The Brendan Voyage".

 The Piper's Call (Tara, Ireland).

All of O'Flynn's piping skills are on display, magisterial solo playing on the airs, one arranged by Mícheál Ó Súilleabháin and played with the Irish Chamber Orchestra and by contrast a gritty soulful air accompanied by Mark Knopfler.

Brendan Power

New Zealand-born harmonica player, Brendan Power adds his name to a small but illustrious list of harmonica master players. In his case virtuoso technique combines with a sympathetic approach to traditional music informed by jazz and blues. All the bent or blued notes are effortlessly expressed, while the ornamentation intrinsic to traditional music is perfectly executed.

 New Irish Harmonica (Punchmusic, Ireland).

If it has to be done at all, it might as well be done like this.

Micho Russell/Russell Family

Micho Russell, master of the tin whistle and of the Co. Clare tradition, both musical and folkloric, played in a plain and direct style, with tremendous charm.

 Ireland's Whistling Ambassador (Pennywhistle Press, US).

Recorded shortly before his untimely death in a car crash at the age of seventy-nine, and including further material, this CD, along with its handsomely produced and informative accompanying booklet, stands as a fitting memorial to a much loved figure.

THE RUSSELL FAMILY

 Traditional Music from Doolin, Co. Clare (Ossian, Ireland).

Recorded in O'Connor's pub in 1974, this is music as it used to sound in Doolin before the tourists arrived, rough around

the edges, but a vibrant testimony to the West Clare musical tradition embodied in the three brothers – Gussie and the late Micho and Pakie.

Sharon Shannon

Virtuoso Sharon Shannon is one of the brightest stars on the traditional music horizon, whose accordion and fiddle playing brings a questing, unpredictable intelligence to re-interpreting the tradition.

 Out of the Gap (Solid, Ireland).

Several of the tracks on this, Shannon's second album, were produced by famed dub producer Dennis Bovell, and it shows to good effect as the accordionist turns her hand to traditional Irish versions of reggae tunes in addition to her usual spirited renditions of traditional melodies.

Sharon Shannon (Solid, Ireland/Philo, US).

A sparkling 1993 album featuring tracks from traditional Irish to Cajun, French Canadian, and contemporary arrangements. The contributions of some fine trad and not-so-trad musicians (including Adam Clayton of U2) adds to the fun.

Davy Spillane

Uillean piper Davy Spillane was a focal member of Moving Hearts and, since their demise, his outstanding solo technique and sensitive accompaniment has been in much demand on sessions for everyone from Kate Bush to Steve Winwood.

 Out of the Air (Tara, Ireland/Cooking Vinyl, UK).

Spillane has never released his own live album, but this is the nearest thing to it. Half consists of sessions for BBC Radio One and truly captures the sheer verve of his then (1988) touring band, while the remainder adds the guitar and electric sitar (!) of famed (and, sadly late) Donegal blues-man Rory Gallagher. Spillane's low whistle duet with Gallagher's driving acoustic guitar is an eclectic gem.

Groups

Artists

Afro–Celt Sound System

A fusion project to end them all, the Afro-Celts mesh Irish (and Celtic) music with West African and techno rhythms – and to surprisingly good effect, with sean nós singer Iarla O Lionáird, especially, shining through.

 Volume 2: Release (RealWorld, UK).

The band's second (1999) album reflects an easier approach to the material, forged from some hard gigging. The disc includes some wonderful Irish singing and piping, and a guest spot from Sinead O'Connor.

Alias Ron Kavana

Now back as a solo artiste, guitarist Ron Kavana's 1990s band produced some of the most eclectic music of the decade, drawing upon influences as wide as blues, cajun, country and, of course, Irish music.

 From Galway to Graceland (Ark, Ireland).

Kavana's finest album wears its heart on its sleeve, a mixture of his own compositions, interpretations of some traditional tunes and an extraordinary traditional cover of The Rolling Stones'

"19th Nervous Breakdown". This must be the only album ever dedicated to both Micho Russell and Champion Jack Dupree.

Altan

Altan have been a key band of 1990s traditional music, taking the place of the old guard of The Chieftains and Clannad. They had recorded the landmark *Island Angel* when flute player and musical lynchpin Frankie Kennedy died tragically early (in his 30s). The Band rallied from the blow, adding virtuoso Donegal box player Dermot Byrne, and remain a major force on disc and live.

 Island Angel
(Green Linnet, US).

The classic album, before Kennedy's death, saw the band tap into the deep roots of the Ulster tradition, particularly that of Donegal, for a set that was both coherent and fresh. Their re-interpretation of regional style in contemporary idiom informs this set of great tunes and five beautiful songs from Mairéad Ní Mhaonaigh, who also plays masterfully on fiddle.

⊚ **The First Ten Years: 1986/1995**
(Green Linnet, US).

The sheer breadth of Altan's music is well-represented on this magical collection of highlights from the first decade of the band's recording career and includes Mairead's fabulous interpretation of "Dónal Agus Mórag", a wedding song from Rathlin Island.

Anam

Anam is Irish for 'soul' or 'life' and it's an obvious factor in the music produced by this young mixed Irish-Scottish-Cornish quartet whose sparky blend of self-penned and traditional material has proved popular as far afield as Japan.

⊚ **First Footing** (JVC, UK).

The addition of Cornish bouzouki player Nigel Davey has added an extra dimension to Anam's sensuous sound while Brian ó hEadhra's songwriting skills are strongly in evidence.

Anúna

Michael McGlynn formed and directs this well-respected 22-voice mixed choir whose material ranges from traditional Irish songs to Latin requiems via polyphony and McGlynn's own compositions in Irish.

⊚ **Omnis** (Danú, Ireland).

The choir's voices combine and contrast to great effect on this uplifting recording over an atmospheric backing of chants, drones and occasional percussion.

Bohinta

English-based Bohinta are a loosely-knit group led by singers Martin and Áine Furey (of the famed Furey family) who mainly perform their own material – strangely ethereal lyrics in a traditional setting.

⊚ **Bohinta** (Velo, UK).

This debut album spanned six years of recording and six different studios as the band sought a record label, but it's hard to spot the cracks in the delicate treatments of these songs and Martin and Áine Furey possess two of the most haunting voices in contemporary Irish music.

The Bothy Band

The Bothy Band, the template band of the 1970s and breeding ground for a whole tribe of musicians, featured fiddler Kevin Burke, flute virtuoso Matt Molloy, piper Paddy Keenan, and the visionary innovator Donal Lunny on bouzouki and guitar.

⊚ **The Best of the Bothy Band** (Green Linnet, US).

This representative selection of material from the band's career is probably the best place to start.

Calico

This young instrumental foursome created a storm with their debut album, and uilllean piper Diarmaid Moynihan's material has already been covered by Lúnasa and Déanta.

⊚ **Celanova Square** (Ossian, Ireland).

A grand mix of traditional Irish and Breton tunes, and Moynihan's own, played with panache and no small sense of humour with pipes and Tola Foley's fiddle well to the fore. Donncha Moynihan (guitar) and Pat Marsh (bouzouki) are no mean accompanists, either.

The Chieftains

Under the leadership of piper Paddy Maloney the Chieftains, undoubtedly one of the best-known and most entertaining of all Irish groups, have filled the role of semi-official ambassadors for Irish music for the past thirty years. Their music ranges from the almost purely traditional to lengthy suites that owe much to Western classical music, but they rarely lose their gift for presenting accessible music without compromising their dedication to tradition.

 Chieftains Four
(Shanachie, US).

This all-time favourite is a classic slice of Chieftains, dating from 1973. It was the band's international breakthrough album and the first to feature harpist Derek Bell.

⊚ **Santiago** (BMG/RCA Victor, US).

In recent years The Chieftans have done some collaborative concept albums. This 1996 recording makes a sort of imaginary pilgimage to Santiago de Compostella forging links between the Celtic music of Ireland and Galicia. Guest artists include Linda Ronstadt with Los Lobos, Ry Cooder, and Galician pipe player Carlos Nunez, 'the seventh Chieftan'.

WITH VAN MORRISON

⊚ **Irish Heartbeat** (Phonogram, UK).

Van employs his legendary Irish soul to wonderful effect on a set of largely traditional material.

Clannad

From the Donegal Gaeltacht (Gaelic speaking area), Clannad take their name from a conflation of words *Clann as Dobhair* meaning 'family from Dobhair'. Originally comprising three siblings – Máire, Paul, and Ciarán Brennan, and cousins Noel and Padraig Duggan – they have always been a strongly song-based band, reworking regional repertoire in a fresh, inventive manner. They were the first band to have a No 1 in the UK with a Gaelic language song – "Theme from Harry's Game".

⊚ **Dúlamán** (Gael Linn, Ireland).

A 1976 album of syncopated, jazz-influenced arrangements from this highly influential band.

 Macalla
(RCA, UK).

Clannad's sound changed indelibly in the mid-1980s and this is the transitional album which many still regard as their finest

PHONOGRAM

Van Morrison and The Chieftains,1988

hour. Certainly, all subsequent releases have been based on the same characteristic elements: Máire Ní Bhraonáin's ethereal voice, multi-tracked and blending with lush (and increasingly synthesised) arrangements of traditional and Celtic-inspired music.

Cran

Individually, Cran's three members have been around for some time (singer/bouzouki player Sean Corcoran recorded an album as long ago as 1977), but the band itself was only formed in the mid-1990s. Corcoran, Ronan Browne (pipes) and Desi Wilkinson (flute and whistles) produce exuberant music with an astonishing degree of technical accomplishment.

 Black Black Black (Claddagh, Ireland).

It's difficult to imagine how Cran could possibly surpass their debut album, a marvellous concoction of music and songs with an occasional Breton influence, produced by the band themselves with the surprising assistance of American rock legend Shel Talmy.

Déanta

Déanta, a band of young, mainly women virtuosos from County Antrim, bring a subtle sense of musicality and cunning to the performance of Irish classics.

 Ready for the Storm (Green Linnet, US).

The group's second album, a thoughtful tapestry of voice and instruments, demonstrates that the delicate approach pays dividends.

De Dannan

There have been many changes in the line-up of De Dannan band but the two central figures of fiddle player Frankie Gavin and bouzouki player Alec Finn remain the drving creative force behind the band. Gavin is one of the finest players of his generation while Finn stands as a pioneering player of the bouzouki, his playing characterised by elegant counter melodies and an exquisitely developed sense of timing.

De Dannan (Polydor, Ireland).

The mighty Galway band at their awe-inspiring best. Flying dance music and great singing from Mary Black, Dolores Keane and Maura Ó'Connell.

Dervish

Formed in the 1980s, Dervish are one of Ireland's most interesting bands, always tasteful and musical, without the breakneck 'look three hands' approach of some of the better-known musicians, and with the plus of the remarkable voice and musicianship of Cathy Jordan, whose singing in both English and Gaelic is mature and expressive.

 At the End of the Day (Whirling Discs, Ireland).

Dervish's best album to date. While the debt they owe to their predecessors is clear and freely acknowledged, they have managed to break free of the lurking cliché to find their own voice. Some wonderful singing is backed by skillful arrangements, beautifully played, and the dance tunes aren't half bad either.

Goats Don't Shave

The Goats are currently on an extended furlough, while singer/lyricist Pat Gallagher explores solo projects. Catch them live and you'll rarely hear a finer, more raucous blend of traditionally inspired contemporary music. Undoubtedly, the best band ever to come out of Dungloe, Co. Donegal.

 The Rusty Razor (Cooking Vinyl, UK).

The Goats' finest hour contains twelve of Gallagher's songs, including the infectious "Mary Mary", satirising the Mary from Dungloe festival, and "The Evictions", a moving account of the events that took place in 1861 in nearby Derryveagh.

Horslips

Horslips singlehandedly invented 'Celtic Rock' in the 1970s and the band is still remembered fondly for its treatments of Irish myths in a rock setting.

The Tain (Oats, Ireland).

The first and the best of the band's mythological concept albums sees them taking on "Tain Bo Cualighe" (The Cattle Raid of Cooley), the centrepiece of the Ulster cycle of Heroic Tales. The story is told inventively as the band draw inspiration from traditional tunes. This was probably also the first album ever to feature the uillean pipes in a rock setting.

Kilfenora Ceili Band

Hailing from the North Clare village of Kilefenora, this Ceili Band has been going since the 1920s (with changing membership, of course) and its distinctive style has gained both widespread popularity and an unprecedented seven all-Ireland championships.

Set on Stone (Torc, Ireland).

The core of the Kilfenora Band's unique sound are its three fiddlers – and they're prominent in this dynamic collection of dance tunes. Listeners are defied to stay immobile.

Moving Hearts

Moving Hearts were yet another of Donal Lunny's projects, which he started with a view to marrying traditional (and not merely Irish) music with the rhythmic energy of rock, to considerable success. The contribution of piper Davy Spillane (who took his first steps on the road to iconhood with this band) was vital to the sound of this wonderful band.

The Storm (Tara, Ireland).

This instrumental compilation released after the band broke up boasts a heady mixture of traditional and contemporary tunes on a grand collection of instruments: saxophone, pipes, percussion, electric guitar, bouzouki and bodhrán.

Nomos

A Cork-based group featuring the explosive talent of Niall Vallely on concertina and Vincie Milne on fiddle, enhanced by the lyrical songwriting skills of bass player John Spillane, the driving percussion of Frank Torpey, and Gerry McGee on bouzouki.

 I Won't Be Afraid Anymore (Grapevine, UK).

An impressive debut, voted 1995 Album of the Year by *Folk Roots* magazine, this set Nomos at the cutting edge of contemporary traditional music. The words daring, risky, and dangerous all apply. A purist's nightmare, an iconoclast's dream, outstanding playing throughout, and featuring on fiddle the Donegal player Liz Doherty (now a member of the all woman group The Bumblebees).

Planxty

Most of those that served their apprenticeship with Planxty – Andy Irvine, Christy Moore, Liam O'Flynn and others – have gone on to become household names. The refined and cunningly balanced sound that they pioneered remains attractive to this day.

 The Well Below the Valley (Shanachie, US).

Although every Planxty album has something to recommend it, this is perhaps the pick of the bunch. The title song alone is practically worth the price of admission.

The Pogues

The Pogues, with their unpredictable lead singer Shane MacGowan, became immensely popular in the late 1980s with their punk-rock influenced approach to Irish music. MacGowan remains a singer to be reckoned with his current band, The Popes.

Rum, Sodomy and the Lash (WEA, UK).

This early Pogues album was a perfect rendering of their London Oirish punk-roots sound.

The Saw Doctors

The band that put Tuam, County Galway on the map with their infectious and quintessentially Irish blend of folk and rock, still worth seeing for their jubilant stage act.

If This is Rock and Roll, I Want My Old Job Back (Solid, Ireland).

The Saw Doctors have never matched this priceless debut, containing the hugely successful "I Useta Lover" (sic) and their Galway eulogy and Route 66 parody "N17".

Sliabh Notes

Sliabh Notes are three individually acclaimed musicians who combined to produce their interpretation of West Cork's Sliabh Luachra music. The band consists of Donal Murray (accordion), Tommy O'Sullivan (guitar and songs) and Matt Cranitch (fiddler and one-time member of Na Fili who recorded a number of albums in the 1980s.

Gleanntán (Ossian, Ireland).

There is an easy lilting quality to the Sliabh Luachra style of music which belies the ability to play it as tremendously well as this trio, supported on a couple of tracks by the Sliabh Notes Trad Big Band. There's a fair smack of tunes from the area, too, mixed in with jigs and reels from around the country and a couple of fine contemporary songs.

Solas

This Irish-American quintet forged a formidable reputation for its tight ensemble playing, centred on the multi-instrumental talents of Seamus Egan, and delicious vocals of Karan Casey (who left in 1999).

Summer Spells and Scattered Showers (Shanachie, US).

A grand mix of songs, airs and dance tunes – Karan Casey's vocals on the opening track "The Wind That Shakes the Barley" could melt butter.

The Waterboys

Some cynics claim that Scotsman Mike Scott decided to give Irish music back to the Irish when he set up camp in Spiddal, County Galway in the late 1980s, but his impact can't be underestimated. Formerly a purveyor of epic rock anthems, Scott drew an assortment of traditional musicians to his band's new incarnation and for a while turned Spiddal into a musical magnet. He's since moved on, found God, and moved on again.

Fisherman's Blues (Ensign, UK).

The Waterboys' tour de force included two songs that have subsequently entered the canon of Irish music (as Scott remarks in a later song, "City of Ghosts" – "Dublin is a city full of buskers singing old Waterboys hits"): the lazy swing-along, sing-along title track, dominated by Steve Wickham's tasteful fiddle; and the upbeat "And a Bang on the Ear" where Scott catalogues his ex-lovers supported by a backing band including De Dannan's accordionist Mairtin O'Connor.

Thanks to Geoff Wallis for revising this discography

Italy

tenores and tarantellas

Italy only became a unified country in 1860 and its constituent parts still retain their regional – and often much more local – identities. Yet while regional specialities in food and drink are justly celebrated, Italy's regional and roots music awaits wide recognition at home or abroad. **Alessio Surian** sets out on a *giro* of the regions.

Traditional music is one of Italy's best kept secrets. You hear it in the hip-hop of Almamegretta, one of the most thrilling of Neapolitan bands, and in the soundtracks of Ennio Moricone, but it gets little recognition from the Italian press or even its music industry. Indeed, Italy's mainstream record industry has little idea of 'roots' music beyond TV events like the Sanremo national song contest, preferring to play safe with its staple of singers – the jazzy Paolo Conte, or poppier artists like Lucio Dalla, Claudio Baglioni and Pino Daniele, who can attract a hundred thousand people to a concert and sell a million copies of a new CD. Like many Italians, they probably haven't heard of most of the musicians in this article, who flourish on what at present is a lively but very local and independent roots music scene.

Rescuing the Past

Franco Coggiola, who did extensive research into regional music until his death in 1996, said he'd like to disguise himself as a peasant in a remote valley and wait for an ethnomusicologist so as to confuse him by singing songs in a dozen different styles. He and other collectors such as **Alan Lomax** (the American Library of Congress archivist), **Diego Carpitella** and **Roberto Leydi** made important field recordings in Italy from the 1950s on, when many regional styles and traditions could still be found. Carpitella also captured Italian musical traditions on film, including such events as the Montemarano Carnival, Holy Week in different parts of Sardinia, and the possession rituals of Puglia. In the 1950s he teamed up with anthropologist **Ernesto De Martino** for groundbreaking work on the magical aspects of traditional culture – particularly Puglia's *tarantolati*.

The **Istituto De Martino**, named after Ernesto and based in Sesto Fiorentino, near Florence, was established in the early 1960s to research and document Italian oral culture and traditional music. It also spawned the group **Nuovo Canzoniere Italiano**, which has brought together traditional musicians such as **Giovanna Daffini** (from Reggio Emilia) and young composers and singers from different regions such as **Paolo Pietrangeli** (Rome) and **Gualtiero Bertelli** (Venice). Among its leading figures was **Giovanna Marini** who, combining traditional music and protest songs, literally documented Italian history in the 1960s and '70s.

Between 1962 and 1980 the group produced 276 records, mostly for the Dischi del Sole label, and played about 3500 concerts. Their live works included *Ci ragiono e canto* (1966 and 1969) which brought together young musicians and traditional groups, including the striking voices of **Aggius** (from Sardinia) under the direction of Dario Fo. He added a theatrical dimension to the interpretation of a traditional repertoire ranging from Piedmont to Sicily.

Fo's show was one of the few attempts to unite traditions from various Italian regions, which otherwise can be loosely divided into four areas – the north, centre, south, and the island of Sardinia. Broadly speaking, **northern Italian music** has many features in common with Celtic music, a dominance of the major mode, and songs in a narrative, ballad-like style. The **south of Italy** shares many (minor) modes with the Middle East and generally favours melody over words in its chants; its traditions are most active in Naples. The **central region** combines northern and southern musical elements, though it retains some original features, for example singing in *endecasillabo*, a songform based on phrases of eleven syllables. And then there is **Sardinia**, which more than anywhere else in Italy retains a strong and autonomous cultural and musical identity.

Sardinia

A mountainous, isolated island off the west coast of Italy, **Sardinia** has retained a distinctive and archaic musical culture. This includes striking and active traditions of **polyphonic singing – a tenore** – performed by singers in a circle, and *launeddas* piping. Most Sardinian dances, too, are circle dances, rotating in the direction of the movement of the sun. They may well have prehistoric roots, dating right back to the *nuraghi*, the fortified stone houses dating back to 1500 BC, probably the era from which much of this music originates.

Launeddas

Launeddas are like a set of bagpipes without a bag: three different-sized reeds played by means of circular breathing. The instrument is peculiar to Sardinia and very ancient, appearing on votive statues from the eighth century BC.

It is played during religious processions or to accompany **su ballu** (popular dances), which today offer the best chances to hear them. It is played using a complex technique which allows the player to produce infinite variations on the basis of few melodic phrases. One song can last over an hour and include several melodic motives. Their sound is one of the most elemental and resonant in European music.

The village of Samatzai, in Cagliari province, is famed as the birthplace of the best launeddas players of the last two centuries and it is there that **Dionigi Burranca** was born in 1913. He studied the instrument with Peppe and Francischeddu Sanna, the two last masters of the school of Figus, established in the seventeenth century. Burranca was playing the launeddas professionally by the age of fourteen and went on to work with Ravi Shankar and jazz composers Ornette Coleman and David Liebman. After an outstanding career drawing international attention to the instrument, he dedicated his last years until his death in 1995 to his school-workshop in Ortacesus where today the association *Sonus de Canna* continues his work.

Two other important launeddas players of this century were **Antonio Lara** (1886–1979) and **Efisio Melis** (1890–1970), masters from the Sàrrabus region. A professional player from the age of sixteen, Melis made some of the best recordings of the instrument, including an exceptional duet with his musical 'rival', Antonio Lara in 1961. The two were the teachers of today's most outstanding player, **Luigi Lai** who has enriched the Sàrrabus tradition with his own virtuoso approach. He teaches the launeddas in Suelli.

Tenores

Sardinia's **polyphonic chant**, especially that of the **tenores** from the rural areas in the centre of the island, is an equally startling sound. Is origins are probably shared with the triple-voice shepherds' *paghjella* from neighbouring Corsica. In Sardinia, though, there are usually four male voices: *boghe* (leader and soloist), *mesa boghe* (middle), *contra* (counter) and *bassu* (bass). The leader begins with an introductory phrase and then the other voices enter with a rich chordal harmony. It has a soulful appeal akin to the Georgian male (or Bulgarian female) voice choirs, although its harmonies tend to be more consonant. Its repertoire includes evocations of rural life as well as religious, love, and satirical songs, sometimes in verse.

The most distinguished contemporary group is the **Tenores di Bitti** who have been together for over twenty-five years and enjoyed a fair bit of international exposure. Recently they have

REALWORLD

Tenores di Bitti

started a school to ensure their art is passed on to the next generation. Daniele Cossellu, one of the group's lead singers remembers how in the first years after the second world war everybody in Bitti, a village of 3000 people, would gather in the evening to sing *a tenore*, both the youths and grown men, but he fears the art could easily be lost with emigration and TV unless the school takes root. Other fine *a tenore* groups include the **Tenores de Oniferi** and **Tenore "Su Cuncordu" de Orosei**, from two villages near Nuoro (with a different approach to the bass sounds), and the **Tenore Antonia Mesina**, from Orgosolo.

The vocal traditions of Sardinia also include the **gozos** – sacred songs. This polyphonic singing can be heard during the Christian rituals of Lent, Holy Week and Christmas. The best-known choir (which also performs secular songs) is **Su Cuncordu 'e su Rosariu** from Santulussurgiu; it was founded in 1605. Many other male choirs perform throughout Sardinia and can have up to thirty voices; **Coro Ortobene** and the **Coro Gabriel** are notable.

Singers and Groups

Sardinia's leading female vocalists are **Maria Carta** and **Elena Ledda**. In a career of over twenty-five years, Maria Carta has sung various Sardinian traditions from ancient chants to religious music and popular lullabies. Elena Ledda, working with composer, guitar and *mandola* (a cross between the guitar and mandolin) player **Mauro Palmas**, has gone further, combining traditional music and jazz improvisation in the group **Suonofficina** and, more recently, with their own compositions and new arrangements of traditional songs, in the group **Sonos**.

In a region with a strong living tradition it's not surprising to find one of Italy's best regional **organetto** (accordion) players, **Totore Chessa** (see Organetti feature box). And on the Sardinian contemporary music scene, **Alberto Balia**, **Massimo Nardi** and **Gesuino Deiana** have been able to bend guitar techniques to the specifications of Sardinian styles. Together they perform as **Abbanegra**, sometimes including the launeddas of **Carlo Mariani**, a former pupil of Dionigi Burranca. Each of them also has his own group. Deiana's **Cordas et Cannas** has been together for almost twenty years performing material rooted in Sardinian traditions, with rock and jazzy elements.

Some interesting instrumental explorations combining Sardinian traditional forms and jazz have also come from composer and sax player **Enzo Favata**, composer and trumpet-player **Paolo Fresu**, and the **Meta Quartet** led by Antonello Salis on piano and accordion.

Naples

Naples is another part of Italy rich in live roots music, from sentimental song to roots-rock re-interpretations of traditions. As elsewhere in southern Italy, it's a place that is at its best arond events like saints' days, or Holy Week, when the devotional music and dances bring together pagan and Christian roots.

Canzone napoletana

There is a song from 1839 – "Te voglio bene assaie" (I love you so much) – which is still very popular in Naples and throughout Italy and has been re-interpreted by countless people. It is often considered the starting point of **canzone napoletana** (Neapolitan Song), the unique mix of popular and classical elements that cuts across Naples' social classes and musical styles.

Canzone napoletana has roots in the *villanella* of the sixteenth century, a rural style which influenced the cultivated Neapolitan composers with its polyphonic vocal harmonies and often satirical lyrics. The writers and composers of the urban canzone napoletana were poets and intellectuals as well as un-trained popular authors. Some of their songs achieved international fame thanks to performances from tenor **Enrico Caruso** (1873–1921) onwards.

In recent years this vast repertoire has found sober and yet passionate new voices in **Sergio Bruni** and **Roberto Murolo**, who interpret the traditional songs as well as new compositions such as "Carmenla" (Sergio Bruni and Salvatore Palomba) and "O ciucciariello" (Roberto Murolo). Through the popular themes of canzone napoletana they sing of the everyday life of Naples – a city of many faces, with a strong musical language and many dialects.

Sepe and Roots Groups

While Murolo's canzone napoletana shows the city's traditional face, **Daniele Sepe** and his group's cosmopolitan sound represent Naples'

Danielle Sepe

musical versatility. Sepe is a classical flautist, jazz saxophonist and percussionist. What is most remarkable though, is his ability to find protest songs from Italian and world traditions and to attract to his musical projects the most inspired musicians from the Neapolitan scene.

Sepe began playing in the 1970s with **Gruppo Operaio di Pomigliano d'Arco** (also known as **E' Zezi**). At that time, he recalls, "there were two different views on popular music. One of them was for more or less philological research. For others, such as E' Zezi, traditional music was less serious so we were convinced it was legitimate to create new texts and new sounds. It was a more political way of interpreting things." **Nuova Compagnia di Canto Popolare**, founded in 1967 by **Roberto De Simone**, was in the other camp, a roots music group who kept things pure. They have achieved national fame and are still active today with the powerful voices of Fausta Vetere and Giovanni Mauriello, while De Simone continues to pursue his own research, often as a source for stage productions.

Other contemporary sounds come from jazz pianist and composer **Rita Marcotulli** and singer **Maria Pia De Vito**, who recently toured and recorded the project "Nauplia", a marriage

between improvised music and Neapolitan traditions, including the great classics of canzone napoletana. Another distinctive trend is the **neomelodici**, the pop-oriented love and satirical songs which are making singers such as **Ciro Ricci** and **Ida Rendano** the new stars of weddings and street parties.

In the Neapolitan area and in much of southern Italy there is still a living tradition of dancing and singing to the accompaniment of a frame drum – the large **tamura** or *tammorra* and smaller *tamburello*. This has been adopted and updated in the music of groups such as **Nando Citarella**, **Tamburi del Vesuvio** and **Tammurriata di Scafati**, or that of **Marcello Colasurdo**, previously with E' Zezi.

Another leading tamburello musician is the Sicilian (but largely Naples-based) **Alfio Antico**. He learned to play frame-drums – which are also a common feature of Arabic and Sicilian music – from his shepherd grandparents and has developed a technique which bridges many styles, including the widespread *tarantella*.

The **tarantella** – a lively 12/8 dance – is common to many regions of southern Italy and has many local forms. It can have a syncopated rhythm, smooth modulations into different keys, and can be accompanied by melodic variations on the organetto.

Marcello Colasurdo with a tammorra

Organetti – Italy's accordions

For anyone who's seen Fellini's film *Amarcord*, the melodies of the blind organetto player will evoke the mood of Italian celebrations and intimate storytelling. This little diatonic accordion or melodeon has become one of the most popular instruments in Italian traditional music, sometime substituting for, or teaming up with, instruments like the zampogna (bagpipe), launeddas or violin. It is especially widespread in the central and southern regions of the country though even in the north many traditional groups have adopted it. It's used by most of the new fusion groups and even rock bands and singers have introduced it on some of their records.

The first organetto player they usually think of inviting to join them is **Ambrogio Sparagna**. The son of traditional musicians from Maranola (Latina), Sparagna made field recordings with the late Diego Carpitella, Italy's leading ethnomusicologist. A virtuoso organetto player, in 1984 he founded the **Bosio Big Band**, an orchestra of thirty organetti and percussion. Following Roberto Di Simone's example of "La Gatta Cenerentola" Sparagna has composed several theatrical works for the orchestra including "Trillilĺ", "Giofà" and "La via dei Romei", featuring the voice of the famous Rome-based songwriter Francesco De Gregori.

One of the most gifted pupils of Ambrogio Sparagna is **Clara Graziano**. A member of the Bosio Big Band, she has teamed up with outstanding jazz players such as Toni Germani (reeds) and Giovanni Lo Cascio (percussion). The compositions she writes for her group, **Circodiatonico**, are all instrumentals centred on a

theme of circus life, and the band's members interact on stage with the theatrical clown Augusto.

Also based in Rome, **Mario Salvi** has been playing organetto and tamburello for over twenty years and has specialised in the various forms of tarantella. He can play dozens of different traditional tarantellas and has composed several himself. Although his own recordings are fairly recent, he can be heard on the first record by Riccardo Tesi in 1983 where he plays tamburello, the frame drum which he also teaches, drawing from the techniques of different parts of Italy.

The virtuoso player is **Riccardo Tesi**, who has collaborated with French mandolin virtuoso Patrick Vaillant and the jazz reeds of **Gianluigi Trovesi**. Based in Pistoia (Tuscany), he is a great interpreter of the repertoire of the Apennine mountains between Tuscany and Emilia, usually involving violin and organetto ensembles. In 1995 he gathered together outstanding folk, classical and jazz musicians for a project centred on the **liscio**, a dance born in the wake of nineteenth-century waltzes and polkas, which is probably the only style which can be found in all Italian regions.

Amongst organetto players working in regional traditions, one of the most accomplished is **Totore Chessa** from Irgoli in Sardinia, where the instrument was first introduced around 1870 and has partially replaced wind instruments such as the launeddas. Chessa has mastered organetto styles from different parts of the island and develops the heritage of the virtuosi of the recent past, such as Francesco Bande, Pietro Porcu and Tonino Masala, supporting the melodies with his extraordinary talent on the bass parts.

PAOLO BENVENUTI

Ricardo Tessi

ITALY

Sicily

More riches here: from religious song to roots jazz and new compositions from Franco Battiato.

Devotional Song

Holy Week is the best time to visit Sicilian villages to hear music traditions. In **Montedoro**, for example, devotional songs connected with the passion of Christ are sung a cappella by male singers, with moving four-part harmonies. **Brass bands** (baride) are also a frequent feature of religious festivities and they have developed a rich repertoire often based on compositions from the late nineteenth and early twentieth century. A collection of Easter and funeral marches from southern Italy was recently recorded by the twenty-piece brass band, the **Banda Ionica**, including some of the best Sicilian musicians led by Rosario Patane and Roy Paci.

But religious singing has never been confined to churches and processions. Along with Puglia, Sicily has been for a long time 'Italy's granary' and traditionally **harvest times** have brought together religious and work songs as reapers gather from different parts of the island. Polyphonic singing in the devotional style of "Sarvi Rigina" and "Razioni di lu Metiri" blend with party songs such as "A Nicusiana", often accompanied by guitar or organetto.

Storytellers and Songwriters

The guitar and sometimes a series of drawings have been the working tools of the traditional storytellers and popular historians such as **Ciccio Busacca** who have been singing until recently of the island's social struggles. Busacca worked with Dario Fo on a stage show, but his art was probably at its best in his setting of the poems of the late **Ignazio Buttitta**, a poet with a genuine passion for the Sicilian language who has remained a source of inspiration not only for traditional groups but also for new bands such as **Agricantus** from Palermo (check their electric version of Buttita's "Li vuci de l'omini") and the seminal **Kunsertu** from Messina, a group open to many world beats and languages, featuring the superb voice of **Fahisal Taher**.

Listen out too for the voices of the **Fratelli Mancuso**, the two brothers Enzo and Lorenzo from Sutera who continue to develop a Sicilian tradition with exclusively acoustic instruments. They draw upon vocal styles such as the peasant *lamentazioni* and monodic chants called *alla carrettiera* (a chant sung coming back from the fields riding a mule in the evening), which they heard as children.

Shamal and Battiato

Sicily has some of Italy's best instrumentalists, thanks to a lively jazz scene which interacts with the local musical traditions. Based in Palermo, **Enzo Rao** (violin, electric bass and oud) is a skilled composer and musician. His group **Shamal** (aka Ettna), with Glen Velez (percussion) and Gianni Gebbia (saxophones) has drawn on Sicilian traditions and the Arab influence which is so much part of the island's history. They are a kind of Italian couterpart to the Spanish group Radio Tarifa.

Another significant musician and composer is the Catania-born **Franco Battiato**, whose work bridges classical, traditional and rock music. He came to fame in Italy with a pop-oriented trilogy – *L'era del cinghiale bianco*, *Patriots* and *La voce del Padrone* (1979–81) – which sold over one million copies. Battiato demonstrated his talent for co-opting traditional music through his long-term co-operation with virtuoso musicians such as violinist and composer **Giusto Pio**, and through his work in such diverse fields as sacred music and opera (notably "Gilgamesh" in 1991). He is a radical humanist. In the aftermath of the Gulf War, he took an orchestra to Baghdad to play together with the Iraqi National Symphony Orchestra – an attempt to try and break through the wall of hatred and indifference.

Calabria and Puglia

Calabria is the 'boot of Italy' – a region where agricultural cycles and festivals remain very much a part of life.

Bagpipes and Languages

An instrument which occurs throughout the southern (and central) Italian regions is the **zampogna** (bagpipe). It comes in different varieties and in Calabria alone – where it is usually called *ciaramedda* – there are five different types.

Ettore Castagna and Sergio di Giorgio of the group **Re Niliu** (King of Wax) have been actively documenting and reviving the tradition since 1979. The group has its roots in the music of Calabria, which retains a strong agricultural life and a large number of festivals, both religious and secular, an as well as bagpipes, they have researched and revived the *lira* (ancient Calabrian violin) tradition. More recently, they have concentrated on original compositions featuring acoustic and electric instruments, with brilliant lyrics in Calabrese, as well as in ancient Greek and Albanian – the minority immigrant languages still spoken in Calabria.

Another group which makes use of different languages for their lyrics is **Al Darawish**, a multicultural outfit from Bari, Puglia, on the east coast. A very energetic, electric live act centred on the voice of Palestinian Nabil Ben Salaméh, they were probably the best-known roots band from this region, although they have recently divided into two separate groups. Also mixing traditional roots with modern sounds and instruments is **Tavernanova**, while other groups have explored specific local traditions such as **Canzoniere di Terra d'Otranto** (Salento) and **Uragniaun**, with the moving voice of Maria Moramarco.

Brass and Jazz

Puglia also has a lively brass band tradition, probably best represented by the **Banda Ruvo di Puglia**, an ensemble which sometimes collaborates with the iconoclastic jazz trumpet-player and composer **Pino Minafra**. They play compositions during Holy Week of great beauty and slow passion, with rhythm, as Minafra puts it, "practically suspended" and "a sweet, spiritual sound, with sweeping melodies, where there is no crisis of doubt or scepticism, because this music is addressed to believers."

In recent years, the passion for brass bands has involved many other outstanding jazz players – **Enrico Rava, Battista Lena, Eugenio Colombo** and even **Daniele Sepe**, who felt a brass band was essential for his passionate arrangement of "Padrone mio" by **Matteo Salvatore**. Salvatore, who was born in Foggia in 1925, was a seminal folk song revivalist, having learnt, revived, and popularised a canon of traditional songs – some perhaps dating back to the thirteenth century, as a child.

Tarantolati

Traditional music from Puglia is best known for the healing ritual of the **tarantolati**, a complex tradition which can still be witnessed today. It has ancient roots and many syncretic elements, centred around the figure of Saint Paul, a fact which makes some Christian chapels a favoured place for the healing ritual. The tarantolati – usually women believed to have been bitten and poisoned by the poisonous tarantula – are healed through long hours or even days of dancing to the insistent rhythms of the *tarantella* or *tarantata*. The music is usually performed with *tamburelli* (small frame drums) and guitar, organetto or violin, depending on the local ensemble.

Its modern master of ceremonies is **Antonio Infantino** who founded the group **Tarantolati di Tricarico** in 1975 to perform and further explore this possession music, alternating the obsessive percussive patterns of tarantella with more soothing melodies.

Central Italy

As you would expect, the more cosmopolitan and sophisticated central Italian provinces have less in the way of roots music. But there is an interesting vocal tradition – ottava rima – and some roots revivalist bands.

Ottava Rima and Saltarello

The medieval tradition of **ottava rima** is a way of singing widespread in Lazio, Tuscany and the Abruzzo. Sometimes called the chant of the *poeti contadini* (peasant poets), it can be based on the poetic texts of Homer, Dante and Ariosto, it can address social and political issues, or it can be totally improvised, often as a competition between two singers. The singers take turns in improvising a new eight-line stanza. But the difficulty lies in having to begin the new stanza with the last rhyme of the previous singer.

The **saltarello**, a rather solid 4/4 dance, is probably more ancient still. The most widespread dance in central Italy, it is traditionally accompanied by zampogna and tamburello. Among its different forms, the saltarella from Alta Sabina (Lazio) is considered the liveliest and most complex. It is usually structured in four different parts to be danced in couples.

The Folk Revival

The saltarello and other local traditions are well captured by various new folk groups in central Italy, and especially by some outstanding organetto players such as **Riccardo Tesi, Ambrogio Sparagna** and **Mario Salvi**.

Rural revivalists La Ciapa Rusa

The roots scene here, however, was perhaps more active during the Italian 'folk revival' movement at the end of the 1960s. The best-known of the groups formed at this time was **Canzoniere del Lazio**, who worked closely with filed-recordist Sandro Portelli. Their versions of central Italian traditions on the classic *Quando nascesti tune* included popular and political songs. Their vocalist, Piero Brega, went on to form, with Demetrio Stratos of the fusion group Are, **Carnascialia**, an explosive mix of young jazz and traditional musicians who played roots material and original tunes in an almost entirely acoustic setting.

Other folk revival voices are still active today, including **Gastone Pietrucci**, the leader of **La Macina** (Ancona) and **Sara Modigliani**, today with **La Piazza** (Rome). Their arrangements are often based on the repertoire of traditional singers such as **Pietro Bolletta** for La Macina, and **Italia Ranaldi** for La Piazza. La Piazza has also performed original music by **Giovanna Marini**, who brings together contemporary music and popular traditions – as well as a passion for polyphonic singing in her own female vocal group, **Quartetto**.

A member of Giovanna Marini's Quartet for seventeen years, **Lucilla Galeazzi** has gone on to work in two outstanding trios: one with Carlo Mariani and Massimo Nardi, integrating different Italian and Sardinian roots elements, and a second named **Il Trillo** with the virtuoso percussion player Carlo Rizzo and Ambrogio Sparagna, exploring different types of traditional song-formats.

Acquaragia Drom, based in Rome, is a group focusing on Gypsy music which adds to the basic line-up of voice, organetto, guitar and violin other traditional instruments such as the tammorra.

The North

As in central Italy, most northern Italian folk and dance traditions disappeared as the twentieth century progressed. However, here, too, there have been revivalists, often recreating the music and traditions – mainly on stage at festivals – from the tales of old folk and musicians. And Genoa has its own tavern-song tradition.

Rural Revivalists

Based in Padua, the group **Calicanto** grew out of the research and field recordings of multi-instrumentalist Roberto Tombesi. After five records presenting for the most part the traditional repertoire of the **Veneto**, their recent concerts and recordings feature new compositions open to other Mediterranean influences.

In Piedmont, **La Ciapa Rusa**, founded by **Maurizio Martinotti** (hurdy gurdy) and **Beppe Greppi** (organetto), has been active since 1977 mixing northern Italian traditional music and original material, latterly as an all-acoustic group.

The folk and political song traditions of **Lombardy** (and neighbouring regions) are well captured by **Baraban**, a group which has been active for over fifteen years, slowly introducing electric instruments. As the Associazione Culturale Baraban (ACB) they have promoted extensive research ranging from the chants of rice-field workers to the dances collected by **Compagnia Strumentale Tre Violini** which reminds us of the importance of the violin in the dances and styles of the Po Valley region. Another group with deep roots in the tradition of this region and in the Emilian Apennine is **Piva dal Carner** (Bagpipe), an acoustic ensemble which is rapidly establishing a reputation on the Italian folk circuit.

The **Piedmont** region has a dynamic and multicultural young group, **Mau Mau**, mixing the Piedmont language and organetto patterns with world beats and particularly African percussion. The region offers a wealth of excellent and diversified musical traditions and interpreters, from the singer **Vincenzo 'Ciacio' Marchelli**, the heart of **Tre Martelli**, a group with deep roots in the Lower Piedmont area, to **La Cantarana**, whose repertoire draws from the Pinerolo Valleys which are close to the French border and open to the influences from Occitane and the French Alps.

But many northern Italian groups' repertoires cut across different regions. The group **Sentiero del Sale** have a repertoire of Genoese and Lombard songs, while **I suonatori delle quattro province** and **Voci del Lèsima** draw from the traditions of four northern Italian provinces: Piedmont, Liguria, Lombardy and Emilia Romagna. Voci del Lèsima take particular inspiration from Bogli, a village that gives its name to the *buiasche*, a way of polyphonic singing which is called *fermo* (still) as it lacks a clear beat.

Genoese Songs

Genoa, the great seaport on the Ligurian coast with its twenty-two kilometres of docks, has a tavern song tradition called **trallalero** – an onomatopoeic name from the 'tra-la-las' of the songs. It is again a polyphonic vocal style, possibly related to the nearby Sardinian and Corsican varieties, involving a complicated counterpoint by five male voices: tenor, baritone, alto, *chitarra* (guitar) and bass. The 'guitar' singer imitates the sound of the instrument by singing in a nasal voice and putting the back of his hand over his lips. The sound of trallalero is one of the most ornate and haunting in the Mediterranean. And it's unusual amongst polyphonic singing styles for being urban rather than rural.

Trallalero thrived in the taverns where the men met after work and in its heyday in the 1920s over a hundred groups existed in Genoa. At that time the café-bar *Tugini's* was a famous trallalero venue.

Today, the *Porto Franco* bar, on Via Sottoripa under the arcades of the port, hosts the leading group, **La Squadra – Compagnia del Trallalero**, led by Francesco Tanda and **La Squadra di Canto Popolare di Valpolcevera.**

Recently, a female singer has found her way to break the male-monopoly over the trallalero. It took the passion and the powerful voice of **Laura Parodi** to do so but she is now accepted by fellow male trallalero singers, and also sings with **La Rionda**, a group that borrows its name from the *ballo tondo* which was traditionally played in Genoa during the Carnival.

Genoa is also the home of some of the best 'modern' ballads, written by the likes of **Gino Paoli** and **Fabrizio De André**. De André knew national fame back in 1968 through the interpretation of his song "La canzone di Marinella", by top woman singer, **Mina**. Many more of his songs became classics and often served as a poetic means to raise awareness on social and political issues. His collaboration with multi-instrumentalist, composer and arranger **Mauro Pagani** brought together the Genoese language with various Mediterranean traditions.

Genoa is home, too, for a number of young roots groups seeking new directions, from the dub of **Sensasciou** to the vocal gymnastics of **Le Voci Atroci**.

JEAN-LUC FAUQUIER/ANITA CREATIONS

La Squadra – Compagnia del Trallalero down at the docks

discography

Compilations

 Atlante di Musica Tradizionale: Vols 1 & 2 (Robi Droli, Italy).

There are two of these sampler releases from Robi Droli and both give an excellent introduction to Italy's acoustic and roots groups. Vol 1 includes Baraban, Calicanto, La Ciapa Rusa, La Piazza, Re Niliu, Ritmia, Tenores di Bitti, Tre Violini, and others. ⊚ *Italia 2* (even stronger) includes Aquaragia Drom, Totore Chessa, Efisio Melis-Antonio Lara, La Piva del Carner and, once again, La Piazza and Tenores di Bitti.

⊚ **Folk Music and Song of Italy** (Rounder, US).

Recordings made in 1953 by Alan Lomax and Diego Carpitella from the Alps to Sicily when regional traditions were still very much alive.

⊚ **Italie: Musiques populaires d'aujourd'hui** (Buda/Musique du Monde, France).

One of the best current Italian compilations giving a good survey of music both north and south. Includes La Ciapa Rusa, Calicanto, Il Trillo, Riccardo Tesi, Daniele Sepe, Fratelli Mancuso, E' Zezi and others. Recommended.

⊚ **Italian String Virtuosi** (Rounder, US).

Ever wondered how that Captain Correlli actually sounded on his mandolin? Well, this is a pretty authentic soundtrack: 25 tracks, recorded in Italy and the US, of mandolin, banjo and guitar virtuosi from the 1920s and '30s.

⊚ **Zampogne en Italie** (Auvidis/Silex, France).

An impressive anthology of different types of zampogne (bag-pipes) from central, southern Italy, Sicily and of the *piva* from Istria (Croatia) edited by the ethnomusicologist Roberto Leydi. With twenty-four field recordings from between 1969 and 1990 and examples of both the 'double oboe' and the 'double clarinet' families of zampogne.

Sardinia

Compilations

⊚ **Ballos Sardos: An Anthology of Sardinian folkdances, Vol 1** (Ethnica/Robi Droli, Italy).

A fine sampler featuring some of the most outstanding Sardinian musicians, often recorded during ceremonies and village dances, between 1987 and 1996 by Giuseppe Michele Gala. Twenty-five different types of dances and, among others, the launeddas of Dionigi Burranca, the organetto of Totore Chessa, the tenores groups from Oliena and Oniferi, and a bena solo by Antioco Pinna.

⊚ **Corsica/Sardinia: The Mystery of Polyphony** (World Network, Germany).

A good disc for comparing and contrasting the vocal polyphony of neighbouring Corsica and Sardinia. The latter sounds a lot more rugged and rough hewn. Groups include Canta u Popolu Corsu, A Filetta and Donnisulana from Corsica and various groups including the Tenores di Bitti from Sardinia. Luigi Lai on launeddas is an added bonus.

⊚ **Sardaigne: Les Maîtres de la musique instrumentale** (Al Sur, France).

A unique sample of old field recordings by Gianni Secchi, Diego Carpitella and Roberto Leydi who adds terrific photos and liner notes. It includes the organetti of Pietro Porcu, the accordion of Raimondo Vercellino, the launeddas of Dionigi Burranca, Luigi Lai, and Aurelio Porcu.

Artists

Antonio Lara and Efisio Melis

Considered the two greatest players of the Sardinian launeddas this century and the masters of the Sàrrabus region. Both from Villaputzu, Antonio Lara (1886–1979) always remained faithful to the old tradition while Efisio Melis (1890–1970) was more inclined to innovation.

⊚ **Launeddas** (Robi Droli, Italy).

The best introduction to the instrument, both as traditional solo instrument and in rare duets. The oldest recordings date back to 1930 and on each track the launeddas play a different *cunzertus* (tonality).

Tenore de Orosei

Four relatively young voices devoted to an ancient local tradition: Patrizio Mura (voche), Salvatore Mula (mesu voche), Luca Frau (cronta, and Mario Siotto (bassu). They grew up in the 1970s learning to sing a tenore from the unique voice of Vissente Gallus in Orosei (Nuoro). In this village the more cultivated religious (Cuncordu) singing and the popular a tenore style have always borrowed from each other.

⊚ **A su primu ispuntare** (CNI, Italy).

Recorded in an Orosei cellar by Enzo Favata in 1996, the six tracks are dedicated to traditional songs and dances from Orosei. The CD begins with a moving rendition of one of the most difficult a tenore singing styles and includes "Voche `e notte antica" (the Song of the Ancient Night), by one of the greatest Sardinian poets of the nineteenth century, Luca Cubeddu.

Tenores di Bitti

Founded in 1974, the group is a cornerstone of Sardinian traditional music with outstanding recordings for Robi Droli (1986 and 1990) and Amori (1993). It includes the voices of Piero Sanna, Daniele Cossellu, Tancredi Tucconi and Mario Pira who recently replaced Salvatore Bandinu after his death. The official name of the group is Remunnu 'e locu, after a satirical poet who lived in Bitti in the nineteenth century.

 S'amore 'e mama (RealWorld, UK).

Producer Michael Brook captured one of the finest Sardinian tenores at home in Bitti in 1995. Excellently recorded in churches, bars, the countryside and an ancient nuraghe.

Naples

E' Zezi

Neapolitan folk music and a working-class revolutionary message are the vital elements which have made E' Zezi a cult group both in Italy and France with a variable ensemble usually featuring some fifteen musicians and a large number of percussion instruments. Reluctant to participate in the market economy, E' Zezi have only produced three CDs in over twenty years.

Auciello ro mio: Posa e sorde (Tide Records, Italy)
Pummarola Black (Lyrichord, US).

Two different names for the same disc, first released in 1994 to celebrate the band's twentieth birthday. Ten tracks swimming in Naples' diversity of sounds and featuring the sax of Daniele Sepe and the voices of Raiss (Almamegretta) and Marcello Colasurdo in a most inspired tribute to Vesuvio.

Zezi Vivi (Il Manifesto, Italy).

If you like a smashed glasses and marketplace atmosphere don't miss this recording that captures Zezi live in Napoli at the end of 1996, with a breathtaking sequence of trance-like tammuriatas.

Roberto Murolo

Born in 1912, the son of the poet Ernesto, Roberto Murolo is a veteran interpreter of the canzone napoletana repertoire in a style that is both restrained and moving.

Roberto Murrolo (Ricordi/BMG, Italy).

A 1995 compilation that provides a concise introduction to the art of Murolo.

Nuova Compagnia di Canto Popolare

Since 1967 the group has changed many of its members but still retains a powerful frontline with the voices of Fausta Vetere and Giovanni Mauriello and the guitar and arrangements of Corrado Sfogli.

Incanto Acustico (CGD, Italy).

Live recording, entirely acoustic, celebrating almost thirty years of Neapolitan music with an outstanding balance between traditional songs and original compositions.

Daniele Sepe

Sepe's relentless musical and poetic search brings together Gato Barbieri and Matteo Salvatore, Tacit and Mayakovsky. With a sound training as classical and jazz flute and saxophone player, and a passion for traditional songs and instruments, his albums are never less than compelling.

 Vite Perdite
(Piranha, Germany).

This is where you want to start your Italian trip. Meet the iconoclastic Naples music scene in Sepe's visionary and fascinating patchwork featuring the hip-hop of Bisca and 99 Posse, the tradition and political commitment of E' Zezi, the vocal abilities of Quattro Quatti and Mariapia De Vito, the sixteen-piece roots orchestra of Tuba Furiosa and many more.

Sicily/The South

Compilations

Calabre: Musiques de fêtes (Inédit, France).

Atmospheric field recordings of traditional festivals in Calabria between 1983 and 1993. Processions, tarantellas and religious music with plenty of zampogna, organetto and drums.

Sicily. Music for the Holy Week
(Auvidis/Unesco, France).

Songs, chants and laments in Sicilian, Latin and Italian, played and sung by different traditional ensembles reflecting the living tradition of Sicilian ceremonial music. Polyphonic chant (which some may find hard-going), brass bands and vocals with harmonium with a real sense of occasion.

Sutera. La tradizione musicale di un paese della Sicilia (SudNord, Italy).

A thrilling and varied sample of the Sicilian rural repertoire, drawing from the traditions which are still alive in the village of Sutera. Featuring Enzo and Lorenzo Mancuso, Nonó Salamone and traditional singers and choir singing religious, labour and love songs.

Violini e Serenate a Canosa
(Ethnica/Robi Droli, Italy).

One of the most beguiling of Robi Droli's traditional "Ethnica" series featuring mainly string band (violins and chitarra battente – folk guitar) music from Canosa in Puglia. Waltzes, quadrilles and the occasional tarantella mostly recorded in the 1980s in a beautiful down-home style.

Artists

Banda Ionica

Twenty-piece band actually made up of musicians from four traditional Sicilian brass bands formed and directed by members of Turin group Mau Mau.

Passione (Dunya/Robi Droli, Italy).

Funeral marches for religious processions in southern Italy idiomatically played. A good example of the Italian brass bands' tradition.

Antonio Infantino e i Tarantolati di Tricarico

In the region around Taranto (Puglia) lives the infamous tarantula spider. The poison left by its bite can only be overcome by means of trance-like dancing, but only a few know the right tarantella. Among its best interpreters is Antonio Infantino (guitar and voice), active since 1975. His group currently includes five percussion players and vocalists.

Tarantella Tarantata (Amiata, Italy).

Recorded in 1996, these nineteen tracks are a thrilling introduction to the tarantella rhythm with the five percussionists beating out rhythmic ostinati. The music is closely connected with the taranta ritual, with tunes such as "Psatura" intended to modify the heartbeat.

Kunsertu

Based in Messina (Sicily), Kunertu has been active since the mid-1980s staging a front line with two powerful singers, Pippo Messina and Faisal Taher, a funky rhythm section and a passion for opening up Sicilian traditions to numerous other Italian and world beats.

Shams (NewTone/Robi Droli, Italy).

Melodies from southern Italian and Middle-Eastern traditions. Lyrics in Sicilian, Sardinian, Neapolitan, Italian, Arabic and Wolof with an energetic beat and a mix of traditional and rock instruments. Recorded in 1989, it captures the group in a funky 'Mustaphas' mood.

Re Niliu

Based in Catanzaro (Calabria), Ettore Castagna (strings and toothbrush), Sergio Di Giorgio (vocals and reeds) and fellow musicians have been researching, documenting, teaching, performing and innovating Calabrian traditions for twenty years.

⑩ Pucambu (Pontesonoro, Italy).

After two records dedicated to Calabrian traditions, Re Niliu perform their own compositions finding a delicate balance between roots and innovation, minority languages and visionary texts, subtle irony and plenty of energy.

Shamal

Violinist and bass player Enzo Rao from Palermo brings together Gianni Gebbia (saxes) and Glen Velez (frame drums and percussion). Rao draws on native Sicilian music plus jazz and Arabic influences which are strong in Sicilian culture.

⑩ Acqua di Mare (Pontesonoro, Italy);
⑩ Ettna (Music of the World, US).

The same (1993) disc under different names. Partly Sicilian jazz, partly Mediterranean fusion, this album has some strong dance rhythms alongside somewhat New-Age doodlings.

Central Italy

Compilations

⑩ La Saltarella dell'Alta Sabina
(Ethnica/Robi Droli, Italy).

This disc brings you to the mountains of the Central Apennines, for centuries a region of cultural exchanges, beginning with the salt road between Rome and the heart of the Apennines. The saltarella is the region's most characteristic folk dance and it is performed here by zampogna, organetto and tamburello. Almost eighty minutes of twenty-four field recordings from 1989–1992.

Artists

Giovanna Marini

Based in Rome, Giovanna Marini is by far the most important singer of the last three decades of Italian roots music, always combining her research, teaching and performing activities with concern and personal involvement at the social level. She has specialised in polyphonic singing, with new compositions especially suited for female quartet.

⑩ La vie au-dessus et en-dessous des mille mètres
(Auvidis/Silex, France).

Traditional roots and contemporary compositions rendered with passion and ability by this exceptional female vocal quartet including Lucilla Galeazzi, Patrizia Bovi and Patrizia Nasini.

La Piazza

The group produced its first CD in 1993 as a quartet centred around the voice of Sara Modigliani, former member of Canzoniere del Lazio. Over the years it has turned into a septet.

⑩ Milandè (Robi Droli, Italy).

This 1997 album achieves a good balance between traditional songs and original compositions, including the opening, striking track written by Giovanna Marini "Pi' lontano di così", with a reference to a traditional song from Calabria. The repertoire is roóted in the traditions of the Lazio region though it features also some 'classics' which cut across different Italian traditions such as "Mampresa", "Donna Lombarda", "La Pastora e il Lupo".

The North

Baraban

A sextet which has been active since 1983 researching and performing the roots music of Lombardy: Guido Montaldo, Paolo and Diego Ronzio (wind instruments), Vincenzo Caglioti (organetto), Aurelio Citelli (guitars and mandolino), and Giuliano Grasso (violin).

⑩ Live (Robi Droli, Italy).

A selection of sixteen live recordings from 1989–1993, including Apennine dances, carnival tunes, narrative and religious songs, mixing the original acoustic traditional sound with a discrete use of electronics.

Calicanto

Padua-based band led by multinstrumentalist Roberto Tombesi. Very active since 1981 in field research, they have made several albums of largely traditional Veneto music and since 1986 have started generating their own repertoire.

⑩ Diese (Robi Droli, Italy).

An anthology of some of the best arrangements of traditional repertoire from the first five Calicanto recordings, featuring the collaboration with Commedia dell'Arte theatre groups and the use of ancient instruments such as *piva* (traditional Veneto and Istrian bagpipe), concertina and popular strings.

La Ciapa Rusa

Led by Maurizio Martinotti (hurdy-gurdy, percussion, violin, vocals) and Beppe Greppi (organetto, vocals), this group has been researching and performing traditional Piedmont and original music for over twenty years, establishing itself as one of Italy's leading roots bands.

⑩ Antologia (Robi Droli, Italy).

A selection of twenty tracks from the first four records of La Ciapa Rusa, entirely acoustic and dedicated to the rich traditional music repertoire of the Piedmont region, from rice-fields chants to epic songs.

Compagnia Strumentale Tre Violini

The violinists Bernardo Falconi, Giuliano Grasso (also with Baraban) and Giulio Venier are three outstanding performers from Lombardy and Friuli, supported by the guitar of Oliviero Biella and the bass of Paolo Manfrin.

⑩ Matuzine (Robi Droli, Italy).

A convincing anthology of northern Italian violin repertoire.

Fabrizio De André

Born in Genoa in 1940, De André recorded his first songs in 1958. His voice and compositions are still a point of reference within the Italian music scene.

⑩ Creuza de ma (Ricordi, Italy).

An exciting musical trip, sailing from Genoa to other shores of the Mediterranean. Seven original tracks with the arrangements of Mauro Pagani and offering a poetic rendition of the Genoese language, a turning point for the Italian roots scene.

La Squadra
(Compagnia del Trallelero)

In the best tradition of trallaleri, most members of La Squadra are or were Genoan dock workers; they have no formal music training and an average age of sixty. Led by Francesco Tanda they have revived this Genoan tradition with a repertoire of sixty songs.

 Italy: Genoese Polyphony
(Buda/Musique du Monde, France).

The manual workers of the Genoa docks know their tavern tra-la-las. Haunting vocal harmonies in traditional trallalero.

Chansons Génois
(Buda/Musique du Monde, France).

Composed songs in trallalero style from the 1920s, recorded in a wine celler a few kilometres away from Genoa. The 'sixth voice' in this polyphony is supplied by a popping cork.

Squadra di Canto Popolare di Valpolcevera

Based in Campomorone, a small town northwest of Genoa, the seven members of the Valpolcevera specialise in the oldest songs of the trallalero repertoire. They formed in 1983 as heirs to the legendary Nuova Pontedecimo and Vecchia Pontedecimo groups.

Trallalero (NewTone/Robi Droli, Italy).

Eighteen classic trallaleri from one of the most representative groups.

Voci Del Lèsima

Six male voices from the northern Apennines in the Bogli vocal style with two soloists, Attilio 'Cavalli' Spinetta and Stefano Valla, also a member of the Valpolcevera.

Splende la luna in cielo (Robi Droli, Italy).

A lively trip to Bogli, on the borders of Piedmont and Liguria, where history is written in the *buiasche* (popular polyphonic chants), reminiscent of the Genovese vocal style, with deep drones sung in parallel fifths and the higher voices imitating string and wind instruments.

Organetti

Compilations

Organetto e Tarantelle (Ethnica/Robi Droli, Italy).

Edited by Giuseppe Michele Gala, this includes field recordings made between 1979 and 1991 in the southern Italian regions of Basilicata and Campania where the organetto traditionally performs various tarantellas and other dance rhythms. Also featured are traditional songs of the shepherds, carnival, and courting repertoires.

Artists

Totore Chessa

Born in 1959, Totore Chessa is considered today the best player of Sardinian organetto, a style characterised by acrobatic finger work and powerful bass lines, with the instrument usually featuring eight to twelve bass notes.

Organittos (NewTone/Robi Droli, Italy).

A selection of virtuoso solo dances, though the disc also features three guests: Annamaria Puggioni (voice), Luigi Lai (launeddas), and Nicola Loi (jew's harp).

Mario Salvi

Born in Rome in 1956, Mario Salvi has been active for over twenty years researching, interpreting and teaching southern Italian musical traditions.

Caldèra (Finisterre, Italy).

A mature work presenting both traditional songs and original compositions. Featuring classical tarantellas such as "Pizzica Pizzica" and "Tarantella di Montemarano", and a wide range of traditional and electric instruments such as the flutes of Cristina Scrima, the powerful tammorra of Raffaele Incorra and the bass of Erasmo Petringa.

Ambrogio Sparagna

Born in Maranola (Lazio) in 1957, the son of traditional musicians, Sparagna has always combined his activities as musician and composer with field research and took his MA in ethnomusicology with Diego Carpitella in 1982.

Invito (BMG, Italy).

Produced in 1995 after numerous live performances, this disc offers some of the best composition by Sparagna and his organetto with various instrumental collaborations ranging from the Villa Carpegna Polyphonic Choir directed by Anna Rita Colaianni to the thirty organetti of the Bosio Big Band. Also featuring the powerful voices of Lucilla Galeazzi and Nando Citarella.

Riccardo Tesi

Italy's leading organetto player has mastered styles as different as Central Italy's saltarello, Southern Italy's tarantella and Sardinian ballu tundu, and produced the first of a series of brilliant recordings in 1983.

Un ballo liscio (Auvidis/Silex, France).

Tesi brings unexpected new life to the neglected liscio dance style. An inspired interaction between the organetto and the rest of the twelve-piece ensemble featuring diverse instrumentalists such as jazz and classical pianist Mauro Grossi and mandolin player Patrick Vaillant.

Macedonia

tricky rhythms

The Former Yugoslav Republic of Macedonia – to give it its official title – is one of the musical powerhouses of the Balkans, with unstoppable sounds and rhythms coming from a prodigious mix of nationalities. Sometimes known as Vardar Macedonia, after the river that runs from north to south, the Republic is, in fact, a part of a much larger area that bore the name Macedonia during the Ottoman occupation, which was divided between Serbia, Bulgaria and Greece by the 1913 Treaty of Bucharest. To the south, it is bordered by Aegean Macedonia (part of Greece), and to the east by the Bulgarian territory of Pirin Macedonia. **Kim Burton** looks at the mix of ingredients that are the essence of Macedonian music.

S it down at a café in Skopje, Macedonia's capital, and you will hear conversation switching between Macedonian, Albanian and Turkish as people join or leave the company. For a state of under ten million population, Macedonia has an amazing cultural and ethnic diversity. It contains a large Albanian minority (considerably increased during the 1999 war in Kosovo), as well as Turks, Cincars (Vlachs), Roma (Gypsies), Serbs, Greeks and others – even a small group who claim Egyptian origin. Around 65 percent of the population, however, are of Slav 'Macedonian' stock: a people only recognised after World War II when the new Yugoslav Communist government created a Macedonian Republic, declared that its language was separate and distinct, and decreed a Macedonian nationality.

Naturally, the ethnic mix finds its reflection in the musical make up of the area. Macedonian Albanians take part in the mainstream of Albanian music (see p.1); the Turkish minority maintains it own repertoire, often with a strong local accent; and there are significant contributions from the Roma, or Gypsy, communities. The music of the Macedonians themselves, meantime, has a startling richness and range of mood. Many of their folk songs are historical – mournfully referring to the country as *Jadna Makedonija* (Sorrowful Macedonia), or dealing defiantly with heroic deeds from the past – but just as many are love songs, while others have a lightness of touch and a humour that on occasion tips over into the bawdy.

Old-style **dancing** remains an important social activity, even among the young urbanites who frequent the techno clubs of downtown Skopje, and at weddings or village celebrations everybody from toddlers to grannies ends up in a big circle jigging happily to rhythms that are quite baffling to the unfamiliar ear.

Signatures for Swing

As usual in Eastern Europe, the music of the towns differs considerably from that of the villages, but there is one thing they have in common: an extraordinary **complexity of rhythm**. Much music around the world, whatever its origin, can be understood as combinations of equal beats or of long and short beats in the ratio of two to one. But in Macedonia (and to a lesser extent in neighbouring countries) there are many more ways of dividing a bar.

In western music, a **bar of triple time** – such as a waltz – has three equal beats; but in Macedonia it may be a bar of 7/8 divided up as 3–2–2 (eg. the dance tune "Potrcano oro") or 2–2–3 ("Staro Komitsko Oro") or 2–3–2 ("Baba Djurdja") and so on. The dance song "Pominis li libe Todoro" is in 22/16 played as 2–2–3–2–2–3–2–2–2–2!

As well as this, some of the older musicians have a habit of playing in slow tempos in a fashion which subtly **stretches the time**, so that one beat lasts fractionally longer than it would if counted strictly. The feeling of suspense and tension imparted by this technique is hard to describe, but can be heard on older recorded performances of such dance melodies as "Ibraim Odza" and "Berance", where it generates a swing that answers perfectly the demands of the dancers.

Instruments and Ensembles

Macedonia's quintessential, or more accurately, traditionally sanctioned village instrument is the

gajda bagpipe, as proverbs such as 'Without a gajda it's no wedding' bear witness. Although at one time very widespread, it's now rarely heard outside concert presentations and the majority of younger players are schooled – and conscious of their part in preserving the tradition. Many of them are one-time pupils of **Pece Atanasovski**, until his recent untimely death the finest gajda player in the country, and leader of the very fine Radio Skopje (now Macedonian TV-Radio) ensemble, the **Ansambl na Narodni Instrumenti**, with which he recorded frequently.

Other traditional village or small-town instruments include the double-course **tambura**, a Balkan variant on the strummed string instrument; the rim-blown **kaval** flute, slenderer and longer than the Bulgarian model and made of a single piece of wood; the **supelka**, the kaval's baby cousin; and almost extinct now, the fiddle-like **cemane** with its three strings, bowed and held upright on the knee.

Particularly in the eastern and southern parts of the country festivals and weddings are often marked by the appearance of wild-sounding (and generally Gypsy) ensembles of two *zurli* and a *tapan*. The **zurla** is a large but simple oboe with a piercing nasal sound at its best in the open air. The Macedonian variety is large, and relatively deep in tone. Always played in pairs, the first plays the lead while the second accompanies, normally holding a drone, but sometimes joining the first in a rough unison. The **tapan**, a large cylindrical drum played with a heavy stick in one hand and a light switch in the other, drives the dance along with a flurry of syncopations. Towards the end of a party, young men carried away by drink and emotion approach the musicians, press bank notes upon them and kneel so that the zurla can be played directly into their ears.

After World War II the state sponsored the creation of professional ensembles – such as the Radio Skopje ensemble mentioned above and the group of instrumentalists connected with the **Tanec Ensemble** – which performed arranged versions of folk melodies. Local folk groups, known as **KUDs**, were also formed under state aegis. Unlike similar ventures elsewhere in eastern Europe, the arrangers took care not to introduce a harmonic language unsuited to the genre, allowing the original rhythmic drive and emotional directness of the songs to come through. Some urban and village KUDs – the **KUD Niko Pusoski** and the **Ansambl Pance Pesev** are good examples – feature small instrumental groups to accompany singers, but the majority of the KUDs are essentially clarinet and accordion bands – *narodni orkestri*, or folk orchestras.

At least one source for the sound of these bands is the traditional urban music performed by the groups known as **calgii**. The classic line-up of a calgia is violin, clarinet, *kanun* (Turkish plucked zither) and *ut* (lute), with a percussion section of *def* (a large tambourine with jingles) and *tarabuka* (small hourglass drum). Providing entertainment for the urban merchant class, who sometimes built low stages on their verandas for calgii to perform on, and later in cabarets similar to the Greek *café-aman*, where they would accompany *čoček* dancers or play the slow tunes known as *na trapeza* (at the table) intended for listening, calgii were the Macedonian version of a type of ensemble found from Albania to Istanbul.

The calgia sound is romantic and passionate, sometimes tinged with a typical Macedonian melancholy, sometimes fiery and mysterious, and the melodies are either adaptations of Macedonian folkloric melodies (versions of zurla tunes are not uncommon) or point back toward a Turkish classical or light-classical origin, with plenty of room for improvisation. Macedonian Radio and Television still maintains a calgia of the old style, as do some of the folklore groups, but despite the beauty of the music, today it's pretty much on a life-support system, and modern instrumental groups have a quite different sound.

One of the few clarinettists to have performed successfully both with a calgia and in the more modern style is **Tale Ognenovski**, born in 1922 and one of the most influential musicians of the post-war era. He was a member of the Tanec group during the 1950s and lead clarinet of the Radio Skopje calgia. The composer of many tunes that have become standards, he is today the leader of his own group, and a master of the more Westernised style that became prominent in the 1940s and '50s. This is the style that still holds sway, and which is the basis for Macedonia's own new-composed folk music.

New Folk Music

The **narodni orkestri** or folk orchestras have a line-up of clarinet (more recently saxophone), accordion, guitar, bass and drum kit, with synthesiser and drum machine becoming ever more common. They have a more direct and less dark-hued sound than most calgia, which to many ears is less 'oriental', although like most modern Balkan music it gathers material and influences from all sorts of places. Their music is hugely popular and a vast number of ephemeral cassette releases serve the needs of cafe habitués, bus and taxi drivers and hard-pressed radio programmers. Musicians arrive and disappear from the scene with frequency but clarinettist **Miroslav Businovski** and brilliant accordionists **Milan Zavkov** and **Skender Ameti**, the latter with a striking command of any number of idioms, are names that look to be fixtures for years to come.

As well as the enormous body of folk song collected from the villages and still sung in something like its pristine form, either solo or by a group of singers in a simple drone-based polyphonic texture, Macedonia has a thriving industry based on arrangements of such songs, either using folk instruments or factory-made ones. Singer **Vaska Ilieva** has made a very successful career performing such arrangements, although she is probably at her best as a singer of slow, highly decorated ballads like "Air da ne storis, Majko" to the accompaniment of a pair of *kavals*.

Ilieva, along with her male counterpart **Aleksander Sarievski**, is also one of the best-loved singers of newly composed songs based on a folk idiom. These parallel the *novokomponovana* music of Serbia (see p.273) and have followed the same pattern of development, becoming harder edged and nowadays drawing on the rhythms of house and techno music.

Anastasia, a trio who are able to play a wide variety of folk instruments and are competent singers as well, have chosen yet another direction. They seem to have little interest in preserving folklore but instead transform it, using the resources of the recording studio and an impressive dramatic sense to produce a sort of Macedonian Gothic, well-represented by their soundtrack for the Macedonian film *Before The Rain*.

The new-composed music exists alongside a well established Macedonian tradition of local **rock bands**. By far the most important of these is **Leb i Sol**, a group founded in the late 1970s and still active, who leaven their basic rock instincts with a yeasty brew of local rhythms and scales. Their version of the traditional "Uci me, Karaj me", with rock guitar laid out over a grandiose keyboard riff, stands good comparison with the mass of progressive music that has influenced them.

The audience for such groups is and has been since their inception, the children of the urban professional classes – many of whom are now parents themselves. On the other hand, professional music-making, when it comes to providing entertainment for the average Macedonian, is overwhelmingly in the hands of Roma, the Gypsies.

Electric Gypsies

The **Gypsies** are thought to have arrived in the Balkans about 600 years ago, originating from Rajasthan in the Indian subcontinent (see Gypsy Music article p.146). They seem to have swiftly established a reputation as skilled and adaptable musicians, and they hold a musical reputation that is out of all proportion to their numbers. In some places they are practically the only musicians available for weddings and feasts, and more or less hold a monopoly over musical life.

This is particularly true of Macedonia where Gypsies are a substantial minority. The settlement of Shuto Orizari outside Skopje – the setting for Emir Kusturica's film *Time of the Gypsies* – is the largest Roma town in the world, and there is a Romani-language newspaper as well as radio and TV broadcasts.

The Gypsies owe their commanding position first to their undoubted skill as performers, and secondly, and regrettably, to their low social status. As foreigners of suspect origin they were forced into jobs thought to be dirty or dangerous, either physically or for magical reasons or both: for example executioner or metalworker. Music is a job in the second category, the magical. In the Balkans as in many other parts of the world, instrumental musicians are considered to be in contact with the unseen and risky world of spirit forces, and a travelling musician is still more of an outsider. The status of being a traveller and professional, however, had benefits. Gypsy musicians were first to adopt the clarinet and violin – instruments that require more time and skill to master than was available to the peasants – and their relative lack of ties to land or territory allowed them to travel from place to place as the need for musicians ebbed or flowed. One authority estimates that in the heyday of the calgia 65% of the musicians were Roma, 35% Macedonian and 5% Turkish.

These days, in the bars of Shuto Orizari (known affectionately as Shutka) you can hear different styles of Gypsy music, especially on **Gjurgjevden**, the sixth of May and the feast of St. George, which the Roma have adopted as the most important of their festivals. The typical orchestra is fronted by a singer, backed by electric guitar, synth or electric organ, drum kit, and maybe a saxophone or clarinet. Highly coloured, passionate, even erotic, the music may sound very Indian, particularly in vocal quality and phrasing. The Romani language is related to Hindi, and Indian film musicals are popular with the Gypsy population; some songs have firmly entered the repertoire.

FOLK ROOTS

Esma Redžepova

The most traditional Macedonian Gypsy style is associated with **Stevo Teodosievski** and his wife **Esma Redžepova**. Clarinettist Stevo died recently, but Redžepova remains Macedonia's most celebrated Gypsy performer. She has a powerful voice and vast repertoire, and an undoubted passion and ability, sometimes undermined by her glossy cabaret approach.

A much more modern approach is employed by the clarinettist, saxophonist and composer **Ferus Mustafov** from Strumica – arguably the greatest Macedonian virtuoso. He comes from a musical family: his father Ilmi Jasari reputedly introduced the saxophone to the southern Balkans, and the young Ferus was classically trained, turning professional in his late teens and soon establishing a reputation as a brilliant, adaptable instrumentalist. His music is a fascinating fusion of Macedonian, Turkish and Gypsy influences and many of his tunes have become standards. He can frequently be found playing in and around Skopje. Although sometimes his accompanists fall short of his high standards, in the right company he is unrivalled.

Although **brass bands** have not taken root in Macedonia to the same extent as they have in Serbia, they are

an increasing part of the musical landscape. Once again, many of them are Gypsy, although not exclusively so. One band that has made it beyond the borders of the country and into the World Music scene is the **Kočani Orkestar**. Drawing on popular song, traditional melodies, and Bollywood film tunes this band from Kočani, a town about 70 kilometres east of Skopje is typical in its determined swing and readiness to adapt melodies from all over to its purposes.

The most intriguing singer to have emerged over the last decade or so is **Džansever**, a woman who first came to prominence in the 1980s, and who unusually writes her own words to most of her songs. She has a magnificent voice, and a deeply serious and eclectic approach to her art; unlike most of her predecessors she gives short shrift to the idea of simply being an entertainer. She has also made an impact on the Turkish market, and has recorded a couple of CDs singing Turkish songs, which she also does superbly.

CRAMMED DISCS

Kočani Orkestar

discography

Compilations

 Anthology of Macedonian Folk Song (Mister Company, Macedonia).

These 20 songs are absolute classics, and include examples by some of the finest singers of the last 30 or more years. Highly recommended.

⊚ **Folk Music of Yugoslavia** (Topic, UK).

A splendid choice of village music from all over former-Yugoslavia collected and annotated in 1969 and 1970 by Wolf Dietrich. It includes some startling Macedonian tracks – the Robanovski brothers on clarinet and violin, and fine gajda bagpipe playing by Ilija Poljakot who also sings while playing, "having drunk half a dozen glasses of good, home-made red wine". The survey also includes Croatian diaphonic songs, a Serbian kolo and some sweetly romantic Bosnian singing.

⊚ **Gypsy Music of Macedonia and Neighbouring Countries** (Topic, UK).

For fans of the typical outdoor duo of zurna and drum, this is the essential compilation. But its title is rather misleading as it features only one track from Macedonia, but plenty more from Kosovo (Serbia), Romania, Greece and Turkey. Wild stuff recorded in the 1970s and '80s.

⊚ **Gypsy Queens** (World Network, Germany).

This double CD set includes fine Gypsy music from Hungary, Romania and Spain, as well as some of the best recent recordings from Esma Redžepova, and it marks the first appearance in the western market place of the brilliant younger singer Džansever, recorded on top form with a hot band and some splendid Romani songs.

⊚ **Makedonski Folklor so Zurli i Tapani, Svadbeni Običai** (Mister Company, Macedonia).

If you feel like developing a taste for the wild sounds of zurla and tapan (it may take time, but it's well worthwhile), this is the place to start. Featuring the great Mahmut Muzafer and companions, this is a collection of melodies traditionally played during the wedding festivities, including an over-whelming version of the long and intricate showpiece (for dancers and musicians alike) "Teškoto".

Artists

Anastasia

Anastasia combine a decent understanding of popular western music with a thorough grounding in traditional styles. Their dramatic flair has led to them being involved in a number of theatrical performances.

⊚ **Before the Rain** (Philips, Greece).

This film soundtrack, using bagpipe, kaval and kanun among other instruments supported by keyboards is atmospheric, evocative and effective.

Vaska Ilieva

Singer Vaska Ilieva is one of the older generation, who came to prominence following World War II. Her style remains close to the village tradition, but her experience of café performances and big festival stages brings her a confident professionalism. Her voice is still unrivalled in traditional and 'newly composed' folk song.

⊚ **Zemljo Makedonsko** (MRT, Macedonia).

This excellent and resonant selection of love songs, folk melodies, and historical songs illustrates the emotional range of Slav Macedonian music.

Kočani Orkestar

This is one of Macedonia's best brass bands – largely Gypsy, typically rumbustious, and featuring zurla as well as the brass. They are from a town in eastern Macedonia and are led by Naat Veliov.

⊚ **L'orient est rouge** (Cramworld, Belgium)

This is the disc to go for – a vast improvement on their first album (on Long Distance). It is a collection of traditional dances and song melodies, mostly Macedonian although from as far afield as China, and concluding with the Romani anthem Djelem, Djelem.

Ferus Mustafov

Clarinettist and saxophonist Ferus Mustafov, a breathtaking performer with a seemingly inexhaustible flow of inspiration, is the leading figure in modern Macedonian Gypsy music.

 King Ferus (GlobeStyle, UK).

Recorded in Berlin with a top class band, this is a splendid collection of old and new favourites.

Esma Redžepova

Esma Redžepova remains the reigning queen of Romani song, a stirring performer whose voice is still capable of the subtlest inflections and wildest passions.

⊚ **Songs of a Macedonian Gypsy** (Monitor, USA).

The 21 tracks on this disc are mainly Romani, including the fabulous and deservedly popular Čaje Šukurija, but they also include Macedonian songs.

Netherlands

tilting at windmills

The Dutch have a tendency to embrace every other music but their own. There is a lively World Music scene in all the main cities of the Netherlands – including some interesting music from the former Dutch colonies – but these days, outside of the province of Friesland, you can count yourself lucky if you hear one single original Dutch melody. Nonetheless, **Wim Bloemendaal** tiptoes through the surviving remnants and revivalists.

As in Britain and Germany, the Netherlands had a folk revival of sorts in the late 1960s, as groups like **Wolverloi** and **Fungus**, and singer **Gerard van Maasakkers** (who sang in Brabant dialect), explored the songs of a pre-war generation. These had been collected and championed by radio producer Ate Doornbosch, who had for years broadcast them in his programme *Onder de groene linde* (Under the Green Lindentree), and by Cobi Schreijer, who played host to Dutch folksingers and musicians in his *De Waag* club in Haarlem. Both, however, are long retired.

Frisian Folk

As the folk movement lost momentum, and rock took over, many Dutch performers began performing in English. However, the trend was bucked somewhat in the northern province of **Fryslân** (Friesland), where a handful of folk groups continued to express themselves in Frisian – a separate language, older than Dutch and related to Anglo Saxon. In the mid-1970s, the group **Irolt** (named after a Frisian mythological figure), influenced by British bands like Fairport Convention and Steeleye Span, created music based on Frisian stories and folktales.

Nanne Kalma, one of the founding members of Irolt, remains a driving force behind Frisian folklore, and there are today quite a number of active groups and soloists singing in Frisian. It is, inevitably, though, a small scene. Since Frisian is only spoken in Fryslân (by around half a million people) the music is largely confined to that province.

For a sample of Frisian music, it's worth heading for the little village of Nylân (between Sneek and Bolsward) on Easter Monday when the **Aaipop Festival** takes place. Performers might include singers like **Piter Wilkens**, **Doede Veeman**, **Ernst Langhout** or **Doede Bleeker** and groups like **Reboelje**, **Briquebec**, **Sebeare**, **Om 'e Noard** and **Adri & Sa**. Each of the six hundred inhabitants of Nylân has a role in Aaipop and the festival is attended by close to three thousand people each year.

Since 1955 the village of **Joure** has organised an annual revival of a traditional Frisian farmer's wedding on the last Wednesday in July. While it's obviously an artificial event – with everyone dressed in nineteenth-century costume – it's been a focus for the revival of the Frisian *skotsploech* (traditional music and dance group). There are now around ten *skotsploegen* in Friesland with the Ljouwerter Skotsploech now fifty years old. They can feature from two to six musicians (playing fiddles, accordions and percussion like a 'stamping stick' or *rommelpot*) and up to thirty or more dancers. The music dates from the nineteenth century, when the rise of national feeling amongst the Frisians developed, and includes popular European dances like the *wals* (waltz), polka, galop and particularly the *skots* (schottisch). There's also a surviving fiddle and old-style melodeon scene on the island of Terschelling – off the northern coast of Fryslân.

Dutch Revivalists

There is hardly any other original Dutch roots music left elsewhere in the Netherlands. However, there is an active if low-key revivalist scene, with bands singing in Dutch or a regional dialect, recreating old forms.

One of the surprise roots hits of 1998 came from the band **Törf** (Turf) in Groningen, featuring bagpiper Flip Rodenburg. They discovered some tunes from the early nineteenth century and recreated them in an imaginative and refreshing way on bagpipes, bazouki, accordion and euphonium. Another lively group is **Twee Violen en een Bas** who play dance music from Dutch pubs of the 1700s, on violins and a sawing bass, in a popular, earthy style.

Other roots revivalists include the quartet **Folkcorn**, centred on Jitze Kopinga and multi-instrumentalist Laurens van der Zee, who sing and play dance music, songs, ballads and madrigals from the Low Countries. Another group reviving traditional Low Countries music is **Pekel**, five musicians led by Theo Schuurmans playing bagpipes, guitar, accordion, hurdy-gurdy and other assorted instruments. They take their source material from written collections and music recorded by collectors in the 1950s, but their arrangements are a little over-scholarly.

There's also been something of a revival in **bagpipe playing**. The *doedelzak*, *pijpzak* or *piepzak* has an honourable history in the Low Countries, as can be seen in the sixteenth- and seventeenth-century paintings of Brueghel and Steen with chubby peasants clutching bagpipes at village fairs. Bagpipes feature heavily in Törf and Pekel's music and there's an annual bagpipe festival in June.

One good sign for those interested in the surviving traditions of the Netherlands is the new series of CDs started by Music & Words (MW Records). They've released a disc of archive and contemporary accordion players, followed by songs of traditional netmenders from Vlaardingen. Future plans include dance music with fiddles and melodeon from Terschelling.

Moluccans and Surinamese

What has most enhanced the Dutch roots music scene is the influx of people from the former colonies, particularly the Moluccas (Indonesia) and Surinam (Dutch Antilles).

The **Moluccan Islands** are a largely forgotten international issue. They were due to be a federal state of Indonesia in 1950 but Suharto reneged on the agreement, the South Moluccans declared independence, and their uprising was crushed. The Netherlands has a sizable exile community, whose music has Polynesian as well as Indonesian influences. They include a strong choral tradition, carried on by bands like **Tala Mena Siwa**, and a more pop-based music, whose best exponent (until his death in a plane crash in 1988) was guitarist **Eddie Lakransy** and his **Moluccan Moods Orchestra**.

Holland has even more substantial communities from the former colonies of Dutch Antilles and in particular **Surinam** (a historic part of the Dutch West Indies but actually on the northeast coast of South America). The dominant music from Surinam is known as *kaseko* – an energetic and irresistible fusion of marching band, New Orleans jazz, diverse Caribbean styles, and West African influences (the latter rooted among the maroons – the colony's one-time African slaves). Several of the top kaseko groups are resident in the Netherlands – which has over a quarter of the Surinamese population – including groups led by **Carlo Jones** and **William Souvenir**. Their music is joyously infectious. Jones also plays in a group called **De Nazaten van Prins Hendrik** (The Offspring of Prince Hendrik), a lively Dutch-Surinam outfit that promote themselves as 'purveyors of bastard music'.

discography

Compilations

Achterhoekse harmonikamuziek (MW Records, Netherlands).

Melodeon music from Achterhoek, a region in the east Netherlands. Old-style dance music from veteran players like Jan Klein Hesseling and Gerrit Klompenhouwer. Polkas, waltzes, mazurkas with some German influences from over the border.

It's Dawning in the East: Bagpipes of the Low Countries (Pan, Netherlands).

For those interested in the lesser-known bagpipes traditions of Europe. Bagpipe music of the Low Countries from five of the best soloists and ensembles of the current revival.

Jouster Boerebrulloft (Pan, Netherlands).

This is a recording of the Farmer's Wedding festival in Joure.

PAN 2004CD

Jouster Boerebrulloft

Farmer's Wedding in Joure

It's inevitably artificial – people in nineteenth-century costume playing at serious folk revival – but introduces music from Ljouwerter Skotsploech (from Leeuwarden), Snitser Skotsploech (from Sneek) and Aald Hielpen, a folklore group going back to 1912.

⊚ **Zingt zo lekker weg** (MW Records, Netherlands).

Songs of female netmenders from the fishing town of Vlaardingen, near Rotterdam. Recorded at a reunion where they sang spontaneously all the songs they used to sing – popular and religious.

Artists

Doede Bleeker

Frisian singer-songwriter Doede Bleeker earned notoriety in the late 1980s making fun of bourgeois types. He comes from the city of Staveren where he owns a fish shop.

⊚ **Mengde Gefoelens/Mixed Feelings** (Marista, Netherlands).

On this 1997 CD, Bleeker shows he can write and perform emotional material as well as the satire for which he is known.

Folkcorn

Formed in the early 1970s, this quartet – Jitze Kopinga, Anneke Rot, Marja van der Zee and Laurens van der Zee – perform at historical parties and give educational performances at home and abroad. They get their material from Dutch collections like the Haarlems Lietboek and the Oude en Nieuwe Hollantse Boerenlieties.

⊚ **Jan de Mulder** (Clipsound, Netherlands).

The group's 1997 album is perhaps the best of their output, featuring a wide collection of dances from Holland and overseas, plus sailors' songs.

Irolt

Active from 1974–86, Irolt were Fryslân's most successful group, led by Nanne Kalma with a shifting cast in support.

⊚ **Ier of Let/Early or Late** (Universe Productions, Netherlands).

A four-CD collection of all of Irolt's recorded music, together with a book including lyrics and music – in Frisian!

Kikstra Brothers

Wytze Pieter and Jan Foeke Kikstra started playing melodeons in 1985 when they were respectively fifteen and thirteen years old. Their first inspiration was the accordion music of the Frisian island of Terschelling; later they made their name in Scandinavia, as the Bröderna Kikstra, playing music from Norway and Sweden.

⊚ **De Boerenbruiloft (The Farmer's Wedding)** (Syncoop, Netherlands).

On this mid-1990s disc the Kikstra Brothers play – with companions on fiddle, clarinet, guitars, bass and percussion – waltzes, polkas and mazurkas plus music picked up by sailors from Scandinavia and the British Isles. Includes a few songs in Frisian and Dutch.

Ernst Langhout

Langhout originally sang in English, but is now one of Fryslân's best singer/songwriters in his native language.

⊚ **Nea Foar Altyd/Never for Always** (Marista, Netherlands).

Recent album containing "Fryslân moat stikken", about developers who ruin Fryslân's beautiful countryside.

Ljouwerter Skotsploech

The skotsploech dance team of Leeuwarden, half a century old, are one of the vintage groups of Frisian dance music. They feature fiddles and accordions and focus on wedding music from the mid nineteenth century.

⊚ **Ljouwerter Skotsploech** (Pan, Netherlands).

This includes historical material, plus a version of *Fryske Trou*, a musical play written around the turn of the century depicting traditional Frisian life and customs.

De Nazaten Van Prins Hendrik

Prins Hendrik (1876–1934), the husband of Dutch Queen Wilhelmina, was infamous for his promoscuity and this band of Dutch, Surinamese (Carlo Jones – see overleaf – is a member) and Antillean musicians is named after his bastard offspring. With a line-up of saxes, trombone, guitar and percussion, they explore music from all over the Dutch-speaking/colonised world.

⊚ **Kownu Boy E Dansi (The Prince is Dancing)** (Pan, Netherlands).

This is a fine dance record, mixing influences from the Dutch Antilles, creole music, dixieland and even a combination of Balinese gamelan and Surinam kaseko. As inventive a World Music fusion as you could hope to find.

Törf

This Groningen band including bagpipes, guitars, bouzouki, accordion, cowhorn, whistle and euphonium. They play real Dutch music, imaginatively re-worked.

 Törf speelt Beukema (Törf, Netherlands).

This is the best Dutch roots record yet – a recoding of dance tunes by one Jakub Pietrs Beukema (1782–1859), arranged from a manuscript discovered by Törf bagpipe player Flip Rodenburg on the piano of an open-air museum. (Available from Visserstraat 19A, 9712 CR, Groningen, The Netherlands).

Twee Violen En Een Bas

Ilans Troost, Jos Koning and Willem Raadsveld started in 1978 under the name Knerp (Creak). They began playing nineteenth-century music, but then started digging deeper into history.

⊚ **Amsterdam 1700** (Syncoop, Netherlands).

Instrumental repertoire as it might have been performed in the city's pubs in 1700. The tunes come from rural, classical and theatre traditions.

Gerard van Maasakkers

Van Maakakkers is an enduring (and funny) singer/songwriter, who released his first album in 1977.

⊚ **20 Jaar Liedjes Live!** (I.C.U.B4.T, Netherlands).

A double CD recorded in concert featuring fresh arrangements of his classic songs with a fine band.

Doede Veeman

Veeman lives in rural Fryslân, earns his living by teaching

Dutch and sings Frisian songs in his spare time. The *éminence grise* of the Frisian folkscene, he is a real old-time performer, full of songs and anecdotes.

⊕ **Húske/Outhouse and c Frustraasjebloes**
(Universe Productions, Netherlands).

Both these dialect albums are extremely funny – though you need to understand the language. Vocals and guitar with occasional guest musicians.

Piter Wilkens

Wilkens, a former-carpenter, is now one of the best-known performers in Fryslân.

⊕ **Timmermants joender/Carpenter Magician**
(Achterdyk Produksjes, Netherlands).

These are peculiarly Friesian songs – for example, about the sheep that live on the dykes with their legs shorter on one side than the other to stay upright.

Dutch-Moluccans

Moluccan Moods Orchestra

A band of South Moluccan expatriates, led by guitarist Eddie Lakransy until his death in 1988.

⊕ **Wakoi** (Piranha, Germany).

An addictive disc of Moluccan songs given a contemporary jazz-funk treatment by Holland-based expatriates. Guitar, keyboards, sax, flutes and percussion plus some wonderful harmony singing from the three female vocalists.

Tala Mena Siwa

A ten-piece band of expatriate South Moluccans based in Nijmegen. Their name means 'a breakthrough' and features rich, choral-style singing from the six women.

⊕ **Sae Ena** (MW Records, Netherlands).

This material is much more traditional than the Moluccan Moods Orchestra above, based on romantic or moralistic *kapata* songs and epic *legoe* songs.

Dutch-Surinamese

Carlo Jones & the Surinam Troubadors

Surinam-born saxophonist Carlo Jones has played music since childhood, graduating through police and military brass bands at home. Now settled in the Netherlands, he leads the Surinam Kaseko Troubadors, a highly seductive big band, whose line-up includes alto sax, sousaphone, trumpet, trombone, banjo and marching drums.

 Carlo Jones and the Surinam Kaseko Troubadors (SPN, Netherlands).

A compulsive initiation into the kaseko sound, this has a real humour and bounce that owes a good deal to New Orleans. Carlo takes the lead with squealing sax, but there are wonderfully agile and punchy sousaphone riffs from André Jones, and it's all powered on by the marching drums.

William Souvenir

Souvenir was born of Aucan and Saramaccan parents, in the Paramaribo area of Surinam. A self-taught guitarist, he has played in kaseko and calypso groups, and is much influenced by Haitian music. He moved to the Netherlands in 1970 and has worked with Mighty Botai, Surinam's foremost calypso singer.

⊕ **A tin télé** (MW Records, Netherlands).

A 1990 retrospective of Souvenir's varied but always highly danceable sounds, including zouk, merengue, kaseko and calypso. The songs – mostly love songs, but also addressing environmental concerns – are in Sranang Togo dialects.

Norway

fjords and fiddles

In Norway some of Europe's most distinctive traditional music and innovative musicians meet face to face. Many might have learned their craft listening and playing American music, but they have now turned their attention towards home, meeting their equals among fiddlers, traditional singers and Sámi joikers to evolve new Nordic jazz and rock forms. These often draw in ideas, sounds and musicians from other world traditions, particularly those which derive their energy not from Western classical harmony but from the interweaving of linear melody and rhythm which is at the heart of the old and new Nordic music. **Andrew Cronshaw** explores Norway's burgeoning scene.

Roots music in Norway is experiencing a surge in popularity and media coverage, but it is not exactly mainstream. Many Norwegians seem to regard such things as Hardanger fiddling as a bit hokey in a modern, oil-rich nation. When asked if they had any Norwegian roots music, the head of A&R at the Oslo office of a major label replied: "No, but there's this American singer who records over here with Norwegian musicians – he's very good, like Bob Dylan." And when I mentioned to a TV company marketing manager the magnificent Lillehammer 1994 Winter Olympics opening spectacular – skiing Telemark fiddlers, music from Knut Reiersrud and Iver Kleive, Bukkene Bruse, Nils Aslak Valkeapää and others – his response was "Hmm, too many fiddles." He went on to enthuse about Cajun music. As musician and Norwegian Radio producer Leiv Solberg, editor of NRK/Grappa's important ten-CD archive set *Norsk Folkemusikk - Norwegian Folk Music*, says: "It's what we call 'The Norwegian Problem'".

Borderlands

Nearly half of Norway lies north of the Arctic Circle, but the majority of its 4.5 million population lives in the southern part. The country borders Finland and Russia in the far north, but the thousand-mile south-east border is with Sweden, with which Norway was politically united until 1905. A much longer union with Denmark – Scandinavia's dominant power in the Middle Ages – lasted from 1380 until Napoleon's defeat in 1814.

Since 1917 there have been two official Norwegian languages. The 20 percent minority *Nynorsk*, based on Norwegian dialects, is found in inland valley and mountain communities, while the more Danish-rooted *Bokmål* prevails in all the cities and many other country areas.

Despite its former Danish and Swedish links, Norway has always had a distinct culture, or rather a patchwork of cultures, which are largely the result of its mountainous topography. The high tops of the Scandinavian spinal mountain range discourage east-west communication across the border with Sweden, and north-south travel is impeded by a corrugated pattern of steep valleys. Water has been a more convenient route, and styles and fashions from outside have tended to spread up the fjords from the west and south, not always penetrating the remoter areas.

As a result, forms of music very different from the European mainstream have persisted among the rural population of Norway, and their isolation even from one another has resulted in greater divergence. Much fiddle-playing and traditional singing shows the influence of the **natural scale** and may use non-fixed and microtonal intervals; it can sound either out of tune or exquisitely 'on the edge' to those accustomed to twelve mathematically equal semitones. There's also an appreciation in Norwegian music, particularly apparent in the sound of *hardingfele* (fiddle) and *seljefløyte* (flute), of the high, silvery frequency ranges.

Indeed, there's generally an open, airy sound to much Norwegian roots music. As in Sweden, calls such as *lokking* (cow-calling), and *laling* (vocal signalling) are striking features still used by singers, though no longer needed in their original environment – the high summer pastures.

Kveding

The overall word for Norwegian traditional vocal music is **kveding** (*kvede* means 'sing'). Short songs known as **stev**, some dating from the middle ages, are still sung, particularly in Setesdal, where they're still being improvised. The much longer narrative **ballad** is a major part of Norway's song tradition and it's likely that these songs of epic and magical tales were once danced, as they still are in the Faroes.

Some of the old ballad stories were printed as broadsheets, **skillingstryk**, which were sold in Norway as in other Nordic countries from the seventeenth to the beginning of the twentieth century. Other skillingstryk were topical, and many of the last published (before they were replaced by records) related to the late nineteenth and early twentieth century emigration of about 75,000 Norwegians to North America.

Norway has its share of traditional **lullabies** (*bånsuller*), **children's songs** and **work songs**, and also of **hymns** which managed to maintain a good deal of their traditional melodic characteristics despite the introduction of harmonium or organ with their equal temperament scales.

Tralling is the equivalent of Scottish or Irish 'diddling' – vocalising a dance tune - with the difference that it isn't only a vocal substitute for the instrument but is performed by some fiddlers as an accompaniment to their playing. The name derives from the predominant 'tra-la' vocables.

Fiddles

The best-known Norwegian instrument is the **hardingfele** or Hardanger fiddle (see box) with its distinctive high-ringing sound. It gets its name from the Hardanger area of southwest Norway where it originated, though exactly when is uncertain. It seems to have been in use by the middle of the seventeenth century, while the present-day form evolved in the mid-nineteenth century.

Hardingfele territory is roughly to the west of Oslo as far as the sea and as far north as Ålesund, with the triangle made by inner Hordaland, Valdres and Telemark usually regarded as the instrument's heartland. In other areas the prevailing fiddle remained the **vanleg fele** (ordinary fiddle), also called the **flatfele** because of its longer neck and lower tuning. Sometimes, even ordinary fiddles have their necks shortened and bridge flattened, making it possible to play in a hardingfele style. Others are fitted with resonant strings, making what's now known as the **Setesdals-fele**. Players of vanleg fiddle, like Hardanger fiddlers, use a variety of tunings, and in the solo styles of both there is much ornamentation and little vibrato.

Like the hardingfele, ordinary fiddles reached Norway in the seventeenth century, and both suffered a setback as a result of religious revivals during the nineteenth century. Fiddles were seen as instruments of the devil, and in western Norway many were destroyed or hidden away. Fortunately, fiddle-burning was by no means universal.

The hardingfele attracted more musical converts later, when its players were seen to be winning in the competitions, **kappleikar**, which began at the end of the nineteenth century. These gave a new lease of life to fiddling, and the many local kappleikar and the national contest, the **Landskappleik**, remain a major feature of the fiddle scene today. They are rather formal guardians of the tradition, with judging systems which are geared more to past than present innovations. Until recently the hardingfele was inseparable from its traditional repertoire, and anything outside that was considered a degradation. Well-known and progressive hardingfele player **Annbjørg Lien**, who always lost the points assigned for playing a tune from one's local tradition

ANDREW CRONSHAW

Annbjørg Lien

Hardingfele

A hardingfele is a beautiful object, usually with black pen-drawn acanthus patterns on the body, mother-of-pearl inlay on the fingerboard and a carved head, often in the shape of a lion or dragon. Compared to an ordinary fiddle, the neck is shorter, and the bridge flatter. In addition to its four playing strings, it has four or five resonating strings passing under the fingerboard and bridge.

Such sympathetic strings were found on the English viola d'amore in the seventeenth century – it's thought the idea came from the East where several Asian instruments feature them. They ring unchecked even when the bowed strings have been damped, so the hardingfele generates a ringing, silvery high overtone drone, while the fingered strings can produce a lower unstopped drone or a double-stopped effect; the flat bridge facilitates the bowing of two or more strings at once. The tuning itself is drone-oriented. There are said to be twenty-four different tunings; the standard is A D A E (starting with the lowest string), with the resonating strings D E F# A.

The 'non-standard' tunings change the apparent tonal centre of a tune and therefore its whole feeling. The playing styles of different regions favour particular modalities, and so use particular tunings. Some have mood associations, and are named to match – for example, *grålysing* (dawn; A E A C# – one of the 'troll' tunings). Another, *gorrlaus* (very slack) – in which the A is tuned right down to F and so wows in pitch as it's bowed hard – is associated with the three Setesdal *Rammeslag* (strong tunes) only resorted to by a fiddler in times of extreme emotion. Reidar Sevåg, in his notes to a CD on which Vidar Lande plays these Rammeslag, describes the effect:

"Discomfort and horror would strike both listeners and fiddler, and the latter would bow like a madman until somebody cut the strings or ripped the bow from him. Then he would cry ... it is evident that the fiddlers did not resort to Rammeslag until alcohol had its effect and unless somebody had annoyed or teased them."

because her family home just south of Ålesund wasn't in hardingfele territory, nevertheless sees the value of a strongly defended tradition: "Some fiddlers don't want to play in competitions, but it's there you find young people starting to play the Hardanger, and it's there they get their inspiration, so it's a pity if the best players don't show up. Competitions are good for young players, who can then move on to concerts, and they're one way of keeping the musical dialects alive. If there weren't some kind of rule, so that you have to play at least one traditional tune, you'd probably find them gradually disappearing."

Lien herself is no stranger to disapproval; she received a mixed reaction to her first major album, *Annbjørg*, made in 1989 when she was eighteen, which surrounded her hardingfele and *nyckelharpa* (Swedish keyed violin) with arrangements by Helge Førde (of category-crossing brass and reeds band Brazz Bros) for reeds, percussion and Frode Fjellheim's synths. Nevertheless, the album won many friends for the hardingfele, and Annbjørg continues to make connections, including regular collaboration with the brilliant and equally dynamic Shetland fiddler Catriona Macdonald. (Shetland fiddling has much in common with Norwegian, a fact recognised in the 1983 album project *Ringing Strings*, which united Shetland's Tom Anderson and his young pupils Catriona Macdonald and Debbie Scott with Norway's Knut and Hauk Buen and Vidar Lande.)

Dance Fiddling

Though in concert performance the music of solo fiddlers may be highly expressive, it is virtually all based on dance rhythms. The rhythms can be stretched and complex, but the player's footstamp is a guide. In some recordings players have been discouraged from stamping, in case it swamped the recording levels. Well-recorded though, in a nicely reverberent space, the footstamp is a key component.

Norwegian folk-dance music can be divided into two ages. The old dances, known as **bygdedans**, are done to an older stratum of tunes known as *slåttar*, and these make up most of the solo repertoire of hardingfele and fiddle. Slåttar subdivide into two-beat dances, including *halling*, *gangar*, *rull*, *brurmarsj*, and three-beat, which include *springar*, *springleik* and *pols*. The halling is a male solo dance involving displays of prowess, including kicking a hat from the top of a stick held by a woman standing on a chair – the sort of thing beloved of dance-display teams. The rest, apart from the stately *brurmarsj* (bridal march), are normally couple dances.

The old, straightforward way of playing the tunes is as a short series of themes, each repeated, with small variations but nothing very elaborate. But during the nineteenth century some players began to play in a more personally expressive way, exploring and developing the themes, turning them from

SIGNE DONS

Hallvard T. Bjørgum with a hardingfele

dance tunes into more evocative works. The leading name in this progression was **Myllarguten** (Torgeir Augundsson, 1799–1872), from Telemark, who was a great innovator and also travelled a good deal spreading his ideas. Though he did play for dances, he was one of the first masters of hardingfele to perform in a concert situation, to a non-dancing audience. The Norwegian classical violinist **Ole Bull** recognised his skill, and they sometimes shared a concert platform. Bull was also influential in the musical education of composer **Edvard Grieg** (1843–1907), who incorporated hardingfele music in works such as the piano piece "Slåtter", based on transcriptions of the playing of **Knut Dahle** (1834–1921). Another frequent visitor to Hardanger was **Ola Mosafinn** (1828–1912) from Voss, and his creative developments of Hardanger ideas, particularly his springar style, had considerable influence on fiddling back in his home area in the west.

The tradition has continued unbroken from the famous fiddlers of the nineteenth century, and today fine players of hardingfele are legion. Leading present-day players include **Knut** and **Hauk Buen**, **Hallvard T. Bjørgum**, **Håkon Høgemo**, **Knut Hamre**, **Leif Rygg** and, moving increasingly into the creation of new material in different styles, **Annbjørg Lien**. Notable players of ordinary fiddle include **Hans W. Brimi**, **Susanne Lundeng**, **Per Sæmund Bjørkum** and **Arne M. Sølvberg**. All of these, and many more, have recorded CDs.

Fiddlers frequently acknowledge the influence of preceding maestros and they'll often play a tune in the style of a particular predecessor. Of course, intentionally or not, subtle touches of their own creep in. That's the nature of this deeply expressive music, and one of its most alluring aspects.

Gammeldans and Accordions

During the nineteenth century increasing numbers of people moved from the country to the cities where they had fixed working hours and regular leisure time. Before long, new dances, such as *vals*, *reinlender*, *masurka*, *polka*, *polkett*, *skotsk*, *englis*, *hamburger*, *galopp*, *sekstur*, *hopsa*, *fandango* and *feier* became fashionable. These were collectively called *runddans* (round, or turning dance), but when the next new wave arrived in the 1920s runddans became known as 'old dance' – **gammeldans**.

Gammeldans is still popular, and its music is dominated by the **trekkspel** (accordion), an instrument that also first appeared in the nineteenth century and to an extent ousted the fiddle. First came the diatonic **enrader** or **torader** (one or two-row melodeon) and later the bigger chromatic forms.

A typical modern gammeldans band may or may not have a fiddler, but it will certainly have accordion (usually chromatic), probably double or electric bass and perhaps guitar. Accordions – particularly these large ones when insensitively played – tend to make fiddlers pack up and walk away. Not only are the fiddle's tone and most of its stylistic turns obscured by volume, but the fixed-pitch and equal temperament tuning, and the frequently used musette detuning of reeds to create a thicker, beating effect, are in direct conflict with the subtleties of the 'floating-tone' scales of the old fiddling, in which the exact pitch of some notes varies according to the feel of the piece and whether the phrase is ascending or descending.

Largely outside the gammeldans scene, however, there are sensitive modern accordionists working harmoniously with fiddlers (for example, **Kristin Skaare** on **Susanne Lundeng**'s CD *Drag*, or **Jon Faukstad** playing with **Hans W. Brimi**), and others are coming to understand the subtlety necessary for a good relationship. A whole other approach to accordion is taken by the witty and eclectic accordion and drumkit duo **Fliflet/ Hamre Energiforsyning** and the stunning playing of Farmers Market's **Stian Carstensen**.

Other Instruments

Although the hardingfele gets most of the attention, Norway has other distinctive instruments. The **langeleik** is a variant of long box zither, bearing melody strings which run over frets and unfretted drone accompaniment strings. Dating back to the sixteenth century or earlier, it was once widespread, with regional forms including the dramatic Telemark design which has a high head scroll reminiscent of the prow of a Viking longship. The instrument has been undergoing a renaissance, but the only unbroken tradition of slåttemusik played on the langeleik is in Valdres, where the best-known player today is **Elisabeth Kværne**.

There has also been some revival in the playing of the elegant, clean-lined, metal-strung **Norwegian harp**, led by singer/harpist **Tone Hulbækmo**. Her partner in many musical projects is multi-instrumentalist **Hans Fredrik Jacobsen**, who is a particularly fine player of **seljefløyte**. The word 'selje' means 'sallow', and that's what the flute – earlier called *borkfløyte* (bark-flute) – was originally made from, by animal-herders here and in other north and central European countries. In Norway it was particularly used in the high pastures where animals were moved for summer grazing. There are no finger-holes – the flute, or really whistle, plays two harmonic series of overtones, one made with the end open, the other, a tone or less lower, made by covering or part-covering the end with a finger. Thus a natural scale is playable; it's only complete

above the first octave, so the tone is high and whispery, with a playing style of tonguing and fast shivering grace-notes.

Like many of the new ideas reaching Norway, the first European recorders arrived by sea, and that's probably how the **sjøfløyte** (sea-flute) – a huskier-toned whistle with many of a recorder's design features – got its name. It was considered more on the side of the angels than fiddles, and so survived when they were suppressed. Notable present-day players of Norwegian folk-flutes include **Steinar Ofsdal**, **Tellef Kvifte**, **Hans Fredrik Jacobsen** and **Per Midtstigen**.

Various **clarinets** have been used in Norwegian folk music - an unkeyed shepherd's instrument known as the **Meråker** clarinet, the **tungehorn** made from an animal horn, and versions of the orchestral instrument. Herders' instruments included a range of trumpets, among them the long **lur** and smaller ones made from animal horn. The **bukkehorn** (goat-horn), with finger-holes, is occasionally used again in contemporary music – for example by saxophonist **Karl Seglem** in the powerful trio **Utla**.

Alongside the drum tradition that was a spin-off from military drumming into the civilian population – just drums, beating out rhythm tunes, traditionally played at weddings and other social events – Norway also has a distinctive sound in its contemporary percussion styles. Utla percussionist **Terje Isungset** (now also a member of Swedish roots band Groupa) – whose fascinating organic kit throbs like an animated pile of jetsam – is a prime example of this new Norwegian approach to percussion. Isungset's kit ("I wanted something I couldn't buy in a shop") takes advantage of the hands-free machine of bass drum and hi-hat pedal, but the bass drum is not rock music's tight, damped thud but a huge, heartbeat-booming item, evocative of a fiddler's footstamp. The hi-hat itself is replaced by a tangle of bells and jingles, attached by string to lines bearing slates, wooden boards and barked-stripped branches. Other prime exponents of the emerging new styles are Mari Boine band drummer **Helge Norbakken** (who sadly seems to have forsaken the bucket of water which was previously part of his kit) and **Paolo Vinaccia**.

Guitarist **Knut Reiersrud**'s musical grounding has been in American music but, particularly in the music on his first album *Tramp*, based on the footstamp of its title and featuring Vinaccia and African musicians, he shows how even the guitar can develop a sparse, spacious Norwegian sound in which chords aren't the key.

Church Connections

Norway is unusual in that there's a great deal of connection between folk music and church music, and on into art music, new contemporary song and settings of poems. It's hard to find parallels in other countries for a singer such as the resonant-voiced tenor **Sondre Bratland**, who moves between all three (and a recent album shows him exploring Indian and Irish sean-nós stylistic ideas). He's often accompanied by the likes of Reiersrud and Vinaccia, Hardanger fiddler **Einar Mjølsnes**, Hans Fredrik Jakobsen and **Oslo Kammerkor** (chamber choir). A younger singer following a similar path is **Arve Moen Bergset**, who as well as his solo work has made two albums and high-profile appearances singing and playing hardingfele in the group **Bukkene Bruse** together with Steinar Ofsdal and Annbjørg Lien.

Equally hard to categorise is **Ola Bremnes**, whose works include setting the religious texts of seventeenth-century pastor Petter Dass to original and folk tunes, with choral, rock and folk-instrument arrangements.

The voices of several leading female singers of folksong, too, such as **Tone Hulbækmo** or **Sinikka Langeland** (who comes from the old Finnish enclave of Finnskog, and plays a Finnish concert kantele with high technique and energy), have a hint more of the sort of voice production to be found in classical or choral music than is usually to be found among contemporary European folk-rooted singers.

Another link with the church is in the work of two organists, **Iver Kleive** and **Kåre Nordstoga**, both of whom use the church organ in accompanying fiddlers (Kleive with Annbjørg Lien and others, Nordstoga with **Per Sæmund Bjørkum**). Kleive in particular takes the organ into new territories, combining its mighty sound with Hammond organ, piano, the electric, acoustic and slide guitars of Knut Reiersrud (with whom he is a very regular performer) and thunderously reverberating percussion from Vinaccia or from Jan Garbarek percussionist **Marilyn Mazur**.

Jazz and World Connections

There's a healthy respect between many traditional and jazz musicians of one another's musicianship, and collaborations are between equals, not simply a borrowing of one another's clothes. The jazz saxophonist **Jan Garbarek** has included Norwegian and Sámi musical references, and singers such as **Agnes Buen Garnås** and **Mari Boine** in some of his musical explorations. He's far from alone, in the creation of new Nordic and European musics which use the jazz approach of twisting and turning a thematic idea but are no longer tied to American blues or even bebop roots. Another leading inhabitant of this new nordic-jazz world is bassist **Arild Andersen** who has collaborated in particular with the majestic-voiced **Kirsten Bråten Berg**, sensitively and atmospherically working with traditional themes. And then there is **Chateau Neuf Spelemannslag**, a swingy folk big-band, with hardingfele, a reed section of saxes and clarinets, plus accordion, guitar and a rhythm section, with tralling group vocals.

Norway is also home to a number of leading musicians from other parts of the world. The **Frå Senegal Til Setesdal** group combines the voices and instruments of kora player **Solo Cissokho**, **Kouame Sereba** on mouth-bow and djembe, with **Kirsten Bråten Berg** and **Bjørgulv Straume** playing an instrument that has been made and used in Setesdal for a thousand years – the **Jew's harp**. (When not performing, Bråten Berg continues another Setesdal metalwork tradition, that of fine silversmithing).

Another leading roots fusion band is **Farmers Market**, who feature 'speed/Balkan/boogie' and the music of the invented islands of Hybridene. The group are four Norwegians and a Bulgarian and they indulge in rapid-fire flickering between Bulgarian sounds (sometimes with guests from the Le Mystère des Voix Bulgares ensemble) and a myriad of other forms, including snatches of corny pop classics. It is all played and sung with unerring accuracy and switches so quickly and often that the mind approaches multi-cultural meltdown.

The Sámi

Sámiland spreads across north Norway, Sweden and Finland, and on into northwest Russia. A unified section on the remarkable Sámi musical culture, distinct from but influential in much modern Nordic roots music, is to be found in a separate article (see p.255). Norway, with the largest Sámi population, is the home of such leading musicians and bands as Mari Boine, **Berit Nordland**, **Ailu Gaup**, **Orbina** and **Transjoik** as well as leading Sámi record labels DAT and Iðut.

The main international folk music festivals, with a lot of Norwegian traditional and progressive roots music, are **Førde** (four days at the beginning of July) and **Telemarksfestivalen** (at Bø in Telemark, four days at the end of July and/or beginning of August).

There are numerous regional kappleikar throughout the summer, and going to one of these is an excellent way to get the feel of the local music. For example, **Setesdalskappleiken** is at the end of June, **Buskerud** at the beginning of September, and **Porsgrunn** in Telemark has its **Folkemusikkdagarna** (Folk Music Days) at the end of August. The **Landskappleik**, the national competition, moves to a different area and date each year. There's also a national gammeldans festival, and the World Music festival **Världen i Norden** at the end of October.

The national folk music magazine is **Spelemannsbladet** (Hellandtunet, 3800 Bø in Telemark ☎ (47) 35 95 35 50; fax 35 95 15 93).

discography

A UK/international supplier of most of the recordings below is *ADA*, 36 Saturday Market Place, Beverley, E.Yorkshire HU17 9AG, ☎/fax 01482 868 024.

Compilations

◎ **Meisterspel** (Heilo, Norway).

Twenty-three players of hardingfele accorded the title of Master, recorded solo between 1937 and 1997; includes the Buens, the Bjørgums, Leif Rygg, Knut Hamre, Håkon Høgemo, Eivind Mo, Torleiv Bolstad, Alf Tveit, Sigbjørn Bernhoft Osa and many more.

◎ **Norsk Folkemusikk** (Grappa, Norway).

A ten-CD series of recordings, dating from the 1930s to the 1990s, from Norwegian Radio's archives of instrumental and vocal traditional music. Vol 1 is an overview from before WWII, and each of the others deals with a different county. Notes in Norwegian and English, written by regional experts.

Artists

Kirsten Bråten Berg

A singer rooted in the Setesdal tradition, Berg was a member in the late 1970s and early '80s of the group Slinkombas, and a regular collaborator with leading jazz bassist Arild Andersen. She has also worked with the Norwegian-Senegalese group Frå Senegal til Setesdal.

◎ **Min Kvedarlund** (Heilo, Norway).

CD reissue of 1988 album featuring Slinkombas members Hallvard T. Bjørgum (hardingfele and fiddle) and Tellef Kvifte (flutes & reeds), plus Swedes Ale Möller (bouzouki and synth) and Per Gudmundson (fiddle and bagpipe) with ten tracks from her 1980 first album and three from Slinkombas albums.

WITH ARILD ANDERSEN

◎ **Arv** (Kirkelig Kulturverksted, Norway).

A 1993 album featuring traditional songs from Bråten Berg among slowly unfolding shapes of double bass, sax, keyboards and percussion.

Hallvard T. & Torleiv H. Bjørgum

Father (the late Torleiv) and son, from Setesdal – both prime exponents of the essence of hardingfele.

 Dolkaren
(Sylvartun, Norway).

A fine display of the strong Setesdal tradition, and recommended as a pathway into the sound, depth and uniqueness of unaccompanied Norwegian traditional music. Solos from each on hardingfele, plus some ordinary fiddle, Jew's harp and singing from Torleiv.

Per Sæmund Bjørkum

Bjørkum's playing of ordinary fiddle is rooted in the tradition of Vågå in Gudbrandsdal.

◎ **Den Våre Fele: The Delicate Fiddle**
(Heilo, Norway).

Music based on the playing of Bjørkum's mentor Pål Skogum (1921–1990). Solo, and accompanied by prominent Norwegian modern roots musicians: Knut Reiersrud, Kåre Nordstoga, Jon Faukstad, Hans Fredrik Jacobsen, Bjørn Kjellemyr.

Kari Bremnes

Bremnes is a world-class singer with a voice roughly in Judy Collins' territory and a large catalogue of albums of intelligent music to her name, including settings of poems by artist Edvard Munch.

◎ **Spor** (Kirkelig Kulturverksted, Norway).

Released in 1991. Not tradition-rooted as such, but nevertheless a prime example of the new Norwegian music, and featuring such ace cross-disciplinary musicians as Knut Reiersrud, bassist Stan Poplin, accordionist Kristin Skaare and percussionist Finn Sletten.

Knut Buen

The Buen family of Telemark has been musicians for generations. Brothers Knut and Hauk are leading players of hardingfele, and their sister, Agnes Buen Garnås, is a leading traditional singer. Hauk also makes the instruments, and Knut's Buen Kulturverkstad company releases hardingfele CDs and books.

◎ **As Quick As Fire** (Rounder/Henry Street, US).

A compilation from Knut's albums on Buen Kulturverkstad. Includes such classic tunes as "Fanitullen", "Nordfjorden" and "St.Thomasklokkene på Filefjell". Largely solo, but some accompanied on church organ by Kåre Nordstoga, and one with Erik Stenstadvold's lute.

Agnes Buen Garnås

A singer with a deep tradition, one of the first traditional performers to blend her art with that of jazz musicians in the creation of the new Nordic-rooted music.

Rosensfole (Kirkelig Kulturverksted, Norway).

A 1989 collaboration with the great Norwegian saxophonist on a set of traditional songs, largely ballads, with occasional herding-calls, all with a spacious, drifting, lyrical sound. Buen Garnås also appears in later Garbarek projects including 1993's album **Twelve Moons** (ECM, Germany), while her solo works include **Draumkvedet** (Kirkelig Kulturverksted), an epic treatment of a ballad with brother Knut's hardingfele, plus organ, Celtic harp, flute and sax.

Oslo Kammerkor

Choirs, church music and folk song link up in Norway. Oslo Kammerkor has collaborated regularly with the roots mafia.

 Dåm (Kirkelig Kulturverksted).

Featuring soloists Sondre Bratland and Berit Opheim in choral arrangements of folk songs – no, don't stop reading. After the rather unpromising jolly tralling opening track there's much here of drifting, misty beauty, and of the shape and tonality of Norwegian music.

Iver Kleive

Kleive is probably the world's rockiest church organist, combining the big pipes with Hammond B3, piano, Paolo Vinaccia's resounding percussion, Knut Reiersrud's guitar and hot gospel choirs, as well as accompanying hardingfele and many other musical forms. He and Reiersrud typify the best Norwegian crossing of disciplines.

 Kyrie (Kirkelig Kulturverksted, Norway).

An extraordinary, massive-sounding album, largely recorded in Odense cathedral, using Norwegian traditional and other church music and some enormous grooves, stinging slide guitar, soaring vocals and power percussion.

Annbjørg Lien

Lien, from Sunnmøre, first recorded at the age of thirteen; five years later in 1989 she made *Annbjørg*, her first major album, controversial but widely appreciated. She has become a prominent figure in the increasing popularity of hardingfele among a younger audience.

 Prisme
(Grappa, Norway; Shanachie, US).

Lien's 1996 third album. The material here isn't from the traditional hardingfele repertoire but is virtually all her own tunes, showing her to be a richly melodic composer drawing on a wide range of influences. Full of exuberance and elegance, it features guitarist Roger Tallroth and viola player Mikael Marin of Swedish band Väsen, keyboardist/arranger Bjørn Ole Rasch, percussionist Rune Arnesen and Hans Fredrik Jacobsen on flutes and bagpipe.

Susanne Lundeng

Lundeng, from north of the Arctic Circle, is an outstanding player of the ordinary fiddle with silky smooth tone or huge drive as the tune demands and an engagingly eccentric and energetic stage manner. Her first album, *Havella* (Heilo, Norway) was solo fiddle; for the following two, *Drag* (1994) and *Ættesyn* (1997) she brought in top cross-cultural musicians on wonderfully subtle accordion, organ, bass and percussion.

 Drag
(Kirkelig Kulturverksted, Norway).

Polsdanses, stately bridal marches, compelling hallings, and hypnotic, ecstatic pieces such as her own classic "Hav", as well as occasional, unexpected serene singing, and an underlying subtle wit. Equally recommended, and with the same basic approach and sound, is her most recent, **Ættesyn** (Kirkelig Kulturverksted, Norway).

Knut Reiersrud

A guitarist and singer who might be put loosely into the Ry Cooder category, but with very much his own voice, linking slide guitar and blues with Norwegian traditional and west African musics, and a distinctive session player on many albums.

 Tramp (Kirkelig Kulturverksted, Norway); remixed as **Footwork** (Shanachie, US).

Dedicated to the footstamp – a beautiful airy, powerful recording, perfectly and naturally crossing textures, grooves and cultures with Alagi M'Bye's kora and vocal, Juldeh Camara's vocal and riti (African fiddle), Iver Kleive's church organ and Hammond, percussionist Paolo Vinaccia, bassist Audun Erlien, plus the Five Blind Boys of Alabama et al. Full of wit and surprise.

Tango For 3

Yes, Norwegian tango – it didn't only take root in Finland – and in the hands of Tango For 3 it has a dazzling virtuosity, ingenuity, strength and lightness of touch. Odd Hannisdal (violin), Per Arne Glorvigen (bandoneon), Sverre Indris Joner (piano), Steinar Haugerud (bass).

 Soledad (Majorselskapet, Norway)

Argentinian and new-composed tangos, and the splendidly witty "Gringos" – an acute tango take on three of his tunes that Grieg hadn't envisaged.

Utla/Karl Seglem

Saxophonist Seglem is a prime example of the transformation of Norwegian jazz by musicians drawing on roots traditional music. He, fiddler Håkon Høgemo and percussionist Terje Isungset are collaborators on a series of projects which explore the rawness and airy beauty at the heart of the Norwegian tradition, a music not of chords and vertical harmony but something much older.

UTLA

 Dans (NOR-CD, Norway).

The most recent album by the trio, in which the hardingfele of Landskappleik winner Høgemo, occasionally kicked into screeching Marshall overdrive, unites with Seglem's soaring sax or bukkehorn and Isungset's extraordinary organic percussion. Ideally this is a band to experience live, enveloped by the full primitive hypnotic energy, the spirit of Rammeslag.

KARL SEGLEM AND SOGN-A-SONG

 Rit (NOR-CD, Norway).

An archetypal meeting of new Norwegian jazz and traditional music. Wide airy sounds, floating modal tunes, Berit Opheim's singing, Seglem's yearning sax, Isungset's rattling percussion, plus bass, keyboards, electric guitar and Høgemo's hardingfele.

Poland

hanging on in the highlands

Traditional music in Poland isn't exactly widespread. The country has Westernised rapidly and the memory of Communist fakelore has tainted people's interest in the genuine article. But there are pockets of Poland that boast some of the most distinctive sounds in Europe, and the experience of a górale (highland) wedding – fired by furious fiddling, grounded by a sawing cello and supercharged with vodka – is unforgettable. **Simon Broughton** outlines the background and highlights some of the new developments.

n Poland, as elsewhere in eastern Europe, an interest in folklore emerged in the nineteenth century, allied to aspirations for national independence; folk music and politics in the region often have symbiotic links. The pioneering collector of songs and dances from all over the country was **Oskar Kolberg** (1814–90). His principal interest was in song; it's thought that instrumental music was fairly primitive until towards the end of the nineteenth century. From the 1900s on progress was rapid, fueled by gramophone recordings. However, the wartime annihilation and shifting of ethnic minorities in Poland severely disrupted folk traditions, and postwar, the Communist regime, as throughout eastern Europe, co-opted folk culture as a part of its own ideology, as a cheerful expression of healthy peasant labour.

Communist Folk

The Communist espousal of folk music was a near killer blow for the traditon. Both folk music and traditions were sanitised almost to irrelevance, emerging mainly through presentation by professional folk troupes – most famously the **Mazowsze** and **Sląsk** ensembles – who gave (and still give) polished virtuoso performances with massed strings and choreographed twirls, whoops and foot stamping. Their repertoire was basically core Polish with a slight regional emphasis (the Mazowsze territory is around Warsaw, the Sląsk around Wrocław), but the overall effect was homogenisation rather than local identity.

Smaller, more specialised groups, like **Słowianki** in Kraków, were also supported and kept closer to the roots, but for the most part the real stuff withered away as the image of folk music became tarnished by the bland official ensembles.

Nonetheless, there was just about enough slack in the system for local bands to keep some genuine traditions going.

Polish Dances

Thanks mainly to Chopin, the **mazurka** and **polonaise** (*polonez*) are Poland's best-known dance forms and stand at the core of the folk repertoire. Both dances are in triple time with the polonaise generally slower and more stately than the mazurka. The polonaise is particularly associated with the more ceremonial and solemn moments of a wedding party. It was taken up by the aristocracy from a slow walking dance (*chodzony*), given a French name identifying it as a dance of Polish origin and then filtered back down to the lower classes.

In addition to these triple-time dances, which are associated with central Poland, there are some characteristic five-beat dances in the northeastern areas of Mazury, Kurpie and Podlasie. As you move south, somewhere between Warsaw and Kraków, you find duple-time dances like the **krakowiak** and **polka**. Generally speaking the music of central Poland is more restrained and sentimental than that of the south, which is more full-blooded. The krakowiak is named after the city of Kraków and the polka is claimed by both the Poles and the Bohemians as their own, although it was in Bohemia that it became most widely known.

Of course, these dances are not confined to their native areas, and many have become staples across the country and abroad.

Folk Music Today

Today, with the notable exception of the Tatra region and a few other rural pockets, traditional music has virtually ceased to function as a living tradition and has been banished to **regional folk festivals**. Several of these are very good indeed, with the **Kazimierz Festival** at the end of June foremost amongst them (see p.223).

But the best way to hear this music is out in the countryside, at the sort of occasion it was designed for – a village **harvest festival** (*dozynki*), for instance, or a **wedding** (*wesele*). At such occasions, lively tunes are punched out by ad hoc groups comprising (nowadays) clarinet, saxophone, accordion, keyboard and drums. At country weddings there is often a set of traditional dances played for the older people, even when the rest of the music is modern. In the rural areas people tend to be hospitable and welcoming and, if you've shown an interest in music, a wedding invitation is often extended.

Typically, the areas where the music has best survived tend to be the remoter regions on the fringes – Kurpie and Podlasie in the northeast, around Rzeszów in the southeast (where the *cimbały* – hammer dulcimer – is popular in the local bands), and the Podhale and highland regions in the Tatras along the southern border. Among

good, active regional bands are the **Franciszek Gola Band** in Kadzidło (Kurpie); the **Kazimierz Meto Band** in Glina and the **Tadeusz Jedynak Band** in Przystałowice Małe (Mazowsze); the **Edward Markocki Band** in Zmysłówka-Podlesie and the **Stachy Band** in Haczów nad Wisłokiem (Rzeszów region); the **Kazimierz Kantor Band** in Głowaczowa (Tarnów region); the **Swarni Band** in Nowy Targ; the **Ludwik Młynarczyk Band** in Lipnica; the **Trebunia Family Band** in Poronin and the **Gienek Wilczek Band** in Bukowina (Podhale).

Podhale

Podhale, the district around Zakopane, which has the most vibrant musical tradition in the country, has been one of Poland's most popular resorts for years – so it defies the rules, being in no way remote or isolated.

The Podhale musicians are familiar with music from all over the country and beyond, but choose to play in their own way. This sophisticated approach is part of a pride in Podhale identity which probably dates from the late nineteenth century when several notable artists and intellectuals (including the composer **Karol Szymanowski**; 1882–1937) settled in Zakopane and enthused about the folk music and culture. Music, fiddlers and dancing brigands are as essential to the image of Podhale life as the traditional costumes of tight felt trousers, broad leather belts with ornate metal clasps and studs, embroidered jackets and black hats decorated with cowrie shells.

Podhale music has more in common with the peasant cultures along the Carpathians in Ukraine and Transylvania than the rest of Poland. While traditional music in lowland Poland has tended to keep its simple drone accompaniment (where it survives at all), in Podhale there's a strong chordal harmony – probably a result of the intellectual presence.

The typical **Podhale ensemble** is a string band (the clarinets, saxophones, accordions and drums that have crept in elsewhere in Poland are much rarer here) comprising a lead violin (*prym*), a couple of second violins (*sekund*) playing accompanying chords, and a three-stringed cello (*bazy*). The music is immediately identifiable by its melodies and playing style. The tunes tend to be short-winded, angular melodies in an unusual scale with a sharpened fourth. This is known to musicians as the 'Lydian mode' and gives rise to the Polish word *lidyzowanie* to describe the manner of singing this augmented interval.

POLSKIE RADIO

Mato polska fiddler

A Podhale Wedding

Believe it or not, **górale weddings** are often held in the local fire station. There's room enough for feasting and dancing and it provides useful extra income for the fire brigade. It was to one such station on the outskirts of Zakopane that I was invited.

There the family assembled and the couple were lectured by the leader of the band on the importance of the step they were taking – an indication of how integral the band is to the event. Then came the departure for the church in a string of horse-drawn carriages – the band in one, the bride in another and the groom following in another behind. At the front, the *pytacy*, a pair of outriders on horseback, were shouting rhymes to all and sundry. The band played the couple into the wooden church and (unconventionally) played "Krywan" from the gallery inside the church while communion was taking place. Then it was back to the fire station for the party.

The incredible thing was the way the band kept going for hours, substituting different players from time to time to give themselves a short break. Quite unexpected until you get used to it is the way the górale dances and songs are superimposed, often with no relation to each other. A fast up-tempo dance will be in progress when suddenly a group of women will launch into a slow song seemingly oblivious to the other music. I was putting it down to the vast quantities of vodka consumed or perhaps a serious underlying quarrel between family groups who wanted different sorts of music. But no, it is typical of the way music is performed in these circumstances and the tensions between the instrumental music and song are obviously calculated.

Among the dances the local *ozwodna* and *krzesany* figure highly, begun by one of the men strutting over to the band and launching into the high straining vocals that cue the tune. The man then draws a girl onto the floor, dances a few steps with her before handing her over to the man on whose behalf he originally selected her. All this is part of a carefully structured form which culminates late in the evening with the ritual of the *cepiny* (or *cepowiny* as it's known in Podhale), the 'capping ceremony'. This is one of those peasant rites of passage, which happens all over Poland, when the bride has a scarf tied round her head symbolising her passage from the status of a single to a married woman.

The music whirls on throughout the night and extends well beyond the Podhale repertoire. There are romantic waltzes and

Podhale wedding band outside the church

mazurkas, fiery polkas and *czardasz* – tunes that you might hear in northern Poland, Slovakia, Hungary or Romania, but always given a particular Podhale accent. The górale people are famed for keeping themselves to themselves and mistrusting outsiders, but there's no puritanism. They take and enjoy what they want from outside, confident and proud of the strength of what they have.

POLAND

The **fiddlers** typically play these melodies with a 'straight' bowing technique – giving the music a stiff, angular character as opposed to the swing and flexibility of the usual 'double' bowing technique common in eastern Europe and typified by Gypsy fiddlers. The straining high **male vocals** which kick off a dance tune are also typical.

At the heart of the repertoire are the *ozwodna* and *krzesany* couple **dances**, both in duple time. The first has an unusual five-bar melodic structure and the second is faster and more energetic. Then there are the showy Brigand's Dances

(*zbójnicki*) which are the popular face of Podhale culture – central to festivals and demonstrations of the music. Danced in a circle by men wielding small metal axes (sometimes hit together fiercely enough to strike sparks), they are a celebration of the górale traditions of brigandage – full of tales of colourful robberies, daring escapes, festivities and death on the gallows for anti-feudal heroes. "To hang on the gibbet is an honourable thing!" asserted the nineteenth-century górale musician Sabała, "They don't hang just anybody, but real men!"

The songs you are most likely to hear in more tourist-oriented performances are those about **Janosik** (1688–1713), the most famous brigand of them all. Musically these are not actually Podhale in style, but are lyrical ballads with a Slovakian feel; countless tales of the region's most famous character are sung on both sides of the border. The most played songs are "Idzie Janko" – whose tune seems to be used for many other Janosik songs – and "Krywan", which is a celebration of one of the Tatra's most famous mountains.

The mountain regions **around Podhale** also have their own, less celebrated, musical cultures. To the west there is **Orawa**, straddling the Polish/Slovak border and the Beskid Zywieckie to its north, with an annual festival in the town of **Zywiec**. To the east of Zakopane, the music of the **Spisz** region has more Slovak bounce than the Podhale style and boasts an excellent fiddle-maker and musician in **Woytek Łukasz**. Even if you don't make it to a highland wedding, music is relatively accessible in Zakopane. Many of the restaurants have good bands that play certain nights of the week; there are occasional stage shows; and there's the Festival of Highland Folklore in August.

Ethnic Minorities

Post-Communism, there's been something of a revival in the music of some of the **national minorities** living in Poland. There is now a more liberal climate in which to express national differences and travel is easier across the borders between related groups in Lithuania, Belarus and Ukraine.

Poland's **Boyks** and **Łemks** are ethnically and culturally linked to Ukranians and the Rusyns of Slovakia, and their music betrays its eastern Slavonic leanings in its choral and polyphonic songs. Recently some fascinating work has been done by the **Kresy Foundation** based in Lublin, who have gathered diverse groups of musicians from several territories to play together and compare their music in informal gatherings. Boyk and Ukrainian groups are now also a regular feature of the **Kazimierz Festival**. Look out for the group led by singer **Roman Kumłuk** who, with fiddler Wołodymyr Bodnaruk, performs music of the Hucul people of the Carpathian mountains. You can hear the common heritage with types of Romanian, Ukrainian and Jewish music. The singer **Maria Krupowies**, born in Vilnius, Lithuania, but raised in Poland, has sung Lithuanian, Belorussian and Polish songs exploring the connections and differences between them.

World War II saw the effective extermination of **Jewish** life and culture in Poland along with the exuberant and melancholy **klezmer** music for weddings and festivals that was part of it. The music had its distinctive Jewish elements, but drew heavily on local Polish and Ukranian styles. Thanks to emigration and revival, it now flourishes principally in the US (it is covered in depth in *The Rough Guide to World Music Volume 2*) and is barely heard in Poland except at the annual **Festival of Jewish Culture** in Kraków. The city is, though, home to its own klezmer band, **Kroke**. This trio, led by violinist Tamasz Kukurba, started off playing schmaltzy standards, but has evolved into an inventive and exciting band who've proven their ability on tour (at WOMAD, for example). Two of the band's members are Jewish, although one of them didn't discover the fact until they'd been playing klezmer for several years – which says something about the pressure to assimilate in post-war Poland.

Revival and New Music

It is perhaps not over-optimistic to sense a picking up of interest in Polish traditional music as the exhortations of the Communist troupes slip further into the distance. In the western region of Wielkopolska there's been something of a revival in **bagpipe** (*kozio* – 'goat') playing, a tradition reaching back to the Middle Ages in Eastern Europe. And in the last few years a number of good **contemporary folk groups** have emerged.

Not surprisingly, some of the most interesting developments have come out of Podhale – in particular the **Trebunia** family band of Poronin. Here

Polish reggae with the Trebunia family

the stern fiddler Władiław Trebunia and his son Krzysztof are both preservers of and experimenters with the tradition, as well as being leaders of one of the very best wedding bands around. In the early 1990s they joined up with reggae musician Norman 'Twinkle' Grant to produce two albums of **Podhale reggae**, or perhaps more accurately, reggae with a Polish backing. Surprising as it might seem, once you get used to the rigid beat imposed on the Polish material, the marriage works rather well. In 1994, the Trebunias teamed up on another project with one of Poland's leading **jazz** musicians, saxophonist Zbigniew Namysłowski. Here the usual górale ensemble meets saxophone, piano, bass and drums in an inventive romp through classic Podhale hits such as Zbójnicki tunes, "Krywan" and "Idzie Janko".

Elsewhere, contemporary folk bands to look out for include **Orkiestra Św Mikołaja** and, particularly, the **Kwartet Jorgi**. Based in Poznań, the latter group takes its music from all round Poland and beyond, with many of the tunes coming from the nineteenth-century collections of Oskar Kolberg. The group's leader, Maciej Rychły, plays an amazing range of ancient Polish bagpipes, whistles and flutes which are sensitively combined with guitars, cello and drums. The music is inventive and fun and shows how contemporary Polish folk music can escape the legacy of fakelore.

In a similar spirit, following the Hungarian dancehouse movement (see p.161) a **Dom Tańca** has been started in Warsaw to play and teach authentic Polish folk dances. This is the place to go to learn your mazurkas and obereks.

With thanks to Krzysztof Cwizewicz

Festivals and Events

Kazimierz Dolny. This Festival of Folk Bands and Singers, held on the last weekend in June, is Poland's biggest traditional music festival. Contact: Helena Weremczuk, Wojewódzki Dom Kultury, ul. Dolna Panny Marii 3, 20-010 Lublin, Poland. ☎ (48) 81 532 4207; fax 81 532 3775.

Meeting of Folk Bands in Przysucha (Radomskie). A more down-home festival held over the the first weekend in June.

Dom Tańca (Dance House) in Warsaw takes place every Thursday evening (except during the summer) and mainly focuses on the central traditions of Mazowsze, Małopolska and Roztocze. Warszawski Ośrodek Kultury, 12 Elektoralna Street, Warsaw. ☎ (48) 22 870 0384.

discography

An excellent survey called *Sources of Polish Folk Music* has recently been issued by Polish Radio. With recordings from the 1960s to the mid-90s, many of them recorded at the Kazimierz Festival, the series currently runs to ten volumes. Each disc focuses on a different area and comes with good notes in Polish and English on the characteristics of the region, the vocal and instrumental music and biographies of the musicians. *Vol 1: Mazovia; Vol 2: Tatra Foothills; Vol 3: Lubelskie; Vol 4: Małopolska Północna; Vol 5: Wielkopolska; Vol 6: Kurpie; Vol 7: Beskidy; Vol 8: Krakowskie Tarnowskie; Vol 9: Suwalskie Podlasie; Vol 10: Rzeszowskie Pogórze.* Contact: Polskie Radio SA, Biuro Promocji I Handlu, al. Niepodległości 77/85, 00-977 Warszawa, Poland. Fax (48) 22 645 5901.

Compilations

◉ **Polish Folk Music: Songs and Music from various Regions** (Polskie Nagrania, Poland).

An excellent cross-section of Polish Radio recordings from eight different regions all over the country, from Kaszuby in the north to Podhale in the south.

◉ **Poland: Folk Songs and Dances** (VDE-Gallo/AIMP, Switzerland).

A more hardcore selection of field recordings compiled by Anna Czekanowska. Includes some recent recordings of music by ethnic minorities, and informative notes.

◉ **Polish Village Music: Historic Polish-American Recordings 1927–1933** (Arhoolie, US).

Recordings from old 78s of Polish bands recently arrived in the US. Most still have a great down-home style. Górale fiddler Karol Stoch ("Last Evening in Podhale") was the most highly regarded of his day and the first to record commercially. His music sounds astonishingly similar to that which can still be heard in the region today. Not true for the bands from elsewhere in Poland. Very good notes and translations.

 **Pologne: Danses** (Arion, France).

The cover suggests one of those fakelore ensembles, but

this is actually a very good collection of instrumental polkas, oberek and other dances from southeastern Poland. Two family bands from Rzeszów district and the third, the celebrated Pudełko family, from Przeworsk. Includes several solo tracks on the cimbały hammer dulcimer.

Pologne: Instruments populaires (Ocora, France).

Predominantly instrumental music ranging from shepherds' horns and flutes, fiddles and bagpipes to small and medium-sized ensembles. A compilation, by Maria Baliszewska, of field recordings of the real thing in the best Ocora tradition.

Sources of Polish Folk Music 5: Wielkopolska (Polish Radio Folk Collection, Poland).

The area of 'Greater Poland' around Poznań is famous for its bagpipes and you hear a good many of them on this disc, solo and in bands. Some of the ensembles, like the Krobia Band of bagpipe and violin, sound quite medieval and outlandish. The notes profile the region's celebrated pipers, although few actually appear on the disc.

Sources of Polish Folk Music 8: Krakowskie – Tarnowskie (Polish Radio Folk Collection, Poland).

The discs with a good dose of instrumental music tend to be the more accessible in this series. This features music from the areas of southern Poland around Kraków and Tarnów. Lots of krakowiaks, of course, and other dances from string bands often with added clarinets or trumpets.

Sources of Polish Folk Music 10: Rzeszowslie – Pogórze (Polish Radio Folk Collection, Poland).

Not surprisingly this disc, featuring music from the southeastern region of Rzeszów, kicks off with the famous Sowa Family Band (recorded in 1976) but includes many other local bands such as the Pudełko family and cymbały players. Mostly peformances at the Kazimierz Festival.

Artists

Kwartet Jorgi

Strangely enough the Jorgi quartet usually seems to have just three members: Maciej (the leader) and Waldemar Rychły with Andrzej Trzeciak. Maciej plays an astonishing range of old Polish pastoral instruments, pipes and flutes. His classical background is evident in the arrangements of tunes from all over Poland.

JAM (Jam, Poland).

The quartet's first release from 1990 remains their best CD, featuring lots of old tunes collected by Kolberg. (Available from Jam Phono Co. (48) 22 830021).

Sowa Family Band

A famous family band (with over 150 years of history) from the village of Piątkowa in the Rzeszów region in southeast Poland, this was led for many years by Wojciech Sowa (1911–1977), one of Poland's great peasant fiddlers. His brother Józef Sowa (1904–1983) played second violin or cymbały and Piotr Sowa (1911–1997) played bass.

Songs and Music from Rzeszów Region (Polskie Nagrania, Poland).

A wonderful disc of authentic village dances – sztajereks, waltzes, polkas and slowies. Sometimes strings and cymbaly, some tracks with clarinet. The 1970s recordings are rather harsh, but splendid all the same. Sadly, the band is no longer playing.

Trebunia Family Band

Without doubt, one of the leading bands of Podhale based in Poronin near Zakopane with four or five fiddles and basy. Fiddler Władysław Trebunia is the father-figure and the band includes his son Krzysztof (who often leads in his own right), daughter Hania and several other family members. They play for local weddings, make recordings and have an adventurous spirit for collaborations.

Music of the Tatra Mountains: The Trebunia Family Band (Nimbus, UK).

An informal gathering recorded in their home village of Poronin. Dances with stamping feet, whistling and seemingly spontaneous outbursts of song. Real interplay between dancers and musicians. Includes examples of all the core górale repertoire plus some lighter waltzes, polkas and tunes from neighbouring Spisz. Good notes.

TWINKLE BROTHERS AND TREBUNIA

Twinkle Inna Polish Stylee: Higher Heights (Ryszard Music, Poland).

Reggae musician Norman Grant is the Twinkle Brother bringing the reggae ingredient into this suprisingly infectious collaboration. The strong backbeat sometimes threatens to destroy the intrinsic flexibility of the Trebunia's music, but on the whole this "góralstafarianism" works. Fans can also try the equally successful **Comeback Twinkle 2**. (Both available from Poland's Caston distribution (48) 27 642 3221).

WITH Z. NAMYSŁOWSKI JAZZ QUARTET

Z. Namysłowski Jazz Quartet & Kapela Góralska (Folk, Poland).

The Trebunias meet Zbigniew Namysłowski, one of Poland's leading jazz saxophonists, with piano, bass and percussion. Pleasant jazz versions of Podhale's dances and famous songs – "Idzie Janko" and "Krywan". The cassette is readily available in Zakopane, but probably hard to find elsewhere.

Gienek Wilczek

The fiddler Gienek Wilczek was born in 1943, but seems older. He was taught at a young age by the woman-brigand Dziadonka, the only recognised woman-musician in the area. He has worked mostly as a shepherd, but spent much of his free time playing the violin.

Music of the Tatra Mountains: Gienek Wilczek's Bukovina Band (Nimbus, UK).

An eccentric peasant genius, Wilczek's style is idiosyncratic, ornamented and sometimes wayward, but has all the depth and excitement of a real, intuitive peasant musician. This is a disc to savour once you've absorbed the basic characteristic of highland music. Like the other Nimbus disc above, recorded at an informal party which includes "Oh, Susanna" like you've never heard it before. A real treat.

Portugal

traditional riches, fate and revolution

Musically, Portugal is best known as the home of the passionate and elegant vocal and instrumental fado of the cities of Lisbon and Coimbra, but its regions boast varied traditional musics that show attributes reaching far back into European history, and the country forged a politically influential new song movement before, during and after the 1974 demise of the Salazar dictatorship. Today's evolving musics draw on all these strands, as well as that of the former colonies, notably the fado-like morna of Cabo Verde's Cesaria Evora (see p.451). Below, **Andrew Cronshaw** explores Portuguese roots and developments, while **Paul Vernon** tells the story of fado.

Regional Traditions

Social and economic change has removed much of the role for Portugal's old traditional musical cultures, but there's a surprising amount that continues in its original context and which also provides a wellspring for new Portuguese musics.

Trás-os-Montes

One area in particular, that of **Trás–os–Montes** in the northeast – as its name says 'behind the mountains', a ravine-carved high plateau of burning summers and icy winters – still retains ways of making and hearing music which survive in few other regions of Europe. Neither the bagpipes found there (*gaita-de-foles*), nor the older traditional unaccompanied singers, use the equal-temperament scale of equal semitones which has come to dominate the musics of the world.

The **songs** of Trás-os-Montes, and some of the other remote areas of the mainland and also the Azores, draw on the oral ballad repertoire that was once widespread across Europe with stories going back to the Middle Ages. Iberia has its own specific group of ballads, the *Romanceiro*, which were sung in the royal courts from the fifteenth until the

seventeenth century, but continued in use in the fields and villages long after that, and in some cases up to the present day. While for the nobles these songs were just polite amusements, for the rural population they had a vital function, including religious celebrations, festivals and work, particularly the work of harvesting.

In some of the ballads found in Trás-os-Montes there persists the old language of Mirandês, derived possibly from an early language of Spain's León or from Low Latin. An interesting aspect is that specific ballads are associated with specific canonical hours, giving fixed points dividing up the reapers' long back-breaking day.

Portugal came into existence as a country in the twelfth century, but its language, and aspects of the

ANNE CAUFRIEZ & MICHAEL PLUMLEY/OCORA

Trás-os-Montes group with drums and gaita-de-foles

Portuguese Instruments

Portugal is home to a remarkable variety of instruments, most of them associated with particular regional traditions.

Guitarra Portuguesa

The best-known Portuguese regional tradition is **fado**, and be that the Lisboa or Coimbra tradition its dominant instrument is the **guitarra**. Though sometimes called the Portuguese guitar, its body isn't 'guitar-shaped'; it is a variety of the European cittern, which arrived in Portugal in the eighteenth century in the form of the 'English guitar' via the English community of Porto, where it was used in a style of art-song ballad known as *modinha* which was popular at that time in Portugal and Brazil.

The instrument caught on in Lisboa, and from there spread to Coimbra. Two forms evolved – the Lisboa guitarra used for accompanying singers, and the larger body and richer bass of the Coimbra version more suited to that city's instrumental fado. Both have six pairs of steel strings tuned by knurled turn-screws on a fan-shaped machine head. The traditional tuning is B, A, E, B, A, D. The bottom three pairs have one of the pair an octave lower than the other, giving a chiming resonant bass supporting the silvery singing vibrato and fluid runs of the unison-tuned top three pairs.

"Violas"

In fado, the guitarra is usually accompanied by a six-string guitar of the Spanish form which, like all fretted instruments of that waisted body-shape, is known in Portugal as a **viola**. Though the **viola de fado** is usually a normal Spanish guitar, there is a remarkable range of other specifically Portuguese violas found in regions of the mainland and islands. They're virtually always steel-strung, and most have soundboards decorated with flowing tendril-like dark wood inlays spreading from the bridge, and soundholes in a variety of shapes.

The version encountered most often, particularly in the north, is the **viola braguesa**, which has five pairs of strings and is usually played rasgado (a fast intricate rolling strum with an opening hand). A slightly smaller close relative, from the region of Amarante, is the **viola amarantina**, whose soundhole is usually in the form of two hearts; a similar soundhole pattern is found on the **viola da terra** of the Azores.

Other varieties include Madeira's **viola d'arame**, a kind of slim guitar; the ten or twelve-stringed **viola campanica alentejana** which has a very deeply indented waist, almost like a figure of eight; and the **viola beiroa**, which is distinctive in having an extra two pairs of strings, besides its other five pairs, which run from the bridge to machine heads fixed on the body

where it meets the neck; these are used in a way similar to the high fifth string on an American banjo.

Cavaquinhos and Bandolims

One popular Portuguese stringed instrument has taken root across the world. The **cavaquinho** looks like a baby viola with four strings, and is played with an ingenious fast strum akin to the braguesa's rasgado. It spread from Portugal to the Azores and Madeira, and travelled onwards with Portuguese migrants from the Atlantic islands to Hawaii, where it became, with very few changes, the ukulele. Indonesia has the *ukélélé*, also called *keront jong*. Cavaquinho is much-used in the biggest Lusophone country, Brazil, and the South American *charango* shows strong similarities.

The Portuguese form of mandolin, the **bandolim** or **banjolim**, is much used; a particularly fine player is **Júlio Pereira**, who is also an expert exponent of cavaquinho and the range of violas.

GHAITA

Júlio Pereira on a bandolim

Hurdy-gurdys and pipes

The **sanfona** (hurdy-gurdy), fell out of use in the early twentieth century but it is now being built and used again by such present-day groups as **Realejo** and **Gaiteiros de Lisboa**. The **rabeca** or **ramaldeira** of Amarante and Douro is a short-necked folk rebec, and in Madeira the extremely primitive one-stringed **bexigoncelo** functions as a bowed bass with a pig's bladder as its soundbox.

The **gaita-de-foles** is the Portuguese bagpipe (the word *fole* means "bag"). Its chanter uses a double reed, while its normally single drone has a single reed. It is the main melody instrument of Trás-os-Montes music, accompanied by bombo and caixa. Many European bagpipes use a scale different from modern equal temperament; the chanter of the gaita-de-foles diverges more than most, and each bagpipe is likely to be tuned in its own way, as it can afford to be, since it's not played ensemble or with other pitched instruments. As revival groups have taken up the gaita-de-foles they have had to decide whether to alter its scale or to give it its own pitch freedom within the band and allow it to speak for the old ways.

The **flauta pastoril** (three-hole whistle) and **tamboril** (tabor drum with snares) are played together by a single musician, the *tamborileiro*, particularly in Trás-os-Montes and eastern Alentejo. The three-hole whistle is sometimes called *pifaro*, a term that also applies to a fife or whistle, an instrument found in several regional traditions including that of Beira Baixa, where it's accompanied by caixas and bombo in groups called *zés-pereiras*.

Drums

A feature of Beira Baixa music, and found elsewhere too, is the **adufe**. Introduced by the Arabs a millennium ago, it is a square double-headed drum usually containing pieces of wood or pebbles which rattle. Held on edge and tapped with the fingers, it's played by women, often in groups, to accompany their singing. Also found in several traditions is the clanking **ferrinhos** (triangle), played pretty much as in Cajun music.

Bombo, caixa, adufe, **pandeiro** (small drum) and **pandeireta** (tambourine) or occasionally **cântaro com abanho** (a clay pot struck across its mouth with a leather or straw fan), provide the thump of Portuguese traditional music, while the clatter comes from the likes of the **cana** (a split cane slap-stick), **trancanholas** (wooden 'bones'), **castanholas** (castañuelas, or in Madeira a chain of ten flat shell-shaped boards), **reco-reco** or **reque-reque** (a scraped serrated stick), **conchas** (shells rubbed together), **zaclitracs** (a form of rattle), **genebres** (a wooden xylophone hung from the neck, a feature of the dança dos homens (men's dance) in Beira Baixa) and, lost from the mainland but still found in Madeira, the **briquinho**, a cluster of wooden dolls each with a castanet on its back, mounted in circles on a pole.

In Alentejo there's a grunt, too - that of the **sarronça**, a friction drum made from a clay pot with skin stretched over the mouth; rubbing a stick set into the skin produces the sound, as with the higher-pitched Brazilian cuica.

culture of its northern parts, show its even longer connections with Galicia to the north. The **gaita-de-foles** and the Galician *gaita* are closely related forms of bagpipe, and several dances, such as the *murinheira* (milkmaid) are found in varying forms on both sides of the border. There are also links across the eastern border into such Spanish regions as Zamora – for example, in the occurrence of the **dança dos paulitos**, a stick dance for men only, which like several Iberian dances is strongly reminiscent of an English morris-dance. Such dances are typically played by a gaita accompanied by a *bombo* (bass drum) and *caixa* (snare drum), or alternatively by a solo musician (*tamborileiro*) playing with one hand a three-hole whistle and with the other a small snare drum (*tamboril*). In the absence of instruments their tunes are sung, using ballad lyrics.

Alentejo

The south of Portugal has a very different singing style. In the province of **Baixo Alentejo** there is a surviving tradition of **polyphonic vocal groups** – a vibrant Mediterranean sound comparable to that of the vocal ensembles of Corsica and Sardinia. The ensembles are usually male. A solo singer (the *ponto*) delivers the first couple of verses, setting the song and pitch, then a second singer (the *alto*) takes over the theme, usually singing it a third above the ponto's preamble. After only one or two notes he's joined, in the ponto's pitch, by the full chorus, over which the alto sings an ornamented harmony line. As the song (*moda*) proceeds the powerful group vocal alternates with expressive solo verses from the alto and sometimes the ponto.

Essentially, this is spontaneous rather than chorally directed music-making, but there exist named performing ensembles, and it is these that most available recordings feature. They may be organised to a degree, but they're not professional entertainers, they're the real thing.

Ranchos Folclóricos

The strongest survivals of old-rooted material in Portugal are in the rural areas away from the sea such as Trás-os-Montes, Beira in the central east, and Alentejo, but each region of Portugal has its distinctive living traditional forms and instruments. Quite a number of villages and towns have folklore ensembles known as **ranchos folclóricos**. These were encouraged by the dictatorship as exemplars of the happy colourful peasantry, and were therefore somewhat disapproved of by musicians who were opponents of the regime.

Emerging from those associations, the ensembles continue to exist, and indeed in the last couple of decades they have increased in number. Most are a worthwhile and genuine part of folk culture and its festive occasions.

Fado

The dictionary definition of the word **fado** is 'fate'. The meaning invested in this small word by the Portuguese, however, is rich, deep and complex. The music, at least in Lisbon, could be defined as an urban café style and parallels can be drawn with Greek rembétika, American blues and original tango. Like rembétika, its subject matter is life's harsh reality, and its instrumental accompaniment is largely stringed – in this case the Portuguese guitarra and Spanish guitar. But unlike rembétika its approach is more about the graceful acceptance of destiny than a garrulous resistance to it. The fado speaks with a quiet dignity born of the realisation that any mortal desire or plan is at risk of destruction by powers beyond individual control.

Fado Origins

There are many theories of fado's origins and almost all of them contain some essential truths, for the fado is an old tree of music, with deep and tangled roots. They are bound in Portugal's early imperial expansion, which ensured that the home country was exposed to a broad wedge of other cultures, principally African. The Portuguese style of imperialism was an odd mix of arrogance and humility – arrogance in assuming that parts of the world were just waiting to become Portuguese, humility in Portuguese readiness to settle, to mix and to leave the home country for good. Intermarriage was common and the goal of Portuguese citizenship through achievement – becoming *assimilado* – was a permanent fixture in the culture of Portuguese-colonised peoples.

By the beginning of the nineteenth century a substantial African and mixed-race population, often from Brazil (which became independent in 1822 and was soon substantially richer and more important than Portugal), was firmly ensconced in the Alfama district of Lisbon. The **dances** most commonly associated with this cultural group were the *fofa* and the *lundum*, a song and dance exchange for a couple in which lewd comments, expressions of desire and outrageous insults were traded. It was described with contemporary horror as 'the most lascivious thing I ever saw'. Later, elements of lundum and fofa came to be known as the fado, which in this proto-form seems to have been a guitar-accompanied and essentially African dance.

A second factor in fado's creation was the long Portuguese tradition of poetry and literature, both academic and folk. Both the **quatrain** (rhyming couplet) and **modhina**, or ballad tradition, were part of Portuguese culture in the early nineteenth century. The popular folk quatrain was used in many forms by a largely rural community to celebrate calendar events, preserve folk wisdom, tell children's stories and declare undying love – all the usual concerns – and it served as the lyrical genesis of the fado, taking over from the strong lyrical meat of its old African precursors.

These three basic ingredients – dance, modhina and quatrain – supplied rhythm, form and content. At some point lost in the fog of history the parts gelled together and matured to form the fado.

Early Fado: Maria Severa

Maria Severa is where the enigmas really begin. According to most dependable contemporary accounts, she was the first great exponent of the fado and the originator of the female fadista tradition of wearing a dramatically draped black shawl while performing. Born and raised in the Alfama district of Lisbon, she and her mother ran a small tavern in which the embryonic music was performed. In 1836, her fado was heard by the Comte de Vimioso and they entered into what observers of the time referred to as a 'tempestuous love affair'. The impact on Lisbon society of this scandalous, high-profile 'mismatch' was considerable, with the result that the fado received widespread public attention for the first time. Sheet music was published, newspaper articles were written and the whole matter was hotly debated. The controversy was similar in essence to the emergence of the tango in Buenos Aires.

For how long before these events the fado had been an identifiable song is uncertain. There is some evidence to suggest it was known in Brazil a few years earlier, in 1829, but it is clear that the fado we hear on record from at least as far back as 1910 – the fado that is still nightly practised in Lisboa – is the same fado that emerged from this nineteenth-century scandal.

It is still possible to hear the older styles of Lisbon fado if you take the trouble to look. Ignore the expensive restaurants offering evenings of 'fado and folclórico', they are ersatz experiences that will disappoint. However, in a back street of the Alfama district, tucked away at the edge of a courtyard, at Beco de Espírito Santo, stands the *Perreirinha de Alfama*, a restaurant owned and run by the redoubtable **Argentina Santos**. It has been there from 1952 and ever since it began Argentina has taken time, every evening, from running her business to sing fados for the patrons. Even now, in her seventies, her voice retains remarkable timbre. Hers is the authentic sound of traditional professional fado and she is a direct descendant of the great café singers of the first half of the century.

You can hear her and immerse yourself in that tradition for the price of a decent meal, and it's one of the unmissable experiences of this ancient and beautiful city.

Other hunting grounds could include the oldest fado house in Lisbon, *A Severa*, at Rua das Gavaes 51, and *Senhor Vinho*, at Rua das Praças; these are both upmarket restaurants but book good and authentic singers for local aficionados. Elsewhere you might find people like **Carlos Zel** singing in one of the old flagstone-floored bars tucked away down narrow cobbled streets of the Bairro Alto, that old proletariat quarter that sits above the Rocio, or in the ancient Mouraria district. At some bars you can maybe find an impromptu early-evening session conducted not by professionals but by working folk, who simply find that a drink and a fado are the two classic ways to unwind from their day. If you're lucky enough to catch such a session, you'll have an ideal insight into what the fado actually means, and its function as a kind of catharsis in Portuguese life.

Saudade and Fadistas

There is a Portuguese word, **saudade**, that has no direct equivalent translation in English. The closest definition is 'yearning'. It is that spirit which lies at the very heart of the fado. Its emotional parallel is the Spanish *duende*, but the direction it takes is different. It's perhaps the Portuguese equivalent of whatever it is that fuels deep Mississippi or Texas blues – a measure of the understanding that passes between performer and audience.

Fado must possess saudade to be considered genuine: a singer will not last long before a Portuguese audience without it. Audience behaviour is crucial to a live performance and the rules for the audience are at least as strict as for the singer. In the typical Lisbon situation, the audience will not suffer a poor performance to the end, nor tolerate interruption during a good one. Noisy patrons are physically jostled from the room, and poor singers rudely halted in mid-song. At the end of a song it is perfectly acceptable to indulge in applause, whistling, stamping, shouting, table-banging and beer-spilling. Indeed they're all expected. For especially fine renditions the phrase "fadista!" (pronounced "faaadeeshta") is acclaimed.

The term **fadista** has deeper layers of meaning than 'singer of fados'. From the mid-nineteenth century until at least the early 1900s it was a term applied to a picaresque section of Lisbon society. Fadistas were the Portuguese counterparts of Athenian *mánges* – people whose dress, attitude and pocket knives spoke eloquently of their disdain for ordinary society. A contemporary description is worth noting for its refined sense of outrage: "Fadistas wear a peculiar kind of black cap, wide black trousers with close-fitting jacket, and their hair flowing low on the shoulders – they are held in very bad repute, being mostly *vauriens* of dissolute habits". (Lady Jackson in *Fair Lusitania*, 1874).

Coimbra Fado

There is another side to the fado story – the fado of **Coimbra**, which shares the origins and keeps the basic form, but is recognised by both devotees and critics alike as essentially divorced from the barrel-house style of Lisbon. Among the narrow streets of Coimbra, Portugal's old university city, a tradition of literature, song and poetry has been quietly and lovingly nurtured for more than five centuries. The fado and the guitarra were brought here from Lisbon in the second half of the nineteenth century by students.

The attitude of Coimbra fado is markedly different from that of Lisbon, and those who practise the fado de Coimbra are a very different breed from the bus drivers, barbers, labourers and shoeshiners who use it in Lisbon for release. It has been called a more refined strain of fado, but this empty phrase does not accurately reflect the majesty and emotional summits – like a fusion of blues and opera – that a good singer can reach. However, a Coimbra fado would be deemed unseemly if it were not highly rehearsed and stylised. Rodney Gallop, writing in 1936, succinctly defined the difference: "It is the song of those who retain and cherish their illusions, not of those who have irretrievably lost them".

While in Lisbon the guitarra's main role is that of accompanying singers, Coimbra, and in particular its university, also has a strong tradition of its use in instrumental pieces, usually called *guitarradas*, in which one or two guitarras are accompanied by one or two Spanish guitars. This tradition flowered most famously in the 1920s and '30s around a group focused on **Dr Antonio Menano** that included singing doctors **Edmundo de Bettancourt** and **Lucos Junot** and guitarristas of astonishing virtuosity such as **José Joãoquim Cavalheiro** and **Artur Paredes** (1899–1980). They drew on fado and also interpreted other Portuguese song forms from rural regions such as the Beira Baixa and Alentejo. Coimbra fado was also at the root of the hugely influential music of singer **José Afonso** (of whom more below).

There have emerged from Coimbra such luminary players and composers for the guitarra as **António Portugal** (1931–1994), and Paredes' son **Carlos Paredes** (b.1925), and their legacy is strongly upheld by today's most prominent guitarra soloist and composer **Pedro Caldeira Cabral**, whose music reaches far outside fado into semi-classical territories.

The tradition of **student fado** also continues in Coimbra. You can go to the *Bar Diligencia* on Travessa da Rua Nova or the *Café Santa Cruz* at Praça 8 de Maio, tuck yourself in a corner and just observe and listen. Depending on who's there

– everyone is an amateur – the musical experience could be good or mediocre but the cultural experience will be enlightening. Students sing of the beauty of Portugal, their love of poetry and academia, their longing for the unattainable. Their style, pioneered in the 1890s by Augusto Hilario, remains completely unaltered. It's a time warp that co-exists surprisingly well with the present.

Fado Stars

Fado is not just about star performers, but the music has produced a number of key singers – and none more so than **Amália Rodrigues**, who has had an immeasurable impact upon the direction of the fado through her recordings. Like Maria Severa (who never had the chance to record her art), Rodrigues was born (in 1920) into the poverty of the Alfama district of Lisboa. In a long career that started in 1939, she not only sang but acted in a number of films. Her style has defined and crystallised the fado and if you've had only a passing

THE ART OF *Amália* RODRIGUES

acquaintance with the music, it's likely to be hers you have heard. The later, more popular pieces with orchestral accompaniment can be a bit middle of the road; there are, however, early recordings that not only illuminate the roots but also reflect the heights to which a real fadista can rise. Intense, heartfelt, deeply traditional and strikingly innovative, they represent a pinnacle of development in fado's history.

Rodrigues, however, is in semi-retirement these days and the need for a new fado icon has been obvious for some time. Perhaps it's a shade early to begin drawing conclusions as to who that might be, but **Misia** is a clear front runner in the current stakes. Born of a Portuguese father and Catalan mother, she lived in Porto for the first twenty years of her life before moving to Barcelona. Now, having absorbed both sides of the Iberian cultural coin, she has chosen Portugal as her home and the fado as her life's work. That work is refreshingly different. Her music is still very obviously fadistic, but displays the influence of a wider experience. Beginning in 1991, with her first CD for EMI Portugal, she has now moved through the BMG stable to Warner, developing her style at every turn. She looks set to be the first major fado star of the twenty-first century and, along with others like **Mafalda Arnauth** – a fine and underrated singer who deserves wider recognition – should ensure that the fado has a future in the new millennium.

José Afonso

José Afonso, New Song and Modern Fusions

In the second half of the twentieth century, and particularly in the years following the Portuguese revolution of 1974, fado combined with other influences – folk, rock, Latin American nueva canción – to form a style of 'new song'. The great figure in this movement was José Afonso. From the 1970s onward, too, groups have emerged in Portugal re-exploring and fusing regional traditions with jazz and rock influences.

José Afonso and New Song

The giant of twentieth-century Portuguese popular and roots music, **José Afonso** was born in 1929 in Aveiro, later moving to Coimbra. He had a classic soaring fado voice and his first recording (with **Luís Góis** in 1956), *Fados de Coimbra*, was, as its title suggests, fado, though it included two of his own songs. During the years to and through the 1974 revolution he was the leading figure in the reinstitution of the ballad – in the sense of a set of artistic, poetic, usually contemporary lyrics set to music.

It was Afonso's songs, and his choice of songs by others, and his evolving musical framework drawing on regional traditional musics and fado,

---

Tudo isto é Fado (All this is Fado)

You asked me the other day
If I knew what fado was.
I said I didn't know,
You said you were surprised.
Without knowing what I said,
I lied then,
And said I didn't know.

Vanquished souls,
Lost nights,
Strange shadows
In the Moorish quarter.
A whore sings,
Guitars weep,
Ashes and fire,
Pain and sin.
All of this exists,
All of this is sad,
All of this is fado.

If you want to be my man
And always have me by your side,
Don't speak to me of love
But tell me about fado.
Fado is my sentence,
I was born to be lost.
Fado is everything I say,
And everything I cannot say.

Amália Rodrigues, composed by Anibal Nazaré
F. Carvalho, translated by Caroline Shaw.

that provided a rallying point in the development not only of new Portuguese musics but also of a new democratised state. In the final years of dictatorship, censorship and the restriction of performing opportunities caused some songwriters to move and record abroad, but Afonso remained, when necessary masking social and political messages with allegory. Though he died in 1987 his albums keep his music and ideas very much in the forefront of Portuguese musical thinking.

The work of Afonso and his contemporaries such as **Sérgio Godinho** (b.1945) and **Luís Cília**, working both individually and often in collaboration, came to be called **nova canção** (new song) After 1974 there was a need for songwriters to move from protesting under oppression to exploring the needs and possibilities of the new democracy; nova canção evolved into *canto livre* (free song) and other categories and sub-movements.

In shaping the new forms songwriters drew on influences from both within and outside Portugal. **Vitorino**'s lyrics, and particularly his titles, often have a surreal tinge, suggesting the work of such South American writers as Gabriel Garcia Márquez, while his music is strongly linked with the traditions of his native Alentejo. His brother **Janita**

JOÃO CASTEL-BRANCO/CBS

Fausto

Salomé brings in the Arab influence of the south of Portugal. Both are well known as solo performers, and for performances with José Afonso, and together they have performed intermittently with the vocal group **Lua Extravagante**.

Fausto's first album appeared in 1970, and he has gone on to become a major songwriting force, using traditional forms and instrumentation as well as a rock sensibility in such major projects as 1984's double LP about the voyages of Fernão Mendes Pinto, *Por Este Rio Acima*. This and a string of other albums feature many other leading musicians, including **Júlio Pereira**, who began as a songwriter, played with José Afonso, and has become a fount of knowledge and skill on traditional Portuguese stringed instruments.

Roots Groups

It wasn't just individual songwriters who drew on Portuguese traditional musics. Groups began to form in the 1970s which devoted their attention either to the research and performance of traditional music from one or more regions, or to the construction of new musics with folk roots. While sometimes such work is viewed as a quest for a lost ruralism, in a newly democratised state it is often an important part of self-rediscovery.

Portugal's rich rural musical traditions were, and to varying extents still are, alive and functioning, so the gathering of material involved a trip not to dusty archives but to the villages. *Ranchos folclóricos* might have had the residual scent of dictatorship-approval, but the new groups were closer to the spirit of nova canção, and their members often appeared on the recordings and in the bands of the singer-songwriters.

This socially-aware connection is seen most obviously in the name of the pivotal roots-with-evolution group **Brigada Victor Jara**, formed in Coimbra in 1975. Today it contains none of the original members, but it continues to be a major force, and former members have gone on to create new projects. In finding material the band collaborated with a man who did a huge amount to document traditional music and make it available to listeners, ethnomusicologist **Michel Giacometti** (1929–1990), who together with **Fernando Lopes Graça** made a large amount of field recordings throughout Portugal which were released on various labels from the late 1950s onwards.

Some bands such as Brigada Victor Jara have been a fairly steady presence, while others wax and wane, almost disappearing from view and then

Brigada Victor Jara

returning with a new line-up or new album. Notable names over the years include **Raízes**, **Ronda dos Quatro Caminhos**, **Trigo Limpo**, **Terra a Terra**, **Trovante**, **Grupo Cantadores do Redondo**, **Almanaque**, **Romanças** and **Toque de Caixa**.

Today's leading traditional-roots groups include Brigada Victor Jara, **Vai de Roda** and **Realejo**. All have moved on to a more detailed exploration of sound and the possibilities for development than that which prevailed in the first wave. A powerful and innovative recent arrival is **Gaiteiros de Lisboa**, based around the sound of gaitas and other wind instruments with drums and Alentejo-style vocals, bypassing the Western tradition of chordal music and making a modern context for the much older layer of music that's still to be heard in Trás-os-Montes and some other Portuguese traditions which is governed not by harmony but by rhythm and melody free from the rigidity of the equal temperament scale.

With a different approach – closer in sound and spirit to fado but not bound by its traditions – is the very popular **Madredeus** (a band which gets its name from the Lisbon neighbourhood of Madre de Deus where it rehearsed and where its first album was recorded) which set out in 1985 to make new compositions for classical guitars and synthesiser. The addition of an accordionist, and,

crucially, a year later of seventeen-year-old fado-style singer **Teresa Salgueiro**, completed the sound. Early success was later boosted further by a central role for the band, playing themselves and creating the music in Wim Wenders' 1994 film *Lisbon Story*. There has been a line-up change since then, and only leader Pedro Ayres Magalhães and Teresa Salgueiro remain of the original members.

Exploring new compositions for an instrument widespread in Europe but used distinctively in some Portuguese traditions, such as those of the Minho region, is the diatonic accordion quartet **Danças Ocultas**, which draws music not just from the reeds of the instrument known in Portugal as *concertina*, but from its less obvious aspects such as the panting of the bellows.

A former member of Brigada Victor Jara and, briefly, Trovante, as well as of studio project Banda do Casaco, singer **Né Ladeiras** went solo in 1983, and has made a string of notable albums in both pop and roots genres since then, including one devoted to Trás-os-Montes music and another – her most recent – featuring the songs of Fausto (one of her strongest influences) and drawing them closer to traditional instrumentation and feel.

Also moving between pop and largely fado roots is one of Portugal's current biggest stars **Dulce Pontes**. That her credibility doesn't seem to have been damaged by representing Portugal in the

Eurovision Song Contest is demonstrated, for example, by her appearance on Euskal trikitixa player Kepa Junkera's 1998 major double album project *Bilbao 00:00h*.

Misia is, as mentioned earlier, a major fadista, and is being heard increasingly widely abroad as a strong Portuguese contribution to the World Music cast list. Somewhere between the fado tradition and nova canção in terms of song content, and both with fine fado voices, are **Amélia Muge** and **Teresa Silva Carvalho**.

Gaiteiros de Lisboa member **Rui Vaz**, a name to watch in new roots music, produced the 1996 *Amai* album, released on David Byrne's Luaka Bop label, by fado singer **Paulo Bragança**. Bragança doesn't have the breadth in his voice of the great fadistas, but the project, patchy as it is, shows that fado can move far from its traditional instrumentation and still project a unique identity.

On the Atlantic islands of **Madeira** and the **Azores** there are also signs of new interest among musicians in their cocktail of musical traditions, which show influences not only from Portugal but also from Africa and from just about any musical sailor who passed through on a trade ship. In Madeira, for example, the recent establishing of the record label Almasud has created a new outlet for musicians such as those in the roots–fusion band **Almma**.

Meanwhile, of course, transnational pop is as all-pervading in Portugal as elsewhere. It's not all import, though – the rap-based music of Porto-born **Pedro Abrunhosa** has sold hugely at home and internationally.

Some contacts

Discantus/Mundo da Canção, Rua Duque de Saldanha 97, 4300 Porto. ☎ (351) 2 51 93-100, fax: 2 51 93 109, email *discantus@mail.telepac.pt* Promoter of roots and World Music events such as the *Festival Interceltico* in Porto. Also distribute and retail Portuguese roots CDs.

Etnia, Calçada Marquês de Abrantes 10–3 esq., P-1200 Lisboa. ☎/fax (351) 1 396 1355. Arts organisation promoting Portuguese roots music and bringing other world roots performers to Portugal.

Portugal 600, Palingswick House, 241 King St., London W6 9LP. Tel: ☎ (0)20 8748 0884, fax: 8748 4187; email *mail@portugal600.demon.co.uk* Website *www.portembassy.gla.ac.uk/info/port600.html* An organisation for the promotion of Portuguese arts in the UK and Ireland, connected to the Portugal-based Calouste Gulbenkian Foundation. It publishes an English-language magazine, *Cultura*.

discography

General Compilations

Both the compilations listed here are very listenable and give a good range, but they reflect the commercial end - they contain virtually no regional traditional material, so they don't give any sense of the differentness of such traditions as Trás-os-Montes, nor show Alentejo polyphonic singing (the Smithsonian box is good on this, though, and even better on Trás-os-Montes is the Ocora). Compiled largely from material on the major Portuguese labels EMI-Valentim de Carvalho and Movieplay, the Hemisphere and Rough Guide discs also miss out on such major forces as Gaiteiros de Lisboa, Fausto, Pedro Caldeira Cabral and Júlio Pereira, and singers such as Paulo Bragança or Amélia Muge.

Music from the Edge of Europe
(EMI Hemisphere, UK).

An excellent taster, with the limitations noted above. Includes one or more tracks from Madredeus, Carlos Paredes, Vitorino, Danças Ocultas, Amália Rodrigues, Sérgio Godinho, Ala dos Namorados, Trovante, Né Ladeiras, Lua Extravagante, António Pinho Vargas.

The Rough Guide to the Music of Portugal
(World Music Network, UK).

With tracks taken from the catalogue of the Portuguese record company Movieplay this fills some of the gaps in the Hemisphere compilation, with José Afonso, Dulce Pontes, Ronda dos Quatro Caminhos, Realejo, Vai de Roda, Terra a Terra, Teresa Silva Carvalho, Carlos Paredes and others and a clutch of fine fado singers including Amália Rodrigues, Carlos Zel and the magnificent Maria Teresa de Noronha and Maria da Fé.

Regional traditions

Les Açores – The Azores (Auvidis/Silex, France).

Azorean music is a blend of south-west European and northwest African roots. The most obvious flavour in the cocktail is Portuguese; there's a caressing, passionate vocal style, and instruments include the specifically Azorean version of the *viola*, the twelve or fifteen-stringed *viola da terra*, whose use was dwindling but is now reviving somewhat. In 1994 Jacques Erwan recorded individual singers and musicians, music at traditional celebrations, dance music, a brass band, and organised folklore groups.

Musical Traditions of Portugal
(Smithsonian Folkways, US).

This 2-CD box has recordings (plus substantial notes) of a selection of regional traditions: from Bragança in the northeast there are dances with gaita-de-foles or flauta and tamboril with caixa and bombo, and a solo ballad; from Monsanto in the central east ritual songs and chant accompanied by adufes; from the village of Cuba in the Alentejo secular and religious songs. The Quarteto de Guitarras de Coimbra plays instrumental compositions by Artur Paredes, António Portugal and others, and three ranchos folclóricos from the Tejo valley and the north-west show that there's much more to them than colourful costumes.

Música Tradicional: Vol. 6 – Terra de Miranda
(Tecnosaga, Spain).

A follow-up rather than first buy. Songs and romances, and instrumentals on gaita-de-foles with caixa and bombo, or on flauta and tamboril, from the Miranda region, north of the Douro on the eastern edge of Trás-os-Montes. Notes in Castellano and Portuguese.

Portugal - Trás-os-Montes: Chants du blé et cornemuses de berger (Ocora, France).

The ever-reliable Ocora gets to the heart of the differentness of Trás-os-Montes music with recordings (with notes in French and English) made in 1978 of a fine spread of the regional traditions - gaita-de-foles with caixa and bombo, flauta and tamboril, and songs, including several romances going back to the Carolingian Cycle and other medieval bodies of tales. Lest any consider that the gaitas are just 'out of tune', listen to the remarkable pitching of the overlapping duet singing by Antonio Evangelista Marao and Antonio das Horas de Sousa of "O Conde de Allemanha" – an education in the old music of Europe.

Fado and Guitarra

Though they may require some searching out, there are a large number of recordings of fado available on CD, many on international labels including an archive series - Arquivos do Fado (Heritage, UK) – and a series of more recent recordings – Un Parfum De Fado (Playasound, France) – and a whole lot of Amália Rodrigues and other fadistas on a range of labels. Plunge in and listen: as with flamenco, if it moves you that's the fado for you.

Compilations

 Portugal – The Story Of Fado
(EMI Hemisphere, UK).

A widely available and well-chosen collection that makes an excellent introduction.

□ **A History of the Portuguese Fado**
(Ashgate Publishing Ltd., UK).

Actually a 140-page book, by Paul Vernon (author of the Fado section of this article), which includes a 24-track CD compilation of classic vintage-era fado.

Artists

Pedro Caldeira Cabral

Cabral is a dazzlingly skilful guitarra virtuoso (and multi-instrumentalist) who has worked as accompanist and arranger with the likes of Vitorino, Fausto, Sérgio Godinho, Luís Cília and Júlio Pereira.

□ **Variações** (World Network, Germany).

A live recording of a concert in Köln for WDR in 1988 (released 1992), featuring largely his own compositions, accompanied by Francisco Perez on guitar. The two of them make a very full sound.

Misia

Misia is the 'new voice' of the fado, increasingly being taken to the heart of the World Music touring circuit.

 Garras Dos Sentidos
(Erato/Detour, France).

Wonderful contemporary renderings of classic songs and themes. They feature, among other musicians, Manuel Rocha & Ricardo Dias of Brigada Victor Jara (violin & accordion – a sound used in fado at the turn of the century), with Custodio Castelo on guitarra.

Carlos Paredes

Born in Coimbra in 1925, the son of famous guitarrista and instrumental fado composer Artur Paredes, Carlos in turn became a leading guitarra virtuoso, further developing the scope of the instrument. As well as solo performance, and the recording of, for such an important musician, relatively few albums, he played and recorded with José Afonso (see below).

WITH CHARLIE HADEN

□ **Dialogues** (Antilles, UK).

A late surprise, a duet album with jazz bassist Charlie Haden. For a view of Paredes' talent in a less shared context, try any album of his you can find.

Júlio Pereira

Virtuoso stringed instrumentalist, and producer of the recordings of others within and outside Portugal.

□ **Acústico** (Sony, Portugal).

After exploring the uses of synthesisers and other musical technology, Pereira has in recent years tended to focus on the acoustic sound. This 1994 album comprises his compositions for braguesa, cavaquinho, guitarra and bandolim, sometimes solo and sometimes multitracked or with guitarist Moz Carrapa and singer Minela.

Amália Rodrigues

The most famous singer of fado, Rodrigues has forged a star-crossed path, recording 'standards' as well as fado, and turning for a while to film acting. But the two albums below show why she surpassed all others.

□ **The First Recordings** (EPM, France).

Beautiful, soulful performances that redefined the genre in the post-war era. Some might say that this was her truest period, before she branched out into other instrumentation and material, but many of the greatest musicians are not slaves to someone's idea of their tradition – they carry it with them into whatever they do.

 The Art of Amalia
(EMI Hemisphere, UK).

Early in the 1950s, already a big star, Amália was signed via Valentim de Carvalho to EMI, where she remained, so Hemisphere had the run of most of her catalogue. Here are eighteen well-chosen tracks, in which she's finely accompanied by guitarra and viola, from sessions between 1952 (at Abbey Road) and 1970.

New Song and Roots Groups

José Afonso

The giant of Portuguese popular song, Afonso died in 1987 but his huge influence lives on in recordings and in the work of present-day musicians. He was the figurehead of nova canção, which bridged the change from dictatorship to democracy and was a focus of Portuguese social and political thinking during that period. A fine singer and innovative musician, even for a non-speaker of Portuguese his music - drawing together the romance tradition, fado, regional tradition and European songwriting - is highly accessible and perpetually contemporary.

□ **Cantigas do Maio** (Movieplay, Portugal).

An influential album from before the revolution.

◎ Fados de Coimbra e Outras Canções
(Movieplay, Portugal).

A revisiting of the musical territory where he began.

Brigada Victor Jara

A leading roots band since its formation in Coimbra in 1975, and showing no sign of weakening. The musical paths of many leading musicians pass through this band.

◎ Danças e Folias (Farol, Portugal).

The 1995 album. By now none of the original members are among its eight musicians. Lead vocals are by Aurélio Malva and guests Margarita Miranda and the wonderfully gruff José Medeiros (who sings the balho "A Fofa", from the Azores to an accompaniment reminiscent of the style of Cesaria Evora's band). The material comes from Bragança, Douro Litoral, Terra de Miranda, Azores, Gândara, Beira Litoral, Beira Baixa and Estremadura.

Gaiteiros de Lisboa

Gaiteros are a constantly innovative band making the links from roots to new Portuguese musics, using magnificent, vibrant Alentejo-style male singing (comparable to, and to a degree influenced by, Corsican vocal groups), with drums and gaitas de foles or Galician bagpipes. These are sometimes played together, with a non-standard intonation that nevertheless feels in tune, plus trumpet, flügelhorn, and ethnic flutes played percussively. There are no chordal instruments, no stringed instruments except sanfona, which anyway sits more comfortably with pipes. Both albums are excellently recorded, upfront, modern and impeccably powerful.

 Invasões Bárbaras
(Farol, Portugal).

The band's 1995 debut album. Material from Ribatejo, Alentejo, Trás-os-Montes, and by band members J.M. David, Carlos Guerreiro and Rui Vaz.

◎ Bocas do Inferno (Farol, Portugal).

The second album in 1997 shows them exploring the new sounds of invented instruments such as the plumbing-tube serafina in more traditional and new music, and also wrapping kazoos, panpipes, trumpet and another invention, the orgaz, round a tune by the Portuguese/German-American J.P. Sousa.

Madredeus

Widely known Portuguese band led by Pedro Ayres Magalhães, centred on two guitars and the voice of Teresa Salgueiro.

◎ O Espírito Da Paz
(EMI Valentim de Carvalho, Portugal).

Released in 1994, the year the band and its music featured pivotally in Wim Wenders' film *Lisbon Story*. Changes since then have left only Magalhães and Salgueiro from the original line-up.

Né Ladeiras

A member of the original Brigada Victor Jara, and briefly of Trovante, singer Né Ladeiras has a serene voice with a hint of fado passion. In the course of a range of projects she has combined her fondness for traditional musics with elegant arrangements, while retaining the sounds and skills of traditional instrumentalists.

◎ Traz os Montes
(EMI-Valentim de Carvalho, Portugal).

A 1994 album devoted to traditional songs from Trás-os-Montes, giving them modern settings without losing their melodic essence. Features former Brigada Victor Jara colleagues Ricardo Dias and Manuel Rocha, plus Fausto and others. Several of the songs are to be found as field recordings on the Ocora album above, and the final track here consists of that album's recording of Adélia Garcia singing "A Fonte do Salgueirinho".

Romania

taraf traditions

Wild, raw, exuberant, tragic and fuelled by litres of home-brewed plum brandy: that's the essence of both Romania and its music. Despite the (half-witted) political and industrial schemes of the Ceaușescu years, the country remains predominantly a rural, village-based society – one with a peasant economy and deeply rooted customs. Musically, this means a strong showing for roots, and with its village *taraf* ensembles, and its large minority populations of Gypsies and Hungarians, Romania has riches to rival anywhere in Europe. **Simon Broughton** explores a resolutely living tradition.

Each of the regimes in eastern Europe has left its legacy and Nicolae Ceaușescu's twenty-five years of dictatorship are still a dark shadow over Romania. As the country struggles to catch up with the rest of Europe, the effects of a centralised economy and a feared secret police are hard to shake off.

The legacy extends, too, to the country's folk music, which was manipulated to glorify the dictator and present the rich past of the Romanian peasantry on which Ceaușescu's future was to be built. The regime created huge shows called *Cîntarea Romaniei* (Singing Romania), which involved thousands of peasants dressed in traditional garb being bussed out to picturesque hillsides to perform songs and dances. These were filmed, appallingly edited, and shown on television every Sunday. The words of songs were shorn of anything deemed to be religious or which questioned the peasants' love of their labours and replaced with bland patriotic sentiments or hymns to peace.

This gave folklore a pretty bad name amongst the educated classes, though the peasants were hardly bothered. They just did what they were told for Cîntarea Romaniei and got on with the real music in the villages. Today, traditional music still flourishes throughout Romania – and perhaps more than anywhere else in Europe. The isolation of the country and its almost medieval lifestyle preserved traditions that have been modernised out of existence elsewhere.

As Romania now catches up with the West, just how long its amazing musical culture can survive is a thorny question. However, the music is not ready to wither away just yet, and its joy is its spontaneity and authenticity. It has a life, function and identity all its own, and it can absorb outside influences with ease.

Romania lies across a geographical, historical and cultural barrier that separates central Europe from the Balkans. The line is that of the Carpathian Mountains, which sweep across the country and sharply divide the musical styles. In **Transylvania**, in the northwest, the music is audibly central European, on the other side of the mountains it is distinctly **Balkan**. Of course, such borders are not impermeable; the same Latin-based Romanian language is spoken on either side and there are plenty of musical cross-fertilisations.

Transylvania

People sometimes imagine that Transylvania, the land of Dracula, is an imaginary location. Lying within the sweep of the Carpathians, it was an independent principality back in the sixteenth and seventeenth centuries, while Hungary and Romania were under Turkish rule, and then became part of the Hapsburg Empire. Its character is thus more central European than other parts of Romania and Transylvanians consider themselves more 'civilised' than their compatriots in Moldavia and Wallachia. The architectural styles belong to the Austro-Hungarian Empire and the medieval Gothic buildings come straight out of the world of Grimm's fairytales. The music of Transylvania feels equally exotic, though it is recognisably part of a central European tradition.

If you want to experience a living European folk tradition, there is no beating Transylvania. Home to an age-old ethnic mix of **Romanians, Hungarians** and **Gypsies**, the region's music is extraordinary: wild melodies and dances that are played all night (and beyond) at weddings and other parties. Music is still a part of everyday life the way it

Dumitru Vranceanu with his home-made violin with gramophone horn

must have been hundreds of years ago all over Europe. The older men and women know the old songs and still use them to express their own personal feelings.

The Hungarian composers **Bartók** and **Kodály** found Transylvania the most fertile area for their folk-song collecting trips in the first decades of the century, and they recognised that the rich mix of nationalities here had a lot to do with it. For the communities of Romanians, Hungarians, Saxons, Gypsies and others, music forms a part of their individual identity, as well as that of Transylvania as a distinct culture. The Romanian music of Transylvania is closer to the Hungarian than it is to the Romanian music outside Transylvania. And the Hungarian music of Transylvania sounds much more Romanian than the music of Hungary proper.

In fact within Transylvania the Romanians and Hungarians share many **melodies and dances**. A particular melody may be described as Hungarian in one village and Romanian in another village over the hill. The Romanian dances often have a slightly more irregular rhythm than the Hungarian, but often the only difference between one tune and another is the language in which it is sung. There's a recording of an old man from the village of Dimbău (Küküllődombó) singing an example of a song with the first half of each line in Hungarian and the second half in Romanian!

The traditional ensemble is a **string trio** – a violin, viola (called a *contra* in Romanian, *kontra* in Hungarian) and a double bass, plus a cimbalom in certain parts of Transylvania. The *primás*, the first violinist, plays the melody and leads the musicians from one dance into another while the contra and

the bass are the accompaniment and rhythm section of the band. The contra (also known as *braci*) has only three strings and a flat bridge so it only plays chords on the off-beat, and it's the deep sawing of the bass and the rhythmic spring of the contra that gives Transylvanian music its particular sound. Often the bands are expanded with a second violin or an extra contra to give more volume at a noisy wedding with hundreds of guests. The dances are generally strung together into suites, lasting anything from five to twenty minutes, generally starting slow and increasing in speed towards the end.

Wedding Parties

Music in Transylvania fulfils a social purpose – nobody would dream of sitting down and listening to it at a concert. In some areas there are still regular weekly dances, but everywhere the music is played at weddings, and sometimes at funerals and other occasions, as when soldiers go off to the army.

Wedding parties last a couple of days and if you're lucky you'll find yourself in a specially constructed wedding 'tent' built from wooden beams and tree fronds. The place is strung with ribbons and fir branches, tables are piled high with garish cakes and bottles of plum brandy and various courses are brought round at regular intervals. There's a space cleared for dancing and a platform is erected for the band of musicians sawing and scraping away at battered old fiddles and a bass making the most mesmerising sound. The bride and groom, stuck up on their high table, look a little fed up while everybody else has the time of their lives.

The wedding customs vary slightly from region to region but generally the band has to start things off at the bride's or groom's house, accompany the processions to the church and possibly play for one of the real emotional high spots, the bride's farewell song (*cîntecul miresei*) to her family and friends. Whilst the marriage takes place inside the church, the band plays for the young people, or those not invited to the feast, to dance in the street outside. Once the couple comes out of the church there's another procession to wherever the wedding feast is being held – either in the village hall or the 'tent' erected at the house of the bride or groom. There the musicians will have a short break to get something to eat and then play music all Saturday night, alternating songs to accompany the feast and dances to work off the effects of the food and large quantities of plum brandy. There are even particular pieces for certain courses of the banquet when the soup, stuffed cabbage or roast meat are served!

Late in the evening comes the bride's dance (*jocul miresei*) when the guests dance in turn with the bride and offer money. Things usually wind down by dawn on Sunday; people wander off home or collapse in a field somewhere and then around lunchtime the music starts up again for another session until late in the evening.

With the trend toward larger weddings and an influx of new music, all sorts of instruments have started to find their way into the bands. Most common is the piano accordion, which, like the contra, plays chords, though it lacks its rhythmic spring. Very often you hear a clarinet or the slightly deeper and more reedy *taragot* which sounds wonderful in the open air. Sadly, as young people have moved away to work in towns, they also often demand the guitars, drums and electric keyboards of the urban groups – along with appalling amplification, which is increasingly brought in, too, by traditional acoustic bands.

Some band leaders might regret this trend but they are obliged to provide what the people demand. With the newer instruments the quality of the music is often lost, and, paradoxically, the combination of guitar and drum kit is far less rhythmic than the contra and bass in the hands of good musicians. It's still possible to hear first-rate traditional bands, but they are probably now a disappearing phenomenon. The 'Final Hour' project and Fonó Records, based in Budapest, Hungary (see Hungary – p.159), aims to record and document the remaining traditional bands in Transylvania before it's too late.

Gypsy Bands

Most of the village musicians in Romania are Gypsies. In the villages, Gypsy communities all tend to live along one particular street on the outskirts, and it's amazing how often you find these streets are called Strada Muzicanților or Strada Lăutari – both of which translate as 'Musicians' Street'. The Gypsy musicians will play for Romanian, Hungarian and Gypsy weddings alike and they know almost instinctively the repertoire required. Children often play alongside their parents from an early age and grow up with the music in their blood.

There's no doubt the Gypsies have some special aptitude for music, and perhaps the job suits their social position on the edge of village life. Playing music, too, can be an easy way to earn good money. The best bands command handsome fees, plus the odd chicken and bottles of plum brandy 'for the road', but they certainly have their work cut out over the weekend. It's also an indication of the value of music in this society that the musicians are not only well rewarded but also well respected. When the old primás of the Pălatca band (one of the most celebrated of the traditional bands) died, all the people he had played for in the village came to pay their respects.

It's difficult to highlight the **best bands** – there are dozens of them – but in addition to the Pălatca band you can hear great music from bands in the following villages of central Transylvania (the names are given in their Romanian form with the Hungarian, where appropriate, in brackets): Mera (Méra), Almaşu (Váralmás), Vaida-Cămăras (Vajdakamarás), Suatu (Magyarszovát), Soporu de Cîmpie (Mezőszopor), Sîngeorz-Băi (Oláhszentgyörgy), Ceuaş (Szászcsávás) and Sic (Szék), a virtually 100 percent Hungarian village and one of the great treasure houses of Hungarian music.

A glance at the engagement book of one of these bands will show them booked for months ahead. Yet most of them confine their playing to quite a small area as travel is relatively difficult. Some tunes are widely known right across Transylvania but many are distinctly local and a band playing too far from its home village will simply not know the repertoire. It will be interesting to see what happens now that local bands are travelling to Hungary and beyond on tour. Foreign audiences demand a variety of styles which sophisticated groups like Muzsikás from Budapest can readily supply. But if the village bands from Transylvania start doing the same thing then the music's strong local identity could easily break down.

The Hungarians

There are about two million Hungarians in Transylvania and seven million Romanians, but it is the music of the Hungarian minority that has made most impact outside the region. The Hungarian group **Muzsikás** have recorded and toured extensively and have been the leading ambassadors of Transylvanian music. During the Ceauşescu years the Hungarians consciously promoted the culture of their brethren in Transylvania to highlight their suffering.

Transylvania has always held a very special place in Hungarian culture as it preserves archaic traditions that have disappeared in Hungary itself. While Hungary was occupied by the Turks for one hundred and fifty years and its villages destroyed, Transylvania remained an independent principality with its own cultural identity. The old medieval settlement patterns changed very little under Ceauşescu's isolationist policies and much of it seems like a lost world. As a minority, the Hungarians in Transylvania felt threatened, and there was a deliberate move to wear their traditional costumes, sing their songs and play their music as a statement of identity, even protest. These days, national costume and dances are much more visible amongst the Hungarian minority than the majority Romanians.

The regular visits of folklorists and tánchaz musicians have also helped reinforce the musical culture. Transylvanian music is the staple diet of the Budapest tánchaz clubs (see p.161), and once the peasants saw these educated city folk taking an interest they took more of an interest themselves. Now there are two opposing trends at work in Transylvania: the continuing interest in this unique tradition and the inevitable effect as the country catches up with the times.

Regional Styles

Within the overall Transylvanian musical language there are hundreds of local dialects: the style of playing a particular dance can vary literally from village to village. But there are some broad musical regions whose styles can be quite easily distinguished.

Bartók gathered most of his Romanian material in the area around **Hunedoara**. The area is still musically very rich though, strangely enough, a recent musical survey found that virtually the entire repertoire had changed. Surprisingly little is on disc.

Further north is the area the Hungarians call **Kalotaszeg**, and which is home to some of the most beautiful music in the region. This area lies along the main route to Hungary and central Europe, and the influence of Western-style harmony shows itself

in the sophisticated minor-key accompaniment – a development of only the last twenty or thirty years. Kalotaszeg is famous for its men's dance, the *legényes* and the slow *hajnali* songs performed in the early morning as a wedding feast dies down. These have a sad and melancholy character all their own. One of the best of all recordings of Transylvanian music includes both these forms, featuring the Gypsy primás **Sándor 'Neti' Fodor** from the village of Baciu (Bács). There is also some fine Romanian music in this area, particularly in the Sălaj district, around the town of Zalău.

Also in western Transylvania in the **Bihor region** around the city of Oradea there's a strange hybrid instrument to be found, the *vioară cu goarnă* (violin with a horn). This isn't a cow or ram's horn, but a horn from an old gramophone. Often there's no body to the violin at all, just an old-fashioned acoustic pick-up which transmits the vibrations into the horn. It's thought the instrument was developed in the 1930s (as you might expect from the technology involved) so that violins could compete with the louder wind instruments like clarinets. The sound is rather harsh and wiry, but it certainly cuts through the dancing feet, particularly when you get three or four playing together.

Probably the richest area for music, and where many of the best bands come from, is known to the Romanians as **Cîmpia Transilvaniei** and to the Hungarians as **Mezőség**. This is the Transylvanian heathland, north and east of Cluj, a poor, isolated region whose music preserves a primitive feel with strong major chords moving in idiosyncratic harmony.

Further east is the most densely populated Hungarian region, **Székelyföld**. The Székelys, who speak a distinctive Hungarian dialect, were the defenders of the eastern flanks of the Hungarian kingdom in the Middle Ages, when the Romanians, as landless peasants, counted for little. Rising up towards the Carpathians, their land becomes increasingly wild and mountainous, and the dance music is different once again with eccentric ornamentation and very often a cimbalom in the band.

For Hungarian speakers the songs are fascinating as they preserve old-style elements that survive nowhere else. In one village I heard a ballad about a terrible massacre of the Székelys by the Hapsburgs in 1764, sung as if it had happened yesterday. Fleeing this massacre, many Székelys escaped over the Carpathians into Moldavia, where they preserved music and customs that are no longer found in Székelyföld itself. In those outer reaches the string bands of Transylvania have given way to a solo violin or flute accompanying the dances.

On the eastern side of the Carpathians, and actually outside Transylvania in western Moldavia, live the Hungarian-speaking **Csángós** whose songs leave Hungarians misty-eyed for their distinctively archaic language and expression. The Csángós living in the high valley of Ghimeş (Gyimes) also play an ancient instrumental music on the remarkable duo of violin and *gardon* – an instrument shaped like a cello but actually percussive and played by hitting its strings with a stick. The 'pipe and drum' nature of the music suggests Moldavian, pastoral origins. The fiddle playing is highly ornamented and the rhythms complex and irregular, showing the influence of Romanian music. One of the most celebrated musicians is the veteran fiddler **Mihály Halmágyi** in the village of Lunca de Jos (Gyimesközéplok) who was accompanied on gardon by his wife until her recent death.

Maramureş

In the far north of Transylvania, sandwiched between Hungary, the Carpathians and the Ukrainian border, is Maramureş one of the most extraordinary regions of Europe. It has beautiful wooden churches, carved gateways, watermills and villages perched in the rolling foothills of the Carpathians . . . and a living traditional culture. Village costumes are worn for everyday life and music forms an accompaniment to every stage of life, from birth, through courtship and marriage to death. There are magic songs and spells of incantation against sickness and the evil eye, and you still find Sunday afternoon village dances, either on the streets or on wooden dance platforms.

The music, while recognisably Transylvanian, sounds closer to that of Romanians outside the Carpathians. As often happens in the highland regions of Romania, it is played predominantly by Romanians, not Gypsies. The instrumental group is a trio of violin (locally called *cetera*), guitar (*zongora* – with only four or five strings tuned to a major triad) and drum (*doba* – usually an old military style drum with a little cymbal on top struck with a screwdriver). The music has a fairly primitive sound, lacking the beguiling harmonies of elsewhere in Transylvania, and with a repeated chord on the zongora played as a drone. Hundreds of years ago all the music of Europe probably sounded something like this.

There are many extraordinary fiddlers in the region and in 1997 there was a French and Belgian-organised festival, **Maramuzical**, which took place in different villages highlighting the local violin traditions and inviting other musicians from Romania and abroad. Whether it will become a regular event is unknown, but it was repeated in July 1999.

The small district of **Oaş**, to the northwest, is separated from Maramureş by a range of hills. Here the musical style is even more outlandish. The ensemble is reduced to a duo of fiddle and zongora – the violin strings are tuned up several tones to make the sound project better and the melodies are all played 'double-stopped' on two strings at the same time. The sound is high-pitched and harsh, as is the local singing style. It takes some getting used to, but has captivating power and unsettling, tragic quality. There's still a regular Sunday dance held in the early evening on a wooden platform in the village of Certeze.

SIMON BROUGHTON

Village dance in Maramures

 ROMANIA

KLAUS REIMER/CRAMMED DISCS

Taraf de Haidouks

Lowland Romania

Outside the Carpathians, Romania is for the most part fertile lowland. There are three broad cultural regions: **Banat** in the west, **Moldavia** in the northeast, and **Wallachia** in the south, around the capital, Bucharest. It is Wallachia that is home to the quintessential Romanian band, the **taraf**.

The Wallachian Taraf

As in Transylvania most village bands in **Wallachia** are made up of Gypsies: the groups are generally named 'Taraf of' the village name. The word *taraf* comes from Arabic and suggests the more oriental flavour of this music, which sounds altogether different from that of their Transylvanian counterparts. Songs are often preceded by an instrumental improvisation called *taksim*, the name again borrowed from the Middle-East. The staple dances are the *hora, sîrba*, seven-beat *geamparale* and *brîu* – all of which are danced in a circle.

The taraf *lăutari* (musicians) are professionals who play a vital function in village life at weddings and other celebrations. The lead is, as ever, provided by the **fiddle**, which is played in a richly ornamented style. The middle parts are taken by the **ţambal** (cimbalom), which fills out the harmony and adds a plangent rippling to the texture.

At the bottom is the double bass, ferociously plucked rather than bowed Transylvanian style. In the old days you'd always find a *cobză* (lute) in such bands but their place has given way to ţambal, guitar and accordion. Both the cobza and ţambal probably came to Romania from the Middle-East, the latter with the Gypsies. Never slaves to tradition, the young Gypsies, in particular, are always keen to try new instruments and adopt modish styles.

Whereas in Transylvania the bands play exclusively dance music, the musicians in the south of the country have an impressive repertoire of **epic songs** and **ballads** as well. These might be specific marriage songs or legendary tales like "Sarpele" (The Snake) or exploits of the Haidouks – the Robin Hood brigands of Romanian history. One of the instrumental tunes you hear played by lăutari all over Romania is **"Ciocărlia"** (The Lark), which has also become a concert piece for the stage ensembles. Reputedly based on a folk dance (although attributed by others to composer Grigoraş Dinicu; 1889–1949), it is an opportunity for virtuoso display culminating in high squeaks and harmonics on the violin to imitate birdsong, followed by the whole band swirling away in abandon on the opening theme. It was incorporated by George Enescu (1881–1955) into his first Romanian Rhapsody.

Internationally, the best-known Romanian group is the **Taraf de Haidouks**, from the village of Clejani, southwest of Bucharest. These musicians were first recorded in 1988 on the French label, Ocora, and, enthused by this disc, Belgian Gypsy music enthusiasts Michel Winter and Stéphane Karo went to the village in 1990 and struck a lasting relationship with the group. They have successfully produced the Taraf into a first-class recording and touring ensemble of about a dozen musicians – all of them Gypsies. They remain, however, a real working band, playing wedding music for locals. So often this music is stultified or just picturesque when it reaches the stage, but the Taraf bring it off. They sub-divide into small ensembles for different parts of their stage show and the traditional-style of the old men contrasts with the flashier playing of the younger musicians who also bring in jazz-style walking basslines and tricksy Bulgarian or Turkish rhythms.

The band's success has brought a new lease of life to the old musicians, too. The bright-eyed singer and fiddler Nicolae Neaşcu, now in his late seventies, had virtually retired until his ornamented fiddle style brought him international attention. His party piece is to tie a length of horse's hair to the lower string of the violin and pull it rhythmically through the fingers of the right hand creating a very moving, deep gutteral sound. The Kronos Quartet, who have worked with the group, have since used the technique.

Other noteworthy Gypsy bands – who might equally have accomplished the Haidouks' fame – can be found in the Wallachian villages of **Mîrşa**, **Dobroteşti**, **Suteşti** and **Brăila**.

Moldavia

The culture of Moldavia extends across the border to the former Soviet Republic of Moldova. Both places share similar Romanian traditions and are largely pastoral. No surprise, then, that you often hear a **shepherd's flute** in place of a fiddle, as lead instrument in an ensemble.

There is also a Moldavian tradition of **brass bands**. They derived from the Hapsburg and Turkish military bands (*mehter*) and are part of a brass band tradition right across the Balkans, notably in Serbia and Macedonia. The bands (*bantă*, although now the French term *fanfare* is more common) became popular in the 1940s, replacing the traditional fiddle groups. They feature clarinets and saxophones, trumpets, tenor and baritone horns and a tuba or euphonium, and the same drum with a little cymbal found in Maramureş. The tradition, sadly, has rapidly declined in the last few years, with the band from Zece Prăjini, who've toured abroad as the **Fanfare Ciocărlia** (named after that tune), pretty much the last in active service.

Typical **Moldavian dances** are the *bătută* (stamping dance) and *rusasca* (Russian), both circle dances, as well as the *sîrba*, *hora* and *geamparale* popular elsewhere in Romania.

The Banat Beat

The Banat, in Romania's western corner, is ethnically very mixed, with communities of Hungarians, Serbs, Germans and Gypsies living alongside the Romanians. The province's largest town, Timişoara, is famed as the birthplace of the revolution that brought down Ceauşescu, and the protests there were due largely to the presence of these ethnic minorities.

The Banat has developed a modern-sounding urban music with clarinets, saxophones and brass. It is a fast, exciting, virtuoso style – well exemplified by the Silex CD of the **Taraf de Carancebeş** – and has absorbed much from the *novokomponovana* (new folk) music of neighbouring Serbia. It is extremely popular, played all the time on the national radio stations and by Gypsy bands everywhere.

Other traditions are to be found, too. Working in Timişoara is the fine Gypsy singer **Nicolae Gutsa** who's become a very popular performer in Romanian and Romany working with a band of stunning players. Their music is modernised to a degree, but grows unmistakably out of the Romanian and Gypsy tradition.

The Doina

The **doina** is a free-form, semi-improvised slow song heard all over Romania. With poetic texts of grief, bitterness, separation and longing, it's the nearest Romania gets to the blues. *Dor*, in Romanian, is a pleasant feeling of melancholy which this music tends to evoke. Its melodies usually follow a descending pattern, and very often different texts are sung to the same melody, which may then take on a contrasting character.

Taragot player from Taraf de Carancebes

Doina is essentially private music, sung to one-self at moments of grief or reflection, although nowadays the songs are often performed by professional singers or in instrumental versions by Gypsy bands. Old doinas of the traditional kind can still be found in Oltenia, between the Olt and Danube rivers in the south of the country. This one is typical:

I don't sing because I know how to sing
But because a certain thought is haunting me
I don't sing to boast of it
But my heart is bitter
I don't sing because I know how to sing
I'm singing to soothe my heart
Mine and that of the one who is listening to me!

Lost Sheep

The pastoral way of life is slowly disappearing and with it the traditional instrumental repertoire of the **fluier** (shepherd's flute). But there is one form – a sort of folk tone poem – that is still regularly played all over the country: "The shepherd who lost his sheep". This song was referred to as early as the sixteenth century by the Hungarian poet Bálint Balassi. I've heard it on the flute in Moldavia, the violin in Transylvania and on the violin and gardon in Gyimes. It begins with a sad, doina-like tune as the shepherd laments his lost flock. Then he sees his sheep in the distance and a merry dance tune takes over, only to return to the sad lament when he realises it's just a clump of stones. Finally the sheep are found and the whole thing ends with a lively dance in celebration.

Some of the professional bands have adopted the lost sheep story and embroidered it so that during his search the shepherd meets a Turk, a Jew, a Bulgarian, and so on. He asks each of them to sing him a song to alleviate his suffering and promises to pay them if they succeed. No one succeeds until he meets another shepherd who plays a *ciobaneasca* (shepherd's dance) and cheers him up. In the end he finds his sheep devoured by wolves.

Rituals

Many of the ritual customs that survive all over Romania, particularly around Christmas and New Year, have their origins in pre-Christian rites. **Carol-singing** takes place just before Christmas as bands of singers go from house to house with good-luck songs (*colinde*). The custom is something like wassailing in Britain but the songs are nothing like the religious carols of the West. These are pagan songs for the celebration of the mid-winter solstice: Christ does not feature, and the tales instead are of such things as legendary battles between folk heroes and lions or stags. What is remarkable is that so many of the pagan texts have survived undisturbed. In performance they have a fiery character rather than a pious or religious one and are sung with a strong, irregular rhythm. The tradition predominates in the western half of the country.

The coming of New Year is traditionally celebrated with **masked dances** and the **capra** or goat ritual. The goat is both a costume with hair and horns and a musical instrument as the animal's wooden muzzle is articulated so its jaws can clack together in time with the music. The ritual goes back, like similar customs all over Europe, to ancient fertility rites as the old year suffers its death agony. The noise of bells and clappers was supposed to frighten evil spirits and drive them away. The goat is also mirrored in the devil figures painted in local churches.

The goat dances are most thriving in Moldavia where the custom has expanded into full-scale carnivals with music, costumes and political satires bringing its message very much up to date. In the towns, groups of costumed youths have taken to leaping on board trains and intimidating passengers with performances.

The Pipes of Pan

Romania's best-known musician on the international stage is **Gheorghe Zamfir**, composer of the ethereal soundtrack of the film *Picnic at Hanging Rock*. He plays *nai*, or **panpipes**, which are thought to have existed in Romania since ancient times – there's a famous Roman bas-relief in Oltenia. The word nai, however, comes from Turkish or Arabic, so perhaps an indigenous instrument existed as well as a similar one brought by professional musicians from Istanbul where they were used in classical ensembles.

In the eighteenth century, Wallachian musicians were renowned abroad and the typical ensemble consisted of violin, nai and cobză. But by the end of the following century the nai began to disappear and after the First World War only a handful of players were left. One of these was **Fanica Luca** (1894–1968), a legendary nai player who taught Zamfir his traditional repertoire. Nowadays, Zamfir plays material from all over the place, often accompanied by the organ of Frenchman **Marcel Cellier** (of Bulgarian mystery voices fame). In other hands, the nai has become largely associated with tatty urban orchestras.

Festivals

Bucharest Sărbătoarea muzicii (Musical Feast). 21 June at the Muzeul Țăranului (Peasants Museum). Although the idea of a festival in the capital is rather artificial the music is always good, as Speranța Rădulescu, who works at the Peasants Museum, is the leading Romanian ethnomusicologist and knows the best musicians. Details: fax (40) 1 312 9875

Regional Festivals: There are numerous regional festivals, although many verge on the kitsch. Information should be available from the Centrul de Conservare a Tradițiilor; fax (40) 1 222 7706

discography

General Compilations

Romania: Musical Travelogue
(Auvidis/Silex, France).

An excellent disc in this series with music from Banat, Maramureș, and Wallachia. It incldues good examples of a 'violin with a horn', some ethnic minorities music, and beautiful cobză playing by Dan Voinicu; the disc is weak, however, on the main Transylvanian and Wallachian styles.

Romania: Wild Sounds from Transylvania, Wallachia & Moldavia
(World Network, Germany).

Number 41 in Network's global survey, this is the best overall anthology of Romanian music. It includes a few examples of rather arranged Communist-style performances, but there are great ensembles from Transylvania and Wallachia (including the Taraf de Haidouks), the Moldavian Fanfare Ciocărlia, and samples of taragot and a 'violin with a horn'.

Village Music from Romania
(AIMP/VDE-Gallo, Switzerland).

A three-CD box produced by the Geneva Ethnographic Museum. Archival recordings of specialised interest made by the musicologist Constantin Brailoiu in 1933–43 on his travels around Moldavia, Oltenia and Transylvania.

Transylvania

Fonó Records of Budapest (fax (36) 1 206 6296, email *fono@mail.c3.hu*) have a series of discs called 'New Patria', documenting the last remaining Hungarian Transylvanian bands.

Compilations

The Blues at Dawn (Fonó/ABT, Hungary).

A beautifully produced CD of the slow, melancholy *hajnali* (morning songs) from Kalotaszeg. They are sung by two native Kalotaszegi singers with guests Márta Sebestyén and András Berecz from Budapest. The excellent fiddler Sándor 'Neti' Fodor leads the band.

The Edge of the Forest: Romanian Music from Transylvania (Music of the World, US).

There are two good Music of the World discs of Romanian music, this one covering Transylvania and the other Wallachia. Included here are dances from southern districts of Maramureș (Codru and Chioar) where the style belongs to the central Transylvanian tradition, several lyrical songs and a couple of tracks from Maramureș proper and Oaș.

Fiddle Music From Maramureș (Steel Carpet, UK).

An excellent survey of different fiddle players of the Mara Valley, recorded by Lucy Castle who is playing and studying the music of the region. Real peasant fiddlers, recorded in their own homes – a great way inside this musical microcosm. (Steel Carpet Music, 190 Burton Rd., Derby DE1 1TQ ☎ 01332 346399).

Magyarszovát – Búza (Fonó, Hungary).

A double CD featuring Hungarian music performed by village musicians and singers from two villages in Mezőség. It features dance sequences and many unaccompanied songs which are, perhaps, more of an acquired taste.

Musiques de Mariage de Maramureș
(Ocora, Franco).

A good selection of Maramureș dance music, captured at three village weddings.

Musiques de Mariage et de Fêtes Roumaines
(Arion, France).

Here is the largest selection of the extraordinary music from Oaș on disc played by the Pitigoi brothers. Also a good selection of music from Maramureș and Bihor.

Musiques de Transylvanie (Fonti Musicali, Belgium).

One of the best introductions to Transylvanian music featuring a mostly Hungarian repertoire played by the best musicians on Budapest's tánchaz scene. Includes great music from Kalotaszeg, Mezőség, Gyimes plus Romanian dances from Bihor and Moldavia.

Romania: Music for Strings from Transylvania
(Chant du Monde, France).

A great collection of dance music played by village bands from the Cîmpia Transilvaniei, Maramureș and Oaș. Excellent notes and photos, too.

La Vraie Tradition de Transylvanie
(Ocora, France).

A pioneering disc when it was first made in the 1970s as it highlights real peasant music from Maramureș and Transylvania when sanitised folklore was prevalent. It features some excellent ensembles, bagpipes and a violin with a horn, and from Maramureș there's a track from Gheorghe Covaci, the son of a fiddler Bartók recorded in 1913.

Artists

Budatelke Band

The village band from the village of Budatelke (Budești in Romanian) in northern Mezőség, led by Ioan 'Nuncu' Hârlet.

Budatelke – Szászszantgyörgy (Fonó, Budapest).

The second of the New Patria series archiving Transylvania's village bands. The band play mainly Romanian repertoire plus

Hungarian, Gypsy and Saxon tracks. Includes a version of the ubiquitous shepherd searching for his sheep.

Sándor 'Neti' Fodor

Neti Fodor (born 1922) is the most respected Gypsy fiddler of the Kalotaszeg region.

 Hungarian Music from Transylvania: Sándor Fodor (Hungaroton, Hungary).

On this compelling disc of both Hungarian and Romanian music from Kalotaszeg, Neti plays with some of the best tánchaz musicians from Budapest – who've become his disciples. The energy and bite is fantastic. One of the essential Transylvanian records.

Mihály Halmágyi

Halmágyi is a veteran player of Csángó violin music from Gyimes. He plays a five-stringed fiddle, the extra string running under the playing strings to add overtones and fill out the sound. He was for years accompanied on the gardon by his wife Gizella Adám, who recently died.

🔘 **Hungarian Music from Gyimes: Mihály Halmágyi** (Hungaroton, Hungary).

Dance, wedding and funeral tunes played on fiddle and gardon. Strange and wild music. A great performance of the shepherd and his lost sheep.

Iza

This Maramureş-based group led by zougoră-player Ioan Pop, with various fiddlers and drummer Ioan Petreuş, is trying to keep the traditional style intact.

🔘 **Christmas in Maramureş** (Buda/Musique du Monde, France).

Although recorded in Bucharest, this disc has all the flavour of a real Maramureş occasion. It comes with excellent notes and translations.

The Mácsingó Family

One of the important musical Gypsy families from central Transylvania based in the villages of Báré (Bărăi in Romanian) and Déva. György Mácsingó leads the band.

🔘 **Báré – Magyarpalatka** (Fono, Hungary).

Of the 'New Patria' recordings released so far this is the place to start. It may be too raw for some tastes – the bass saws, grates and often slides onto its notes and the lead fiddle is heavily ornamented drawing energy and emotion out of every note – but this is the real thing. The band comprises two fiddles, two contras and bass and offers up Hungarian, Romanian and Gypsy dance sets plus a couple of songs.

Muzsikás

Hungary's leading tánchaz band and the leading ambassadors of Transylvanian music. See Hungary discography (p.165) for more recommendations.

🔘 **Máramaros – The Lost Jewish Music of Tansylvania** (Hannibal/Ryko, UK).

Music from a tragically vanished people in Transylvania revived with the help of two veteran Gypsy musicians who played alongside Jews before the war. For more on this and the Jewish music of eastern Europe see the Klezmer article in *The Rough Guide to World Music Volume 2*.

Ökrös Ensemble

Csaba Ökrös is a tremendous fiddler and his traditional ensemble is one of the best Budapest tánchaz groups. They often work together with village musicians from Transylvania.

🔘 **Transylvanian Portraits** (Koch, US).

A fine survey of Transylvanian music from one of Budapest's best groups, the Ökrös Ensemble, with vocals by Márta Sebestyén. Mainly Hungarian repertoire including violin and gardon music from Gyimes and Csángó songs. The fiddle-playing of Csaba Ökrös on the last track ("The shepherd losing his Sheep") is stunning.

Palatca Band

Probably the most celebrated band of central Transylvania, led by members of the Codoba family in the vilage of Magyarpalatka.

🔘 **Magyarpalatka – Hungarian Folk Music from the Transylvanian Heath** (Hungaroton, Hungary).

A beatutiful selection of traditional dance sets recorded over the years by this seminal band. Their typical line up comprises two fiddles, two contra and bass.

Soporu Band

Soporu are one of the fine Gypsy bands from the Cîmpia Transilvaniei, led by Şandorică Ciurcui.

🔘 **Taraful Soporu de Cîmpie** (Buda/Musique du Monde, France).

Several suites of dance tunes and songs sung by Vasile Soporan.

Szászcsávás Band

Szászcsávás (Ceuaş in Romanian) is a predominantly Hungarian village in the Kis-Küküllő region of Transylvania. Their Gypsy band, led by István "Dumnezu" Jámbor, is one of the best in the region.

🔘 **Folk Music from Transylvania: Szászcsávás Band** (Quintana/Harmonia Mundi, France).

This is a great recording of a real village band with a wide dance repertoire, including Hungarian, Romanian, Saxon and Gypsy tunes.

Váralmási Band

This band from Váralmási (Almaşu in Romanian) was one of the last old-time groups of the Kalotaszeg region.

🔘 **Váralmási Pici Aladárés bandája** (Fonó, Budapest).

The first recording in the New Patria series of 'Final Hour' recordings of Transylvanian bands. Includes Hungarian and Romanian dances plus a bizarre Jewish tango. Zágor Aladár, the *primás* (leader), died shortly after the recording was made in October 1997.

Lowland Music

Compilations

🔘 **Romania: Wedding Music from Wallachia** (Auvidis/Ethnic, France).

A selection of songs and dance tunes from various bands including members of the Taraf de Haidouks and more urban repertoire from Ion Albeşteanu. The Music of the World disc below covers similar repertoire and is more attractive.

⊚ **Taraf: Romanian Gypsy Music**
(Music of the World, US).

Companion to the Transylvanian disc above and a very good selection of tracks from various Wallachian Tarafuri including members of the Taraf de Haidouks. Mostly small ensembles of a couple of violins, ţambal and bass. The cobză lute appears on a couple of tracks.

Artists

Ion Albeşteanu

Albeşteanu (born in the 1930s, died 1998) was born into a large family of lăutari and learned to play all the instruments, although he became known as a violinist and singer. He worked in Bucharest in the officially promoted folklore of the Ceauşescu period, but was also able to maintain the genuine style. Good notes.

⊚ **The Districts of Yesteryears**
(Buda/Musique du Monde, France).

The pieces on this disc aim to recreate the music of the out lying districts of Bucharest in the years 1920–70. Albeşteanu is a good singer, with a pleasant and idiomatic voice, an expressive fiddler and is accompanied by a good band of musicians with beautifully textured ţambal, accordion and the fine cobză playing of Marin Cotaoanţă. "At the Reed House", sung in an intimate, "head voice" is quite beautiful.

Taraf de Caransebeş

A five-piece Gypsy band from a town in the Banat region in the western region of neighbouring Serbia, led by saxophonist Constantin Ciurariu.

 Musiciens du Banat
(Auvidis/Silex, France).

Some stunning virtuoso playing of dance tunes which is enough to explain the popularity of the Banat style. The line-up includes saxophone, trumpet, clarinet, accordion and bass, plus occasional taragot and nai.

Taraf de Haidouks

Romania's most recorded Gypsy band from the village of Clejani near Bucharest. In a succession of discs from 1988 to 1998 you can trace the dynamic development of Gypsy music in Wallachia as new styles are absorbed without ever diluting the distinctive flavour of the taraf.

 Honourable Brigands, Magic Horses and Evil Eye (Crammed Discs, Belgium).

It's hard to choose between any of the Taraf's discs – every one has its strengths: 1998's *Dumbala Duma* for its contributions from the Ursari Gypsies with their vocal percussion and female vocalist Viorica Rudăreasa, and 1991's *Taraf de Haidouks* with its inimitable "Ballad of the Dictator" and old-style playing of Nicolae Neaşcu. But the 1994 release, *Honourable Brigands* is most essential, for its beautiful old-

style songs and dances and wild Geamparale and Turcească from the new generation.

⊚ **Roumanie: Les Lăutari de Clejani** (Ocora, France).

This was the disc that started it all off, recorded in 1988. Great songs, doinas and dance music before the taraf were sharpened up by international touring.

Fanfare Ciocărlia

This brass band from the Moldavian village of Zece Prăjini are perhaps the last representatives of a tradition.

⊚ **Radio Pa cani** (Piranha, Germany).

A frenetic romp, punchily recorded, through some fearsomely fast dance numbers – rusasca, sîrba, bâtută, geamparale and a wonderful foxtrot plus "Nicoleta" which sounds like it's straight from the repertoire of Serbian or Macedonian bands. And of course Ciocârlia, from which they take their name. The pace occasionally breaks for a doina.

⊚ **Zece Prăjini's Peasant Brass Band**
(Buda/Musique du Monde, France) .

This more traditional set, with a slightly different line-up, is also pretty good.

Nicolae Gutsa

A Gypsy singer, Nicolae Gutsa was born near Petroşeni in 1967 and now works in Timişoara in the Banat region of western Romania. A very popular singer, he performs traditional music in a contemporary style.

⊚ **The Greatest Living Gypsy Voice**
(Auvidis/Silex, France).

Despite the absurd title, this is a great disc with excellent vocals and some wild instrumental playing, notably from Ion Trifoi on violin and Remus Kiroaci on sax in a band that also includes piano accordion, guitar and synth.

Trio Pandelescu

Vasile Pandelescu (born in 1944) is a virtuoso accordionist who played for many years in a group with Gheorghe Zamfir. His trio includes double bass and Vasile's son Costel on ţambal.

⊚ **Trio Pandelescu** (Auvidis/Silex, France).

A really attractive disc recorded live with high-quality, intimate playing, delicate moments of real poetry, and all the requisite fire. It includes a couple of beautiful solo ţambal tracks.

Gheorghe Zamfir

Born in Bucharest in 1941, nai panpipe player Zamfir must be Romania's most recorded musician. He has literally dozens of albums with panpipe arrangements of anything from Vivaldi to Andrew Lloyd Webber.

⊚ **The Heart of Romania** (Pierre Verany, France).

Easy-listening, Romanian style. Zamfir's music has little to do with the traditional music of Romania, but his arrangements of doinas and folktunes have an ethereal beauty. Accompanied by Marcel Cellier on the organ.

Russia

music of the people

"Music is created by the people, we artists only arrange it," said the nineteenth-century Russian nationalist composer Mikhail Glinka, a sentiment taken to extraordinary lengths by Communist ensembles like the Red Army Choir to make a national music. This, of course, has little to do with the people's real music – the songs that grew naturally out of their lives, their dances, shamanistic rituals, bylinas and epic songs. Amazingly, some of that deeply rooted music has survived seventy years of Communism and state interference – and there's a growing interest in ethnic and regional sounds in concert. **Simon Broughton** and **Tatiana Didenko** chart the uneasy relationship between the people's music and the state.

t's hard to generalise about the music of a country that stretches about 7500 km from St Petersburg in the west to the icy Kamchatka peninsula in the east. But the very size of this terrain is perhaps the chief reason why more than remnants of authentic traditional music endured through collectivisation, industrialisation and seventy years of Communist ideology.

The traditions of the Soviet Republics, music included, had an obvious political dimension and were pressed into service by the state, from the revolution on. But the rural customs of Russia itself were less pressured. You can go out into the Russian countryside today – and all Russians will tell you that the countryside is the *real* Russia – and find groups of babushkas singing seasonal songs at village parties or local folk ensembles, much as they did a century ago. There are even a few folk instrumentalists to be found, playing traditional melodies on flutes, horns, violins and accordions, though the dominant strand of Russian folk music, however, is choral singing – usually by women.

This singing takes on different styles depending on the region; the voices tend to move together in the north and divide into solo and chorus in the south. The repertoire ranges from plaintive laments (*plachi*), wedding songs and lyrical songs to the humorous and satirical *chastushki*, often with backing from accordion or balalaika, while the chief dances are the funky, foot-stomping *khorovodi* round-dances.

The areas where the strongest regional traditions survive are southern Russia (the districts of Belgorod, Voronezh and Kursk); the north around Archangelsk; the central Volga region; and Siberia (see box on p.252), where extraordinary shamanist rites and musical styles persist.

There is also a strong and distinct musical tradition in the autonomous republic of **Tuva**, which lies within the Russian Federation, though its celebrated music and overtone singing – hugely successful on the World Music circuit – is Central Asian in character. (It is dealt with in an entry on Mongolia and Tuva in *The Rough Guide to World Music Volume 2*).

Roots and Composers

You're very unlikely to encounter any of the real Russian traditional music unless you arrange to go with somebody who knows when and where to find it. What you can hear easily enough, on a visit or on disc, are the versions of Russian folk played by **professional groups**. These are by no means all Communist fakelore; indeed, they have a surprisingly long pedigree of their own, rooted in the whole development of Russian music – folk, religious and classical.

Going back to medieval times, the first **church singers** who turned into 'composers' and used a primitive hook-like system of notation for their chants were the same rural people who were creating the folklore. These original composers started their 'professional' composing equipped with the modes and intonations they inherited from calendar and ritual songs.

This is why the modal structure of monophonic church singing is so similar to that of folk tunes. Such 'professional' musicians travelled as their lords' serfs to distant lands and brought foreign influences into their tunes, performed on traditional instruments like wooden pipes and *gusli* (a folk zither or psaltery). Out of this came the first 'professionally trained' Russian composers like Maxim Berezovsky (1745–1777).

Most of the famous Russian composers of the nineteenth century maintained close ties with the rural tradition – this is true of Glinka, Balakirev, Tchaikovsky, Rimsky-Korsakov, Musorgsky and Stravinsky. Well-to-do children tended to spend their summers in the country, immersed in the natural sound environment of folk tunes, and in the nineteenth century country people were regular visitors to city markets and fairs. Each of these composers' experience was strongly enriched by a substantial stream of folklore.

State Ensembles

As early as the mid-nineteenth century Russian folklore came under the guardianship and protection of the state as part of the so-called 'national revival' and Count Uvarov's patriotic campaign of Orthodoxy-Autocracy-Nationality.

At the end of the century, in the wake of this national cultural revival, the musician **Vassily Andreyev** founded the first professional orchestra of traditional Russian instruments. He'd heard a **balalaika** (the three stringed triangular guitar) in a village somewhere and decided to reconstruct it. He made a few models in different sizes, taught a company of grenadiers to play the instrument and took them to Paris to display Russian exotica. The repertoire of Andreyev's orchestra was based on his arrangements of Russian folk songs and dances.

This was not authentic folk music performed by peasants, but arrangements performed by musicians far from the genuine tradition. As such it was a direct antecedent to the Communist 'fakelore'. Indeed, the famous Red Army Choir which (vocally) conquered the world in the 1960s and '70s was a fairly logical development from Andreyev's Orchestra.

In the early 1900s **Mitrofan Pyatnitsky** – a great connoisseur and admirer of Russian folk song – formed what was later to become the **Pyatnitsky Choir**. This originally recruited only genuine peasant singers and its repertoire and performance was a reflection of a vibrant and living musical culture, but in time it became just another state ensemble performing compositions *à la russe*. By the 1940s such **pseudo folk music** was institionalised and the country was flooded with folk music and dance ensembles singing "Kalinka", "Katyusha" and the "Volga Boatman" – popular Russian songs taking their place alongside the ubiquitous Matriozhka dolls.

It's sad that this attitude to tradition – servile to officialdom – prevailed despite a profound perception of folk music by Russian composers and ethnomusicologists. At the end of the nineteenth century oral musical tradition was attracting the attention of both practising musicians and music scholars. The advent of the phonograph made it possible to document the music of Russian peasants in its full authenticity. From 1899 expeditions resulted in field recordings which were regularly published with academic commentaries. But despite this, the gap between genuine folklore and its official presentation was growing and the genuine forms, having been plundered for their melodies, were increasingly left out in the cold.

Reviving the Tradition

Luckily, an interest in the revival of the real tradition did not have to wait for the fall of Communism, although perhaps the death of Stalin in 1953 helped things along. In 1958 a young singer called **Vyacheslav Shchurov** came back from a field trip with his teacher Anna Rudneva, a folk researcher. A gifted singer with a strong voice, Shchurov was so charmed by the singing of Arkhangelsk peasants that he took it up himself. He joined forces with two friends who put on performances as a trio and, without quite realising what they were doing, instigated a small revolution of authenticity.

In 1966, Shchurov, who by then had become a professional ethnomusicologist, organised a series of concerts in the Composers' House in Moscow to which he invited authentic singers from all over Russia. In 1968 he went on to create his own ensemble with graduates of the Gnesin Musical Institute in Moscow. They were all involved in recreating authentic singing and performed songs from various regions of Russia.

The Dmitri Pokrovsky Singers

JAK KILBY

Sergei Starostin and a Trinity Sunday Trip

An overnight train southwest from Moscow with musicologist Sergei Starostin and TV-producer Tatiana Didenko to hear music over the weekend of Trinity Sunday in the Kaluga district. In the countryside there's no mistaking Russia's expanse – the endless forests and plains, baking in June sunshine under a vast sky with puffy clouds. We stop in a wooded glade beside a small pond. I've never seen so many mosquitoes in my life. While I'm swotting them off my face and neck, Sergei pulls out a pocket knife and cuts young branches from a 'wolf berry' tree. He cuts away at the branches to find the right one to make a reed for the *rozhok*, a cow's horn he has in his pocket. Shaving the reed down to the right size, he inserts it and the horn sounds bright and strong – a sound that has echoed across these lands for centuries. Starostin plays a wonderful assortment of home-made horns and flutes, as well as one of the oldest instruments of medieval Rus, the gusle, which he also made himself.

Sergei Starostin

During the Soviet period many of these seasonal events managed to continue, Starostin explained to me. "Very often they just changed the names, so instead of a 'Trinity celebration' it was called the 'Birch tree celebration'. This is the time of year when the new leaves are appearing on the birch trees. The irony is that many years ago religious festivals of the Orthodox Church often coincided with the older pagan ones, with the result that a great many Russian traditions have Christian names, but pagan contents. For seventy years it was really difficult to actively celebrate Easter, Christmas and Trinity – although the Communists tolerated Maslennitsa (Shrove Tuesday) because it was purely pagan. Now a lot of folk festivals have appeared around Christian events. Just in the Kaluga district there are seven Trinity festivals."

On the tour bus

Although a good deal of music seems to have survived the Soviet system, the state system has had far-reaching effects. For years music has been organised by 'folklore collectives' and they continue to organise it. Even when there are more spontaneous musical events it's usually members of the folklore collectives who are responsible. Also, Starostin says, the influence on the repertoire has been a lasting one: "The authorities always had a view about what you should sing in a village, in a city or in a factory. For the village they created *kolkhoz* (collective farm) songs about the wide fields, beautiful rivers and how well they were living thanks to the Party, etc. It may seem strange, but many of these songs became very popular in the villages – and still are – although they have nothing to do with the traditional or local styles. In fact, because Russia is so vast the styles of singing vary enormously. Sometimes in neighbouring villages they do not sing the same way and between southern and central Russia there may be no points of contact at all, except the type of song."

The Trinity celebrations took place in a lush meadow beside a river. There was a market with bread, cheese, drinks and trinkets sold from the backs of vans. At the climax a young birch tree was launched into the river and wreathes of yellow flowers thrown after it. This was the farewell to spring and the beginning of summer. Away from the festivities we listened to small groups of old ladies singing the songs – in their wooden houses, in the fields, in a coach. It was extraordinary. There was a grandmotherly love for, and familiarity with, this music and the singing often broke into hilarious laughter. It was an important reminder of just how different this music is to that presented on stage, something Starostin links to the symbolic importance of the circle in Russian culture: "The circle is the basis of most Russian dances and songs. The circle holds the energy of the performance and it is directed towards the centre. The audience is the performers themselves. On stage you need to face the audience – then you break the circle, the energy goes away and practically nothing is left."

Simon Broughton

Shchurov paved the way for the **Dmitri Pokrovsky Ensemble** which was formed a few years later. The Ensemble's repertoire consisted of Russian peasant songs brought back by its members from their field expeditions. Pokrovsky's musicians talked to peasant singers, recorded their singing and transcribed their songs. By immersing themselves deeply in the authentic scene, they drew upon its wealth and were able to transfer the genuine folk tradition onto the professional stage. The Pokrovsky Ensemble also influenced other spheres of music. There were memorable collaborations, for instance, with jazz groups Arkhangelsk, Arsenal and the Ganelin Trio. Musicians of different persuasions instantly found a common language, not in the *à la russe* cliches, but in the spirit of collective improvisation.

In the 1970s and '80s the Dmitry Pokrovsky Ensemble was very active. The new wave of 'singing' ethnomusicologists, initiated by Shchurov, gave birth to a new trend among young urban intellectuals. First informally and then on a more organised level, folk ensembles went out to research folk music in the countryside and came back to recreate it in the cities. In Moscow these ensembles united into the **Union of Amateur Folk Ensembles**. The movement remained grassroots and made no attempt to make it onto the professional scene.

AZZURO MATTO/VDE-GALLO

Pesen Zemli Ensemble

At the same time another generation of professional 'folk artists' was gaining prominence with state backing. These ranged from out and out kitsch – chief offenders here included Lydmila Zykina, Russkaya Pesnya Ensemble, and Zolotoye Koltso – through ensembles who kept a respectful attitude to their material. The latter included Evgenia Zosimova's **Karagod**, Gennady Rudnev's **Slavichi**, Maria Chekareva's **Slavyanskaya Kumirnia**, Marina Kapuro's **Yabloko** and Evgenia Smolianinova, all of whom managed to retain the charm of genuine and authentic musicmaking.

New Russia

In the late 1980s two more authentic-minded groups appeared on the scene: **Pesen Zemli** (aka Narodnyi Prazdnik), and **Kazachy Krug**, specialising in Cossack songs. Both based their work on studies of authentic folk music. The leaders of Narodnyi Prazdnik, Ekaterina Dorokhova and Evgenia Kostina, are professional ethnomusicologists who each year embark on expeditions to research and record folk songs in the regions of Kursk, Bryansk and Belgorod, transcribing songs and later including them in the repertoire of their ensemble. Most importantly, they sing together with authentic folk singers. It's amazing that the authentic tradition still survives, but it does, particularly in these regions, and it's likely that the revivalists are saving the traditional songs. Even in the countryside there are less and less people who remember and sing the genuine folk music.

The **Pokrovsky Ensemble** is also slowly coming back to life. After the untimely death of its leader the musicians split into two halves, led by Tamar Smyslova and Olga Yukecheva, and these have since led to further offshoots. They include Andrey Kotov and his group **Sirin** who specialise in recreating early religious Russian Orthodox singing, as well as non-religious songs such as the so-called 'spiritual verses'. Another former member of the

Pokrovsky, singer and instrumentalist **Boris Bazurov**, is an exceptional connoisseur of old Russian instruments. He develops and expands the possibilities of these not just as a musician but as an instrument-maker. He restores old instruments he can find, and also reconstructs instruments known only through reminiscences and descriptions. Bazurov writes music for his own group **Narodnaya Opera** and provided music for the soundtrack of Andrey Konchalovsky's film *Kurochka Ryaba*.

Far removed from the traditional revival is the **Terem Quartet** from St Petersburg who have played great concerts at WOMAD events and recorded for the RealWorld record label. Their music doesn't try to be authentic or traditional. It's just wild, eclectic and great fun. The four members of the band trained at the (then) Leningrad Conservatoire and play their instruments – accordion, two *domras* (a three-stringed mandolin and the forerunner of the balalaika) and a huge bass balalaika – with astonishing panache and virtuosity. Their repertoire includes Russian popular songs, pastiches, classical arrangements and their own compositions.

Folk rock singer Inna Zhelaniya

Another current name on the folk-rock scene is **Inna Zhelaniya**, who again has recorded and toured abroad. Her songs cut a path between archaic Russian singing and the spirit of Joan Baez. The ethnic beauty of her band is strongly enhanced by specifically Russian instrumental arrangements with **Sergei Starostin** on various flutes and pipes (see box on p.250).

One of Russia's leading folk instrumentalists, Starostin is also a singer, arranger and member of the **Moscow Art Trio** (with pianist Mikhail Alperin and French horn player Arcady Shilkloper). He's also been behind several fusion projects such as the collaboration between Tuvan group Huun-Huur-Tu and the Bulgarian female choir Angelite (see Bulgarian discography), and the multi-ethnic group **Vershki da Koreshki**.

Sasha Cheparukhin, a promoter staging World Music gigs in Moscow, is optimistic about this new scene, and has noticed a change of attitude and new openness to this music: "There used to be a Moscow arrogance and chauvinism. They would be interested in John Zorn, Michael Nyman or Nick Cave, but not in something from a remote

Siberia's Indigenous World

There are over twenty ethnic groups living in *tundra* (steppe) and *taiga* (forest) in the north of **Siberia** and on the **Sakhalin islands**. They number less than half a million in an area of nearly 17 million square kilometres amongst a Russian population of twenty-five million. Some of the ethnic groups comprise no more than two or three hundred people.

The Soviet system relocated the Siberian villages, brought universal education and collectivised the reindeer farming, breaking the traditional way of life. The music, as elsewhere, was 'folklorised' and 'desacralised' as much of it was connected to shamanism which was forbidden. But **shamanism** is still very much a part of life here, as an enactment of the traditional relationship between nature and its inhabitants. People worship their environment through singing and drumming. They defy the permafrost, wind and thunder through songs, drums and instruments. With their voices and simple accompaniment they are the best imitators in the world, recreating the sounds of the forest, the steppe and the

animals they hunt. They drink too much and have a high suicide rate, but they keep on singing of their lives.

The 400,000 **Yakuts** (or Sakhas) live in a republic the size of India and are the biggest indigenous group in Siberia. They are famed for playing the *khomus* (jew's harp) and for their *olonkho* epic songs. The **Buriats** in south Siberia, the other large group, sing unaccompanied songs and play a stately spike fiddle related to central Asian instruments. The various **Tungus** people in the far east can produce extraordinary imitations of animals and nature with voice, horns and drums. And the **Nganasan** in the far north are best known for their shamanistic practices.

Over the past few years the French musicologist Henri Lecomte has been working on a series of recordings for the Buda label, presenting a detailed musical survey of Siberia's ethnic groups; it runs so far to six CDs.

Etienne Bours

undeveloped region of Russia. In fact, folk music is much more popular in Moscow than I thought and we've filled the Tchaikovsky Concert Hall for these fusion events. I'd say there's a revitalisation of interest in a diversity of music."

This article is in memory of Tatiana Didenko who died in 1998. She devoted so much of her time and energy to bringing Russian traditional music to a wider audience through her 'Global Village' series on Russian TV (which was always under threat from the bosses) and always knew how to make the most of the good things in life. With thanks to Alexander Kan for the translation.

discography

Compilations

Chants des femmes de la vielle Russe (Inédit, France).

Women's choirs from Bryansk (in the west), Kieba (in the north) and a village in Siberia near Lake Baikal where the women are descendants of prisoners exiled in Tsarist days and who have kept a rich harmonic music distinct from the surrounding Buriat people. Strong unaccompanied performances.

Old Believers: Songs of the Nekrasov Cossacks (Smithsonian Folkways, US).

Liturgical songs, spiritual verses, bylinas (epic songs), laments, wedding and lyrical songs from an amazing group of Don Cossacks who fled Russia (as Old Believers) during the religious reforms of the seventeenth century and returned to their current home near Stavropol in southern Russia in 1962. The recordings, of male and female singers, made by Margarita Mazo in 1989 and 1990 are by no means easy listening but are of great historical and musical importance, and accompanied by a detailed booklet.

Sigrai, Vanya: Play Vanya (Pan, Netherlands).

A pretty rare recording of Russian traditional instrumental music played by village musicians. Folk flutes, pipes and horns from the south, a couple of violinists from Smolensk district, and balalaika musicians playing dance tunes, chastushki and so on. Good notes, but a shame that the cover photos on these two Pan discs seem to have got mixed up so that the full-throated babushkas appear on the instrumental disc and the accordionist on the vocal one.

Tam Letal Pavlin: A Peacock Once Went Flying (Pan, Netherlands).

The second of a pair of discs of the vocal and instrumental music of southern Russia. This features vocal music sung by various local groups from the Belgorod region invited to record in Moscow by Shchurov. Outdoor songs for festivals, Christian ritual songs, wedding songs and songs for evening gatherings.

Artists

Moscow Art Trio

The Moscow Art Trio unites three musicians from three different musical disciplines: folk singer and instrumentalist

Sergei Starostin, jazz pianist and composer Mikhail Alperin, and classical French horn player Arkady Shilkloper. As a group they've worked with Tuvans Huun-Huur-Tu and other groups.

Prayer (Auvidis/Silex, France).

A slightly New Age evocation of the ancient depths of Russian music – Starostin plays some of his home-made flutes, a slow Russian melody on the horn emerges over a jazz piano ostinato and Russian folk singers and Tuvan throat singers also get in on the act.

Pesen Zemli Ensemble

This ensemble (the name means Voices of the Earth) was founded in Moscow in 1982 by Ekaterina Dorokhova and Evgenia Kostina. Where possible, the ten (or so) women members of the choir learn the songs directly from the village singers.

 Russia: Polyphonic Wedding Songs (VDE-Gallo/AIMP, Switzerland).

It's indicative of just how difficult it is to get good quality field recordings in Russia that this label (which usually features the real thing) has gone for a trained ensemble. But these wedding songs are very hard to hear in Russia now – and here there's a good spread from western, northern and southern Russia.

Dmitri Pokrovsky Ensemble

Founded in 1973, the ensemble led by Dmitri Pokrovsky (until his death a few years ago) was the best-known group of revivalists trying to recreate an authentic village style. Pokrovsky also released an interesting disc of Stravinsky's "Les Noces" (The Wedding) including village songs musically related to the score.

Faces of Russia (Trikont, Germany).

This recording has the edge over the RealWorld disc (below), for its wider repertoire – including Cossack songs, harvest and wedding songs, religious music and a bizarre instrumental of jew's harp, whistle and clanging rhythms hammered out on a sickle.

The Wild Field (RealWorld, UK).

Another good recording, but one with a limited repertoire, concentrating on vocal music from southern Russia.

Vyacheslav Shchurov

Shchurov (born 1937) was a pioneer in creating a choral group to perform Russian music with some fidelity to the original folk style. He took the recordings or transcriptions of the village songs as his score and refused to arrange them or beautify them as other ensembles did. He started his group Solovka (Nightingale) in 1968.

 Solovka (Pan, Netherlands).

A collection of Melodiya recordings from 1978–85, plus new tracks recorded in 1995, principally of south Russian and Siberian Russian choral songs and some good Chastushki. Shchurov sings lead and solo on several tracks. Real village singing can be quite demanding to listen to, so this makes a good introduction. Several tracks can be found in authentic, village-style performance on Pan's other Russian discs.

Terem Quartet

Created in 1986, the Terem Quartet's four instrumentalists were first spotted on a talent show on Russian TV. Andrei

The Terem Quartet work out

Konstantinov plays soprano domra, Igor Ponomaremko alto domra, Andrei Smirnov accordion and Mikhail Dziudze the huge bass balalaika.

 Terem
(RealWorld, UK).

Post-modern Russian music – the stereotypes and clichés of Soviet style folk music turned on their head. Instead of a vast balalaika orchestra, here is an inventive, witty and nimble chamber group racing through traditional and professionally composed Russian music. Typically St Petersburg.

Volnitza Ensemble

A small group based in Rostov collecting Cossack songs in Russian and Ukrainian in the Don region.

◎ **Chants Cosaques** (Inédit, France).

There's no mistaking that these are formal stage performers, but this disc has a good varied repertoire and committed performances, including some percussion accompaniment.

Inna Zhelaniya

The current folk-rock star of Russian music. She has a strong, warm voice with a cutting edge.

◎ **Inozemetz (Farlanders)** (Green Wave, Russia).

A more adventurous album than her debut *Vodorosl*, with

Sergei Starostin on various conventional and folk winds. Includes a rocked up version of a Christ has Risen Easter song and some much more quirky numbers with distinctive woody and reedy contributions. Worth exploring.

Siberia and Other Minority Groups

Compilations

◎ **Korjak Kamchatka:**
Dance drums from the Siberian Far East
(Buda/Musique du Monde, France).

This is perhaps the most accessible of Henri Lecompte's Siberian series, with its physical dance music from the Kamchatka peninsula in the far east. None of these discs are exactly easy listening but they are well recorded and document music otherwise unavailable to the wider world. Of the other volumes:
Vol 1 features shamanistic and narrative songs of the Nganasan.
Vol 2 Yakut songs, epics and some delicate and skilful overtone playing on the khomus.
Vol 3 songs of nature and animals from people of the Kolyma river in the northeast.
Vol 5 shamanistic songs from the Amur basin.
Vol 6 music from the island of Sakhalin, north of Japan.

◎ **Mother Volga: Music of the Volga Ugrians**
(Pan, Netherlands).

Music of the Finno-Ugrian Mari people and Turkic Chuvash living in the Kazan district on the Volga. Some really archaic instruments, notably the gusle zither and various bagpipes – valuable ethnographic stuff.

◎ **Musiques de la Toundra et de la Taiga**
(Inédit, France).

A selection recorded in Paris of music from the Buriat, Yakut, Tungus, Nenets and Nganasan peoples of Siberia. Includes some stirring Yakut jew's harp playing, and Tungus music imitating the forest and shamanistic tracks.

◎ **Songs of the Volga** (Auvidis/Ethnic, France).

Songs and accordion music from the Turkic Chuvash people and polyphonic songs of the Finno-Ugric Mordvin people from the Volga region. Recordings made in situ with local groups. Includes good notes and lyric translations.

Sámiland (Lapland)

joiks of the tundra

In just about every European country there's a region where things are seen as distinct and somehow more in contact with nature. In Britain it's the Celtic areas. In the Nordic countries they look north to what was known by foreigners as Lapland and is now more usually called Sámiland or Sápmi. Not only is the Arctic tundra here one of Europe's most extreme environments but there's the indigenous Sámi people, with their reindeer-centred lifestyle, and their music which – as **Andrew Cronshaw** finds – can at its most traditional seem so minimalist it could almost be avant-garde, or in the hands of a modern singer like Marie Boine can rock with the best of them.

The last couple of decades have seen a flowering of Sámi music, both traditional and boldly progressive. This and the equally unique visual art are strong foci of modern Sámi identity, both for the people themselves and for foreign perceptions. Despite the relatively small number of Sámi, their art, indeed their very existence, has a far-reaching influence.

The Land and the People

'Sámi' is the name for their people used by Sámi themselves. The word 'Lapp' is thought to derive from an archaic Finnish word with connotations of 'outcast'; it was used by foreigners but not the people themselves, and its use is diminishing.

The Sámi arrived in the far north, it's thought, from the eastern fringes of Europe at least two thousand years ago, probably long before. A thousand years ago they still populated most of Finland, but Finnish tribes, who moved in like the Sámi from the southeast, displaced them from the southerly territories. Present-day Sámiland includes most of the areas of Norway, Sweden, Finland and the Kola peninsula of northwest Russia that lie north of the Arctic Circle, and also territory well south of that in Norway and Sweden. By no means everyone who lives there, though, is Sámi. Estimates vary, but there are 50-75,000 people who might claim that distinction in terms of heredity, lifestyle or language.

These days the traditional occupation of **reindeer-herding** is followed by far fewer people, and the movement with the herds from winter to summer pastures and annual roundups are accomplished to the roar of snowmobiles. Nevertheless, the relationship with reindeer is still an iconic defining feature of the Sámi; indeed in Sweden the Sámi are the only ones legally allowed to own the animals.

The several **Sámi languages**, spoken today by about 20-30,000 people, are Finno-Ugrian, related to Finnish but not understandable to a Finn nor even necessarily to one another – they fall into three mutually non-comprehensible regional groups. The majority speak North Sámi, a language of the Central group.

There has never been a Sámi nation with its own political identity, but there is a considerable sense of solidarity and communication, with a Sámi Parliament in each Nordic country, and the cross-border umbrella organisation of the Nordic Sámi Council. Norway has the largest Sámi population of about 40,000, the majority living in its northernmost county, Finnmark. (Yes, to add further confusion, the Norwegian word for Sámi is 'Finn'!).

The Joik

While individual Sámi might play instruments such as fiddle or accordion – and nowadays also draw on the whole contemporary instrumental range – there is no tradition of Sámi instrumental music, nor any traditional instruments except for the **drum** (see box overpage).

The musical focus is on song – *lavlu* or *laavloe* in Sámi. The most characteristic type of singing is the improvised **joik**, also called in North Sámi *luohti* or in South Sámi *vuolle*. It's hard to give a watertight definition of a joik – there are wide regional differences and it is perhaps more definable by what it isn't than by what it is. It's not a rhyming, formal structured song. The tune can wander, usually with some phrases recurring. A singer improvises a joik to go with whatever he or she is

The Sámi Drum

The word 'shaman' originates with the Tungus people of Siberia but what is generally accepted as shamanism is found in many parts of the world, and drums are widely used to induce the trance under which the shaman makes a spirit journey.

In Sámi custom, there is a second use of the drum, found in few other shamanic traditions – that of divination. The skin of the oval single-headed drum (**kobdas**, or in South Sámi **gievri**) bore pictographic symbols drawn in the red juice from chewed alder-bark. The layout of these varied regionally. A small bone or metal pointer, sometimes with attached chains and charm-shapes, was laid on the skin, which was vibrated with a small T- or Y-shaped hammer so that the pointer moved across it, and the shaman (**nåjde** or **noaite**) drew conclusions from its movement relative to the drawn symbols.

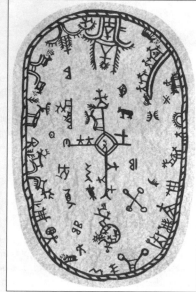

Sami drum skin

The practices of the preceding religion were firmly discouraged by the propagators of Christianity, so by the eighteenth century most of the drums had been destroyed, and the remainder spread across the world in ethnographic collections; only about seventy of these still exist. Nowadays many new ones are being made, but their use is musical or symbolic rather than religious.

Sámi graphic art has a very strong identity, and artists frequently use symbols from the drums. One, the sun and moon circle usually drawn in the centre, is the basis of the Sámi flag, which uses the bright colours of the striking traditional costume. The flag was adopted in 1986 – as was the national anthem, a setting by Arne Sørlie of Isak Saba's 1906 poem *Same soga lavla* (The Song of the Sámi Family).

doing or thinking, or performs it about a person, an animal or a place. Sometimes it'll be a one-off, sometimes parts of it will be remembered and repeated on another occasion and it will become more fixed in form. The singer explores vocal textures – thin, thick, high, low – normally using just a few different notes, sliding between them, chopping them with glottal stops. Sometimes there will be words, perhaps just one, a name for example, repeated from time to time, its sound explored and reinterpreted. There aren't usually a lot of words, or a story, but then again there can be. There are no absolute fixed rules – self-expression is the key.

Though a joik may be sung to or for another person, it's not a performance in the modern sense. A singer will make one which somehow typifies a person, living or dead, and helps remember them. It's a difficult concept to grasp, but joiks are usually said not to be *about* their subject, but rather in some way to *be* the subject. A joik may be a gift, for example to a new-born baby. As a leading modern joiker, **Wimme Saari**, explains: "The mother or father can do it. Then, as the child grows up, more is added to the joik – it grows up as the

child grows up. A joik is like life". Though largely expressive, joiks could also have a function, for example making a sound to discourage wolves from attacking the herd, or attracting a girl across the marketplace.

The joik isn't a creature of the concert hall; its natural environment is outdoors, sung by a person alone while working or travelling, or perhaps over the usual Sámi drink – coffee – at the fireside. When Matts Arnberg, Håkon Unsgaard and Israel Ruong were recording joiks for Swedish radio in the 1950s and '60s (see discography), it was clear, as it had been to others before them (sound recordings were made as far back as 1906) that as far as possible they had to take their bulky equipment to wherever the singers felt most comfortable if the stream of consciousness was to be prompted.

As with many folk forms, researchers have regularly been told that joiking is dying out or is already dead in a particular district. It's true that religious fundamentalism – in northern Sámiland largely Laestadianism, which still has its adherents – often took a dim view of a custom which once had associations with magical, shamanistic practices. Lars

Levi Laestadius of Karesuando, who preached in the nineteenth century – though mostly targeting fiddling and other modern pleasures – sometimes condemned joiking, partly because of the type of joik that tended to emerge under the influence of drink, and many followers regarded it as sinful.

Overall, Sámi art and music these days is a strong force, and a central feature has been widespread interest in *joiku*. The main focus has been on North Sámi luohti, while Swedish South Sámi vuolle has diminished, and the music and culture of the East Sámi of the Russian Kola peninsula are close to extinction. **Wimme Saari**, who comes from Kelottijärvi in northwestern Finnish Sámiland, describes the situation: "In the border areas like ours where there are more Finns and Swedes, joiking has a tendency to vanish, but in the middle, in Sámi areas like Kautokeino, naturally it has been able to survive better, and it's very strong with young people too. Since we've been doing the new modern styles more young people have paid attention, and it's opened their eyes to the old joiking too."

Wimme himself had to piece together his own family tradition: "I started working at the Finnish Broadcasting Company in 1986. There I found some tapes including my uncles joiking. With the help of those tapes I learned some of the old tradition. Although my mother comes from an old joiking family, the direct connection from one generation to another had already been broken. Due to religious fundamentalism there was no joiking at home."

New Developments

What Wimme Saari learned was the North Sámi tradition of luohti, in which the joik normally describes a specific person or animal and the melody sticks fairly rigidly to a pentatonic scale. Since then, however, he has also moved into a freer form, and also joiks over instrumental and electronic textures and rhythms. He has had collaborated in this with Finnish traditional band **Tallari**, Swedish/Finnish roots-rock band **Hedningarna**, and predominantly with Finnish saxophonist **Tapani Rinne** and members of his ambient techno band **RinneRadio** where the sound of the instruments becomes an environment within which to joik:

"When working with musicians, often I close my eyes and listen to what comes from the instruments and samples. Then it's like a building, a dream building in my mind. I can perhaps see a lake, or a tree, or I'm underwater like a fish, swimming against the stream. Sometimes I'm in space,

with the stars. Sometimes it's colours and shapes, and I'm following them with my voice. What I do is the same as the older joikers did, but I'm in the sound world of the instruments, and I must listen."

Since the 1970s the name of poet, designer, artist and singer **Nils–Aslak Valkeapää**, otherwise known as **Áillohaš**, has been at the forefront of Sámi joik and other aspects of Sámi contemporary culture. He has focused attention on its minimalism, simultaneously modern and archaic. His musical collaborators have been saxophonist **Seppo 'Báron' Paakkunainen**, **Esa Kotilainen** and other members of the Finnish exploratory-roots band **Karelia**. Being traditionally a largely outdoor activity, several recordings of joiking feature the natural or contrived sounds of nature. Áillohaš has incorporated them as accompaniments, and on his 1994 album *Goase Dušše* (The Bird Symphony) they constitute the whole piece. In 1992 he produced **Johan Anders Bær**'s album of person-joiks – *Máhkaravju* – which had the continuous accompaniment of a noisy gannet-colony.

These and many other recordings are on one of the leading Sámi record labels, DAT, based in Guovdageaidnu (Kautokeino) in Norwegian Sámiland, which has an ever-growing catalogue of both progressive and traditional unaccompanied joik recordings by Valkeapää, Bær, **Ingor Ántte Áilu Gaup**, **Inga Juuso** and others.

Also working with powerful modern instrumentation is the best-known Sámi singer (though not a joiker as such), **Mari Boine** (see box overleaf). Other singers include **Inga Juuso** – a former journalist with NRK Sámi Radio and ex-member of the Sámi theatre company **Beaivváš** – who has recorded an album of solo joiks and is

Mari Boine

The only way to fully experience **Mari Boine** is live. Her figure in the centre of the band's spacious sound becomes magnetic – the intense bright focus, her wheeling dance with outstretched arms evocative of a gliding bird. Her on-stage persona, the culture she reflects, the sound of her North Sámi language, her joik-rooted exploration of vocal sounds and the powerful, vibrant minimalism, rock-stripped-bare, of the band all contribute to her distinctive position in European music.

Boine belongs very much to the radical Nordic remodelling of jazz and rock and its open relationship with traditional music: a move that involves a shift from the harmonic, chordal structure which has prevailed in Europe for so long, back towards forms drawing their richness from the texture and shape of the note, and their energy from rhythmic stresses and balances. It pulls in ideas from other traditions, many of them fundamentally linear, predominantly monophonic or duophonic, and there are glimpses in the Boine band's instrumental work – only fleetingly discernible and never creating a detour – of Indian, Arabic and Native North and South American musics.

Mari Boine came to the notice of a non-Nordic audience when the album *Gula Gula* was licensed by the Sámi label Iðut to Peter Gabriel's RealWorld. About the same time she was a part of a live worldwide TV musical special. But, as she told me, that wasn't the beginning:

"I started in the late '70s, and I think I started to sing and make music as a therapy for myself. I never planned to be an artist; sometimes, when I think about it, it's crazy that I'm here, and I'm touring, and I'm doing what I'm doing.

"I think I realised, at teachers' training school, that I felt that the culture that I came from, the Sámi culture, was not good enough, so I wanted to be Norwegian or European, I wanted to forget the culture. And then I had to ask myself 'why is this, and what does all this come from?' And after that came a lot of songs. Actually I made my first lyrics to John Lennon's "Working Class Hero"! At that time I don't think I quite understood what he was singing about, but there was something in the music, and I think also my unconscious understood, and I wrote a song about how it was for Sámi children to be placed in the Norwegian school and learn to hate their own background."

But that's changed now hasn't it – there are Sámi schools?

"Yes, there are some Sámi schools, and there is more room for the Sámi culture in the schools. I can see many changes in a good direction. I was working in a school in the Sea Sámi area before I started to sing,

and then there were only a few children who learned the language. These days, there are many more."

Your songs are not traditional joiks – but is it a major influence on your music.

"It's always there. Influences from joik and influences from the Christian hymns (I was brought up in a very Christian family), and I like this mixture. Actually we made a new piece out of six Christian hymns, and then I mixed it with a shamanistic beat, because I like this meeting, when things that you'd expect to be very different, to find the meeting points."

'Shaman' seems to be a word that blurb-writers utter whenever a Sámi bangs a drum.

"Yes, I feel that. I also was afraid of the word shamanism, and I see this stereotype. But I want to fill this word with meaning, because I think through my music I learn to understand, a bit of it, and to get in touch with the spirituality that was in our culture before. I think you can find elements of the shamanistic tradition, of shamanistic music, in my music – the beat, the spirituality. This trance, or this good feeling that I'd call it, it's a way . . . if you go there you can get new energy, but it's not something you just play with.

"For me, I want to have this down-to-earth relationship with the shamanism, because this is what my people had, and also other people who had this religion. I don't want to let it be something mysterious, not able to be caught, not able to be understood. There are some very healing parts in this religion, and I learned something about this in my music but I can't express it in words, I am expressing it in my music."

JAK KILBY

Mari Boine on the drum

a member of Swedish sax and flute player **Anders Hagberg**'s band, which draws on Sámi and Swedish traditional forms and Nordic jazz. She also guested on the album by **Orbina**, a joik-rock band featuring three Mari Boine band members which formed as a result of the meeting in a Beaivváš project of singer **Leif Isak Eide**, Mari Boine guitarist **Roger Ludvigsen** and Norwegian keyboardist **Bjørn Ole Rasch**.

There are meetings of joik and jazz, too. The **Frode Fjellheim Jazz Joik Ensemble** bridged the distance between joik and a Miles Davis kind of approach to jazz-rock with tremendous success. Now renamed Transjoik, it has moved in a more ambient-groove direction. **Johan Sara Jr**. leads a joik-rock band which includes a West African percussionist. **Pål Torbjörn Doj** joiks in South Sámi on Swedish roots techno-rock band Garmarna's *Guds Spelemän* album.

Annel Nieiddat/Angelin Tytöt (girls of Angeli), originally a trio of young Sámi women singers, now consisting of sisters **Ursula** and **Tuuni Länsman** with guitarist **Alfred Hakkinen**, perform an audience-rousing mix of joik-influenced and more conventional rhyming-structure songs. Former member **Ulla Pirttijärvi** has gone on to solo work featuring members of Transjoik and leading Swedish saxophonist Jonas Knutsson.

discography

There's more to traditional solo joik than just the way it sounds, and it's hard to get a real sense of it from a studio recording. Accompanied joik isn't the heart of the tradition, but it can make a much easier access point. If you have difficulty obtaining the discs, try ADA (36 Saturday Market Place, Beverley, Yorks HU17 9AG, UK; ☎/fax 01482 868 024), or *Digelius* (see Finland), or *Rotspel* or *Multikulti* (see Sweden).

Unaccompanied Joik

Compilations

◉ **Yoik: A Presentation of Saami Folk Music** (Caprice, Sweden).

This is unrivalled as a window on the essential nature of joik: a boxed set including a 300-page book in Swedish and English and a triple CD containing all the recordings made on two field trips to Swedish Sámiland in 1953 for the Swedish Broadcasting Company by Matts Arnberg, Håkan Unsgaard and Israel Ruong – 195 joiks, all in all, from 33 Forest and Mountain Sámi. The book puts it all in context and reveals much of the beautiful imagery of the joiks and their insights into the old ways of life.

Dagny Biti Green

Dagny Biti Green is a female joiker from Kárášjohka in northern Norway.

◉ **Bávttajohka** (DAT, Norway).

Twenty-nine solo person-joiks, recorded beside the sea. There's an increasing tendency to record traditional joikers outdoors; as the producer put it – "in a studio the voice becomes narrow."

Johan J. Kemi, Marit Berit Bær and Berit Inga Bær

◉ **Dejoda** (DAT, Norway).

One man and two women performing pentatonic solo joiks. Recorded in Norway in 1993, outdoors.

New Sámi Music

Artists

Johan Anders Bær

Bær is a joiker who has collaborated in many Nils-Aslak Valkeapää projects, and is emerging as a strong voice in contemporary joik.

◉ **Guovssu** (DAT, Norway).

Hefty modern sounds involving musicians, including other Valkeapää collaborators, whose long work with joik forms has given them considerable experience of ways of blending instruments with the elusive essence of joik.

Mari Boine

Mari Boine (Persen) is a riveting live performer and a modern Sámi figurehead, both outside and within Sámiland. She makes no claim to perform joik, but her songs and voice are replete with its spirit. Her band is a real powerhouse, featuring Roger Ludvigsen (guitars), Hege Rimestad (violin), Carlos Quispe (South American notch flutes and charango), Gjermund Silset (bass, hackbrett), Helge Norbakken (percussion).

 Eallin (Antilles, UK; Sonet, Europe).

This is the best introduction: a 1996 live album, with her splendid, intense band. It includes the popular title track of the first of her albums to be released worldwide, 1990's ◉ **Gula Gula** (Iðut, Norway; remixed for RealWorld, UK).

Frode Fjellheim Jazz Joik Ensemble/ Transjoik

The Ensemble (now renamed Transjoik) are an effective meeting of gutty joik with jazz-rock, heartbeat grooves, pinched harmonics, strength, subtlety and variety of texture. They comprise keyboardist/vocalist Fjellheim, guitarist/vocalist Nils Olav Johansen, Håvard Lund (reeds), bassist Torbjørn Hillersøy and percussionists Snorre Bjerck and Tor Haugerud.

FRODE FJELLHEIM JAZZ JOIK ENSEMBLE

 Saajve Dans (Iðut, Norway).

From almost inaudible to threatening, from limpidly melodic to tortured, touching many bases including Miles Davis territory. Largely based on joiks transcribed between 1910–1913. Not rooted exclusively in Sámi music, but too classic to miss.

TRANSJOIK

⊙ **Mahkalahke** (Warner/Atrium, Sweden).

The new band has less eccentricity, personality, variety and surprise, and more emphasis on heavy ambient grooves.

Annel Nieiddat/Angelin Tytöt

Originally three tytöt (girls) from Angeli, now two – Ursula and Tuuni Länsman (vocals and drum) – with Alfred Hakkinen on guitar and drum. They are joik-imbued, but essentially Sámi folk-pop.

⊙ **Skeaikit** (Mipu, Finland).

The group's third album features some straightforward, singing, but has more technological influence than before, with the keyboards and programming of producer-engineer Kimmo Kajasto (of RinneRadio). Also hints of native North American music.

Orbina

Orbina are joiker Leif Isak Eide, Mari Boine band guitarist Roger Ludvigsen, and Sissel/Annbjørg Lien keyboardist Bjørn Ole Rasch.

⊙ **Orbina** (Iðut, Norway).

Big, spacious joik rock on new and traditional themes. With saxophonist Bendik Hofseth, guest joiker Inga Juuso, Mari Boine band rhythm section et al.

Ulla Pirttijärvi

This singer was originally the third member of the group Angelin Tytöt, and now has a solo career.

⊙ **Ruossa Eanan** (Warner/Atrium, Sweden).

An impressive and appealing album with support from a trio from Transjoik, plus leading Swedish saxophonist Jonas

Knutsson, cellist Ørnulf Lillebjerka, and bassist/producer Manne von Ahn Öberg.

Wimme Saari

Wimme is a fine traditional joiker who re-learned the art upon hearing recordings of his uncles. His recorded and live work, with the ambient and techno approaches of RinneRadio and his own band, have made considerable waves in Scandinavia.

⊙ **Gierran** (RockAdillo, Finland).

This 1997 album is a robust and meaningful interaction between voice and strong sounds, with more varied joiking and less drifting ambience than its 1995 predecessor *Wimme*.

Johan Sara Jr. & Group

Sara's group are a five-piece and use largely non-chordal instruments and percussion to accompany traditional and new joiks.

⊙ **Ovcci Vuomi Ovtta Veaiggis** (DAT, Norway).

The instrumentation flows into the joiks, drawing out rhythmic motifs and giving a contemporary accessibility, without cluttering their freedom.

Nils-Aslak Valkeapää

Valkeapää is a major figure in Sámi music, poetry and visual art, and a pioneer of the current creative climate. His regular collaborators have been Finns Seppo Paakkunainen and Esa Kotilainen, who surround his joiks with sound textures of woodwind and reeds, subtle synth and trickling, rattling percussion.

⊙ **Dálveleaikkat: Wintergames** (DAT, Norway).

A good gathering together of what Áillohaš and associates have been evolving over the years. With Paakkunainen and Kotilainen, and fellow-joiker Johan Anders Bær. Centred on music they made for 1994's Lillehammer Winter Olympics.

Scotland

from strathspeys to acid croft

Scottish music is in better health than for decades, with a bedrock of Celtic groups – the likes of Boys of the Lough, Silly Wizard, Tannahill Wavers, and Runrig – storming through traditional material in a blaze of bagpipes and flying fiddles. **Pete Heywood** and **Colin Irwin** survey a new roots culture that seems to have finally shaken off the image of Andy Stewart and Jimmy Shand, with their accordions and sentimental songs of the highlands.

Scotland through the 1980s and '90s saw an explosion of roots and dance music, and, at the same time, a renewal and revisiting of traditions that had seemed perilously close to the edge. As the '90s close, there are a half a dozen Scottish labels devoted entirely to local music; there's a monthly roots magazine, the aptly titled *Living Tradition*, and there's a real sense of a scene – from Glasgow right up to the Shetlands. A new generation of bands and musicians can wear their Scottishness on their sleeves, confident that this is a music at last commanding as much respect as the traditions of Ireland, or even England.

That Scots music had been troubled in the years of Anglo pop and rock dominance was in part, perhaps, due to its nature. A precision is required in traditional Scottish performance – especially in piping – that irons out much of the individual flair of a solo player. But the broadening of the music in the new roots scene, with 'non-traditional' influences coming from Ireland in particular, and from the folk scene in general, has allowed the virtuosity of individual artists to come through.

The Celtic Folk Band Arrives

As in much of northern Europe, the story of Scotland's roots scene begins amid the **'folk revival'** of the 1960s – a time when folk song and traditional music engaged people who did not have strong family links with an ongoing tradition. For many in Scotland, traditional music had skipped a generation and they had to make a conscious effort to learn about it. At first, the main influences were largely American – skiffle music and people like Pete Seeger – but soon people started to look to their own traditions, taking inspiration from the Gaelic songs of **Cathy-Ann McPhee**, then still

current in rural outposts, or the old **travelling singers** – people like the **Stewarts of Blairgowrie**, **Isla Cameron**, **Lizzie Higgins**, and the greatest of them all, Lizzie's mother, **Jeannie Robertson**.

On the instrumental front, there were fewer obvious role models despite the continued presence of a great many people playing in **Scottish dance bands**, **pipe bands** and **Strathspey and Reel Societies** (fiddle orchestras). In the 1960s the action was coming out of Ireland and the recorded repertoire of bands like The Chieftains became the core of many a pub session in Scotland. Even in the early 1970s, folk fiddle players were rare, although **Aly Bain** (see box overleaf) made a huge impression when he came down from Shetland, and soon after, Shetland Reels started to creep into the general folk repertoire.

The 'Celtic Folk Band' was a creation of the 1960s. Previously the art of a traditional musician was essentially a solo one. These days, there is a more or less standard formula with a melody lead – usually fiddle or pipes – plus guitar, bouzouki and a singer. The singer is often just another sound in the band whereas before it was the song that was the focus. Instrumental in these developments was a Glasgow folk group, **The Clutha**, who in a folk scene dominated by singers and guitarists, boasted not one but two fiddlers, along with a concertina, and four strong singers – including the superb **Gordeanna McCulloch**.

The Clutha were hugely influential and became even more successful when **Jimmy Anderson** introduced a set of chamber pipes into the line-up. Jimmy was not only a great piper but was also a pipe maker and he 'invented' a set of pipes to be played in the key of D and which sounded much quieter than the highland pipes. This was essential at that time, as virtually all the venues were acoustic and sound systems were not up to the job

Aly Bain and Shetland Magic

Boys of the Lough with Aly Bain (2nd from left)

Aly Bain has been a minor deity among Scottish musicians for three decades. A fiddle player of exquisite technique and individuality, he has been the driving force of one of Scotland's all-time great bands, Boys of the Lough, throughout that time, while latterly diversifying roles as a TV presenter and author. In these guises, he has been instrumental in spreading the wings of Scottish music to an even greater extent. First and foremost, though, Bain is a Shetlander and his greatest legacy is the inspiration he has provided for a thriving revival of fortunes for Shetland's own characteristic tradition.

Aly was brought up in the capital of Shetland, Lerwick, and was enthused to play the fiddle by **Bob Duncan** – who endlessly played him records by the strathspey king Scott Skinner – and later the old maestro **Tom Anderson**. Duncan and Anderson were the last of an apparently dying breed, and the youthful Aly was an odd sight dragging his fiddle along to join in with the old guys at the Shetland Fiddlers Society. Players like Willie Hunter Jnr and Snr, Willie Pottinger and Alex Hughson were legends locally, but they belonged to another age and the magic of Shetland fiddle playing – one inflected with the eccentricity of the isolated environment and the influence of nearby Scandinavia.

By the time the teenage Aly was persuaded to leave for the mainland, Shetland was changing by the minute, and the discovery of North Sea oil altered it beyond redemption, as the new industrial riches trampled its unique community spirit and sense of tradition. The

old fiddlers gradually faded and died, and Shetland music seemed destined to disappear too.

That it didn't was largely down to Aly. After a spell with Billy Connolly (then a folk artist, before finding comedy success as a professional Glaswegian) on the Scottish folk circuit, Aly found himself working with blues iconoclast Mike Whellans, and then the two of them tumbled into a link-up with two Irishmen, Robin Morton and Cathal McConnell, in a group they called **Boys of the Lough**. The last thing Aly Bain imagined was that he'd spend the next quarter of a century answering to this name. But he did, and his joyful artistry, unwavering integrity and unquenchable appetite and commitment to the music of his upbringing kept Shetland music alive in a manner he could never have imagined. Even more importantly, it stung the imagination of the generation that followed.

These days, Shetland music is buzzing again, with its own annual festival a treat of music-making and drinking that belies the impersonal industrialisation of Shetland. There are young musicians pouring out of the place, and a plethora of bands of all styles, including pop-oriented groups such as **Rock, Salt & Nails** and more recently **Red Vans**. The pick of the roots players, currently, is **Catriona MacDonald** – who was also taught by Tom Anderson, in his last days. She is adept at classical music, and is fast becoming an accomplished mistress of Norwegian music, and her mum went to school with Aly Bain – which in Shetland these days counts for an awful lot.

of balancing out the sounds of pipes, fiddle and voices. Such a development was to come later, in the late 1970s, with bands like Battlefield Band, The Tannahill Weavers and Ossian.

Key, too, to developments were **The Boys of the Lough**, a Scots-Irish group led by the Shetland fiddler **Aly Bain** (see box) and **The Whistlebinkies**. Developing in the Glasgow folk scene alongside The Clutha, both these groups took a strong instrumental line, rather than The Clutha's song-based approach. These two bands were in many ways Scotland's equivalent to The Chieftains and through their musical ability and recognition outside the folk clubs, played an important part in breaking down musical barriers.

The Whistlebinkies were notable for employing only traditional instruments, including fine *clarsach* (Celtic harp) from **Judith Peacock**. However, the most important, and definingly Scottish, element of all three of these bands was the presence of **bagpipes**. Clutha had piper **Jimmy Anderson**; the Whistlebinkies featured **Rab Wallace**, who had a firm background in the Scots piping scene; while The Boys also had an experienced piper in **Robin Morton**. They were pioneers for what was to become a revolution.

Pibroch: Scots Pipes

Bagpipes are synonymous with Scotland yet they are not a specifically Scots instrument. The pipes were once to be found right across Europe, and pockets remain, across the English border in Northumbria, all over Ireland, in Spain and Italy, and in eastern Europe, where bagpipe festivals are still held in rural areas. In Scotland, bagpipes seem to have made their appearance around the fifteenth century, and over the next hundred years or so they took on several forms, including quieter varieties (small pipes), both bellows and mouth blown, which allowed a diversity of playing styles.

The highland bagpipe form known as **pibroch** (*piobaireachd* in Gaelic) evolved around this time, created by clan pipers for military, gathering, lamenting and marching purposes. Legend among the clan pipers of this era were the MacCrimmons (they of the famous "MacCrimmon's Lament", composed during the Jacobite rebellion), although they were but one of several important piping clans, among which were the MacArthurs, MacKays and MacDonalds, and others. In the seventeenth and eighteenth centuries, through the influence of the British army, reels and strathspeys joined the repertoire and a tradition of military pipe bands emerged. After World War II they were joined by civilian bands, alongside whom developed a network of piping competitions.

The bagpipe tradition has continued uninterrupted, although for much of this century under the domination of the military and the folklorists Piobaireachd Society. Recently, however, a number of Scottish musicians have revived the pipes in new and innovative forms. Following the lead of Clutha, The Boys of the Lough, and The Whistlebinkies, a new wave of young bands began to feature pipers, notably **Alba** with the then-teenage **Alan McLeod**, the **Battlefield Band**, whose arrangements involve the beautifully measured piping of **Duncan McGillivray**, and **Ossian** with **Iain MacDonald**. These players redefined the boundaries of pipe music using notes and finger movements outside of the traditional range. They also showed the influence of Irish Uillean pipe players (particularly Paddy Keenan of the Bothy Band) and Cape Breton styles which many claim is the original, pre-military Scottish style.

In 1983 Robin Morton released *A Controversy of Pipers* on his Temple Records label, an album featuring six pipers from folk bands who were also top competitive players in the piping world. Up until this point, pipers in a folk band could be considered second class by some in the piping establishment. This recording made a statement and soon the walls began to crumble!

MARC MARNIE/TEMPLE RECORDS

The Battlefield Band

Alongside all this came a revived interest in traditional piping, and in particular the strathspeys, slow airs and reels, which had tended to get submerged beneath the familiar military territory of marches and laments. The century's great bagpipe players, notably **John Burgess**, received a belated wider exposure. His legacy includes a masterful album and a renowned teaching career to ensure that the old piping tradition marches proudly into the next century.

Folk Song and the Club Scene

Whilst the folk bands were starting to catch up on the Irish and integrating bagpipes, folk song was also flourishing. The song tradition in Scotland is one of the strongest in Europe and in all areas of the country there were pockets of great singers and characters. In the 1960s the common ground was the folk club network and the various festivals dotted around the country.

The great modern pioneer of Scots folk song, and a man who it is perhaps no exaggeration to say rescued the whole British tradition, was the great singer and songwriter **Ewan MacColl**, born in Perthshire in 1915 (see feature box). He recorded the seminal *Scottish Popular Ballads* as early as 1956, and founded the first folk club in Britain. After MacColl, another of the building blocks of the 1960s folk revival were the Aberdeen group, **The Gaugers**. Song was the heart of this group – Tam Speirs, Arthur Watson and Peter Hall were all good singers – though they were also innovative in using instrumentation (fiddle, concertina and whistle) without a guitar or other rhythm instrument to tie the sound together.

Other significant Scots groups on the 1960s scene included the **Ian Campbell Folk Group**, Birmingham-based but largely Scots in character (and who included future Fairport Daves, Swarbrick and Pegg, as well as Ian's sons, Aly and Robin, who went on to form UB40). They flirted with commercialism and pop sensibilities – as virtually every folk group of the era was compelled to do – and were too often unfairly bracketed with England's derided Spinners as a result. So too were **The Corries**, although they laced their blandness with enterprise, inventing their own instrumentation and writing the new unofficial national anthem, "Flower of Scotland".

Other more adventurous experiments grew out of the folk and acoustic club scene in mid-1960s Glasgow and Edinburgh. It was at *Clive's Incredible Folk Club*, in Glasgow, that **The Incredible String Band** made their debut, led by **Mike Heron** and **Robin Williamson**. They took an unfashionable glance back into their own past on the one hand, while plunging headlong into psychedelia and other uncharted areas on the other. Their success broke down significant barriers, both in and out of Scotland, and in their wake came a succession of Scottish folk-rock crossover musicians. Glasgow-born **Bert Jansch** launched folk super-group Pentangle with Jacqui McShee, John Renbourn and Danny Thompson, and the flute-playing **Ian Anderson** found rock success with Jethro Tull. Meanwhile, a more traditional Scottish sound was promoted by the likes of **Archie, Ray and Cilla Fisher**, who sang new and traditional ballads, individually and together.

The great figure, however, along with MacColl, was the singer and guitarist **Dick Gaughan**, whose passionate artistry towers like a colossus above three decades. He started out in the Edinburgh folk club scene with an impenetrable accent, a deep belief in the socialist commitment of traditional song, and a guitar technique that had old masters of the art hanging on to the edge of their seats. For a couple of years in the early 1970s, he played with Aly Bain in The Boys of the Lough, knocking out fiery versions of trad Celtic material. Gaughan became frustrated, however, by the limitations of a primarily instrumental (and fiddle-dominated) group and subsequently formed **Five Hand Reel**. Again playing Scots-Irish traditional material, they might have been the greatest folk-rock band of them all if they hadn't just missed the Fairport/Steeleye Span boat.

Ewan MacColl: The Man from Auchterarder

The single most gifted, influential and inspirational figure in modern British folk song was a man from Auchterarder, Perthshire, called **Ewan MacColl** (1915–89). He was enthused with the unique spirit and dignity of Scottish music by his parents, both lowlanders, and became a superb ballad singer, devoting himself to the music with such zeal and political sense of purpose that it still colours people's thinking years later.

He is perhaps best remembered now as a gloriously evocative songwriter – with the ability to switch from tender love songs to crushing political venom without apparent change in demeanour. But it was his revolutionary championing of indigenous folk song that caused such a furore, and played such a fierce role in the preservation of folk song wherever it came from. Singers and musicians, decreed MacColl, should only play music of their own country: a rule he gained much notoriety for imposing at his own folk clubs. It seems a ludicrous notion in hindsight but with American music sweeping the world in the late 1950s/early '60s it may well have saved large swathes of traditional British folk music.

Initially MacColl made his mark in the theatre ('apart from myself, he is the only man of genius writing for theatre in Britain today' asserted George Bernard Shaw), and later moved to the BBC, where he allied his theatrical leanings with his love of folk music in a series of documentary dramas in which the lives of people in different industries were illustrated by the shrewd interspersal of his own songs, written in a folk idiom for the series. These eight 'radio ballads' were major breakthroughs for folk music, and from that point on MacColl was a central figure in the evolution of British roots music. He continued to perform with his American wife Peggy Seeger almost to his death in 1989, his hatred of the Thatcher government inspiring him to ever greater heights of savagery in his songwriting.

Elvis Costello made his public debut down the bill at a Ewan MacColl gig. Shane MacGowan of The Pogues says the only time he ever set foot in a folk club was when MacColl was appearing. And both Elvis Presley and Roberta Flack recorded one of his songs – the superlative "First Time Ever I Saw Your Face". They should be thinking about building some kind of statue up there in Auchterarder.

Leaving to pursue an independent career, Gaughan became a fixture on the folk circuit and made a series of albums exploring Scots and Irish traditional music and re-interpreting the material for guitar. His *Handful of Earth* (1981) was perhaps the single best solo folk album of the decade, a record of stunning intensity with enough contemporary relevance and historical belief to grip all generations of music fans. And though sparing in his output, and modest about his value in the genre, he's also become one of the best songwriters of his generation.

Crucial contributions to folk song came, too, from two giants of the Scottish folk scene who were probably more appreciated throughout Europe than at home – the late **Hamish Imlach** and **Alex Campbell** – and from **song collectors** and academics such as **Norman Buchan**, with his hugely influential songbook, *101 Scottish Songs*, and **Peter Hall**, with *The Scottish Folksinger*.

Gaelic Rocking and Fusions

Scottish music took an unexpected twist in 1978 with the low-key release of an album called *Play Gaelic*. It was made by a little-known ceilidh group called **Runrig**, who took their name from the old Scottish oil field system of agriculture, and worked primarily in the backwaters of the highlands and islands. The thing, though, that stopped people in their tracks was the fact that they were writing original material in Gaelic. This was the first time any serious Scottish working band had achieved any sort of attention with Gaelic material, although Ossian were touching on it around a similar time, as were Nah-Oganaich.

Runrig have since marched on to unprecedented heights, appearing in front of rock audiences at concert halls around the world where only a partial proportion of the audience are jocks in exile. Their Gaelic input is marginal these days, but they started a whole new ball rolling, chipping away at prejudices, adopting accordions and bagpipes, ever sharper arrangements, electric instruments, full-blown rock styles, surviving the inevitable personnel changes and the continuous carping of critics accusing them of selling out with every new market conquered. They even made a concept album, *Recovery*, which related the history of the Gael in one collection, provoking unprecedented interest in the Gaelic language after years of it being regarded in Scotland as moribund and defunct.

Of course, not everyone applauds. Critics point out that many singers using the language are not native Gaelic speakers and only learn the words phonetically, while further controversy has been caused by the 'sampling' of archive recordings for use in backing tracks. For many people these songs are important and personal, and in the case of some

Ceilidhs, Festivals and Contacts

Dances, Ceilidhs and Festivals
Scottish dances thrived for years under the auspices of the RSCDS, the Royal Scottish County Dance Society. Their events tended to be fairly formal with dancers who were largely skilled but in the 1970s and 80s more and more Scottish dances, or **ceilidhs**, adopted the (English barn dance) practice of a 'caller' to call out the moves. Nowadays there are two types of traditional dance events: **ceilidh dances**, usually with a caller and perhaps a more folky band, and Scottish Country Dances, usually with a more traditional Scottish dance band line-up and an expectation that the dancers will know the dance forms.

Scottish **music festivals** range from the **Celtic Connections Festival** (January at The Glasgow Royal Concert Hall) where you can catch many of the top names in the Celtic music world in a comfortable concert setting, to lots of smaller festivals which offer a mix of concert, ceilidh and informal sessions. In recent years there has been an increase in the number of festivals where teaching takes a central role. Many of these are in the Highlands and Islands where the **Feisean** movement has introduced thousands of people to traditional music-making.

The Feisean Movement
Scottish bands such as Capercaillie and Runrig feed the notion that folk music can be exciting, electric and diverse, without losing sight of its roots. However, the survival of traditional music depends on support from young players: they need to play it, listen to it, and take it forward. In Scotland, change is coming from a grassroots **Feisean Movement** (*feis* is Gaelic for festival). These festivals, held during summer months and school holidays, involve children receiving tuition in traditional music, drama, art, dance and Gaelic singing, with evening gigs in local venues. The teachers (and performers) are often leading musicians.

The idea began on the island of Barra, in the southern Hebrides, in 1981 and has spread to many parts of the Islands and Highlands. Its results have been remarkable. Beginners on the fiddle, clarsach, guitar, tin whistle or accordion have now begun to form bands and teach others. And the sheer numbers of young people coming through the Feis throughout the Highlands has resulted in more and more communities holding workshops and ceilidhs: In small communities there are great economic spin-offs for instrument makers, music shops and for teachers of traditional music.

Tuition projects have not been limited to the Highlands. In Edinburgh Stan Reeves has made remarkable progress with The **Scots Music Group** within **The Adult Learning Project**, leading to several hundred people learning traditional instruments and an annual festival of fiddle music. In Glasgow, **The Glasgow Fiddle Workshop** under the guidance of Ian Fraser, has made similar progress and is starting to widen its brief beyond fiddle tuition.

Feisean Nan Gaidheal: Nicolson House, Somerled Square, Portree, Isle of Skye IV51 9EJ; ☎ 01478 613355, fax 613399.
Adult Learning Project/Scots Music Group: 184 Dalry Road, Edinburgh, EH11 2EP; ☎ 0131 337 5442, fax 337 9316.

The Living Tradition
The Living Tradition is a traditional music magazine published from Ayrshire. It covers music from Britain and Ireland, with a focus, obviously, on Scotland. They also run a mail order service for traditional recordings, and their website offers a reasonable starting point for issues arising from this article.
The Living Tradition, PO Box 1026, Kilmarnock, Ayrshire KA2 0LG; ☎ 01563 571220; email *living. tradition@almac.co.uk* Website *www.folkmusic.net*

The Piping Centre
The place to visit for anybody with an interest in piping. They have an exhibition, a teaching programme, concert space, café and even a hotel.
The Piping Centre: 32 McPhater Street, Glasgow; ☎ 0141 353 0220, fax 353 1570.

SCOTLAND

DAVE PEABODY

Snooglenifty

of the religious singing, they felt very strongly that this use was in bad taste.

Nonetheless, the popularity of Gaelic roots bands undeniably paved the way for 'purer' Scots musicians and singers: *clarsach* player **Alison Kinnaird**, for instance; or singers **Savourna Stevenson**, **Christine Primrose**, **Flora McNeill**, **Cathy-Ann MacPhee**, **Heather Heywood**, and **Jock Duncan**; or the **Wrigley sisters** from Orkney – who started out as teenagers playing traditional music with technical accomplishment and attitude and are now the core of the band **Seelyhoo**.

And among the ranks of the roots or fusion bands, each with their own agendas and styles, have passed many – perhaps most – of Scotland's finest contemporary musicians. **Silly Wizard**, especially, featured a singer of cutting quality in **Andy M. Stewart** (and did he need that M.), while **Phil and Johnny Cunningham** have gone on to display a pioneering zeal in their efforts to use their skills on accordion and fiddle to knit Scottish traditional music with other cultures.

Mouth Music, too, were innovative: a Scots-origin (but recently Canadian) duo of **Martin Swan** and **Talitha MacKenzie**, who mixed Gaelic vocals (including the traditional 'mouth music' techniques of sung rhythms) with African percussion and dance sounds. Talitha MacKenzie later went solo, radically transforming traditional Scottish songs, which she clears from the dust of folklore with wonderful multitracked vocals and the characteristic Mouth Music African rhythms.

Another development was the fusion of traditional music and **jazz** by bands such as **The Easy Club** and the duo of piper **Hamish Moore** and jazz saxophonist **Dick Lee**. Moore has since come full circle, now taking his inspiration from a parallel Scottish culture which has developed in **Cape Breton**. Scottish interest in Cape Breton music (covered in *The Rough Guide to World Music Volume 2*) has also led to the more or less lost tradition of Scottish step dancing being reintroduced.

At the end of the 1990s, however, the two most interesting Scottish roots groups are sure-

ly **Capercaillie** and Shooglenifty. The former, based on the arrangements of **Manus Lunny** and the gorgeous singing of **Karen Mattheson**, rose from Argyll pub sessions to flirt with mass commercial appeal, reworking Gaelic and traditional songs from the West Highlands. **Shooglenifty** meanwhile captured the imagination of a new audience with a style they described with their tongues in their cheeks as 'acid croft'.

discography

In addition to the disc reviewed below, see the box overleaf for details of the remarkable Scottish Tradition Series of CDs and cassettes. For more information, check out the 'Scottish Music Links' at www.netreal.co.uk – a wonderful site with links to many label and artist pages, and even a gallery of Aurora Borealis photos!

General Compilations

The Caledonian Companion (Greentrax, Scotland).

A 1975 live recording of four of Scotland's most respected traditional, north-east musicians – Alex Green, Willie Fraser, Charlie Bremner and John Grant – featuring solo fiddle, mouth-organ, whistle and diddling.

The Rough Guide to Scottish Music (World Music Network, UK).

A terrific compilation, this is strongest on the new roots bands – with good selections from Battlefield Band, Capercaillie and Wolfstone, among others – but it also delves iinto folk (Dick Gaughan) and traditional singing (Catherine-Ann McPhee, Heather Heyward) .

The Nineties Collection (Greentrax, Scotland).

Sixteen artists, including four pipers and well-known names such as Aly Bain and Phil Cunningham play all-new tunes in a traditional style. Also available, is a companion book containing over 200 tunes (Canongate Books, Scotland).

Traditional

Singers

Jock Duncan

Duncan is an authentic bothy ballad singer from Pitlochry who gets to the heart of any song. He made his recording debut aged seventy on the album below, backed by musicians including his son, the piper Gordon Duncan.

Ye Shine Whar Ye Stan (Springthyme, Scotland).

Some of the traditional singing on this album is truly remarkable and the production from Battlefield Band founder **Brian McNeill** is impressive, too, creating an atmosphere that only falls a little short of the experience of a live performance.

Heather Heywood

Heywood, from Ayrshire, is reckoned by many Scotland's foremost traditional singer of her generation. She performs largely core Scottish ballads and songs.

The Scottish Tradition Series

Scottish traditional music – in its deepest, darkest manifestations – has been superbly documented in a series of archive recordings produced by Peter Cooke and others at Edinburgh University's School of Scottish Studies. The highlights of this collection have found their way onto a series of a couple of dozen cassettes and/or CDs, which, if you're seriously interested in the roots of many of the musicians covered in this article, are nothing less than a treasure trove.

The first volume in the series, **Bothy Ballads**, is one of the most important and fascinating. These nar-

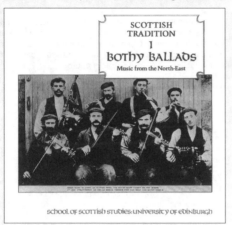

SCOTTISH TRADITION
1
BOTHY BALLADS
Music from the North-East

School of Scottish Studies: University of Edinburgh

rative songs were composed, sung and passed around the unmarried farmworkers accommodated in bothies or outhouses in late-Victorian and Edwardian days. The songs were often comic or satirical, such as warnings about skinflint farmers to be avoided at the hiring markets. Under the bothy system, workers would move on from farm to farm after six-month 'fees', so the songs were in constant circulation and re-invention. They include some gorgeous ballads and instrumentals. .

Music from the Western Isles (Volume 2) is another intriguing disc: Gaelic songs recorded in the Hebrides, including some great examples of 'mouth music', the vocal dance music where sung rhythms are employed to take the place of instruments. There are pibroch songs on this disc, too – the vocal equivalent of the pipers' airs and laments. On **Volume 3, Waulking Songs from Barra**, you enter another extraordinary domain, that of Gaelic washing songs, thumped out by women to the rhythms of their cloth pounding. If you were played this blind, you could imagine yourself to be thousands of miles from Scotland. More amazing vocal traditions are unleashed on **Volume 6, Gaelic Psalms from Barra**, with their slow, fractured unison singing.

An equally compelling vocal tradition is that of the Scottish **Travelling Singers**, showcased on **Volume 5, The Muckle Sangs**. This is a delight, including virtually all the greats, Jeannie Robertson, Lizzie Higgins and the Stewarts of Blairgowrie among them.

Fiddle music is also outstandingly represented in the series, with several volumes devoted to the art. **Volume 4, Shetland Fiddle Music**, features classic players such as Tom Anderson and George Sutherland, who were to exert such influence on the likes of Aly Bain and Catriona MacDonald (see box on Aly Bain on p.262). **Volume 9, The Fiddler and His Art**, is a fine overall compilation, showing the different styles prevalent around the country.

Finally, as you'd expect, the Scottish Tradition has recordings of some of the finest **pibroch pipers**, among them **George Moss (volume 15)**, and pipe majors **William MacLean, Robert Brown and R.B. Nicol (volumes 10, 11 and 12)**.

The Scottish Tradition Series discs are available on CD and cassette from the Scottish label Greentrax (Cockenzie Business Centre, Edinburgh Rd, Cockenzie, East Lothian EH32 0HL; ☎01875-814155).

 By Yon Castle Wa'
(Greentrax, Scotland).

A 1993 disc of epic ballads and contemporary songs, produced by Battlefield Band founder **Brian McNeill**. Heywood's forte is traditional song which she usually sings a cappella. **McNeill makes the album** accessible, without compromising the basic style, with the addition of accompaniment, including pipes – something which is difficult to do in live performance. This was a landmark recording in the traditional area.

Catherine-Ann MacPhee

Catherine-Ann MacPhee, from Barra, has a warm yet strong voice and her Gaelic has the soft pronunciation of the southern islands of the Outer Hebrides.

 Canan Nan Gaidheal (The Language of the Gael) (Greentrax, Scotland).

This superb 1980s recording, re-released on CD, shows mature traditional singing from one of the best of the current generation of Gaelic singers.

Gordeanna McCulloch

The lead singer of seminal 1960s band, The Clutha, Gordeanna McCulloch is another of the great voices of the Scottish Folk revival.

⊕ **In Freenship's Name** (Greentrax, Scotland).

Gordeanna's voice is a strong, sweet and flexible instrument, capable of a variety of tones. Here, she is at home among some great Scots songs, all traditional, bar one, and backed by some of Scotland's top musicians.

Jim Reid

With Arbroath's Foundry Bar band, Jim Reid was for many years a weel kent face at festivals and ceilidhs throughout Scotland. One of our finest singers.

I Saw the Wild Geese Flee (Springthyme, Scotland).

A selection of songs ranging from his own compositions to traditional ballads. Jim's version of "I Saw the Wild Geese Flee" alone, makes this re-issued album a classic.

Margaret Stewart and Allan MacDonald

Lewis-born Margaret Stewart is a talented Gaelic singer; Allan MacDonald is one of the famous piping family from Glenuig – his brother was the piper with Ossian and Battlefield Band.

Fhuair Mi Pog (Greentrax, Scotland).

This is a fascinating CD of music and Gaelic song that works as terrific entertainment; lovely singing and great tunes, some of the best written by Allan himself.

Jane Turriff

Jane Turriff is a legendary song carrier. Born into the Aberdeenshire Stewart family in 1915, she grew up in a travelling family.

Singin is Ma Life (Springthyme, Scotland).

A must for anyone interested in traditional song style. Content ranges from the 'big' ballads such as 'Dowie Dens of Yarrow" through to the classic C&W song "Empty Saddles".

Sheena Wellington

Broadcaster and radio presenter, Sheena Wellington is Fife Council's Traditional Arts development officer and one of Scotland's leading traditional singers.

Strong Women (Greentrax, Scotland).

A live recording showing off what Sheena does best, communicating traditional song to an audience.

Mick West

Well-known as a session singer, West is now rated at home and abroad as one of the country's finest traditional singers.

Fine Flowers & Foolish Glances (KRL, Scotland).

One of the most successful albums using jazz musicians with a strong traditional singer. It may prove to be a classic.

Instrumentalists

Aly Bain

Shetland-born Aly Bain (see box on p.262) is one of the great movers in Scottish music's revival, through his band, Boys of the Lough (see p.270), and a panoply of solo and collaborative ventures.

 Aly Bain and Friends (Greentrax, Scotland).

One of the bestselling Scottish albums of modern times, compiled from a TV series Bain produced on traditional

Scottish music. The friends include Boys of the Lough, Capercaillie, Hamish Moore and Dick Lee, and zydeco star Queen Ida and her Bonne Temps band.

TOM ANDERSON AND ALY BAIN

The Silver Bow: The Fiddle Music of Shetland (Topic, UK).

This collection of Shetland fiddle tunes was notable for bringing together Bain with his old teacher, Tom Anderson. They played both individually and together on the album and the effect is never less than enthralling.

WITH PHIL CUNNINGHAM

The Pearl (Whirlie, Scotland).

Bain teams up with Scotland's finest accordion player for some fabulous tunes from slow airs to Shetland reels reflecting the incredible range of styles which this duo have mastered. Phil composed almost half of the tracks and he plays five of the six instruments featured.

John Burgess

The century's greatest exponent of traditional bagpipes.

King of the Highland Pipers (Topic, UK).

The maestro demonstrates his art to devastating effect through piobaireachd, strathspeys, hornpipes, reels and marches. Not for the faint-hearted!

Pete Clarke

A great fiddle player whose skills with slow air playing also makes him in great demand as a song accompanist.

Fiddle Case (Smiddymade, Scotland).

An hour of top-notch traditional music – not all Scottish fiddle though – there are tunes from Europe and the US and even a couple of songs. There's a classical feel to some of the pieces with cello and flute parts which works well.

Gordon Duncan

Gordon Duncan, the son of bothy singer Jock, is one of Scotland's younger generation of pipers who is stretching the boundaries with some breathtaking solo piping.

 The Circular Breath (Greentrax, Scotland).

As well as performing on the Great Highland Bagpipe, Gordon plays the practice chanter and low whistle. He is joined by banjo-player Gerry O'Connor, Ian Carr on guitar, Ronald MacArthur on bass guitar, Jim Sutherland playing clay pots (!) and Andy Cook on Ugandan harp.

Alasdair Fraser

A master fiddler, renowned for his slow airs and now for his leading of The Skyedance Band whose members provided music for the film *Braveheart*.

Dawn Dance (Culburnie, Scotland).

An album of completely self-penned tunes in the traditional style which bounces along, defying you to sit still while you listen! Fraser has a rare clarity of playing, without sacrificing the feel and enthusiasm essential to traditional music.

Mac-Talla

In 1994 this 'Gaelic supergroup' made a small number of

concert appearances and one spectacular recording before settling back into their own individual paths having 'made the statement'. Mac-Talla's members included singers Arthur Cormack, Christine Primrose and Eilidh MacKenzie plus Alison Kinnaird (*clarsach* – small harp), and ex-Runrig musician Blair Douglas.

 Mairidh Gaol is Ceol
(Temple, Scotland).

The one and only album from a 'Gaelic Supergroup' with impeccable credentials. Glorious harmony and solo singing, accordion and harp – you can hear the spirit even if you don't understand the language.

Willie Hunter and Violet Tulloch

Willie Hunter was one of the all-time greats of the Shetland fiddle and Violet Tulloch is one of Shetland's leading piano accompanists.

🎵 **The Willie Hunter Sessions** (Greentrax, Scotland).

A set of recordings made over several years including Scots and Shetland strathspeys, reels and slow airs. 'Traditional chamber music' of the highest order.

William Jackson

Billy Jackson is one of Scotland's best-known traditional composers. He wrote some – and arranged most – of the music for folk band Ossian, and now works solo.

🎵 **Inchcolm** (Linn Records, Scotland).

This album brings Billy's harp playing to centre stage. It is a collection of largely unrelated tracks with some orchestral interludes and forays into Early and Eastern musics.

Hamish Moore

One of Scotland's finest contemporary pipers, Hamish Moore plays Border pipes, Scottish Small pipes and the great Highland Bagpipe.

🎵 **Stepping on the Bridge** (Greentrax, Scotland).

Inspired by the Scottish culture he discovered in Cape Breton, Moore plays Scottish pipes with Cape Breton accompanists to produce a lively glimpse of what piping may have been like before it became regimented.

Iain McLachlan

Iain McLachlan is a well-known and respected accordion player who also plays fiddle and melodeon.

🎵 **An Island Heritage** (Springthyme, Scotland).

From the writer of "The Dark Island", real traditional music from the Western Isles played on accordion, fiddle, melodeon and pipes.

Scott Skinner

Skinner was a legendary, Victorian era fiddler – formidably kilted and moustachioed.

◎ **The Music Of Scott Skinner** (Topic, UK).

An essential roots album, featuring rare and authentic recordings by the elusive genius of the fiddle – and the weird strathspey style in particular – dating from 1908. Some of the quality is understandably distorted, though the collection is supplemented by modern interpretations by Bill Hardie.

'New Roots' Groups

Battlefield Band

The Battlefield Band have been one of the enduring top groups of the last thirty years. Evolving line-up changes have kept a continued freshness with the constant being skilled musicianship and excellent songwriting.

 Rain, Hail or Shine
(Temple, Scotland).

All the Battlefield Band trademarks are here in force – distinctive keyboard playing, well-chosen pipe tunes, guitar and bouzouki injecting excitement and tension, fine singing, and John McCusker's sharp fiddle-playing is a joy throughout.

Boys of the Lough

With the virtuoso talents of Shetland fiddler Aly Bain and singer/flautist Cathal McConnell at the heart of the band, The Boys have been a benchmark of taste for thirty years.

🎵 **The Boys of the Lough** (Shanachie, US).

This was the group's 1973 debut – and remains one of their strongest sets, powered by contributions from Dick Gaughan and piper Robin Morton.

🎵 **The Day Dawn** (Lough Records, Scotland).

Quality, taste, superb singing and the relaxed easy style that comes from skilled musicians with years of experience. Along with the concertina and mandola of Dave Richardson, Aly on fiddle and Cathal on flute, whistle and vocals, this album features singer and uillean piper Christy O'Leary.

Capercaillie

The hugely influential and successful Capercaillie have taken Gaelic music to a worldwide audience in a modern contemporary style from a traditional base. They have in Karen Mattheson one of the best singers around today.

 Beautiful Wasteland
(Survival Records, Scotland/Green Linnet, US).

Flute, whistle and uillean pipes pop up all over the place and a whole host of things are happening with fiddles, bouzoukis, keyboards and percussion, too.

Ceolbeg

Ceolbeg were not a full time band but produced some of the finest albums of the genre, featuring some fabulous songs from their singer, Davy Steele.

🎵 **An Unfair Dance** (Greentrax, Scotland).

An impressive collection of tunes played on a huge variety of instruments, with a great sense of light and shade.

Deaf Shepherd

Following in the footsteps of the Battlefield Band, Deaf Shepherd are a passionate 1990s band, rooted in the Scottish tradition, and getting more skilled all the time.

🎵 **Synergy** (Greentrax, Scotland).

A really varied album, including traditional and new material, and jumps from reels to jigs and back, involving vigorous fiddle playing and powerful bouzouki. Poignant guitar, fiddle and whistle counter-melodies smoothly with the vocals.

The Easy Club

An admirably ambitious and sadly underrated group, the Easy Club took the baton from the more thoughtful Scots bands of the 1970s and ran with it at a pace, injecting traditional rhythms with a jazz sense.

 Essential (Eclectic, Scotland).

Essential it is. MacColl's "First Time Ever I Saw Your Face" never sounded like this before.

Mouth Music

Gaelic nonsense songs – *puirt-a-beul* – met ambient dance, funk keyboards and African sampling in Talitha MacKenzie and Martin Swan's Mouth Music.

 Mouth Music (Cooking Vinyl, UK).

Talitha MacKenzie has gone on to a solo career but this first Mouth Music disc remains her finest hour – one of the best Celtic fusions committed to disc, featuring stunning rhythms, funk, Gaelic sea shanties and puirt-a-beul.

Ossian

This groundbreaking band, formed in the mid-1970s, have recently reformed with a new line-up featuring Iain MacInnes on pipes and Stuart Morison on fiddle alongside founder members Billy Jackson on harp and Billy Ross on guitar and dulcimer.

 The Carrying Stream (Greentrax, Scotland).

A fine album, signalling the welcome return of Ossian's quintessentially Scottish sound. This is a collection of terrific tunes – first rate jigs and reels, both traditional and contemporary, blended with songs in English, Scots and Gaelic.

Runrig

This band of Gaelic rock pioneers were formed in North Uist, Outer Hebrides, in 1973 by brothers Rory (bass/vocals) and Calum MacDonald (drums/vocals), with singer Donnie Munro joining the following year. They worked their way up, over fifteen years, from ceilidhs to stadiums, going Top 10 in the UK charts in 1991. They are perhaps at their very best live, with memorable tunes and vocals, and well-honed, subtle musicianship.

 Alba (Pinnacle, UK).

An excellent 'best of' compilation of this most dynamic Gaelic band.

Mouth Musician Talitha MacKenzie

Seelyhoo

The Wrigley sisters from Orkney have made their own statement with their own recordings. On this album they are joined by several other musicians in a band which came out of the Edinburgh session scene.

 Leetera (Greentrax, Scotland).

A really fresh approach to traditional tunes and Gaelic song using fiddle, guitar, bass guitar, accordion, whistle, keyboard and percussion. Vibrant music from some of Scotland's young rising stars.

Shooglenifty

Shooglenifty are a brilliant, innovative band who have made their mark well beyond the Scottish roots scene with their grafting of Scottish trad motifs and club culture trance-dance. Live, they are unstoppable.

A Whisky Kiss (Greentrax, Scotland).

The album that coined the term 'acid croft', with elements of traditional music and house. A sound here, a strange sound there, a sequence played in an odd way. There's nothing else like it.

Silly Wizard

Silly Wizard were a key roots band, featuring Andy M. Stewart (vocals, bouzouki, guitar), Phil (accordion, etc) and Johnny (fiddle) Cunningham. Their albums are full of fresh, lively takes on the whole traditional repertoire.

 Live Wizardry (Green Linnet, US).

The band at their zenith in 1988, playing traditional and self-composed dance tunes and narrative ballads.

ANDY M. STEWART, PHIL CUNNINGHAM AND MANUS LUNNY

Fire In The Glen (Shanachie, US).

Two former members of Silly Wizard combine with an Irishman in a formidable celebration of Scottish traditional music. Phil Cunningham's brilliance as an accordion player is demonstrated on any number of albums, but it's especially impressive placed against the wonderful, wonderful singing of Andy M. Stewart.

The Whistlebinkies

One of the founding folk groups in Scotland – often dubbed the 'Scottish Chieftains' – the Binkies are still playing music with a difference.

 A Wanton Fling (Greentrax, Scotland).

An album that has all the freshness of early Whistlebinkies recordings – a combination of lowland pipes, clarsach, flute, concertina and fiddle.

Wolfstone

Wolfstone play folk-rock from the Highlands – "stadium rock meets village-hall ceilidh" said one reviewer – full of passion and fire.

 The Half Tail (Green Linnet, Scotland).

This is a more subdued progressive sound than usual for Wolfstone, featuring amongst other tracks, a classic whaling song "Bonnie Ship the Diamond", "The Last Leviathan" and catchy instrumental sets.

Folk/Singer-songwriters

Artists

Eric Bogle

Bogle emigrated from Scotland to work in Australia as an accountant but when he returned home he was hailed for writing one of the great modern folk songs, "The Band Played Waltzing Matilda".

 Something of Value (Sonet, UK/Philo, US).

Bogle's singing doesn't quite match his songwriting, but he has all-star support. Includes the number above.

Archie and Cilla Fisher

The Fisher family – Archie, Ray and Cilla – were mainstays of the 1960s/70s Scottish folk club scene, reviving old ballads and creating new ones.

ARCHIE FISHER

 The Man With A Rhyme (Folk Legacy, US).

Archie's finest hour – 14 tracks from 1976 with the Fisher voice and guitar backed by concertina, banjo, dulcimers, cello, fiddle and flute.

CILLA FISHER AND ARTIE TREZISE

 Cilla and Artie (Greentrax, Scotland).

Released in 1979, this still retains an ease and freshness – and Cilla's imperious rendition of the late Stan Rogers' "The Jeannie C" is worth the acquisition in itself.

Dick Gaughan

Singer/guitarist/songwriter, Gaughan is one of the most charismatic of Scottish performers – an artist who can make you laugh, cry and explode with anger with every twist and nuance of delivery. His new material is still up there with his classic albums of the 1980s.

Handful of Earth
(Sonet, UK/Philo, US).

This is the Gaughan classic: a majestic album of traditional and modern songs, still formidable a decade on. When *Folk Roots* magazine asked its readers to nominate the album of the 1980s, it won by a street – and deservedly so.

Robin Laing

Robin Laing is one of the best songwriters and performers to emerge out of the Scottish folk scene in the 1990s.

 Walking In Time (Greentrax, Scotland).

Includes four re-workings of traditional songs, three by other writers and seven of Laing's own songs, accompanied by his own Spanish guitar. Producer Brian McNeill's multi-instrumental talents are also in evidence on most of the tracks.

Ewan MacColl

MacColl was, simply, one of the all-time greats of British folk song (see feature box on p.265).

In Black and White
(Cooking Vinyl, UK/Green Linnet, US).

This posthumous compilation, lovingly compiled by his family, showcases MacColl's superb technique as a singer, his gift for choruses ("Dirty Old Town"), his colourful observation as a lyricist ("The Driver's Song"), and his raging sense of injustice ("Black And White", written after the Sharpeville Massacre of 1963). A fitting epitaph.

Dougie MacLean

One time member of The Tannahill Weavers, Dougie MacLean is now carving out a successful solo career as a singer-songwriter.

 The Dougie MacLean Collection (Putumayo, US).

A good selection from Dougie's extensive recorded output including perhaps his most famous song, "Caledonia".

Adam McNaughtan

Adam McNaughtan has written many songs rich in Glasgow wit including one which has travelled the world, "Oor Hamlet", a condensed version of Shakespeare's "Hamlet" to the tune of "The Mason's Apron". He has a deep understanding of the tradition and is one of Scotland's national treasures.

 Last Stand At Mount Florida (Greentrax, Scotland).

Adam's comic songs are masterpieces and here he is in excellent voice, accompanied by fellow Stramash members – Finlay Allison, Bob Blair and John Eaglesham.

Brian McNeill

A man of amazing talents, the one time fiddling founder of the Battlefield Band is a multi-instrumentalist and a songwriter of some substance.

 No Gods (Greentrax, Scotland).

An album showing the broadening of McNeill's writing talent both in song and tunes. He is joined by ten backing musicians including masterful guitarist Tony MacManus.

Serbia and Montenegro

balkan beats

The states of Serbia and Montenegro, linked in an uneasy federation, make up the only Yugoslavia that is left, and – at time of writing – find themselves driven to the verge of break-up, due to the policies of Slobodan Milosevic, the Federal President. War with NATO, crippling sanctions, and the burden of a vast influx of ethnic Serbs displaced from Croatia, Bosnia and Kosovo, has, unsurprisingly, created a mistrustful, inward-looking society. In this climate, music is alternatively an opiate, a malleable means of political influence, or simply a means of asserting human dignity. **Kim Burton** reports.

While Westerners tend to associate 'folk music' with traditional tunes sung by revivalists, in societies that retain something of their ancient mores and social relationships, it can equally mean a modern tune sung by ordinary people as a part of their lives. The state of 'folk music' (*narodna muzika*) in Serbia illustrates this in a very direct way. It's possible to find, in more remote areas, survivals of ancient songs and dances from some half-understood ritual, yet when most Yugoslavs talk about *narodna muzika* they usually mean songs written this year or last, and performed in nightclubs or on TV by singers wearing glittering and often skimpy costumes. This *novokomponovana narodna muzika* (newly composed folk music), with its high media profile, its stars and scandals, hit-parades and its own magazine, *Sabor*, is an extremely important strand in Serbia's (and to a lesser extent Montenegro's) musical life.

Country and Eastern

Novokomponovana has transformed traditional village and small-town songs into a music that answers the needs of urban working-class life – particularly that of rural immigrants – and underwrites a huge recording industry. It is comparable in some ways to Country and Western music in the US. Both use a band of traditionally sanctioned instruments – accordion and clarinet in the case of one, fiddle and steel guitar in the other; both use a formalised performance practice derived from true folk roots; both have lyrics dealing mainly with love and its betrayal; and finally, the vast majority of both genres is superficial and written to order.

Still, just as is the case with Country and Western, there are true gems to be found, and ephemeral as these songs may be, some are masterpieces in miniature. **Miroslav Ilić**, **Šaban Šaulić**, **Šaban Bajramović**, **Šemsa Suljaković**, **Vesna Zmijanac** and **Hanka Paldum** are not only great stars but also fine singers, and some are distinguished interpreters of the noble tradition of *sevdalinka* (see Bosnia-Herzegovina, p.33).

At the pop end of the spectrum is **Lepa Brena**, whose posters stare down from bedroom walls all over the Balkans. She presents herself as a girl of the people made good, and remains popular inside the country and beyond. Like many of her colleagues she is of Bosnian origin. Indeed it is from urban Bosnian music, with its Turkish influences, that modern novokomponovana draws much of its style, to the enduring displeasure of the self-appointed guardians of Serbian national and artistic purity.

As in Croatia, the rise of nationalist feeling – never far below the surface if truth be told – has been mirrored in Serbia's music, and its (often racist) expression made more acceptable under the guise of 'patriotism'. From the outset of the war in Yugoslavia, songs associated with the royalist and anti-Communist resistance of the Second World War that had remained underground, and could not have been sung in public without fear of arrest, began topping the charts, and new ones were written to accompany them.

Later, as the fighting in Bosnia-Herzegovina reached a new intensity and rendered Serb society – treated as a pariah by the Western public – yet more paranoid and inward-looking, the production of songs overtly calling for slaughter increased, part of the machinery of war. The same process continued during the war with NATO over Kosovo.

Turbo-Folk

Many young Serbs have had an equivocal relationship with this music. Although some entered whole-heartedly into playing the part prepared for them, others took refuge in a further development of new-composed folk music. In the early 1990s the youth of Belgrade and other industrial towns took the modernisation a stage further with the invention of what was soon dubbed **Turbo-folk**. The beat grabbed influences from garage, house and jungle, producers jumbled sampled guitar riffs, spaced-out synth sounds and heavy bass-lines behind singers whose melodies and turns of phrase owed something to rock and soul, but more to the age-old sound of the village, or the sentimental urban song of the 1950s, '60s and '70s. The grooves got faster, the beats more aggressive and the samples more eclectic, while the costumes shrank to become, if possible, yet skimpier.

The sound of turbo-folk is at its best in noisy company with some form of alcohol abuse and, if chronologically feasible, the angst of puberty. But if you want to wallow, the names of **Ceca**, **Dragana**, **Sneki** and **Nino** are ones worth remembering. Their lyrics, on the whole, eschew nationalism for pop's eternal subject – love and its probable failures. But the apolitical aspect of the music is not necessarily reflected in the lives of the performers. Ceca, one of the better and certainly more popular female singers, is married to the notorious warlord (and arraigned war criminal) Željko Raznjatović-Arkan, commander of a vile paramilitary unit active in the conflicts in both Croatia and Bosnia. She gave a much publicised nation-rousing concert early in the war with NATO.

On the other side of political life, although there has been no protest music as such, a few Serbian groups have used folk-based forms in a mocking way, implicitly criticising the hijacking of the music by nationalists. Others reject folk altogether, sometimes for similar reasons, adopting straight Western rock modes.

There are also a few groups who stand outside of all these strands. **Moba**, for example, are a highly committed and skilled group of women singers – many with an academic background – who simply try to keep the older tradition of village singing alive. Without an overt political stance, they draw on their experiences as folklorists and performers to show that the value of such music is universal.

100 Serbian Dances, c 1910

Traditional Styles

When divorced from the political arena, Serbian music is generally cheerful rather than stately, joyful rather than lamenting (although it has its own satisfyingly miserable *sevdalinka* tradition) and is well represented by the fast two-beat dance called the *kolo*, meaning a wheel or circle. As its name suggests, this is danced by a group of people in a ring, clasping each other's hands and wheeling from right to left and back again. The upper body hardly moves at all; all the hard work is done below the knee and the feet weave the most intricate patterns. A kolo is liable to break out on most social occasions and is obligatory at weddings, whether the music is being supplied by a live band, a single musician or just recordings. At one time the village bagpiper was essential, but nowadays there are few, if any, to be found, and his place is usually taken by an accordionist or keyboard player with a more or less clumpy drum machine.

The most typical peasant instrument today is the *frula*, a small recorder-like flute, which can be played with considerable skill. It was originally a shepherds' instrument with a pure and piercing tone used for pastoral improvisations and to accompany dancing. Its place is now occupied by the accordion, which has become the foremost national instrument since its introduction shortly before

A B C D E F G H I J K L M N O P Q R S

World War I. Most families have one tucked away somewhere, often a child's size. The most usual type has five or more rows of buttons, allowing rapid trills, slurs and repeated notes reminiscent of the articulation of the frula. Modern virtuosi play with breathtaking velocity and precision.

One of the most extraordinary Serbian accordionists is **Mirko Kodić**, who plays with great skill and passion, and is not afraid to mix the frula with the synthesiser and *sa-sa* (a more syncopated rhythm than kolo, of southern origin) with rock music. A less iconoclastic but equally fine player is **Ljubo Pavković** of the Narodni Orkestar of Radio-Television Belgrade, while an older generation is represented by **Tine** and **Radojka Živković**. New stars appear and disappear with remarkable speed.

In the area bordering Croatia and Hungary, the **Vojvodina** (with its capital Novi Sad), large **tamburica orchestras** of the Croatian type are common. The sound of the bands with their complex running countermelodies and driving backbeat, or tear-jerking tremolos is much the same, although the repertoire is different, drawing on local folksong and the café music of nineteenth- and early twentieth-century Belgrade (the so-called *starogradske pesme*). One fine singer from the area is **Zvonko Bogdan**.

Brass Bands

The southern areas of Serbia were freed from Turkish control considerably later than Belgrade, and the music and dance of towns like Leskovac and Vranje have a much stronger oriental flavour than the purely Slav music of northern and central Serbia.

Vranje is also the centre for one of the main schools of **brass band music** in the country (other ex-Yugoslav states have their own brass-band traditions), the other two being in the Vlach country (see overleaf) and around the town of Čačak in central Serbia. These loud, energetic bands of trumpet, euphonium, sousaphone-like bass, and snare and bass-drum, sometimes augmented by saxophone or clarinet, are now the most popular village ensembles and have replaced the traditional instrumental groups. They normally play local music, the straightforward kolo, or the more complex and syncopated *čoček* dance. They also usually play recent hit songs, along with the Lambada and Macarena.

The most famous bandleader, **Bakija Bakić**, died a few years ago but his son carries on the family tradition and has recently regained the status of number-one band from **Fejat Sejdic**, voted top

orchestra six times since 1979 in the annual brass-band festival held in late August/early September in the village of Guca, near Čačak. Many of the best musicians are Gypsies and their sound has inspired the scores written by one-time pop star **Goran Bregović** for Emir Kusturica's award-winning films *The Time of the Gypsies* and *Underground*.

Montenegro and Epic Poetry

The epic figure of the blind travelling **minstrel** accompanying his tales of past heroes on the *gusle*, a type of one-stringed fiddle, features prominently in Serb art and literature as a symbol of national identity and culture unbroken by five centuries 'under the Turkish yoke'. Like all nationalist myths there's a fair amount of truth in it and, although even this particular tradition may only stem from the sixteenth century in its present form, it deals with legends from the remote past as well as historical events dating as far back as the fourteenth century.

Although the tradition of the **sung epic** flourished throughout Croatia and Bosnia-Herzegovina as well as Serbia, in this century it has become particularly identified with the mountain fastness of **Montenegro**, where independence, isolation and an old-fashioned patriarchal society provided the conditions in which it could continue to flourish. The vast majority of present-day *guslari* come from Montenegro.

The poems, which may be thousands of lines long, are intoned in a strained and pinched voice rather than sung. The melody is more a set of patterns to carry the words and aid the performer's memory than it is a tune, and a listener who doesn't understand the words will come away with the impression of unvaried and wearisome monotony. But it is in the words that the interest lies. They speak of entirely legendary subjects, or historical figures become legendary, like the

Jova Stojiljkovic and his Brass Orkestar

prince Kraljević Marko whom they transform from a minor nobleman of doubtful loyalties into a mighty warrior against the Turks, aided by his horse Šarac, who could speak and drink wine like a man; or the hajduks, eighteenth- and nineteenth-century bandits who took to the hills and swept down to rob and murder rich travellers, at the same time providing an unofficial resistance to Ottoman rule.

The most important texts are a loose cycle of poems that cluster around the battle of **Kosovo Polje** when the Serbians were conquered catastrophically by the Turks in 1389. These tales of fate, heroism and treachery set the agenda for much of Yugoslav literature, and were one of the first to be pressed into service with the outbreak of war. Their themes of Islamic conquest and oppression, coupled with the view of Serbia as a 'heavenly country' – favoured by God yet eternally a victim of betrayal and falsehood – were vastly effective in bringing about the state of mind that justified the conflicts in Bosnia and Kosovo. In Bosnia, each of the Bosnian Serb gun crews shelling Sarajevo had its resident guslar who regaled them with epics as they watched the city burn.

Cassettes of guslars continue to be produced, and deal with such diverse subjects as the death of promising young footballers, the progress of the war, and the careers of notorious Belgrade gangsters. They have probably found a wider audience in the 1990s than at any time since World War II.

The Vlachs

The northeastern corner of Serbia, an area known as the Vlaška Krajina (the Vlach Marches), is home to a little-known people, the **Vlachs**. Formerly nomadic shepherds, they speak a language closely related to Romanian but their origin remains obscure. They may or may not be related to the Vlachs of the border regions of Macedonia, Greece and southern Albania, who also speak a version of Romanian; the word Vlach originally had the simple sense of foreign. In general their musical culture is practically identical with that of their surrounding ethnic groups, but they retain a distinct sense of separate identity, even in Greece, where assimilation has gone the furthest. The Vlachs of Serbia retain a unique mixture of customs, some of which are clearly pre-Christian and connected with ancient cults of the forest and the sun and moon, and many of the rituals connected with the customs involve music. At the Whitsuntide festival of Rusalija, for example, women used to fall into

prophetic trances – a custom which is rumoured to still take place in private gatherings.

The funeral rites known as *Pomana* are the most common expression of old Vlach culture; designed to comfort and provide for the departed on their long journey to the other world, they are deeply emotional and rich in musical content. The French record company, Ocora, has released an excellent recording of village music from the Krajina which includes funeral, wedding and dance music from ensembles that range from bagpipe and fiddle duets to large brass bands.

Modern **Vlach popular music** of the sort used in everyday life for dancing and other forms of entertainment bears a strong resemblance to that of Wallachia in southern Romania in its rhythm, harmony and modality. Dance music is energetic and speedy, often in a rapid 6/8 time, but with a melancholic aspect that is more evident in the songs. Vlach music is very popular, not only among the Vlachs themselves, and most Serbian musicians find it worthwhile to have several tunes in their repertoire.

discography

Compilations

🔘 **Folk Music of Yugoslavia** (Topic, UK).

A splendid choice of village music from all over former-Yugoslavia collected and annotated in 1969–70. It includes some startling cuts, including a Serbian kolo.

🔘 **Guslari I and II** (RTS, Yugoslavia).

A collection of some of the better-known historical and mythical epic poems intoned in traditional fashion to the the accompaniment of the one-stringed gusle.

🔘 **Yougoslavie 1: Les Bougies du Paradis** (Ocora, France).

This is a selection of music from the Vlach minority in the northeastern corner of Serbia, featuring energetic dances, contemplative ballads, and music from the rituals of the dead. A rare recording, of striking power, it is a wonderful introduction to the region's extravagant musical riches.

Artists

Jova Stojiljković Brass Orkestar

The Orkestar are a nine-piece Gypsy brass band from the village of Golemo Selo in the Vranje region of south Serbia. Their leader, Jova Stojiljković, is from at least the third generation of musicians in his family.

🔘 **Blow 'Bečir Blow** (GlobeStyle, UK).

Dance music with lots of čoček and plenty of kolo, giving a pretty good idea of what you might hear at a wedding or all-night party.

Slovenia

the sound of austro–slavs

Slovenia was the first member of the Yugoslav Federation to secede, achieving de facto (later fully recognised) independence in July 1991, following a ten-day war which left sixty dead. This secession, benign by Balkan standards, was largely thanks to the (again, relative) cultural homogeneity of Slovenia compared to the other Yugoslav republics and its irrelevance to the plans of the major players in the conflict, Croatia and Serbia. **Kim Burton** introduces the sound of music in this new Austrian-Slavic nation.

Slovenia is (and always was) the most 'Western European' part of former Yugoslavia. It emerged from the federation with a relatively liberal outlook and a well-developed industrial base. Its music, too, looks very much to the West. In the last days of Communism, the Slovene capital, Ljubljana, produced the avant rock band **Laibach**, while today rave and hardcore are dominant in the clubs. There is also a distinctly mainstream and rather uninspired 'national pop music' – *domaca zabavna glasba* – based on more traditional sounds from the country's links with the Alpine region and German-speaking world. This party-time genre encompasses cheerful waltzes and polkas played by accordionists, guitarists, trumpeters and clarinettists in knee-breeches, and romances sung by women in dirndls, with harmonised melodies.

Nonetheless, it's not all beer-and-sausage clichés, and there are a few interesting old-time styles and revivalists.

The Avsenik Sound

Slovenia's musical (and historic) roots are in the Austro-Hungarian Empire, to which it belonged until 1918. As Slovenian conscripts were posted far from home, they learnt tunes from soldiers from Vienna, Prague, or Budapest, and towards the end of the last century, the accordion, clarinet and guitar made their appearance.

Slovenia's dominant style of arrangement and performance, however, was more or less invented by the **Avsenik brothers**, Slavko and Vilko, in the 1950s. Their band attained immense popularity at home and over the border in Austria and southern Germany, where local musicians cover their songs in German translation; still very active, they regularly appear on the radio and TV.

In Slovenia practically every other 'national pop' band conforms to their style and copies their line-up of accordion, trumpet, clarinet, guitar and brass bass, with a vocal trio. Such bands perform at weddings and other celebrations and, during the summer, at the *gasilske veselice* (firemen's merrymaking), events held at weekends and holidays at local fire stations, where there is some space to set up stalls selling food and drink and enough open ground for dancing. As well as local tunes old and new, many also play arrangements of Western chart music, from 1950s rock'n'roll and Beatles tunes to contemporary pop. The singers **Zasavci and Irena Vrckovic** have both recorded examples of this rather camp kind of Slovenian music.

Slavko and his happy troupe

SLOVENIA

Old Styles and Revivals

The popularity and commercial strength of domaca zabavna glasba has swept aside other, older styles of music, although there are some remnants, for instance the so-called **velike goslarije** (big bands) of cimbalom, stringed instruments and woodwind. In this small field, the best exponents are **Marko** and **Beltinska Banda** from the northeast.

Traditional unaccompanied **harmony singing**, once very widespread, can still be found in the villages, and there are a few players of older traditional instruments such as the **bowed zither** and the **panpipes** - although numbers dwindle by the year. However, there is a movement which seeks to preserve and revive these more ancient forms of music. The work of **Mira Omerzel-Terlep** and her husband **Matija Terlep**, who collect and rebuild old instruments, research old songs and perform them, was perhaps the earliest example of this kind of initiative. As well as making a series of field-recordings, some of which have been released by the German company Trikont, they have recorded a series of four discs for the Slovenian company Helidon which, although re-creations, are well worth listening to.

Revival Bands

Since the beginning of the 1990s there has been a rapid growth in the number of such revivalist groups. **Katice** are a group of eleven female singers with a faintly academic bias and a sweet-toned vocal timbre who perform a cappella songs from all over the country recovered from published folk-song collections and field recordings. They have made a couple of pleasant albums and add a little local colour to some records by the pop-oriented **Roberto Magnifico**.

Another well-established revival group with a stronger instrumental bias is **Trinajsto Prase**, a trio of conservatoire-trained musicians whose outlook has something in common with the Hungarian *tánház* movement. Their accordionist **Tine Lesjak** has recorded some of the dance, song and military repertoire from the days of Austria-Hungary in an attempt to show how these tunes gradually took on an ever more Slovenian tinge. **Tolovaj Mataj**, a trio/quartet, take an energetic approach to many forms of Slovenian music, and are also well worth catching live.

These groups have a repertoire that draws on music from the whole of Slovenia, while others have a strong regional bias. **Musicante Istriani** are a revivalist trio dedicated to researching and performing the songs and dances of the Istrian peninsula (the northernmost part of Istria lies in Slovenia, around the town of Koper), which have a strong Italian tinge in the melody, and texts in the local dialect of Italian (related to Triestino). They play some of the area's older instruments, including the droneless double bagpipe called the *meh* and the *sopile* folk oboe (also to be found in Croatian Istria) as well as the more familiar button accordion, mandolin and violin.

discography

Compilations

 Das Bleiche Mond/Bledi Mesec (Trikont, Germany).

These recordings of (mostly) instrumental music are not as old as they sound. Made under what seem to have been sometimes challenging circumstances by musician and musicologist Mira Omerzel-Terlep in 1974, they give a fascinating insight into the range of musical forms once widespread in the Slovenian heartland, even at a fairly recent date. Polkas, waltzes, *csardases* from cimbalom bands, panpipes, zithers and more, including a barrel organ Blue Danube. The title song "The Pale Moon" is a homespun panpipe duet as extraordinary and outlandish as the 1930s bird quills on the Anthology of American Folk Music.

Slovenie: Musiques et chants populaire (Ocora, France).

The most interesting of these recordings, drawn from the archives of Radio Slovenia and mostly recorded in the 1980s and early 1990s, are the various examples of unaccompanied choral singing drawn from various areas of the country. The instrumental music is less powerful, although the melodies played on church bells have a certain charm.

Super Veselica (Sraka, Slovenia).

With a strong bias towards the modern commercial side of folk, some of which may prove a little bland to non-Slovene ears, this 'Super Party-time' compilation contains some fine virtuoso accordion playing from Toni Iskra and Tine Lesjak, as well as some startling bluegrass-tinged zither from the young virtuoso Karli Gradisnik – hear it and believe it!

Artists

Bratov Avsnik

The Avsenik brothers are the most influential exponents of Slovenia's cheery and sentimental *domaca zabavna glasba* (national pop music) and are hugely popular throughout the Alpine region and southern Germany.

40 Let 40 Hitov (Helidon, Slovenia).

The brothers have kept up an unchanging standard for over forty years now, and this compilation ('40 years, 40 Hits' claims the title, which seems if anything a little modest) is as entertaining as anything they have ever done.

Spain | Flamenco

a wild, savage feeling

Flamenco is one of the great musical forms of Europe, with a history and repertoire that few traditional or folk cultures can match. Twenty years or so ago, however, it looked like a music on the decline, preserved only in the clubs or peñas of its aficionados, or in travestied castanet-clicking form for tourists. But in the 1980s and '90s, flamenco has returned to the Spanish mainstream, with styles infused by jazz, salsa, blues and rock making their way in the charts and clubs, and a new respect for the old 'pure flamenco' artists. **Jan Fairley** investigates the state of play.

Scratch a hot night in Andalucía, even on the much-maligned Costa del Sol, and you'll find flamenco. "You carry it inside you", said a man in his sixties sitting next to me at a concert in the local municipal stadium in downtown Marbella. There was not a tourist in sight, it was 2am, the sky was deep blue-black, patterned with stars, the stadium cluttered with families enjoying the most pleasant hours of the Andaluz summer, flapping their fans until dawn, children asleep on laps.

Flamenco is undoubtedly the most important musical-cultural phenomenon in Spain, and its huge resurgence in popularity has seen its profile reaching out far beyond its Andalucían homeland. It owes this in part to the emigration from that province, which has long meant the flamenco map encompasses Madrid, Extremadura and the Levante – indeed, wherever Andalucían migrants have settled. And it perhaps owes something to Spain's unconscious desire, having joined the European Union, to establish its national identity.

But flamenco's resurgence in the last two decades is more than anything else down to the musicians – to the vitality and attitudes of a younger generation of traditional flamenco clans. In the 1980s, the Spanish press hailed the group **Ketama** as creators of the music of the 'New Spain', after the release of their first album which fused flamenco with rock and Latin salsa. They then pushed the frontiers of flamenco still further by recording the two wonderful *Songhai* albums – still perhaps the highpoints of world music fusion – in collaboration with Malian kora-player Toumani Diabate and British bassist Danny Thompson.

Another young group, **Pata Negra** ('black leg' – the tasty bit of an Andalucían leg of smoked ham – and an everyday term used for anything good), caused an equal sensation with their *Blues de la Frontera* album. This time flamenco was given a treatment encompassing both rock and blues.

These developments were not always welcomed by flamenco 'purists', who had kept (and continue to keep) old-time flamenco alive in their *peñas* or clubs. But the new Spain was a much bigger audience. These days, on radio and on cassettes blaring from market stalls across the country, you hear the typical high-pitched treble tones of commercial flamenco singers like **Tijeritas**. And the music has found a fresh market abroad, too, spurred by the global success of the flamenco-rumba of the **Gipsy Kings**, a high-profile gypsy group from southern France (see p.153).

The 'flamenco nuevo' revolution, however, had begun at least a decade earlier, towards the end of the 1960s, with the innovations of guitarist **Paco de Lucía** and, especially, the late, great singer **El Camarón de la Isla** (see box on p.283). These were musicians who had grown up learning from their flamenco families but whose own tastes embraced international rock, jazz and blues. Paco de Lucía blended jazz, salsa

SPAIN

ELNE/LA CAÑA

Camarón, Paco de Lucia and Juan Peña El Lebrijano

and other Latin sounds, including those of Afro-Peruvian music (particularly its percussion), onto the flamenco sound. Camarón, simply, was an inspiration – and one whose own idols (and fans) included Chick Corea and Miles Davis, as well as flamenco artists.

Origins and Laws

The **roots of flamenco** have evolved in southern Spain from many sources: Morocco, Egypt, India, Pakistan, Greece, and other parts of the Near and Far East. How exactly they came together as flamenco is a subject of great debate, though most authorities believe the roots of the music were brought to Spain by Gypsies arriving in the fifteenth century. In the following century, it was fused with elements of Arab and Jewish music in the Andalucían mountains, where Jews, Muslims and 'pagan' Gypsies had taken refuge from the forced conversions and clearances effected by the Catholic kings and the Church. The main flamenco centres and families are still to be found today in quarters and towns of Gypsy and refugee origin, such as Alcalá, Jerez, and Cádiz, Utrera and the Triana barrio of Sevilla.

There are various theories about the origins of the name flamenco. One contends that Spanish Jews migrated through trade to Flanders, where they were allowed to sing their religious chants unmolested, and that these chants became referred to as flamenco by the Jews who stayed in Spain. Another agrees on the derivation from the Spanish word for Flemish but suggests the word arrived to describe the Gypsies who had served with distinction in the Spanish war in Flanders and were allowed to settle in lower Andalucía. A third argument is that the word is a mis-pronunciation of the Arabic words *felag* (fugitive) and *mengu* (peasant), a plausible idea, as Arabic was a common language in Spain at the time.

Legendary gypsy singer Manolo Caracol

Flamenco, from its outset, has been associated closely with the Gypsy – *gitano* – clans of Andalucía, although the singers and players are not exclusively Gypsy in origin. Nonetheless, its whole development and preservation was probably made possible by the oral tradition of the Gypsy clans. Its power, and the despair that its creation overcomes, seems also to have emerged from the gitano experience – from a people surviving at the margins of society and which offers them little or no social status. Flamenco reflects a need to aggressively protect self-esteem.

These days, there are as many acclaimed *payo* (non-Gypsy) as gitano flamenco artists. However, for both sets of artists, the concept of dynasty is fundamental. The veteran singer **Fernanda de Utrera**, one of the great voices of the tradition, was born in 1923 into a Gypsy family in Utrera, one of the *cantaora* (flamenco singer) centres. She was the grand-daughter of the legendary singer 'Pinini', who created her own individual flamenco forms, and with her younger sister **Bernarda**, also a notable singer, has inherited her flamenco, as they say, with her genes. This concept of an active inheritance has not been lost in contemporary developments: even the members of Ketama, the Madrid-based flamenco-rock group, come from two Gypsy musician clans – the Sotos and Carmonas.

It is generally agreed that flamenco's 'laws' – its forms of expression and repertoire – were established in the nineteenth century. From the mid-nineteenth into the early twentieth centuries the music enjoyed a **Golden Age**, the tail-end of which is preserved on some of the earliest 1930s recordings. These original musicians found a home in **café cantantes** – bars which had their own groups of performers (*cuadros*). One of the most famous was the *Café de Chinitas* in Málaga, immortalised by the Granada-born poet García Lorca.

Duende

Duende is one of those mystical, indefinable words that goes deep to the heart of Spanish culture. García Lorca wrote that duende could only be found in the depths of abandonment – " in the final blood-filled room of the soul". Its power is likened to a moment which transcends time – a moment of immortality.

Marío Pacheco, founder of the best contemporary flamenco label, Nuevos Medios, says: "Some artists have it, others don't. It's a quality that has nothing to do with training or technique. It's dragged crying and spitting from the bottom of the soul – a very brief moment of pure communication that takes you out of time. That moment is part of Spanish culture: the audience waits for it in flamenco as they do in the bullfight. The artist becomes what they are singing, they are there, but at one moment they disappear, they are not there – it's beyond words, impossible to describe. You are totally taken up by it then. It's that powerful."

Carmen Linares

Flamenco, Lorca asserted, was a way of breaking out of social and economic marginality, and this was clearly shown in 1922 when he was present, with the composer Manuel de Falla and the guitarist Andrés Segovia, at a legendary *Concurso de Cante Jondo* (Competition of Deep Song). A Gypsy boy singer, **Manolo Caracol**, reportedly walked all the way from Jerez and won the competition with the voice and the flamboyant personality that was to make his name throughout Spain and South America. The other key figure of this period, who can be heard on a few recently remastered recordings, was **Pastora Pavon**, known as **La Niña de Los Peines**, and popularly acclaimed as the greatest woman flamenco voice of the twentieth century.

In the 1950s several crucial events in flamenco history took place, establishing for the music a culture beyond its aficionados in the *café cantantes*. In 1954, the Spanish label Hispavox recorded all the flamenco greats on the *Antología del Cante Flamenco*; two years later the first national contest of Cante Jondo was launched in Cordoba; then in 1958 a Chair of Flamencology was established at Jerez. Each of these events brought media attention (and deserved respectability) and they were accompanied by the appearance of numerous *tablaos* (clubs – heirs of *café cantantes*), which became the training ground for a new and more public generation of singers and musicians.

The Art of Flamenco

In addition to tablaos, flamenco is played at fiestas, in bars, and at *juergas*, which are informal, more or less private parties (see box overleaf). The fact that the Andalucían public are so knowledgeable and demanding about flamenco means that musicians, singers and dancers performing even at the most humble local club or festival are usually very good indeed.

At that local fiesta in Marbella mentioned at the beginning of this article, Tina Pavon from Cádiz sang *fandangos* and *alegrías* (literally happinesses) and *malagueñas* from Málaga: part of the light **cante chico** and intermedio repertoire which pave the way for **cante jondo** (deep song). The latter is the profound flamenco of the great artists, whose *siguiriyas* and *soleareas* are outpourings of the soul, delivered with an intense passion, expressed through elaborate vocal ornamentation. Tina Pavon's improvised sculpting of phrases, which draws attention to certain words and the emotions they evoke, had people on their feet shouting encouragement.

To invoke such a response is essential for an artist, as this 'talking it up' lets them know they are reaching deep into the emotional psyche of their audience. They may achieve the rare quality of **duende** – total communication with their audience, and the mark of great flamenco of any style or generation.

SPAIN

Recording a Juerga

The word *juerga* has no exact equivalent in English but implies a get-together of flamenco singers, guitarists and aficionados: an informal occasion, with an atmosphere of spontaneity, exuberance and gaiety, in which some of the most inspired and cathartic flamenco can be experienced. It is quite the opposite of a performance or 'act'; indeed, the distinction between performers and listeners blurs as all involved contribute, if only by shouts of encouragement.

When an opportunity came to record a juerga in Andalucía for the Nimbus label, I jumped at the chance. I'd been hooked on flamenco for several years and had amassed a large collection of records and cassettes. And with few exceptions the recordings that seemed to give the best impression of flamenco's richness and intensity were not studio recordings but those rare and much-copied tapes generated by some unknown soul who had set up a cheap cassette recorder in a bar or backroom where a juerga was happening.

My Nimbus collaborator, Phil Slight, had been intimately involved with the flamenco scene in the town of Morón de la Frontera. He contacted **Paco del Gastor**, one of the most sought-after accompanists, and found him immediately enthusiastic about the idea of a juerga recording in Morón, his home town. Paco arranged for the use of one of the flamenco peñas (clubs) and started recruiting Gypsy flamenco singers from across Andalucía to take part in our two planned juergas. They included

José de la Tomasa from Sevilla; María la Burra and María Solea from Jerez; Manuel de Paula and Miguel Funi from Lebrija; Gasper de Utrera from Utrera; and Chano Lobato from Cadiz. After some warming up, both sessions went with a typical juerga swing. Like good jazz musicians, flamencos of this calibre are so immersed in their art that there is no need for rehearsal or trying out arrangements, even though they might not have worked together before.

The recording equipment used was an unobtrusive portable DAT recorder using a single point sound-

At the Peña Flamenca in Morón de la Frontera

field microphone for Cante Flamenco and spaced omni-directional mics for Cante Gitano; there was to be no mixing, no re-takes, no editing, nothing to freeze out the essential elements of spontaneity and surprise. Apart from some re-ordering of songs the CD that emerged (*Cante Gitano*) is just as it happened, captured on the wing in the Andalucían night.

Robin Broadbank

Duende is an ethereal quality: moving, profound even when expressing happiness or deep sadness, in one sense mysterious but nevertheless felt, a quality that stops listeners in their tracks, and it can have a profound emotional effect, reducing people to tears. Many of those listeners are intensely involved, for flamenco is not just a music; for many it is a philosophy that influences daily activities. A flamenco is not only a performer but anyone who is actively and emotionally involved. Flamenco was and is still regarded by many as a sacred music. It is said that Tomas Pavón, brother of La Nine de los Peines, would not sing *cante jondo* as an enter-

tainment. Before singing he reportedly meditated in Church and listened to the monks intoning psalms in Gregorian Chant.

For the musicians, this fullness of expression is integral to their art, which is why for as many famous names as one can list, there are many other lesser known musicians whose work is perhaps just as startling. Not every great flamenco musician gets to be famous, or to record, for flamenco thrives most in live performance. Exhilarating, challenging and physically stimulating, it is an art form which allows its exponents huge scope to improvise while obeying certain rules.

The Repertoire

There is a **classical repertoire** of more than sixty flamenco songs (*cantes*) and dances (*danzas*) – some solos, some group numbers, some with instrumental accompaniment, others a cappella.

These different styles or *palos* of flamenco singing are grouped in families according to more or less common melodic themes. The basic palos are **soleares**, **siguiriyas**, **tangos** and **fandangos**, but the variations are endless and often referred to by their place of origin: **malagueñas** (from Málaga), for example, **granadínos** (from Granada), or **fandangos de Huelva**. The Andaluz provinces of Cádiz, Sevilla, Málaga and Granada are responsible for most of the palos, although contributions came from other parts of Andalucía and from the bordering regions of Extremadura and Murcia. Certain *cantes* have achieved prominence by their link with individual singers, for exmaple, *solea* with Tomas Pavon and *siguiriyas* with El Maholito.

El Camarón de la Isla

José Monge Cruz – known throughout his career as **El Camarón de la Isla** – died on July 2, 1992. Flags were immediately dropped to half mast in his home city of San Fernando, near Cádiz, and that morning every single Spanish newspaper, even the Basque journal *Egin*, which held little love for the then socialist stronghold of Andalucía, carried Camarón's photo and obituary on their front pages. The leading Madrid daily, *El País*, devoted no less than four pages of homage to his memory. "Camarón revolutionised flamenco from the point of absolute purity", it concluded.

Only forty-one years old when he died, El Camarón (the nickname referred to his bony frame, likened to the delicious shrimps – *camarones* – of the small peninsular island where he came from, near Cádiz) was acknowledged as a genius almost from the moment he first sang publicly at the end of the 1960s. His high-toned voice had a corrosive, rough-timbred edge, cracking at certain points to release an almost ravaged core sound. This vocal opaqueness and incisive sense of rhythm, coupled with an at times near-violent emotional intensity, made him the quintessential singer of the times, with a voice that seemed to defy destiny.

Even at his gentlest, Camarón's voice would summon attention – "a fracture of the soul", critics called it – and he would phrase and match cadences in astonishing ways, yet always making the song appear as if it was composed for exactly that manner. To his guitarist-collaborator, Paco de Lucía, the voice "evoked on its own the desolation of the people. My soul left me each time I heard him – he gave to flamenco a wild, savage feeling." It was a verdict echoed elsewhere in almost Christ-like terms. As one of the obituaries put it: "Camarón's despair was our consolation. His desperation soothed us. The infinite sadness of his voice gave us tranquility. He suffered for us. His generosity liberated us from misfortune."

Of mythical standing in his lifetime, Camarón has become a kind of flamenco saint, for he seemed to live out the very myths of the music that sprung from him. The anguish of his singing dogged his life and he supported it through enormous quantities of cigarettes, hashish, cocaine, and then heroin. His death has left an unfillable void in the flamenco world which even now continues unassuaged, as vividly expressed by Paco de Lucia in the song "Camarón" on his disc *Luzía* (Polygram, Spain):

con lo mucho que yo quería
se fue para siempre,
Camarón, Camarón

(with all my love for him,
he went forever,
Camarón, Camarón)

PHILIPS SPAIN

In all of these palos, the most common **beat cycle** is twelve – like the blues. Each piece is executed by juxtaposing a number of complete musical units called *coplas*. Their number varies depending on the atmosphere the *cantaor* (creative singer) wishes to establish and the emotional tone they wish to convey. A song such as a *cante por solea* may take a familiar 3/4 rhythm, divide phrases into 4/8 measures, and then fragmentally subdivide again with voice ornamentation on top of that. The resulting complexity and the variations between similar phrases constantly undermines repetition, contributing greatly to the climactic and cathartic structure of each song.

Songs

Flamenco **songs** often express pain, and with a fierceness that turns that emotion inside out and beats it up against violent frontiers. Generally, the voice closely interacts with improvising guitar, the two inspiring each other, aided by the *jaleo* – the hand-clapping *palmas*, finger-snapping *palillos* and shouts from participants at certain points in the song. This jaleo sets the tone by creating the right atmosphere for the singer or dancer to begin, and bolsters and appreciates the talent of the artist as they develop the piece.

Aficionados will shout encouragement, most commonly "¡olé!" – when an artist is getting deep into a song – but also a variety of other less obvious phrases. A stunning piece of dancing may, for example, be greeted with "¡Viva la maquina escribir!" (long live the typewriter), as the heels of the dancer move so fast they sound like a clicking machine; or the cry may be "¡agua!" (water), for the scarcity of water in Andalucía has given the word a kind of glory.

It is an essential characteristic of flamenco that a singer or dancer takes certain risks, by putting into their performance feelings and emotions which arise direct from their own life experience, exposing their own vulnerabilities. Aficionados tend to acclaim a voice that gains effect from surprise and startling moves more than one governed by recognised musical logic. Vocal prowess or virtuosity can be deepened by sobs, gesticulation and an intensity of expression that can have a shattering effect on an audience. Thus pauses, breaths, body and facial gestures of anger, pain and transcendence transform performances into cathartic events. Siguiriyas which date from the Golden Age, and whose theme is usually death, have been described as cries of despair in the form of a funeral psalm. In contrast songs and dances such as tangos, sevillanas and fandangos capture great joy for fiestas.

The **sevillana** originated in medieval Sevilla as a spring country dance, with verses improvised and sung to the accompaniment of guitar and castanets (these are rarely used in other forms of flamenco). **El Pali** (Francisco Palacios), who died in 1988, was the best-known and most prolific sevillana musician. He combined an unusually gentle voice and accompanying strummed guitar style with an enviable musical pace and ease for composing the popular poetry of the genre. In the last few years dancing sevillanas has become popular in bars and clubs throughout Spain, but their great natural habitats are **Sevilla's April Fería** and the spring **Romería del Rocio** – a pilgrimage to a shrine near Huelva. It is during the Sevilla fería that most new recordings of sevillanas emerge.

Another very important but specifically seasonal form is the **saeta**. These are songs in honour of the Virgins carried on great floats in the processions of **Semana Santa** (Easter Week), and they are, traditionally, quite spontaneous. As the float is passing, a singer will launch into a *saeta*, a sung prayer for which silence is necessary and for which the procession will come to a halt while it is sung.

Singers

Camarón – or more fully **El Camarón de la Isla** (see box) – was by far the most popular and commercially successful singer of modern flamenco. Collaborating with the guitarists and brothers Paco de Lucia and Ramón de Algeciras, and latterly, Tomatito, Camarón raised cante jondo, the virtuoso deep song, to a new art. He died in 1992, having almost singlehandedly revitalised flamenco song, inspiring and opening the way for the current generation of flamenco artists.

Among those regarded as the best **contemporary singers** are the male singers Enrique Morente, El Cabrero, Juan Peña El Lebrijano, the Sorderos, Fosforito, José Menese, Duquende, and El Potito, and the women Fernanda and Bernarda de Utrera, Carmen Linares, Remedios Amaya, and Carmen Amaya.

Enrique Morente, in particular, is considered one of the great artists of his generation through his renovation and adaptations of modern and classic poets. Similarly, **Carmen Linares** has been a major female figure of the 1990s, commanding all the cantes and her deep, rich voice expresses melodies with complex attack and searingly intense emotion. Rigorous and uncompromising, like many other great artists of her generation, she works by innovating from within the tradition.

SPAIN

Enrique Morente

Commentators are always searching for the successor to El Camarón and **El Potito**, twenty-four years old, has been tipped as one of the voices to watch, as have **Duquende** and **Remedios Amaya**.

Flamenco Guitar

The flamenco performance is filled with pauses and the singer is free to insert phrases on the spur of the moment. The **guitar accompaniment**, while also spontaneous, is precise and serves one major purpose – to mark the *compas* (measures) of a song and organise rhythmical lines. Instrumental interludes which are arranged to meet the needs of the *cantaor* (as the creative singer is called) not only catch the mood and intention of the song and mirror it, but allow the guitarist to extemporize what are called *falsetas* (short variations) at will. When singer and guitarist are in rapport the intensity of a song develops rapidly, the one charging the other, until the effect can be overwhelming.

The flamenco **guitar** is of lighter weight than most acoustic guitars and often has a pine table and pegs made of wood rather than machine heads. This is to produce the preferred bright responsive sound which does not sustain too long (as opposed to the mellow and longer sustaining sound of classical guitar). If the sound did sustain, particularly in fast pieces, chords would carry over into each other. The other important feature of the flamenco guitar is a diapason placed across the strings to enable retuning. This was an important development for the relationship between guitarist and singer, for before its introduction a singer often had to strain to adapt to the guitarist's tone.

Guitarists

The guitar used to be simply an accompanying instrument – originally singers themselves played – but in the early decades of this century it began developing as a solo form, absorbing influences from classical and Latin American traditions.

The greatest of these early guitarists was **Ramón Montoya**, who revolutionised flamenco guitar with his harmonisations and introduced a whole variety of arpeggios – techniques of right-hand playing adapted from classical guitar playing. Along with **Niño Ricardo** and **Sabicas**, he established flamenco guitar as a solo medium, an art extended from the 1960s on by **Manolo Sanlucar**, whom most aficionados reckon the most technically accomplished player of his generation. Sanlucar has kept within a classical orbit, with no influences from jazz or rock, experimenting instead with orchestral backing and composing for ballet.

The best-known of all contemporary flamenco guitarists, however, is undoubtedly **Paco de Lucía**, who made the first moves towards 'new' or 'fusion' flamenco. A payo, or non-Gypsy, he won his first flamenco prize at the age of fourteen, and went on to accompany many of the great traditional singers, including a long partnership with Camarón de la Isla. He started forging new timbres and rhythms for flamenco following a trip to Brazil, where he fell in love with bossa nova, and in the 1970s established a sextet with electric bass, Latin percussion, flute and saxophone. A trip to Peru introduced him to the Afro-Peruvian box – the kind of crate played, seated, between the legs – which he also incoporated into flamenco.

Over the past twenty years Paco de Lucia has worked with jazz-rock guitarists like John McLauglin and Chick Corea, while his own regular band, featuring his other brother, the singer Pepe de Lucia, remains one of the most original and distinctive sounds on the flamenco scene. Of his fusion, he says: "You grab tradition with one hand, and with the other you scratch, you search. You can go anywhere and run away but must never lose the root, for it's there that you find flamenco's identity, fragrance and flavour."

Other modern-day guitarists have equally identifiable sounds and rhythms, and fall broadly into two camps, being known either as accompanists or soloists. The former include **Tomatito** (Camarón's last accompanist), **Manolo Franco** and **Paco Cortés**. Among the leading soloists are the **Habichuela brothers**, Pepe and Juan, from Granada; **Rafael Riqueni**, an astonishing player who is breaking new ground with classical influences; **Enrique de Melchor**; **Gerardo Nuñez**, **Vicente Amigo**; and **Jerónimo Maya**.

Nuevo Flamenco

One of flamenco's great achievements has been to sustain itself while providing much of the foundation and inspiration for new music emerging in Spain today. In the 1960s rock largely displaced traditional Spanish music, like everywhere else. But the work of Camarón de la Isla (see box on p.283) began a revival of interest in flamenco and in the 1980s flamenco almost reinvented itself, gaining new meaning and a new public through its absorbtion of influences from Brazilian music and Latin salsa, blues and rock. For José 'El Sordo' (Deaf One) Soto, Ketama's main singer, there were implicity connections: "our music is based on classic flamenco that we'd been singing and listening to since birth. We just found new forms in jazz and salsa: there are basic similarities in the rhythms, the constantly changing harmonies and improvisations. Blacks and Gypsies have suffered similar segregation so our music has a lot in common."

As previously noted, Paco de Lucía set new parameters of innovation in guitar-playing, and commercial success, and he was followed by others including **Lolé y Manuel**, who updated the flamenco sound with original songs to huge success; **Jorge Pardo**, Paco de Lucía's sax and flute player, and originally a jazz musician; and **Salvador Tavora** and **Mario Maya**, known for their flamenco-based spectacles.

Meanwhile, **Enrique Morente** and **Juan Peña El Lebrijano** both worked with **Andalucían orchestras** from Morocco, while **Amalgama** recorded with southern Indian percussionists, revealing stylistic unities. Another interesting fusion of forms came with **Paco Peña**'s 1991 *Misa Flamenca* recording, a setting of the Catholic Mass to flamenco forms with the participation of established singers like Rafael Montilla 'El Chaparro' from Peña's native Cordoba, and a classical academy chorus from London.

The encounter with **rock and blues** was pioneered at the end of the 1980s by Ketama and Pata Negra. **Ketama**, as noted before, used rock and Latin sounds, and added a kind of rock-jazz sensibility, a 'flamenco cool' as they put it. **Pata Negra**, a band led by two brothers, Raimundo and Rafael Amador, introduced a more direct rock sound with a bluesy electric guitar lead, giving a radical edge to traditional styles like *bulerías*.

These young and iconoclastic musicians became known in the 1990s as *nuevo flamenco*: a movement associated, in particular, with the Madrid label **Nuevos Medios**. They form a challenging, versatile and musically incestuous scene, in Madrid and Andalucía, with musicians guesting at each others' gigs and on each others' records. Members of Ketama crop up, for instance, along with the astonishing guitarist Tomatito on an album by **Duquende**, another powerful singer of flamenco's 'new wave'.

Pata Negra brothers Raimundo and Raphael Amador

Flamenco Dance

Most popular images of flamenco dance – twirling bodies in frilled dresses, rounded arms complete with castanets – are *sevillanas*, the folk dances performed at fiestas and, in recent years, on the disco and nightclub floor. 'Real' flamenco dance is something rather different and, like the music, can reduce the onlooker to tears in an unexpected flash, a cathartic point after which the dance dissolves. What is so visually devastating about flamenco dance is the physical and emotional control the dancer has over the body: the way the head is held, the tension of the torso and the way it allows the shoulders to move, the shapes and angles of seemingly elongated arms, and the feet, which move from toe to heel, heel to toe, creating intricate rhythms. These rhythms have a basic set of moves and timings but they are improvised as the piece develops and through interaction with the guitarist and singers.

Dance engraving by Gustav Doré

Flamenco dance dates back to about 1750 and, along with the music, moved from the streets and private parties into the café cantantes at the end of the nineteenth century. This was a great boost for the dancers' art, providing a home for professional performers, where they could inspire each other. It was here that legendary dancers like **El Raspao** and **El Estampío** began to develop the spellbinding footwork and extraordinary moves that characterise modern flamenco dance, while women adopted for the first time the flamboyant *bata de cola* – the glorious long-trained dresses, designed to show off the the sensuous movements of the upper torso, and which cut high at the front, today expose fast moving ankles and feet.

Around 1910, flamenco dance had moved into Spanish theatres, and dancers like **Pastora Imperio** and **La Argentina** were major stars. They mixed flamenco into programmes with other dances and also made dramatic appearances at the end of comic plays and silent movie programmes. A period of theatre flamenco, with light comedy dramas known as *Sainetes* (one act farces) offered brief moments of flamenco song and dance.

In 1915 the composer Manuel de Falla composed the first **flamenco ballet**, *El Amor Brujo* (Love Bewitched), for the dancer Pastora Imperio. **La Argentina**, who had established the first Spanish dance company, took her version of the ballet abroad in the 1920s, and with her choreographic innovations flamenco dance came of age, working as a narrative in its own right. Another key figure in flamenco history was **Carmen Amaya**, who from the 1930s to the 1960s took flamenco dance on tour around the world, and into the movies.

In the 1950s, dance found a new home in the *tablaos*, the aficionado's bars, which became enormously important as places to serve out a public apprenticeship. More recently the demanding audiences at local and national fiestas have played a part. Artistic developments were forged in the 1960s by **Matilde Coral**, who updated the classic dance style, and in the 1970s by **Manuela Carrasco**, who had such impact with her fiery feet movement, continuing a rhythm for an intense and seemingly impossible duration, that this new style was named after her (*manuelas*).

Manuela Carrasco set the tone for the highly individual dancers of the 1980s and '90s, such as **Mario Maya** and **Antonio Gades**. These two dancer-choreographers have provided a theatrically inspired staging for the dance, most signifcantly by extending the role of a dance dialogue and story – often reflecting on the potency of love and passion, their dangers and destructiveness.

Gades has led his own company on world tours but it is his influence on film which has been most important. He appeared with Carmen Amaya in *Los Tarantos* in 1963, but in the 1980s began his own trilogy with film-maker Carlos Saura: *Boda de Sangre* (Lorca's play, *Blood Wedding*), *Carmen* (a reinterpretation of the opera), and *El Amor Brujo*. The films featured **Paco de Lucía** and his band, and the dancers **Laura del Sol** and **Christina Hoyos** – one of the great contemporary dancers, who has herself created a superb ballet, *Sueños Flamencos* (Flamenco Dreams).

The top flamenco dancer of the moment – and a real phenomenon, reaching completely new audiences across Europe and the US – is **Joaquín Cortes**. Rather in the manner of a flamenco Michael Flately (*Riverdance*), Cortes has introduced a new balletic and jazz-dance element into the flamenco repertoire. It is revolutionary stuff – and quite stunning. He is also, of course, exceptionally cute.

Radio Tarifa

Flamenco is now also a regular sound in nightclubs, through the appeal of young singers like **Aurora**, whose salsa–rumba song "Besos de Caramelo", written by Antonio Carmona of Ketama, was the first 1980s number to crack the pop charts, while pop singer **Martirio** (Isabel Quiñones Gutierrcz) is one of the most flamboyant personalities on the scene, performing dressed in lace mantilla and shades, like a cameo from a Pedro Almodovar film. Martirio has recorded songs that are Almodovar-like, too, with their ironic, contemporary lyrics, full of local slang, about women's lives in the cities. One set of sevillanas revealed a splash of music hall style, delivered with a powerful passionate voice.

Martirio's producer, **Kiko Veneno**, who wrote one of Camarón's most popular songs, "Volando voy", is another key artist on the scene. His own material is basically rock music but it has a strongly defined sense of flamenco, as has that of **Rosario**, one of Spain's top woman singers, who brought a flamenco sensibility to Spanish rock music.

Other more identifiably nuevo flamenco bands and singers to look out for include **La Barbería del Sur** (who add a dash of salsa); **Wili Gimenez** with **Raimundo Amador** (of Pata Negra fame), and **José El Frances**, from Montpelier in France. In the mid-1990s **Radio Tarifa** emerged as an exciting group who started out as a trio, expanding to include African musicians. Mixing Arabic and medieval sounds onto a flamenco base, they also have a fine feeling for the popular song side of the genre, bringing flamenco to an even wider World Music audience.

discography

In addition to recommendations below, enthusiasts should be aware of four major series: EMI-España's *Antologia de cantaores* (25 volumes), the Hispavox *Magna antología del cante flamenco* (10 volumes), RCA España's *Gran antología flamenco* (10 volumes), and the French label Chant du Monde's *Grandes Cantadores du Flamenco* (12 volumes). Discs in each of these series are available individually, and between them they cover most historic figures, styles, and epochs.

Compilations

◉ **Cante flamenco** (Nimbus, UK).

The best of both worlds: live recordings of an intimate, emotionally intense juerga, an informal meeting of singers, musicians and aficionados, followed by a full-scale public recital. See the feature box about this recording on p.282.

◉ **Cante gitano** (Nimbus, UK).

José de la Tomasa, María la Burra, María Solea and Paco and Juan del Gastor recorded live at a juerga. Again, these are exemplary atmospheric performances.

◉ **Duende: The Passion and Dazzling Virtuosity of Flamenco** (Ellipsis Arts, US).

This is a terrific introduction to flamenco: an excellent and well illustrated booklet offering a succinct introduction to the tradition, genre, singers and musicians, and 3 CDs covering pretty much the full range of artists from La Niña de los Peines to Radio Tarifa.

◉ **Early Cante Flamenco: Classic Recordings from the 1930s** (Arhoolie, US).

A great selection of the earliest recordings of seminal artists of the first half of the twentieth century, including La Niña de los Peines, her youger brother Tomas Pavón, Manuel Vallejo, one of the first non-Gypsy singers hailed as king, and the great voice of the flamboyant Manolo Caracol.

Los jóvenes flamencos: Volumes I–5
(Nuevos Medios, Spain).

From a pioneering label, the very best of the innovative young artists on the 1990s scene who have brought jazz, blues and a rock sensibility to the flamenco tradition. Each artist can be followed up through their own various solo albums.

The Story of Flamenco (EMI Hemisphere, UK).

The songs on this budget-priced CD were chosen as a 'primer for beginners'. As such, it succeeds brilliantly well with examples of all the major styles performed by a selection of splendid singers and virtuoso guitarists.

Artists

Remedios Amaya

One of the hottest female singers of the late 1990s, Remedios Amaya has a contemporary but essentially traditional style.

Me voy contigo (EMI Hemisphere, UK).

This was one of the most popular flamenco discs of 1998, with Vicente Amigo, Carlos Benavent and others accompanying the startling voice of Amaya.

Agustin Carbonell 'Bola'

Born in 1967 into a family of flamenco artists (related to Sabicas), Carbonell has accompanied singers Enrique Morente, Chocolate, Rafael Romero 'El gallina' and 'El chato de la isla', and bailores such as 'El Guito', Manolete and Farruco. Already one of flamenco's top new solo guitarists, he has a cool, innovative style often backed by piano, double-bass and violin.

Carmen (Messidor, Spain).

Modern, often experimental playing of great skill, accompanied by other instrumentalists and singers.

Duquende

Duquende is one of the singers most often described as a successor to El Camarón.

Duquende y la guitarra de Tomatito
(Nuevos Medios, Spain).

Duquende is accompanied here by Tomatito, Camarón's last accompanist, and one of Spain's most respected young flamenco guitarists.

El Camarón de la Isla

Spain's greatest flamenco singer of the second half of the twentieth century, El Camarón de la Isla (Jorge Monge Cruz) was unsurpassed for interpretation, tone, and for pushing flamenco into new areas. With a voice of unrivalled passion and flair, he died tragically in 1992 at the age of forty-one. All of his discs are worth hearing, from pared down voice-and-guitar to those with orchestral accompaniment.

 Autorretrato (Self-Portrait)
(Philips, Spain).

A compilation showing Camarón's genius at both ends of the flamenco scale – the deeply traditional and infectiously commercial. It includes the fabulous tango "Soy gitano" (I am a Gypsy) with the Royal Philarmonic Orchestra, as well as some heart-stopping unaccompanied solos such as "Las doce acaban de dar" (Twelve has just struck).

Camaron Potro de Rabía y Miel (Polygram, Spain).

The disc includes a heroic poetic tribute to Camarón from Joaquin Albaicin which really states just how significant the singer was for flamenco. This, one of his last recordings, is for many the most cherished.

El Indio Gitano

El Indio Gitano has a voice like bitter chocolate that can deal with anything from tangos to granadínas.

Nací gitano por la gracia del Díos
(Nuevos Medios, Spain).

El Indio is accompanied here by the jazz-sensitive guitar of Gerardo Nuñez.

Ketama

One of the cutting edge groups of the 1980s. Obliquely named after a North African village, centre of the hashish network, these guys rocked and Latinised flamenco without losing its roots, bringing it right into the late twentieth century to inspire rock and pop audiences. The group have also collaborated with Malian kora player Toumani Diabaté, bassist Danny Thompson and others to produce the two Songhai discs – the most sensitive and satisfying of all World Music crossover projects.

Ketama (Ryko/Hannibal, UK).

This innovative, groundbreaking album never fails to suprise with its confident use of blues and rich themes and textures.

WITH TOUMANI DIABATE AND OTHERS

 Songhai I and 2
(Nuevos Medios, Spain; Ryko/Hannibal, UK).

For *Songhai I* Ketama get together with kora player Toumani Diabaté and British bassist Danny Thompson, exploring all sorts of string sounds and African-Spanish interconnections. *Songhai 2* features Malian singer Kassemady Diabaté, jazz bassist Javier Colina (in place of Thompson) and flamenco's first violinst, Bernardo Parilla. Both discs are treasures.

Carmen Linares

Linares is one of the top contemporary female singers, a counterpoint to El Camarón with a fierce edge to her voice, a passion that borders on anger and fury before catharsis. Her concerts are a stunning live experience, not to be missed.

Cantaora (Riverboat, UK)
La luna en el río (Auvidis, Spain).

It is difficult to choose between these two albums. Both feature rich, emotional and dynamic flamenco singing.

Lolé y Manuel

Lolé and Manuel are scions of long-established flamenco families and were harbingers of the current generation in their challenge to the traditonal scene in the 1980s. Hugely successful as traditional musicians, they were inspiring in their crossover experiments – moving flamenco into a kind of singer-songwriter mode. Lole's voice is replete with register and power, yet retains an undeniable contemporary attitude and sensibility.

Lolé y Manuel (Gong Fonomusic, Spain).
Grandes Exitos (CBS, Spain).

The first was a groundbreaking record which firmly launched the duo onto the scene; the second is an album of their greatest hits, including the seductive "Tu Mira" (Your Look).

Martirio

Martirio (Isabel Quinones Gutierrez) is a pop singer who has flirted with flamenco and sevillanas, appearing in mantilla and dark glasses in the 1980s like a symbol of the new Spain.

 Estoy mala and **Sevillanas de los bloques** (Nuevos Medios, Spain).

The lyrics expose the hardship and frustrations of life (particularly for women) at the margins of Spanish society and the hypocrisy of both bourgeois society and Catholicism in relation to both women and the female experience. Using untranslateable local slang with great verve and humour.

Federico García Lorca and La Argentina

Lorca, the poet and playwright killed by Franco's men, was a keen flamenco enthusiast and excellent pianist, who worked hard to win intellectual respect for this unique genre and whose interest brought it to new audiences in the 1930s.

Colección de Canciones Populares Españolas (Sonifolk, Spain).

Here García Lorca accompanies singer La Argentina on piano with a repertoire of ten classic Spanish songs, including flamenco numbers, recorded in 1931.

Paco de Lucía

Spain's leading and best-known flamenco guitarist, Paco de Lucia has a unique intuitive style, whether playing solo, accompanying, or working out on jazz- or Latin-inflected material with his sextet. He worked closely with El Camarón and has often collaborated with jazz guitarists such as Al di Meola, John McLaughlin and Pat Metheny.

Sirocco (Philips, Spain).

A landmark album which set new standards for solo flamenco guitar and even now has few rivals.

Luzia (Polygram, Spain).

This recent (1998) solo outing is a reflective and potent set, including pieces inspired by the memories of the late Camarón and by his own mother, Luzia.

Paco de Lucia

Live – One Summer Night (Phonogram, Spain).

An irresistible, innovative recording that, for all its fusion with jazz and Latin music, and its big concert audience, still captures the essence of all that flamenco can be. If you prefer this material in the studio, plump for **Solo quiero caminar** (Philips, Spain).

WITH PACO PEÑA

Doble (Philips, Spain).

Two of the great guitarists of their generation join forces.

Enrique Morente

Enrique Morente is considered one of the great artists of his generation as a result of his renovation and adaptations of modern and classic poets.

Negra, si tú supieras (Nuevos Medios, Spain).

Innovative arrangements of lyrics by various important poets.

WITH SABICAS

New York and Granada (BMG, Spain).

This was one of Sabicas's last recordings – and an instant classic.

Gerardo Nuñez

Generado Nuñez, from Jerez, is one of the great guitarists of the present generation. He studied in the 1960s at the Collegio Flamencologia

Flamencos en Nueva York (Accidentales Flamencos, Spain).

Nuñez shows his stunning technique: there are few faster guitar runs to be heard on any disc.

Pata Negra

The Amador brothers took their name from the key phrase for something tasty and extremely good, (originally the best slice of locally cured ham). In the 1970s they worked together at the innovative edge of new flamenco before going their separate ways.

Blues de la Frontera (Nuevos Medios, Spain/Hannibal, UK).

The cast of Pata Negra's seminal disc, incorporating an intoxicating mix of blues and rock sensibility, reads like a who's who of musicians who would later emerge in the new flamenco movement.

El Pelé

El Pelé is an excellent contemporary singer.

Poeta de esquinas blandas (Pasión, Spain).

Terrific singing from El Pelé and superb accompaniment from the talented, young Vicente Amigo.

Juan Peña 'El Lebrijano'

Gravel-voiced singer Juan Peña, from a family of Gypsies from Lebrija, has long been one of flamenco's most important voices. He's a good guitarist, too.

WITH THE ORQUESTRA ANDALUSI DE TANGER

 Encuentros
(Ariola/GlobeStyle, UK).

At the end of the 1980s, Juan Peña joined forces with the scratchy strings of the Arabic Orchestra of Tangier to explore flamenco's Arabic roots, reuniting the musics of Andalucía and the Maghreb. An enchanting disc, as is its 1998 follow-up, **Casablanca** (EMI Hemisphere, UK).

Manuel Soto 'El Sordero'

Manuel Soto is another great flamenco voice.

 Grandes cantaores du flamenco: Manuel Soto 'El Sordero' (Chant du Monde, France).

This is music to bring tears to your eyes and features a breathtaking recording of a Holy Week *saeta*.

Tomatito

Virtuoso guitarist Tomatito remains best-known for having been El Camarón's last accompanist, which is reason enough to cast him as one of the most fluent, imaginative and fiery contemporary guitarists.

 Barrío negro (Nuevos Medios, Spain).

A superb solo album.

Fernanda and Bernarda de Utrera

Grand-daughters of the legendary 'Pinini', the two Utrera sisters are fabulous both live and on disc, with a natural, earthy passion and lyricism.

 Cante Flamenco
(Ocora, France).

These brilliant recordings made for French radio include the Cantinas de Pinini, plus siguiriyas, bulerías, por solea and fandangos, with Paco del Gastor accompanying on guitar.

Pastora Pavon

Pastora Pavon – aka La Niña de los Peines – was one of flamenco's most important early twentieth-century singers, indeed reckoned by many to have been the music's classic female voice.

 La Niña de los Peines: Antologia de cantaores Vol. 3 (EMI, Spain).

An important archive compilation.

Paco Peña

Córdoba-born Paco Peña is a largely London-based guitarist, though he still organises the annual Córdoba guitar festival. He plays in various guises: with Paco de Lucía, with his friend and colleague, the classical guitarist John Williams, with his own music and dance company, and on occasion with Chilean group Inti Illimani. He is also reported to have given flamenco guitar classes to British Prime Minister Tony Blair. Through it all, he has retained an intense, classically-inspired style.

 Azahara (Nimbus, UK).

A disc that shows Peña at his striking and solo best.

 Misa Flamenca (Nimbus, UK).

A beautiful and arresting flamenco-mass performed by Peña with a host of extraordinary singers and guitarists and the choir of The Academy of St. Martin in the Fields.

El Potito

El Potito is another young singer tipped to be following in the footsteps of El Camarón.

 Andando por los caminos
(Sony, Spain).

The raved-about debut album demonstrating Potito's astonishing vocal skill.

Radio Tarifa

Radio Tarifa draw on the entire Mediterranean region and medieval sounds for their sultry Arab-influenced take on flamenco. Their first self-produced disc, *Rumba Argelina*, became one of the World Music hits of the mid-1990s.

 Rumba Argelina (World Circuit, UK).

Radio Tarifa's sensitive excursion into flamenco's roots with rumba and Arabic rhythms, exploring Spain's popular music past. The record, made under their own steam, first brought them to everyone's attention. They continue in much the same vein on **Temporal** (World Circuit, UK).

SPAIN

Spain | Regional musics

a tale of celts and islanders

Spanish music is known almost universally for flamenco but – popular though it is – for many of the country's musicians (and listeners) it's an exotic, almost alien strain. The 'new Spain' of the 1990s and beyond is very much about its regions, and music is an integral part of the country's multiple identities. There are bagpipes and Celtic sounds to be heard in the northwest; accordionists in Euskadi, the Basque provinces; and, dotted around, fine singer-songwriters like the Catalan Lluís Llach or Mallorca's Maria del Mar Bonet, and even a raft of medieval revivalists. **Jan Fairley** takes a tour, with thanks to **Manuel Domínguez**.

Spain is in some ways a rather closed world: less than in the years of Franco, of course, but still remarkably resistant to Anglo-US culture. And as you go down a level, to the **autonomous regions**, the resistance steps up a gear in rejecting the dominance of Madrid. As a result, there is quite a healthy tradition of local music, particularly where its preservation is a matter of political and cultural significance, notably in **Euskadi** (the Basque provinces) and **Catalunya**. Spain also has a tradition, as in Latin America, of **political song**, forged in the 1970s in opposition to Franco, which has a legacy in singer-songwriters like Lluís Llach.

The regions have in many cases centuries-long traditions of folk song and dance. Some dances – such as the *jota*, *fandango* and *seguidilla* – cut across several regions. Others are unique to (and often emblematic of) particular communities: for example, the *muiñeira* for Galicia; the *zortziko* for Basque country; the *sardana* for Catalonia. These have acquired a certain mythology of 'ancientness', although in fact they are not so old as people like to think. Still, the new regional councils are receptive to supporting or reviving their own folklore traditions and the country has an unrivalled concentration of fiestas, all vigorously popularising traditions, and well supported by their 'exiles' who return to their villages to take part and celebrate familial and historic bonds each year.

Galicia and Asturias

Currently, folk or regional music is at its most developed in the northwest, in the region stretching from Galicia to Euskadi – **Celtic Spain**. The **Festival del Mundo Celta** at Ortigueira has played a leading role in this revival, and there is a regular summer scene of local festivals in the Basque country, Asturias and Galicia. Spain's Celtic musicians also take an active role in pan-Celtic festivals across Europe.

Galician music is in particularly fine fettle, rooted in ensembles of pipes, bagpipes and drums. The best-known of such groups is **Milladoiro**, who are regulars on the European festival scene. The music of Galician bagpiper **Carlos Nuñez** (see box) and **Xosé Manuel Budiño** and exemplifies that of a new generation who have grown up steeped in tradition and adopted wider influences. Nuñez served a kind of touring apprenticeship with the Irish super-group, The Chieftains, and constantly searches out collaborations which bring out different aspects of Galician music.

Other Galician musicians who have helped revitalise the scene include **Na Lua** (who combine saxophones with bagpipes); **Doa**, **Citânia**, **Trisquell**, **Fía Na Roca** and **Xorima** (all traditional and acoustic); **Palla Mallada** (hyper-traditional), and **Alecrín**, **Brath** and **Matto Congrio** (electric folk). **Emilio Cao** switches back and forth between traditional folk and more modern singer-songwriting.

A Celtic movement also exists in the neighbouring province of Asturias. Most groups there are fairly traditional, but **Llan de Cubel** can be challenging. There are also some talented Asturian harpists, among them **Herminia Olivarez** and **Fernando Largo**.

Euskadi (Basque Country)

Euskadi (as Basques call their land) is home to an accordion music called **trikitrixa** (literally 'devil's bellows') – a traditional pipe music transposed for

Carlos Nuñez

Bagpiper **Carlos Nuñez** is an ascending star in the firmament of Galician music. His 1997 *A Irmandade das Estrellas* (Brotherhood of Stars) album went platinum in a matter of months in Spain and included guest performances by North American guitarist Ry Cooder, Cuba's Vieja Trova Santiaguera, and Ireland's The Chieftains. Nuñez is at the forefront of a generation of musicians gaining world-wide fame as a result of his exceptional technique, talent, passion and inspired attachment to his Galician and Spanish roots.

A great enthusiast, Nuñez's pivotal achievement has been to reconstruct the **Galician piping tradition**. Convinced that Galician and Scottish pipes were the same a few centuries ago but have developed differently, he has restored the nuance and detail to Galician playing by listening to Irish and Scottish players:

"The origin and sound is basically the same. Nowadays, we Galicians use the normal scale but the old pipers used the modal scale, like the Scots, just as they used the close-fingered way of playing. And old bagpipes in Galicia had a bigger interior diameter which made them more powerful, with a deeper sound, tuned like the Scottish ones.

"But essentially, what was missing was the ornamentation. More or less from the time of Franco's dictatorship, traditional music became folklore, considered quaint, and the tradition of bagpipes being a professional instrument – the piper playing for a living – was broken. The chain of tradition was broken. What we are seeing now, with the help of other Celts, is the rebirth of it all."

Nuñez has revived Galicia's Celtic background, including in his repertoire Irish tunes possibly brought by Irish regiments to Pontevedra, which have been reconstructed with flute and fiddle with the help of members of The Chieftains. Having learned flute and bagpipe from the age of eight, followed by studies of Baroque music at the Madrid Conservatory, he has an astonishing ability to move fluently from one instrument to another in concert, often at an extraordinarily fast pace, without losing pitch. "They complement each other like fire and air, full of sensations," he explains. "Now I am applying the ornamentation and grace notes of the bagpipe to the flute."

Carlos Nuñez

With Galicians scattered all over the world, Nuñez had the opportunity in Havana to meet the oldest piper in the world, Clemente Brañas, over one hundred years old, playing pipes made from a rubber inner tube. The visit made a deep impression: "The Galicians took their bagpipes with them when they emigrated to Cuba and their music is steeped in the music of the island. That's how I play 'Para Vigo me voy' – it's Cuban but our pipers always played it."

Nuñez has recently worked with a *pandereta* (tambourine) group and singers, **Cantegueiras Xiradella**, from near La Coruña on the Galican coast, reviving traditional work songs and *jotas* sung by old women in the countryside, some of them with *coplas verdes* (picaresque verses with double meaning). His current project is a collaboration with **flamenco** musicians, exploring the age-old links between these two key musics of Spain through a repertoire of traditional tunes, and with vintage nineteenth-century bagpipes and flutes.

Kepa Junkera

the accordion. Trikitrixa maestro, **Josepa Tapia**, who was taught the instrument by his uncle and who now plays with *pandereta* (tambourine) player Leturia in the **Tapia et Leturia Band**, is one of the most popular stars in this genre. **Kepa Junkera** has taken trikitrixa further afield, working with Carlos Nuñez, and in 1998 playing live, and creating an exciting disc, *Bilbao 00:00 hrs*, in collaboration with musicians from Madagascar, Sweden and beyond.

The best-known Basque roots band, **Oskorri**, are a politicised electro-acoustic group. They were instrumental in keeping Basque music publicly alive in the latter years of Franco and have since gone from strength to strength. Also impressive are **Ganbara** and **Azala** and the singer-songwriter **Benito Lertxundi**, whose energies are generally devoted to traditional Basque music but who has also recently experimented with the Celtic sounds of the northern coast. **Ruper Ordorika** is another singer-songwriter, with a rock edge, who has recently worked on a collaborative venture using the poetry of **Bernardo Atxaga** (the first Basque to win Spain's National Prize for Literature). Atxaga has written lyrics previously for rock and folk bands.

There is also a thriving Basque tradition of **bersolari** – improvising rural poets – and now a younger generation move freely between village and city, encouraged by Basque radio and TV competitions and festivals.

Catalunya

Catalunya shares with French Rousillon the roots of a language and a number of music and dance styles, including **Rumba Gitana** (Gypsy Rumba), made famous by the Perpignan-based Gipsy Kings (see p.153). Catalunya's top star in the genre is **Peret**, who opened the Barcelona Olympics. The late **Gato Perez** was also hugely popular, producing a kind of rock-rumba.

The province also has a couple of national (and indeed international) stars – **Lluís Llach** and **Joan Manuel Serrat**. Serrat sings in both Catalan and Castilian, and enjoys a huge reputation in both Spain and Latin America. Llach started out in a group called **Els Setze Jutges** before going solo as a singer-songwriter, and was a political writer in the late Franco years, composing songs in the repressed Catalan language – songs such as the clandestinely distributed "País Petit" (My Small Country). He lived out four years of exile in France. These days he leads a village life and his lyrics have an acute political awareness of the problems of life in rural areas, notable in his 1997 suite of songs, *Porrera*. He tours with a superb group and mixes elements of jazz and rock in his arrangements.

Catalonia also has a number of orchestras who play traditional dance music: some closer to salsa like the **Orquesta Platería** and the **Salseta del Poble Sec**, others more traditional like **Tercet Treset** and the **Orquesta Galana**.

Lluís Llach

The emblematic **sardana dance** remains important, too, in every local festival, as does a tradition of popular singing known as **habanera** which thrives today on the coast in summer festivals, linking Catalonia with Cuba. The maritime connections through merchant seaman and the navy have been strong throughout the nineteenth and twentieth centuries, the music of *ida y vuelta* – coming and going, of greeting and farewell.

Mallorca

In Catalan-speaking **Mallorca** singer-songwriter **Maria del Mar Bonet** was, with Llach, a part of the 1960s singer-composer group Els Setze Jutges, and a prominent figure in the *nova cançó* (new song) movement which incurred the displeasure of Franco's censors: "At that time the sheer fact of singing in Catalan was a political act in itself," she recalls. "If you spoke Catalan in public the dictatorship treated it as an act of disobedience. But in general songs weren't directly social or political. They were poetry, mostly love songs, for our country. What united us in Els Setge Jutges was our desire to use our language – on the streets, on radio, in literature, in theatre."

Bonet's most popular songs include Mallorca's unofficial hymn, "La Balanguera", as well as lively dances like "La Jota Marinera" and the apocalyptic medieval "La sybilla", sung only on Christmas Eve in certain churches in Mallorca. Some of her arrangements of Mallorcan work songs have been choreographed as ballets. "Mallorcan songs are rooted in nature, partly because in the past each job had its rhythm", she explained. "There is music for sowing, harvesting olives and grapes, getting water from the well, for all sorts of fiestas, religious and secular, and lullabies. When people worked alone they sang of their body as they worked, accompanied by the sound of the animals. People came to work from all over and songs were brought from southern France, Catalunya and Andalucía in the last century. They sang in the fields: *"Me gusta coger la aceituna* – I love to pick the olives, hold firm friends, life cannot be bought with money. ("Tonada de cuillir olives")."

Bonet has delved into Mallorca's Mediterranean connections, into what Turkish poet Omar Zülfü Livaneli has decribed as the 'sixth continent', linking all the countries embraced by the sea, from Mallorca to North Africa and the Maghreb, Sardinia, Sicily, Italy, Greece. As well as recording Livaneli's' songs, she has worked closely with Greek composer Mikis Theodorakis.

Maria del Mar Bonet

Other Mallorcan musicians of interest include the superb guitarist **Joan Bibiloni** who embraces folk, jazz and picking styles, and the singer-songwriter **Tomell Penya**, always disguised wearing a cowboy hat.

Andalucía

Andalucía is home not only to flamenco. Musicians like **Kiko Veneno** and **Joaquín Sabina**, for example, play a witty, catchy rock with lyrics younger musicians identify with. Andalucía also has two further significant singer-songwriters, the popular **Carlos Cano**, who has revived the traditional Andalucían *copla*, and **Javier Ruibal**.

Sephardic (medieval Iberian Jewish) music is also to be found in the region – a cross between folk and traditional styles. **Rosa Zaragoza** and **Aurora Moreno** are two female singers who have produced interesting work in this field, as has the outstanding musician **Luís Delgado** (see article on Jewish Sephardic music on p.370). Moreno has also recorded Mozarabic *jarchas* (Arabic-Christian verse set to music), while the groups **Els Trobadors** and **Cálamus** have, like Radio Tarifa (see Flamenco article) experimented with medieval traditions.

Elsewhere

Other renowned singer-songwriters dotted across the country include **Luís Eduardo Aute**, based in Madrid, who has enjoyed a wonderfully creative relationship with Cuban trovador Silvio Rodríguez, and the long-standing partnership of Asturian **Víctor Manuel** and **Ana Belén**. Belén's songs – popular settings of the poems of Cuban poet Nicolas Guillen – are unsurpassed, her mobile, lively voice forging a new Spanish–Cuban style.

From Valencia, **Al Tall** is an interesting band whose last major project was a joint effort with the Moroccan Berber group, Muluk El Hwa. From Aragon, roots groups include **Hato de Foces**, **Cornamusa** and the **Orquestina del Fabriol**, while the Zamora-based **Habas Verdes** perform spirited, vivid versions of traditional tunes on instruments such as the hurdy gurdy, the *dulzaina*, as well as cello, organ and guitar.

Lastly, singer **María Salgado** deserves a mention. She who has made fine recordings of the habanera tradition found outside Catalunya, and has worked on *La sal de la vida* (The Salt of Life) with two other women musicians, Uxía from Galicia and Rasha from the Sudan, exploring the similarities and differences of each other's cultures through recordings of largely unheard songs from Galicia and Asturias, from lullabies to songs of leaving for Havana.

discography

Compilations

▣ **Hent Sant Jakez** (Shamrock, Austria).

Bleizi Ruz (Brittany, France), Leilía (Galicia, Spain), La Musgana (Castille, Spain) – three groups join together to map the European journey of pilgrims to Santiago de Compostela in music and song, patterning the journey of souls, the stars of the milky way (those who make the journey after death) from Brittany through the Vendée and Landes through Spain to Santiago. A superb disc.

Artists

Habas Verdes

Based in Zamora, this is an interesting new group exploring their local music on cavaquinho, zanfona, rabel, dulzaína, pipes and more.

▣ **En el jardin de la yerba buena** (Gam, Spain).

Habas Verdes' debut disc has established quite a reputation for the band.

Kepa Junkera

The virtuoso accordion player of Basque trikitrixa is unusual for achieving success while not being a native Basque speaker.

▣ **Bilbao 00:00 Hr** (Resistencia, Spain).

The trikitrixa ace successfully collaborates with veteran Basques Oskorri, Portuguese singer Dulce Pontes, The Chieftains' Paddy Maloney, Swedes Hedningarna and Madagascar's Justin Vali.

Leilía

All-women group Leilía are reviving the Galician rural tradition of *pandeireta* (women tambourine players) and their repertoire of dance songs, many with double-entendre. A band with great energy and sense of innovation.

▣ **Leilía Exuberant** (Discmedi, Spain).

A disc of *jotas*, *muineiras* and *mazurcas*, with the original six women joined by various guests including the six-man Pandeiromus group.

Lluís Llach

Llach is a key singer of Catalan *nova cançó* (new song) who has succesfully moved from embodying the spirit of opposition to Franco to success with new themes and audiences in the 1990s.

 Ara, 25 anys en directe (Picap, Spain).

Rivaling Bonet, this is a concert celebrating twenty-five years in the music business. It includes most Llach classics and many love songs, celebrating jazz-rock influences while still producing songs of integrity with a political conscience, rooted in the Catalan way of life.

Llan de Cubel

A band headlining the Celtic movement in Asturias with challenging versions of traditional music.

L'otru llaou de la mar (Fono Astur, Spain).

A lively introduction to this exciting group.

Maria del Mar Bonet

The Mallorca Maria del Mar Bonet celebrated thirty years singing in 1997, and continues to go from strength to strength.

 El cor del temps
(Picap, Spain).

A superb live recording of Bonet's 30 Years anniversary concert held in Barcelona's Palau San Jordi for a public of 14,000, with guests Serrat, Llach, Martirio, Ensemble de Musique Traditionnelle de Tunis, Paco Cepero, Lautaro Rosas, Nena Venetsanou, Joan Ramon Bonet.

Milladoiro

Galicia's band extraordinaire with many years' experience of pioneering the Gallego sound on a multiplicity of pipes and other instruments.

 As fadas de estraño nome
(Green Linnet, US).

Recorded live in April 1995 in Buenos Aires, Argentina, to an audience including many Argentine-Gallegos. A brilliant set of invigorating tunes and rhythms.

Carlos Nuñez

Galicia's – and Spain's – foremost bagpiper and flautist, Nuñez has a feel for the diaspora of Spanish and Galician music reaching to Cuba and back.

A Irmandade das Estrelas
(Ariola, Spain).

A superb disc of lively and moving melodies with a great band and terrific arrangements, this established Nuñez's potential for worldwide fame.

Ruper Ordorika

Ordorika is a Basque singer-songwriter with a fine ear for language and melody who embraces rock influences.

Hiru truku (Nuevos Medios, Spain).

An excellent introduction to this poetic songwriter.

Oskorri

Oskorri are the Basque country's essential folk group, forging a clear musical identity for themselves at home and abroad over the past couple of decades.

Badok hamahiru (Elkar, Spain).

Just one of Oskorri's many excellent discs.

Port-Bo

Port-Bo are one of several Costa Brava groups singing the surviving habanera tradition which links these Catalonian fishing villages with Cuba.

Arrel de tres and Canela y Ron (Picap, Spain).

Celebrated in annual festivals held on the beaches of Catalonia these are old and new, mostly romantic *habaneras*.

FOLK ROOTS ARCHIVE

Oskorri singer Anton Reixa

María Salgado

One of mainland Spain's most interesting, contemporary singer-songwriters.

WITH UXIA AND RASHA

La Sal De La Vida (NubeNegra, Spain).

Castilian María Salgado, Galician Uxia and Sudanese singer Rasha come together to sing their own traditions and exchange songs.

Joan Manuel Serrat

Serrat is one of Spain's key singer-songwriters with a huge international following in Spain and Latin America.

Nadie es perfecto (Ariola, Spain).

A 1994 live album that found Serrat in exuberant, serenading form.

BELÉN, RIOS, MANUEL, SERRAT

El gusto es nuestro (Ariola, Spain).

Ana Belén, Miguel Ríos, Víctor Manuel, Joan Manuel Serrat: four of Spains's top singers joined together for an exciting world tour with songs including stunning covers of American 1960s rockers, revealing their true eclecticism.

Tapia Et Leturia

This is a Basque trikitrixa duo – the masters of the genre, carrying on and revitalising the tradition.

Nueva Etiopia (Colleccion Lcd el Europeo, Spain).

Sub-titled 'Songs, Conversations and Poems', this is an exciting collaboration, with texts by Basque and Spanish national prize-winning author, poet and lyric writer Bernardo Atxaga. Music from Tapia, Leturia, folk-rocker Ruper Ordorika, giant Basque singer Mikel Laboa, Itoiz and Gari. Inspiring medieval troubadour music.

Sweden

a devil of a polska

Sweden has made more of an impact on the global pop/rock scene than the other Nordic countries, but only recently has its new roots music begun to find an international audience. It balances an image of folkloric legend with dynamic modernity, has rich fiddle traditions and distinctive uses of the voice, alongside jazz, multi-ethnic fusion and the wildest of folk-rock. Pervading much of it are the devilish polyrhythms of polska. **Andrew Cronshaw** takes a journey of discovery.

As elsewhere in Europe, it was the youth radicalism of the late 1960s that sparked a revival of interest in Sweden's roots music. A new wave of young musicians took up the fiddle and other instruments historically used for traditional music, in particular the characteristic Swedish **nyckelharpa** (keyed fiddle). Many of them joined a **spelmanslag** (traditional musicians' club) or started new ones, learning where possible from exponents of the tradition; courses were established for playing and making traditional instruments; and roots music began increasingly to appear live and on radio and TV.

By the 1980s there was a thriving scene of Swedish roots bands and musicians. Their emphasis was on instrumental music, centred on the country's dominant folk dance form, the **polska**, but during the 1990s singing became more popular. Powerful, original and influential bands have emerged, many of them comprising Swedish-traditional stylists who draw freely on musical ideas from outside to create new perspectives.

From a traditional standpoint, Sweden is a patchwork of **regional styles** of dance and music, with varying degrees of intercommunication depending on the topography. The most famous fiddling region, for example – and still the area of most intense folk music activity – is **Dalarna**, and in particular the townships of **Rättvik**, **Boda** and **Bingsjö**.

Fiddling

The **fiddle** in its present form arrived in Sweden in the seventeenth century and was widespread within a hundred years, though it suffered a setback in some areas in the nineteenth century as a result of religious fundamentalism; some preachers saw music and dancing as ungodly and fiddles especially so.

The styles of individual fiddlers were major shaping factors in the way Swedish fiddling evolved. Notable fiddlers of the nineteenth century, whose names are still associated with particular tunes or versions, include **Lapp-Nils** (Nils Jonsson, 1804–1870) from Jämtland, **Lejsme-Per Larsson** (1822–1907) from Malung, and **Pekkos Per** (d.1877) of Bingsjö.

These fiddlers' music is only known from reputation and the playing of those who knew them, but the next generation lived into the era of sound recording. Most famous by far was **Hjort Anders Olsson**, (1865–1952), who came from Bingsjö and played many of Pekkos Per's tunes. His success in a fiddle competition launched his concert career, and he became well known in Stockholm as the resident player at Skansen outdoor museum. And it is Hjort Anders' striking figure in long black coat and wide-brimmed hat that forms the logo of Sweden's largest folk festival at Falun in Dalarna. He made many radio broadcasts, and a number of records. The next generational link in the chain was his grandson **Nils Agenmark** (1915–1994), who regularly travelled to visit his grandfather, and tried to reach back in his playing to the style of Pekkos Per.

Another highly influential old-time player – still active – is **Päkkos Gustaf** (b.1916), who continues to draw many modern players to his home in Bingsjö. Gustaf is the subject of a brilliant modern wood-sculpture in Falun's Dalarnas Museum

FALUN FOLK FESTIVAL

Veteran Swedish
fiddler Hjort Anders

Per Gudmundson and the Polska

Between sets performed by Norwegian folk big-band Chateau Neuf Spelemannslag and high-energy Haitian-Swedish dance-band Simbi in Falun's Grand Hotel during the Norrsken conference, **Per Gudmundson** plays solo fiddle – unassuming, skilful and subtle. Before long, a large circle of couples gathers in front of him, including leading musicians, swirling in a quiet **polska**. Here, in this shared moment between musician and audience, is the heart of Sweden's present-day roots music.

Polska's unsettling polyrhythms make perfect sense when you dance them. Though there are endless variations to the form, it's not hard to accomplish the basic hesitating walk and wide-stepping turn, and then a world of satisfaction, understanding and possibility opens up.

The music itself works at various levels: be it solo fiddle, two fiddlers interlocking lines and rhythms, or the enormous sound of the amplified bands, the dance is still there. Indeed one of Swedish roots music's strongest aspects in terms of wide-world appreciation is that however far it's taken into heavy rock (and in some cases that's very far indeed, into realms much wilder and all-out than anything in British folk-rock) it still retains its character.

which deserves to be on a list of the world's great artworks for capturing the essence of the old fiddlers, their work-hardened hands pouring out music of great subtlety and complexity.

Unlike many countries, there is no rigid folk tradition and many of the best-known present-day fiddlers play or have played in progressive roots bands and projects, as well as in traditional music. One such performer is **Ola Bäckström** from the Dalarna region. He has moved back and forth between **Den Fule**'s heavy rock outfit, **Simon Simonsson's Kvartett**, the traditional and new music trio **Triptyk**, the Anglo-Swedish quartet **Swåp**, and duets with veteran Päkkos Gustaf.

Forms of fiddle with drone-enhancing sympathetic strings – modern developments of the viola d'amore akin to the Norwegian *hardingfele* – with various names including *stakefiol* and *låt fiol*, are used increasingly by such present-day players as **Mats Edén** and the dynamic fiddle duo **Magnus Stinnerbom** and **Daniel Sandén-Warg**.

Nyckelharpa

The folk revival was the perfectly-timed salvation of Sweden's most distinctive indigenous instrument, the **nyckelharpa** (keyed fiddle). In size and construction, it's some way from a standard fiddle – more like a thinner hurdy-gurdy without a wheel; it has a long, boat-shaped soundbox tapering to a thick neck bristling with rows of keys operating tangents which press against one or more of the bowed strings. Its sound is enriched by a set of sympathetic strings which produce a sustained ringing.

The first depiction of the instrument is a carving of circa 1350 on a gate at Kälunge church in Göt-land. It is also depicted in murals in late fifteenth-century churches in Denmark and Uppland. The oldest preserved nyckelharpa is dated 1526: its body shape is waisted like a guitar's, but during the seventeenth century the boat shape came to prevail. The sympathetic strings were added in the eighteenth century.

The county of **Uppland** has been a nyckelharpa stronghold right through to the twentieth century, and is also the centre of the instrument's modern renaissance. The best-known nyckelharpa spelman of the nineteenth century was **Byss-Calle** (Karl Ersson Bössa, 1783–1847) from Älvkarleby. In 1925 fiddler **August Bohlin** built a chromatic nyckelharpa; player and maker **Eric Sahlström** (1912–1986) of Tobo made further developments and so emerged the form of the instrument now most commonly played. Whereas the old forms had an arched bow – with the tension adjusted by thumb pressure making it well suited to bowing several strings at once to create drones – this new one uses a straight, violin-type bow which picks out a clearer melody with occasional double-stopping or chords.

This more flexible instrument created new enthusiasm, crucially boosted by Eric Sahlström's energetic ambassadorship for it – he organised and led players' and makers' courses and displayed the nyckelharpa's possibilities in his very skilful, fluent playing. However, despite his work, the number of social occasions at which the instrument was needed were diminishing by the end of the 1960s – it was becoming an old curiosity only seen at competitions organised to keep traditions alive. Then along came the "tok vogue" and keen new makers and players went to learn from Sahlström, who received a state artist's salary from 1977. Player numbers have risen from probably under twen-

Väsen trio: Roger Tallroth, Olov Johansson and Mikael Marin

ty in the 1960s to tens of thousands worldwide, and the level of skill continues to escalate.

The best-known nyckelharpa-powered band is **Väsen**, which features Olov Johansson with viola player Mikael Marin and guitar/octave mandolin/bouzouki player Roger Tallroth, recently augmented by percussionist André Ferrari. Apart from their own dance-compelling new polska, Väsen took the nyckelharpa to a long stay at the top of the Swedish pop charts as members of the group **Nordman**.

Anders Norudde (aka Anders Stake) of leading roots band **Hedningarna** has made a series of instruments which he calls *moraharpor* – based on the old 1526 nyckelharpa but extending the principle as far as a bass model – and their exciting sound has been a major feature of the band since its inception. Several other players have also turned for a thicker, deeper, more dronal sound to older variants of the instrument, such as the *silverbasharpa* (so named because of its silver-wound gut bass string) and the *contra-drone*. These instruments give more meaning to old tunes written before the chromatic nyckelharpa was invented, and their deep drones and rawness suit the feel of much new Swedish roots music.

The field of fine play increases constantly. **Trio Patrekatt** shows the powerful blend of nyckelharpa, in the hands of Johan Hedin and Markus Svensson, with Annika Wijnbladh's driving cello. Svensson's nyckelharpa also takes what would probably otherwise be the fiddle's place in roots band **Kalabra**, while Hedin leads his own band

which is built around the wild amplified sounds the instrument can make.

Others include the all-nyckelharpa band named in memory of Sahlström, the **Till Eric Group**, a new power-chamber-music of exciting complexity, with a rich low end from Hedin's tenor version of the instrument. **Åsa Jinder** made several popular CDs with nyckelharpa in a more commercial keyboard-oriented setting, and played with Secret Garden in Norway's Eurovision-winner. Other leading players include **Peter Hedlund** and, using the nyckelharpa in a Baroque/classical context, **Kersti Macklin**.

Piping

Playing of the Swedish **bagpipe** (*säckpipa*) persisted longest in Dalarna; the unbroken tradition finally expired with the death of Gudmunds Nils Larsson in 1949. Its revival gathered steam when the construction work of Per Gudmundson and Leif Eriksson resulted in a reliably playable instrument, which includes the innovation of a tuning slide, a feature absent on the dozen or so old preserved instruments. Dalarna pipes, which have a fairly sweet reedy tone, are small and simple, mouth-blown with a cylindrical-bored chanter and a single drone, both having single reeds made of a tubular section of reed with cut tongue. There are now a number of able players, among them **Anders Norudde**, always a champion of raw, wild sounds, who when playing with Hedningarna is prone to wave the chubby little bagpipe around like a squealing piglet.

The **spelpipa** or **spilåpipa** is a small wooden whistle, usually with eight equal-sized, equally spaced fingerholes; it's one of the instruments associated with animal herders on the high summer pastures, and they would normally play alone for their own amusement. It persisted longest in Dalarna, and since the 1970s has been taken up by new players. Until the 1950s Härjedal had a tradition of playing a cylindrical-bored spelpipa with six finger-holes. Its leading present-day player is the multi-talented **Ale Möller**.

Another pastoral whistle is the **sälgpipa** (willow pipe), the no-holed overtone whistle originally made by sliding the bark off a willow stick, cutting a notch, and re-inserting a short length of the wood with a slice removed to make an airway to the notch. It was played in Sweden and Norway into the twentieth century, and its natural scale and wild sound fit well with the return to dronal music. Anders Stake made many of those played today from plastic plumbing tubing and he and Möller also use longer 'drone-flute' versions.

Pastoral instruments used on the hills for amusement, predator-scaring or communication had lost their role until taken up in the revival. Others include the finger-holed **cow-** or **goat-horn trumpet**, and **birch-bark trumpets** (*näverlur*) related to the bronze lurs found by archaeologists.

Striking sounds and textures are characteristic of modern Swedish roots music. Instruments known in Swedish tradition and now reborn include hammered dulcimer (*hackbräde*), jew's harp (*mungiga*), hurdy-gurdy (*vevlira*), bowed lyre (*stråkharpa*), shawm (*skalmeja*), chord zither (*ackordcittra*) and hummel (a strummed zither related to Norwegian *langeleik* and Appalachian dulcimer).

Accordions and Free-reed Instruments

Free-reed instruments made their appearance in the nineteenth century. The first **harmonicas** and **accordions**, both invented by C.E.L. Buschmann in Berlin, were expensive, but mass-production brought the price down, and large numbers of both were sold in Sweden. They became the dominant instrument here, as in Norway, for playing the popular dance tunes of the turn of the century – the music now known as **gammeldans**. **Carl Jularbo** (1893–1966), a very skilled player with 1500 compositions and vast numbers of record-

ings to his credit, was immensely popular in the first half of the twentieth century and remains Sweden's most famous accordionist.

All types of accordion (*dragspel*) have often been viewed with suspicion in folk music revival circles, but even the most distrusted, the big shiny chromatics, feature in spelmanslag ensembles, and they remain at the heart of gammaldans bands. Playing of one and two-row diatonics gained more acceptability, and in 1970 their popularity led to their being allowed in auditions for the Zorn Badge, the award given to folk musicians – who then merit the title *riksspelman*. The first musician playing diatonic accordion to become a riksspelman was **Mats Edén** in 1979, and since then **Erik Pekkari**, in particular, has emerged as a fine sensitive player.

Singing: Kulning and Ballads

Song was the most prevalent traditional folk music in Sweden, accompanying ceremonies, work (including songs of the railway navvies and Swedish versions of sea shanties), religion, dancing games, drinking and the enforced sedentary occupations of long dark winters. Singing was unaccompanied until the advent of such instruments as the chord zither, harmonium, piano, guitar (used in the home long before the folk revival) or accordion.

Two particular styles stand out among today's singers. One is impossible to miss. The penetrating, high-pitched **kulning** was originally a cow-calling cry on the high summer pastures, and was still to be heard in some areas into the 1970s. In its revival, kulning has become one of the most striking elements of contemporary Swedish vocal music – show-stopping in performance and a socially-sanctioned opportunity to let fly an expressive, cathartic sound. It's practised by women; indeed most of the notable singers in Swedish roots music are women, the foremost being **Lena Willemark**.

The other prominent vocal tradition is the **ballad**. Sweden has its share of variants of the great ballad stories found across northern Europe, many of which are traceable back to the middle ages or earlier, with such eternal themes as love, heroic exploits and magic. Old ballads regularly appeared, together with topical songs and whatever else would sell, in the precursor to the record – the printed street-ballad, *skillingtryck*, sold throughout Norden until as late as 1910 by itinerant ballad mongers. Tunes used for a particular ballad story varied according to singer and region.

Lena Willemark & Ale Möller: Bringing the Big World Home

Singer and fiddler **Lena Willemark** learned the old ways of traditional music as a child in Dalarna, and has taken them right to the heart of new Swedish music. Her wide-ranging work embraces the strongly tradition-rooted trio **Frifot** with Ale Möller and Per Gudmundson, the ballad-centred **Nordan** project, the fusion-improvising **Enteli**, and the more mainstream-jazz piano-led **Elise Einarsdotter Ensemble**. With her voice moving from mellow breathiness to ecstatic soaring or hovering on microtonal ledges, she exemplifies the uniqueness of her tradition, and the fresh power it can bring to other musics, as for example when her kulning is chased by saxophonist Jonas Knutsson's soprano, like two birds tumbling in a windblown sky, the two sounds becoming almost indistinguishable.

Frifot: Lena Willemark with Ale Möller (left) and Per Gudmundson

The daughter of a forester, hers was an early-to-rise rural childhood, growing up in those traditions and speaking a dialect which even now causes the occasional Swede to think she's some kind of foreigner. "I grew up in the northwest of Dalarna, in a little village called Evertsberg. I spent a lot of time with old people, strong personalities who meant a lot to me and have been my teachers – for example, Märta Eriksson, who taught me singing, tales and kulning, and Ekor Anders Andersson, a truly original person, both fantastic and strange, a painter as well as a musician, a 'life-artist'.

"So it was very natural for me to learn how to call for the animals, or to take the fiddle and sit down with Anders and learn a polska; and at the same time I then went home and painted my eyes turquoise, tuned in to Radio Luxembourg to hear Wings and went out to go berserk with the kids in the village. So there were two worlds that were both very natural to me.

"I moved to Stockholm when I was eighteen, when I went to music school where I studied for some years. During that period I lived together with a jazz musician who played records by Keith Jarrett, Jan Garbarek and Miles Davis. It was like another door opening for me. Later I met people at the school working with jazz music, and played with them. And about this time, the late '80s, I met Elise Einarsdotter, who I've worked with a great deal."

An aspect of Swedish traditional music is the use of micro-tones. In order to fit with those in Lena's singing, **Ale Möller** has extra quarter-tone frets on his flat-back mandola/bouzouki. It's an instrument which evolved during the Celtic revival of the 1960s and '70s but is natural for him to use. He studied from 1976 with bouzouki player Christos Mitrencis, and for several years played *rembétika* and more modern Greek music, including shows with Mikis Theodorakis. His current mandola includes more of his special requirements, such as extended bass strings and stud-capos for individual pairs of strings. Möller's a genuine multi-instrumentalist, a skilled player of a range of instruments including hammered dulcimer, keyboards, accordion and wind-instruments such as whistles, shawm, cowhorn and trumpet, and his playing and his tunes crop up all over the Swedish and wider Nordic music scene.

He was born in Sweden of a Norwegian mother and Danish father. "I'm from the town, from Malmö, and grew up with rock-'n'roll, and jazz has always meant a lot to me because it was the music of my teenage years. Then I became passionately in love with Greek culture, and from that I learned how important it is that people have some kind of pride in their own history, and self-confidence that doesn't have to lead to picking on those that are different. That way I first became theoretically curious about Swedish folk music, and had to search for it. When I finally met it I, luckily, fell in love with it. But it was a music that I almost didn't know existed."

Modern Sweden is a multicultural society, home to leading musicians from other cultures, and Ale is active in the creation of new cross-cultural links in the Swedish music of today. Currently amongst his major projects is the 14-piece **Stockholm Folk Music Big Band** led by Möller and Jonas Knutsson and involving local musicians from Europe, Africa, Asia and Latin America.

"If you look at other folk music groups, like for example Norrlåtar, they too have travelled a path beginning with a local musical language and later increasingly reaching out into the world. I think we have a powerful longing to bring the big world home to Sweden. Folk music isn't much interested in borders on maps drawn by politicians and generals; influences creep in, even in traditional music."

In the 1970s and '80s some of the new folk music bands began to introduce songs between the instrumental dance tunes. **Folk och Rackare**, partly inspired by ideas emerging from the British folk-rock scene of the time, was one of the first to concentrate on ballad material. Echoes of that approach to ballads can be heard in such present day bands as **Garmarna** and the Finnish-Swedish **Gjallarhorn**. Garmarna singer Emma Härdelin is also a member of the acoustic vocal, fiddle and harmonium trio **Triakel**, again with a strong quota of ballads, and **Susanne Rosenberg** brings them to the repertoire of the trio **Rotvälta** and her larger vocal and bowed strings group **Rosenbergs Sjua**, as does Sjua member **Ulrika Bodén** to **Sälta** and **Kalabra**.

Written collections are a major ballad source, as are the recordings of twentieth-century singers, most notably **Svea Jansson** (1904–1980), the source of over 600 songs and ballads, **Lena Larsson** (1882-1967) and **Ulrika Lindholm** (1886–1977), all three recorded by Matts Arnberg in the 1950s and '60s.

As Lena Willemark and Ale Möller, speaking at the first press conference of their Nordan ballad project, put it: "Many of these songs had hundreds of verses; it must have taken hours to sing them, without instruments, so the stories must have meant a great deal to people. They entice one into a new world, one which doesn't feel completely unfamiliar because there are things that still concern us today - man in relation to nature, to life and to the other worlds one should care about. You don't think 'this is important because it's old' - it's born anew each time you sing it."

Swedish Finland, Finnish Sweden and Sámiland

Svea Jansson was born in the slew of islands off the Finnish city of Turku/Åbo, and later moved to its western neighbour in the Gulf of Bothnia – the self-governing Finnish archipelago province of Ahvenanmaa/Åland. Both of these areas, and some parts of the western Finnish mainland, are mainly Swedish in language and culture. Music that had disappeared from the Swedish mainland has been collected and recorded there from Svea and others throughout the twentieth century, and has been a source for both Swedish musicians and the Vaasa-based Finnish-Swedish band **Gjallarhorn**.

Conversely, there are Finnish-speakers in a large area of the far north of Sweden. Two mod-

ern northern Swedish bands in particular, **Norrlåtar** and the fiddles-and-harmonium **JP Nyströms**, show distinct Finnish characteristics. Despite official pressure against the Finnish language on the Swedish side of the border until well into the twentieth century, it persisted in the home. The religious fundamentalist followers of such nineteenth-century preachers as Lars Levi Laestadius of Karesuando discouraged the use of instruments for entertainment, and also to

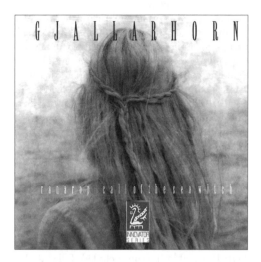

some extent suppressed radio and records, diminishing modern influences on singing. Consequently, there persisted a joik-like gutturalness in vocal style, audible in field recordings and in the singing of former Norrlåtar member (and now a presenter of folk music on Swedish radio) **Hans Alatalo**.

Sámiland spreads across north Norway, Sweden and Finland, and on into northwest Russia. The remarkable Sámi musical culture, distinct from but clearly influencing much modern Nordic roots music, including that of Sweden, is covered in a separate article (see p.255).

New Roots Bands, Fusion and Multiculturalism

Swedish folk music had inspired classical composers in the past, and in the 1960s some Swedish jazz musicians began to explore the possibilities of using folk songs and dance tunes as themes. The most influential of these was pianist **Jan Johansson** (1931–1968), whose work, capturing the nuances of live traditional performance, was the path into traditional music for many of today's folk-influenced jazz musicians.

Coinciding with and intensifying the folk music vogue of the early 1970s, a series of enthusiast-run, admission-free, all-music festivals in Stockholm launched what came to be known as the **Swedish Music Movement**, in the course of which new, largely musician-run recording labels dedicated to Swedish rock and roots music came into being. They included many of today's folk-oriented record companies.

Since learning a tune by ear usually involves playing with another fiddler, duos become a natural performing unit – not simply playing unison but finding lines and parts to draw from the tune – adding complexity to the sound and sharing a musical communication. Fiddle duos emerging in the 1970s included **Pers Hans Olsson & Björn Ståbi**, and **Mats Edén & Leif Stinnerbom** (a duo which expanded in the '80s into Groupa).

Some fiddlers worked with jazz or rock musicians. Rock band **Contact**'s collaboration with fiddle trio **Skäggmanslaget** resulted in a number one hit for them. Kalle Almlöf, Ole Hjorth, Alm Nils Erson, Pers Hans and Björn Ståbi all played at various times with Hammond organist **Merit Hemmingson**'s 'Svensk folkmusik på beat' band. Influential improvising band **Arbete & Fritid**'s flexible line-up included Kalle Almlöf and Anders Rosén and saxophone players Kjell Westling and Roland Keijser – the saxophone was to become a strong factor in later roots bands. Even **Abba**'s **Benny Andersson**, returning to his roots, wrote a set of tunes which he recorded with great success in a collaboration, continuing today, with **Orsa Spelmän** (a leading Dalarna fiddle club).

Folk och Rackare, Swedes Ulf Gruvberg and Carin Kjellman with Norwegians Trond Villa and Jørn Jensen, picked up on the approaches of such groups as Britain's Steeleye Span in their pathfinding treatments of ballads. The touring collective band **Kebnekajse**, with Kenny Håkansson on lead electric guitar, delivered largely instrumental rock arrangements of traditional dance tunes.

From the north came Norrbotten's Norrlåtar, founded on the Finnish-accented styles of the north, Västerbotten's **Burträskar'a**, and the fiddles and harmonium band with a Finnish Ostrobothnian sound, JP Nyströms. Västergötland trio **Forsmark Tre** inspired a whole new direction for the Finnish band **JPP**, influencing the Finnish revival at the beginning of the eighties.

In the 1980s **Filarfolket** and **Groupa** made another major click of the evolutionary ratchet.

Both put together the likes of fiddle and flutes with bouzouki or lute, trumpet and the deep honk of bass clarinets and baritone or bass sax in very muscular, danceable and intricate polskas and hallings. 1990's **Folkmusiktältet** – a touring circus-tented show presenting the new roots music for both listening and dancing – pitched camp around Sweden. It featured the core of Sweden's roots scene, including Möller, Willemark and Hedningarna.

As the 1990s progressed the ideas and live and recording innovations intensified. **Hedningarna** gained two Finnish singers, a hugely powerful technologised sound and a wide, increasingly international audience. Together with **Hoven Droven** (of which a founder member was ex-Groupa trumpeter Gustav Hylén), **Den Fule** and **Garmarna**, they demonstrate how electrifying can be the meeting between the power of technology, the raw textures of amplified traditional instruments and the wild, syncopated drive of Swedish traditional dance or the differentness of the old ways of song.

In today's scene many of the aforementioned musicians and bands are still to the fore, but it's not a case of plodding on with the same formula; there are constant developments and new formations, and a flow of emerging new names. New innovative bands, fully formed and impressive, such as **Kalabra** and **Sälta** are constantly emerging. **Enteli** and the work of saxophonists **Jonas Knutsson** and **Anders Hagberg** show the links with the new Nordic roots jazz. Möller and Willemark's **Nordan** project takes the oldest Swedish music and words, in particular ballads, into a new international territory, while the nyckelharpa is taking more and more of a leading role in the hands of such as **Olov Johansson** and **Johan Hedin**.

Links with other world musics have produced the Swedish-Indian **Mynta**, the Haitian high-energy of **Simbi**, the Balkan sounds of **Orientexpressen**, the **Eric Steen Flamenco Fusion**, the tango of **Katzen Kapell**, and many more. Sweden has become a meeting place for musicians from all over the world, sometimes, as in the pan-South American **Cressento**, developing new sounds not heard in their native countries. In the making of new Swedish roots music immigrant musicians are embraced and welcomed, as in the fourteen-piece **Stockholm Folk Music Big Band** led by Ale Möller and Jonas Knutsson. There's a strong feeling among leading musicians that today's living Swedish tradition cannot be a recreation of the past but must draw on present-day multicultural society.

Festivals

Gatherings of spelmän for individual and ensemble concerts and informal music are called **spelmansstämmor**, and there are many of them, mostly in the summer, all over Sweden. The biggest is at **Bingsjö** (Dalarna) in early July, which attracts about 10,000 people for its 24 hours. Others include **Delsbo**, in Hälsingland (also early July) and **Ransäter** in Värmland (early June). The dominant instrument is usually fiddle, with nyckelharpa and other instruments according to region and event. Space, and a quiet place, is often made for singing.

Rättvik Folklore Festival in Dalarna in late July gathers musicians, dancers and singers beside Lake Siljan. It's primarily a festival of customs and costumes rather than a folk festival in the usual present-day sense of bands and international names. Nearby **Falun** hosts Sweden's largest international folk music festival for five days in mid-July, with performances by a large number of the new roots bands, and some others from abroad, plus a lot of spelmän and sessions. Falun Folkmusik Festival also organises the January **Norrsken/Nordic Lights** Nordic and Baltic roots music conference.

Further north **Urkult Folkfest vid Nämforsen** at Näsåker in early August is a World Music festival including Swedish and Nordic roots bands, Finally, at the end of February there's the **Umeå** folk music festival, which features performers mainly from Sweden and the other Nordic countries in indoor venues.

Contacts

Information about musicians and events can be found in the bi-monthly *Lira* **magazine**, Tullkammaregatan 1, S-791 31 Falun, ☎ (46) 23 633 77, fax 23 638 88; *www.lira@lira.se* Also worth checking is Izzy Young's small magazine *Folklore Centrum:* with useful listings and adverts for folk music events, tour-lists, radio broadcasts and the like, it is published eight times a year by Folklore Centrum, Wollmar Yxkullsgatan 2, S-118 50 Stockholm, ☎/fax (46) 8 643 46 27.

The quarterly magazine for members of **SSR (***Sveriges Spelmäns Riksförbund***)** gives information on spelmansstämmor and other spelman-related doings. **RFoD (Riksföreningen för Folkmusik och Dans)** publishes a biennial directory of organisations, institutions, musicians and teachers called *Folkmusik Katalogen*, distributed by Svenska Rikskonserter, Nybrokajen 11, S-111 48 Stockholm, ☎ (46) 8 407 16 00, fax 407 16 50. The Katalog is also searchable online, at *www.rfod.se/fkatalog.html*

Many relevant **Internet site links** are to be found at *www.home3.swipnet.se/~w-33552/links/folk_sv_links.htm*

discography

Good sources for Swedish roots releases are *Rotspel* (Tulegatan 37, 113 53 Stockholm ☎/fax (46) 8 16 04 04; *www.rotspel.a.se*) and *Multikulti* (St. Paulsgatan 3, 118 46 Stockholm ☎/fax (46) 8 643 61 29; http://home3. swipnet.se/~w-3932); or *Digelius* in Helsinki (see Finland). In Britain, ADA and Direct Distribution represent a number of labels.

Compilations

⊚ **Musica Sveciae: Folk Music in Sweden – Vols 1–25** (and growing!) (Caprice, Sweden).

This series is one of the most comprehensive surveys of any national music, a remastered CD reissue of LPs covering the whole gamut of Swedish traditional music (excepting the present-day roots/fusion scene), using archive recordings and some new material. The plan was for 25 volumes, but it looks like growing beyond that. Those already released are:
1–2 The Medieval Ballad: recordings from the 1950s and '60s by Swedish and Finland-Swedish traditional singers.
3 Traditional Folk Music: archival and contemporary recordings.
4 Adventures in Jazz and Folklore: interpretations of traditional themes by some leading Swedish jazz musicans.
5 Folk Tunes from Orsa and Älvdalen: featuring Dalarna fiddlers born in the 1870s and '80s. **6 Rhymes and Lullabies**.
7 Harmonica and Accordion: on the dance floor and at home.
8 Ancient Swedish Pastoral Music: including lockrop herding calls, flutes and horns.
9–10 Three Traditional Folk Singers: Lena Larsson, Ulrika Lindholm and Svea Jansson recorded 1952-63.
11 Fiddlers from Five Provinces: featuring **Eric Sahlström** and others from the 1950s.
12 Songs of Tornedalen: the meeting of Swedish and Finnish cultures.
13 Nordic Folk Instruments: including bowed lyre, bagpipes, kantele, langeleik etc.
14 Folk Tunes from Jämtland: performed by two diddlers, a clarinetist and five fiddlers.
15 Songs of Sailors and Navvies.
16–17 Folk Tunes from Rättvik, Boda & Bingsjö.
18 Folk Tunes from Dala-Floda, Enviken & Ore.
19 Blood, Corpses and Tears: featuring bloodcurdling broadsheet ballads.
20 Folk Songs and Tunes from Bohuslän.
21–23 Joik – A presentation of Sámi Music: with 195 joiks recorded in 1953.
24 Chorales & Wedding Music from Runö: an island off the coast of Estonia.
25 Folk Music in Transition: including jazz and orchestral arrangements and Hedningarna.

 Årsringar (MNW, Sweden).

This double CD compilation gives a very clear overview of Swedish roots music 1970-90, compiled from many labels by Ale Möller and Per Gudmundson. It includes many leading fiddlers plus Filarfolket, Simon Simonsson's Kvartett, Lena Willemark, Folk och Rackare, JP Nyströms, Trio UGB, Orsa Spelmän with Benny Andersson, Arbete och Fritid, Groupa, early Hedningarna and much more.

⊚ **Nordic Roots** (NorthSide, US).

A great budget-priced 1998 sampler from this US label specialising in licensing prominent Nordic new-roots music. It's largely Swedish – Väsen, Hedningarna, Hoven Droven, Den Fule, Swåp et al – plus some Finns and Norwegians.

 Traditional Folk Music (Caprice, Sweden).

This is volume three of the *Musica Sveciae – Folk Music in Sweden* outlined above and is particularly recommended. A rich selection includes lockrop herding calls, Sámi joiks, nyckelharpa, accordions, lots of fiddles and today's groups Frifot and Hedningarna. Recordings from the 1940s to the '90s.

 Xourcism!
(Xource, Sweden).

Much has happened since *Årsringar* (above) was compiled, a substantial proportion of it released by Xource/Resource. This is a 1997 label sampler in which folk-rock and polska/halling driven groove features strongly. Bands include Garmarna, Hedningarna, Hoven Droven, Väsen, Trio Patrekatt, Dan Gisen Malmquist, Urban Turban, Folk & Rackare, Kenny Håkansson, JP Nyströms et al.

Artists

Ola Bäckström

Bäckström is a leading modern Dalarna fiddler who began playing in the 1970s and moves freely between the old tradition and modern bands, exemplifying the continuity between the old masters and new evolution.

 Ola Bäckström (Giga, Sweden).

Traditional and new tunes, playing solo and with Carina Normansson (his fiddler colleague in the English/Swedish quartet Swåp). The Giga label focuses almost entirely on fiddlers, particularly solo, and includes a 3-CD set of all Hjort Anders' recordings. It's fair to say that some of this music played solo by the old masters can be difficult listening for inexperienced ears; Bäckström's album, varied with duo and ensemble items as well as fine classic solo playing, is both the real thing and an accessible entry point.

Mats Edén

The memorable, shapely tunes written by Mats Edén of Groupa, the Nordan Project, etc., have become widely played in the new Swedish music and also picked up by foreign musicians.

 Struling (Amigo, Sweden).

Largely Edén compositions; he plays fiddle and stakefiol, with fiddler Ellika Frisell, percussionist Tina Johansson, Rickard Åström's synths and Stefan Ekedahl's cello.

Filarfolket

This was a band which, with Groupa, marked a transition in the 1980s for Swedish roots music. It included Ellika Frisell, Katarina Olsson, Ale Möller, Sten Källman, Dan Gisen Malmquist, Lasse Bomgren, on bowed strings, saxes, bass clarinets, trumpet, flutes, harmonica, bouzouki, guitar, bass, percussion etc. in polska frenzy.

 Vintervals (Resource, Sweden).

A compilation from the band's series of albums – still richly melodic, energetic, fresh and relevant.

Den Fule

Hefty, brooding rock-polska, with hints of Arabic feel. Henrik Wallgren's vocals, fiddler Ellika Frisell or later Ola Bäckström, Sten Källman (saxes), Jonas Simonsson

(flutes and bass sax), Henrik Cederblom (guitars), Stefan Bergman (bass) and Christian Jormin (drums).

 Skalv (Xource, Sweden).
 Quake (NorthSide, US).

Skalv is the 1995 album; *Quake* is a US compilation of it and predecessor *Lugumleik*.

Garmarna

Garmarna specialise in ballads and instrumentals with a wild, dense pulsing bowed-string and sampling drone-based foundation. Singer/fiddler Emma Härdelin with viola, guitars, hurdy-gurdy and drums.

 Guds Spelemän
(Massproduktion and Xource, Sweden; Omnium, US).

The second album, with a guest vocal on one track from Sámi singer Pål Torbjörn Doj.

Gjallarhorn

Gjallarhorn are actually a Finnish band, but from Finland's Swedish-speaking minority, and play Swedish music from the archipelagos of the Gulf of Bothnia and other Finlands-Svenska regions of the western mainland.

 Ranarop: Call of the Sea-Witch
(Warner Finlandia Innovator, Finland).

Strong melodies, finely poised microtonal singing from Jenny Wilhelms with fiddle and viola dancing together over rippling didgeridoo and deep percussion. An exquisite balance between beauty and guts.

Groupa

Groupa have always been trail-blazers, their changing line-up comprising prime movers in the new music over the years. The current members are Mats Edén, Jonas Simonsson, Rickard Åström, Norwegian percussionist Terje Isungset and, new in 1998 and opening up yet another interesting phase, singer Sofia Karlsson.

 Månskratt
(Amigo, Sweden).

A classic 1990 album, featuring Lena Willemark. For me personally, a turning point in listening to Swedish music; the extraordinary wild intensity of Willemark's singing with Mats Edén's driven bow, Totte Mattsson's furious lute, Gustav Hylén's cornet, the grunting block bass of Bill McChesney's bass clarinet and Jonas Simonsson's bass sax, over Tina Johansson's energetic percussion.

Hedningarna

Hedningarna began as an instrumental trio – Anders Stake, Totte Mattsson, Björn Tollin – then added two Finnish singers – Sanna Kurki-Suonio and Tellu Paulasto (now replaced by Anita Lehtola), and now also bass lute player Ulf Ivarsson. A massive-sounding band, they combine the raw, wild sound of amplified old instruments, Tollin's unique sample-expanded percussion, and Finnish vocal, linguistic and melodic input, with dynamic stagecraft and high-tech production.

 Trä (Xource, Sweden; Northside, US).
Fire (Sony/Tri-Star, US).

Kaksi and *Trä*, the band's second and third albums, delivered the full-blown and overpowering Hedningarna sound. *Fire* is a compilation of 13 tracks from *Trä* and *Kaksi!*

ous projects, all finely-wrought and richly interesting. Try anything with their names on it.

FRIFOT

 Järven
(Caprice, Sweden).

Frifot are a trio of Möller and Willemark with Per Gudmundson, a master Dalarna fiddler and bagpiper. This, their second album (1996) of tunes and songs, traditional and by Möller and Willemark, exemplifies the rhythmic and melodic excitement, skill and open-ended possibilities of Swedish traditions.

NORDAN

◉ **Agram** (ECM, Germany).

The Nordan group, formed for ECM, comprises Möller, Willemark, fiddler Mats Edén, saxophonist Jonas Knutsson, bassist Palle Danielsson and percussionist Tina Johansson. *Agram* is their second (1996) album, in which traditional music combines with spacious Nordic jazz developments, centred around Willemark's compelling singing of ballads and Möller-composed and traditional music.

Hoven Droven

Hoven Droven are a stunning, screamingly high-energy rock-polska band with deep traditional skill; Kjell-Erik Eriksson (fiddle), Jens Comén (saxes), Bo Lindberg (guitars), Pedro Blom (bass), Björn Höglund (drums). Trumpeter Gustav Hylén left in 1998, and was replaced by Janno Strömstedt on Hammond organ.

◉ **Grov** (Xource, Sweden).
◉ **Groove** (NorthSide, US).

Grov is the 1996 second album; *Groove* is a US-licensed compilation of it and predecessor *Hia Hia* with two extra live tracks. Either serves up the raw meat.

Kalabra

This is a fast-rising, ingenious young band, particularly good live, featuring singer/flautist Ulrika Bodén, saxist Amanda Sedgwick, nyckelharpor Markus Svensson with Eric Metall's bass guitar, Sebastian Prinz-Werner's percussion and Simon Stålspets' harmonica, sälgflöjt, jew's harp and bouzouki.

◉ **Kalabra** (Caprice, Sweden).

Songs and dance tunes traditional and new-made, a varied, flexible open sound with great lift and swing whose instrumental aspects continue on the trail blazed by the likes of Filarfolket and Groupa.

Jonas Knutsson

Knutsson is a leading new-Nordic-jazz soprano saxist with strong traditional connections in Enteli, Nordan, Stockholm Folk Big Band etc.

◉ **Vyer: Views** (Caprice, Sweden).

An album that demonstrates just how far the new Nordic jazz forms have diverged from American music – airy and slowly unfolding, with influences from Swedish tradition, Sámi joik and Icelandic poetry.

Ale Möller and Lena Willemark

Ale Möller is a multi-skilled instrumentalist: mandola with quarter-tone frets, trumpet, wind instruments, etc. Lena Willemark is a unique, magnificent, intense singer and a dynamic fiddler. Separately and together – in the groups Frifot and Nordan – they are constantly involved in numer-

Norrlåtar

An innovative band from Norrbotten in northern Sweden formed in 1972 and achieving breakthrough album sales with ever-changing approaches. Founder-member Hans Alatalo, who left in the mid-'90s, is from the region's Finnish-speaking population.

◉ **En Malsvelodi** (MNW, Sweden).

A classic album, from 1990. Huge quirkiness, wit and variety, wide instrumentation, unusual vocals in Swedish and Finnish.

Orsa Spelmänslag

A famous Dalarna fiddling club, a sub-group of which is the fiddles, clarinet, guitar, accordion and bass group Orsa Spelmän which is even more famous for collaborations with Abba's Benny Andersson.

◉ **Orsa Spelmanslag 50 år** (Giga, Sweden).

The distinctive Orsa polskas and other tunes, the big silvery-ringing sound of the full group plus items by Orsa Spelmän, duets, solos by Bjorn Ståbi, Jonny Soling, Olle Moraeus and others, and three herding tunes on willow pipe and horn. The spelmanslag's 1998 50-year anniversary album.

Trio Patrekatt

This nyckelharpa-dominated trio comprises Markus Svensson and Johan Hedin (nyckelharpas and tenor nyckelharpa) with Annika Wijnbladh (cello).

◉ **Adam** (Xource, Sweden).

The rich deep ringing counterpoints of nyckelharpas and cello in ingenious bow-driven traditional and new tunes – in no way dinner-jacketed, but it would make waves in the classical world too.

Väsen

Väsen are a very popular instrumental trio from Uppland : Olov Johansson (nyckelharpa), Mikael Marin (viola) and Roger Tallroth (12-string guitar, bouzouki, octave mandolin), now joined by percussionist André Ferrari.

 Världens Väsen (Xource, Sweden) or
Whirled (NorthSide, US).

Acoustic, but as thick and powerful as rock, with furious Swedish dance swing and drive.

SWEDEN

Ukraine

the bandura played on

Ukraine, the largest of the non-Russian states to emerge from the wreckage of the Soviet Union, has a vast heritage of traditional music. Much has been lost in the twentieth century as war, collectivisation, and rapid industrialisation have taken their toll on the social fabric of the Ukrainian village, but all across the country there are places where unique regional vocal and instrumental styles survive. **Alexis Kochan** and **Julian Kytasty**, continuing a tradition in exile, explore the roots of their music.

G iven Ukraine's position, it's not surprising that it shares Carpathian musical traditions to the west with Romania and Poland, and rich polyphonic song styles with southern Russia to the east. But it also has music uniquely its own, notably the impressive **bandura** – a cross between a zither and lute – and its associated bardic repertoire. A strong village **instrumental tradition** also persists in the western part of the country, although the customary ensemble of fiddle, *tsymbaly* (hammer dulcimer) and drum – a combination known as **troista muzyka** – is rapidly losing ground to drum machines and synthesisers.

At the turn of the century a wave of emigrants from western Ukraine brought the troista muzyka tradition to **North America**, where its most famous exponent was **Pavlo Humeniuk**, 'King of the Ukrainian Fiddlers', who recorded in New York in the 1920s. Even today on the Canadian prairies no Ukrainian wedding band is complete without a tsymbaly, and a small local recording industry there continues to produce cassettes of hybrid **troista–country** bands.

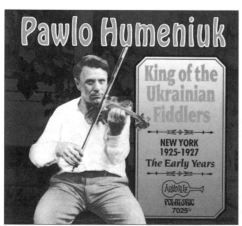

Hutsul Melodies

The prairies aside, the best place to hear real Ukrainian roots music is in the Carpathians, where the **Hutsuls**, a mountain people speaking an archaic Ukrainian dialect, have clung tenaciously to their distinctive music. This is the home of the *kolomeyka* (named after the town of Kolomyya), a widespread circle dance in duple time, and in the highland villages around the towns of Rakhiv and Kosiv, the full assortment of Hutsul instruments can still be heard.

These include not only fiddle and tsymbaly, but a bewildering array of flutes (*sopilka, frilka, floyara, tylynka*) reflecting the Hutsuls' traditional pastoral occupation. The *trembita*, a long mountain horn, has a repertoire of calls used for signalling between mountaintops. The melody instruments play in a wildly ornamented unison over the rhythmic underpinning of the tsymbaly, creating an instantly recognisable sound.

Many of the ensembles in this region – as elsewhere in Ukraine – are organised around multi-generational families of master musicians. Among them, the **Tafichuk Family** ensemble from Bukovets is especially highly regarded.

Choirs and Rituals

Elsewhere in Ukraine, **vocal music** predominates. 'Bring together two Ukrainians and you have another choir' – so goes an old Ukrainian saying – and despite everything that the twentieth century threw at the country, those choirs have survived, or are sprouting anew.

In **Polissia**, a region of forests and swamps northwest of the capital Kyiv (Kiev), an archaic repertoire of seasonal **ritual songs** dating back to pre-Christian times has been preserved. In **western Ukraine** choral singing is in unison, while in **eastern and** central **Ukraine** there's a rich tradition of, mainly two-part, **folk polyphony**, sung mostly by women.

In the latter tradition, the beginning of a verse is often sung by one or two singers (the *zaspiv*) and then the verse, or chorus, is taken up by the rest of the choir (*pryspiv*). The solo lines are more ornamented and sometimes improvised, while the lower choral lines take the melody. The traditional singing style is strong and open-throated and the harmony quite bare.

Sadly, the elderly grannies heard on today's field recordings are in most cases the last carriers of the tradition in their village and will have no successors. However, recently several excellent ensembles of university folklore students have begun performing and recording recreations of regional vocal styles based on fieldwork and archival recordings. **Drevo** from Kyiv and **Hilka** from Kirovohrad can be heard on the French label Silex, and both also have locally produced recordings.

Eastern Ukrainian polyphonic singing was also exported, to the Kuban region in southern Russia, settled by descendants of Ukrainian cossacks from the eighteenth century. Striking examples can be heard on the recordings of the professional **Kuban Cossack Chorus**, which had professional status in the Soviet era.

Another big Soviet group, based in Ukraine, was gathered by folklorist and composer Hryhory Veriovka, who in 1944 followed the advancing Red Army westward across Ukraine, picking the best singers from the ruined villages for a State Folk Chorus. For forty years, this group – known after the founder's death as the **Veriovka State Folk Chorus** – was practically the only recorded source of Ukrainian traditional music, showcasing stunning examples of women's polyphonic singing and brilliant instrumental soloists.

Singer **Nina Matvienko** began her career as a soloist with the choir in its heyday in the 1970s. She has gone on to record on her own and with her vocal trio Zoloti Kliuchi on the new Ukrainian Symphocarre label.

The Bandura

The **bandura**, a kind of zither, is unique to Ukraine and is considered the national instrument. Unlike the Scandinavian and Baltic zithers, it is plucked held upright and has a lute-like neck for the longest bass strings.

The bandura owes its special position in Ukrainian culture to its association with a tradition of epic songs – *dumy* – that survived into the twentieth century. Most of them were historical tales of Turkish captivity, daring escapes and the deeds of Cossack heroes. Their performance was the special province of the *kobzari*, blind singers formed into secretive guilds. The bandura was the accompanying instrument of choice, though at least one prominent nineteenth-century kobzar still used the older lute-like *kobza*, whiled **hurdy gurdy players** – *limyky* – performed a similar repertoire of dumy and religious and moralistic songs.

At the turn of the century urban musicians took up the instrument and by the time of the Russian revolution there were professional ensembles in Kyiv and Poltava performing choral music with bandura accompaniment. The subsequent history of the bandura is a case study in the way the cultural politics of the Soviet regime could shape and deform the development of a musical tradition. The one or two blind singers who survived the Stalinist terror of the 1930s (there is considerable evidence of a Congress of Traditional Singers from which the participants did not return) paid for their survival with pseudo-dumas about Stalin and Lenin. Meanwhile, the Kyiv and Poltava ensembles were lumped together into a **State Bandurist Chorus** performing party anthems and merry folk ditties

After World War II the bandura, like other folk instruments in the Soviet Union, was 'developed and improved' to a standard 60-plus string chromatic instrument with complex and bulky key change mechanisms. Conservatoire courses in Kyiv and Lviv trained many technically proficient players, but neither the instrument nor the playing technique – still less the repertoire, heavily oriented towards classical transcriptions – has much connection with the earlier tradition.

In fact, a more traditional take on the instrument can be heard today in Detroit or Cleveland. There, an instrumental style evolved out of the style of exile players from the Kyiv ensemble. The **Ukrainian Bandurist Chorus**, a group containing most of Ukraine's best surviving players, made its way west in an incredible wartime odyssey that included forest concerts for Ukrainian insurgents, close calls from Allied bombing, and hungry months in a Nazi labour camp. Coming to the US in 1949 and settling in Detroit, the group maintains an unbroken performance tradition going back to the original Kyiv and Poltava ensembles and has issued a steady stream of recordings (over twenty at the last count) beginning with albums of 78s in the 1940s and now including several CDs.

The long-time director of the group **Hryhory Kytasty** (1907–1984) and other original members trained a generation of North American-born play-

Heorhiy Tkachenko (3rd left) with students at his 90th birthday concert

ers. Today's North American bandurists cultivate a repertoire and a style of playing based on the professional school of the 1920s and '30s and markedly different from that taught in Ukraine. New York-based **Julian Kytasty**, a third generation bandurist, has built on his great-uncle's work to create new music for the instrument. He has made several recordings including a recent independently produced CD of Hryhory Kytasty's solo music.

In terms of re-discovering an older style, the Smithsonian Folkways Institute is carrying out restoration work on a priceless archive of wax cylinder recordings of *kobzari* from the turn of the century and there is work being done on recordings of **Zynovij Shtokalko** (who died in New York in 1968), arguably the one bandurist of this century who achieved a professional standard of performance without in any way classicising the instrument or the music.

New Ukrainian Music

The contemporary Ukrainian **pop scene** was conjured into existence in the space of one September week in 1989 in Chernivtsi. The occasion was **Chervona Ruta** (named after a red flower in the Carpathians that is said to bloom just once a year), the first festival of modern Ukrainian music. Surmounting considerable obstruction from the authorities – performers had to thread their way to venues through rings of military checkpoints – the festival assembled hundreds of musicians from every corner of the country, performing in genres ranging from singer-songwriter to heavy metal.

Since independence, Chervona Ruta has been repeated, each time in a new city, at two-yearly intervals. Although in recent years the protest songs of 1989 have given way to a predominance of techno-oriented dance genres, the organisers of the festival continue to seek out and showcase new music that connects to traditional roots. A 1997 prize-winner was the Kharkiv based group **Radoslav**, which bases its vocal style on an authentic treatment of local polyphonic singing. Another recent laureate, **Katya Chilly**, combine drum-and-bass with vocals from the ancient ritual songs of Polissia.

Today the most interesting traditional music is happening where efforts are being made to bridge the gaps and disruptions of the Soviet period: for example, the revival of the **epic singing tradition**. This is centered on the single performer who carried its unbroken thread into the 1990s: **Heorhiy Tkachenko** (1898–1993), who learned the art of duma singing in his youth from blind kobzari. In his old age, he passed on his songs and an authentic style of accompaniment on a traditional twenty-one-string bandura to several students. The movement has since spread to include several informal kobzar schools and workshops building traditional banduras and other ancient instruments. The best performers are Tkachenko's student **Mykola Budnyk** and lirnyk **Mykhailo Khai** (who can both be heard on the Silex CDs), and kobza player **Volodymyr Kushpet**.

Some of **Ukraine's minorities** have been engaged in bridging formidable cultural disruptions of their own. A **Jewish cultural revival** is under way, but the music of the Jewish towns and *shtetls* (villages) in western Ukraine did not survive the

Holocaust. New Jewish culture in Ukraine is largely an urban phenomenon in Kyiv and Odessa.

In 1944 the entire **Crimean Tatar** nation was loaded into cattle wagons and deported to Uzbekistan and other parts of the Soviet Union. Since Ukraine's independence in 1991, hundreds of thousands have returned to the Crimea, many living in shanty towns outside their ancestral villages. One of their number, **Enver Ismailov**, a brilliant self-taught guitarist, has toured in Europe and made several recordings, recently teaming up with wind player Narket Ramazanov and percussionist Rustem Bari in jazz-tinged compositions based on Crimean Tatar melodies.

Bridges of a different kind have been built by a new generation of Ukrainian musicians in the diaspora by fusing Ukrainian music with Western styles. These include the British group **The Ukrainians** which was formed by musicians of Ukrainian descent from the rock band The Wedding Present. They adopted traditional instruments, alongside a rock rhythm section, and went back to old recordings of Ukrainian country dances and melodies for inspiration.

Other musicians, from the larger, North American Ukrainian community, include the mandolin virtuoso **Peter Ostroushko**, and Canadian born jazz pianist **John Stetch**, who draws on the Hutsul music of the Carpathians in his improvisations and original compositions. Another Canadian, singer **Alexis Kochan**, discovered the depth of the Ukrainian folk song tradition while on a six-month internship with the Veriovka State Chorus. Her recordings have combined seemingly contradictory elements, putting together Ukrainian musicians from the Canadian prairies and the Carpathian mountains, and more recently working with bandura player Julian Kytasty alongside jazz and African drums.

COOKING VINYL

British band The Ukrainians get back to their roots

discography

Mykhailo Khai at the Ukrainian Experimental Laboratory of Folklore in Kyiv has produced a series of cassettes of field recordings of both vocal and instrumental music. Everything from old babushkas singing, to Hutsul fiddlers and bandura revivalists. Each cassette (there are currently seventeen) focuses in depth on a specific region, group or performer. Ukrainian Experimental Folklore Laboratory, Ukraine 252143 Kyiv, vul. Metrolohichna, 6, apt. 89.

Compilations

Diakouyou (Auvidis/Silex, France).

A rather wonderful contemporary fusion album with three vocalists from the Drevo ensemble accompanied by French percussion group Baron Samedi. Village polyphony interwoven with a raw, rhythmic interplay.

 Musiques Traditionelles d'Ukraine: Vols 1 & 2 (Auvidis/Silex, France).

These two CDs of recent field recordings (mainly by Hubert Boone) provide a valuable picture of traditional music in Ukraine today. **Vol 1** includes polyphonic singing from central Ukraine including the Hilka choir, excellent Hutsul music from the Tafichuk family and string bands from western Ukraine. **Vol 2** features excellent tracks by the Drevo choir, various old singers, the rare sound of the *lira* (hurdy gurdy) and intimate old-style bandura playing by Mykola Budnyk.

**Ukrainian Village Music:
Historic Recordings 1928–1933** (Arhoolie, US).

Down-home recordings by fiddlers and bands fresh off the boat from western Ukraine: polkas, kolomeykas and the odd Jewish number.

Artists

Cheres

Cross the soul of a village musician with Conservatoire-trained musicianship and that's the Cheres ensemble. Leader Andriy Milavsky (sopilka and various winds) spent his childhood traipsing between village weddings in western Ukraine with his musician grandfather, then trained at the Kyiv Conservatory as a folk instrument specialist. Along with tsymbaly player Alexander Fedoriuk, he formed this ensemble dedicated to the (then-revolutionary) idea that folk instrumental music sounded better in its original *troista muzyka* instrumentation than in the lush orchestration of Soviet Folk Instruments Orchestras.

**From the Mountains to the Steppe:
Village Music of Ukraine** (Cheres, US).

Now based in New York, Milavsky and Fedoriuk add a fiddle and bass to recreate the raucous textures of the Carpathian village bands they grew up with. The CD's four vocal tracks are a marked contrast, featuring the haunting folk-style vocals of American-born Lilia Pavlovska over the ensemble's minimalist soundscapes. (Available from Cheres, 24 5th Ave. No 919, New York, NY 10011; *CheresCD@juno.com*)

Ensemble Berehynia

The Berehynia are a Ukranian-based ensemble of singers and instrumentalists. Their name refers to a woman who preserves hearth, home and traditions.

Vorotarchyk (The Gatekeeper) (Pan, Netherlands).

A good sample of songs, rituals and instrumental pieces – although some tracks are rather over-polished. Bandura playing by Roman Hrynkiv, various flutes, and several Cossack songs, including a spirited finale.

Pavlo Humeniuk

Born in western Ukraine around 1884, Pavlo Humeniuk, 'King of the Ukrainian Fiddlers', left over 250 recordings by his death in 1965. He went to America around 1902 and started recording 'village style' music in 1925.

 King of the Ukrainian Fiddlers
(Arhoolie, US).

These are recordings made for Columbia and Victor in New York in the 1920s. Quite a few include urban instruments like piano or trombone, but the best, with tsymbaly and double bass or violins and accordion, are classic examples of the old village style.

Alexis Kochan

Born in Winnipeg, Canada, singer Alexis Kochan has a particular interest in the older layers of Ukrainian song.

Paris to Kiev (Olesia, Canada).

An unlikely but successful fusion. Kochan puts together musicians from the Canadian prairies with others who grew up in the Carpathians to come up with some fizzing polkas, marches and kolomeykas.

Paris to Kyiv Variances
(Olesia, Canada; Ladyslipper, US)

Music from the deepest layers of the Ukrainian tradition – with a contemporary twist. Kochan and bandurist Julian Kytasty weave a multi-layered fabric of voices and instruments, incorporating pre-Christian ritual songs, fragments of medieval chant, jazzy improvisations and African drumming.
Olesia productions, PO Box 2877, Winnipeg, Manitoba R3C 4B4. ✆/fax (204) 338 3385.

Kuban Cossack Chorus

The Kuban state choir, under the Ukrainian director Victor Zakharchenko, used the freedoms of the 1990s perestroika era to stretch the boundaries of the form. They spent a lot of time in the villages collecting material and stimulating a revival of village singing in the region. In their own work, the Chorus had an intensity and commitment that occasionally allowed one to forget that it was a show song and dance chorus like all the rest.

In the Kuban: Folk Songs of the Black Sea and Linear Cossacks (Melodiya, Russia).

Ukrainian folk song repertoire of the Black Sea Cossacks with Nina Matvienko as a soloist on two of the cuts.

Julian Kytasty

Julian Kytasty is an American-Ukrainian bandura player, actively exploring the old tradition. Based in New York, he is the grand-nephew of Hryhory Kytasty, the great bandurist who emigrated to the US after World War II.

Hryhory Kytasty: Music for Solo Bandura/Songs
(Kytasty, US).

A tribute to Hryhory Kytasty, these works develop the bandura style of the first generation of professional players of the 1920s and '30s which was subsequently lost in Ukraine. Although composed for a classicised chromatically-tuned

instrument they are informed by the modes, ornamentation, and textures of the kobzar tradition. A nice unmannered vocal style too.
Available from: Julian Kytasty, 138 2nd Ave, New York, NY 10003.

Nina Matvienko

Originally a soloist from the Veriovka State Folk Chorus, Matvienko now pursues a solo career as the diva of Ukrainian folksong.

Zolotoslov (Symphocarre, Ukraine).

Features a contemporary choral composition from Kyiv composer Lesia Dychko, and twenty-one unaccompanied folksongs. The interpretations are unrivalled.

Peter Ostroushko

Mandolin, guitar and fiddle player Ostroushko was born in northeast Minneapolis to parents from Ukraine. For many years he was a regular performer and then music director of Garrison Keillor's radio show, *A Prairie Home Companion*. A fine mandolin player, he blends American and Ukrainian sensibilities.

Down the Streets of My Old Neighbourhood
(Rounder, US).

A 1986 recording in tribute – loving, humorous, sentimental – to the people, food and music of his immigrant neighbourhood. Some Ukrainian love songs, a drunken polka, and the memorable "B-O-R-S-C-H-T" dedicated to the women of the local Orthodox Church.

Sluz Duz Music (Rounder, US).

Marginally less Ukrainian, perhaps, but available on CD.

John Stetch

Born in Edmonton (one of Canada's strongly Ukrainian cities) in 1966, jazz pianist Stetch grew up in a Ukrainian musical environment. He currently lives in New York.

Kolomeyka Fantasy (Global Village Music, US).

Carpathian polkas and other tunes in solo piano arrangements (with some bass and drums), and with excursions into Bartók, boogie-woogie, blues and impressionism.

The Ukrainians

Active in the early 1990s, The Ukrainians were a British band, led by guitarist Pete Solowka, that evolved from rock band The Wedding Present. Their albums featured songs inspired by old-style dances, and used a mix of traditional and rock instruments. The songs are in Ukrainian, sometimes using traditional melodies, and sometimes their own authentic-sounding compositions.

 The Ukrainians
(Cooking Vinyl/BMG, UK).

The band's first eponymous album was their most Ukrainian in style, with some furious dances tunes (like "Hopak" fired by Solowka's mandolin) as well as more rock numbers. "The Glory of the Kobzar" with its bandura sound also harks back to the tradition.

Kultura (Cooking Vinyl/BMG, UK; True North, Canada).

A 1994 album provided a more cynical and contemporary look at corrupt politicians and the issues of Ukrainians at home and in exile.

Wales

harps, bards and the gwerin

Welsh music tends to conjure up images of miners raising the roof of their local chapel – and, indeed, despite the near-obliteration of the mining industry, male voice choirs remain a dominant, if declining, feature of life across the Valleys and rural Wales (mixed choirs are in the ascendant today). But Welsh music extends out into village halls, clubs, festivals and pubs, where Saturday nights often resound with impromptu, but naturally-understood, harmonies. In quieter venues, harp players repay their musical debt to ancestors who accompanied the ancient bards, while modern folk draws directly from the broader Celtic musical tradition. There's an exciting new buzz, too, spurred in part by the success of new Welsh rock bands, in a nation whose music has too often been commercially over-shadowed by the Celtic giants of Ireland, Brittany and Scotland. **William Price** reports from the valleys.

The Welsh word *gwerin*, the closest approximation of 'folk', has a much wider meaning than its English counterpart, taking in popular culture as well as folklore. At a **gwyl werin** (folk festival), you're as likely to encounter the local rock band as the local dance team, and the whole community will be there – not just the committed specialists. If you're roaming around Wales, look out, too, for the word **twmpath** on posters – it's the equivalent of a barn dance or ceilidh and is used when Welsh dances are the theme of the night (in the west and the north the calling is likely to be exclusively in Welsh, too). Some of the best twmpathau can approach the hedonism of a Breton *festou-noz*.

It's often said that the Welsh love singing but ignore their native instrumental music. Certainly, Welsh **folk song** has always been close to the heart of the culture, acting as a carrier of emotions, political messages and social protest, while traditional Welsh music and dance have had the difficult task of fighting back to life from near-extinction following centuries of political and religious suppression. Unlike their Celtic cousins in Ireland, Scotland and Brittany, folk musicians in Wales largely learned their tunes from books and manuscripts rather than from older generations of players, although in recent years a surprising and encouraging series of links with 'source' performers has been revealed.

Language has traditionally been more of a divider in Wales than in other Celtic countries, and the picture for many years has been that of a Welsh-speaking 'Taffia' controlling many key areas of life in the country to the exclusion of the English-speaking majority, who have felt disenfranchised and debarred from their national culture as a result.

Today, the Welsh language is spoken by half a million of the country's 2.5 million population, and the national attitude to the language has undergone a remarkable renaissance in the past twenty years. In some parts of the anglicised south, up to 33 percent of children now attend Welsh-language schools and their monoglot parents are rushing to evening classes in a bid to keep up.

Rock and folk are both great pillars of the Welsh language, but English speakers have not received the same encouragement to explore their own heritage within the Welsh framework. The preservation and nurturing of Welsh-language songs, customs and traditions is vitally important, but the folklore of English-speaking Gower and South Pembrokeshire and the rich vein of industrial material from the valleys is actually in much greater danger of being lost to posterity.

The most exciting move of recent years has been the emergence of **Fflach Tradd**, a label devoted to capturing the key roots sounds of Welsh music and giving it the same international profile as that enjoyed by the Celtic giants. A string of excellent albums has been released and actually made it on to the shelves of shops in Brittany and elsewhere in the Celtic world, to the delight of musicians who have been frustrated at the lack of sales outlets for their work outside Wales. At last, the inward-looking establishment has been challenged and the world may well get a chance to find out about Welsh music.

Sadly, though, the biggest-selling Welsh-language act of all is country-and-western duo **John Ac Alun**. The inflections of this noble, ancient tongue simply do not sit happily on the metrical simplicities of Nashville. Equally bizarre, but much more fun, is the Welsh-Louisiana music of **Cajuns Denbo**.

Welsh Harps

Historically the most important instrument in the folk repertoire, the **harp** has been played in Wales since at least the eleventh century. In recent years craftsmen have recreated the ancient *crwth* (a stringed instrument which may have been either plucked or bowed), the *pibgorn* (a reed instrument with a cow's horn for a bell) and the *pibacwd* (the primitive Welsh bagpipe). Some groups have adopted these instruments, but their primitive design and performance means they rarely blend happily with modern instruments.

The simple early harps were ousted in the seventeenth century by the arrival of the **triple harp**, with its complicated string arrangement (two parallel rows sounding the same note, with a row of accidentals between them), giving it a unique, rich sound. The nineteenth-century swing towards classical concert music saw the invasion of the large chromatic pedal harps that still dominate today, but the triple, always regarded as the traditional Welsh harp, was kept alive, as a portable instrument, by Gypsy musicians. It has been making a mighty comeback in gwerin circles over the past decade.

Ar Log with Welsh harpists Dafydd Roberts (left) and Gwyndaf Roberts.

Bards and Eisteddfods

The **bardic** and **eisteddfod** traditions have long played a key role in Welsh culture. Medieval bards held an elevated position in Welsh society and were often pure composers, employing a harpist and a *datgeiniad*, whose role was to declaim the bard's words. The first eisteddfod appears to have been held in Cardigan in 1176, with contests between bards and poets and between harpists, players and pipers.

It was a glorious but precarious tradition. Henry VIII's Act Of Union in 1536 – designed to anglicise the country by stamping out Welsh culture and language – saw the eisteddfodau degenerate, and the rise of Nonconformist religion in the eighteenth and nineteenth centuries, with its abhorrence of music and merry-making, almost sounded the death knell for Welsh traditions. Edward Jones, Bardd y Brenin (Bard to the King), observed sorrowfully in the 1780s that Wales, which used to be one of the happiest of countries, "has become one of the dullest".

Folk music, however, gained some sort of respectability when London-based **Welsh Societies**, swept along in a romantic enthusiasm for all things Celtic, revived it at the end of the eighteenth century. Back in Wales, in the 1860s, the **National Eisteddfod Society** was formed, the forerunner of today's eisteddfod societies. These days three major week-long events dominate the calendar: the **International Eisteddfod** at Llangollen in July, the **Royal National Eisteddfod** in the first week of August and the **Urdd Eisteddfod**, Europe's largest youth festival, in May. The National and the Urdd alternate between north and south Wales.

Eisteddfodau have always tended to formalise Welsh culture because competitions need rules, and such parameter-defining is naturally alien to the free evolution of traditional song and music. When Nicholas Bennett was compiling his 1896 book *Alawon Fy Nghwlad*, still an important source of Welsh tunes, he rejected a great deal of good Welsh dance music because it did not conform to the contemporary high art notion of what Welsh music ought to sound like. Despite this often-heard criticism, eisteddfodau have played a major role in keeping traditional music, song and dance at the heart of national culture.

Today a host of non-competition festivals champion Welsh music alongside the best from around the world, including **Mid Wales May Festival** at Newtown (last weekend in May), **Gŵyl Werin y Cnapan** at Ffostrasol, Dyfed (second weekend in July), **Sesiwn Fawr** at Dolgellau (third weekend in July) and **Pontardawe International Music Festival** (third weekend in August).

Gwerin Sounds

In terms of world popularity, two Welsh names stand out today — **Robin Huw Bowen** and the group Fernhill. Triple harpist Bowen is the most influential traditional Welsh musician of recent years, reviving interest in the instrument with appearances throughout the world and doing tremendous work in making available unpublished manuscripts of Welsh instrumental music. He started out in the late 1970s with a pioneering roots band called **Mabsant**, who introduced a jazz sensibility to the Welsh folk tunes he unearthed, before concentrating on a solo career. He also works, mainly abroad, with the quartet **Cusan Tân**.

Maboant (Robin Huw Bowen centre)

Fernhill is a gloriously eclectic quartet which sprung out of the ashes of **Saith Rhyfeddod**, featuring singer **Julie Murphy**, pipers Ceri Rhys Matthews and Jonathan Shorland, plus ubiquitous young English diatonic accordionist Andy Cutting. They sing in Welsh, English, Breton and Gallo and strip well-known songs down to the bare bones, refurbishing them ready to face a new Millennium.

Bob Delyn

Within the Welsh language scene, bands can be hugely popular without ever breaking through to the wider world outside. **Ar Log**, with the wonderful harp-playing brothers **Dafydd** and **Gwyndaf Roberts**, were the first to cross the divide more than twenty years ago, and their occasional concerts today can still whip up a fury even if the original bleak wildness of their sound has been replaced by a smoother big-band approach. Dafydd and Gwyndaf were taught by the legendary Nansi Richards, and another triple harpist who has recently started to excite UK-wide attention (in her late fifties) is **Llio Rhydderch**, also a pupil of Nansi's.

In north Wales, **Bob Delyn A'r Ebyllion** led by the enigmatic Twm Morys, plough a unique path fusing Welsh, Breton and rock influences, fascinating, visionary and uncompromising. Other northern bands include **Moniars**, who have a raucous electric bass-and-drums approach to Welsh language song, and **Gwerinos**, descendants of the late lamented Cilmeri, who have produced a couple of great albums and who play for concerts and for twmpathau. Southern bands breaking through to an international audience from the Welsh-language scene include Cardiff-based **Carreg Lafar** and Ammanford dance band **Jac y Do**.

On the more traditional gwerin scene, the acknowledged father of Welsh folk is politician, songwriter and Sain Records founder **Dafydd Iwan**. He began as a singer-songwriter in the Dylan/Pete Seeger mould in the mid-1960s and has been popular and prolific ever since, providing a musical voice for the nationalist movement. From the same school, singer-songwriter **Meic**

Dawns, Dawns . . .

Traditional dance in Wales has been revived over the past fifty years after a long period of religious suppression. It plays a big part in the folk culture of Wales, and the top teams are exciting and professional in their approach. Dances written in recent years, often for eisteddfod competitions, have been quickly absorbed into the repertoire.

Cwmni Dawns Werin Canolfan Caerdydd, Cardiff's official dance team, are the leading group, and their musicians are recommended for a hearing as well. **Dawnswyr Nantgarw**, from the Taff Vale village that was the source of the country's romantic and raunchy fair dances, have turned Welsh dance into a theatrical art form: concise, perfectly drilled and very showy; while the theatre show "A Tale Of Two Rivers" has given birth to the exciting, stage-oriented **Dawnswyr Tâf-Elai**.

Dawnswyr Gwerin Pen-y-Fai, from Bridgend, always come up with a good twmpath night, while Anglesey-based **Ffidl Ffadl** also boast an excellent musician in fiddler Huw Roberts, formerly with the early 1980s bands Cilmeri and **Pedwar yn y Bar. Dawnswyr Brynmawr** also have a capable band who play for twmpath dances as Taro Tant.

The major dance festival is **Gŵyl Ifan**, held in Cardiff on the closest weekend to midsummer's day with displays and special events held across the city and at the Museum of Welsh Life, St Fagans.

Stevens has consistently produced good work on the borderlines of folk, blues and acoustic rock.

Singer/harpist **Siân James**, from Llanerfyl in mid-Wales, has produced three albums which have won the acclaim of Welsh and English speakers alike and have now been released in Japan. Her influences are wide-ranging and her pure-voiced harp pieces were always offset by sporadic appearances with the rock-oriented **Bwchadanas**. She even cropped up playing harp with the London roots-reggae band, One Style. Rich-voiced singer **Siwsann George**, from Rhondda, appears more often in her own right these days than with her band Mabsant. Another quality Welsh-language singer is Cardiff-based **Heather Jones** who works solo and alongside fiddlers Jane Ridout and Mike Lease, uillean piper Alan Moller and harpist Chris Knowles in the five-piece **Hafren**.

SIÂN JAMES

cysgodion karma

SCD 4037
ADD

Harmony songs in three or four parts were a traditional feature in mid-Wales, where the *plygain* carol-singing tradition still survives at Christmas. Small parties of carol singers, each with its own repertoire, would sing in church from midnight to dawn on Christmas morning. The group **Plethyn**, formed in the 1970s to adapt this style to traditional and modern Welsh songs, still perform occasionally and singer Linda Healey has also developed a solo career.

Wales' busiest and furthest-travelled band is probably **Calennig**, from Llantrisant in Glamorgan, who blend fiery Welsh dance sets with English-language songs from the Valleys and Gower, much of it stemming from their own research. They tour regularly in Europe, America and New Zealand and have helped to popularise Welsh dance worldwide with a punchy collection of *twmpath* tunes and up-front calling from Patricia Carron-Smith. They are also moving into the fields of theatre and new music creation, with a string of shows that are winning critical praise such as "A Tale Of Two Rivers" and "Caradog: The First Welsh Hero!"

On the straight folk circuit, **The Hennessys**, led by broadcaster, TV personality and songwriter Frank Hennessy, still have a huge and well-deserved middle-of-the-road following in the south, twenty-five years after joining the procession of Irish-influenced trios in the folk clubs. Frank, too, has done great work by bringing Welsh and other Celtic music to mainstream attention with his various radio and TV programmes.

Singer-songwriters **Huw** and **Tony Williams**, from Brynmawr in the Gwent Valleys, are popular on the folk circuit across Britain, though their following, like other English-language performers, is greater away from home than it is inside Wales. Huw's songwriting, notably songs like "Rosemary's Sister", has been embraced by Fairport Convention and a string of other big-name performers. In Wales, he is best known for his Eisteddfod-winning clog dancing.

The guitar and fiddle playing **Kilbride Brothers** trio, long an institution in Cardiff ceilidh bands, have released a highly acclaimed CD and started playing far and wide outside Wales. Other notable performers have never been recorded, such as the Welsh-Irish couple John and Briege Morgan, Bargoed songwriter Jeff Hankins and Cardiff harpist Elonwy Wright.

Contacts

Colfyddydau Mari Arts: Research, information, education and creation of new work based on traditonal Welsh themes. Studio 4, Model House Craft and Design Centre, The Bullring, Llantrisant CF72 8EB. ☎/fax 01443 226892; email *mari.arts@argonet.co.uk*; Website *www.argonet.co.uk/users/mari.arts*

COTC (Cymdeithas Offerynnau Traddodiadol Cymru): The Society for the Traditional Instruments of Wales. Good for information on the ever-growing number of regular Welsh music sessions around the country. 8 Bron Arfon, Llanllechid, Gwynedd LL57 3LW.

Taplas – the Voice Of Folk In Wales: Magazine published every two months, £1.50 from Keith Hudson, 182 Broadway, Roath, Cardiff CF5 2YQ. ☎ 029 2049 9759, fax 2048 4882.

TRAC (Traddodiadau Cerdd Cymru/Music Traditions Wales): Newly formed body aiming to be a point of contact enabler, pointing enquirers in the right direction and keeping nationwide information exchanges up-to-date and on the ball. Contact Phil Freeman, ☎01686 688102.

discography

For Welsh music by mail order, try *Cob Records* in Porthmadog ☎01766 512170.

Compilations

◎ **Blas** (Fflach Tradd, Wales).

The new face of tradition in Wales, fourteen tracks from projects like Ffidil (fiddles), Datgan (female voices) and Pibau (bagpipes) and from artists including KilBride and I lio Rhydderch. Scintillating stuff.

◎ **Carolau Plygain** (Sain, Wales).

Few CDs are available of Welsh 'source' performances, the older generation who handed down their songs, but this

album of Christmas carols from a surviving mid-Wales tradition is a gem.

 Ffidil (Fflach Tradd, Wales).

An in-depth look at the work of thirteen of Wales' leading fiddlers, almost all of excellent quality. The range of styles, from north to south and from old to innovative, stands out particularly well.

◎ **Goreuon Canu Gwerin Newydd: The Best of New Welsh Folk Music** (Sain, Wales).

Sain, the biggest record label in Wales, has released many of the better-known Welsh artists and bands, and this compilation of eighteen tracks from Ar Log, Aberjaber, Calennig and less well-known names such as Ogam and Pigyn Clyst, is a good place to start if you're interested in the field.

Artists

Aberjaber

Aberjaber was formed by Cardiff jazz/roots/world musician Peter Stacey, Swansea harpist Delyth Evans and Oxford music graduate Stevie Wishart (viol and hurdy gurdy), and reformed in 1997 with Stevie replaced by Ben Assare on African percussion.

◎ **Y Bwced Perffaith** (Sain, Wales).

Experiments with traditional music from Welsh and other Celtic sources plus a swathe of original writing.

Ar Log

Ar Log, originally put together artificially in the 1970s to play at the Lorient Interceltic Festival when Wales couldn't raise a group, went on to give Welsh music its first major foothold on the world scene. They have remained the kingpin band within Wales ever since.

 Ar Log VI (Sain, Wales).

The band's sixth album celebrated their twentieth anniversary by gathering together all their members old and new to produce a party-atmosphere trawl through a familiar selection of songs, spiced up with some sparkling tune sets given extra lift by the unusual amount of new material. Members include fiddler Iolo Jones, who deserves a medal for services to Welsh music – he not only contributes a large amount of new tunes to the repertoire but also plays for Calennig, The Hennessys, Siwsann George and Mabon as well.

Bob Delyn A'r Ebyllion

Bob Delyn, led by Twm Morys and Gorwel Roberts, blend Welsh and Breton influences with rhythms and attitude fostered from rock and roll.

◎ **Gwbade Bach Cochlyd** (Crai, Wales).

Celtic harp meets the bardic beatbox on the band's most recent album, which has won praise from many corners, much of it from English-speaking reviewers.

Robin Huw Bowen

Harpist Robin Huw Bowen is not merely a virtuoso on the national instrument of Wales, but also a researcher responsible for bringing much dormant music into the light through his own publishing company.

These two self-produced albums contain dance music and airs for the triple harp, the latter examining the gypsy tradition and including tunes from the still-living Cardiff triple harpist Eldra Jarman.

Calennig

Calennig, from Glamorgan, are both a fiercely propulsive dance band and concert performers with a long international record, known worldwide for their research work in the South Wales folklore field.

⒪ **Dwr Glan** (Sain, Wales).
⒪ **Trade Winds** (Sain, Wales).

Two very different albums. Rocky Welsh dance sets rub shoulders with songs tinged with Breton and Galician influences on the first, while *Trade Winds* is part of an on-going research project into the sea songs and shanties of the sailors of the South Wales ports.

HTV WALES

Calennig

Carreg Lafar

A young Cardiff band which has taken off with the city's hip community and has also made it to America.

⒪ **Ysbryd Y Werin** (Sain, Wales).

Strong female vocals make up for a lack of weight in the instrumental department.

Cilmeri

Sadly defunct Gwynedd band which was the first to put a harder, Irish-style edge on Welsh music.

⒪ **Cilmeri** (Sain, Wales).

Thoughtful, politically edged songs and tune sets driven along by insistent fiddle, guitar and bodhrán.

Cusan Tân

This quartet, including Robin Huw Bowen, are a vehicle for the highly-individual songs of Ann Morgan-Jones and Sue Jones-Davies.

⒪ **Yr Esgair** (Sain, Wales).

Floaty, ethereal and hypnotic lyrics and tunes with a real sense of mid-Wales earth consciousness about them. But do not file under New Age Hippie Nonsense there are some challenging ideas here.

Delyth Evans

Aberjaber's harpist, from Swansea, is in great demand as a solo performer for events of many different kinds in Wales.

⒪ **Delta** (Sain, Wales).

Music for the Celtic harp from Wales and other parts of the Celtic world, an entrancing blend of traditional material and new tunes.

Fernhill

Fernhill are an adventurous, multi-lingual band which developed out of Saith Rhyfeddod. They have only one Welsh-born member, but Essex-born Julie Murphy sings strongly and confidently in Welsh (and in Gallo, Breton, French and English as well). Bagpipe experts Ceri Rhys Matthews and Jonathan Shorland are joined by diatonic accordion master Andy Cutting to produce a sound which is refashioning familiar Welsh songs and giving them a stark new beauty.

 Llatai (Beautiful Jo Records, England).
Ca' Nos (Beautiful Jo Records, England).

Two musical adventures which approach Welsh music from a new direction and slot it into place alongside material from other sources. Destined to raise the profile of Welsh music outside the country but likely to be too revolutionary (and too linguistically wide-ranging) for the internal Welsh market.

Siwsann George

George is a Rhondda-born singer who has worked with the trio Mabsant as well as in her own right.

⒪ **Traditional Songs of Wales** (Saydisc, England).

Part of a series of albums of British music which saw Siwsann working alongside Ray Fisher and Jo Freya in a series of 'Songs Of Three Nations' concerts around the UK.

Gwerinos

Gwerinos are the descendants of Cilmeri, equally at home playing for concerts or for twmpath dance nights. The seven-strong Gwynedd band includes Tudur Huws Jones, one of the major contributors to Welsh music over the past two decades.

⒪ **Seilam** (Sain, Wales).

A rumbustious package of songs and tunes which isn't afraid to have fun, including a wonderful reggae-style treatment of one of Wales' favourite sea anthems. Another band which is writing prolifically and usefully.

Dafydd Iwan

Dafydd Iwan, the godfather of Welsh folk music, is a singer-songwriter who has played an important role in the arts wing of the nationalist movement. His performances are basic yet charismatic.

◉ Dafydd Iwan ac Ar Log: Yma O Hyd (Sain, Wales).

This compilation uses material from two great mid-1980s albums which celebrated legendary joint tours around Wales by these performers.

Siân James

Classical and traditional harpist, singer and keyboard player with a wonderful and at times spine-tingling voice. Her atmospheric music has won her deserved praise beyond Welsh-language circles.

◉ Distaw
◉ Gweini Tymor (Sain, Wales).

Very different albums, *Distaw* offering some challenging new songs and *Gweini Tymor* concentrating on well-known traditional songs, both presented with silky, cabaret-style feel.

Kilbride

The three Kilbride brothers from Cardiff have played widely in different bands and in different musical fields over the years, and now they have teamed up to create a powerful new force on the Welsh music scene. Bernard and Gerard's flailing fiddles get a firm foundation from Danny's inventive guitar.

◉ Kilbride (Fflach Tradd, Wales).

Storming trip through a welter of tunes from Wales and from other sources which they picked up from their parents and along the way. One for playing loud at parties.

Meredydd Evans

Evans has been a lifelong activist for Welsh song, in collaboration with his American-born wife Phyllis Kinney. He has always resisted the fusty, antiquarian attitude that surrounded folk song in Wales for many years and has done much to further its cause, both through his former work at the BBC and outside.

◐ Mered (Sain, Wales).

From the 1970s, but still a wonderful and enlightening lesson in the art of unaccompanied singing. Sounds as fresh today as it did then.

Moniars

Moniars are quirky, visual folk-rockers from Anglesey with the world's shortest fiddler, a blind sax player, an ultra-hip second singer, a drummer and a percussionist all backing the powerful vocals of the redoubtable Arfon Wyn.

◉ Y Goreu O Ddau Fyd (Sain, Wales).

Can't-go-wrong party selection from the band's first two CDs. Lots of thrashing, heads-down fun with hints of cajun, hillbilly and jazz thrown into the Welsh mix.

Tudur Morgan

A founder of bands like Cilmeri and Pedwar yn y Bar, Tudur Morgan has brought a range of new ideas and projects to Welsh music.

◉ Branwen (Sain, Wales).

Songs and music based on the Mabinogi legend, produced by Irish musician Donal Lunny and featuring a glittering collection of Welsh names including Linda Healey.

Pedwar Yn Y Bar

Anglesey four-piece which arose from the ashes of Cilmeri and added American and other international influences to Welsh music. The band included Tudur Morgan, Tudur Huws Jones and highly-entertaining Llangefni fiddler Huw Roberts.

◑ Byth Adra (Sain, Wales).

The band's second and last vinyl outing matched excellent playing with a creative approach which was ahead of its time.

Llio Rhydderch

Rhydderch is a triple harp player who is at last being recognised for her remarkable talent – in her fifties. Her vibrant, rhythmic style comes straight from her teacher, the late, great Telynores Maldwyn.

 Llio Rhydderch (Fflach Tradd, Wales).

A must for those who treasure the long-deleted vinyl album of Nansi Richards and for anyone who still believes that the harp is a classical and not a folk instrument. An enthralling trip round a range of styles and including a contribution from Llio's young pupils – the next generation in the Celtic world's only unbroken harp tradition.

TWO

Middle East

This map is drawn on the Peters' projection
which shows the correct relative size of countries

partner of poetry

Egypt – and, specifically, Cairo – is the heart of the Arab musical world. For an Arab singer (and it is singers who are accorded overriding respect) to make it, she or he must do so in the Egyptian capital. And so it has been since the 1920s, when the gramophone and radio meant that the Arab World, with its shared language, religion and culture, was once again listening to the same music. Below, **David Lodge** and **Bill Badley** look at the traditions of Classical Arab song, and profile its superstars.

Because of the elevated place given to the word in Arab culture, where poetry is the highest of all art forms, the role of the singer has always been to take the word to the people. Arab song and musical expression reached its first golden age between the eighth and twelfth centuries, followed by a long period of stagnation and Turkish influence under Ottoman rule. It was reborn this century against a background of nationalist fervour and political instability, and developed amid a modern age of radio, films and cheap cassettes.

The Arab world's singers and writers, through the language and emotional power of popular song, have been influential in determining the identity of nations, expressing the hopes of their people and on occasions threatening their states. Music has retained a unique power in the Arab world, and it offers listeners a window to its personality. The survey that follows looks at the region's shared classical music, and its superstars.

Classical Arab Music

Classical Arab music is enjoyed throughout Arab society and transcends all ages and social barriers. It is a musical arena that, ever since the first recordings, has been dominated by a small coterie of **pan-Arab superstars**, adored by the masses. Their popularity has given these giants of the stage enormous cultural significance. They have been, in their time, more influential than presidents - swaying the moods of society at large by touching the lives of almost every individual with their poignant lyrics and sultry melodies. From humiliation in military defeat to the personal wounds of love, their music has provided sustenance during long periods of pain and introspection.

Typically, Classical Arab singers will perform pieces up to an hour in length, in highly charged melancholy tones, dwelling on the themes of tragic fate, or love – forbidden or unrequited – beckoning the listener to wallow in metaphor and listen as the lyrics unfold to the story of his or her own life. As the greatest of all Arab singers, **Umm Kalthum**, sang in "Enta Umri" (You Are My Life):

Your eyes brought me back to my lost days.
They have taught me how
to regret the past and its wounds.
What I experienced before my eyes
saw you is wasted time.
How could they count it as my age?
You are my life, whose morning
started with your light.
You are, you are, you are my life.

(Lyrics by Ahmed Shafik, music by Mohammed Abd el-Wahab, 1965).

Shared Roots

Love, wine, gambling, hunting, the pleasures
of song and romance, the brief pointed
elegant expression of wit and wisdom.
These things he knew to be good. Beyond
them he saw only the grave.

Arabic original, anonymous

From a thousand years or more before Islam, the **nomadic Arab tribes** had firmly established the hedonistic character of their music. In nomadic days, music was primarily a job for women. Female **singing slaves** were brought to the cities to entertain the noble houses and caravanserais, both as prostitutes and artists.

These women singers would accompany warriors onto the battlefield, banging *duff* and *tabla* and singing war songs of **rajaz poetry** while the combat ensued, and en route would be always at the ready to stir the spirits of the soldiers. At tribal

Koranic Recitation: the Non-music of Islam

In Egypt, a **Koran reciter** who wants to broadcast on the radio will first have to be judged worthy by a committee of religious scholars. He is tested on the complexity and subtlety of the *maqamat*, and in his agility in dispensing, through it, the words of God. By protecting the Arabic 'scales' throughout the ages in this way, a religion which shuns music has in effect kept the music alive. Today Islam's 'non-music' still plays this role by continuing to demand only the most perfect rendition of ancient Arabic modes from the most able voices – a sure defence against encroaching Western influence. The full resonance of the call to prayer from some of the finest and most accomplished singers in the world is sheer delight.

There are two types of Koran recitation: **tartil**, a musically simple rendition of Koranic text adhering strictly to the rules of reading, and **tajwid**, which is musically elaborate and involves intricate melodic and cadential formulae and ornaments. Here there is room enough for individual styles, and many popular reciters have crossed over to pursue very profitable careers in the secular field (most notably **Sayed Darweesh** – see p.327).

Religious, but non-Koranic, **devotional chanting** lies between the secular song and Koranic recitation. A musical ensemble will be led by a Western-style conductor, and the solo singer of the secular field is replaced by a chorus of twelve men. Religious chanting is performed during Ramadan, at local weddings and at **Sufi celebrations** around mosques on the birthday of the saint.

---

nuptials the women singers and musicians led the celebrations, and they were there too on the *haj* to Mecca – which was in those pre-Islamic days a pagan pilgrimage – where they would sing and dance around the *kalabba*.

The principal male performers of the time were **mukhanathin** – transvestite slaves – from whose ranks came the majority of male musicians well into the early days of Islam. They suffered the wrath of the more orthodox Muslims, and ridicule from society at large, but their skills were nurtured in the protective courts of certain less pious caliphs who appreciated their outrageous antics at feasts and banquets.

With such decadent roots, it is hardly surprising that when **Islam** arrived in the seventh century, the singing and the playing of musical instruments were considered sins, and swiftly banned. Yazid III, a noted Umayyad caliph, warned in 740 AD: "Beware of singing for it will steal your modesty, fill you with lust and ruin your virtue." Unlawful instruments were destroyed, singers were considered unworthy witnesses in court, and female slaves who turned out to have a vocal inclination could be taken back to market and exchanged. Still today in the practice of Islam there is no music. The **call to prayer** by the **muezzin**, while being a supreme example of the complex *maqamat*, the Arabic scales on which Arab music is based, is not itself considered music.

This is because the emotional input of a sheikh in the recitation is guarded by strict rules about pitch and tempo. A celebrated Cairo court case in 1977 ruled: "The Holy Koran contains the words of God, who recited it in a manner we do not comprehend. Koran recitation is an act of compliance and does not involve innovation." To induce *tarab* – enchantment – through delivery of the Koran is a sin, indicative of the fear in Islam of the influence of music on human nature. Music in most of the Islamic Arab world is a singularly secular pursuit. (Although a very different view prevails in Pakistani/North Indian qawwali: see *The Rough Guide to World Music Volume 2*.

Denied figurative expression in Islamic art, the Arabs reserve special importance for their language, which has been the control point of their culture throughout history. In pre-Islamic nomadic times, the poet was magnificent; a spokesman on policy, judge in dispute, a voice to praise heroes and scorn enemies. As cultural ambassadors, the Arab poets wrested the limelight from the brilliant cultural centres of Baghdad and Damascus. With the arrival of Islam, the Koran's rich language, rhythm and rhyme struck a chord with the Arabs, and it became the textbook of artistic creation. Today the special place of **poetry in Arab music** is proudly guarded. Songs are judged primarily on their words, and music without them is considered a 'religion without a scripture.'

Soon after the birth of Islam, Arab music gained a suitor from an unexpected quarter. The Arab musical world was under the protection of the caliph's court in Baghdad, where away from the jurisdiction of the Islamic purists, enjoyment and creativity reigned. This was the hedonistic world of Harun el-Rashid (786–809) and the *Thousand and One Nights*. The environment proved to be a highly productive one, nurturing such visionaries as the musician and theorist **Ishaq al-Mawsili** (767–850), famed for knowing every line of poetry ever written in Arabic, and whose antics are celebrated in fable. It is said he once found himself in the charge of a previously deaf and dumb consul, whom he succeeded in inciting to tears at the beauty of his voice.

This was an age of great advances for the Arabs, an era of intellectual order and discovery that abounds with tales of superhuman feats, and which pushed Arab culture to the forefront of medieval art and science. At a time when Europeans were clubbing each other on the dark plains of Christendom, the Arabs were living their golden age, worrying about the power of imagination and the effects of music on the human soul.

Emerging Traditions in the Twentieth Century

The brass bands marching at the head of colonial advances into Egypt in the 1850s, and the tantalising operas of Verdi and Mozart playing in the new Cairo Opera House, were a rude awakening for an Arab world that had, for 500 years, been shrouded under the Ottoman mantle. Intellectual and artistic life ignited as this sudden clash with

modernity shook the Arabs out of a deep-rooted complacency.

Egypt, fired by nationalism after 2000 years of foreign rule, emerged to lead the quest for an **Arab renaissance**, and soon was recognised as Arab cultural heartland and the focus of musical innovation. Turkish sounds dipped out of favour and Arab music was heard again in the streets and theatres. In attending this rebirth of music and song, and attempting to bring Arab music into the modern age, the **Cairo music scene** struck a dynamic balance between tradition and the seductive promise of Western advances.

Arab culture was vulnerable to the sophistication and technical know-how of Europe. Despite having invented a musical notation as early as the ninth century, Arab music was rarely written down, and by the late 1800s musicians had moved a long way from established theory. In 1932 at an extraordinary pan-Arab conference in Cairo (supported by the composer Bartok, an enthusiast for Arab music), Arab musicians gathered to take stock of their musical output. They found a wide diversity from one end of the Arab world to the other. Thus began a campaign to rekindle an interest in tradition, and to search its roots for guidance.

Theory, Scales & Rhythm in Classical Arab Music

The musical knowledge and theories of the Ancient Greeks have come to us largely through the surviving works of early Islamic writers. Chief among them was **Abu Nasr Al Farabi** – one of the greatest philosophers and scholars in Islamic history. Born in Transoxiana around the year 872, he studied and taught in the three cities that are to this day the exalted triumvirate of classical Arab music: Baghdad, Cairo, and Damascus. He wrote on numerous subjects but is best known for the *Kitab al-Musiqa al-Kabir* (Grand Book of Music), a work which sets out tonal systems (*maqamat*), metrics (*iqa*), different kinds of melodies (*alhan*), instruments (*al-alat al-mashhura*) and their tunings (*taswiya*).

Much of what he wrote is still relevant. **Melody** is still organised into a series of **maqamat** (melodic modes), any given one of which (*maqam*) has a distinctive scale which is based around 24 quarter notes – as opposed to the twelve semitones of Western music. Each mode then has its own ethos and is often associated with a particular mood, season or body humour: Safi el-Din, in the ninth century, devised one for every hour of the day. Today there are estimated to be about forty in use in Egypt, and about twenty oth-

ers elsewhere. This wide range of modes means an Arab singer has a highly complex job and it is this wide spectrum of musical colours that makes Arab music so infinitely fascinating.

Rhythm theory is complex but easier to get a fix on. Perhaps the most basic rhythm is **rajaz** – the metre of a camel's hooves on sand. With this beat nomadic Bedouins developed **al-Huda**, the caravan song, capable of distracting their beasts from the burden of heavy loads so effectively that, so the story goes, the animals would arrive frisky after a long journey to the rhythm of the drum, and then drop dead of fatigue.

Centuries of music have produced a sophisticated range of rhythms, and the old camel song is no longer very high up the list. Today, rhythm patterns vary greatly in length, from two beats to 88 beats. Of the 111 rhythms, or **iqa'a**, recorded in the Middle East and Egypt, only about ten are commonly used. Among these are the **matsoum** in 4/4 time, the most broadly used rhythm in pop music, where it is frequently slowed down, mid-song, to make the **masmoudi** rhythm, which is 8/4. You'll hear both of these in Egyptian *al-jil* (street music). Classical song tends to use the **samaai**, a 10/8 rhythm.

The West was seen as a source of inspiration. Composers were keen to make the most of Western advances, many of whose root ideas had passed from Arab hands a thousand years earlier – like the *rabab* fiddle which had evolved into the violin, or the concept of harmony, which gradually crept back into Arab composition. Entirely **new instruments** were greeted with unguarded enthusiasm. For example, the introduction of the cello – which one Western musician at the conference thought would overwhelm the Arab ensemble and bring on tears – was welcomed by Egyptian musicians who thought that was the very reason to have it.

As the century progressed, oboes, the double bass, and electric guitars were added to the traditional five-piece Arab **takht** (ensemble), which soon became a full-blown orchestra. Studios were re-equipped with the latest technology, and composers plagiarised melodies from Beethoven to Bartok, giving them form with a jazz back-beat or Hollywood rumba. In many songs of the 1960s there is a strong hint – a kind of proto-sampling – of **Western classical melodies**, notably in the works of **Mohamed Abd el-Wahaab** and his poet-mentor **Ahmed Shawki**. Yet this was no

Mohamed Abd el-Wahaab

imitation. Foreign themes were woven into dense layers of drones, unisons and parallel octaves of the lush Arab orchestra, and the Eastern feel was maintained.

Despite these modernising trends, many traditional themes remain in Arab music from its distant heritage. Arab music still centres on **the singer**, whose vocal ornamentation and improvisation skills enrich the song from 'merely a chicken, without the nice fat which gives it taste', as one local saying puts it. The live *hafla* (party) atmosphere, with repeated shouts of praise and demands for encore from the audience, is still vital to the performance. Music continues to be the partner of poetry, while vibrant rhythm, fine melody and ancient instruments remain pivotal to the sound. Ironically, in the computer world of today's generation of 'classical' composers, sampled sound and Arabic programs are maintaining the traditional character in their contemporary music, and manage to fool even the critical Arab listener.

Along with technical advances came the **media**, which has played a dominant role in the music of the Arab world. The big Western music companies moved in on Cairo early in the century, and before long entrepreneurs were touting village café-goers with the new phonograph, which they would operate for a fee. The piercing voices that emerged from the whirling contraptions at their feet seemed to pronounce that life was never going to be the same again. Yet the three-minute phonograph was hardly suited to the tradition of the long Arab song, and music had to wait for radio in the late 1920s before it discovered the new opportunities offered by technology. Film, and later television, provided a stage for popular song, which found an expanding record-buying public.

By the 1920s more or less the whole Arab world was listening to the same Arab music for the first time. With its mass appeal, a **superstar industry** developed fast. Through these publicly adored giants of song arose the cult-hero poet-lyricists like **Ahmed Ramy** and the 'prince of poets' **Ahmed Shawki**, spreading revolutionary new messages that implied the right to personal fulfilment and expectations alongside the duties of family and Islam.

But what proved the most revolutionary of media innovations was the least spectacular. The **tape cassette** appeared in the early 1970s and put the music industry into the hands of the public, turning its control from businessmen to the streets (though the men in suits have been staging something of a comeback lately). Suddenly everyone could make music, and it sometimes seemed nearly everyone did. Coinciding with a period of dramatic social change – the 1980s arrival of Arab youth culture and pure pop music – the cassette offered a format for a new wave of popular aspirations and opened the floodgates to songs moving away from acceptable musical standards. It allowed the working class for the first time to voice their discontent, and with a contemporary breed of urban folk music they have successfully embarrassed traditional Egyptian good taste (for more on which, see the article on p.338).

It was not an entirely willing process. In the early 1970s, as the new street music took over, Mohammed Abd el-Wahab, who carried the torch for classical song until his death in 1991, insisted: "There should be a distinction between the great singers, like Abd el-Halim Hafez and Umm Kalthum. In Europe, they are not attempting to replace classical music with modern." He was quite right, of course. Hafez and Kalthum – and other Superstars of Cairo – have, through their voices and personalities, left an imprint on Arab culture with which there are few parallels anywhere in the world.

Superstars of Cairo

The Arab Classical musical arena – and Cairo as its fulcrum – has always been dominated by a clutch of iconic singers, enjoying huge popularity and influence across the Arab world.

Profiled below are seven of the finest: **Sayed Darweesh** (1891–1923), **Abd el-Halim Hafez** (1922–77), **Mohammed Abd el-Wahaab** (1910–91), **Farid el-Atrache** (1914-74), **Asmahan** (1917-44), the now-legendary **Umm Kalthum** (1904–75), and the woman who carries her beacon, **Warda** (born 1940).

Sayed Darweesh

At age 25, **Sayed Darweesh** (1891–1923) was a travelling actor fallen on hard times. At 30 he was hailed as the father of the new Egyptian Arab music, and hero of the renaissance. He rose to fame with his controversial **'innovation' musical movement** of the 1910s and '20s, in which he blended Western instruments and harmony with forgotten Arab musical forms and Egyptian folklore. More importantly, he wrote words for the Egyptian people: dedications for the tradesmen, operettas for the hashish dealers, and daring anti-

British nationalism for the masses, like "Bilaadi Bilaadi" (My Country, my Country), which became the national anthem.

My country my country,
my love and heart is for you.
Egypt, the mother of countries,
You are my wants and desire,
And your Nile has given
so many gifts to your people.

After a composing career of just seven years, Darweesh died of a cocaine overdose, aged 32. Mourned by thousands, he now lies in the Garden of the Immortals in Alexandria.

Abd el-Halim Hafez

Abd el-Halim Hafez (1927–77) was known as the 'Nightingale of the Nile'. In a society that generally reserves true respect for the old, it surprised everyone when Halim Hafez took over the musi-

EMI ARABIA

"Nightingale of the Nile", Abd el-Halim Hafez

cal arena in his early twenties to became the golden boy of the nationalist revolution of 1952. He came at the right time with short patriotic songs that pleased President Nasser as well as the young generation of the day who embraced him as their spokesperson.

By the 1960s his new, short, light songs, with their distinct melodic style, gave way to a partnership with Mohamed Abd el-Wahaab and a return to the long classical form. He was ill with bilharzia almost all his life, and involved the nation in his ongoing fight for good health with a vulnerability that charmed everyone in Egypt. For men, he offered a rather camp alternative role in an oppressively macho society. And his little-boy-lost image had women crooning to mother him. He died in 1977, perhaps the last superstar of the great artists' era.

Farid el-Atrache and Asmahan

Farid el-Atrache (1914-74) and his sister **Asmahan** (born Amal el-Atrache in 1917, died 1944) were born to noble Druze parents in the Syrian/Lebanese border area of Jebal Al-Druz. Due to political upheavals in the region, their early years were spent travelling around the major cities of the Levant, but after their father's death they finally settled in Cairo. Living in new-found poverty, the children received their early musical education in this crucible of Arab music while their mother supported the family by playing the oud and singing in night clubs.

The pair's musical talent was quickly recognised and soon they too were making a living playing in Cairo's numerous clubs and radio orchestras. However, it was the birth of the **Egyptian film industry** in the 1930s that launched them as household names throughout the Arab world: *Intisar Al-Shabab* (The Triumph of Youth) was the first of many films in which they starred, with Farid also writing the music. Their rise was tragically terminated when Asmahan mysteriously drowned - numerous conspiracy theories, laying the blame at the feet of everyone from a jealous Umm Kalthum to Allied spies, have circulated since. In the great tradition however, an untimely demise has done nothing to dim her fame and Asmahan is still fondly remembered as the tragic femme fatale cut down in her prime.

Farid's enforced solo career got off to shaky start, but a string of films with his lover, the dancer **Samia Gamal**, re-established his reputation and he continued to perform to great acclaim right up to the end of his life. His later films, when he often appears as an oily old smoothie who ought to know better, belittle the remarkable legacy of his earlier work. He was a virtuosic oud player with an alluringly rich voice, and one of the Arab world's most inventive composers to boot.

Mohamed Abd el-Wahaab

Mohamed Abd el-Wahaab (1910–91) was dubbed the 'artist of generations', as the last remaining figure from the old guard, of which he was the most controversial and respected member. His achievements spanned a long career from the 1920s as a singer, film star and eventually composer – a talent crowned when Umm Kalthum agreed to sing his "Enta Omri", a song which featured an electric guitar for the first time in her career.

As a composer, Abd el-Wahaab is remembered as the moderniser of Arabic music, liberating it, as his supporters see it, from the limitations of the takht ensemble and allowing it to embrace Western-style tangos, waltzes and instrumentation. Others criticise his music for overt plagiarism. He stood by his vision for modernisation of the music all his life, demanding that "the artist is the creator and has the full right to introduce new elements into his music as he sees fit. We must always be open to new ideas and not resist change. Change is inevitable in everything."

Ironically, in his later years Abd el-Wahaab became so contemptuous of other modernisers that he took his initiative a step further. In 1990 he released a classical song into a market awash with the bleeping synths of the new youth pop. It was the first occasion in 32 years that he had sung his own composition and the song, "Minrear Ley" (Without why), was a blatant test of popular loyalty. It was viewed by many as the final gasp of a wounded musical genre but its immediate success went some way to prove that his vision for Arab music lived on.

Umm Kalthum

Umm Kalthum (1904–75) was indisputably the Arab world's greatest singer. Stern and tragic, rigidly in control, this was a woman who, in her heyday, truly had the Arab world in the palm of her hand. With melancholy operettas that seemed to drift on for hours, she encapsulated the love lives of a nation.

Rumour had it that Umm Kalthum inhaled gulps of hashish smoke before performing and that the scarf trailing from her right hand was steeped in opium. Her stage presence was charged by a theatrical rapport with the audience: a slight nod of the head or a shake of her shoulders and they were in uproar. She learned to sing by reciting verse at cafés in her village, and sometimes dressed as a boy to escape the religious authorities.

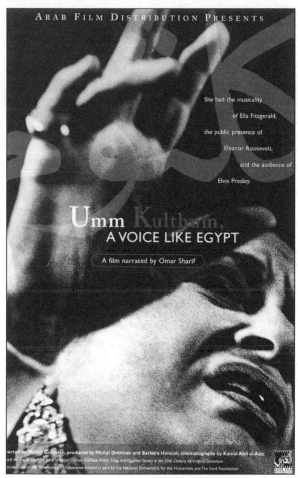

ARAB FILM DISTRIBUTION PRESENTS

She had the musicality
of Ella Fitzgerald,
the public presence of
Eleanor Roosevelt,
and the audience of
Elvis Presley.

Umm Kulthum,
A VOICE LIKE EGYPT

A film narrated by Omar Sharif

Directed by Michal Goldman, produced by Michal Goldman and Barbara Holecek, cinematography by Kamal Abd al-Aziz
based on the book of the Voice of Egypt: Umm Kulthum Arabic Song and Egyptian Society in the 20th Century, by Virginia Danielson
a production of the Filmmakers Collaborative funded in part by the National Endowment for the Humanities and The Ford Foundation

Umm Kalthum, about whom all Arabs agree

It was to her training in religious chanting that she owed her stunning vocal agility and her masterful command of the complex maqamat. She was educated in the secular field by the poet Ahmed Ramy and of her total output of 286 songs, 132 were his poems.

Kalthum's voice was the epitome of the Arab ideal – saturated with *shaggan*, or emotional yearning, and powerful enough on occasion to shatter a glass. In her long career, she specialised in love songs that sometimes lasted an hour, improvising and ornamenting on a theme that would bring the audience to a frenzy. She was once asked to sing a line 52 times over, which she did while developing the melody each time. Of this ability she said: "I am greatly influenced by the music found in Arabic poetry. I improvise because my heart rejoices in the richness of this music. If someone went over a song which I sang five times, he would

not find any one like the other. I am not a record that repeats itself, I am a human being who is deeply touched by what I sing." As a childless mother, her songs were her offspring given to the people. For these gifts they returned total adoration.

Apart from Allah, they say, Umm Kalthum is the only subject about which all Arabs agree, a fact that has always given her special political significance. She embraced Nasser's pan-Arab ideals and drew Arabs together by extending a pride to them during their most difficult period in history. Nasser used her nationalist songs to keep the masses behind him, and timed his major political speeches carefully around her broadcasts. The less prescient Anwar Sadat once addressed the nation on the same day as her concert, and ended up without an audience, a mistake he only made once.

She remained a great campaigner for the traditional Arab song, leaving behind an orchestra, the **Arab Music Ensemble**, dedicated to maintaining the pure heritage of *al turath*, from the eight and ninth centuries.

At Umm Kalthum's funeral in February 1975, attended by many Arab heads of state, over three million people followed her through the streets of Cairo. At 10pm on the first Thursday of every month, all radio stations still play Umm Kalthum in memory of her momentous live radio concerts of the 1950s and '60s. To this day, Israeli broadcasters seduce Palestinians to their stations with the music of Umm Kalthum, duly spliced with propaganda.

Warda al-Jaza'iriya

Although definitely viewed as one of the Cairo superstars, **Warda al-Jaza'iriya**'s more pan-Mediterranean roots set her apart. Born near Paris in 1940 to a Lebanese mother and Algerian father, she learned to sing from her mother – who taught her Lebanese songs – and took her first steps to stardom in her father's prestigious Paris night spot, *TAM TAM*. This club (named after the initials of the three Maghreb countries, Tunisia, Algeria and Morocco) was the meeting place both for the top names in Arab music whilst passing through the city, and for supporters of the FLN (Front de

Libèration National, a group dedicated to Algerian independence from France). Both of these were to shape her musical identity: it was in this club that she was first heard by the Godfather of Arab music, Mohamed Abd el-Wahaab; and she has always been associated with her Algerian roots – her name means 'The Rose of Algeria'.

When her family was deported from France to Lebanon, Warda continued to sing in clubs; but her real break came with a move to Cairo at the beginning of the 1960s. Here, through the considerable influence of Umm Kalthum's musical collaborators, Mohamed Abd el-Wahab and **Riyad Al Sumbati**, her 'Parisian' style quickly became popular.

Aside from a ten-year break from singing – at the insistence of her first husband – Warda has remained at the forefront of Arab music. Aided by a close team of exceptional composers, lyricists, musicians and producers, she has built one of the most lucrative and long-lasting careers in recent years. She has wisely shunned the 'new Umm Kalthum' tag - partly out of respect for the undisputed diva, but also because the comparison is inaccurate: whereas Umm Kalthum's singing has an aching intensity that can be quite startling to the uninitiated, Warda's style is altogether more cosmopolitan and optimistic.

Thanks to Zein al-Jundi for additional input on the Classical singers

discography

With the notable exception of Warda – who is still working at a furious rate – most of the Cairene superstars recorded their best work in the relatively early days of audio technology. However, though the sound quality may leave something to be desired, there is often a gripping intensity about these live or one-take performances. The longer playing time of CDs is far better suited than cassettes to the extended Arab songs at which these singers excelled, and a burgeoning industry of re-issued and re-mastered collections has sprung up. There have also been a number of good recent compilatuions of Classical Arab music on various Western labels.

Compilations

 Arabian Maters – Les Plus Grandes Classiques de la Musique Arabe (Virgin, France).

A double CD set with classic performances by many of the legends: Warda, Mohamed Abd el-Wahaab, Abdel Halim Hafez & Umm Kalthum from Egypt, Fairouz from Lebanon, Saudi's Mohammed Abdu and the Iraqi Kasim El Saher. As good a starter pack as you are likely to find – even if the explanatory notes are a bit skimpy.

 Les grands noms de la musique du monde arabe (NFB, France).

Another excellent 2-CD set, highlighting the great Arab singers. Classical Egyptian traditions are represented by tracks from Hafez, Farid el-Atrache, Asmahanm, Mohamed Abd el-Wahaab, Oum Khalsoum, and Warda. And there are equally strong showings from the rest of the Arab world.

The Music of Islam (Celestial Harmonies, US).

Recently released, this is an extraordinary 17-CD boxed set of recordings made over 10 years throughout the Islamic world by New Zealander, David Parsons. Whilst it's worth remembering that not all Muslims are Arabs – and not all Arabs are Muslims – this is one of the most thorough trawls through Arab music available. It also includes religious music from non-Arab countries like Pakistan, Turkey, Iran and Indonesia. It is well recorded and beautifully presented. For those on a budget, there is an excellent single-CD sampler.

Music in the World of Islam (Topic, UK).
Vol. 1: The Human Voice/Lutes
Vol. 2: Strings/Flutes & Trumpets
Vol. 3: Reeds & Bagpipes/Drums & Rhythms

Originally issued as six LPs – now on 3 CDs – these gritty recordings made by Jean Jenkins and Poul Rovsing Olsen in the 1960s and '70s have some great moments, and the discs constitute the best survey of its kind.

La Musique Arabe (FNAC, France).

This is a useful and instructive sampler from the French megastore: a booklet and disc, including tracks from Mohamed Abd el-Wahaab, Abdel Halim Hafez and Umm Kalthum from Egypt, as well as contemporary sounds from around the Arab world.

Artists

Farid el-Atrache & Asmahan

The late Farid el-Atrache and Asmahan – a brother and sister team – are claimed by the Syrians and Lebanese (they were born on the border), but they are Egyptian by adoption. Asmahan died tragically young. Farid had a longer career and is still honoured as 'al-Malek al-Oud' (the King of the Oud).

FARID EL-ATRACHE

 Farid el-Atrache: Les Années '30 (Club du Disque Arabe, France).

This selection of remastered songs from the 1930s show Farid as a young, potent performer – as opposed to the smoochy crooner he became in later life. Although many of the featured songs (with their then-fashionable strains of tango and lush European strings) might now sound quaint, they were right at the cutting edge in their day. On the basis of this CD it is easy to see how the melancholy Druze with matinée idol looks took the Arab world by storm.

Best of Farid el-Atrache Live (Voice of Lebanon, Lebanon).

Farid was obviously a phenomenal live performer, and his often professed love of playing the oud is well to the fore on this collection: the dazzling *taqsim* (improvisation) at the beginning of his most famous work, "El Rabaïï" (The spring) is the standard by which all others are now judged.

ASMAHAN

 Asmahan (Baidaphone, Lebanon).

Few recordings survive from Asmahan's short career but this includes many of her best loved songs. The waltz, "Layalil uns fi Vienna" (Delightful nights in Vienna) was a hit in the late 1930s and is guaranteed to get old Cairo hands misty eyed . . .

Sayed Darweesh

Sayed Darweesh lived fast and died young – the hero and founding father of the Arab music renaissance. His patriotic "Bilaadi, Bilaadi" (My country, my country) is the closest thing to a national anthem for Arab brotherhood and is played by marching bands all over the Middle East.

 Cheikh Sayed Darwiche – L'Immortel (Baidaphon, France).

Because he died in the early 1920s, there are only a handful of Sayeed Darweesh's recordings in existence. This short disc shows his passion rising above the crackly recording, with three songs full of thrilling vocal improvisation, throwing in snatches of European flavour that at the time was completely revolutionary.

Mahmoud Fadl and Samy El Bably

Egyptian trumpeter Samy El Bably is the only horn player to have mastered the microtonal intricasies of Arabic music. He has recently teamed up with music director and drummer Mahmoud Fadl.

Mahmoud Fadl

 The Love Letter from King Tut-Ank-Amen (Piranha, Germany).

One of those surprise delights that pop up in the World Music world. Featuring the trumpet of Samy El Bably, with backing from oud, zither, accordion and swooping strings, this album reinterprets Cairo love classics originally sung by Umm Kalthum and Mohamed Abd el-Wahaab. For anyone struggling to appreciate the subtle nuances of the original lyrics, these seductive instrumentals are just the job with stimulating rhythmic diversions and great solos.

Abd el-Halim Hafez

The pallid 'Nightingale of the Nile', Abd el-Halim Hafez rose to fame on the wave of Egyptian patriotic zeal after the Second World War, aided by a successful career in the emergent movie business as he struggled against the effects of bilharzia. The soundtracks to all his films are at last being re-released.

 Abd el-Halim Hafez – Twentieth Anniversary Memorial Editon (EMI Arabia, Dubai).

This double CD includes a disc of early and late material. The former has seven film-score songs from the early 1930s, with classic Egyptian movie orchestration. The latter includes his best known song, "karia el-Fingan" (The Fortune Teller).

Umm Kalthum (Oum Khalsoum)

No-one has yet come close to Umm Kalthum, who is still considered the Arab world's primary diva. Her dramatic, angst drenched performances may not be to everyone's taste, but to ignore her is to disregard one of the world's 20th century icons.

 Al-Atlaal (EMI, Egypt),

This song-album – *Al-Atlaal* (The Ruins) – is Kalthum's most acclaimed work, full of melodrama and suspense. For "Enta Omri" (You are my life), she was greatly criticised at the time on account of its electric instruments.

 Hajartek (EMI, Egypt).

The (Saudi-spelled) title-song is the centrepiece of this CD – a passionate rendering of "Hagartak, yimkin ansa hawak" (I've left you and perhaps I will forget your love). It is as essential as anything in the Kalthum canon.

Mohamed Abd el-Wahaab

Mohamed Abd el-Wahaab was the colossus of Egyptian music from the late 1920s until his death in 1991. For 60 years, there was hardly a single performer of note whose career was not in some way blessed by his magic touch.

 Treasures (EMI Arabia, Dubai).

The best introduction to Abd el-Wahaab, this is a a double CD with a selection of pieces from the master's better periods. Most notable is the astonishing 40-minute "Al Dooa' al Akhir" (The Last Blessing).

 Volumes I–X (Club des Disques Arabes, France).

The godfather of the Egyptian musical revival's huge output is slowly being released in its entirety on CD: Volume X only takes us up to 1939 and el-Wahaab lived until 1991 . . .

Warda

Warda ('The Rose') is a true child of the Mediterranean; born in France of Algerian/Lebanese parents, she found fame in Cairo. She is still in good voice, and in fact, much of her more recent work surpasses the bleeping synthesiser songs she recorded in the 1980s. Her recordings are legion and pretty easily available worldwide.

 Warda (EMI Hemisphere, UK).

This mid-priced compilation is an excellent introduction to Warda's more recent work: it is hard not to be seduced by the diva's creamy, mature voice.

> See also the Syria/Lebanon discography.

Armenia

the sorrowful sound

An Armenian legend tells of God allocating land to the various peoples of the world. The Armenians turn up late and God says, "sorry but all that's left is this pile of stones". It is an apt description of this rugged land in the foothills of the Caucasus – a land that has had an often bleak history, punctuated by massacres and earthquakes. When Djivan Gasparyan, Armenia's most famous traditional musician, was asked why so many of the tunes he plays on the *duduk* sound so melancholy, he said that it was a reflection of the fate of the people. This 'sorrowful sound' has an unparalleled beauty and, as **Harold Hagopian** explains, Armenian music can also demonstrate an awesome vigour and fire.

The Armenian musical heritage spans many centuries and much of the globe, thanks to its resilient traditions and cultural diaspora. Its characteristic melodic elements can be traced from pre-Christian modal music to contemporary middle-eastern pop, and variants of the music can be heard from the Armenian monasteries of the Caucasus to local weddings and dances in New York, Boston and especially Fresno – the grape-growing valley of central California where many refugees fled after the Turkish massacres of 1915.

Religious Music

Traditional Armenian music consists mainly of folk melodies performed by ensembles at community gatherings and celebrations, and religious chants sung by the clergy.

St Gregory the Illuminator converted the Armenian king to Christianity in 301 AD and Armenia became the world's **first Christian state**. Whether or not the Armenians, who had lived on the Anatolian plateau at the base of Mount Ararat since the eighth century BC, were descendants of Noah's son, Hayk, as was claimed, Armenia in the early Christian period certainly developed one of the richest traditions of liturgical music.

Melismatic **chants**, each composed in one of eight modes, made up the largest body of sacred chants, or *sharakans*. Medieval Armenian musical notation, known as **khaz**, allowed singers to improvise ornate embellishments around established melody types. Some of the oldest of these melodies can be traced back to pagan times, while new Christian chants were composed as early as 405 AD by **Saint Mesrop Mashtots**, the Armenian priest who brought literacy to Armenia by inventing the country's unique alphabet, still used today. Other notable priests whose music has survived include Movses Korenatsi (fifth century), Grigor Narekatsi (tenth century) and Neses Shnorhali (twelfth century).

One of the most renowned interpreters of the sharakan is the late soprano, **Lucine Zakarian**, who served as soloist at the **Holy Cathedral of Etchmiadzin**, the seat of the Armenian Church.

Old-time Armenian ensemble

If you visit Armenia, it's certainly worth the trip to Etchmiadzin (20km outside the Armenian capital, Yerevan) to hear the Divine Liturgy sung by the choir there, which is made up of Armenia's best vocalists. Those willing to head further should venture out to the monastery of **Geghard**, a fourth-century structure carved into the side of a mountain. Acoustics within produce a reverberation of up to a minute. If you are lucky you can catch the local choir but even in their absence it's a glorious experience. The Celestial Harmonies CD collection of Armenian music includes sacred music recorded there.

All Armenian liturgical music remained monophonic until the latter part of the nineteenth century, when the renowned Armenian priest and composer **Komitas Vartabet** (1869-1935), who was schooled in Europe, introduced polyphony and Western-style composition into Armenian music. His arrangement of the Divine Liturgy in four-part harmony is still considered a master work, maintaining the Armenian spirit within the context of Western musical practice. Besides composing sacred music, Komitas travelled throughout the Armenian countryside from 1899 to 1910, collecting and notating more than 3000 folk tunes, some of which he arranged for performance with Western instruments such as the piano.

The Massacres and the Diaspora

It is fortuitous that Komitas researched and collected that folk music when he did, since a few years later the Armenian population of historic Armenia (now part of eastern Turkey) was violently uprooted. The towns of Erzerum, Kars, Diyarbakir, Van, and Harpoot were home to more than two million Armenians before the **1915 Massacres** by the Young Turk regime – an act of brutal 'ethnic cleansing' preceding the formation of the modern Turkish state by Mustafa Kemal Ataturk. After the massacre, most of the surviving Armenian population went into exile. Today scarcely any Armenians remain in the region.

As a result, Armenian folk music from this area has been more difficult to document than the music of the foothills of the Caucasus to the east, the region of present-day Armenia. Though the American-born children of those who fled the massacres preserved some of the Anatolian dance tunes and wedding songs of their parents and grandparents, hardly a native recording exists of Armenian traditional music. It is instead second- and third-generation Armenian-Americans who have actively struggled to preserve this musical heritage. In particular, the oud player **Richard Hagopian**, born in Central California's large diaspora community in 1937, has endeavored to document and pass on the music of Anatolian Armenians.

Preservation and performance of this music has been complicated by the fact that many Armenians from Anatolia spoke, and sang, not only in Armenian (an ancient language which is its own branch of the Indo-European language group), but Turkish as well. This has led to disagreements within the Armenian community itself over what precisely constitutes its musical heritage.

Folk Music

All Armenian folk music shares fundamental features with its middle-eastern neighbours, including modal scales, the use of quarter tones and the importance of improvisation within the traditionally established modes. The melodies are monophonic and played against a continuous drone, rather than chordal harmonies. The attempt to determine the ultimate origin of a particular Armenian melody may be impossible, however, since Kurdish, Turkish, Persian, Armenian and Gypsy musicians of Anatolia all intermingled under the Ottoman Empire for several hundred years.

What can be identified as Armenian are the styles of playing **instruments** such as the *tar* (short-necked lute), *kanon* (dulcimer), *oud* (unfretted lute), *kamancha* (upright fiddle), *zuma* (shawm) and *davul* (double-headed hand drum), especially the ways in which they have been played in modern times within the former Soviet Republic of Armenia.

Soviet-style **conservatoires** taught these instruments with the same rigour as the violin and piano, producing a number of renowned musicians whose performances are virtuoso, if controlled, versions of the 'folk' repertoire. Unfortunately, in today's Armenia, you are unlikely to see or hear these traditional songs and dances outside of State Ensemble performances. Ironically, Armenians in the US are more likely to dance the traditional dances such as *shalako* (solo dance in 6/8) or the *kochare* (men's line dance) at celebrations like weddings or family gatherings. Nevertheless the choreographed versions produced by Armenia's folk ensembles are stunning to watch. The choir of zurnas performing together, though not exactly as it was practiced in the villages, is one of the most exhilarating sounds you will ever experience.

Djivan Gasparyan and the Duduk

If there's one instrument emblematic of Armenia, it's the **duduk**, whose soft, plaintive, reedy tone seems to express the soul of the country and its often tragic history. The most celebrated duduk maestro is **Djivan Gasparyan**, born in 1928 in Solag – a village close to the Armenian capital Yerevan.

"My father was a fine duduk player," Gasparyan remembers. "I was his apprentice and I taught myself at his side." But Gasparyan's initial inspiration came from the cinema. "I was fascinated by the duduk players accompanying the film. Their ability to play a suitable melody for a sad or romantic scene and also to burst in with vivacious folk dances when the film demanded more dynamism. The film didn't interest me much. I was riveted by the music and its extraordinary ability to express the right feelings through the duduk."

The young boy returned to the cinema day after day, got in without paying and befriended the old musicians who explained the process of circular breathing necessary to play the accompanying drone part, or dam. He collected empty bottles and sold them to buy himself an instrument and joined the musicians at the cinema as a *damkash* (drone player). At the age of twenty he joined the Tatoul Altounian National Song and Dance Ensemble. He then completed his studies at the Conservatoire, became a soloist, and started touring internationally in the late '50s.

The duduk has eight holes, plus a thumb hole rather like a Western recorder. It is made of apricot wood with a cane reed. Its range is no more than an octave, but it is capable – as Gasparyan learned at the cinema – of the most powerful expression. The instrument goes at least as far back as the fifth century, although some Armenian scholars believe it existed more than 1500 years before that. Duduks always come in pairs, or larger groups, with the soloist playing over a held drone which occasionally moves, but more usually stays fixed. The duduk repertoire is made up of instrumental versions of Armenian folk songs or ashoug songs, special duduk melodies, folk dances (usually accompanied by a two-headed drum (dhol)) or improvisations.

Not surprisingly, the art of making the instrument is a highly skilled one. Gasparyan's prefered craftsman is Karlen Matevossian. "He finds the right apricot tree, but I choose the particular piece of wood according to its size. The wood must be left for two years to dry before the master puts it on the lathe. The final positioning of the holes and tuning must be done by the musician himself. A good instrument can last 300 years. Of course, lots of melodies are dedicated to the apricot tree. In my concerts I like to include "Tsirani Tsar" (The Apricot tree)" – a famous folksong collected by Komitas.

Of those duduk musicians who have had a major influence on his playing, Gasparyan cites **Levon Madoyan** (1909–1964) and **Vatche Hovsepian** (1925–1978), but he sincerely believes that the standard of musicianship is better now than it's ever been. This is one of the effects of the conservatoire training where study of the instrument was placed on a par with Classical instruments. One of the things that distinguishes a good player is the ornamentation of the notes and the oriental colouring of the scale with semitones and quarter-tones which gives the music its expressive power. Gasparyan gives an impressive demonstration of how it's done, by half or fractionally covering the finger holes.

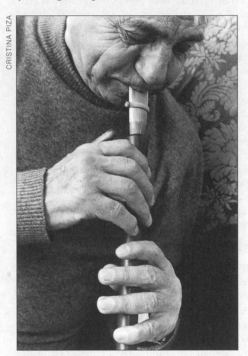

CRISTINA PIZA

Djivan Gasparyan

Having taught at the Conservatoire in Yerevan for over thirty years, Gasparyan has recently left to pursue a more international career. He has developed a duduk quartet with instruments of different sizes, including a large "bass duduk", and has been working with prominent figures in the World Music scene like the Kronos Quartet, Peter Gabriel and Canadian guitarist and producer **Michael Brook**, with whom he collaborated on a 1998 album for RealWorld. "The duduk is an amazing instrument," says Brook, "it was the sensuous expressiveness and nuance that attracted me."

Simon Broughton, with thanks to Alessio Surian

While most of these instruments are common throughout middle-eastern music, there is one – the **duduk** (double reed flute) – which is indigenous to Armenia, and its sound is something of a symbol of the country. Carved from apricot wood, the duduk has a beautiful melancholy timbre, which has found its way from the Armenian countryside to Hollywood soundtracks such as Peter Gabriel's *The Last Temptation of Christ*.

The best-known and probably the greatest contemporary duduk player is **Djivan Gasparyan** (see box), although there are other fine players such as **Gevorg Dabagian** and **Yeghish Manoukian**. The dudk's modern repertoire tends to be made up either of rhythmic songs and dances, or slow, suite-like fantasies, perhaps including improvisation, exploiting the emotive nature of the instrument. Many melodies that seem mournful to Western ears, however, just don't sound that way to Armenians.

Ashoughs

Like the Medieval French troubadours and the Turkish *asiks*, Armenian **ashoughs** travelled the countryside in the seventeenth and eighteenth centuries carrying news and messages from afar through song. The most prolific and celebrated of them, **Sayat Nova** (1717-1795), served as court singer and musician to the Persian Nadir Shah and later to the Georgian ruler Iraklii II. His favourite instrument was the **kamancha** and one of his most famous songs is dedicated to this instrument which he said could "console the broken-hearted, cure the sick and be fully appreciated only by a true artist."

Ashough songs are traditionally accompanied by the kamancha, tar, kanon and duduk, and Sayat Nova's songs are still regularly performed today. Modern singers of the ashough are highly respected artists who specialise in the genre and hardly an Armenian citizen exists who does not know the voices of legendary **Rouben Matevosian** and **Hovhaness Badalian**. They sing songs of love and tragedy, usually accompanied by large folk orchestras such as Tatoul Altounian's Ensemble – one of the most famous in the country.

Classical Music, Cabaret and Pop

Istanbul was the intellectual and cultural centre for Armenians in the Ottoman Empire, and before the nationalist ethnic purification, the work of a number of Armenian composers and musicians was absorbed into the standard repertoire of late Ottoman music. The most notable was **Kemani Tatyos Ekserciyan** (1863-1913), one of the finest composers of Ottoman classical music.

Armenians (and other ethnic minorities) were also prevalent in Istanbul's burgeoning nightclub and cabaret scene in the 1920s and '30s – one of the greatest being the blind oud master **Udi Hrant Kenkulian** (1901-1978). Armenian women, joined by other minorities as well as the least intimidated Turkish Muslim women, also became popular nightclub singers in this period – **Suzan Yakar** was one of the best known.

With much of the Armenian community dispersed throughout America and Europe after 1915, some of the most innovative interpretations of Armenian music have occurred in open dialogue with modern Western genres. The most famous twentieth-century Armenian classical composers – including **Alan Hovhaness** and **Aram Khatchaturian** – have reworked and incorporated Armenian musical idioms, while Ara Dinkjian's group **Night Ark** has linked Armenian folk music and instruments with jazz and New Age styles.

There are also various strands of Armenian pop/rock music, the most interesting of which are to be found among the Armenian immigrant communities in **Los Angeles**. They include a rock-infused pop music with hints of folk melodies, and a more Arabic-influenced style, favoured by Armenian immigrants from Lebanon. **Adiss Harmandian** has been the top seller in this style for twenty-five years.

Since the break up of the Soviet Union, pop culture has also emerged in Armenia itself, as in most of the other former Soviet republics, with musicians and pop groups mimicking American styles. This often means a lot of echo and digital delay superimposed upon synthesisers and drum machines – not very inspiring. But there are a handful of innovators, such as **Harout Pamboukjian**, **Gagik Gevorkian** and a current favourite female pop-star known as **Gayane**, who have used older Armenian modal influences with hip new arrangements. The newest CDs have sampled duduk and kanon sounds.

discography

The most comprehensive survey of Armenian music is a six-volume, seven-CD **Music of Armenia** set from Celestial Harmonies (US). **Vol 1** includes choral and church music, ancient and modern; **Vol 2** sharakan chants in beautiful arrangements by Komitas and others; **Vol 3** focuses on the duduk; **Vol 4** is an album of kanon music; **Vol 5** is folk music played by the Shoghaken and Sasus folk groups; and **Vol 6** features music from the Armenian-inhabited region of Nagorno-Karabagh within Azerbaijan. The discs are well recorded by David Parsons and come with very informative liner notes. As they are available separately, as well as in a set, some also feature in the individual recommendations below.

Church Music

Compilations

⊙ Arménie 1: Chants Liturgiques du Moyen Age et Musique Instrumentale (Ocora, France).

The first half of this disc concentrates on church music including sharakan by Mesrop Mashtots. Most of it is solo chant, some performed by Lucine Zakarian. The instrumental folk music features small ensembles of kamancha, duduks, zurnas and so on, including duduk player Vatche Hovsepian.

⊙ Music of Armenia: Vol 1 Sacred Choral Music (Celestial Harmonies, US).

A very beautiful collection of religious music recorded by the Haissmavourk Choir (with men and women's voices) in Geghard Monastery and Etchmiadzin Cathedral. Some of the tracks have fantastic clashing drones and harmonies. The most attractive introduction to Armenian church music.

Artists

Komitas

Komitas (1869–1935) was born Soghoman Sogomanian in Ottoman Turkey and adopted his pseudonym from a seventh-century Armenian poet and musician. He was orphaned at an early age, studied liturgical music and became a vartabet (priest). He undertook the most important collection of Armenian folksongs and melodies, made musical arrangements of them and worked on his Divine Liturgy for over twenty years. In 1915, during the Ottoman genocide against the Armenians he was deported and imprisoned. He escaped with his life, but much of his work was destroyed and, after a mental breakdown, he spent most of the rest of his life in asylums in France.

⊙ The Voice of Komitas Vardapet (Traditional Crossroads, US).

Of rather specialised interest perhaps, but these solo recordings of Komitas singing were made in 1912 in Paris. He has a strong baritone voice that is very moving through the crackles, particularly in one of the most beautiful and touching Armenian harvestsongs, "Kali Yerg". At the piano, Komitas also accompanies one of his pupils, the rather operatic tenor Armenak Shahmuradian in some of his song arrangements.

⊙ Komitas: Divine Liturgy (New Albion, US).

A full-bloodied performance of Komitas' *Divine Liturgy* from the (all male) Choir of St.Gayané Cathedral. A major work of Armenian liturgical music.

Folk Music

Compilations

⊙ Armenians on 8th Avenue (Traditional Crossroads, US).

New York's 8th Avenue was the centre of the city's Armenian and Greek communities and a taverna culture thrived there, reaching a peak in the 1950s. This CD, re-issuing recordings from the 1940s and '50s, reveals a little-known world of classical and popular musicians like kanon player Garbis Bakirgian, oud player Marko Melkon and singer 'Sugar Mary'. A musical curiosity, but a fascinating one.

⊙ Arménie 2: Musique de tradition populaire et des Achough (Ocora, France).

A companion disc to the Ocora release above with various folk songs and ashough pieces by Sayat Nova and more recent troubadours accompanied by small instrumental groups and a couple of dubious, Soviet-style big ensembles.

⊙ Haut-Karabagh: Musiques du Front (Auvidis/Silex, France).

An imaginative musical postcard from the war-stricken region of Nagorno-Karabagh. Includes laments in a cemetary, songs about the struggle and military leaders and wonderful instrumental groups of clarinets, duduks, accordion and drums. Folk music that deals with contemporary realities.

⊙ Kalaschjan: Rural and Urban Traditional Music from Armenia (Schott Wergo/Weltmusik, Germany).

A good cross section of folk and ashoug music from a concert at the House of World Cultures in Berlin. There's an outdoor ensemble of zurnas and dhol and a more refined ensemble of oud, kanon, kamancha, duduk and dhol.

⊙ Music of Armenia: Vol 5. Folk Music (Celestial Harmonies, US).

A 2-CD set maintaining the high standards of the Celestial Harmonies series. There are two ensembles, the Shoghaken with a larger ensemble of 'refined' instruments adopting a sort of 'early music' approach for a more authentic pre- or post-Soviet style (making it perhaps less accessible to first time listeners), and the Sasun group with a more vernacular duduk and dhol line up. Slightly dour performances, but good sleeve notes.

Artists

Gevorg Dabagian

The leader of the Shoghaken Folk Ensemble, Dabagian is one of the best duduk players in Armenia today. Like Gasparyan he learned (and now teaches) at the Yerevan Conservatoire.

⊙ Music of Armenia: Vol 3 Duduk (Celestial Harmonies, US).

A rich variety of duduk music, some of it with moving and harmonic drones. Very fine playing which repays careful listening. Includes a couple of pieces appropriately about the apricot tree.

Djivan Gasparyan

Born in 1928, Armenia's most famous duduk player (see

box on p.334) has pushed the boundaries with his various collaborations and is still going strong.

 I Will Not Be Sad in This World
(Land Records, UK; Warners, US).

The recording that brought Gasparyan to fame from Melodiya recordings released in 1983. A beautiful rich tone, but unremittingly melancholy. The unlikely-sounding title is actually from one of Sayat Nova's most famous tunes "I Will Not Be Sad In This World (If I Have You)". Also full of the soulful stuff is *Ask Me No Questions* (Traditional Crossroads, US). There are more interesting tonal inflections, but a thinner sound.

Heavenly Duduk
(World Network, Germany).

A great introduction to Gasparyan's art. The opening numbers have all the melancholic longing that typifies the instrument, with some seductive microtones. But there are also some lively dance numbers with *dhol* accompaniment, songs (Gasparyan has a moving voice), and more classical arrangements of Komitas tunes for a duduk trio. Another good balance of meditative and dance music is to be found on **Apricots from Eden** (Traditional Crossroads, US).

WITH MICHAEL BROOK

Black Rock (RealWorld, UK).

With some beautiful melodies and transparent arrangements, this collaboration with Michael Brook is the album for those wary of a duduk solo album. Its impact is diluted by occasional doodling but there are real highlights in the more traditional moments and Gasparyan's singing.

Richard Hagopian

Born in 1937 in the grape-growing area of Fresno, California where many Armenians settled, Hagopian learned the oud from Garbis Bakirgian (see above) and has extensively studied and played Armenian folk and classical music.

Armenian Music through the Ages
(Smithsonian Folkways, US).

A stylishly performed selection of folk and classical pieces for oud, kanon, violin and hand drum. Excellent accompanying notes.

Night Ark

Four-piece band led by American-born Armenian Ara Dinkjian. Alongside piano, bass and percussion Dinkjian plays oud, saz and kanon and draws on jazz and blues as well as Middle-Eastern influences. He's also collaborated with noted singers Elefteria Arvanitaki in Greece and Sezen Aksu in Turkey.

In Wonderland (Emarcy/Polygram, Greece).

The disc provides a colourful and tasteful merging of East and West. What many New Age and World Beat drums try to achieve is naturally blended here by artists who have been raised with both cultures.

Muradian Ensemble

Armenian folk ensemble led by veteran kamancha player Hratchja Muradian. They are a typical Soviet-style group, with an arranged and polished style, but very compelling.

Muradian Ensemble and Hayastan
(Pan/Van Geel, Netherlands).

These two CDs are excellent collections of Armenian folk music at its most accessible. Each have slow meditative duduk pieces and a couple of songs, as well as wilder, up-tempo dances.

Egypt | Popular/street music

cairo hit factory

Egyptian – and Arabic – music has moved on apace in the 1980s and '90s. The established tradition of Classical song (see p.323) exploded, mainly through the cassette culture, into the street styles of *shaabi* (a kind of blues-folk) and *al-jil* (Arabic pop). What didn't change, however, was the dominance of Egypt (and Cairo) in the Arab musical world. Turn on the radio or TV or go to the cinema in any Arabic-speaking country and it's almost certain to be an Egyptian show on offer. Not all the stars are Egyptian – there are top Cairene singers from Syria, Lebanon, Algeria and Moroccan – yet working with Egyptian composers and musicians, and singing in Egyptian Arabic (the lingua-franca of Arab culture) their music is to all intents and purposes Egyptian. **David Lodge** and **Bill Badley** take the pulse of contemporary Cairo, and look at popular Egyptian roots and rural folk traditions.

The size and confidence of the Arab market is partly responsible for Egyptians' emphatic rejection of music from other countries – which means the streets of Cairo are

DAVID LODGE

Cairo

blissfully unpolluted with Western pop. The rejection of things foreign extends somewhat to Arab neighbours, too; cassettes from the Middle East (and even Algerian rai) are not common in the kiosks of Cairo. But the city is a supreme gathering point for **Egyptian roots**, a musical playground of cross-cutting influences and inspiration. The brassy jazz of Nubia from the hot African south plays alongside the haunting clarinet of the desert Bedouin; comic rap monologues of the Nilotic Saiyidis mix with the heart-rending tones of Classical song.

In this unique auditory environment – at venues ranging from the giant Sufi *zikr* street festivals to football stadium extravaganzas, from the raw theatre of a working-class wedding to a belly-dance nightclub down Pyramids Road – Cairo offers Arab composers an extraordinary atmosphere for their inspiration. A word of warning, however, to anyone approaching Egyptian music for the first time. The scene is so diverse and moves so fast that almost everything changes by the time you've heard about it! If you can imagine coming to British or American music – in its entirety – as a total novice, you'll have some idea of the vista laid out before you.

Sufi Music and Trance

When the heart throbs with exhilaration and rapture becomes intense and the agitation of ecstasy is manifested and conventional forms are gone, that agitation is neither dancing nor bodily indulgence, but a dissolution of the soul.

Ibn Taymiya, writer and theologian (1263–1328)

While the religiously orthodox have long worked to keep music out of Islam, the Islamic mystics, the **Sufis**, instead sought to harness its power and turn it to the service of God. According to the ninth-century Baghdad philosopher Abu Suliman al-Darani, Sufis believe that "music and singing do not produce in the heart that which is not in it", and music "reminds the spirit of the realm for which it constantly longs". They assert that if you have moral discipline, you need have no fear of it. The Sufis thus helped to nurture Arab music through ages when all around were doing their best to suppress it.

This 'heretical' alliance of music and Islam is most intensely displayed at the giant **mulids** – festivals to celebrate the saint of a mosque – when upwards of a million worshippers and hangers-on gather together in defiance of fundamentalists and authorities alike. The union of body and music is encapsulated in the **zikr**, a dramatic ritual which uses song and dance to open a path to divine ecstasy. Sufis explain the alarming spectacle of entrancement with characteristic spiritual logic: "Music is the food of the spirit; when the spirit receives food, it turns aside from the government of the body."

To a binding hypnotic rhythm, heaving movements and respiratory groans, the leader conducts the congregation, reciting Sufi poetry, guiding them from one *maqam* mode to another. Bodies sway, heads roll upward on every stroke as they chant religious devotions with spiralling intensity. The *nay* (flute), played in a style depicted in the pharonic tombs, alternates short, two-beat pulses on a simple melody line. Lifeless arms dangle, saliva slaps from open mouths, and eyes stare without seeing. Men collapse, convulsing, on the floor, while others run to lift them up, reciting to them verses from the Koran. The beat slows, and rows of sweating heads drop their gaze to the floor. Slowly, exhausted, the ecstatics return to the fray.

For the practising Sufi clans who have marched behind their flags and banners all the way from their village, the event is a display of clan loyalty, piety and pride. For the musicians who roam from one mulid to another throughout the year, turning popular village songs about secular love into an adoration of Mohammed the Prophet, it can also be a good living. In adaptation, these songs lose little of their earthly sexual passion: "It is he, it is only he who lives in my heart, only he to whom I give my love, our beautiful Prophet, Mohammed, whose eyes are made-up with kohl."

JAK KILBY

Mulid folk band

Rural Folk Music: the Nile, the Desert and the Copts

Egypt is a land of many environments. The archetypal image is that of the crowded towns, villages and farmland of the Nile valley, but mountain wilderness and arid desert cover 96 percent of the country. The diversity also ranges from the European colour of the northern, Mediterranean coast lands to the African resonances of the south. From each geographically distinct area comes a distinct music.

Folk music in Egypt still performs a vital role in recording a popular version of history. With their own characteristic rhythms, instruments and voices, there is music to accompany almost every event, from the harvest to circumcisions. There is social criticism in the monologues about village goings-on, worship in the festival songs for Ramadan, and mayhem in activities at weddings and mulids.

Saiyidi is the folk music of the **upper Nile valley**. Saiyidis (the name applies to the musicians as well as their music) are famous for their clever use of words and for their playful monologues set to music. The music features two instruments in particular – the *nahrasan*, a two-sided drum hung across the chest and played with sticks, and the *mismar saiyidi* trumpet. The characteristic rhythm of saiyidi, to which horses are traditionally trained to dance, is one of the most successful styles used in modern al-jil pop.

Among the best-known of saiyidi stars are **Les Musiciens du Nil**. The 'Musicians of the Nile', a name given to them for overseas promotional purposes, are led by the singer **Met'al Gnawi**, the charismatic head of a Luxor-based gypsy family. The group were unexpectedly chosen by the Egyptian government to act as Egypt's official folk group abroad. In Egypt he is best-known for the saucy hit "Ya faraula" (My strawberry); Egyptians are fond of using fruit in sexual allegory. Another saiyidi star is Omar Gharzawi, known for his monologues defending saiyidis and their culture – they are traditionally the butt of Egyptian humour. Other names worth listening out for include

Sohar Magdy, **Ahmed Mougahid**, **Shoukoukou** and **Ahmed Ismail**.

The folk music known as **sawahili** comes from the Mediterranean coastal area, and is characterised by the use of a guitar-like stringed instrument, the *simsimaya*, though the style found in Alexandria features the accordion. Famous sawahili singers include **Aid el-Gannirni** from Suez and **Abd'l Iskandrani** from Alexandria.

As well as the various kinds of folk music, Egypt has two important ethnic musics – Bedouin and Nubian (see separate box on p.345). **Bedouin music** comes from the western, Libyan desert, and the eastern arid

The Musicians of the Nile

zones of Sinai and the Eastern desert. The main instrument is the bedouin *mismar*, a twin-pipe clarinet which enables the player to produce a melody line and a drone simultaneously. Perhaps the best-known Bedouin singer is **Awad e'Medic**.

There is also an ancient liturgical music belonging to Egypt's **Coptic Christians** – sung in the ancient Coptic language. Its melodies and rhythm are closely linked to that of the *felahin*, the farmers of the Nile delta who have been toiling the soil for millennia, and it has been suggested that the extrapolated syllables of Coptic song recall the hymns of the ancient Egyptian priests. If this is so, then the melodies passed on by oral tradition, and the use by the Coptic Church of triangles and small cymbals, are the closest thing to the music of the pharaohs.

Bride and Home

A working class (*baladi*) **wedding** in a cramped alley in central Cairo is possibly the finest exhibition of spontaneous musical theatre you can witness anywhere. On Friday and Saturday nights, the city becomes a patchwork of pulsing coloured light and searing noise, as the elaborate ritual of the marriage party gets underway.

JAK KILBY

Cairo wedding

vides an outlet for the tensions that build up in the tight-knit community.

It is on these occasions that men may choose to settle lingering disputes, dedicating their advice, threats and guarded insults via the stage to their rivals in a furiously fast interchange. Up leaps a boy with a fistful of banknotes held high: he makes his greeting, echoed by the MC in a rapid, musical rap. "Greetings to the police, especially the police of Saiyida Zeynab who are our friends, greetings to the youth of Alaa, greetings to the people of Hussein. We want this wedding to be nice with no trouble." After a stream of appeals to family and friends, and a short break of music from the five-piece band lining the back of the stage,

Belly-dance music

another singer, dressed in evening suit and tie, takes over, slowly wailing "Ya leil ya ein" (Oh! the night, Oh! my eyes!), a wild improvisation that pierces the dark from a deafening, distorted PA.

First comes the *Hassabala* troupe, bugles and trumpets blaring (a style inspired by imperial British marching bands), who form a circle of up to 25 thundering wooden drums. Into this vortex of chanting and deafening rhythm go the whirling dancers and a stick-cracking folklore troupe from Upper Egypt. Once the bride and groom have been escorted away in a cacophony of noise, the music stops abruptly and the group dashes hurriedly into a waiting Toyota van which takes them hooting across town to their next appointment, possibly their fourth or fifth of the night.

Then the real party begins. A riotously made-up dancer laden with glittering sequins takes to the small stage, cavorting with the master of ceremonies, lifting her dress a little, pushing out her leg, lying on the floor and gyrating, rubbing up against him, playfully controlling the arena. This is **raks sharki – belly dancing**. The dancer sings with flaying alto vocals – pop songs, classical songs, traditional songs all made raw and raunchy. The makeshift stage becomes a platform too for the guests who wave banknotes in their bids to stay in the limelight, to dance, sing or play the fool, with unselfconscious bravado and humour. More than just honouring the bride and her father, this stream of musical cameos is all part of the drama that pro-

Music of the Youth

In Cairo, until as recently as the late 1980s, from every taxi radio-cassette deck and every street corner kiosk, day and night, emerged the haunting voice of Umm Kalthum or other Classical Arab superstars (see article on p.323). While this music has far from disappeared, it is not as ubiquitous as it once was (though Umm Kalthum is still listened to constantly by expat Egyptians in the Gulf). Today cassette shops and fast cars are stocked up with other types of music and commercial competition is intense among the hundreds of artists. The new sounds of Egyptian youth – **shaabi** and **al-jil** – are the music of two social revolutions shaping the nation's modern outlook.

Pressure for change in the musical world of Cairo had been building up for some time, and the established music order could do little more than look on as an entirely new Egypt unfurled before them. Since the mid-1970s Sadat's 'open door policy' had welcomed Western business, which gave birth to a new enterprise culture in the big cites. In addition, the Gulf states and Iraq provided new work for millions of Egyptian labourers, craftsmen and technicians who sent back their pay cheques to create, in effect, a new urban middle class.

With their new-found spending power, this rapidly expanding social group has reinvented Cairo in their own image, complete with take-out food stalls, ear-splitting in-car hi-fi, and of course street-corner kiosks crammed with their music. And their music, while taking inspiration from Arab Classical song, is essentially a reassertion of folk traditions, reaffirming Egyptian identity at a time of momentous and rapid change.

Shaabi – Art from the Workers

The humiliating defeat by Israel in 1967 shattered the pan-Arab dream of President Nasser, forcing Egyptians to face stark reality. From this abject poverty and humiliation they escaped into a new **'light song'**, which drew on folkloric themes to reassert a proud Egyptian identity. It was a movement away from the serious classical hue of tradition and towards a more humorous, even salacious spirit. At first this was a middle-class initiative, with singers like **Layla Nasmy** and **Aida al-Shah** popularising these forms for the respectable community. But soon it gave way to working-class singers – and words from the present-day. This was **shaabi** – people's – music, and it found its heart in the working-class areas of Cairo – some of the most overcrowded communities in the world.

Shaabi singers specialise in the **mawal**, a freely improvised vocal in which the singer impresses on the listener the depth of his or her sorrowful complaint. It's a form which is found widely in Classical Arab music, although in a more refined style, and bears comparison with other 'folk-blues' like fado or rembetika. But shaabi songs aren't all sorrow: the traditional progression has a fast rhythmic beat emerging from the improvisation, to take the song through chorus after chorus to climax in a rousing dance tempo. These make the form perfect for both wedding celebrations and nightclubs.

The first shaabi singer to break into the mass market, in 1971, was the charismatic **Ahmed Adaweyah**. His lyrical irreverence, using the rough dialect of the streets, was the essence of his revolution. This kind of language had never been heard in song before and it came over, essentially, as a weapon of the working class, affirming their own values while mocking respectable society. Adaweyah's song, "Setu" (composed by Farouk Salama with lyrics by Hassan abu-Atma), is a good example, poking fun at a middle-class lifestyle:

Fast asleep he's fasting,
He doesn't want to bother.
And his granny and mummy are mothering
  him
With honey and butter.
Finally, but not that final,
He's a weapon without a bullet,
A failure at school and no good at work.

Full of metaphor and comical twists, Adaweyah's songs stamped shaabi character with the release of every cassette. His lifestyle and personality matched them; coming from a poor and uneducated background, he was a true working-class hero.

Adaweyah's provocative social commentaries served to hang Egypt's dirty linen in public, which didn't go down well with the government and ruling class, fearful that it would reinforce the popular Gulf Arab image of Egypt as an uncultured society. When in 1991 Adaweyah received a surprise invitation to appear on TV (for the first time), his remarks were bleeped out, while songs with suggestive lyrics, or those that implied an immoral lifestyle, were banned.

One 1992 shaabi song, with the lines – "Her waist is like the neck of a violin, I used to enjoy apricots but now I would die for mangoes!" – caused an outcry among the middle class, raised on the sung poetry of Umm Kalthum. The song was banned but the cassette was nevertheless available everywhere, sold upwards of half a million, and, with its euphemistic fruitiness, became a favourite of the gay community.

Equally unpopular with the censors is the recurring lyrical theme of working-class pride. In a driving rap on his album *Akhar Sa'ar* (The Last Hour), **Shaaban Abd el-Rahim** affirmed shaabi music as real Egyptian music unadulterated by the outside world. Again, the cassette, and all others by him, were promptly banned. This is an example of the lyrics:

There is foreign music,
We sleep and dream, it's all foreign.
If we imitate, it will never help us,
Have nothing to do with foreign.

Shaabi Superstars

Shaabi stars tend to break through at local weddings and festivals, then, as they become famous, move on to engagements at nightclubs and big private weddings in Egypt and the Gulf. Below is a round-up of the main figures and some ideas on recordings to seek out. Note that although there are many shaabi cassettes (and CDs) available in Cairo, they tend to be transitory compilations, and you usually need to ask for a particular song rather than an album title.

Shaabi's first superstar was **Ahmed Adaweyah**, who remains the finest exponent of the thick, soulful tones of mawal. There are also numerous tapes of his with the title *Mawal Adaweyah*, each featuring a lengthy, heart-rending vocal improvisation. *Al-Tarik* (The route) is one of his finest cassettes. Another pioneer of shaabi was **Kat Kut el-Amir**, who is remembered chiefly for the song "Ya Gazelle el-Darb il-Ahmar" (You Gazelle of Darb il-Ahmar – an old quarter of Cairo), composed for a big private wedding.

The working class hero **Shaaban Abd el-Rahim** is famous for rapping wisdoms about his life, as he cel-

Ahmed Adaeyah – fruity irreverence

ebrates his rise from ironing man to superstar. Despite selling upwards of 100,000 copies of each cassette, fame has yet to change him. He lives in his 'village' on the outskirts of Cairo, where he maintains a traditional lifestyle and keeps chickens and goats on his roof. In his community he is idolised and if you see him in the village or one of the shaabi areas of Cairo, he is constantly surrounded by a group of devotees and extended family. Of his cassettes, *Akhar Saah* (The Final Hour) is highly recommended – but it is banned and not easy to get hold of.

Amr Diab and **Hakim** have both been very successful at taking the raw energy of shaabi and cleaning it up for mass appeal. They have continued the shaabi tradition of street wisdom, but there is also a worldliness about their songs. Amr Diab, in particular, has capitalised on his boyish good looks (tastefully set off by billowing silk shirts) and thoughtful posturing. For a poor boy from Port Said who arrived in Cairo on the bus he has done amazingly well and is a role model for a thousand wanna-bes: he now flies to his sell-out arena concerts in a helicopter.

Thank God I can't find anyone to copy.
Listen to me, my country bumpkin,
All art comes from the workers,
And now all the people are saying,
Look, the ironing man is singing . . .

In the late 1980s, as Japanese VCRs and American films became established in back-alley society, so the younger generation was seduced into a world of foreign, modernising values – one where Shaaban's beliefs might seem no longer appropriate. Younger singers developed a fascination with the musical gadgetry of the West, and synthetic sounds began challenging the claim that shaabi was the only authentic Egyptian music. In the 1980s, on top of the traditional violins, tabla and squeezebox were added drum kit, organ, synthesiser, saxophone and electric guitar. In the 1990s, beat boxes and samplers became more commonplace than traditional Arab instruments.

As the shaabi stars attempt to reach a wider public with their increasingly slick product, production values are more and more critically assessed. The shaabi form has also been 'cleaned up' for radio consumption by artists like **Amr Diab** and **Hakim** – the new mainstream Egyptian popular artists.

Al-jil

In the 1970s, fed up with listening to the Beatles, Abba and Bony M in a language they couldn't understand, the youth of Egypt decided they could do better. With the aid of samplers and quartertone programmes, Egyptian pop music – **al-jil** (generation) music – was born. It was a revolutionary development. The dance music that they produced bore the hallmarks of the Arab sound – trained, controlled voices sliding through infectious happy melodies, and distinctive, clear-as-a-bell backing chorus – but it was performed to a punchy tech-no-Arab beat.

Central to the movement was a young Libyan, **Hamid el-Shaeri**. Fleeing one of Gaddafi's anti-Western purges, Hamid came to Egypt in 1974 and started working with Egyptians on a new sound. He finally hit golddust in 1988 with the song "Lolaiki" (the word is meaningless), recorded in a back room, which sold in the millions. It was sung by a friend, **Ali Hamaida**, who to the great relief of many turned out to be a one-hit wonder (the song was okay once or twice, but all over town for a year . . .):

Without you I'd never sing,
Without you I'd never fall in love.
I have nobody without you.
You are my light and my sight,
My song is only for you,
Lolaiki lo lo lo lo lo lo lo lo

Lyrical themes of 'boy flirts with girl, girl leaves boy, boy is miserable/finds new girl' did little to win over the older generation, but the popularity of the new feel-good scene couldn't fail to impress upon the established cultural guardians the strength of this new youth movement. The rags-to-riches story of "Lolaiki" also impressed the back-street entrepreneurs, and the new industry exploded overnight.

To the older generation, the new music-makers were little more than businessmen selling cheap produce in the market. Gone were the intricate melodies, beautiful poetry, sympathetic use of *maqamat* and natural sounds, and in came the rasping synthesiser and the three-minute pop-song format. The official media turned against al-jil and, while Western pop songs were featured on the radio and TV, the younger generation were for many years denied media access to their own music.

Al-jil singers are the first to admit they're in the business of entertainment, not art, but that is not to dismiss the genre's importance as a cultural force. In many Arab countries, people under twenty-five account for three-quarters of the population. More than merely giving people a tune to dance to, al-jil music has (like Algerian rai) become a focus for young people breaking free from the constraints of traditional society. It

finds ready markets everywhere from the Atlantic to the Euphrates, and by doing so it exports its visions to a wider Arab youth.

The singer is crucial to the success of al-jil songs, less these days for a good voice than for straightforward sex appeal. The singer and musicians typically have little say in the music-making process: there are few singer-songwriters and

COLIN HAWKINS/MANTRA

Adoptive Egyptian Natacha Atlas

groups have never caught on. Instead performers are supplied songs by a producer who has collected the melody, lyrics and rhythm from different sources and arranged them in a formula dedicated to the market. The financial rewards can be great. From a successful cassette (and video), the singer may earn spectacular money from headlining at live concerts in Egypt, the

Arab capitals and private parties in New York, London and Paris, where tickets rarely cost less than £200 ($300).

The top al-jil stars include **Hamid el-Shaeri**, whose treatment of the highly infectious melodies is unrivalled, and his protégé, **Ehab Tawfik**. The stars are almost exclusively men, although there is one exception in **Hanan** – a classically trained singer who began her career in the Arab Music Institute Ensemble. Her highly controlled, squeaky voice sounds, at its best, stunningly wild.

The al-jil scene has also impacted on the European dance scene, in a number of crossover projects. Chief among them is the work that has been done by Tim Whelan and Hamid Mantu of London-based **Transglobal Underground**, who have immersed themselves in the Cairo music scene to great effect, as shown by their production contributions to **Natacha Atlas**'s CDs and a **remix** album of Hakim's best known songs. Natacha Atlas (whose family is originally from North Africa) has herself spent the last few years based in Cairo, soaking up the city's music. Her recent albums have developed this West-East synthesis. Never one to miss out on a marketing opportunity, Amr Diab has also put out a dance-remix album based on his ubiquitous hit, "Habibi".

New Nubian, old Nubian

Nubian music has its origins in the African south of Egypt, among the now displaced Nubian people. The construction of the second Aswan dam in the early 1960s – which created Lake Nasser, the largest artificial lake in the world – effectively drowned their civilisation, as over 100,000 people were forcibly removed. In the wake of the flooding, the communities were transplanted south into Sudan and north into Egypt, including a significant community who moved to Cairo.

Nubian village music remains traditional, with ritual songs supported by a duff and hand-clapping. In Cairo, it has deveoped in new directions, forged by two opposing voices – Ali Hassan Kuban and Mohammed Mounir – who mirror the diverging paths of the city's Nubian migrants.

The original urban sound of Nubia came about through the music of **Ali Hassan Kuban** – who tells a story of overhearing a jazz band in a Cairo nightclub, and deciding at once to add brass to his then-folk based music. Although unknown in Cairo outside the Nubian community, Kuban's unique music has taken him on many European tours and put two CDs onto the World Music market. In Egypt, he campaigns tirelessly for the Nubian language, and insists that members of his musicians' cooperative sing in one of the two Nubian dialects. His brash, urgent musical style has inspired many others in Cairo, most notably **Bahr Abu Greisha** and **Hussein Bashier**. They specialise in wild, wailing brass which lends a New Orleans feel to their sound.

Mohamed Mounir is a modern Nubian, who has produced some of the most sophisticated modern pop music in Egypt. He came to study in Cairo in the 1970s, already speaking Arabic as his first language, and considers himself an Arab Egyptian. Indeed, he is highly critical of the popular Nubian movement for a return to the homeland. His songs look for solutions to the problems of the wider Arab world – of which he feels Nubia is a part – such as the future of the Palestinians and the dilemma of Jerusalem. His home audience is dominated by students who appreciate his lyrics.

In the wider World Music market, **Hamza el Din** is synonymous with Nubian music – in no small part due to the fact that he has been resident in the West for the last 30 years. Like Ali Hassan Kuban, his songs are deeply affected by the sense of alienation that many Nubians feel. He has collaborated with a number of Western musicians, notably the Kronos Quartet whose arrangement of his "The Water Wheel" is one of the highlights of their delightful *Pieces of Africa* album.

A younger Nubian fusionist is **Mahmoud Fadl** – an incredibly accomplished percussionist. He has worked with musicians from varying backgrounds and draws on South American influences as well as his own Arab/African roots – an alluring brew that has been particularly well received in Europe.

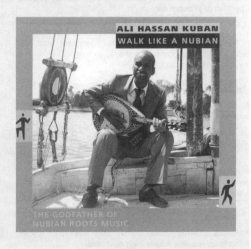

ALI HASSAN KUBAN
WALK LIKE A NUBIAN

THE GODFATHER OF
NUBIAN ROOTS MUSIC

discography

To get contemporary Egyptian releases, you'll need to check Arab-owned stores in major cities, or, of course, buy in Cairo. Even so it's hard to make recommendations as they tend to be ephemeral compilations.

Compilations

 Egypt – Music of the Nile from the Desert to the Sea (Virgin, France).

A tall-format box-booklet, with 2 CDs, that sets out to cover Egyptian music in all its forms, historic and present. It does a pretty good job, featuring singers from Umm Kalthum to Hamed, and a good range of instrumentalists, including Ali Hassan Kuban and the Musicians of the Nile.

 Sif Safaa: New Music from the Middle East and **Camelspotting** (EMI Hemisphere, UK).

These two sampler discs of pop music from around the Arab world provide a great introduction to what's hot. EMI Arabia in Dubai handle many of the finest stars in the region and these are well chosen selections – laudable for being wide ranging (singers from Yemen, Saudi and the Maghreb, as well as Egypt) and reasonably priced.

⊚ **Yalla! Hit List Egypt** (Mango, UK).

This is a terrific introduction to shaabi, al-jil and Nubian styles, compiled in the early 1990s and featuring songs by Mohamed Mounir, Ehab Tawfik, Shaaban Abd el-Rahim, Magdy Talaat, Hanan and others. It is shamefully out of catalogue.

Artists

Natacha Atlas

The British-born singer has been working in Cairo in recent years, developing a remarkable fusion sound.

⊚ **Gedida** (Mantra Records, UK).

This is Atlas's most deeply Egyptian record to date – and is building her a following in both the Middle East and Europe.

Amr Diab

Like him or not, Amr Diab is the contemporary face of Egyptian al-jil pop music.

⊚ **Habibe Remix** (EMI, Arabia).

All the permutations of Amr's hit you could ever wish for – even if much of it sounds like the Gipsy Kings let loose in a very big recording studio.

Soliman Gamil

Gamil is an avant-garde folk/classical composer who trained in both Western and Eastern traditions.

⊚ **A Map of Egypt before the Sands** (Touch Music/Sterns, UK).

An instrumental work, with Arab folk instruments and a classical orchestra, that aims to capture the atmosphere of the pharaonic world centuries before the arrival of Islam and the Arabs in Egypt.

Hakim

Hakim is another million-selling al-jil teen heart-throb, with rather rougher edges than Amr Diab.

⊚ **Haleel** (Slam Records, Egypt).

Although Hakim's image is that of a cheesy, boyish pop star, you can certainly hear the street 'shaabi' origins of his style on many of these tracks.

Les Musiciens du Nil

The Musicians of the Nile, drawn mainly from a Luxor Gypsy family, are stars of the rural *saiyidi* style. They are regulars on the international World Music festival circuit.

⊚ **Luxor to Isna** (Real World, UK).

The *rababa* fiddle rasps and strange oboes and clarinets hoot and buzz through mostly instrumental tracks, interspersed with street-sound interludes.

Mokhtar al-Said & El Ferka el-Masaya

Mokhtar al-Said is a top Cairene arranger; El Ferka el-Masaya (Orchestra of Diamonds) have accommpanied many of the great classical singers.

⊚ **Amar 14: Jalilah's Raks Sharki 2** (Piranha, Germany).

Raks sharki is belly-dance music, and this is the classic orchestral 'oriental' sound, by turns portentous and playful.

Nubian music

Hamza el Din

A Europe-based fusionist, Hamza el Din's performances are much more sparse than many of his fellow Nubians. He has worked with The Kronos Ensemble, and others.

⊚ **Escalay – The Water Wheel** (Nonesuch, USA).
⊚ **A Wish** (Sounds True, USA).

Both these CDs are fine examples of Hamza el Din's poised oud playing and rich voice.

Ali Hassan Kuban

Ali Hassan Kuban was a pioneer of urban Nubian music, introducing brass and other jazz elements. He has become quite a star on the World Music circuit.

⊚ **From Nubia to Cairo** ⊚ **Walk Like a Nubian**
⊚ **Nubian Magic** (Piranha, Germany).

A trio of tough, Cairo-Nubian music releases.

Mohamed Mounir

Mounir is a kind of singer-songwriter, with political pan-Arab lyrics. He sings in Arabic rather than Nubian.

⊚ **Wast el-Daira** (Monsun-Line, Germany).

Mounir at his most intricate and sophisticated.

Salamat

A Nubian group featuring Mahmoud Fadl and others, some of whom also appear with Ali Hassan Kuban. With lyrics in Arabic, this is a less politicised, more good-time sound than Kuban's.

⊚ **Mambo El Soudani - Nubian Al Jeel Music from Cairo** and **Ezzayakoum** (Piranha, Germany).

Strong whiffs of Sudan drift through these thumping songs, dense with hysterical alto-sax, tenor sax and trumpet.

Georgia

a feast of songs

As the locals tell it, when God was distributing land amongst the peoples of the earth, the Georgians were too busy drinking and feasting to turn up on time. When they arrived there was nothing left. "But Lord", they protested, "we were only late because we were toasting You." God was so touched by this that he gave them the land he was keeping for Himself – warm, fertile and fringed by the spectacularly beautiful Caucasus mountains. With feasting celebrated in a national myth, it's not surprising that it's the principal occasion for music-making. **Simon Broughton** raises a glass to Georgia's spectacular polyphonic singing and other musical traditions.

ike their neighbours the Armenians, the Georgians were one of the first nations to adopt Christianity – St Nino of Cappadocia converted the Georgian king in 330 AD. But unlike the Armenians and the other surrounding peoples, the Georgians have a rich tradition of vocal polyphony in both religious and folk music. As Byzantine music is monophonic, it seems likely that Georgia's polyphonic church music grew out of its indigenous folk tradition.

Table Songs

Today, the best place to hear Georgian music is at **a feast**. The country produces fantastic food and wine and people will gather for lavish picnics and celebrations at the slightest excuse. And when you get a group of Georgians round a table, the chances are you'll also get some music. A proper feast is led by a toastmaster (*tamada*) who proposes toasts according to certain accepted rules and customs. The first toast is always to God (not surprising given the national myth) and if there's music the first song will be in praise of God. The second toast is to long life and goes hand in hand with the ubiquitous "Mravaljamieri", a hymn of praise to life. The alternation of toasts and songs continues as the tamada embroiders each toast with philosophical statements or snippets of wisdom.

After the essential toast to 'our ancestors', our tamada

announced that one of the things that distinguishes human beings from animals is the fact that they remember and celebrate their forbears. This was followed by "Zamtari", a song about winter, the notion being that we were honouring our grandmothers and grandfathers, people in the 'winter' of their life. Often the association between toasts and songs is poetic rather than literal.

As well as religious songs and specific table songs, **work songs** that were originally for harvesting or ploughing are now sung around the table. There's a beautiful type of ploughing song, *orovela*, that is found only in eastern Georgia. It's not polyphonic and sounds distinctly Armenian in character with a narrow-range, melancholic solo line over a drone bass. When I heard it sung at a feast, it ended in chuckles as the last line which should have been telling the oxen to work harder was changed to

SIMON BROUGHTON

Svanetian singers with Changi

one urging everyone to drink more. A demonstration, if one was needed, of the transposition of work song into table song.

Polyphony

Georgian **polyphony** is usually in three parts and is generally sung by men, although women's groups do exist. Mixed groups are unusual since Georgian music tends to end on a unison note and the octaves produced with mixed voices are usually avoided. Often the main 'melody' of the polyphony is sung by the middle voice with the upper and lower voices either supporting it or weaving complex countermelodies around it. In a mountainous country where contact is often difficult, styles vary from region to region, but the clearest differences can be heard between the east and the west.

The richest, most sonorous style is in the eastern region of **Kakhetia**, famous for its wine, so it's not surprising that the best table and drinking songs originate here. Kakhetian singing has two solo voices intertwining with each other – like tangled vines – over a slowly moving drone bass sung by the rest of the singers. There are shimmering clashes and dissonances, tensions and releases, as the harmonies collide like slowly moving tectonic plates. "Chakrulo", one of the most beautiful of Kakhetian drinking songs, was one of the pieces of earthly music chosen to go into space on the *Voyager* spacecraft in 1977. Almost a re-run of that national myth.

In the Western regions of **Guria** and **Mengrelia** the bass lines are much more athletic and the whole style more virtuoso. Here the dissonances that sound so strange to Western ears and are so beloved in Georgian music seem even more acute. The men sing in a higher 'head-voice' and a soloist indulges in a spectacular yodelling called *krimanchuli* with striking leaps and rhythmic pat-

The Georgian Music-o-Gram

On an old winding street above the Metekhi church in old Tbilisi there's a place that looks like a cross between a tea-house and a taxi firm. You can't miss it because above the entrance are vivid paintings in the naïve style of Georgia's most famous painter, Pirosmani. The pictures show musicians with pink and bulging cheeks blowing into duduks and striking drums. A notice declares it to be the "Centre for Players of Oriental Instruments".

Going in, it's much quieter than you expect. No puffing cheeks or wild drumming. Not an oriental instrument to be seen. Just a few guys drinking tea, reading the paper or playing dominoes. A man at a desk by the door is on the phone and jotting down notes in a ledger. But when the call comes to say, "We're having a little get together to celebrate my son's engagement. Could you send some of your lads over to get things going?" these musicians will be round faster than a kiss-o-gram. For Georgians, music is an essential ingredient of any celebration. You can see them at the weekend dining al fresco in local beauty spots and, if they're not bursting out with their own homemade polyphonic singing, there'll be an instrumental trio wandering from group to group. This

The Bureau: Dial-A-Duduk

office in Tbilisi is here to provide music for weddings, birthdays – in fact, any sort of celebration.

The 'oriental' instruments are duduks, clarinets and drums – instruments the Georgians have picked up from their Transcaucasian neighbours to the east, the Armenians and Azeris. The tunes range from wild dances on the clarinet and accordion with an insistent rhythm beaten out on the drum, or soft, reflective songs played by a couple of duduks. The instruments themselves are kept in the wooden lockers that line the walls, so they can be grabbed quickly when the musicians are needed in a hurry.

terns. The ancient Greek historian Xenophon wrote in the fourth century BC that the Georgians prepared themselves for battle by singing, and maybe this is the sort of thing he had in mind. These songs, which may include four independent voice parts, have become favourite showpieces for the professional choirs that perform Georgian songs on the concert platform. There are many historical songs and epics in this western style.

In the remote, northern region of **Svanetia** the oldest traditions have survived. High in the Caucasus and cut off by snow for seven or eight months of the year, Svan culture escaped many of the invasions that affected the rest of Georgia throughout the centuries. The villages of Upper Svanetia still have spectacular medieval-style towers, as well as customs and rituals that have their origin in pre-Christian times. At a wedding feast here, toasts were drunk from a ram's horn – as depicted in the canvases of Georgia's celebrated artist Pirosmani – a practice that tends to be purely nostalgic elsewhere in the country. The music sounds distinctly archaic and severe. The harmony – angular and unpredictable – is in three parts with the middle voice leading. The range of each voice is narrow and all three parts move together syllable by syllable. Ritual songs to the sun and to St George are hugely popular in Svanetia and the Svans are famous both for their rhythmic round dances and, in a completely different character, their moving funeral laments. There's also an ancient Svanetian harp (*changui*) and a bowed viol (*chuniri*) which are sometimes used to accompany the voices.

Professional Choirs

Other old instruments like the three-string lute (*panduri*) of eastern Georgia and four-string lute (*chonguri*) of Western Georgia that are no longer

used in practice are often used by **professional choirs** in Georgia who've taken up this repertoire. The most celebrated and prolific is the **Rustavi Choir**, created in 1968 by **Anzor Erkomaishvili**. He is careful to gather members from all the regions of the country to keep the singing styles as authentic as possible. Of course, the performances are rather polished, but to hear them in concert (or on disc) is a surprisingly impressive experience – although not quite the same as hearing the music while sampling delicious walnut chicken (*satsivi*), shashliks (*mtsvadi*), cheese bread (*khatchapuri*) and fresh herbs washed down by potent wine (*gvino*).

Suliko

I was looking for the grave of my beloved
It was difficult to find.
With sorrow in my heart I cried:
Where are you, my Suliko?

The nightingale pining away
Concealed herself in the leaves of a tree.
I asked her in a sweet voice:
Is it you, Suliko?

The poetess shook her wings
And lightly touched a blossom with her beak
Sighing and chirping
As if she wanted to tell me: Yes, I am!

Words by Akaki Tsereteli

Urban Songs

Although polyphonic songs can be heard round the table of a high-rise flat in Tbilisi as well as at a village wedding in Svanetia, there's a very different style of **'urban music'** to be heard on every car radio-cassette player in Georgia or in the bars of downtown Tbilisi. Replacing the idiosyncratic harmonies of Georgian polyphony are sentimental songs – with infectiously hummable melodies, simple Western harmony and guitar accompaniment. The most famous song of the genre is **"Suliko"**, a sad ballad of lost love immortalised as Stalin's favourite song (Stalin was a Georgian and is not unadmired, even now). Several groups play this style of 'urban music' and it also appears on a couple of Western recordings. If you're in town try and pick up a recording of the Tsisperi Trio, the performers of 'urban music' par excellence.

A rougher and livelier sort of music is played (and sung) by instrumental groups around Georgia. They often feature a clarinet or a pair of duduks (*duduki*, soft reedy oboes of Armenian origin) accompanied by an accordion and a double-headed drum (*doli*). The music is wild, raucous and very compelling. Similar groups can be found throughout the Transcaucasian region.

discography

Compilations

⊚ Georgie: Chants de travail – Chants religieux (Ocora, France).

Work songs and religious music recorded in 1977. Not easy listening, but the real thing. Rarely heard intensely rhythmic *naduri* work songs, hymns and ritual songs from various districts, and Svanetian hymns to the sun and St George as well as a funeral lament. The notes verge on the unintelligible.

⊚ Georgia: Polyphony of Svanetia (Chant du Monde, France).

Quite a specialised, but fascinating collection of field recordings made in 1991 by Sylvie Bolle-Zemp. The best survey of genuine Svanetian music on disc with comprehensive notes.

⊚ The Golden Fleece: Songs from Abkhazia and Adzharia (Pan, Netherlands).

Rare recordings of music from two distinct regions of Western Georgia. Recordings made in Abkhazia in 1987 and 1991 with various folklore ensembles featuring instruments and repertoire different from other regions of Georgia. This is the land of plenty where, according to legend, Jason went in search of the Golden Fleece. The Adzharian repertoire, recorded in 1971, is closer to the Georgian style. Good notes.

℗ Soinari: Folk Music From Georgia Today (Welt Musik/Schott Wergo, Germany).

The best collection of 'urban music' available in the West, featuring three ensembles. Soinari play duduks, accordion and doli drum; Mzetamze is a group of women who perform "Suliko" amongst other songs; and Mtiebi is an excellent group led by Edisher Garakanidze who perform urban songs as well as traditional polyphonic songs in a less professional, more authentic style.

Artists

Kolkheti Ensemble

The ensemble was founded in 1980 by Givi Shanidze of the State Philharmonic Society of Georgia. The seven singers and instrumentalists come from various parts of the country.

⊚ Oh, Black-Eyed Girl (Pan, Netherlands).

This disc takes its title from the name of a song "Shavtvala Gogona". Most of the music is popular and urban in style, but features a wide range of traditional instruments including the various Georgian lutes, duduk and bagpipes. A good contrast to the usual polyphonic tradition, although the inclusion of the Gypsy band favourite "The Lark", wrongly attributed to Enescu, was a mistake.

Rustavi Choir

Georgia's most famous choir (about twelve-strong), the Rustavi is renowned for its professional performances of polyphonic songs from all over the country. It was founded in 1986 by Anzor Erkomaishvili who still leads the ensemble.

⊚ Georgia (World Network, Germany).

Vol 2 in World Network's global survey. It features eighteen folk and religious songs from various parts of the country, a couple with changui or chonguri accompaniment. As an added bonus there are six tracks from the Duduki Trio featuring mainly urban repertoire. A good combination.

℗ Georgian Voices (Nonesuch Explorer, US).

Fourteen tracks giving the best introduction to the various styles of Georgian singing. A couple of beautiful church chorales, Kakhetia's best drinking song, "Chakrulo", an orovela, Svanetia's strange "Lashgvash" march and spectacular vocal acrobatics from Guria. All songs a cappella.

⊚ Mirangula: Georgian Folk Songs (St. Petersburg Classics/Sony, UK).

This collection of eighteen songs takes its name from a sad Svanetian song accompanied here by chuniri and changui. Other songs from Western Georgia are accompanied by chonguri. Another good introduction to the different styles of Georgian singing.

Tsinandali Choir

A professional ensemble based in Kakhetia, the winegrowing area of eastern Georgia. Tsinandali is one of the best white wines of the region.

⊚ Table Songs of Georgia (RealWorld, UK).

An excellent programme of songs you might hear during the course of a slap-up feast in Kakhetia from the opening "Mravaljamieri" to the closing spectacular "Chakrulo". Actually recorded by Melodiya in 1988, but a great disc of Georgia's richest music. Crack open the wine, settle down and enjoy.

The Gulf & Yemen

sounds of the arabian peninsula

Set against the great nexuses of Cairo, Baghdad and Damascus, the Gulf countries have long thought of themselves, culturally at least, as poor cousins. However, economic wealth and a new-found pride in *khaleeji* (Gulf) traditions are contributing to something of a renaissance in the region's culture, including its music. And for some decades, the Gulf has been a melting-pot of influences, as the huge numbers of expatriate workers have brought with them their own sounds and tastes. **Bill Badley** looks around the traditions and contemporary music of the Gulf States and their more anarchic neighbour, Yemen.

The Gulf has its distinctive musical traditions and a growing number of artists are aware of them; helped by ever improving marketing and recording facilities, there are a few names being made, in the region, at least. The most significant style is **khaleeji**, which, with its emphasis on oud ('ud or lute), drums and hand-clapping, has its roots primarily in the traditional music of the region's settled, urban populations. There are other roots influences from the Bedouin of the desert and the fishing communities along the coast. With musicians striving to make themselves popular to a wider audience, Egyptian pop can also be heard in many recordings.

Saudi Arabia

Music occupies an uneasy position in **Saudi Arabia**, as it is considered *haraam* (heretical) by the Islamic establishment. As a result, recording studios are officially illegal, so the majority of successful singers travel to Cairo, Dubai or Kuwait to lay down tracks.

Despite such strictures, there is a fine musical tradition – particularly in the Western province of Hejaz – of which the Saudis are justly proud. The father of modern music in the kingdom is **Tariq Abdul Haqim**, a distinguished multi-instrumentalist who wrote the national anthem and now curates his own museum!

The most influential Saudi artist in recent years is **Mohamed Abdu**, who with his legion recordings has done more than anyone to open up the wider Arab market to Saudi sounds. For religious reasons, he took a five-year sabbatical from music, but he is now back in business. Presently making waves in the local scene are **Abadi al Johar** – nicknamed 'The Octopus' for his virtuoso 'ud playing – and **Abdu Majeed Abdullah**, who has become Saudi Arabia's first true pop star.

Mohammed Abdu – volume 55!

Bahrain

The tiny island of **Bahrain** has been at the crossroads of important trade routes for thousands of years and its music reflects the numerous cultures that have passed through and left their mark: East African, Persian, Indian and sundry Arab traces can all be heard. Along with Kuwait, it is the major centre of the **sout** – a kind of urban Arabian blues. Two of the finest exponents of this are the charismatic **Khalid al Shaikh**, who has recently started to blend in other World Music influences, and the defiantly traditional **Sultan Hamid**.

Kuwait

One of the less reported tragedies of the Gulf War was the loss of **Kuwait**'s national sound archive, which held a treasure trove of Gulf music recordings. Massive investment in state-of-the-art recording facilities, both before and after the Iraqi invasion, have ensured that the country is one of the most important players in the Gulf music scene.

The distinctive Kuwaiti style of **sout** was made popular in the 1970s by Abdul Aziz al Muzaraj, better known as **Shadi al Khaleej** (Bird Song of the Gulf). It has younger exponents in **Abdullah Al-Ruisheed**, who combines sout with a light techno-pop, and the rotund, high-voiced **Nabeel**. Both of them are stars throughout the Gulf.

UAE

The **United Arab Emirates** have traditions of desert Bedouin and fishermen's **dance songs**. They can, frankly, sound rather dull on record but witnessed live the music is a revelation – stirring, muscular, drum-driven spectacles. The UAE is also notable for **Ahlam**, the first woman singing star in the Gulf. She has had a hard path to stardom and, even now she is established, many will deny that she is Emirati.

The most famous UAE singer is – or was – **Ali Burroghr**. However, he has for some years been *matowr* (leading a strict Islamic lifestyle) and, at his request, the sale of his cassettes was banned. Following his musical inspiration, there is an increasing number of local singers working within their own tradition and consciously shunning the Egyptian model. **Mehad Hamid** writes cheery anecdotal songs that are hugely popular amongst Emiratis; **Al Ameri** (from one of the region's leading families) is also a name to watch.

Yemen

Yemen is quite different from the rest of the Arabian peninsula, not least because its oil revenues are a fraction of its neighbours. However, it has one of the most vibrant music scenes in the region and musicians from across the Arab world – and Israel, too – acknowledge its profound influence. As in all Arab countries, there is a pronounced difference between urban and rural music. In the cities a sophisticated tradition of composed **poetic songs** with 'ud accompaniment dominates, whilst in the country music is still more closely associated with **ceremonies and work**.

There is an undeveloped professional music scene, so you may well find that the singer you've just been enjoying is actually a postman or tax collector. Much of the most interesting music making takes place at intimate **ghat chews**, when the mild narcotic inspires performers to dazzling heights. Ghat chewing takes place after lunch and it appears as though everyone, including lorry drivers and the traffic police trying to direct them around a major roundabout, is indulging.

Aden   Arab Dance

Early 20th century Yemeni trio

To participate, you'll need to be invited to a home session, where men or women (seldom the two together) meet together in the *mafraj* – a window-lined room at the top of the house. Seated on cushions around the room, the assembled company pick off the small leaves and chomp them into a ball that is kept in the side of the mouth. Initially the effect of chewing is enlivening: conversation is animated and the 'ud playing can be furious. However, as afternoon gives way to evening a mellowness falls upon the room and the pace slows until a sublime moment of blue evening light as the sun falls beneath the mountains around Sana'a, and the gathering breaks up for the call to prayer. It would be hard to imagine Yemeni music (or life) without ghat.

On a more professional base, Yemeni musicians (indeed, Yemenis in general) often travel to other Gulf countries for work. Both the highly regarded Oud player, **Ahmed Fathey**, and the singer **Osama al Attar** are now resident in the United Arab Emirates.

discography

Gulf artists are incredibly prolific, but finding their music outside of the region can be hard. Even though many musicians have now moved over to CD, there remains a refreshingly unfussy approach to packaging and presentation: the majority put out one release each year and simply call it '99, or whatever, and people are apt to talk about them much like wine vintages. There is also a pretty relaxed attitude to copyright and pressing, with individual distributors making up their own compilations, so the exact contents of a CD can come as a surprise.

Saudi Arabia

Compilations

Musique de Unayzah: Ancienne Cité du Najd (Inédit, France).

An ethno-musicological recording but not inaccessible – with some fine Bedouin singing and drumming from central Saudi. Its clear explanatory notes, and translations of the all important poetry, will be useful to anyone wanting to tackle this underated genre.

Artists

Mohamed Abdu

The towering presence of Saudi music, Mohammed Abdu has done more than anyone to raise the profile and confidence of Gulf music.

Abaa'd (Virgin Arabia, France).

This is a rare issue of a Gulf artist by a Western record company – though it is but one of his 100 plus discs!

Abadi al-Johar

Al-Johar ('the Octopus') is a traditional-style singer and 'ud player.

 Abadi al-Johanr '99 (Music Box, Saudi Arabia).

Traditional material with some imaginative contemporary touches. A good first stop on the Gulf music trail.

Abdu Majeed Abdullah

Abdu Majeed Abdullah is extraordinarily successful and much admired by young Gulf women for his sensitive, smooth renditions.

Saleeb Al-Qaleb (Rotana, Saudi Arabia).

His best-selling release to date.

Kuwait

Artists

Nabeel

A big star in every sense of the word; Nabeel is immediately recognisable for both his high rasping voice and the fact that he looks like he has spent many hours in Kuwait City's numerous burger bars!

Nabeel '98 (Rotana, Saudi Arabia).

A good year for the big man.

Abdullah al-Ruisheed

In recent years, Abdullah has moved further away from his *sout* (Gulf blues) origins, to a mixed reception. Nonetheless, he is still a masterful singer and 'ud player.

Wainak (Rotana, Saudi Arabia).

A fairly roots-style disc.

Bahrain

Artists

Khalid al Shaikh

Khalid is Bahrain's most popular singer and his songs are covered by many of the region's other singers. He is never afraid to branch out into new directions, whilst keeping one eye firmly on his island roots.

Mastaheel (Rotana, Saudi Arabia).

The title means 'impossible'.

United Arab Emirates

Artists

Ahlam

Ahlam is the Gulf's first lady of song – not least of all because when she started there were no others.

Ahlam (Funoon Emiraat, UAE).

Many Emiratis voice the opinion that Ahlam is a good singer who could choose better material but this is pretty good.

Al-Ameri

Al-Ameri is the Gulf's new kid on the block, with a vocal control and imaginative ideas that belie his years.

 '99 (Funoon Emiraat, UAE).

Al-Ameri fulfills his promise with some great moments.

Al Ameri's 1999 offering

Mehad Hamid

Mehad Hamid is a very popular, homespun artist, whose songs are engaging stories of local life.

Wail Qalbee (Funoon Emiraat, UAE).

Gulf family favourites.

Yemen

Artists

Ahmed Fathey

Ahmed Fathey is one of the most impressive oud players around. He has left his native country for fame and fortune elsewhere.

La T'saafar (Sidi, Saudi Arabia).

This is a recording of his purely instrumental work.

Hamud al Junayd

The singer Hamud al Junayd was born in the mountain region of 'Udayn in 1956 but has lived in the capital, Sana'a, for the last twenty years. He has slightly updated the traditional sound but keeps rigorously to its forms.

Hamud al Junayd: Traditional Yemeni Songs (Nimbus, UK).

In Europe and the US, this is the most widely available and accessible CD of music from Yemen and, even without a mouthful of ghat, it makes entertaining listening.

Iran

the art of ornament

Iranian music presents ancient and modern faces – both highly rewarding. The Persian classical tradition with its mystical and contemplative melodies is no concert hall heritage music but an intimate part of the culture, performed with an almost blues-like intensity. It is currently in revival at home, while in exile there is an equally vibrant Iranian pop scene, highly distinct with its pulsating dance rhythms. As you'd expect from a huge and predominantly rural region, ranging from the mountains of Iranian Azerbaidjan, through desert expanses to the Caspian Sea, there are also numerous folk traditions. **Laudan Nooshin** takes the pulse.

Iranians often say that their music is imbued with a sense of the vast desert, the mountain landscapes and the very ancient and turbulent history of the country. It is certainly imbued with politics. The 1979 Iranian Revolution, which created the Islamic Republic, was cultural as well as religious, and was accompanied by a strong 'return to roots', and a re-awakening of interest in Iranian traditions. In the backlash against Western culture, directly after the revolution, pop music was banned – some of Iran's own pop musicians eventually found a new home base abroad. But Iran's classical music has experienced an extraordinary renaissance – as have many of the arts – bringing new life and ideas to a musical tradition that goes back centuries.

This article focuses on the three main types of Iranian music: classical, regional folk musics, and pop music at home and in exile.

Classical Iranian Music

Musiqi-e assil (classical music), which in Persian means 'pure' or 'noble' music, was originally a royal or aristocratic entertainment. Some people trace its origins back several thousand years, although there isn't much evidence before medieval times. For Iranians, it is an important symbol of their culture – an intense, private expression, refined, contemplative, historically rooted, and with a close relationship to poetry.

Classical pieces range through slow, quiet, contemplative passages – usually in the lower part of the singer's range – to melismatic displays of virtuosity known as **tahrir**. These are very fast and ornamented passages, usually high in the vocal range and often compared with the singing of the

nightingale. Their typical sound is that of a soulful and intense, slightly nasal solo voice projecting a highly ornate melodic line, accompanied by one of the classical instruments. The result is a mesmerising arabesque, as voice and instrument speak to each other in turn.

Poetry and music go hand in hand in Iran, and much of the classical music is set to the words of medieval Persian mystic poets such as **Jalal-e Din Rumi** (1207–73) and **Hafez** (1325–1389). Music is an important medium through which people experience this ancient poetry, whose messages are often seen to have contemporary significance. Poetry in turn gives music a respectability, since the written word has a higher status within Islam; in fact, much of the Islamic proscription of music is directed towards instrumental music. Today, it's still unusual to hear a performance of Iranian classical music without a vocalist, although there have been moves in the past decades to emancipate music from words and to give instrumental music a validity in its own right.

From Courts to Cassettes

Until the beginning of the twentieth century, classical music was heard mainly at the **royal courts** of the Qajar monarchs who ruled Iran from 1794 to 1925, and in the homes of wealthy amateur players. This intimate music, with its close relationship to mystical Sufi poetry and philosophy, was well-suited to such gatherings, and it remained sheltered there until the 1900s.

The decline in the influence of the royal courts, in the 1900s, coincided with the opening up of classical music to a wider audience,

Classical Iranian Instruments

The **classical instruments** of Iran belong to a family of instruments found widely in the Middle East, neighbouring Turkey and Central Asia.

Tar and Setar

The *tar* and *setar* are both long-necked lutes whose strings are plucked and strummed. The tar is larger, with a relatively loud, more resonant and tangy sound, partly because the belly of the instrument on which the bridge rests is made of skin (rather than wood) and the strings are plucked with a metal plectrum. The sound of the setar, on the other hand, is soft and refined. It is often said to embody the spirit of Iranian music and is difficult to hear in a large concert hall without amplification.

Santur

The *santur* is a dulcimer, usually positioned on a small table in front of the musician who strikes the strings with two felted hammers. This instrument has grown in popularity this century, partly because it enables musicians to display their virtuosity to an extent which is not possible on any of the other classical instruments. This kind of technical display is fairly new to a music whose aesthetic ideals lie more in the spirit and 'soul' of the music rather than musical 'fireworks'.

Ney

The *ney* is an end-blown flute with a very soulful and breathy sound, originally said to have been a shepherd's instrument. When you hear it, it's not hard to imagine the vast and lonely expanses of desert and mountains where a shepherd might play to himself and his animals to while away the time.

The sound of the ney is often said to be a lament for its separation from the reed bed from which it was cut, and this image is used as a symbolic metaphor for the pain of separation from the loved one. This theme was expressed by the poet Rumi in a well-known verse which begins: "Listen to the ney as it speaks to us, for it cries out against separation"

Kamancheh and violin

The *kamancheh* is a bowed spike-fiddle played in front of the musician, on the lap or kneeling on the floor. It has a very distinctive taut nasal sound, rather like the singing style heard in much of the classical music. Before 1979, the smoother sounding European violin was threatening to replace it, but since 1979 the kamancheh has regained its popularity. The violin is still popular and it is now regarded as an Iranian instrument in its own right, but is heard less often in classical performances than it was in the 1960s and 1970s.

Tombak (zarb)

The *tombak* (or *zarb*) is a goblet drum played with the fingers and palms of both hands and held diagonally across the player's lap. It rarely plays as a solo instrument and in classical performances is usually heard accompanying sections of the music with a regular pulse. A good tombak player can perform a stunning range of sounds, timbres and rhythms and it's become very popular this century with the growing preference for music with a regular pulse.

---

through recordings and Western-style public concerts, and eventually through the important medium of radio. A further boost came with the arrival of cassettes, from the 1960s, which meant that music could be carried around discreetly – an important consideration in Islamic society. The rapid pace of Westernisation, however, meant that by the 1970s classical music was still a minority taste. There was a feeling that it belonged to a past age and was out of step with the modernising nation state.

Prominent classical musicians of pre-revolutionary Iran include the singer **Gholam Hossein Bana**, probably the most-recorded voice in the country prior to 1979, and instrumentalists **Ahmad Ebadi** (setar), **Faramarz Payvar** (santur) and **Abol Hassan Saba** (violin, setar, santur).

Post-revolutionary Revival

Culturally, the immediate post-revolutionary period was an extraordinary time, and for Classical Iranian music, it was nothing short of a renaissance. The movement was led by a number of (mainly) younger musicians, many of whom are still active performers and composers. What's more, they weren't willing to follow tradition for its own sake and wanted to make classical music relevant to a contemporary audience. They included the male singers **Mohammad Reza Shajarian** (see feature box opposite) and **Shahram Nazeri**, female vocalist **Parisa**; and the instrumentalists **Mohammad Reza Lotfi** (tar, setar), **Hossein Alizadeh** (tar, setar), **Parviz Meshkatian** (santur), **Jamshid Andalibi** (ney), **Kayhan Kalhor**

Mohammad Reza Shajarian

Mohammad Reza Shajarian is the nightingale supreme of Iranian music, a living legend whose superb technical skill, warm vocal style and vast knowledge of classical Iranian poetry have made him the most successful classical singer in the country.

Born in Masshad (northeastern Iran) in 1940, Shajarian comes from a family with a long musical tradition. He began his singing career at the age of eighteen with the local radio station in Masshad and moved to Tehran eight years later where he performed regularly on Iranian Radio until 1986 (many of these broadcast programmes were subsequently released as commercial recordings).

Following his appearances on national television in the early 1970s, Shajarian become a household name. But it was the musical renaissance which followed the 1979 Revolution, and his close creative work with other musicians at this time, which consolidated his position as the foremost musician of Iranian classical music.

Shajarian has given concerts around the world and worked closely with the most prominent contemporary classical musicians such as Mohammad Reza Lotfi and Parviz Meshkatian. As well as his busy performing and recording career, he devotes a considerable amount of time and energy to teaching and to research into the music of his native Khorasan.

Shajarian (left)

(kamancheh), and the (Kurdish) **Kamkar family** who have toured widely.

While there was a spirit of optimism surrounding this revival, and opportunities for recording and live performance, it all happened largely in spite of the official policy. Whilst more moderate politicians cautiously welcomed the return to traditional culture, the conservative elements viewed even classical music as a potentially corrupting influence. New laws also limited women's public musical roles. Women singers were not allowed to perform in public and could only be heard (but not seen) on TV and radio. Oddly, though, women instrumentalists were allowed to perform.

The situation for musicians became particularly difficult during the Iran-Iraq war (1980–88) when it was felt that live musical performance and the associated expression of joy was inappropriate. Since the early 1990s, however, there has been a renewal, with the emergence of many young musicians and an even wider audience for classical music than before.

One significant development has been the increased number of **women classical musi-** **cians**. Although there have been important female classical singers in the past, the instrumental tradition was almost exclusively a male one. That is now changing, and it is no longer unusual to see a woman classical instrumentalist. Since the landslide election of the moderate President Khatami in May 1997, women musicians have also been allowed to sing in public for the first time since 1979 (but still only to female audiences).

Another recent development is a new satellite television channel, *Jam-e-Jam*, which broadcasts from Iran to Iranians abroad. Its programming schedule includes classical music performances.

How to Listen: Modes and Improvisation

Iranian classical music is a largely improvised music, and this improvisation is based on a series of modal scales and tunes which musicians spend many years memorising as part of their long training.

Traditionally, there was a very close relationship between a pupil and his master or *ostad* (a word which, along with other Persian words, was also taken up by musicians in North India) and teaching would usually take place in the ostad's home. During the course of the twentieth century most teaching was taken over by conservatoires and universities.

The music is largely an oral tradition and its emphasis is still on strict rote memorisation. Musicians never perform from notation, since each individual performance is a spontaneous expression by the musician – but one firmly rooted in the memorised repertoire. In other words, a unique 're-creation' of the tradition at each performance. A metaphor for this is the nightingale, a bird regularly encountered in the visual arts and poetry of Iran. According to popular belief, the nightingale (*bolbol*) has the most beautiful voice on earth as it sings for its unrequited love for the rose (*gol*), a flower which has grown in Iran for hundreds of years. Moreover, it is believed that the nightingale never repeats itself in its song. In practice, of course, both nightingales and Iranian musicians do repeat themselves in performance, but the metaphor is important for its ideal.

The repertoire is a collection of some two hundred pieces collectively known as **radif** (series), and the training of a classical musician essentially involves memorising and being able to play these pieces precisely. The individual pieces of the radif are known as **gusheh** (corner) – a short piece or melody, lasting from as little as fifteen seconds to as long as two minutes, with its own modal identity and often particular turns of phrase. It is these individual gushehs that are memorised strictly by musicians and after many years of training form the starting point for creative improvisation in performance. The gushehs are in turn arranged into twelve **dastgah** (systems). These are ordered collections of modally related gushehs (rather like a Baroque suite), and a performance will usually be in one of the twelve dastgahs.

Each of the two hundred or so gushehs and the twelve dastgahs of the complete radif repertoire are individually named. Some of the names indicate a particular sentiment or emotion while others are names of towns or regions of the country. Some of these names are also found in the *maqams* or *makams* of Arabic and Turkish music, the two other important classical traditions of the Middle East. Historical contact between these cultures has resulted in cross-influences in the modes and their names, as well as in the instrument types already mentioned.

There are also significant differences between Iranian classical music and its neighbouring traditions. There are no rhythmic cycles in Iranian music as there are in Arabic and Turkish (and the even more distantly related Indian), and much of the unmeasured material of Iranian classical music is based on the metrical structure of the poetry that is being sung (or implied in the case of the instrumental accompaniment).

When **listening to this music**, bear in mind that it is the intricate beauty and ornamentation of the solo melody line (usually with no regular metric pulse) that is of the utmost importance, inviting more of a philosophical than physical response. The musical interest is almost totally linear – there is no harmony and only a light drone serves to ground the music from time to time. People often draw parallels between the highly detailed melodic lines and the intricate designs of Iranian carpets. As in the carpets, the movement is meandering, as the musician exhaustively explores the melodic potential of a defined area before moving on to the next.

The length of a **dastgah performance** is largely up to the musician, taking into consideration the particular context of performance. Each individual gusheh, which in the studied repertoire might last thirty seconds, will be expanded in performance to last for several minutes, and often longer. A complete dastgah performance can last for several hours in informal settings, although nowadays something between thirty minutes and an hour is more usual.

Until the 1960s, a typical performance would have comprised a voice and a solo instrument, the latter supporting the vocal sections and playing short **instrumental interludes**, with the addition of a tombak for the sections with a regular pulse. In the last thirty years or so, it has become common for performances to be given by an ensemble of musicians, usually including one of each of the main classical instruments, each musician taking it in turn to accompany the solo voice and to play solo interludes between the vocal phrases. It's also become common for performances to begin and end with a precomposed ensemble piece with a regular pulse. These pieces provide a frame for the main part of the performance, which is usually unmeasured and improvised.

Simplifying somewhat, a **typical classical performance** begins with the opening (*daramad*) section of the chosen dastgah, followed by a progressive development of the material of each individual gusheh. As the performance continues, there is a gradual increase in pitch and tension – each gusheh is based around a slightly higher pitch range than the preceding one – until the music reaches the climax or *owj* of the dastgah. At this point there is usually a descent and return to the opening pitch area and 'home' mode of the dastgah as heard at the beginning to conclude the performance. There may also be a concluding ensemble piece to round the performance off.

The important things to listen out for are the rising pitch level and the resulting overall arch shape of the performance, the alternating (or answering) of instruments and voice, and the explorations of the musicians reinterpreting the underlying tradition each time they perform.

Folk Music

Iran has numerous ethnic minorities, each with their own language, culture and music. For example, **Iranian Kurds** live in the west of the country (bordering on Iraq and Turkey), Iranians of **Turkish origin** live in Azerbaidjan in the northeast, and **Baluchis** live in the southeast area (which borders on Pakistan). Even among the Persian-speaking population, there are many regional variations in dialect, lifestyle, culture and music, one example being the nomadic **Bahktiari** people.

Regional folk music is widely performed in Iran, but is little known abroad, and few recordings are available.

Regional Musics

In contrast to the mainly urban classical music, **musiqi-e mahali** (regional musics) tend to belong to agricultural or nomadic herding communities who comprise a substantial proportion of the population – 46 percent of Iranians live in rural areas and 25 percent of the working population are involved in agricultural work.

It is difficult to generalise, since each region has its own styles and instruments, but the music is often associated with dancing (particularly group dances), with events in the agricultural year (such as harvest time), with the life cycle (birth, marriage, death), or with religious ceremonies. The **instruments** are different from, but related to, those heard in classical music, and include the long-necked lutes of Khorasan, the ney (reed flute), the *ney-anban* (bagpipe), and zurna-type instruments, usually played outdoors and accompanied by the double-headed *dohol* drum and var-

ious other types of percussion, such as the large daff frame-drum. Particularly rich musical regions are Khorasan in the northeast and Kurdistan in the west.

In **Khorasan** you can still hear traditional Turkoman epic poets who perform in local tea houses (the article on Central Asia in this book has more on this) and who accompany themselves on long-necked lutes like the *tanbur* or *dotar* (closely related to the classical setar). One of the best-known singers is **Sima Bina**, who is also an active folk-song collector. Her repetoire is the songs of Khorasan, which have a true earthiness about them, speaking of the harsh life of the nomadic horse people of this region. Another fine, less commercial singer is **Yeganeh**.

Kurdish music is another important regional tradition, including energetic compositions for the famous circle dances. Typical instruments for this music are the double-reed *duduk* which has a beautifully languid sound, and the daff. Musicians to listen out for are singer **Aziz Shahrokh** and the **Kamkar family** (for more on these traditions, see the article on Kurdish music – p.378).

Another very distinct regional music is that found on the **southwestern coast**. This is a fusion of African rhythmic patterns and Iranian melodies played by the descendants of African slaves now fully assimilated into Iranian society.

Iranian Pop

In the early twentieth century, there were various types of traditional urban music styles in Iran, but from the 1950s musicians began adopting Western musical styles and instruments. By the 1970s a strong **pop industry** had emerged – along with a core repertoire of nostalgic love songs – and this was the music that most people listened to at a time when classical music was generally regarded as out of touch with a modernising country.

Iranian pop music drew – and draws – on elements from folk and classical traditions but using Western instruments such as electric guitar, keyboards, bass and drums. Its stars are exclusively **singers**, and their repertoire comprises largely love songs and nostalgic ballads.

With the banning of all pop music (both Iranian and Western) after the 1979 Revolution, many Iranian musicians abandoned the country and settled in Europe or North America. The biggest influx was to **Los Angeles** – Tehrangeles to the million-strong immigrant Iranian population – where a thriving music scene has developed.

Pop Artists

The most popular pre-Revolution pop singer was a women called **Googoosh** – who has chosen to stay in Iran even though she is unable to perform at home. Other important singers, who moved to Los Angeles, and have kept the old ballad tradition alive there in performance and on cassette, include the women singers **Homeirah**, **Hayedeh** and her sister **Mahasti**; and male singers **Shahram**, **Morteza** and **Hodi**.

Alongside them, a **new generation of LA-based musicians** (many of whom have never been to Iran) have created more up-tempo songs with driving rhythms, or experimented mixing Iranian styles with rap and dance music. Their instruments are all Western, except for occa-

The much-loved Googoosh

sional use of an Iranian drum, but the rhythms are often based on folk and popular Iranian rhythms, and it is this, as well as the melodies and lyrics, which gives the music its particularly Iranian feel. It is music to dance to, characterised by pulsating, hip-moving rhythms, and it forms an essential ingredient at any Iranian social gathering.

American-based singers and groups to listen out for include **Siavash**, whose production is always good, although he tends to overdo the synthesised sounds; **Moeen**, always a favourite with his warm vocal sound; and **Andy**, strongly influenced by Western pop, as are the more recent **Black Cabs** and **The Boys**.

These days, Iranian pop music – old style ballands and new wave alike – reaches audiences across the ex-pat communities, and also back in Iran through tapes, CDs and satellite television, as does the music of Western pop stars.

discography

You may need to go direct for discs to the US labels *Kereshmeh Records* (12021 Wilshire Blvd #420, Los Angeles, CA 90025, US ☎ (310) 470 5177, fax 470 5117; *www.kereshmeh.com*); and Caltex Records (9045A Eton Avenue, Canoga Park, CA 91304, US ☎ (818) 700 8657, fax 700 0285) is more promising for pop.
  For discs, in Europe, try *Shahram Video* (13a Hereford Road, London W2 4AB, UK ☎/fax (020) 7221 6296 or *Markaz Nava* (Stolberger Str 1, 50933 Köln, Germany ☎ (49) 221 546 5657, fax 221 546 5658).

Classical

Compilations

Classical Music of Iran: The Dastagh Systems (Smithsonian Folkways, US).

Short performances recorded in Iran in the mid-1960s by some of the principal performers of the classical music at that time (including Ahmad Ebadi), featuring a range of modes and musical instruments. This was the first recording of all the twelve dastgahs, intended to illustrate the tradition to non-Iranians, although it doesn't give a good idea of what an extended performance really sounds like – the extracts are just too short to convey the feeling of the music.

Iran: Persian Classical Music (Nonesuch Explorer, US).

A select group of musicians, including female vocalist Khatereh Parvaneh, plus tar, kamancheh and led by one of the most important santur players, Faramarz Payvar. A disc made in 1973, aimed at demonstrating a range of modes and instruments to a non-Iranian audience, but with more continuity than the Smithsonian recording.

Artists

Hossein Alizadeh

Born in Tehran in 1951, Alizadeh began his professional career at only fifteen years old. He is considered one of the most important figures in contemporary Iranian music and is also a composer, writing both for traditional instruments and for combinations of traditional and Western instruments.

Iranian Music: Săz-é Nô (Buda/Musique du Monde, France).

An excellent single disc with stunning instrumental playing from Alizadeh on *tar*, *tanbur* and *setar* plus a couple of ghazals to words by Rumi sung by one of the finest female vocalists, Afsaneh Rassa'i. Music full of exciting instrumental textures and a pure, meditative vocal quality.

Improvisations (Buda Musique du Monde, France).

A double CD recording of a concert given in Paris in 1994. Alizadeh plays tar and setar in the dastgahs "Nava", "Bayat-e Tork" and "Homayun" with Majid Khaladj on tombak.

 Ney Nava (Kereshmeh Records, US).

"Ney Nava" is one of Alizadeh's most popular compositions – a one-movement concerto for ney (played here by Jamshid Andalibi) and orchestra.

Kayhan Kalhor

Kalhor was born in Tehran in 1963 into a musical family and studied Iranian classical music with some of the great masters, as well as Kurdish folk music in Kermanshah. He's performed with top musicians such as Alizadeh, Shajarian and Nazeri. He now lives mainly in the US.

 Scattering Stars Like Dust
(Traditional Crossroads, US).

Kalhor's innovative approach to the kamancheh – this recording starts with novel pizzicatos – gives his debut disc a freshness and verve. A whole disc of solo kamancheh (and tombak) can be daunting, but the intensity and drama here is captivating. Some unusual time signatures come from Kurdish music and the album's title from a poem by Sufi mystic Jalal-e Din Rumi.

Mohammad Reza Lotfi

Born in 1947 in Gorgan, northern Iran, he studied at the National Conservatoire in Tehran. Regarded as one of the greatest contemporary masters of the tar and setar, he has taught many of Iran's leading young musicians.

 Mystery of Love, Live in Copenhagen
(Kereshmeh Records, US).

One of Lotfi's finest performances accompanied by tombak and daf. In his notes to the recording, Robert Bly writes: "Lotfi is a great musician. He pours his intense, astonishing music into the spiritual ear."

Parviz Meshkatian

Born in 1955 in Neyshabour northeastern Iran, Meshkatian is the best santur player of the post-Revolutionary period. His unrivalled technique is simply extraordinary – he moves the hammers with such speed and subtlety that they can hardly be seen. What's more he looks like a prophet. He was a founding member of the celebrated Aref Ensemble with whom he's performed extensively throughout the world.

 Pegah (Dawn)
(Kereshmeh Records, US).

Dazzling performances in dastgahs "Segah" and "Homayun" with tombak players Nasser Farhangfar and Jamshid Mohebi.

Shahram Nazeri & Ensemble Alizadeh

Shahram Nazeri, born in Kermanshah in 1949, is one of Iran's top classical/Sufi singers, famed for his warm vocal style and technical mastery; he is generally considered second only to Shajarian. Ensemble Alizadeh is one of the best groups of instrumentalists in the country.

 Nowruz: Traditional and Classical Music
(World Network, Germany)

Most of the music here is Persian classical music along with a few Kurdish tunes andl folksongs from Nazeri's native region. A fine recording all round.

IRAN: SHARAM NAZERI & ENSEMBLE ALIZADEH

Hossein Omoumi

Born in 1944 in Isfahan, Omoumi started studying the ney at the age of fourteen. He taught at the National Conservatoire and at the University of Tehran. Since 1004 he has worked in France as a performer and teacher.

 Persian Classical Music (Nimbus, UK).

Stunning performances recorded in France in 1993. Omoumi performs in dastgahs "Homayun", "Dashti" and "Chahargah" accompanied by Majid Khaladj on tombak. Good notes.

Mohammad Reza Shajarian

Born in 1940 in Mashad, Khorasan province, Shajarian (see feature box on p.357) is the undisputed master of Persian traditional singing – technically flawless, powerful and emotional. A major source of inspiration in Iranian music.

WITH ENSEMBLE AREF

 Iran: Mohammad Reza Shadjarian and Ensemble Aref (World Network, Germany).

A live recording of a concert in Germany in 1987 with some of the finest Iranian musicians: Parviz Meshkatian (santur), Dariush Pirniakan (tar), Ardeskir Kamkar (kamancheh) and Jamshid Andalibi (ney). Dastgah "Chahargah". Listen out for excellent contributions from Meshkatian and Andalibi who produce a light, translucent sound on their instruments. Strong folk influences in the lively ensemble sections framing the central section where the solo voice is accompanied in turn by each of the main instrumentalists.

WITH MOHAMMED REZA LOTFI

 The Abu-Ata Concert (Kereshmeh Records, US).

A great performance by two of the finest musicians in Iran: Mohammad Reza Lotfi is considered the best tar and setar player of the post-Revolutionary period. The concert took place in 1981 at the German Cultural Centre in Tehran, one of the few performance platforms in Iran at that time.

Dariush Talai

Born in 1952, Talai is a tar and setar player and has spent much of the post-Revolutionary period in France where he has been active in promoting Iranian classical music.

Iran: Les maitres de la musique traditionelle Vol 1 (Ocora, France).

This Ocora series is one of the best of Iranian music released on a Western label. Talai, on tar, performs with Mohammad Musavi (ney) and Majid Kiani (santur) – three leading virtuoso musicians of the younger generation.

Folk Music

Compilations

Baloutchistan: Bardes du Makrân (Buda Musique du Monde, France).

A wonderful survey of the music of the Baluchis, who some believe to be the ancestors of the Gypsies, invited to play music for the Persian Shah Bahrâm Gur. Instrumental music on the expressive *sorud* fiddle, plus epic songs and ghazals.

Iran: The Music of Lorestan (Nimbus, UK).

Rousing dance music from the southwestern province of Lorestan, featuring the loud outdoor instruments: sorna, like the *zurna* and *dohol* drum common throughout the Middle East. Played by Shahmirza Moradi and his son Reza.

Folk Music of Iran (Lyrichord, US).

Recorded in 1972 by Verna Gillis, the recording includes solo singing and dance music from the regions of Lorestan and Fars. The latter is the birthplace of the Persian language and home of the classical poets Hafiz and Saadi.

Music of the Bards of Iran: Northern Khorasan (Kereshmesh Records, US).

The bardic tradition of Central Asia extending into northeast Iran. Performed by Haj Ghorban Soleimani (vocals and dotar lute), part of a long line of epic story-tellers and singers. A mixture of solo instrumental pieces and songs with Alireza Soleimani on *dotar*.

Artists

Sima Bina

Born in Birjand in 1944, Sima Bina was the daughter of a leading classical musician. She collects and performs folksongs from Khorasan in the northeast, but also sings classical repertoire. In 1994 she was the first Iranian woman singer to tour Europe and the US since the Revolution.

Sima Bina (Caltex, US).

A live recording (in Germany) of some of the most beautiful folk songs from the Khorasan and Lorestan region, accompanied by kamancheh, dotar, ney and percussion. The kamancheh player, Faraj Alipour is a master folk musician in his own right. Bina's more classical-style recordings on Nimbus and Musique du Monde are also recommended.

Kamkars

Kamkars are a Kurdish family of seven brothers and a sister from Sanandaj in western Iran. They were taught by their father, the late Ustad Hassan Kamkar, one of the master musicians of the region. They play both Kurdish folk and Iranian classical music and have brought some of the folk modes and instruments into the classical tradition. They have toured extensively and appeared at WOMAD festivals.

Nightingale with a Broken Wing (RealWorld, UK).

The album takes its title from a melancholy and beautiful song, one of four songs about nightingales in this collection. Reflective love songs and energetic dance pieces giving a good sample of Kurdish folk music, well performed.

Pop Music

Artists

Dariush

Famed for his nostalgic songs, Dariush's best work dates from before 1979, although he is still recording in Los Angeles.

Sal-e-Dohezar (2000 Years) (Caltex, US).

This is Vol 6 of a collection of Dariush's greatest hits – a mix of pre- and post-Revolutionary songs, including the beautiful "Khouneh" (Home).

Googoosh

Googoosh was Iran's most popular singer of the pre-Revolutionary period but, living in Iran, she has recorded nothing since the Revolution in 1979.

Pol (Bridge) (Taraneh, US).

Googoosh has a lyrical, breathy voice accompanied by soft strings and an easy listening beat. The title track here is one of her most celebrated love songs in a good collection of hits.

Siavash

A young singer popular among teenage Tehrangeles. The music is Westernised Iranian pop.

Hamsayeh Haa (Neighbours) (Caltex, US).

One of his best recent CDs with cheerful up-tempo songs, plus the more ballad like "Dokhtar Irani" (Iranian Girl).

Moeen

Moeen is a forty-something singer with a modernised acoustic backing, including traditional instruments like violin, tar and dombak.

Panjereh (Window) (Taraneh, US).

1997 album representative of his popular, but distinctively Iranian, style.

Israel

a narrow bridge

"The whole world is a narrow bridge and the most important thing is not to be afraid," said the eighteenth-century Polish Rabbi Nahman. The whole world is also a global village (was it Rabbi Marshall McLuhan?) and in the small state of Israel you can find Jewish immigrants from 127 countries all round the world. They started to return in 1882 after two thousand years of exile in the Diaspora, and they brought with them their traditions, languages and, of course, their very different traditions of music. Israel, asserts **Dubi Lenz**, is the natural home of global fusion.

The **Altneuland** in Israel was the dream and Zionist vision of Theodor Herzl, fulfilling the long yearning for a 'promised land'. From 1882 the waves of immigration started, mainly from Eastern Europe, but also from Yemen, North Africa and Asia. With the declaration of the State of Israel in 1948 the influx escalated, and there were countries – Yemen, Libya, Iraq, Bulgaria – from where the whole Jewish community (or what remained after the Holocaust) came as one to their old-new homeland. In the fifty years since then, Jews have continued to make *aliya* (from the Hebrew word 'to go up'), particularly when circumstances grew difficult in their old homeland. Most recently, thousands have come from the Former Soviet Union and Ethiopia.

Songs of the Good Old Land

An Israeli born in Israel is called a *sabra* (literally the fruit of the prickly pear cactus – prickly on the outside and sweet inside) and conventional wisdom has it that if, on a Friday evening, you put a guitar in a sabra's hand, a harmonica in their mouth and add an accordion, song will fill the air. Those songs are known in Hebrew as *Shirei Eretz Israel Hay'shana Ve Hatova* – **Songs of the Good Old Land of Israel**. The words 'old' and 'good' are synonymous here – it is nostalgia which fills the throat (not that old times were much better – but then that's the nature of nostalgia). These are songs born of the youth and kibbutz movements, songs thick with the dust of the road, redolent of suffering and, of course, love.

Many of these Hebrew songs are set to **Slavic and Russian melodies** adopted by the earliest Israeli songwriters from Eastern Europe. Most of the songs of the youth movement date from that

time, and the best of them are known to everyone: for example, the Hebrew version of the famous Russian song "Katyusha".

For political reasons, those new Israeli songs were written in Hebrew – the language of the new country. Yet Hebrew was also the holy tongue, sacred and honourable and for many it was unthinkable that songs about mundane human affairs should be sung in the language in which men and women communicated with their God. Nonetheless, from 1948 there was a deliberate policy to encourage Hebrew at the expense of the languages of exile that the immigrants brought with them – principally **Yiddish** and **Ladino**, from the Ashkenazi and Sephardic communities respectively.

Today it's hard to find an Israeli musician dedicating him or herself to Yiddish or Ladino songs, although some of Israel's best singers have released occasional albums in Yiddish (Chava Alberstein, Mike Burstein) or Ladino (Yehoram Gaon, Lolik, Esther Ofarim). However, the main exponents of both the Yiddish and Ladino musical traditions are not working in Israel (for more, see the article on 'Sephardic music' following; and for more on the traditions of Klezmer music, see the US section in *Volume 2* of this book.

In the early years of the state of Israel, attempts were made to forge a specifically national style as well as a language of expression. It was said that Israeli music should be a bridge between the many musical cultures that had arrived on these shores, and it was felt that a new music should emerge free from the smack of exile. Deliberate attempts were made to **integrate Eastern and Western music**, but the results were somewhat forced – oriental (Middle Eastern and North African) rhythms and motifs not lending themselves easily to orchestration in a classical Western style.

Chava Alberstein: Israel's Joan Baez

Chava Alberstein has been an important figure in Israeli music since the 1960s when she modelled herself on American singer-songwriters like Joan Baez and Pete Seeger. "It was part of my growing up as a human being," she admits. "From a distance, I was involved with all kinds of rights movements in America. In my soul I was there. In the eternal argument about whether an artist should actively take part or sit in their room and write about lofty things, I've always believed in taking part."

Alberstein started to get involved in politics at home when Egyptian President Sadat first visited Israel in 1977 to begin peace talks and she became a vocal part of the Peace Now movement, a tendency which takes her beyond the arts pages of the Israeli newspapers. During the years of the Palestinian intifada she wrote "Chad Gadya" (One Goat), a song the authorities tried to ban from the radio: "I based it on a traditional song we sing at Passover when we sit down to eat together. It is something like "The Woman Who Swallowed a Fly". In this version a dog bites a cat, a stick beats the dog, fire burns the stick, water puts out the fire, an ox drinks the water, a butcher kills the ox and then the Angel of Death comes, and so on. It is a circle of violence, and I wanted to make a modern song about this, and how you can get drawn into violence. Israeli soldiers in the occupied territories were behaving very brutally towards Palestinian women and children which was something new and shocking in Israel. This wasn't necessarily the soldiers' fault – it was the fault of the situation. To stop these people behaving like animals the occupation needed to be stopped."

This is a song that Alberstein still sings at every concert as that circle of violence is still turning. "The terrible assassination of Prime Minister Rabin was like the climax of what I was afraid we could become. The only solution is to let the Palestinians have their own country and this will happen in the end. Most of the Left in Israel – and I am one of them – feel guilty now about not supporting Rabin and his government more vociferously because we were so sure that everything was going to be all right." Alberstein dedicated the song "Artzi Artzi" (Oh My Country, I Suffer So), on her 1996 album *Horaot Bimvi* (Stage Directions), to the memory of Itzhak Rabin.

Alberstein sings with a voice that is soft, but precise and clear, a pleasure to listen to even without under-

Chava Alberstein

AVIV PRODUCTIONS INC.

standing the words. And she is a powerful performer on stage, thanks, she says, to her years of military service. "We have groups of artists in the army. I did my military service and sung with a guitar, three or four times a day for soldiers. We performed everywhere. Sometimes it was for five soldiers in a small place in the desert, or sometimes in the dining hall of a horrible camp where they just wanted to laugh at you – a frightened girl with big glasses and a guitar. You had to make them listen to you. The army was a great school for me."

Alberstein was born in Szczecin, Poland where her parents spoke Polish and Yiddish, and arrived in Israel as a baby. "We came in 1950 to Haifa and were brought to a camp – it was a very poor camp with tents and it reminded many people of the concentration camps they'd been in during the war. It was very frightening for them because this was supposed to be a new country and a new beginning, but the beginning was very sad and hard. One of the first songs I wrote was "Sha'ar Haalia" (Gate of Immigration). My story is the story of many new immigrants – combining the vision of both outsider and insider: Part of my subject in music is the fact that I'm a mixture of Diaspora and Israel. I've been described as the 'most Jewish of Israeli singers'. Israel is a new nation in the world, but in my music it is always the past and future together."

For many years Alberstein has performed and recorded Yiddish songs. "People always think of Yiddish as a language for humour and making jokes, but they don't realise there is a wonderful world of literature and poetry." She recently recorded *The Well*, a ground-breaking collaboration with New York klezmer group the Klezmatics featuring new settings of Yiddish poetry. On the other side of the culture, she also sings old Hebrew *nigunim* (religious songs), which brings her into conflict with the Orthodox community: But, she says, "For me Hassidic and religious songs are not a ritual thing, but part of my heritage and collective memory. I need them like I need Beethoven, Mozart and Shakespeare. It is very beautiful poetry and I get sad when Orthodox people want to restrict it to their own religious use. Judaism doesn't only belong to the Orthodox people, it belongs to me also."

Simon Broughton

The more successful composers in this 'orientalist' style were **Mordechai Ze'ira**, **Moshe Wilensky** and **Sasha Argov** – all of whom were immigrants from Russia.

Yemenite Songs

From the 1930s to '50s, real **oriental singers**, most of them **Yemenite** – such as **Bracha Zefira**, **Esther Gamlielit** and **Shoshana Damari** – began to play an important part in Israeli music.

Yemenite singers have been hugely important in the development of Israeli music – the Jewish community in Yemen kept its tradition and way of living longer than any other community in the Diaspora (from the first century AD until the end of the nineteenth century). Immigration from Yemen began in 1882 and concluded between 1948 and 1950. The Jews in Yemen had a very rich musical tradition. They sang on every occasion – in moments of sorrow and joy, songs of everyday life and prayer. Families used to gather and sing the old traditional songs with beautiful clear voices, mostly unaccompanied, as musical instruments were banned by the Muslims of the Arabian peninsula.

In contemporary Israel, Yemenite Jews are amongst the leading popular artists. Current stars include **Noa** (Achinoam Nini), **Gali Atari**, **Boaz Shar'abi**, **Zohar Argov**, and **Ofra Haza** – the best-known singer outside of Israel, through the success of her traditional *Yemenite Songs* album

Fifty Gates Of Wisdom   *Yemenite Songs*

(1985) and her soundtrack for Spielberg's *Prince of Egypt* animation (1998). Haza's recordings drew on the **Diwan repertoire** – devotional songs that cover both religious and secular subjects and are performed at weddings and other celebrations.

Noa's music has an interesting take on the Yemenite tradition, combining elements of jazz with a marvellous voice and musicality; she has worked with Sting, Zucchero and Pat Metheny. For Boaz Shar'abi influences include Western music and Songs of the Good Old Land of Israel, as well as the Yemenite musical tradition.

Roots and Fusions

Yemenite roots were not the only ones to resurface in the 1980s and '90s, as a new *sabra* generation looked to air their inherited music beyond the synagogues or family celebrations. Many musicians started to record 'hard core' oriental music, often cheaply produced on small independent labels, as an alternative to mainstream Israeli rock and pop. A semi-underground cassette culture developed for their music, along with a few dedicated pirate stations.

Many major Israeli artists started their careers on the indie labels, being taken up by the mainstream labels once they'd made it. Their number include **Zehava Ben**, **Chaim Moshe**, **Margalith Zan'ani**, the late **Zohar Argov**, **Eli Luzon**, **Avner Gedassi** and the Israeli-Arab violinist and singer **Samir Shukri**.

For many of these and other contemporary Israeli artists, a fusion of Eastern and Western elements is a natural part of their creative processes and family history. **Ehud Banai** and his cousin **Me'ir Banai** offer rhythms and melodies from their Iranian heritage. **Yehuda Poliker** – one of the most popular rock artists in Israel – adds his Greek roots to his music, while **Miki Gavrielov**, who has written some of the best-known Hebrew songs, incorporates his Turkish ancestry. There is a particularly rich strain of musicians proclaiming their Moroccan heritage, among them **Sfatayim**, **Tanara**, **Sahara**, **Marakesh**, and the singer **Yosefa**, who mixes her family's musical heritage (a Yemenite father and Moroccan mother, both born in Israel) with modern dance music.

Other notable fusionists include the violinist and oud player **Yair Dalal** and his group **Al Ol** (see box overleaf), who have forged a successful mix of Jewish, Arabic and other traditions; the **Trio Ziryab** (comprising oud, violin and Arabic percussion), who explore the traditions of Arabic and Turkish classical music; and **Tea Packs**, who with leader Kobi Oz, create an oriental pop akin to groups like Les Negresses Vertes. Then there is

ISRAEL

Yair Dalal: Israeli Oud

Composer, violin and oud player, **Yair Dalal** is one of the leading Israeli musicians making new music from the diverse roots of the country's population. His own parents immigrated from Iraq and, he explains, "I used to hear Iraqi and Arabic music in my house and my father took me to the synagogue where I heard liturgi-

cal music from Iraq. But in Israel all our education directs you towards the West so you need to have the self-confidence to say 'I left something behind' and it's beautiful."

Dalal took up music as a career in 1982, after playing music with the bedouins in Sinai: "I played the violin while they played the *rabab* (spike fiddle). And it was very strong and they were amazed how I knew their songs – the same traditional songs as in the desert of Iraq." What he plays today, however, with his **Al Ol** ensemble, has evolved from those traditional roots into something more global – drawing on the music of neighbouring countries like Turkey and the Middle East "and of course a large part of our Jewish tradition like klezmer from one side and Iraqi from the other side. But I don't know if I ever thought about combining it all together – it just came out like it is."

In 1994 Dalal was invited to Oslo to perform at a celebration of the first anniversary of the Peace Accords. His song, "Zaman el Salaam" (Time for Peace), was performed by fifty Palestinian children, fifty Israeli children, Norwegian children and the Norwegian Philharmonic Orchestra conducted by Zubin Mehta. "Shimon Perez and Yassar Arafat were there, but they weren't speaking. After hearing the song they signed a contract they hadn't signed before. Perhaps it's a bit naïve to believe that music can influence the Peace Process, but I believe it."

Simon Broughton (with thanks to Roger Short)

the cantor **Emil Zrihan** who combines the Arab-Andaluz tradition with the Hebrew liturgy; **Ilana Eliya** singing the Kurdish songs of her father; the **Alayev Family** blending the music of Tajikistan with Israeli songs. **Nash Didan** perform ethno-ambient music sung in the biblical Aramaic language that Jesus spoke (preserved for two thousand years by the Nash Didan Jewish tribe on the borders of Azerbaidjan, Iran, Turkey and Russia). **Shlomo Gronich** sings Israeli-Ethiopian songs with the Sheba Choir. **Atraf** even have a Hebrew take on Latin salsa.

The most significant fusion group, however, active for the past twenty or so years, are **Habrera Hativeet** (The Natural Gathering). They shook up Israeli music in the 1970s by forging a mix of Moroccan, Yemenite and Hassidic songs, and over the years have added influences from Africa, Blues and Classical music. They had to struggle for acceptance (the majority of Israel media

people were raised on Western music), but they have become one of the most influential forces in Israeli culture. **Shlomo Bar**, the group's moving spirit, is an eclectic spirit. He sings texts from the Old Testament and contemporary protest songs about the government's attitude towards new immigrants from North Africa.

A much more recent ensemble following a similar line is **Bustan Abraham** (Garden of Abraham), founded in 1991 by **Avshalom Farjun**. The group combines seven distinguished Israeli musicians – both Jews and Israeli-Arabs – who draw on oriental, Indian, classical, jazz, flamenco and American folk music in an original and compelling way. They are a group who are not only building musical bridges between East and West, but creative bridges between Arabs and Jews.

Others have thrown even more ingredients into the melting pot – **Esta** have added jazz and melded country and western with Hasidic chant.

Bustan Abraham

And Yisrael Borochov's **East West Ensemble** has embraced pretty much everything from Western classical to rock and jazz to Far Eastern music.

What's going on underlines the riches that Israel has within its borders from over a century of immigration. Unlike Paul Simon, David Byrne or Hector Zazou, Israeli musicians have no need to travel very far to find their inspiration – everything is on hand. What's more, the fire under the melting pot is getting stronger and stronger. It's a matter of time before Israel wins recognition as one of the most fruitful sources on the World Music scene.

discography

Compilations

 Homeland: 22 Beautiful Songs of the Land of Israel (NMC, Israel).

A compilation of Israel's best-known stars doing the evergreen Songs of the Good Old Land of Israel. Typically soft, a bit melancholy and in a minor key, they are love songs – to people or to the land of Israel and its landscapes. Everyone in Israel knows them and can join in from beginning to end.

 World Music in Israel (Frémeaux, France).

A collection of music from various immigrant groups recorded in Israel by Deben Bhattacharya in the late 1950s. Includes traditional music from Morocco, Yemen, Uzbekistan plus Ashkenazi liturgical music, Sephardic songs and a police band playing, amongst other things, Israel's most famous tune "Hava Nagila".

Artists

Chava Alberstein

The "First Lady of Israeli Song" was born in Poland and came as a baby to Israel. Strongly influenced by American folk singers like Joan Baez, she has been a dramatic force on the Israeli music scene for over thirty years, and a political one, too, as a vociferous champion of the peace process.

Crazy Flower: A Collection (Shanachie, US).
Yiddish Songs (EMI Hemisphere, UK).

These two internationally released compilations of Alberstein's music are equally good. The Shanachie collection includes her classics "Ghad Gadya", "Old Violin" and "Song Chases the Darkness Away". The EMI disc is a new selection of Alberstein's Yiddish songs.

WITH THE KLEZMATICS

 The Well (Green Linnet/Xenophile, US).

Chava has been back to her roots in five albums of Yiddish song, but here she teams up with the cutting edge New York

Israel 367

klezmer band, the Klezmatics, in brand-new musical settings of classic Yiddish poetry. Excellent.

Zehava Ben

Zehava Ben is an Israeli vocalist of Moroccan heritage, born in 1970 and brought up in a poor neighbourhood in the southern city of Beersheba. She started her career recording many low budget 'Indie' albums ignored by the media, but recently she's become one of Israel's biggest stars. Her voice is mesmerising.

 Zehava Ben sings Umm Kalthum (Helicon, Israel).

Accompanied by the Haifa Arab Music Orchestra conducted by Suheil Raduan, Zehava Ben wins over even the fanatic fans of the Egyptian singer Umm Kalthum.

Bustan Abraham

Established in 1991 by Avshalom Farjun, Bustam Abraham (Garden of Abraham) is made up of seven Israeli Jews and Palestinians. Instrumentation includes oud, kanun, Arabic percussion, flute, violin, banjo, classical and flamenco guitar and more – all combined with great musicality.

 Fanar
(Nada Productions, Israel; Crammed World, Belgium).

Bustan's fourth album and the most varied. The compositions clearly reflect the members' different musical orientations as well as the cohesiveness of working together for six years. Among the special guests are the Indians Zakir Hussain and Hariprasad Chaurasia, and Israeli Yemenite singer Noa with Gil Do (her musical partner and guitarist).

Yair Dalal

Composer, violin and oud player Yair Dalal was born in Israel in 1955 to parents from Iraq. His musical skills range from European classical music to jazz, blues and Arabic music. He's a strong advocate for peace in Israel and has been actively involved in a number of Palestinian music projects. He works with his own Al Ol Ensemble, SheshBesh (a quartet of classically trained musicians exploring oriental music) and with a wide range of musicians around the world.

Silan
(Najema Music, Israel; Amiata, Italy).

The Al Ol ensemble (violin/oud, flute/clarinet, guitar, tabla and percussion) kicks off with the very catchy "Acco Malca" (Queen of Acco), a city where Jews and Arabs "live together in harmony". Other treats include a wonderful Turkish-style klezmer fantasy and an equally inventive treatment of a tune by qawwali master, Nusrat Fateh Ali Khan.

 Azazme (Magda, Israel).

In this 1999 release Dalal plays with musicians of the Azazme bedouin in the Negev desert. A rare chance to hear the disappearing traditions of a people marginalised in Israeli society.

The East–West Ensemble

A really multi-ethnic group – which changes personnel from album to album – combining all sorts of musical styles. The driving force is Yisrael Borochov who plays synth, bass guitar, tabla and various percussion.

 Zurna (ITM, Israel).

Named after the Central Asian oboe that is found from China to the Balkans, this recording includes the Alayev family (from Tadjikistan) playing the doira frame drum and accordion. A tasty blend of classical, oriental, jazz and Jewish styles.

Esta

The four-piece world-beat/jazz-fusion explorers Esta combine Middle-Eastern and Mediterranean modal styles with elements of jazz, Celtic music, rock, and funk.

 Mediterranean Crossroads (NMC, Israel).

A remarkably successful music from such a radical mix. "Go-Go" combines Scottish music and funk, while "Deror Yikra" is a Yemenite song with Celtic touches.

Yehoram Gaon

Yehoram Gaon was born in Jerusalem fifty-odd years ago to a Sephardic family of Turkish origin. He was a member of the two most famous vocal groups of the 1960s – The Roosters and The Yarkon-Bridge Trio – and has recorded dozens of albums of romantic love songs and songs about Israel, as well as making occasional roots excursions into Ladino ballads. He is one of Israel's most loved singers – almost the country's Frank Sinatra.

 Sung in Ladino (NMC, Israel).

Judeo-Spanish ballads from the last five hundred years. Love songs for Zion, the Promised Land and Jerusalem. These have had such a strong impact in Israel that many have become part of the religious heritage and are sung in prayer. Gaon is accompanied by a symphonic orchestra.

Habrera Hativeet

Fort over twenty years, Habrera Hativeet have been at the forefront of Israel's melting-pot music – and one of the country's most consistently inspiring bands. They've gone through a series of incarnations but their leader Shlomo Bar has always imprinted his open-minded personality on the music.

 Origins (Isradisc, Israel).

The group's first album was pretty revolutionary for Israeli music. Shlomo Bar and three other members (percussion, Indian violin, guitar and cello) play traditional Yemenite Jewish song (Deror Yikra) along with original songs about Jewish life in Morocco, and Hassidic tunes.

Barefoot
(Hed Arzi, Israel).

Their ninth album (1996) in which they reach a new phase of their musical development with six members and three guest players. Written under the transcendental influence of Bar's visit to Morocco, it includes songs from Morocco, Yemen, Hassidic and Israeli poetry, with asymmetric rhythmic accompaniment plus the influence of Africa, Blues, Jewish soul and classical music.

Ofra Haza

Ofra Haza was born in 1957 in Israel (her parents emigrated from Yemen) and as a teenage pop singer represented Israel in the Eurovision Song Contest. Her incisive voice and slightly ornamented singing style project her Yemenite songs with great power, but her success in Israel was built on poppy love songs, and in Israel that is how she is still best known.

Yemenite Songs
(Hed Arzi, Israel; Shanachie, US).

A classic Israeli roots/fusion album, featuring songs from the Yemenite Diwan repertoire – most of them with lyrics by sixteenth-century Sephardic Rabbi Shalom Shabazi expressing love for God, love for the Promised Land and just love. "Galbi" and "Im Nin'alu" were the most successful tracks that got re-mixed for the dance clubs.

Minuette

One of Israel's best jazz groups, Minuette employ flutes, saxophones, guitars, bass and percussion of all kinds. They tend to play their own material, but in the past few years they've discovered oriental material and are performing miracles with it.

◉ **The Eternal River** (MCI, Israel).

The fusion all began for Minuette with an innovative project at the Jewish-Arab Music Festival in Jaffa, for which they were asked to perform arrangements to the famous Egyptian composer Mohamed Abdel Wahab, Egypt's best-known composer. This is the record that came out of it.

Amal Murkus

Amal means hope in Arabic, and 29-year-old Israeli-Arab singer Amal Murkus is full of it. She's already performed and recorded with Israel's best artists, appeared on TV, in films and is now doing the new Israeli-Palestinian 'Sesame Street' collaboration.

◉ **Amal** (Highlights, Israel).

"A white dove, a flower in its beak, in its eyes an unbreakable oath – never to let blood be shed between people" – lyrics from one of Amal's songs in her marvellous first album collaborating with the best Israeli musicians (Jews and Arabs). Reason enough to hope for peace love and understanding. Warmly recommended

Nash Didan

Nash Didan (Our People Have Arrived) was established to preserve the group's Aramaic language. In 1929 immigration started from their villages on the borders of Azerbaidjan, Persia, Turkey and Russia and this community of 30,000 people came to Israel on camels, donkeys and by foot.

◉ **Nash Didan Idaylu** (Phonokol, Israel).

If you want to dance to the old language spoken in the Bible – well, here it is. Mysterious voices, sounds mixed with operatic voices and instruments reaching back two thousand years.

Sfatayim

Sfatayim ('lips' in Hebrew) come from the southern immigrants' village of Sderoth. They play traditional music from Morocco and original songs in Moroccan style.

◉ **Moroccan Party** (Phonokol, Israel).

The very danceable greatest hits of Sfatayim. A real Moroccan Hafla with traditional and Western instruments. Sung mostly in Moroccan Arabic.

Tea Packs

Another group from Sderoth who make everybody smile with joyous lyrics (about love, life and politics) and with their Mediterranean-North African rhythms. Kobi Oz, the group's leader (of Tunisian origin) is one of the most colourful of Israeli artists.

◉ **Your Life in Laffa** (Hed Arzi, Israel).

Laffa is a kind of pitta bread – and you can put your whole life with your troubles, with your happy moments into it, to taste it and to see if you like it. This album from 1995 is their best – a touch like the French group Mano Negra.

Yosefa

Yosefa Dahari was born in 1971 of a Yemenite mother and Moroccan father. She began singing, like many Israeli musicians, while in the army. Most of her songs are in Hebrew, and she adds 1990s dance rhythms and production techniques to her dual inheritance.

◉ **The Desert Speaks** (EMI Hemisphere, UK).

An undemanding blend of Arabic and Western styles including music by Alon Oleartchik and Shlomo Gronich. Traditional instruments rather swamped by synthesisers and electronics. An evocative title track about the end of a relationship.

THE DESERT SPEAKS
Yosefa
HEMISPHERE

Ziryab Trio

A spin-off from Bustan Abraham – a trio of first class musicians from Arabic and Turkish backgrounds. Oud player Taiseer Elias leads the ensemble, with Nassim Dakwar (violin) and Zihar Fresco (a very great percussionist in international demand).

◉ **Oriental Art Music** (Nada Productions, Israel; Crammed World, Belgium).

Clear textures and sensitive playing of music by Tanburi Jemil Bey and twentieth-century Egyptian composers in a live concert. The trio are joined by Avraham Salman on kanun and Emmanuel Mann on bass for one of the most compelling recitals of classical Arabic and Turkish music around.

> **For more on Jewish music from outside Israel, see the following article on Sephardic Music, and for Palestinian Music, see p.385. The predominantly American revival of Klezmer Music is covered in Volume 2.**

Jewish Music | Sephardic

ladino romance

There are two great diaspora traditions of Jewish music – Klezmer and Sephardic – the first born in Eastern Europe and largely recreated in the US (see *Volume 2* of the *Rough Guide*), and the latter born in Spain and developed in exile in other parts of the Mediterranean. The roots of Sephardic music are popularly thought to be the music and romances of the Spanish Jews, prior to their expulsion in 1492. However, the story is more complex than that as different cultures and layers of history have left their mark. The word Sephardic itself refers to the Biblical *Sefarad*, traditionally thought to be the Iberian Peninsula, though the place actually mentioned in the Old Testament (Obadiah 1:20) was probably somewhere else. As **Judith Cohen** explains, the making of Sephardic music involves the recreation of several traditions and the creation of a few myths in the process.

The year 1492 marked the final Christian *reconquista* of what is now Spain, when Ferdinand and Isabella's troops took Granada, the last Moorish stronghold. In the same year, they proclaimed the Edict of Expulsion of the Jews who had lived in the Iberian peninsula for over a millennium. Jews were given three months to arrange their affairs, sell off their homes and goods, and leave – or convert to Catholicism and stay on as **conversos** or 'New Christians' – in danger of being denounced as secret Judaisers by the Inquisition and tortured, imprisoned or burned at the stake. No one has really figured out how many left but historians estimate the Jewish population in Spain just before the Expulsion as somewhere between 100–200,000. Five years later the process was repeated in Portugal, where a number of the Spanish Jews had moved.

Most of the exiled Sephardim made their way to establish communities in northern **Morocco** or the **Ottoman cities** of Constantinople, Thessaloniki and Jerusalem. There they continued to speak their language, now known as **Judeo-Spanish** or **Ladino** (though strictly speaking the latter refers to a word-for-word translation from Hebrew religious texts). The language and the name given to it differs from one place to another, but it generally includes archaic forms going back to medieval Spanish languages (Castilian, Catalan, Galician-Portuguese), mixed in with bits and pieces of Hebrew, Greek, Turkish, Arabic, and later on, Italian, French and modern Spanish.

These days 'Sephardic' is often used to refer to almost any Jewish group which is not Ashkenazi (basically, of Eastern European origin), but here we'll concentrate on the original meaning, and songs in Judeo-Spanish/Ladino.

La yave de Espanya (The Key of Spain)

Where is the key that was in the drawer?
My forefathers brought it with great pain
From their house in Spain
Dreams of Spain

Where is the key that was in the drawer?
My forefathers brought it with great love.
They told their children, this is the heart of
  our home in Spain.
Dreams of Spain

Where is the key that was in the drawer?
My forefathers brought it with great love.
They gave it to their grandchildren for them to
  keep in the drawer.
Dreams of Spain

Music and lyrics by Flory Jagoda (1984)

Musical Crosscurrents

Sephardic songs reflect the same mixture of cultures as the language itself. Those songs which the exiles took with them were adapted and changed over the centuries, often absorbing melodies from local Greek, Turkish or Moroccan songs. Songs were also borrowed from these new environments and, of course, new ones were composed. The story of Sephardic songs is further complicated by the fact that some of the *conversos* and their descendants left Spain and Portugal much later than the Expulsion, not as Jews but as Christians who then resumed their Jewish identities. Other Sephardim actually returned to Spain, either for business or to stay on as New Christians. Thus the songs of the Sephardic tradition don't necessarily hark back to medieval Spain – and many of them have travelled from one Jewish community to another.

Some song texts, especially **romances** (narrative ballads) and **wedding songs**, can indeed be traced back to medieval or Renaissance Spain, but their **tunes** are not often medieval. Some Sephardic romance tunes share musical traits with ballads in the *cancioneros* (Spanish courtly songs) of the late Middle Ages and the Renaissance, but as a group, the tunes are exuberantly eclectic, reflecting five centuries of exile. They include adapted melodies and styles from classical Ottoman *maqamat*, Moroccan rhythms, Argentine tangos, Istanbul Gypsy and *gazino* songs, Greek operettas, Maurice Chevalier tunes, the Charleston, popular nineteenth-century Spanish melodies. One of the best-known songs in the Ladino repertoire is "Adio querida" ("Farewell my love; life has lost its attraction for me, you've made it bitter"). Its tune appears to have come from the "Addio al passato" in the last act of Verdi's *La Traviata*.

Very broadly, Judeo-Spanish songs can be divided into three groups: the **romances**, songs for **religious and life-cycle** occasions, and **lyrical, topical or recreational** songs. There are also Sephardic religious songs sung in **Hebrew**, often to melodies from the Judeo-Spanish/Ladino tradition. Most scholarly work has concentrated on the romances, with their tantalising ties to old Spanish literature. But most of the songs featured in concert and on disc are **canticas** – lyrical songs and love songs. most of them from the eastern Mediterranean, rather than Morocco, and dating to the second half of the nineteenth century.

Contemporary composition in Judeo-Spanish has been scanty: the only ones which have really entered the folk repertoire are in a light traditional style by Bosnian **Flory Jagoda**, a gifted musician, singer, composer and grandmother living in Washington DC.

Western and Eastern Traditions

The two main areas where Judeo-Spanish song flourished over the centuries were **northern Morocco** – often called the Western tradition – and the former **Ottoman lands** of Turkey, Greece, the Balkan countries, Jerusalem and Alexandria – the Eastern tradition. "Whichever wagon you get on, sing the same song" runs a Sephardic proverb, but actually the repertoire across the diaspora is markedly different.

Sephardic wedding songs in **Turkey and Bulgaria** may be sung to a typically Balkan 9/8 rhythm (2-2-2-3), while **Moroccan Jews** adopted a local 6/8 rhythm and the women trilled the high-pitched ululation common throughout the Middle East and much of Africa. In **Turkey**, melodies from the older genres were often sung in *maqam*, the Turkish modal system, and (especially *romances*) in a melismatic style with one syllable stretched out over several different pitches. In both eastern and western repertoires, the **vocal style** was usually similar to that of the host culture – Turkey, Greece or Morocco – though in recent decades, especially among younger singers, it has become more Westernised.

Women have been the main carriers of the song tradition – it's a predominantly **domestic repertoire**. The older among them generally sing in a fairly low range (sometimes higher when they're younger), in a strong, focused voice, with rapid, but clear vocal ornaments. Judeo-Spanish songs aren't harmonised, though in this century Bosnian Sephardim was sometimes sung in parallel thirds. Sadly, one rarely hears the old styles now.

Traditionally, most songs are unaccompanied – women's hands were busy with various domestic tasks while they sang – except for **wedding songs**, which the women accompanied on percussion (usually tambourines). One of the few things we know about Jewish women singers in medieval Spain is that they played various kinds of hand percussion: a chronicle of the Expulsion even tells us that the rabbis told the exiles to sing and play their tambourines and frame drums. When men performed the songs, they usually added local **stringed instruments** such as the *oud* (lute) or *kanun* (plucked zither). Today, recording artists experiment with instruments from all sorts of traditions – medieval and Renaissance, Middle Eastern, Western Classical, jazz and folk.

The **eastern repertoire** is far better represented on commercial recordings, and it's the one most people with a casual knowledge of Judeo-Spanish songs have heard. The early twentieth century commercial recordings of Sephardic songs were from **Turkey and Greece**, and the first Israeli singers to popularise the repertoire came from Sephardic families in **Jerusalem**. The popular lyric songs never really developed in Morocco.

Musically, Eastern lyric songs are quite different from the older genres (the romances and life-cycle and calendrical songs). They're much shorter than the narrative ballads, their melodies are often influenced by Western European music, and their texts are usually romantic or amusing. They were probably easier on unaccustomed ears (before the World Music scene turned our notions of the familiar upside down) and easier to adapt for concerts and recordings. As the most recent part of the repertoire, it's ironic that they're often assigned exotic medieval Spanish associations.

When songs exist in both the Moroccan and eastern repertoires (usually with different melodies), it's tempting to conclude that they go back to pre-Expulsion Spain. In some cases – certain ballads and wedding songs – the words do go back (although not the tunes). But often these songs simply left Spain much later than the Expulsion, or were composed in one area and then learned from travellers in others. The well-known "Cuando el Rey Nimrod" (When King Nimrod) about the birth of Abraham, with other Biblical episodes mixed in, is probably one of these relatively recent travelling songs.

Portugal: the Crypto Jews

The community of so-called **Crypto-Jews of Portugal** (also known as *Marranos* although this carries pejorative connotations) were the result of the 1497 Expulsion which turned out to be

The Three Main Types of Judeo-Hispanic Song the Sephardic Repertoire

Some of the **Sephardic 'Spanish' Romances** go back to the early Middle Ages, others derive from later broadside ballads or later still, were adapted from the local (for example, Greek) repertoire. The older ones tend to feature queens, kings and other members of the old nobility, or famous historical characters such as El Cid, and stories of encounters among the three cultures, Christian, Jewish and Muslim. Love, seduction, rape, heroism, poisoning, rescue, sailors and such familiar figures as the warrior maiden and the disguised husband home from the wars abound. There are also Old Testament romances. Some are still sung in Spain, Portugal or Latin America; others have been kept in oral tradition only among the Sephardim. Most of them are in a standard form of an indefinite number of eight-syllable lines all sharing the same assonance.

The romance **"Gerineldo"**, one of the best-known Moroccan Judeo-Spanish songs, is still heard in Spain and Portugal (now very rarely, if at all, in the eastern Judeo-Spanish repertoire). Briefly, a princess invites one of the king's pages, Gerineldo, to sleep with her. The king finds them and – in the Jewish version – decides against the more common Hispanic solution of killing one or both of them to maintain honour, and instead marries them off to each other. This has led to the unique Moroccan Sephardic expression, "el mazal de Gerineldo", the good luck (from Hebrew *mazal* - star, fortune - as in *Mazal tov!* - Congratulations!) of Gerineldo.

Wedding songs (in the eastern repertoire known as 'canticas', in Morocco 'cantares de boda') are by far the most numerous and popular of the **life-cycle songs**, and tend to pick up local rhythms – Moroccan,

Turkish, Greek. The bride in one Moroccan wedding song compares life in her father's home ("I looked in the mirror") with life in her husband's ("I look in his wallet") but concludes on a sincerely pious note of praise. Other songs describe the dowry and trousseau, and some include erotic references ("clouds wander through the sky and the groom gets wet"), especially those traditionally sung among women only.

There are also a few **birth songs**, which privilege the birth of male babies; "Cuando el Rey Nimrod", about the birth of Abraham, is often used as a birth song. **Laments** (*endechas*) were traditionally sung only on suitable occasions of mourning; otherwise, it was considered bad luck to sing them. The calendar cycle songs, mostly known as *coplas*, follow the religious year, although several are on religious themes but not associated with any one holiday. **Songs for Purim** are especially popular in both Judeo-Spanish repertoires.

Lyrical, love and recreational/topical songs are mostly from the eastern repertoire. Many developed in the mid-to-late nineteenth century or afterwards, as love marriages, rather than arranged marriages, became a possibility. Some are from Spain, but not medieval or Renaissance Spain; some are adaptations from Turkish or Greek songs, some are even translations from tangos, operettas and other 'modern' sources. They range from the very romantic ("Yo m'enamori de un aire" – 'I fell in love with an air') to local events such as the Great Fire of Salonica in 1917 ("Dia de Shabbat, mi madre") to out-and-out gossip ("Esterina Sarfatti's in love...") and satire ("Me vaya kappará" talks about the fashionable Andalusian mineral springs for liver ailments).

more of a forced baptism (some 20,000). These instant New Christians were not permitted to leave the country and many continued to identify with Judaism, or practice it in secret. Since 1996, the author of this piece has been working with these communities as part of an ethnomusicology project. Their songs are in Portuguese, rather than Ladino or Hebrew, though they have learned some songs and prayers in these two languages from visitors. Their prayers, and some Old Testament Biblical ballads on themes of escape – Jonah, Isaac, Daniel, the crossing of the Red Sea – are now mostly recited rather than sung. The very few songs in Portuguese which are specifically theirs were probably composed in the early twentieth century. Once again much of this repertoire is more recent than is popularly imagined.

Archive Recordings

With its historical roots going back half a millenium, it's all too easy to think of Sephardic music as a dead art enjoying revival. But in fact, the diaspora communities hung on to their traditions tenaciously and their singers maintained a living tradition into the twentieth century. A good number of singers are still performing, and many others have been captured on disc.

As with Klezmer music, the first 78rpm recordings of Sephardic music appeared in the early years of the century – mainly in **Turkey**. The artists were mostly men, usually singing with *ud* or *kanun* accompaniment; the same men were often also respected performers of Turkish classical music, and sometimes synagogue cantors. Among them were **Haim Efendi**, **Jack Mayesh** and **Yitzhak Algazi** (many of the latter's virtuoso performances were re-issued on cassette in the 1980s by Israeli ethnomusicologist Edwin Seroussi). The principal woman recorded was **Victoria Rosa Hazan**, born in 1898 in Turkey. She emigrated to the US in 1920, and continued to advise and coach aspiring singers of Judeo-Spanish song. **Roza Eskenazi**, who despite her name was also a Sephardic Jew, was one of the best-known Greek *rembétika* singers of the 1920s (see p.128), although she didn't actually record any Judeo-Spanish repertoire.

Written collections of Judeo-Spanish songs were made early this century by Manuel Manrique de Lara, Alberto Hemsi and other musicologists in the eastern and western areas. Since then important documentary recordings of living singers have been made by **Henrietta Yurchenco** (romances and wedding songs from women in the Moroccan town of Tetouan in 1956); **Edwin Seroussi** (Turkish and Bulgarian singers in Israel); and most extensively by **Shoshana Weich-Shahak** (who's recorded both eastern and western repertoire – including the Moroccan singer Alicia Bendayan, who'd appeared on Yurchenco's recordings of a quarter of a century earlier). These have all found CD re-issues.

Sephardic Performers

Ironically, many of the most popular singers of Sephardic music are not themselves Sephardic, but a number of important performers are. Several of them modify the traditional style – often they've skipped a generation of direct oral transmission, and have learned their songs in other ways – but all the same, these performers tend to stick to the repertoire of their own community.

Amongst singers from the **eastern tradition**, **Gloria Levy** in New York exerted considerable influence over later performers. She learned her songs from her mother, Emilie Levy, who grew up in Alexandria, and continued, well into her eighties, to sing in a choir and coach aspiring performers of Judeo-Spanish song. Her songs are mainly quite modern lyric songs, in *a la franca* (European, as opposed to Turkish) style, performed with guitar and mandolin accompaniment. Another major influence and teacher has been **Flory Jagoda**. Known as 'La Nona', Flory performs with her three grown children, and her recording *La Nona Kanta* (The Grandmother Sings) is aimed affectionately at children. In Turkey, the best-known group is the **Pasharos Sefardíes** (Sephardic Songbirds). Karen Gerson and Izzet Bana infuse the quartet's lively performances with characteristic expressions and gestures, and are accompanied by traditional string instruments. Their repertoire consists largely of late nineteenth-century lyric and topical songs, often learned from older members of the Istanbul community. **Jak and Janet Esim** also perform similar repertoire.

There are few performers of Moroccan Sephardic descent and the **western tradition** is principally represented by the Montreal, Canada-based group **Gerineldo**, led by Oro Anahory-Librowicz, of which Judith Cohen is the only non-Sephardic member. Gerineldo's songs, sung in traditional style, are from their own field recordings and family memories, and mostly of the endangered species of older romances and wedding songs. The name 'Gerineldo' is taken from a romance whose story goes back to Carolingian times (see box on p.372).

Israel considers Judeo-Spanish song as part of its heritage and for a long time most performers learned their repertoire principally from **Isaac Levy**'s four-volume anthology. Levy, himself from a Jerusalem Sephardic family, collected a huge corpus of songs, pioneered Judeo-Spanish music on Israeli radio, and also performed and recorded the songs. His performances and transcriptions are Westernised, sacrificing the oriental maqam to well-tempered piano accompaniment and often simplified rhythms. He has probably been the single most influential figure in the revival of Judeo-Spanish song, while the best-known Israeli performer is **Yehoram Gaon**, an Israeli singing star from a Jerusalem Sephardic family. Gaon's records have played a central role in disseminating songs from the eastern lyric and light religious repertoires, usually backed up by a small Western orchestra.

Many of the early performers recorded on 78rpm such as Yitzhak Algazi also sang in **Hebrew**.

PAUL HENSELS

Emil Zrihan

These pieces are usually prayers, *piyyutim* (songs of praise) or other religious texts. The tradition has continued with Moroccans – like **Jo Amar**, **Haim Louk** and recently **Emil Zrihan** – functioning as cantors for their own congregations. In the right hands, the music has that heightened intensity that characterises much devotional music round the globe. Zrihan's backing includes oud, violin, accordion and *darabouka* (goblet drum) giving the music a real Moroccan sound and, like many cantors, he's successfully taking it into the concert hall.

A particularly convincing Israeli performer from outside the tradition is **Ruth Yaakov**, who specialises in Balkan and Turkish Sephardic songs. She is one of the rare singers who combine Western concert training with a traditional style, in her case a clear, low-to-middle range timbre with a strong edge. She performs with a trio of Middle-Eastern musicians based in Israel.

Spaniards and Fusions

Spanish singers often see Judeo-Spanish song as part of their own heritage and have recorded much of the material. The first Spanish artists to record Judeo-Spanish songs were both women trained in Western concert music: **Sofía Noel**, and the renowned **Victoria de los Angeles**. Folklorist **Joaquín Díaz** was the first to record the repertoire in a non-classical style, in the 1970s. His vocal technique wouldn't be mistaken for Moroccan or Turkish, but his warm voice and extensive background in regional Spanish folk traditions have influenced many other singers.

Folklorist **Angel Carril** and the groups **Raices** and **La Bazanca** (led by Paco Díez) have experimented with Spanish traditional singing styles and a mixture of Spanish and Middle-Eastern instruments. **Rosa Zaragoza** has recorded combinations of songs from the 'three cultures' of Spain (Jewish, Muslim and Christian). Definitely worth noting are two recent recordings (*Arbolera I* and *II*) by Spanish singers **José-Manuel Fraile** and **Eliseo Parra**. These are directed by Israeli ethnomusicologist **Shoshana Weich-Shahak**, who plays *kanun*, coached the singers in authentic performance style, and brought an intriguing selection of songs from her own field recordings.

Several groups performing Sephardic music have ignored the living tradition and have chosen to re-invent an 'historical' one. This has been fertile ground for early music specialists from the Western classical tradition and their **'Medieval-Sephardic fusion'** comes from romantic misconceptions about a body of music going back to Medieval Spain. **Alia Musica** in Spain, **Accentus** in Vienna and **Altramar** in the US are among the groups who perform this sort of material. They're good musicians, and have done reasonable research, but the main part of the tradition is vocal, and that's where they fall down, relying on classical training even if they do try to modify it, so that it contrasts even more oddly with the instrumentals. They tend not to have fun with those songs which invite it; and overall they're short on warmth and spontaneity.

While there are many well-established Sephardic communities in North America, the best-known performers of Judeo-Spanish songs there are rarely Sephardic. One group currently specialising in Judeo-Spanish songs is **Voice of the Turtle**, whose director, Judith Wachs, has worked with

VOICE OF THE TURTLE
Balkan Vistas - Spanish Dreams
PATHS OF EXILE
QUINCENTENARY SERIES, VOLUME III

MUSIC OF THE SPANISH JEWS
OF BULGARIA AND YUGOSLAVIA

scholars and documentary sources to develop a wide repertoire across the various Sephardic traditions. The quartet uses an eclectic assortment of medieval, Renaissance, early music and Middle Eastern instruments, though their vocals give little idea of what a traditional Sephardic male or female singer would sound like.

Other US groups include **Alhambra**, led by Isabelle Ganz, and David Harrison's **Voices of Sepharad**, both of whom combine classical and cantorial training and independent research. Harrison's singing is backed up by a flamenco guitarist an eclectic percussionist and a dancer/ dance scholar, Judith Brin Ingber (although there is no such thing as specifically Sephardic dancing). The singer **Judy Frankel** has also recorded Sephardic songs.

In Europe, there's a large crop of French singers – including **Jacinta**, **Héléne Engel**, **Françoise Atlan**, **Sandra Bessis** and **Esther Lamandier**; **Liliana Treves Alcalay** is working in Italy, and **Jana Lewitová** in the Czech Republic; while popular Greek artist **Savina Yannatou** has recorded Greek Judeo-Spanish songs with appropriate instrumental accompaniment.

The future of Judeo-Spanish/Ladino/Sephardic songs probably depends on these performers from outside the tradition. Over the past few years, their choices of repertoire and approach to singing styles have become quite open and flexible. And though the language is spoken by very few young people, the songs seem to have taken on a life of their own in a series of new voyages and diasporas.

discography

For details of record labels and developments, there's an interesting Sephardic music website at *www.geocities.com/Paris/6256/pizmonim.htm*

Compilations

◉ **Chants judéo-espagnoles** (Inédit, France).

These are unaccompanied solo recordings of two elderly women – Berta (Bienvenida) Aguado and Loretta (Dora) Gerassi – made in Israel in 1993. Aguado, born in Turkey in 1929 is an especially subtle performer of the old Ottoman Judeo-Spanish tradition. Gerassi was born in Bulgaria in 1931 and sings in a more Westernised style. The songs range through old romances, holiday songs, wedding songs and love songs. Informative notes, though only a few of the songs are translated.

◉ **Cantos Tradicionales y Romances Judeo-españoles de Oriente** and **Cantares y Romances Tradicionales Sefardíes de Marruecos** (Tecnosaga, Spain).

Since the late 1970s, Israeli ethnomusicologist Shoshana Weich-Shahak has collected and Sephardic songs, mainly using elderly traditional, Israeli-resident singers. The performers are mostly women, a cappella except for some percussion on wedding songs. The Oriente disc here comprises Romances and wedding songs, plus some liturgical songs which are models for *mode* (*maqam*), ornamentation and vocal timbre (i.e. expert singing without the interference of classical training.) The Moroccan disc is the real stuff, including Tetouan romances sung by Alicia Bendayan and a medly of wedding songs. Notes are in Spanish.

◉ **Duelas y Alegrías de la Novia** (Global Village, US).

These 1956 recordings by Henrietta Yurchenco are important early documents. They include good a cappella singing from women (including Alicia Bendayan) in Tetuan. Notes are minimal but song texts and translations are included.

Artists

Rabbi Isaac (Yitzhak) Algazi

Yitzhak Algazi was a Turkish Sephardic singer, revered for his virtuoso performances of synagogue singing, Judeo-Spanish songs and Turkish classical music. He died in Uruguay in the 1960s.

🎼 **Cantorial Compositions, Piyyutim, and Judeo-Spanish Songs** (Renanot, Jerusalem).

Reissued 78s, on two cassettes, accompanying the book *The Life and Music of Rabbi Isaac Algazi from Turkey* by Edwin Seroussi published in 1989.

Arbolera

An intriguing group made up of Spanish singers and instrumentalists José-Manuel Fraile Gil and Eliseo Parra with Israeli specialist Shoshana Weich-Shahak directing the recordings and playing kanun.

🎼 **Arbolera I & 2** (Tecnosaga, Spain).

Two recordings drawing on Weich-Shahak's extensive field recordings. The first volume covers various genres (with male vocals), while the second (featuring romances) is let down by a rather anodyne female vocalist. Good instrumentals (kanun, oud, saz, percussion) and thorough jacket notes.

Henriette Azen

Azen is a veteran Paris-based singer from the Moroccan Judeo-Spanish tradition.

🎼 **Desde el Nacimiento hasta la Muerte (From Birth to Death)** (Sacem/Vidas Largas, France).

1991 recording of a cappella renditions from Mme Azen's family repertoire.

Joaquín Díaz

Folklorist, musician and author Diaz is Director of his own Ethnographic Museum, northwest of Madrid.

🎼 **Kantes judeo-espanyoles** (Tecnosaga, Spain).

A 1996 recording of many well-known songs, others less so from the Ottoman and Moroccan repertoires. Some a cappella others with guitar. It's not a Sephardic vocal style, but warm, subtle vocals, based on decades of working with traditional village singers.

Gerineldo

Formed in 1981, Gerineldo is the only performing group specialising in the Moroccan Judeo-Spanish repertoire and performance style. The quartet is led by Oro Anahory-Librowicz, including Kelly Sultan Amar, Solly Levy and Judith Cohen. Their repertoire is learned from oral tradition, backed up by extensive research.

 Me Vaya Kappar· (Tecnosaga, Spain).

The best introduction to the Moroccan repertoire. A cappella performances with occasional oud and percussion.

🎼 **En Medio de Aquel Camino (Midway Along the Road)** (Gerineldo, Canada).

Includes both western and eastern repertoire, including different versions of the same romance, wedding and religious songs. Also includes Charly Edry on oud, violin and darabouka (goblet drum).

Flory Jagoda

One of the most influential figures in the renaissance of Judeo-Spanish song, Jagoda was born in Sarajevo, Bosnia and is now resident in the US. Her repertoire is from the eastern Mediterranean tradition; her own compositions have entered the folk tradition.

🎼 **La Nona Kanta (The Grandmother Sings)** (Global Village, US).

Flory Jagoda is joined by her adult family. Few of the old ballads or life-cycle songs, but a musical window on pre-war Jewish Sarajevo.

Los Pasharos Sefardíes

This Turkish Sephardic group, based in Istanbul and directed by Karen Gerson with vocalist Izzet Bana, have been influential in disseminating the lighter Turkish Judeo-Spanish repertoire, and in setting new compositions by Israeli Sephardic poet Avner Perez.

🎼 **La Romanza de Rika Curiel** (Gozlem, Turkey).

Very little of the old romance and life/calendar cycle repertoire, but engaging Turkish style music with santur and oud.

David Saltiel

David Saltiel, in his sixties, was born in Salonica and never left it. He is probably the last singer in the old Salonica style, harking back to the old 78s released between the wars. Subtle ornamentation in the vocal delivery, and the modes and rhythms are those of the early twentieth century, well before the commercialisation of Judeo-Spanish song.

 Jewish-Spanish Songs of Thessaloniki (Oriente, Germany).

This is *the* recording of Judeo-Spanish music from Salonica and the wider Ottoman tradition. Saltiel is accompanied by expert Greek musicians on oud, qanun, violin, lyra and frame drum – perhaps heavier instrumentation than would originally have been used. Life-cycle songs, calendar songs, love songs and topical humorous songs – no ballads/*romances*. A few well-known songs such as "Morena me llaman" and "La serena" as they're meant to sound, as well as less familiar ones, from moving stories to sly double-entendres. Excellent notes and song texts in English, Spanish and Greek.

ΔΑΥΙΔ ΣΑΛΤΙΕΛ — DAVID SALTIEL

JEWISH-SPANISH SONGS OF THESSALONIKI

WITH THE KIND SPONSORSHIP OF THE JEWISH COMMUNITY OF THESSALONIKI

Voice of the Turtle

Voice of the Turtle are probably the best-known group performing Sephardic repertoire – a Boston-based quartet directed by Judith Wachs with Lisle Kulbach, Derek Burroughs and Jay Rosenberg. On the scene since the early 1980s, they have released a well-planned *Paths of Exile* series including music from Turkey, Morocco, the Balkans and Jerusalem, all with lyrics, translations, and good notes.

Balkan Vistas: Spanish Dreams
(Titanic Records, US).

Repertoire from Yugoslavia and Bulgaria based largely on collections by Shoshana Weich-Shahak, plus the Flory Jagoda song "La yave de Espanya" (Dreams of Spain).

Full Circle: Music of the Spanish Jews of Jerusalem (Titanic Records, US).

The Jerusalem repertoire means it includes songs from different parts of the Sephardic diaspora except Morocco. The disc includes more of their own collections and mixes old favourites ("Adio kerida") with lesser-known songs ("Yo era un leoniko") and a rarely recorded romance ("Delgadina").

Ruth Yaakov

From Jerusalem, Ruth Yaakov's considerable training in Western concert music hasn't stopped her from developing a clear timbre with a satisfying traditional edge to it.

Her ensemble consists of Armenian oud and saz player Juan Carlos Sungurlian, Albanian violinist Shkëlzen Doli and Turkish percussionist Levent Tarhan.

Shaatnez: Sephardic Songs of the Balkans
(Piranha, Germany).

Good strong vocals and excellent instrumental contributions make this a compelling collection of songs (and a couple of instrumental pieces) from Turkey and the Balkans. Several songs taken from the repertoire of Berta (Bienvenida) Aguado and 78rpm recordings. Lyrics and translations.

Emil Zrihan

Born in Rabat, Morocco in 1954, Zrihan moved to Israel as a child where he has become a successful cantor and performer of sacred and secular music in the Moroccan tradition.

Ashkelon
(Piranha, Germany).

Named after the city in Israel where Zrihan lives, and one of the oldest in the world. A brief introduction on the oud, then the darbouka drums kick in, and wave upon wave of ecstatic praise-music in Moroccan, Arabic and Hebrew follows. Zrihan has a voice that cuts and soars and the ensemble of oud, violin, flamenco guitar, accordion, percussion and backing vocals drives this music in an unstoppable frenzy. The disc includes both Moroccan folk repertoire and Judeo-Moroccan religious *mawals*, a compelling juxtaposition of the Mediterranean and the Orient.

Kurdish Music

songs of the stateless

To the Kurds, the world's largest nation without a country, cultural identity is the essence that fuels the struggle for survival. An ethnic and historic entity since the 7th century BC, and a territory as large as France, Kurdistan was in 1923 divided up amongst its neighbours – Turkey, Iran, Iraq, Syria and the Soviet Republic of Armenia. Ever since, thirty-five million Kurds have become all too familiar with the techniques states can deploy to suppress language and culture to make a people disappear. **Eva Skalla** and **Jemima Amiri** listen to the sounds that give a voice to the Kurdish people.

Music is integral to Kurdish identity – and there are few places on earth where it has more meaning, as an assertion and expression of a culture. Historically, too, it has a central role in Kurdish society. In a land of mountains and high plateaux, lying between the Black Sea, the Iranian Plateau and the steppes of Mesopotamia, music has for centuries been the means of oral transmission of chronicles, epics and lyrical poetry. In a non-country, whose language and literature is suppressed, everything is sung and put to music to be committed to memory, to be passed down.

The music sings of the joy and sorrow of everyday life, gives rhythm to the labour of the field, magnifies mystic and erotic rapture, and helps the listener to relive the tales of the wars and insurrections that still punctuate the life of the Kurds. The Kurdish prince Salahaddin – the Saladin of the Crusades – is one of the principal heroes whose exploits feature in **epic songs**, though other sung events date back to the time of Alexander the Great, and seem scarcely less current than those describing the Gulf War. The epic song is a constant call to battle and a glorified, nostalgic reminder of the past, arming its listeners against the harsh realities of modern life, and defending their beliefs and identity. Even today when a *peshmerga* (Kurdish freedom fighter) dies in the hills, his comrades sing and dance, long into the night, to express their grief and say their farewells.

Bards, Minstrels, and Songs

Traditionally Kurdish folklore is transmitted by **dengbej** (bards), **stranbej** (minstrels) and **chirokbej** (story tellers), usually from families of musi-

cians. The feudal structure of society, however, in which every feudal lord would have his dengbej and would compete with fellow lords for the best, has changed greatly in this century. The systematic destruction of Kurdish villages by the Turkish, Iranian, Iraqi and Syrian governments has resulted in a considerable movement to the towns and cities where a different kind of music scene has evolved. Nonetheless, the majority of Kurds are still rural people, and some are still nomads.

In Kurdistan one sings, if not of heroic deeds, then of unhappy, unrequited love, and unusually it is the woman who compose and sing the **songs of love**, at least within their own village or valley, before the wandering minstrels – men – take up these songs and perform them on their travels. The repertoire of these *stranbej* also includes **erotic poetry**, which is passionate and direct despite the Islamic culture. These singers are judged by their creativity, the beauty of their poetry and their ability to stir emotions.

There is also a strong body of **work songs**, used to accompany spinning wool and weaving rugs, or the threshing, winnowing and herding that is part of agricultural life, or the shearing of sheep and the birth of lambs that puntuates nomadic life. In addition, music is central to **weddings, births, funerals and feasts**. At all such events, young and old dance for hours – men and women together in long lines, arms linked. There are hundreds of different **dances** and they vary from region to region. The music is provided by village musicians who sing traditional or newly created songs, accompanied on the *zurna* (wooden shawm), *dhol* (drum) and *bloor* (flute).

A celebration of great importance to the Kurds is **Nawroz**, the New Year, held on March 21st. Bonfires are lit in every village, picnics are eaten and everyone dances till dawn. The lighting of fires harks back to the pre-Islamic times and the Zoroastrian religion, which together with its forerunner, the ancient Yazidi religion, still survives amongst the Kurds. Yazidis are found both in Iraqi Kurdistan – around their sacred shrine of **Shekan Baazra** – and in Armenia, where there is relative freedom for Kurds. Their religious music, mostly sacred chants, survives although no recordings are currently available. There is religious music, too, among the various **dervish and Sufi cults** that proliferate amongst the mountain valleys; hypnotic and trance inducing, its origins are ancient and predate Islam. As elsewhere, the **daf** (frame drum) and **shimshal** are used by Kurdish Sufis as part of their ceremonies in order to induce trance.

Instruments and Rhythm

The **voice** takes the leading role in Kurdish music so instruments are secondary. Most of them are also found in the neighbouring musical traditions of Turkey and Armenia to the north, and Iran and Iraq to the south. The **duduk** (soft reedy oboe) and **bloor** are more common in the north and in the mountains, as are the **doozela** (double reed flute) and the **shimshal** (ney, long flute) – both very much folk instruments. Amongst the stringed instruments the **tenbur** (saz) is more common in the north whilst the **kamanche** (spike fiddle), which is thought to originate from Kurdistan, is more of a southern instrument. The **oud** also features in the south as do the **santur** (zither) and **tar** (lute) in more urban sophisticated contexts.

While the content of Kurdish music and songs is very varied, the words are usually set to one of five different **rhythmic patterns**. One is based on a Zoroastrian *chatta* (chant) with either eight or ten syllables in each line. The other four styles are simply three verses with lines of eight syllables, or two verses with lines of seven, ten or twelve syllables. The form containing two verses with lines of ten syllables is the most frequently used. Songs which are based on these five rhythmic patterns are considered to constitute the most ancient and traditional part of the repertoire. The **melodic line** is simple, its range consisting of only three or four notes, which are repeated as the different verses are sung. The form of the songs is strophic – one identical line of poem and music recurs at the end of each stanza like a refrain.

Kurdish music is **modal**, with the mode or *maqam* known as *Kurdi* throughout the Arab world being, as you might imagine, predominant. How-

ever, all the different types of modal schemes which are found in Persian traditional, classical and folk music also exist in Kurdish music in Iran; in fact, it has been suggested that Kurdish music is one of the roots on which Persian classical music has been built. As so much has been made of the influence of surrounding nations on the culture of the Kurds, it is important to consider how much the influence has been the other way. Kurdish musicians, especially within the diaspora, emphasise the independence of Kurdish music from Persian or Arab music, whilst national authorities prefer to marginalise Kurdish music as being a local species of another nation's music.

Partition States

Since partition in the 1920s the culture of the Kurds has been strongly disrupted. Travel between the various Kurdish regions has been – and is – severely restricted, while mass media has helped to impose dominant national languages even in the furthest-flung villages. Music has undergone different changes in the different countries, though it has remained in clandestine circulation between them through smuggled and copied cassettes.

Turkish Kurdistan

Until recently, in **Turkey**, all songs in Kurdish were banned on pain of imprisonment, torture or death, both for musicians and listeners. Throughout the last seventy years the Turks have been the most ruthless in their attempts to destroy all Kurdish culture. Many musicians have been imprisoned, killed or have fled into exile; others – such as the popular Arabesk singer **İbrahim Tatlıses** – have taken the easier path of singing in Turkish.

Despite the risks, Kurdish pirate radio stations have flourished, mostly run by partisans in the mountains, and a huge underground market for tapes of forbidden singers, passing from hand to hand, smuggled through from one part of Kurdistan to another, has grown up. It is in this atmosphere that **Şivan Perwer** (see interview box overleaf), the most famous and popular Kurdish singer today, came to the fore. Born in Urfa in Turkish Kurdistan, into a family of musicians, his earliest memories are of songs of loss and of longing, always filled with the desire to live in a land free from persecution. From an early age his wish was to be the best *dengbej* and already as a child, composing his own songs, he was singled out for his remarkable voice.

Şivan Perwer

As a passionate defender of his people and their music, Şivan Perwer travels the world in an untiring effort to make his music heard – the mythical minstrel of an entire people. Political song forms a good part of his repertory but it is in traditional, epic and love songs that he excels, accompanying himself on the tenbur (saz); his repertoire now includes nearly five hundred songs, drawn, to some degree, on poetry from the seventeenth century. He has made the tenbur he plays the symbol of the struggle and in many homes a tenbur hangs on the wall making a clear statement of defiance. Simon Broughton talked to him:

What does it mean to be 'The Voice of the Kurdish People'?

We have problems with politics, freedom, human rights and democratic rights. When you are a Kurdish singer or artist you have to talk about those. They affect your life and you cannot separate them from what you do. You need morals and strength to do this.

Is it your role to draw attention to the Kurdish problems?

I try to bring a message into every song, for example human rights, equality, justice, freedom, peace. Not just about Kurds, but for everybody in the world. I'm from Turkish Kurdistan, but I never wanted the Turks and Kurds to fight each other. I hate war and I want them to live together in brotherhood.

Is that a message that you try and give to the Kurdish people?

Yes. In Turkey, the government promotes very nationalistic ideas and tells the people to be proud they are Turks. In my songs I tell the Kurdish people you have to be proud to be a good human being. You have to respect people and love them, then you can strive for peace and be a good human being. No matter what language and culture you grow up with.

So you would never sing a song against the Turks?

No never. I just sing songs against the government, because they occupied, colonised and killed Kurdish people. I give a message to the Turkish people saying this government makes you guilty by what it is doing

Şivan Perwer

to the Kurdish people. I am telling Turkish people don't kill your friends, because that is what they are required to do in the army. Don't kill human beings. A Turkish mother is the same as a Kurdish mother. I would never condone killing Turks.

Now that Kurdish music can be played in Turkey [the government has legalised Kurdish language 'in private', legalised sale of some tapes, and set up a state radio station broadcsting in Kurdish], would you go back?

I have been nearly twenty three years in exile. Imagine what that's like. I am a well-known singer and people would love to hear me, but I can't go. It's just not safe. The government has killed Kurdish businessmen and other visitors. They might pretend to welcome me, but they would never let me sing my songs there. The sale of Kurdish cassettes is just for show.

Şivan rose to fame rapidly in 1972 at Ankara University, at the time of the Kurdish uprising in Iraqi Kurdistan. Cassette tapes made on the simplest equipment were smuggled into Iraq and to Iran at great risk. Thousands were inspired listening to his songs, thousands came to hear this charismatic and controversial figure with a breathtakingly beautiful voice, sing live, always illegally and often at gatherings of *peshmerga* before they went into battle. In 1976 he had to escape Turkey and fled to Germany, where he continued recording.

Şivan came to world notice when he took part in the Simple Truth concert at London's Wembley Stadium in 1991, an event he organised with Peter Gabriel and the Red Cross to raise funds for the Kurds in the aftermath of the Gulf War.

It is remarkable that Şivan should have such great popularity in all parts of Kurdistan and with the Kurdish diaspora as well as with Azeris, Turks and Persians given he is banned from radio and television across the whole region. Possession of one of his political cassettes can lead to a long prison sentence in Iran or Iraq, and only a few (of traditional songs) are permitted for sale in Turkey.

Iraqi Kurdistan

Until the emergence of Saddam Hussein, Iraqi Kurdish musicians had a better situation than in Turkey. Urban Kurdish musicians were able to study music in Baghdad and perform on Baghdad or Kirkuk radio, and they were permitted to take a limited part in the cultural life of Iraq as long as there was no hint of anything political.

One of the great names of the century was the legendary **Ali Mardan** (1914-1980) from Kirkuk, an urban musician, singer and composer whose music sometimes showed Arab influences (he played with Arab orchestras), but was much appreciated and played by many other Kurdish musicians. Other important musicians include the first two Kurdish women singers to be recorded and to work on Baghdad radio, **Ayse San** and **Miryem Xan**; and **Mohammed Arif Jesrawi**, another influential figure, whose music was taken up by Kurds not only in Iraq but also in Iran.

In time, simple recording facilities became available, although a government licence was necessary to make any recording. Getting this licence could take several months as the poetry was heavily scrutinised by the censors for any political references, and so a highly symbolic language evolved, a flower or a beautiful girl would symbolise Kurdistan, the partridge the struggle for freedom. Many cassettes were recorded illegally on portable equipment and distributed clandestinely with the result that numbers of musicians and poets were imprisoned or put to death for their defiance. **Karim Kaban** from Sulemaniyah was hanged, **Tasin Taha** was blown up, **Tahir Tafiq** 'vanished'.

In 1974, after a popular uprising that cost many thousands of lives, the Kurds managed to win a degree of autonomy. They were allowed to publish in their own language; the radio stations in Erbil, Sulemaniyah and Kirkuk played Kurdish music; schools, universities and music schools, teaching in Kurdish, were established; and there was a prolific output of cassettes. However within just a few years the situation deteriorated, Kurds would not abandon the idea of independence and when one of the Kurdish political parties sided with the Iranians in the Iran-Iraq war, wooed by hopes of independence, the Kurds experienced the horror of chemical bombing. During the Gulf War thousands of villages were destroyed and their menfolk 'disappeared' by Saddam's secret police.

Since the establishment of the so-called Safe Haven, after the Gulf War, the Kurds have had more freedom, but in a climate of full economic sanctions and constant internal struggle and turmoil there are no funds for developing an infrastructure for recording. The radio and TV stations, run by the different political factions, each champion and promote 'their' artists.

Iranian Kurdistan

In Iran subsequent regimes have dealt harshly with any Kurdish attempts at politics, whilst allowing Kurdish language newspapers and radio stations. Musicians have at times been imprisoned, as elsewhere, but there is a rich tradition in this region and some of the most sophisticated musicians have always come from this part of Kurdistan.

A leading figure of recent decades has been **Hassan Kamkar**, who collected and arranged over four hundred songs from the villages, founded a school of Kurdish music in Sanandaj and trained many of the musicians, including his eight children, who have been in the forefront of urban musical tradition. The Kamkars are unique. Keeping well clear of any political involvement, they have made a considerable name for themselves in the mainstream of Iranian music, playing and composing within both Iranian and Kurdish traditions. The exceptional singer of Iranian classical music, **Sharam Nazeri** is also Kurdish and frequently includes Kurdish material in his performances.

Other important figures include the singer-composer **Said Asghar Kurdistani**, who contributed much to Iranian classical music; the singer and poet **Abbas Kamandi**; and **Hassan Zirak**, an illiterate genius who composed over a thousand songs. Famous for his often erotic and sensual lyrics coming straight out of the village tradition, Zirak travelled all over Kurdistan in the 1960s and '70s and rare recordings of his, from various radio stations, have survived. **Hama Mamlê** and **Aziz Shahrokh** are also renowned for their remarkable

The Kamkars

voices. Mamlê is now in his eighties, but Aziz Shahrokh is still singing and is considered a living legend, perfoming his own music and also some of the songs of an earlier generation, in particular the music of **Jesrawi**.

Syrian and Armenian Kurdistan

Only in **Armenia** have the Kurds been free of the fear and restriction that pervades elsewhere, although their numbers are small. In Yerevan, there is a Kurdish faculty at the university where research has been done into Kurdish music, and there is a flourishing Kurdish radio station with a rich archive of recordings.

In **Syria**, the Kurds are an isolated and suppressed minority.

The Diaspora

Faced by repression, war and destruction, over half a million Kurds have been forced to flee their homelands – many of them in 1974 and 1991 – but also on a continuing basis. The largest concentrations are in Germany, followed by Sweden,

Britain, France, USA and Australia. Among the exiles is a considerable musical community. At every major gathering of Kurds whether for Nawroz, weddings or political events, musicians play and people dance their traditional dances. Audiences are eager to hear singers from all regions of Kurdistan.

In Paris the **Kurdish Institute**, set up with the help of the Mitterands, does much to promote Kurdish culture. It has an archive of old recordings and has re-issued many of these as well as some new recordings. In **Sweden** where several musicians including Şivan have settled, there is a thriving musical community. It is here that young musicians have started to experiment, adding elements from Western pop, Western classical, jazz, and Indian music to traditional Kurdish music.

Şivan's later records reflect these influences as does the music of **Naser Razazi** and his wife Marzia, exiles from Iran, with a big following at Nawroz parties and gatherings. **Najmeddin Ghulami** is another urban singer who has settled in Scandinavia. He has produced several recordings using traditional instruments, but also experiments with other formations and has recently introduced a synthesiser to his line-up.

Ciwan Haco, originally from Turkish Kurdistan, now living in Norway and playing with Norwegian musicians, sings in Kurdish, and with some reference to Western rock music (Bruce Springsteen springs to mind) draws his inspiration from traditional music of Northern Kurdistan (Turkey).

The freeing up of strictures in exile has led to a generation of women singers becoming established. In traditional Kurdish society they were unable to make music a profession. Besides Marzia Razazi, there is **Gulestan**, Şivan's wife, who has recorded and performed with him but is now making her own records of traditional and new songs accompanied on the saz. Meanwhile, two newcomers worth mentioning are **Nilofar Akbar**, whose operatic training has influenced the way she performs, and **Nazé**, who lives in Denmark, whose first record mixes traditional instruments with synthesiser and guitar more successfully than most.

Gulestan also has a show on the new Kurdish satellite TV station, **MEDTV**, which has a head office in Brussels and others in London and Stockholm. Although threatened with closure on a number of occasions through pressure from the Turkish government, the station has become a major influence over the last five years with transmissions all over the world. Most of the musicians based in Europe and the US have played on MEDTV and the recordings of these shows have become a valuable archive. These transmissions reach Kurdistan where they feed new ideas into a young generation of musicians.

discography

A few recordings of Kurdish music (Şivan, the Kamkars and the French anthologies) are now available from the megastores, but the majority can be found only at specialist outlets and in Kurdish organisations, and then mostly on cassette, although the numbers of CDs is growing all the time. Stran Music in Sweden and Bahar Video in Green Lanes, London (see p.727) are useful, while in Turkey *SES Plak* (WMÇ Blok No. 6410, Unkapani, Istanbul, Turkey; ☎ (90) 212 527 5261, fax (90) 212 513 5087) has an extensive selection of Kurdish pop music.
Kurdish music information and discs are available online at the *Global Heritage* Website: *www.terranovamusic.com*

Compilations

📼 **Yaşlılar Dersim Türküleri Söylüyor**
(ADA Müzik, Turkey).

The title means 'Elders Sing Dersim Songs', and the tape is made up of a number of excellent field recordings of amateur performers from the town of Dersim (known in Turkey as Tunceli) where there was one of the biggest Kurdish revolts

against the Turkish Republic in 1938. However, this is just excellent singing and saz playing with some wild dances thrown in. Authentic and listenable.

◉ **De Soran a Hawraman – Songs from Kurdistan** (Al Sur, France).

Mostly traditional and folk music recorded in France by musicians from both Iran and Iraq, featuring the kamanche, tanbur, daf, ney and duduk. Good notes in French and English.

◉ **Kurdish Music** (Auvidis/Unesco, France).

Field recordings made in Kurdish villages in Syria with instruments that include the tanbur (saz), zorna (shawm), zil (copper cymbals used by Kurdish nomads) and tabalak (clay kettledrums). Interesting notes in English.

Artists

Dilshad

Considered by many in Iraqi Kurdistan to be a significant influence on contemporary Kurdish music, Dilshad studied violin and composition in Eastern Europe and then returned to Kurdistan to encourage development in music education. He now lives in Austria and has composed and arranged for many other musicians including Sivan.

◉ **Kurdish music for Violin** (Stran Music, Sweden).

This recording, of Kurdish melodies on the violin, is a good example of musicians – including the Tipi Sulemaniah (Sulemaniah Orchestra) – playing Kurdish music in Western classical style.

Ilana Elia

Ilana is a singer, the daughter of a Kurdish/Jewish musician from Iraq, and now lives in Israel.

◉ **Ilana Eliya** (MCI, Israel).

Ilana attracted much attention with this, her first record, in 1996. She sings in Kurdish accompanied by an ensemble of musicians playing oud, saz, ney, zurna, cello, clarinet, flute, dhol and keyboards.

Ciwan Haco

A refugee from Turkey, Ciwan has settled in Norway and is one of the bright stars of contemporary Kurdish pop.

◉ **Dûrî-Carcira** (SES Plak, Turkey).

Ciwan plays with Kurdish and Norwegian musicians on this debut album which has been a big hit with the younger Kurdish audience.

The Kamkars

The Kamkars are a group of seven brothers and a sister from Sanandaj in Iranian Kurdistan and are certainly the most polished of Kurdish musicians. They are considered amongst the very best of musicians in Iran today for both their classical Persian and Kurdish repertoires. Many of the group members play several instruments, they are gifted soloists in their own right and prolific composers. They are responsible for bringing Kurdish music into the mainstream in Iran.

 Nightingale with a Broken Wing
(RealWorld/WOMAD Select, UK).

A good collection of vocal and instrumental tracks showing the group's virtuosity on oud, rabab, kamanche, tar, santur, setar, daf, gaychak and tombak. Instantly appealing music with exuberant and joyful dance rhythms plus some lilting and reflective songs. Very polished.

⊚ **Living Fire** (Long Distance, France).

This live recording, recorded in Paris, has a darker feel and perhaps more atmosphere and intensity. There are many other Kamkar CDs available, including their classical performances, in Persian music shops in many large cities in Europe, the US and Australia.

Adnan Karim

Adnan Karim is one of a generation of musicians who developed their style in Iraqi Kurdistan but fled the oppression of the Iraqi government. He has now settled in Sweden.

⊚ **The Longest Night** (Stran Music, Sweden)

Adnan is the singer and composer of most of the songs on this recording in the traditional style. It was made in Sulemaniyah (Iraqi Kurdistan) by the music group of the Kurdish Fine Arts Society and remixed in Sweden.

Hama Mamlê

From a traditional family of musicians, now in his eighties and considered one of the great old singers, Mamlê is renowned for his beautiful voice. He was deported by the Shah's regime and now lives in Sweden.

⊚ **Zemane** (Stran Music, Sweden).

A collection of classic recordings on which he is accompanied by violin, flute, santur, tar, oud and zarb (tombak drum).

Sharam Nazeri & Ensemble Alizadeh

Sharam Nazeri, born in Kermanshah in 1949, is one of Iran's top classical singers and the Ensemble Alizadeh one of the best groups of instrumentalists in the country. Nazeri is famed for his Sufi singing.

⊚ **Nowruz: Traditional and Classical Music** (World Network, Germany)

Most of the music here is Persian classical music plus various Kurdish tunes, including several folksongs from Nazeri's native region. A fine recording nevertheless.

Nazé & Newroz

Both young musicians, Nazé and her husband Newroz are refugees living in Denmark. She has a rich, dramatic voice and their music is a good example of new popular Kurdish music with Western influences that is popular at parties.

⊚ **Ax Kurdistan** (Own label, Denmark).

Nazé and Newroz head up Oriental Mood, the group of Kurdish and Danish musicians featured on this recording playing a collection of traditional and new songs composed by Nazé and Newroz.

Şivan Perwer

The inspiration of a whole generation of young musicians, Şivan was exiled by the Turkish government as the voice of a people demanding their independence. He is noted for his emotive and passionate style. At least half of his Turkish CDs on SES Plak, the label with the best collection of Kurdish pop, are banned in Turkey. While most of Şivan's discs are traditional in style, others have him experimenting with synthesisers and electric guitars. He tours constantly and is based in Sweden.

⊚ **Chants du Kurdistan** (Auvidis/Ethnic, France).

This collection of mostly traditional songs is a good introduction to Şivan's earlier music, accompanying himself on saz.

 Kirive Volumes 1 & 2 (SES Plak, Turkey).

Şivan has sixteen CDs on SES Plak and these volumes are best of collections and a good place to start. They include many of his most famous political songs and some folk songs. Şivan accompanies himself on the saz, other instruments include duduk, bloor, oud and kanun.

Naser and Marzia Razazi

Both Naser and his wife Marzia were born in Iranian Kurdistan and fled at the time of the Iranian revolution. Very popular among the Kurds in Europe, they live in Sweden and have made several recordings of dance melodies and folk songs, accompanied on traditional and electric instruments. Nazir is now talking of returning to his acoustics roots and moving away from his synthesiser.

⊚ **Piroz** (Stran Music, Sweden).

This album (or equally Be, Gome Sin or Nayale Cudayi) gives you the inside track on dance music, a very important feature, at every Kurdish party.

Many thanks to Hooshang Kamkar, Arsalan Kamkar, Sivan Perwer, Kendal Nizam, Ahmed Nejad, Newroz and Sheri Laiser for their help in preparing this piece.

Palestinian music

the sounds of struggle

As an uneasy peace persists between the Palestinian National Authority (which administers the Gaza and Jericho territories vacated by Israel) and the Israeli Government, Palestinian music is still as much a statement of identity as it's ever been. In the years of the Intifada, music played a substantial part in the movement, but today the beginnings of a more stable musical life are underway. **Andy Morgan** and **Mu'tasem Adileh** chart the background and explore the current Palestinian music scene.

Before the creation of the state of Israel in 1948, **Palestine** comprised a multifaceted collection of creeds, religions and races, all of whom had coexisted in relative peace for hundreds of years – at least until the turn of this century. Christians from Nazareth and Galilee, Druze people from the Lebanon and the Golan Heights, indigenous Jews, nomadic tribes who roamed the great deserts between the Mediterranean and the Gulf, Arab farmers and townspeople, Egyptians, Turks, Cypriots and Greeks – all were part of the cultural crossroads of the Holy Land.

Rural Songs: Dabka and Qawaali

Although the great city ports of Jaffa and Haifa were already sizeable commercial centres in the first half of the twentieth century, most Palestinians were rural people who had either settled to become **felahin** (farmers), or who still pursued a nomadic, Bedouin lifestyle. The music of the felahin comprised mainly functional songs for harvesting, tending the flocks, fishing, grinding coffee or making olive oil. There were also epic songs about old heroes and legends sung by itinerant storytellers or improvisers – **zajaleen** – who travelled from village to village with their box of tricks and retinue of players.

The most important occasions for music and merrymaking were **weddings** and their associated feasts. After the immense platters of meat and rice had been cleared away the party-goers would sing and dance. The dances were collectively known as **dabka**, which literally means 'foot-tapping'. They consisted of precise steps and jumps performed by linked chains of dancers. The music was provided by village musicians who sang traditional airs, accompanied by traditional instruments such as the *shababi* and *ney* (short flute and long flute), the *mijwiz* and *yarghoul* (shawms), the *tabla* and *duff* (drums), *rebab* (fiddle) and oud.

Certain songs became so ingrained and widespread that they mutated into distinct song-forms with fixed melodies and verse structures over which new lyrics could be improvised. In terms of their rooted structure and versatility, these song-forms are comparable to the twelve-bar blues or even, lyrically speaking, to the limerick. The most common types of song-form, then as now, were the **dalauna** and the **meyjana**. Singers were judged as much by their word-play skills as by their vocal prowess. The ability to juggle words and phrases to fit the form brought local fame.

Nowhere are these skills more pronounced than in the art of the **qawaali** or **zajal**. The singers who practise this art engage in a kind of musical debate, each participant often representing one of the families at a wedding where they would discourse on the virtues and qualities of their patron families, or argue over the relative merits of dark- or light-skinned women. These punning, rapping, word-tussling sessions were always sung rather than merely recited.

In recent times certain qawaali and zajal, most notably **Abu Leil**, **Haddaji Rajih el-Salfiti** and **Mousa Hafez**, have achieved fame across the Palestinian communities.

Songs of Partition

The tumultuous events of the late 1940s which led to the partition of Palestine and the creation of Israel in 1948 did not destroy the culture of the felahin. The many thousands of Palestinians who fled to the refugee camps of the West Bank and

Gaza Strip took their musical traditions with them and kept them alive in their hostile new surroundings. The Arabs who stayed behind and continued to live in the new state of Israel, collectively known as 'the Arabs of the 48', also clung tenaciously to their heritage.

Around the period of partition, the songs and dances of the felahin did not form part of the commercially exploited and recorded body of Arabic popular music. This area was dominated by the great Egyptian and Lebanese singers and songwriters of the day such as Umm Kalthum, Mohamed Abd el-Wahaab and Sayed Darweesh (see 'Arab World' article, p.323). The felah music was a hidden heritage, a common cultural bond among the Palestinian people completely unknown outside their own sphere of existence.

Nevertheless Palestine did have a musical scene of sorts based in the northern Israeli towns of Haifa and Nazareth, the only active, cosmopolitan centres for Palestinian music-making until the early 1970s. In these towns, songs were composed, performed and recorded. This urban genre of music was performed by small groups consisting of a singer and a few instrumentalists and was far removed in its complexity and sophistication from the country 'folk' style of the felahin. Instead, these city musicians were attuned to the sounds coming from Damascus and Cairo, where the intricate art of classical Arabic music was still revered and practised as it had been for centuries.

It was the versatility of the song-form that allowed the roots music of the felahin to survive the political upheavals of the late 1940s and develop a stage further. In the new climate of fear, anger and alienation, the gist of the **improvised lyrics** that accompanied the *dalauna* and the *meyjana* began to reveal a harder edge. Instead of songs about the slender stalk of wheat swaying in the wind like the lithe body of the dancing woman, the newly dispossessed sang about the power of the gun and the dream of nationhood. Heroes and martyrs of the struggle such as the great Arab leader Cheikh L'Hezedin el-Kassam – who vowed to be the first to shoot the God of the British colonialists – were lauded in popular song. Even non-Arab figures like Che Guevara became part of the new folklore. Every significant event in the life of post-partition Palestine – the Six Day War, the Yom Kippur offensive, Arafat's speech to the UN in 1974, the belligerence of Saddam Hussein and the Intifada – has at one time or another been celebrated or mourned in song.

The first singer to score a hit with a collection of essentially Palestinian songs was **Mustafa Al Kurd**, whose cassette release *Kullee Amal* (Full of Hope) enjoyed fervent popularity all over Palestine in the early 1970s. He sang of the daily suffering of the Palestinians living under occupation, using a radical new concoction of local folk forms, Egyptian and Lebanese pop and Western rock.

The dearth of recording studios and commercial infrastructure accessible to Palestinians in Israel and the Occupied Territories meant that the

Mustapha Al Kurd, full of hope in the 1970s

growth of modern Palestinian pop was slow and arduous. At first, singers found their concerts and recordings subject to censorship but eventually the Israelis gave up trying to control the clandestine Arab cassette industry and recordings became readily available even if they had to be sold under the counter. In the late 1970s and early 1980s a new movement of political theatre began to make its mark. Playwrights were often forced to use highly symbolic language to convey their defiant message, and theatrical performances were subject to much closer scrutiny than the playing of music, which continued more or less unheeded in the privacy of Palestinian homes. These theatre companies made much use of music and foremost among them was the group **El-Funoun**, founded in 1979.

JAK KILBY

After Al Kurd's success in the early 1970s, Palestinians had to wait until the end of the decade before other groups made a similar impact at home and abroad. One of the most successful pop acts was **Al Ashiqeen** (The Lovers), who achieved fame all over the Arab world, a rare thing for a Palestinian artist. The theme of their most famous cassette release, *Sirit Izz Deen El Kassam*, was the colourful life of holy man and freedom fighter El Kassam. This period also saw the creation of **Sabreen** which has become the most internationally successful Palestinian group. Founded by Said Murad in 1980, 'Sabreen' means 'People who are Patient' – a precondition for Palestinians.

The Intifada

The energy devoted to music-making intensified in the mid-1980s, especially among the youth of the occupied territories. The **Intifada uprising**, a youth-led, stone-throwing revolt initiated in the Gaza strip in December 1987, fuelled the desire to express political woes in song, and groups like El-Funoun and Sabreen carried the hard-edged sentiments of revolt to a receptive audience. Sabreen's album *Mawt a'nabi* (Death of a Prophet) is one of the lasting musical products of that time. "The Intifada started while we were in the studio making this album", remembers Said Murad. "We saw young men throwing stones – and people got killed for that. We felt these people were the

prophets of our new history and we named this album after them." Musically this album is very strong, with urgent, mournful vocals and a rich, plangent plucked accompaniment on instruments of the classic Arabic tradition: *kanun* (plucked

zither), oud, *buzuk* (strummed instrument related to the Greek bouzouki) and guitar.

Much Intifada music was simple, disposable and worked like a newspaper, but it was effective. One of the most important figures was the songwriter **Suhail Khoury**: "It was a very powerful time, a very revolutionary time. People were in the streets every day. Ordinary people were fighting the occupation. And music was a part of this. I did a tape called *Sharrar* (Spark). The lyrics were very powerful, talking about things that had happened just a few days before. How they'd kicked the Israelis out of Nablus and so on. It was describing the daily life of the Intifada and it was a very powerful tool." After making the tape Khoury was stopped at a checkpoint in his car and arrested. The car and the tapes were confiscated. "Somehow one tape leaked out to the community and it was copied in tens of thousands, one to another. We estimated that at least 100,000 were made. A big number in a small state. And the Israelis did quite a good marketing service for me because they announced on the radio and TV that I was arrested for making music and could be imprisoned for ten years. So everybody wanted to know what kind of tape that was. Of course, I'm laughing now, but I was tortured for twelve days. They wanted to know who composed, who sang, who played. I didn't tell them anything and I was sentenced to six months imprisonment."

Most of the Intifada music was unsophisticated – usually based on well-known folksongs – but it carried great power in spreading the feeling of opposition amongst the people. One of the most important tapes was *Doleh* (Statehood), produced in 1988 during the first year of the Intifada. The key figure behind it was **Thaer Barghouti** (himself a zajjal improviser) and it was a collection of songs by various singers recounting deeds of the Israeli soldiers and everyday events of the rebellion. The title track became very popular because it coincided with the announcement that the Intifada would not stop until there was a state.

Beginnings of a State

In 1993 a Declaration of Principles was signed by Israel and the PLO, and in May 1994 the **Palestinian National Authority** was set up in the Gaza Strip and parts of the West Bank with Yasser Arafat as its President. As the turmoil of the Intifada subsided and the situation stabilised, it became easier for musicians to work. For instance, **wedding bands** reappeared, having been put out of business during the fighting. Using shababi and mijwiz

El Funoun – Palestinian Art-Music

The road to success is never easy for folkloric ensembles anywhere in the world. They won't see their videos on MTV, and young musicians in most countries are generally more interested in trying to be the next Madonna, Spice Girls or Pearl Jam than learning the music of their grandparents. In Palestine, these obstacles seem trivial. Since their inception in 1979, **El Funoun** (The Arts) have faced repeated border closings, the arrest of many of its members, travel restrictions, and even bans on public performances. Why risk arrest simply to sing and dance? For El Funoun, the

EL-FUNOUN
فرقة الفنون الشعبية الفلسطينية

ZAGHAREED

answer was easy. They realised that half a century on the losing side of history has left many Palestinain folk arts facing extinction.

The group of fifty singers, dancers, and musicians began with a mission to revive regional folklore as a form of Palestinian identity. El Funoun's early works were the result of extensive research in Palestinian villages, preserving centuries-old songs and dances, including the dabke using traditional Arab instruments (oud, nay, and kanun). "This was very controversial," explains El Funoun's Omar Barhgouti. "According to the Israelis, we were supposed to be a people without a culture. Over the years, we have faced numerous attempts to suppress it."

"During the Intifadah, our rehearsals were clandestine," Barghouti remembers. "We would rehearse underground. We had to play the music quietly. Imagine, trying to play music as quietly as possible. Everyone would whisper. At the time, these activities were banned,

and we all knew that we faced being arrested every time an Israeli patrol passed by." Over the past two decades, numerous members of the ensemble have been arrested. El Funoun's co-founder Muhammad Atta has been jailed four times "for posing a security risk and inciting violence", says Barghouti. "Still, life continues, and we adapt. Not just us, Palestinians in general. Local concert organisers know that they are taking a risk when they arrange one of our concerts."

Border closings have become a fact of life in the Palestinian territories. After scores of accolades and awards, the group has still never played in Gaza or to many Palestinian communities within Israel. As Barghouti says: "We've played in the United States, Spain, Sweden, throughout the Middle-East, and even Expo '98 in Portugal, but I think we'll get to perform on Mars before we ever get permits to go to Gaza. Even dancing itself is controversial to some – you see, traditionally, in our culture, dancing is for fun, for happiness. People used to say, 'we are working so hard to defend ourselves against the occupation. Two people died yesterday, and you are dancing?' But we dance because we want to express ourselves."

In addition to the Israeli occupation, El Funoun faces countless obstacles in age-old local traditions. "The purpose of El-Funoun is to challenge traditions, not just to preserve them," says Barghouti. Their 1997 project, *Zaghareed* (Ululations), tells the story of a modern Palestinian wedding, where a young woman confronts her father as he discovers that she has a lover. The argument gets heated as she wants to break with tradition and defy her parents' wishes for an arranged marriage. "Everyone is entitled to the right to choose, (a marriage partner)," explains Barghouti. "This was very controversial when we first performed it, but we are used to defying traditions."

Zaghareed is the cry of joy that Arab women make during weddings and each region in Palestine has its own particular style. For their production El-Funoun collected ululations from Acre, Safad, Ramallah, Jerusalem and Bir Al Sabe. The ululations, they say, represent the unity of Palestinian culture, despite the disunity in Palestinian geography – the PNA administered areas, Israel, and the refugee camps in Lebanon, Syria and the rest of the diaspora.

Daniel Rosenberg

alongside modern instruments, they generally perform the most popular songs of Egyptian and Lebanese singers – happy, good-time music. Some of the Intifada singers faded away with the establishment of the PNA, and Al-Ashiqeen disbanded. But Suhail Khoury and Sabreen have continued making music, and Mustafa al Kurd is still composing songs, albeit without the profile or impact he had in the 1970s.

The Doves are Coming

Your food is a locust
Dipped in a drop of honey
Your dress, burlap and camel hair
Your shoes are thorns,
Your path is thorns, its flowers few.
O moon on the outer edge
O prophet exiled
Calling in the wilderness:
Widen the roads
For the deer of love and peace
Widen the roads,
The doves are coming from the mountain,
The doves are coming.

Lyrics by Hussein Barghouthi of Sabreen

A new post-Intifada addition to the music scene was the 'chanson' soprano **Tania Nasser** who returned from Jordan in 1993 after nineteen years in exile with her husband Hanna Nasser, a former member of the PLO executive committee and now President of Birzeit University near Jerusalem. Her first appearance before the Palestinian people after returning was with songwriter **Rima Tarazi**. As a feminist and political activist, Tarazi's songs are mostly true stories of the struggle and those involved in it. Similarly **Reem Banna**, a singer/songwriter musically educated in Russia, focuses on the Palestinian-Israeli struggle. She has a distinctive, ethereal voice and while her melodies are clearly Arab in character, the arrangements are mostly in popular Western style.

One interesting, if short-lived group was **Washem** (Tatoo), named after the decoration frequently used by Bedouin women. They made a strong album, *Ashiqa* (Lover – of one's country and freedom), with an Arabic/Western fusion sound and vocals by soprano Reem Talhami. The songs, composed by group member Suhail Khoury, were about prison, the popular revolt and the siege of east Jerusalem which is still going on.

Continuing in the political theatre tradition, **El Funoun Palestinian Popular Dance Troupe** (see box opposite) draws on traditional music and dance. They started out with folk dances, but their choreography now includes non-traditional mixed (male and female) dances. Their theatrical production *Haifa, Beirut wama ba'ad* (Haifa, Beirut and Beyond) was an interpretation of the Palestinian experience and its extrapolation into the future, while their latest, *Zaghareed* (Ululations) moves away from folklore and tries to appeal to a younger audience. Another group, **Yuad**, led by composer Nabil Azer, turned towards stage productions in 1997 with a musical, *Katr e Nada*, about the Palestinian's suffering under fifty years of Israeli oppression. Based in Galilee (Israel), this is one of the few groups still performing resistance music.

The most interesting contemporary Palestinian group, though, remains **Sabreen** who, since the 1980s, have been adding elements of jazz, Western classical and Indian music to Arabic forms. They are fronted by the charismatic Galilean soprano **Kamilya Jubran** and their instrumentation includes oud, kanun, buzuk, Arabic percussion and drums, plus violin, guitar and bass. Like many groups in Israel they are concerned with building a bridge between East and West and making peace. In Said Murad's words: "In the East you have to be in the music – it's not on paper outside you. When you play the oud or the mijwiz you improvise, you make your own music yourself. This is the philosophy of Eastern music. In Western music you have to be organised and the score is outside you. They are two different ways of thinking. What we are trying to do is find a common language between both. Our message from the beginning was how to make people live together."

One thing that still inhibits the production of Palestinian music is the total lack of proper recording studios and facilities – Sabreen's studio in East Jerusalem is the only one. The options open to Palestinians wishing to study the Arab musical tradition were, until recently, also very limited. Travel within the Arab world can be difficult, particularly for Palestinains from Galilee who have no option but to hold Israeli passports.

One remarkable gifted young oud player from Nazareth, **Samir Joubran**, succeeded in attending the renowned Abd el Wahaab Institute in Cairo. Since his graduation in 1993, he's begun to build a career with concerts in Palestine, Jordan and France and a solo CD, *Taqsim*. He's already been acclaimed as one of the important new oud players in the Arab world. Another notable oud player who went abroad to study – this time in Baghdad – is **Adel Salameh**. Born in Nablus, but now resident in the UK, he is a distinguished performer of classical Arabic music who has taken the oud into new areas, forming interesting collaborations with Indian sarod player Krishnamurti Sridhar and flamenco guitarist Eduardo Niebla. He has toured widely and played at WOMAD festivals.

The founding of the **National Conservatoire of Music** in 1993 was an important development for Palestinian musicians. The first of its kind in Palestine, the Conservatoire was established to give the opportunity to a new generation of students to receive a high standard of musical instruction. Originally based in Ramallah, but now with branches in Jerusalem and Bethlehem as well, it has an enrollment of some four hundred students and is still growing. It's hoped that home grown musical talent in the West Bank will rapidly develop as students finish their studies and start groups and musical careers. This has already begun with the creation of the **Oriental Music Ensemble** at the Conservatoire, a group re-establishing the Palestinian contribution to classical Arabic music – something that has suffered in the last fifty years. Comprising six professional musicians with acoustic, instruments hand-made by Palestinian craftsmen, it's led by **Khaled Jubran**, teacher of Arabic music at the NCM and a virtuoso oud and buzuk player. It also includes nay player **Suhail Khoury**, Intifada singer, turned director of the NCM.

Thanks to Roger Short,
Bill Badley and Suhail Khoury

discography

Discs below are available from: **Popular Art Centre** (PO Box 3627, El-Bireh, West Bank, Palestine; *pac@palnet.com*); **Sabreen** (PO Box 51875, 91517 Jerusalem) and **Washem** (PO Box 19106, Jerusalem). For information on new developments, check the Website of the **Jerusalem Festival of Arabic Music** (*www.yabous.org*).

Compilations

Traditional Music and Song from Palestine (Popular Art Centre, Palestine).

The best introduction to Palestinian folk music, thirteen tracks from recordings made by the Popular Art Centre in El-Bireh on the West Bank. The disc includes five tracks featuring the powerful voice of Mousa Hafez, the leading Palestinian poet-singer, who lives in the refugee camp in Jineen.

Artists

El Funoun

El Funoun literally means 'the arts' and the group was founded in 1979 to present Palestinian song, music and dance. They are one of the country's leading theatrical and musical ensembles.

Zaghareed (Sounds True, US).

The title of this show means 'ululations', the traditional cry of celebration, and the music and lyrics describe the various stages of a wedding ceremony. It all feels a little rehearsed and formal, but the musicianship on acoustic instruments like oud, buzuq, mijwiz and others is excellent and it adds up to one of the better examples of traditional Palestinian music.

Sabreen

Formed in 1980, the Jerusalem-based Sabreen are still the best Palestinian band and the most internationally famous. Music by Said Murad, lyrics by Hussein Barghouthi and the ravishing vocals of Kamilya Jubran. Like many Israeli bands they have drawn on a range of cultural sources for their music – tabla and reggae as well as Arabic music. They have always been at the forefront of the Palestinian peace movement, and also perform music for films and theatre.

 Death of the Prophet (ACT-AIN, Japan).

The CD features early songs from the 1980s. Wild oud playing by Murad and a tragic tone to Jubran's vocals – in "A Song for Childhood", for example. Very musical and very expressive.

Here Come the Doves (Sabreen, Palestine).

The title of their most recent (1994) album suggests a longing for peace, but the title song is enigmatic. Less passion and more slickness than the album above, but a combination of Arabic and Western influences that is quirky, but powerful when it works.

Adel Salameh

Born in Nablus in 1966, Salameh spent time learning the Fragiond style in Baghdad and has become a leading player. He is now based in the UK and has taken the oud into new areas with collaborations with Indian sarod player Krishnamurtri Sridhar (RealWorld) and flamenco guitarist Eduardo Niebla.

Mediterraneo (Riverboat, UK).

Many consider the Spanish guitar to be descended from the Arabic lute, so there's an enjoyable musical anachronism in this lively collaboration with flamenco guitarist Eduardo Niebla. Salameh's disc of traditional improvisations in Arabic music **Solo** (Pastorle, Japan) is also recommended.

Washem

Washem are a seven-piece band led by nay, sax and piano player Suhail Khoury with vocalist Reem Talhami.

Ashiqa (Washem, Palestine).

A 1995 album that's an intriguing combination of Arabic melodies, Western harmonies, plus a touch of the operatic from lead singer Reem Talhami. The songs talk of Palestinian resistance, expressed in the traditions of Arabic poetry: "Jerusalem, where is the soul? Where is the open-ended expanse? This space is in flux".

Syria, Lebanon & The Levant

europe meets asia

The Levant – Syria, Lebanon, Jordan and Iraq – has for centuries been described as the crossroads between Europe and Asia: a fertile basin for musical influences. Syria, ever the dominant power in the region, has a respected Classical tradition. However, for popular song, this century, it is Lebanon that has been most influential. Before the civil war of the 1970s, Beirut rivalled Cairo as a centre for Arab music, and in Fairouz, the country produced the superstar who took over from Umm Kulthum. **Bill Badley** and **Zein al Jundi** take a look at the Levant's past glories and its diverse contemporary scene.

Syria

Damascus has been considered one of the Arab world's great cultural cities since the early days of Islam, and members of the older generation reminisce wistfully about its classical tradition of music. Modern visitors to the city are liable to be disappointed, however. Even though there are some fine players living in the city, there are few opportunities for them to perform. The old Andalusian repertoire with its complex rhythmic and melodic patterns has largely given way to Egyptian style al-jeel dance music, played on mainly electric instruments. Long musical apprenticeships and vocal training have lost out to looks and charisma.

In popular Arab song, the biggest Syrian star in recent years is the singer **George Wasoof** – though he made his reputation in Beirut (in the early 1980s) and he has subsequently set up base in Cairo. He draws upon Syrian and Levantine folk melodies, however, mixing them with classic Egyptian song.

Two younger, Damscus-based performers are **Nur Mahana** and **Mayada el Hennawy**. Nur's infectious pop sound, exemplified by his hit "Jameel al Ruh" (Beautiful Soul), has made him a widely travelled star, entertaining Syrian communities all over the globe. Mayada's style is truly *shamee* (Syrian): shades of Egypt and Turkey combine with a home spun glamour that is instantly recognisable to anyone who has spent a few days in the country.

Syria's sophisticated northern second city Aleppo has a reputation for fine musicians; its soirées in the 1920s and '30s were legendary and it is still said that any singer who meets with approval in

Aleppo is assured success elsewhere. The city has a tradition of singers specialising in the Andalous **muwashshah** (decorated) – sung poetry that draws on the Levantine *mawlawi* sufi ideology. Its chief exponent is octogenarian **Sabri Moudallal**, a national treasure with an extraordinary vocal technique. Any chance to see him in action should not be missed.

Aleppo is also home to **Sabah Fakhri** (born in 1933), who is considered Syria's pre-eminent singer

Sheikh Hamza Chakour and Ensemble Al-Kindi

– and is the major Syrian musical export to the Arab world. He has also probably done more than anyone alive to keep the flame of traditional Andalusian music alive, with his abundant recordings of *nagham al ams* (melodies of the past), and his international tours.

After Fakhri, the most active exponent of **Syrian classical music** in recent years has been the **Jalal Edinne**, a Frenchman (born Julien Weiss) who converted to Islam and has studied the *qanun* (arab zither) to a very high standard. His discs and tours with **Ensemble Al-Kindî**, sometimes featuring the singers **Sabri Moudallal** or **Sheikh Hamza Chakour**, and whirling dervishes, are as fine a representation of Syrian art music as you are presently likely to find.

Out in the villages, both Syria and Lebanon share the muscular **dabka** dance-song tradition: an energetic communal celebration with strong Turkish overtones.

Lebanon

In its heyday after World War II, **Beirut** was known as the 'Paris of the Middle East': a chic, Eurocentric home to artists and intellectuals escaping despotism elsewhere. This cosmopolitan centre produced an intense, glamorous scene, in which the great stars were the woman singers **Fairuz** (the

biggest living star in the Arab world – see feature box opposite), **Sabah**, the singer and oud player **Wadih al-Safi**, and the Syrian-born George Wassouf (see previous page).

During the terrible seventeen-year civil war, the Lebanese music scene moved largely to Cairo and Paris. However, since 1992, enormous effort has been put into rebuilding Beirut, and it is surely regaining its reputation as the pleasure dome of the Levant. French influence has always been very strong in Lebanon and there is a Gallic smoothness to much of the city's music. Stars tend to come and go according to the whims of the night club audiences, though **Walid Tawfiq** (who sings in a mix of Arabic and French) and **Rageb Alama** (who is best at poppy rather than Classical Arab songs) are two that have stayed around for a while.

Jordan

Jordan's Bedouin heritage is the primary influence on the local music. Travellers in the countryside are likely to hear the improvised poetry of **zajal** songs accompanied by the *mijwis* or *yaghul* reed pipes or the single-stringed rabab.

The young Bedu pop singer **Omar Abdullat** scored a rare homegrown hit with his patriotic "Hashemi, Hashemi". His style owes as much to

Fairuz and the Rahbanis

The Arab world superstar **Fairuz** (Huhad Haddad) was born in 1934 to a Christian Maronite family in Beirut. While a teenager, the tender quality of her voice brought her to the attention of the newly founded Lebanese Radio Beirut, which she joined as a chorus singer. There, she soon became a leading solo singer, known for her interpretations of Classical Arab song. There,

to the orchestration, combining the piano, guitar, violin and acordion with the ney and Arab percussive instruments. They even created hybrids with tango and rumba, and produced an Arabised version of Mozart's 40th Symphony. No Arab composer before or since has been quite so innovative. But the trio's most remarkable achievements were the huge musical plays that they mounted together at the Baalbek Festivals – elaborate, operatic spectacles that drew heavily on the folk culture of rural Lebanon. Certainly the region has seen nothing on such a scale before or since, and these productions became a recognised showcase for other emerging Lebanese talent.

Two of the many faces of Fairuz

During the civil war, Fairuz's refusal to leave Beirut even during the worst of the conflict became a symbol of hope, and her first peacetime performance in the city was hailed as a landmark. She remains hugely popular with Lebanese diaspora communities all over the world, and she can fill any concert hall in Europe or the US, where there are Lebanese or Arab communities.

too, she met the bothers, **Asi** and **Mansour Rahbani**, struggling composers who at the time were earning their living as policemen. Fairuz and the two brothers (Fairuz and Asi married in 1954) worked together for the next thirty years. Asi composed the music; Mansour wrote the words – which in the early part of her career were largely nostalgic and romantic; Fairuz sung, sweeping all before her.

The Fairuz/Rahbani team was incredibly prolific and diverse. They reinterpreted Classical Arab song, bringing in Western and Eastern European styles (and keys)

Fairuz and Asi parted in the early 1980s (Asi died in 1986) but she has continued to work with Ziad, the son from their marriage, as her musical director. Their 1990s collaborations have brought a new, more adventurous direction to her career. **Ziad Rahbani** (born 1957) has pioneered his own particular brand of Arab Jazz, a distinctly Lebanese synthesis of East and West. He has also continued the family tradition of music and drama, scoring the music for several plays and films.

the Arabian Peninsula as to the Levant – though this is hardly surprising, as traditionally the Bedouin have moved throughout the region with scant regard for national boundaries.

Iraq

Iraq is the historic home of deep, Classical Arabic music, a cultural heritage that Iraqis are very

aware and proud of; indeed many of the most promising young players from all over the Middle East still come to study at the Baghdad Institute. In recent years, Iraq's musical profile was kept in view chiefly by the virtuoso oud player, **Munir Bashir** This master player did more than anyone else to champion Arabic classical music in Europe and the US, and in this respect it would be valid to compare him to Ravi Shankar. His

Munir Bashir

death in 1997 robbed the Arab world of a major figure.

Iraq has also produced a major contemporary star in popular Arab song – **Kazem al Saher**, who is lauded throughout the Arab world. However, he was forced to leave the country in the early 1990s, and remains in exile; when he tried to return recently, he was shot and wounded.

discography

Syria

Artists

Ensemble Al-Kindî

French-born Muslim Jalal Eddine heads up a brilliant ensemble in Syria, exploring Classical Arabic music in collaboration with the region's top singers.

⊚ **The Allepian Music Room – The Art of Classical Arab Singing** (Le Chant du Monde, France).

A lavish CD package, presented with photos that will make you want to jump on the next plane. Jalal Eddine and his ensemble accompany the dazzling Sabri Moudallal and Omar Sarmini in a selection of *wasla* (suites of songs and improvisations).

Sabah Fakhri

The Syrian master of traditional Arab song, Sabah began singing on Damascus Radio in the 1940s. He has made hundreds of recordings and is also notable for his place in *The Guinness Book of Records* – he once sang non-stop for 10 hours.

⊚ **Au Palais des Congrès** (Club du Disque Arabe, France).

Recorded live in 1978, this gives a good account of Sabah's masterful control of melody, which has enchanted the Arab world for decades.

Mayada el-Hennawy

The woman singer Mayada is the toast of Damascus' flashy post-civil-war night clubs.

⊚ **Bayent al-Hob Alaya** (EMI Arabia, Dubai).

This album (I declared my love to him) is Mayada's most popular release, and widely available around the world.

Nur Mahana

Nur Mahama is Damascus's king of good time pop. Though extremely popular in Syria, his cassettes can be tricky to find outside the country, and hard to identify if you don't read Arabic. Look out for the dapper, bank-manager-as-pop-star covers!

⊚ **Hafla Amreeka** (Various cassettes available).

This 'American Concert' recording shows Nur on fine form and includes most of his hits. It gives a good idea of what you can expect in Damascus's more upmarket nightclubs!

George Wasoof

Having flirted with a rough-hewn, George Michael image, Wasoof has gone MOR and is now firmly entrenched in the Cairo hit factory. He is perhaps rather less interesting for it, though still a voice to be reckoned with.

⊚ **Kalem al-Nas** (Relax In, Kuwait).

A recent, Cairo-recorded album but one that still retains some charming Syrian touches.

Lebanon

Artists

Rabih Abou-Khalil

Rabih Abou-Khalil is very much in the modern Lebanese tradition of East/West pick'n'mix. An inventive oud player, he has teamed up with an international band of jazz musicians to play his own compositions.

⊚ **The Sultan's Picnic** (Enja, Germany).

Rabih's compositons take the oud into previously uncharted territories here, and there's no doubting the calibre of musicianship on display.

Fairuz

Fairuz is the reigning queen of Arab song – the successor to Umm Kalthum. Her work harks back to the folk song of her native Lebanon and has touches of jazz and Western classical music thrown in, with intentional disregard for authenticity.

⊚ **Le Cristal de l'Orient** (Virgin Arabia, France).

A newly issued collection of early recordings, including some songs by Mohammed Abd el-Wahaab, that show a youthful Fairuz at the peak of her powers.

JAK KILBY

SYRIA, LEBANON & THE LEVANT

A B C D E F G H I J K L M N O P Q R

Kifak inta (Relax In, Kuwait).

This is one of Fairuz's jazz tinged projects with her son, Ziad. The new direction divided her traditional fans but the album remains a landmark in her career.

 The Legendary Fairuz (EMI Hemisphere, UK).

These live recordings from 1990s shows are ample proof that the great lady is still in good voice.

FAIRUZ AND SABAH

Dabke - Folk songs & Dances from Lebanon (Voix de l'Orient, Lebanon).

The contrast of Fairuz's plaintive voice, Sabah's throaty roar and the Rahbani Brothers spirited arrangements make this anthology of live performances required listening. There's probably no better introduction to Lebanese music.

Matar Muhammad

Matar (who died in 1995) was from Lebanon's small Gypsy community and played *buzuq* (Arab bazouki).

 Matar Muhammad – Hommage à un Maître du Buzuq (Inedit, France).

Recorded live in Beirut in 1972, this is a wonderful memorial to a rare talent – and one of very few solo *buzuq* recordings.

Ziad Rahbani

Opinion seems divided between those who feel that the scion of Fairuz and Asi Rahbani is a genius, and those who just think he's crazy combining jazz with Arab song.

 Houdou Nisbi (Relax In, Kuwait).

This music, from a play performed at the height of the Beirut conflict, is typical of Ziad's Arab-Jazz style.

Iraq

Artists

Fawzy al-Aiedy

Fawzy's highly individual compositions are delightfully dotty; Arab songs in the classical mould, with sundry European influences – from Ravel to cabaret – flying in from left field.

 Le Paris Bagdad (Buda, France).

Fawzy's quirky material is mixed here with a dignified rendition of the traditional muwashshah song, "Layali".

Munir Bashir

Bashir (who died in 1997) was an oud player, considered the supreme master of the Arab maqamat scale system.

Live in Paris (Harmonia Mundi, France).

This disc really launched Bashir on the international scene, and if you are going to only ever buy one oud CD, it is the one above all others to go for.

Kazem el Saher

Kazem el Saher is considered by many to be the best young singer in the Arab world. His virtuosic technique and easy style is wholly Iraqi, though his arrangements tend towards Egyptian synth pop.

 La Ya Sadiki (No, my friend) (Virgin Arabia, France).

In comparison to some of his more recent releases, this tour de force performance of "La Ya Sadiki" – clocking in at over 40 minutes – is a better reflection of Saher's true vocal talent.

Jordan

Compilations

 Bedouin Songs, Wedding Songs, Fisherman's Songs from Aqaba (Inedit, France).

This ethnological disc is not easy listening but it has intriguing textures which techno-samplers as well as those interested in the roots of Arab song might find inviting.

Artists

Omar Abdullat

Jordan's only home grown, household name, Abdullat is an admirable singer. His songs have a strong Bedouin flavour – reminiscent of the Gulf – laced with a typical Jordanian fusion of pan-Arab popular culture. It may be difficult to get his music other than on a cassette.

 Haan Waqt al-Safar (Al Zarabia, Jordan).

'The Time Has Come to Leave' is the title of this collection. It is at times quite roughly recorded but the Bedu spirit of this young singer shines through.

Turkey

sounds of anatolia

Outside the country, Turkish music is known mainly for its Mevlevi (Whirling) Dervishes and for laughably unsuccessful efforts in the Eurovision song contest. Yet it has been highly influential in the eastern Mediterranean, and the music is widely popular with the Turkish and Kurdish diaspora. **Martin Stokes** shows the way in to an enticing variety, from refined classical forms to commercial arabesk, from rural bards to wild Gypsy ensembles.

Turkish music is a battlefield. The state invested great efforts to construct a unitary national culture since the establishment of the modern Turkish republic in 1922 by Kemal Atatürk. Great stress was laid on Turkish ancestry in Central Asia and, conversely, on the cultural distance of Turkey from neighbouring Middle Eastern and Arab countries. It was an exercise that involved some far-fetched flights of historical imagination and the often brutal repression of rival claims to legitimacy within the Turkish state – particularly those associated with Kurdish nationalism (see p.378) or, to a lesser extent, Sufic Islam (whirling dervish sects).

Although privately an aficionado of Turkey's urban classical music, Atatürk and his ideologues deemed it too tainted by 'Arab' civilisation to carry the weight of national culture. "The capacity of a country to change is demonstrated by its ability to change its music", he once said, and he set about doing exactly that: he prohibited the circulation of Arabic language musical films, and initiated a process of collecting, archiving and recording orchestrated versions of exemplary folk musics from the Anatolian countryside, known as **halk music**. A generation of musicians was trained to propagate it, through the Turkish Radio and Television station (TRT) and elsewhere.

This policy ran aground. The classical art music genre known as **sanat** (or *klasik* – or just *Türk Musikisi*), associated with the cosmopolitan Ottoman cities of Istanbul, Izmir and Bursa, underwent a process of regeneration, culminating in the foundation of the State Conservatoire in Istanbul

Sufi musicians, early 20th century

COLLECTION CHRISTOPH WAGNER

in 1976, where Turkish classical musicians were given the same quality of training as the previously privileged folk musicians, and they gained an increasing share of radio and television airtime.

Then in the 1980s, the liberal President Turgut Özal deregulated the media. Pop, rock and *arabesk* (a supposedly Arab-inspired popular genre) began to fill the private FM radio stations, satellite and cable TV channels. The TRT made efforts to update their large orchestral formats, too. And at the more radical end of things, Kurdish-language folk music could for the first time be heard in public – even in cafés in Istanbul's entertainment districts, and purchased in recorded form.

So too could religious and Sufi music. In 1923, Mustafa Kemal Atatürk, the founder of the Turkish Republic, had closed the lodges of the **Sufi sects**, amongst them those of the **Mevlevi** order whose members had been great patrons of music across the Ottoman empire. Overnight, a widespread base of dynamic classical music was lost, and for many years the **Mevlevi ayin** (the main ritual musical form) was 'performed' in public only as a kind of tourist attraction in the home of the order, **Konya**, in Central Anatolia.

Under Özal's policies, which allowed Islam a public face in Turkey, the Mevlevi were significant beneficiaries. In Istanbul, they now perform to tourists and interested Turks in their newly-restored lodge at Galata, and even in the Byzantine cisterns in Sultanahmet.

Turkish Folk

Turkish folk music is domianted by the music of the **saz**, a long-necked lute with a varying number of strings, also known as the *bağlama*. It's played in a wide variety of styles and constitutes the old 'official' folk music of Turkey.

Saz Music and the TRT Sound

Large orchestras of the saz, heavily miked to boost the body of its sound, dominate the **TRT folk music style**. Performers associated with this and the urban popular folk music market may release up to two cassettes a year – often the same recordings heard on the radio, but with a few Western rock instruments grafted onto the commercial mix. These can be found in their hundreds in music shops and mobile street stalls. All bear the mark of **Belkis Akkale's** tremendously successful style of the mid-1980s; large, buzzing, busy saz orchestras,

driving rhythms, and a deep, soulful voice singing a *türkü* (folk song). Current exponents include **Güler Duman**. A slightly older generation, including charasmatic and highly talented musicians such as **İbrahim Can** (from the Black Sea) and **Nuray Hafiftaş** (from the Central Eastern area), record and appear on TV.

Played as a solo instrument accompanying the singing voice, the saz has an intricate, silvery tone, providing not just notes and rhythmic patterns, but an ambience; it's a partner in a complex dialogue with the singer. Listen to **Ali Ekber Çiçek**'s "Haydar Haydar", an old recording by a TRT musician, a complex and dramatic creation largely of his own inspiration, but anchored in the expressive techniques of the aşık and Alevi mysticism (see overleaf). It's hard to say whether the instrument is accompanying the voice, or vice versa. And then listen, for con-

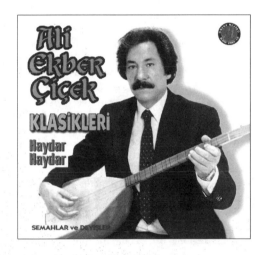

trast, to **Talip Özkan's** intricate and idiosyncratic solo style, embracing a variety of Anatolian tunings and plectrum techniques, but with each musical phrase embellished and nuanced to the utmost degree.

There are those who favour playing saz with a plectrum and those who play without (*selpe*), plus many regional styles (*tavir* – attitudes) of playing and tuning (*duzen* – orders). Some players strive to maintain the regional tavir, others support a national style. Though a simple instrument, the saz is capable of enormous variety.

Regional Folk

Despite the heavy colonisation of saz-based music by the TRT, many other varieties of folk music exist in Turkey today, recognisable largely by the instruments and the dances associated with them.

Outside the large cities in the west of Turkey, or in their squatter suburbs (*gecekondu*), one can hear the quintessential rural **Turkish ceremonial music** combination, the **zurna and davul** (the shawm and drum duo to be found in Turkey and the Balkans and as far afield as Central Asia and China) at almost any wedding or circumcision celebration, their enormous, unamplified volume indicating to all and sundry that something important is taking place.

Away from the city centres, any weekend, keep your ears open, follow the sound, and you will almost certainly find yourself the object of warm hospitality (language no barrier) and treated to a display of regional dance styles in somebody's house or backyard, or at wedding salons rented for the occasion (known as *düğünsalonu*).

In eastern areas of the country this will most usually be the stately chain dance known as the **halay** (arms linked or on shoulders); on the Aegean coast the macho **zeybek**, and elsewhere, and more or less everywhere, the **çifte telli** and **karşilama**, both dances for couples.

You will know if you are among **Black Sea Turks** or **Laz** people if you hear a small upright fiddle (*kemençe*), the bagpipe (*tulum*), or a smaller and shriller version of the zurna and davul. They will be dancing the **horon**, whose quick movements are said to imitate the wriggling of the *hamsi* – the anchovies that are such a conspicuous feature of their diet.

Most of Turkey's rural population (approximately half of the total) know, at least passively, these regional dances, and the music that goes with them. In **provincial cities**, the *elektrosaz* and *darbuka* (goblet drum) constitute the main proletarian musical fare for ceremonial occasions, and electric keyboards are now quite widespread.

Cassette recordings of all of these kinds of music can be picked up from roadside stalls and the stall-owners are usually well informed on the currently highly-rated, local musicians. Regional genres and instruments are well represented in this local cassette culture: look out for the music of the *sipsi* (a plaintive double reed instrument) in the southwest; the *mey* in the southeast (lower and more mellow than the sipsi, like the Armenian duduk); accordion music played by Circassian migrants in the northeast; and Gypsy music to the sound of darbuka, metal clarinet, violin and *çümbüş* (a metal-bodied lute) from the west.

All around the country there are contemporary musicians updating and re-inventing the local styles. Many of them are of only local interest, but others are making very fine music like the Laz *kemençe* player, **Birol Topaloğlu** from the Black Sea coast who has collected local songs and arranged them into a striking album.

Aşık Music

There are said to be twenty million **Alevis** in Turkey today (in a total Turkish population of 63 million), so it is little surprise that the best-known regional music is associated with the **aşık**, folk bards from these heterodox Muslim communities, originally from the central northeastern provinces of Sivas, Tunçeli, Çorum and Erzincan.

Aşık sing a repertory of songs of mystical quest, interspersed with invocation to the Alevi saints, and to Mohammed's brother-in-law, Ali, whom they regard as the rightful heir to the Prophet's spiritual tradition (this is the belief of the Shia Muslims, although they have different practices from the Arab or Iranian Shiites.).

Traditionally aşık favour the three-string saz for its symbolism of the trinity of Allah, Mohammed and Ali and they sing to the solo saz, which is virtually a sacred object to the Alevi, rich in spiritual significance. Many of the aşık's songs have words by or about **Pir Sultan Abdal**, an aşık martyr of the sixteenth century executed for his involvement with a rebellion against the Ottoman authorities. His birthplace, the village of Banaz near Sivas, is a place of pilgrimage.

Today's flourishing aşık revival was encouraged in the early 1970s by the opera singer **Ruhi Su**, a fine saz player. He was not an Alevi, but was forcefully left-wing and lost his job at the opera as a result. While the mainstream performers had to compromise he demonstrated another way. His albums sold in large numbers, and still do although they remain banned on state radio. Today's top names – **Arif Sağ**, **Yavuz Top**, **Musa Eroğlu** and **Muhlis Akarsu** – have made excellent recordings both as a group, **Muhabbet**, and solo. A fire in Sivas, started by orthodox Sunni extremists during an Alevi festival in 1993, killed several distinguished musicians, including Akarsu.

Aşık music has always had a political edge. **Ali İzzet** and **Mahsuni Şerif** brought out its latent political protest in songs which ranged from passionate denunciations of social and political injustice to gentle satires on Turkish football. They were lionised by the urban Turkish left in the late

1960s. **Feyzullah Çınar** is a slightly more recent representative of this tradition.

The politics of others has been more collaborative. **Aşık Veysel**, a blind troubador from Sivrialan, in the province of Sivas, is a household name in Turkey. His most famous songs, such as "Dostlar Beni Hatırlasın" (May My Friends remember Me), and "Uzun Ince Bir Yoldayim" (I'm on a Long and Difficult Journey) circulated widely around the country both in written and recorded form, and are still well known. In comparison to Şerif and İzzet, he sang a gentler poetry expressing humanistic sentiments. Like many Alevi he endorsed the secularist politics of the Turkish state, and participated heavily in the state's efforts to teach and disseminate Anatolian music in Anatolia. His fellow singer Aşık Ihsani, rigorous about his principles, said of Veysal "he was born one of us, but died one of them."

Aşık music is generally easy to identify, even to those unfamiliar with Turkish music. It is one of the few studio recorded genres featuring only the voice and the saz though there is a small number of experimental orchestral versions, notably by Yavuz Top and Arif Sağ. The saz is tuned differently, resulting in a particularly somber and intense sound, with complex chord patterns emerging from the shifting drones. Elsewhere, the instrument is tuned in open fifths, and played with more attention to flamboyant melodic lines.

Two exceptions are worth mentioning, one of which is music associated with Alevi communities in Western Anatolia, notably a form of free rhythm, semi-improvised declamation of scorching emotional intensity, somewhat akin to flamenco, and known as **bozlak**. The singer sings, literally, at the top of his voice, and the saz is tuned in the 'open fifths' manner, allowing for dramatic melodic flourishes, and a sparse, astringent sound. Perhaps the greatest exponent in recent years was **Neşet Ertaş**, from Kırşehir, a cult icon amongst folk music enthusiasts in Turkey and the son of **Muharrem Ertaş**, another bozlak singer of mythic reputation. **Ekrem Çelebi** is perhaps the best known of a younger generation of bozlak musicians, and an extraordinary virtuoso.

The aşık tradition takes on a second distinct form in the far northeast of the country, in the city of **Kars**. Here, the singers are considered to have fallen into a trance in which they receive gifts of musical and spiritual knowledge, and henceforth wander the countryside in search of their lovers, revealed to them by the prophet Elias.

They make their living as entertainers and storytellers in cafés of the cities of the northeast. Audiences particularly enjoy the ritualised exchange of insults, which follows a preordained rhyme and musical scheme. No detail of appearance or character is spared and the event ends when one musician is too tongue-tied to come up with a witty riposte, which, by the end, is often graphic sexual innuendo.

Few recordings of these events are available, even in Turkey, but contests can be observed every year in the Gülhane Park festival in Istanbul involving some of the very best performers, such as **Aşık Seref Taşlıova**. **Murat Çobanoğlu**, also from the area, is perhaps the most widely recorded of these musicians, and you can visit his aşık's cafe in Kars. Even if you can't follow the words, it is worth seeking these events out just to enjoy the sense of occasion, and the tears of laughter rolling down the cheeks of the listeners.

Aşık's still have a role in the regular **Alevi religious ceremony** (*cem*) which includes prayers, recitations, singing and culminates in a circular dance, the *semah*. Alevi music (and the whole orientation of the sect) is far more rural and folk-like than the more classical, high art Mevlevi. It's possible to attend cem services at the Şahkulu Sultan (Merdivenköy) and Karacaahmet Sultan (Üsküdar) mosques in Istanbul on Sundays and Alevi holidays. Recently several cafés featuring singers with saz or a small band have appeared in Istanbul, off İstiklal Cadessi in Beyoğlu, notably the *Jasmine Café Bar* in Arkası Akarsu sok. and others in Hasnun Galip sok.

Classical Traditions

Urban Turkish musics divide into three genres: **religious** (*sema*), **classical** (*klasik* or *sanat*), and **nightclub** (*fasıl*). Definitions are, of course, not watertight, and they have overlapping repertories of song and instruments (urban and Middle Eastern instruments quite different from those found in the countryside), and share the compositional rules known as *makam*.

The **makam** are musical modes or scales (with associated rules governing melodic flow and prominent notes) in which the musicians compose their songs and instrumental pieces and, more importantly, weave their **taksim** (improvisations) which are central to classical music performance. The makam currently practised in Turkey have a lot in common with those of the Arab world; the Iranian *dastgah* are more distantly related.

The Tradition

The taksim improvisation usually precedes, and also punctuates, long suites of music which begin with an instrumental prelude (*peşrev*), end with a postlude (*saz semaisi*), and consist mainly of songs, known as **şarkı**. Most of those sung today date from the late nineteenth century, and the time of one of the great songwriters, **Haci Arif Bey**. Some are much earlier, though. The tradition dates back at least to the fourteenth century and its theoretical base took shape at the end of the seventeenth century, when a Romanian princely enthusiast, **Demetrius Cantemir**, was resident in Istanbul and began to notate it.

These classical genres are, essentially, chamber genres, where the instruments play as a loose collection of soloists, each taking turns at improvising taksim, and each elaborating the melodic and rhythmic line as they see fit. Songs and instrumental numbers thus differ greatly from performance to performance.

Typical **instruments** are the *ud* (lute), the *ney* (end-blown flute), the *tanbur* (long-necked lute, with frets), the *kanun* (a zither, played on the knees), and *klarnet* (a metal clarinet appropriated from military bands at the end of the nineteenth century). *Usul* (rhythm) is provided by the *def* (a frame drum, sometimes with small cymbals attached, as on a tambourine) or the *darbuka* (the omnipresent goblet drum). Many famous virtuosi are associated with particular instruments, and recordings of them can be found easily: **Tanburi Cemil Bey** (1871-1916) and **Necdet Yaşar** (born 1930) on the tanbur; **Yorgo Bacanos** (1900-1977) and **Udi Hrant** (1901-1978) on the ud; **Şükrü Tunar** (1907-1962) on the klarnet; **Ahmet Meter** aka Halil Karaduman (born 1959) on the kanun.

Many instrumentalists and composers inhabit the world of professional **secular music** making, whose association with the profanities of drink and dance led this music to become the preserve of Istanbul's **Armenian, Greek and Jewish minorities**, and others, notably **Gypsies**, who could operate comfortably outside bourgeois Muslim respectability. A list of Armenian, Greek and Jewish musicians would include a very large proportion of all significant names in the Turkish

musical world of the nineteenth and early twentieth century. It would be hard to imagine the contemporary classical repertoire without the work of **Tatyos Efendi** (1863-1913) or **Lavtaci Andon**, or the extraordinary contributions to contemporary instrumental performance styles of **Udi Hrant** or **Şükrü Tunar**.

Classical Stars

The theory and history of classical Turkish music is taught in private conservatoires, of which perhaps the most highly esteemed is the **Üsküdar Musiki Cemiyeti** in Istanbul. There are others in most major cities and musicians gather there to socialise or give regular public concerts. Many, if not all, of the top echelon of recording artists are conservatoire-trained, and singers, too, tend to have at least passing connections with the conservatoires.

The voice lies at the heart of all classical genres. Since the time of **Münir Nurettin Selçuk** (1900-1981), 'the Turkish Umm Kalthum', singers have assumed most of the trappings of the Western star system. Münir Nurettin Selçuk was the first solo artist to stand up at the front of the stage, with the other instrumentalists reduced to a backing role. He is now undergoing a major nostalgic re-appropriation by the Turkish intelligentsia, after being somewhat forgotten. A dashing figure, his exquisite bel canto style was the perfect complement to his dandified Western dress sense.

Zeki Müren, perhaps the highest-rated vocalist in the latter half of this century, studied with Refik Fersan and Şerif İçli, and worked extensively with the composer **Müzaffer Özpınar**, who, in turn, was trained at the Eminönü conservatoire. Müren made his name with versions of Egyptian and Lebanese musicals, and with performances in Istanbul's burgeoning gazino clubs in the 1970s. He made a decisive turn to arabesk (see p.403) with "Kahır Mektubu" in the early 1980s, but throughout his career turned out austerely classical recordings.

Bülent Ersoy, Turkey's most famous transsexual, studied with **Müzeyyen Sennar**. She continues to produce songs in a restrained classical idiom: her recent *Orkide* recordings are particularly fine examples, following on from her reinterpretation of the turn-of-the-century repertoire in a striking recording, *Alaturka 95*. This caused outrage to devout Muslims in Turkey for the inclusion of a real call to prayer on the opening track sung by Bülent herself – the association of religion with this outrageous figure was too much for some.

Recordings of classical songs often add lavish accompaniments, often heavily harmonised, and with the metallic ticking of drum machines replacing the lively rattle of the darbuka. **Metin Milli** and **Zekai Tunca** pioneered this style in the 1980s; more recent exponents include **Mustafa Keser**, whose crooning, silky style also takes in songs from the arabesk and folk repertoire, and **Ebru Gündeş**.

Mevlevi: Whirling Dervishes

Classical religious music is almost the exclusive preserve of the **Mevlevi (whirling) dervishes**. Whilst the order has no official existence, public performances are put on, as indeed they were in Ottoman times, for foreign observers in Konya, and at the Galata lodge in Istanbul.

Mevlevi performances consist of long **ayin** – complex yet delicate compositions. They are preceded and followed by instrumental and vocal pieces with words from the thirteenth-century Sufi poet **Jelaleddin Rumi (Mevlana)**, the order's founder, and interspersed with taksim, particularly on the *ney,* the end-blown flute.

Major musicians associated with the Mevlevi order, notably **Kudsi Ergüner** (born 1952) and **Necdet Yaşar** (born 1930), record outside Turkey, and their CDs reflect Western interests in Sufi and Ottoman high culture more than popular religious expression in Turkey. Versions of the Mevlevi repertory can be heard at the lodge of the Halveti-Cerahi sect, with a heavier emphasis on the practice of *zikr*, a trance-inducing repetition of various of the ninety nine names of God, and the collective singing of *ilahi* (hymns). This practice has been freed from the censorship of earlier years but is still somewhat clandestine, although one of the greatest Halveti-Cerahi sheikhs, **Müzaffer Ozak** made a superb recording of Mevlevi ayin with **Kudsi Ergüner** in the late 1970s.

Gypsies and Fasıl Music

As so often, **Gypsies** (Roma, or Roman as they are called in Turkish) are an important presence on the music scene, and they are responsible for some of Turkey's most thrilling sounds – a music often referrred to as **fasıl**.

This has sleazy associations with **gazino nightclubs** and **belly dancing** but it is also performed in more respectable restaurants. Down market *gazinos* can be found anywhere, particularly around Beyoğlu, in Istanbul. Their seedy reputation has changed in recent years as a result of the Islamist municipality's efforts to 'tidy up' Istanbul but it is still best to stick to the clubs around Istiklal Caddesi. The renovated Çicek Pasajı and the clubs around it are well worth a visit. Here, the music incorporates recent songs, and makes less effort to stick to classical formula. This is, after all, music to drink and dance to.

Though many areas of nightclub repertory overlap with what you might hear in a radio concert, or in the conservatoire, this is a very different kind of music. The classical values of precision and dutiful respect to past times are replaced by a demonstrative, present tense music. The klarnet and darbuka dominate and many if not all of the most noted instrumentalists are Gypsies from nearby Tarlabası. They play with great skill and passion. Tunes are tossed around with breathless ease, long notes are held on the klarnet for extended yet exquisitely poised moments during improvisation, kanun and violin decorate and interrupt; noise and gestural energy flow across the musical event like a torrent, carrying all before it. Violinists spice the music up with lightning fast glissandos that swoop and squeak, and clarinettists favour the low G-clarinet which has a really throaty sound that gives this music its special character.

Perhaps the most famous of all fasıl musicians is the clarinettist, **Mustafa Kandıralı** (born 1930), the so-called 'Benny Goodman of Turkey'. He worked

Amongst the Dervishes

I'm sitting amongst eighty or so dervishes in a small, hidden mosque in Istanbul as they begin to lean forward together rhythmically and chant the name of Allah. It's one of the most powerful sounds I've heard and speeds up like an express train to paradise. There's a violin weaving through the sonic picture and a *kanun* (zither) doing runs that send chills down your spine. Out of nowhere comes a solo voice – similar to the muezzin's call from the minarets – that is so full of longing it breaks your heart open. This is serious blues music.

Just when you think you can't take any more, twelve dervishes file into the room and take off their black cloaks – they're wearing white robes underneath – and in unison they start spinning with incredible lightness and grace. This angelic whirling is a perfect counterpoint to the earthy chanting. As a spectacle photographs can't prepare you for the disorienting feeling that the dervishes are defying gravity. It takes months of training before you learn not to get dizzy. Like much of Sufism, the performance works on different levels and is heavy with symbolism. The funereal black cloak is a tomb which the dervishes cast off with all worldly ties. They spin with their right arms extended to heaven and the left to the floor – grace is received from Allah and distributed to humanity. The dancers themselves represent the heavenly bodies circling the sun, personified by the Sheikh, the spiritual leader.

The Sheikh of this gathering possessed a quiet authority and many have stories about them which suggest highly developed psychic powers. After the ceremony, the translator I was with looked shocked and refused to continue translating. Later he told me that the Sheikh had quoted a poem from the fifteenth century which was in detail what he had dreamed about the previous night.

The ceremony is called a *zikr*, which simply means 'remembrance' and the ceremony is not about entertainment or aesthetics, but about spiritual purification and reconnection to the divine. Officially, the zikr is illegal in Turkey. The Sufi sects were suppressed by Atatürk in his creation of a secular state. But the dervishes are also mistrusted by the fundamentalists, as they don't toe the strictest Islamic line – in their use of music for one thing – and appeal to many artists, intellectuals and bohemian types.

There are some dervish performances, however, which are legal and can be seen easily. The largest of them is the celebration of the death of **Jelaleddin Rumi**, the founder of the Mevlani sect, who called the night of his death (December 17th) his wedding night; this takes place every year in sub-zero temperatures in Konya. But none of the zikrs had the beauty of the one in Istanbul. I asked the Sheikh there for the meaning of the ceremony and he said "The purpose of life is to remember Allah. Every electron and proton is whirling round a nucleus, the planets whirl about the sun – and all of them are chanting for Allah. Even your heartbeat – and here he thumped his chest – is chanting All-lah, All-lah".

Peter Culshaw

Whirling Dervishes

for the TRT and has recorded widely. No fasıl player approaches his knowledge of the repertoire and fiery improvisations which wring every possible tonal nuance. Other celebrated Gypsy musicians include the **Erköse brothers** (clarinettist Barbos Erköse is still performing), violinist **Kemani Cemal** and **Burhan Öçal**, renowned for his epic darbuka solos. There's more of the wider concept of Roma music in the Gypsy music article on p.146.

Burham Öçal's Istanbul Oriental Ensemble

Arabesk and Pop

Arabesk – Turkey's dominant popular music – draws on folk, classical and fasıl traditions, though it takes its name from its predominantly Arabic rather than Turkish melodies. Turkish nationalists made strenuous efforts to exclude Turkey's 'Arab' history and cultural links, but for most people Arabesk is simply Turkish music in its most basic and appealing form.

Arabesk is a working class and to an extent outsiders' music which addresses everyday realities and the problems of the *garihan*, the poor and oppressed. Its CDs and cassettes outsell any other genre by far – a star name will reckon on selling a million cassettes in a year – and fill a good half of any street stall. If you visit Turkey, look out for concerts and festivals, like the one held in Istanbul's Gülhane Park on a weekend in late August; it attracts artists like Ferdi Tayfur or Müslüm Gürses and crowds of up to 80,000 from some of Istanbul's poorest suburbs. Alternatively, just keep your ears open in taxis, or buses: you'll be listening to arabesk.

Oriyental Roots

Arabesk has its roots in Egyptian 'Oriental' dance music – **Raks Şarkı**, or **Oriyental**, often misleadingly known as 'belly dancing' music – which has been of enduring popularity in Turkey. It was introduced in the 1940s by **Haydar Tatlıyay** (1890-1963), who had worked in Egyptian groups, and returning to Turkey set up a large dance orchestra as used in Egyptian film. When the Turkish state attempted to ban Arabic language music and film in 1948, and began in earnest to establish a national alternative through the TRT, people voted with their radio dials, tuning to Radio Cairo.

Turkey's nascent recording and film industry subsequently invested heavily in recording versions of Egyptian hits, particularly those associated with Mohammed Abd el-wahaab and Umm Kalthum and later the Lebanese star Farid al-Attrash. **Zeki Müren** and **Münir Nurettin Selçuk** made their names, initially as film stars, in this way in the 1940s and '50s, singing, in front of large string-based orchestras, dramatic solo vocals of unrequited love.

Arabesk is not simply derivative Egyptian music, however, and from the 1940s its songs addressed specifically Turkish problems such as rural–urban migration. Many popular films, particularly those of Baha Gelenbe, began to deal with themes of rural life, accompanied by rural music, and urbanised rural genres began to appear in the cities and on record. **Dıyarbakırlı Celal Güzelses** and **Malatyalı Fahri Kayahan** were amongst the earliest to record popularised folk-based forms for an urban audience, drawing heavily on the musical styles and repertories of the southeast.

Ahmet Sezgin took this one step further, bringing urban and rural styles into a creative mix in the mid-1960s. Recordings from this period illustrate the enduring Turkish fascination with the art of vocal improvisation, or **gazel**. Singers such as **Hafız Burhan Sesiyılmaz** and **Abdullah Yüce**, both with electrifying voices, did much to popularise the genre, which otherwise did not find much favour amongst the reformist intelligentsia.

Arabesk Goes Big Time

In the 1960s Turks bought into Anglo-American rock music, and some singers adopted elements into their music. The first figure of interest to do so was **Orhan Gencebay**, born in 1944 on the Black Sea coast, who began his career with Ahmet Sezgin. His first solo recording, "Bir Teselli Ver" (1969) related to the classical form, but the sobbing intensity of the voice owed much to the gazel, and frank lyrics addressed the plight of the lonely lover – a far cry from the heavy metaphors and archaic language of the classical song style. A more eclectic set of references, including rock and flamenco, was in evidence by his 1975 album *Batsın Bu Dünya*, and a creative and playful eclecticism has marked his career to date. He is also a top saz player and a leading film actor.

Despite Gencebay's colossal status, it is the voice which defines Arabesk aesthetics, and those of **İbrahim Tatlıses**, **Müslüm Gürses** and **Ferdi Tayfur** – again, these are also film actors – are the most significant. Their songs tell of self-pity and humiliation in the big city, experiences close to most Turkish hearts. Another noted Arabesk singer and actor, **İbrahim Tatlıses**, himself migrated from the impoverished southeastern town of Urfa, and many of his films and song-texts allude to his story. He was a huge star in the mid- to late-1980s, with a series of albums featuring well-drilled orchestras, danceable tunes and his electrifying voice, heard to best effect in the rural *uzun hava* (long, semi improvised pieces, accompanied by a solo saz) that have an almost ritual place on every cassette. Ferdi Tayfur's voice also has strong resonances with southeastern vocal styles, and his reputation, like that of Tatlıses', rests heavily on his portrayal of a poor villager made good in the big city. Müslüm Gürses is still adored by his fans mainly for his older hits, mournful, fate-obsessed numbers inviting the listener to light another cigarette ("Bir Sigara Yak"), to pour another glass ("Bir Kadeh Daha Ver"), and to curse the world ("Yeter Allahım").

Arabesk was legitimised by Özal's government, as part of a general back-tracking on the republican political tradition, and many Arabesk stars were quick to take advantage. Private FM radio and TV gave the music a new lease of life, and it is now possible to see classic Arabesk films from the 1970s on a more or less daily basis. Some younger stars are getting a look in, too. Sales of **Mahsun Kırmızıgül**'s "Tam 12'den" almost doubled those of İbrahim Tatlıses's "Klasikler" in 1995. Singers with classical backgrounds, notably **Bülent Ersoy**, **Muazzez Abacı**, **Nese Karaböçek** and most recently **Muazzez Ersoy** and **Yilmaz Morgül** continue to drift in and out of Arabesk. Many in Turkey assumed that with legitimacy and patronage in high circles, Arabesk would disappear. But, if anything, the reverse is the case. Arabesk shows absolutely no signs of going away.

Rock, Pop and Özgün

Rock and **pop** have leapt to enormous prominence since 1990, as part of the liberal revolution that has transformed Istanbul and Ankara. But they had long been influential. Turks have always made versions of 'international' genres: Tango was enormously popular from the 1930s to '50s; French *chanson* (Jacques Brel had huge influence in Turkey) had Turkish exponents such as blonde bombshell **Ajda Pekkan** (who still performs); and Elvis Presley spawned a wave of imitators in the late 1950s, most notably **Erol Büyükbürç**.

Somewhat away from the mainstream, a number of musicians began to try to reconcile Anatolian folk and Western rock. Most of these musicians were from the bourgeoisie, and despite the phenomenal difficulties involved in procuring instruments and recording, an Anadolu (Anatolian) Rock movement gathered pace. The music was banned from the official media, and became increasingly politicised. When the generals took over in 1980, most of the groups promptly disbanded, and **Cem Karaca** – who had worked with nearly every significant Anadolu rock band – fled to Germany, returning only in 1987.

Cem Karaca was and is the most interesting voice of the genre, combining rock histrionics with a cultivated art music bel canto; live, his voice sounds capable of filling an entire auditorium with or without amplification. His songs combined a taste for highbrow literature with social realism – Dervisan's *Safinaz*, recorded in 1979, was a kind of rock opera about a poor girl's struggle with honour and blood feuds. He has also superbly recorded the poetry of Nazım Hikmet (who died in exile in the Soviet Union) and Orhan Veli. Today, he performs in small clubs in Beyoğlu, with his old accomplice Uğur Dikmen at the keyboards.

Karaca's political reputation, for many, was undermined by his accommodation with Özal's regime, and he doesn't command the attention he once did. However, the group **Moğollar**, formed and reformed under his direction, have kept a political edge very much to the fore, alongside an up-tempo stadium rock style. Others who have kept a counter-culture tag include **Yeni Türkü** and **Bulutsuzluk Özlemi** (longing for blue skies). Yeni Türkü, inspired by the Latin American New Song movement, were one of the first groups to use traditional Turkish instruments in rock, and enjoyed great popularity amongst the intelligentsia towards the end of the 1980s for their versions of old Istanbul songs and Greek rembetika numbers. **Zen**, another band drawing on indigenous styles and instruments, as well as technological bric-à-brac and avant-garde theatre, are interesting, too.

Other established groups, worth checking out on cassette or CDs include **Erkin Koray**, **MFÖ** (one of the few to survive the generals), **Okay Temiz**, **Edip Akbayram**, and **Barış Manço**.

In the mid-1980s, there was a radical impulse connected with mainstream Arabesk which combined rural melodic forms with guitar-based harmonies and an intimate, mellow vocal style, dubbed **özgün** (original) music. The austere figure of **Zülfü Livaneli** – best-known outside Turkey for his work with Greek composer Mikis Theodorakis and singer Maria Farandouri for the music to Yılmaz Güney's film *Yol* – dominated the genre. As befitted the time, the lyrics were politically cautious, but the Kurdish-born **Ahmet Kaya**'s renditions of the work of banned leftist poet Nazım Hikmet had enormous resonance amongst the Turkish left. The gentle, literary lyricism of Kaya's thoughtful and social-realistic love songs, however, was not enough to sustain the genre and, despite some quite popular Kurdish practitioners, notably **Hasan Hüseyin Demirel** and **Umut Altınçag**, özgün has practically disappeared from circulation.

Turkish pop, on the other hand, is resolutely mainstream. At the heart of Turkey's indigenous pop music is one figure: **Sezen Aksu**. She trained as an art music singer in her native Izmir and her current prominence owes much to her partnership with the late **Onno Tunç**, an Armenian church musician who embraced soul and jazz in the 1960s, and had the challenging task of overseeing Turkey's Eurovision song contest entries in the 1980s. Aksu's soulful voice, owing much to traditional Turkish urban music, and Tunç's eliptical arrangements and keyboard-based harmonic style, made for a winning combination.

Aksu is also a political figure, embracing concerns and campaigns, including Bosnia, feminism, ecology and human rights, and particularly the plight of the Cumartesi Anneleri, 'Saturday Mothers' – a Turkish women's protest against the refusal of the judiciary to investigate the 'disappearance' of their sons. Her CDs anticipate the political zeitgeist, and each one, in recent years, has been a national media event. When *Işık Doğudan Yükselir /Ex Oriente Lux* came out in 1995, evoking the cultural mosaic of Anatolia in gentle feminist terms, at a time of intercommunal religious rioting in Istanbul and the worsening crisis in the southeast of the country, the album's release was the first item on the TRT's evening news programme. On the disc, Aksu brought her idiosyncratic vocal style to bear on regional songs, popular urban dance genres and the religious repertoire. Her recent album, *Düğün ve Cenaze*, is a collaboration with Bosnian Serb musician Goran Bregovic, reworking popular tunes currently circulating around the Balkans.

Aksu's 'students' dominated the pop scene at the end of the 1980s and early 1990s. **Levent Yüksel**, a multitalented instrumentalist and singer, has produced carefully crafted CDs which connect quite explicitly with indigenous Turkish traditions and Turkish literature. More recently the singer **Candan Erçetin** has drawn on a wide range of Anatolian, Balkan and Mediterranean styles.

In recent years, a newer genre of pop has come to the fore, with driving rhythms and a melodic style that is, if anything, close to arabesk, but with an attitude of hedonism. **Mirkelam**, **Tarkan**, **Rafet el Roman**, and **Mustafa Sandal** produce energetic and danceable music in this idiom, while **Volkan Konak** has come up with an engaging hybrid for the Black Sea community in Istanbul.

Rapping in Germany

The music of the large Turkish diaspora in Germany erupted in Turkey itself with rap group, **Cartel**'s 1995 CD. Cartel's lyrics explicitly equate the Turkish and Black American ghetto experiences, sampling Anatolian sounds (saz, zurna and davul), parading the Turkish flag, and appropriating the hyper-macho posturing of their US models. They rap in Turkish, German, Spanish and English and are a multicultural group, though their message is very clear: that Turks in Germany should unite (a hand of brotherhood is extended to Kurds, Circassians and Laz) against German racism. Cartel galvanised debate in Turkey and received, disturbingly, a warm welcome from Turkish fascists on their Istanbul debut.

Other Turkish-German rappers, for example the Frankfurt based **DJ Mahmut**, **DJ Volkan** and **KMR**, pursue a style which is simultaneously mellow and avant-garde, mixing German and Turkish in complex lyrics which are more about urban dislocation than racial conflict. **Aziza-A**, based in Berlin, raps on feminist issues. Arguments will continue to rage about what is and what is not Turkish, and what is and what is not 'mere' imitation; what is appropriately 'political' and what is not. Turkish rap poses the question in stark terms, but also indicates the inventive dynamism that is going to take this music into the next century, and beyond.

With thanks to Ferhat Boratav

discography

In Turkey the leading label for folk and classical recordings is Kalan (İMÇ 6. Blok No. 6608, Unkapanı, Istanbul) who release an unrivalled range of archive recordings of classical instrumentalists, contemporary folk and popular singers, aşık bards and the music of minority groups in Turkey. Outside Turkey, Traditional Crossroads (PO Box 20320 Greeley Sqare Station, New York, NY 10001-9992 USA) has an excellent catalogue of archive and contemporary recordings. One of the best record shops in Istanbul is Lale Plak, Tünel, Galipded Caddesi No.1, 80050 Beyoğlu, Istanbul (☎(90) 212 293 7739).

Folk and Aşıks

Compilations

🔊 Gaziantep Türküleri (Kalan, Turkey).

An idiomatic collection of songs and instrumental music from the Gaziantep region of south Turkey performed by local musicians on vocals, saz, zurna and davul.

🔊 Music and Throat Playing of the Yörük in Anatolia (Kalan, Turkey).

Kalan have several discs of minority groups in Turkey (another features the *Pomak* Bulgarian Muslims) and this is a fine example of the music of the pastoral Yörük people of the Taurus mountains. Beautiful string instruments and flutes, songs to the animals and throat playing (a custom peculiar to the Yörük) with the fingers on the throat to change the note while singing. Some extraordinary instrumental sounds. Notes in English, a rarity on a Kalan recording.

🔊 Saz (Kalan, Turkey).

A compilation tracing examples of the various types of saz from Central Asia to Turkey and beyond to Greece. The Uzbek dutar, Tadjik tambur, Kyrgyz komuz, Kazakh dombra, Iranian tanbur, Azeri saz, various Turkish varieties including Ali Ekber Çiçek playing "Haydar" on the big divan saz. A useful and listenable survey with photos and a few notes in English.

🔊 Song Creators in Eastern Turkey (Smithsonian Folkways, US).

Four aşıks from Kars and Erzurum in north eastern Turkey recorded in aşıks cafés in the early 1990s. Excellent notes about the singers, tradition and repertoire, with translations.

🔊 Turkey: Anatolian Village Music (VDE-Gallo/AIMP, Switzerland).

A good selection of field recordings – music from village festivals, 'personal repertoire' and women's music. Includes zurna and davul, a horon dance on the kemençe from the Black Sea, several uzun hava, an aşık's song, lullabies and love songs. Great notes and photos.

💿 Turkish Village Music (Nonesuch/Explorer, US).

There are plenty of field recordings of Turkish rural musics, but this is the best, recorded by ethnomusicologist Laxmi Tewari in two villages in North West Turkey. The aşıks' songs are heart rending, and represent the repertoire as heard and performed in villages – a long way away from the TRT's idea of what it should sound like. The disc also contains good examples of zurna and davul.

🔊 Turquie: Aşık (Inédit, France).

This is probably the best introduction to aşık music, featuring three singers including the celebrated Ali Ekber Çiçek and one of the few female aşıks Nuray Hafiftaş plus a spectacular saz solo from Arif Sağ. Good notes and translations.

🔊 Turquie: Musiques des Yayla (Ocora, France).

Jerome Cler's excellent recordings from a mountain village in the south west of the country. Instrumental dance tunes on various types of saz and violin predominate, ranging from the sprightly "teke zortlatması", representing the skipping of mountain goats, to the ponderous and macho "zeybek".

Artists

Belkis Akkale

Akkale is a TRT (Turkish Radio) vocal artist specialising in the Alevi repertory, though she is not herself from this community. She set the agenda for an entire decade of popular folk music recording in the 1980s with "Türkü Türkü Türkiyem", and a style characterised by an earthy voice, and driving saz rhythms.

Güvercin (Raks/Midas, Turkey).

This 1986 recording contains perfect examples of her renditions of the popularised Alevi repertory, poised, grave, and passionate in tone. Note the brief excursion to Azerbaijan in "Bu Gala Dasli Gala", characterised by a 6/8 rhythm unusual in western or central Anatolia.

İbrahim Can

Born in Besikdüz, Trabzon, Can (pronounced Djan) is one of the younger TRT singers who has done most to render the folk genre meaningful to contemporary listeners. He studied at Trabzon Lycée, and was recruited into the Istanbul TRT in the early 1980s, since when he has established himself as a major recording artist, specialising in the music of the Black Sea area.

Bir Avuç Türkü (Coskun Plak, Turkey).

His efforts to reconcile the kemençe of his native Black Sea music, rock and mainstream Turkish popular music on this 1996 recording are utterly compelling.

Ali Ekber Çiçek

Çiçek is an aşık from Erzincan in eastern Turkey, famed for his singing and saz playing.

Haydar Haydar (Mega Müzik, Turkey).

A collection of classic songs. Haydar is the name given to Ali meaning the 'lion of God'.

Neşet Ertaş

Son of bozlak genius, Muharrem Ertaş, Neşet, resident in Germany, set down his own hat with some haunting compositions and passionate bozlak improvisations. The street language and blunt emotional style of arabesk is never far away (he directly addresses German migrant experience). He has always been held at some distance from the state's media machine, but versions of his songs have been recorded by an astonishing number of singers.

Kova Kova Indirdiler Yazıya (Raks/Müziksan, Turkey).

The title song on the second side is one of a number of classics on this recording. Three vocal improvisations (two uzun hava and a bozlak) take the rural genre to extremes. The rural Turkish expression for singing is 'to burn', and this recording leaves one in no doubt as to why.

Erkan Oğur

Vocalist, guitarist and saz player Oğur grew up in eastern Turkey and listened to the local aşıks as well as Jimi Hendrix on the radio. He studied ud before building himself a fretless guitar and working in the rock and folk scene.

Gülün Kokusu Vardi (Kalan, Turkey).

A delicate and rather aescetic disc of traditional songs from all over Turkey with fellow singer and instrumentalist İsmail H. Demircioğlu and other guest musicians. Exquisite instrumental playing and good listening even if you don't understand the lyrics (which are not translated). The title track ('The Rose had a Smell') regrets the lost riches of tradition.

Talip Özkan

Born in 1939 in southwest Turkey, Özkan worked for many years at TRT before settling in France. He is not a traditional musician, but an intellectual and fine player who's mastered many of Turkey's different types of saz.

L'art vivant de Talip Özkan (Ocora, France).

Eight great tracks covering different regional styles and instruments from the large *divan saz* to the small *cura bağlama*.

Bayram Bilge Toker

Toke is a singer and saz player from Yozgat province in central Anatolia.

Bayram: Turkish Folk Songs and Sufi Melodies (Music of the World, US).

A strong collection of türkü folksongs, improvisations, dances and Sufi ritual songs like "Haydar, Haydar". Idiomatically performed.

Birol Topaloğlu

Born in Rize on the Black Sea in 1965, Topaloğlu is an engineer who had no formal musical training, but learned kemençe, the local instrument.

Lazuri Birabape Heyamo (Kalan, Turkey).

A very listenable album of vocalists from the Black Sea Laz minority, Topaloğlu on kemençe and musicians from the popular Grup Yorum. The title track is a well-known work song and sounds like it could be Bulgarian in this arrangement.

Aşik Veysel

The paradigmatic Turkish aşık, who was born in Sivrialan, Sivas, in 1894 and died there in 1974. Veysel, blind from birth, became a national institution, and was awarded a pension for his services to the state in 1965. His songs, mystical contemplations on the human condition, are thus known throughout Turkey.

Voyages d'Alain Gheerbrant en Anatolie (Ocora, France).

Veysel recorded widely, and studio-recorded cassettes of his music, simply called 'Aşık Veysel' can be found on street cassette stalls almost anywhere. These field recordings, made by French musicologist Alain Gheerbrant who travelled with him in 1957, are a chance to hear him in a more natural setting, and include one of his emblematic songs "Bülbül" (The Nightingale).

Classical/Religious Music

Compilations

The Bektashi Breaths (Cemre, Turkey).

The Bektashi are a Turkish sect with musical rituals and dances in which the hymns are called *nefes*, breaths. This is an extraordinarily powerful disc which exudes a real ritual solemnity and power. The melodies sigh expressively with an ensemble of ney, kemençe, kanun, ud, cello and drum.

Istanbul 1925 (Traditional Crossroads, US).

Despite the title, this covers the early years of the Turkish recording industry up to the 1950s. It features excellent examples of popular classical instrumentalists, (Udi Hrant,

ISTANBUL 1925

Classic Recordings from the Middle East made from the Original Metal Parts

Şükrü Tunar) and the precursors of arabesk (Mahmut Celallettin, Kemani Haydar Taltlıyay).

🔘 **Gönül Telimizi Titreyenler** (Coskun Plak, Turkey).

A compilation from the old Turkish-HMV catalogue, working from early recordings by one of the first female vocalists, Safiye Ayla to pre-Arabesk club stars of the 1950s and '60s, notably Zeki Müren, Münir Nurettin Selçuk and Suat Sayın.

🔘 **Mevlana** (EMI Hemisphere, UK).

A good example of the classical music for the Sufi Mevlevi ceremony re-issued from Turkish Kent recordings. Four hymns in different makams featuring an introductory taksim improvisation on ney (played by Suleyman Ergüner), a selam with soloist Nizeh Uzel, and preludes and postludes for an ensemble of ney, rebab, tanbur, kemençe and drum.

🔘 **Women of Istanbul** (Traditional Crossroads, US).

A companion selection to Istanbul 1925 featuring an archival collection of the greatest female singers from the golden era of cabaret-style nightclubs from 1920 to the mid-'40s. Excellent notes and photos.

Artists

Kudsi Ergüner

Ergüner was born in Istanbul in 1952 and is one of the leading Turkish ney players, from a long family tradition. He learnt from his father Ulvi, who was music director at Radio Istanbul for many years. He settled in Paris in 1975.

🔘 **Dervisches Tourneurs de Turquie** (Arion, France).

A serious recording of the music of the Mevlevi (Whirling) Dervishes, a genre with which Ergüner is closely associated. With the voice of the now deceased Sheikh of the Halveti order, Muzaffer Ozak. The recording covers the ceremony as a whole, including parts other recordings often miss out, such as the opening recitation in praise of the prophet (the Na'at-i Mevlana), the entire sequence of vocal sections (the *selams*), and the recitation of the Koran.

📀 **The Works of Tatyos Efendi**
(Traditional Crossroads, US).

One of the best discs available of classical Ottoman music. Music by Armenian composer and violinist to the Sultan,

Kemani Tatyos Efendi (1863-1913). With an ensemble of ney, violin, kanun, clarinet, ud, tanbur and drum, this disc includes Tatyos' complete instrumental music, while a second volume includes his sarkı songs.

Bülent Ersoy

Singer in the art and arabesk genres; student of Muzeyyen Senar. Underwent sex change surgery in London in the early 1980s, and spent much of this decade resident abroad, unable to perform in Turkey. Since her return, Bülent has been associated primarily with the recording company Raks, who have done much to engineer her megastar status in Turkey today.

📀 **Alaturka 1995**
(Raks, Turkey).

The singer's interpretation of the popular classics from the 1880s to the 1950s and '60s. Conceived as a tribute to her mentor, Muzaffer Özpınar, this is definitely Bülent's best recording in recent years. The CD contains some gazels of scorching intensity, marking the comeback of this semi-improvised classical vocal genre.

🔘 **Seçmeler** (Raks, Turkey).

If you're hooked by the disc above, this is a collection of all-time greatest hits from Bülent Ersoy's prolific Arabesk output, including "Biz Ayıılamayız", "Geceler", and "Sevgi Istiyorum".

Udi Hrant

One of the most important players and composers on the Turkish ud. Hrant (1901-1978), from an Armenian family, was born blind and started playing cafés before making it on the radio. He became one of the most popular performers in Istanbul's nighclubs and toured widely.

🔘 **The Early Recordings Vol. 1**
(Traditional Crossroads, US).

This might seem a specialised disc of tracks from early 78rpm recordings, but there are storming and touching performances (some including the celebrated Şükrü Tunar on clarinet) that leap out at you. Exemplary remastering and good notes, photos and translations of lyrics. There are two other volumes of later recordings on the same label.

Zeki Müren

Born in Bursa, Zeki Müren (1931–96) first came to public attention through his radio concerts in the early 1950s as an interpreter of the contemporary art music, although his repertoire also covered Turkish versions of Tango, Chanson, and the work of Arab singers such as Umm Kulthum and Ferid al Attrache (notably his version of the latter's "Zennübe"). His fame was established by some eighteen musical films, from Beklenen Sarkı in 1953 to Rüya Gibi in 1971, and by his live performances in Istanbul's gazino clubs, characterised by their elaborate decor and Müren's increasingly camp costumery.

🔘 **Kahır Mektubu** (Türküola, Turkey).

Originally recorded in 1979 this was composed, by Zeki's long term associate Muzaffer Özpinar, as a result of a formative encounter with Egyptian star Umm Kulthum's later, monumental style. Simultaneously vast in scope and intimate in style, it was a landmark in Arabesk's history.

🔘 **Türk Sanat Müziği Konseri** (Coskun Plak, Turkey).

Remastered from the old HMV catalogue, this recording is a near perfect example of Zeki's elegant mastery of the classical lyric style.

Münir Nurettin Selçuk

Born Istanbul 1900, died 1981 Selçuk was dubbed 'the man who put Turkish music in Western dress'. He established the idea of the star vocalist in Turkish popular music in a concert given in the French Theatre, Istanbul, in 1930 but was famous primarily for his recordings, which ranged from light classical to tango.

 **Bir Özlemdir** (Coskun Plak, Turkey).

One of a series of re-issues of old HMV recordings of the bel canto master of the Turkish classical style. Bir Özlemdir contains some of the enduring classics: "Aziz Istanbul", "Kalamış", "Endülüste Raks" (a Turkish view of Flamenco), and an electrifying improvised gazel, "Aheste Çek Kürekleri".

Fasıl/Gypsy Music

Kemani Cemal

Born in Thracian Turkey, the heartland of Turkish Roma music in 1928, Cemal learnt music from his father specialising in the violin (keman). He has played in many of Istanbul's nightclubs and gazinos.

🔘 **Sulukule: Rom Music of Istanbul** (Traditional Crossroads, US).

A splendid selection of instrumental numbers and songs really evoking the earthy character of urban Roma music. Good notes and translations of lyrics.

Erköse Ensemble

One of the veteran Turkish Gypsy musical families, three brothers and two cousins on clarinet, violin, ud, kanun and darbuka. The clarinet player Barbaros Erköse now performs with his solo band.

🔘 **Tzigane: the Gypsy Music of Turkey** (CMP, Germany).

An instantly appealing welcome into the fiery world of fasıl music with a tight virtuosic ensemble.

Istanbul Oriental Ensemble

This ensemble of Roma musicians, led by percussionist Burhan Öçal, is currently top of the pile as far as recordings are concerned. The traditional line-up of clarinet, violin, oud, kanun and darbuka drums.

🔘 **Gypsy Rum** (World Network, Germany).

Fourteen tracks of tight instrumental playing. Emotional twists and lighting virtuosity will have your belly dancing – listen for the screaming shrieks from Fethi Tekayğil's violin. Once you've tried this, move on to their follow-up album, 🔘 **The Sultan's Secret Door** (World Network, Germany).

Mustafa Kandıralı

Born in Kandıralı in 1930, this Gypsy clarinet player toured the USSR and USA as a band leader in the 1960s, and there had his formative encounter with jazz, which earned him the nickname of 'Turkey's Benny Goodman'. Charlie Parker would not be a bad point of comparison either. Kandıralı's performances have a quiet radicalism to their melodic invention and improvisations.

🔘 **Caz Roman** (World Network, Germany).

This is the epitome of instrumental fasıl, including some of Turkey's best known fasıl instrumentalists, Ahmet Meter (kanun), Metin Bükey (ud) and Ahmet Kulik (darbuka). The last section of dance tunes is from a live recording at a concert in Düsseldorf in 1984.

Karşilama

A group of Istanbul Gypsy musicians led by Selim Sesler on clarinet with Canadian vocalist Brenna MacCrimmon.

🔘 **Karşılama** (Green Goat, Canada; Kalan, Turkey).

Roma music from western Turkey and the Balkans, played with real panache and good to have some of the vocal repertoire – gleaned from archive recordings and manuscripts – expertly sung. Recommended.

Arabesk

İbrahim Tatlıses

Tatlıses' poverty stricken life in Urfa in the far southeast of the country, his mixed Arab-Kurdish family background, and his turbulent domestic life, is a matter of public mythology in Turkey today. His early recordings (many associated with films) alternated traditional folk and Arabesk; many have circulated widely outside Turkey as well.

🔘 **Fosforlu Cevriyem** (Emre, Turkey).

This live recording is a rare chance to hear what Arabesk sounds like in the flesh, with some of his all-time favorites ("Beyaz Gül", "Kırmızı Gül", "Fosforlu Cevriyem", "Beyoglu", "Yooil Yooil"), and some superb *uzun hava*. It was a huge hit in Turkey in 1990, and gives some sense of Tatlıses' phenomenal vocal presence.

Müslüm Gürses

Gürses, like many Arabesk singers, is from Adana, in the southeast of the country, but has lived in Istanbul, where he records, makes films and has run a gazino for many years. His Arabesk has stood for many of its critics as an extreme manifestation of the lugubrious self-pity inherent in the genre, and his fans are drawn from the poorer and younger ranks of Turkey's urban proletariat. His complete discography would be impossible to compile.

🔘 **Insaf/Kahire Resitalı** (Ugur, Turkey).

Gürses's collaboration with Egyptian musicians, billed as his 'Cairo recital', but in fact a tight studio recording. The inspiration of Egyptian dance orchestra musicians on the genre as a whole is immediately obvious from this recording. Contains perfect examples of his intense vocals and despairing lyrics.

Orhan Gencebay

Gencebay was born in Samsun, northern Turkey in 1944; receiving a musical training in folk, classical and Western art music genres. He was associated with Arabesk's emergence as a popular genre addressing rural-urban migrant experience. Most of his early recordings accompanied musical films, and most can still be found in either cassette or CD form.

🔘 **Yalnız Değilsin** (Kervan, Turkey).

This recording, one of his most recent, demonstrates his unflagging and wide-ranging musical curiosity, taking in Middle Eastern, European and American popular and classical genres in a magisterial sweep. His own virtuoso saz playing, as ever, is to the fore. Listen out for the thunderous belly dance number ("Gencebay Oriyentalı") and a mock baroque overture ("Nihavent Üvertür").

Pop, Rock and Rap

Compilations

The Best of Turkey (Atoll, France).

Just what it says, a cheap and cheerful compilation of Turkish pop featuring İbrahim Tatlıses, Bariş Manço, Cem Karaca and Zeki Müren.

The Other Side of Turkey (Feuer und Eis, Germany).

A good 1991 compilation of music from Bulutsuzluk Özlemi, Mozaik and Bülent Ortaçgil and Erkan Oğur.

Turkish Hip Hop (Looptown, Germany).

Produced by musicians heavily involved in Frankfurt's multi-cultural underground scene, these Turkish rappers (DJ Mahmut, DJ Volkan, DJ Murat) escaped the hype that have surrounded rappers such as Cartel and Aziza A. Sampling from Turkish classical music to cool jazz, they rap mainly in Turkish, in a thoughtful and esoteric manner.

Artists

Sezen Aksu

Aksu trained in the classical genre in her native Izmir. She has dominated the world of Turkish pop since the mid-1970s, but her distinctive style emerged through her subsequent collaboration with Onno Tunç. She has recently begun to explore musics outside of the Turkish popular mainstream, notably Anatolian folk genres, and Balkan music.

Işık Doğudan Yükselir/Ex Oriente Lux
(Foneks, Turkey).

The release of this album made headline news in Turkey. Despite the hype, it is an intriguing CD, from the overblown orchestral opening (worked out with Onno Tunç), to the intimate and sparse style which characterises all of her recent work. It makes playful reference to a variety of urban and rural Turkish genres, some self-consciously 'authentic' in spirit, others in a more abstract and allusive style.

Düğün ve Cenaze (Raks, Turkey).

A collaboration with Yugoslav musician Goran Bregoviç, translating the music from Emir Kusturica's films, *The Time of the Gypsies* and *Underground* into Sezen Aksu's distinctive idiom, with a Serbian brass band thrown in for good measure. A superb slow tango kicks off a successful experiment and engaging curiosity.

Cem Karaca

Born in Bakırköy in Istanbul in 1945, Karaca has been a leading figure in Turkish and 'Anatolian' rock through his work with bands such as Apaşlar, Kardaşlar, Moğollar and Dervidan. His work became progressively more radical throughout the 1970s and he left Turkey in 1979, shortly before the military coup, and returned, after a big public display of reconciliation with the liberal-rightist regime of Turgut Özal in 1987. Whilst (some would argue) his politics have lost their way, his music has lost none of its jagged intensity and literary intelligence.

Cemaz ül-Evvel
(Kalan, Turkey).

This is a retrospective of all of Karaca's major work with his early groups, particularly Apaşlar and Kardaşlar, and thus

traces his experiments through a variety of Western pop and rock genres, and his emerging political radicalism. The story of Turkish highbrow rock, in its entirety, on one disc.

Ahmet Kaya

Since the early 1980s, Kaya has been one of the main figures associated with so-called 'independent' ('özgün') music; a guitar-oriented genre with radical aspirations, and much reference to indigenous traditional musics (especially that of the saz). Kaya is a Kurdish Jacques Brel, and the blend of saz and guitar with Kaya's deep, melancholy voice and the political tone of the lyrics has an enduring appeal amongst many of the Turkish and Kurdish intelligentsia to this day.

An Gelir (Taç, Turkey).

Plangent saz, and up-tempo Halay dance numbers, radical in gesture, but social-realist weltschmerz in content. Nothing that Kaya did subsequently lived up to the enormous vitality and lyricism of this early album.

Zülfü Livaneli

Composer, saz player and vocalist, born in the eastern Black Sea region. As a leftist intellectual he spent several years in exile in Sweden where he hooked up with the like-minded Greek composer Mikis Theodorakis. Since his return to Turkey he's been an important opinion maker and one-time candidate for mayor of Istanbul. Recently he's been through a New Age phase, but his 1998 album *Nefesim nefesime* (Breath to Breath) showed him back on better form.

Maria Farandouri Söylüyor
(Raks, Turkey).

From the early 1980s, this is one of the great Turkish albums of all time, Maria Farandouri sings Livaneli. Beautiful melodies, exquisitely sung in fine arrangements, in Greek and Turkish, but equally appealing if you understand neither.

Mirkelam

Mirkelam is a foremost representative of the newer generation of Turkish pop stars (including Tarkan, Rafet el Roman, Mustafa Sandal, Izel).

Mirkelam (Istanbul Plak, Turkey).

Featuring the song that launched Mirkelam in 1995, "Her Gece", this CD illustrates, for Turkish listeners, all of the virtues and vices of contemporary Turkish pop. It is, effectively, turbo-charged Arabesk, with a distinctly Turkish sound to the melodic line and vocal style, but with a pounding dance/techno pulse.

Yeni Türkü

The group's name means 'new song' and betrays the influence of South American groups like Inti Illimani and Greek musicians like Manos Laizos. Since the late 1970s their music has been characterised by fine instrumental arrangement featuring traditional Turkish instruments. The key musicians have been Derya Köroşlu (lead vocal and saz), Murat Buket (vocals and ud) and Selim Atakan (keyboard and guitar), but the group has now reformed with new members under Derya Köroşlu. They have many excellent releases on BMG.

Her Dem Yeni [New Every Time] (BMG, Turkey).

The greatest hits album with twenty of their songs. Excellent listening even if you don't speak a word of Turkish.

Africa

This map is drawn on the Peters' projection which shows the correct relative size of countries

Algeria | Rai

music under fire

Like almost every other aspect of life in modern Algeria, music has been caught in the fire of civil war in recent years. The blood of several famous musicians has been added to that of politicians, journalists, clerics, union leaders and ordinary citizens, victims of a vicious conflict between the military-backed regime and terrorists who kill in the name of fundamentalist Islam. The horror of this war hasn't managed to annihilate musical activity entirely and many varied styles with long histories and deep cultural associations continue to thrive within the borders of this huge country – as well as in exile in Paris and elsewhere. **Andy Morgan** takes a look at two of the most important: rai and (in the following article), the music of the mountainous region of Kabylia.

ndulge in a little lateral thinking and it's easy to draw parallels between **Algerian rai** and that other hugely successful and influential style of late twentieth-century urban music with which it shares all but one letter. American rap and Algerian rai are both styles born out of a strong local culture which use the language of the street to express opinions about street life. They value lyrical improvisation and 'borrow' musical ideas from many sources if and when necessary. They antagonise the values of 'decent' society and the cultural mainstream. They are the musical styles most favoured by the dispossessed in their respective countries, by those who have little to loose and a lot to say. And for both, their paths to international fame have been littered with controversy and misunderstanding. Just as folk who live comfortably within the cultural pale in America wince when they hear words like 'bitch' and 'uzi' coming from the mouth of a rap artist, so the cultural muftis of the Maghreb turn red when they hear tales of drunkenness, despair, sex and hedonism from the lips of a teenage *cheb* (youth).

Oran: Where it all Began

Wind your way back in search of the roots of rai and you'll find yourself in the west of Algeria with its lush cultivated coastline and harsh arid interior, peppered with the towns whose names echo throughout the history of the genre; Ain Temouchent, Relizane, Saida, Tlemcen, Mostaganem, Sidi bel Abbes, Mascara and, of course, the city where it all started and whose name is synonymous with rai itself, **Oran**.

DAVID BROWNE

Khaled

Oran is a modern seaport and the capital of the colonial province of Oranie in western Algeria. Known as the 'little Paris' of North Africa, it has had a reputation for being one big fun-house ever since the Spanish invaded it centuries ago and kept women there to entertain the troops. Before Algerian independence in 1962, the city was divided into separate quarters – French, Jewish, Spanish and Arab – each with its own atmosphere and music.

The Jewish quarter was known as the *Derb* where Jewish musicians like **Saoud L'Oranais**, **Larbi Bensari** and **Reinette L'Oranaise** performed every night in the cafés and cabarets of the quarter. The Spanish, mostly fisherman whose numbers were swelled by refugees after the fall of the Spanish republic in 1939, lived in Sidi el Houari. Spanish songs and melodies have always been tightly woven into the musical fabric of the city. The French lived in the best accommodation the old town had to offer and went to the Jewish cafés to get their shot of oriental dancing and maybe a little something else. The old Muslim quarter was known as Medina Jedida (new town). Muslims were forbidden by the French administration to sell alcohol in their own cafés so they crossed to the Jewish and Spanish quarters to get it. The various communities, between whom music was often the best point of contact, coexisted peacefully enough, hustling for their daily bread, watched over by their French rulers.

At the end of World War I, Arabic music in western Algeria was dominated by two main strands. The strictly regulated 'classical' style known as *al-andalous*, which was imported into North Africa from southern Spain after the expulsion of the Moors way back in 1492, had evolved into various local hybrids: *hawzi* (from the Tlemcen area), *aaroubi* (from Algiers) and *maluf* (from Constantine in the east). This was the music of the elite performed by painstakingly trained musicians who were taught to respect the rigid melodic and tonal structures of classical arabo-andalusian music over which they sang in the refined and symbolic language of classical Arabic poetry. Between the wars, many of the stars of hawzi were women and the roll-call of the *grandes dames* of this genre includes **Maâlma Yemna**, **Cheikha Tetma**, **Myriam Fekkai**, **Fadila D'zirya** and the aforementioned songstress, **Reinette L'Oranaise**.

Meanwhile out in the streets, music with its roots in the age-old rural chants of the local bedouin tribes was being performed for the masses. Dressed conspicuously in long white jellabas and turbans, the *cheikhs* (the word 'cheikh' is a venerable title meaning something like 'honourable sir') used a more populist form of poetry known as *melhûn*, set to a very basic two- to three-chord rural music with strong pounding beats. While they sang the long epic sagas of the melhûn canon they would bang out the beat on a small metallic drum called the *guellal*, accompanied by two players of a hard rosewood desert flute called the *gasba*. Their stage was any café in the Arabic quarter (the *Café Bessarhraoui* was a favourite haunt), a marriage, a circumcision ceremony or any busy marketplace such as the *tahtaha* of Medina Jdida where they performed among magicians, story-tellers, political agitators, beggars, teeth-pullers, snake-charmers and the rest of the motley crew that frequented such places.

The music of the cheikhs was known as *bedoui*, *gharbi* (meaning 'from the West') or *folklore Oranais*. The cheikhs guarded their skills jealously and their circle was a hard one to enter. The works of the great melhûn poets like Zenagui Bouhafs or Mestfa ben Brahim were long, complex and difficult to learn. The aspiring bedoui artiste would have to suffer a long apprenticeship under the strict supervision of a 'master' and then pass a test before he could grace his name with the title 'cheikh'. The cheikhs, men such as **Cheikh Hamada**, **Cheikh Khaldi**, **Cheikh Mohamed Senoussi** (who made the first bedoui recording in 1906), **Cheikh Madani** or **Cheikh Hachemi Bensmir** were somewhat stuffy and retro. They were from society's 'guardian' class, men with strong standards of morality and decency. Despite the fact that the French authorities distrusted melhûn, with its eulogies to the great muslim saints and freedom-fighters of yesteryear, they looked benignly on the activities of the cheikhs who they considered to be a healthy bulwark against lewd talk in the local arts.

Many cheikhs were refined city-dwellers who led a comfortable coexistence with their French overlords and were even collaborators, generally loath to step out of line. Hamada, to be fair, was an exception, and became a stern critic of the colonial administration. One of his sons was executed by the French. The cheikhs were popular but their language was not populist.

Women, Dock-workers and Street Urchins

The early decades of the century were a time of great change and social upheaval in Algeria. The traditional patterns of society, based on land and tribal allegiance, had been broken down by the land-grabbing policies of the colonists which resulted in a new urban underclass of poor factory workers, for the most part illiterate and rootless.

The venerable cheikhs seemed unprepared to sing about the stresses of poverty, rural immigration, colonial misrule, unemployment, overcrowding, crime, prostitution and other daily concerns of this new group of people. This job was left to the street poets who sang *zendanis* (from *zendan* meaning 'cellar') or bar songs which stitched together snippets of melhûn, bawdy rhymes and patches of improvised street wit covering every topic of momentary concern in the community of the dispossessed.

The musicologist, Jules Rouanet, writing for *La Revue Musicale* in 1905, described these forerunners of rai music in these damning terms: "The zendani are the musical airs which can be found right at the bottom of the Arabic musical repertoire. Any self-respecting musician does not sing the zendanis. He leaves them to women, dock workers and street urchins, and the people take their revenge by giving themselves whole-heartedly to the culture of this pariah style. They pepper these short melodies with all kinds of lyrics, fugitive improvisations and, in moments of inspirational weakness, with 'ahs' and 'ya lallas' ... sufficient to fill the gap."

He might also have mentioned that these inspirational hiatuses were often filled with the cry 'ya rai' or 'errai errai'. The word rai covers a vast expanse of meaning and loosely translates as an opinion, choice, advice, or point of view. Momentarily stumped for the right phrase or rap with which to continue, the singer would simply intone this all-encompassing word as if to say "This is how I see the world."

In the topsy-turvy society of 1920s Oran, **Muslim women** were the exploited of the exploited. If you had the misfortune to be born poor and female you had to learn survival in hostile surroundings. The constant struggle to preserve female honour was lost by many unsuspecting young women and social ostracism was the usual result. If a young female had a mind to pursue a career in singing or dancing then polite society would usually turn its back on her. Traditionally, a women who had lost her ticket to social respectability, for whatever reason, or who simply craved the opportunity to sing for a living, could join one of the groups of itinerant female singers who sang the *medh* – popular poetic songs in praise of the prophet performed on a bed of basic pounding percussion and sometimes accompanied by a flute or violin. The *meddhahates* would tour the region, strictly supervised by their leader or *m'allma*, and perform to female-only audiences at marriages, ramadhan gatherings and circumcision feasts.

For a woman who found herself on the dangerous periphery of society, membership of a meddhahate group offered companionship, support and a meagre means of survival. Although most meddhahate groups kept a low profile, only performing 'standards' and never their own material, some medh singers like **Soubira bent Menad**, **Les Trois Filles de Baghdad** and the great poetess, **Kheira Essebsadija**, did acquire notoriety in the inter-war years. Meddhahate groups still exist today and, at the last count (1988), more than three hundred were registered with UNAC (Union Nationale des Arts Culturels) in Oran.

The crucial link between the 'low-life' zendani songs and modern rai however is not the meddhahates but the **cheikhas**. These women were generally the daughters and wives of peasants or manual labourers, or orphans who had survived the harshest of upbringings and opted for the life in music as the only way to keep on living with some kind of dignity. Known as the 'women of the cold shoulder' – because they had a Maddonna-esque approach to clothing and were beyond the pale of 'decent' society – they had a lot to say and very little to lose. They adopted the rural bedoui style of the cheikhs, mixed it with the style of the meddhahates and came up with a truly individual, rough-neck, free-speaking and generally 'shocking' approach to poetry and music.

Whereas the meddhahates performed only for women, the cheikhas would sing for all and sundry and especially for men, in the steamy world of hash dens, cantinas, Moorish cafés, bars and bordellos in Oran and other towns. Quickly ditching the classical and poetic language of the cheikhs, which was purely men's talk anyway, the cheikhas adopted a patchwork of Oranian street slang, interwoven with bits of French and clichés of the melhûn canon.

The music of the cheikhas is considered to be as far removed from what might be politely described as 'family entertainment' as is feasibly possible. When they 'went public' they severed all ties with their previous existence and gave up their family name. They shrouded themselves in a carefully woven veil of mystery and anonymity, never allowing their images to be portrayed on the covers of records or cassettes, adopting colourful nicknames which often alluded to their place of origin and travelling from village to town to village with their male retinue of gasba players and a *berrah*, a kind of MC who performed the introductions and shouted dedications to members of the audience in return for money.

Cheikha Remitti el Reliziana from Reziliana (see box overleaf) is the most notorious, outspoken and oldest surviving member of the

Cheikha Remitti

Cheikha Remitti, the grandmother of **Algerian rai music** has spent most of her bitter-sweet existence walking on the wild-side of life. This seventy-six-year-old mother of ten was already a school-of-hard-knocks graduate when she recorded the infamous "Charrag Gatta" for Pathé Marconi in 1954. The title of the song means 'Tear, lacerate!', a completely unveiled message to female virgins to do the deed.

Remitti's orphaned childhood in the western Algerian town of Relizane not only taught her how to survive, but to do it with style and panache, sleeping rough in *hammams* (local Arabic bath-houses) and the tombs of local marabouts, singing with groups of itinerant female musicians called *meddhahates*, or dancing past exhaustion through until dawn at all-night *wa'adat*, the local marriage or saint-day feasts. The young Saadia (The Blessed or Happy One), as she was then known, earned her nickname in a bar-tent at the annual festival of Sidi Abed. When her entourage suggested that she buy a round for her assembled fans, many of whom were French, the singer overcame her dire ignorance of the language of the colonial masters by singing the words of a popular tune to the bewildered French barmaid "Remettez panaché madame, remettez!" (Another shandy barmaid. Another!), and she was baptised Cheikha Remitti Reliziana.

Remitti is the greatest of all the *cheikhas*, the women singers of western Algeria who sing and improvise their raunchy lyrical snapshots of daily low-life in a thick, highly flavoured dialect unique to the country around the great sea-port of Oran. Her notoriety is founded on her remarkable skill with words, her acute improvisational abilities and her fearlessness. Only those ears tuned in to the cheeky and comical patois of Oranie can appreciate her razor sharp talent for satirical impro-

Cheikha Remitti

ABSOLUTE RECORDS

visation. Inspiration comes to her at night and, in her words, "like a swarm of bees attacking my head." She sings about the pleasures of booze ("Some people adore God. I adore beer"), the repugnant attitude of old men towards their young brides ("Who would bring repugnant old saliva together with sweet young saliva"), the pleasures of sex ("He scratched my back and I gave him my all"), about cars, telephones, the TGV and the homesick agonies of the emigrant.

All this verbal wizardry is belted out in a voice that could grate the hide off a rhinoceros, a deep souful rasp that pulsates to the raw rhythmic trance of the metallic *guellal* drums and interweaves with the swirling barren wail of the *gasba* (a rosewood desert flute). On stage, Remitti flirts outrageously with her audience, distilling all the sexual power of an Elvis groin thrust into the rhythmic hike of her eyebrows and the flutter of her shimmying shoulders, the glint of her gold teeth vying with the wicked sparkle in her eyes.

Despite enjoying a respect and love that unites Algerians in this present era of murder and political chaos, official recognition has been painfully slow in coming. Remitti maintains that her "lust for life" sits easily with heart-felt religious convictions. She has performed the sacred duty of pilgrimage to Mecca and earned herself the respected title of *hadja*. Official acceptance of her music had to wait until 1994 when she performed at the temple of all things culturally acceptable in the Arabic music world, the Institut du Monde Arabe in Paris. Later that year her collaboration with Robert Fripp and Flea (of the Red Hot Chilli Peppers) on the album *Sidi Mansour* proved that her mojo doesn't only work on her fellow Arabs, but a much wider range of cultures and ages. If rai is the blues of North Africa, then Remitti is the Bessie Smith of the genre.

cheikhates and claims to be *el ghedra* (the root) of modern rai. She is the visible tip of the cheikha phenomenon, which is peculiarly Oranian and much misunderstood, even maligned in other parts of the country. Behind her are other great cheikhas, like the comparatively young **Cheikha Djenia** (from the word *djinn*, or evil spirit), **Cheikha Kheira Guendil**, **Cheikha Grélo** (cockroach) **el Mostganmia** (from Mostaganem), **Cheikha Bachitta de Mascara** (from the town of the same name) who caused a scandal in the forties by wearing trousers and a cap, **Cheikha el Ouachma** (tattooed) **el Tmouchentia** (from Ain Temouchent) and **Cheikha Zohra el Reliziana**.

At the inspirational source of the cheikates' art is the concept of *mehna* which has close affinities to the elusive *duende*, so cherished by the great singers of Flamenco. Cheikha Djenia gives this definition of mehna: "Mehna is hard and terrible. Mehna is strong and dangerous. She who has never experienced it is lucky. It's better for her, for her peace of mind. Mehna is the love that hurts, the love that sickens. Mehna, God preserve us, is like a tumour, an evil that envelopes your being. That's mehna, that's suffering, that's life. A woman's mehna is different from that of a man. A man, even if he suffers from it, will never show it".

Independence and the Jazz Age

In the 1930s, the underground agitators and muja-heddin of the emerging independence movement considered the rai of the cheikhas anti-revolu-tionary and a-political, drugging the people with retrograde thoughts of debauchery and alcoholic oblivion. Remitti and others could not have cared less and continued defiantly to expound the every-day woes and occasional pleasures of the workers and peasants who flocked to the cafés where they performed. Around this time, too, 78rpm records by the great Egyptian artists Umm Kalthum and Mohammed Abd el-Wahab were beginning to find huge popularity all across the Maghreb and new styles of city music were evolving.

In Oran the Egyptian sounds were blended with a little classical andalous and a measure or two of rai and the result was *wahrani*, a new urban hybrid whose greatest exponent was **Blaoui Houari**. Sailors fresh in port would come and sell records in Houari's father's café featuring the latest French pop tunes by the likes of Edith Piaf, Tino Rossi and Josephine Baker. These sounds became very popular with young urbanites and this popularity grew stronger in the period when American troops were stationed in Oran during the World War II. Seduced by the music and culture of the jazz age, Houari and a group of talented contemporaries including **Ahmed Wahby**, **Djelloul Bendaoud**, **Maurice El Médioni** and **Mohammed Belar-bi** incorporated Western instruments like the piano and accordion into the local musical language. Wahby's song "Ouahrane Ouahrane" (Oran Oran), became a classic anthem of the new Oranian folk-lore, or *bedoui citadinisé* as it was also known.

Ever since the early 1930s, the battle for an inde-pendent and free Algeria had been gathering pace. In the mid-1950s the volcano of revolutionary fer-vour erupted and insurrection gripped the country. The cheikhas and the urban wahrani stars were quick to add their voice to the protesting chorus. Some, like Blaoui Houari and the outspoken **Ahmed Saber**, ended up in jail whilst others like Ahmed Wahby escaped to Tunisia to join the FLN (Front de Libération National) in exile.

In the words of Remitti: "The FLN didn't have to contact me. Straight after the uprising of Novem-ber 1, 1954 I began to sing about the armed strug-gle. For we, the generation of cheikhs Hamada and Madani, were prepared for the armed struggle." In the bitter heat of the war of independence many rai artists managed to make their first records. The French company Pathé, who seem to have dominated the music industry in Algeria until the late 1950s, gave Blaoui Houari, Ahmed Wahby and Cheikha Remit-ti their first breaks during this period.

Hick Music Goes Pop

With the eventual capitulation of the French under De Gaulle and Algerian independence in 1962 there was a brief period of nationwide jubilation, street partying and riotous merrymaking. Very soon, however a cloud descended on the young nation. The Marxist theoreticians of the Boume-diene regime were not partial to outspoken liber-tine musicians championing sexual freedom and the good life. Their cultural policy was to promote a respectable 'national' musical genre and not sur-prisingly they opted to place the classical andalous style mixed with a little of the local chaabi music of Algiers on this vaulted pedestal. Rai was, after all, hick music, sung by a bunch of hooligan yokels with stiff Oranian accents who were unworthy of any role in the sacred Algerian patrimony.

In Oran, things were seen a bit differently. One artist in particular, **Ahmed Saber**, continued to parody the shortcomings of the new government in songs like "El Khaïne" (The Thief – a diatribe against official corruption) or "Bouh bouh el khedma welat oujouh" (Oh, oh, you get a job by pulling strings) which mixed rai, wahrani, jazz and a little rumba. He dared even to criticise Ahmed Ben Bella, Algeria's first President and the hero of the revolution, and spent several periods in jail, eventually dying in poverty in 1967. Boumedi-enne, Ben Bella's successor, shut the regional TV station of Oran, prohibited alcohol and put a ban on large concerts or gatherings of rai musicians. Rai was locked behind closed doors.

Bellemou Messaoud

Redding. This was the hey-day of 'Yé Yé', that particularly French twist on beat-mania and the youth of Oran, Algiers and other big cities were rolling and shaking with the rest of the world.

Rai had to be made danceable to retain its appeal. Bouteldja, alias 'Le Joselito', hit the big time in 1964 at the tender age of fourteen, taking songs from the cheikhates and melhûn repertoire and spicing them up with modern instrumentation and arrangements. Messaoud started experimenting by substituting the gasba with sax or trumpet and the small guellal with the much larger, booming tabla drum. Around the same time, Bouteldja was customising an accordion so that it could play the quarter-tones so characteristic of Arabic music in general.

The post-revolutionary generation of young musicians, which included Belle-mou, Bouteldja, **Boutaïba Sghir** and **Benfissa** started to formulate a modern **pop-rai**. Their influences ranged from rock to flamenco, from jazz to bedoui and the rai of the cheikhas. Spanish artists had been visiting Algeria for decades to play for the large Spanish community of Oran. Their music was very popular, especially with the young Bellemou who had studied at the Spanish music school in his hometown of Ain Temouchent.

After a few years testing their new sounds on the Oran wedding, cabaret and café circuit, Belle-mou and Bouteldja had achieved local fame, not to say notoriety. Trumpets, saxophones and accordions in rai music? They left audiences speechless. Cheikha Remitti, jealous and proud by nature, was furious at her baby being stolen from her. "I built the house and they stole the keys and moved right in", she declared angrily.

In the slip-stream of Bellemou's and Bouteldja's success a new generation began turning to the rai hybrid to provide a soundtrack to their lives. Among these 'midnight' children were two child singers from Oran who were becoming a popular attraction at wedding and circumcision feasts – the singers who were to become known as rai's biggest stars, **Chaba Fadela** and **Cheb Khaled**.

Fadela Zelmat's family house in the seedy former Jewish quarter was a stone's throw from the municipal theatre and she had always had her heart set on a stage career. Nicknamed 'Remitti sghira' (little Remitti) by the theatre's director, the young Fadela starred in Mohamed Ifticène's 1976 film

This was not an unfamiliar place for rai to find itself. Rai was always most comfortable in small gatherings such as marriages, circumcision feasts or simple family get-togethers in which the singer would improvise stories about the lives of the people present, all of whom she or he knew personally, and the berrah would go around cajoling tips out of the audience. In these surroundings rai could be poured out uninhibited without fear or recrimination. Apart from anything else, the *gasba* flutes and *guellal* drums of the traditional rai orchestra were totally unsuited to large concert halls.

This fact hadn't escaped the attention of the younger generation and especially of two young musicians from Oran, multi-instrumentalist (but mainly trumpeter) **Bellemou Messaoud** and singer **Belkacem Bouteldja**. Independently, both dreamed of updating the rai sound to make it more suitable for the youth of the mid-1960s who were getting hooked on the latest sounds from Europe and America. The French *beau mec* Johnny Halli-day played the Regent cinema on Oran's corniche or seafront strip and dozens of hopeful 'rocker' combos – with names like The Students or The Vultures (the latter fronted by the Ahmed brothers, later key rai producers) – began boogying to the beat of The Beatles, James Brown and Otis

JAK KILBY

Chaba Fadela and Cheb Sahraoui

Djalti at the green age of fourteen, where she played the role of a smoking, drinking, bikini and mini-skirt wearing local girl. She also performed as a backing vocalist on various recordings by Boutaïba Sghir and Cheikha Djenia.

Khaled Brahim came from the Echmuhl district in Oran's new town where his father was a mechanic in the local police garage. Like all his contemporaries, Khaled was mad for the sounds of the Moroccan new wave, groups like Nass el Ghiwane and Jil Jilala who were busy moulding a hard, modern style of Arabic music and becoming popular all over the Maghreb. With his Nass el Ghiwane sound-alike group **Noujoun el Khams** (The Five Stars), Khaled would play anywhere and everywhere, beginning the evenings with Moroccan and rock influenced songs and later, when only the intimates were left in the house, finishing off with some down home rai.

The 1970s were a bad time for the youth in Algeria. The previous decade had exacerbated the problems of poverty, homelessness and unemployment which had plagued the country since independence. When President Chadli took over from the long-standing leader Boumedienne in 1977, corruption became almost endemic. The young people of cities like Algiers and Oran, too old for school and too young for military service, existed in an aimless limbo, denied sexual freedom or the chance to travel abroad, and continually preached to about religion and morality by the authoritarian central government. Frustrated as they were, they were not oblivious to the gener-

al radicalisation of Third World culture which was implicit in the music of Bob Marley, the Moroccan new wave and the plight of the Palestinians.

The mid-1970s also witnessed another development that was to be crucial to the pop-rai boom of the 1980s. For decades, record producers in Algeria had released their material on 45rpm vinyl singles which were relatively expensive to produce. After 1974 cheap cassette recorders became available and the vinyl era rapidly ended. Producers, or *éditeurs* as they're known in French, sprang up like flowers after a freak flood, ranging from two-bit sharks with a microphone and a beaten-up cassette player, to the likes of brothers **Rachid** and **Fethi Baba Ahmed** who ran a studio and production centre in Tlemcen, or the talented arranger-producer **Mohammed Maghni**, all survivors of 1960s rock groups who strove to develop new sounds and styles.

Cassette Chebs

For the emerging generation of chebs and chebas, royalties were unheard of. Candyfloss contracts were confected and then ignored. When Cheb Khaled eventually hit the big time, a number of producers claimed to have an exclusive deal with him. His reply was: "My only contract is with God".

The cassette revolution allowed rai to circumvent the traditional disinterest and elitism of the state-run media giant RTA (Radio Télévision Algerienne) with whom many of the young rai singers had a love-hate relationship. On the one hand they despised the haughty indifference of the media cadres far away in Algiers, and on the other they craved the fame and potential fortune which might result from TV coverage.

According to Bouziane Daoudi and Hadj Miliani, the authors of *L'aventure Rai*, one of the few books on the subject, it was a desire on the part of the musical scene in Oran to be considered on a par with the lucky few who appeared on television that the title **'cheb'** – meaning 'young' or 'charming' – was adopted. The presenters of musical shows on TV would intone a formula to introduce the next act which consisted

One of the first Khaled cassetes

of the anodyne phrase "Wa el an nouqadim lakouni éch-cheb…" (And now please welcome the young ...). The éditeurs in Oran, in a calculated game of one-upmanship – and also, it must be said, to differentiate their young recording stars from the cheikhs and cheikhas of old – persuaded and cajoled all and sundry to become cheb this and chaba that.

The modern rai era was born when Chaba Fadela recorded **"Ana ma h'lali ennoum"** (Sleep doesn't matter to me any more) in 1979. The song was a hit, and more importantly, a hit all over the country. It was the first time that rai had really gone out beyond its western Algerian stronghold and seduced the whole nation. All the elements that had made the rai of the cheikhas so controversial – the plain speaking, the realism, the love of life, the lack of concern for accepted mores – were at its heart.

Not every singer was prepared to jump on the cheb bandwagon, however. The silver-tongued exponent of 'clean' rai, **Houari Benchenet**, whose popularity rivalled that of Cheb Khaled's in the early 1980s, resolutely refused to adopt the cheb moniker and preferred the more socially palatable and elegant wahrani style to the new rai.

Nevertheless, without any official sanction from government or media, rai continued to grow in popularity. In 1983, Chaba Fadela teamed up with the talented classically trained musician and arranger **Mohamed Sahraoui** to record **"N'sel Fik"** (You're Mine), one of the anthems of modern rai, under the supervision of producer **Rachid Baba Ahmed**. Shortly afterwards the pair got married and became the most famous man and wife team in Arabic music. **Cheb Hamid**, whose singing style owed a lot to flamenco, scored huge hits in the early 1980s with "El Marsam" and "Maandiche maa" before going back to his job as a hospital technician.

Another burgeoning star was **Cheb Mami**, who was only fourteen when he burst onto the scene in 1982 after coming second in a televised talent contest and went on to blaze a trail of firsts – first to move to France in 1985, first to play at Paris' most prestigious rock venue L'Olympia in 1989, first rai singer to perform in the USA three months later and first to record an album outside France or Algeria (*Let me Rai*, 1990, produced by Hilton Rosenthal in Los Angeles).

1986 was the year when rai became a truly international phenomenon. The more progressive organs of the French cultural media like the magazine *Actuel* or Radio Nova had been giving the phenomenon some scant coverage in the early years of the decade. Meanwhile back home, the Algerian establishment had finally relented (in summer 1985) and the first ever official **festival of rai** was staged in Oran. Cheb Khaled, already a superstar in his own country, was crowned King of rai. In the summer of 1986 the cultural organisation Riadh el Feth, led by the ubiquitous Lieutenant Colonel Hocine Snoussi, staged a Festival of Youth in Algiers at which many of the emerging Algerian 'World Music'

JAK KILBY

Cheb Mami

stars performed. Rai was represented at the festival by the group **Raina Rai**, from Sidi bel Abbès, a weak choice in the eyes of the hardcore rai congnoscenti at the time who considered the group to be a pale imitation of the 'real' rai – although these days their album *Hagda* is now universally included amongst the great recordings of the genre.

With World Music becoming a force in the French and international music scene the stage was set for rai to join the party. In January 1986, the working class Parisian suburb of Bobigny staged a festival of rai which showcased the talents of Cheb Khaled, Chaba Fadela and Cheb Sahraoui, Raina Rai, Cheikha Remitti and others to an intrigued and delighted audience of north African immigrants and French journalists. The word was out and the word was rai.

Khaled, the King of Rai

In spite of the successes of Cheb Mami, Fadela and Sahraoui, Cheb Tati et al, no one has achieved fame and fortune on the international stage to rival **Khaled**. When still known as Cheb Khaled he was signed in 1991 to a worldwide recording deal by the legendary French label and Polygram subsidiary, Barclay.

When Barclay took on the challenge of spreading the rai-gospel throughout the world, the idea of investing large amounts of cash in the career of an Algerian singer was viewed as a huge risk by many. In the event, the pay-off was handsome. Their first album release, *Khaled* (1992), produced by Don Was and featuring the smash hit "Didi", went gold in France (over 100,000 sales) and sold respectably in many other countries. The follow-up, *N'ssi N'ssi* (1993), featuring songs from the soundtrack of Bertrand Blier's film *1-2-3 Soleil*, sold less well but compensated by earning Khaled a *César* (the French equivalent of the Oscar) for best soundtrack album.

In 1996 Khaled released his third Barclay album, *Sahra*, which featured a song co-written with France's answer to Neil Diamond, Jean-Jacques Goldman, entitled "Aïcha". This innocuous love-ballad, dedicated to the younger of Khaled's two daughters, was a huge hit in France, far outselling anything the stars of variété Française had to offer at the time.

Although Khaled's international progress has been patchy – astounding success in India on the one hand and slow, arduous development in the USA on the other – in France he's a one hundred percent crossover success, a name who gets invited onto chat shows and sells out the massive Zenith venue in Paris for two to three nights in a row.

It's as if there was only ever room for one North African to become a name in French households (and beyond) and Khaled, with his radiant smile and happy-go-lucky unthreatening demeanour, earned himself the job. The other big names of the genre, Mami, Fadela and Sahraoui have had to content themselves with fame amongst the World Music cognoscenti in addition, of course, to their huge and abiding popularity amongst North Africans.

Many people back in Algeria who had followed and idolised Khaled throughout the 1980s felt that he lost touch after his departure for France and seemed intent on fuelling his rapid rise to international fame with rehashed versions of old worn-out standards rather than producing a new and exciting material. His departure left a vacuum which was eventually filled to overflowing by the Casanova of rai-sentimentale, **Cheb Hasni**. Hasni's sweet-as-syrup language of love proved to be even more popular than Khaled and his cassettes sold in their tens of thousands. Ironically, two of his most famous songs, "Baraka" which launched his career in 1989 and "N'châf Lhaziza", also known as "Visa", are amongst the most crude and real of pop-rai. However, his fame rests on his seductive celebrations of love and women. Together with **Cheb Nasro** and **Cheb Tahar**, he dominated the rai scene in the early 1990s.

Cheb Hasni
Lover's Rai

Courage Under Fire

This is where the story of rai crashes into the tragedy that is modern Algeria in a terrible and dramatic head-on collision. On 29 September 1994, **Cheb Hasni** was gunned down by commandos of the Armed Islamic Group near his home in Oran. His death, and that of the legendary producer **Rachid Baba Ahmed** in similar circumstances a few months later, dealt a blow not only to rai but to Algerian culture in general that many continue to feel deep inside.

The irony of these events is painful. Here was a young singer, at the height of his fame, who preached in the language of earthly love and paid for it with his life. In many ways Hasni's death symbolises the struggle that rai has been engaged in throughout its existence. Intensely hedonistic and apolitical by nature, rai has always been ensnared in politics despite itself. Whilst the zendani crooners, the cheikhas, the masters of wahrani and the chebs have concentrated on singing truthfully and passionately about the life which they lead, warts and all, a cultural polemic has raged all around them led by the self-appointed guardians of tradition, morality and the 'spirit' of Islam.

Speaking only months after the riots which shook Algeria in 1988, Cheb Sahraoui put rai in its proper perspective: "There's absolutely no connection between rai and the violence of last October. Rai does not incite revolt. It's just a youth thing designed to let you have fun and forget your troubles. Rai is all about partying and nothing to do with politics." But in a country like Algeria – torn between religious fundamentalism, social traditions and the glare of modernity – having fun can all too often be in itself a political act and a singer of rai can, without intention, be considered a political animal, suitable for brutal and senseless elimination.

Considering the horror of Hasni's death it is extraordinary that rai continues to be performed and recorded in Algeria. New stars like **Cheb Hassan**, who performs in a suave tuxedo to rapturous audiences, accompanying himself on a single solitary synth-keyboard, or the latest female rai sensation, **Kheira**, are keeping the genre alive and the cassette vendors in business. Nevertheless, there is a sense of crisis in the scene. The generation of Khaled and Fadela are now in their thirties, long past their "cheb" phase and struggling with the mundane realities of

surviving and rearing families in the suburbs of Oran, Algiers, Paris, Lyon and Marseilles. The next generation, born and bred in France, have little time for the record-em-quick-and-sell-'em-cheap philosophy of the éditeurs in Barbès, the African 'ghetto' of Paris. They're too busy getting down to the breakbeats of the French rap explosion and, more importantly, they expect to buy well-produced and well-packaged music on CD.

Faudel, the latest rai sensation to hit France, is typical of this new generation. Born and bred in the charmless Parisian suburb of Mantes-la-Jolie, he demonstrates a concern for quality, both in terms of recording and musicianship, totally out of keeping with the old values of the éditeurs. "I grew up in the *quartiers* of funk and rap, which changes everything," he says. "The Barbès circuit doesn't interest me. It's a closed world which caters

Faudel

CHRISTOPHE GSTALDER/SANKARA

only for North Africans." His debut album, *Baïda*, was released to huge critical acclaim in 1998 before he'd even reached his twenties. Similarly, Parisian star **Rachid Taha** (who notably shared a supergig stage with Khaled and Faudel in 1998) plays rai as just one of many styles, given a techno gloss, with sampled backing vocals.

The old-style producers thus face a change-or-die ultimatum which few show signs of heeding. Ask any of the Arab cassette-shop owners in Paris how business is going, and you get bowed heads and tales of woe. Nevertheless, it is with the few younger *beur* (children of North African immigrants) producers and musicians who are aware of the need for change – who can adapt rai's sound to the tastes of the new generation, and take on board the notions of proper investment in recording, marketing and publicity – that hope must lie. As one prominent rai producer said recently: "The beurs are rai's best hope."

discography

There's a fair amount of rai available on CD these days, though many of the latest releases still appear first (and in some cases only) on cassettes issued in France or Algeria. If you want to track these down, get yourself to Paris and scour the cassette shops near the Barbès Rochechouart metro station, or the shops *Bouarfa* (32 rue de la Charbonière) and *Laser Video* (1 rue Caplat).

See also the France discography (p.111) for 'not quite rai' French-Algerian artists such as Rachid Taha and Orchestre National des Barbes.

Compilations

⊚ **Maxi Rai** (Dèclic, France).

A bumper four-CD collection of pop-rai sounds featuring the who's who of pop-rai with the conspicuous exception of Khaled. Some great songs including a couple of classics from the incomparable Chaba Zahouania.

⊚ **Pop-Rai and Rachid Style**
⊚ **Rai Rebels** (Earthworks, UK).

These two compilations feature the work of the late Tlemcen-based producer Rachid Baba Ahmed, in whom many hoped they had at last found the Lee Perry of rai. Although Rachid didn't fulfil his early promise before his tragic and untimely death there are some seminal tracks here including Fadela and Sahraoui's rai standard "N'sel Fik" (on *Pop-Rai*) and excellent contributions by Cheb Khaled and Cheb Anouar.

Artists

Cheb Anouar

The young Anouar – whose contribution to the Earthworks' compilation *Pop-rai Rachid Style* (above) stood out a mile – has always been among the most promising artists from Rachid's stable.

⊚ **Laaroussa** (Etoile d'Evasion, Algeria).

A charged recording, on which Anouar's husky singing style is aptly accompanied by a simple violin-driven backing-track.

Cheb Djellal

Djellal is a much underrated Moroccan rai singer from Oujda, close by the Morocco-Algeria border.

⊚ **Le Prince de la Chanson Maghrebine** (Boualem, Algeria).

This set demonstrates to full effect Djellal's pared down and menacing Moroccan-rai style with its hypnotic call and response vocal arrangements, without a tacky synth sound in earshot. Absolutely captivating.

Chaba Fadela and Cheb Sahraoui

This husband and wife team was one of the most enduring names in pop-rai and was responsible for many classic recordings of the genre. Now separated, they are both still live active on the international concert circuit.

⊚ **You Are Mine** (Mango, UK).

The best of a pair of albums recorded by the duo for Mango in the UK. On this solid collection the duo perform one of their many versions of "N'sel Fik". The other Mango disc is Fadela's *Hana Hana*.

Faudel

Born of Algerian parents and brought up in the grim Parisian suburb of Maintes-la-Jolie, Faudel looks set to inherit the mantel of 'rai boy-wonder' which has passed from Joselito to Cheb Mami to Cheb Anouar. Faudel shuns ways and values of the traditional rai 'ghetto' in France and sets his sights firmly on seducing "le grand publique" in the manner of his childhood hero, Khaled.

 Baïda (Sankara/Mercury, France).

"To warn people of the worst, that's my mission", declares the young and precocious Faudel who reaped plaudits from both the French and North African media with this his first release. The musicianship and arrangements here are excellent and Faudel's voice, nurtured from an early age on both North African and Western influences in equal proportions, is a joy to hear.

Cheikh Hamada

One of the greatest, if not THE greatest of all the roots rai male vocalists, Cheikh Hamada made his first recording in the 1920s and continued to record in Algeria, Paris and Berlin until his death in 1968. He has left a rare and priceless body of material which is one of the best illustrations of modern pop-rai's ancestral roots.

⊚ **Le Chant Gharbi de l'Ouest Algérien** (Les Artistes Arabes Associes, France).

Roots rai in all its rough and ready glory. Hamada's raucous wail jerks along over the rhythmic wail of the gasba flutes and the guellal drums. This is no slick hi-fi experience and one for people who like their rai raw, rootsy and unadulterated.

Cheb Hasni

Hasni Chekroune was the leading figure of so-called 'soft rai', featuring amorous and romantic lyrics directed at female and family-oriented audiences. He'd released a prolific 150 cassettes before his death, gunned down by fundamentalists, in 1994.

⊚ **Lover's Rai** (Rounder, US).

An excellent 'best of' collection with translations of lyrics and full notes.

(Cheb) Khaled

Khaled was crowned 'King of Rai' when he was still a cheb, at the first rai festival in Oran in 1985. Since then he has continued to extend his dominance, not only over the rai genre, but also over Arabic music in general. He is rai's only true crossover star, loved and respected both by North Africans and by the wider French and international public.

 Hada Raykoum (Triple Earth/Sterns, UK).

This is pop-rai in its raw mid-1980s state with Khaled singing like the rebel he was reputed to be. Although the sound of his music became slicker in his later productions, the raw sound of the Maghreb blues was never better showcased than on this seminal release.

⊚ **Fuir mais où?** (MCPE, France).

Recorded in 1991, when tensions in Algeria were reaching dangerous new levels, this album found Khaled in a fiery and thought-provoking mood.

 Khaled (Barclay, France).

Produced by Don Was this album blew rai wide-open for

thousands of non-Maghrebis throughout the world. Featuring the bombastic bass-driven "Didi", which was rai's first international 'hit' in the strictest sense of the word.

 N'ssi N'ssi (Barclay, France).

Although many of the songs are old rai standards, the production of Don Was and Philippe Eidel is of the highest quality with beautiful lush string sections recorded in Cairo.

 Sahra (Barclay, France).

This lushly produced 1996 outing divided fans. It is Khaled at his most accessible – and at times a little over-easy. But there are some gorgeous ballads and one absolute stunner of a track, "Oran Marseille", opening with the funkiest kazoo solo known to man.

CHEB KHALED AND CHABA ZAHOUANIA

 A Ya Taleb (MCPE, Algeria).

The King of Rai has often teamed up with the genre's most durable and impressive female star for a quick cassette release or two. Zahouania is one of the rare singers who has successfully mastered both the folk-rai style of the cheikhas and the pop-rai of the chebs and chebas. This duo recording is fantastic, rootsy, raw rai, featuring a great tribute to one of Algeria's all-time heroes "Sidi Boumedienne".

CHEB KHALED, RACHID TAHA AND FAUDEL

 1, 2, 3 Soleils (Barclay, France).

The King, the Revolutionary, and the Young Pretender shared a stage at the Bercy Stadium in late 1998 for a gargantuan celebration of rai, peace and Algerianité. The three nabobs put on an unforgettable show, backed by an orchestra of more than 40 musicians, including a 28-piece Egyptian string section, all under the musical direction of (Taha's producer) Steve Hillage. All three delivered their best-loved hits to an ecstatic and riotous assembly of fans, with a devil-may-care passion stoked by the occasion. The concert marked the symbolic arrival of rai (and Algeria) at the summit of French pop culture and the CD is a fitting memento.

Cheb Mami

Since causing a sensation, aged 14, on the Algerian TV talent show *Alhan wa Chabab* (Melodies of Youth) in 1982, Cheb Mami has fought hard to earn international recognition with a string of well-produced releases. His lyrics have always been less crude and abrasive than those of many other rai contemporaries, which makes him popular with young women and their anxious parents. Universally acknowledged as one of the greats of the genre, Mami has suffered from playing the role of 'Prince' to Khaled's 'King of Rai'.

 Let Me Rai (Totem/Virgin, France).

The superb voice of Mami is at times here shanghaied by bland production: at others it's done full justice by subtle use of violins and accordion. A mixed bag, but significant for the fact that it reveals the musical ambitions of the most realistic pretender to Khaled's throne.

 Meli Meli (Totem/Virgin, France).

An older and maturer prince of rai explores various eclectic avenues on this 1998 release which features fusions of rai and rap, rai and flamenco and rai and funk. A collection of fine well-produced tunes.

Maurice El Médioni

As a young Jewish piano-player in pre-independent Algeria, Médioni made the clientèle of a pied-noir bar in Western Algeria swing. He is now an esteemed veteran living in Marseilles.

 Café Oran (Piranha, Germany).

Marvellous revival of the post-World War II hey-day of El Médioni with his captivating blend of indigenous Andalusian music and raï, Cuban rumba, and North-American jazz and boogie-woogie.

Bellemou Messaoud

The trumpeter Messaoud is one of rai's pioneers, having updated it from folk to pop form in the 1960s.

 Le Père du Rai (World Circuit, UK).

As an example of Messaoud, this album should be included in any self-respecting rai collection, though its fine moments are sadly accompanied by a rather flat production.

Reinette l'Oranaise

The great Jewish diva, Reinette l'Oranaise, loved equally by Jews and Arabs from her native North Africa, was one of the great exponents of *hawzi*, a hybrid of the Classical music of the Maghreb known as al-Andalous. Blind from the age of two, she studied with her mentor, Saoud l'Oranais, and the two were regular performers in the cafés of Oran's Jewish quarter. After Independence in 1962, Reinette fled the anti-semitic new regime and settled in Paris, where she lived in obscurity until in her 80s, when a French journalist tracked her down and she relaunched her career. She recorded several discs and continued to perform until her death in 1998.

 Mémoires (Blue Silver, France).

Reinette's final recording distills both the dark and radiant memories of a long, eventful life into five songs full of dignity, passion and soul. Accompanied by the great Algerian pianist Mustapha Skandrani, and playing oud herself, she pours out her wistful words in a voice too rough for sentimentality and too sweet for bitterness. North African blues at its best.

Cheikha Remitti

The diva of folk rai, Remitti is still strutting about the stage, singing deeply suggestive songs, in her 70s. She is a nut with an acquired taste – but hypnotic once cracked.

 Rai Roots (Buda/CMM, France).

This compilation features Remitti in all her lustful, rasping, pounding glory.

 Sidi Mansour (Absolute Records, France).

Who could have imagined this? Remitti – at 70 – recorded in Paris and LA with youngblood Algerian producer Houari Talbi, along with Robert Fripp, Flea (Red Hot Chilli Peppers), and a host of LA sessionmen.

Cheb Zahouani

Grim-faced Zahouani has a 'local hard man' look and sings in a suitably rasping no-nonsense style.

 Moul El Bar (Bouarfa, Algeria).

Hardcore rai, set to hard bass-heavy rhythm tracks.

bards of immigritude

Since the late 1980s, the immense international success of Khaled, Mami, Fadela, Sahraoui et al has established rai as the dominant Algerian musical genre but there's another altogether different style which has held fast against the hegemony of the chebs and chebas from Oran, especially in the eyes and ears of North African immigrants in France and elsewhere. This is the music of **Kabylia**, a remote and beautiful mountainous region which lies just to the east of the Algerian capital Algiers. **Andy Morgan** takes a look.

The population of Kabylia are Berbers, descendants of the indigenous people who inhabited North Africa before the arrival of the Arabs in the seventh century. They speak a Berber dialect called 'Amazight' ('Tamazight' in its written form) and their history is one of a continuous struggle for the survival of their culture and language against the Romans, Arabs, French and most recently both the socialist leadership of independent Algeria and their violent Islamic fundamentalist enemies.

More than a century ago, in pre-colonial times, music in Kabylia was tied to the ebb and flow of village life. Songs and dances were performed on a powerful rhythmic bed comprising *t'bel* (tambourine) and *bendir* (frame-drum) with added colour from the *ajouag* (flute) and *ghaita* (bagpipe). The French colonisers realised that it would be easier to do business with the traditionally democratically minded and liberal Kabyles than with their Arab neighbours and practised a policy of divide and rule, favouring Kabyles when it came to education, the civil service and emigration to France. The earliest North African émigrés in France were Kabyles and by the 1980s forty-six percent of all Algerian immigrants in France originated from the Kabyle provinces of Setif and Tizi Ouzou.

Exile and Protest

The story of **modern Kabyle music** really starts in Paris in the 1930s where a small Kabyle community was already well established and a network of cafés run by Kabyles provided a convenient place for Kabyle musicians to perform. An early pioneer was Cheikh Nourredine who helped to adapt traditional Kabyle melodies to modern 'café' instruments like the violin, banjo, guitar and double bass.

> **L'Hirondelle (The Swallow)**
> *Go beautiful bird*
> *I'm sending you back to my country*
> *Go and beat your wings*
> *In the skies of Kabylia*
> *Go, fly over the mountains and plains*
> *To the country of the Berbers*
> *To the place of Saint Abderrahmène*
> *Who looks at the sea*
> *Tell him of my pain*
> *In this bitter state of exile.*
>
> Slimane Azem

His song "Alouk Tricité" was a creative catalyst for **Slimane Azem**, a young Kabyle who had arrived in Paris in 1937 to become a musician. Inspired by the work of the great nineteenth century Kabyle poet, Si Mohand Ou Mohand, Azem sought to tackle the pain and homesickness of his immigrant countrymen in plain simple language which often employed imagery from the animal kingdom to

Vol. 3

LES GRANDS MAITRES DE LA CHANSON KABYLE
SLIMANE AZEM

AAA 135

Texte de présentation français et anglais :
A. HACHLEF

express deep intense emotion. Like many other Kabyle musicians he was a passionate supporter of the struggle for Algerian independence and his song "Fegh Ay Ajrad Thamourthiou" (Locusts, leave my Country) delivered a barely veiled message to the French colonial overlords in Algeria, bringing the singer into direct conflict with the French police. Another big presence in the 1940s was **Cheikh El Hasnaoui**, nicknamed 'The Bard of L'Immigritude' whose song "La Maison Blanche" (The White House) describes the deathly silence of the white-washed buildings in a Kabyle village, emptied of life by poverty, emigration and war, and remains a classic of early Kabyle pop.

In the 1950s, Egyptian music took over the Arabic world and Kabyle singers began to accompany their songs with lavishly orchestrated scores, aided in Paris by two Arabic geniuses of orchestration – **Amraoui Missoum** and the Tunisian **Jamoussi**. Singers and composers such as **Cherif Kheddam**, **Alloua Zerrouki** and **Akli Yahiatene** all released hit records and their popularity lasted well into the 1970s.

Cherif Kheddam is an especially influential figure in the modernisation of the Kabyle sound. As presenter on the Kabyle service of Radio Algiers after independence in 1962, Kheddam helped develop the careers of the new generation of Kabyle singers who were to put Kabyle music on the international map in the 1970s. During the 1950s the careers of three female singers from Kabylia also took to the air, often in the face of considerable hostility on the part of their families who considered singing ignoble and an anathema to womanhood. **Cherifa**, **Hanifa** and **Djamilla** all made a lasting impression on Kabyle song, and their songs inspired contemporary female artists like **Malika Domrane** and the group **Djurdjura**.

At the end of the 1960s, young Kabyles were disenchanted with the broken promises and corruption of the regimes of Ben Bella and Boumedienne, both of whom stifled any moves towards cultural or linguistic freedom for Algeria's Berber minorities in the two decades after independence. The music of counter-cultural revolution –

LES GRANDS MAITRE DE LA CHANSON KABYLE VOL. II
CHEIKH ELHASNAOUI

Texte de présentation français - anglais : A. Hachlef
Traduction : M. Stoffel

AAA 044

Dylan, Joan Baez, Brassens, Sylvio Rodriguez and Victor Jara – was a huge inspiration for many young Kabyle singers including a geology student called **Idir** who recorded a track called "A Vava Inouva" (My Little Father) in 1973 and scored Kabylia's first international hit, selling previously unheard of quantities both in Algeria and Europe.

Together with contemporaries **Aït Menguellet** and **Ferhat**, Idir is one of the great truimvirate of modern Kabyle pop. Whilst Idir is the thinker, Aït Menguellet is the poet, who in the eyes of many has inherited the mantle of Si Mohand Ou Mohand. He still lives in the village of his birth in the Djurdjura mountains, stubbornly refusing to leave Algeria, despite the tragic fate of many of his fellow musicians. On his rare visits to Paris, Aït Mengullet can fill the 6000-seater Zenith hall for three nights in a row, a feat no other Algerian artist, with the exception of Khaled, can hope to achieve. Ferhat is the revolutionary, who retired from performing in 1989 after a decade in which he had been arrested four times for subversion.

In the early '80s, after the momentous events of 1980 when the whole of Kabylia rose up against the Arab socialist government in Algiers in what became known as the 'Kabyle Spring', other artists like **Matoub Lounes**, **Djamel Allam** and **Abdelli** stepped into the limelight with ever more ambitious fusions of progressive Western pop and traditional Kabyle music. Abdelli was taken up by Peter Gabriel's RealWorld, recording a fusion album for the label. In 1986 rai music exploded on the scene with its brash hedonistic stance and stole the limelight. Suddenly the cultural and political radicalism of Kabyle music seemed unfashionable. A Kabyle group called **Takfarinas**, led by **Hassen Zermani**, managed to adapt to the new ethos and their tale of teenage love pangs "Weytelha" (She's Beautiful) was a huge success in the late 1980s. Since that first onslaught of rai, Kabyle music has re-established itself as one of the main musical exports of Algeria. The two styles are opposite and complementary, rai expressing the need to party against all odds and Kabyle music a more radical, socially aware and 'conscious' stance.

As with so many chapters in the history of modern Algeria, this one must end on a sorrowful note. On 27 June 1998, **Matoub Lounès**, whose radical and uncompromising stance was a powerful inspiration to Kabyles the world over, was ambushed and killed in the mountains of Kabylia. His death sparked widespread riots throughout the region and many suspected that the government, who were preparing to pass a new arabisation law to further curtail the freedoms of the Berber minorities, were reponsible for this senseless act of brutality. At Matoub's burial service in the village of his birth, Taourit Moussa, which was attended by thousands upon thousands of mourners, his sister Malik said: "The face of Lounès will be missed but his songs will dwell forever in our hearts. Today is a day of great joy. We're celebrating the birth of Matoub Lounès."

discography

Compilations

 Les Maitres de la Chanson Kabyle:
Vol 1 Slimane Azzem; Vol 2 Cheikh El Hasnaoui;
Vol 3 Cherif Kheddam; Vol 4 Alloua Zerrouki.
(Les Artistes Arabes Associes, France).

This is an extensive series covering the roots of modern Kabyle music. The artists covered on the first four volumes were all crucial players in the development of the music and the CDs feature compilations of their most important tunes, delivered in the heavily Egyptian influenced style that prevailed in the 1950s.

 Planète Kabylie
(Declic, France).

A popular compilation of some of the best names in modern Kabyle music, appropriately kicking off with Idir's "A Vava Inouva" which launched the music internationally. The disc also includes Slimane Azem, Cherifa, Aït Menguellet, Ferhat, Djamel Allam, Matoub Lounès and Abdelli.

Artists

Djurdjura

An all-female Kabyle group, whose lead singer has dedicated herself to the crusade for women's rights. Songs on this album are dedicated to "all women deprived of love, knowledge and freedom".

 Adventures in Afropea 2:
The Best of Djur Djura (Warner/LuakaBop, US).

An excellent compilation by David Byrne of hauntingly beautiful

songs, fusing modern with traditional styles. The album includes the songs "Heirs to the future'" – a stirring hymn of the War of Liberation, and "King of the Broom", a poignant tribute to a road-sweeper replaced by a machine. (Note: this compilation, possibly out-of-stock, draws on songs featured in four albums still available under the French Musidisc label: *Le Printemps*, *Asirem*, *A Yemma*, and *Le Défi*).

Idir

Idir's gentle and lyrical style, which owes more to French singers like Brassens than to the Egyptian models which had held Kabyle music in their tight grip in previous decades, was a complete revelation when he emerged on the scene in the 1970s.

 A Vava Inouva (Blue Silver, France).

It was the title song of this album that launched Kabyle music onto the international stage. "A Vava Inouva" describes a winter scene high in the Djurdjura mountains where a group of villagers huddle around a fire contemplating the stillness of the cold snow bound night and the dangers that threaten their existence. The song was a thinly veiled parable about the precarious state of Kabyle culture and language. It takes centre stage on this compilation.

Matoub Lounès

Lounès was one of the big names of kabyle music from the 1980s until his assassination in 1998. He had an uncompromising commitment to the struggle of the Berber people for democracy and tolerance in a bitterly divided Algeria.

 Tigri G-Gemma (Blue Silver, France).

The list of song-titles on this album ("The Revolutionary", "The Widow's Revolt"', "Remorse and Regret", "The Spoils of War") testifies to Matoub Lounès' commitment to the struggle. The music is an intelligent blend of Kabyle melodies and rhythms with Western rock and funk.

Aït Menguellet

Born in 1950, Lounis Aït Menguellet hit fame after appearing on a talent contest on Algerian TV at age seventeen. He quickly made a name for himself with his heartfelt poetic lyricism and passionate insights into society and Berber culture. He still lives in the village of his birth high in the Djurdjura mountains, despite the tragic fate of many of his contemporary musicians, although he refuses to perform live in Algeria fearing his appearance might provoke a massacre. He is a huge figure not only amongst Kabyles but North Africans as a whole.

 Chants & Poesie de Kabylie
(Blue Silver, France).

A compilation which features many of the important moments in the career of this icon of modern Kabyle music. These are the songs that have inspired a generation of Kabyles for the past three decades, and the soul seeps easily into the comprehension of a non-Kabyle listener. Aït Menguellet's rough and ready guitar vocal style is very well showcased here. You can almost imagine you're hearing a Celtic echo in the way his moody bluesy voice and rasping single-string guitar plucking weave in and out of base notes over a sparse metallic percussion accompaniment. Kamel Hamadi, another big name in the Kabyle scene, adds oud and bouzouki parts to some of the songs.

Angola

struggle and talent

If you are familiar with any Afro-Portuguese music at all, odds are it's that of Cape Verde and its global diva Cesaria Evora (see p.45). If talent and energy are anything to go by, Angola's musicians are surely next in line for greater recognition. As **Christian Hyde** and **Richard Trillo** discover, Angolan music, after two decades of isolation caused by civil war and a Marxist regime, is making up for the lost years, with a crafty variety of style, instruments and voices . . . and if a visit isn't top of your agenda, there is a bevy of mesmerising CD issues to prove the case.

A ngola feels like the country that Kafka built, with its strange brand of order by decree superimposed on chaos. Civil war and nightmarish living conditions are enduring, as is a lunatic bureaucracy. This is a country that has been under siege ever since its independence in 1975, when the democratically elected MPLA government of Eduardo Dos Santos was militarily challenged by UNITA. A peace treaty signed in 1994, known as the Lusaka Accords, has led to mostly broken promises by UNITA to disarm and hand over the 50 percent or so of the country under its control. But things aren't quite as bad as they were.

In terms of music, bright notes are the return of many Angolan exiles and the end of the government's monopoly on musical production. This has led to the emergence of some dynamic music studios, including singer **Teta Lando**'s *Teta Lando Produções* and *Kanawa*. These might just allow some new voices to come through, and

there are certainly enough styles to keep the interest up. Distinct Angolan musical trademarks include an artful leading voice calling on a slow chorus for its sexy or mournful rejoinder; tragedy sung with defiant joy as well as aching lamentation; and spicy traditional tunes threaded with percussion backgrounds, guitars and the rasp of the *reco-reco*.

On many of the country's releases, you'll find various national languages featured, most commonly *Kikongo* and *Kimbundu*, alongside Angolan-flavoured Portuguese. Helpfully for an international audience, recent CDs more often than not include translations of the lyrics.

Early Waves

The first Angolan musicians to make much of an impression outside Africa were the **Kafala Brothers**, who toured Europe in 1988 and 1990. Their CD *Ngola* (from the Kimbundu language for 'King', which gave the country its name) sold modestly well, but enthusiasm for their mournful acoustic guitar duets didn't endure much beyond the brothers' departure. They are, however, said to be working on a new release.

More promising (indeed the promise was fulfilled decades ago) was the upbeat, tropical dance band splatter of the **Orquestra os Jovens do Prenda** (the 'Prenda Boys Band' – Prenda is a poor suburb of Luanda) who were formed in the mid-60s, peaked in 1971, then disbanded in 1975, until being re-formed by two original members in 1981. With a large team of musicians, including four guitars, two trumpets and a sax, and half a dozen percussionists and drummers, they produced a generous fast-paced wall of sound, whistled along at key moments.

ORQUESTRA OS JOVENS DO PRENDA
The Irresistible Kizomba Beat of Angola
BERLIN FESTA!
recorded live at Heimatklänge

The core of their style, which had much in common with Brazilian samba, was a sound they called **kizomba**, rooted in the two-person *marimba* xylophone: the four guitars ('solo', 'contra-solo', rhythm and bass) played the parts of the marimba to achieve the sound of a single instrument. Meanwhile, the trumpets and sax interrupted in fanfare unison and the pile of drums – *tumba*, bongo, *buita*, *bate-bate* – punched out more rhythms than you could keep up with.

Orquestra os Jovens' lyrics became increasingly politicised in Portuguese times, but with the sour background of civil war at the time of their re-formation, the band's second-incarnation lyrics became the conventional staples of love and fortune – often forcefully expressed, as in the sulky "Manuela":

You Manuela
You are very old-fashioned.
Manuela, if you have a good heart,
Let's go home and talk about it
And if you don't like good advice
Then get the fuck out of here.

Nowadays Manuela has changed.
She passes and she doesn't
greet me anymore.

Mind you, in paranoid Angola, as Portuguese-born Angolan writer José Luandino Vieira might put it, even that could somehow be considered political.

Unfortunately, the Orquestra os Jovens do Prenda has now disbanded, with some of its members joining new bands.

New Styles

While some of its different styles are audibly related to popular African sounds such as soukous or to Brazilian rhythms, Angolan music comes into its own with distinct home-grown creations. Despite having to slowly pick up the pieces of a broken economy and cope with the results of a massive influx of people fleeing unrest in the vast countryside, the capital, Luanda, is as much a powerhouse of musical creation as any city on the continent.

The city has seen the birth of such styles as **Kilapanda** (for a sample of which you might try the band **Afra Sound Star**), Angolan **Merengue** and **Semba**. Angolan Semba comes from an Angolan word meaning 'navel' and came to describe the circling dance step associated with that rhythm. While Semba's name might excusably lead you to believe it is an offshoot of Brazilian samba, proud Angolans might tell you it was born from a musical tradition carried over to Brazil by

Angolan slaves, transformed there and then brought back to its original home.

Even the narrow stretch of an island which juts out across the bay from Luanda, the *Ilha do Cabo*, came up with its own brand of sound, **Rebita**, a rolling accordion and harmonica-packed invitation to dance which explains why Luanda's music clubs are bursting at the seams until the small hours.

More traditional forms of music include those from the singer **Kituxi** which, like his cosmopolitan counterparts, rely on such Angolan favourites as conga drums, *reco-reco* (a bead-wrapped cylinder giving a washboard-like effect), *ungo* (a one-string instrument shaped like a bow, also known as the *berimbau* in Brazil), and various shakers.

Perhaps due to the political commitment of several Angolan artists, such as **Bonga** and **Teta Lando**, both of whom at one time made Paris a home-in-exile, a common feature of the latest crop of releases is a conscious attempt to showcase the variety of Angolan styles, musical languages and cultural heritage. This effort is apparent, for example, in Bonga's release *Roça de Jindungo* (Hot Pepper Plantation), which includes such songs as a festive mix of traditional Angolan Semba rhythms "Potpourris do Semba" (Semba Mix), or puts on a slow-burning rendition of Rebita in "Rebita H", which features lyrics such as as: "Here we are – Rebita will rise again, we are keeping the tradition alive."

Waldemar Bastos has been playing music since 1961. In the early 1980s he went to Brazil, where he recorded his first album, *Estamos Juntos*, in 1986. Although now long based in Portugal, his wide-ranging song-writing skills remain popular in Angola. His latest release, *Pretaluz*, was

produced in the US with the innovative New York guitarist Arto Lindsay.

Recent CD issues also include compilations by Teta Lando and **Carlos Lamartine**, both titled *Memórias*. Here, the aim of the compilation is not so much to present a 'greatest hits' selection as a desire to promote the cultural heritage, threading through songs from the past quarter century, and combining a variety of sounds from Angolan Semba, such as in the upbeat "Vunda ku Muceque" (Jumble in the Ghetto) featuring an itching mix of voice, percussions, bursts of trumpet and guitars against African–Cuban beats, to such gems as the bolero-flavoured lament, "Africa chora pena" (Africa cries its sorrow).

Musicians from several musical bands from the 1960s to the '90s have come together to form **Banda Maravilha** (The Wonder Band). In addition to the musicians from the band proper, Carlos Vieira-Dias, Moreiro Filho, Rufino Cipriano and Marito Furtado, this band includes renowned guest Angolan artists, such as Mestre Geraldo on the accordion, a legendary figure in the rebita movement. For its first CD, entitled *Angola Maravilha*, the band reached into Luanda's ghettos to share some of the classics of ghetto gossip and hard truths, with its cast of miserable husbands and ridiculed spinsters, as in the lightly sardonic "Mana" (Sister), which tells of a woman with a sharp tongue and no friends, or the sad trumpet-introduced and chorus-led "N'Zala" (Hunger). The band's emphasis on Angolan culture is also apparent in its musical rendition of "O meu amor da rua 11" (11th Street Love Affair), a rhythmic, trumpeting song based on lyrics by Aires de Almeida Santos, a revered twentieth-century Angolan poet from the southern coastal city of Benguela.

Another name to watch for is **Carlos Burity**, whose latest and very popular release was in 1996. He is reputedly still going strong, with a new CD expected soon.

discography

Compilations

 Angola '90s
(Budd, France).

Excellent compilation of most of the current names mentioned in this article plus new bloods Pavlo Flores and Simmons.

 Telling Stories to the Sea (Luaka Bop, US).
25 anos de independência (Tinder Records, US).

These two valuable compilations showcase Luso-African music from Angola, alongside that of Guinea-Bissau, Cape Verde, São Tome and Mozambique.

Artists

Banda Maravilha

This group is a get-together of musicians from some of the major bands of Luanda stretching from the late 1960s to the early '90s. It is comprised of Carlos Vieira-Dias, Moreirao Filho, Marito Furtado and Rufino Cipriano, and features some renowned Angolan guest musicians.

Angola Maravilha (Kanawa, Portugal).

A shaking, snaking, trilling mix of semba, rebita and other Angolan gems, with the first track "Rebita" a remake of a tune originally played by the group Os Merengues in true axiluanda style – that of the fishermen from Luanda's harbour island.

Waldemar Bastos

Born in 1954 in the northern town of Mbanza Congo, Waldemar Bastos travelled widely in Angola with his parents, and picked up a variety of regional musical influences as he grew up – as well as an acute awareness of the country's suffering under the Portuguese.

 Pretaluz
(Luaka Bop, US).

Bastos's yearning, tremulous voice is beautifully aired on this largely acoustic CD – guitars, percussion and bass – produced by New Yorker (and honorary Brazilian) Arto Lindsay.

Bonga

Standard-bearer of Angolan artists and political activists, Barceló de Cavalho ('Bonga') was born in Luanda in 1942, pursued a career in Portugal as a footballer (for Benfica), and then got on the wrong side of colonial authorities at home with his anti-Portuguese songs. Forced into exile, he eventually settled in Paris in the early 1970s. His first release was in 1972.

Roça de Jindungo
(Vidisco, Portugal).

This is the CD to get if you want a good sample of Angolan Semba, featuring Bonga's trademark raspy voice and songs

of oppression, including the lament in the Kimbundu language, "N'gongo Jetu" (Our torments), decrying the ongoing misery in Angola.

 Swinga Swinga: the Voice of Angola 102% Live
(Piranha, Germany).

Gruff vocals with a variety and exuberance of expression that's deeply satisfying. The Brazilian influences and counter-influences blend seamlessly into the whole.

The Kafala Brothers

The 'Brothers Kafala', as they are internationally known, are sons of a pastor assassinated by the Portuguese. They started singing in the same church choir their mother conducted. Although their cultural roots are with the Kimbundu people, the family travelled all over the land.

 Ngola (Anti-Apartheid Enterprises, UK).

Acoustic guitars back heavy, poetic lyrics, somewhat after the manner of Agostinho Neto, Angola's first poet-president.

 Identi-kit (Anti-Apartheid Enterprises, UK).

Their song-ballads, heavily inspired by the nhatcho and kilampanga beats are sung either in Portuguese or Kimbundu. Through their harmonies it is easy to observe not only the pain and sadness, but also the vigour of a people that has suffered thirty years of war. The ballad "Ngola" is a lament of

an individual whose family, in the Balombo area, was killed by the South African army.

Carlos Lamartine

Already a main figure of the Angolan musical scene in the late 1950s, Lamartine came out with his first CD in 1975 – and his second (Memórias, below) in 1997. In the '70s, he shared cultural stage with such artists as David Zé, Artur Nunes and Urbano de Castro, all of whom were murdered in 1977, after having been suspected of involvement in anti-governmental activities. Lamartine is now back in his native Luanda, apparently working for the Ministry of Culture.

 Memórias
(Kanawa, Portugal).

Twenty-two years after his first release, *Angola Ano 1*, Lamartine has come out with a masterful compilation, collecting in this CD a rich variety of Angolan styles, languages and instruments. Semba, Kilapanda, ballads, Angolan Merengues and African-Cuban beats, among others.

Teta Lando

Teta Lando is from northern Angola, and is now back in Luanda after over a decade of exile in Paris. In Luanda, he runs Teta Lando Produções, probably the only other significant Angolan music production outfit aside from Kanawa (formerly R.M.S.).

 Memórias (1968–1990)
(Teta Lando Produções, Angola).

A musical activist, Lando has put together an impressive collection of thirty-four songs in two CDs, showcasing a career which spans over two decades, with songs in Portuguese, Kikongo and, Kimbundu. One of the more overtly political of the recent crop of records, it features strumming guitars and plaintive tunes, with such songs as "Angolano segue em frente" (Angolan, keep forging ahead) and "Irmão ama teu irmão" (Brother love your brother).

Orquestra os Jovens do Prenda

This band, whose musical trademark is a style known as *quilapanga*, was formed in 1965, disbanded during the civil war, reformed in 1981 and again disbanded a few years ago. Their album *Berlin Fiesta* was released by Piranha in 1990.

 Berlin Fiesta (Piranha, Germany).

Bounces along happily, but doesn't leave much trace in the ear of the listener.

Benin and Togo

afro-funksters

The neighbouring West African countries of Benin and Togo are similar in many respects. Both French-speaking, they also have relatively small populations – 5m and 3.8m people respectively, as compared, say, to Ghana's 16m. Togo is still lumbered with its tyrant leader of thirty years, while Benin, one of the forerunners of Africa's democratic movement of the early-1990s, has recently elected its former dictator as head of state. Music has not been given a high profile in either country, yet it's there in the people. Witness the exiles: Benin boasts Angélique Kidjo, a veritable superstar on the World Music stage, while Togo has a past great in Bella Bellow (once a diva in Paris) and a major talent in the currently Paris-based King Mensah. **François Bensignor** takes a look around, with guidance from **Eric Audra**.

Togo and **Benin**'s music scenes could be utterly different to present realities. In the mid-1980s, the Togolese capital of **Lomé** could boast one of the most sophisiticated 24-track recording facilities in Africa at its **Africa New Sound** studio, where records by **Abeti** and **Dr. Nico** were produced. But life has become a struggle under President Eyadéma's regime, with social unrest collapsing any semblance of a music scene at home.

Things aren't so bad for musicians in Benin these days but the nation's stars – **Wally Badarou**, **Nel Oliver**, **Tohon Stan** and the superstar **Angélique Kidjo** – probably owe something to Mathieu

Kérékou's dictatorship (1972–90) in so far as it encouraged them to seek work abroad and to reject a homeland where artists were only expected to praise the revolution and its leaders.

Benin

From 1960–1972, in the first years of independent Dahomey (as Benin was called before Kérékou changed its name), the music scene was quite vibrant – strongly influenced by Ghanaian and Nigerian highlife, Cuban music, Congolese rumba, American soul and French song.

JAK KILBY

Angélique Kidjo

At that time, the late **Ignacio Blazio Osho** and his **Orchestra Las Ondas** could fill any club they played, while other popular dance groups included **Ignacio de Souza and the Black Santiago**, **Pedro Gnonnas y sus Panchos**, **El Rego et ses Commandos**, **Picoby Band d'Abomey**, **Superstar de Ouidah**, **Les Volcans de la Capitale**, and some time later **Anassua Jazz de Parakou** and **Poly Rythmo de Cotonou**. But with the Kérékou government, the scene ground to a halt. There was no more wild nightlife, as clubs and bars were forced to observe a strict curfew. Musicians, when they could, moved abroad to play, settling in Paris and elsewhere.

Benin Rockers

The first Benin musician to emerge with an international reputation was **Nel Oliver**, who debuted in France in 1976. He absorbed a range of Afro-American influences to create a powerful 'Afro-akpala-funk', and continues to pound away a message: "Démocratie" was the title track of his 1997 album, sung in Yoruba, Goun, English and French. He has become an important producer in the 1990s, with a studio in the Benin capital, Cotonou. His success, however, does not even compare with that of **Angélique Kidjo** (see box overleaf), who started out her career in Holland, before going solo at the end of the 1980s, and cracking the international dance market with "Ayé" in 1994. Currently based in New York, she goes from strength to strength.

Among other Benin artists, **Pedro Gnonnas** stands out. He joined the Afro-salsa super-band **Africando** in 1995, following the death of its lead singer and founder Pap Seck.

Other Benin musicians like **Cella Stella**, **Vivi l'Internationale**, **El Rego**, **Ambroise Coffi Akoha** and **Bluecky d'Almeida** have followed a more mainstream African-pop direction, which eases their way onto radio and TV airplay lists in various African countries, mostly in Abidjan – the gateway to West African (and then maybe world) recognition.

Outside influences have also hit Benin in the 1990s. **Yaya Yaovi** planted the rasta seed here, launching a **reggae** group, after a trip to Jamaica

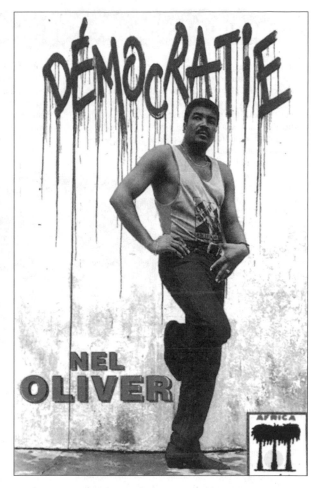

and a visit to the famous Bob Marley Tuff Gong studio. Recently, **rap** has also found its niche with the musical youth. Most groups have a rather derivative American-style (with French lyrics), though the **Ardiess Posse** do it fresh, adding a distinct style of their own.

Traditions

But where are the real and original Benin sounds to be found? Perhaps the one good thing that came out of Kérékou's 'Marxist' regime was that artists were encouraged to seek their own traditions and make something out of them, albeit for the government's benefit. Thus **Tohon Stan** created his **tchink-system**, a musical style that derives from the local funeral music known as *tchinkoumé*, traditionally played with 'water percussion' – half-calabashes sitting in water-filled larger half-calabashes which are whacked with a sandal or other handy item.

Angélique Kidjo: Keep On Moving

Life hurls a welter of different circumstances at the artists engaged in creating the CDs found in the World Music stacks. Some, on the more ethnographic recordings, may be barely aware that their voice or instrumental skills are reverberating in the living rooms of the Western world. Others, having secured much sought-after recording deals, cling to signs of success, and wait for modest royalty cheques. Of the successful few, a tiny minority return home to reinvest skills and money in the local recording industry, as Youssou Ndour has done. Most successful artists, however, having served their time on the fringes of the global recording industry, settle more or less permanently in Europe or America, reaping the rewards of hard work and talent and generally giving short shrift to purists who pick holes in their widely acclaimed crossover productions.

If any female artist embodies this kind of World Music it's **Angélique Kidjo**. The diva from Benin, signed since 1989 to Island Records, has done more to popularise African music than any other woman. Her music combines a broad spectrum of genres from soul to funk-rock, always with firm, high-tech production by Parisian producer (and Mr Kidjo) **Jean Hébrail**. The common factor is Angélique's angelic voice – a vocal style not so much honeyed as darkly caramelised, and given full rein on every album. She has a staggeringly powerful voice, coached by jazz training in Paris and the influence of *zilin* – a blues-like vocal technique from Abomey, the Fon heartland in central Benin. She still sings almost exclusively in Fon, a tonal language, like the closely related Yoruba.

Kidjo's albums range widely in style, from her debut *Pretty*, which used Beninois rhythms like the *gogbahoun*, tapped out with a coin on a bottle, to the 1989 *Parakou* (her first international release), to *Logozo* and *Ayé*, dancehall fusions tearing away from her roots, and then the innovative masterpiece of 1996, *Fifa*, incorporating field recordings in Benin and ranging from taut-muscle dance tracks to heart-dissolving ballads.

Born in 1960, Angélique was brought up in an artistic household in Ouidah (the voodoo capital of Benin) by the kind of parents who helped create a quartier latin image for the country, as the seat of Africa's intellectual and creative avant garde. She performed from the age of six as an actor and dancer in her mother's theatre group, and they provided unusual support for her stage-struck ideas. As a child, she listened to James Brown and the Beatles, and sang her own words, in Fon, to the tunes, and when she joined her brothers' band, Simon and Garfunkel and Santana were her favourites (Carlos

Pretty: Angélique's debut

Santana was later to take a guest spot on *Fifa*).

By the time Kidjo was twenty, she was already working as one of the country's very few professional female singers. She moved to Holland to sing with the afro-jazz-weirdness fusioneers **Pili Pili**, led by Jasper Van t'Hof, and then to Paris, where she first recorded as a solo artist. Unlike most Benin or Togo musicians based in Paris, who tend to produce discs of largely roots appeal with Ivoirian and Gabonese artists, Angélique went for a crossover music from the outset. She put her remarkable vocal talents to work with a loose and eclectic community of French, Caribbean, African and American musicians, and over the years she has travelled between Paris, London and America to record, with musicians of the calibre of Manu Dibango and Branford Marsalis in support.

Although Angélique Kidjo keeps a strong note of social concern in her lyrics – hunger, homelessness, AIDS, injustice – she always denies being a political person. In Africa's new, multiparty states, most artists are anxious to avoid any suggestion of political ambition. Pan-African idealism is more her marque. She still rates Miriam Makeba as a role model, and, fittingly, one of her best songs is haunting rendition of the love-song, "Malaika" that helped make Miriam Makeba famous.

With her internationalist outlook, flat-top hairdo, unique, strident voice and exhausting on-stage dynamism, Kidjo has become by far the most popular African woman singer. She has an inspired realism, rejecting roots purists who would have music stay within its borders, yet continuing to draw inspiration from Africa as well as Europe and the US. On her 1998 CD, *Oremi*, she explored musical branches of the black diaspora. "The whole idea of Oremi goes back to my childhood," says Angélique, talking on her website (*www.imaginet.fr/~kidjo*). "Since I was a little girl I wondered how it would feel to explore the African heritage of American Music". *Oremi* might be sub-titled 'Explorations Volume 1: R&B'. Funky numbers with a whisper of Africa jostle with melting lullabies and lively asides, like the cover version of Hendrix's "Voodoo Child". While the sound sometimes strays into the more mainstream R&B territory of, say, Nigerian singer Sade, every track includes South African backing vocals recorded in Johannesburg, adding remarkable texture to a sophisticated and subtle production.

"Oremi could be the first part of a trilogy I would like to make", says Angélique, "the second stop being Brazil, the third Haiti and Cuba. My head is always turning, but I will learn and try hard to challenge myself, keep on learning, keep on moving."

Even more traditional, **Danialou Sagbohan** has gained a great respect and local success with his intense 'kaka' rhythms. Working on the rich Goun tradition, he takes *hongan* and *kakagbo* percussion, ritually used by the Zangbeto guardians of the night, and creates new patterns to give them expression in the modern world.

Many artists from the Ouémé region, like **Adjassa**, **Amangnon Koumagnon** or **Gankpon Gbesse** on the Nel Oliver Production catalogue, carry on the complex **Yoruba traditions** much as their fellow Yoruba-speakers do in Nigeria; indeed, they were separated only by the colonial boundaries instigated at the Berlin Congress in 1885.

Denagan Janvier Honfo has probably demonstrated the most exquisite approach to voodoo tradition in Benin, despite living in Germany. His two CDs, *Aziza* and *Bolo Mimi*, recorded with his group **Kelebe**, draw on the finest research on voodoo rhythms, using a wide and colourful range of traditional percussion, including numerous rattles, gourds, water drums, and a kind of thumb piano known as *guidigbo*.

Benin in the 1990s

The music scene in Benin's capital, Cotonou, has improved considerably since the end of the (original) Kérékou regime, with a couple of active studios again in business. **Nel Oliver's studio** has been dynamic through the 1990s, while **Oscar Kidjo**, Angélique's brother, built his own upmarket digital recording facilities in 1997. Other smaller studios use mostly Q-base systems on computers for their productions. Their problem is distribution. Benin is flooded with pirate cassettes, mainly from Nigeria, making life hard for the real labels.

On the live front, there are a number of good **music venues**, including the 2500-seat *Halle des Arts* and the long-established *So What!* jazz club, run by Loïc Martin, where these days you can have dinner and even surf the Internet, and a trio of vibrant dance clubs, *La Cabane*, *Djonke* and the upmarket *2001* disco club, where wealthy Benin society gathers.

Music is also beginning to get more **media exposure**, through a new private TV channel, LC2, launched by ex-professional football player Christian Lagnidé, who became the new government's minister of Youth and Sports in 1998. The station produces music videos, and hopes to become an important promoter of West Africa's music industry. As a result of Kérékou's new government policy (the old dictator was legally elected in 1997), private music radio stations are also booming.

Togo

There seems little light at the end of the tunnel for **Togo**, where President Eyadéma's government has been in place since 1967, making life increasingly difficult. Since the begining of the 1990s, social unrest and military violence have shaken the country, hitting Togolese youth in particular. People who once loved to celebrate now think twice before having a party at their home, fearing the militia's punitive expeditions. The situation has hindered the careers of talented musicians on the national scene, many of whom have moved to Europe, or, in recent years, across the border to Benin, or to Cameroon.

The best-known contemporary Togolese musician is **King Mensah**, who in the early 1990s joined the Ki-Yi M'Bock Theatre in Abidjan. He toured as an actor and a singer in Europe and Japan between 1992–1993, then created his own show in French Guiana and finally settled in Paris where he formed his own group, **Favaneva**.

Turning to the past, it is impossible to avoid the aura of light left by the Togolese singer, **Bella Bellow**. Often compared to Miriam Makeba, her West African career began in 1966, when at the age of twenty she represented her country at the Dakar Arts Festival. Her soft voice, made for love songs, had a strong seductive power, at its best on slow ballads. With the release of her first single, produced in 1969 by the Togolese Paris-based producer, Gérard Akueson, she was invited to perform on French national radio's most prestigious musical programme which in turn led to her appearance at the famous Paris music hall Olympia. Bellow then travelled and performed as far afield as Rio. Her death in a car accident in 1973, having just recorded the hit "Sango Jesus Christo" with Manu Dibango, made her a legend.

Bella Bellow's success story inspired many Togolese female singers, such as **Ita Jourias**, **Mabah**, the 1980s 'sentimental queen', **Afia Mala**, and the voice of the 1990s, **Fifi Rafiatou**, who has had some international success, singing in Ife and Ewe dialects.

Another Togolese voice is that of **Jimi Hope**, who has forged his own heady mix of rock and tropical rhythms. Always a rebel, he is not afraid to denounce power abuse whenever necessary through his extremely cutting lyrics. An artist in every sense of the word, his strange paintings and surreal sculptures express this same desire to break the bounds of convention and explore new ground.

discography

Benin

Compilations

 Yoruba Drums from Benin, West Africa
(Smithsonian Folkways, US).

Drum ensembles of bata and dundun (hourglass tension drums) demonstrate the rapid-fire ritual percussion – including plenty of 'talking drum' – of the Yoruba religion. Recorded in 1987, with detailed liner notes and analysis.

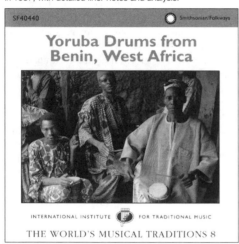

Artists

Denagan Janvier Honfo

Probably because he lives in Europe, far from his beloved country, Honfo takes Benin's percussion tradition very seriously and pushes it to an exiquisite refinement.

 Bolo Mimi
(DJH, Germany).

This is Honfo's second, very nicely self-produced CD, adding some vocal polyphonies to the subtle polyrhthmics he already developed on his previous outing, *Aziza*.

Angélique Kidjo

Brought up in an artistic household in Ouidah by parents who provided unusual support for her stage-struck ideas, Angélique Kidjo made her name first of all in Paris. Now settled in New York, she is probably the most popular woman singer on the World Music stage (see feature box on p.434).

Logozo
(Island, UK).

On this, her second international CD, Kidjo shows the extent of her vocal range. With tributes to Miriam Makeba ("Malaïka") and Bella Bellow ("Sénié"), she shows that she is firmly up there among the great international singers.

Ayé (Island, UK).

Containing the world hit "Agolo", some of this powerful album was recorded at Prince's Paisley Park studio in Minneapolis. It includes, of course, the huge hit "Ayé" – a dancefloor killer.

Fifa (Island, UK).

In 1995, Angélique and her husband, bass player Jean Hébrail, travelled through Benin recording some traditional music that inspired the songs on this album.

Oremi
(Island, UK).

This is a remarkable disc for Kidjo, exploring the music of the African diaspora – and in particular, American R&B. She covers Jimi Hendrix's "Voodoo Child", employs jazz saxophonist Branford Marsalis, and generally funks things up big time. With South African backing vocals adding timbre and texture, her art has never been more mature and sweetly inspired.

Nel Oliver

A renowned producer, as well as performer, Nel Oliver has always loved funky music. It inspired his first 1976 recording in France with the American band Ice and still motivates his music in Cotonou, where he settled back in 1987.

Démocratie (Africa Distributions, Benin).

With its 'Afro-akpala-funk' this 1997 production easily reaches international standards and gets you dancing instantly.

Cella Stella

Born in Cameroon, Stella has built her career from Benin, singing in Fon, Mina and Douala, as a mainstream vocalist in the 1970s African style.

Sensationelle Cella Stella Charme & Voix
(Nelric's Production, France).

Produced by Toto Guillaume (a leading Cameroonian figure in the Paris studios), this album goes from speedy dance tunes to very melodic songs. No special Benin blend, but a very professional and slick sound.

Stan Tohon & the Tchink System

With his wild stage act Stan has led his Tchink System to popularity all over West Africa, since the late 1970s.

Tchink Attack (Donna Wana, France).

This may lack some of the spontaneous power of the Tchink System's stage performances, but it's a vibrant disc, nonetheless, with some very interesting rhythms on the hit song "Dévaluation".

Togo

King Mensah

Mensah Ayaovi Papavi has performed on stage since he was nine years old. A singer with Les Dauphins de la Capitale, he is also a story-teller, has been part of the Ki-Yi M'Bock Theatre in Abidjan, and is today the most popular musician in Togo.

Madjo
(Bolibana, France).

Driven by powerful percussion deeply rooted in African traditions, King Mensah's music, moving from Afrobeat to reggae, is also strongly influenced by jazz and jazz-rock.

Burkina Faso

hidden treasure

Even African music enthusiasts are hard-pressed to name a band from Burkina Faso – an omission due in part, perhaps, to the richness of the music cultures surrounding the country. But it's an omission nonetheless. Burkina has musics aplenty of its own, reflecting its cultural diversity. **François Bensignor** uncovers some of these hidden treasures.

The phrase 'cultural diversity' is no cliché in relation to **Burkina Faso** (the former Upper Volta – renamed after the 1984 revolution of Thomas Sankara). This is a country of some sixty different ethnic groups, bordered by the influential nations of Mali, Côte d'Ivoire, Ghana, Togo, Benin and Niger. The result, for the country's music, is that no significant national style has emerged. However, there are some definite national stars, such as **Black So Man**, **Simporé Maurice**, **Traoré Amadou Ballaké** and **Kaboré Roger**. Oddly, the Burkinabé artists who have made an impression abroad – WOMAD-sponsored **Farafina** and the Italian-based singer **Gabin Dabiré** – would ring few bells back home.

A Multitude of Traditions

West and southwest Burkina Faso is mostly under the influence of **Mande culture**, which is shared with both Mali and Côte d'Ivoire. The Dioula people settled their capital there, in Bobo-Dioulasso, still a strategic commercial and cultural centre. Musically, its strongest traditions are those of **balafon** (xylophone) and percussion.

Living in the centre of the country, the **Mossi people** represent half of Burkina's population and have a strong *griot* tradition. The **Larle Naaba**, traditional head of all the Mossi griot musicians, still retains his traditional function towards Mossi kings as a genealogist, counsellor, historian and musician. He has his own troup and teaches musicians in his own royal court.

The northern part of Burkina is the home of the **Fulbe people** (also called Fula and Peul), who are closely linked to their cousins across the Mali and Niger borders. Their traditional music is splendid, with incredible voice techniques and fabulous hand clapping rhythms. There are also strong musical

Not your average night out in Koudougou

FRANÇOIS BENSIGNOR

Kaboré Moussa at Bazar Musique

traditions among the **Senoufo**, **Gourounsi**, **Bissa** and Nankana people in the **south** along the borders of Côte d'Ivoire, Benin and Ghana, but little is recorded.

This multitude of musical traditions has had its profile raised through a variety of different Festivals. Every two years since 1983, the **Semaine Nationale de la Culture** is held in Burkina's second city, Bobo Dioulasso, where traditional and modern musicians from all over the country come to compete for awards. Since 1996, the capital, Ouagadougou, has held modern music yearly awards, **Les Grands Prix Nationaux**. And lastly, there is the **Nuits Atypiques de Koudougou**, held every year in Burkina's third city, Koudougou. This non-competitive international festival mixes traditional and modern acts. It was launched in 1996 by Koudbi Koala, founder of the dance and percussion troup, Saaba, with support from French and Dutch World Music festivals.

All Kinds of Styles

There is view held in the African music business that people in Burkina have never really cared to listen to artists from their own country. Stars from Côte d'Ivoire are superstars in Ouagadougou. Artists from Mali also have a great impact in the west of Burkina. And from every cassette shop, radio and bar, you can hear the never-ending pulse of Congolese rhythms.

Pick up the *Best of Burkina Compilation* CD and you will certainly hear all kinds of styles. There is modern Mandingo from **Abdoulaye Cissé** and **Burkina Band**; Congolese soukous from **Thomas Tiendrebeogo**; Cuban dance from **Tidiane Coulibaly**; afro-pop from **Pierre Sandwidi** and **Amety Meria**; reggae from **Jean-Claude Bamogo** and **Black So Man**; soul-funk from **Georges Ouédraogo** and **To Finley**; and ethnobeat from **Nick Domby**.

These are the country's best known artists – and none plays an original sound taken from Burkina's musical traditions, principally because most of the radio stations play ninety percent foreign music, according to Kaboré Moussa, director of the record company, Bazar Musique. In 1998 radio DJs were asked by the Minister of Culture to play 38 percent local artists but they don't seem ready to do so, and national TV shows include no more than one or two national artists a day among many foreign bands and singers. People know how to dance to Congolese *dombolo*, or *mapouka* or *zouglou* from Côte d'Ivoire, but when it comes to music from Burkina . . . well, they just can't do it.

Bazar Musique

When founding **Bazar Musique** in 1989, **Kaboré Moussa** determined to promote Burkina's culture and music. For five years, he had imported foreign cassettes from Mali, Congo, Guinea, Cuba and Côte d'Ivoire, and sold them all over the country. He realised that it was almost impossible to find any Burkina artists' cassettes on the local market so he launched a record company dedicated to national artists. He produced traditional music from every region, in every language spoken throughout the country – 239 albums by 113 different artists in his first ten years.

Following his lead, three other companies have followed suit: **Sika Sound** and **Africa Musique** in Ouagadougou, and **Faso Ambiance** in Dédougou. Maybe things are looking up. The main problem, however, remains the very limited choice of professional studios. In Ouagadougou there are just two 24-track studios: a busy one owned by **Désiré Traoré**, leader of **Dési et les Sympathiques**, the best-known backing group for afro-pop artists, and another built by local star **Nick Domby**, equipped with new technology.

Another initiative has come from Seydoni Productions, founded in 1993 by **Seydou Richard Traoré**, a Burkina musician based in Sweden. They have been promoting Côte d'Ivoire singer **Aïcha Kone**'s shows, organising concerts in Burkina Faso for other West African stars, and also creating the first national, live modern music contest (subsequently taken over by the government's cultural department). Even more crucial, Seydoni set up the country's first cassette duplication unit, combatting the flood of pirate tapes. This could well make a big change to Burkina's music scene at a time when modern musicians are beginning to use the country's diverse traditions for creating original new styles.

discography

Compilations

 Best of Burkina Compilation
(Bolibana, Burkina Faso/France).

This panorama of Burkina's modern music is a good way to get to know the sounds of leading artists like Tidiani Coulibaly, Georges Ouédraogo, Roger Kaboré, Pierre Sandwidi, Amadou Balaké Traoré, Nick Domby.

 Burkina Faso - The Voice of the Fulbe
(Le Chant du Monde, France).

These recordings made by ethnomusicologist Sandrine Loncke in different locations of northern Soum province in 1992-93 and 1994-95 present the extraordinary voice technics of *doohi* and *gude worbe* sung by men and *jimi rewbe* and *gude rewbe* sung by women. A very interesting and detailed booklet accompanies the splendid music.

Artists

Gabin Dabiré

Based in Europe – currently Italy – since the mid-1970s, this veteran singer-songwriter is a revelation.

 Kontomé (Amiata Records, Italy).

Some of Dabiré's work sounds like Uganda's Geoffrey Oryema in folksie mode, but his more complex choral arrangements, such as "Mariam a në Awa", have a carefully architectured beauty entirely their own.

Farafina

The musicians of Farafina have been touring Europe and America since the mid-1980s, driving the public to dance to their complex but clearly structured polyrhythms. Members have changed through the years but the music is still enjoyable.

 Faso Denou
(RealWorld, UK),

Feel the percussive power of the two balafons (xylophones), bara-skinned open callabash, *doumdou'ba* tall drums and voluble *djembe*.

Japanese imports...Farafina at The Cay Club in Tokyo, 1000

Nemako (Intuition, Germany).

An interesting short, but effortlessly lively set from the consummate performers, with a high-tech studio sound. There's more to please here than skillful percussion, including kora, some delicate arrangements and striking vocals.

WITH JOHN HASSELL

Flash of the Spirit (Intuition, Germany).

An interesting encounter between the talented British trumpet player and this strongly rooted percussion troupe.

Fomtugol

This facinating musical and dance troupe from the northeastern town of Dori presents a repertoire rooted in Fulani traditions. Lutes, flute and calabash are the main instruments accompanying the voices.

Haji Pendo (Daqui, France).

This is one of the first CDs presenting this beautiful Sahel nomads' music to be distributed worldwide.

Les Frères Coulibaly

The Coulibaly *griot* family belongs to the Bwa people living in the north of Burkina. Brothers Souleyman, Lassina and Ousséni lead a standard percussion orchestra with *djembe*, *bara*, *tama* and *kenkeni* drums, *barafile* rattle, *balafon* xylophone and *kamele ngoni* harp-lute.

Musiques du Burkina Faso & du Mali
(Musiques du Monde/Buda, France).

This features brother Lassina Coulibaly with his traditional acoustic group Yan Kadi Faso. Beautiful kora playing is the standout, but there's also a great balafon duo "Massoum pien", complete with wooden 'buzz', a spookily vocal fiddle (the *soukou*) on "Bri kamaye" and a flute solo on the affecting final track, "Ba mana sa" (The Death of a Mother).

Anka Dia (Ethnic/Auvidis, France),

A good drumming record, well recorded.

Cameroon

music of a small continent

'Africa in miniature' is how people in Cameroon often describe their country. There's nowhere on the continent with such abundance of languages, cultures and religions — nor the diversity of Cameroon's geography. It has even been colonised by four nations: the Portuguese, Germans, French and British. All contributed to the culture, which is nominally bilingual, with French and English as official languages, although more than 250 ethnic groups speak their own dialects. From the francophone side Cameroonians have acquired an urbanity of style, fashion and smooth musical delivery (witness jazz giant, Manu Dibango). **Jean-Victor Nkolo** and **Graeme Ewens** explore the legacies – and the latest sounds.

Cameroon, like other francophone nations in the CFA currency zone, has had a hard time in the 1990s, and the faltering economy has been reflected in its music output. At the begining of the decade, things looked bright, with Cameroon's **pop–makossa** style one of Africa's hottest dance genres. But makossa got tied into the zouk scene in Paris, and when that lost its edge, so did makossa. The craze which followed, **bikutsi**, simmered for a while, and helped to inspire Paul Simon's *Rhythms of the Saints* album. But it, too, seems to have lost its fire. In fact, there's a sense, these days, of looking back, with few professional bands active at home, and current releases tending to be greatest hits, or re-issues of old favourites recorded in Paris. However, the prolific and evergreen **Manu Dibango** goes from strength to strength, albeit based abroad, and *kalimba*-player **Wes Madiko** had a European chart success in 1997/98, with the platinum single "Alane". Maybe it's all just a lull.

There is certainly enough indigenous music and rhythms in Cameroon for a multitude of popular styles to surface. Among those already in the pop sphere are the **tchamassi**, popularised by the blind singer **Andre-Marie Tala**, and the **mangambe**, a Bamiléké folk rhythm popularised in its modern form by the bass player **Pierre Didy Tchakounte**, who had a string of popular album releases during the 1970s. In recent years mangambe has been the pulse of a new jazz-fusion notably championed by **Brice Wassy**, the drummer who spent several years at the core of Manu Dibango's always-impressive rhythm section. Then there is the Bassa people's **assiko** on the coast and a **fast,** guitar-based street music called **ambasse bey**. Many Cameroonian musicians also play highlife, soukous or juju music – styles imported from neighbouring Nigeria and Congo/Zaire.

Travel around the country and you will find further traditional elements still very much alive. There are traditions of **kalimba** (sanza/thumb piano) music; talking drums; the **balafon** (xylophone) and **accordion**; **Islamic music**; huge **religious choirs**; **a cappella**; traditional **horn trumpeters** in the Bamoun country. And then there are those pygmies.

> ### LOOKING BAKA
> Cameroon is also the home of the **Baka pygmies** — the culture which provided the group Baka Beyond with such huge success in the 1990s. For a separate article on Pygmy music, see p.601.

Recording Roots

In the 1930s, various record companies such as Pathé imported primitive equipment and persuaded local musicians to record; they had to sing in one take, after briefly introducing themselves. The recordings of those early years are so bad it's difficult to know the composition of the band or the lyrics, or even what type of instrument is being played. You hear something like: "It's me, Thimothé Essombé, from Yabassi, near Douala, and I am happy, today, in the year nineteen-something or other, to sing this song for my loved one. La la la Jules et Mambo . . . Thimothé . . . Chérie . . . Jules et Mambo . . . la la la". It was all over in less than two minutes.

Back then, Cameroon's urban pop music was American, French or British, and eventually artists such as James Brown, the Beatles, Chuck Berry, Johnny Haliday and Sylvie Vertan inspired an internationalism. But in the 1950s the fledgling music industries in Nigeria and Congo had an important influence as 78rpm discs by **highlife** and **rumba**

Manu Dibango and Francis Bebey

Sax-player, composer, singer, pianist and arranger, **Manu Dibango** is Cameroon's musical superstar. He is at heart a jazz player, but he has carried makossa (and other West African styles) to a world audience, and has collaborated with players from Johnny Pacheco to Fela Kuti, the Fania All-Stars and Don Cherry. He is truly international in his orientation, having gone to college in France in 1949, and spent periods since then living in Brussels, Paris, Kinshasa and Côte d'Ivoire.

Dibango's early musical influences were jazz, mainly from the Brussels jazz-club scene of the early 1950s. He forged a career of his own in Congo/Zaire, where he played with the legendary **Kabasele** in the early 1960s and ran a band called **African Soul**. But it was the release of **"Soul Makossa"** in 1973 that made his name and propelled him into the ranks of Africa's big-name musicians. The song was actually recorded as a B-side – to "Mouvement Ewondo", a praise song for Cameroon's football team – but it was picked up by a New York radio station, becoming a massive hit worldwide, with nine different versions in the *Billboard* chart at one time. Its rhythm was even adopted by Michael Jackson on his *Thriller* album.

Back home, "Soul Makossa" paved the way for a new generation of artists to combine traditional inspiration with hi-tech recording facilities. The public, however, seems always to have had a rather ambivalent relationship with Dibango. They respect and admire his international status but his music has never been a regular feature in the clubs or on the dance floors. "Soul Makossa" itself was a very untypical makossa track.

Still, Dibango more than paid his dues to Cameroon in the early 1980s when he produced, arranged and performed on the three-album boxed set *Fleurs Musicales du Cameroun*, a collection which gathered the country's best veteran and new popular musicians, alongside unsung traditional artists, to give a panoramic soundtrack to the country. The discs included most of the diverse rhythms which have informed the 1980s and '90s styles of pop-makossa, mangambe, assiko and bikutsi.

Manu Dibango

An early buddy and collaborator of Dibango's, in the jazz bars of Brussels and Paris, was **Francis Bebey** – Cameroon's other great musical ambassador. A multi-talented character, Bebey is a novelist, storyteller, filmmaker, and musicologist, but primarily a guitarist and composer. He sings in English, French and Douala, experimenting with styles ranging from classical guitar and traditional rhythms to makossa and straight pop, and has released some twenty albums since 1969 . He's also the author of a seminal music book, *African Music: A People's Art* (Lawrence Hill, US).

artists were being broadcast across Africa on the radio. Following behind came the traders who supplied original discs and later made licensing agreements to re-issue popular records.

The only developed city in Cameroon at the time was the port of **Douala** and it was low-key compared to its neighbours. Prevailing musical styles included the frenetic guitar action of **ambasse bey**, while **accordion** players bridged the gaps between folk songs and French *chansons*. In the international hotels, white clients expected to hear the latest American swing, or local versions of it.

Singer/guitarists were the first to create something approaching a local sound, with artists such as **Lobe Lobe**, **Ebanda Manfred**, **Nelle Eyoum** and **Ekambi Brillant** among the pioneers. A musically progressive artist, Brillant more or less created **makossa**, and his single "N'Gon Abo" was such a hit that, to this day in Cameroon it'll have everyone on the dance floor in seconds, shaking their waists.

In those days, music was not as politicised or tribalised as it has become. Just as Brillant did a song in the Ewondo language of the Beti people from the Yaoundé district, so **Messi Martin** also made attempts to sing, quite beautifully, in the Douala language, thanks to the collaboration of Nellé Éyoum, himself from Douala and another of the fathers of modern makossa.

Before independence in 1960 there were no recording opportunities, although some Cameroonians did appear on Congolese and Nigerian labels – such as **Herbert Udemba**, whose songs were released on the Nigerphone label as 'Ibo minstrel style'. The opening of a radio station in Douala finally made recording possible. In 1962, **Eboa Lotin**, 'The Lion', made his recording debut for Phillips. His style, based on guitar and harmonica riffs, was a precursor of makossa, named after a children's dance. He was followed by **Misse Ngoh**, a member of Los Calvinos band, who developed a more flamboyant finger-picking style.

The most popular form around the time of independence was **assiko**. Played on acoustic guitar accompanied by percussion and bottle, this was a local variant of **palm wine music** (see Sierra Leone) with an up-tempo beat. Leading protagonists were **Dikoume Bernard** and **Jean Bikoko**, who recorded a national hit "A ye pon djon nì me" in 1960 for the Samson label and went on to form a forty-strong troupe of assiko dancers. The fifty-year-old **Oncle Medjo** also found fame with a similar line-up.

GRAEME EWENS

Moni Bilé

Makossa

The Doula-based style of **makossa** has dominated Cameroon's pop scene since the 1960s, and with Manu Dibango's funky hybrid "Soul Makossa" in 1972 (see box on previous page) it briefly reached an international audience. In its earliest form, it was a folk dance and music, evolving out of the mission schools of Douala, where it was played on guitars and accordions. Perhaps the best early exponent was **Eboa Lotin**, who has been much anthologised on cassette in Doula.

In the early 1970s, makossa became an increasingly urban, electric style, with a dance rhythm precisely cut for the nightclubs. Then in the 1980s it was transformed into **pop-makossa**, and produced largely from Paris. Most of the effective music of this new style was played by the so-called **National Team of Makossa** – a clique of Paris-based musicians directed by bassist **Aladji Toure** with **Toto Guillaume** and **Ebeny Wesley**.

The best singers of this era were the sophisticated **Moni Bilé** and **Moundy Claude** (known as 'Petit Pays'). For a flavour of the early 1980s, and some spine-tingling, high-note vocals, you should also check out "Ami", the international success by **Bébé Manga**. And try **Ben Decca**, or the elegant makossa mix of the group **Esa**. Or **Prince Eyango**, **Doleur** or **Misse Ngoh**.

Other must hears for the full Cam makossa treatment are: **Sam Fan Thomas**, whose *African Typic* collection made him the biggest Cameroonian name abroad after Dibango; guitarist **Toto Guillaume**, who has backed just about everyone (including Miriam Makeba) and was one of the main engineers of the explosive affair between Antillean zouk and African music; and **Lapiro de Mbanga**, who achieved fame with his anti-ruling-party, pidgin-English vitriol in song, then, to the bafflement of all, started praising President Biya's regime.

Bikutsi's Essential Thrust

Cameroon's dictatorial President Paul Biya is a great aficionado and dancer of the rival musical style of **bikutsi**, which has its power-base in the city of Yaoundé. With his patronage, it has flourished on the (heavily state-censored) radio and TV. A story that hit the drinking parlours of Yaoundé a few years back – part-joke, part-rumour – went like this: the archbishop of Douala, Monseigneur Jean Zoa, goes to the president's palace, hoping to get the latest bikutsi song – "The Lift", by the raunchy **Katino Ateba** – banned. But as the arch-bishop enters the president's living room, he hears Biya himself asking his wife to "play that song again". The Monseigneur has to change his tune and throw in the towel before uttering a word.

Katino Ateba's songs are often crude, porno-graphic and anticlerical. But such themes are the essential thrust of **bikutsi**, a style whose origins lie in a blood-stirring war rhythm – the music of vengeance and summoning to arms, sounding through the forest. Tra-ditionally, it used rattles and drum and the *njang* xylophone or balafon. And, for decades, if not centuries, Beti women tricked the Christian church, as well as their own men, by singing bikutsi using complex slang phrases reserved for women. While clapping out the rapid-fire rhythm, they sang about the trials and tribulations of every-day life; they discussed sexuality; and they talked about sexual fantasies and taboos. In the middle of the song, a woman would start a chorus leading to a frenzied dance of rhyth-mic foot-stamping and shaking: shoulders-back-bottom-clap-clap-clap-clap-clap. The whole thing was accompanied by strident screams and whistles.

Many women still perform the old folk dances across the sprawling hills of Yaoundé city and beyond to the south. One of the stalwarts of bikut-si was **Anne-Marie Nzie**, 'The Queen of Cameroonian music' who kept the form popular from the 1940s until the '80s, recording on the Pathé Marconi label. Another historic group was the **Richard Band de Zoetele** – which employed a six- to eight-piece balafon orchestra.

The inventor of 'modern bikutsi', as a staple of mainstream Cameroonian pop, was **Messi Me Nkonda Martin**, founder of the band **Los Camaroes**, whose tunes were played incessantly on provincial radio stations in the 1960s and '70s. Messi Martin came up with an idea that translat-

Ascenseur: Le Secret de l'Homme

Action 69!
The lift, every male's secret
I like men who are no fools
Those who know how to
*   press my sensitive button*
The lift, that's every male's secret
I like a man who is no fool
I like a man who will suck me downstairs
I like a man who will suck me upstairs too
I like men who sin on earth
I like men who sin in heaven too
Even the parish priest loves that
Instead of giving me a private service
He comes home to sin downstairs
And I like the priest who sins upstairs too
And his mass will not be sad
*   as a funeral ceremony*
Because, every male is a boss
Even in his pyjamas
But only when he's strong and big
With his prick as solid as a man's gun
Solid as a church's big candle
And I'll lick him up and down
And then, and only then, I'll ask him
To press the button in my lift
Every male's secret...

Katino Ateba

ed the sound and magic of a traditional balafon to a new era, linking together some of the strings of an electric guitar with lengths of cotton cord, to give a damper tone and a slight buzz. Other bikut-si performers soon followed his example, notably the singer **Maurice 'Elamau' Elanga**.

If bikutsi's sound is characterised by screaming, clapping, stamping, and balafon-playing (or bala-style guitar), its acclaimed superiority over makos-sa lies in its heavily charged content: where there's bikutsi, there must be dance, controversy, social debate and sex, either implied or explicit. Messi Martin has been a master of all that, with his mellow voice, liberal doses of social commentary and eternal womanising. When he stopped composing and performing, his younger brother **Beti Joseph** took over. His "N'Son Anyu" was a rant against local journalists, who make London's tabloid reporters look like angels. **Mbarga Soukous** and a handful of others also found momen-tary fame with overtly 'pornographic' lyrics.

Gradually, bikutsi musi-cians improved the techni-cal quality of their music and began to challenge the commercial success of makossa. Maurice Elanga shrewdly added brass in the 1970s. **Nkondo Si Tony** used electronic keyboards and synthesisers, and brought state-of-the-art production to bear. His output on the local cassette market was impressive and he acquired something of a cult status among Yaoundé youth. Later, the long-established bikut-si/rumba big-band, **Les Veterans**, began to make themselves heard in Europe with some bikutsi album releases. It was a man called **Mama Ohandja**, how-ever, who truly popularised the bikutsi in the 1970s, with a string of releases on the French Sonodisc label and a touring band called **Confiance Jazz**.

In the 1980s, Ohandja's success was followed and surpassed by **Les Têtes Brulées**, at least out-side Cameroon. This was a band who looked great, and whose stylish (almost easy listening) appeal

Burnt-out Heads

Les Têtes Brulées, the first bikutsi band to appear on CD, brought a dramatic new global awareness to Cameroonian music. On stage, their wild, cross-cultural appearance – body paint, sculpted hair, layers of clothing and clumpy trainers – comes over as a kind of tribal pantomime. Their initial gigs abroad whipped up a whirlwind of media attention and earned them equal measures of censure and adulation at home. The name was provocative enough – what could they mean by 'Burnt Heads'? It implied hyperactive self-indulgence, burnt-out, blown minds…. they didn't sit comfortably in the pantheon of African music stars. The Têtes' publicity files filled up early on after the release of the well-made *Man No Run* film of their first French tour, directed by the Cameroon-born maker of *Chocolat*, Claire Denis. And an interesting and relatively young Cameroonian cinéaste, Jean-Marie Teno, made a rather good docudrama on the politics of water in Cameroon, starring Théodore Epémé – aka Zanzibar, founder member of the Têtes – entitled *Bikutsi Water Blues*. Tragically, the sensitive young lead guitarist committed suicide shortly afterwards.

Les Têtes Brulées in characteristic low-key stage make-up

soon won them festival slots in Europe and the US. Cameroonians were less enthusiastic, in part due to the political affiliations of the band (they were presidential favourites). But there's no doubt that they took bikutsi to a new audience, just as Manu Dibango had done with makossa.

More roots bikutsi performers in the 1980s and '90s included the experienced musicians **Uta Bella**, **Marilou & Georges Seba** and **Jimmy Mvondo Mvelé**. All of them grew up in the Yaoundé area, and found work as producers, session and concert musicians in Paris and New York. Others included **Sabbal Lecco** and **Vincent Nguini** – who made huge (and undervalued) bikutsi contributions to Paul Simon's *Rhythm of the Saints* album – and the singer **Sissi Dipoko**. In Cameroon's musical-political mix, Dipoko, being from Douala (makossa-land), would not have been expected to perform bikutsi. But she had extensive experience singing with Dibango's band and her recording "Bikutsi Hit" signalled an easing of the clash between bikutsi and makossa.

Cameroon Now

Cameroon was one of the last African countries to get a TV station – which began broadcasting in 1985. The guitarist and composer **Elvis Kemayo** returned from Gabon, where he had been artistic director of their TV station, to present the '*Telepodium*' show which gave exposure to many of the country's artists – especially the President's favourites. It hasn't helped a great deal. In the 1990s, the lack of a music infrastructure, economic decline and the inability of musicians to maintain working bands, have combined to mute the production of home-grown music. Many of the old-school musicians, including **Prince Eyango**, **Tom Yom's**, **Lapiro** and **Solo Mouna**, have left the country, while at home, ground-breaking veterans are sliding into obscurity and poverty.

Which is not to say that nothing new has emerged in the 1990s. **Bend-skin** is a recent kind of street-credible percussion-led folk music, pioneered as a pop music by **Kouchoum Mbada**. Another style which owes something to folk roots, and something to bol (from 'bal' accordion-playing), is **Bantowbol**, championed by **Gibraltar Drakus** with Nkondo Si Tony. And then there's a lesser-known rhythm from Northern Cameroon – the **nganja** – which was exposed in Britain during the mid-1980s by the eccentric dancer/singer **Ali Baba** and is getting a new contemporary run-out from **Le Groupe Kawtal**. There is also a kind of Congo/Zairean **'new rumba'**, and a **makossa-soukous** fusion, popularised by **Papillon**, **Petit Pays**, the late **Kotto Bass**, and newcomer **Jean Pierre Esssome**. A dance called the *zenge* has evolved to accompany this recent beat.

But for all this music, Cameroon desperately needs another global hit such as "Soul Makossa" to liven things up and restore some confidence, among musicians, producers and listeners alike.

Thanks to Prince Eyango

discography

Compilations

O Fleurs Musicales du Cameroun
(FMC/Afrovision, Cameroon).

An authoritative and comprehensive three-album boxed set, produced, arranged and musically directed in the early 1980s for the government by Manu Dibango, to showcase the country's musical vitality. One disc of folk songs and two of makossa, mangambe, bikutsi and assiko – and a 12" booklet. Long since deleted but one to scour the record fairs for.

Makossa Connection Vols 1–4 (TJR, France).

Four-hour makossa celebration, with everyone you can think of and many you won't – Guy Lobé, Emile Kangué, Manulo, Moni Bilé, Ben Decca, Salle Jean, Lapiro de Mbanga, Hoigen Ekwalle, Epée et Koum, Ndedy Dibango and Gilly Doumbé.

Artists

Kotto Bass

The late Kotto Bass was a popular, witty and engaging artist whose soukous fusion provided an antidote to straight makossa.

Soukous Fusion (Kouogueng Fils, France).

This was the second, and last, release, showcasing his nice voice and round, fulsome sound.

Francis Bebey

'Africa's Renaissance Man', Bebey has worked his way through jazz and most of his country's roots music. A multi-instrumentalist and musicologist, amongst other things, he defies categorisation.

Nandolo/With Love: Francis Bebey Works 1963–94 (Original Music, US).

This retrospective features Bebey on bamboo flute, kalimba and acoustic guitar. It is highly, and frequently, commended.

Moni Bilé

Smooth, suave but excitable, Bilé really maximised the enjoyment potential of makossa. He was the most influential artist of the 1980s, whose hi-tech productions outsold all others.

 10th Anniversary: Best of ...
(MAD Productions/Sonodisc, France).

Enjoy the mellow growl and revisit those great, dance-floor stirrers, "Bijou" and "O Si Tapa Lambo Lam".

Manu Dibango

The 'makossa man' has maintained his output into the late 1990s and has about a dozen CDs on the market. The perceived 'African' content ebbs and flows but, call it what you will, Manu's music always swings.

Live '91 (Stern's, UK).

The catalogue of Africa's foremost jazz sax-player is so vast, it's hard to know where to begin. If you find nothing to please among the eclectic set on this old but representative CD you probably don't like him.

 Homemade
(Celluloid/Melodie, France).

Classic cuts from the 1970s when Manu was really blowing up his own kind of Afrofusion into a massive sound. Includes the often reprised "Ah Freak son fric".

CubAfrica (Celluloid/Melodie, France).

Really mellow versions of Cuban classics, accompanied on acoustic instruments by Cuarteto Patria and Manu's eternal guitar partner, Jerry Malekani. As sweet as can be.

Guy Lobe

Lobe arrived on the Paris scene in the mid-1980s just as Antillean musicians were 'zouking' up makossa.

◎ **Dix Ans Vols 1 & 2** (Tandem/Blue Silver, France).

A double-barrelled collection of straight ahead, no nonsense makossa that takes you dancing through a decade.

Wes Madiko

Wes Madiko's career went ballistic when his single "Alane" sold millions in Europe in 1997, followed by a chart entry in Britain. The grandson of a griot, he seemed on a mission.

◎ **Walenga** (Epic/Sony, UK).

Twelve tracks of 'music therapy' including his platinum hit, from the 'rootsman' kalimba player teamed up with French composer Michel (*Deep Forest*) Sanchez.

Lapiro de Mbanga

A master of political rap, Lapiro was hugely controversial – a tough blend of politics, rhythm and hot language made him a big name in Cameroon.

 Ndinga Man Contre-Attaque: na wou go pay? (Label Bleu, France).

Here – with a hard mix of makossa, zouk, soukous and Afro-beat – Lapiro rebuts the criticism that he sold out to the powers that be.

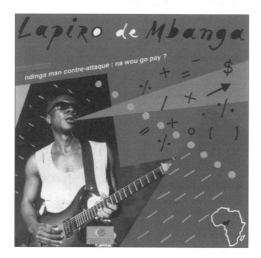

Charlotte Mbango

A serious makossa singer who can work just as well with other rhythms, Mbango was introduced to international audiences in the early 1990s as part of the Manu Dibango roadshow.

◎ **Konkai Makossa [Makossa New Form]** (Touré Jim, France).

Backing Mbango, you hear Sissi Dipoko, Aladji Touré and Toto Guillaume. If you want to know what hi-tech, 1990s makossa means, venture no further.

Sally Nyolo

Sally Nyolo came out of the Belgium-based, world-babes band, Zap Mama (see p.28), and has been the first of the group to make a solo breakthrough.

◎ **Tribu** (Lusafrica, France).

Her first solo release: twelve songs which showed off her superb voice and individual treatment of bikutsi, amongst other things.

◎ **Multi Culti** (Tropical, France).

Polished, soul-inflected, vocal-led package that represents Cameroon's roots music in a worldly, accessible fashion. No sign of the makossa team on this one.

Anne-Marie Nzie

Known as 'The Golden Voice of Cameroon' and the 'Queen Mother of Bikutsi', Anne-Marie Nzie is still pumping out some pretty robust music with her quavering Edith Piaf-like voice. She made her recording debut in 1954 on the Congolese Opika label, playing Hawaiian guitar, but had only released one album of her own, *Liberté*, on the Pathé Marconi label, between then and 1998.

◎ Beza Ba Dzo (Label Bleu, France).

Produced by, and featuring, the drum motivation of Brice Wassy, Anne-Marie's second album renders her folklore-based material with power and energy. Her semi-acoustic amalgam of traditional and modern instrumentation, and the variety of rhythms and moods make a welcome change from makossa. Her guests include Manu Dibango, Jean-Philippe Rykiel and Marcelin Ohanda, guitar maestro of Les Vétérans.

Papillon

Papillon is a popular new makossa singer, bringing a zenge, zouky, soukous shake-up to liven up the scene.

◎ **Homme Fort** (Gazon Synthetique/TJR, France).

Sounds more zouky than makossa, and thus a bit of a manufactured sound for some tastes.

Paris Africans

This group is the latest creation of Toups Bebey, nephew of the great Francis Bebey, and fusionist extraordinaire – a saxophonist who doubles/triples up on keyboards, percusion, vocals, etc. The Parisian element includes accordion and some space-rocky guitar.

◎ **Paris Africans** (VEK/Melodie, France).

The PAs provide a good mantra for World Musicians everywhere. "We are nearly stateless, our country is music". Not surprisingly, given Bebey's first language and instrument, this contains many Manu Dibango-isms, and some confounding fusions.

Petit Pays

As a young artist, PP (aka Moundy Claude) gave to the makossa scene one of its best successes with his first work *Ça Fait Mal*, a great local cassette release.

◎ **Avant Gout** (Melodie, France).

With his band Les Sans Visas, PP gets down a zouk/soukous/makossa blend, complete with shouted animations.

◎ **Le CV de Petit Pays (10 Ans, 10 Hits)** (Melodie, France).

Another decade under the bridge on this fine compilation.

Les Têtes Brulées

The Têtes Brulées came to Europe on a high note, just when the national football team was showing promise in the 1994 World Cup. Early reports had them playing football on stage. They caused a flash of excitement, but subsequently seem to have burnt out.

ⓒ **Les Têtes Brulées** (Bleu Caraibes/France).

The CD which Stern's licensed by the band that broke bikutsi to the world in 1990, now available on French import only. Lots of energy but little depth.

Sam Fan Thomas

'Mr Makassi' had a truly phenomenal success with "African Typic Collection" – what many don't know is that the closing refrain [words and music] is lifted straight from a song by Franco, called "Boma l'Heure".

ⓒ **The Best Of Sam Fan Thomas** (TJR, France).

Thomas ran out a string of sound-alike records following that first big hit and tried to trademark makassi. Here we have an hour and a quarter of bright, perky, singalong tunes.

SAM FAN THOMAS & CHARLOTTE MBANGO

ⓒ **African Typic Collection** (Virgin Earthworks, UK).

Four Cameroonian songs (and one stray Cape Verdean number via Paris) packaged around the mega-hit title song.

Brice Wassy

Manu Dibango cohort, Brice Wassy is a consummate session drummer and a producer with a pan-African CV. His own material, like Dibango's, is jazz fusion.

ⓒ **Shrine Dance** (M.E.L.T. 2000, UK).

Brice draws on a full palette of textures for his second album with an international jazz line-up. The set includes everything from a bikutsi version of Miles Davies to the mangambe and mevum – yet another dance rhythm.

Tom Yom's

Yom's (yes – that's his name) is a revolutionary part-bikutsi artist with an exceptional, high, clear voice, singing compositions by, among others, Eboa Lotin.

ⓒ **Tom Yom's and the Star's Collection, Sunny Days** (TJR, France).

Ignore the naff packaging and a few duff numbers: Yom's is a singer and musician of real power and range.

Cape Verde

music of sweet sorrow

Two hours' flying time west of Dakar — and exactly midway between Portugal and Brazil, lie the Cape Verde islands, a unique archipelago adrift in the Atlantic Ocean, and an island group whose population is now outnumbered by its overseas communities. **Susana Máximo** and **David Peterson** explore the homeland of World Music superstar Cesaria Evora.

C ape Verdean music has gained quite a high profile in the past decade, through the success of **Cesaria Evora**, the unlikely 'barefoot diva'. She sings the bluesy songs known as **morna**, one of a number of styles unique to her island archipelago home.

The Republic of Cape Verde is a group of ten islands of volcanic origin, 600km off the coast of Senegal. An Atlantic world apart, Cape Verde is an ex-Portuguese colony, independent since 1975, not quite African, but scarcely European. Named after Cap Vert, the peninsula of Dakar, this small country is anything but green – in fact, for ten months of the year, it is dry, dusty and windy, essentially a maritime extension of the Sahel. It is prone to catastrophic droughts, which, together with the islands' isolation, and lack of opportuties, have driven very large numbers to emigrate.

The islands were uninhabited when the Portuguese arrived and settled in 1462, but with the arrival of African slaves and sailors, they became quite mixed racially. The bulk of the modern population is composed of the descendants of African slaves; the everyday language is Kriolu – a creole language which blends old-style Portuguese with West African languages. In the five hundred years of its occupation, Portugal almost totally ignored the islands' development. Thousands perished in famines, went to São Tomé as plantation workers, or emigrated overseas. Of a million people who call themselves Cape Verdean, only about a third actually live on the islands. The remainder are scattered in the US (mostly New England), Europe (mainly Portugal, France, Italy and the Netherlands) and Africa (Dakar). There is even a flourishing community in Cardiff, Wales. Almost every family has relatives overseas.

The islands' music is coloured by this history of separation and longing, by the creole culture, and by the mix of Europeans and Africans. Cape Verdean music is influenced both by the waltz and the contre-dances of the old continent; and by rhythms from Africa, Brazil and the Caribbean. There is a variety of unique styles, some of which have changed little over the centuries. Some, such as the **morna**, sound quite European, while West African elements are more to the fore in **batuco** and **funana**.

PIERRE RENI-WORMS

Cesaria Evora: "I only regret my success has taken so long"

Sodade	Nostalgia
Quem mostra' bo Ess caminho longe? Quem mostra' bo Ess caminho longe?	Who showed you This far journey? Who showed you This far journey?
Ess caminho Pa São Tomé.	This journey To São Tomé.
Sodade, sodade, Sodade Dess nha terra São Nicoloau.	Sodade, sodade, Sodade, For my land of São Nicoloau.
Si bô 'screvé' me, 'M ta 'screvé' be. Si bô 'squecé' me, 'M ta 'squecé' be.	If you write to me, I'll write to you. If you forget me, I'll forget you,
Sodade, sodade, Sodade, Dess nha terra São Nicoloau.	Sodade, sodade, Sodade, For my land of São Nicoloau.
Até dia Qui bô voltá.	Until the day On which you return

By Luis Morais and Amandio Cabral (from Cesaria Evora: Miss Perfumado; Mélodie, France); translated by Caroline Shaw.

Music is an essential cultural expression of the life of Cape Verdean communities, an integral part of family and social celebrations, and of popular festivals. Each island is proud to have its own music. Brava sees its men emigrate, thus the morna there is sad and slow; in Santiago people dance as on the African continent, demonstrating their African roots; in São Nicoloau, a very religious island, people sing above all at funerals and for their saints.

The Morna

What tango is to Argentina, or fado to Portugal, the **morna** is to Cape Verde. This national song form, the most popular of the archipelago, is at least a century and a half old and is part of nearly every Cape Verdean band's repertoire. It represents the soul of the people.

Hovering on the borderline between music and poetry, the morna is both a lyrical song with a profoundly melancholic flavour and a dance. Almost always written and sung in Kriolu, mornas are slow and have minor-key melodies. The lyrics are the heart of the matter and can stand alone as a poetic form. They speak of love and longing for one's distant *cretcheu* (beloved), of the beauty of the archipelago, of departure and separation and sufferings in the new land, of death. It is the music of *sodade* – an intense melancholy – of a people who want to stay on in their island home, yet must leave to survive.

As one of the oldest musical genres of the archipelago – it developed in early nineteenth century dance halls – the morna's origins are a subject of ongoing debate. There are theories that it was influenced by the Luso-Brasilian *modinha*, the Portuguese *fado* or perhaps African rhythms from Angola. The fado-modinha-morna triangle is so clearly drawn that it is obvious they are all interconnected.

In its earliest form, on the island of Boavista, the morna was a cheerful and satirical musical form. It developed its classic themes of love, emigration and nostalgia in the hands of the Brava-based composer **Eugénio Tavares** (see box overleaf). Later, in São Vicente, with **B. Leza** and **Manuel de Novas**, it changed its tone once again into a lively, happier form. The great mornas sung today are by Tavares, but the form is still actively composed.

Until the advent of electric instruments in the 1960s, mornas were performed by a solo singer accompanied by string ensembles of different sizes. These consisted of at least one guitar, often a fiddle, and sometimes bass, and a piano or accordion. The high-pitched strumming that is an identifying feature of many mornas was provided by the

Eugénio Tavares: Composer of Morna

Morna composers are as important to Cape Verdeans as their singers, and there is huge respect for the likes of **Luis Rendall**, **Olavo Bilac**, **Abilio Duarte**, **Manuel de Novas**, **Teófilo Chantre**, and **Ramiro Mendes**, and especially for **B. Leza** (Francisco Xavier da Cruz), who died in the 1980s, having written some 1700 songs.

But the truly great figure is **Eugénio Tavares**, the composer of many of Cape Verde's best-loved mornas. Born in 1867, Tavares was a native of Brava. and is a romanticised figure in Cape Verdean lore. Working most of his life as a journalist and civil servant, he was a champion of Kriolu language and culture, and one of the first to compose poetry in Kriolu instead of Portuguese.

Most of his mornas dealt with the pain and spirituality of romantic love. One of his most popular, "O Mar Eterno", is the tale of his romance with a wealthy young American woman who was visiting Brava by yacht. She was impressed by Tavares'

poetry, and the two fell in love, but her disapproving father doused the affair by setting sail one night. Tavares found out the next morning that she had gone, and set down his sadness in a morna that is still often performed.

A number of his compositions also portray the sadness of those emigrating from the islands, such as "Hora di Bai" (The Hour of Leaving), his most famous song. It is a morna traditionally sung at the little dock at Furna, in Brava, as people boarded America-bound ships, and it is also often sung to signal the end of an evening's festivities.

On his death in 1930, Tavares' body was accompanied to its resting place by crowds of people singing and playing his mornas. He was the interpreter *par excellence* of the soul of Brava's inhabitants, poignantly exploring the aspirations and feelings of his people. *Mornas e Manijas*, by Osorio de Oliveira, is a collection in Portuguese of many of his morna lyrics.

---

cavaquinho, an instrument popular in Portugal and Brazil, from where it was introduced to the islands. The cavaquinho is much like a ukulele, with four strings, tuned like the top four strings of a guitar. Another instrument used was the twelve-stringed Portuguese or tenor guitar called the **viola**, which is a little shorter than a standard guitar. Its rhythmic role was supplanted by the maracas, but it is still used on occasion. Contemporary mornas make use of trumpet, sax, clarinet or electric guitar – which often state the melody or play an instrumental break – backed by a piano, synths, a string section, and maybe a jazz drum kit.

Among the most famous performers of morna are **Cesaria Evora** (see box opposite), **Djosinha**, a

PIERRE RENÉ-WORMS

Bana, giant of the morna

great musician and talented violinist who died a few years back, and **Bana**. The latter is a singer with a magnificient voice from Mindelo, the town of São Vicente. He worked for many years with the disabled composer **B. Leza**, whom he transported from gig to gig. After stints in Rotterdam and Paris, he is now based in Lisbon and is beginning to perform again thanks to a helping hand from the Mendes Brothers.

Other well known morna singers include **Ildo Lobo**, one-time leader of the group Os Tubarões; and the female singers **Maria Alice**, **Celina Pereira, Titinha**, and **Sãozinha**. Among instrumentalists, the great virtuoso was the late **Travadinha** (Antonio Vicente Lopes), who was a legendary performer on cavaquinho.

Barefoot Diva in Paris

Cesaria Evora (Cize among her own people), or the 'Diva aux Pieds Nus' as the French named her, is the best-known Cape Verdean artist in Europe. The niece of the composer B. Leza, Cesaria began performing in her late teens in the handful of bars in her native Mindelo, the town of São Vicente island, Cape Verde's liveliest cultural centre. She was accompanied by the celebrated clarinettist **Luis Morais** and by the age of twenty was the darling of the local radio station.

It was not until her mid-forties that Cesaria decided to leave the islands, travelling to Lisbon with the singer Bana to give a few performances. There she met the agent José da Silva (known as Djô), who organised for her to tour, together with Bana. In Paris Cesaria recorded her first solo album *Distino di Belita* on the Lusáfrica label, which brought her some attention in France and Portugal. But it was her fourth album for the label — the acoustic *Miss Perfumado* — which achieved global success, leading to international tours and sales across Europe and the US.

In concert, Cesaria's trademark is singing barefoot. It is her mark of solidarity with those left behind, with the ragged children of the island interiors for whom even a trip to Praia (the little capital on Santiago) is just a dream. Her new audiences might not understand the song lyrics, but they respond to the passion and bluesy immediacy of her gutsy, acoustic songs about the country's hardship and her own heartbreak. She has subsequently recorded a string of good-selling albums on the Lusáfrica label, most recently *Café Atlantico* (1999) a collaboration with Cuban musicians.

Her albums are distinguished by her extraordinary voice and most include one or more morna compositions by Uncle B. Leza, as well as composers such as Manuel de Novas, Teófilo Chantre, Amandio Cabral, and Ramiro Mendes. Her current musical director is the pianist **Paulino Vieira**, and her band includes **Morgadinho**, the original guitarist from the Holland-based band A Voz de Cabo Verde.

A former whiskey-drinking, cigarette-puffing grandmother, married three times, thrice deserted and now scornfully independent, Cesaria is an unlikely diva. Despite her worldwide fame today, she still leads the simple life she always led. At her age she has little interest in the frills and thrills of stardom: "I wasn't astonished by Europe and I was never that impressed by the speed and grandeur of modern America. I only regret my success has taken so long to achieve."

Coladeira

At the more African end of the Cape Verdean musical spectrum is the **coladeira**, faster in tempo than the morna, less involved lyrically and melodically, but generally more rhythmically complex. The form probably derived from the morna, with some South American input, in the 1930s.

Coladeiras are mainly songs of humour, joy and sensuality, more whimsical (and sometimes satirical) than the morna, with a tight, sexy rhythm. They are usually performed late in the evening, when the atmosphere heats up and dancers call for the band to play coladeiras. The term itself refers to the manner of dancing – man and woman move as if glued together ('cola' being the Portuguese word for glue).

The creators of modern coladeira were **Ti Joy** (Gregório Gonçalves), **Djosa Marques**, **Luis Morais** and – above all – **Frank Cavaquim** and **Manuel de Novas**, whose texts have enriched this São Vicente music genre. The best-known coladeira group was **Os Tubarões**, a six-piece outfit fronted by the vocalist **Ildo Lobo**. They recorded eight albums, and played in the US and Europe, before finally splitting in 1994. Other popular performers include the group **Mendes Brothers** (currently living in the US), **Cabo Verde Show**, **Gardenia Benros** and **Tito Paris**.

Funana

Closer still to African mainland roots is **funana**, an accordion-led music and dance where the rhythm occupies a central position. Unlike the morna and coladeira typical of São Vicente, funana is mainly a rural art, typical of **Santiago**, the most African of the islands. It conveys a strong eroticism through exaggerated dance rhythms, though it can also be just as expressive as any morna. The words are often about special events in local everyday life or the past. Like Cape Verdean poetry, these texts are based on double entendres and allusions.

Again the origins of this music are uncertain. It was perhaps imported from São Tomé, where a similar musical form is performed, along with the accordion at the beginning of the twentieth century. Originally, the accordion was accompanied by just a metal scraper (*ferro* or *ferrinho*), and this traditional funana bears a very strong imprint of West African traditions, particularly in terms of rhythm and vocal technique.

Funana was for a long time looked down upon by both the Church and the colonial government. Exposed to contempt and prohibitions because of its 'primitivism', it was forced underground until independence. Since then, however, it has been incorporated, revitalised and in some cases 'modernised' by many of the pop bands of the islands in a movement similar to those in other African countries.

The band who started this was **Bulimundo**. They studied the rhythms and melodic structure of funana and succeeded in adapting it to electronic musical instruments, bringing it from the experience of rural peasants to the towns. In the following decade, many bands followed their lead, notably **Finaçon**, formed in Santiago in the late 1980s by brothers Zeca and Zeze di Nha Reinalda. The band is no longer around, but it is remembered for an album produced in Paris with the ground-breaking Congolese musician Ray Lema, and for the creation of *funacola*, a mix of coladeira and funana. Another very successful group from Santiago is the **Ferro Gaita**, a trio playing accordion, ferrinho and bass.

The major singer of rural, traditional funana is acknowledged to be **Kodé di Dona**. Born in 1940 in the heart of Santiago, the first years of his life coincided with the country's worst famine which lasted until 1947 and his song "Fomi 47", which has been covered by many other groups, is his own testimony to a tragedy ignored by Portugal, which saw people dying at the roadside. A working farmer today, Kodé is remarkable for his talent as a composer and his ability to turn his own experience into song. His sense of poetry illustrates perfectly the allegoric spirit of the *badiu* peasant culture of Santiago island. His voice is broken with the misery which is described in his songs. Hoarse with (sugar cane) alcohol abuse, it changes from mumbled pain to lively mockery. He recorded only one album, *Cap Vert*, which was released in 1996.

SUSANA MAXIMO

Kodé di Dona

Batuco and Finaçon

The **batuco** is essentially women's music from the Santiago countryside. Again considered an African legacy – there are similar forms on the mainland – it fulfils a ritual role. Traditionally it accompanied the ceremonies of the *tabanka* (a processional festival dance), weddings and christenings. Today every festivity is a good occasion for batuco – women sing together for relaxation during a break, after work, or at a feast.

The batuco is usually performed by a female soloist who sings the verse, and a group of other women who sing the refrain. When the music becomes more animated everyone present repeats a line. *Batuqueiras* (women who perform Batuco) are generally illiterate, but witty and endowed with poetic gifts; they are usually older women, though a noted exception is **Nacia Gomi** who at the tender age of ten demonstrated her extraordinary talent for poetry. She has become a unique representative of Cape Verdean culture and has been selected as her country's representative at international events such as the 1992 World Exhibition in Seville.

The batuco performance is made up of songs which are nearly always improvisations, with verses satirising or criticising social or personal events. The *tchabeta*, which is the main part of the batuco, involves keeping time by clapping and beating a rolled-up cloth placed between the legs to form an acoustic box; the *torno* is a typical African dance involving the wriggling of the buttocks in a simulation of the sexual act; and the *finaçon* is the serious moment of the performance when everybody remains silent and only the *cantadeiras* (women singers) are allowed to sing; it is the moment for them to convey their particular message.

The batuco and the **finaçon**, though different forms, complement each other – batuco is the rhythm and finaçon the text. Both are African in origin and old musical forms. The finaçon includes compliments to party-givers, matrimonial advice, condemnation of loose behaviour, comments on political issues, criticism against those in power, maxims and advice on social issues, and even saucy allusions.

The rhythmic support for finaçon is provided only by hand clappers. The style of singing is both mumbled and shouted, and the songs are often of substantial length. It requires a very special lead singer, combining musical talent with considerable philosophical and poetic qualities. Among its most famous performers, alongside Nacia Gomi, were the late **Nha Gida Mendi** and **Bibinha Kabral**.

There is one man known as **Denti d'Oro** (Gold Teeth) who performs finaçon, with a group comprising women, men and children. Having had permission from his mother to perform a music mainly confined to women, he says he was obliged to play finaçon to keep the tradition alive. Although his texts are shorter

and less witty than Nacia Gomi's, he is well known in Santiago and has just recorded his first album, at the age of seventy.

International Stars

In addition to the major star **Cesaria Evora** (see box on p.451), there are a number of groups and singers in Cape Verde who regularly release recordings on labels in Portugal, France and Holland, where most of the music is recorded. Many of them divide the year between Cape Verde and either Portugal or New England, playing to large audiences at independence festivities held in the Cape Verdean enclaves.

The sax-player and clarinettist **Luis Morais** and multi-instrumentalist **Paulino Vieira** have produced and played on many albums by Cape Verdean artists, as well as their own projects. Vieira, in particular, is a musical explorer who has brought together various overseas influences (reggae, country, R&B) and merged them with home-grown rhythmic and instrumental roots. A long-established group of artists that have achieved big success in Paris is **Cabo Verde Show**, a dance music vehicle for musicians and singers Manou Lima, Luis da Silva, Serge da Silva and Rene Cabral. Often labelled as zouk-derivative, they say their music was a precursor of Jacob Desvarieux's Antillean sound, and claim it was he who was influenced by the sounds of the islands, rather than the reverse.

Denti d'Oro (right) with his group

Among other musicians and groups living abroad in Holland and Lisbon are **Gil & the Perfects**, **Dina Medina**, **Grace Evora**, **Djoy Delgado**, **Os Rabelados Splash**, **Dany Silva**, **Tito Paris**, **Maria Alice** and **Bana**.

Other current popular musicians on the islands include **Bau** (an excellent violinist and guitarist who plays in Cesaria Evora's band but who already has albums of his own), **Vasco Martins** and **Simentera** (see box below).

Cape Verdeans in America

Throughout the nineteenth century, each year saw a few Cape Verdeans escaping poverty by fleeing to New England with whaling ships, and islanders began to move to America in large numbers from the beginning of this century. Today there are more Cape Verdeans and people of Cape Verdean descent living in the US than in the islands themselves. California and Hawaii both have big Cape Verdean communities but by far the largest concentration is in

New England. With the decline of the whaling era, many of the old ships were bought by Cape Verdeans and sailed back and forth between the US and Cape Verde, delivering supplies to the islands and transporting emigrants to America.

The emigrants, of course, brought their music with them, playing it at social gatherings and on special occasions. Early **Cape Verdean string bands** included the **B-29s**, the **Cape Verdean Serenaders**, and groups led by **Augusto Abrio** and **Notias**. Cape Verdeans also contributed to the Big Band era, with orchestras such as Duke Oliver's **Creole Vagabonds**, and the **Don Verdi Orchestra**. These groups played mostly the swing music of the day, but also included their arrangements of Kriolu songs.

At present, there's a good number of groups and musicians playing in New England, mostly based in Boston. **Rui Pina** grew up making drums and singing in the neighbourhood. He was influenced by Ildo Lobo and Zeca di Nha Reinalda – and later by Prince and Phil Collins. Pina's first album, *Tchika*, in 1985, was backed by the Guinea-Bissauan group **Tabanka Djaz**, while his 1992

Simentera: Return to Roots

In 1992 a number of professional artists and musicians gathered together in the capital of Praia, united by a passionate interest in Cape Verde's traditional music and musical history. The result was the establishment of a permanent cultural group, **Simentera**, which began cultivating traditional forms. Since the very beginning, the organisation was characterised by its innovative work – new concepts of composition, new techniques for musical arrangement and elaborate research into Cape Verdean music, rescuing musical genres and styles almost forgotten.

The group can now look back on a number of successful performances in their own country and widely acclaimed international tours. In 1994 they recorded an album *Music from Cape Verde* with other Cape Verdean artists, and a year later recorded their first solo album, *Raiz* (Root) on the Lusáfrica label. It was followed by a second solo album *Barro e Voz* (Clay and Voice) in 1997, a disc which **Mario Lucio**, the group's leader, described as music which "mirrors the music of our islands in its various rhythms and origins, calling up old folk-songs with both African and European roots.

Through the different Cape Verdean musical types, one is telling the history of Cape Verde's identity formation itself."

The impact of Simentera on the Cape Verdean music is a source of great pride to its leader. "Simentera is a turning point in Cape Verdean music", Mario explained. "Most recently, we have revived the funana, and we have rescued the acoustic instruments. Before, all Cape Verdean music was played with electronic instruments. Simentera is completely acoustic and plays old traditional themes with modern arrangements. It was necessary to return to our roots in order to understand and play better music, and this attitude has had a big effect. For example, Cesaria Evora recorded three albums with electronic instruments and then a year after Simentera's appearance she made *Miss Perfumado* with acoustic instruments. Nowadays almost every group pays great attention to the vocal work, to the chorus. We planted the roots and even the children are now singing in chorus and using acoustic instruments. Simentera is well aware of its responsibility."

release, *Irresistible*, included contributions from another Boston-based artist, **Norberto Tavares**. A native of Santiago, Tavares and his group Tropical Power play both Cape Verdean and Brazilian music. Also based in Boston is singer-songwriter **Frank de Pina**. Born in Cape Verde in the 1950s, he and his brothers formed his first group, Os Vulcanicos, in 1971. Later, he left for Portugal and, ultimately, the US, where he has made four albums. Also New England-based are the **Creole Sextet**, who specialise in the older Cape Verdean styles, and have been playing parties, benefits and dances in the area for many years.

Perhaps the leading names on the US-based Cape Verde scene are the **Mendes Brothers**, Jo and Ramiro. Ramiro is a veteran strings arranger and producer, having worked on most of Cesaria Evora's releases and those of many other Cape Verdean musicians such as Bana. The Mendes Brothers group display an eclectic mix of styles, including explorations of the Luso-African music of Angola.

The brothers also run their own label, MB Records, whose Cape Verdean roster includes **Gardenia Benros**, a relatively young singer based in Rhode Island, the very danceable **Mirri Lobo**, and the morna-singer **Saozinha**, with whom they released a CD of beautiful old Eugénio Tavares songs.

Festivals

The **Baia das Gatas Music Festival** on the island of São Vicente has been getting ever more ambitious since its launch in 1984 to promote musicians from Mindelo. These days it hosts artists from across the islands and the Cape Verdean diaspora, and has grown into Cape Verde's major summer attraction, with 30,000 people attending for the three days in August. Many expatriate Cape Verdeans time their summer holidays to coincide with the festival, and the area jostles with reunited families and the noise of long-lost friends bumping into each other. A village of wood and sackcloth bars and restaurants comes into existence (it never rains), buzzing with merry-makers every night until 3am. The quality of the music is variable, it has to be said, but anything from a dozen to twenty local and visiting acts perform, so there are always highlights.

In **Praia**, a smaller – but ever-growing – festival takes place on Gamboa beach during three days in May and includes performances by Cape Verdean musicians from home and abroad.

Other summer festivals take place on almost every island in August, with music mainly from local artists. Those to look out for include: the **Boavista** festival, a week after Baía das Gatas, on Cruz beach; the **Brava** festival in Furna; the **São Nicolau** festival on Prainha beach; the **Santo Antão** festival at Ponta do Sol and, in September, the **Sal** festival at Santa Maria.

discography

Compilations

Cape Verde: Anthology 1959–1992
(Buda Musique du Monde, France).

A splendid historic 2-CD compilation, ranging from the first professional recordings in 1959 to the post-Cesaria boom of the early '90s, featuring morna, coladeira and funana. It runs more or less chronologically from early tracks by Fernando Quejas, through early Bana and Voz di Cabo Verde to the romantic violin of Travadinha, the funana of Zeca e Zeze di Nha Renalda and classics from Cesaria, Bana and Finaçon. Great photos and notes on the history of the music.

Cape Verde Islands: The Roots
(Playa Sound, France).

Mornas, coladeiras, and funanas with *cavaquinho*, the old-style viola and accordion. There's also a tune for the *cimbo*, a kind of fiddle used to accompany the batuco. Intriguing CD, recorded in 1990.

Funana Dance, Vols 1–3 (Mélodie, France).

Interesting compilation of hi-tech funanas by several different groups.

Music from Cape Verde (Caprice Records, Sweden).

Fourteen tracks, on the more rustic side, recorded in Cape Verde in 1993. Coladeiras from the group Simentora, batuco prodigy Nacia Gomi, traditional funana with gaita, accordion and ferro and some languorous mornas. Good notes and biographies.

Musiques du Monde: Cap Vert (Buda, France).

A recent collection of traditional Cape Verdean musicians. Includes Kodé di Dona, Augusto da Pina, Mino de Mama and the group Pai e Filhos.

The Soul of Cape Verde
(BMG/Lusafrica, France).

A great introduction to some of the best names in Cape Verdean music. It opens with a soft sultry track from Cesaria and follows up with Maria Alice, Bana, Celina Pereira, the bird-like voice of Titina, the exquisitely out of tune violin solo of the Mindel Band, guitar playing by Bau, Voz de Cabo Verde and lots more. Melancholy, seductive and highly recommended.

The Spirit of Cape Verde (Lusafrica, France).

A slightly less characterful collection than the one above, but with more of a contemporary feel. Includes Cesaria, Bau, Tito Paris, the up-and-coming singer Fantcha and old favourites like Simentera, the Mindel Band, Celina Pereira and Voz de Cabo Verde.

Artists

Bana

Bana is one of the most amazing voices from Cape Verde, and a father figure for artists like Cesaria and Tito Paris. He settled in Portugal in 1975 and invited musicians to perform with him there giving them international exposure. Now in his late sixties, he still performs at the café B. Leza in Lisbon.

 Bana chante la Magie du Cap Vert (Lusafrica, France).

In this 1993 recording Bana exercises his vocal chords around a sweet, classic selection of mornas and coladeiras with a band that understands the old style.

O Ritmos de Cabo Verde (Movieplay, Portugal).

The best Cape Verdean attempt at soukous you're likely to hear.

 Gira Sol (Iris, France).

Songs about life in Cape Verde. After a few years of recording inactivity, Bana released this acclaimed CD in 1997.

Bau

A frequent performer in Cesaria's band, Bau is a top instrumentalist on cavaquinho, guitar and violin (he makes many of the instruments himself).

 Jaílza (Lusafrica, France).

Beautiful playing, if slightly soft-centred, on fourteen instrumental tracks with that unmistakable sighing Cape Verdean melancholy.

Gardenia Benros

Born in Cape Verde's capital, Praia, Gardenia spent her childhood in Portugal and the USA, and is currently based in Rhode Island, the heartland of the American Cape Verdean community. The first female artist from Cape Verde to graduate with a professional music industry qualification, she is in the process of starting her own label.

 Mix II (MB Records, US).

Gardenia's most recent release encompasses medleys of the whole range of Cape Verdean styles, including some fine B. Leza mornas.

Cesaria Evora

Cape Verde's barefoot musical ambassador, born in Mindelo on the island of São Vicente in 1941. She began singing with her mother (a cook) and father (a musician and cousin of morna composer B. Leza). Her father died when she was seven, she spent time in an orphanage and went on to sing on the streets and then in bars. In 1975, with the disappearance of nightlife after independence, she gave up singing and raised her children as a single mother. In 1987 she was invited to Portugal by the singer Bana and went on to record a series of discs which, with the release of *Miss Perfumado* in 1992, brought international fame. Now she has a handful of exquisite albums to her credit, alongside collaborations with Brazilian Caetano Veloso, and seems to revel in her late-flowering fame.

 Miss Perfumado (BMG/Lusafrica, France; Nonesuch, US).

The album which swept Cesaria to international attention. Its appeal lay partly in its acoustic approach, which allowed the chanson-like mornas to emerge in sharp focus, backed by some wonderful piano and guitar playing.

 Cesaria (BMG/Lusafrica, France; Nonesuch, US).

This 1995 album was Cesaria's follow-up to *Miss Perfumado*, and many rate it even higher. "Petit pay", which opens, is a delicate love song for Cape Verdean music and, apart from one dud track ("Flor na Paul"), the rest of the disc complements it splendidly with some great musical arrangements.

Mendes Brothers

The Mendes Brothers are an influential group from Fogo, now living in the USA, whose music is mainly coladeiras.

 Palonkon (MB Records, US).

An album named after their home village on the volcanic island of Fogo, this is a first CD for veteran music-fixer Ramiro and brother João. Unclassifiable, but spends most of its time animatedly on the dancefloor.

Os Tubarões

A group from Santiago known for its coladeiras, its wonderful vocalist, and lively concerts. Unfortunately, they stopped performing and recording in 1994.

 Os Tubarões ao vivo (EMI Valentin de Carvalho, Portugal).

Perhaps the best of the band's eight albums, this is a recording of a live concert in Lisbon in 1993.

Sãozinha

A superb singer of mornas living in the US.

 Sãozinha canta Eugénio Tavares
(MB Records, US).

Sãozinha sings classic and beautiful mornas by one of its pioneers – Eugénio Tavares.

Simentera

A renowned group of ten musicians living in Santiago, Simentera have been instrumental in rediscovering the country's musical history. They cultivate the traditional forms, playing only acoustic instruments and presenting polyphonic compositions.

Barro e Voz'
(Melodie, France).

The all-acoustic Barro e Voz (Clay and Voice) confirms the talent of Simentera on a kind of auditory tour of the essence of Cape Verde, using sponges, cans, water vessels, bits of wood, x-ray negatives, bottles, plastic, bamboo, pods and a good number of catchy tunes.

Antoninho Travadinha

Born Antonio Vicent Lopes, violinist Travadinha was one of the great self-taught instrumentalists of Cape Verde. He started performing at local dances aged nine, but didn't win real recognition until his forties when he went on tour to Portugal. An expressive, sensitive player, he died in 1987.

Travadinha: The Violin of Cape Verde
(Buda Musique du Monde, France).

Yearning and nostalgic violin over a shimmering accompaniment of guitars and cavaquinho. A beautiful disc recorded in 1986. He's accompanied by guitarist and cavaquinho player Armando Tito (who also works with Cesaria) and laid-back percussionist Micau. Coladeiras, traditional mazurkas, and a couple of mornas with the soft voice of Ana Firmino.

Congo

heart of danceness

Congolese music – rumba, soukous, call it what you will – has been the core African dance sound for more than thirty years, influencing just about every other African pop style in existence. From Roots Rumba to Nouvelle Generation, **Graeme Ewens** follows the streams and tributaries of Central African musical culture.

The **rumba** of **Congo** (or Zaire as it was known in the aberrant Mobutu years) is a musical form that has hit a nerve throughout Africa, animating dancers of all ages and social classes in a way that no other regional style, not even Ghanaian highlife, has come close to matching. With its spiralling guitars and hip-swinging rhythms, **soukous**, as it's commonly known to the rest of the world, has also had a bigger cumulative effect on Western dance floors than any other African music.

Since colonial times, Kinshasa (known as Leopoldville in the days of the Belgian Congo) has been the musical heart of the continent, pumping out a flow of life-giving 'Congolese' music by great dance bands like **African Jazz**, **Franco's OK Jazz**, and **African Fiesta**. And it's an evolving and current tradition as their descendants from the 'new generation' – the **Zaiko Langa Langa** family, who blended rumba with rock during the 1970s, or big 1980s/90s stars such as **Papa Wemba**, **Pepe Kalle**, **Bozi Boziana** and **Koffi Olomide** – consolidate appreciative audiences in Europe, North America and the Pacific rim as well as across Africa.

To delineate musicians and groups, however, is only half the story. Despite severe social, political and economic difficulties, the Congolese have maintained a reputation for knowing "how to enjoy" – and dance has been a crucial form of self-expression. The early **rumba dances** such as the *maringa* and *agbwaya* were 'cool' expressions of physical grace involving subtle hip moves and shifts of balance, rather than fancy footwork and pirouettes, and this understated style has remained the basis, seasonally adjusted with a few new gestures or arm movements. The passing of time can be easier measured by memories of seductive rhythms such as the *rumba-boucher*, *kiri-kiri*, *cavacha*, *kwasa-kwasa*, *madiaba*, *sundama* and *kibinda nkoi*, rather than particular song titles.

Rumba Roots and Branches

In the aftermath of World War II life was sweet for the new Congolese urbanites, attracted to **Kinshasa** by well-paid work, public health and housing – and by its reputation as a 'town of joy'. Following independence from Belgium, the town quickly grew into the largest French-speaking city outside France, with a population now estimated to be over four million. But Zaire, as the second largest country in Africa became known in 1971, was never French; it has its own flamboyant identity subtly different from the 'French' cousins across the river in Congo-Brazzaville. Musicians from Brazza may have been heavily involved in many of the musical initiatives of the past thirty years, but Kinshasa has provided most of the Congolese superstars.

Congolese music is renowned for the stylish intricacies of electric guitars which combine melody and rhythm in a way that is both mellow and highly charged. But creative excellence apart, it has had practical advantages which made it an

GRAEME EWENS

Zaiko Langa Langa - 1970s 'new generation'

Soukousemantics

There is really no generic term used by the Congolese themselves to describe their music. People speak of miziki na biso (our music) to distinguish it from imported sounds, but even that phrase relies on the French word *musique* rendered into Lingala. African languages have many words for different dances and song forms but rarely a single term for music. Various styles of congolese music have been named over the years after the dances from which they sprang, or which they generated, but none of them applies to the whole, expansive genre. Western recording industry professionals, promoters and marketing people can't stand this sort of thing: they seem unable to function without a brand name with which to label their product. The bland rumba-rock, with its suggestion of Cuban accessibility, has rather stuck as one catch-all moniker for Congolese styles, but to combine a Cuban word with an American word to describe something distinctively African seems doubly inappropriate and it's not a term that any local musician or music fan would ever use. The seemingly more politically correct (and sweet-sounding) soukous has been the tag of recent years, even since before the existence of that other dubious handle, World Music, and at least serves to locate the music and to some extent identify it for Western ears. But in Congo, soukous refers to a particular dance style popular in the late 1960s; and it's also in use as a football term, describing when a player feints and dribbles the ball around an opponent. Using the word soukous to describe music as different as Joseph Kabasele's classics and Papa Wemba's latest offering is like referring to everything from "Why Do Fools Fall in Love?" to "Cop Killer" as twist.

Ken Braun

internationally viable popular music. Firstly, it was 'non-tribal': it used the interethnic trading language of **Lingala**, a melodic tongue which has been the vehicle for some of the sweetest singing voices in Africa. And secondly, the distinctive **guitar style** was an amalgam of influences brought to the lower Congo from the west coast of Africa and the Central African interior, and thus struck a chord across the continent.

The dance format which stormed West and Central Africa before and after World War II was the **Afro-Cuban rumba**. Itself a new-world fusion of Latin and African idioms, the rumba was quickly reappropriated by the Congolese, most notably by adapting the piano part of the son *montuno* to the guitar and playing it in a similar way to the *likembe* or *sanza* – the thumb piano. Although Ghana's highlife beat it to the post as the first fusion dance music with pan-African appeal, Congolese music was less influenced by European taste than highlife and it was in many ways more African, even though Western instruments were preferred.

The music also appeared in the right place at the right time. The post-war Belgian Congo was booming and astute Greek traders in Kinshasa saw the commercial potential of discs as trade goods to sell alongside textiles, shoes, and household items, including, of course, record players. Inspired by the success of the GV series of Cuban records distributed by EMI, the **early Congolese labels** – Ngoma, Opika, CEFA and Loningisa – released a deluge of 78rpm recordings by semi-professional musicians of local rumba versions alongside releases of folklore music. **Radio Congo Belge**, which started African music broadcasts in the early 1940s, provided the ideal promotional medium. While live performance remained more informal, the record companies maintained their own house bands to provide backing for singers. The CEFA label employed Belgian guitarist and arranger **Bill Alexandre**, who brought the first electric guitars to the Congo and who has been credited with introducing a finger-picking style at a time when most guitarists strummed. The rival Loningisa label recruited **Henri Bowane** from the Equatorial region, who injected even more colour into the style.

The forefathers of Congolese popular music included the accordionist **Feruzi**, often credited with popularising the rumba during the 1930s, and the guitarists **Antoine Wendo**, **Jhimmy**, and **Zachery Elenga**. These itinerant musicians entertained in the African quarters at funeral wakes, marriages and casual parties. In more bourgeois society, early highlife, swing and Afro-Cuban music were the staples of the first bands to play at formal dances where the few members of the elite 'evolués' could mix with Europeans. While many of the pioneers came to Kinshasa from the interior, others turned their sights east. One of the first guitarists to become known in the eastern regions was **Jean Bosco Mwenda** from Katanga, who was recorded in the field by the South African musicologist Hugh Tracey and later made his career in Nairobi.

In the capital, Kinshasa, life was cosmopolitan: French-style *variété* or **cabaret music** made its mark, while other ingredients which combined to form the classic Congolese sound included vocal harmonic skills learned at church and, later, a tradition of religious fanfares played on brass–band instruments. All these elements can be clearly heard in the last and greatest of the big bands, **OK Jazz**, while only the horns are missing from the modern variations of the Zaiko generation, sometimes replaced by synthesiser or voices.

The Belle Époque

The Congolese music scene really came alive in 1953 with the inauguration of **African Jazz**, the first full-time recording and performing orchestra, led by **Joseph 'Le Grand Kalle' Kabasele**. In the same year fifteen-year-old prodigy **'Franco' Luambo Makiadi** (see box on p.462) first entered the Loningisa studio to play with his guitar mentors Dewayon and Bowane. Three years later Franco and half a dozen colleagues from the studio house band branched out to form Orchestre Kinois Jazz (a Kinois is someone from Kinshasa) which soon became known as **OK Jazz**.

Kalle's African Jazz, which included the guitar wizards, **Nicholas 'Dr Nico' Kasanda** and his brother **Dechaud**, alongside singer **Pascal Tabu Rochereau** and the Cameroonian saxophonist and keyboard player **Manu Dibango**, ensured themselves musical immortality with the release in 1960 of "Independence Cha Cha Cha", which celebrated the end of colonial rule in the Belgian Congo and became an anthem for much of Africa. Kalle was a showman as well as composer and arranger, and he created an international-sounding fusion, which gradually re-Africanised the popular Latin rhythms. Franco and the school of OK Jazz also started from the same points of reference but their music was rootsier, drawing on traditional folklore rhythms and instrumental techniques, and the songs were more down to earth.

1970s Congolese single sleeve

During the 1950s and '60s there was a constant movement of musicians between the Belgian and French colonies where the proliferation of 'Congo bars' and a mood of optimism gave the region its good-time reputation. Across the river, in Brazzaville, a founder member of OK Jazz, **Jean Serge Essous**, and fellow sax player **Nino Malapet**, soon set up the equivalent Congolese big band institution, **Les Bantous de la Capitale**, with **Papa Noel**, **Brazzos** and a few others who later returned to Kinshasa to play with Franco. In the decade following independence both cities spawned hundreds of dance bands, releasing 45rpm singles on dozens of record labels.

By now the music had evolved a stage further and, thanks largely to the extended playing time of the 7-inch discs, more emphasis was placed on the exciting instrumental section known as the **seben**, when the slow rumba breaks, singers stand back and the multiple guitars go to work on the dancers. Franco was a master of the seben and his style was mimicked (though never matched), throughout Africa.

COLLECTION OF GRAEME EWENS

Joseph 'le Grand Kalle' Kabasele – father figure of modern Congolese music

For several years the careers of African Jazz and OK Jazz ran parallel, but African Jazz disbanded in the mid-1960s after recording some 400 compositions. Pascal Tabu Rochereau, who later took the name **'Tabu Ley'**, set up **African Fiesta** with **Dr Nico**, whose rich, florid, solo style gained him a huge following of his own. What came out of the relationship was something new and slightly experimental, with a greater diversity of rhythm and melody and occasional hints of Western soul and country music. African Fiesta rapidly garnered a rather urbane audience. Regrettably, for the many fans of this new fusion, they also separated after two years, but Tabu Ley eventually formed **Afrisa**, which maintained the allegiance of a 'sophisticated' audience and for some time was the only serious rival to OK Jazz. Both Kalle and Nico faded during the 1970s, Nico dying in 1982, followed a year later by Kalle.

Key figures who emerged from the growing ranks of these great dance bands included the raucous, honking sax player **Kiamanguana Verckys**, who spent six years with OK Jazz before setting up **Orchestre Veve**, and went on to produce some of the hard core bands of the new wave. Others also found varying levels of solo fame after working in both camps, notably the erstwhile co-president of OK Jazz, **Vicky Longomba**, as well as **Ndombe Opetum**, **Dizzy Mandjeku** and **Sam Mangwana**.

Mangwana's smooth, sympathetic vocal style endeared him to followers of both camps and all ages. He started out in the early 1960s with **Vox Africa** and **Festival des Marquisards** before joining Tabu Ley's Afrisa. In 1972 he switched allegiance to OK Jazz for three productive years before returning to Afrisa. Eventually he set up a splinter group in West Africa called **African All Stars**, with whom he developed a pan-African sound with pop and Caribbean rhythmic undertones, which has been the basis for a successful globe-trotting solo career.

A one-time colleague in OK Jazz, the guitarist **Mose Fan Fan** was Franco's deputy and co-soloist for several years, introducing a tougher, rock inflection to the OK Jazz rumba. In 1974 he took his fate in his hands and moved to East Africa with **Somo Somo**, where he fed the craze for Congolese music, before settling in Britain.

By the 1970s, the Kinshasa scene was getting crowded and many Zaïrean musicians appeared in other parts of the continent. Among the first wanderers had been **Ryco Jazz**, founded by Bowane, who brought Congolese rumba to West Africa and the French Antilles during the 1960s and early

1970s. In East Africa, too, the likes of **Baba Gaston**, **Real Sounds**, **Orchestra Makassy**, **Orchestre Maquis** and Samba Mapangala's **Orchestre Virunga** all enjoyed more acclaim outside the Congo homeland than they might have done in Kinshasa. Musicians from the Brazzaville side of the river were more likely to move west, with artists from Les Bantous de la Capitale such as **Pamelo M'ounka** and **Tchico Thicaya** establishing a fan base in Abidjan and feeding into the wider francophone economy.

CONGO

JAK KILBY

Tabu Ley Rochereau

Francofile

The continuity of Congolese music was broken in 1989 with the death of **Franco Luambo Makiadi**, leader of **OK Jazz** and the last surviving giant of the Belle Époque. As well as being a stunning guitar stylist with a hard, metallic urgency, Franco had a relationship with his audience that remains unmatched. More than any other public figure he accompanied his country's progress from the colonial repression of village society through independence and statehood to the constricts of military rule and the first murmurings of democracy.

Born in 1938, Franco had grown up alongside his mother's market stall, among the 'Yankees' and 'bandits', and he was always more in tune with the street people of Kinshasa who liked their music hard and their songs to deal with day-to-day realities. His first instrument was a homemade, tin-can guitar with stripped electrical wire for strings, but at the age of eleven he was given his first real guitar and came under the tutelage of **Paul Dewayon**, one of the early recording artists who also moved among the market people rather than the intellectual *évolués* (literally 'evolved') classes.

Franco's fancy finger-picking, his street-cred and boyish good looks made him an almost instant success. He was quickly hailed a 'boy wonder' and, by the age of fifteen, was a popular recording star and member of the **Loningisa** label house band, in demand for modelling the latest clothes, and a heart-throb for the women of Kinshasa. In 1956 he helped found OK Jazz and, although he was only third in seniority, his organisation and commitment, combined with star quality, made him very much the leader.

When independence came to the Belgian Congo in 1960, the founder of the first dance orchestra and acknowledged 'father' of Congo-rumba music, **Joseph Kabasele**, set up a recording deal for OK Jazz in Europe, and through the 1960s the band evolved into the biggest, most effective music machine in Africa. By then known as the 'Sorcerer of the Guitar', Franco re-Africanised the Afro-Cuban rumba by introducing rhythmic, vocal and guitar elements from Congolese folklore. Although primarily a dance band, OK Jazz was also a vehicle for Franco's observations and criticisms of modernising society, and his songs had more information and educational value than other any medium. His sternest morality lecture was "Attention Na Sida" (Beware of Aids), in 1987.

Like many African superstars, Franco had an ambivalent relationship with the state. He was a true patriot, but he also felt compelled to speak his mind and, while he was an essential element in Mobutu's *authenticité* (authenticity) programme, he was also reprimanded and jailed more than once and several of his records were banned. Although he was a stern moralist, he could slip quite easily into obscenity in his declared mission to provoke and tell the truth. The meanings of his songs are often opaque, with layers

GRAEME EWENS

Franco Luambo Makiadi

of allusion covering a subtext or hidden agenda. His own constituents, however, have always known exactly who and what Franco was criticising.

Franco also pumped out standard African praise and memorial songs, and covered a whole range of topics from football to commercial endorsement. But the theme to which he constantly returned was the conflict between men and women, and he couched many of his messages in a soap-opera style. The format reached a peak in 1986 with the episodic "Mario", about a lazy but educated young man and the older woman he lives with and exploits (until she eventually gets fed up and kicks him out of the home).

More than any other African musician, Franco transcended the boundaries of language, class, nationality and tribal affiliation. His music was as hugely popular in anglophone Africa as in the French-speaking countries, and OK Jazz records have been licensed almost worldwide. He also had considerable international succes, though he played only once in Britain and once in America. During a career which lasted nearly forty years, he released over 150 albums and composed some 1000 songs, while the band's complete repertoire was closer to three thousand. In mid-life, he developed the bulk to match that reputation, weighing around one hundred and forty kilos (more tan 300 pounds) at his peak. The band too was massive, with up to forty musicians on call and over one hundred families dependent on their fortunes.

When Franco died after a long illness in October 1989, Zaïre spent four days in national mourning, while the radio played nonstop OK Jazz. His long-time rival, Tabu Ley Rochereau, said at the time he was "like a human god". Sam Mangwana said he was the kind of man who appears only once in a hundred years and compared him with Shakespeare or Mozart combined with Muhammad Ali or Pele.

Riding the New Wave

RETROAFRIC

Thu Zahina

The classic Congolese sound was a rich tapestry of vocals, guitars and rhythm instruments, embellished with full-blown horn arrangements which became more prominent after James Brown visited Kinshasa in 1969 and 1974. During that time, however, a new stream of pop music had sprung from the students at Gombe High School, who had picked up on the Western rock group format and, independently of the older-generation musicians, started doing their own thing. One group of graduates known as **Los Nickelos**, was able to experiment and record in Brussels, while their juniors back home formed **Thu Zahina**, which influenced a whole generation during its brief existence. As their early recordings, which have recently come to light, show, Thu Zahina were the band who really took rumba to the edge. Horns were not part of the original live line-up – although they were used on recordings, they make the band sound like OK Jazz on acid.

The new music, of which Thu Zahina was a leading exponent, was raw and energetic, with emphasis on spiralling, interactive guitars and rattling snare drums during the seben, and hardly a horn to be heard. Taking elements of the animation (shouting) from strident forms of shanty-town music, and also from the wordplay used at Bakongo funerals, the new bands brought an extra vitality to the music, adapting traditional dances like the soukous and inventing new ones such as the *cavacha* to accompany the extended seben.

The groups which capitalised most on the new wave were **Stukas**, led by the outrageous showman Lita Bembo, who played with a frenetic intensity, and **Zaiko Langa Langa**, which was to lead the way for the whole post-independence generation. Zaiko Langa Langa was founded by conga player DV Moanda with lead singer **Nyoka Longo**. The name was constructed from 'Zaire ya Bakoko' (Zaire of our Ancestors); Langa Langa is the name of a people in the Equator region. They also added the prefix Tout-Choc-Anti-Choc (aka 'Untouchables').

Within months the band had expanded to take in a line-up of singers and guitarists who helped to redefine soukous. Among the early members were **Papa Wemba**, who eventually formed **Viva La Musica**; **Evoloko Jocker** of **Langa Langa Stars**; **Bozi Boziana** who joined Choc Stars before setting up the rival **Anti-Choc**; **Pepe Feli Manuaku** of **Grand Zaiko Wa Wa**; and dozens more. Unlike other bands, Zaiko was not the personal property of one leader. It was always a group,

totalling over twenty musicians. Following a serious rupture in 1988, one group remained with Nyoka Longo, who adopted an old ZLL slogan **Nkolo Mboka** (Village Headman), while the defectors set up Zaiko Langa Langa Familia Dei (Family of God), which also splintered soon after. By now Zaiko was a national institution and although the prodigals rarely return to the fold, they can always evoke the Zaiko name.

A host of rival new-wave groups had appeared in the early 1970s, including **Lipua Lipua**, **Bella Bella**, **Shama Shama**, **Empire Bakuba** and **Victoria**. The music had a rough, sweaty feel, while most of the singers, with the exception of husky-throated 'elephant' Pepe Kalle, compensated with honey-toned vocals. Many of the new-wave bands were promoted by Kiamanguana Verckys, who turned to record production and created a kind of Kinshasa 'garage-band' sound. From the ranks of these bands and their subsequent offshoots came Kanda Bongo Man, Nyboma, Pepe Kalle and Emeneya.

GRAEME EWENS

The hugely successful Pepe Kalle

IMAM/FOLK ROOTS ARCHIVE

Mbilia Bel and Rigo Star

Soukous really took hold in international markets during the mid-1980s when musicians began recording in Europe, and the cleaner Paris sound edged out the less polished Kinshasa variants. Among the early successes were the **Four Stars (Quatres Etoiles)**, whose smooth arrangements and streamlined presentation offered a direct challenge to the more ornate big bands – although the top two orchestras were still thriving, with Franco and Tabu Ley releasing international albums at a prolific rate.

During the mid-1980s Tabu Ley boosted the effectiveness of Afrisa with the introduction of **Mbilia Bel**, an attractive young singer with a dreamy, creamy voice who became one of Africa's first female superstars. Bel had started her career as a dancer with **Abeti Masekini**, who, along with **Vonga Aye**, had paved the way for female singers a decade before. While the male bands were obliged to stick to their winning dance formulas, women artists were able to experiment with European-style ballads and a variety of regional rhythms. One of the most versatile and charming was **M'Pongo Love**. Until her untimely death in 1990, Love, 'La Voix Limpide du Zaire', enjoyed a glittering career, despite the disabling effects of polio.

The women's contribution has been maintained by **Tshala Mwana**, who debuted as a dancer in M'Pongo Love's band Tsheke Tsheke before finding fame as the Queen of *mutuashi*, the funk-folk rhythm of the Baluba people. A whole string of young women singers has been introduced more recently through Anti-Choc, notably **Jollie Detta**

Deyess – a new wave of women singers

and the angel-voiced **Deyess Mukangi**. Kinshasa is also home to **TAZ Bolingo**, one of Africa's rare all-female bands, who play a particularly languid, smoochy soukous under the slogan 'self-control'. Others who have achieved a degree of international success during the 1990s include **Yondo Sister** and **Nimon Toko Lala**.

An aspect of the new-wave phenomenon which brought soukous to international attention was the **fashion** ingredient. Inspired by Papa Wemba, the cult of *kitende* celebrated cloth and cut and promoted style consciousness to the rank of a religion. Wemba's followers – the *sapeurs* – took their name from an informal but highly competitive group of poseurs who called themselves the 'Société des Ambianceurs et des Personnes Elegants' (the Society of Cool and Elegant People). Reminiscent of eighteenth-century dandyism and of the 1960s British mod scene, the sapeur movement was viewed as the antithesis of hippiedom.

Although any new-rumba music provided the soundtrack for sapeurs' fashion battles, the main style icons were individuals such as Wemba, Emeneya and Koffi Olomide, while the deities were Japanese and European designers – above all, at least in the early years, Yohji Yamamoto and Jean-Paul Gaultier. Like the mods, the sapeurs' look was adapted by mainstream culture while the main proponents toned down their flamboyance. The hippest sapeurs have long since publicly claimed "Sape is dead", but true believers can still be identified by the way they wear their gear.

Party time in Paris

By the end of the 1980s the 'classic' era was over, and the Zairean music business had fragmented. Of the big three, Franco was dead, Tabu Ley was semi-dormant (with Afrisa having partially disintegrated), and Verckys' business influence was waning. The Zaiko generation still appealed to Congolese who weren't even born when they started, but international listeners favoured the more minimal studio sounds coming out of Paris.

There were more pressing, non-musical reasons, too, for a shift of scene, as Zaïre lurched deep into anarchy and economic chaos amid the death throes of President Mobutu's corrupt regime. Many bands quit a muted Kinshasa, going on extended foreign tours, or settling in the US, London, Brussels, Paris or Geneva.

Spearhead of the new **Parisian soukous** scene was **Kanda Bongo Man** who, with commercial foresight, cut back on the fancy choral parts and architectural arrangements to create fast-track party music which he has brought to audiences around the world. Other key Paris players included **Pepe Kalle**, who found greater album success with sparser Paris sessions, and the guitarist **Rigo Star** who came out of Wemba's Viva la Musica in the early 1980s. Star, with his clean, crisp guitar contribution, accompanied Kanda on tour from 1983, and then appeared on countless records, often as arranger, with a galaxy of star names including Wemba, the camp crooner **Koffi Olomide**, Madilu System and Mbilia Bel, with whom he teamed up when Bel quit Tabu Ley's band.

Kanda Bongo Man - the sound of Congo all over Africa

DAVE PEABODY

Another guitarist in Kanda's first touring group, **Diblo Dibala**, went on to form **Loketo**, whose crossover sound, packaged for young, pop-wise Western audiences, made them dancefloor darlings. In 1991, Diblo regrouped with **Matchatcha** in which his devilish licks featured even more prominently. **Lokassa Ya Mbongo's Soukous Stars** offer a similar fast-food version of Congolese musical cuisine. This type of easy, sleazy medley package was advanced somewhat by **Awilo Longomba**, son of OK Jazz original Vicky, who brought guest singers into his line-up and won the Kora African Music Award in 1996.

One of the few new bands to make a real go of it in Europe was **Nouvelle Génération**. Comprising several defectors from Wemba's Viva clan, the new boys created a dynamic, danceable sound around voices and upbeat rhythms. They did not move the music forward a full generation, but did give a pointer to new possibilities. Their recordings hit the spot, but the band found it hard to grind out a living in Europe.

Kinshasa in the 1990s

In Kinshasa in the early 1990s, the continuity maintained by young bands such as Wenge Musica, Rumba Ray, and Zaiko veterans Bimi Ombale and Dindo Yogo was threatened by the social upheavals. With Verckys' Studio Veve inactive, the only operational studio in Africa's music city for a couple of years was the 16-track Bobongo studio. Artists who stayed home included Zaiko Langa Langa, **Bana OK** – the OK Jazz survivors under the leadership of Simaro Lutumba – and the Choc Stars' offshoot **Big Stars**, led by Defao. These groups recorded over in Brazzaville at the revamped 48-track IAD studio.

While the number of Zairean releases on the market slumped during the early 1990s, in December 1993 a showcase event in Kinshasa demonstrated that the music had not been silenced. The remaining big bands were brought together with artists like **Koffi Olomide** and Papa Wemba, who had been recalled from Europe to show that soukous was alive and well. An interesting departures from the established

Papa Speaks...

Radio journalist Dan Rosenberg talked to Papa Wemba Congo's biggest international star, about roots, influences and his country of birth.

Tell us about your earliest singing experiences.
I started singing at my Catholic church, and my mother used to sing at funerals. When I was ten, I sometimes used to go with her. I've always said she was my first singing teacher, and she was also my first audience. Whenever I made a mistake, she corrected me, and when I got it right, she was always there to applaud.

In Zaire in the 1960s, there was a lot of rock-'n'roll, but Mobutu was imposing his authenticity programme. How did that work out?
When 'authenticity' was initiated, many people failed to understand it. But a little later, we realised Mobutu was right about rediscovering our traditions. That doesn't mean we were supposed to live in grass huts, no – or dress in raffia skirts. It allowed us musicians to come back to our traditional songs and dances and rythms again. Congo is a huge country, with 450 different peoples, and each one has its own musical genre. I think it's the motherland of African music.

What did you listen to when you were young?
Well, I grew up in an epoch that was a musical crossroads. I listened to Franco, Kabasele, Wendo, Afro-Cuban music, black American music from the likes of James Brown, Otis Redding, Wilson Picket, Aretha Franklin, plus the Beatles, the Rolling Stones, then here in France there was Johnny Halliday, Claude François, Richard Anthony, and in Africa a huge star was discovered, Miriam Makeba . . . plus of course my own traditional music.

Your first group, Zaiko Langa Langa, was formed in 1969...
Yes, it was a group composed of students, and we wanted to do what our compatriots were doing, those who pursued their studies in Belgium, and who formed groups to play in their leisure time. We started out pretty naïvely, but in our case it became a profession.

And then later you formed Viva La Musica, which incorporates a lot of Cuban, Caribbean, Rock, Funk and other influences. Tell us about the differences between your music with that band and soukous music.
Well obviously, when you refer to soukous music like that I have to laugh because we, in Congo, don't know about soukous music. We know Congolese rumba. And this rumba started around the 1950s and was influenced by Afro-Cuban music and the Spanish guitar. Our first modern musicians incorporated a little of the rhythms of Cuba, and that's how our modern Congolese rumba started.
Soukous was a dance of the late 1960s, and it became a style, like a fashion or a trend. We soon forgot the word. But French journalists applied the word to Congolese music that was being created in Paris – music with a tempo that was regular from the beginning to the end, like Kanda Bongo. In the country at the time we didn't know this kind of music. We knew modern Congolese music, which you can divide into three sections with different time-signatures. The first is the introduction, second is the verse, with very nice lyrics, the refrain, and finally leading into the part you'd call soukous, the part where you really dance hard.

How did the album *Wake Up*, with Koffi Olomide, come about?
Well, we say that Congolese musicians are never together and we were thinking, well, we should try to be a bit above all that, you know. We ought to make it understood to music lovers and to all our musician friends that music is, above all, a tool of our country. We have to all work in unison. And that's the reason why we did that album, my brother Koffi and me.

Does music have anything to say about Africa's problems?
Well, we musicians should speak out about what we think – the things that are just whispered about – but politics in Africa are still not the politics as practised here in the West where you really do have freedom of speech. As for me, I can't sing bad of my country, I would be seen in a very very bad light by my brothers for a start, but also I'd be viewed in a very bad light in the political sense. But I just know that for our children, we must try to build a country where they can live in calm and peace, and unity.

Classic Swede Swede - raw folk, electrified

guitar-based line-up was **Swede Swede** – whose name is cryptically translated as 'mouse hole', but which could also be the sound of sex. They were the rhythm revelation of the early 1990s, using a variety of drums, percussion, vocals and harmonicas to created a sound, both postmodern and neo-traditional, which recalled the raw, rhythmic charge of pre-electric music. But to most ears, Congolese music should be all about guitars, and Swede Swede were unable to crack the international market.

As Congo enters the 21st century, at last free from the monopolising patronage of Mobutu's entourage, the scene has witnessed a gradual revival: Wemba spreading the word globally; Koffi becoming a household name throughout Africa; individualists like **Ray Lema** holding their own in fusion circles; and the star bands reformed, with Simaro leading Bana OK and Youlou Mabiala maintaining the name of OK Jazz. New bands, meanwhile, have come and gone, while a raft of re-releases has made almost all the great period pieces available on CD. Video, too, has become huge, with 'playback' concerts of Congolese stars finding a ready market in bars throughout Africa. For all its formulaic conventions, Congolese music remains the only truly pan-African favourite.

discography

Compilations

⊚ **Congo Compil** (Syllart, France; Stern's, UK).

Part of the *Rendezvous* series, this compilation contains good examples of Kinshasa kitsch, mostly licensed from other labels, and not tainted with Syllart's fast-food tag – though many tracks share a synthetic keyboard sound. Eleven tracks from the likes of Koffi, Zaiko, Kalle, Madilu, Wenge, Wemba and Defao put the emphasis on vocal expression. It's good to hear people like ex-OK Jazz guitarist/composer Simaro and Choc Stars charmer Carlito get another outing, while Emeneya's "Nzinzi" still stands proud.

⊚ **Ngoma: Souvenir ya l'Indépendance** (Pamap, Germany).

Ngoma was one of the earliest and most influential labels in post-World War II Léopoldville – now Kinshasa. This is the second of three compilations from the German label containing the melodies, instruments and grooves that moved the nation through the 1950s – folk ballads, early urban fusions and proto-rumba, as well as a soul number from Manu Dibango.

⊚ **Revue Noir à Kin, Zaire '96** (Revue Noir, France).

Recorded 'in the field' during the last dark days of Mobutu's reign, this release is a compilation soundtrack for issue No 12 of the prestigious French art magazine. With less emphasis on rumba but more of the shanty town sound, this just shows how life was bubbbling away despite restrictions and repression. Raw, urgent and refreshingly unsophisticated.

◎ **Soukous Paris (Syllart, France/Stern's, UK)**

Collection of hot snacks, best taken with a couple of cold drinks, a cement dancefloor and some heady atmosphere. Although the fast, curly guitar action, simple melodic mantras and whipcrack drum machines sound a bit dated now, the line-up includes Lokassa, Dally Kimoko, Diblo, Kanda, Kass Kass, Nyboma, Yondo Sister and the late, lamented Mpongo Love.

Artists

Bantous de la Capitale

The Brazzaville band, Les Bantous, was formed by ex-members of OK Jazz in the late 1950s to become virtually the official Congo-Brazzaville state orchestra. There is a series of Bantous CD compilations which documents this great Congo orchestra.

⊙ **El Manicero** (Soul Posters, France).

This deleted LP is a showcase for Essous and Malapet, subtitled the *Best Saxes in Central Africa*. Mellow, big-band backing and some actual 'Latin' rumba, dating from 1970. Includes the rumba anthem "El Manicero" (Peanut Vendor).

Mbilia Bel

Mbilia Bel rose to fame with Tabu Ley's Afrisa band, and as a solo singer became one of Africa's first women superstars.

⊙ **Keyna** (Genidia, Zaire/France).

Bel at the peak of her career with Tabu Ley – great songs, creamy vocals and fine dance action. The title song is not a misspelled tribute to East Africa, although she does sing about going to Nairobi. At this point in 1985 Bel and Ley were treated like royalty across the continent. Soon after the thrill had gone — and so had she.

Bisso na Bisso

A group of Congo/Parisian twenty-somethings brought together from different hip-hop crews under the direction of top French rapper Passi. Their background is Brazzaville, rather than Kinshasa, and they're clearly at the forefront of a new music.

◎ **Racines** (V2, France).

Take some cool Parisian hip-hop beats, soulful voices and meaningful lyrics, blend them with samples and reworkings of classic African pop hits from the past and deliver with panache. Three or four of the 15 tracks here are all-time great tunes, and there are only a couple of duds. High production values and a classy guest list lift this debut release well above most attempts at finding mainstream approval. The album scored in a big way in France and quickly inspired a new generation of African-language rappers.

Bozi Boziana & Orchestre Anti-Choc

After quitting the Zaiko Langa Langa offshoot Choc Stars, Bozi Boziana created Anti-Choc to provide a faster power source for his energetic compositions.

◎ **Emenya 'Manhattan' & Anti-Choc 'Sissi Nguema'** (Ngoyarto, France).

A 1988 Verckeys production from Emeneya, complete with radio ad, combined here with one of the best Anti-Choc collections. With bubbling guitars, skippy rhythms and Deyess in fine form, "La Sirène" is a real flyer.

Choc Stars

Founded in 1984 by Ben Nyamabo with musicians from Zaiko and Langa Langa Stars, Choc Stars developed a sound that was mellow yet passionate. The songs are generally slower than other bands' but the arrangements add up to cool seductive soukous. They faded out in the early 1990s but singer Defao's Big Stars now carry the flag.

◎ **Les Merveilles du Passé, Choc Stars Vol 3** (FDB, France/Zaire).

Verging on the sleazy side of good taste with the right amount of studio ambience and production values that sustain the camp delivery. "Celio" is a special fave. This collection does them proud.

Deyess

The former singer with Bozi's Anti-Choc band, Deyess has one of the great Congolese female voices.

◎ **Little Goddess** (Stern's, UK).

Deyess's first solo album after leaving Bozi, produced by top Senegalese producer, Ibrahima Sylla.

Mose Se Sengo 'Fan Fan'

Thirty years ago, Fan Fan was playing guitar with Franco, writing some material and taking his place in rehearsals or when the big man was unavailable. Following some hits of his own, he headed east to conquer Tanzania and Kenya. Since arriving in England in 1984, he's become known and loved for his hard-charging guitar style.

◎ **The Congo Acoustic** (Triple Earth, UK).

The usual attitude has been moderated, and a more relaxed Fan Fan delivers contemplative, mellow music with an unplugged warmth that spreads from low-volume exposure. "Sikulu" pays urbane homage to Fela Kuti's Afrobeat, with horns chirruping politely.

Franco and OK Jazz

Franco – Le Grand Maître – is the outstanding figure in Congolese music, indeed perhaps Africa's greatest star. His career (see box on p.462) encompassed over 150 record releases, and, since his death in 1989, there have been more than 60 compilations issued on Sonodisc alone, many of them bearing the titles of original discs but with completely different tracks. Below are just a few of the highlights.

 Originalité
(RetroAfric, UK).

A terrific re-release of the very first recordings of OK Jazz. This was the point where classic rumba began the long journey into soukous. You enter OK, you leave very KO'd.

⊙ **Mario & Réponse de Mario** (Sonodisc, France).

A long, soap-opera CD: even without understanding the dialogue the man's charisma is tangible.

⊙ **Azda** (Sonodisc, France).

This was actually an advert-disc, for the local VW distributor, hence the unambiguous chorus. Every member of the band got a VW Passat – and in return VW were given the complete big-band treatment with wonderful horn arrangements.

 Likambo Ya Ngana
(Sonodisc, France).

A classic 1971 release in which Franco reprised the 1940s accordion sound of Feruzi, before grinding into some of the most classic big band rumba. Packed with exemplary guitar picking.

⊙ **Mabele** (Sonodisc, France).

A fulsome treatment of folklore dating from 1974, including the classic title track ballad, composed by 'vice-president' Simaro Lutumba and sung by Sam Mangwana.

⊙ **Attention na Sida** (Sonodisc, France).

Franco's famous beware-of-AIDS sermon – powerful oratory set against a memorable folklore rhythm.

Evoloko Jocker

A classy singer with a taste for theatricality, Evoloko was one of the true eccentrics of the Zaiko Langa Langa family, making his mark with Langa Langa Stars. He lost a few years' momentum when he got stranded in London in the eartly 1990s.

⊙ **Mingelina** (FDB, France).

A vocal curiosity so sweet it sticks to you, this was a fine, if belated, come-back release in the early 1990s.

Pepe Kalle

The 'elephant' brought Empire Bakuba to the verge of true stardom during the 1980s. One of the most 'typical' Kinshasa bands, Bakuba combined Kalle's husky voice with the stage antics of his dwarf friend, Emoro, and requisite wild guitars. Kalle is a crowd pleaser, who remains, as they say, big in Africa.

⊙ **Gigantafrique** (GlobeStyle, UK).

A collection that packs a double ration of Kalle dance tracks. Now somewhat dated but it includes the original and biggest kwassa kwassa hit "Pon Moun Paka Bougé".

Emeneya Kester

As one of the original new-wave singers, Emeneya was a first generation sapeur, playing florid, posey soukous as leader of Victoria Eleison.

⊙ **Nzinzi** (Gefraco, France).

At the time this was a major breakthrough for Zairian music. In a radical departure from the norm, producer Verckeys added a 'Zulu' bass beat and hi-tech production to generate a pan-African hit.

Ray Lema

Ibrahim Sylla, the ubiquitous Senegalese producer of African music, once remarked in discussing his artists that he could not work with this idiosyncratic fusionist: "Ray Lema's music is completely denaturé. He calls it 'open' but we Africans can't relate to it. It doesn't interest us at all". Sylla was perhaps overstating the case: Lema, long a successful overseas recording artist, may have gone distinctively his own way, but the path is unquestionably worth following.

⊙ **Stoptime** (Buda, France).

Delightfully individual and hyper-inventive set of chansons, jazz studies and time-signature jokes. All in a very chilled mode, there are echoes here of Brazil, Keith Jarrett, David Byrne and, even, occasionally, Congo.

Sam Mangwana

Sam Mangwana formulated his own 'international' sound in Abidjan after quitting the Rochereau/Franco nexus. With his African All Stars he took on the world with soukous-based pan-African pop.

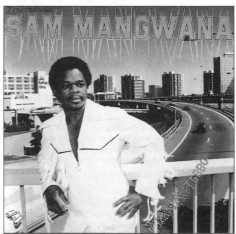

Maria Tebbo
(Stern's, UK).

From the first, excited guitar licks you're moving. This is delightful, positive, happy music of the first order, recorded in the late 1970s at a time when Africa was still going forward. Enduring songs.

Antoine Moundanda

A consumate master of the giant thumb piano, from Congo-Brazzaville, who learnt learnt the instrument as a therapeutic device for chasing evil spirits out of the afflicted.

⊚ **Likembé Géant** (Indigo, France).

Live showcase for Moundanda's agile thumbs and those of his elderly accomplices. The fact that Congolese rumba – soukous – originated in part with these lush, equatorial notes, later adapted to the guitar, signifies no greater recommendation needed.

Tshala Mwana

From dancing girl with Mbilia Bel to Queen of Mutuashi, Tshala's career progressed smoothly during the 1980s, making her the brightest female lead in the country.

 Mutuashi
(Stern's, UK).

An outstanding set of mutuashi songs with an irresistible driving pulse that pushes the tripping (in the dance sense) funk-folk rhythm of the Baluba people into the realm of Afro-Cuban. It's a whole lot different from the steam-rolling guitars of soukous.

Jean Bosco Mwenda

Bosco was picking out delicate melodies on his guitar in his own two-finger style in Katanga province of the Belgian Congo in the late 1940s. It is cleaner cut and morer reflective than the Kinshasa style.

⊚ **African Guitar Legend: The Studio Album**
(Rounder, US).

This release gives Bosco an audience at last among people who may only have ever heard him on a WOMAD compilation tape from the early days of 'World Music': here's that song again – Masanga. Listen and melt.

Nouvelle Génération

Ex-Wemba musicians, keeping the new wave rolling on. The band was short lived, but their perky, confident handling of Kinshasa street rhythms brought a blast of fresh air in the mid-1990s.

⊚ **Porokondo** (FDB, France).

Their hot debut album still swings the feet into action.

Koffi Olomide and Quartier Latin

Since learning his trade in Papa Wemba's Viva la Musica, Koffi has combined a distinctive, smoochy style of singing with dynamic arrangements that are instantly recognisable. During the 1990s he has grown to become probably the most popular artist in Central Africa.

 V-12
(Sonodisc, France).

Koffi's tour de force — he even announced it in 1996 as his last release before retiring (what a wind-up). Here he concentrates on vocal delivery and smooth arrangements with less emphasis on the frenzied sebens served up by his

band Quartier Latin. Great songs frustratingly truncated to fit a dozen tracks on the CD.

Quartier Latin

⊚ **Ultimatum** (Sonodisc, France).

Quartier Latin's 1997 release didn't carry Koffi's name but he participated and directed everything, and saw that disc become the last big hit from the country called Zaire. Fast track sebens all the way through.

Tabu Ley Rochereau

The man's voice shone out from African Jazz, African Fiesta and Afrisa, making him the country's favourite singer, but Ley's career has slumped recently — especially following his bust-up with Mbilia Bel and subsequent problems with the old regime. He has since re-opened contacts with the new Congo, so maybe there is a comeback just around the corner.

⊙ **En Amour y a pas de Calcul**
(Genidia, Zaire/France).

This was Ley's first release on his own label in 1983 – a career highspot for a breathtaking singer and great bandleader. Classic tunes, florid arrangements and masterly voice.

Ry-Co Jazz

Founded by Franco's first bandleader, Bowane, Ry-Co Jazz left Congo in 1959, just before independence, for a tour of West Africa and stayed on the road as a quartet or quintet for 11 years.

⊚ **Rumba'round Africa** (RetroAfric, UK).

Ringing guitar and jive action with catchy songs in French, Spanish, Lingala and pidjin English. Ry-Co brought Congo music to West Africa and blended it with rock'n'roll and Latin/Caribbean grooves.

Swede Swede

For a while, in 1989, it looked as if a whole new genre was about to re-define Zairean music. But Swede Swede fell into the familiar trap of splitting up once too often, then hanging out in Europe for too long. It is hard to sustain a Congolese band without guitars but somewhere these guys are still trying.

⊚ **Toleki Bango** (Cramworld, Belgium).

Their first CD on the Belgian label is still available. Although this one doesn't quite capture the rowdy energy of a live show it marks an interesting attempt to take a new direction.

⊚ **Mokili Etumba** (UMWE Records, UK).

A later release, recorded in London, which added sampled marimba/xylophone to their usual percussion in a less raucous, more mature development.

Papa Wemba

As a member of the original Zaiko line-up, Wemba helped set the pace of modern music. Then, with the establishment of Viva la Musica, he refreshed it with hard-core folklore rhythms and churning guitars, before setting a smoother course with his solo career, accompanied by his band for the international market, Molokai.

 Papa Wemba
(Stern's, UK).

Wemba's unique, yearning, almost hymnal voice is his best

asset. On this stylish 1988 outing, still one of his best albums, Rigo Star's guitar work bursts through.

 Dernier coup de sifflet/Epeak Ekomi na Douzieme Espiode (Americano/ FDB, France).

A mellow foray with the late Stervos Niarchos – the king and crown prince of sapeurs together. Niarchos composed a couple of tasty rumba ballads on this for his sartorial hero. Recommended but hard to find.

 Molokai (RealWorld, UK).

Glorious as-live studio set for the World Music market, that shows off Wemba's extraordinary voice, one of Africa's very best, with mesmerising, slow-burn impact. It opens with a sweet a cappella number, "Excuse Me", and closes with a heartstoppingly beautiful arrangement of his signature "Esclave".

Wenge Musica

Wenge Musica came to prominence in 1988 under the musical direction of multi-instrumentalist Alain Makaba but never improved on the excitement of their original release. Moving to Europe, where the band split in two, was part of their downfall.

 Bouger Douger (Natari, UK).

Their debut album, since re-mastered in England. It's high-grade Kinshasa soukous with classy segues, synths and a nice line in shouting.

Thu Zahina

The new wave started here. Formed in 1967 by a group of high school students, Thu Zahina was the first 'pop group' to challenge the big Congo bands. As wild as they were young, the boys bent the rumba into a pop format.

 Coup de Chapeau (RetroAfric, UK).

Teenage voices run the gamut of emotion: guitars wail and reverberate, stretching the confines of classic rumba, and the recently discovered snare drum rattles like a calabash of cowries carried by a drunken sorcerer. Seminal, soul-stirring stuff.

Zaiko Langa Langa

From the end of the 1960s, the Zaiko extended family was the driving force of the guitar-powered 'new generation'.

 Zaire–Ghana (RetroAfric, UK).

Recorded in Ghana back in 1976, this includes "Zaiko Wa Wa", the band's theme song. Raw and sweaty, it was produced by Bowane with the only example of horns on a ZLL recording.

 Jetez L'Éponge (Carrere, France/deleted).

A Kinshasa classic from the madiaba era – 1989 – this is Nyoka Longo's response to the Zaiko split-up. Probably their strongest album yet, with hard guitars, thoughtful arrangement and powerful ambience.

Côte d'Ivoire

heart of the african music industry

Bordering Côte d'Ivoire's Ebrié lagoon lies the city of Abidjan, a modern metropolis with the rough, grey Atlantic on one side and cocoa plantations and savannah on the other. The city's fast, noisy downtown district – Le Plateau – caters to transient business types while the street life of the city happens in the low-rent Treichville district, with its teeming market, cheap bars and seedy hotels. **François Bensignor** and **Brooke Wentz** check out the buzz of a city at the heart of the West African music industry (after Paris, of course).

Abidjan's technically sophisticated **studios**, and the diversity of talent attracted by them, have established the Côte d'Ivoire capital as a hub for musical and cultural exchange. Musicians from all over West and Central Africa – Guinea, Mali, Niger, Cameroon and Congo – come to absorb new rhythms and try out their own beats in the hope of landing a record deal. **Salif Keita**, **Kanté Manfila** and **Mory Kanté** all refined their talents playing the Treichville clubs before venturing on to Paris in the early 1980s. The sax player and 'Soul Makossa' man, **Manu Dibango**, directed the Ivoirian TV orchestra in 1975, and four years later another

Cameroonian, **Moni Bilé**, ventured to Abidjan to record his first album. Malian producer/arranger **Boncana Maïga** has been working mostly in Abidjan studios for almost twenty years. And then there are the established local artists – like **Alpha Blondy**, **Meiway**, **Monique Séka** and **Gadji Celi** – all of whom hold international recording contracts and have their music heard over the airwaves throughout Africa.

As if to emphasise Abidjan's pre-eminent position in the African music industry (a position contested only by Johannesburg), the city hosted the first *Marché des Arts du Spectacles Africains* (MASA) in 1993. This week-long trade fair and showcase event, held every two years, attracted entertainment executives from around the world in February 1999.

Radio Solo – and Mapouka

Every day, from 6.30am to 7.45am, **Soro Solo** (he changed his name from Souleymane Coulibaly because he wanted to get back to his African roots) presents the morning show on the government-sponsored **Radio Côte d'Ivoire** (RCI). Soro will play anything from Roy Ayers, Cameo and Michael Jackson to the newest releases of Ismael Lô, Femi Kuti, Youssou N'Dour and Papa Wemba, or emerging local talent like reggae artist **Tiken Jah**, a cappella singing group **Kajim** and Afrozouk star **Monique Séka**. In between request spots, Soro reviews concerts, interviews artists and highlights new releases. It's important to get on the show. If you don't make it here, you're unlikely to progress further.

A bit of a star in his own right, Soro's musical knowledge is encyclopedic and he's constantly on the move, meeting musicians and checking out the newest clubs in town. Interviewed in 1998, he pronounced **Mapouka** to be the big new Côte d'Ivoire music, with top bands like **Nigi Saff** and **Génération Mot à Mot**. "It takes its inspiration from village traditions," he explained, "but it is basically an erotic dance. In fact, it was promoted on TV to challenge *dombolo*, the Congolese rhythm danced in an erotic maner all over Africa. People were complaining about the suggestive dance movements shown on TV, and dombolo and mapouka were banned by the government from the national screen. But some journalists went to the villages and filmed traditional dancers, arguing mapouka was directly taken from the Ivorian traditions. They won the battle and mapouka came back on TV. But there are now two forms of mapouka: the one they play in private clubs, called *mapouka serré* (close mapouka), which is extremely erotic, almost strip tease, and the one they show on TV which is much softer."

Business

EMI Pathe Marconi was one of the largest and most powerful record companies in West Africa, but in 1995, when it appeared that EMI International was on the verge of creating a huge, powerful network, the decision was taken to shut down the African branch. In Abidjan, **Jat Music** bought EMI shares, while in Bamako they were bought by **Ali Farka Touré**. EMI-Jat music still signs local musicians and licenses foreign material from all over Africa and even Europe, the US and the Caribbean.

Other important players in Abidjan's music industry are the recording studios **JBZ**, **Sequence** and **Nefertiti**. JBZ, located in lush, palmy Cocody, is one of the oldest studios in West Africa. A one-room facility, this studio has been responsible for some of the best African recordings, including releases by Nahawa Doumbia, Pepe Kalle, Sam Mangwana and Lokassa. American blues guitarist Johnny Copeland discovered JBZ and recorded here while on tour in Abidjan; Youssou N'Dour used it to record some of his early material at a time when no other facilities were available in West Africa; and Toumani Diabaté's successfully eccentric "Shake the Whole World" was put together here too. The more recently established **Nefertiti** studio is also worth a visit. Opened by Stevie Wonder's engineer of fifteen years, **Abdoulaye Soumaré**, Nefertiti is in the heart of the bustling Plateau district.

The big studios may be where most of the money gets spent, but a lot of new little studios, like **Touré Sound** or **Studio Grenier**, have now sprung up in the cheaper Yopougon area. And if you're looking for the fruits of big studios' labours, every Friday evening, a bunch of fresh new productions can be found in the little cassette stalls on Abidjan's street corners.

Live and Local

Côte d'Ivoire is home to more than sixty native ethnic groups, and more than a hundred others that have migrated here. Among them, some carry specific and moving musical traditions.

In the centre of the country, the **Baoulé**, who came from Ghana, developed characteristic **vocal polyphony**, famed all over Côte d'Ivoire. Northeastern **Lobi** have strong **xylophone** traditions. In the north, **Senoufo** have intense initiation and funeral ceremonies, from which **Aïcha Koné**, one of the local stars for years, has borrowed and modernised the **poro** rhythm.

In the West, the **Dan** have a very impressive mask tradition. From the southwest traditions, **Zagazougou** took the **gombe polyrhythmics**. On the southeast coastal area, **Appollo** people use **edongole talking drums** for their annual ritual *abissa* purification dance. The musician **Meiway** has taken up abissa from his people's coastal traditions as well as *grolo*, *fanfare* and *sidder*, to create his sweet and sensual white handkerchief **zoblazo dance** – one of the most impressive stage acts from the Ivorian scene. But those attempts to bring up some real Ivorian traditional sounds into modern music continue to be subverted by mainstream Afro-pop and Afro-zouk productions with drum machine and synthesiser backing.

Le Zagazougou - unplugged and very, very fast

In the 1960s, with Côte d'Ivoire newly independent, **Baoulé artists** were heard from transistor radios in every bar. The twin vocal sounds of the **Soeurs Comöé** were partly driven by the local *gbégbé* rhythm. Then, in the 1970s, the new dynamism of **Sery Simplice** and his **Frères Djatys** bubbled up, based around the same heavy-duty *gbégbé* rhythm. Today's veteran of the local scene, **Bally Spinto**, still plays a modern music strongly rooted in gbégbé.

Among this first generation, some names still mean good music, like **Anoman Brou Félix**, **François Lougah** or composer **Jimmy Hyacinthe**, who created the *goly*. Another celebrity in the 1960s, **Mamadou Doumbia** toured all over West Africa and even the US. Today, he prefers to live the poor life of the simple people in Abidjan, rather than use his vocal skills to serve the new rap trend, as some producers urge him to. He has set up a home studio and continues to help young musicians get started, charging ten times less for a demo tape than most other outfits around town.

Ziglibithy

The real father of Ivorian modern pop is the internationaly renowned **Ernesto Djédjé**. He consciously took a traditional rhythm of the Bété people as a base upon which to build the giggling, frenzied guitar sound of his **ziglibithy**, putting dancers in a joyous trance all around Africa and further afield. Everyone in Côte d'Ivoire thanks him for giving the country its first modern musical identity.

Djédjé's teacher, local 1960s superstar **Amédée Pierre**, had himself used a strong Congolese rumba flavour in his self-titled **dopé** style. But Djédjé, whom he cherished as his young guitar player, declared in a radio interview in 1975, seven years after he had left Amédée's band Ivoiro-Stars, that he didn't like the 'congolisation' of Ivorian music. In 1977, Djédjé's album *Gnoantre-Ziboté*, recorded in Nigeria, was an instant hit throughout West and Central Africa and crossed the oceans to Paris and Montréal.

Ernesto Djédjé's sudden death at the age of thirty-five, while recording his sixth album, made him a legend. A great many musicians have tried to follow in his footsteps, but none of them have achieved quite the same sucess. The late **Gnaore Djimi**'s *polihet* style, or **Luckson Padaud**'s *laba laba* – both deriving directly from ziglibithy and keeping up its traditional Bété spirit in today's society – can still be a great experience for any listener or dancer trying to get close to that deep African feeling. If you want to hear this music live in Abidjan, you'll find it in the far northern suburb of Yopougon, where it has given birth to the fresh **zouglou** rhythm.

Zouglou

The new sound of **zouglou** emerged in the early 1990s in the midst of a university crisis perpetuated by the aged president Houphouët-Boigny: the man who spent US$200m building a Vatican-modeled church as a gift for the Pope while students were turned into squatters on the university campuses. In the Baoulé language, they say 'Be ti le zouglou' (stacked like a rubbish heap!) to describe student life in **Yopougon** where four people share one miserable single student room.

This is the place where the satirical and ironic zouglou music began, danced as a form of appeal to some fictitious god, crammed with humorous lyrics exposing the harsh reality of student life. **Didier Billé,** the unrivalled zouglou leader, soon became the focus of his generation with his caustic, witty songs. Fellow students raised money to enable him to record with his band **Les Parents du Campus**, who were pushed to a dazzling success when they appeared on the Podium TV programme.

The most interesting thing in zouglou is that it has created a new language that combines French, Pidgin and Baoulé words given special meanings. Students have a lot of fun developing their own dictionary: *caillou* or *peeble* – to vandalise property; *coco* – a student who lives off his friends; *koun* – drunk; *libérer* – to liberate, or in other words, to dance zouglou.

The zouglou craze was at its peak in the mid-1990s, spreading to Burkina Faso and even to Mali. Although overtaken now by mapouka in Côte d'Ivoire, it is still very popular and one of the best-selling musics in the country, mostly because of its sharp lyrics. Didier Billé remains a major figure but with his move to Paris he has loosened his grip on zouglou jive. Once very successful, the group **Les Cocos** have split, but their singer **J Marcial 'Bobby' Yodé** is recording good cassettes. The most popular new zouglou generation are **Les Poussins Chocs**, **Espoir de Yop** and **Petit Denis**.

Reggae

For the past fifteen years reggae has played a leading role in Côte d'Ivoire's music scene. **Alpha Blondy**, who like many of the country's artists sings in the Mande trading language, Dioula, was

JAK KILBY

Alpha Blondy

the first on the African scene to use reggae as a means to express his concerns on African urban youth. Born Seydou Koné, his life is something of a legend. He never knew his natural father, and grew up playing French pop and rock as a teenager. He discovered reggae when he was twenty at a New York Burning Spear concert and began to experiment with the music and rastafarianism. Taken back to Côte d'Ivoire, he was locked up by his stepfather, but managaed to escape and change his name to Alpha Blondy. In 1983, Fulgence Kassy turned him into an instant young urban star when he invited Blondy to appear on his TV programme *First chance*. Signing with EMI France in 1984, he recorded in Jamaica at the Tuff Gong studio with the Wailers, then gained international recognition with some powerful stage performances with his band **The Solar System**.

Based in Paris for years, Blondy settled back in Abidjan in the mid-1990s. His flourishing record and stage career boosted reggae's appeal in Côte d'Ivoire with many reggae singers attempting to emulate his success. Some, like **Ismaël Isaac** have achieved a certain international success; others, like **Serge Kassy**, are well received on the local scene. The newest, most popular Abidjan reggae singer, **Tiken Jah**, is now making his presence felt abroad with messages of unity and good acoustic arangements.

Rap

Despite the fact that **rap** was growing among Côte d'Ivoire's youth from the mid-1990s on, local producers showed little interest in making albums. Until that is, a sell-out concert at one of Abidjan's biggest venues, the Palais des Congrès, where the two local leaders of the rap scene were called to a challenge. After this event, rap was taken more seriously by the local music businessmen and you can find more and more rap cassettes in the stores.

Topping the bill and singing a form of gangsta rap, or Stezo, in French is **All Mighty**, who comes from the Adjamé quarter, and who had a big success with a song calling the people to protect themselves from AIDS. Ange Romain Agou, aka **Angelo**, is another player, and includes Ebrié and Adioukrou rhythms in his **rap dogba**. His collaborations with hip-hop radio DJ **M.C. Claver** in 1992 brought him success and his stage act at the Masa '97 opening concert, with sexy dancing girls, consolidated things. Angelo now drives a red Ferrari and presents *Rapattack*, a Saturday hip-hop programme on TV2 with music videos and chat.

discography

Compilations

Côte d'Ivoire Compil (Syllart, France).

Part of Sylla's grand, 1999 release of a dozen modern African compilations. Little info can be gleaned from the liner notes, but it's no less musically recommended and danceable for that, and includes tracks by Meiway, François Lougha, Jimmy Hyacinthe and an excellent Monique Seka number, "Missoumwa" – a bumper 75 minutes in all.

Anthology of World Music: the Dan
(Rounder US).

Rare insight into the music of one of the country's most culturally exciting ethnic groups – part of the southern Mande language group, famed for their exhilarating mask dances. Originally released on vinyl by Bärenreiter Musicaphon, the detailed booklet documents their music culture as it was in the early 1960s. Songs, percussion, and an amazing orchestra of six ivory trumpets.

 Maxi Ivoire
(Déclic, France).

A 2-CD compilation released in 1997 showing a wide panorama of Abidjan's productions at that time. Moving from Afrozouk star Monique Seka to king of polihet Gnaore Djimi, it also includes music from popular young zouglou band, Les Poussins Chocs.

Super Guitar Soukous (EMI Hemisphere, UK),

A fine album with a misleading title, as the best tracks are wild Ivorian polihet. Just listen to Zoukunion's "N'Nanale"!

Artists

Angelo

Angelo is Côte d'Ivoire's main rap star – and presenter of the local hip-hop TV show.

🎵 **Represent** (Showbiz, Côte d'Ivoire)

Accomplished rap and ragga sung in English and French, plus some more interesting material in Adioukou using some deep traditional percussion and singing styles.

Nyanka Bell

With her splendid voice, Nyanka – half-Corsican, half-Touareg – earned the nickname of the 'African Barbara Streisand' singing as a teenager in the RTI orchestra. Her first solo album was released in 1983. She has always been influenced by American soul and soft funk.

🎵 **Visa** (Sonodisc, France).

Nicely produced by Boncana Maïga and recorded in Paris, this album shows Nyanka's wide range, singing in a variety of different languages.

Alpha Blondy

Seydou Koné was struck by reggae in the early 1980s while living in New York. Back home, he took the name Alpha Blondy and his first song ever recorded, "Brigadier Sabari", was an instant hit in 1983. Since then, he has come to represent West Africa's young generations who have never known colonisation, and he is still the leader of a powerful West African reggae stream.

💿 **The Very Best Of Alpha Blondy**
(Une Musique/EMI, France).

A real best of, including most of Alpha's personal statements recorded throughout his ten years of success, and showcasing the diversity of his inspiration.

🎵 **Yitzhak Rabin** (Stern's, UK).

Blondy's tuneful 1998 album is muddied slightly by dubious 'agit-pop' themes, gently espoused in French, English and Dioula.

Gadji Celi

Former football player Gadji Celi has now secured for himself a very successful singing career on the Ivorian showbiz scene.

🎵 **Elephant's Story** (Syllart, France).

A funny, gimmicky CD, where every song tells part of Les Elephants national football team's saga, driven by zouk-like Ivorian rhythm.

Ismaël Isaac

The day Isaac discovered young Alpha Blondy on TV, he knew exactly what he wanted to do. He has gone on to develop a style of his own with his sweet voice.

🎵 **Treich Feeling** (Misslin, France).

Having recorded three cassettes with the Keïta brothers (1986–89), Ismaël's first CD was produced by Boncana Maïga on the Sylla label in 1990. A second CD released on Island in 1993, and a third in 1996, are evidence of his increasing popularity and talent.

Aïcha Koné

Aïcha learned the tricks of her trade in the 1970s as a singer with the Orchestre Radio Television Ivoirienne, initially under the leadership of Boncana Maïga, then Manu Dibango. Influenced by Miriam Makeba, she is one of the first international female pop singers from Côte d'Ivoire.

 Adouma
(Bolibana, France).

Recorded in 1983 under guitarist Jimmy Hyacinthe's artistic guidance, this album shows a mature artist achieving fulfilment among the great performers of African song.

🎵 **Mandingo Live from Côte d'Ivoire**
(Weltmusik, Germany).

Very solid set of dancefloor grooves, featuring Miriam Makeba's famous paean to pan-Africanism, "Kilimanjaro".

Meiway

Originally from the colonial coastal town of Grand-Bassam, Frederic-Désiré Ehui, alias Meiway, created *zoblazo* in the early 1990s, borrowing dance rhythms from his Appolo people's traditions, but making abundant use of digital instruments. He has created a powerful stage act with his group Zo Gang.

 200% Zoblazo
(Sonodisc, France).

Released in 1991, *200% Zoblazo* was a club and radio power hit all over West Africa and still remains some DJ's chosen trick to wake up sleepy dancers. Has to be played loud and danced waving white handkerchiefs!

Monique Séka

Making her first appearance on the Abidjan scene in the mid-1980s with her Afro-zouk style, Monique Séka has slowly gained celebrity status not only in Africa but in the Caribbean and in the African diasporas.

🎵 **Okaman** (Déclic Communication, France).

Released in 1995, this album earned Séka an African Music Award and a best performance award at Ngwomo '96. It has achieved platinium in her own country.

Le Zagazougou

Zagazougou's style derives from a country, happy-go-lucky music invented during the first half of the century. In 1990, it was reintroduced, entirely refreshed, to modern audiences and was as readily adopted.

🎵 **Zagazougou Coup** (Piranha, Germany).

Ivory Coast unplugged: all accordions and percussion, and very, very fast.

Equatorial Guinea

malabo blues

The problems facing musicians and singers in Equatorial Guinea, rooted in extreme poverty and isolated by thirty years of corrupt dictatorship, are countless. There is no real market for cassettes, few places to perform, and a severe lack of instruments and equipment for recordings. Pretty much the only concert venue and studio is run by the *Centro Cultural Hispano Guineano* in EG's capital, Malabo, which does its best on limited funds. The only radio station is run by the president's close family and has a playlist of self-congratulatory songs. Still, Spanish record label chief **Manuel Dominguez** is undeterred, in part because there is excellent Equato-Guinean music to be heard in the suburbs of Madrid, where a considerable exile community is based.

There is no doubt that Equatorial Guinea, formerly Spain's only colony in sub-Saharan Africa, has a rich traditional music. You can hear it on the compilation *Calles de Malabo*, which showcases the music of the Fang and Bubi, Equatorial Guinea's dominant ethnic groups. And you can hear it in EG's capital, Malabo, where people ease the pain of a repressive regime with a thriving culture based around beer and music. Any night after 10pm music of all kinds thumps out from the city's main nightlife street, Calle Nigeria, which throngs with bars, cafés and street vendors. Discovering just what it is you're hearing is a little trickier: this is one of the world's less documented musics, or, come to that, nations.

Equatorial Guinea is, in fact, a pretty strange construct, comprising three of Spain's former colonies in sub-Saharan Africas: Bioko (formerly Fernando Pó), a lush little volcanic island off the coast of Cameroon; Rio Muni, a strip of mainland Africa sandwiched between Cameroon and Gabon; and the tiny island of Annobón, far out in the Atlantic. All in all, they have a population of 400,000, governed (if that's the word) from Malabo, on Bioko island. For the most part the territories consist of thick rainforest.

The Spanish handed over power of these enclaves in 1968 to Macias Nguema, a mild-mannered civil servant who rapidly degenerated into a dictator with few equals. By the late 1970s, a third of the population had fled the country, disappeared, or been killed. After a coup in 1979, Nguema senior was replaced by his nephew Lt-Col Obiang Nguema, who, while not exhibiting the same genocidal tendencies, has starred in a number of Amnesty International reports.

Fang Traditions

Most people in EG speak languages from the huge **Bantu** group. The dominant groups are Fang and Bubi, with smaller populations of Ndowe (on the mainland coast), Annobónese (from Annobón island), Combe, Bujeba and Bisio. The **Fang**, the largest ethnic group, originally lived only on the mainland, but they have emigrated to Bioko in such

numbers that Fang is now the dominant language and culture of the island, while the **Bubi**, the island's indigenous language group, are in decline.

The Fang have a vigorous song tradition. The main local instrument is the **mvet**, a harp-zither fashioned from a gourd, the stem of a palm leaf and strings woven from plant fibre. Mvet-players have evolved a musical notation disclosed only to initiates of the *bebom-mvet* society, a kind of fraternity of griots responsible for maintaining folk traditions. In Fang culture, the mvet plays a similar role to that of the kora in Mali, used for accompanying epic songs of history. Like the kora, too, it has a two-sided bridge with the string plucked with both hands.

Most villages, plantations and urban barrios have a traditional **chorus and drum group**, the dominant form of traditional music. The style of these groups, much of it in call-and-answer form, has a choral quality. When performing, members wear traditional, two-piece straw dresses.

The most important musical figure in the Fang tradition is **Eyi Moan Ndong**, from Mongomo, on the mainland,. On his recommended, locally available, cassette entitled *Asongono Ncogo*, he sings a series of stories accompanied by the mvet, which form a traditional epic.

There is also a CD of this music, *Mbayah*, recorded in the Muséo de Antropología in Madrid. Based on a myth revised by **Maria Nsue**, "La leyenda del sauce lloron", Mbayah is a collaborative effort by musicians from different tribes. Grounded in a polyrhythmic bass line played on a host of traditional Equato-Guinean percussion instruments, it incorporates elements of Catholic and Protestant choral traditions, as well as tribal initiation rites.

EG Pop Styles

Back in EG, there are few opportunities for musicians, traditional or modern. Malabo's three discos – and another trio in Bioka's other town, Bata – have a highly precarious existence. The one small beacon for music is the *Centro Cultural Hispano Guineano* (CCHG), an old colonial building in the centre of Malabo, which puts on a couple of concerts a month, power cuts permitting. In addition, it maintains a small recording studio, and organises, every two years, a contest with awards for the best song in a local language and the best song in Spanish.

The dominant style among EG-based bands is Cameroonian **makossa**, though Congolese **soukous** and rock can also be heard. And the colonial heritage has spawned an engaging acoustic music that blends Spanish folk styles and guitar music with the local fondness for stringed instruments.

The finest of these acoustic guitar bands is **Desmali y su Grupo Dambo de la Costa**. They're now based in Malabo, but they come from the remote island of Annobón and are legendary throughout EG. Desmali's voice is full of delightful contradiction, sweet, but with a ragged edge echoing the pain of exile – especially on songs like "Lament for our Village". He's also a great guitar player. Accompanying percussion, and harmonies sung in thirds, elegantly complement and fill the songs. Another good acoustic group is **Dambo de La Costa**, who use a square frame drum, called the *pandero*.

Other Malabo-based artists include **Elvis Romeo**, also from Annobón, who fuses rap and traditional music; the Fang artists **Maruja and Yoli Miski**; **Lily Afro**, who has recently recorded a CD; **Chiquitin**, who has produced her own version of Jimmy Cliff's "The Harder they Come"; **Ngal Madunga** from the mainland Bisio people; the Bubi artists **Luisira**, **Sita Richy** and **Samuelin** (who sings a delirious song about polygamy on the *Calles de Malabo* CD); and **Chucunene**, a young Bubi artist on whom everybody is betting.

In the backwater town of **Bata**, on the mainland, it's worth mentioning the work being put into developing **Luna Loca**, a group who mix song with theatre.

EG in Madrid

It is little surprise that EG musicians, if they get the chance, look abroad to make a living. In the 1980s, a few artists – among them **Maele**, **Bessoso** and **Efamba** – made it to Paris where they recorded albums, though they seem to have faded from the scene. Others, notably Malabo's most important backing band, the **Bisila Sytem**, have left to forge their careers in Spain, leaving a real vacuum back home.

The most significant Equato-Guinean exile community is based on the outskirts of **Madrid** where a small suburb has been named **Malabo Dos** by the Guineans. The community includes many of the best Equato-Guinean musicians, and a real star group in **Las Hijas del Sol**.

With their harmonious voices, Las Hijas have a unique beauty, well captured on their 1995 disc, *Sibèba*, a sparse production with just voices, drums and guitar – the latter from the late, great **Super Momo** (he died in 1996), a guitarist who started

Las Hijas del Sol

his career in 1983 leading the Café Band Sound in Malabo. On their second, Spanish-produced, CD, *Kottó*, the Hijas follow Bubi tradition by singing a cappella, while also incorporating reggae, makosa and other rhythms. Their songs deal with themes such as immigration, racism and the environment.

Another fine Madrid-based artist, about to release her first CD in Spain, is **Muana Sinepi**, who collaborated on the soundtrack for the film *Lejos de Africa*, made in Equatorial Guinea. Her stage name means 'small singer' – she first went on stage at the age of nine. Muana usually accompanies herself on guitar, though she has also been working recently with former members of the Bisila System in a group. She has a very sensual voice with a soft pop tone.

Baron Ya Buk-Lu, a Fang, has had different luck around the Malabo Dos disco scene. He continues to persevere in his search for a style, and continues to turn out new, Spanish-produced records. The most obvious pop representatives, however, are the Zamora brothers, the musicians who make up **Mascara**; originally from Annobón island, they had a hit back home in the early 1990s with their album *Bi Mole*.

discography

Compilations

 Calles de Malabo (Nubenegra, Spain).

Get to know the new generation of musicians in Equatorial Guinea: Chiquitin, Nona de Macha, Sindy, Elvis Romeo, Pola, Yoli Miski, Luisira, Nuresu, Samuelin, Aniobe and Charlot Zemba. A variety of modern styles.

CAS Revelations 2000 (Eko Music, Cameroon).

A production by ICEF and CICIBA featuring Apolonio Mba, Jose Siale, Paco Bass, Kouki, Isabel Idjabe, Gady Bass and Hijas del Sol.

Mbayah (Nubenegra, Spain).

A CD-ROM compilation of traditional music, interpreted by amateur musicians and singers from the Fang, Ndowe and Bubi peoples, using indigenous instruments. Guest players include Hijas del Sol, Muana Sinepi and Baron Ya Buk-Lu.

Artists

Baron Ya Buk-Lu

The Baron is a Fang pop artist based in Spain, who in the 1990s has played in a variety of styles.

B.B. Project (Ngomo, Spain).

Disco music with Fang roots.

Las Hijas del Sol

Their name means 'daughters of the sun', though the duo of Piruchi Apo and Paloma Loribo are really aunt and niece. They are Bubi-speakers – native Bioko islanders – and their songs are very different from those of other tribes due to the isolation of the island from the mainland.

Sibèba (Nubenegra, Spain).

A brilliant first international release from EG and very in tune with tradition on this 1995 debut, with the Hijas' voices stripped down against a jungle of percussion and a little electric guitar (the latter from Armando 'Super' Momo — who, alas, died the year after its release). Extensive liner notes, in Spanish.

 Kottó (Nubenegra, Spain).

Varied, inventive, constantly surprising in its shifts of rhythm and colour, *Kottó* is a masterpiece with songs in Bubi and Spanish, and traditional rhythms mixed with makossa and bikutsi. It combines the startling vocal talents of the Hijas with ambitious arrangements and pointed lyrics: "You, who changed my paradise [by drilling for oil] have a desert in your heart. Stop to listen to my song before making any decisions." Fat chance.

Mascara

The Zamora brothers' group from Annobón island are expected to make a comeback with a new CD after the success of their last release.

Bimole (Twins, Spain).

Tradition-laced pop music which had a major impact in EG when released in the early 1990s.

Ethiopia

land of wax and gold

Ethiopia is one of Africa's most fascinating countries — musically and in every other respect — and after years of civil war and dictatorship it is once again open to foreign visitors. An ancient mountain kingdom, it is dominated by the Amhara language group – one of the world's oldest Christian communities. Modern Ethiopian music is dramatic and soulful, based on a five-note scale, and irresistible in the hands of key singers like Aster Aweke or Mahmoud Ahmed. **Francis Falceto**, long-time aficionado, tours the land of Ras Tafari.

As you get off the plane at Addis Ababa, you are greeted by a sign that reads "Welcome to Ethiopia, Centre of Active Recreation and Relaxation". It is a sentiment sublime in its optimism but perhaps no more or less the truth than all of the disaster-laden clichés that have been the currency of Ethiopian reportage for the last two or three decades. And with a new millennium beginning, the ancient land of Ethiopia could just be in line for worldly rehabilitation. The ongoing dispute with Eritrea, which still sporadically simmers into war, continues to cast a pall, but the country has come a long way since it shed its 'Marxist' dictorship in 1991 and brought to an end thirty disastrous years of civil war.

Frew Hayln and The Imperial Bodyguard Band

COLLECTION FRANCIS FALCETO: ETHIOPIQUES

The civil war – and Mengistu's 17 years of dictatorship – had a profound effect on Ethiopia's cultural and musical life. For most of the Mengistu years, a continuous curfew deprived a whole generation of Ethiopians of any kind of nightlife. To these restrictions was added a censorship of nightmarish pedantry that picked through song lyrics before recording sessions could be licensed, and

put overseas visitors through painstaking inspections of locally bought cassettes before allowing them to leave the country. Little surprise then, that those musicians who could emigrate did so, opting for a precarious exile in the US, Sudan, Saudi Arabia or Europe. Their number included Aster Aweke, Ephrem Tamru, Kuku Sebsebe, Menelik Wossenatchew, Teshome Meteku, the producer Amha Eshete . . . a roll call of the leading artists of the day.

All this has changed and at the close of the 1990s music feels omnipresent in Addis Ababa, the capital, honking out of battered tape decks in buses and taxis, drifting from stores and markets and pumped up loud at the innumerable little restaurants (*tedjbets* or *bunnabets*), guesthouses and semi-private drinking parlours. These nerve centres of national vitality had a buzz about them even during the years of dictatorship – and they have burgeoned since its demise.

Trad/Mod and the Golden Age

Traditional music forms the basis of all Ethiopian styles. Even the most famous contemporary singing stars like **Tlahoun Gessesse**, **Mahmoud Ahmed** and **Neway Debebe** have two repertoires, one modern, the other rooted in tradition. Ethiopians buy modern and traditional cassettes with equal enthusiasm, and the modernity in question is essentially that of the 'modern' Western instruments which have been introduced.

The first Western imports were **brass bands**, brought in by the military under Haile Selassie. Performers tried out their instruments on traditional material and by the late 1940s there were full **orchestras** to accompany fashionable singers. The first among them were the **Imperial Bodyguard**

Aster Aweke

Ethiopia's most successful World Music star, **Aster Aweke** was born in 1961 near Gondar, the ancient capital of the country. In the aftermath of the overthrow of Haile Selassie in 1974, she was already preparing herself for a life of music. Strongly influenced by an Addis musical idol of the time, Bezunesh Bekele, she sang first in 1977 with various groups, then went solo and was 'discovered' by the producer and record shop owner Ali Tango for whom she released several cassettes and a couple of 45rpm singles.

Her exceptional voice became well known, and she joined the famous **Roha Band** in 1978. By 1979, however, the revolutionary climate in Ethiopia had become intolerable for free spirits like Aster and she fled the country to the US. She eventually settled among the diplomatic and African exile community of Washington DC, where she set about re-establishing her musical career on the club and restaurant circuit. A formidable careerist ("I have never been in love"), she has cleaved a straight path to World Music stardom by never allowing her superbly vocalised and fiery – often pretty raunchy – lyrics to be swamped by arrangements. She is currently based in L.A.

Band**, the **Army Band** and the **Police Band**, trained initially by professionals, often Armenians, brought in from Europe, but gradually private orchestras grew up alongside. In Addis, you can occasionally come across the odd back-street shop full of old 45s from the 1970s in which these orchestras accompany stars like Tlahoun Gessesse and Mahmoud Ahmed. And they remain popular, copied to order on cassette.

The special characteristic of Ethiopian music is the use of a five-note, pentatonic scale with large intervals between some of the notes, giving an unresolved feeling to the music, like waiting for a stone to hit the bottom of a well, and not hearing it. These modes create an intensity of performance not unlike soul music – especially in the hands of a singer like the Los Angeles-based exile **Aster Aweke**. The limping asymmetrical rhythm of much of the music is also highly characteristic.

Shopping around for CDs – or if you're lucky enough to visit, for local cassettes – pretty much all the recordings of the 1960s and '70s pioneers are worth getting hold of. Premier league names include **Tlahoun Gessesse**, **Bezunesh Bekele**, **Hirut Bekele** (no relation), **Mahmoud Ahmed**, **Ali Birra**, **Alemayehu Eshete**, **Muluken Mellesse** and **Ayalew Mesfin**. Try to get your hands on the five *Ethiopian Hit Parade* LPs, compilations which comprise, apart from the stars mentioned, traditional musicians such as **Kassa Tessema**, **Mary Armede**, **Ketema Makonnen**, **Asnaketch Worku** and **Alemu Aga**.

Instrumental music also has its key figure in the shape of **Mulatu Astatke**, promoter and sole exponent of **Ethio-jazz** and the king of arrangers through this golden, pre-revolutionary age. Another superb figure, though seemingly forgotten these days, was **Getatchew Mekuria**, a saxophone and clarinet player.

The main body of Ethiopian records was produced in just one decade, from 1969–1978. In all, some 500 singles, and just thirty LPs were released in this 'golden age'. Pressed first in India, then in Lebanon, Greece and finally Kenya, up to 3000 copies were produced for big hits – serious numbers at the time. And by the end of this period, with the advent of a local cassette industry, there were tape pressings of 20–30,000, while the biggest hits sold more than 100,000.

Wax and Gold

During the dark years of the dictatorship in the 1980s, the cassette industry continued, and new singers emerged besides the veteran artists. Most stayed in the country as it had become virtually impossible to emigrate. The top local stars of the decade included the singers **Ephrem Tamru**, **Kuku Sebsebe**, **Netsanet Mellesse**, **Teshome Wolde** and **Amelmal Abate**, and they shared the trio of professional orchestras for recording sessions. Three historic groups were also important in this era – the **Wallias Band**, the **Roha Band** and the **Ethio Stars**.

In the late 1980s, however, one figure eclipsed them all: the singer **Neway Debebe** became an idol, bringing a new freshness which reminded his public of the vocal prowess of the early Tlahoun Gessesse. Alongside a generation of young singers, Neway renewed interest in the poetic style of **semenna-werq** (wax and gold), an old Abyssinian tradition of double entendre which half-fooled the censors, or at least allowed a safety valve whose presence they could sometimes ignore without incurring the wrath of the military chiefs.

Wax and gold meanings were carried to the public through apparently innocuous love songs. Here, for instance, is "Altchalkoum" (Can't take any more), created by Tlahoun Gessesse on the eve of an abortive coup against Haile Selassie (it was performed by him with the backing of the Imperial Body Guard Band, implicated in the coup attempt); it fooled nobody and was quickly banned – and was banned again by Mengistu.

How long are you going to make me suffer?
I can't take any more, I've had enough.
I'm up to here with it,
  I'm more than up to here.
I can't take any more,
  how can I put up with it?
I can't put up with your torments
I don't know what more I can do.

New Styles

At the turn of the millennium, with the establishment of a fragile democracy and the return of freedom of expression, it's not unreasonable to hope for a creative renewal for Ethiopian music: less of the one-two beat immediately danceable stuff, and a renewal of inspiration from the old style, rythmically formidable *tchik-tchik-ka*, with its unfettered lyrics, controlled synthesisers, and supreme horn sections. New talents are already jostling in an exciting field – **Gera Nekatibeb**, **Fikreaddis**, **Solomon 'Houloum zero zero' Tekalegn**, and **Hebiste Tiruneh**, a brilliant woman singer tipped as the successor to Aster Aweke. A number of bands, too – the **Abyssinia Band**, the **Medina Band** and the **Axumite Band** – are waiting in the wings.

Also getting a hearing is **Tigrinya music** from Eritrea and Tigray. It is characterised by repetitive, throbbing, camel-walk rhythms. There was a stunning recent CD, *Kozli Gaba*, by Abraham Afewerki, one of the best singers, released in Italy.

Don't look for Ethiopian reggae, though. It's true the word 'Rastafari' comes from Ras Tafari Makonnen, the title and surname of Haile Selassie, the last emperor of Ethiopia, but rasta fetishism has no special meaning in Ethiopia, despite the admiration for Bob Marley common to the whole of Africa. There is a community of Jamaican rastas at Sheshemene, 200km south from Addis Ababa, but they're viewed as an imported phenomenon. Nor is there any discernible relationship between Ethiopian music and reggae. This part of the world has never fuelled the African diaspora.

Live in Addis: Azmaris

The best live venues in Addis Ababa are the music bars or **azmaribets**, or the local **tedjbets** – where *tedj* (honey beer) is consumed. They're to be found absolutely everywhere and you can just look in to see if you like the atmosphere. Apart from a dozen or so main roads, the streets of Addis have neither names nor street numbers, and to give directions people refer to a district, then to a handy point of reference, like the post office, a pharmacy, a garage or an embassy. It's difficult, therefore, to be precise about addresses: but the taxi drivers know nearly all the music places (book a taxi for the whole evening). As Ethiopians are absolute strangers even to the music of the rest of Africa, they're invariably amazed when foreigners show interest in their music. You can be sure you'll be adopted and guided, and introduced to all the best sounds and experiences.

Ali Tango

Every taxi driver in Addis knows the location of the cramped little *Tango Music and Video Shop*, in the heart of the Piazza, the base of **Ali 'Tango' Kaifa**, who has played an essential role in the Ethiopian music scene over the last two decades.

A smart talent scout and an inventive producer, Ali Tango pioneered the cassette industry after having produced some fifty records, including cult classics like Mahmoud Ahmed's "Ere Mela Mela", Muluken Mellesse's "Jemeregne", Alemayehu Eshete's "Wededkuh Afkerkush" and Ayalew Mesfin's "Gunfan". He also 'discovered' Aster Aweke, Amelmal Abate, Neway Debebe and most recently the teenage singer Hebiste Tiruneh, the first great success of the post-dictatorship era. An enthusiast for technology, Ali Tango was the first to use

"Music this way: azmaribet sign"

digital recording equipment and he has opened a private studio – a high-performance set-up, even if it's not close to European standards.

The respected and envied godfather of a passionate industry, Ali Tango has always defended the freedom of expression of singers and independent orchestras – sometimes with great cunning during the dictatorship. And he enthuses over all the regional rhythms of Ethiopia – Gurague, Tigrinya, Gondar, Kotu, Oromo – and even takes an interest in Yemenite and Somali music – a rather unusual path in such a culturally self-sufficient country.

Lastly, but significantly, Ali Tango introduced the concept of affordable **video rental** before anyone else, and the Western TV shows he offered proved stiff competition to the indigestible diet of TV-Mengistu.

You'll meet all sorts of musicians in azmaribets – players of *krar* (lyre), *masenqo* (one-string fiddle), *washint* (flute) and *kebero* (percussion), even accordionists. These musicians are **azmari**, equivalent to the griots of West Africa or the wandering *taraf* musicians of Romania, privileged carriers of popular music, mediators of collective memory. They have an ambivalent reputation among Ethiopians – a mix of suspicion at their bohemian life and respect for the power of the word.

Azmari depend on tips – given to sing what one feels deep down, be it sadness, nostalgia, praises or veiled criticism. As such, they had a particularly hard time during the dictatorship. But since the end of Mengistu, they – and the azmaribets – have had a spectacular return. The clubs sprang up throughout the capital, with concentrations in the areas of Kazentchis and Yohannès Sefer, and a whole new generation of talented, non-conformist, sarcastic azmaris burst upon the scene. Most arrived in the capital for the first time from their distant provinces, and the style of this new wave became known as **bolel** – literally 'car exhaust fumes' – the putt-putt-putt of jabbering and nonsense. Bolel is a mix of azmari traditions (praise or sarcasm at will, depending on the tip) and of modern urban culture (the country/city divide, TV, international references).

In the Kazentchis area you will meet the greatest Ethiopian voices and characters of bolel: **Abbebe Fekade** (*Bati Restaurant*), **Betsat Seyoum** (in Yordanos Hotel Street), **Adaneh & Malefya Teka**, **Tigist Assefa**, **Mandelbosh 'Assabelew' Dibo**, **Tedje**, to name a few of the hippest. In Yohannes Sefer, you'll find musicians in every house on the street. Try also just off Bole Road, next to *Torero Bar* and *Ibex Hotel*, for the amazing 'sisters' **Zewditou Yohannes & Yezinna Negash**. In Datsun Sefer, just ask for **Admassou Abate**. You'll find him: he's modest but he's really the blues itself.

Whether you find the atmosphere in your azmaribet bluesy or not, the alcohol flows freely and the atmosphere gets very hot, very quickly. Better put on your seat belt when they unleash the *eskista* – a dance style in which the shaking of shoulders and chests would melt a statue.

Future Shock

Ethiopian musicians are still in many ways reeling from the effects of the changes since the flight of Mengistu and the onset of democracy in 1991. The end of the civil war resulted in a new country on their northern border – Eritrea – and the first taste of personal freedom for a whole generation. Travel

Hanna Shenkute of The Abyssinia Band

is much easier than before, so musicians and bands are able to play and record overseas - and return without a problem – and the opportunity to listen to other African and European music is beginning to have an effect on their own.

Contemporary bands are also influenced in the same direction by the demands of Addis Ababa teenage culture, keen to make up for lost exposure to global youth fashions over the last two decades. Western music, reggae, rap and the sounds of Kenya and Congo (Zaire) are all increasingly popular.

The **Abyssinia Band** was formed straight after the end of the war and is currently one of the hottest groups in Addis. As musician Abiy Solomon remarked, "We don't exactly want to be Westernised – we're just trying to produce music of equal quality to the rest of the world. We're working hard to make the sound richer and change the traditional arrangements a bit to make them more modern." They are now experimenting with bubbling guitar tunes and writing songs in the seventone Western scale rather than traditional pentatonic. Ironically, of course, it's pentatonic, polyphonic music that jumps, that the global audience is really attracted to, never mind what the young trendies in Addis yearn for. If Abyssinia Band and their like can bridge the two views, that would be some success to sing about.

Abiyou Soloman of The Abyssinia Band

Music Shops in Addis Ababa

If you're looking for recorded music in Addis Ababa, you'll find the city full of '**Music Shops**' – cassette-copying stores where you can get customised tapes for about £1/$1.60.

At the entrance to the Mercato quarter, near the Great Mosque, the noteworthy **Marathon Music Shop** and **Alem Music Shop** stand out, in an area where music stores run to dozens. Not far from Mercato, the Piazza quarter is also the base for a number of bigger centres for music production, in particular **Tango Music Shop** and **Mahmoud Music Shop**, the latter belonging to the singer Mahmoud Ahmed, on the corner of Cunningham Street and Adwa. Close by on the other side of the square is **Ayalew**, owned by Ayalew Mesfin, a singer who was a big star in the 1970s. He's always there, ready with anecdotes about the good old days and unofficial recordings of wild Ethiopian Radio sessions available for fans who call by. His group, the Black Lion Band, had one of the most rapid-fire horn sections on the pre-Mengistu nightlife scene.

To close this shopping trip, there are two stores situated outside the strategic centres of Mercato and Piazza: the first, **Ghion Video**, by the entrance to the

VÉRONIQUE GUILLIEN, CRAM WORLD

Mahmoud Ahmed,
singer extraordinaire and shopkeeper

Ghion Hotel, belongs to the former lead sax-player from the Roha Band, Fekadou Amde Meskel. The second, **Selamino**, on Bole Road, is owned by the Roha's former guitarist, Selam Seyoum, a remarkable instrumentalist and the living memory of modern Ethiopian music (he has written the first study of it for Addis Ababa University). He's a mine of information for anyone who wants to know more about the evolution of one of Africa's most engaging musical cultures.

discography

If your local record store can't help, the best place to find recorded Ethiopian music, and have an unusual meal at the same time, is your local Ethiopian restaurant. If you don't have one yet, you may not have long to wait – they seem to be opening all over the world. For Addis Ababa shops, see the feature box above.

Contemporary

Compilations

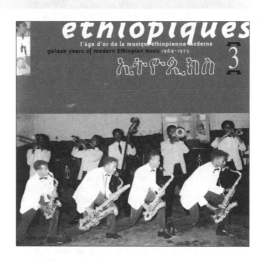

◉ **Ethiopian Groove: The Golden '70s**
(Dona Wana/Blue Silver/Stern's, UK; Abyssinian, US).

This 16-track introduction to the golden age of Ethiopian music brings together artists unheard outside Ethiopia (Bezunesh Bekele, Hirut Bekele, Ayalew Mesfin, Tamrat Ferendji) as well as the earliest recordings of Aster Aweke and two hits from Alemayehu Eshete.

◉ **Éthiopiques 1: Golden Years of Ethiopian Modern Music 1969–1975** (Buda Musique, France).

The first of the compilation series executive-produced by the author of this article, this features Muluqen Mellesse, the great Mahmoud Ahmed, Seyfu Yohannes, Teshome Meteku and a track from Gétachew Kassa.

 Éthiopiques 3: The Golden Age of Modern Ethiopian Music 1969–75 (Buda Musique, France).

Volumes 1 and 3 of Buda's superb series feature bands and artists of the early 1970s: the years of flares and afros and African unity, before the relatively healthy turmoil of life under

the uncertain thumb of King Haile Selassie was thrown aside by the arrival of Mengistu's brutal military dictatorship in 1974.

◉ **Éthiopiques 2: Tètchawèt!: Urban Azmaris of the '90s** (Buda Musique, France).

Azmaris are the folk musicians of Addis's hole-in-the-wall clubs or azmaribets, the dens where alchohol and live music combine in a smoky atmosphere and the performers work up a sweat in delivering a richly codified social commentary in exchange for the tips which are their only pay. Azmaribets have proliferated in the capital since the fall of Mengistu's regime and this CD features tracks from ten of their most accomplished performers.

Artists

Mahmoud Ahmed

One of modern Ethiopia's greatest voices, Mahmoud Ahmed has been at the top for thirty years. His sound is beautiful, sad, and always danceable.

 Éthiopiques 7: Erè Mèla Mèla (Buda Musique, France).

Recorded in Addis in 1975 with the Ibex Band – most of whose members went on to found the Roha Band – this was the first modern Ethiopian recording to be released in the West (by Crammed Discs in 1986) and became something of a cult album, a collection of all Mahmoud Ahmed's singles released by Ali Tango's Addis-based Kaifa Records. This remastered re-release not only contains the original Kaifa 45s, but also four bonus tracks. ◉ *Éthiopiques Vol 6* is also a Mahmoud Ahmed record, the superb *Almaz*.

◉ **Soul of Addis** (Earthworks, UK).

A good album from the 1980s.

Mulatu Astatke and Ethio-Jazz

As a teenager in the early 1960s, Mulatu Astatke studied music in England and the USA. No other musician in Ethiopia is anything like Mulatu, and it looks like his style will die with him.

◉ **Éthiopiques 4: Ethio-Jazz et Musique Instrumentale 1969-1974** (Buda Musique, France).

Chronologically, part of the same early-1970s era as Vols 1 and 3 of Buda's series, but the sound here is very different, with two LPs' worth of instrumental tracks from the superbly brooding, and – unique in Ethiopia – Latin-influenced tones of Mulatu (on keyboards) and his Ethio-Jazz Band.

Aster Aweke

The first Ethiopian artist (after Mahmoud Ahmed) to crossover into the Western market, Aster Aweke has a voice that kills you. She emigrated to the US in the late 1970s but remains hugely popular at home.

 Kabu and **Aster** (Triple Earth, UK; Columbia, US); **Ebo** (Barkhanns/Stern's, UK).

These CDs, recorded in the US and London between 1989 and 1993, are notably Westernised in the brass section arrangements, but still a formidable introduction to the Ethiopian feeling. *Aster* is perhaps the first choice.

Alemayehu Eshete

Alemayehu Eshete introduced the languid poses of rock into his country's music but it's his profoundly Ethiopian, soul/blues style which knocks out his home audience.

◉ **Alemayehu Eshete Addis Ababa** (Dona Wana/Musidisc Stern's, UK; Shanachie, US).

Recorded in Paris, this CD introduces some of the hits with which Eshete has built his reputation. Listen to the pianist, whose keyboard style is unique in Africa. Guest clarinettist is big Ivo Papazov from Macedonia.

Ethio Stars & Tukul Band

Two bands here: one a modern group (formed in 1981) based around the trumpeter Shimeles Beyene and the singer Getatchew Kassa, the other a traditional ensemble.

ILPO SAUNIO/PIRANHA

Krar, drums and washint from the Tukul Band

◉ **Amharic Hits** (Piranha, Germany).

This CD brings together some of the best instrumentalists in the business (particularly Kut Ojulu on bass krar). All produced by the dynamic Global Music Centre in Helsinki.

Netsanet Mellesse

Netsanet is from the young generation of artists who have emerged over the past decade and, with his soulful voice, has become one of the top post-Mengistu stars.

◉ **Dodge** (Dona Wana/Stern's, UK; Shanachie, US).

Mellesse's exceptional voice is served perfectly by the sophisticated arrangements of Yohannes Tekola – the trumpeter and leader of the Wallias Band.

Roha Band

For more than twenty years the Roha Band has been the top Ethiopian group, as well as backing most of the country's recording artists at one time or another.

◉ **Roha Band Tour 1990** (Aman Int, US).

Featuring the legendary Neway Debebe, Amelmal Abate and Berhane Haile, this is mainly an electric set, with several traditional pieces as bonus.

Teshome Wolde

Born in Shoa province in 1955, Teshome began his musical career in the Addis City Hall Theatre in the early years of the Mengistu dictatorship. Following in the footsteps of Mahmoud Ahmed, he sings traditional compositions to a modern backing, and also writes his own.

Ethiopian Soul Revue (Rags Productions, UK).

With the famous Ethio Stars band behind you, it's hard to go wrong. Teshome Wolde's first CD release (following nine Ethiopian cassette recordings), presents love songs in various arrangements, from jazz to funk and rock, but always with a hypnotic, swinging beat.

Folk and Traditional

Compilations

Ethiopie: Love Songs
(Inédit, France).

Two male and one female singer perform exquisite songs accompanied by Krar (Lyre) and masengo (fiddle). Traditional material compellingly recorded in Paris.

Ethiopie: Polyphonies of the Dorze
(Chant du Monde, France).

This discography would be incomplete without paying homage to one of the most outstanding aspects of the numerous 'tribal' musics found in Ethiopia. Part of the World Music heritage.

Harp of Apollo (JVC, Japan).

Unpromising ethnomusicological packaging, but this repays a good listen: check out the wonderful voice of Tayech Berhanu on "Gurague Song" and the kebero-drumming of Getachew Abdi. Also features nice tom (thumb piano) playing and the young krar maestro Kut Ojulu.

Music from Ethiopia (Caprice Records, Sweden).

Recordings made in Addis with Swedish assistance, bringing together traditional and modern songs. Includes some beautiful traditional examples (especially Lemma Gebre Hiwot, Alemayehu Fanta and Asnaketch Worku) and unusual ceremonial flute music from Tigray, in which each flute plays only certain notes of the melody. The modern songs aren't representative of the best of Ethiopia but are still a reasonable showcase for what's around. Good accompanying booklet by Anu Laakkonen and Sten Sandahl.

Music of Wax and Gold (Topic, UK).

Ethnic field recordings by the late, respected ethnomusicolo-

gist Jean Jenkins. Previously three LPs on the Tangent label, now available on one wonderful, bumper CD.

Eritrea

Compilations

The Best of 18 Eritrean Singers in Europe
(Rags Productions, UK).

With solid, bang-bang-bang beats and an almost Chinese sound (from the electric krar harp), Eritrean songs, as typified by the persistent rhythms of Tigray, have a sparser feel than neighbouring Ethiopia's more familiar Amhara sound. But they share that halting, off-beat style that makes you want to dance with a limp. Proceeds from sales of this CD go to supporting orphans and disabled children through The Eritrean Relief Association.

Éthiopiques 5: Tigrigna Music
(Buda Musique, France).

A compilation devoted to recordings from Tigray (northern province of Ethiopia) and Eritrea, from 1970-75, this includes tracks by a number of artists who joined the anti-Mengistu resistance, and three songs from Eritrean drummer and singer Teklé Tefsa-Fzighe which were suppressed when first recorded in 1975 and got their first airing on this 1998 release. As in all the *Éthiopiques* CDs, excellent, illustrated liner notes complement.

Artists

Abraham Afewerki

Afewerki divides his time between Eritrea and Italy (you can hear it in Paolo Modugno's production). His music is a good introduction to today's Eritrean beat, following in the footsteps of the late, great Yeamane 'Baria' Gebre-Michael.

Kozli Gaba (Stile Libero/Virgin, Italy).

Eritrean music (or to be more precise Tigrinya music) could merit a chapter of its own, so greatly does it differ from Ethiopian – it has a very specific rhythm, intoxicating and persistent. This disc is the first Western outing for music from Africa's newest nation.

Ghana

gold coast: highlife and roots

Ghanaian music dominated Africa at independence with its highlife styles – and it is possibly the best researched on the continent. But it had a hard couple of decades, as the economy collapsed and the bottom fell out of the record industry. Is a long-awaited resurgence at hand? **Ronnie Graham** and **John Collins** check in.

ighlife – Ghana's urban, good-time music – has had enormous influence throughout West Africa, but its roots are firmly embedded in the clubs and dancehalls of the **colonial Gold Coast**. Here, in the early years of Ghana's independence in the late 1950s, it effectively became the national music, and for the fifty years since, it has proved one of the most popular, enduring, and adaptable African styles.

Highlife Roots and Palm-wine

The highlife story begins in the early years of this century, when various European influences – church music, military brass band music, sea shanties – and African influences from along the coast in Liberia were introduced to the Gold Coast's own local rhythms and idioms. Forms that went into the mix included *osibisaba* (a Fante rhythm from southwest Ghana); *ashiko*, originally from Sierra Leone; *mainline*, *fireman* and *dagomba* guitar styles from Liberia; and, perhaps most important, *gombe*. Gombe was introduced to Ghana from Sierra Leone, which in turn had acquired it from freed Maroon slaves from Jamaica in the early nineteenth century. All in all, a pretty complicated picture.

Instrumentation depended on what equipment was available and, out of a welter of neo-traditional variations there gradually emerged a form known generically as **highlife**. The term, coined in the 1920s, is a reference to the kind of European-derived evening of dressing-up and dancing (the high life), to which the local elites aspired and to which new immigrants to the towns of West Africa between the wars were quite unaccustomed – but which they soon made their own.

Highlife has emerged in many shapes, but initially there were two key varieties. At one extreme was the high highlife of the ballroom – a **dance orches-**

1960's GUITAR BAND HIGHLIFE of GHANA

It's all Yaa Ampansah: classic acoustic highlife

tra style favoured by the coastal elite (toppers and tails and much ceremony, according to means). The bands were large-scale string and brass orchestras, playing the full array of foxtrots, waltzes, quicksteps and ragtimes. At the other extreme were the poor, often rural, **guitar bands** playing a neotraditional African style for less Westernised audiences (often dubbed, especially when least respectable, as **palm-wine music**).

Initially a coastal music of the Fante people, this latter (low) highlife spread inland after World War I and thereafter focused on the Asante, Kwahu and Akwapim areas around Kumasi, Ghana's second city and capital of the Ashanti region. In the early days the instruments were simple acoustic guitars, often homemade, plus a tapped wooden box, a beer bottle hit with a stick or coin and, of course, voices. The vocals were often pitched high and had a nasal quality. In time, the bands acquired electric guitars and more sophisticated percussion.

Although there's plenty of room for argument

about which category each Ghanaian artist and band belongs to, the broad dance band/guitar band distinction quickly took hold, and was given official sanction in 1960 when separate musicians' unions were set up for the dance and guitar bands.

During the 1930s and '40s hundreds of highlife 78rpms were released and the style spread to Sierra Leone, Nigeria and even as far south as the Belgian Congo where musicians remember it for its simple appeal and attractive, two-finger guitar lines. By the end of World War II, highlife was established in West Africa and the UK as typifying virtually all modern African dance music.

Dance-band Highlife

The already exuberant dance-band style was further enriched during the war by elements of **swing** and **jazz**, introduced by British and American servicemen, to produce what many consider to be classic highlife. These dance bands emerged from the pre-war dance orchestras and flourished during the rapid process of urbanisation and social change unleashed by the nationalist struggle of **Kwame Nkrumah**.

With independence, in 1957, Nkrumah's socialist-aligned government actively encouraged indigenous music. Apart from funding dozens of state bands, the president frequently travelled to neighbouring countries with a full dance band – often the **Tempos** – in his retinue. Ghana's music reflected the assertive self-confidence of Ghana at the time – newly independent, reasonably prosperous and widely respected in the pan-African struggle. Showy, dance-band highlife went from strength to stength. The top highlife orchestras composed original material in English and all the local languages, incorporating traditional rhythms into new arrangements. This framework was augmented by forays into 'Congo' music, calypso, and any other style which grabbed the bandleader's fancy. The result was a lilting, relaxed, sophisticated dance style with enduring appeal.

ET Mensah (see box on p.491) led the charge with his talented **Tempos** band. A consummate musician, equally at home on sax or trumpet, he brought a new level of professionalism to African dance music and popularised it throughout the region.

ET Mensah took over the Tempos' leadership and direction in the late 1940s from the master

Rural Roots

Highlife is far from the only Ghanaian style. The country has a strong, living tradition of indigenous rural music, which continues to feed into urban sounds. These folk/roots sounds include court music played for chiefs, the ceremonial music of special occasions, work songs to accompany agriculture and domestic chores, as well as music played for pleasure when the day is done.

In Ghana, although musicianship tends to be inherited, musical output is not the prerogative of a particular social caste, as it is in the Mande-speaking world to the north and west. However, as in Mali, Senegal and Guinea, a particular ethno-linguistic group does hold cultural sway over other communities – the **Akan** language group of central and southern Ghana. Akan nationalities include Fante and Asante (or Ashanti), while on the coast of Ghana, the main groups are the Ga-Adangme and the Ewe. All are part of a broadly related family of languages. They have an elaborate **court music** using large drum ensembles and groups of horns. Another great spectacle is the huge **log xylophone** played in **asonko**, a form of recreational music.

Northeastern Ghana is home to a cluster of Voltaic-speaking peoples – the **Dagomba**, **Mamprusi** and **Frafra**. In this area the instruments are mostly fiddles, lutes and wonderful, hourglass **talking-drum** ensembles. It's customary for musicians to perform frequently for the local chief – in the Dagomba country each Monday and Friday. Passing through towns like Tamale and Yendi you might find something going on because professional musicians, although attached to chiefs, regularly perform for the public. Dagomba drummers are always a great spectacle, their flowing tunics fanning out as, palms flying, they dance the *takai*.

In the **northwest**, the **Lobi**, **Wala**, **Dagarti** and **Sissala** make music with the **xylophone** – either played alone or with a small group of drums and percussion instruments. Finger bells and ankle bells are often worn by the dancers.

The **Ewe** populate **southeastern Ghana**. Their music is closer to the traditions of Togo and Benin than to that of other Ghanaian peoples and, with their enthusiasm for music associations and drum dance clubs, they've developed many different kinds of recreational music, like the **agbadza**, which evolved out of a traditional war dance in the 1920s or 30s, and the **borborbor**, which is a fusion with **konkoma highlife** that was put together in the eastern town of Kpandu in the early 1950s. The leader of the first borborbor group was the policeman **FC Nuatro**. His band consisted of young musicians, who were also supporters of Kwame Nkrumah. Almost inevitably, the band became known as Nkrumah's Own Borborbor!

Palm-Wine Music: Buy the Man a Drink

In Ghana, **palm-wine music** was the forerunner of guitar-band highlife, and it remains the popular street and house music of the Akan people – a relaxed, rural, acoustic guitar style. It takes its name (and purpose) from late afternoon drinking sessions at palm-wine bars in the bush – usually simple, outdoor affairs under a big tree. A musician would turn up with his guitar and play for as long as people wanted to buy him drinks. This is music purely for entertainment, and such palm-winers, like the best drinkers anywhere in the world, tend to be comedians as well as parodists of the local scene.

Palm-wine guitar music is fast dying out in Ghana, partly because musicians are enticed into the electric guitar bands and concert party groups (or overseas if they're really good, and lucky), and partly due to the lack of instruments. In many places, still, someone will be able to point you in the direction of a palm-wine musician, but you may have to find an instrument for him to play on. Buy the man a drink and you may well find your name included in the current number.

In a professional setting, Ghana's long-time palm-wine star was undoubtedly **Kwaa Mensah** (no relation to ET), who was taught the two-finger guitar-picking style by his uncle, guitar-highlife pioneer, 'Sam' Kwame Asare. Mensah released hundreds of 78s in the 1950s, and a decade later his style (and many of his songs) were copied by dozens of highlife guitar bands. By then he had withdrawn from the limelight, though he had a brief return in the late 1970s, when he toured the US with the Ga roots troupe, Wulomei, and made an album, *Wawo Christo*. He died in 1991.

The prolific Kwaa Mensah in regal mode

King Bruce

drummer **Guy Warren**. The young Warren, aka Kofi Ghanaba (son of Ghana), was a precocious talent, responsible for introducing hotter **Afro-Cuban rhythms** into the more relaxed highlife groove. Following a trip to London, where he met Caribbean musicians, he was also responsible for the introduction of **calypso** throughout West Africa, playing it live with the Tempos whilst widening its appeal on his radio programmes. In 1953 he began to redirect his efforts and moved, via Liberia, to the US where he released a series of radical albums combining modern jazz with African percussion and aiming to reintroduce black Americans to their African roots – legendary recordings now worth their weight in gold.

Another major figure in classic era big-band highlife was **King Bruce**, whose trumpeter's taste was for jazz and swing. He established a stable of dance bands, which included his own, famous Black Beats, the Barbecues, the Barons and five other groups, all beginning with B and mostly playing 'copyright' – in other words covers. In the mid-1990s King's son, Eddie Bruce, re-released two professional quality cassettes of Black Beats' evergreens. This was followed by a CD and a biography (John Collins) jointly released in 1997. Sadly, King Bruce died in September 1997.

Yet another B band – the Broadways, led by the guitarist Stan Plange, and not part of the King Bruce stable – went on to become the big-band **Professional Uhuru Band** in 1965. Stan is currently the Director of the Ghana Broadcasting highlife band.

The other big highlife dance band was Jerry Hansen's **Ramblers International Dance Band**,

formed in 1962 by Hansen and nine other Black Beat escapees and eventually consisting of a fully professional, fifteen-man line-up. Almost uniquely, they made a living from their shows and records for nearly twenty years (and, in a second-generation, Jerry-Junior incarnation, are still going about it in the 1990s).

Yet fashions were changing and a foretaste of highlife's decline came in 1966 with the CIA-inspired overthrow of Nkrumah and the first in a long line of corrupt, military juntas. By the 1970s, dance-band highlife was on the way out, undermined by new, imported pop styles and the near-impossibility of maintaining large, full-time groups in a declining economy.

ET Mensah: King of Dance-band Highlife

Emmanuel Tettey 'ET' Mensah – the 'King of Highlife' – was born into a musical family in Accra in 1919. He learned the fife and played in the huge school band run by the legendary Joe 'Teacher' Lamptey. At secondary school, in the 1930s, he learnt organ and sax before forming the Accra Rhythmic Orchestra. But it was World War II which marked the turning point in his career. In 1941 Accra had the busiest airport in the world, as the Allies mobilised forces for the Middle East campaign. Thousands of European and American soldiers (among them many musicians) passed through Ghana and introduced modern jazz and swing into the indigenous highlife style. ET joined forces with Scottish trumpeter Sergeant Jack Leopard, who encouraged him to notate his music, tighten up the arrangements and accommodate new influences.

JAK KILBY

No money troubles for ET Mensah (right)

After the war ET joined the famous **Tempos**, then under the joint leadership of Guy Warren and bassist Joe Kelly. ET, with a more disciplined approach to band management and a masterful touch with arrangements (not to mention several armloads of instruments), gradually assumed control of the band, and by 1952 they were ready for their first studio venture. Featuring trumpet, trombone, saxes, double bass, drums, congas,

clips (claves) and maracas, ET and the Tempos cut a swathe through the competition with hit after hit, including "Schoolgirl", "You Call Me Roko", "All For You", along with a variety of calypsos, cha-cha-chas, boleros and charangas. The band toured regularly and made an enormous impact in West Africa.

When highlife big bands proved impossible to maintain, ET Mensah went into musical semi-retirement, earning his living as a government pharmacist. He was called back into action during the mid-1970s roots revival, recording several golden oldie albums for Afrodisia producer Faisal Helwani, and performing regularly in Accra. He made further comebacks in 1982, with a trip to Nigeria and the release of "Highlife Giants of Africa" with Nigerian trumpeter Victor Olaiya, and in 1986 when a batch of original recordings from 1956 were reissued on the London-based RetroAfric label. Anyone privileged to see one of his live performances in London or Amsterdam, performing in a wheelchair, the golden tones and classic arrangements intact, couldn't fail to appreciate his contribution.

ET Mensah died in June 1996 from a long and debilitating illness. He was accorded a state funeral.

Guitar-band Highlife

The African Brothers give it the grand calabash

Guitar-band highlife first achieved big popularity in the 1930s, when the top guitar band was **Sam's Trio**, led by **Jacob Sam** (Kwame Asare). His Trio first recorded in 1928 for Zonophone, in London, and put out three versions of his famous song "Yaa Amponsah", the structure of which runs through many a great highlife number.

A key figure in the music's development was **EK Nyame**. In the early 1950s, he was in the vanguard of the folk-guitar scene. He pioneered singing in the local language of Kumasi (Twi) and developed the guitar band repertoire by adding jazz elements, including double bass and Latin percussion. As leader of the **Akan Trio**, the most popular of all guitar highlife bands, he also grafted highlife onto Ghana's popular vaudeville concert shows, or '**concert parties**', which, with guitar bands, combined music, dance and drama into an all-night extravaganza. The trio played stock roles from the repertoire – 'Bob' (a joker), 'the gentleman', and 'the woman' (a man dressed in women's clothing), mounting semi-improvised plays (intended to be hilarious as well as topical), and breaking to take up their instruments. They were a huge success everywhere they played. In 1975, Nyame recorded a set of old numbers to keep for posterity what had only been recorded previously on fragile shellac. He died in 1977 and was given a state funeral for his contribution to the nation.

In the 1960s, highlife guitar bands all went electric and the rootsier, older styles vanished for a decade, until Ghana's **Roots Revival** of the mid-1970s. This adopted several guises but it's hard to overstress the importance of the 1971 *Soul To Soul* festival in Accra which featured Santana, Wilson Picket and Ike and Tina Turner on the same bill as home-grown highlife and drum bands. The presence of internationally successful black musicians acted as a major stimulus, almost seeming to legitimise Ghanaian musical endeavour. Equally, however, the contrast between the local and the imported, for those who attended, and its subsequent reverberations through the Ghanaian music scene, looked for a while like wiping out indigenous sounds altogether and replacing live music on the dance floor with imported vinyl.

But the threat acted as a spur. The guitar-band variety of highlife – still a vibrant, popular style in the hands and voices of **Nana Ampadu and the African Brothers**, the **Ashanti Brothers**, the **City Boys**, **Alex Konadu's Band** and dozens of others – received a new lease of life. **F Kenya**, **CK Mann** and **Eddie Donkor** all had big hits with new variations on the highlife theme as they responded to the rising challenge of disco and, later, reggae.

An evolving approach to highlife was adopted by a number of bands promoted by the forward-looking music entrepreneur **Faisal Helwani**. Helwani supported innovative fusion groups like **Hedzolleh** ('Peace-Freedom' in Ga, the language of Accra), **Basa-Basa** (Chaos) and the **Bunzus**, who dug into Ghanaian culture and presented it in a sophisticated package. At the same time, he tried to repackage giants of the past, promoting ET Mensah, the Uhurus and the palm-wine acoustic guitarist Kwaa Mensah in a series of weekend variety shows.

Another initiative came in the form of the **Ga cultural revival** spearheaded by the neotraditional cultural troupe **Wulomei** (Ga for 'Fetish Priest') – to encourage pop-minded young people "to forget foreign music and do their own thing", in the words of leader Nii Ashitey. They toured with Kwaa Mensah and were soon followed by other Ga bands such as **Dzadzeloi**, **Blemabii**, **Abladei** and **Suku Troupe**. These groups were characterised by powerful Ga drumming, sweet female harmonies and exciting floor shows, yet they were as comfortable in hotel cabarets as they were in downtown Accra compounds. The Ga cultural

Classic Guitar-band Highlife

Some of Ghana's greatest bands reached maturity in the 1970s, creating classic guitar-band highlife.

Nana Ampadu and his African Brothers International Band, formed in 1963, are still one of the country's most innovative and enduring guitar groups. They had their earliest and one of their best-loved hits in 1967 with "Ebi Tie Ye" – a plea for democracy in the dark days following the fall of Nkrumah – and had released over 100 songs on singles before 1970 and the release of their first LP, *Ena Eye A Mane Me*. Since then they've made nearly sixty albums and twice as many singles. Always a group to mix street wisdom with thinly veiled political comment, they never let this interfere with good music, and are forever trying something new.

Unlike most Ghanaian bands, they play entirely their own material. During the 1970s they experimented with a variety of styles including reggae, rumba and what they called **Afro-hili**, a James Brown-inspired beat which was a challenge to Fela Kuti's Afro-Beat and was supposed to embrace all African forms. In recent years they have returned to a more refined highlife with strong rhythms and sparkling guitars.

An early stalwart of the band was the late **Senior Eddie Donkor**, who established his own **Simple Seven** band in the mid-1970s and had a series of pidgin English hits like "Na Who Cause Am?" and "Asiko Darling".

Another major highlife star – and often dubbed a purist – is **Alex Konadu**. He and his band play music firmly rooted in Ghanaian traditions and he is today the uncrowned king of guitar-band highlife, with a dozen albums to his credit. He has enjoyed massive sales throughout anglophone West Africa with his

highly personal, reflective songs, mostly sung in Twi, the Asante language. But it's in his charismatic live shows that Konadu's "one man thousand/one man bulldozer/one man army" personality is most clearly released. It is said that he has played in every town and village in Ghana and his loyalty to the country and to guitar-highlife music is legendary.

A third figure in classic highlife was **CK Mann**, one of the most influential African guitarists of the 1970s. He graduated out of Moses Kweku 'Kakaiku' Opong's

JAK KILBY

Alex Konadu – one man and his band

band (**Kakaiku's**) in the 1960s and, in his own band, Carousel Seven, started composing songs with a close version of the traditional osode beat and a single guitar – his own. The slightly melancholy results were enormously popular and CK more or less had the rootsier end of the Ghanaian highlife market to himself in the mid-1970s. But, with commercial success came a steady dilution of what made the sound really distinctive and, by the mid-80s, CK Mann had retired into relative obscurity. Now based in Canada, he attempted to revive his career with the 1995 album, *Timeless Highlife*, and by guesting as a vocalist on the *Con Ghana Cuban* release of the same year.

troupes still play in Accra and it is always worth checking a troupe known as **Bukom**, led by Bi Boy Nii Ashitey (formerly of Wulonei).

Highlife guitar styles were revitalised by Daniel **'Koo Nimo'** Amponsah. He absorbed the guts of his finger-picking, palm-wine guitar style from Kwame Asare, Kwaa Mensah and EK Nyame, but learnt classical guitar in his late twenties, and brought in all kinds of European and American

jazz and classical influences. He has been a source of inspiraton to Ghanaian musicians trying to graft new musical stock onto old roots, and, now in his early sixties, continues to perform regularly with his all-acoustic **Adadam** band. He recently incorporated the Akan *seprewa* harp-lute into his group and arranged for this almost extinct instrument to be taught at the University of Ghana's School of Performing Arts.

The Highlife Diaspora

For almost two decades – the golden era of Nkrumah's Revolution – Ghana was the very heart of Africa and African music. However, with Nkrumah's overthrow in 1966 the country began a downward spiral of political instability, corruption and economic collapse. Musicians suffered alongside everyone else and their livelihoods were in jeopardy when the clubs and dancehalls began closing, the instruments and equipment broke down and the beer dried up.

Many musicians left to seek work abroad. The nucleus of **Osibisa**, for instance, who were the most prominent African band in Europe in the 1970s (see box), left Ghana shortly after the 1966 coup. Through the 1970s, and particularly during the early 1980s, when Ghana reached an all-time low, many others joined them, leaving to seek work in Europe or, closer to home, **Nigeria**, which was enjoying a period of booming oil prosperity.

Many Ghanaian highlife bands flourished in Lagos and in Nigeria's eastern, Igbo regions. **Okukuseku** became the best-known but dozens of others – among them the Canadoes, the Opambuas, Odoywewu, the Kuul Strangers, the Beach Scorpions, the Golden Boys and Citystyle – also made their mark in Nigeria, often recording only one album before returning to Ghana. A specific example of a well-travelled professional musician was **Mr TO**

Jazz (of Ampoumah's Guitar Band) who spent seven years in Zaire playing with Franco and the OK Jazz. Later, in the 1970s, he spent two years in Onitsha, with the Igbo highlife guitar master, the late Stephen Osadebe. Most recently, TO has turned his hand, back home, to highlife-gospel music.

Ghana's relationship with **Britain** was, of course, long established. The folk musician Kwame 'Sam' Asare had sailed to England as early as 1928 to make the first-ever highlife recordings, and during the 1930s all the country's top musicians made the pilgrimage to Decca's London studios. Ghanaians also started to put down roots in Britain: many arrived as students and seamen and ended up settling as musicians. An early arrival in the 1930s was **Cab Quaye**, who joined Billy Cotton's Big Band; in the 1940s **Guy Warren** played bongos with Kenny Graham's Afro-Cubists. By the 1960s, a new generation was arriving, while British tours by ET Mensah, Jerry Hansen's Ramblers and even the Gold Coast Police Band served to keep expat Ghanaians in touch with home.

In the early 1980s scores of talented Ghanaian musicians arrived in Britain to add momentum to the burgeoning interest in African music, making their presence felt as sessionists, teachers and bandleaders. Important contributions were made by Kwabena Oduro-Kwarteng, Kofi Adu, Herman Asafo-Agyei and Sam Ashley, the core members of **Hi-Life International**, a successful London-based

Osibisa

In Britain at the end of the 1960s, pop audiences were presented for the first time with African music: the "criss-cross rhythms which explode with happiness" of Osibisa. Formed in London in 1968 by Ghanaians **Teddy Osei**, **Mac Tontoh** and **Sol Amarfio**, and with a mixed African and Caribbean line-up, Osibisa's 'Afro-rock' singles climbed the British charts and in the 1970s three of them – "Dance the Body Music", "Sunshine Day" and "Coffee Song" – made it into the UK Top Ten (still almost unheard of for African musicians).

Osibisa took their name from *osibisaba*, a pre-war proto-highlife rhythm, which they chose to reflect the coming-together of African roots and foreign pop. They were, for many years, the world's best-known African band and they made a lasting impact throughout Africa. As the situation deteriorated back home in Ghana, Osibisa became a beacon of hope to musicians struggling to keep body and soul together.

But Osibisa were, perhaps, a decade too early. Criticised by purists for muddling African rhythms with Western rock, but asked repeatedly by record companies to adjust their style and presentation to the needs of America's burgeoning soul and disco markets, they switched from label to label and steadily lost momentum. By the early 1980s, at a time when Sunny Ade's undiluted juju was making headlines for Virgin Records, Osibisa's popularity had largely melted away.

Yet their music was so innovative and influential that it was a prime candidate for re-release. Between 1995 and 1997 the Red Steel label did the honourable thing and re-issued the entire eight-album Osibisa canon.

band with two albums on Stern's. Other Ghanaian arrivals became core members of busy touring and recording groups like **Orchestra Jazira** and **Kabbala**, while **Dade Krama** ploughed a lonelier furrow with an innovative, more arty approach. And there were dozens of other Ghanaian musicians on the session music scene, like guitarist **Alfred Bannerman**, keyboard specialist **Jon K** and vocalist **Ben Brako**.

In the mid-1980s, due to changes in British immigration laws, Ghanaians began to focus their attentions on **Germany**. Here, highlife was being fused with funk and rock to produce a new, harder-edged, studio sound. **George Darko** led the way and his song "Akoo Te Brafo" (recorded in Berlin but a big hit in Ghana) gave rise to the term '**burgher highlife**'. He claimed Koo Nimo as a major influence, although, in truth, it's hard to hear many traces of the classical/palm-wine guitarist. He returned to live in Ghana in 1989. Meantime, members of his band had formed **Kantata** in Berlin, releasing a successful album of dance floor highlife including the song "Slim Lady", which was a huge success back in Ghana. In the 1990s, computer sourced 'burgher' highlife takes a huge slice of the Ghanaian popular music market, purveyed by leading exponents, **Daddy Lumba** (ex-Lumba Brothers) and **Nana Acheampong**.

Towards the end of the 1980s, **Canada** – in particular Toronto, where there was an established Ghanaian community – started to attract Ghanaian musicians. **Herman Asafo-Agyei**, the bass player, composer and leader of the Afro-funk outfit **Native Spirit**, led the way and he was later joined by drummer **Kofi Adu** and star vocalists **Pat Thomas**, **AB Crentsil** and **Jewel Ackah**. Pat Thomas, one of Ghana's premier highlife vocalists, sang with many of the country's great dance bands in the 1970s before going solo in the following decade. He gained international recognition with 1980s albums such as *Highlife Greats*. AB Crentsil's band, the **Sweet Talks**, was one of Ghana's top highlife groups, and in 1978 they went to LA to record the classic *Hollywood Highlife Party*. Soon after the group's split, Crentsil formed the new **Ahenfo Band**, which again won international acclaim with discs like *Tantie Alaba*.

In addition, the Ghanaian musical diaspora includes individual artists based in other countries – **Kumbi Salleh** in Holland, **Mustapha Tettey Addy**, who commutes between Ghana and Germany, **Andy Vans**, based in Switzerland and **Obo Addy** in the US. And everywhere they go, Ghanaians become effective music teachers, planting deep roots in host communities through their work in schools, clubs and social centres.

Gospel and Reggae

At home, Ghanaian music entered the 1980s in much the same shape as the country itself – hungry, revolutionary and weakened by a decade of neglect. Cassette piracy undermined the motivation to record, while only two studios had survived the degradations of the 1970s. Those musicians remaining at home began to organise and lobby for government support and had some success, with, for example, the criminalisation of tape piracy, and state copyright protection. Musically, meantime, **gospel** and **reggae** were the new forces.

With economic decline came a rise in religion, and especially pentecostal and evangelical churches, and as secular nightlife took a dive, many musicians were hired by churches to promote the message. By the 1990s, there were an estimated 800 gospel groups, many of them playing variants of highlife. While few records are made, cheap cassettes are ubiquitous. Top groups include the wonderful **Genesis Gospel Singers**, one of seven bands of the Christo Asafo mission.

Ghana's local gospel music now represents around 60 percent of the country's commercial pop output and airplay. Many churches have their own recording studios (note the Jesus Above All studio in east Legon, outside Accra) and in 1987 a **Gospel Musicians Union** was established. An important consequence of the gospel revolution was that, for

JAK KILBY

AB Crentsil

the first time, a substantial number of women entered the popular dance music arena. The result was the rise to prominence of such great voices as **Helen Rhabbles, Mary Ghansah, Diana Akiwumi,** the **Tagoe Sisters** and the **Daughters of Glorious Jesus**. In the old days a woman on stage was considered 'loose', but who could stop their daughter or wife from singing for Christ.

Reggae, with its strong appeal for the disenfranchised underclass, understandbly resonated heavily throughout Ghana in the late 1970s and 1980s, boosted by football stadium gigs from Côte d'Ivoire's reggae star **Alpha Blondy**. The reggae boom shows no signs of abating. **Kojo Antwi**, originally a singer with Classique Vibes, is now a successful solo singer specialising in soft reggae songs sung in Twi. **KK Kabobo** sings a kind of reggae highlife, also in Twi. Another name to listen out for is the **Fish Band**. There are even a few artists beginning to rap in Twi; **Daddy Lumba** is one, with gospel rap not far behind. Ghanaian music comes full-circle.

State of the Art

At the start of the new century, with Jerry Rawlings' relatively stable government, and a renewed entrepreneurial spirit, an atmosphere has been established in which Ghanaian musicians can look to the future. Hopefully, they will get more international exposure. It seems that the rise of gospel and reggae in the 1980s meant that overseas audiences lost sight of just how much good Ghanaian music was around.

Highlife is certainly not extinguished. In addition to stalwarts like Nana Ampadu and Alex Konadu, there are new quality bands and musicians such as the **Western Diamonds, Marriots, NAKOREX, Papa Yankson, (Gyedu) Blay Ambulley, Nana Tuffuor, Golden Nuggets,** and, most crucially, **Amekye Dede**. Through the 1990s, Dede rose through the ranks to become the single most popular musician in Ghana. He started his career with the Kumapim Royals before moving to Nigeria in the early 1980s to try his luck with the Apollo High Kings. In 1987 he returned home and released the sensational *Kose Kose* which established a truly national reputation for the young guitarist. Playing in a **highlife-reggae** idiom which seemed to capture the musical mood of Ghana, Amekye went on to release an astonishing 15 albums in the 1990s, and made enough money in the process to set up his own Accra nighclub, the *Abrantie Spot*, one of the few venues in Accra that guarantees regular live music.

discography

Ghanaian music deserves a lot more CD re-releases. At present, you may have to hunt specialist vinyl stores for many classic highlife discs.

Highlife

Compilations

● **Akomko** (Afrodisia, Nigeria).

This compilation of early 1950s items is, despite its poor pressing quality, still one of the best introductions to dance- and guitar-band highlife.

 Classic Highlife (OsibiSounds, Germany).

A veritable tour de force featuring the very best of late 1980s/early '90s international highlife – Crentsil, Agyeman, Darko and, almost inevitably, Osibisa. Required listening for anyone who thought that highlife died in the '70s.

◉ **Giants of Danceband Highlife** (Original Music, US).

A great stack of old dancehall highlife numbers featuring ET Mensah, Ramblers and Professional Uhuru, recalling the days when highlife reigned supreme.

◉ **I've Found My Love** (Original Music, US).

Another top selection, featuring classic guitar-band highlife in a succession of Yaa Amponsah-style rural shuffles.

Artists

Jewel Ackah

Jewel Ackah is one of the 'Big 3' contemporary Ghana vocalists, along with Pat Thomas and AB Crentsil. Jewel served the full musical apprenticeship in Ghana before travelling the world in search of success.

● **Electric Hi-Life** (Asona, UK).

A personal favourite from 1986 – mellow, melodic and mature – awaiting CD reissue.

African Brothers

Led by Nana Ampadu, the African Brothers have held sway as the top highlife guitar band for over thirty years. At their peak in the 1970s and 1980s the band recorded prolifically and toured incessantly.

● **Agatha** (BNELP01, Ghana only).

A West African hit in 1981, this was perhaps their best album – although their singles of the mid-1960s and late '70s would give any band a run for their money.

King Bruce & the Black Beats

King Bruce (1922-1977), was a major figure of the classic highlife era, a trumpeter who formed the Black Beats, the first of a string of successful dance bands in Accra, in the early 1950s.

◉ **Golden Highlife Classics from the 1950s and 1960s** (RetroAfric, UK).

Superb introduction to the sound of Ghana nearly half a century ago – all laid-back grooves and claves and slightly pear-shaped horns.

AB Crentsil & The Sweet Talks

AB Crentsil's Sweet Talks, who split soon after this recording to spawn a host of solo stars, including Agyeman and Frempong, were one of the most popular highlife acts of the 1970s, with a string of hit singles and a successful excursion to the US.

◉ **Hollywood Highlife Party**
(World Circuit, UK).

Recorded in 1978, this is beyond a doubt the best Ghanaian album of the last twenty years.

◉ **The Lord's Prayer** (Stern's Africa Classics, UK).

Classic reissue of 1970s gospel-style highlife and a serious lesson in sexy religiosity – the opening bars of the title track lift you straight onto your feet. Just great.

George Darko

George Darko the original 'Burgher King', acquired his nickname during a protracted stay in Germany, where he co-opted funk and rock into highlife, producing a darker, hard-edged style known as 'Burgher Highlife'. George is a true master guitarist whose overseas success enabled him to return home and live in some style, performing very occasionally.

◉ **Highlife Time** (Oval, UK).

A blend of highlife and funk whose hit song "Akoo Te Brofo" (Parrot speaks European) made an international impact.

Alex Konadu

Alex Konadu is the uncrowned 'King of Highlife', and master of sweaty, good-time music. The live shows of the 'one man bulldozer' are justly celebrated.

◉ **One Man Thousand Live in London**
(World Circuit, UK).

No less than what it says – infectious tunes that come back to you months later.

Koo Nimo

One of the few remaining masters of the 'palm-wine' style of rural highlife, Koo Nimo is a remarkable all-round guitarist, bringing a wide range of styles, including jazz and classical to his astonishing technique. He is equally at home playing alone or with his six-piece drum and string ensemble.

◉ **Osabarima** (Adasa/Stern's, UK).

This 1976 recording remains Nimo's only commercial release to date, although local cassette recordings are occassionally available.

ET Mensah and the Tempos

ET Mensah learned his trade during the 1930s in the Accra Rhythmic Orchestra to such effect that when he joined the already famous Tempos in the late 1940s he soon assumed control of the band. His first big-band highlife recording in 1952 led to a string of hits, and had an enormous impact on West African musical life. ET received many awards during his long and illustrious career, finally hanging up his horn in 1996, and he was honoured with a state funeral.

◉ **All For You**
◉ **Day By Day** (RetroAfric, UK).

These excellent compilations of 1950s and '60s numbers were remastered from original 78s. The songs demonstrate the full richness of the dance-band highlife idiom, augmented by forays into calypso, cha-cha-cha and other Latin styles and performed in a wide range of languages.

EK Nyame

A pioneering musician equally at home in concert party or guitar band, EK was enormously influential and highly respected by colleagues during the 1950s and '60s. His recordings are now almost impossible to find although a brief renaissance in the mid-1970s, shortly before his death, did encourage a new appreciation of his massive contribution.

◉ **Sankofa** (RAL, Ghana).

The Sankofa (Go Back and Retrieve) collection was put together to preserve the greatest songs for posterity. It is hard to find but repays the effort.

Okukuseku

Formed in 1969, this highlife guitar band from Koforidua had huge success at home, and then spent many years in Nigeria when Ghana in the 1970s turned into a curfew nightmare. They are now back home but rarely perform.

◉ **Take Time** (Rogers All Stars, Nigeria).

This 1983 recording doftly demonstrates the many Igbo highlife touches – a top-drawer Ghanaian guitar band at the peak of their powers.

Osibisa

No review of modern Ghanaian music could possibly be complete without Osibisa and the 'criss-cross rhythms which explode with happiness.' In terms of both sales and influence, Osibisa's international impact has never been surpassed by any other African band. Combining highlife veterans with Caribbean musicians, they ruled the roost in the late 1960s and '70s, moving on to countless world tours and a place in history.

◉ **Fire – Hot Flashback Vol 1** (Red Streel, UK).

All the hits are here from "The Coffee Song" to "Sunshine Day". If your're too young to remember what all the fuss was about, move heaven and earth for this collection. Red Steel have also re-issued all seven original LP recordings on CD.

The Ramblers
International Dance Band

The Ramblers were one of the best and most resilient of the highlife orchestras. They finally called it a day in the early 1980s when leader Jerry Hansen moved to the US.

◉ **The Hit Sounds of the Ramblers** (Decca, Nigeria).

Classic highlife from this fifteen-member orchestra.

The Western Diamonds

The Western Diamonds, from the twin cities of Sekondi-Takoradi, are the best of the current crop of highlife dance bands. Formed in the late 1980s by veteran star, Papa Yankson, they are dynamic stage performers who guarantee a good time whether storming Accra or on one of their regular European tours.

Diamonds Forever (Sterns, UK).

A benchmark album of 1990s highlife.

Papa Yankson

The lead singer of The Western Diamonds (above) also has a solo career.

o **Wiadzi Mu Nsem** (Flying Elephant, UK/Germany).

This fine disc was the critical success of 1996.

Folk, Roots and other Music

Compilations

Music in Ghana (PAM, Germany).

A carefully chosen representative selection of traditional styles picked from the archives of the Institute of African Studies, Legon, near Accra. The only modern track is, significanty, "Bra Ohoho" by EK Nyame!

Artists

Mustapha Tettey Addy

Mustapha Tettey Addy is a master drummer from the Ga tradition of Accra. During a long and illustrious career, he has covered all the bases, from pure Ga percussion to jazz ensembles and drumming workshops for the thousands happy to put skin to skin, and batter along with one of the most infectious rhythmic styles in Africa. He owns a popular drumming school and hotel at Kokrobite, west of Accra.

Mustapha Tettey Addy (Tangent, France).

This 1972 recording, still widely available, demonstrates the wide variety of Ga drum styles and why Mustapha is so highly regarded at home and abroad.

Mustapha Tettey Addy (centre)

JAK KILBY

Alfred Kari Bannerman

Bannerman is a master guitarist, veteran of a thousand studio sessions and a member of almost every serious UK based highlife band since the days of Osibisa.

 Ghana Gone Jazz (Blueprint, UK).

At last a Bannerman solo album: jazzier than one perhaps expects from his numerous public performances, and an absolute essential for any African music collection.

Dade Krama

Dade Krama, a short-lived but highly influential London-based neo-traditional outfit, took the city's African circuit by storm in the mid-1980s with their powerful, atmospheric percussion-based sound.

o **Ancestral Music** (Own label, UK).

A reasonable representation of their stunning live show and a unique reminder of how far Ghanaian music can go to explore the frontiers of skill and imagination.

Jacob Sam & Kumasi Trio

Sam and the Kumasi Trio are almost legendary figures from the dawn of Ghanaian popular music – in fact from the days when it still figured on classroom maps as the Gold Coast. These are the true pioneers of the guitar band tradition as this remastered 1928 recording reveals.

Jacob Sam and Kumasi Trio Vols 1 & 2 (Heritage, UK).

Music from a vanished world. Guitar and percussion music with much more than an academic interest.

Guy Warren (Kofi Ghanaba)

No understanding of modern Ghanaian music is possible without reference to Guy Warren's singular effort. Starting as the Tempos' drummer and leader in the mid-1940s, he gave way to ET Mensah and moved to pursue his jazz interests in the US. Along the way, he pioneered cu-bop and released half a dozen classic albums before returning home and changing his name to Kofi Ghanaba. Considered by many as Africa's finest drummer, Ghanaba now performs infrequently and lives on his farm.

o **Africa Speaks: America Answers** (EMI Regal–Zonophone, US).

Guy Warren at his cu-bop best. A serious collector's item – check the archives!

Wulomei

In the early 1970s, Ga drumming and folk music underwent a cultural revival, pioneered by the twelve-strong Wulomei cultural troupe. Often followed, never surpassed.

o **Drum Conference** (Phonogram, Ghana).

A bit too 'sweet' perhaps on first hearing and difficult to find, but perseverance is rewarded.

Guinea-Bissau

the backyard beats of gumbe

Guinea-Bissau is a small patch of jungle, grassland and mangroves, wedged between Senegal and Guinea-Conakry. While it is one of Africa's poorest countries – and since 1998, has been embroiled in a civil war* that has made a third of its one million inhabitants homeless – its *gumbe* music provides a defiantly upbeat contrast. Gumbe embraces many West African traditions – the kora is said to have originated here – and has the added bonus of being perhaps the most joyful sound to be heard anywhere on the African continent. **Guus de Klein** is completely enraptured.

I t is a shame that commerce stands in the way of wider exposure for Guinea-Bissau's music. Even African specialist shops have difficulty unearthing it. How many people know the music heroes of Bissau – or any heroes from the country, come to mention it? Maybe some might remember the name of Amílcar Cabral, one of the great men of Africa's decolonisation, killed shortly before independence. The Bissau bands have always sung about him, but since most venues have been destroyed in the recent fighting, those few musicians left in Bissau nowadays sing along with the women cooking in the open air, about the waste of Cabral's revolutionary heritage by the ousted president Nino Vieira.

People still cherish some of the symbols of the 1974 revolution but what preoccupies them now is survival. Yet the people of Guinea-Bissau *are* survivors and in the midst of hardship their music has taken on a vital role.

Guinea-Bissau's special music is **gumbe**. It combines a contemporary sound with the ten or more musical traditions that survive in the area. Some compare it to the samba, though it's much more polyrhythmic. Bissau, the capital, has had a few electric bands for some years, but most are unplugged; indeed, at most music venues (and there are many) there is not a plug in sight. The lyrics of gumbe are in Kriolu, a creole synthesis of African languages and the colonial Portuguese; it is said to have sprouted on the Portuguese ships where local sailors worked. Kriolu is an integral part of gumbe music. And it has a lot to tell.

* As much of the Bissau City's infrastructure was destroyed in 1998/99 and the country's future was still uncertain when this book went to press, some elements of Guus de Klein's enthusiastic description may have ceased to exist.

Backyard Beats

If you walk a little in Bissau, before the hot sun disappears behind the mango trees, and head off the sidewalks into the *bairros*, you are almost bound to stumble upon a small backyard where fifty or so people have gathered to hear music. A group of women will be sitting in a circle, boys and girls around them. In the centre stands a big bucket filled with water and in it a *calabash* turned upside down. A boy slides one palm over the surface of the calabash, the other hand slaps it; the sound given off is like an early disco rhythm box. Soon, other calabashes are being played with wooden objects, spoons and other instruments resembling cooking implements. At a certain point the tempo of spoons and wood is about eighty beats per minute, as if people are waiting for something. And they are. A girl jumps into the circle and all at once, in time with her dancing – hands low, knees high – the wood musicians double their speed and the spoon–players treble their pace.

And what do they sing about? They sing about cars they will never own. They make jokes about the owner of the newest Nissan Patrol ("The chef will have to wait like us when the station has run out of gas, both his Nissan and his Patrol!"). They sing about their hard life and about Amílcar Cabral and the *Tuga*, the former Portuguese rulers. They sing love stories their grandparents sang, and they sing about the *irão* – mysterious forces found in trees, water, stones and in certain individuals. They sing about AIDS and about their hope that peace will return to the country. They know all the songs by heart and have no need to rehearse. The rhythm will change while the beat keeps steady. Occasionally, a worn-out guitar will add some chords the player has heard .

outside a disco where he hangs around at night – without money to pay the *entrada*. And whatever they're singing about, there's always fun in gumbe music.

When they're in town, those few musicians who have a more or less professional status, will come and sit down at the outskirts of the circle and fit in with what is happening. Of course, when there's electricity, they plug in. And they'll add some lyrics about the thirty-five-storey buildings they have seen abroad.

Ethnic Traditions

Gumbe is a catch-all word for any kind of music in Guinea-Bissau. But technically, it is just one of several Kriolu mixtures of ethnic and modern culture. In Bissau city you will also find **tina** and **tinga** – more acoustic than gumbe, but very Kriolu, with lots of spoons and calabashes. And there are other more ethnic styles like **kussundé** and **broxa**, or **brosca**, from the Balanta people; **djambadon** from the Mandinga people; and **kundere** from the remote Bijagos islands. Like gumbe, all these musical styles are performed and shared around the Bissau cooking pots.

The ethnic styles are close – in their musical structure – to the traditional sounds that bound up with **ceremonial activities**: funerals, the calling up of spirits, initiation rituals, and the request for good harvests. These very traditional musical styles are precarious, and there have been some efforts (notably by the teacher João Neio Gomes at the Instituto das Artes) to record them before they're forgotten.

Music
and Independence

Kriolu music played an important role in the Guinea-Bissau struggle for independence. It brought people together, perhaps more successfully than political rallying, and gumbe, as the common ingredient flavouring the country's many different dishes, could in some manner be called the voice of unification, the multicultural life which no policy could introduce.

With the departure of the Portuguese in 1974, Guinea-Bissau was left with literally no musical heritage (beyond ceremonial music) after more than three hundred years of colonial domination. Even the fado, which influenced so many musicians in the lusophone areas of Angola, Mozambique and Cape Verde hadn't penetrated the local culture of Bissau. So it is

possible to pinpoint exactly when the modern music of Guinea–Bissau started.

It began with the production of the first vinyl record by a Guinea–Bissau musician: a 45rpm single recorded in Portugal in 1973, just one year before independence. The two songs – gumbe style with acoustic accompaniment – were sung in Kriolu by **Djorçon (Ernesto Dabó),** who had just left the Lisbon marine band. The A-side was "M'Ba Bolama" (I'm going to Bolama), its lyrics loaded with double meaning, speaking loud and clear to young Africans living in Portugal as well as in Bissau and the liberated zones, to declare that freedom was coming. One year later, the record was used as part of the celebrations of the country's liberation and independence.

The producer of this first record was the poet and composer **Zé Carlos** (José Carlos Schwartz). He was the charismatic leader of what is recognised as the mother of all contemporary Guinea–Bissau bands, **Cobiana Djazz**. The group was already very popular in 1972, inspiring a great many school-goers in Bissau to join the liberation forces in the forest. That year, Zé Carlos and other members of the band were expelled by the colonial police (the PIDE) and sent into internal exile on the tiny Ilha das Galinhas. Carlos remembered the happiness on the island in a song called "Djiu di Galinha" (Song of Galinha), which is also the title of the album he later recorded in the US at the invitation of Miriam Makeba, who had met him when she performed in Bissau after the liberation.

Cobiana Djazz were the first band to achieve recognition on a national level. With their Kriolu music they literally accompanied the Guinea–Bissau people on their way to freedom. In the euphoric post-revolutionary period that followed, the band was closely associated with the new government which promoted its music as the banner of a new national culture. In spite of this, Cobiana Djazz released just one LP, *Zé Carlos e Cobiana Djazz*, in 1977. It was produced in Portugal: there was still no local music production or distribution.

Cobiana Djazz did not remain art-of-the-state for long. Within a few years the socialist government, deprived of the charismatic leadership of Amílcar Cabral, slid into incompetence and nepotism. It was criticised by Carlos (then a member of government) in his poetic way, a criticism that led to his falling out of favour and even to a new term of imprisonment. He died in May 1977 in a suspicious plane crash in Havana, where he had travelled as a government representative. After Zé's death, Cobiana Djazz went downhill and by 1982 most of its members were abroad. The group was revived briefly in 1986 with new musicians.

There are remarkable political and musical parallels between Cobiana Djazz and the band **Bembeya Jazz National** (see p.547) of neighbouring Guinea-Conakry. Musically, both groups – Bembeya a decade earlier and doubtlessly inspiring Cobiana – used their ethnic background as ingredients for the Kriolu musical soup they created, adding a strong rhythmic basis in their *kabas-garandi* (great calabashes). Politically, both lost faith with their governments, after having been an integral part of the movement for independence.

The other early group to attain star status in Guinea-Bissau was **Super Mama Djombo**. Formed shortly after independence, they were the icon of the socialist party, even accompanying the president on visits abroad. Their first album, *Cambança*, recorded in Portugal and released in 1980, dazzled the public. The people knew all the songs by heart already but the more sophisticated arrangements on the record, and the electric guitar accompaniment, greatly added to the band's success.

The government, however, was unamused by the lyrics on some of the tracks – and even more so by the group's follow-up release, *Festival*. Songs which glorified the PAIGC party were juxtaposed with songs mocking corruption within the very same party, with titles like "Ramedi ki ka ta kura" (A Remedy that Does Not Cure). It was hardly surprising when the group began meeting with difficulties – like finding a stage to perform on, or even a rehearsal room.

Other bands in the first decade of Guinea-Bissaun music were less closely alligned to the regime. Among the most popular were **Africa Livre**, **Kapa Negra**, **Tiná-Koia** and **Chifre Preto**. None of these ever recorded on disc, although **Sabá Miniambá** – a group formed in 1978 with ex-members from almost all the aforementioned bands – did get a vinyl release.

The '80s on a Shoestring

There was a growing number of solo careers among this intermingling of groups. **Zé Carlos** was the first to have his own album, supported by Miriam Makeba. He was followed by **Kaba Mané**, who recorded an infectious kussundé style album entitled *Chefo Mae Mae*, sung in the Balanta language with kora-like electric guitar, and

by **Sidónio Pais**, Kapa Negra's vocalist. **Ramiro Naka** switched between solo projects and playing African covers with his band **N'kassa Cobra**.

In the 1980s, revolutionary enthusiasm was no longer the only stuff of lyrics but social and political concerns seeped into even the hottest dance music. There was reason enough for it. The country was in dire financial straits, the shops virtually empty, with hardly enough food to go round. The musicians lived through what the people lived through and have often reflected their concerns. **Zé Manuel**, Djombo's drummer, who recorded "Tustumunhus di aonti" (Yesterday's Testimony) in 1983, was forbidden to perform in public because of the lyrics of his songs, written by the poet Huco Monteiro. The singer **Justino Delgado** was arrested for making President Nino Vieira the target of his sarcasm and his records became very popular as a result.

In the 1980s – and even today – professional Bissau musicians probably number no more than a hundred, so working temporarily with members of other bands is the norm. Many performances are simply small projects, while most recordings can only be done abroad. So the 1980s saw Sidónio and Justino Delgado leaving for Lisbon, and Ramiro Naka and his band settling in Paris. The scene was – and is – one of musicians more or less commuting between Bissau and Portugal, where they had small contracts and sometimes a gig.

Even the few Bissau producers, notable among them the filmmaker Flora Gomes Jr, are forced to record in Lisbon. In Bissau, there is just one small studio at Rádio Difusão Nacional, the state radio-station, which produces a few cassettes for local release. Instruments and equipment have to be bought outside the country, often with help from *cooperantes* (development workers) from Holland or Scandinavia.

The 1990s: Survival and War

In the first half of the 1990s, things did not improve much for Guinea-Bissau's economy, despite IMF loans and market liberalisation. Sure, the stores became better stocked, but with goods most people were unable to buy. The music scene, however, benefited from a more open market, and had no shortage of inspiration.

Most visible was the opening of a cluster of private open-air clubs in Bissau, and a little more money invested in the discos – *Cabana*, *Capital* and *Hollywood*. These played a wider range of music than of old – a lot of soukous and other African dance music, a little Stevie Wonder and salsa. But the main dish here, and on Radio Pidjiguiti, a new private station, was still gumbe.

As the decade progressed several of the country's top musicians became established in France – **Ramiro Naka** and **Kaba Mané** – and Portugal – **Sidónio Pais** and **Justino Delgado** – where they released albums. Their sound grew more sophisticated, still narrative, but attuned to the demand for a faster disco tempo. Back home, **Tabanka Djaz** became the first really commercial band, with a polished sound, while **Gumbezarte**, a nine-piece multicultural band led by **Maio Coopé**, brought together different ethnic styles in a funny and exciting Kriolu style. Both toured abroad but recording and distribution, however, remained major problems. Most releases were produced in Portugal, with very little money, or in Conakry (Guinea) with even less.

In the chaos of the war, during 1998–99, most local bands disintegrated and in some cases members lost touch with each other. Among the handful who chose, or were forced, to sit out the conflict in Bissau were Miguelinho N'simba, Narciso Rosa and Sidia Baio. Gumbezarte's drummer, Ernesto da Silva, was last heard of in a refugee camp in Dakar. In Bissau, right now, there is currently no intact band, and the opportunities for any musicians left in the capital to perform for cash have competely dried up.

To Portugal's credit, most Bissauans who could afford the journey found a relatively welcoming reception in **Lisbon**. Here, the musicians in exile meet every day at the Praça de Figueira, many of them between shifts on construction sites or office-cleaning. And they manage to find gigs here and there, playing together quite frequently (at the Praça Sony, for example, on the former Expo site, which is quite popular at weekends).

Meanwhile, back home, the people in the countryside are somehow holding life together, receiving refugees from the fighting around the capital, and reinvoking old ties of family and kinship to avert total disaster.

discography

There are few Guinea-Bissau CDs and cassettes even in the best World Music stores. One specialist on the Web is *Balkon Zuid* at *www.balkon.zuid@inter.nl.net*

Compilations

 Popular music from Guinea Bissau (Intermusic, South Africa).

A decent compilation with songs from Tabanka Djaz, Justino Delgado and Rui Sangará, Néné Tuty and others, most of them interesting, though offset by misleading liner notes.

 Guiné Lanta (Atlantic Music, Netherlands).

A collective record from the Guinean and Cape Verdean community in Rotterdam (the title means 'Guinea Stand Up'), with Tino Trimo, Dina Medina and others. It showcases various styles, including rap, and a children's song.

Artists

Aliu Bari

Aliu Bari was one of the founders of Cobiana Djazz, who pre-war had seemed a bright hope.

 Tributo ao Cobiana Djazz Nacional (Sons d'Africa Portugal).

Bari delicately brings some of the group's older traditional sounds to the urban surface, avoiding electronic boobytraps, with a lofty, nostalgic voice and occasional fine electric guitar solos by Manecas Costa. A worthy tribute to the first band of independent Guinea-Bissau, released in 1998.

Bidinte's *Kumura* album

Bidinte

Jorge da Silva Bidinte was born in Bolama, the old capital. When he was eleven, he got hold of a mandolin and began to pick out gumbe tunes, to his father's disapproval. "In the end", he remembers, "I had to seek refuge in the church and convert to Catholicism so that I could play the guitar with the priest". Moving to Bissau for secondary school, he met Maio Coopé and began composing music for Maio's lyrics. He later emigrated to Europe, played in a band, Docolma, led by Justino Delgado, and was drawn to the flamenco.

 Kumura (Nubenegra, Spain).

Subtle and distinctively coloured music reflecting a multiplicity of sources and influences, from David Byrne (who was present through most of the recording) to flamenco, with melting Kriolu lyrics delivered with tender skill. After this beautifully produced album – nowhere better than on the effortless guitar-and-voice blend of "Ke cu minino na tchora?" (Why does the child cry? with its lyrics, sadly apposite for G-B today, by poet José Carlos Schwartz) – Bidinte ought easily be able to step into the long-vacant shoes of former international stars from Guinea-Bissau, Ramiro Naka and Kabá Mané.

Zé Carlos

Poet, singer and leader of Cobiana Djazz, Zé Carlos died at the age of twenty-seven in a mysterious plane accident, having made albums critical of the regime he had supported through the liberation struggle. He was a major talent, and was persuaded by Miriam Makeba to go to the US for a recording session.

O Djiu di Galinha (Comissariado de Estado da Guinea-Bissau, Guinea-Bissau).

Poetic and narrative, with soft American blend – the album was arranged by William Salter. Though Carlos is occasionally out of tune, he is an inspired artist. Makeba provides the backing vocals.

Cobiana Djazz

Cobiana Djazz were literally 'a revolutionary band' in the 1970s, though not a jazz one. They inspired all modern Guinea–Bissau bands despite the fact that they only released one album in 1978.

🎞 Zé Carlos and Cobiana Djazz (Comissariado de Estado da Guinea–Bissau, Guinea-Bissau; Valentim de Carvalho, Portugal,

Only worn-out cassette copies are available, but just about every adult in the country knows all the songs by heart.

Justino Delgado

Born on one of the small isles of the Bijagos archipelago, Delgado has been active in many Bissau bands, but he is mostly popular for his narrative, sarcastic sung stories. In the late 1980s he was arrested for offending the president, but later he made up by performing a song called "Gabi" (former president Vieira's nickname).

O Casamenti D'haös (Vidisco, Portugal).

Rhythmic singing of daily life (the title song is about marriage today). Delgado is surrounded by too many synthesisers but an acoustic guitar comes to the occasional rescue.

🎵 Toroco (Sonovox, Portugal).

Delgado continues the narrative sarcasm of his former recordings in this 1998 album. No great musical developments, but popular for its inside-scoop lyrics – Delgado delights his audience by singing as if he were in the Bissau presidential palace inner circle.

Mama Djombo

Mama Djombo, who put gumbe on the World Music map, were a favourite of the first independent government, but like Cobiana Djazz, soon fell out with them. They were never touched by sophisticated producers and their 1980s recordings still sound remarkably fresh.

O Festival (Debilo, Min. da Cultura da República da GB, Guinea-Bissau).

Exulting voices, clear electric guitars, and fine compositions.

Check out the super soprano of a then very young Dulce Neves, who was later to go solo.

Gumbezarte

Gumbezarte were the most interesting band to emerge from Bissau in the 1990s. Led by the witty and inventive Maio Coopé, this multicultural group included veterans from Cobiana Djazz and Mama Djombo (Miguelinho N'simba and Narciso Rosa), as well as young talents like Sanha N'Tamba on bass and Ernesto da Silva on drums.

 Gumbezarte Camba Mar (Balkon Zuid, Guinea-Bissau; Lusafrica, France).

A 1998 release, with gumbe in the name and in several of the songs, but the album is really an electrifying tour of lesser-known music styles, including *kussundé* and *djambadon*. No synths or drum machines; the album was mixed as the group wanted it to be, with lovely shifting rhythms.

Iva & Ichi

Lisbon-based duo with a wide-ranging repertoire of styles, and excellent voices – including Ichi's superb fruity baritone.

🎵 Canua ca na n'kadja (Nelson Pais Quaresma, Portugal).

Loads of drive on a musical trip round the whole country. Listen out, in particular for the title track, which means 'If the canoe doesn't capsize (we'll arrive)' and the 'bush' (*brosca*) song from the Balanta, track 12, 'Paga Rabada'. In spite of the somewhat irritating electronic base drum, the style of this song is immediately recognisable if you have Gumbezarte's CD *Camba Mar-* compare it with the latter's track 4.

Juntos Pela Guiné-Bissau

An ad hoc group of musical refugees currently based in Lisbon, including nearly all the big names, as well as Portuguese and Cape Verdean artists.

🎵 Mom na mom (Vidisco, Portugal).

Collective wail of grief ('Mom na mom' means hand in hand) over the destruction of Bissau, including songs and poems – the latter both in Kriolu and Portuguese – and beautifully produced by Juca Delgado.

Kaba Mané

Born into the Beafada – a Mande people – Mané is master of a variety of ethnic styles. He learned the kora when young and plays electric guitar in kora style.

⊚ **Best of Kabá Mané** (Mélodie, France).

This has good tracks from Mané's delightfully infectious *Chefo Mae Mae* album – in the *kussundé* rhythm of the Balanta people, this was the first to dent overseas charts – and its equally seductive follow-up, *Kunga Kungake*.

Zé Manuel

Zé Manuel is Mama Djombo's drummer – but his solo effort concentrated on his voice.

◐ **Tustumunhus di Aonti**
(Casa da Cultura, Guinea-Bissau).

The slow songs from this 1983 album are particularly good, politically sharp, poetically soft, guitars mourning without pedal effects, and Manel's terrific voice.

Ramiro Naka

Naka is an exuberant talent who makes gumbe rock without destroying its uniqueness. Though living in Paris, he remains very popular in Bissau.

◐ **Naka & N'kassa Cobra**
(N'Kassa Cobra Productions/Volume, France).

It's heavy, it swings and what's more, with his own little company Ramiro stays out of the hands of the Paris commercial sound producers.

⊚ **Salvador** (Mango, UK).

Showcase album with material ranging from upfront rock on the title track to Kriolu/Cape Verdean inflection on "Tchon Tchoma" and "Rabo de Padja" and an appealingly offbeat roots sound on "Nha Indimigo".

⊚ **Po di Sangui** (Naka Production, France).

Part filmtrack album of the emponymous movie about the relation between culture and nature (directed by Flora Gomes, and co-starring Naka) and part compositions inspired by traditional melodies recalled while Naka was on the film set in eastern Guinea-Bissau. Check out track 8, his version of "Canua ca na n'cadja".

Dulce Neves

As a teenager, Neves had a bewitching influence on Mama Djombo's music with her extremely high voice. She gets better and better as a solo artist.

⊚ **N'ha distino** (Sonovox, Portugal).

There have never been many female singers on Bissau stages and Dulce's voice can compete with the strongest male ones. This album was one of the hits in Bissau just before war broke out in 1998.

Sidónio Pais

With his early band Kapa Negra, Sidónio Pais was perhaps the most melodic interpreter of gumbe. The group was marvellous, with a terrific pair of competing guitars.

⊚ **20 Anos de Capa Negra** (Discos, Sidó Portugal).

Mainly due to its over-use of rhythm boxes, this 1992 CD (with the variant spelling of the band) doesn't match the quality of the live band.

Rui Sangará

Sangará is one of the angry young men who use gumbe for storytelling – without making it less danceable.

⊚ **Sanguis n'consola** (Spa, Portugal).

Eight little gumbe stories, some full of melancholy, like "credifone" about living abroad. Unfortunately, there's little live drumming on the album.

Janota Di Nha Sperança

Sperança was involved in an effort to re-establish Cobiana Djazz in 1986 and now makes his own records.

⊚ **Senhorío** (Atlantic Music, Netherlands).

An album with an autobiographical theme. Janota went to Europe to make a living, with the firm intention of returning. Being a construction worker in Portugal paid a lot better than being a top musician in Bissau but when money was stolen from him and he couldn't pay the rent, nor buy a ticket back home, he realised that he was no better off than a slave.

Tabanka Djaz

Bissau's bestselling band, the group started in the mid-1980s, in a Bissau restaurant called Tabanka ('Village'), and was an instant hit with its customers. Tabanka Djaz has since gone on to success as far afield as the USA.

⊚ **Sperança** (Sonovox, Portugal).

Commercially produced dancehall music, but gumbe none the less.

Tino Trimo

Tino Trimo is an artist with the voice – and the ambition – to cross some borders. To date, however, he's been less successful than his colleagues in Tabanca Djaz, whom he reproaches for stealing some of his songs.

⊚ **Kambalacha** (MB Records, US).

An album for gumbe fans – traditional songs played 'live' in the studio. Strong album, great voice.

⊚ **Katoré** (Vidisco, Portugal).

A nicely-produced, very danceable disc. There's a drum machine, of course, but it's unobtrusive.

Indian Ocean

a lightness of touch

The music of tropical islands often seems to have a lightness of touch compared with mainland forms. Unselfconscious borrowings, sometimes dating back centuries, and disparate influences which have at one time or another been cast ashore, create accessible creole blends, full of common musical demoninators and no longer so firmly rooted in their original soil. Nowhere is this more the case than in the western **Indian Ocean**, as **Graeme Ewens** and **Werner Graebner** discover.

T he Indian Ocean washes the coasts of three continents. In its western half, the monsoon winds once blew the sailing dhows in a back-and-forth pattern that took them from East African coastal waters to the Gulf and on to India and beyond and then back again. The old trading routes have made connections between many varied cultures, and on the thinly dispersed islands descendants of African, Arabic, Indian, Polynesian, Far Eastern and European forebears have lived for centuries with differing degrees of cooperation and assimilation.

The Comoros

The tiny **Comoros Islands**, lying between the north coast of Madagascar and the mainland, are one of World Music's minority territories. As in their dominant neighbour, the former colonial language is French, and one of the islands, Mayotte, remains an outpost of France. There is a huge Malagasy influence but the dominant cultural millieu, especially of the poorer people, is closer to the Swahili world of East Africa.

Twarab – similar to the taarab of Zanzibar (see p.690) – is the most popular music on the islands, and especially on Grand Comoro. It differs from the classic Swahili music in having more Western instrumentation, in place of the Arabic flavours of qanoon and violin, resulting in a funkier and very dance-driven sound. The leading groups are **Sambeco** and **Belle Lumière**, electric ensembles using keyboards, guitar, drums and percussion. Like most of the local groups, they are run and backed by village youth associations, and they play mainly at weddings, occasionally in a concert setting. An older twarab artist – whose hits are being reissued on CD by the Dizim label – was **Mohammed Hassan**. He was a local star in the 1950s and 60s, and was unusually a professional musician. He sung and played 'ud – twarab at this stage was still based on 'ud and violin, with local *msondo* drum and tambourine – at Comorian weddings as far away as Madagascar.

On the islands of **Moheli** and **Anjouan**, a favourite type of musical entertainment are topical songs accompanied on the *gabusi* (a lute related to the yeminite *qanbus*). **Boina Riziki** from the Mohelian town of Fomboni is considered to be the leading gabusi player on the islands, leading a trio with **Soubi**, who plays the *ndzendze*, a self-styled box-shaped instrument derived from the malagasy *valiha*. Their music is situated somewhere between Zanzibar taarab and Malagasy, the latter most evident in the vocal harmonies.

INEDIT

COMORES

Musiques traditionnelles de l'île d'Anjouan

Two younger Comoros musicians are **Maalesh** and **Salim Ali Amir**, both of whom are fusing local traditions and international styles. Salim Amir leans heavily on studio production, playing all instruments himself and creatively mixing local rhythms and melodies with those of reggae, zouk or soukous. Maalesh's is a more subtle synthesis; accompanying his songs by using just one or two acoustic guitars and quiet percussion, he evokes local *ngoma* melodies and *qasida* chanting, and incorporates regional musical experiences from his time working on the Kenya coast and in Saudi Arabia, all resulting in a softly floating style akin to Brazilian cançao.

In France, the leading Comoran artist of recent years – releasing a series of discs in Paris – has been the dreadlocked singer-guitarist **Abou Chihabi**, who composed the first Comoros national anthem in 1976, but had to flee two years later following a coup. He plays a style of music known as **Variet** – an upbeat sound featuring horns, keyboards and electric bass – that is popular mainly among the francophone middle class, at home and in France. He paid his artistic dues on the African mainland, building up a fund of techniques and influences to add to his own reggae-tinged delivery. His most recent 1999 release, *Swahili Songs*, on the Paris-based Evasion label, is dedicated to his father, who played accordion with **Orchestre ACM**, bringing together African, Arabic and Western elements. Chebli brought this blend up to date with songs recorded in Marseille. The end result, filtered through the francophone consciousness, would be hard to locate.

A more identifiable sound is provided by the ambience of tropical birdsong and crickets which introduces *Kaul/Word*, a recent album by another French-resident Comoros artist, **Mikidache**. This also features a traditional bow harp, although the band quickly move into a more orthodox mainstream type of folk-pop.

Mauritius

Further out in the Ocean, **Mauritius** has yet to make much of a mark on the musical map, although there has been a series of CDs released over the past few years by the London-based Tambour label (these are now hard to find). Mostly licensed from the island-based Sonolynn Productions, Tambour's catalogue included cultural music, Chutney/Bhojpuri releases for the Indian community, and **sega**, the popular music common to Mauritius and Réunion, which is also enjoyed in Madagascar and Comoros.

Sega evolved out of European polkas and quadrilles, and is nowadays reminiscent of Haitian compas, or something like a thinner version of the stomping zouk beat from the French Antilles, without the same level of intensity or sophistication. The evocatively named **Les Windblows** typify the music, combining light-stepping, upbeat rhythms with perky creole lyrics, an acoustic guitar/ accordion/ keyboard feel that resembles Tex-Mex music, and some fruity Central African style guitar playing. Playasound have released several CDs of sega, which might be easier to find than the Tambour releases. Other national stars include the slower-paced **J-P Boyer** and top female artist, **Marie-Jose Coutonne**. A development of the sega genre has been championed by musicians like **Ras Natty Baby** – no prizes for guessing which genres he combines on his *Seggae Time* album.

The top Mauritian star of recent years was the dreadlocked singer **Kaya**, who died, tragically, in police custody in 1999. His death made international headlines in 1999 when it sparked three days of rioting and looting.

La Réunion

The smaller island of **La Réunion**, which lies to the west of Mauritius, is a *département* of France (like France's Caribbean possessions, Martinique and Guadeloupe). Réunion is a popular holiday destination for well-off French vacationers and there are regular international music festivals which celebrate *francophonie* as much as local culture. The black population who work the sugar plantations are mostly descended from slaves, rather than indigenous peoples. Réunion is also rich in voodoo tradition and preserved Africanisms but these are not always officially approved of, and the creole music known as *maloya* has been in danger of disappearing along with other oral traditions.

Firmin Viry is credited with preserving this African heritage which survived as an underground expression of faith and communication with the ancestral spirits. He plays the *kayamb*, a shaker made of a flat wooden box filled with seeds. Drums, musical bow, triangle and female chorists complete the sound, which moves to rhythms of Bantu origin. His simple songs of love and everyday life are delivered against a backdrop of 'silent history' – subtle references to conflicts with the *Malbar* culture of the slave-owners, who are largely of Indian origin.

The 'sorceror', **Granmoun Lélé**, is a truly exotic figure, who also runs his own church. In

1998 he released his third CD of voodoo trance music similar to the *tromba* spirit possession cult of Madagascar, and including Tamil expressions linked with fire-walking rituals. Foreign observers and participants at his *maloya* ritual performances report a heavy atmosphere involving a good deal of rum. Lélé claims ancestry from Zanzibaris, Kilimanians (from Quelimane, now Mozambique), Somalis, Anjouans and Malagasy people. Sometimes you'd swear the rhythms and vocalising are direct from Cameroon or Congo (Swede Swede leaps to mind, especially with the cry of "bougé, bougé"). Occasionally, in some of Lélé's pieces, there is a whispering echo of *taarab*, the great classical music of the dhow countries. Taarab uses instruments found throughout the Islamic world, such that similarities can be heard in music not only from the Gulf but also from Uzbekistan and Indonesia.

The Seychelles

There is little apparent musical identity, these days, on the islands of the **Seychelles**, a frail archipelago a thousand miles off the East African coast. But the islands once had an eclectic mix of styles and influences, and a form of percussion and vocal music known as **contonbley**. An Ocora release of the late 1980s showcased a folklore music with elements of creole, sega, and a host of retentions from *contredanse* (English country dance), polka, mazurka, Polynesian, French Arcadian and even Scottish sources. By the 1970s when the tracks were recorded, so-called 'prestige' music was taking over and the plantation workers' folklore was being repressed as too lewd.

One of the few more recent stars of the Seychelles was **Patrick Victor**, whose style of *montea*, mixing Kenyan *benga* guitar with the folkie, vocal, rhythm was pretty hot in the 1980s.

discography

Comoros

Compilations

◉ **Chamsi Na Mwezi –**
Gabusi and Ndzendze from Moheli, Comoros
(Dizim Records, Germany)

This is a lot less impenetrable than the title suggests, featuring Boina Riziki and Soubi on several tracks.

◉ **Musiques traditionelles de l'île d'Anjouan**
(Inédit, France).

Comorians from the island of Anjouan trace their origins back, like the east African Swahili, to mythical 'Shirazi' ancestors who arrived from Persia in the twelfth century. In fact, Anjouan society, like that of the Swahili, is a composite, and musically there is a multitude of references here – to taarab, not surprisingly, but also to Moroccan *milhûn* songs, and to Malagasy traditions. Varied, trance-llike and quite compelling.

Artists

Salim Ali Amir

A young multi-instrumentalist, fusing Comoran rhythms with reggae, zouk and soukous.

◉ **Ripvirwa** (Studio 1, Comoros).

An interesting and good-time danceable debut outing for this new Comoran fusion.

Abou Chihabi

This guitar-playing Comoran rastaman began with the Dragons, then moved on to the Angers Noirs, before forming his own more avant-garde group Folkomor Ocean, with which he scored a major success in France.

◉ **African Vibrations** (Playasound, France)

Abou fronts a fully-functional, five-piece group, which oozes sophistication – slightly experimental, perhaps, but nothing too extreme.

Maalesh

Like Salim Ali Amir, Maalesh is part of a new wave of Comoran musicians, looking to fuse local melodies and rhythms with international styles.

◉ **Wassi Wassi** (Melodie, France).

An interesting debut album of this new Comoran fusion, with softly floating style akin to Brazilian *canção*.

Mikidache

Mikidache is a singer-songwriter and bandleader, again based in France.

◉ **Kaul/Words** (Long Distance/Wagram, France).

Birdsong and insects herald a prelude on bow harp, leading into some some spirited acoustic guitar interplay, accordion colour washes, flute and pleasant enough singing, with a vocal mix that is bright and poppy.

Mauritius

Compilations

◉ **Les Ségatiers de l'île Maurice:**
Mauritius Island Ségadance (Playasound, France).

An old-time curiosity compilation from the mid-1970s, which is still available. The intro ballad io extremely turgid, although the rhythms warm up with a string of creole variety numbers and some more African folklore items. Overall it sounds like the exotic soundtrack of a B-movie comedy. You half expect Bob Hope to come hoofing by at any minute.

Artists

Jean Uranie

A singer, arranger and producer from Mauritius.

 Angeline (Tambour, UK).

Up-tempo dance beats from band Les Windblows, with Uraine's creole lyrics, and a couple of vocal and percussion folklore pieces which almost take you back to the Congo. There is also some gaucho-like whistling – another one to play 'spot the roots' with.

Artists

Granmoun Lélé

Lélé, the 'sorcerer' of maloya music, grew up on Réunion considering death as an occasion to celebrate. Customs have adapted to modern life, but his gruff, no-nonsense voice can still span worlds of understanding. His family group provides the chorus and a drum sound deep in both tone and meaning.

Namouniman
(Label Bleu/Indigo, France).

Most of Lélé's music has evident mainland roots, sometimes reminiscent of Congo or Cameroon, but at times here you also hear uncanny echoes of Haiti – a similarly mistreated, former French colony (slavery, sugar, sea....), alongside a variation of the more sedate East African taarab.

Firmin Viry

Credited with keeping *maloya* alive, Fermin Viry plays *kayamb*, a shaker made of a flat wooden box filled with seeds, to accompany simple songs which refer to deeper themes. He also runs his own church.

 Ti Mardé (Label Bleu/Indigo, France).

Drums, musical bow, triangle and female chorists accompany Viry's chants, which again echo to rhythms of Bantu origin. After a short reprise, each song seems to end up with the same encouragement to dance. And it obviously works.

Kenya

the life and times of kenyan pop

It's 8am on a Monday morning. Late to be setting off, and the equatorial sun is already shining fiercely above the highland metropolis of Nairobi. In an alley off River Road, **Doug Paterson** jumps in a *matatu*, a shared taxi, and heads out of the city, first-stop Ukambani, at the start of a musical tour of Africa's number-one tourist destination – and not a safari suit in sight.

Matatus are the common man's disco, the small trucks, Peugeot station wagons, vans and minibuses pressed into service as public transport in Kenya. They're more expensive than the buses, unreliable and dangerous – and they play music. Typically overloaded, folks don't have much to say about matters of comfort or safety in a matatu but they do vote for their favourite music by their patronage. Take, for example, the small town of Masii in Machakos District, the heart of Ukambani (the region of the Kamba people). As one resident explained to me, "People here are completely nuts about Katitu Boys Band". Every day at the bus stand or along the highway, it's a battle of the bands as matatu operators vie for customers, trying to lure them in with the latest sounds from bands performing Kamba styles in the Kamba language. Although the music sounds pretty similar from song to song (at least to the untrained non-Kamba ear), the words amuse the people waiting. More than that, the lyrics describe events that every Kamba can relate to in some way. The common person's disco is a commentary on life, and if the music's right, people will gladly squeeze in.

Throughout Kenya, the scene is reproduced over and over again from dawn to dusk. Each of Kenya's major language groups has its own musical style. In the cities, though, it's a different story. 'People's music' there is somewhat harder to find. Maybe it's a status issue or a statement of values, but whatever the reasons, music in Kenya's local languages is largely absent in the night clubs. It's even difficult to pick up on the radio, local language music having been shunted to the obscure vernacular service that devotes just a few hours a day to Kenya's major languages. In Nairobi, the average disco now plays reggae, Congolese music, or various strands of Euro-American pop, meaning that Kenyan musicians and the music business seem to be in a perpetual struggle for survival against imported sounds.

Guitars: the Common Denominator

There is no single identifiable genre of 'Kenyan pop' but rather a number of styles that borrow freely and cross-fertilise each other. Many Kenyan musicians direct their efforts towards their own linguistic groups and perform most of their songs in one of Kenya's **indigenous languages**, while others, aiming at national and urban audiences, sing in Swahili, or the Congolese language Lingala. What is defining about Kenyan music, though, is the **interplay of guitars**, prominent guitar solos, and the **cavacha** rhythm – the Bo Diddley kind of beat, popularised in the mid-1970s by Congolese groups such as Zaiko Langa Langa and Orchestra Shama Shama. This rapid-fire percussion, usually on the snare or high hat, quickly took hold in Kenya and continues to underlie a great sweep of Kenyan music from the Kalambya Sisters to Les Wanyika and Orchestre Virunga.

GRAEME EWENS COLLECTION

Early Kenyan recording artists,
Fadhili William (left) and Fundi Konde

Even before 1900, guitars were being played among the freed slaves around Mombasa, and by the 1920s there was a group of quite well-known players, including such names as **Lukas Tututu**, **Paul Mwachupa** and **Fundi Konde**. Their songs

Kenya's Tribal Music

All the people of Kenya have tribal (a term used widely in Kenya) musical cultures, some of which have survived more intact than others into the twenty-first century. Throughout the country, music has always been used to accompany rites of passage, from celebrations at a baby's birth to songs of adolescence and warriorhood. There were songs for marriage, harvests, solar and lunar cycles, festivities, religious rites, and death. Nowadays, however, the majority of Kenyans are Christian, and **Gospel** now reigns supreme – sadly not the uplifting version of the US or South Africa, but a tinny, synthesised and homogenous form.

Gospel has all but obliterated traditional music and among the Kikuyu (Kenya's largest tribe) or the Kalenjin (who comprise much of the government), the old tribal music is almost extinct. Elsewhere, to hear anything you need a lot of time and patience, and often a local family's trust, before being allowed to witness what can still be very sacred events.

The following is a very brief tribe-by-tribe rundown of more easily encountered traditional music and instruments. Obviously, there's much more available if you know where to search and what to ask for: essential reading for this is George Senoga-Zake's *Folk Music of Kenya* (Uzima Press, Nairobi, 1986).

Akamba

Best known for their skill at drumming, the Akamba tradition is sadly now all but extinct. There's only one commercial cassette available, *Akamba Drums* (Tamasha); it covers many styles and can be ordered from the *Zanzibar Curio Shop* in Nairobi.

Bajuni

The Bajuni are a small ethnic group living in the **Lamu** archipelago and on the nearby mainland, and are known musically for an epic women's work song called "Mashindano Ni Matezo". One of only very few easily-available recordings of women singing in Kenya, this is hypnotic counterpoint singing, punctuated by metallic rattles and supported by subdued drumming. You can find it in Lamu, Kilifi or Mombasa.

Borana

The Borana, who live between Marsabit and the Ethiopian border, have a rich musical tradition. The Arab influence is readily discernible, as are more typically Saharan rhythms. Most distinctive is their use of the **chamonge guitar**, a large cooking pot loosely strung with metal wires. On first hearing, you'd be forgiven for thinking that it is funky electric guitar, or some earthy precursor to the blues.

Chuka

Once again, sadly practically extinct, Chuka music from the east side of Mount Kenya – like that of the Akamba – is drumming genius. Your only hope is to catch the one remaining band, who currently play at the *Mount Kenya Safari Club* near Nanyuki.

Gusii

Gusii music is Kenya's oddest. The favoured instrument is the **obokano**, an enormous version of the Luo *nyatiti* lyre which is pitched at least an octave below the human voice, and which can sound like roaring thunder. They also use the ground bow, essentially a large hole dug in the ground over which an animal skin is tightly pegged. The skin has a small hole cut in the centre, into which a single-stringed bow is placed and plucked: the sound defies description. Spread the word and you should be able to pick up recordings in Kisii easily enough.

Luhya

Luhya music has a clear Bantu flavour, easily discernible in the pre-eminence of drums. Of these, the **sukuti** is best-known, sometimes played in ensembles, and still used in rites of passage such as circumcision. Tapes are easily available in Kakamega and Kitale.

Luo

The Luo are best-known as the originators of **benga** (for more on which see the main article). Their most distinctive musical instrument is the **nyatiti**, a double-necked eight-string lyre with a skin resonator which is also struck on one neck with a metal ring tied to the toe. It produces a tight, resonant sound, and is used to generate complex hypnotic rhythms. Originally used in the fields to relieve workers' tiredness, a typical piece begins at a moderate pace, and quickens progressively, the musician singing over the sound. The lyrics cover all manner of subjects, from politics and change since the *wazungu* arrived, to moral fables and age-old legends.

Maasai

The nomadic lifestyle of the Maasai tends to preclude the carrying of instruments, and as a result their music is one of the most distinctive in Kenya, characterised by astonishing **polyphonous multi-part singing** – both call-and-response, sometimes with women included in the chorus, but most famously in the songs of the morani warriors, where each man sings part of a rhythm, more often than not from his throat, which together with the calls of his companions create a pattern of rhythms. The songs are usually competitive

continued overleaf

(expressed through the singers alternately leaping as high as they can) or bragging – about how the singer killed a lion, or rustled cattle from a neighbouring community.

The Maasai have retained much of their traditional culture, so singing is still in use in traditional ceremonies, most spectacularly in the *eunoto* circumcision ceremony in which boys are initiated into manhood to begin their ten- to fifteen-year stint as morani. Most tourists staying in big coastal hotels or in game park lodges in Amboseli and Maasai Mara will have a chance to sample Maasai music in the form of groups of morani playing at the behest of hotel management. Cassettes are difficult to find.

Mijikenda

The Mijikenda of the coast have a prolific musical tradition which has survived Christian conversion and is readily available on tape throughout the region. Performances can occasionally be seen in the larger hotels. Like the Akamba, the Mijikenda are superb drummers and athletic dancers. The music is generally light and overlaid with complex rhythms, impossible not to dance to.

Samburu

Like their Maasai cousins, whose singing is very similar, Samburu musicians make a point of not playing instruments, at least in theory. They do play small pipes, and also a kind of guitar with a box resonator and loose metal strings – though these are played just for pleasure, or to soothe a crying baby, and are thus not deemed 'music' by Samburu. Listen out also for the sinuously erotic rain songs sung by women in times of drought. For cassettes, ask around at the lodges and campsites in Samburu/Buffalo Springs National Reserves, or – better still – in Maralal.

Turkana

Until the 1970s, the Turkana were one of Kenya's remotest tribes, and in large part are still untouched by Christian missionaries. Their traditional music is based loosely on a **call-and-response** pattern. The main instrument is a kudu antelope horn but most of their music is entirely vocal. A rarity to look out for are the women's rain songs, sung to the god Akuj during times of drought. Visitors are usually welcome to join performances in Loiyangalani for a small fee.

Jens Finke

dealt with secular topics but were similar in form to church music with several verses and a refrain.

In a separate development, from around the mid–1920s there were several dance clubs in the Mombasa area playing music for Christian Africans to do European dancing. The **Nyika Club Band** was one such house band, a group comprising guitars, bass, banjo, mandolin, violin and sax/clarinet. As for the rest of Kenya, there's little in the historical record of this period about what was happening musically, apart from singing and drumming – and a bit of accordion among the Kikuyu.

During World War II, many African soldiers were sent to fight in Ethiopia, India and Burma, and some of the coastal musicians were drafted into the Entertainment Unit of the King's African Rifles. With a couple of Ugandan recruits, the group comprised guitars, mandolin, accordion and drums, and after the war they continued as the **Rhino Band**. Based at first in Kampala, they soon worked their way down to Mombasa. After they split in 1948, some of the members formed the distinguished **Kiko Kids**, and other dance bands.

From the early 1950s, the spread of radio and a proliferation of recording studios pushed genuinely popular music across a wide spectrum of Kenyan society. Fundi Konde was a prominent broadcaster and also recorded on HMV's Blue Label series. His early songs, and especially his chord sequences, were closely allied to those of contemporary European dance bands, and it's a fair guess that if they had been in English rather than Swahili, much of his tight, melodic, very rhythmic output would have found favour with the pre-rock'n'roll tastes of Europe and America.

Finger-pickin' Good

While Fundi Konde's urbane style was much in demand, the 'second generation' of Kenyan guitarists were making their names, often with a different playing technique – the thumb and forefinger **finger style** first heard in the music of eastern Congolese players like **Jean-Bosco Mwenda** and **Edouard Massengo**. Bosco's recordings were available in Kenya from 1952 and by the end of the decade he and Massengo had moved to Nairobi.

Finger-style music has a lively, fast-paced bounce, especially where a second guitar follows the lead guitar with syncopated bass lines. The Kenyan finger-pickers sometimes pursued solo careers, but more usually they formed small guitar-based groups, with two-part vocal harmony and simple percussion using maracas, a tambourine, wood-blocks or even soda bottles. From the mid-1950s, this new sound gained a huge following and produced spectacular record sales. AGS, the African Gramophone Store, one of the bigger labels, claims to have sold 300,000 copies of **John Mwale**'s "Kuwaza Sera" 78 rpm.

By the mid-1960s, finger-style acoustic guitar bands were losing ground to other electric guitar styles. The rhythms of the new urban Swahili music were also influenced by Congolese rumba and South African kwela, or what was locally called **twist**. Twist's underlying rhythm is the beat of 'Mbube' (The Lion), better known internationally as 'Wimoweh' but played faster.

The old styles were absorbed in part into the new music, and many ideas taken up by the electric bands were based on the finger-picking and soda bottle percussion. One of the most important groups of the new electric era of the 1960s was the **Equator Sound Band**, first formed in 1959 as the Jambo Boys, a studio and performing combo for the East African Records company. Led by **Fadhili William**, they went on into the 1970s as African Eagles and Eagles Lupopo. Some of the most famous names of the period – Daudi Kabaka, Gabriel Omolo, Sylvester Odhiambo and the Zambian émigrés Nashil Pichen and Peter Tsotsi – distinguished the line-up. Typical Equator elements were the two-part vocal harmony, a steady, often 'walking' bass and a bright, clean lead guitar. There's often a strikingly American feel in the guitar solos and chord formations, suggesting pervasive rock and country influences.

Abana Ba Nasery (Nursery Boys) strike that Fanta

Benga Wizards

The late 1960s and early '70s was a time of transition in Kenyan music. While the African Eagles and others continued to play their brands of Swahili music, many top Kenyan groups, such as the **Ashantis**, **Air Fiesta** and the **Hodi Boys**, were playing Congolese covers and international pop, especially soul music, in the Nairobi clubs. But it was also at this time that a number of musicians were beginning to define the direction of the emerging **benga style**, which became Kenya's most characteristic pop music.

Although benga originated with the Luo people of western Kenya, its transition to a popular style has been so pervasive that practically all the local bands play variants of it and today most of the regional or ethnic pop groups refer generally to their music as benga. As a pop style, it dates back to the 1950s when musicians began adapting traditional dance rhythms and the string sounds of the *nyatiti* and *orutu* to the acoustic guitar and later to electric instruments. During its heyday, in the 1970s and into the 1980s, it dominated Kenya's recording industry and was exported to west and southern Africa where it was very popular.

By any measure, the most famous benga group is **Shirati Jazz** led by **D.O. (Daniel Owino) Misiani**. Born in Shirati, Tanzania, just south of the Kenyan border, he has been playing benga since the mid-1960s. His style is characterised by soft, flowing and melodic two-part vocal harmonies, a very active, pulsating bass line that derives at least in part from traditional nyatiti and drum rhythms, and stacks of invigorating guitar work, the lead alternating with the vocal.

Shirati have been one of the few Kenyan bands able to make things work as full-time musicians. For most, music is a part-time job in addition to the homestead farm, wage employment, or a small business. Nonetheless, other pioneering Luo benga names include Colella Mazee and Ochieng Nelly – either together or separately in various incarnations of **Victoria Jazz** and the **Victoria Kings** – as well as **George Ramogi** and his **Continental Luo Sweet Band**. All are still active in Kenya except for Ramogi who passed away at the end of 1997.

Another significant Luo musician, who died the following year, was **Ochieng' Kabaselleh** – who led his **Luna Kidi Band** through the 1970s and '80s. His songs were mostly in Luo, but with a seasoning of Swahili and English, and to benga melodies and harmonies he grafted on rhythm guitar and horns from the Congolese sound. Kabaselleh languished in prison for several years (for 'subversion') but returned to the music world with a flood of releases in the 1990s, and in 1997 had a US tour and his first international CD release, *From Nairobi with Love*.

Nursery Boys

The Luhya highlands to the north of Luo-land are home to many of Kenya's most famous guitarists and vocalists. They include **Daudi Kabaka**, who had a renowned early career but struggles today with only the occasional hotel gig; **Sukuma bin Ongaro**, famed for his humorous social commentary; and **Shem Tube**, whose music straddles past and present – though it's his past which has given him a popular following in Europe, following the 1989 GlobeStyle Records release *Abana ba Nasery* (The Nursery Boys), a compilation of songs by Tube and his group in the **omutibo** style.

The **Abana ba Nasery** collection offers a glimpse of a musical era of the 1960s and early '70s which has largely vanished. Coming together as a trio in the early 1960s, the group blazed a path for Kenyan pop to follow. While using traditional Luhya rhythms and melody lines, their two-guitar line-up and three-part vocal harmonies (and the Fanta bottle) were a hint of things to come, containing all the main elements of today's contemporary pop sound in Kenya. The central position of the solo guitar in Kenya's electric groups is anticipated in Shem Tube's solos of twenty-five years ago. Justo Osala's guitar parts in the lower ranges are like the rhythm and bass parts in today's electric bands. Even Enos Okola's Fanta rhythms are a precursor of the modern drum kit.

While Abana's CD reissue created overseas interest as a rootsy and very accessible African sound, the compatibility of their music with strands of European folk tradition is clear in their 1990s release, recorded by GlobeStyle in London: *Nursery Boys Go Ahead!* Guest artists included members of the Oyster Band and Mustaphas as well as Ron Kavana and Tomás Lynch.

Although they've never earned enough money to buy their own electric guitars and amps, Abana ba Nasery have had a string of local hits as an electric band under the stage names **Mwilonje Jazz** and **Super Bunyore Band** (listen, for example, to Super Bunyore's "Bibi Joys" on the *Nairobi Beat* compilation). If the Nursery Boys have their way, it won't be long before audiences outside Kenya get a taste of their electric music too.

Kikuyu: Prayers for the Country

As Kenya's largest ethnic group, the **Kikuyu-speaking people** of Central Province and Nairobi are a major market force in Kenya's music industry. Perhaps because of this built-in audience, few Kikuyu musicians have tried to cross over into the national Swahili or English-language markets.

Kikuyu **melodies** are quite distinct from those of the Luo and Luhya of western Kenya and their pop manifestations also differ significantly in harmonies and rhythm guitar parts. In contrast to Luo and Luhya pop, **women vocalists** play major roles as lead and backing singers and many of the top groups have women's auxiliaries – duos and trios invariably called the something-or-other sisters. Most often, Kikuyu pop takes the form of the benga/cavacha style, but popular alternatives are also based on country and western, reggae, and Congolese soukous.

The king of Kikuyu pop is **Joseph Kamaru**, who has been making hit records since the release of "Celina" in 1967, performed, on one guitar and maracas, with his sister Catherine Muthoni. Since then he has carved a small empire – including his **Njung'wa Stars** band and the Kamarulets dancers,

Joseph Kamaru"s raunchy pop – he gave it up for gospel!

two music shops and a recording studio. He sees himself as a teacher, expressing the traditional values of his culture, as well as contemporary social commentary, in song. In the early 1990s his recording, "Mahoya ma Bururi" ("Prayers for the Country"), gently criticised the Kenya government but resulted in his shop being raided and the banning of the song from the airwaves. Kamaru takes pride in his lyrics for going beyond trivial matters. "My songs are not like other peoples' – 'I love you, I love you,' they keep on singing – No, no, no! My songs are not that way. I can compose a love song but very deep, a grown-up loving."

In the period following "Mahoya ma Bururi," Kamaru's popularity was steadily on the rise, his band was fully booked, playing his regular and 'X-rated, Adults Only' shows to packed nightclub crowds. Thus his announcement in 1993 that he had been 'born again' came as a bombshell for his fans. Much to their disappointment, Kamaru abandoned the pop scene to devote his efforts to evangelical activities and gospel music promotion.

Kamaru may not write songs for teenage lovers but someone who does, and who became famous in the process, is hit-maker **Daniel 'DK' (Councillor) Kamau**. Kamau released his first three records in 1967 while still at school and continued with a highly successful career through the 1970s. He is regarded as having brought Kikuyu music into the benga mainstream, but it was not until 1990 that he returned to the stage with a new **Lulus Band**. In Kenya's rapidly changing political climate, the councillor struck a responsive chord with his fans and the population at large with his Top Ten hit, "FORD Fever" (about the newly formed opposition party). DK has continued to address political and human rights issues, sometimes in partnership with singer-composer **Albert Gacheru**.

With Kamaru's departure from the pop market, at least part of the void has been filled by one of the rare female headliners in Kikuyu pop, **Jane Nyambura**. Known these days simply as Queen Jane, she's a staunch advocate for the inclusion of traditional folk forms and local languages within contemporary pop. Her use of tribal languages has limited her radio exposure (such music is deemed 'tribal' in official circles) but Jane and four of her brothers and sisters now make their living from her band.

Merry-go-round Style

East and southeast of Nairobi is a vast, semi-arid plateau, the home of the **Kamba** people, linguistically close relations of the Kikuyu. Kamba pop music is firmly entrenched in the benga/cavacha camp, though there are special Kamba features. One is the delicate, flowing, merry-go-round-like rhythm guitar that underlies many arrangements. While the primary guitar plays chords in the lower range, the second guitar plays a fast pattern of notes that mesh with the rest of the instrumentation to fill in the holes. This gentle presence is discernible in many of the recordings of the three most famous Kamba groups; the **Kalambya Boys & Kalambya Sisters**, **Peter Mwambi and his Kyanganga Boys** and **Les Kilimambogo Brothers Band**, fomerly led by Kakai Kilonzo.

These groups dominated Kamba music from the mid-1970s. Mwambi, although he can get into some great guitar solos, has a following that comes largely from within the Kamba community: his musically simple, pound 'em-out, pulsing-bass drum style may not have enough musical variation to keep non-Kamba speakers interested.

The Kalambya Sisters are a different story. Backed by Onesmus Musyoki's Kalambya Boys Band, the Sisters (now disbanded) were famous, even notorious, throughout Kenya and they even had a minor hit in Europe with "Katelina". This related the comic plight of a young woman, Katelina, who likes to drink the home-brew *uki*, but gets pregnant with annual regularity in the process. The soft, high-pitched, feline voices of the Sisters whine engagingly in unison over the delightfully sweet guitar work of Musyoki and the Boys. After a ten-year absence from the studio, Musyoki returned to record "Sweet Sofia" in 1993, while founding sister, Mary Nduku, now leads the **Mitaboni Sisters**.

To reach a larger audience, a number of local-language artists have turned to Swahili, which is widely spoken throughout east and central Africa. Kakai Kilonzo and Les Kilimambogo Brothers band were always identified as a Kamba band, but once Kakai started recording in Swahili, the group enjoyed widespread popularity in Kenya. With socially relevant lyrics, a good dose of merry-go-round guitar and a solid dance-beat backing, Les Kilimambogo were national favourites until Kakai's death in 1987.

These days, a generation of musicians, relative newcomers to the Kamba hall of fame, is drawing most of the limelight away from the old guard. The **Katitu Boys Band** have come to dominate the Kamba cassette market. Leader David Kasyoki, a former guitarist with Mwambi's Kyanganga Boys, won the 1992 Singer of the Year award for "Cheza na Katitu" (Dance with Katitu). Other groups of the new Kamba generation include **Kimangu Boys Band**, **Kiteta Boys**, and **Mutituni Boys Band**.

Congolese and Swahili: Big-name Bands

The **big-name bands** in Kenya can usually muster sufficiently large audiences for shows in sprawling, ethnically diverse towns like Nairobi, Nakuru or Mombasa. Unlike the groups with a particular ethnic leaning, the national performers can appeal to a broad cross-section of the population with music which tends to be either a local variant of the **Congolese** sound or **Swahili music**, a Kenyan-Tanzanian hybrid sound, unique to Kenya.

In both Congolese and Swahili popular music, **rumba** has always been a major ingredient. Songs typically open with a slow-to-medium rumba that ambles through the verses, backed by a light percussion of gentle congas, snare and high hat. Then, three or four minutes into the song there's a transition – or more often a hiatus. It's goodbye to verses and rolling rumba as the song shifts into high gear. A much faster rhythm, highlighting the instrumental parts, especially solo guitar and brass, takes over with a vengeance.

There are some significant points of divergence in the Swahili and Congolese styles. The tempo of Swahili music is generally slower, even in the fast section. Swahili music over the last twenty-five years has been particularly faithful to this two-part structure although, today, both Swahili and Congolese musicians often dispense with the slow rumba portion altogether. While the Congolese musicians are famous for their vocals and their intricate harmonies, Swahili groups are renowned for their demon guitarists and crisp, clear guitar interplay.

While Swahili pop is usually associated with Swahili lyrics, it isn't distinguished by the language. In fact one of the greatest Swahili hits of all time, the Maroon Commandos' "Charonyi Ni Wasi" is not in Swahili but in the closely related Taita language. Similarly, Nairobi's Congolese scene has become less Lingala as it has moved from the near-exclusive use of that Congolese language twenty-five years ago to a preponderance of Swahili lyrics today. Nearly all the songs on the recent *Feet on Fire* CD from the immensely popular **Orchestre Virunga** are in Swahili, helping to guarantee popularity with a mass audience. As for Lingala songs, while few Kenyans understand the lyrics, their mysterious incomprehensibility and a veneer of Gallic sophistication gives them a certain sex appeal.

Most of the Swahili and Congolese music produced in Kenya originated with the multinational giants like Polygram and CBS/Sony or was put out by independent labels run by British or Asian Kenyans. When European and American interest in African music began to emerge in the early 1980s, it was these companies with their international connections that released the first, tantalising sounds from Nairobi. These early Kenyan recordings released in London were drawn from the big names and featured artists such as **Super Mazembe**, **Orchestra Makassy**, **Orchestre Virunga**, **Lessa Lassan**, **Issa Juma**, and **Lovy Longomba**. Of these, all but the Tanzanian-born Issa Juma came from Congo (then Zaire) – there wasn't a Kenyan among them – and it was not until several years later, after Shirati Jazz had done their first British tour, that Kenya achieved an international reputation for its indigenous benga dance music.

Immigration Department

Congolese musicians have been making waves in Kenya since the late 1950s. It was the **Congolese OS Africa Band** that opened Nairobi's famous *Starlight Club* back in 1964. But it wasn't until the mid-1970s, after the passing of the American soul craze, that music from Congo began to dominate the city nightclubs. One of the first musicians to settle in Kenya during this period was **Baba Gaston**. The rotund Gaston had already been in the business for twenty years when he arrived in Nairobi with his group Baba National in 1975. A prolific musician and father (he had twelve children), he stole the scene until his retirement as a performer and recording artist in 1989.

In the mid-1970s, at about the same time Baba Gaston was just getting settled in Nairobi, the Congolese group **Boma Liwanza** was already on the scene at the *Starlight Club* and the popular **Bana Ngenge** were about to leave Nairobi for a year in Tanzania. **Super Mazembe** had just completed their migration from then Zaire to Kenya by way of Zambia and Tanzania, and soon to follow were **Samba Mapangala and Les Kinois**.

IAN ANDERSON

One of Africa's all-time best voices:
Samba Mapangala

JOHN CLEWLEY

Vundumuna during their Japan period

The latter were an early prototype of **Orchestre Virunga**, which Samba Mapangala put together with the Super Mazembe singer Kasongo wa Kanema. In 1984, however, Virunga ran into problems with work permits, and broke up, leading to a new all-star group, **Ibeba System**, led by ex-Virunga guitarist Sammy Mansita. When Ibeba first took over from Virunga at the Starlight, the group was a virtual clone of the Virunga sound but over several years performing at the JKA Resort Club they became one of Nairobi's most accomplished club acts with a good mix of their own soukous and covers of African pop.

The ultimate Congolese crossover band in Nairobi, and darlings of Kenya's young elite, were **Vundumuna**. The group formed in 1984 with guitarist **Tabu Frantal**, Ugandan vocalist Sammy Kasule, and bassist Nsilu wa Bansilu (another ex-Virunga player), and quickly gained institutional status at the *Carnivore* packing in the crowds with their performances. With the best equipment in the city, they presented a clean, hi-tech sound fusing Congolese soukous, benga rhythms, and elements of Western jazz. Their flawless horn arrangements blended beautifully with the keyboard-playing of leader **Botango Bedjil** (BB Mo-Franck) and Frantal's guitar. After three LPs and riding a crest of popularity, the future was looking bright until, once again, the Immigration Department struck. The group played its farewell concert at the *Carnivore* in late 1986 and since then have worked abroad in places as far afield as Japan and Oman. Between jobs, they return to Kenya – several band members have Kenyan wives and children – and they have been allowed to play short stints as guest performers. BB Mo-Franck and sax

player Tabu Ngongo have stayed on in Japan playing African music in BB's groups, **Bitasika** and **MAMU** (Modern African Music), releasing a couple of nicely produced CDs in Japan.

The loss of Vundumuna set the stage for the return of Orchestre Virunga, and when they took up a residence in *Garden Square* club in Nairobi in 1988 they were greeted with the same abundant enthusiasm they had left behind three years earlier. With a captivating stage show, they played dazzling renditions of all their familiar hits, and new compositions like "Safari" and "Vunja Mifupa" joined the list of favourites. Sadly, in 1993, Samba gave up on the local nightclub scene and disbanded the group, though he still performs for special events in Kenya, tours abroad and makes records. Although the musicians continue to change, nothing has altered Samba Mapangala's formula – a catchy, not over-complex melody, faultless vocal harmonies, innovative, interlocking guitar lines and superbly crafted horns floating over light, high-tensile percussion.

Samba Mapangala was not the only one disillusioned by the business of music in Nairobi. By the early 1990s, Nairobi's status as an island of opportunity for Congolese musicians had fallen flat. With harder economic times, a declining record industry, fewer live venues and restrictive work rules, Nairobi had become a departure point for greener pastures rather than the promised land itself. Some musicians headed to Tanzania and other neighbouring countries while others followed Vundumuna's lead and signed up to play outside Africa. In recent years, Japan has been a destination for a number of Nairobi's Congolese musicians, who form touring groups such as **Angusha Band**.

Since the mid-1990s, however, the Congolese music scene has been on the upswing once again with a host of new names and new places to work. Congolese names on the current scene include **Senza Musica**, **Choc la Musica**, **Station Japan**, **Tshiakatumaba International**, and **Bilenge Musica**. The latter have a CD release called *Rumba Is Rumba* that, in terms of quality, places them among the top soukous bands anywhere. The vocalist **Coco Zigo Mike** would have been in this list, too, as leader of Losako la Musica. Sadly, he died in 1998 at the age of 39. 'Prince Cocozigo', as he was known, sang in the late-1970s band Viva Makale and, later, in Orchestre Virunga, Ibeba System, and Moreno Batamba's Orchestra Moja One.

Wanyika Dynasty

Songs with **Swahili lyrics** are part of the common currency of East African musical culture. Kenya's own brand of Swahili pop music has its origin in the Tanzanian pop styles of the 1970s but, since that time, the Kenyan variety has followed a separate evolutionary path. In addition to the stylistic features it shares with the Congolese sound (light, high-hat-and-conga percussion and a delicate two/three-guitar interweave), the Kenyan Swahili sound is instrumentally sparse, allowing the bass to fill in gaps, often in syncopated rhythms. Trumpets and saxes are common in recorded arrangements but usually omitted in club performances because of the expense.

One of the first Tanzanian groups to migrate to Kenya was Arusha Jazz, the predecessor of what is now the legendary **Simba Wanyika Original** (Lion of the Savanna). Founded by Wilson Peter Kinyonga and his brothers George and William, the group began performing in Mombasa in 1971. The following year, they began recording for Phonogram, making a name for themselves with single releases, and in 1975, with Tanzanian recruit Omar Shabani on rhythm and Kenyan Tom Malanga on bass, shifted their base to Nairobi and released their first album, *Jiburudisheni na Simba Wanyika* (Chill Out with Simba Wanyika). Over their twenty-year history in Nairobi, the group were favourites of the city's club scene and made scores of recordings. They broke up in 1995 after the deaths of first George (in 1992) and then Wilson Kinyonga.

Interestingly, Simba Wanyika's international releases present a rather different sound from their typical recordings for Polygram in Nairobi. In both *Simba Wanyika Original: Kenya Vol I* and *Pepea*,

the group has taken a page from the benga handbook and quickened the pace considerably – though the vocal and instrumental parts are still their 'original' sound of great guitars, creamy sax (on *Vol I*) and pleasing, listener-friendly vocal lines. For purists interested in their local, live sound, the albums *Haleluya* and *Mapenzi Ni Damu* are more representative.

The Wanyika name is famous in East Africa for several other related bands that emerged from the family line. The group's first big split occurred in 1978 when the core of supporting musicians around the Kinyonga brothers left to form **Les Wanyika**. Among those who made the move were rhythm guitarist 'Professor' Omari Shabani, bass player Tom Malanga, drummer Rashid Juma, and vocalist Issa Juma, who had only joined Simba Wanyika a month before. The group added another crucial member in Tanzanian lead guitar player **John Ngereza**, who had been playing in Kenya with the Congolese group Bwambe Bwambe. After six months' practice, they began performing at *Garden Square* and soon found fame across Kenya with their massive hit "Sina Makosa" (It's not my fault). Under Ngereza's leadership, they have remained one of Nairobi's top bands, distinguished by imaginative compositions and arrangements, a typically lean, clean sound and the delicious blend of Professor Omari's rhythm guitar mastery with Tom Malanga's bass. Their vocals are great, too, handled by lead guitar player Ngereza, with solid multipart harmonies from Mohamed Tika and other Swahili session vocalists.

The group was not afraid to adapt to changing times. In the early 1990s, as Kenyan tastes embraced disco music, they were in there with a disco medley of their greatest hits, *Les Les Non-Stop '90*, a formula carried over into their next album, *Kabibi* – rather dire international disco. Mercifully, Ngereza abandoned this course on his following cassette releases and, in returning to classic Les Wanyika form, has consistently been in Kenya's Top Ten charts with each new release. His inclusion as a guest artist on Orchestre Virunga's 1997 US tour finally brought him some international exposure outside Africa as well as his first international CD in 1998, *Amigo*. Sadly, 1998 saw the death of Professor Omari, who had composed many of the group's early hits such as "Sina Makosa", "Paulina" and "Pamela".

An important figure in the Wanyika story is Tanzania-born **Issa Juma**, who quickly established a name for himself in Kenya as a premier vocalist in the early days of the band. Mention his name today and many Kenyans will immediately think of 'Sigalame', a character from his 1983 single of the same name and now a part of Kenyan vocabulary. Sigalame is a mysterious character who has disappeared from family and friends but is rumoured to be living in Bungoma doing 'business'. What kind of business? ("Biashara gani?") With so many illegal activities to choose from, it was up to the listener to answer.

Issa formed **Super Wanyika** in 1981 and over the next few years had a series of hits featuring half a dozen variations on the Wanyika name – Super Wanyika Stars, Wanyika Stars, Waa-Nyika, L'Orchestra Waanyika and Wanyika Super Les Les. As one of the most productive artists of the 1980s, he released many numbers in the style of Swahili-benga fusion heard in "Sigalame". Yet, he has been perhaps the most versatile and creative of the Swahili artists in his willingness to take his music in different directions. With producer Babu Shah, some of his songs sound very much like the Conglese music of the time. Others are more in the old rumba style of Simba Wanyika.

Although the Wanyika bands have been dominant in Swahili music, it is not their exclusive domain. Foremost among other Tanzanians and Kenyans performing in the Swahili style are the **Maroon Commandos**. Members of the Kenyan Army, the Commandos are one of the oldest performing groups in the country. They first came together in 1970 and were intitially mainly a covers band playing Congolese hits. But by 1977 they had come out as a strong force in the Swahili style with the huge Taita-language hit "Charonyi Ni Wasi." Within their genre, the Commandos do not limit themselves to any sort of rigid formula. Like many of the Swahili groups, they use trumpets and sax liberally but they're also quite experimental and have at various times added a keyboard and innovative guitar effects and, at their most creative, mingle Swahili and benga styles.

KELELE RECORDS

Them Mushrooms

Hakuna Matata . . .

International influences have always been a part of Kenyan music but where Kenyan pop meets the tourist industry, at the resorts to the north and south of earthy Mombasa, another distinct style can be heard in all the hotels. Here, a band can successfully make a living just playing covers at hotel gigs. **Tourist pop bands** typically have highly competent musicians, relatively good equipment and, overall, a fairly polished sound. In live performances, the best of them play an eclectic selection of old Congolese rumba tunes as warm-ups, popular international covers, a few Congolese favourites of the day, greatest hits from Kenya's past, and then some original material that leans heavily towards the American/Euro-pop sound but with lyrics relating to local topics.

The most successful Kenyan group in this field has been the oddly named **Them Mushrooms**. Strictly speaking, the Mushrooms graduated from the coastal hotel circuit when they moved to Nairobi in 1987. Their music, however, lives on at the coast, highlighted by their crowning achievement, the perennial tourist anthem "Jambo Bwana" with its unintentionally ironic refrain, "Hakuna Matata" – no problems. TM have several different versions of the song and while they are proud to take credit for this insidiously infectious bit of fluff, they have much more serious intentions in the world of music.

At the time of their formation, in 1972, Them Mushrooms were a reggae band without an audience. However, as they gravitated toward the hotel circuit for work, they changed their style to a more commercial sound encompassing international covers, African pop standards, a little soca and reggae, and some Kenyan variants of benga and the coastal chakacha rhythm. By the time they had moved to Nairobi's *Carnivore* restaurant in 1987, their polished sound quickly established them as a favourite among the affluent nightclub set.

Them Mushrooms are without doubt Kenya's most active band today with at least fifteen albums to their credit. Over the best part of thirty years, they have produced a series of successful collaborations, highlighting diverse artists, and including pioneering musician Fundi Konde, taarab star Malika and the Kikuyu singer Jane Nyambura. They now own and operate one of the best studios in the country, and their recent work has taken them back to their first love, reggae with the CD *Kazi Ni Kazi* (Work Is Work), released internationally on the Kelele label.

The Mushroom's long-time counterpart in the hotel circuit, **Safari Sound**, have also joined the reggae brigade with another Kelele release called *Mambo Jambo*. This group already has the distinction of having Kenya's best-selling album ever in *The Best of African Songs*, a veritable greatest hits of hotel classics that includes *Malaika*, a beautiful composition about ill-starred love, first sung by Fadhili William and rarely given the soulful treatment it deserves.

Labour of Love

For the great majority of Kenyan musicians, the music business is a labour of love. This is not to say they wouldn't love to have money, but that very few can even support themselves and their families without other income. Although Kenya has a rich musical tradition, musicians have always struggled to gain recognition and respect. Kenyans speak fondly of the great artists and songs in Kenyan pop, and they relish all the local music around them on the streets – in matatus, restaurants and bars. On the other hand, they often speak disparagingly about Kenyan music in comparison with music from Tanzania, Congo, Europe or America. Institutionally, little has been done to help Kenyan

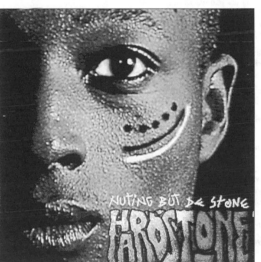

musicians. Cassette piracy and the unaffordable cost of instruments and supplies are two of the major problems. Kenyan radio doesn't give them much support either, especially if their songs are recorded in a local language.

These days, musicians playing benga, Swahili pop, or Congolese music face stiff competition on the airwaves and in the music shops from American and European sounds: mainstream pop, hip-hop, reggae, R&B, the whole lot. As the audience for these types of music has grown (including in its number plenty of Kenyan musicians), many Kenyan artists have decided it's time to bring these international styles into their own compositions.

The Nairobi production company, **Synch Sound Studio**, has been active in promoting international styles for distribution abroad in con-

junction with the German label **Kelele Records**. Among the first performers releasing CDs with Kelele were Them Mushrooms, Safari Sound, Hart, Shadz O'Blak, and Hardstone. Harrison Ngunjiri, alias **Hardstone**, has been particularly successful in Kenya with his hit song "Uhiki", from the CD *Nuting but de Stone*. This appropriates Marvin Gaye's "Sexual Healing" and mixes it with Kikuyu folk music and rap – a strange combination but one Hardstone pulls off nicely. The song earned him the "Best New Artist of the Year" award in 1997, in Nairobi's Kisima Awards.

Over the last few years, many of Kenya's younger generation of musicians have taken inspiration from rap, R&B, house, reggae, and dancehall genres, blending elements of Euro-American pop with local Kenyan melodies, lyrics and rhythms. There's genuine enthusiasm for local music in this niche, and a sense of anticipation of much greater things to come. The 1998 CD, *Kenyan: The First Chapter*, seems to be an expression of such optimism. The disc is a showcase for several of the pioneers in this new music. It includes Swahili rap from **Kala Mashaka**, Swahili language ballads from **Nikki** and **Shadz O'Blak**, R&B from **Jimmi Gathu** and the female duo, **IN TU**. In separate recordings, **Pox Pressure** (Prechard Pouka) has emerged a radio favourite with his Luo language reggae, raggamuffin, and dance hall styles and, from Mombasa, **Malkia Rukia** mixes taarab and hip-hop in her hit song "Anipenda Nakupenda" (He loves me, I love you).

It is difficult to predict where this new direction in Kenyan pop will eventually lead and which of these artists will be around in the coming years. For the moment, however, it's one of the bright spots in the local scene. With innumerable variants of local benga styles, Swahili rumba, Congolese soukous, international (tourist) music, gospel, and the new emerging fusions, Kenya's musical diversity is both a strength and a problem – as the market for each style is small. Still, there's some great music emerging: explore and enjoy . . .

discography

A number of tape compilations of traditional music are available in Kenya. CDs below are mostly available from African specialists worldwide.

Compilations

 Before Benga Vol. 1: Kenya Dry and **Vol. 2: The Nairobi Sound** (Original Music, US).

Both the acoustic collection on *Kenya Dry* and the electric *Nairobi Sound* provide an excellent cross-section of guitar music from the 1950s to the '70s. These are styles that have largely disappeared in Kenya.

⑩ **Guitar Paradise of East Africa**
⑩ **Kenya Dance Mania** (Earthworks/Stern's, UK).

These two CDs range through Kenya's various styles, although not always featuring the best or most representative material from the artists. Highlights on *Guitar Paradise* include the classic hit "Shauri Yako" by Super Mazembe as well as Ochieng' Kabaselleh's "Achi Maria." *Kenya Dance Mania* includes Kenyan classics of the 1970s and '80s like Les Wanyika's "Sina Makosa" and the Maroon Commandos' "Charonyi Ni Wasi" (recently revived in Kenya).

⑩ **Kapere Jazz Band & Others**
⑩ **Luo Roots: Musical Currents from Western Kenya** (GlobeStyle, UK).

Today's versions of the traditional music of the Luo people, suggesting the foundations of the benga style.

⑩ **The Most Beautiful Songs of Africa** (ARC Music, UK).

The naff title aside, this is a rather good collection of largely 1970s Kenyan and Tanzanian music. The mix is totally eclectic with the Congolese dance sounds of Super Mazembe (with "Kasongo" and "Shauri Yako") and Bopol Mansiamina, taarab music of the coast, Tanzanian dance music from Afro 70 and Western Jazz, and a top version by Miriam Makeba of the haunting "Malaika" (the version that served as the model for Angelique Kidjo's rendition).

⑩ **The Nairobi Beat: Kenyan Pop Music Today** (Rounder, US).

First-rate collection of mid-1980s music compiled by the author of this article and showcasing a cross-section of musical varieties covering some of the best examples of regional benga styles: Luo, Kikuyu, Kamba, and Luhya; plus a couple of Swahili and Congolese dance tunes for good measure.

 The Rough Guide to the Music of Kenya and Tanzania (World Music Network, UK).

Okay – you'd expect us to like it, but this really is a superb collection of Kenyan and Tanzanian music, sampling traditional and popular styles, including taarab from the coastal region. Kenyan artists include Simba Wanyika, Victoria Kings, DO Misiani and Shirati Jazz, Abana ba Nasery, Henry Makobi, Ogwang Lelo Okoth with Paddy J Onono, and Zein Musical Party.

⑩ **The Secret Museum of Mankind, Music of East Africa, Ethnic Music Classics: 1925–48** (Yazoo, US).

With selections from across East Africa, this provides a fascinating window onto traditional and popular sounds reflecting local styles of the 1930s and '40s. Of the eleven selections from Kenya, most feature guitar accompanying traditional songs. On some tracks there's a sense of the precursors to the Luo benga that emerged two or three decades later.

Artists

Abana Ba Nasery

From western Kenya, this trio keeps alive a style of music they pioneered in the 1960s and early '70s. As one of the first groups to produce a two-guitar weave, their sound was innovative. To this they added three-part harmony and a rhythm line created by scraping the ribs of a Fanta bottle with a metal rod.

⑩ **Abana Ba Nasery: Classic Acoustic Recordings from Western Kenya** (GlobeStyle, UK).

Original thirty-year-old recordings – a charming collection of finger-picking acoustic guitar music from Bunyore, Kenya.

⑩ **!Nursery Boys Go Ahead! The Guitar and Bottle Kings of Kenya** (GlobeStyle, UK; Xenophile, US).

This CD captures the crisp ABN sound in recordings made on their 1991 tour to the UK. It also places the trio in some interesting collaborations with European artists, some of which really get rockin'.

Bilenge Musica

This group of eight Congolese musicians came together in Nairobi in 1996 under the leadership of Didie Doubleweight. Individually, they've played with some of Congo's most famous musicians and groups including Sam Mangwana, Koffi Olomide, Viva la Musica, and Tanzanian-based Maquis Original and Carnival Band.

⑩ **Rumba is Rumba** (Kelele, Germany).

But for Swahili language lyrics in several of the songs, this is mainstream Congolese soukous all the way – and that's not bad. The sound is reminiscent of Wenge Musica. Production, at Sync Sound Studios, Nairobi, is first-rate, as usual.

Oguta Bobo

Not much is known about the late Oguta Bobo Otange but that he's a compelling accordion player from among the Luo of Western Kenya and his music covered the gamut of topics from serious social commentary to the lighter side of love.

⑩ **Rujina Kalando** (Equator Heritage Sounds, US).

A chance for squeeze-box fanatics to get some rare recordings of African accordion with Oguta Bobo singing and playing. The songs are traditional in melody and rhythm but contemporary in lyrics of the time (the 1960s) and filled with humour for those who understand Luo.

Sam Chege's Ultra–Benga

Raised by his grandmother in rural central Kenya, Chege received a solid grounding in Kikuyu music and oral tradition before going to study in Nairobi and the US. A music journalist by profession, his own music is rooted in Kikuyu musical traditions which have been fused with other local Kenyan and Congolese styles.

 Kickin' Kikuyu-Style (Original Music, US).

Kickin is a great example of Kikuyu benga music with its solid pulsing kick drum, interlocking guitars (with seriously delayed reverb), providing an interesting contrast to the Luo benga of DO Misiani, George Ramogi, or Victoria Kings. Lively, fun music with excellent sound quality.

Hardstone

Born in 1977, Hardston is a rapper in Kikuyu and (Jamaican-sounding) English – one of the new breed of young Kenyan artists. He's a solo performer (with borrowed crews) but in studio he works in partnership with Tedd Josiah. He won the 'Best New Artist of the Year' award at Nairobi's Kisima Awards in April, 1997.

 Nuting but de Stone (Kelele Records, Germany).

Caribbean ragga, American urban sounds, and African lyrics and rhythms come together in a superbly produced mix, with many stopping points along the way.

Jabali Afrika

This ensemble was originally brought together for the Kenya National Theatre, whereupon they developed a repertoire and a following, and formed Jabali Afrika. Currently based in the US, they have toured extensively in America and Europe.

 Journey (Jabali Afrika, Kenya).

This is a gem of a CD – entirely acoustic, as is all Jabali's music. Beautiful harmonies, flowing percussion and brilliant sound quality. Vocals are a cross between choir and work (or play) songs and percussion includes various African drums, congas, bells and shakers, as well as drum kit.

Ochieng' Kabaselleh & the Luna Kidi Band

Kabaselleh (d.1998), from the area around Lake Victoria, was a great Kenyan bandleader whose music was always a little bit different – an interesting mix of Luo benga, Swahili rumba, and Congolese influences.

 Sanduku ya Mapendo (Equator Heritage Sounds, US).

Thiis collection of five double-sided singles from the 1980s is a fine example of Kabaelleh's fusion of benga, rumba, and soukous, with superb guitar, some tasteful horns and sax, and long tantalising grooves. Beware that it is hugely preferable to **From Nairobi with Love** (Equator Heritage Sounds, US), which lacks almost all of its musical variation, and has annoyingly saccharine keyboards.

Fundi Konde

One of Kenya's renowned early guitarists and the creator of many of what Kenyans consider classics, Konde's heyday was the 1950s but he was rediscovered by Kenyans forty years later through his collaboration with Them Mushrooms in new releases of his music. Recently, he has enjoyed another renaissance performing with the Tanzanian veteran musicians, Shikamoo Jazz.

 Fundi Konde Retrospective Vol. 1 (1947-56) (RetroAfric, UK).

Enticing, historical Kenyan pop from one of the country's most famous guitarists and singer-songwriters. Many of his tunes are rumbas, though a couple sound like reggae precursors. Imagine a vocal line like a mellow, two-part "Chattanooga Choo Choo"; add a smooth, jazzy electric guitar, bass and clarinet and you have the ingredients for the typical Konde recipe.

Les Wanyika

Les (pronounced 'lace') Wanyika were the last of the great Swahili rumba bands in the 'Wanyika' lineage, dating back to the early 1970s. They have been one of Kenya's most

creative groups since 1978, when they were formed by John Ngereza out of Simba Wanyika. Sadly, most of the other founding members, including the superb rhythm guitarist and composer 'Professor' Omari, have now died.

 Amigo (Clifford Lugard Productions, US).

After years of hits on cassette and LP, John Ngereza's band have finally broken through with a CD of classic Swahili rumba with the great guitar interweave and some very cool horn/sax combinations. Old numbers include such famous tunes as "Sina Makosa", "Pamela", "Paulina", "Afro" and "Nimaru". You can check out their early sound on *Kenya Dance Mania* (see 'Compilations' above).

The Magazines Band

Originally from Nairobi, this quartet migrated to the coast in 1992 to play in the Malindi and Watamu tourist hotels.

 Muche Marinda (Kelele, Germany).

Talented musicians play upbeat music with local flavour and plenty of international pop influences.

Henry Makobi

Makobi is renowned for superb finger-picking guitar – a form rarely recorded since the 1950s.

 New Memories: Guitar Music from Kenya (MW Records, Netherlands).

Recorded in 1991 in a Nyahururu hotel room, Makobi brings the finger-picking era alive with his fine renditions of old George Mukabi, Losta Abelo, Ben Blastus, John Mwale and Jean Bosco songs.

Ali Mula Maneno & Grand Magoma

Ali Maneno grew up in Morogoro in Tanzania, the home of East Africa's most famous musician, Mbaraka Mwinshehe (see Tanzania). He joined Mbaraka's band, Morogoro Jazz, on leaving school and went on to develop his skills in several other Tanzanian bands. In 1985, he moved to Nairobi, playing with Les Volcano, one of Mbaraka's successor groups. By 1987, he had released his first LP with the Nairobi-based group, Isse Isse and since 1991, he has led various versions of his own group, Grand Magoma.

 Zetty (Equator Heritage Sounds, US).

Ali Maneno's first CD release is a cross between classic East African rumba and the contemporary Congolese sound, with keyboards mimicking horns in the style of Quatre Etoiles or Soukous Stars, while the guitar retains the local element of delicate detail. Varied and musically interesting songs are complemented by a refreshingly raw sound, aided in part by guitars that can't quite stay in tune and Ali's appealingly raspy, unpolished voice. With heavy bass and solid rhythm, this is great dance music.

Samba Mapangala & Orchestre Virunga

From their early days at the famous Starlight Club to their triumphant stint at Nairobi's Garden Square, Orchestre Virunga have long been one of Kenya's most exciting groups and Samba one of the most gifted talents in Kenya. Since the early 1990s when he disbanded his group, he has moved back and forth between the low-tech, essentially live, Kenyan sound using East African musicians and a more hi-tech Paris-soukous style, with keyboards and programmed percussion.

Virunga Volcano
(Earthworks/Stern's, UK).

Although not representative of Kenyan music, the band's first CD was in a class of its own – the perfect album. Six, superbly crafted songs, each like a story allowed to develop over a ten-minute period, exploring different combinations of rhythm, melody, and harmony right through to the finish. As fresh and enticing today as it was when first released on vinyl back in the early 1980s.

Feet On Fire (Stern's Africa, UK).

First-rate Samba Mapangala in the East African groove, recorded on the 1991 UK tour.

Vunja Mifupa (Lusam, US).

Samba's latest CD is almost as good as *Virunga Volcano*. Five songs were recorded in 1996, the other three in Paris back in 1989. They are in the vein of the group's earlier Nairobi recordings: great guitars, driving rhythms, and the superb saxes of Rama Athumani and Twahir Mohamed. It's soukous alright, but the sweet East African version. Listen out for "Wabingwa", with cute little guitar riffs evolving throughout its nine minutes.

D.O. Misiani & Shirati Jazz

One of the founding fathers of benga, Daniel Owino Misiani has been doing this so long – still playing after more than thirty years – it's probably time to refer to him as a grandfather.

Benga Blast! (Earthworks/Stern's, UK)

A fine collection of songs from the definitive name in Luo benga, this presents the rough, unpolished sound of the old Pioneer House studios – and, yes, it's in mono.

Piny Ose Mer/The World Upside Down (GlobeStyle, UK).

An original GlobeStyle recording made in Nairobi – clean, polished, and stereo. While the musical content is pure Shirati, the mix is unusual for the group.

Ayub Ogada

Ayub Ogada has been exploring and bridging cultural boundaries over the last two decades, mingling cultures in his musical productions at Nairobi's French Cultural Centre in the 1970s, in the renowned African Heritage Band, which he co-founded in 1979, and in the London scene with the group Taxi Pata Pata in 1986. He is still at it today, giving solo performances on the *nyatiti*, the traditional Luo harp.

En Mana Kuoyo (RealWorld, UK).

A quiet, largely acoustic CD with beautiful melodies and captivating rhythms that starts with nyatiti, praise songs and local rhythms. "Chiro" is a new rendering of the popular and lively Kenyan tune "Western Shilo" (performed by Daudi Kabaka and George Agade's on *Before Benga Vol 2* – see 'Compilations', above).

Original Zengela Band

The Original Zengela are a bit of a mystery group from the Kenya coast: seven members, all of them unknown in Nairobi and other places upcountry.

Original Zengela Band (Kelele, Germany).

Classic Swahili rumba, with great interlocking guitars and bass meshing with flowing rhythmic grooves, displaying a kinship with the Wanyika groups, though a couple of the tunes are delightfully reminiscent of the great Equator Sound Band era. First-rate production – pity the songs aren't longer.

George Ramogi & CK Dumbe Dumbe Jazz Band

Since the early 1960s, George Ramogi has helped fashion the sound of Luo pop with his benga and rumba styles. He started the Luo Sweet Band in 1965, later renaming it the Continental Kilo (CK) Jazz Band. The nucleus of the group performed together, on and off, right up to Ramogi's death in 1997 at the age of 52.

1994 USA Tour-Safari ya Ligingo.
(Dumbe Dumbe Records, US).

In 1994, a group of US Kenyans pooled their resources to fly Ramogi and band over to perform. The recording isn't very polished, perhaps, but authentic benga none the less, with moments of greatness.

Simba Wanyika Original

Simba Wanyika were one of Kenya's favourite Swahili rumba bands from the early 1970s up until they stopped in 1995, after the deaths of both founding brothers, George and Wilson Peter Kinyonga.

 Pepea
(Kameleon Records, Holland; Stern's, UK).

Although they recorded many albums in Kenya, this 1992 release, recorded in Holland, is Simba Wanyika's only solo CD. It's superbly produced, allowing the band to shine on some of their biggest hits of the previous two decades. Highly recommended.

Them Mushrooms

Them Mushrooms have sprouted in several forms over their twenty-five-plus years, starting as a reggae band then working international pop sounds together with local chakacha into their music for a ten-year stint on the coastal hotel circuit. Now based in Nairobi, they're also active in music production with their own Mushrooms sound studio. The early 1990s found them in interesting collaborations with other Kenyan artists such as Malika, Jane Nyambura, and Fundi Konde.

Them Mushrooms (Rags Music, UK).

After the first two songs, "Jambo Bwana" and "Mushroom Soup", a set of remakes of classic Kenyan tunes from the 1950s and '60s. Popular in Kenya with those who grew up with this music, it's beginning to sound pretty cheesy to the rest of the world now.

Kazi Ni Kazi (Kelele Records, Germany).

Mushrooms in reggae mode, and they certainly sound at home. A CD of mainstream material with lots of catchy numbers and lyrics dealing with everything from women's rights and Rwanda to Italian style, the wonders of Dubai, or inviting their "Swiss Lady" to come to Africa.

Victoria Kings

Victoria Kings were one of the great benga groups from Luo-land. They started in the 1970s with Ochieng Nelly as bandleader and, joined by long-time musical partner Collela Mazee, became one of the top-selling recording groups of the benga's golden age in the late 1970s and early '80s.

The Mighty Kings of Benga (GlobeStyle, UK).

A different perspective on benga (ie not Shirati Jazz) and a very good compilation of energy-packed hits.

Madagascar

ocean music from southeast africa

When the island of Madagascar broke away from East Africa many millions of years ago to exist in relative isolation in the Indian Ocean, it prepared the way not only for separate evolution of its unique fauna and flora, but eventually for a distinct cultural development as well. Just as the geography of this huge 'island continent' (it's 1600km long, two-and-a-half times the area of Britain, half as big again as California) can vary from rain forest to thorny cactus desert, from high, barren mountains to palm-fringed beaches, so the culture is multifaceted, with around eighteen distinct tribes. The music sounds like everywhere and nowhere else at the same time, and **Ian Anderson**, who has been married into it for nearly a decade, knows he's still only scratching the surface.

Madagascar is an island of puzzles and surprises. Even around the capital, the varied landscape and architecture could convince you that you were in central Europe, or West Africa, or the high Andes, or maybe Asia with its terraced rice fields. You look at the people and they could possibly be Indonesian, Asian, African or South American. Then you hear the music, which contains little clues, passing sounds, harmonies, riffs, playing styles and instruments that all seem to be related to other parts of the world. But it is audibly unique.

The island's earliest inhabitants, the Vazimba, were of Malayo-Polynesian origin (as is the consonant-rich Malagasy language), arriving, from the third century AD, via southeast Asia and East Africa rather than directly across the Indian Ocean. There are still some distant cultural connections with parts of Indonesia and these racial origins explain the almost Polynesian harmonies that are found in the music of the Merina, the highland people. Undoubtedly more can be traced back to the slave trade, Arab sailors, Welsh missionaries and the long period of French colonisation. The proximity of East Africa and its airwaves has had a strong influence, too, notably on the coastal styles of electric guitar dance music called **watcha watcha** (in the northwest) and tsapika (in the southwest) which are first cousins of **Kenyan benga** and **South African township music** respectively.

But that still doesn't explain why the musicians who accompany the travelling players called **hiragasy** – the most popular of current troupes being the Ramilison, Razafindramanga and Rakoto Kavia – so puzzlingly resemble Mexican street bands, or display a myriad of other connections to anywhere and everywhere. Has all the music in the world bumped into Madagascar at some time in history? Or did it all start here and wander off somewhere else?

Highland Hitmakers

In the 1960s a Malagasy pop group called **Les Surfs** had a string of French chart hits with Francophone covers of Spector and Beatles songs. But they were a one off, and the first major modern group in Madagascar was **Mahaleo**. Emerging at a time of student unrest in the early 1970s, they fused Western soft-rock with typical Malagasy harmonies, rhythms and traditional instruments like the *kabosy*.

IAN ANDERSON

Rossy – modern and multi-talented

Combined with complex, meaningful lyrics addressing many aspects of the lives of Malagasy people, their music became enormously popular and their songs known by everybody. Though no longer a full-time band, they occasionally re-form for big concerts. Their leader, Dama, is still a strong musical force, though his music career is somewhat restricted by his role as an elected government deputy.

Following Mahaleo's lead came multi-instrumentalist Paul Bert Rahasimanana, otherwise known as **Rossy**, who formed the group that bears his nickname. They became the most successful band of the 1980s, touring in Europe and evolving a dynamic, fairly hi-tech stage act that mixed roots styles from the island with the latest trends in the world's music. Rossy is skilled at tailoring things to the audience: European pop, Johnny Clegg and zouk influences for the home crowd, where they have a following from all echelons of society, and conversely a more Malagasy roots repertoire abroad. The band remain powerful at home – the re-emergence as an elected president of former dictator Ratsiraka, for whom Rossy has publicly campaigned, is unlikely to harm this – but have somewhat disappeared from the international stage in recent years.

In the 1990s, the biggest name – on the international circuit and recently with a series of hits at home, too – has been **Tarika** ('group'), who emerged in 1994 following a split in the well-respected folk revival band, **Tarika Sammy**. Fronted, unusually, by women – sisters **Hanitra Rasoanaivo** and **Noro Raharimala** – this younger band mix the instruments and styles from other areas and tribes with the distinctive,

melodic vocal harmonies of the Merina, incorporating the results into a live act high on energy and visual impact. Their three albums to date are notable for songs, particularly those written by leader Hanitra, which combine controversial and hard-hitting political subject matter with upbeat, danceable music. Tarika have been Madagascar's most successful musical export in recent years, topping World Music charts and touring extensively on the European and North American club, concert and festival circuits.

Another important contemporary group are **Solo Miral**, who play a music they call *vakojazzana* – a fusion of *vakodrazana* traditional music and jazz. They are a quintet of, mainly, brothers and their leader, Haja, is a staggering and totally original electric guitarist in marovany style, one of Madagascar's best. The hardworking members of Solo Miral are also often seen in other bands, in demand to accompany many of Madagascar's domestic superstars. International recognition, long-overdue, has eluded them, although they showcased at the 1997 *Womex* (the annual World Music industry-fest) in France and finally completed their first album in nearly two decades – one of the best modern Malagasy recordings to date and deservedly one of the few to get domestic release on CD as well as cassette.

With local newspaper headlines like 'Rickymania!', **Ricky** (Randimbiarison) has been in the spotlight for years, though his uncompromising career approach always denied him international recognition and his first record deal only came in 1998. Malagasy singing is usually at its strongest in harmony but Ricky is one of the island's best ever solo vocalists. Locally, he often works with an electric band who include the finest musicians in town, particularly **Tôty**, who pioneered an extraordinary bass guitar style based on the marovany, and some of the members of Solo Miral. Abroad, Ricky has toured with marovany player Matrimbala and a cappella group Salala, but his more typical work is revealed in all its glory on the recent MELT 2000 album *Olombelona Ricky*.

IAN ANDERSON

Malagasy roots quintet, Tarika

Traditional Instruments

Traditional instruments are a major feature of Malagasy roots bands – and they are stunning in their variety and imagination, both in look and sound.

The most famous instrument is the **valiha**, a tubular zither made from drainpipe-diameter bamboo with around 21 strings running lengthways all around the circumference, lifted and tuned by small, moveable pieces of calabash. Traditionally the strings were strands of bamboo skin lifted from the surface but nowadays they tend to be unbraided bicycle-brake cable, giving a sound similar to a harp or the West African *kora*. The leading player is **Sylvestre Randafison**, an almost-classical virtuoso who was once a member of the celebrated traditional music ensemble Ny Antsaly, the first Malagasy group to tour extensively abroad. Other masters include **Zeze** (Zeze Ravelonandro, who died in 1992), **Tovo**, **Rajery**, Paris-based **Justin Vali** (Justin Rakotondrasoa), and the late **Mama Oana**, an incredible old singer from the west coast who wore coins braided into her hair and attacked her instrument with the ferocity of a Mississippi blues guitarist.

Madagascar's other zither is the **marovany**, a suitcase-like wooden box with two sets of strings on opposing sides. One of the best and most influential players was the late, legendary **Rakotozafy**, but once again it's a common traditional instrument, particularly in the south. Virtuosos abound among traditional players, including Masikoro musician **Bekamby**, Tulear's **Madame Masy**, **Matrimbala** from the Antandroy tribe and younger city players like Tarika's **Donné Randriamanantena**.

The traditional, end-blown flute is the **sodina**, whose undisputed master is **Rakoto Frah**. A charming old man with an impish twinkle in his eye, he has represented Madagascar all over the world and his picture appeared on the local 1000-franc banknote. However, he still lives in a tiny house in Isotry, the capital's poorest area.

The **kabosy** (also known as *mandoliny* in the southwest) is a small guitar with four to six strings and partial frets. It's a relatively easily made instrument – the body is often just a rectangular box and the strings fishing line or those unbraided bicycle-brake cables – but it's played to a high standard. It's not uncommon to encounter small groups of boys on street corners

or country roadsides playing with the drive of electric guitar bands, sometimes even including a larger, bass version. The best-known exponents are **Jean Emilien** – who, like many other players, also utilises harmonica on a neck rack – and **Babata** from the west coast.

The **jejy voatavo**, mostly used by the Betsileo tribe, has a large calabash resonator, a neck with huge block frets and two courses of strings on ninety-degree opposed sides. Its sound can be reminiscent of the Appalachian dulcimer.

Finally, the **lokanga** is a three-string fiddle, once again often with a simply made box-style body, played mainly by the Bara and Antandroy tribes from the south.

Imported instruments have also been adapted for local use. The **accordion** is found all over, if less so these days because of difficulties in getting spare parts

Traditional flautist in the money

for repairs. The most famous younger player, **Regis Gizavo**, now resides in Europe. The **piano** has long been an upper-class favourite for accompanying choral singing, and **guitars** are found everywhere. Along with fiddle and accordion, it's **brass and woodwind** instruments that are the characteristic sounds for the hiragasy, the popular mixture of street theatre, oration, opera and dance. The same brass players make the joyful noise for Madagascar's extraordinary *famadihana* or re-burial ceremonies.

'Tourist' instruments, especially *valiha* and *jejy voatavo*, are offered for sale in the markets, hotels and on the street. But if you're visiting Madagascar and in the market for musical instruments, beware. They look pretty hanging on the wall but they are rarely very playable (and often harbour fearsome Malagasy woodworm). It's better to seek out and buy from a good musician or instrument-maker. There's a notable shop run by musician Rajery at Lot IVP3ter Ankadifotsy, Tana 101, or you can contact Valiha High, a training scheme for young musicians that is in touch with local makers, c/o Lot VR 103 Fenomanana, Tana 101, ☎22 60202.

Half-green and Salegy

The electric dance band music called **watcha watcha**, similar to Kenyan benga, comes from the northwestern coastal region (which like Tulear in the south receives clear mainland African radio signals) and is popular in places like Mahajanga. But the island has a number of other modern dance styles, including the lilting **sega** (also common in nearby Mauritius) and most characteristic and omnipresent of all, the driving 6/8 **salegy** rhythm. This is heard all over Madagascar, though the electric version is generally connected to the north, particularly the Sakalava people in Diego Suarez and Mahajanga.

Back in the 1970s, there was a thriving record industry in Madagascar, in the course of which hundreds of salegy and watcha watcha seven-inch singles of vibrant dance music were produced, some of which reputedly sold over 60,000 copies. But the last local singles were pressed by Disco-Mad in the mid-1980s. The record plants closed in the deteriorating economic climate, and masters have been lost or destroyed. Now, even in the capital, you can barely find a few very scratchy, secondhand copies on market stalls. Yet singles by **Orchestre Liberty**, **Jaojoby**, **Jean Fredy** or **Abdallah** rivalled the recordings of famous bands from mainland Africa. Many have a distinct Malagasy style, a few directly absorbing East African and South African sounds (particularly those produced by the influential **Charles Maurin Poty**).

There was a hiatus in the late 1980s and early 1990s when that whole genre of music – known colloquially as **tapany maintso** (half-green) because of the half-green labels of the old, long-defunct Kaiamba label which produced the wildest of these discs – was in danger of vanishing into undocumented history. But as production changed to cassettes, eventually a new generation of recordings came onto the market, and in 1992 Jaojoby was recorded in Madagascar for a Western-label CD, and **Tianjama** (ex-Orchestre Liberty) made the first successful new salegy cassettes in the classic style for Mars (DiscoMad's successor).

These days there are more and more regular local cassette releases by names like **JB & Batmen Music**, **Mily Clement**, the heavily soukous-influenced **Dedesse,** the wildly raw **Lazan'i Maroantsetra** and the first female salegy star **Ninie**. Whilst touring regularly in Europe, Jaojoby has recorded several more CDs for Indigo in France, and in 1998, as CDs finally made sufficient inroads into the local market, Mars released a great compilation of current bands. So salegy finally made it to the CD generation.

Kaiamba label, "half-green" singles

THOMAS DORN

Njava

Sounds of the South

Although Madagascar is theoretically united by a national language, in practice tribal cultural differences are quite profound and have been maintained by vast distances and poor communications – a journey by road from the central capital to Tulear in the southwest takes several days, and national radio transmissions cannot penetrate the mountains. In Tulear, as in many distant population centres, the only way to get a tape distributed is often to record it yourself and give it to the many street-market bootleggers to copy and copy again. The omnipresent sound is of **tsapika**.

Leading local bands playing tsapika include **Orchestre Rivo-Doza**, **Tsodrano** and **Safo-Drano**. Their unmistakeable Malagasy groove is layered with blockbuster township drive, whilst lead guitarists scatter dazzling, fractured lines over the top of full-scream female voices.

Tulear was also the place where **D'Gary** grew up – a stunning guitarist who has evolved a complex style based on the sound of the marovany and other local instruments like the lokanga bara. Many consider that he surpasses other African acoustic guitar greats such as Ali Farka Touré or Jean Bosco Mwenda, First recorded by Mars in the early 1990s, he has released a series of increasingly excellent albums into the international market for some years now on French label Indigo.

Njava, a family band from the Antemoro tribe in the southeast of Madagascar, have come a long way in recent times. Evolving from a fairly dull electric band, they relocated to Belgium, went

Famadihana: Reburial Parties

The Malagasy people have enormous respect for their ancestors, who are considered to exist still on a spiritual level. This is reflected in the huge amount of money that an extended family will invest in their tomb – sometimes a far more substantial dwelling than the house for the living – based on the logical theory that the amount of time to be spent there will eventually be far greater than the insignificant period of passage through the mortal world. A man is traditionally entombed in his native village, whilst a woman will be buried with her in-laws.

Equally large amounts of money – sometimes stretching a family's resources to the limits – are spent on the traditional **famadihana** or re-burial parties. These are not held at fixed intervals: perhaps a person may have expressed a wish as to frequency before their death, or a living relative may receive a hint from the ancestor that the tomb is cold and they need new

clothes. The event will last a whole day and involves much feasting, drinking, dancing and merry-making by the entire extended family and local village. Musicians, usually a hiragasy troupe playing instruments like trumpets, clarinets and drums that can be heard above a rowdy crowd outdoors, will be hired to play nonstop to drive the affair on. The party will process to the tomb, disinter the remains of the loved one, rewrap them in fresh cloth (traditionally known as *lamba mena* – red cloth – even though it is rarely red these days), carry them around the area on their shoulders to see the new local sights, provide them with food and drink, and finally put them back to rest, resealing the tomb.

The whole affair is totally joyous, not the least bit macabre, and the music is wild and glorious. Outsiders – if officially invited – can be made very welcome. The best time of the year for maximum famadihana yield is September.

Malagasy Guitar: A Word with Bouboul

There is no single, uniform Malagasy guitar style. Between the almost mainland African lead guitars of the electric salegy and watcha-watcha bands from the north, through courtly, classical highland plateau playing with echoes of nineteenth-century parlour music, Hawaiian slack key and ragtime, to the dauntingly dense flurries of the marovany-inclined players like D'Gary, N'Java's Dozzy, Solo Miral's Haja and the tsapika players from the southwest, there are major gulfs.

Etienne Ramboatiana, aka **'Bouboul'**, is a legend among Malagasy musicians. He was Madagascar's first electric guitarist in the early 1950s, and later toured the world with a circus. Now a captivating, sparkling-eyed gentleman in his sixties, he is a mine of information that could fill a book about the history of the guitar in Madagascar and the origins of the high plateau style in Antananarivo. The following is a short extract from an interview with Ramboatiana on the subject of Malagasy guitar, first published in *Folk Roots* magazine, in April 1998.

"As we all know, the guitar is a foreign instrument but in the time of Ranavalona III [the last Queen of Madagascar], the guitar, viola, 'flûte traversière' and mandolin all arrived together. The vazaha played those instruments and people just watched. We realised that the guitar was only an accompaniment to the mandolin. So the Malagasy wanted the guitar to be independent. We wanted it to sing a song not to only accompany. The Malagasy sang in harmony a lot, with breathing technique and lots of melodies, so we wanted the guitar to do all these. The Malagasy guitar style was born!

"There was a competitive spirit because of the piano. The piano was brought here before the guitar by missionaries and its place was always in the royal court. In La Haute Ville, people had piano, while 'les grand bourgeois', in Ambatovinaky and Faravohitra, had harmonium, saxophone and accordion, and in Ambodin'Isotry [the poor part of Antananarivo] they had the guitar wizards. If you went down still further, what you would find in people's homes were traditional instruments.

"When people down here heard that the piano made a really high sound, they put the capo on their guitars. When there was a very bassy sound they changed the bass strings by re-tuning it into C and G to get what we call today Malagasy style. I changed my bass string into D because it's just too much to change it to C. In Antananarivo, some people would even change that string into a piano wire to get that big bass note.

"Since the piano was used for theatrical pieces, that's what guitarists translated onto their guitars. In 1942, these guitarists would go out serenading. They wore caps, big clothes and scarves, and girls would come out. They had to stop around Faravohitra because if they continued upwards, they would get soaked because people from La Haute would throw dirty water on them. La Haute is a piano place. Faravohitra was the highest area a guitarist could go up to and then they had to go back to Ambodin'Isotry where they came from.

"If you really want to find out about the Malagasy guitar style, it came from the way the Malagasy played the piano, but the piano was only copying the valiha. So the valiha is the origin of it all, then on to the piano and then on to the guitar.

"Things changed around about the second world war. The Malagasy got some style out of Charlie Kunz's songs, a German who ran away to England. Then Randrianarivelo arrived. He brought another style of guitar. Then I arrived. One day, around 1951, Harry Hougassian, a Hawaiian guitar-player and Mounitz (a Jewish player) played here in Madagascar. I was really taken by their whole way of playing. Harry played one of those guitars you put on your lap and slide it across and Mounitz accompanied him. [Hougassian was a celebrated Armenian player of the Hawaiian guitar, still alive and now running a restaurant in Paris]. Every time a new guitarist arrived and brought a new style, others just took an inspiration from it."

acoustic and back to their traditional roots. They were one of the hits of the 1995 Brussels *Womex*, with a very professional showcase that won them many fans, a lot of subsequent festival work, and the attention of legendary Japanese producer **Makoto Kubota** (whose credits include work for Shoukichi Kina, Sandii and Detty Kurnia) for their debut album released in 1997.

Regis Gizavo is Madagascar's best accordion player. With a formidable reputation already in the bag before winning the RFI *Decouvertes* and

emigrating to France in 1990, he developed a sophisticated technique on the chromatic button accordion, working sessions with Manu Dibango, Ray Lema, Les Têtes Brulées and Corsica's I Muvrini before finally launching his solo career with a debut album in 1997.

Tirike are the best-known tsapika band on the island. Their music hurtles along at a frantic pace, with call-and-response lyrics driven by some great marovany-styled electric guitar, flutey/township keyboards and really tight, kicking bass and drums.

MADAGASCAR

A B C D E F G H I J K L

Their 1995 cassette was Mars' biggest seller of that year, though oddly the national label hasn't delved much further into the tsapika genre.

Tsimihole are a powerful group playing the music of the Antandroy people from the far south, and very influential – often copied, but rarely bettered. They were one of the first Malagasy acts to have released independent tapes, though they're quite hard to find.

Salala are another Antandroy group. Usually an a cappella trio with strong vocal harmonies – including a lead singer who could be ranked alongside Aaron Neville – they also sometimes appear as part of an eight-piece band. Their line-up has fluctuated in recent years, but they have still managed to release CDs on German and French labels and to tour Europe on occasions.

Poopy Pop and Beyond

What happened with music in Madagascar in the late 1980s and 1990s was a mirror on the whole culture. With the opening up of the economy, TV beamed Western styles into the wealthier homes, while the rich few, making their shopping pilgrimages to Paris, brought back synthesisers, drum machines and European fashion. *Vita Gasy* (Made in Madagascar) had become synonymous with 'worthless'.

A new breed emerged of rich-kid pop stars and artists with wealthy patrons. They included Europop chanteuses with names like **Bodo**, **Poopy**, **Landy**, **Mbolatina** and **Tiana**; a style of bubblegum salegy (all Mickey Mouse synths and drum machines); and embarrassing mainstream rock bands like **Apostol Rock**, **Kadradraka 2000** (Cockroach 2000), **Tselatra** and **Green**.

These days, nearly a decade after the years of isolation ended, it is still the height of chic to ape all things European and especially American, and the standard multi-national hits soon find their way onto local radio. Judging by the piped music in hotel restaurants in the more remote parts of Madagascar, it sometimes seems as if this is where old rock albums go to die.

Some artists managed to retain a Malagasy character in their music better than others. Charles Maurin Poty's protégés **Feon'ala** and regional groups like **Zaza Club** from Tulear and **Clo Mahajanga** all released better-than-average tapes. **Tata Rahely**, a female singer once in D'Gary's band, was making a very good job of it, sadly cut short by her death in 1999. At the time of writing, the hottest-selling tape was by **Samoela**, a younger singer-songwriter straight out of the Dama/Mahaleo Malagasy soft-rock mould, but with altogether racier lyrics that have polarised local audiences to his benefit.

Back to the Roots

In the early 1990s, it looked for a while like curtains for Malagasy roots. However, outside influence has had a beneficial effect. The catalyst was GlobeStyle Records' 1985 recording trip which produced two classic compilations that set the stylistic and artistic agenda for other Western producers. Among these were the Henry Kaiser and David

Where to Hear Music in Tana

Finding live music in Madagascar is a hit-and-miss affair. There are concerts – often open-air – in the summer months, but on the whole it's hard to plan to hear music. You may run into traditional performances unexpectedly in the streets, as part of a ceremony or celebration, or simply in someone's home; or you might take a daytrip and accidentally encounter wild village ceremonies with full-tilt electric bands, and kabosy players or hiragasy musicians strolling by the roadside.

In **Tana**, Madagascar's capital, there's a more of an established infrastructure. A good bar venue for salegy bands is the funky *Hotel Glacier* in the Avenue de l'Indépendance, run by Charles Maurin Poty. More formal concerts take place at the *Roxy Cinema*, *Centre Culturel Albert Camus* in Analakely, the *Cercle Germano-Malagas*, also in Analakely (at the foot of the steps leading to Antaninarenina) and at the newly built

Alliance Français (Ampefiloha Andavamamba). Restaurants and hotels such as *La Résidence* (Ankadindramano Ankerana), *Le Palmier* (Ankadilalana Tsimbazaza), *Misty* (Antsakarivo), *Le Chapiteau* (Ankorondrano), *Le Damier* (Ankadimbahoaka Androndra), *Hotel Rubis* (Ankorahotra Ampasanimalo) and *Caf' Art* (Ambatonakanga) are worth keeping an eye on.

Oddly enough, the best bets for a good selection of original (ie non-pirate) **cassettes and CDs** of local music are the growing number of huge supermarkets that have opened up for the better-off – and you compensate for their higher prices by the diminished likelihood of having your pockets picked, as may well happen in the street markets. You can find a good range at *Magri*, *Géant Score*, *Conquette* and *Champion* (near the central Post Office in Antaninarenina), and stock up on other fine Malagasy produce at the same time.

Lindley recording, *A World Out Of Time* (1992), on which the American guitarists played local material with many of the island's leading and emerging roots musicians.

In the wake of all this, the 1990s saw a considerable amount of international touring, recording by European and American labels, and festival appearances, spearheaded by **Tarika**, **D'Gary**, the **Justin Vali Trio**, **Njava**, **Jaojoby** and **Regis Gizavo**. Back home, the message that the West liked all this music helped to reinvest pride in the culture. Traditionally rooted musicians could, suddenly, not only aim to make a living from music (something almost unheard of before) but travel abroad as well. So the musical climate changed again: at the end of the long national strike in early 1992, one local newspaper pointed out that while Madagascar was in desperate straits, at least Malagasy musicians were achieving something in the wider world.

Madagascar's musical individuality is certainly not at risk any more. As artists go out and enjoy success around the world, playing Malagasy roots music, even the snobby rich are beginning to think that Malagasy culture is okay after all. The Malagasy haven't yet got their equivalent of a Youssou N'Dour or Thomas Mapfumo – a national superstar making new music out of traditional styles that translates to the international market. But surely on a huge island where the most important people are your ancestors, can it really be impossible to preserve your roots?

Thanks to Hanitrarivo Rasoanaivo

discography

Amazingly, there are now well over 100 CDs available of Malagasy music and the task of recommending a selection gets ever harder. You can find a complete non-annotated listing at *www.froots.demon.co.uk/madagcd.html* but the following are particularly worthy of investigation.

Note that the review (and star-rating) of the Tarika album below is the opinion of the editor of this book. The author of this article, Ian Anderson, being married to the group's leader, opted out.

Compilations

 Big Red: Music of Madagascar (Nascente/MCI, UK).

This is an essential, budget-priced sampler of Malagasy sounds, featuring most of the contemporary bands mentioned in this article. Released in 1999, it covers styles from solo marovany, valiha and kabosy to tsapika, salegy and vakojazzana.

 Destination Madagascar (Mars, France/Madagascar).

In contrast to the more traditional content of many of the available Malagasy compilations, this is an across-the-board selection of current and recent hits from the only national label. High on salegy (notably Jaojoby, Jean Fredy, Ninie and Jidhe) and local pop, it is a disc made in Madagascar for the Malagasy.

Les Grands Maîtres Du Salegy (Sonodisc, France).

Skittering, up-tempo 6/8 pumped out by bands with guitars, keyboards, bass, drums and percussion, all made for local consumption and culled from releases by the only national record label. Lazan'i Maroantsetra, Tianjama, Liberty, JB & Batmen Music, Pascal & Jidhe and more. The sound of Madagascar dancing!

Madagasikara One: Current Traditional Music
Madagasikara Two: Current Popular Music
(GlobeStyle, UK).

GlobeStyle's two anthologies, recorded by Ben Mandelson and Roger Armstrong in 1985, led the way for most other Western recordists' activities later on. Featured names included Rossy, Tarika Sammy, Mahaleo, Rakoto Frah, Zeze, and salegy band Les Smokers. Both sets sound just as fresh today as ever, and have excellent notes.

Madagaskar 1: Music From Antananarivo
Madagaskar 2: Music Of The South
Madagaskar 3: Valiha: Sounding Bamboo
Madagaskar 4: Music Of The North
(Feuer & Eis, Germany).

After GlobeStyle, next to hit the field was the first of these four fine thematic acoustic sets from Birger Gesthuisen's label, now also available as a boxed set. Vol 1 introduced the best of remarkable kabosy player Jean Emilien and featured more Rossy, Sammy, and Rakoto Frah & Zeze together as Kalaza. Vol 2 went on to showcase the intriguing southern traditions which GlobeStyle hadn't been able to reach, while Vol 3 collected together the very best players of the valiha, notably Sylvestre Randafison, the stunning Tovo and the last recordings of Zeze. Vol 4 again fills previously undocumented areas with some exceptional recordings of Sakalava rapping and unique instrumentalists.

Madagascar Open Notes – Fruits De Voyages (Musikela, France).

Another two-CD set, one of current tracks by first-rate roots musicians including a particularly fine duet by Ricky and Solo Razafindrakoto, the other of field recordings from 1959-63. A good tour d'horizon of Madagascan sounds.

The Marovany Of Madagascar (Auvidis/Silex, France).

Staggering, pulse-quickening playing of the local box zither, well-recorded in the field, centred on the amazing Madame Masy and Bekamby.

The Music Of Madagascar: Music Of The Coast And Tablelands 1929-31 (Fremeaux, France).

A double CD, well re-mastered from old 78s originally recorded in Madagascar, particularly featuring the golden age of valiha orchestras, singing troupes and some local field recordings. Plus excellent notes, rare photos, recording memorabilia and discographical info.

Prophet 6: Madagascar (Philips/Kora Sons, France).

Charles Duvelle field-recorded some excellent sets for the renowned Ocora label in the early 1960s, and this beautifully packaged compilation — some really classy photos and good bilingual notes – consists of previously unreleased gems from the same sessions. First class marovany, valiha, lokanga and jejy voatavo players, plus some superb examples of hiragasy troupes in full flight.

 **A World Out of Time –
Kaiser and Lindley in Madagascar** (Shanachie, US).

This 1992 recording saw the American guitar duo of Henry Kaiser and David Lindley playing an accompanying role to showcase many of the island greats – Rossy, Tarika Sammy, Rakoto Frah, Mahaleo, Mama Sana, D'Gary and Voninavoko.

Artists

Bemiray

Bemiray play hiragasy – the style of music which accompanies performances by troupes of travelling players.

 Polyphonies Des Hauts-Plateaux (Auvidis/Silex, France).

A really lively set, including some remarkable a cappella singing. Notice the inexplicable echoes of Mexico…

Dama

Dama, leader of the legendary band Mahaleo from the early 1970s, is now out on his own, both as a solo singer, and pursuing a political career.

 Mélodies De Madagascar (Playasound, France).

Beautiful, contemporary, acoustic-guitar singer-songwriter music.

D'Gary

The brilliant D'Gary is a guitarist with a dazzling technique based on the style of the marovany (box zither) and lokanga (local fiddle).

Mbo Loza (Label Bleu/Indigo, France).

D'Gary's third album displays his skills to the full.

Feogasy

Feogasy feature various veteran ex-members of Mahaleo and Lolo Sy Ny Tariny plus flute man Rakoto Frah.

Tsofy Rano (Les Nuits Atypiques/Melodie, France).

Showcases grand old-style highland harmonies and the guitar of Erick Manana.

Regis Gizavo

Regis Gizavo is the undisputed squeezebox boss of Madagascar, up there in the world rankings with the likes of Flaco Jimenez.

Mikea (Label Bleu/Indigo, France).

Named after his tribe, this CD features Regis accompanied by superb percussionist David Mirandon.

Jaojoby

Jaojoby is the king of kings of salegy and leads one of the world's great live bands – a recent WOMAD hit.

 Salegy!
(Xenophile, US).

The first Western-released salegy CD, rough'n'ready but including versions of all Jaojoby's greatest hits.

Njava

Njava are a family quintet from the southeast, now relocated in Belgium and a big success on the Euro-festival circuit.

 Vetse
(EMI Hemisphere, UK).

A 1999 re-package of their 1997 Japan-only debut, beautifully produced by Makoto Kubota, to bring out every nuance of Monika's soulful vocals and Dozzy's virtuoso guitar work.

Rakotozafy

Dubbed 'the Robert Johnson of Madagascar', Rakotozafy was an equally legendary, mysterious and toweringly influential marovany player – one of the most important figures in the recent history of Malagasy music.

 Valiha Malaza – Famous Valiha
(GlobeStyle, UK).

A lovingly prepared re-issue, taken from surviving Malagasy master tapes, and enhanced by Ben Mandelson's excellent sleeve notes.

Ricky Randimbiarison

One of Madagascar's most inspiring modern male singers, Ricky is backed by a first-rate team of players including influential bassist Tôty and members of Solo Miral.

Olombelona Ricky (MELT 2000, UK).

Tracks on this long-awaited international debut (produced by Airto Moreira) range from the out-and-out rootsy to some with a strong jazz rock influence, but it's all uncompromisingly Ricky.

Rossy

Madagascar's biggest star of the 1980s is a musical jack-of-all-trades, with an ability to mould all sorts of influences into music that remains his while consistently hitting the populist button.

 Island Of Ghosts
(RealWorld, UK).

This was a TV film soundtrack, but of the five CDs Rossy has available, it gives probably the most enjoyable across-the-board representation of his band's music.

Mama Sana

Mama Sana was a remarkable, utterly wild valiha player and a fearsome singer – with coins jingling in her hair.

The Legendary Mama Sana (Shanachie, US).

Undisputable proof of why she's a legend, and why it is such a tragedy she passed away before getting the chance to tour abroad.

Solo Miral

The band Solo Miral includes some of Madagascar's finest modern musicians, including the stupendous marovany-style guitarist Haja.

 Gasikara
(Mars, Madagascar).

The first album in 20 years by this renowned band features traditional instrumental sounds and local rhythms updated onto electric instruments with skill, taste and imagination. Truly, the bee's knees!

TARIKA : SON EGAL

Tarika

Formed out of Tarika Sammy (below), this multi-instrumental roots dance band is led by sisters Hanitra (Rasoanaivo) and Noro (Raharimalala). They have had huge success in Europe and the US with their albums and live shows, and in 1999 topped the Malagasy charts.

 Son Egal (Xenophile, US).

"A huge work of fire and zest, blending dance compositions for traditional instruments, guitar and electric bass with the passions of lead artist Hanitra in addressing the issues of Malagasy corruption and racism." *Richard Trillo, Editor*

Tarika Sammy

Tarika Sammy, featuring multi-instrumentalist Sammy Andriamalalaharijaona, emerged in the 1980s as a fine folk revival band of fluctuating personnel, first heard on the GlobeStyle anthologies. Their most successful line-up split in 1993, out of which emerged both Tarika (above) and another Tarika Sammy, led by Sammy.

 Beneath Southern Skies (Shanachie, US).

A highly enjoyable CD that shows Sammy's latest grouping returning to their gentler, earlier style.

Tianjama

Alongside Jaojoby, Tianjama is another major veteran from the golden age of salegy 45s, and still leading a great current band.

Best Of Tianjama (Mars, Madagascar/France).

Includes most of their recent hits from cassettes made for the home market.

Tirike

From the dry, thorny south, Tirike produce a bush-party sound quite different to that from the rest of the island, and one which became massively popular across the island in the mid-1990s.

Hot Tsapiky From The South Of Madagascar (Mars, France/Madagascar).

A wild electric band driven by speedy marovany-style electric guitar and, once again, compiled for CD from local masters.

Justin Vali

Valiha virtuoso Justin Vali is based in Paris, from where he continues to regale the world with his gifts.

The Sunshine Within (Bush Telegraph, UK).

Valli's latest, 1999 outing finds him on top form, exploring new styles as well as his usual energetic, almost classical approach to acoustic Malagasy roots music.

Malawi

sounds afroma!

Malawi was the country where visiting gentlemen were asked to shave off beards, ladies had to keep their skirts below the knee and everyone had to measure their jeans for signs of illegal flare. Until 1994. Then, a new, democratically elected government booted out the sagging, apartheid South African-aligned dictatorship of 'Life President' Hastings Banda. Though the poverty remains – this is a country where 'as heard on radio' is still more common than 'as seen on TV' – Malawi is once more a free and vibrant nation – and music is everywhere, as **John Lwanda** discovered.

One hundred and twenty years before the first CDs, in 1859, David Livingstone heard the xylophone music of southern Malawi and, with typical Scots enthusiasm described it as "wild and not unpleasant" – one of the first World Music reviews. Through the next century, this little country has had a strong, if underrated influence on Southern and East African music. You can hear Malawian strands in musicians as diverse as Jairos Jiri, Robson Banda, Dorothy Masuka and Devera Ngwena from Zimbabwe; Ray Phiri from South Africa; Sam Mangwana from Congo; and Alick Nkhata from Zambia, to name just a few. And despite its many problems – cassette piracy, a lack of studios, and a shortage of electric instruments – Malawi, itself, has strong traditions, and some individual and vibrant contemporary bands.

Banjos, Jazz and the Malawi Beat

Malawians are great travellers and have taken their music to every city from Nairobi to the Cape. Malawian soldiers served in Central and East African British battalions during World War II and, as well as spreading their music, a number brought back guitars and new musical ideas. From the late 1940s to the early 1960s Malawian **banjo and guitar** duos were a dominant dance format, usually with the banjo leading and the guitar playing rhythm. This style was followed in the late 1960s by South African **kwela** music, popularised by migrant workers returning from South Africa, and whose most notable exponent was **Daniel Kachamba and his Kwela Band**.

The next craze was '**jazz bands**', a tradition that remains very active. Malawian jazz is not exactly jazz in the Western sense. Bands are made up of rural or semi-rural popular musicians using acoustic instruments – imagine an acoustic Kanda Bongo Man or Shirati Jazz and you have an idea of their sounds – and musicians take a pragmatic attitude to instruments, using home-made or imported ones as need or affordability determine. Leading groups have included Alan Namoko's **Chimvu Jazz**, the **Jazz Giants**, the **Mulanje Mountain Band**, the **Mitoche Brothers**, the **Ndingo Brothers** and the **Linengwe River Band**. Alan Namoko, who died in 1995, was a great figure – a blind bluesman who turned out a stack of earthy roots music on acoustic banjo, guitar and percussion.

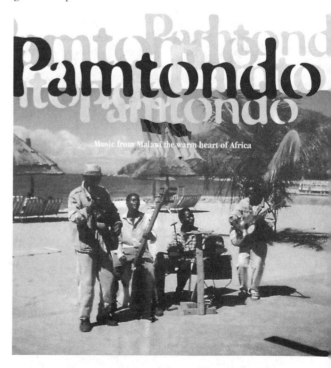

Pamtondo

Music from Malawi the warm heart of Africa

Ethnographer's Corner

Malawi is a small landlocked country dominated by the beautiful Lake Malawi. The country's eleven million inhabitants are packed into a largely rural 94,000 square kilometres – an area little larger than Scotland or Maine – but there are nine tribal and linguistic groups, of which the **Chewa** is the largest and the national lingua franca.

The ethnic diversity means that there are numerous **traditional dances and rhythms**. These include the Chewa and Nyanja masked *gule wa mkulu* (the big dance); the Ngoni's *ingoma* war dance; the *likwata* and the *beni* 'military' dance among the Yao; the highly stylised and chic *mganda* among the Tonga; *tchopa* among the Lomwe; the healing *vimbuza* of the Tumbuka and Henga; and the Nyanja's *likhuba* and *chitsukulumwe*.

Many local songs and dances were recorded in the 1940s and 50s by **Alick Nkhata** and **Hugh Tracey** (see p.669), and can still be heard in the villages today. A common source of such songs is **women at the mortar**. As they pound the staple maize their thumping produces various complex *pamtondo* rhythms which serve as the accompaniment to their songs of lament, blues, gossip or celebration. Popular musicians are influenced by these long-standing traditions and although most performers are male, many of the songs sung by young bands are pamtondo or *kumpanda* songs – music traditionally sung by women as they work or tend their children.

During the Banda period the most popular non-commercial music in Malawi was also created by women, the **mbumba** (women) music – songs of celebration and praise with drum accompaniment, based on traditional dances, sung at ruling party and state occasions and always carefully colour-coordinated. Mbumba was also played widely on the radio, but with Banda's demise it is now mostly heard on hawkers' cassettes. New political parties, however, are showing signs of introducing their own yellow-themed (UDF) and blue-themed (AFORD) mbumba dances, to add to the established red, green and black mbumba of the former ruling MCP. As the UDF are now in power, expect more yellow mbumba music!

In the late 1960s and 1970s, as in Zimbabwe and Zambia, urban musicians began electrifying various traditional rhythms. This resulted in the **afroma** – the afro-rock-Malawi beat – whose best exponents were the band **New Scene**, led by Morson Phuka and Daniel Kachamba. **Morson Phuka**, who died in 1991, had been the leader of the Jazz Giants and was a father figure for Malawi popular music. A talented vocalist, composer and arranger, he trained countless musicians through his bands. **Daniel Kachamba** (1947–1987) was an influential folk guitarist whose innovative guitar style fused kwela, local rhythms and his own Chileka ideas into a style he called *sinjonjo*.

Other bands – **Makasu**, **Love Aquarius**, **Mikoko**, **Mitondo**, **Fumbi Jazz** and Bernard Kwilimbe's **Rain Seekers** – followed in New Scene's footsteps.

Kwasa Kwasa and Current Sounds

In the 1980s and '90s Congolese soukous-style music took hold across Malawi in a local form called **kwasa kwasa**. The kwasa kwasa rhythms and melodies blended particularly well with local time signatures. So too did **ska and reggae** –

Alleluya Band

which also became a popular part of the mix. The current prime exponents are **Sapitwa**, a band led by keyboardist Patrick Tembo and guitarist Tepu Ndiche and distinguished by gorgeous vocals.

The contemporary scene also features Anglo-US pop; rural folk groups; guitar-and-banjo singer-songwriters such as **Stonnard Lungu** and **Snodden Ibu**; jazz groups – the **Jazz Giants** and **A Touch of Class**; and big bands like the **Army and Police String Bands**, both of which are well-equipped and would give the increasingly techno-dependent Congolese combos a run for their money in live shows.

Perhaps the dominant music, however, is **gospel**, which has been big since independence, often employing traditional rhythms and instruments, and has created the biggest current draw in 1990s Malawi in the **Alleluya Band**. Led by the multi-talented **Paul Banda** – a composer and producer, as well as a hot guitarist and pianist – along with his younger brother Lucius, they per-

formed before the Pope during his 1989 visit – a visit that combined with the poverty and misery of the time encouraged a mushrooming of gospel. But the Alleluyas are poppy as well as popey, and play everything from reggae to soukous and jazz. Their blend of traditional rhythms and melodies with reggae, gospel, soukous and pop, is irresistible.

The other top Malawian band, through the 1990s, has been the **Kasambwe Brothers**, Isaac and Frank Chikwata, from the Thyolo district in southern Malawi. They started in 1987, singing and playing home-made instruments and were joined in 1989 by their (then) nine-year old cousin, Kennedy Nagopa. Their folk-based material is startlingly original with strong lyrics (see below) about matters like family life, separation and survival, marriage and duty in a matrilineal society – and of course love and alcohol.

Newer arrivals on the 1990s scene include the **Acacias Band**, led by Ben Michael, who have taken the live scene by storm, playing excellent blues, jazz,

Live in Malawi!

If you're visiting Malawi, check out some of the following bands and venues:

Chief Chipoka Band at *Nkopola Lodge*. An acoustic mixture of pop, reggae and folk against the delightful Nkopola beach.

Bolingo Stars at the *Bamboo Bar and Grill* in Lilongwe. Hot live kwasa kwasa music mixed with Malawi traditional fare. Also **Ethel Kamwendo**, a rare female performer, at the same venue.

Gotani Sounds – ex-Mulangeni Sounds exponents of Malawi home-grown kwasa kwasa – at *Gotani's* in Mzuzu. **Kalimba**'s jazz sessions on Sunday afternoons at *Lingadzi Inn* and every Friday night at the *Capital Hotel*.

The Roots and **Masaka** at the *Lilongwe Hotel*.

A Touch of Class for Malawi jazz, and **Tiakalulu** for multi-ethnic music, both at the *French Cultural Centre*.
Bright Nkhata and **Makasu & the Love Aquarius** in hotels around Blantyre.

Lucky Stars Band – a guitar duo formed in 1971 and still playing folk blues and drinking songs – at the *Shire Highlands* and *Ryalls* hotels. Also **Wyndham Chechamba**, a 64-year-old pianist at the *Ryalls Hotel*.

Mulangeni Sounds at the *Mulangeni Lakeshore Resort*.

In the more highly populated townships you may find **Robert Fumulani** and **Likhubula River Jazz Band**, **Maurice Maulidi** and his **Songani Swing Stars**, the **Ndingo Brothers Band** and a host of others.

Chief Chipoka Band

reggae and soukous inflected with traditional rhythms; **Pearson Milanzie**, who writes songs with polemical lyrics and takes rhythms from Yao and Chewa traditions, as well as reggae; and **Ned Mapira**, who plays a bubbling guitar–based afroma music.

Female singers have been under-represented in Malawi music, though notables have included the **Chichiri Queens** of the **MBC Band** (the national broadcasting corporation's house band), **Mary Chidzanja Nkhoma** (Malawi's answer to Miriam Makeba), **Rose Juma**, **Rose Chipembere** and **Ethel Kamwendo**. The latter two came to prominence in the kwasa kwasa boom. A current star is **Molly Kachale**, who has a strong gospel-influenced voice, and performs in a mix of styles encompassing ska, South African mbaquanga and the Balaka beat.

**Thanks to George Claver
for additional information.**

discography

In Malawi, the availability of recorded local music has increased greatly in recent years, though sadly most of it appears on pirate cassettes, sold by street hawkers. Legally issued cassettes, usually of better quality, are retailed by the *Clifton Bazaar* in Limbe, *OG Issa* and the *Portuguese Shopping Centre* in Blantyre, as well as the licensed hawkers in Lilongwe city and old towns. Look for a 'Copyright Society of Malawi' stamp.

Overseas, the best source is the pioneering small Malawian label *Pamtondo*, 4 Gailes Park, Bothwell, Glasgow G71 8TS, Scotland; fax 01698 854472; *http://pamtondo.virtualave.net*. Apart from their own releases Pamtondo (which is run by the author of this article) import cassettes from time to time.

Compilations

 Music from Malawi
(Pamtondo, UK).

Excellent compilation featuring an up-to-date array of Malawi musicians and styles, including Charles Sinetre, Paul Banda, Lucius Banda, the Jupiters, Allan Ngumuya, Alan Namoko, Love Aquarius, Kalimba, Overton Chimombo and a rare female artist, Ethel Kamwendo. What more could one ask?

◉ **Music From Malawi: The Last Pound**
(Pamtondo, UK)**.**

Another wide-ranging Malawian sampler, including styles from gospel with the Katawa Singers to 70-year-old Luka Maganga on the banjo, a tough, electric sound from New Scene and guitar duos like Lucky Stars.

 Music Tradition of Malawi
(Avididis/Unesco, France).

A CD of traditional music from Malawi which includes examples of chimtali, tchopa, ingoma, gule wamkulu, vimbuza; as well as bangwe, beni, mganda and other traditional musical traditions. Excellent value and good introductory notes.

◉ **Songs from Malawi** (Pamtondo, UK).

Compilation cassettes of acoustic and electric Malawian music. A wide variety of music from the rural guitar sounds of the late Dr Daniel Kachamba, to the blues from Alan Namoko and Chimvu Jazz, to more sophisticated grooves of top club acts Kalimba and Masaka.

◉ **Sounds Eastern and Southern** (Original Music, US).

Original Music's African Acoustic series has two tracks from Malawi: "Ndiza Fera Chuma" by Sitero Mbewe & Frank Mukweza and "Elube" by SR Chitalo & the De Ndirande Pitch Crooners – fantastic name, delightful song.

Artists

Acacias Band

This very popular new band are versatile stylists, led by Ben Michaels. They play an afroma style which, on their recordings, has a strong reggae slant.

▦ **Tilire** (High Density Records, Malawi).

The sound of Malawi at the end of the 1990s: catchy soukous/afroma/reggae rhythms, and songs with social metaphor and humour.

Alleluya Band

Malawi's leading band play mainly electric gospel. They are led by Paul Banda and his younger brother, Lucius.

 Mtendere
(Sounds of Malawi, Malawi).

Features the awesome "Mudzisankire njira" (Choose your destiny). Crisp, intelligent arrangements, tasty guitar and heavenly voices.

Lucius Banda

The Alleluya vocalist has a side-career as a reggae artist, with polemical songs much influenced by Lucky Dube and Bob Marley. He gets braver by the month.

▦ **Take Over** (Zembani, Malawi).

A danceable and highly political album castigating poor leadership. Features brother Paul producing and playing guitar.

Paul Banda

Malawi's answer to Stevie Wonder, Paul Banda is also a prolific solo artist.

▦ **The Best of Paul Banda** (Sounds of Malawi, Malawi).

Sweet voice, clever and subtle production and a fully digested mixture of electronics and Malawi and foreign rhythms.

Brothers and Sisters Choir

A youthful and exuberant choir, comparable to the Holy Gospel Choir from South Africa.

▦ **Brothers and Sisters Choir** (Vol 1–2, Malawi).

Rousing hymns, huge volume and a range of vocal tones with various Malawi rhythms. Irresistible.

Chief Chipoka Band

Formerly Makazi Band and now the resident band at Nkopola Lodge, the Chipokas produce an engaging and

complex melodic and rhythmic stew. A more friendly band you would be hard put to find.

 Rhythms of Africa (Protea Hotels, Malawi).

Well recorded traditional acoustic music

Overton Chimombo

Chimombo is a veteran of the Malawi music scene, who achieved solo success in the early 1990s.

⏩ **Zasintha**
(Scan Music UR2, Malawi).

Overton hit the mark (at the onset of democratic change in 1994) with this, a brilliant Studio K production, that bubbles with clever lyrics, jumpy Lomwe, manganja and Sena rhythms. Musicians like veteran bassist Lester Mwathunga and D Nyirenda on keyboards make this one of the most accessible of the cassettes to foreign ears.

Goodson Gomonda

Goodson Gomonda is a singer, songwriter and producer who gives a modern twist to his traditional music, augmented by a clean, clear sound.

🎞 **Kaduwa** (Gomonda Music Enterprises, Malawi).

Engagingly deft, poetic tunes combining old rhythms with new melodies. Accessible to all.

Daniel Kachamba

Dr Daniel Kachamba (1947–87) was Malawi's premier folk musician from the 1960s until his death – a talented guitarist who formed the roots-oriented band New Scene with Morso Phuka, fusing kwela and local rhtyhms into his own unique 'sinjonjo' style.

🎞 **Dr Daniel Kachamba's Memorial Tape**
(University of Malawi).

Kachamba's spiritual side comes across strongly in the lyrics on this recording of haunting tunes and guitar playing.

Donald Kachamba

Donald Kachamba (Daniel's brother) has been playing kwela flute since the mid-1960s and has toured all over Europe and Africa.

⏏ **Malawi Concert Kwela**
(Le Chant du Monde, Germany).

A delightful and individual adaptation of the kwela.

Kasambwe Brothers

One of Malawi's leading bands since their formation in 1987, the Kasambwes feature brisk guitar work and snappy percussion on their folk-based material.

💿 **Ndilibe Ambuye**
(Pamtondo, UK).

A refreshing acoustic set from the Brothers, along with Alan Namoko and gravel-voiced Jivacort Kathumba – billed as Malawi's Mahlathini.

Malawi Police Orchestra

The Police Orchestra combines big band sophistication with sparkling batteries of guitars, keyboards and horns. Originally formed to entertain at state occasions, the need to alleviate official function fatigue thrust them into the dancehalls.

🎞 **Police Strings** (Malawi Music, Malawi).

If you can find an original copy, the policemen's ska-tinged version of the Yao "Ajendeje mbole mbole ndi wanache wangune" and their polemic against too much uncritical modernity, "Ndachita manyazi", set against traditional rhythms, are both dynamite.

The MBC Band

The MBC (Malawi Radio) band was started soon after independence and has been a training ground for many musicians, playing everything from South African mbaqanga to afroma, cabaret jazz and Lucky Dube-style reggae.

⭕ **Kokoliko ku Malawi** (MBC Music, Malawi).

This LP remains the only commercially available recording from the band; and even then as a collectors' item. A groundbreaking and intelligent mixture of traditional and mod-

The Kassambwe Brothers Band

ern instruments, it is streamlined into an afro-jazzy groove by producer Frank Dlamini.

Mhango Salvation Singers

A top-notch gospel group from the north of Malawi, active since the early 1980s.

📼 **Mhango Salvation Singers** (Mhango Salvation Singers Vol 1–2, Malawi).

Well arranged, well produced, uplifting gospel, with smooth and sophisticated harmonies.

Wambali Mkandawire

Artist, keyboardist and fine vocalist Wambali Mkandawire, has recorded and travelled widely. He specialises in soulful renditions of traditional tunes and hymns, singing a cappella or backed by acoustic or electric bands. Wambali was one of the first musicians to dare to refer to 'departed heroes' in his music during the one-party era.

📼 **Kavuluvulu** (Jump Productions, Scotland).

Features hymns, traditional tunes, melodies and rhythms from northern Malawi.

Alan Namoko & Chimvu Jazz

Blind blues player Nakomo was one of Malawi's major figures of the 1970s and '80s with his rootsy, acoustic 'jazz band'.

💿 **Ana osiidwa** (Pamtondo, UK).

A classic Namoko recording of raw guitar and vocals with tea chest percussion.

Allan Ngumuya

Allan Ngumuya is a gospel singer and preacher and one of a staple of artists at Patrick Khoza's Studio K. He is one of Malawi's most prolific artists.

📼 **Umkonde Yesu** (Malawi Gospel Sounds, Malawi).

The emotive singing is first-class, backed simply by guitars, drums and keyboards, plus occasional sax.

Saleta Phiri

Something like Malawi's answer to Zimbabwe's John Chibadura and the Tembo Brothers, Saleta Phiri's Amulamu (in-laws) Band plays ska-coloured, Zomba-beat, neotraditional electric music, full of country music-style social-issue and family lyrics.

📼 **Saleta Phiri and the AB Sounds** (Saleta Phiri Vol 3, Studio K, Malawi).

Crisp, catchy, country ska and roots rhythms combine with lyrics of social angst.

Sapitwa

Sapitwa, currently Malawi's top home-grown soukous, manganja and tchopa band are led by keyboardist Patrick Tembo and guitarist Tepu Ndiche (the son of the late Niche Mwarare, a pioneer slide and acoustic guitarist).

📼 **Sapitwa presents** (SAP 1, Malawi).

Good introduction to Malawian soukous, with crisp guitar, lovely singing and frequent rhythm changes, offset by some rather slack production.

Tiyamike Band

Tiyamike is an electric gospel band led by Sydney Kapyola and produced by the Alleluya firm at their Balaka studio.

📼 **Mudaona Kuwala** (Sounds of Malawi, Malawi).

Blistering, as-live, electric gospel. The title track alone is worth the price of this cassette.

Mali/Guinea | Mande Sounds

west africa's musical powerhouse

The states of **Mali** and **Guinea** formed the heartland of the historic Mande Empire and through the Mande (or Manding) language they have strong cultural and linguistic bonds – not least in one of Africa's oldest and most absorbing musical traditions. This is a real musical powerhouse, with its traditions of *kora* and *balafon* (xylophone) players, its *jeli* (or griot) minstrels and wassoulou praise-singers, and, not least, its mesmerising dancebands. There may be few recording studios or live venues, and little money to go round for equipment, yet this is a region that has produced some of the great superstars of modern African music: kora players Mory Kanté and Toumani Diabaté, golden-voiced singers Salif Keita, Kasse Mady and Oumou Sangaré, supreme dancebands Bembeya Jazz and the Super Rail Band, and the great river-bluesman Ali Farka Touré. **Lucy Duran** checks the pulse of Mali's capital, Bamako, and surveys an extraordinary culture.

amako is a dusty city hugging the banks of the Niger River, and one of the most musical capitals you could hope to find. Music is as much a part of its scenery as the neo-Sudanic architecture, the haze of red dust and wood smoke, the pervasive smell of incense, and the silvery waters of the river. It wakes the city up. At 5am, the cries of the muezzin from the mosques – "God is great!" –

echo through each other across town in a kind of random counterpoint. Women begin the food preparation for the day and the rhythmic beat of millet-pounding thuds out from every compound, mingling with Radio Mali's morning sounds – haunting Bamana music from Segou, soaring Mande voices with rolling harmonies accompanied on electric guitars, and punchy rhythms from Wassoulou.

JAK KILBY

Kandia Kouyaté 'la dangéreuse' - Mali's most exalted singer

Drive through the city on a Thursday or Sunday, and you're bound to come across a wedding party – a crowd of vibrantly dressed women sitting under an awning stretched across the street in front of the bride's or groom's house, with, at one end, an ensemble of amplified guitars, banjolike *ngoni* or *balafon* (traditional xylophone) backing one or more women singers, belting out arrangements of classic Mande tunes through massive amps. These are the **jelis** (or *jalis*) – hereditary musicians known elsewhere in West Africa as *griots* – who for centuries have monopolised professional Mande music.

At night, when the dust settles, the fires for cooking are extinguished, and the air is transparent and soft, Bamako resounds to the voices of a host of Malian singers played through a thousand ghetto-blasters and taxi cassette decks.

Malians love their own music more than anything, and for sheer beauty of melody, there are few if any traditional musics to rival it.

Mande Culture

The closely related **Mande** (or Manding) languages are spoken by peoples who trace their ancestry to the Mande Empire, based in the savannah region of present day western Mali and eastern Guinea from the early-thirteenth to late-fifteenth centuries. It was founded by a warrior-hunter prince, **Sunjata Keita**, who remains a powerful symbol of Mande culture. The epic song "Sunjata", which in its full version tells the story of how Sunjata rose to power by uniting the many small kingdoms into one mighty army, is still today the most important piece in every traditional musician's repertoire. All Mande peoples trace their common ancestry to Sunjata and his generals.

The Mande peoples and three major languages are today found in seven West African countries. Maninka is the language of the heartland of Mande culture in western **Mali** and eastern **Guinea**; Bamana (or Bambara) is spoken in central Mali and is also Mali's lingua franca; and Mandinka is spoken in **The Gambia**, southern **Senegal** and eastern **Guinea–Bissau**. Mandinka, the most different of the three, is about as close to Bamana as Spanish is to Italian.

Maninka, **Bamana** and **Mandinka** are often used interchangeably in talking about Manding music. It is true that all three cultures are characterised by the presence of jelis, and they have a common origin in the ancient heartland of Mande, but over the centuries they have developed distinct musical styles. These differences have come

about partly as a result of differing contacts with various neighbouring peoples, and partly through different colonial and post-colonial experiences. Thus, today, each of the three languages also defines a musical style, with its own repertoires, vocal delivery, lyrics and tunings and preferences for certain instruments.

Maninka

Maninka represents the most classical musical style of Mande. It is the style and language of Malian singers like **Ami Koita**, **Kasse Mady Diabaté** and **Salif Keita**, characterised by a medium tempo with catchy rhythms, ornamental melodies over static harmonies, and sweet, long, flowing seven-note (heptatonic) vocal lines.

Dance is an important part of Maninka style, and women are the preferred singers. The **ngoni lute** is the traditional accompanying instrument, along with the **tamani** (talking drum) and **doundoun** (cylindrical) drums.

Maninka is also the style of **eastern Guinea**, epitomised by the music of singers like **Sekouba Bambino Diabaté**. In Guinea the rhythms are a little faster, and the music seems to float with more rolling vocal lines and harmonic changes, creating a circular, rippling effect. This has something to do with the local importance of the **guitar**, and its adaptation of **balafon** melodies and techniques.

The guitar has been the favourite instrument in Guinea since the late 1940s. Indeed many of the best-known Guinean guitarists, such as **Kanté Manfila**, came from balafon-playing families. The guitar has also become widespread in Mali since the 1950s. At wedding and child-naming ceremonies, jelis play the guitar alongside the traditional instruments. Since the late 1980s, the electric guitar has replaced acoustic guitar in these ensembles, and it goes hand in hand with drum machines and most recently, sequencers.

Bamana

Bamana melodies are more stark, with mostly five-note (pentatonic) melodies, and tend to be in slow tempo, linking them more closely to music of the northern desert regions. The best-known traditional singer of Bamana music is **Fanta Damba**, who was one of Mali's first female jeli stars in the 1970s. **Mah Damba** and the late **Hawa Drame** are other well-known female exponents of the Bamana style. Bands that have specialised in it include the **Super Djata Band** and **Super Biton de Ségou**, Mali's oldest dance band.

Since Malian independence (1960), Bamana and Maninka musicians in Mali's cities – especially in the capital Bamako – have created a synthesis of the regional styles into a form of guitar-based music sometimes called **bajourou** after a famous eighteenth-century jeli song in honour of a king, Tutu Jara. Fanta Damba made this song so famous in the 1970s, that it was nicknamed bajourou – 'mother of tunes'.

Mandinka

The music of the **Mandinka** people of **Senegal** and **The Gambia** (for more on which see p.617) also has a very distinctive style, determined largely by their favoured instrument – the **kora**. Mandinka music is also increasingly influenced by the rhythms and drum patterns of neighbouring peoples like the Wolof (in northern Senegal) and the Jola of Casamance in southern Senegal. Two of the best-known performers of Mandinka music, distinguished by their lively, highly syncopated and fast, hard-driving rhythms, are the Gambian duet **Dembo Konteh** and **Kausu Kouyaté**.

Unlike in Mali, where women are the preferred singers, men do most of the singing in Gambia and Senegal, and their voices are usually high-pitched and very nasal. Since the mid-1980s, one of the most influential of the Gambian kora players has been **Jaliba Kuyateh**, who has introduced a new type of kora playing which is relentlessly fast with a strong Senegalese mbalax influence.

Mande Music Meets the World

With independence (Guinea 1958, Mali 1960), new political and cultural ideologies, the advent of radio, TV and a local cassette industry, and opportunities for performing and recording abroad, have brought about many and sweeping changes in Mande music.

The most exciting developments in the 1970s were the creation of **dance bands** that drew on the jeli tradition, the two great pioneers being **Bembeya Jazz** in Guinea, and the **Rail Band** in Mali. These groups made an enormous impact on the development of local forms of popular dance music. The 1980s was notable, above all, for shifts in **recording locations**, from a largely home-based industry to locations such as Abidjan, Dakar and, inevitably, Paris. Consequently, the most successful dance bands, especially from Mali and Guinea – countries undergoing severe economic and political difficulties at the time – moved abroad.

The subsequent involvement of international record companies with the music of such artists as **Salif Keita** and **Mory Kanté**, who resettled in Paris, and **Foday Musa Suso**, living in Chicago since the late 1970s, has given the music of Mande jelis worldwide exposure, and they have had opportunities to create new fusions with other types of music. Meanwhile, back home in West Africa, locally based Mande musicians cultivated a more local style for a local market, at more functional occasions such as weddings and child-naming ceremonies.

At the end of the 1990s, dividing lines – between acoustic and electric, traditional and popular – have become ever more difficult to draw. Increasingly popular in Mali and Guinea are small, semi-acoustic ensembles featuring traditional instruments combined with electric guitars and a drum machine. And venue is more important as a marker than instruments: **'modern' music** is that of nightclubs and restaurants, while **'traditional' music** is heard at weddings and naming ceremonies. But there are a few almost-rules: 'modern' music tends to include horns and is usally fronted by male singers, while 'traditional' music – even if it involves electric instruments – is invariably led by women, the famed *jelimusolu*.

The Jelis

Common to all Mande music is its virtually exclusive performance by a group of professional musicians – the **jalis** or **jelis** – or **jelimusolu** in the case of women – who are born into a social group or caste, and whose musical and verbal art is called *jaliya* or *jeliya*.

Traditionally, Mande society is hierarchical. At the top are the nobles or freeborn (*horon*), descended from Sunjata Keita and his generals. They are the patrons of the jelis, who are part of a category of craftsmen called *nyamakala*, which include hereditary musicians as well as blacksmiths and leatherworkers. Traditionally, the nyamakala are expected to marry within their caste and even today those born into a jeli family are regarded as jelis whether or not they have ever touched an instrument or sung a note. Marriages between jelis and horon are rare.

All the caste professions have **surnames**. For example, the Kantés are blacksmiths (though many are also musicians), and the Kouyatés are exclusively jelis. The surnames Diabaté (spelt Jobarteh in Gambia), Koné, (a variant of Konté), Sissokho or Cissokho (with variants Suso in The Gambia, and Damba and Sakiliba for women), Kamissoko, Soumano, Dambele and Sacko are also commonly, though not exclusively, found among jelis.

There are many legends of how jelis originated. Some musicians recount how a certain Sourakata, while mocking the Prophet Mohammed in disbelief, was frozen in his tracks three times. After the third time, he realised the power of the prophet, and his taunts became praises. From then on, the principal role of the jeli has been that of 'praise singer'.

Until the end of the nineteenth century, when colonial rule put an end to traditional kingship, the jelis were attached to the courts of local kings (*Mansa*). They entertained the nobility with their epic songs and stories about the major events in Mande history. They guarded the knowledge of genealogies and the complex **'praise names'** attached to every surname.

Although their status is not as high as the freeborn, skilled jelis have always been and remain highly respected for their prowess as musicians and entertainers, and as trusted messengers and advisors. As the late Gambian kora player Jali Nyama Suso explained: "a member of the nobility will not talk freely to someone of the same class, who might be a rival, whereas musicians can be trusted because they are no threat ... They're journalists, they interpret events of now and of the past. The art of the jelis lies in their ability to praise, which gave our kings the courage to fight battles." Nowadays, they may sing for politicians or businessmen instead of kings, but they function in very similar ways. Their gift of speech has made them ideal go-betweens – they patch up quarrels and feuds, arrange marriages, and negotiate the most delicate economic and political matters. In the words of Toumani Diabaté, one of Mali's most brilliant young kora-players: "They are the needle that sews."

The jelis operate like a closed trade union, and guard their profession and knowledge with jealousy and some secrecy. Until recently it was difficult for a non-jeli to take up music as a profession, and in practice very few have done so. One of the best-known exceptions is **Salif Keita**, a noble by birth who chose, against his parents' wishes, to sing professionally and who makes it clear that he is an artist and does not have the specific social obligations of the jeli.

The influence of Mande musicians in West Africa goes far beyond the Mande peoples. Some **Wolof griots** trace their ancestry from Mande. In Siné-Saloum, a region in Senegal just north of the Gambia River, most of the older traditional griots include the classic Mande songs in their repertoire and even sing partly in Maninka. Senegalese superstars Youssou N'Dour, who is Wolof, and Baaba Maal, who is Tukulor, have both recorded versions of many Mande tunes.

The jelis traditionally make their living on the generosity of **patrons** or *jatigui*. In precolonial times, the patrons were kings, or otherwise members of the freeborn including farmers, traders and *marabouts* – Muslim holy men. Until independence – when jelis were first employed as part of government-sponsored ensembles – they were never paid as such but instead received gifts, sometimes of extraordinary generosity, which might include land, animals, a house, cloth, gold, wives and slaves. Still today, the jelis praise their patrons with phrases like "the hundred-giver" (*kemenila*), meaning someone who gives a hundred of something.

Patron and jeli have a close, trusting and mutually dependent friendship. In precolonial times, if the jatigui died, the jeli might even commit suicide. "Lanaya soro man di" (It's not easy to find a trustworthy person) is a constant refrain of Mande songs, reminding both jeli and patron of their duty of loyalty to each other.

Those who consider themselves patrons rely heavily on the advice and diplomacy of their jeli. The presidents of Mali, Guinea and Senegal have had thousands of songs dedicated to them. But while the jelis are praise-singers, their relationship is not based on deference. In the words of Jali Nyama Suso: "I may have patrons, but no one is my boss."

The Jeli Repertoire

Despite its different regional styles, Mande jeliya is unified by a basic **repertoire of songs** that dates back to precolonial days and which is common to all the Mande regions. These serve as the core or classic repertoire, and they are performed for special occasions such as the re-roofing of the sacred hut in the old capital of the Mande empire, Kangaba, every seven years.

The most important songs in this repertoire are "Sunjata" (which has many variants); "Lambang", one of the oldest songs in the repertoire, in praise of music ("O, jaliya-o, Allah le ka jaliya da": 'Ah music! God created music'); and "Tutu Jara", a song composed for an eighteenth-century Bamana king of Ségou. The melodies of these songs are used over and over again in different arrangements and with new lyrics. Older singers such as Fanta Damba and Tata Bambo Kouyaté use "Lambang" and "Tutu Jara" as the basis for a great deal of their music, though they may change the vocal choruses and the arrangements; to this extent these tunes are more like basic melodic structures for improvising rather fixed tunes, a bit like twelve-bar blues.

Younger singers tend to use newer songs of twentieth-century origin. Favourites include "Kelefa" and "Jula Jekere" (Baaba Maal recorded these on his album *Baayo*); the Malian songs "Kaira" and "Jawura" (a song and dance from Kita); the Gambian kora song "Alla l'aa ke"; and "Apollo" – named after the Apollo space missions. A recent version of this can be heard on Sekouba Bambino Diabaté's beautiful 1992 semi-acoustic album *Le Destin* (World Circuit) in the opening song "Ka Souma Man", in praise of tailors.

All these songs, whether in purely traditional versions, semi-acoustic, or accompanied by a full electric dance band, tend to follow the same structure. The singing is divided into two sections, a choral refrain or *donkili* which is pre-composed, and improvisation.

Jeli **vocal improvisations** are formulaic, consisting mainly of **praising family surnames** and reciting their ancestors. Every family name has an epithet or *jammu* which tells something of its origin. The name Musa, for example, is praised by saying "Jealous and able Musa, four-eyed Musa; Bala, the adventure-seeking Musa", which were the praises for Musa Molo, last king of the Mandinka, who died in 1931. The Tourés are "The holy nobles from Mande" and praised with the name Mandjou. There is a small repertoire of songs in praise of specific jeli family names – for example, "Tessiry Magan" on Kasse Mady Diabaté's album *Kela Tradition* (Stern's) is dedicated to the Kanoutés.

Proverbs and pithy sayings are also important. The lyrics are quite moralistic, warning against betrayal, hypocrisy and obsession. Sayings like "Silver and gold cannot buy a good name" permeate lyrics as they do conversation. Even Youssou N'Dour, who doesn't speak Bamana, used the well-known jeli cliché "Saya Man Nying" (Death is terrible) as the title for a ballad.

Mostly, the jelis direct their songs at a single person. In the opening lines of a song by **Kandia Kouyaté**, which she recorded in 1986 for Zoumano, one of her main patrons, she sings many of the standard jeli phrases:

Zoumano, the hundred-giver,
Kandia Kouyaté is singing for you.
Don't force me to become someone else's jeli,
The life of a jeli patron and that of someone
  with no jeli
Are not to be compared.
Cool down the instruments!
Don't let the music make me lose my head!
Betrayal is bad,
And so is obsessive thinking.
The hundred-givers have not vanished
  completely,
But there are certainly very few left.

She then goes on to recite the names of all Zoumano's family as well as his ancestors and all his deeds of generosity towards her and other jelis.

The **instrumental accompaniment** of the Mande repertoire is a two- or four-bar phrase. This riff, as in jazz or blues, serves as the basis for improvisation and provides the framework for the song. The accompaniment is called 'the main way' or 'big meeting', and the variations are known in Mandinka as *birimintingo*, an onomatopoeic word imitating the sound of the kora strings, and in Maninka as *teremeli*, meaning 'to bargain' – in other words, to take the notes higher and lower.

The Kora and other Jeli instruments

Jeli have three traditional instruments : the **kora** – a cross between harp and lute with 21 to 25 strings; the lute-like **ngoni**; and the **balafon**, a wooden xylophone. The kora is by far the most popular of the three and, unlike the others, is traditionally not played by any other ethnic group.

With its striking appearance, beautiful ringing sound, and versatility, the kora has also come to symbolise Mande music abroad. No other African instrument has had the same impact on the international scene. The work of **Foday Musa Suso** with Herbie Hancock and Bill Laswell, the flamenco and classical crossover albums of **Toumani Diabaté**, and the amplified rock style kora of **Mory Kanté**, have all helped to establish it as one of the world's great solo instruments.

Although some of the most famous kora players are from Mali, the kora is said to come originally from the area which is now Guinea-Bissau. The Scots explorer Mungo Park reported seeing an 18-string *korri* played for one of the Mande kings in 1796. But the kora only came into its own in the twentieth century. Although there have been various innovations, the standard 21-string kora's most distinctive feature is its wide-notched bridge dividing the strings into two parallel rows at right angles to the sound table, and a large gourd resonator.

Two main **kora-playing styles** are recognised – eastern, from Mali and Guinea, and western, from Casamance in southern Senegal and The Gambia, where most of the famous players originally came from. The **western style** is 'hotter' and more percussive, with more cross-rhythm, lots of strumming and pinching of the strings, and rhythmic tapping of the handles – players talk about 'beating the kora' (*ka kora kosi*). Some use up to 25 strings to increase the bass range and allow for

Masters of the Kora

Below are brief notes on some – though by no means all – of the great kora players, from Mali, Guinea, Senegal and Gambia. For a selection of CDs, see the discographies at the end of this feature and that of Senegal and The Gambia (p.629).

Cissoko, Soundioulou (Senegal). From a dynasty of kora players and influential in the 1960s and '70s. His best-known song, the joyfully melodious "Mariama", exists in many local dance-band versions and has been covered by Baaba Maal.

Diabaté, Sidiki (The Gambia/Mali). Developed a solo instrumental style where the kora plays both melody and accompaniment – a tradition followed by his son Toumani.

Diabaté, Toumani (Mali). Virtuoso Malian artist who has made the kora one of the world's great solo instruments and has also shown its enormous crossover potential – for example with flamenco on the *Songhai* albums.

Drame, Lalo Keba (The Gambia; died 1974). Prolific composer, whose songs are still played frequently on Radio Gambia. His dizzily fast technique remains a model of the Gambian style for young musicians. Pirated tapes circulate endlessly.

Jobarteh, Amadu Bansang (The Gambia). The first kora musician to tour Britain, in 1980. His lyrical style and precise technique reflect his Malian heritage.

Jobarteh, Malamini (The Gambia). Adoptive son of Alhaji Bai Konteh, he toured the US in the 1970s. His eldest son, Ebrima Jobarteh (aka Tata Dinding), follows the Jaliba Kuyateh style of acrobatic kora playing.

Jobarteh, Wandifeng (The Gambia; died in the 1950s). A legendary kora player and composer of some of The Gambia's most oft-played tunes, such as "Nteri Jato".

Kanté, Mory (Guinea). Originally a balafon player, he developed a unique, almost linear, jazz style on the kora, and with the huge hit song "Yeke Yeke" introduced his sound to the clubs of Europe, giving a robust new edge to perceptions of roots music.

Konteh, Alhaji Bai (The Gambia; died in 1986). A virtuoso in the Casamance tradition, and the first kora player to tour the US, appearing at the Woodstock festival.

Konteh, Dembo (The Gambia). Alhaji Bai Konteh's son, he plays in a similar style, usually in duet with his brother-in-law, the brilliant Kausu Kouyaté.

Kouyaté, Batourou Sekou (Mali). Entirely self-taught, he evolved a unique, highly staccato style and made his reputation as the accompanist to singer Fanta Damba. Hear him with Sidiki Diabaté on the first instrumental kora record, *Cordes Anciennes*, an all-time classic from 1970.

Kouyaté, Kausu (Senegal). Specialist in a Casamance style called "Yeyengo" (named after a song) with its own tuning and much strumming on a 23- to 25-string kora.

Kuyateh, Jaliba (The Gambia). Has built a reputation as a local entertainer, leading a Wolof/Mande ensemble of percussion, amplified kora and electric bass.

Sissoko, Djeli Moussa (Ballaké) (Mali). Born in 1967, the son of one of Mali's greatest kora players Jelimadi Sissoko, and cousin of Toumani Diabaté (with whom he has recorded kora duets), Ballaké is the regular accompanist to singer Kandia Kouyaté.

Sissoko, Jali Mori (Senegal; died in the late 1970s). Best-known of the super-strung kora players: his instrument had twenty-five strings and he played in a very bluesy tuning, with a strummed technique.

Suso, Foday Musa (The Gambia). One of the earliest kora masters to quit Africa in the late 1970s, when he went to the US and formed the Mandingo Griot Society with Don Cherry. More recently, he has been involved in collaborations with the Kronos Quartet.

Suso, Jali Nyama (The Gambia; died in 1991). One of the most influential of Gambian kora players in the 1960s and 1970s, he was the first kora player to teach in the US, was favoured by former President Jawara's first wife, and also provided the idea for the Gambian National Anthem (a version of the kora piece, "Fode Kaba"). He was shunned after Jawara's divorce and rarely performed in his later years.

Mory Kanté – from Rail Band to world stage

MALI/GUINEA

more change of key. Men do the singing – though women may sing the chorus. The **eastern style** is more vocally oriented with a slower, more linear and staccato 'classical' sound, borrowed from the ngoni and balafon. They talk about 'speaking the kora' (*ka kora fo*), which is seen more as an instrument of accompaniment. Women do most of the solo singing.

It is said that all great kora players are likely at one point or another to be possessed by *djinns* or spirits (much in the way that some blues players are said to have made a pact with the devil), especially if they play late at night. Jeli folklore is full of stories of players being bewitched or possessed; too much virtuosity is believed to make a musician vulnerable to illness.

The **ngoni** is another prestigious Mande instrument, an oblong lute which has three to five strings, a resonator carved from a single piece of wood, and a skin sound table. In Bamana and Maninka it is called *ngoni*, in Mandinka *konting*; it is also played by griots from other peoples such as the Wolof, who call it *khalam* (*xalam*) and the Fula and Tukulor, who call it *hoddu*. The instrument is an ancient one. The Moroccan traveller Ibn Battuta, who visited the court of Mali during the reign of Mansa Musa in 1352, described such an instrument, embedded with mother-of-pearl and silver. West African slaves re-created this instrument in the New World, as the **banjo**.

Today, the ngoni – which is technically quite difficult to play, and also a very quiet instrument – is not often heard in Senegal and The Gambia, though it is still extremely popular in Mali and Guinea, where it is usually played with an electric pick-up as accompaniment alongside acoustic and electric guitars. The **electric guitar** itself, which is now the ubiquitous Maninka instrument, is played with almost exactly the same technique and often with a variety of unusual tunings.

Another instrument reported by Ibn Battuta at the fourteenth-century Mali court was the xylophone, called **balafon** or *bala* in Maninka. The balafon usually has 18 to 21 keys cut from rosewood, suspended on a bamboo frame over gourd resonators of graduated sizes. It is often played in pairs, one musician performing the basic riff while the other improvises.

The **Susu people** of western Guinea, who are linguistically part of the Mande family, are experts on this instrument. In the story of Sunjata Keita, the bala originally belonged to Sunjata's rival Sumanguru Kanté, king of the Susu people, and still today, the greatest balafon players are from Guinea, such as **El Hadj Djeli Sory Kouyaté**,

leader of Guinea's National Ensemble and a legendary virtuoso. The Guinean superstar **Mory Kanté**, a blacksmith by birth from a musical family, famous for his hit song "Yeke yeke", started his musical career as a balafon player. Malian singer **Salif Keita** has also used the balafon in his otherwise purely electric band.

There are three Mande **drums**: the **tama**, or variable-pitch drum (talking drum); the **djembe**, a single-headed goblet-shaped drum with a high-pitched tone, played with the hands, which is the drum par excellence of the Wassoulou region; and the **doundoun**, a large double-headed drum which is played with a heavy stick, once used to announce the arrival of the king.

Guitars, Dance Bands and Cuban Sounds

After World War II and the return of African conscripts, the **guitar** quickly became a symbol of neotraditional music. In **Guinea**, **Kanté Facelli**, his younger cousin **Kanté Manfila** and **Sekou 'diamond fingers' Diabaté** forged a local style of playing. They introduced love lyrics and a new harmonic element of constantly shifting chords under strong melodies. Songs like "Tallasa" (Put the light out, my love) and "Lanaya" (The one you trust) came out of this period and remain eternal favourites.

In **Mali**, in the decade before independence, a number of regional towns, in particular Kita (birthplace of many of Mali's best-known musicians) and Ségou, had their own **dance bands**. Kita's orchestra was led by **Boureima 'BK' Keita**, Mali's first professional saxophonist. Kita was an important colonial centre, and every Saturday people would take the train from Kayes and Bamako to hear the town's modern orchestra.

Another of Mali's early bands was **Afro-Jazz de Ségou**. Founded in 1952, under the leadership of trumpeter Amadu Ba (nicknamed 'Armstrong' for his admiration of Satchmo), their repertoire throughout the 1950s consisted of waltzes, tangos, paso dobles, rumbas, and French chansons. By 1964, they had joined with a rival band under the name **Alliance**, and became the official orchestra of the region. They dropped the ballroom songs and, influenced by Guinean dance bands, cultivated a more **Afro-Cuban sound** – then, in pre-Castro days, a dominant influence in jazz and dance music generally.

As in Guinea, state-subsidised **orchestras** were a prominent feature of Mali's first years of independence under President Modibo Keita; they

Les Amazones de Guinée

were established in Kayes, Ségou, Sikasso, Gao and Mopti, of which the first three were predominantly composed of Mande musicians. Modibo Keita also founded the **Orchestre Nationale A**, Mali's first national electric dance band. Led by Keletigui Diabaté on guitar and Tidiane Kone on sax, it had a standard Latin-jazz line-up.

In Bamako an orchestra was founded for each section of the capital. The most popular of these district bands was **Pioneer Jazz** of Missira. **Jalimadi Tounkara** (today the lead guitarist of the famous Super Rail Band) was a member of Pioneer Jazz in the early 1960s, his first experience away from purely traditional Mande music: "At that time our bands weren't using folklore, just Latin American music, some jazz, and some rock. I especially liked Chuck Berry and I tried to imitate his style." Other Malian bands of the time, like the **Harmonie Soudanaise**, **Sinfonia**, **Fiesta Tropical**, and **Askia Jazz**, were independent, and mainly played cover versions of Latin music learnt from imported records. Like the state orchestras, disbanded with the downfall of Modibo Keita, those early groups are now mostly forgotten.

Throughout the 1960s the biggest outside influence on Malian pop – as in the rest of Francophone Africa – was **Cuban dance music**. The rhythms and musical structures of Cuban *son* and rumba are remarkably close to those of Mande music: indeed the characteristic *clave* of Cuban music, or 'Bo Diddley rhythm' ("Shave and a hair-

cut, two bits"), may well have been taken to Cuba by Mande slaves. When dance bands performed Mande tunes they were almost invariably given Latin arrangements, and Latin music has remained extremely popular in Mali even today. Salif Keita's greatest hit of the 1970s, "Mandjou", has a clear Latin tinge. In an interview for BBC TV in 1989 he remarked: "I used to sing in Spanish – or at least I think it was Spanish, because I didn't actually speak it. I love Cuban music, but more than that, I consider it a duty for all Malians to love Cuban music, because it's through Cuban music that we were introduced to modern instruments."

The 1960s were the golden years for **Guinea's dance bands**. More than a dozen first-rate orchestras sprang up around the country: **Keletigui et ses Tambourins**, **Balla et ses Balladins**, **Les Amazones de Guinée** (West Africa's first all-woman dance orchestra, recruited from the police), **Lanaya Jazz**, **Horoya Band**, **Super Boiro** – all immortalised on a series of superb LP records on the Syliphone Conakry label.

The majority of their repertoire was Mande, the lyrics political and exhortatory in true cultural-revolutionary style, but the Cuban influence, especially in the rhythms and arrangements, was strong. It tended to be reinforced by the close political ties between Guinean dictator Sekou Touré and Fidel Castro, and by the popularity of **Congolese rumba** (see p.462); the Congolese musician Joseph Kabasele – 'Le Grand Kalle' – played in Guinea in the early 1960s and made a lasting impression.

The most important and famous band of the time was **Bembeya Jazz National**. Specialising in arrangements of Mande classics, with the rolling harmonies of Guinean guitar, they featured a Latin-style horn section and percussion, with **Sekou Diabaté** on guitar, and the sweet voice of **Aboubacar Demba Camara**. Founded in 1961 in Beyla (eastern Guinea), they won Guinea's national *Biennale* festivals in 1962 and 1964, where regional bands competed with each other, and in 1966 were declared the 'National Orchestra'.

The year before, Bembeya had made a memorable visit to Cuba. The well-known Cuban singer Abelardo Barroso was reportedly moved to tears by the voice of Bembeya's lead singer, Aboubacar Demba Camara. Tragically, Camara was killed in a car accident while on his way to a concert in Dakar in 1973, an event which plunged Guinea into nationwide mourning. Bembeya subsequently went into a decline and – combined with increasing political and economic problems in Guinea – never quite recovered their popularity. By 1991 they had dispersed completely, though **Sekouba Bambino Diabaté** (not to be confused with his older, guitarist colleague Sekou Diabaté) has now become Guinea's most popular singer of semi-acoustic Mande music.

Return to Roots

Throughout the 1970s in Guinea, Sekou Touré continued to subsidise music, organising huge concerts for state occasions and awarding medals and 'National Orders' to preferred singers and instrumentalists. The kora player **Sidiki Diabaté** was awarded the National Order, and **Salif Keita** was given a gold medal for his concert with the Rail Band in Conakry in 1976. In return, Keita dedicated his song "Mandjou" to Sekou Touré – a leader now viewed as a despot. Asked two decades later if he regretted having sung a praise song to the dictator, Keita was pragmatic: "I don't have any regrets, it was a different time. From the moment I knew what dictatorship meant, I hated it. And I never criticise someone who is dead."

Mali's second president, Colonel Moussa Traoré, maintained close political links with Guinea and followed its example by encouraging musicians in the *Biennale* festivals to draw on local music. Under the entry rules, each band had to perform music based on local folklore. Thus the **search for a more traditional idiom** began. Gone were the

Sékou 'Diamond Fingers' Diabaté of Bembeya Jazz dispenses with the amp

imitation Cuban costumes, now replaced by tunics of tie-dyed damask or the black-and-white patterned mud-dyed cloth of the Bamana.

The **Super Biton de Ségou** – a new incarnation of Alliance and Afro-Jazz, and named after the founder of the Bamana kingdom – won first prize twice in a row. The driving dance rhythms of their Bamana music translated powerfully onto guitars and horns, creating a new style, refreshingly different from previous Mande pop. "We made the big changeover in 1970", recalls Amadu Ba, Super Biton's trumpeter and founder member, now retired. "At first we encountered lots of difficulties because it involved a change of attitude. It was hard to break with the colonial mentality. Even when we musicians accepted a return to a more indigenous style, we had to struggle to convince our audience. It was a long process but eventually it worked." Super Biton's example was followed by other bands like **Super Djata** – led by the percussionist and guitarist Zani Diabaté – and **Kené Star** of Sikasso.

Tidiane Koné was another of the major figures in the campaign to 'return to folklore'. His wizardry on the ngoni was legendary – he was said to play so fast that his fingers disappeared completely from sight. But he also learnt to play most other dance-band instruments, and was the mentor of many musicians. In 1969 Koné set up a new band, the **Rail Band du Buffet Hôtel de la Gare**, which was to launch the careers of two of West Africa's most internationally successful singers: Mory Kanté and Salif Keita.

The Rail Band v Les Ambassadeurs

The distictively albino **Salif Keita**, Mali's best-known singer since the late 1970s, has, more than any other individual, been responsible for fusing Mande music with world beats. Being an albino carries a stigma in most African countries and Salif's youth in his native Djoliba, a village west of Bamako, close to the heartland of the old Mande empire, was not easy. On both his mother's and father's side he is a Keita and there was no precedent for someone of such high lineage to take up singing as a profession. His mother had a fine voice, though she never sang in public. His father and he communicated little. Salif trained as a schoolteacher but poor eyesight prevented him from teaching as a profession, and so, despite his family's disapproval, he began to sing for a living in the streets and bars of Bamako.

RICHARD TRILLO

Jalimadi Tounkara, Rail Band lead guiarist

When Salif was first approached by Tidiane Koné to join the Rail Band he refused: "I don't do modern music, and anyway I'm not supposed to sing." But he was persuaded: "My family opposed me, but isn't it true that the evolution of civilisation is marked all the time by revolution? It was necessary to mark a century that wasn't that of the ancestors."

In 1971 another band formed in Bamako, **Les Ambassadeurs du Motel**, the resident band of a small hotel in Bamako with a flourishing nightclub. While the Rail Band was known for its Mande roots repertoire, with songs like "Sunjata", at least half the Ambassadeurs' numbers were foreign-style pop – rumbas, foxtrots, French ballads, Cuban and even Senegalese Wolof songs, sung particularly well by their lead singer, **Ousmane Dia**. Les Ambassadeurs was one of the few bands who were not government sponsored.

Both groups began to attract big followings. And two Guinean musicians now arrived on the scene who were to become very important: the singer **Mory Kanté**, a balafon player from an illustrious musical family from Kissidougou in eastern Guinea; and his cousin **Kanté Manfila** (or Manfila Kanté), an innovative guitarist who had learnt to play in Côte d'Ivoire. Manfila was invited to become leader of the Ambassadeurs, while Mory became a second singer in the Rail Band. (During the early 1970s, Mory also studied the kora in Bamako and after he moved to Paris in the 1980s, it was as a kora player that he became famous).

In the Rail Band, Mory Kanté was immediately seen as a potential rival to Salif. They both had powerful, inspirational voices and were adept at praise lyrics. During 1972 Salif made a brief trip out of the country, and on his return found Mory doing the lead singing. Snubbed, Salif's response was to 'defect' to the Ambassadeurs, which created an uproar among his fans and even greater rivalry between the two bands.

The relative merits of each band were soon put to the test. President Traoré – in one of his more enlightened programmes – had launched an adult literacy campaign called *Kibaru* (News) aimed at the vast majority of rural Malians who were unable to read. In order to attract attention to the campaign, Traoré invited the Rail Band and the Ambassadeurs to perform in a Kibaru concert to be held at the National Sports Stadium.

By the morning of what was immediately billed a contest, a huge crowd had gathered outside the stadium. The atmosphere was as tense as at a major football game. The Rail Band, fronted by Mory Kanté, were first to go on. "Our first piece was 'Soul Makossa' by Manu Dibango", recalls the guitarist Jalimadi Tounkara. "We had really rehearsed well, so from the first note the public went wild. At that time, singers didn't dance, they would just stand still. It was Mory Kanté who started to dance in the modern orchestras." Mory was wearing a *grand boubou*, a traditional robe notoriously diffi-cult to dance in; but his performance of the grace-ful *jalidong* was breathtaking. It drove the audience to a frenzy.

Then it was the Ambassadeurs' turn. The line-up of the band included many of those who have continued to work with Salif Keita even after its break-up – the Guinean guitarist **Ousmane Kouyaté**; **Keletigui Diabaté**, the left-handed virtuoso whose main instrument is the bala; **Cheikh Tidiane**, the keyboard player; and **Kanté Manfila** on guitar. Salif and Manfila had written a song for the occasion called "Kibaru", starting out with a slow section encouraging farmers and workers to take reading classes, and concluding with a fast, humorous passage where the word "Kibaru" was broken into syllables, as in a spelling lesson. Later, when this song was recorded, it took up the whole side of an LP.

Salif Keita, twenty-three years old, came on defi-antly, not in the expected grand boubou but in the traditional garb of Mande hunters: a rough, undyed, home-spun cotton tunic sewn with all kinds of magic charms. It was a costume that reflected his ancient and noble ancestry, similar to the one he wears on the cover of *Amen*. There was uproar: here was an educated albino of noble ances-try, dressed like a hunter, singing – in the style of the jelis – a song about literacy.

There was no winner – it was considered a draw – but to this day 'the contest' is remembered as a showcase event for modern Mande music and a stimulus for other bands to look to tradi-tion for their sources.

The competition between the two bands continued throughout the 1970s, turn-ing Bamako into one of West Africa's most exciting cities for dance music. Mean-time, another band entered the scene: the **National Badema**, formerly the **Mar-avillas de Mali**, composed of a group of musicians including **Boncana Maiga**, who had been studying music in Cuba for eight years. They were joined in the mid-1970s by the singer **Kasse Mady Diabaté**, a jeli from Kela near Kangaba, as

part of a drive to introduce traditional Maninka praise-singing to their charanga-style arrangements. Their biggest hits were "Nama" and "Fode", a song which, in the late 1980s, Kasse Mady re-recorded in Paris for the Syllart label.

The Rail Band remained the most traditional of the three bands, often inviting guest singers such as **Djelimadi Sissoko** to join them for special recordings. Throughout the 1970s, the Rail Band played at the Buffet Hotel almost every night of the week and it was always full. On Saturday nights you couldn't get in. "But in 1979", recalls lead guitarist Jalimadi Tounkara, "I left for Abidjan with Mory Kanté. We left because we had asked for a pay rise and didn't get it. We were on low wages and our fees always went to the Rail company, so we got discouraged. In Abidjan we formed our own band, the Rail Band International. The atmo-sphere in Abidjan was hot!"

The Ambassadeurs had also left Bamako for Abidjan in 1978 to record their album *Mandjou*. "Mandjou" had almost become the group's sig-nature tune, demanded by their audiences every-where (though according to Kanté Manfila, the track on the album that the group itself preferred was "Ntoma", which reappeared on Salif's *Amen* album as "M b'i fe"). "Mandjou" was recorded in the rehearsal room of the Ivoirian TV station, and transformed Salif into a star overnight.

ROBERT URBANUS/STERN'S

Kasse Mady enjoys his success

Jelimusolu: Mali's Women Singers

Since Mali's independence, the most consistent stars of the local scene have been the **jelimusolu** – the famed women jelis. Their status as local superstars, who take the lion's share of fees and command adoring audiences, is unique in West Africa, where in general popular music is male dominated. Their flamboyant personalities and independent life-styles have made them the subjects of intense, often malicious, gossip. "It's brought us many problems from jealousy and intolerance", says singer Ami Koita, "but personally I have had no choice but to go ahead anyway; this is my destiny."

One of the first women singers to become popular after independence was **Fanta Sacko** from Kita. She called her style *jamana kura* (new age), delivering light, rhythmic and melodious love songs, accompanied on two acoustic guitars in non-standard tunings, with a capo high on the neck, imitating the kora and the insect-like sound of the ngoni. Referred to in Bamana as *bajourou*, this represents the most popular trend of guitar-based music in Guinea and Mali since the 1970s. Her most famous song, "Jarabi" has been recorded in dozens of cover versions by most of Mali's best-known artists. Apart from being a beautiful minor-key tune, "Jarabi" was a local hit because of its lyrics, which advocate passionate love above all other feelings.

Love is an illness no doctor can cure.
Wait for me, my love, for I cannot live without you.
Loves knows no father, no mother,
no brother or sister.
Love is blind and deaf to all this.
What counts alone is what you have said to me.

In many ways Fanta Sacko paved the way for a whole new generation of Mali's women singers. But she paid bitterly for her fame when in the early 1980s she burned herself with skin bleach (many Malian women singers still believe that pale skin is a shortcut to success). And she was never paid for her record, which is still sold on bootleg cassettes.

Probably the most respected of all the jelimusolu was the late **Sira Mory Diabaté** (Kasse Mady's aunt) from Kela, an imposing, nearly blind woman with a moving alto voice, and composer of several famous songs such as "Bani" and "Sara". Unlike many of today's jelimusolu her voice is low-pitched and leisurely, her lyrics more moralistic than praising. In "Sara", a tune later made famous in a stunning arrangement by the Guinean band Balla et ses Balladins, she sings, "sara (popularity) is not sung for those who have money, sara is sung for those who keep their word." It is a song about a woman who was forced to marry someone she did not love; but at the last minute she decides not to go through with the marriage, and remain faithful to her true love. Sira Mory had uncompromising principles: she was favoured by President Modibo Keita but neglected by his successor Moussa Traoré because she did not sing praise songs for him.

The first Malian jelimuso to tour Europe as a solo artist, in 1975, was the Bamana singer from Ségou, **Fanta Damba**, who sings in the cool, classic Bamana style of Ségou, accompanied on ngoni, kora and guitar. Her voice became something of a cult, much admired by musicians such as Youssou N'Dour, whose song "Wareff" was a reworking of her material.

A World Stage: Salif Keita and Mory Kanté

The 1980s saw a shift of the musical scene – at least for the dance bands – away from Conakry and Bamako, initially to Abidjan, and from 1985 onwards, to Paris. When Mory Kanté left the Rail Band, he was replaced by **Lafia Diabaté** (younger brother of Kasse Mady), whose lyrical voice is less classical than that of his brother and was perfectly suited to the band's new lighter repertoire. Renamed the **Super Rail Band**, they recorded their superb album *Foliba* in Abidjan in 1980 (subsequently re-released by GlobeStyle as *New Dimensions in Rail Culture*).

The **Rail Band** still survives, but they've not had an easy time. They continued to be sponsored by the Malian rail company through the 1980s, but audiences at the *Buffet de la Gare* began to decline and by the late 1980s they were only playing once a week, competing with Bamako's discos and video clubs. They have since gone independent, following the political upheaval that led to Mali's new democratic regime under President Alpha Oumar Konaré. There are few other dance bands in Bamako, though since 1996 the scene has shown some healthy growth.

The Ambassadeurs, renamed the **Ambassadeurs Internationaux**, only survived as a band until the mid-1980s. In 1980, **Salif Keita**, together with Kanté Manfila and two other musicians from the Ambassadeurs, had spent four months in the US making another of their classic records, *Prinprin*, working with local session musicians. But in 1982, conflict between Salif and Manfila came to a head with Salif leaving the band altogether and moving to Paris. Rumours about his health –

Another of the finest women singers of the 1970s was the Guinean **Kadé Diawara**, "the Archangel of Mande". She had a typically Guinean, open-throated, liquid-sounding voice. In the 1980s she stopped singing – the result, so it was said, of witchcraft directed at her by rival singers – but in 1992 she made a strong comeback with her cassette *Kadé Diawara l'Éternelle*, with a semi-acoustic backing ensemble.

TRICIA CHACON

Tata Bambo Kouyaté, praise singer extraordinaire

Of the jelimusolu who have achieved major success as soloists in the last two decades, three stand out: **Ami Koita**, who comes from Djoliba, the village where Salif Keita was born; **Tata Bambo Kouyaté**, from Bamako; and **Kandia Kouyaté** from Kita. Ami Koita is the most innovative: her magnificent album *Tata Sira* became Mali's biggest hit of 1988. Subsequent albums, *Songs of Praise* and *Carthage*, combine synthesisers and electric guitars with the usual jeli instruments of kora, ngoni and balafon. Koita has been criticised by some Malians for going too far down the line of modernisation, something which female singers are not supposed to do. For example, she was severely criticised for recording an album with the Congolese band Afrisa International, using soukous-type rhythms.

Malian TV plays an increasingly important role in the promotion of jelimusolu, as do recordings. "A jelimuso is only as good as her latest cassette", says **Naïny Diabaté**, one of the most popular of the new generation of younger singers in Bamako. Her excellent 1992 cassette, *Farafina Mousso*, showed a less classical approach, more open to new styles, with clear nods to Congolese influence. This trend was followed by others of the new generation of jelimusolu, such as **Babani Koné**, **Yayi Kanouté** and **Astan Kida** who currently dominate the airwaves of Bamako's flourishing local scene.

At the start of the new millennium, however, it's **Kandia Kouyaté** who stands out as Mali's class act. She was born and raised in Kita, the well-spring of so much in the classic Mande musical tradition, and, by eschewing the pull of stardom she has remained close to the hearts of the people. Instead of releasing one album after another, she has honed and polished her expressive contralto vocal skills, and concentrated on making exquisite arrangements for the repertoire. The results finally reached a truly international audience with the release of the highly original and much acclaimed *Kita Kan* (Voice of Kita) in 1999.

always fragile – began to circulate but in reality he was working on a fusion album – *Soro* – with French keyboardist Jean-Philippe Rykiel and Senegalese producer and impressario Ibrahima Sylla, which was to launch Mande music around the world.

Soro marked the coming of age of Mande dance music. With this album, Salif finally abandoned all trace of Latin influence, instead working with contemporary sounds from the world of rock and pop. And he was no longer primarily using the idioms of jeli praise song, but had begun to draw on the wider world of Mande music, especially the melodies of Maninka hunters, which was his real heritage as a Keita. The powerful cultural millieu of Maninka hunters has become increasingly important in Salif's work – he is often depicted wearing the traditional costume of hunters (a mud-dyed cloth strung with amulets and mirrors). His stunning soundtrack for the French feature film, *L'enfant lion*, includes several tracks based on the 10-string melodies of the Maninka hunters' harp.

In the mid-1980s, the Mande dance music scene had shifted to Paris. On a parallel trajectory to Salif, but working in a more straightforward techno-disco mode, Guinean kora player **Mory Kanté** was moving towards stardom with his album *Mory Kanté à Paris*. This was followed by the album *10 Cola Nuts* which, despite its disco beat, still had a strong Mande flavour, especially in songs like "Teriya", a version of the Rail Band's old number "Balakoninfi". In 1988, Mory's version of the classic old favourite "Yeke Yeke" (a love song from Guinea), first launched on his *Mory Kanté à Paris* album, reached number one on several European charts and, remixed, became a standard of the early acid house scene.

Reflective moment for Salif

Many of Salif Keita's original group of musicians – some of whom, like Cheikh Tidiane and Ousmane Kouyaté, had been with him since the days of the Ambassadeurs – left after *Soro* to form their own groups, and a scattering of 'Soro-sound' records came and went, often featuring the same group of musicians. **Kasse Mady**'s excellent album *Fode*, despite his magnificent voice and some fine arrangements, did not make the impact it might have done had *Soro* not existed. Ousmane Kouyate rejoined Salif for the album *Folon*, which represented a rootsier, sometimes semi-acoustic return to Salif's Mande roots.

The beginning of a 'back to roots' movement on the Mande music scene dated back, in reality, to the mid-1980s, hailed by the release of some of the best Mande acoustic albums. The first to receive international attention was the haunting 1983 Abidjan recording *Yasimika*, featuring the young Guinean singer and kora player **Jali Musa Jawara** (half-brother of Mory Kanté), accompanied on balafon and guitar and with a chorus of three women including Djenné Doumbia and Djanka Diabaté. **Kanté Manfila**'s acoustic album

Tradition, which includes Mory Kanté on kora, is another all-time classic acoustic album, as is **Kasse Mady**'s stunning 1990 album *Kela Tradition*.

Another leading light in the forging of new forms of musical expression in Mali has been the kora player **Toumani Diabaté**. His acoustic ensemble, the **Symmetric Orchestra**, brings together some of Mali's finest jeli instrumentalists, including **Keletigui Diabaté** on balafon and the brilliant young ngoni (lute) virtuoso **Batourou Sekou Kouyate**. Their repertoire is loosely based on the established pieces of the jeli, but these are interpreted with a richly textured jazz format, whereby each instrument takes it in turn to do a solo. This gives the old songs a contemporary feel, without signifying a break with tradition. Toumani has influenced a whole generation of young kora players in Mali as well as reaching new international audiences through the two superb *Songhai* flamenco-crossover albums. Most recently, Toumani's album *New Ancient Strings* – instrumental kora duets with his cousin Ballake Sissoko – takes the art of the kora to new levels of virtuosity and expression.

Sekouba 'Bambino' Diabaté, former lead singer with Guinea's Bembeya Jazz (never disbanded, but hardly functional since the early 1990s) is one of the major singers on the contemporary Mande music scene. A jeli from upper Guinea, he began singing professionally in local orchestras even before his teens (hence his 'bambino' nickname). His soaring, romantic tenor voice is nowhere more beautifully showcased than on his 1997 album *Kassa*, in the song "Damansena", for example, a lyrical tribute to Guinea's diamond miners, accompanied on piano by the Cape Verdean Paulino Vieira (from Cesaria Evora's band).

One of the newest entries on the Mande music scene, a rising star both locally and internationally, is **Habib Koité**. Though a jeli (from the northwest of Mali), he makes a break with the well-worn mould of jeli-based praise songs, drawing on different ethnic traditions from the whole country. In his 1998 album, *Maya*, Habib Koité dedicated songs to the Fula and Soninke, using their musical styles as well as singing in those languages. He also emulated the songs of hunters (as in the title track "Maya"). His understated and beautiful arrangements give pride of place to the acoustic guitar, and he makes no use of synthesiser. Habib has created a new category of Malian music in the singer-songwriter tradition, with original compositions and thoughtful lyrics that cover a wide range of social and human issues.

Love, not Praise: Wassoulou Music

In the late 1980s, disillusion with Mali's corrupt military regime at the time, and the severe economic crisis in the country, resulted in a swing away from praise song, with its built-in expectancy of reward and its reinforcement of the status quo. Instead there was an upsurge of interest in different styles of Mande music. The strongest development was the rise in popularity of the music from the region of **Wassoulou**, south of Bamako, which has a completely different social and musical basis from that of the jelis.

The people of Wassoulou are a mixture of Bamana and Fula ethnic groups, originally descended from Fula – as shown by their four main surnames (Sidibé, Sangaré, Diakité and Diallo) – although they speak a local dialect of Bamana. There are jelis in Wassoulou, but they play a rather marginal musical role. Instead, anyone who has musical talent and wishes to sing, dance or play an instrument may do so. To show that they are musicians by choice, not birth, they call themselves *kono* - songbird.

The music which is now known as 'wassoulou' sounds quite traditional, but actually it only dates from the mid-1970s as a named style of music. It was created in Bamako among migrant communities from Wassoulou, and combines two regional types of music. One is the music of the ancient tradition of songs for sacred hunters' societies, accompanied on a smaller version of the six-string hunter's harp, and an iron scraper. These **hunters' songs** are traditionally only performed by men who have been initiated into the society, though ironically in wassoulou music they have been largely appropriated by female singers. The second source of wassoulou is an acrobatic masked dance called **sogoninkun**, in which women sing to the male masquerader, to the accompaniment of two djembe drums and a *dundun* (cylindrical drum). These two traditions provide the basic

Oumou Sangaré - loving, not praising

musical material for today's urban wassoulou, mixed in with electric guitars and certain more pan-Malian musical elements. The music is pentatonic, and has powerful dance rhythms.

Part of the appeal of wassoulou music to Malian audiences is that it preaches a very different philosophy from that of jelis. It is music of social advice to the whole community, rather than praise of individuals and to perform it, the musician must have some birth connection to the region. Many of the songs address women's issues.

The best-known and most successful performer of this type of music is **Oumou Sangaré**, who burst onto the Malian scene in 1989 with her best-selling cassette *Moussolou* (Women), recorded in Abidjan in 1989. Her songs carry a strong message against female oppression. She criticises, either overtly or in more indirect ways, polygamy, arranged marriages, and the ideology whereby women are slaves to their menfolk. The song which rocketed her to local fame was "Diaraby nene" (Love Fever), an overtly sensual piece about the shivers of passion which remains to this date her 'fetish' (most solicited) piece. Sangaré's subsequent albums, *Ko Sira* and *Worotan*, have expressed increasingly overt attacks on polygamy.

"Since childhood, I've always hated polygamy," she explained. "My father had two wives. It was really a catastrophe. From a young age I started to sing, from nursery school, and I said the day that I take a microphone in front of a crowd of people, the first thing I'm going to do is deplore the people who marry four women, who engage in forced marriage. I had a lot of problems at first. At my concerts at the Palais de la Culture, the men used to wait in their cars. Their wives went into the concert and the men stayed outside. But a few men came inside and now more come. Lots of young women understood and really agreed with

me. They had all that in their heads and were refusing forced marriages. When their parents tried they refused, but they could not express the pain they felt. So, now they had someone who could help them to cry out what they felt."

The main aural hook in Sangaré's music is the punchy, nervous and funky sound of the **kamalengoni** (the youth's harp). This harp was created in the late 1950s by Allata Brulaye Sidibí, who appropriated the powerful melodies of hunters' songs, using them for illicit youth entertainment at night outside the village. The kamalengoni has a staccato sound which characteristically drives the rhythm on, punctuated by the scraping of the *karinyan* metal scraper. The women play the *fle*, a calabash strung with cowrie shells, which they spin and throw in the air at weddings in time to the music. Another Wassoulou dance rhythm is the vigorous *didadi*, performed with a scarf in each hand, which is the basis of the music of another wassoulou singer, Nahawa Doumbia.

Several male singers have also made names for themselves as Wassoulou stars – such as **Yoro Diallo**, whose style is similar to that of Oumou Sangaré; and **Abdoulaye Diabaté**, the lead singer of Sikasso's regional band Kené Star. His album, *Kassikoun*, recorded in Abidjan in 1990 with Kené Star and later released in Paris on the Syllart label, features the didadi rhythm on the powerful track "Sissi Kouloun". Otherwise, wassoulou music is dominated by women singers. The pioneers were **Kagbé Sidibé** and **Coumba Sidibé**, both of whom specialised in the sogoninkun style, with an emphasis on djembe percussion combined with electric guitars.

Sali Sidibé, another influential wassoulou singer and a former member of Mali's Ensemble National, has created her own firmly traditional brand of wassoulou. Her ensemble includes the large Senufo bala, the four-string *bolon* bass harp, and the single-string Fula horse-hair fiddle, the *soku*.

Wassoulou music is youth music, a breath of fresh air after the strict conventions of Mande society. "The jelis direct their singing at a particular individual," says Sangaré. "I sing for everyone, about things that concern everyone; not for one person to make them feel superior. At first we had a lot of problems with the jelimusolu, they complained that we were not griottes, so we had no right to sing. Our answer is that all of us in Wassoulou are artists, all our parents are artists. Before, if you weren't a griot you couldn't sing in Mali. It is we, the Wassoulonke, who have turned all that around." It's a mood that's well attuned to an increasingly confident and democratic Mali.

River Spirit Blues: Songs of Ali Farka Touré

JAK KLIBY

Ali Farka Touré (left) with US bluesman Taj Mahal

Ali Farka Touré, from northern Mali, was born into a family of noble origins, who trace their ancestry back to the sixteenth-century migration from Spain of a Moorish army known as the Armas – part Spanish, part African – who crossed the Sahara to take control of the trade in salt and gold. He plays guitar with a highly distinctive style that's earned him the title 'Bluesman of Africa'. An absolute individualist, his music is a passion for him, but not a profession in the manner of the jelis. He plays as if his fingers had a life of their own, and his conversation, in French, can be equally hard to follow. Journalist and broadcaster Andy Kershaw visited Ali Farka Touré while recording a series for BBC Radio.

I was sent one of Ali Farka's recordings out of the blue. I put it on and was stunned. I wasn't the only one. Of all the records I have ever played on the radio this was the one that elicited the most enquiries. With the rhythmic guitar-picking style and the nasal lonesome vocals, it was the West African version of the delta blues of Lightnin' Hopkins or John Lee Hooker.

Ali's musical roots are firmly in the Songhai and Tuareg cultures of the region between Timbuktu and Gao, although on his albums, *The River* (with various Chieftains) and *The Source* (with Taj Mahal) and most famously *Talking Timbuktu* (with Ry Cooder), he has

teamed up with musicians from other traditions. But while these outings are superbly recorded and well produced, and give Ali's music refreshing new perspectives, nothing can beat the sparse combination on the early Sonodisc recording of voice, guitar and insistent rhythm tapped on the calabash. It is this style that he has returned to on his most recent disc, *Niafunké* (1999), recorded at home with a crew from the World Circuit label.

Niafunké is Ali Farka's hometown and it has charm if not much else. There's a dock, shipping office, school, market, flophouse and a few thousand people. Life revolves around the Niger River, especially when the steamer makes its irregular stops and the riverbank is shrill with the noise of commerce.

From his sporadic earnings, from royalties and European tours, Ali feeds an extended family of more than fifty. His mud-walled compound teems with offspring, second cousins, *petit frères*, the elderly, the newborn and Ali's one wife.

Ali didn't touch his guitar once the whole week we were in Niafunké. His mother told us that it was beneath the dignity of her son to play music. "If you want music," she'd say, "go out and hire a musician." Good thing she wasn't on the trip to Timbuktu when he played his ass off, there and back. I'll never forget the searing sound of his voice and guitar, floating into the still spookiness of a night on the Niger.

discography

Mali

Compilations

 Jali Kunda: Griots of West Africa and Beyond (Elipsis Arts, US).

Kora fans looking for a remedy for the blues should snap up this beautiful book-CD package from the company that does it so well. Musically, the discs are a vehicle mainly for Foday Musa Suso, one of the earliest kora masters to quit Africa, in the 1970s, for the USA.

 Musiques du Mali: Banzoumana and **Sira Mory** (Syllart Productions, France).

Two boxed sets of two CDs each, named after great singers and compiling legendary material from the 1970s, including seminal recordings by the Ensemble National Instrumental, the Rail Band featuring Mory Kanté in James Brown mode, the National Badema with Kasse Mady, Orch National A and other regional orchestras of the period. Essential listening for anyone interested in Mali's music.

◉ **Royaume du Mali** and **Mali Compil** (Syllart Productions, France).

Part of Ibrahim Sylla's 1999 12-volume lucky dip release of African compilations, these two discs provide an idiosyncratic introduction to Mande music culture. *Royaume du Mali* has contributions from Sory Kandia Kouyaté, Kasse Mady and Ami Koita as well as comparative unknowns such as Mory Djely and Camayenne Sofas and, from Senegal, Ismael Lô and Coumba Gawlo. *Mali Compil* is another good crop, with the usual suspects, plus unknowns Haïra Arby, Fodé Kouyaté and the wonderful Amadou & Mariam.

◉ **The Wassoulou Sound: Women of Mali** and **The Wassoulou Sound, Vol 2** (Stern's, UK).

Two excellent compilations featuring a range of styles and female voices from Wassoulou. Includes pioneers of the 'Wassoulou electric' sound, Kagbé Sidibé and Coumba Sidibé, plus the haunting semi-acoustic style of Sali Sidibé and Djeneba Diakhité.

Artists

Bajourou

This was a kind of accoustic super group, teaming guitarist Djelimadi Tounkara (of Rail Band fame) and Bouba Sacko, a favourite of the traditional scene with ex-Rail Band singer Lafia Diabaté.

◉ **Big String Theory** (GlobeStyle, UK).

Lilting cadences derived from the kora and ngoni and mellow vocals make for a stunning set.

Afel Bocoum

An associate and protégé of Ali Farka Touré, Afel Bocoum (born 1955) has worked with the river-blues guitarist since he was a young teenager. The magical song, "Dofana", on Ali's *The Source* is his composition.

◉ **Alkibar** (World Circuit, UK).

Recorded locally, at the same time as Ali's *Niafunké* album, this comes from a smaller, understated mould, but the inflec-

tions and swirling rhythms are similar and the deeply spiritual nature of the music is unmistakeable.

Les Ambassadeurs du Motel

Formed as a resident band at a small Bamako hotel, the Ambassadeurs recruited Salif Keita and Kanté Manfila, to become one of the greatest African bands of all time.

◉ **Les Ambassadeurs du Motel** (Sonafric, France).

Dating from the mid-1970s before their departure for Abidjan, this includes three great classic tracks with Salif Keita: "Diandjon", "Wara" and "Kibaru".

Fanta Damba

Maitresse of the austere Bamana style of praise singing, Fanta Damba was a national symbol in the post-independence era.

◉ **Bahamadou Simogo** (Celluloid, France).

Magisterial vocals and double-tracked ngoni create a powerful impact.

Abdoulaye Diabaté and Kené Star

Abdoulaye Diabaté is a top Bamana singer with his Kené Star band from Sikasso.

◉ **Kassikoun** (Syllart Productions, France).

Rousing electric music, including the didadi dance rhythm (from Wassoulou). Recorded in Abidjan, with arrangements by Boncana Maiga.

Adama Diabaté

Griotte Adama Diabaté's name is perhaps the least known on her first solo CD. She and Makan Tounkara were married in their teens and have worked together for many years.

 Jako Baye (Stern's, UK).

Swing-along-a-Mali: a disc that brings rootsy Adama and her husband Makan Tounkara together with international Malian popsters – including the phenomenally talented ex-Rail Band man Zoumana Djarra – in a perfect blend.

Kasse Mady Diabaté

Arguably the best contemporary Mande voice, Kasse Mady Diabaté rivals Salif Keita for beauty and lyricism, but is absolutely rooted in the jeli tradition.

◉ **Fode** (Stern's, UK).

This hi-tech Paris production, directed by Boncana Maiga, is overproduced in places, but saved by Kasse Mady's spectacular improvisations. Includes his big hits "Fode" and "Laban Djoro".

 Kela Tradition (Stern's, UK).

An almost entirely acoustic studio-produced album, featuring ngoni and balafon as well as guitars, and Jean-Philippe Rykiel on keyboards. Long, expansive and gorgeous versions of Mande classics like "Koulandjan" and "Kaira". Essential.

Naïny Diabaté

Naíny Diabaté is a popular Bamako-based jelimuso, born in 1963, who made her first public appearance with the Rail Band and was one of the first Malian griottes to use television in her career rise.

Nafa (Stern's, UK).

As a follower of the modernising tendency from the Diabaté griots, Naïny's songs have won her a mass audience at home for their mixing of traditional themes with upbeat arrangements and contemporary instrumentation. *Nafa* is her debut international release, and displays plenty of examples of Zouk-Mande and Congolese-style Mandé. Roots fans may bridle, but this is the dominant groove of Bamako's streets and airwaves today.

Sidiki Diabaté, Batourou Kouyate & Djelimadi Sissoko

Mali's three greatest kora players of the older generation.

○ Cordes Anciennes
(Barenreiter Musicaphon, Germany).

Classic 1970 recording, featuring rippling instrumental duets by these legendary figures. A privileged view into the past.

Sira Mory Diabaté

The late first lady of Mali's female jelis.

▣ Sira Mori (Syllart, Paris/Mali).

The only published solo recording by this legendary figure. Includes her famous love song "Sara". A historic recording; very poor technical quality, but worth acquiring nonethless for the music and voice.

Toumani Diabaté

Mali's brilliant kora virtuoso, Toumani Diabate is an ambitious and highly creative artist and probably the best young player around at the present time.

 Kaira (Hannibal, UK).

Instrumental solo kora in the classic style. Exquisite melodies like "Alla l'aa ke" and "Jarabi" and superb musicianship. Could hardly be better within its genre.

CD Djelika
(Hannibal, UK).

On this 1998 release Toumani teamed up with some ace contributors – Danny Thompson on bass, Keletigui Diabaté on balafon and Ba Sekou Kouyaté on ngoni – to produce one of the essential instrumental albums from West Africa. A super-good CD.

WITH BALLAKE SISSOKO

 New Ancient strings (Hannibal, UK).

Instrumental kora duets recorded in Mali on state-of-the-art equipment, showing the extraordinary artistry of these two young cousins following in their legendary fathers' footsteps.

WITH KETAMA AND OTHERS

CD Songhai 1 and **Songhai 2**
(Hannibal, UK).

Two extraordinary collaborations between Toumani and new flamenco group Ketama. *Songhai 1* (with delicate bass from Danny Thompson) created a huge impact on the World Music scene in 1987. *Songhai 2* is equally worthy of attention and includes guest artist Keletigui Diabaté on balafon and wizard ngoni player Ba Sekou Kouyaté, with Kasse Mady doing solo vocals on two tracks, and the lush choruses of Djanka Diabaté and Diaw Kouyate. Mali fusion at its finest.

Zoumana Diarra

Diarra is an exceptionally gifted guitarist, composer,

instrument-maker who has paid his dues with Alpha Blondy's band Dafrastar and then with the Super Rail Band, Super Biton and Super Djata.

 Ballad of Manding (Stern's, UK).

Super-sweet guitar – an all-instrumental album from Mali via Holland and Paris.

Mamadou Doumbia with Mandinka

Mamadou Doumbia is another former member of the Rail Band, who has for some time now forged a career in Japan.

 Independence (JVC, Japan).

A mix of hot guitar and kora with Japanese singers. This is different, wake-up music and experimental in the best sense. It doesn't always work but the kora and Okinawan voices blend, heaven-like, more than once. If you're hooked, check out its successor, **Jafa** (also JVC, Japan).

MAMADOU DOUMBIA with MANDINKA

Nahawa Doumbia

A Bamana singer with a pure fresh voice, Nahawa Doumbia was one of the first Wassoulou artists to gain international release.

 Nyama Toutou (Stern's, UK).

Paris-produced electric Bambara and Wassoulou music. Slick, but pleasing.

 Yankaw (Cobalt, France).

Similar material in a more acoustic vein. Recorded entirely in Bamako, with superb solos on balafon and djembe, plus a moving a cappella solo song.

Alou Fane's Fote Mocoba

Acoustic trio led by the late Super Djata Band vocalist, exploring hunters' rhythms of the Bamana and Wassoulou.

 Alou Fane's Fote Mocoba (Dakar Sound, Holland).

Buzzing harp, spiraling balafon and singing that makes you jump out of your seat. Wild and compelling stuff.

Salif Keita

Mali's golden voice and principal musical moderniser, Salif Keita remains totally inimitable. It's hard to narrow the recommendations down, as almost every one of his records remains interesting and enjoyable, as he has traded production ideas with collaborators from Carlos Santana to Steve Hillage.

◉ **Inedits 1969–1980** (Celluloid, France).

An essential collection of early material, including the epic praise song "Mandjou" and the incendiary guitar work-out "N'Toman".

 Soro
(Stern's UK; Mango US).

These breathtaking and seamless hi-tech arrangements of Mande music provided Keita with one of the biggest-selling African recordings ever – and a place on the World Music stage. Guitarist Ousmane Kouyaté and French keyboard player Jean-Philippe Rykiel provided the perfect backdrop to some extraordinary vocals.

◉ **Folon: The Past** (Mango, UK).

More spontaneous and funky than anything he'd done since Ambassadeurs days, this went back to Salif's roots in Mande culture with stunning melodies and vocals. Plus a new more jazzy version of "Mandjou".

◉ **L'enfant Lion** (Mango, UK).

Gorgeous soundtrack to the film (starring the man himself), co-written by Steve Hillage. Highlights include Salif's stunning acoustic version of the love song "Cherie" accompanied on the Maninka *simbin* (ten-string hunters' harp).

◉ **The Mansa of Mali... a Retrospective** (Mango, UK).

This includes highlights from the Mango releases, plus Salif's all-time hit from 1978 with Les Ambassadeurs: "Mandjou". And it's worth getting the album just for this – one of the finest Mande praise songs ever, with remarkable guitar solos from Ousmane Kouyate and soaring, passionate vocals.

◉ **Papa** (Metro Blue/Blue Note, France).

The 1999 album, recorded in Paris, New York and Keita's own Studio Wanda in Bamako, holds few surprises in its hi-tech production values and diverse credits. A deep strand of melancholy runs through this album, even on the bright "Tolon Willy" (The Party's On) where Grace Jones adds a dark tone. The title track is a requiem to his father, who died in 1995.

Ami Koita

One of Mali's top female singers, Koita combines a feisty attitude with a strong melodic sense.

◉ **Tata Sira** (Bolibana, Paris).

Semi-acoustic music in the Maninka jeli tradition, with some powerful and inspiring renditions of classic tunes plus some of her own compositions, for example, "Simba".

◉ **Songs of Praise** (Stern's, UK).

A late 1980s release of semi-acoustic music from two local cassettes. Slightly more hi-tech than *Tata Sira*, but with some belting tunes.

Habib Koité and Bamada

Habib Koité is a fast-rising singer-songwriter jeli who goes well beyond Bamana praise songs to include traditions from across Mali.

 Maya
(Putumayo, US).

Koité's first international release puts his acoustic guitar to the fore and uses no synths. While there are traces of folksiness ("I like technology but fear for our forest") the musicians deliver a subtle and intriguing set of songs with a folkloric sensitivi-

ty to subject matter and roots. Fans of the Senegalese singer and guitarist Ismael Lô will like this a lot.

Babani Koné

Babani Koné is a Bamako-based jelimuso. Born in 1968 in Ségou (home of the classical Bamana style), she combines, like many of her generation of griottes, a large measure of respect for the old traditions (she was trained by Fanta Damba), with a full-on acceptance of Congolese, Antillean and other popular local influences.

◉ **Sanou Djala** (Stern's, UK).

By the measure of this album (first released on cassette in Bamako), Babani is one of the most forward exponents of Mande-pop. Drum machine plugged in, synth set to 'strings', she steams through a set of souped-up praise songs and ballads, including a lovely tribute to women on the title track.

Kandia Kouyaté

Kandia Kouyaté – 'La dangéreuse' – has been Mali's top jelimuso for the past two decades. Her forceful voice and choral arrangements (it was Kandia, in the 1980s, who initiated the use of those dreamlike female choruses which are now the hallmark of much of the best-known Mande music) are in a similar vein to Salif Keita's, and her working of traditional social and court music has earned her huge wealth, including a personal jet, and a status unequalled by any other female artist from Mali.

 Kita Kan
(Stern's, UK).

This, astonishingly, is Kandia's first international release (and first CD). The kora, ngoni, guitars and balafon xylophones just keep on rolling and there are enough lush studio effects – and even full orchestral backing – to qualify Kita Kan for any number of radio playlists.

Tata Bambo Kouyaté

Raw-voiced diva of the Bamako wedding circuit.

◉ **Jatigui** (Globe Style, UK).

Stunning 1985 album of Mande jeli praise song by one of its most dynamic female singers. Acoustic accompaniment from the full range of Mande instruments plus Fulani flute.

Le (Super) Rail Band du Bamako

The Rail Band were the buffet band at Bamako railway station, and have served as a school for many of Mali's finest singers and musicians since 1969, including Mory Kanté and Salif Keita.

LE RAIL BAND DU BAMAKO

◉ **Mali Stars: Mory Kanté** (Syllart, France).

The sound of the Rail Band in the mid-1970s, pre-Abidjan, featuring inspired and relaxed vocals from Mory Kanté, with one track, "Tie diuguya", by a lesser known but superb singer, Jalimadi Sissoko.

LE SUPER RAIL BAND DU BAMAKO

◉ **New dimensions in Rail Culture** (GlobeStyle, UK).

The legendary band at a peak of mellowness, featuring the rich, warm voice of Lafia Diabaté and the rocking guitar of Djelimady Tounkara. Recorded in Abidjan circa 1981.

The train keeps rolling

 Mansa
(Indigo, France).

Immaculately produced French studio set from 1996 that beautifully captures the Rail Band's effortless, floating style of Mande dance music. The title track, taking traditional guitar into psychedlic realms – a kind of Dire Straits injected with African passion – is already a classic.

Fanta Sacko

Fanta Sacko's preference for personal and emotional themes over standard praise-singing, and her kora-inflected accoustic guitar backing were revolutionary and highly influential at the beginning of the 1970s.

O Fanta Sacko (Barenreiter Musicaphon, Germany).

The first album (1970) of bajourou music, featuring love and praise songs. The unaffected emotional singing and simple, but effective, guitar backing are deeply touching.

Oumou Sangaré

Charisma, outspoken views and a stunning voice have made Oumou Sangaré the biggest star of Wassoulou music, while a World Circuit contract has deservedly helped to propel her onto the World Music stage.

Moussolou (World Circuit, UK).

This first album sold 200,000 copies in West Africa and drew worldwide attention to Wassoulou music. Hard-driving semi-acoustic music recorded in Abidjan.

 Worotan
(World Circuit, UK).

On her most ambitious album yet, Sangaré defies tradition with her lyrics ("marry you? why?!"), custom with her musical arrangements (Pee Wee Ellis and others adding funky horn grooves) and stereotyping with her range (funky dance numbers to moody ballads). There are also two tracks in straight acoustic hunters' style, as well as the lyrical ballad with acoustic guitar, "Djorolen" (Anguish). A pretty good CD in other words.

Coumba Sidibé

The queen mother of Wassoulou, Coumba Sidibé was an early moderniser of the music.

Djanjoba (Camara Productions, France).

Her third solo CD on the Paris-based Malian label Camara. Based mainly on the hunters' repertoire with rocking rhythms and her inimitable powerful vocals.

Sali Sidibé

Sali Sidibé is Oumou Sangaré's principal rival as the leading wassoulou singer. She is a slightly older artist, with a wonderfully earthy and emotive voice.

Wassoulou Foli (Stern's, UK).

A medium-tech, but enjoyable outing.

Super Biton de Ségou

This was a pioneering 1980s roots band in the rocking Bamana tradition of Ségou.

Afro-Jazz du Mali (Bolibana, France).

Hard-driving dances rhythms powerfully translated onto guitars and horns create an exciting departure from the more stately Maninka tradition. Early 1980s recordings.

Ali Farka Touré

While Ali Farka Touré's spiritual life plays the major inspirational role in his music, his distinctive guitar style and rough nasal vocals have led to him being dubbed the John Lee Hooker – or simply 'the Bluesman' – of Africa. He has collaborated with some big names from the West, notably Ry Cooder, but always on his own terms.

Radio Mali (World Circuit, UK).

A beautifully produced compilation of radio recordings in Ali's swinging, bluesy style, made from 1970–1978, a decade or more before he achieved international recognition, and at a time when, as he says, "I was an absolute fool for the guitar". The World Circuit team painstakingly trawled Bamako's radio archive and, considering the antiquity of the source material, the results here are little short of miraculous.

Ali Farka Touré (World Circuit, UK).

Ten all-acoustic songs from 1987, coinciding with the first rush of Ali Farka fever. Dig the big blues sound on "Amandrai". Essential.

The Source (World Circuit, UK).

Perhaps almost as essential, this sees Ali link up with Taj Mahal, Nana Tsiboe, and British-Asian Nitin Sawney on tabla. The best of another ten great tracks are "Hawa Dolo" and the upbeat loping river sound of "Mahini Me".

Niafunké
(World Circuit, UK).

Recorded in Ali's home town by the label with the Midas touch, this is a determined return to roots in every sense, allowing the world to hear Ali doing his wonderful stuff in his own backyard. Says producer Nick Gold: "It was done very organically and very fast – Ali's a one-take man. And he's a farmer first and foremost. He'd go off to see if a water pump was working. The crops always had to come first." The relaxed, but impromptu nature of every track bursts out. "I don't feel as good anywhere else as I do at home" is Ali's explanation. The result is a formidable work.

ALI FARKA TOURÉ AND RY COODER

 Talking Timbuktu
(World Circuit, UK).

Topping many indie charts within days of release in 1994, this Grammy Award winner was a World Music CD out of left field. With Ali in seamless slide-blues collaboration with Ry Cooder, it hits with a rawness and conviction underlining the sense that here is simply a group of great musicians listening hard to one another and playing together in a room.

Sidi Touré

Sidi Touré is a songhai singer and guitarist from the medieval city of Gao, on the fringes of the Sahara.

Hoga (Stern's, UK).

Devotees of Ali Farka should not delay in acquiring this from another Touré – most of the songs sound like Ali on speed. They also sound as if a lot of sand was blowing around the studio in Bamako. Atmosphere? Il y en a beaucoup!

Boubacar Traoré

Boubacar Traoré is a veteran Malian music entrepreneur, singer and guitarist from the western city of Kayes.

Kar kar (Stern's, UK).

Traoré creates his own unique non-jeli style of wistful acoustic love songs on this album.

Rokia Traoré

Born in 1973, Rokia Traoré is an innovative young singer-songwriter-guitarist who has made a huge impact wherever she has performed abroad, though she is still relatively unknown at home in Mali. She has forged unusual combinations, for example the *balaba* balafon of her home region in southern Mali and the dry ngoni of the Bamana jeli.

rokia traoré

 Mouneïssa
(Label Bleu/Indigo, France).

Dulcet-voiced and gently lyrical, nine songs to calm the troubled spirit, with the big liquid sound of the balafon and the insect-strum of the ngoni creating a delightful fusion.

Guinea

Compilations

 Guinée Compil
(Syllart Productions, France).

A rare compilation of Guinea's modern musicians which confirms the country's major musical status. Stars like Mory Kanté and Kanté Manfila rub shoulders with the excellent and little known Dourah Barry and others. Fodé Kouyaté's contribution, "Sokho" is a particular muscular dance track, synths and drum machines to the fore, but not omitting that quintessential Mande chorus.

Artists

Balla et ses Balladins

One of Guinea's best ever bands, superbly modernising deep Maninka songs.

 Reminiscin' in tempo with Balla et ses Balladins (Popular African Music, Germany).

Compilation of greats with the classic Guinea-rumba sound of the 1960s and '70s. Includes two stunning versions of one of the greatest Mande love songs: "Sara".

Les Ballets Africains

West Africa's foremost musical ensemble, created in 1952, have made many international tours and perform a spectacular live show.

Héritage (Buda Musique du Monde, France).

Recorded in Conakry in 1995, this production ranges across Guinea's cultural heritage – from the mythical origin of the balafon to family totems and bird-chasing in the rice fields. A richly woven sound tapestry.

Bembeya Jazz National

Guinea's greatest band of the post-independence era, and still the country's defining musical export.

 Live: 10 Ans de Succes
(Bolibana, France).

Atmospheric session, recorded in Guinea at their best period (1971). Some wild solos from 'diamond fingers' lead guitarist Sekou Bembeya Diabaté, and the unforgettable voice of Aboubacar Demba Camara.

Bembeya Jazz National
(Sonodisc/Esperance, France).

Bembeya in the mid-1980s with their classic recording of "Lanaya", featuring the romantic voice of Sekouba Bambino.

Oumou Dioubaté

A griotte of the dancefloor from Kankan in Haute Guinée, and one of Guinea's most succesful artists, Omou Dioubaté has been based in Paris since the 1980s. She earned the soubriquet 'La Femme Chic-Shoc' for her looks and confrontational attitude. In a deeply patriarchal society, her lyrics convey a threat to the establishment.

◉ **Wambara** (Stern's, UK).

Stunning melody lines, irrepressible beats and nice guitar work mark a set of original songs from a real individual. Oumou's inherited jeli background is the soil in which they're planted, not the crop itself.

Sekouba Bambino Diabaté

The young star of Bembeya Jazz, Sekouba is now Guinea's top male vocalist.

◉ **Le Destin** (Popular African Music, Germany).

Bambino leads his own semi-acoustic band through the lighter side of Guinea's praise song tradition. A sweet voice with wonderful arrangements.

 Kassa
(Stern's, UK).

A terrific album produced in Paris by veteran Ibrahima Sylla, this includes some hi-tech dance tracks as well as the stunning tribute to Guinea's diamond miners. Sekouba is accompanied on piano by Paulino Vieira (of Cesaria Evora's band).

Kade Diawara

Guinea's finest female singer in the Mande tradition.

▦ **L'Archange du Manding**
(Bolibana, Guinea-Conkary/France).

Rolling love songs with acoustic guitar accompaniment. Classic 1970s recording.

▦ **L'Eternelle Kade Diawara** (AMC, Guinea-Conakry).

A brillant 1990s return by Guinea's arc-angel, now in semi-acoustic vein.

Jali Musa Jawara

Mory Kanté's kora-playing half brother leads an excellent, all-acoustic ensemble.

 Yasimika
(Hannibal, UK).

Superbly ethereal, flowing music on guitars, kora and balafon, with luscious choruses from Djanka Diabaté and Djenne Doumbia and soaring vocals from Jali Musa himself. Recorded in Abidjan in 1983, this is one of the classics of Mande acoustic music and nothing he's done since has matched it.

Kaloum Star

Founded back in 1969 by Maître Barry, Kaloum Star was the last state-run band to be set up during the rule of Sekou Touré.

◉ **Felenko** (Buda Musique du Monde, France).

Fine, well-developed songs from the veteran Guinean band. The title track carries a strong flavour of Fela Kuti's Afro-Beat.

Mory Kanté

The former Rail Band singer modernised the kora with breathtaking chutzpah and remains unique in having had an acid house kora club hit.

◉ **10 Cola Nuts** (Barclay, France).

Heavy on the drum kit and synthesiser but some superb material, including the beautiful "Teriya" (reworked from an earlier Rail Band song, "Balakoninfi"), plus one song just with kora. One of Kanté's best albums, recorded in 1987.

 Akwaba Beach
(Barclay, France).

Kanté's breakthrough album, with his worldwide hit "Yeke yeke". Hi-tech kora music for the dance floor.

◉ **Tatebola** (Arcade/Missliin, France).

Mory in slightly more mellow mode, with a lovely version of the classic kora song "Alla l'aa ke".

◉ **N'Diarabi** (Celluloid, France).

A completely acoustic outing.

Sory Kandia Kouyaté

Guinea's greatest traditional singer of the post-independence era, Sory Kandia Kouyaté's high and unmistakable voice made him a national institution.

◉ **L'Epopée du Manding Vols 1 & 2**
(Bolibana, France).

Praise songs in the Mande tradition, with acoustic accompaniment on kora (Sidiki Diabaté) and balafon. Recorded in Guinea, around 1969.

El Hadj Jeli Sory Kouyaté

All the most renowned balafon players are from Guinea, and Djeli Sory Kouyaté, the former leader of Guinea's National Ensemble, born in 1918 and cousin of Sory Kandia Kouyaté, is perhaps the greatest of them all.

◉ **Guinée: Anthologie du Balafon Mandingue/ Vol III Le Balafon en Liberté** (Buda/Musique du Monde, France).

Third of a four-volume set, recorded in 1991 at the Palais du Peuple in Conakry, this showcases the luminous talent of the master of the Susu balafon, a type of instrument nearly 900 years old.

MUSIQUE DU MONDE
Music from the World

MOMO
WANDEL
SOUMAH

GUINÉE: "MATCHOWÉ"
Guinea: "Matchowé"

Kanté Manfila

The guitar wizard of the Ambassadeurs, Kanté Manfila is one of Africa's most innovative guitarists.

◉ **Tradition** (Celluloid, France).

Gorgeous rolling acoustic melodies with guitars and balafon, and kora accompaniment by cousin Mory Kanté.

◉ **Kankan Blues** (Popular African Music, Germany).

Probably the best of a trio of acoustic offerings on the PAM label.

Momo Wandel

Momo Wandel was a conservatoire-trained saxphonist who studied jazz and performed with the Orchestre Kélétigui during Sékou Touré's dictatorship.

◉ **Soumah** (Buda/Auvidis, France).

A rich voice to complement a strongly flavoured union of jazz and Guinean music. Mande crossover in the best taste.

Mauritania & Western Sahara

the ways of the moors

Mauritania is the meeting place of West Africa and the Maghreb – a huge country reaching between Morocco and Senegal. Most of it is desert – traditionally barren camel and goat-herding country – and in recent years droughts have caused a steady flow of nomads towards the cities. Now over ninety percent of the population lives in or around the cities and the population of Nouakchott, the capital, has increased from around 20,000 in the 1960s to more than half a million today. **David Muddyman** and **Richard Trillo** listen to the music of a country on the far-western shores of the Arabic-speaking world, and to the related sounds of the Sahrawi refugees from the disputed neighbouring territory of **Western Sahara**, occupied since 1973 by Morocco.

Mauritania's name comes from its dominant ethnic group, the Moors (Maures in French), a people broadly divided into 'white' Bidan (who claim ancestry from north of the Sahara) and 'black' Haratin whose physical ancestry lies in Saharan and sub-Saharan Africa. The Haratin were traditionally vassals of the Bidan noble class, though social status in Mauritania is considerably more than a question of skin colour. Until quite late in the twentieth century, Moorish society had a strict hierarchical class system.

In this system, musicians, known as **iggawin**, occupied the lowest rung beneath the warriors (*hassans*), merchants and others. Being a hereditary caste, their skills were (and are) handed down from generation to generation, from father to son, or from mother to daughter. Marriages almost always take place between people of the same class (the men always have the word *ould* between their names, meaning 'son of'; likewise women are *mint*, 'daughter of'). Despite the rigid social structure, women in Mauritania have more freedom than in most Arabic-speaking countries, reflecting their mixed African and Berber heritage. The Berbers were the indigenous people of Northwest Africa, the lords of the land before the great westerly migration of Arabs and Arabic culture that began in the seventh century.

Iggawin Traditions

One traditional task of the iggawin was to follow the warriors on campaigns and raids, extolling their bravery and encouraging them into battle. At other times the iggawin would entertain their patrons with **praise songs** about the great deeds of their ancestors. And they would also act as social historians, poets and jokers, in much the same way as the griots of Mali and Guinea, and elsewhere. Before the days of radio it was also the job of the iggawin to act as newscasters, touring the villages and reciting news from the outside world to musical accompaniment. And they sang **epic songs** which were used as teaching stories for the entertainment of both children and adults.

Today, professional musicians can be employed by anyone in return for money or other gifts. And since the advent of recording on tape, it has been the custom for patrons to record the entertainment for their own use – the recordings passing into their ownership rather than the musicians'. Many songs of the iggawin repertoire are Middle Eastern in character and others are simple enough for the audience to take up the chorus.

Instruments

There are different sets of instruments for men and women. The traditional **male instrument** is the **tidinit**, a small hourglass-shaped lute with four strings – two long strings on which the melody is played and two short ones which provide a drone-like accompaniment. This is very similar to other lutes found in West Africa, such as the Wolof *khalem* or *xalam*, and the Mande *ngoni*. In recent years the tidinit has increasingly been replaced, or augmented, by the **electric guitar**.

The main instrument used by **women** is the **ardin**, which looks like a back-to-front kora. It has a body made from a large, skin-covered half-gourd, through which a curved wooden pole is inserted, onto which anything from 10 to 14 strings are attached with leather thongs. Other instruments

Khalifa Ould Eide and Dimi Mint Abba

ANNE HUNT

MAURITANIA & WESTERN SAHARA

Dimi Mint Abba and other artists

One of the most successful musicians to have emerged from the Moorish tradition is the female singer **Dimi Mint Abba**. Born in 1958 to musical parents (her father was asked to compose the national anthem when Mauritania gained independence from France in 1960), Dimi sang and accompanied her father and mother on the *tbal* from an early age, and, from the age of ten, was taught to play the *ardin* by her mother.

In 1976 she was invited to sing on Mauritanian radio, and people first heard her stunning voice. This led to her being entered for the Umm Kalthum Contest in Tunis in 1977. Since then she has toured Africa and Europe and has gained a reputation as one of the Muslim world's greatest singers, while remaining a favourite at home.

During her European tour in 1990 Dimi Mint Abba recorded an evocative album for World Circuit. At the time she was touring with her husband Khalifa Ould Eide, who played guitar and tidinit, and two daughters from a previous marriage, Zeyrouz Mint Seylami and Garmi Mint Abba, who dance, sometimes with remarkable eroticism, and play drums.

The song that won the Umm Kalthum Contest, "Sawt Elfan" (Art's Plume), is included on the album. Written by Ahmedou Ould Abdel Qadir, it tells how the artist's work, in many ways, is more important than the work of the warriors:

Art's Plume is a balsam,
a weapon and a guide
enlightening the spirit of men.
Indeed, it is the world of truth
living between the flickerings of visions
and the folds of the imagination.
Indeed, between the flickerings of visions,
the fold of the imagination,
and the eyes of the impossible,
Winged songs in rapture
float aboard a vessel of hopes!

Among other contemporary artists, the most interesting that have been recorded on Western labels are **Tahra** and **Malouma**, both of whom are female singers and ardin-players. Tahra recorded a crossover album, *Yamen Yamen*, in 1989, with songs sung in Arabic, French and English, and with a hi-tech Moorish-tinged backing. Malouma's album, *Desert Of Eden*, released on the US Shanchie label nearly a decade later, took the Moorish ways deep into the land of fusion.

used by the iggawin are the **tbal**, a large kettle-drum, and, occasionally, the **daghumma**, a long hollowed-out gourd covered by a net of beads which acts as a rattle.

Ways and Modes

By tradition, musicians play in one of three **'ways'**; the white way (*al-bayda*), the black way (*al-kahla*), or the spotted or mixed way (*l'-gnaydiya*), which refer implicitly to rank in the Moorish racial or quasi-racial social hiearchy and levels of worthiness and closeness to God. They also have implications of mood: the black way tends to be associated with earthy, masculine qualities, while the white way is more delicate and refined.

Rhythm and key are critical in distinguishing the ways. On commencing a way, the musical progression consists of five **modes** (*bhor*) played in strict order – a sophisticated system derived from Arabic musical theory but, since as far back as the seventeenth century, deeply imbued with Moorish cultural connotations and, as might be expected, also identified to some extent by colour. The first four modes, which are called *karr, fagu* (both considered black), *lakhal* and *labyad* (white) correspond either to a period in the life cycle or to a mood or emotion. The fifth mode, *lebtayt* (white) relates to a higher state of consciousness and, by analogy with the life cycle, to the time after death. The system seems complex enough, but is further elaborated by sub-modes, which qualify the main mode within the way. Female musicians, happily enough for them, are not bound to the same degree by the rules and make free with the ways and modes in the same piece of music.

A B C D E F G H I J K L

Sahrawi Sounds from the Refugee Camps

When the Spanish dictator Franco died in 1975, Spain lost no time in ridding itself of its colonies. **Western Sahara** (Spanish Sahara), a huge tract of desert between Morocco, Algeria and Mauritania, was abandoned. The discovery of phosphate reserves, however, had by then already brought the region to the attention of the UN, as Morocco and Mauritania both staked claims, and in 1973 Morocco's King Hassan mounted a mass march of Moroccans to lay claim to their 'ancestral' right to live there. This led to twenty years of war and, latterly, a decade of stand-off, as the UN brokered a ceasefire between Morocco and the Sahrawis (the Polisario Front) and attempted vainly to arrange a referendum to determine the territory's future. In these years, a generation of Moroccans has grown up having lived all their lives in Western Sahara, and a generation of indigenous Sahrawis have become a state-in-exile in camps in southern Algeria.

Musically, the Sahrawis share the Mauritanian Moorish obsession with form – the **ways and modes** are adhered to, though perhaps less rigidly. But the refugee life has brought significant changes both in the rules of conduct and in the instruments available. Firstly, unlike Mauritanian musicians, who are invariably born into their profession as members of the *iggawin* caste, Sahrawi artists in the camps come from all backgrounds. Music, which they call **hawl**, and in particular the expression of lyricism, is open to all, and deeply appreciated, in a surprisingly unrestrained and democratic way.

Secondly, the Sahrawis use fewer traditional instruments than their Mauritanian neighbours. An uprooted and uncertain life, and dependence on foreign aid, has shaved away some of the more esoteric items in the traditional instrumental range. The **tbal** is still the basic weapon of percussion, but the **tidinit** is heard less often and has been replaced by the **electric guitar**, bringing a harder, funkier edge to the music that makes it all the more accessible to the untrained ear.

Manuel Dominguez, who runs the Spanish label NubeNegra, visited the Sahrawi camps in 1997, to record music at a festival. The result was a three-CD box set called "Saharauis". Richard Trillo spoke to him about the project.

Apart from separate liner notes for each CD, there's a very detailed booklet to go with the whole package...what were you hoping to achieve?

Yes, an important part of the project was to give the listener the opportunity to look at images of the desert and its people. In these pages we find the beauty of the sandscapes, and we also see the children, women, men and the old people from the Sahara, the musicians, their instruments, the dancers and their mysterious sensuality.

A large part of this booklet is given over to detailed descriptions of excursions and tales of what went on during those fifteen days of sun and sand when we were recording. Alberto Gambino and Luis Delgado, the producers, became involved in getting inside the musical theories on which music, song, dance and poetry are based. A brief but I hope interesting account brings us closer to the basis of *hawl* – a commentary about poets, successors to the mythical figure of Igag Yen and near to the contemporary griot idea. We've also included a short introduction to the unique Sahrawi dances. It's hard to find any comparable styles elsewhere in Africa.

There is also an accompanying CD-Rom. What will people find on it?

I thought it was important to make as complete a 'record' as possible, in light of the fact that all over the Saharan occupied territory, cultural manifestations have been persecuted. The refugee camps are responsible for safekeeping traditional culture, but at the same time, due to the current circumstances, all this tradition will be forced to undergo sudden changes.

Tell us about the CD called A Pesar de las Heridas (Despite the Wounds).

It's dedicated entirely to chants by Sahrawi women, with tidinit, tbal and acoustic and electric guitars. Some of these vocalists, like Mariem Hassan, Teita Lebid or Hadhum Abeid are simply amazing. They convey the emotional build-up of years and years of suffering. More modern, happier, lighter but I suppose less revealing are the young voices of Aziza Brahim, Serguela Abdi or Naha Salec. And then somewhere in between, you get these splendid voices of Jeirana Embarec and Faknash Abeid. It's a recording that tries to respect musical tradition.

What about Sahará, Terra Mía (Sahara, My Land)?

Sahara, My Land is intended to present a contemporary panorama of Sahrawi music. So you get the evolution of traditional structure through the contribution of original authors and composers and you can easily hear the key role played by the electric guitar in this development. Other modern instruments are starting to be used more and more frequently, too. Nayim Alal, a fantastic guitarist who's also an excellent composer and a talented singer, is the highlight of this CD.

The last CD is Polisario Vencerá – 'Polisario Will Win'. Do you think they will? What does the future hold?

This disc is actually a re-issue of a recording I made in 1982. It's a collection of epic songs interpreted by the group **Martir Luali**, calling the Sahrawi people to defend their country and to conquer land illegally taken from them. You get to hear younger versions of Hadhum, Teita, Mariem and Mafhud and various others who are on the other CDs.

As for your question, who can say? They deserve to. Perhaps it depends on whatever changes might come in Morocco following the death of King Hassan.

MAURITANIA & WESTERN SAHARA

discography

Mauritania

Compilations

 Mauritanie: Chants de Femmes Nemadi
(Buda/Musique du Monde, France).

A deeply obscure and fascinating recording of women's songs from a remote corner of southeast Mauritania. The Nemadi are a hunting caste, whose origins are old and barely known. Traditionally despised by mainstream Moorish society for their bush knowledge, oblique approach to Islam and close attachment to their hunting dogs, the Nemadi's way of life is threatened by drought and the attentions of law enforcers (hunting is illegal in Mauritania). While the Nemadi sometimes sing their own versions of the Moorish classics, Nemadi hunting songs and competitive love songs, in which two or more protagonists try to outshine each other in eloquence and musical skill, are more representative.

Musique Maure (Ocora, France).

A pleasant and diverse, if not exactly earth-shattering introduction to the ways and modes.

Mauritanie Vols 1 and 2 – Anthologie de la Musique Maure / Hodh Oriental (Ocora, France).

Concentrates on the black and white ways for solo instruments and voice.

Khalifa Ould Eide and Dimi Mint Abba

Khalifa and Dimi, together with Dimi's two daughters, were the first Mauritanian artists to tour in the English-speaking world, back in the mid-1980s.

 Moorish Music from Mauritania
(World Circuit, UK).

A beautiful and evocative CD – if you haven't seen them on tour then this gives some insight into their special sound. Notice the flamenco-style hand-clapping.

Malouma

Malouma is in a league of her own, a hereditary ardine-playing griot and modern singer at the same time, who mixes the Senegalese *mbalax* style with her own Moorish traditions. While singing exclusively in the Hassaniya dialect of Arabic, she shows no obedience to Moorish musical strictures. This individualism, together with her endorsement of the political opposition in Mauritania, has made her artistic life there uncomfortable.

 Desert of Eden
(Shanachie, US).

This jazz-inflected debut CD is highly accessible and even approaches an easy-listening groove on one or two tracks (echoes of C&W on "Maghrour", for example, and of Motown on "Fa Fa Fa Fa"). That may not appeal to all. Nevertheless, the ardin shines through to distinctive effect.

Tahra

Born in Nema in southeastern Mauritania in 1959, Tahra Mint Hembara is a hereditary griot (her aunt was the famed Lekhdera Mint Ahmed Zeidane) who has been steeped in Moorish musical tradition since the age of ten.

Yamen Yamen (EMI, France).

Released in 1989, with Jean-Philippe Rykiel on synth, this was in some ways a forerunner of Malouma's Desert Eden, testing the stretchability of classic musical traditions on the world stage. An intriguing album of Mooro-tech: on first hearing anyone would be forgiven for having no idea where this comes from.

Western Sahara

Saharauis
(NubeNegra, Spain).

A stunningly packaged 3-CD set of music recorded in the Western Sahara refugee camps in Algeria. Complete with colour booklet, detailed liner notes and recordings old and new, this is instructive, hauntingly beautiful – and pretty funky at times. See feature box on previous page.

Morocco

a basic expression of life

Wherever you go in Morocco you are likely to hear music. It is the basic expression of the country's folk culture – indeed to many of the illiterate country people it is the sole expression – and in its traditions it covers the whole history of the country. There are long and ancient pieces designed for participation by the entire communities of Berber villages; songs and instrumental music brought by the Arabs from the east and Andalucían Spain; and in the 1950s, the struggle for independence, too, found celebration in song. In addition, Morocco has an important tradition of trance music, from the gnaouas and other sects; and, since the 1970s it has had a culture of rock-influenced *chaabi* bands, which in recent years has mutated through collision with (Western) dance culture. **Dave Muddyman** slips on his *babouches* . . .

Although the most common musical phenomenon that you will hear is the *muezzin* calling the faithful to prayer, amplified from minarets, most Moroccan music is performed for the sake of entertainment rather than religion. At every weekly souk, or market, you will find a band playing in a patch of shade, or a stall blasting out cassettes they have on sale. In the evenings many cafés feature musicians, particularly during the long nights of Ramadan. TV also plays its part, with two weekly programmes devoted to music, and the radio stations, too, broadcast a variety of sounds.

Festivals are perhaps the most rewarding. Every popular or religious festival (*moussem*) involves musicians, and the larger **moussems** are always rewarding. Keep an eye out for cultural festivals, too, in particular the international **Festival of Sacred Music** held at the end of May in **Fes** (Fez) which is fast becoming one of the key events of the World Music calendar. For details, take a look at its website (*www.morocco-fezfestival.com*).

Berber Music

Berber music is quite distinct from Arab-influenced forms in its rhythms, tunings, instruments and sounds. It is an extremely ancient tradition, probably long predating even the arrival of Arabs in Morocco, and has been passed on orally from generation to generation. There are three main categories: village music, ritual music and the music of professional musicians.

Village music is essentially a collective performance. Men and women of the entire village will assemble on festive occasions to dance and sing

together. The best-known dances are the **ahouach**, in the western High Atlas, and the **ahidus**, performed by Chleuh Berbers in the eastern High Atlas. In each, drums (*bendirs*) and flutes (*neys*) are the only instruments used. The dance begins with a chanted prayer, to which the dancers respond in chorus, the men and women gathered in a large ring in the open air, around the musicians. An ahouach is normally performed at night in the patio of a Kasbah or in a village square; the dance is so complicated that the musicians meet to prepare for it in a group called a *laamt* set up for the purpose.

MOROCCAN TOURIST OFFICE

Village ahouach in the High Atlas

Moroccan Folk Instruments

Lyrichord Stereo LLST 7316

LYRICHORD

Moroccan rabab and lotar

Moroccan folk instruments are very rudimentary and fairly easy to make, and this, combined with the fact that many music cafés keep their own, allows for a genuinely amateur development. Many of the instruments mentioned below are also to be found under the same or similar names (and with slight variations) in Algeria, Tunisia, Libya and even Egypt.

There are a great many stringed and percussion instruments, mostly fairly basic in design, and a fair number of wind instruments. The **Arab flute**, known by different tribes as the **nai**, *talawat*, *nira* or *gasba*, is made of a straight piece of cane open at both ends, with no mouthpiece and between five and seven holes, one at the back. It requires a great deal of skill to play it properly, by blowing at a slight angle. The **ghaita** or *rhita*, a type of oboe popular under various names throughout the Muslim world, is a conical pipe made of hardwood, ending in a bell often made of metal. Its double-reeded mouthpiece is encircled by a broad ring on which the player rests his lips in order to produce the circular breathing needed to obtain a continuous note. It has between seven and nine holes, one at the back. The **aghanin** is a double clarinet, identical to the Arab arghoul. It consists of two parallel pipes of wood or cane, each with a single-reed mouthpiece, five holes

and a horn at the end for amplification. One pipe provides the tune while the other is used for adornments.

The most common stringed instrument is the **gimbri**. This is an African lute whose sound box is covered in front by a piece of hide. The rounded, fretless stem has two or three strings. The body of the smaller treble gimbri is pear-shaped, that of the bass gimbri (hadjuj or sentir) rectangular. Gnaouas often put a resonator at the end of the stem to produce the buzz typical of Black African music. The **lotar** is another type of lute, used exclusively by the Chleuh Berbers. It has a circular body, also closed with a piece of skin, and three or four strings which are plucked with a plectrum.

The classic Arab lute, the **oud**, is used in classical orchestras and the traditional Arab orchestras known as *takhts*. Its pear-shaped body is covered by a piece of wood with two or three rosette-shaped openings. It has a short, fretless stem and six strings, five double and one single. The most popular stringed instruments played with a bow are the **kamanjeh** and the **rabab**. The former is an Iranian violin which was adopted by the Arabs. Its present Moroccan character owes a lot to the Western violin, though it is held vertically, supported on the knees. The rabab is a spike fiddle, rather like a viol. The bottom half of its long, curved body is covered in hide, the top in wood with a rosette-shaped opening. It has two strings. The Chleuh Berbers use an archaic single-stringed rabab with a square stem and soundbox covered entirely in skin.

Lastly, there is the **kanum**, a trapezoidal Arab zither with over seventy strings, grouped in threes and plucked with plectra attached to the fingernails. It is used almost exclusively in classical music.

Rapid **hand-clapping** and the clashes of **bells** and **cymbals** are only part of the vast repertoire of Moroccan percussion. The most common drum is the clay **darbuka**, which is shaped into a cylinder swelling out slightly at the top, and has a single skin that is beaten with both hands. It is used in both folk and classical music. The **taarija**, a smaller version, is held in one hand and beaten with the other. Then there are treble and bass **tan-tan** bongos, and the Moorish **guedra**, a large drum which rests on the ground. There is also a round wooden drum with skins on both sides called a **tabl**, which is beaten with a stick on one side and by hand on the other. This is used only in folk music.

As for tambourines, the ever-popular **bendir** is round and wooden, 40 or 50cm across, with two strings stretched under its single skin to produce a buzzing sound. The **tar** is smaller, with two rings of metal discs round the frame and no strings under its skin. The **duff** is a double-sided tambourine, often square in shape, which has to be supported so that it can be beaten with both hands.

Only two percussion instruments are made of metal: **garagab**, double castanets used by the Gnaouas, and the **nakous**, a small cymbal played with two rods.

Ritual music is rarely absent from any rites connected with the agricultural calendar – such as moussems – or major events in the life of individuals, such as marriage. It may also be called upon to help deal with *djinn*, or evil spirits, or to encourage rainfall. Flutes and drums are again usually the sole instruments, along with much rhythmic handclapping, although a community may engage professional musicians for certain events.

The **professional musicans**, or **imdyazn**, of the Atlas mountains are itinerant, travelling during the summer, usually in groups of four. The leader of the group is called the *amydaz* or poet. He presents his poems, which are usually improvised and give news of national or world affairs, in the village square. The poet may be accompanied by one or two members of the group on drums and **rabab**, a single-string fiddle, and by a fourth player, known as the *bou oughanim*. This is the reed player, who throws out melodies on a double clarinet, and acts as the group's clown. Imdyazn are to be found in many weekly souks in the Atlas.

Rwais

Groups of **Chleuh Berber** musicians, from the Souss Valley, are known as **rwais**; again they are professional musicians. A rwai worthy of the name will not only know all the music for any particular celebration, but have its own repertoire of songs – again commenting on current events – and be able to improvise. A rwai ensemble can be made up of a single-string rabab, one or two *lotars* (lutes) and sometimes *nakous* (cymbals), together with a number of singers. The leader of the group, the *rayes*, is in charge of the poetry, music and choreography of the performance.

INÉDIT/AUVIDIS

The Gharnati Ensemble of Rabat

A **rwai performance** will start with the *astara*, an instrumental prelude, played on rabab, giving the basic notes of the melodies that follow (this also makes it possible for the other instruments to tune to the rabab). The astara is not in any particular rhythm. Then comes the *amarg*, the sung poetry which forms the heart of the piece. This is followed by the *ammussu*, which is a sort of choreographed overture; the tamssust, a lively song; the *aberdag*, or dance; and finally the *tabbayt*, a finale characterised by an acceleration in rhythm and an abrupt end. Apart from the astara and tabbayt, the elements of a performance may appear in a different order. The arrangement and duration of the various parts are decided upon freely by the rwais.

The Andalous Tradition

Morocco's classical music comes from the **Arab-Andalucían tradition**, and is to be found, with variations, throughout North Africa. It is thought to have evolved, around a thousand years ago, in Córdoba, Spain (then ruled by the Moors), and its invention is usually credited to an outstanding musician from Baghdad called Zyriab. One of his innovations was the founding of the classical suite called *nuba*, which forms what is now known as **andalous music**, or *al-âla*. There are, in addition, two other classical traditions, **milhûn** and **gharnati**, each with a distinctive style and form.

Andalous music, far from being the scholastic relic you might expect, is very much alive, popular and greatly loved. Television broadcasts nightly programmes of andalous classics during Ramadan, and people who don't have their own TVs congregate at local cafés to watch the shows.

Originally there were twenty-four **nuba** linked with the hours in the day. Only four full and seven fragmentary nuba have been preserved in the Moroccan tradition. Complete nuba, which can last between six and seven hours, are rarely performed in one sitting and are usually chosen to fit the time of day or occasion. Each nuba is divided into five main parts, or *mizan*, of differing durations. These five parts correspond to the five different rhythms used within a suite. If a whole nuba were being performed then these five rhythms would be used in order: the *basît* rhythm (6/4); *qaum wa nusf* rhythm (8/4); *darj* rhythm (4/4); *btâyhi* rhythm (8/4); and *quddâm* rhythm (3/4 or 6/8).

Traditionally each mizan begins with instrumental preludes – *bughya*, *m'shaliya* and *tuashia* – followed by a number of songs, the *sana'a*. There can be as many as twenty sana'a within a given mizan although for shorter performances an orchestra may only play three or four before going on to the next rhythm.

The words to many sana'a can deal, albeit obliquely, with subjects generally considered taboo in Islamic society like alcohol and sex – perhaps signifying archaic, pre-Islamic and nomadic roots – although others are religious, glorifying the Prophet and divine laws. The fourteenth sana'a of the *basît mizan* in **Al-'Ushshâq** tells of the desire for clarity following an active night entirely given over to the pleasures of sex and wine:

Obscure night steals away
Chased by the light
that sweeps up shadows
The candle wax runs
as if weeping tears of farewell
And then, suddenly and behold,
the birds are singing
and the flowers smile at us.

When the Arabs were driven out of Spain, which they had known as Al-Andalus, the different musical schools were dispersed across Morocco. The school of Valencia was re-established in Fes (Fez), that of Granada in Tetouan and Chaouen. Today, the most famous **orchestras** are those of Fes, led by **Abdelkrim Rais**; Tetouan, led by **Abdesadak Chekara**; and Rabat, which was led by the great Moulay Ahmed Loukili until his death in 1988 and is now under **Haj Mohamed Toud**.

Other cities, however, such as **Tangier** and **Meknes**, have their own andalous orchestras and are just as fanatical about the music. The **Orchestre de Tangier** have their own clubhouse, in the old city Kasbah, where musicians sit with enthusiasts and play most evenings, in between sucking on their mint tea.

A typical andalous orchestra uses the following instruments: *rabab* (fiddle), *oud* (lute), *kamenjah* (violin-style instrument played vertically on the knee), *kanun* (zither), *darbouka* (metal or pottery goblet drums), and *taarîja* (tambourine). Each orchestra has featured unusual instruments from time to time. Clarinets, flutes, banjos and pianos have all been used with varying degrees of success.

Milhûn and Gharnati

Milhûn is a semi-classical form of sung poetry – a definition which sounds a lot drier than it is. Musically it has many links with andalous music, having adopted the same modes as al-âla orchestras and, like them, it uses string instruments and percussion. But the results can be quite wild and danceable.

The milhûn suite comprises two parts: the *taqsim* (overture) and the *qassida* (sung poems). The taqsim is played on the oud or violin in free rhythm, and introduces the mode in which the piece is set. The qassida is divided into three parts: the *al-aqsâm*, being verses sung solo; the *al-harba*, the refrains sung by the chorus; and the *al-drîdka*, a chorus where the rhythm gathers speed and eventually announces the end of the piece. The words of the qassida can be taken from anywhere – folk poetry, mystical poems or nonsense lines used for rhythm.

Al-Thami Lamdaghri, who died in 1856, was one of the greatest milhûn composers. He is credited with many well-known songs including "Al-Gnawi" (The Black Slave), "Aliq Al-Masrûh" (The Radiant Beauty) and "Al-'Arsa" (The Garden of Delight):

Open your eyes
Taste the delights and the generous nature
Of this heavenly garden
The branches of the wonderful
    trees intertwine
Like two lovers meeting again
And totter about, heady with happiness
The smile of flowers,
Mingled with the tears of the dew
Recall the melancholic exchange
Of a sad lover and his joyous beloved
Birds sing in the branches
Like as many lutes and rababs.

The **milhûn orchestra** generally consists of *oud*, *kamenjah*, *swisen* (a small, high-pitched folk lute related to the gimbri), *hadjouj* (a bass version of the swisen), *darbuka* and *handqa* (small brass cymbals). As well as musicians, an orchestra will normally feature a number of **singers**. Some of the best known are **Abdelkrim and Saïd Guennoun** of Fes, **Haj Husseïn** and **Abdallah Ramdani** of Meknes, and **Muhammad Berrahal** and **Muhammad Bensaïd** of Salé.

Gharnati, the third music of Arab-Andalucían tradition, is mainly played in Algeria but there are two important centres in Morocco – the capital, Rabat, and Oujda, near the Algerian border. As with al-âla, gharnati music is arranged in suites or nuba, of which there are twelve complete and four unfinished suites. The gharnati orchestra consists of plucked and bowed instruments together with percussion: the usual ouds and kamenjahs supplemented by the addition of banjo, mandolin and Algerian lute, the *kwîtra*.

Sufi Brotherhoods

Music in orthodox Islam is frowned upon unless it is singing God's praises. As well as the chants of the Koran, which are improvised on a uniform beat, the *adhan*, or call to prayer, and the songs about the life of the prophet Muhammad, there is another entire range of prayers and ceremonies belonging to the **Sufi brotherhoods**, or *tarikas*, in which music is seen as a means of getting closer to Allah. These include the music used in processions to the tombs of saints during moussems.

The aim is for those present to reach a state of mystical ecstasy, often through **trance**. In a private nocturnal ceremony called the *hadra*, the Sufi brothers attain a trance by chanting the name of Allah or dancing in a ring holding hands. The songs and music are irregular in rhythm, and quicken to an abrupt end. Some brotherhoods play for alms in households that want to gain the favour of their patron saint.

The **Gnaoua brotherhood** is a religious confraternity whose members are descendants of slaves brought from across the Sahara by the Arabs. They have devotees all over Morocco, though the strongest concentrations are in the south, particularly in Marrakesh. The brotherhood claim spiritual descent from **Sidi Bilal**, an Ethiopian who was the Prophet's first muezzin.

Most Gnaoua ceremonies, or *deiceba*, are held to placate spirits, good and evil, who are inhabiting a person or place. They are often called in cases of mental disturbance or to help treat someone stung by a scorpion. These rites have their origins in sub-Saharan Africa, and an African influence is evident in the music. The principal instrument, the *gimbri* or *sentir*, is a long-necked lute almost identical to instruments found in West Africa. The other characteristic sound of Gnaoua music is the *garagab,* a pair of metal castanets, which beat out a trance-like rhythm.

Jilala are another brotherhood, who are devotees of **Moulay Abdelkader Jilal**. Their music is even more hypnotic and mysterious than that of the Gnaoua and seems to come from a different plane of existence. The plaintive cycling flute (the *qsbah*) and the mesmeric beats of the *bendir* (frame drums) carry you forward unconsciously. While in a trance Jilala devotees can withstand the touch of burning coals or the deep slashes of a Moroccan dagger, afterwards showing no injury or pain.

Nowadays, Gnaoua music can be heard at festivals and in the entertainment squares of Marrakesh and elsewhere. Many discs have been recorded, too, the most interesting of them by Gnaoua groups led by **Hassan Hakmoun** and **Mustapha Baqbou**; the latter has been superbly recorded by Bill Laswell.

JAK KILBY

Gimbri player Mustapha Baqbou

Master Musicians of Jajouka

During the late 1950s and early 1960s Tangier was as Bohemian a city as any, attracting Beats and, in their wake, rock stars. In 1968 the Rolling Stones paid the first of several visits and their then-guitarist, **Brian Jones** was introduced to the Berber **Master Musicians of Jajouka** in the foothills of the Rif Mountains.

The Master Musicians are essentially trance musicians, producing an awesome sound through a multitude of double-headed drums and the dark drones and melodies of the *ghaita*, a double-reed pipe or shawm similar in sound to the oboe. They are a kind of brotherhood, and the leadership of the group is passed down from father to son. The present chief, **Bachir Attar**, inherited the post when his father died in the late 1980s.

Jones recorded the Master Musicians with the aid of psychedelic sound trickery and produced his strange *Pipes of Jajouka* album. Its heady concoction of hypnotic rhythms, wailing pipes and Jones's heavy sound treatments gave what for many was close to a mystical experience – especially when stoned immobile on kif (grass). For many years this was the only record available of Moroccan music.

Although the Rolling Stones returned to Morocco in the mid-1980s to use Jajouka on their *Steel Wheels* album, the Master Musicians' next 'solo' recording didn't emerge until 1990 when American bassist and composer **Bill Laswell** travelled to Morocco. Using the latest digital technology, he produced an album of purity and power. Since then, Jajouka have experienced a revival of interest, spurred by the World Music scene, appearing at festivals around the world. They have recorded a further CD, and the original Brian Jones album has also been re-released.

Another, rival Jajouka group is also in existence and has made an album and toured. They are not well regarded by the Bachir Attar group . . .

BRIAN JONES
PRESENTS
THE PIPES OF PAN AT
JAJOUKA

Chaabi

All of the musical forms mentioned so far have had their impact on the most popular music of Morocco – **chaabi**, which means simply 'popular' and covers a bewildering mix of styles. The music that takes this name started out as street music performed in the squares and souks, but it can now be heard in cafés, at festivals and at weddings. Many towns have café-meeting places where the locals sing songs in the evenings (some cafés keep their own instruments for musicians who can't afford their own) and, at its more basic level, chaabi is played by itinerant musicians, who turn up at a café and bang out a few songs. These songs are usually finished with a *leseb*, which is often twice the speed of the song itself and forms a background for syncopated clapping,

Jil Jilala

shouting and dancing. Early evening during Ramadan is the best time to find music cafés of this kind in full swing.

During the 1970s a more sophisticated version of chaabi began to emerge, with **groups** setting themselves up in competition with the commercial Egyptian and Lebanese music which dominated the market (and the radio) at the time. These groups were usually made up of two stringed instruments – a *hadjuj* (bass gimbri) and a lute – and a bendir and darbuka or tam-tam as percussion. As soon as they could afford it, groups updated their sound and image with the addition of congas, buzuks, banjos and even electric guitars. The hadjuj and bendir, however, remained – and remain – indispensable.

The new 'group' music was a fusion of Arab, African and modern Western influences, combining Berber music with elements taken from the Arab milhûn and Sufi rituals, Gnaoua rhythms and the image of European groups. Voices played an important part, with the whole group singing, either in chorus or backing a lead soloist. Lyrics dealt with love as well as social issues, and occasionally carried messages which got their authors into trouble with the authorities – even jailed. The three seminal groups were Jil Jilala, Lem Chaheb and Nass El Ghiwane, all from Casablanca.

Jil Jilala (Generation of Jilali) was formed in 1972 as a Sufi theatre group devoted to their leader, Jilali. Their music is based on the milhûn style, using poetry as a reference (and starting) point. More recently they have worked with Gnaoua rhythms and they occasionally use a ghaita in their line-up. The group's central figures are the conga-player and lyricist **Mohammed Darhem**, and

Hassan Mista, who plays an amplified, fretless buzuk. They are rhythmically accompanied by two bendir players – Moulai Tahar and Abdel Krim Al-Kasbaji – and have recorded with a variety of hadjuj players, including **Mustapha Baqbou**.

Nass El-Ghiwane, the most politicised of the three, lay great emphasis on the words of their recitatives and verses and chorus. Their music again combines Sufi and Gnaoua influences while the words may lambast a lazy government official or talk of social injustices. Originally a five-piece band of banjo, hadjuj, bendir, tam-tam and darbuka, the band was fronted by lead singer **Boujmia**, a man with a soaring, powerfully melodic voice. He was killed in a car crash in the early 1980s and the rest of the group have continued as a four-piece since. There has been a retrospective cassette from Boujmia's time released in Morocco on the Hassania label, which includes "The Table", the song that made them famous:

Where are they now?
The friends who sat at my table
Where are they now?
All the friends that I loved
Where are the glasses?
Where are the glasses we drank from?
Friendship can be bitter
But it was also sweet to sit at my table

The third major chaabi group, **Lem Chaheb** is probably the Moroccan group best known abroad, through its work with the German band **Dissidenten** (see p.120), two of whose members play and record with them. Featuring the virtuoso figure of guitarist and buzuk player Lamrani Moulay Cherif, they are also the most Westernised of the three big names in electric chaabi.

In the 1980s another generation of groups emerged, combining traditional and modern influences, this time based in Marrakesh but concentrating on Gnaoua rhythms. The most successful of these has been **Muluk El Hwa** (Demon of Love), a group of Berbers who used to play in the Djemaa El Fna in Marrakesh. Their line-up is totally acoustic: bendir, tam-tam, sentir, buzuk, garagab and hand claps. They have recorded an album in collaboration with the Spanish group **Al Tall** featuring medieval Valencian music and Andalucían Arabic poetry, which deals with subjects still relevant today – the whims of rulers, exile, love and wine.

Another of their contemporaries, **Nass El Hal**, formed in 1986, offer two shows – one using a traditional acoustic line-up with buzuk and violin, the other with drum kit and electric guitar. Their repertoire includes peasant harvest and hunting songs, and religious dances. Two more groups with recordings to their name are **Izanzaren**, of the Casablanca school, and **Shuka**, who do everything from Andalous to Gnaoua.

Other chaabi artists have remained firmly traditional in their use of instruments, but forward-looking in their musical approach. One such is the sensational singer **Najat Aatabou**. She is proud of her Berber heritage and uses traditional Berber rhythms (though she now sings in Arabic or French) and is very outspoken in her lyrics, which address the inequality between men and women and the injustice of traditional family rules. She is equally capable of writing beautiful love songs. When her ensemble use electric instruments they blend beautifully with more traditional oud and bendir.

Aatabou's first release, the eye-opening "J'en ai marre" (I am sick of it), sold 450,000 copies. Her second release, "Shouffi Rhirou" (Look for Another Lover), and every subsequent release have sold more than half a million copies, and she is now a huge star throughout the Maghreb and can fill large venues in Europe. A wonderful compilation CD, *The Voice of the Atlas* (which includes "Shouffi Rhirou"), is available on GlobeStyle records.

Fusion and Dance

Morocco is an ideal starting point for all kinds of fusion experiments. From the 1960s on, such disparate figures as Brian Jones (see Jajouka box), Robin Williamson, John Renbourn and Pharoah Sanders have been attracted by its rhythms, and in in the 1980s and 1990s collaborations came thick and fast.

STEPHEN LOVELL-DAVIS/REALWORLD

Hassan Hakmoun

The most successful, perhaps, has been that of the Berlin-based **Dissidenten**. Before their collaboration with Lem Chaheb (see previous page), they had worked with **Mohammed Zain**, a star player of the nai (flute) from Tangier who belongs to a Sufi sect, and Gnaoua gimbri players Abdellah El Gourd, Abderkader Zefzaf and Abdalla Haroch. Their albums with Lem Chaheb have placed a genuine Moroccan element into a rock context.

A number of Moroccan singers and musicians have also crossed over into 1990s dance music. the Moroccan-Israeli singer **Yosefa Dahari** (see p.365) is a name to look out for in this respect, with her work (sung in Maghrebi and English) on the Worldly Dance Music label with David Rosenthal and Gil Freeman. **Hassan Hakmoun** is another – a New York-based Gnaoua musician who mixes it in the city with all manner of ideas and musicians. Also resident in New York these days is **Bachir Attar**, leader of the **Jajouka** troupe (see box), who has recorded with jazz saxophonist Maceo Parker under the direction of avant garde funk producer Bill Laswell.

Laswell has also been involved in production work with the group **Aisha Kandisha's Jarring Effects** (or AKJE), who mix Moroccan trance sounds with rock, hip-hop and techno. They released an amazing debut CD, *Buya*, in 1991 on the Swiss Barbarity label, and followed up with a techno-driven, Laswell-production, *Shabeesation*. They are only known on a subterranean level in

Morocco and are yet to perform or release a cassette at home. They have an attitude as radical as their music – akin to, say, Cypress Hill or Ice Cube. Their name refers to a female spirit, whose very mention is taboo, and their lyrics question Moroccan social and religious norms.

The **Barbarity label** (aka Barraka el Farnatshi) has now released about a dozen titles by Aisha Kandisha and other like-minded Moroccan bands seeking to fuse Moroccan music with Western electronic and dance influences. Their catalog includes CDs by the AKJE side project **Amira Saqati**, and the bands **Ahlam** and **Argan**, both of which feature AKJE musicians.

Elsewhere, expatriate Moroccans have been active in various new treatments. In Britain, **Sidi Seddiki**, Rabat-born but a Londoner since childhod, produced a seductive blend of Moroccan music and Western pop: strong, catchy songs, drawing on chaabi, and using a classical flautist. Belgium, meanwhile, has provided a base for the blind multi-instrumentalist **Hassan Erraji**, who has released a trio of jazz-flavoured discs with his multicultural groups Belcikal (now disbanded) and Arabesque. He is well worth seeing live, too, with his startling juggling with the bendir.

In **Spain** there have been a couple of notable collaborations between flamenco musicians and Andalous orchestras, notably that of **José Heredia Maya and Enrique Morente** with the **Orchestre de Tetouan**, and **Juan Peña Lebrijano** with the **Orchestre de Tanger**. The Tetouan orchestra have also collaborated in concert with the British composer **Michael Nyman**.

Moroccan Raï

Raï – the word means 'opinion' – originated in the western Algerian region around the port of Oran. It has traditional roots in Bedouin music, with its distinctive refrain (ha-ya-raï), but as a modern phenomenon has more in common with Western music. The backing is now solidly electric, with rhythm guitars, synthesisers and usually a rock drum kit as well as traditional drums. Its lyrics reflect highly contemporary concerns – cars, sex, sometimes alcohol – which have created some friction with the authorities.

Moroccans have taken easily to the music. Algerian raï stars such as **Cheb Khaled, Cheb Mami** and **Chaba Fadela** are to be heard on cassettes in most souks, while home-grown raï stars include **Cheb Khader, Cheb Mimoun** and the mysterious **Chaba Zahouania**. The latter is said to be forbidden by her family from being photographed for her recordings.

Raï influence is also to be heard in the folk music of the **Oujda** area, the closest Moroccan town to Oran, in artists like **Rachid Briha** and **Hamid M'Rabati**.

Sephardic music

Moroccan Jews, many of whom have now emigrated to Israel, left an important legacy in the north of the country, where their songs and ballads continued to be sung in the medieval Spanish, spoken at the time of their expulsion from Spain five centuries ago (see article on Sephardic Music, p.370). Apart from the narrative ballads, these were mainly songs of courtly love, as well as lullabies and biblical songs, usually accompanied on a *tar*.

Moroccan Sephardic traditions and music continue to thrive in Israel. One of the stars of the 1998 *Fes Festival of Sacred Music* was the Moroccan Jewish singer, **Albert Bouhadanna**, who performed with Mohammed Briouels's Orchestra. Meantime, a rising star in World Music circles is **Emil Zhiran**, now resident in Israel but born in Rabat, whose music mixes Arab and Andalucían influences with the Hebrew liturgy.

Aisha Kandisha

discography

There has been quite a boom in CDs of Moroccan music in recent years. Most record stores in Britain or the US with a decent World Music section should yield at least a few discs of ethnic, folk and Andalous music, or fusion with European groups. In Morocco itself, cassettes are the main medium.

Andalous/Classical

Compilations

 Anthologie d'Al-Melhûn
(Inédit, France).

A three-CD set containing performances from many of Morocco's finest milhûn singers. A good introduction to the slow splendours of Andalous music.

Artists

Orchestre Moulay Ahmed Loukili de Rabat

Loukili was a pupil of the great Mohammed al-Brihi of Fes and for many years was a member of the city's Andalous orchestra. He then moved to Tangier and later Rabat, where he led the orchestra until his death in 1988. He is still considered the greatest master of Andalous music of the past half century. Hadj Mohamed Toud, a former disciple of Loukili, currently leads the Orchestra.

Nuba Al-'Ushshâq (6 CDs) and **Nuba Al-Istihal** (7 CDs) (Inédit, France).

These are fairly daunting boxed sets and, priced accordingly, are not for the casual listener: only problem with this superb set is the price (£75/$120). But if you develop a serious interest, you'll want these for a chance to hear elements of the music rarely heard on short interlude suites.

Abdelkrim Raïs et l'Orchestre Al–Brihi (Fes)

Up until his death in 1996, Raïs was one of Morocco's foremost Andalous musicians. He was born in Fes in 1912 and, like Loukili, studied under Mohammed al-Brihi, who taught him the oud. He then took up the rebab and became a conductor. Under his direction, the Fes-based Al-Brihi orchestra became one of Morocco's finest.

Musique andalouse de Fès
(Institut du Monde Arabe, France).

A classic recording of several of the nuba, recently re-issued.

Orchestre de Tanger

The Tanger Andalous Orchestra, led by Ahmed Zaytouni Sahraoui, have taken part in the Maison des Cultures du Monde series of recordings of the complete nuba, and also recorded a couple of discs with flamenco singer Juan Peña Lebrijano, which are utterly enchanting.

Nuba al-Rasd (6 CDs)
(Inédit, France).

One of the boxed sets in the complete nuba series (see also Orchestre Moulay Ahmed Loukili de Rabat, above).

WITH JUAN PEÑA LEBRIJANO

Juan Peña Lebrijano y Orquestra Andalusi de Tanger – Encuentros (GlobeStyle, UK).

Juan Peña joins forces with the stately Arabic chorus of the Orchestra of Tangier to explore flamenco's Arabic roots, reuniting the musics of Andalucía and the Maghreb. **Casablanca** (EMI Hemisphere, UK) delivers more of the same.

Orchestre de Tetouan

The Tetouan orchestra have been led, for the past thirty years, by Mohammed Larbi Temsamani, instrumentalist, conductor, teacher and musicologist, born in 1918 in Tangier.

Nuba al-Isbihan (6 CDs)
(Inédit, France).

Fourth of the boxed sets in the complete nuba series (see Orchestre Moulay Ahmed Loukili de Rabat, above).

Ustad Massano Tazi

Master rebab player and singer Ustad Massano Tazi practises traditional music therapy based on the idea that being healthy corresponds to a harmonious balancing of the humours. This practice includes the *himmara*, an ecstatic dance, and the playing of certain modes to help to heal certain disorders. To achieve this Tazi plays without the intrusion of Western instruments, and has adopted instruments all but lost in the modern world.

Musique Classique Andalouse de Fès
(Ocora, France).

A beautifully recorded and presented Andalous disc. Includes "Nuba Hijaz Al-Kabir" and "Nuba Istihilal".

Folk/Popular

Compilations

Gnawa Night – Music of the Marrakesh Spirit Masters (Axiom, UK).

Gnaoua music at its evocative best, recorded by Bill Laswell.

Moroccan Trance Music (Sub Rosa, Belgium).

Not for the faint hearted, this is intense gnaoua and jilala music, combined on the disc with some of Paul Bowles' personal recordings.

 Moroccan Trance 2 (Sub Rosa, Belgium).

Good atmospheric selections featuring a Gnaoua Brotherhood from Marrakesh, alongside three tracks of the Master Musicians of Jajouka.

Morocco: Crossroads of Time
(Ellipsis Arts, US).

An excellent introduction to Moroccan music that comes with a well-designed and informative book. The disc includes everything from ambient sounds in the Fes Medina, to powerful Jilala and Gnaoua music, Andalous, Rwai, Berber, and some good contemporary pop from Nouamane Lahlou.

Artists

Najat Aatabou (Aâtabu)

Aatabou is a successful Berber woman singer, born into a conservative family in the small town of Khemisset but long resident in Casablanca.

The Voice of the Atlas (GlobeStyle, UK).
Country Girls & City Women (Rounder, US).

These are two equally good collections. Both feature Najat's best-loved song, "Shouffi Rhirou" – which has also been covered brilliantly by the 3 Mustaphas 3.

Ahlam

Stablemates of Aisha Kandisha (see below), Ahlam are a late-1990s band who grab your attention from the first groove.

 Revolt Against Reason (Barbarity, Switzerland).

Moroccan-meets-hip-hop stakes, featuring some wonderfully expressive singing.

Aisha Kandisha's Jarring Effects

Chaabi meets techno (and rock and hip-hop) in this radical and stunning 1990s group, who have collaborated with, among others, Bill Laswell.

El Buya
(Barbarity, Switzerland).

This debut 1991 album has not been bettered, with its intoxicating mix of Moroccan melodies and traditional string instruments with scratching reverb, and rushes of industrial noise.

Hassan Erraji

This Belgium-resident oud player, singer and percussionist fuses his classical Moroccan training with jazz.

 Marhaba (Riverboat, UK).

The latest in a trio of releases on this label from Erraji, this is a more song-based, upbeat and very listenable disc.

Maleem Mahmoud Ghania with Pharoah Sanders

Gnaoua meets with the great sax player from John Coltrane's band.

 The Trance of the Seven Colours
(Axiom/island, US).

Gnawa-jazz crossover, recorded mainly in Marrakesh.

Hassan Hakmoun

Hakmoun arrived in New York in 1987 with a troupe of gnaoua musicians – and stayed on. He has made several albums, both traditional and mixing in Western dance/trance sounds.

 Trance (RealWorld, UK).

Gnaoua rhythms tinged with jazz dance psychedelia, produced by Afro Celt Sound System mainman, Simon Emmerson.

Hmaoui Abd El-Hamid

Hmaoui is a superb Berber player of the traditional Moroccan flute, the ney.

 La Flûte de l'Atlas (Arion, France).

Hypnotic and haunting ney melodies, backed by percussion, oud and zither.

Lem Chaheb

Lem Chabe were a groundbreaking chaabi (popular) group through the 1980s, both in their own right and in partnership with German group Dissidenten.

Lem Chaheb
(Club du Disques Arabe, France).

A compilation from the late 1980s. The band's usual line-up of guitar, buzuk, percussion is augmented by trumpets and synthe-

One of Lem Chaheb's numerous cassettes

sisers provided by two members of Dissidenten. The infectious "Nari Nari" was later covered by Dissidenten as "Radio Arab" – a kind of Moroccan equivalent to the Byrds' jangling guitar sound.

Master Musicians of Jajouka

The legendary group of pan-pipers and drummers, from a village in northern Morocco, whose music has passed down for centuries. Current leader of the main group is Bachir Attar, son of Hadj Abdesalam Attar, leader of the group for many years. There is also a rival, splinter group using the Jajouka name.

🎵 **Apocalypse Across the Sky** (Axiom, US).

Without the electronic trickery of Brian Jones' seminal album, the power and clarity of these remarkable performers stands out all the more on Bill Laswell's outing.

Cheb Mimoun

Morocco's leading rai singer throws all kinds of chaabi influences into the rai mix.

🎵 **Moroccan Rai** (Sounds of the World, UK).

Sweeping strings, rapturous vocals, continuous beat – an album that conjures you straight back to Moroccan taxi rides.

Nass El-Ghiwane

Chaabi fusionists, Nass El-Ghiwane, like Jil Jilala, combined Sufi and Gnaoua influences with modern lyrics con-

cerned with social injustice. Their singer, Boujmia, was killed in a car crash in the early 1980s, since when they have continued as a quartet.

📼 **Nass El-Ghiwane** (Hassania, Morocco).

The group's only remaining recordings with singer Boujmia. Powerful and hypnotic.

Sidi Seddiki

Born in Rabat in 1961, Sidi Seddiki came to live in West London at eleven, where he was exposed to reggae, rock and funk. His songs mix all these elements with his traditional Arabic background into a unique fusion.

🎵 **Shouf** (GlobeStyle, UK).

A fine, early 1990s debut album, recorded by Moroccan and British musicians. It's a shame Seddiki seems to have subsequently disappeared from the recording scene.

Yosefa

Yosefa is an Israeli-resident Moroccan Jewish singer, mixing traditional songs and sounds with dance culture.

🎵 **Dahari Yosefa** (Worldly Dance, UK).

Just what the label says: dance music with English and Maghrebi songs. A bit of an exotica product but one that lives up to its promise.

Mozambique

a luta continua

In the countryside the people sitting around fires hear stories accompanied by one-stringed bowed instruments that can be struck, plucked or bowed. The kids with long sticks under the hot sun are chasing the goats while blowing gourd flutes they have made themselves. And in the towns people put on their best suits, especially on weekends and gather in clubs to dance to tropical sounds like calypso, salsa, rumba and *marrabenta*. Music is everywhere in Mozambique, as **Celso Paco** discovered.

Mozambique, lying on the east coast of southern Africa, was a **Portuguese colony** for five centuries from 1498 to 1975. During the struggle for independence that commenced in earnest in 1964, culture was an integral part of the struggle. Mozambican leaders used Portuguese language, ideas, culture and religion to fight against Portuguese domination. The consequences of regarding culture as a central feature of national liberation and not just as a mechanism to mould people into good shape, came to light in post-independence developments.

In 1975 Mozambique won its **independence**, and the ruling FRELIMO (Frente de Libertação de Moçambique) party came to power. Independence brought to a new generation the discovery of a cultural heritage that had been ignored in the urban areas during the centuries of Portuguese colonisation. Mozambican **bands**, which prior to independence had played European-style music, began to abandon it as they embraced the patriotic spirit sweeping the country. Bands reformed using improvised musical instruments and began to play roots style music similar to that heard and performed in Tanzania, Zambia and other countries in the region. In the centre of Mozambique, a musical style resembling that of Zimbabwe appeared, while southern Mozambique was strongly influenced by the music brought into the country by the returning workers who provided cheap labour in the South African mines. Throughout the country revolutionary lyrics were fitted to these regional melodies along with the usual social commentaries and life stories.

In 1978 the Ministry of Education and Culture managed to organise a **National Dance Festival** involving half a million people from around the country. One result of this festival was the formation of a National Song and Dance Group and a Children's Dance School. Two years later, the Ministry organised a **festival of traditional music** in the capital Maputo. The mere fact that the traditional musicians, with all their local instruments made of gourds, thongs, reeds, horns and skins – such as *timbila* and *valimba* (regional marimbas); *xitende* (gourd bow); *kalimba* (thumbpiano); *xipala-pala* (antelope horn); *xigovia* (gourd flute); *xipendane* and *xizambe* (mouth-bows) and many more – came out of the bush and the shanty towns to perform on public stages to public acclaim, was an act of cultural recognition and national renaissance.

Meanwhile, the **war** between the FRELIMO government and the South African-backed RENAMO rebels, which had started before independence, led to the loss of at least a million lives (out of a population of fifteen million), while millions more were orphaned, displaced or traumatised. The Mozambican people were more than ready for peace and in 1994, the first multiparty elections were successfully held.

Through all of this, Mozambican musicians – like **Chico António**, **Salimo Mohammed** and the band **Ghorwane** – were writing and performing songs that echoed the frustrations of the Mozambican people while encouraging them to act together for a better future.

Coastal Music: Timbila

The range of traditional music and traditional musical instruments found in Mozambique is a reflection of its ethnic diversity and its geography. The best-known style is the **timbila** music of the **Chopi** people of Inhambane – a highly developed and sophisticated music played on the **mbila** (plural *timbila*), a type of xylophone. Found only in Inhambane, timbila have four to sixteen fixed wooden keys, with resonators made from masaala or pumpkin gourds. Their scale is not a familiar one to Western ears and a unique buzzing sound is produced by a plastic (originally animal intestine) membrane placed over a hole in the gourd.

There is a theory, based on the pattern of trade routes and similarities in the musical scales, that the presence of the xylophone in Africa can be accounted for by traders introducing it from Indonesia (home of gamelan orchestras) through Madagascar and East Africa. Whatever the case, the quarter million Chopi people on the Mozambican coast have developed a firm tradition of composing for voice and xylophone which now occupies a hugely important place in their lives.

The spellbinding music of **Venancio Mbande** and his 32-piece timbila orchestra can be heard most Sunday afternoons at his house in Zavala, Inhambane Province – and yes, you really can just turn up to the sessions uninvited. So any trip to the paradisiacal beaches of Inhambane should be timed to enable you to meet this traditional musician who has played in London's Albert Hall. To find his house, take the main road to Inhambane out of Maputo and about 27km north of Quissico (just after the village of Guilundo) you will see a yellow sign for the *Chopi Music Centre* – his house is on the right, about 100m from the road.

Another internationally known timbila player from Zavala, **Eduardo Durão**, shares the same love of this traditional musical form, adding to it a strong desire for experimentation. He has performed a number of concerts where timbila and Western instruments combine to produce a new and very exciting style. Eduardo is the head of the timbila school in Maputo and is also a composer with the National Song and Dance Company.

Several **field recordings** of timbila and other traditional music are now available on CD, and, for those who can't make the trip, a video called *Mozambique Three* has footage of some of the groups featured on the GlobeStyle CDs.

Marrabenta Pulse

Marrabenta music, Mozambique's main urban dance rhythm, was born during the colonial period as a result of external musical influences and attempts to produce foreign musical instruments using locally available materials. To entertain themselves, people who couldn't afford to buy guitars, for example, would create their own versions using 5-litre oil tins, pieces of wood and fishing line. The name marrabenta derives from the method used to play the instruments – the guitars were played with great enthusiasm until the strings broke. In Portuguese, *rebentar* means 'to break' and *arrabentar* is the pronunciation in the local languages Shangana and Ronga. Marrabenta music shares certain similarities with calypso or salsa from Latin America, and with *merengue* from Angola.

During the early years of this music Marrabenta composers used native languages and played simple, repetitive sequences. The key rarely varied from song to song and in general the words delivered messages of social criticism, praise or, more often, love. Marrabenta was mistrusted by the Portuguese as a medium of revolution and a cultural form they were powerless to control. During the war of liberation, the colonial government closed down numerous marrabenta venues on the grounds that they were terrorist centres.

After independence, many young singers emerged to write marrabenta songs which focused on their hopes and feelings, and the style took a lift in the late 1970s when **1001 Music Productions** recorded and promoted a great number of local artists at large concert venues. An LP compilation was released – *Amanhecer* (Sunrise) – of Radio Mozambique recordings, including some of the artists promoted by 1001, and following its success other compilations were produced under the generic title *Ngoma* (Drum).

In the immediate post-Independence period a number of Mozambican artists living outside the country returned, bringing with them other musical influences to add to the existing, somewhat insular, mix. One such was **Fany Pfumo**, who used jazz elements in his compositions to create a unique sound. Born into a poor family, Fany Pfumo was forced to abandon Mozambique for the better working and living conditions of South Africa. Contact with recording companies in Johannesburg saved him from the mines and launched him as a successful singer. "Loko ni kumbuka Jorgina" (When I remember Jorgina), was the first of his recordings to open this door of success. Most of his singles were recorded by HMV in South Africa, many of them combining Mozambican marrabenta with South African *kwela*.

The creation of the **Grupo Radio Moçambique** (the national broadcasting company house band), was the beginning of a new era for Mozambican popular music. Radio Mozambique continues to facilitate the dissemination of Mozambican music by releasing recorded material by local artists.

National Song & Dance Company of Mozambique, Celso Paco on drums

Sounds Today

Traditional rhythms played on traditional instruments can still be heard in the rural areas of Mozambique, and at the same time, they are kept alive in the cities by cultural groups such as the **Companhia Nacional de Canto e Dança** (National Song and Dance Ensemble). This was created as a symbol of national unity, bringing together people from across Mozambique. It represents the country at international events and at home organises educational programmes through song and dance in urban and rural areas. And the music is kept alive in the cities by the new migrants.

Mapiko traditional music and dance, for example, from the Cabo Delgado province in the north, is performed every Sunday at the military compound near the centre of Maputo.

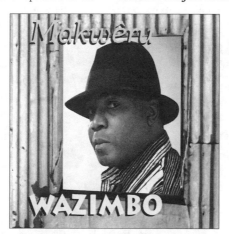

Orchestra Marrabenta Star de Moçambique, formed in 1979, have played an extremely important role in nurturing many of the country's current musicians. Led by **Wazimbo** – previously the lead singer of the Grupo Radio Moçambique – this orchestra was the first to play top-quality marrabenta music, and took it on tour to Europe. Although the orchestra is no longer together, Wazimbo continues to enjoy considerable popularity as a solo artist at home.

Mozambique's most popular male vocalist, **Stewart Sukuma** (Luis Pereira) is among a long list of performers who have come through this orchestra. Sukuma performed as percussionist, and later began recording his own songs. He released his debut solo album, entitled *Afrikiti*, in 1997. **Mingas**, the leading female singer in Mozambique, also began singing with the Star de Moçambique, in the early 1990s. In 1995 she accompanied Miriam Makeba on a world tour, singing her own compositions and traditional and popular songs.

The group's two outstanding trumpeters, **Chico António** and **José Mucavel**, also became successful solo artists following the orchestra's split. Chico António is a modern composer of African fusion, whose song, "Baile Maria", won first prize in the Radio France International competition in 1990. He is now the band leader of **Asaga** and in the late 1990s recorded a compilation of songs at the Radio Moçambique studio. José Mucavele produces his own music which consists of a mixture of the different traditional rhythms from across the country. Although he was born in the south of Mozambique, his commitment to learning and sharing the music from the various regions is a major contribution to the ongoing process of nation-building.

One of Mozambique's best-known and longest surviving bands is **Ghorwane** (named after a small lake in Gaza province that never runs dry, even in the hottest season). **Pedro Langa** played lead guitar with **Salimo Mohammed** in the early 1980s before forming Ghorwane together with the late sax player **José Alage (Zeca)**. The band's music is based on Mozambican traditional songs and rhythms with some South African musical influences mixed in. They feature three guitar players (lead, rhythm and bass), two trumpets, sax, keyboard, a percussion line-up and vocals – a role sometimes taken by **Roberto Chitsondzo**, a fine composer, acoustic guitar player and vocalist, and **David Macucua**, who became the band leader in the mid-1980s. After eleven years as band leader, David gave up his position to make way for other members to take charge and, in 1997, bass player **Carlos Gove (Carlitos)**, took over band leader duties.

Another important artist is **Paulo Miambo**, a veteran solo performer, with a voice which might be mistaken for that of the late Fany Pfumo, and one of the greatest composers of marrabenta music. Paulo recorded songs through the 1980s and in 1996 released an album he produced himself. He is gaining a reputation as a producer of a number of local artists whom he encourages to record and release their music on CD in South Africa.

Most Mozambican bands who have had CDs released come from the south of the country. One important exception is **Eyuphuro**, a band devoted specifically to the promotion of the music of the Macua ethnic group from Nampula province in northeastern Mozambique. They were actually the first group in the country to release a CD, *Mama Mosambiki* (one of RealWorld's earliest releases), which embraces the lightly textured *tufo* rhythm. The band toured Europe for a long period, but split shortly after returning to Mozambique at the end of the 1980s. Their CD, released in 1990, was thus a posthumous glory. Although some of the members are still performing with other local groups, the powerful voice of female vocalist **Zena Bakar** is no longer heard.

The band **Kinamatamikuluty** is the best-known exponent of afro-jazz on the Maputo music scene, using timbila, traditional drums and sax. Most of their music is sung in the Chopi language and accompanied by Chopi rhythms – something along the lines of Venancio Mbande meets John Coltrane. The author of this article, **Celso Paco**, a professional jazz musician who plays the drums and a range of traditional musical instruments, was a founding member of the group but left to teach percussion at the National School of Music.

Celso is also a member of the innovative group **Milho Rei**, who play a fusion of Mozambican and Portuguese popular music – a rare example of such cultural cross-currents. The instruments used by the band include the mandolin, the violin, kalimba, xitende, tambourine, timbila, harmonica, castanets, African drums and acoustic guitar. The lightness and beauty of **Eliana Canteiro**'s voice is the final touch to the band's original music.

Perhaps the best of the country's up-and-coming bands is **K10** (pronounced Kappa Desh) who recently won the Music Crossroads Competition for young musicians in South Africa, Zimbabwe and Mozambique. This group plays a new form of music – a fusion of different aspects of East and West African music – just the latest example of the musical fertility of Mozambique's cultural soil.

Of the Mozambican musicians working outside the country, **Gito Baloi** is one who continues to draw on traditional rhythms for inspiration. He became popular in Mozambique after he had performed and released albums with the South African trio **Tananas**. In 1995, Gito released his first solo album *Ekaya*, featuring his own compositions.

Abdul Remane Gino and Zena Bakar of Eyuphuro

FRANK DRAKE/WOMAD

MOZAMBIQUE

A B C D E F G H I J K L

discography

Compilations

 Arcos, Cordas, Flautas
(C.I Crocevi/Sud Nord Records, Italy).

Musicians from all over Mozambique play all kinds of hand-made friction, wind and string instruments. Rubbing sounds produced by a bow interact with a rattle stick and with over-tones from the mouth which is used as a resonator, while tra-ditional flutes made of hard-shelled wild fruits produce fasci-nating interlocking sounds and rhythms.

Ilha de Moçambique
(C.I. Crocevia/Sud Nord Records, Italy).

A collection of distinct and charming Swahili songs and chants by acclaimed groups from the north of Mozambique present the importance of women in this matrilineal society. The album also includes a song by fishermen at work.

Kerestina – Guitar songs from Southern Mozambique 1955-1957 (Original Music, US).

This, the best available compilation of guitar songs from southern Mozambique, was recorded by ethnomusicologist Hugh Tracey. The musicians are from the countryside and the music is characterised by the powerful sounds of acous-tic guitars and male vocals and, in some cases, backing har-monies of high-pitched female voices. The musicians com-plain and joke about life and changing times in a rap form.

Mozambique One (GlobeStyle, UK).

Mostly acoustic field recordings, partly collected from region-al folk bands playing self-made traditional instruments like the *kanakari* (a four-string banjo with an antelope-skin head), or the *pankwe* (a five-string board zither with two large res-onators) and singing.

Mozambique Two (GlobeStyle, UK).

GlobeStyle's second release – partly set up from regional folk bands, partly stumbled upon – includes songs about social issues and daily life: for example the song "Youth of Today" comments "Friends we are a swarm of bees"; and in another song, "My Bed and my Wife", a husband speaks lovingly of sharing a small blanket with his wife.

¡Saba Saba! (GlobeStyle, UK).

Acoustic dance music from Nyampula in the northeast interi-or, an exuberant kind of afro-skiffle with multi-layered vocals.

Sounds Eastern & Southern (Original Music, US).

This album is full of wonderful acoustic guitar music from the 1940s and '50s, most of it recorded by the legendary ethno-musicologist Hugh Tracey (see p.669).

Artists

Amoya

An orchestra founded in 1979 under the leadership of Chico António. Some of the music played by this band is based on children's games and traditional rhythms from the southern part of Mozambique.

Cineta (Forlane, UMIP/RFI France).

This album is the intriguing result of a joint venture between Mozambican and French musicians and includes powerful synthesiser work along with a full complement of horns.

Gito Baloi

Baloi is an excellent, South African-based composer and bass-guitar master who has performed in Mozambique and around the world with renowned South African and Mozambican musicians.

Na Ku Randza (Sheer-Sound, South Africa).

Wonderful compilation of love songs based on afro-jazz, Latin-beat and other contemporary musical styles. Gracefully floating vocal lines move in unison with the bass guitar. Listen out for the occasional use of compound time as an escape from the normal square time.

Zaida e Carlos Chongo

A husband and wife team who started working together with Carlos as band leader, composer and lead guitar and Zaida as a dancer in the band. He started his musical career at a very young age playing a homemade tin guitar in Gaza province, at a time when he and his young friends were herding cattle. In the early 1980s he recorded his first single, "Timpondo", which became a great success.

Sibo (Orion Trading Lda. Mozambique).

The debut album of Orion Trading, a company formed to pro-mote Mozambique's cultural identity. "Sibo", like many songs on the album, is the result of a mixture of Shangaan tradition-al music with contemporary urban marrabenta dance music. "There are so many beautiful women in the world, why don't you just stick to the one you have?"

Jimmy Dludlu

South African-based Mozambican lead guitarist who taught himself how to play.

Echoes from the Past (Polygram, South Africa).

Studio work based on instrumental guitar music in Afro-jazz and fusion style.

Eduardo Durão

The excellent choreography of the National Song and Dance Company of Mozambique is based mostly on Eduardo Durão's hot repertoire.

Timbila (GlobeStyle, UK).

Modernised recordings of the bittersweet sounds of Mozambican timbila. Some tracks are incorporated into a modern African groove using Western instruments like the bass guitar and the drum-kit.

Eyuphuro

A line-up of roots musicians singing in the Macua lan-guage from the north of Mozambique. This group toured Europe for a long period participating in festivals and recording sessions organised by WOMAD.

 Mama Mosambiki
(RealWorld, UK).

Highly melodic acoustic guitar music with delicious bass-gui-tar lines and a number of carefully pitched traditional hand-drums providing excellent backing to the powerful female voice of Zena Bakar and best when her vocal chords are at full stretch, as on her beautiful composition, "Kihiyeny"

Ghorwane

The masters of Mozambican urban dance music rising from traditional roots to contemporary beats.

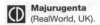 **Majurugenta**
(RealWorld, UK).

A party album par excellence, its big sound demands big speakers. Coloured by the breezy sax of the late Zeca Alage, this one always gets people moving.

🔘 **Kudumba** (Piranha, Germany).

Ten tracks of magically seductive light and breezy dance music – the result of more than ten years of work that always makes everybody jump and jive.

K10 (Kapa Dêch)

A group of young musicians who gained national and international recognition after winning the Music-Crossroads competition in Southern Africa region in 1997.

🔘 **Katchume** (Lusafrica/BMG, France).

A range of dance music based on traditional rhythms and melodies played with Western instruments incorporating influences from East and West Africa. "Sumbi" (a girl's name), they sing, "success is like a coal train that starts slowly but finally gets to its destination. So take it easy."

Venancio Mbande

Venancio Mbande, a much respected traditional music master, is the leader and the composer for a full strength 32-person timbila ensemble. He makes his own instruments and has toured the group in Europe and the US.

🔘 **Mozambique: Xylophone Music from the Chopi People** (Network, Germany).

Powerful music of Mozambique's history, touching upon the struggle for independence and the death of Samora Machel (Mozambique's first president) as well as a song about a miner returning home from the South Africa gold mines. Not easy to get hold of but repays the effort.

Paulo Miambo

Inspired by the late Fany Pfumo's singing style and lyrics, Miambo has done many recordings at the Radio Moçambique Studios since the 1980s.

🔘 **Hayini Unikanganhisa**
(Gresham Records, South Africa).

Dance music based on synthesiser sounds backed by South African female singers.

Chude Mondlane

The first female jazz singer in the country who introduced an innovative way of singing. She stimulated great change and influenced many local young female lead vocalists on the urban music scene.

🔘 **Especiarias do Corao** (Vidisc, Mozambique).

An album that brings together a variety of international styles from heavy Afro-beat to hip-hop, chachacha and jazz lines. "Obrigada Madame Chude" uses a mix of Portuguese and English languages over a strong African beat combined with a loose-limbed melodic line.

José Mucavel

Mucavel is an acoustic guitarist who, since leaving the Grupo Radio Moçambique, is forging a solo career.

🔘 **Compassos 1** (Musicrea, Denmark).

Guitar music with good quota of Mozambique's traditional rhythmic identity. Yodelling vocals, hand-drums and backing harmonies by a wild, high-pitched female vocalist. The soprano sax responds smoothly.

Orchestra Marrabenta Star de Moçambique

A band that brought many changes to Mozambique's music scene in the 1980s, this group toured Europe several times, representing the contemporary sound of Mozambique. Marrabenta Star was the musical nursery for many of the country's top musicians.

🔘 **Independence** (Piranha, Germany).

A variety of joyous compositions ranging across the spectrum – everything from loping dance grooves to brooding songs like the closing track, "Nwahulwana".

🔘 **Marrabenta Piquenique** (Piranha, Germany).

Some of the most popular tunes from southern Mozambique, splendidly rearranged by the orchestra using electric guitars, percussion and horns.

Fani Pfumo

Pfumo, the late, great marrabenta pioneer, started his musical career by entertaining people in the suburbs of Lourenço Marques, now Maputo. He would play his oil tin guitar for small change for the people in the neighbourhood, making them laugh with his witty lyrics.

 Nyoxanine
(Vidisco, Mozambique).

This superb CD is a selection of the most popular music recorded by this master of *marrabenta*.

Stewart Sukuma

One of the most hardworking musicians on the urban cultural scene, Stewart Sukuma (Luis Pereira) started his career around 1980, playing with his school band.

🔘 **Afrikiti** (CCP Record Company, South Africa).

A disc of recordings made with the participation of South African musicians, that covers various aspects of African musical influences from neighboring countries.

Wazimbo

One of the most popular singers in the country, and founder of the Orchestra Marrabenta Star de Moçambique, Wazimbo was previously the lead singer with the Radio Mozambique house band, Grupo Radio Moçambique.

 Makwêru
(Produções Conga, Mozambique).

Rearranged compositions from the time of Grupo Radio Moçambique, sung by an experienced vocalist, these songs have a big nostalgic flavour and texture to draw you in, even though you may not understand the lyrics.

Niger

sounds of the sahel

Muslim Niger is a huge, landlocked nation, with Nigeria to the south and the Sahara to the north, and in musical terms it has tended to be in the shadows of the great musical cultures of West Africa. The Sahel drought of 1973 left an enduring legacy of economic hardship, halting the country's small output of recordings. Yet, although Niger may command a very small space in the CD racks, **François Bensignor** contends that there's a store of good sounds here if you can visit, look and listen.

N iger has a diverse culture, taking in the largely nomadic Tuareg nomads in the north; Hausa in the centre and south; Beriberi in the east, around Lake Chad; and groupings of Djerma and Songhai, and Dendi in the west and south. All have their own distinctive traditional musics.

A Map of Niger

The **Tuareg** comprise only around 3 percent of Niger's population, but their culture is remarkable. They live in the northern regions of the Ténéré desert and Aïr mountains and still travel throughout the Sahel.

The Tuareg of Niger – and the wider Sahel – have kept a vivid and refined kind of **courtly-love poetry**, praising women's qualities in the blooming Tamachek language. Music can be played by anyone, both men and women – there is no professional caste – and, as with most nomadic cultures, there are few instruments. Voices are counterpointed by hand clapping, with the *tinde* drum (a mortar covered with a goat skin) used mostly in women's music and a one-stringed viol in men's songs. On the periphery of the desert, around the town of Tahoua, Hausa influences have crept in, characterised by the art of folk fiddle and calabash percussion.

The **Hausa** people, who make up just over half the country's population, live in central southern Niger, around the town of Maradi. Their music can be recognised by the beautiful melodies of their chordophones, especially on the little two-stringed **molo** lute, and rhythms on the **duma** percussion, played by a seated drumer pressing the skin of the drum with his foot to vary the sound. Music in the southeast area of Zinder is characterised by the big double-skinned **ganga** drum with resonator, the **alghaïta** shawm (trumpet) and the long **kakati** trumpet.

Further eastward, the **Beriberi** people, who live near Lake Chad close to the Tubu people, also play alghaïta but are best known for their beautiful polyphonic singing, comparable to the polyphony of the **Wodaabe Fulani**, whose famous, face-painted dancing ceremony for young men, the *gerewol*, is such an important annual date on Niger's calendar.

The western part of the country along the Niger river is where the capital Niamey is located, and the smaller groupings of **Djerma** and **Songhai** live. Musically, the region is notable for a wide variety of instruments from other parts of the country and across the borders, including lutes, fiddles, flutes, and various percussion instruments. They are usually played solo in their respective home regions but musicians in the western Niger play them together in orchestras.

In the far south-west along the Benin and Nigeria frontiers is the land of the **Dendi** (meaning 'the direction of the current'), who use techniques and instruments from both of the neighbouring countries. They're known for performing some of the finest music in Niger.

Cultural Policy

In strongly Muslim Niger, music as entertainment is not readily accepted, and for many years after independence there was little cultural policy, unlike in Mali or Guinea. However, after the death of the military dictator, Seyni Kounché, in 1987 the new government looked to music as a means of bringing the cultures together. Previously, playing their own traditional music in a non-professional environment meant that each community was largely ignorant of other music in Niger.

The opening for this was a competitve music festival, the **Prix Dan Gourmou**, with a cash prize and a national tour of the youth club circuit for the winner. It was set up by, among others, **Alassane**

Mamar Kassey

The group **Mamar Kassey** was founded in 1995 by singer, dancer and Fulani flute virtuoso **Yacouba Moumouni**. The idea (one repeated often in Africa in recent decades) was to re-work his country's musical traditions in a modern way but keeping the essence of the traditional sound. He gathered three good traditional musicians (on calabash, *komsa* lute and *kalangu* talking drum) whom he knew were open to developing musical traditions beyond the bounds of strict formality, along with two of his fellow musicians in the CFPM house band Takeda – the bass player and director-guitarist. Mamar Kassey's repertoire is based on Fulani, Songhai, Djerma and Hausa traditions, but Moumouni's personality pushes its skills far above the country's average.

Son of a Fulani shepherd, the young Yacouba herded the family cattle in the savannah near the Burkinabe border. After his father's death, he walked the two hundred kilometres to Niamey, trying to find work. The ten-year-old boy finally found work as a houseboy and the woman who opened her door to him was none other than **Absatou Dante** (see main article).

Moumouni, drawn by his passion for music, followed his stint of menial work with seven hard years of training in Dante's Ballet under the instruction of Harouna Maroufa, a master of the Fulani *seyse* flute. He learned to sing and dance and became one of the most impressive members of the National Ballet.

In 1993, he worked as an actor flautist in the theatre show **'Alice en Afrique'**, which took him on tour through West Africa and Europe in 1994 and 1995. During the tour he met Ali Farka Touré and World Circuit producer Nick Gold, who invited him to play his flute on Oumou Sangaré's album, *Worotan*.

Back in Niger, Moumouni knew exactly what he wanted to do: he formed Mamar Kassey, spending a year and a half building its repertoire and rehearsing with the musicians. Their first show. at the **Nuits Atypiques de Koudougou** festival, in Burkina, in 1997, was a revelation. Patrick Lavaud, the director of the French equivalent, *Nuits Atypiques de Langon*, booked the group for his 1998 festival, with resounding success, and they went on to record their first album, *Denke-Denke*, on Langon's Daqui label.

Mamar Kassey

Dante, formerly the National Ballet's director and co-director of the Franco-Nigerien cultural centre, and in his words "it was meant to pay respect to the different musical traditions, and to gather modern musicians together and give them the opportunity to create new music on traditional foundations. The national contest helped form music and dance ensembles in every region. Some wanted to add modern instruments to the traditional ones, so we thought it would be good for the musicians to have a place where they could be trained in modern techniques and instruments." This was the idea behind the **CFPM** (Centre for Musical Training and Promotion) which materialised in 1990 thanks to a six-year grant from the European Fund for Development.

Under the guidance of foreign teachers, most of the experienced musicians in Niamey took courses at the CFPM which was also the first place in the country where they could record in an eight-track studio, and use digital equipment like synthesisers and rhythm boxes. The group **Takeda** was formed with the best musicians working at CFPM and five singers – **Moussa Poussy, Yacouba Moumouni, Adam's Junior, Fati Mariko** and **John Sofakolé**. The European jazz orientation given by CFPM's director was not particularly successful, but when, in 1995, the group was exposed to an international audience at the music business showcase, MASA, in Abidjan, Côte d'Ivoire, some of the musicians were able to make personal progress.

Sylla Checks In

As there was no commercial musical production in the country in the mid-1990s, music from Niger was hardly known. International producer **Ibrahima Sylla** was astonished when his friend and partner Boncana Maïga told him he should check out what was going on in Niamey.

Sylla ended up signing the singers **Moussa Poussy** and **Saadou Bori** to make an album each in Abidjan's JBZ studio, produced by Boncana Maïga and arranged by Abdoulaye 'Abdallah' Alassane, the guitar-player and leader of Takeda. (Most of the tracks from these albums subsequently appeared together on the CD *Niamey Twice* on the Stern's label).

In 1997, Abdallah went to Bamako to produce **Adam's Junior**'s reggae album on Salif Keïta's label. And since 1995, Abdallah has also worked on Yacouba Moumouni's project with the group **Mamar Kassey**, which has the power and talent to represent the voice of Niger on the international World Music circuit. In 1998, just before their first album, *Denké-Denké* was issued, Mamar Kassey shared first place in the public's heart with the group Toubal.

"Niger has something that none of the neighbouring countries has – an active network of youth clubs with viable equipment in each one", says Alassane Dante. "International acts can be sent on tour to every country town all over Niger. Efforts made on music development have recently come to fruition in every region, giving birth to many a new group updating its own local musical traditions. Nowadays, in Niamey, there are at least twenty groups living on their music, playing clubs and touring the country. We hope the world will soon discover the vitality of Niger's culture."

discography

Compilations

Anthologie de la Musique du Niger (Ocora, France).

Wonderful historical recordings made in situ back in 1963 by composer and ethnomusicologist Tolia Nikiprowetsky with Songhai, Djerma, Hausa, Beriberi, Tuareg and Fulani traditional musicians. A must.

Wodaabe Fulani: Worso Songs (Inédit, France).

This record captures most of the strange singing and hand-clapping that accompanies the *worso* ceremonies of the Wodaabe section of the Fulani. Worso is a ritual in which young men compete with their clothes, jewels, painted faces and dancing, over several nights, to be elected the most handsome by the assembled young women.

Artists

Saadou Bori and Moussa Poussy

Two singer-songwriters who worked together in the national music school's house band, Takeda, and went on to bigger things in Abidjan. Both have spiritual backgrounds, Djerma performer Moussa Pousy as the grandson of a traditional healer and Hausa-speaker Saadou Bori as a practitioner of *Dango* (Hausa spirit music) and trance-dancing.

Niamey Twice (Stern's, UK).

A double helping of modern Niger, recorded in Abidjan under the direction of Ibrahima Sylla and previously released in West Africa on two separate cassettes. Six original compositions from each singer swing along happily, Pousy's mostly in Mande style, though with a nod to Blondy-esque reggae. The music of Saadou 'Bori' (his nickname acquired for his Nigérien hit of the same name, after the traditional Hausa spirit possession cult of *Bori*) is more interesting for its rare presentation of Hausa influences and on the more offbeat numbers – "Dango", and "Bori" itself – the spirit-loving polyrhythms bubble through frenetically.

Mamar Kassey

Mostly inspired by Fulani, Hausa, Songhai and Djerma traditional music, Mamar Kassey is the first group from Niger to take their music to an international audience and they can now compete with the best from Mali.

 Denké-Denké (Daqui, France).

Flute, lute, percussion, electric guitars and vocals lead you through old legends and tales from the sixteenth century, when the Songhai empire was the leading power in West Africa.

Nigeria

from hausa music to highlife

The Nigerian musical heritage extends from the stately court drumming of the northern Hausa emirates to the efforts of the late, great Fela Kuti to drum out the military dictators with LPs like *Vagabonds in Power* and *Coffin for Head of State*. **Ronnie Graham** tunes his ear to the beats of Africa's most populous nation, and the home of juju, fuji and highlife.

N igeria is at the heart of African music. The country is large, with a population exceeding one hundred million and it has a cultural heritage as diverse as any on the continent. The music industry is well developed, with numerous recording studios, a thirst for aesthetic and material success and a voracious appetite for life, love and music, born in part of the increasing desperation of everyday existence. Add to this a huge domestic market, big enough to sustain artists who sing in regional languages and experiment with indigenous styles, and it is no surprise that Nigerian musicians constantly reinvigorate their culture with new systems, styles and sounds.

Yet international success remains a fleeting dream for almost all Nigerian stars, however popular they are at home. A number of major musicians have their own labels, live like medieval kings and enjoy all the trappings of success, but they consistently fail to hit home overseas. Corruption, for a start, discourages even the most ardent capitalist from working in Nigeria, severely limiting international business contacts. Political unpredictability and frequent, often violent, changes of government makes even corrupt business a hazardous profession to pursue and while the elections of 1999 were a move back towards democracy after years of military rule, serious doubts were raised about the way they were run.

National success also challenges music stars to make the transition to international languages and performance norms, whilst the sheer numbers involved in a international tour – Nigeria is a land of very big bands indeed, with a 14-musician line-up common and 20-30 none too unusual in juju music – daunt all but the most ambitious promoters.

Modern Roots

The modern musical culture of Nigeria draws on both internal traditional and external influences.

During the second half of the twentieth century, three main types of modern music evolved: highlife, juju and fuji.

Both **juju** and **fuji** are almost entirely sung in local languages, principally Yoruba. They have praise-song vocals and assertive polyrhythmic percussion at their heart. **Highlife**, born in Ghana but finding a new Congolese inflection in Nigeria, flourished between the 1950s and 1980s but is now sadly past its peak. More recently, jazz, rock, soul, reggae, pop and gospel have all played a part in shaping modern music but the results are distinctively Nigerian, reflecting the nation's reality with a force and directness few other countries have been able to maintain.

Sunny Ade and **Fela Kuti** are the most conspicuous figures in the story of contemporary Nigerian music. Both are Yoruba and both have had roller-coaster careers. But while Sunny Ade is very much a society favourite who achieved international success in the mid-1980s, Fela Kuti remained, until his untimely death in 1997, an uncompromising critic of every government Nigerians have suffered since independence in 1960.

The three decades since 1960 have seen several major successes by other Nigerian stars. **Prince Nico Mbarga** and **Rocafil Jazz** enjoyed enormous popularity in 1976 everywhere from Zambia to the Caribbean and throughout West Africa with "Sweet Mother", a musical phenomenon that bulldozed everything in its path. Then there was another pan-African hit in 1978, when **Sonny Okosun** released "Fire in Soweto", a moving tribute to the Black Consciousness Movement set against the driving rock-reggae fusion he called *ozzidi*. But once again, while Okosun maintained an impressive output of music (which appealed particularly to African-Americans) he could not repeat the success of his first hit.

Most Nigerian musicians seem condemned to this one-hit-wonder existence – a paradoxical situation for a country with one hundred million people, arguably the best musical infrastructure on the continent and at least a dozen popular dance styles ranging from the juju of Obey and Ade, to Igbo highlife, *ikwokirikwo* and the many flowerings of Yoruba musical life, including *agidigbo, were, apala, sakara, waka* and *fuji*.

It is a pattern that has been further ingrained by foreign markets. Once the initial excitement over Sunny Ade had worn off, Europe and the US, throughout the World Music boom years of the 1980s and '90s, strangely ignored Nigerian music. One leading World Music magazine went for over three years without reviewing a single Nigerian release – indeed, Nigerian music virtually disappeared from the mainstream record stores overseas. In the last couple of years, however, with the re-emergence of Sunny Ade, the posthumous elevation of Fela to legendary status and the emergence of his son, **Femi Kuti** as a major artist, the pendulum may be swinging back.

Folk Roots

The 'Giant of Africa' is a country of enormous cultural and musical diversity. With over four hundred distinct ethnic groups and a massive internal market, even the most esoteric musical styles find some degree of commercial success.

In the north, **Hausa** music traditionally offered a variety of percussion and **goje** (one-string fiddle) music to accompany ritual and recreational activities – weddings, births, circumcisions and wrestling matches. A strong vocal tradition, invariably in the praise-song category, complemented a range of percussion instruments including hundreds of different skin drums, water drums, xylophones, whistles and bells.

The ruling Hausa-Fulani elite, whose day may be coming to an end with the demise of Abacha, helped establish a courtly trumpet tradition. The Hausa language is a lingua franca across a vast swathe of the Sahel belt, which ensures regional as well as local audiences for songs with Hausa lyrics. Hausa music has flourished since the sixteenth century and the fall of the **Songhai** empire (in present-day Mali), which previously ruled over much of what is now Hausa-land and with whose music there are still many parallels. Today, travellers are unlikely to find much on disc but there is a flourishing cassette market for the big names, who often appear at state occasions, holding audiences enthralled with lengthy praise songs of traditional and modern rulers.

Moving south through the plateau states of minority language groups, instrumentation and performance becomes more varied. Islamic strictures are slightly looser and the Tiv, Idoma and Jukun all enjoy extensive drum and vocal traditions.

The **Igbo** people of the southeast have always been receptive to cultural change. This is reflected in their music (highlife quickly took root in this fertile soil) and in the incredible variety of instruments played in Igbo-land, one of the most pleasing of which is the **obo**, a thirteen-stringed zither, which can be heard at many a nostalgic palm-wine drinking session. In traditional communities, royal music is played every day, when the *ufie* slit drum is used to wake the chief (*obi*) and to tell him when meals are ready, and a group, known as *egwu ota*, which consists of slit-drums, drums and bells, performs when the obi is leaving the palace and again when he returns. The traditional Igbo musical inventory of drums percussion, flutes, xylophones, lyres and lutes was enriched by the arrival of European instruments, producing an important brass band tradition.

Yoruba instrumental traditions are mostly based on drumming. The most popular form of traditional music today is **dundun**, played on hourglass tension drums of the same name. The usual ensemble consists of tension drums of various sizes together with a small kettledrums called *gudugudu*. The leading drum of the group is the *iyalu* (mother), which 'talks' by imitating the strong tonality of Yoruba speech. It's used to play praise poetry, proverbs and other oral narratives. Another important part of Yoruba musical life is music theatre, which mixes traditional music with story telling or live drama.

European and Christian influence, spreading inland from the coast in the nineteenth century, introduced new melodies and rhythms to Yoruba music, together with new brass instruments and written sheet music, early record-players and then, in the 1930s, radio. There was also an important Brazilian contribution which came from the influential Brazilian merchant community of the early nineteenth century. Meanwhile, the southward spread of Islam was accompanied by new percussion styles, new vocal styles and a totally different approach to music and culture.

During the nineteenth and early twentieth centuries, all three traditions were introduced to the Yoruba, and from this hotbed of adaptations and interchange, came a plethora of competing rhythms and idioms. Nowhere is this more evident than in the country's largest city, Lagos which was always at the forefront of musical expression in Nigeria.

Palm-Wine into Juju

From the Lagos melting pot, where indigenous Yoruba people mixed with the descendants of freed slaves from Sierra Leone and Brazil, came new styles and aesthetics. In the palm-wine shacks of the Yoruba neighbourhoods, where men met to drink and socialise after work, an informal style called **palm-wine music** emerged, similar to that developed under the same name in Sierra Leone and Ghana. Played on guitars, banjos or any other available string instrument – backed up by shakers and tapped drinking calabashes – palm-wine was first and foremost a vocal music relying on the vast liturgy of Yoruba proverbs and metaphors to deal with issues of the new urban culture.

By the 1920s several individuals were emerging as popular stars of this music, including **'Baba' Tunde King**, who is credited with coining the term 'juju'. Though its origin is much disputed, one widely accepted explanation is that **juju music** was named for the *ju ju* sound of the small hexagonal tambourine, a popular instrument of Brazilian descent. The word also works as a mild expression of colonial disparagement – musical mumbo jumbo – taken up by juju musicians themselves to subvert it. And *jojo* also happens to be the Yoruba for 'dance'.

Whatever the origins, British record labels like His Masters Voice sensed a commercial opportunity in the budding city of Lagos, recording many early juju musicians and pressing 78s for distribution by local traders. Like the pioneers of any music style, juju's early performers achieved little financial success. However, artists like Tunde King, **Ojoge Daniel** and **JO 'Speedy' Araba** developed a body of work which is still drawn upon by today's stars. The first recordings of this dreamy style started coming out in the early 1930s, but juju really took off, establishing itself as a premier urban dance style, just after World War II, with the introduction of amplified sound.

Tunde Nightingale, a fine palm-wine singer, became juju's first big star. He developed a popular stylistic variant, which dominated the clubs and the record industry of post-war Nigeria, called *s'o wa mbe* (literally 'is it there?' – a reference to the strings of waist beads worn by women beneath their clothes to accentuate dance movements).

In 1957, **IK Dairo** with his band the **Morning Star Orchestra** (later to become the Blue Spots)

Hausa Music

There are two broad categories of **Hausa** music – rural music and urban music of the court and state. The emirates of **Katsina** and **Kano** together with the sultanate of *Sokoto*, and to a lesser extent **Zaria** and **Bauchi**, are the major creative centres.

Ceremonial music, *rokon fada*, of the Hausa states plays a major (if not very musical) role in Hausa traditions, even today. The instruments of ceremonial music are largely seen as prestige symbols of authority, and ceremonial musicians tend to be chosen for their family connections rather than any musical ability – in fact quite often that doesn't come into it at all, with painful results. **Court musicians** and praise singers, on the other hand, are always chosen for their musical skills. Exclusively dependent on a single wealthy patron, usually an emir or sultan, the most talented players are rarely seen in public. The greatest Hausa praise singer was **Narambad**, who lived and worked in Sokoto: he died in 1960.

Ceremonial music can always be heard at the **sara**, the weekly statement of authority which takes place outside the emir's palace on a Thursday evening. The principal instruments accompanying praise songs are percussive – small kettledrums and talking drums. The most impressive of the Hausa **state instruments**, however, is the elongated state trumpet called **kakakai**, which was originally used by the Songhai cavalry and was taken by the rising Hausa states as a symbol of military power. Kakakai are usually accompanied by large **tambura** drums.

Much like elsewhere in Africa, **traditional rural Hausa music** appears to be dying out in favour of modern pop (which still draws inspiration from these roots). The last expressions of rural music are to be found in traditional dances like the *asauwara*, for young girls, and the *bori*, the dance of the spirit possession cult, which dates back to before the arrival of Islam and continues to thrive in parallel with the teachings of the Koran. Zaria is its main stronghold.

Popular **Hausa folk music** thrives both in town and countryside and although it makes little impression outside Hausa-land, musicians can earn a good living satisfying local needs and, as ever, voicing and sometimes moulding public opinion. The leading Hausa singer, **Muhamman Shata**, is always accompanied by a troupe of virtuoso drummers who play *kalangu*, small talking drums. Other leading artists include **Dan Maraya**, an exponent of the *kontigi* one-stringed lute; **Ibrahim Na Habu**, who popularised a type of small fiddle called the *kukkuma*; and **Audo Yaron Goje** who plays (not surprisingly) the *goje* or one-string fiddle.

launched a career that changed juju music. With the development and availability of new technology, Dairo began to infuse elements such as electric guitar and accordion into the music. And although it's not known who was responsible, this era also saw the introduction of the **gangan** (Yoruba talking drum) into the ensemble.

IK Dairo's lyrical skills, short catchy phrases and mastery of the recording technology of the day led to a string of hit records still without equal, and to an appeal that spread to Britain, Europe and even Japan. In 1963, he received a British MBE for his achievements – the only African musician ever to be so honoured – and throughout the 1960s there was no bigger African band than the **Blue Notes**. But by the mid-1970s Dairo's record sales plummeted literally overnight as a younger, style-conscious generation of Nigerians flocked first to Ebenezer Obey and then Sunny Ade – juju's heirs apparent.

Obey and Ade: Juju Goes Global

Ebenezer Obey formed his first group, the **International Brothers**, in 1964, and since then has released over fifty LPs. The success of his blend of talking drums, percussion and multiple guitars had already caught on by the time he renamed his group the **Inter-Reformers** in 1970. With the new band he rose to prominence with exciting bluesy guitar work and lyrics which managed to be steeped in Yoruba tradition and at the same time address issues affecting the new urban elites and impart the conservative Christian values which Obey espoused. *Murtala Muhammed* and *Immortal Songs for Travellers* were among albums he was turning out at a staggering rate in the late 1970s, with advance sales of over a hundred thousand a time.

The rivalry between the chubby joker Ebenezer Obey, dubbed 'Chief Commander' by his fan club, and the more populist, **'King' Sunny Ade** led to fast and furious developments in juju music. Each struggled to be the first to introduce a new instrument, style or sound, with each new development labelled a 'system'. The **juju ensemble**, which had started with four and expanded to over ten musicians with IK Dairo, now pushed over thirty people on stage, with up to four guitars, various keyboards, Hawaiian guitars, trap set, a wide range of traditional and modern percussion and numerous background vocalists.

As technological developments allowed, the recording emphasis shifted from short songs to twenty-two-minute-long, LP-busting tracks. Even in this longer format, juju musicians continued to be prolific in the recording studio, averaging three or four albums each year. And, pulled along in the wake of Ade's and Obey's popularity were several hundred other juju bands scattered throughout southwestern Nigeria.

In 1980 Ebenezer Obey went international with his album *Current Affairs*, and its successors, *Je Ka Jo* on Virgin and the much tougher *Solution* on Stern's. As a result he rose briefly to stardom on the World Music scene in Britain and elsewhere. But by now, **Sunny Ade** (see box overleaf) was already out in the world and, in 1982 he was taken up by the UK-based Island Records as a potential Bob Marley style superstar from Africa. His initial Island release, *Juju Music,* was a huge success in terms of the perceived market at that time for African music in Europe and the US – and his live shows wowed audiences around the world with their complex sound, tight groove and the man's delightful stage presence. A second Island release, *Synchro System*, also sold well.

JAK KLIBY

Chief Ebenezer Obey

King Sunny Ade

Born Sunday Adeniyi to a branch of the Royal family of Ondo town, **'King' Sunny Ade** began his musical career playing in various highlife bands in the early 1960s. By 1966 he had formed his first band, the **Green Spots**, with whom he recorded several modestly successful albums. In 1974 he renamed the band the **African Beats** and released *Esu Biri Ebo Mi* under his own record label, Sunny Alade, which solidified his support and propelled him into the limelight. Other hit albums included *The Late General Murtala Muhammed* (Nigeria's most popular military dictator, remembered almost with fondness), *Sound Vibration* and *The Royal Sound*.

In 1977, a group of journalists and music critics named Ade the King of Juju Music, and Island Records, searching for a replacement for Bob Marley as the standard bearer of tropical music, picked up on him. His guitar line-up, weaving intricate melodic patterns against a background of thundering percussion, the call-and-response 'conversations' of the talking drums, and the infectiously winning, 'African-prince' style of the man himself – all gave off strong commercial signals. As noted, the 1982 release, *Juju Music*, produced by the Frenchman Martin Meissonnier, was a big success, as was its follow-up, *Synchro System*. But Ade failed to gain the global audience demanded by a major, and

his third Island release, *Aura*, bombed. Island dropped him in 1985 and his band subsequently walked out in the middle of a prestigious Japanese tour. It was clear that the international juju boom was over.

Still, King Sunny's short-lived international stardom had secured his position as juju's frontrunner at home, where he continued a full schedule of performances and recording, with occasional overseas sorties on the World Music circuit. His lyrics became more pointed: he started to sing of rumours, jealousy, destiny, new directions – and family planning. This foray into population politics on the 1989 album *Wait for Me*, was not calculated to enhance the domestic reputation of a musician with twelve children.

As the 1990s developed and political repression in Nigeria intensified, Ade, spurned by the global music shakers, withdrew, sallying forth only to deny the latest round of rumours of his death, invariably attributed to some unmentionable or unattributable cause. It was therefore even more of a pleasant surprise when, managed by Seattle-based World Music impresario Andy Frankel, he resurfaced in 1998 with a few shows in Europe before proceeding to the US for a renewed assault on the American market. His shows revealed him to be still on top form.

RICHARD TRILLO

But there were looming doubts: Sunny Ade's Yoruba lyrics and complex rhythms were less readily accessible than the English lyrics and regular rhythms of the reggae greats he was supposed to replace. And the discs encouraged a glut of Nigerian imports. Island's third Sunny Ade release, *Aura*, with Stevie Wonder playing harmonica on the title track, bombed, and he was dropped by the label in 1985. Juju's star had waned, and at home it was beginning to lose out to a new wave of Yoruba music dubbed Yo-pop.

Ade (see box) continued a low-key and erratic career back home, while Obey concentrated his appeal on an older generation of fans, asserting his juju mastery with a series of classic, smaller label albums – *Juju Jubilee* (Shanachie 1988), *Get Yer Jujus Out* (Rykodisc, 1989) and *Juju Jubilation*, (EMI Hemisphere, 1997).

Yo-pop and Afro-Juju

In the mid-1980s, as juju fractured, **Yo-pop** – Yoruba pop music – crashed onto the scene in the person of **Segun Adewale**. All speed, thunder and lightning, it found a huge young audience, especially in Lagos.

Adewale started out as a backup singer, with **Shina Peters,** in the band of Prince Adekunle, a contemporary of IK Dairo's, before splitting off to form their own group which they called, with no trace of irony, **Shina Adewale**. Together they recorded several albums and achieved enormous success, but ultimately individual ambition led each to strike out on his own.

With wealthy Nigerian backers, **'Sir' Shina Peters** combined juju with elements of Fela Kuti's

Afro-Beat style and the upfront drum sounds of fuji music into a style he dubbed **Afro-juju**. *Afro-Juju Series 1*, his 1989 CBS release, became a multimillion seller in Nigeria and abroad and launched a youth craze called Shina Mania. The record's stunning success and Peters' powerful live performances secured him Nigeria's Juju Musician of the Year award for 1990. His follow-up, *Shinamania*, created a modern juju style but despite healthy sales, the result was widely panned by Nigerian critics who damped down the heat of the two-year craze.

Shina's success did manage to open up the juju market to newcomers and in the late 1990s massive plaudits were showered on **Fabulous Olu Fajemirokun**. But in the latter part of the decade, juju was really in the shadows of fuji – of which more below. In the late 1990s, Adewale Ayuba created a kind of juju-fuji fusion, with a twenty-strong band, major chart hits at home, and an underground accreditation abroad for the album *Fuji Dub: Lagos-Brooklyn-Brixton*.

The Eruption of Fuji

Although **fuji** has been around in Yoruba-land for nearly three decades, three top names – Sikiru Ayinde Barrister, Ayinla Kollington and Wasiu Barrister – had come totally to dominate the Lagos scene by the early 1990s. Named, somewhat oddly, after Mount Fuji, the Japanese mountain of love (mostly for the sound of the word, according to originator Sikiru Barrister), the first fuji bands had appeared in the late 1960s.

Early fuji sythesised elements of *apala* – a style with a praise-song core, named after the talking drum – with the sounds of the *sakara* tambourine drum, into a new recreational dance style. It was first popularised by **Ayinla Omowura** and **Haruna Ishola** (a nationally reputed musician and studio-owning entrepreneur).

Sometimes glibly described as juju music without guitars – interestingly, Ebenezer Obey once described juju as mambo music *plus* guitars – fuji is in fact a far more complex style, drawing on Yoruba percussion roots (the small round clay and bamboo *sakara* tambourine-drum and apala talking drum) while adding a specifically Muslim vocal feel. True, there are virtually no stringed instruments involved, apart from the Hawaiian guitar, but it's an overwhelming wall of sound, carved out of silence by percussion and vocals. From a slow start, fuji steadily gained in popularity, overtaking juju by the mid-1980s. It was associated loosely with Islam in the same way that juju tended to be associated with Christianity.

Sikiru Ayinde, better known by his fans as **Barrister**, is the leading Yoruba fuji singer. At the age of ten, he started singing Muslim *were*, the singing-alarm-clock songs performed for early breakfast and prayers during Ramadan. After a brief career in the army, he returned to music and, in the early 1970s, formed the **Supreme Fuji Commanders**, a twenty-five-piece outfit that soon became one of Nigeria's top bands, firing off a battery of hit records.

Ayinla Kollington, popularly known as '**Baba Alatika**' (father of the masses), is ranked second in the fuji popularity stakes behind Barrister. He's very much the source of social commentary in the Yoruba Muslim music scene. His lyrics can be razor-sharp – though he rarely puts himself on the front line of political dissent, as Fela Kuti did, for example. He released over a dozen albums in the 1980s.

As success spawned success, Kollington, Barrister Sikiru and a third major juju name, '**Barrister' Wasiu**, vied with each other to accumulate titles, doctorates and other symbols of status. But the real action was taking place on vinyl. Each fuji leader continued to add new touches to the basic formula – a drop of Hawaiian guitar here, a lone trumpet there; from a subtle synth in the background to an up-front school bell. Proletarian and relentless, the moving percussive force of fuji swept Lagos off its feet and by the early 1990s had become synonymous with dance-floor excitement. Wasiu scored with "Talazo in London" and "Jo Fun Mi"; Kollington with "Megastar", "Fuji Ropopo" and – with the renamed Fuji Eaglets – the 1997 hit "Live in America"; Sikiru with "Extravaganza" and "Fuji Garbage".

"Fuji Garbage" was titled thus to pre-empt any abusive comments from rivals. So, they thought it was garbage? Sikiru would call it garbage himself (if Michael Jackson was 'Bad', Sikiru Ayinde Barrister was 'Garbage'!). It also expressed his contempt for the space taken up in the fuji columns of the Nigerian papers over the alleged gossip and feuding between him and Kollington. Like the term 'fuji', the epithet has worked – especially as the associated dance style swept through Nigeria's Christian and Muslim communities alike – and the 'Garbage' series now numbers many volumes.

Sikiru Barrister's full line-up – when there's room for all of them on stage – is thirty-four. The **fuji percussion orchestras** are a sight to behold. They can occasionally be enjoyed in London and New York when they drop over for shows that are always underpublicised outside an ecstatic Nigerian community. At his overseas gigs, Barrister's stage and line-up resembles a Lagos street scene,

Fela Kuti and the Afro-Beat Revolution

Of all African musicians **Fela Kuti** probably needs the least introduction. He passed his half century with over fifty albums to his credit, and – sweating, naked to the waist, with a massive spliff clenched between his teeth – became the radiant rallying point for the Nigerian underclass, and for political prisoners everywhere. Controversial, stubborn, outspoken, innovative, and always on a track entirely his own, Fela maintained a creative momentum unparalleled in West Africa.

His career, spanning three decades, was repeatedly interrupted by government violence against his musicians, his family and his person. Records were regularly banned, his extraordinary, extended-family base, the self-styled Kalakuta Republic, was destroyed, his mother killed, and the man himself beaten up and imprisoned; yet still he fought on against the corruption, brutality and banal inhumanity of successive regimes, ironically dying a year before the collapse of perhaps the worst of them all, Abacha's ill-fated African reich.

Fela Anikulapo Ransome-Kuti was born into an elite Yoruba family in Abeokuta, north of Lagos. The town, established by the British in the early 1800s for freed slaves, and the home of Nobel-prize-winning novelist Wole Soyinke, was always a creative and radical hotbed. The Ransome family had a history both of anti-colonial, nationalist activity and musical talent. Fela's grandfather was a celebrated composer, his father and mother a piano-playing pastor and a nationalist leader respectively. In the late 1950s Fela moved to London to study music and stayed four years, studying trumpet and music theory at the Trinity College of Music and forming the **Koola Lobitos** in 1961 with his friend and mentor, JK Braimah.

Returning home in 1963 he soon came under the influence of Sierra Leonean soul singer **Geraldo Pino**'s Afro-soul style, itself close to James Brown. Fela combined this innovative style with elements of highlife, jazz, and traditional music and dubbed his sound 'Afro-Beat'.

In 1969 he moved to the US where he read about African-American history and was moved by his contact with the **Black Panthers**. Nigeria was plagued by political instability and military rulers of uncertain calibre. As the plight of the poor in Nigeria worsened, Fela sharpened his wit and honed his musical revolution, recording a number of singles, retrospectively gathered together and released by Stern's as *The Los Angeles Sessions*.

Fela in offstage attire

This was followed in short order by a stint in London, (marked for posterity by *Fela's London Scene*), a new name for the band – the harder hitting **Africa 70** – and then a true purple patch in 1972 with a series of Afro-Beat classics. He then launched into a series of stinging attacks on everything from military governments to skin-bleaching, Lagos traffic to arbitrary arrest and, above all, the political and economic systems which reproduced such grinding poverty. His efforts did not go unnoticed. For him, the 1970s were characterised by police harassment and violence, conflicts with multinational record companies, self-exile in Ghana and, in spite of all this, a growing international reputation.

Afro-Beat emerged as a powerful musical force featuring the fantastic percussionist **Tony Allen** on the drum kit, brooding brass parts, call-and-response vocals, a spectacularly choreographed, twenty-strong female chorus, and of course Fela himself, alternating between tenor-sax, alto-sax and keyboard. Building to magnificent, thundering climaxes, Afro-Beat carved out a niche in the crowded Lagos musical market with best-seller following best-seller.

In 1985, the military government nailed Fela on spurious currency charges and locked him away for a five-year prison sentence. But such was the international outcry and massive protest inside Nigeria that he was eventually released in 1987, weakened but unbowed. Towards the end of the decade he blasted back with classics such as "Army Arrangement" (a stinging indictment of military corruption under the Obasanjo regime), "Beasts of No Nation" (a lashing for the reactionary conservatism of Reagan, Thatcher and Botha in South Africa), and the standing accusation of all Nigerian governments entitled "Which Head Never Steal?".

Accompanied by his forty-strong band, by now known as the **Egypt 80**, Fela was never an easy star to deal with, and he stood accused of racism, extravagant sexism and overweening egoism – all charges which he shrugged off rather than refuted. (In 1986 he divorced his twenty-eight wives, announcing, "no man has the right to own a woman's vagina"). His songs, sung in pidgin English, retained a wide appeal for their humour and clever use of language, but his music was never

dance-oriented and the lengthy on-stage polemics – haranguing captive audiences through a haze of smoke – became legendary.

Fela's lifetime of confrontation, heavy living and personal conviction was taking its toll and when he fell into a coma late in 1997, brought on by AIDS, the end followed quickly. Lagos came to a standstill as he was laid to rest. Fela remains a truly remarkable witness to the realities of post colonial Africa. No system ever broke his resistance, no power broke his bond with the people and no historian will ever capture his true reputation across the continent.

During Fela's periods in jail, his bands carried on, led by his son Femi and others. **Femi Kuti** has now launched a career of his own, escaping from the paternal shadow. Where his father was ranting and polemical, Femi is less vitriolic, more a musician's musician. If he doesn't quite have the old man's voice, his positive approach is a suitable complement to Fela's overpowering political awareness, and his recent (1998) album, *Shoki Shoki*, and tours, show a marked inclination to the dancefloor.

Femi Kuti

COLLECTION GRAEME EWENS

Bobby Benson

as the audience mingle with the orchestra and an organised currency-changing operation is set up on tables and chairs to one side.

By the mid-1990s, all the leading fuji stars were releasing videos mixed from live shows, street theatre and home life. Enormously entertaining and of excellent quality, these fuji videos are now the best way to experience the fuji phenomenon – short of a long weekend in Lagos.

Highlife Rise and Fall

While juju and fuji have ruled among the Yoruba, high-quality **highlife** was the norm in the Igbo east for well over forty years. Light, flowing and eminently danceable, highlife is one of the few core dance rhythms in Africa and it easily took root in **Igbo-land**, where it arrived from Ghana in the early 1950s in guitar and dance bands.

The Igbo have a traditional familiarity with stringed instruments; early 'Igbo Blues' is redolent of later guitar-band idioms and Congolese and Cameroonian guitar bands toured the east from 1959 onwards. Highlife, with its Western and Christian musical links, slotted well into the Igbo cultural framework – non-Muslim, individualist, outward-looking. And the struggle for independence in Ghana, highlife's heartland, was closely watched in Nigeria, where it was branded the cultural expression of West African nationalism, worthy of emulation. **ET Mensah**, the king of Ghanaian highlife (see p.491), toured frequently during the 1950s, and his music struck an immediate chord with southern Nigerians.

Bobby Benson, one of the pioneers of dance band highlife, devoted himself to this style after hearing ET Mensah. In the 1950s, he created Bobby Benson and his Combo, and his early hits went a long way to popularise the style at home. Another pioneer was **Rex 'Jim' Lawson**, who began playing trumpet in bands at the age of twelve, and when highlife took off in the 1950s, he worked with many of the greats. In the 1960s, his eleven-piece group, **Mayor's Dance Band**, produced successive hits including "Jolly Papa" and "Gowon Special". Lawson died suddenly in 1976, at the height of his career. Many of the classics can be heard on his *Greatest Hits* album on Polydor Nigeria which has been re-released on CD by UK label, Flame Tree.

Prince Nico Mbarga and **Rocafil Jazz** are reckoned to have sold some thirteen million copies of "Sweet Mother", making it the biggest-selling African song of all time. Hundreds of bands copied it; radio stations played it incessantly; vinyl copies could only be had at twenty times the normal price. But why? For a song about not forgetting mum, with its vaguely guilt-ridden undertones, and, on first hearing, unadventurous composition, it's hard to see much beyond an innocent charm.

Sweet mother, I no go forget you,
For the suffer wey you suffer for me, yeah,
Sweet mother, I no go forget you,
For the suffer wey you suffer for me, yeah.
When I de cry, my mother go carry me.
She go say, "My pikin, wetin you de cry?, oh,
Stop, stop, stop, stop, stop, stop
Make you no go cry again, oh".

Praise and 'Spraying'

Like all Yoruba music, juju and fuji music is primarily about words. As the Yoruba language is strongly tonal – in other words the pitch of a syllable determines the meaning – lyrics and melody have a peculiarly close relationship. Juju music is steeped in Yoruba oral traditions and its singers draw from the large corpus of proverbs, metaphors and traditional praise poems of the spoken language. While popular juju and fuji musicians play nightclub and theatre shows, the vast majority of performances take place in more traditional contexts such as weddings, naming ceremonies, funeral feasts and other major commemorative events.

The musicians are generally given a guaranteed fee for performing, but the bulk of their earnings come from what is known as **'spraying'**. The lead singer of the band makes sure he collects the names and other pertinent information about prominent individuals attending the event and there is usually a non-performing band member dedicated to this important task. The singer will then praise these individuals one at a time, invoking their heritage, heaping praises on their relatives and, through formulaic proverbs, establishing their great and worthy credentials for all to hear. In response, the patron whose head has 'swelled' with pride will come on stage and slap bank notes onto the forehead of the sweaty musician – quickly collected by a colleague. The more money given, the longer the patron's praises are sung.

At a typical ceremony, the music will begin around 11pm or midnight and the band will play nonstop for two or three hours. It is common for these *inawo* (literally 'something to spend money on') to last until eight o'clock the next morning or later. As long as patrons are spraying, the musicians play. Artists like Sunny Ade, Ebenezer Obey and Sikiru Barrister, who demand guarantees of around $1,000, routinely get sprayed upwards of $10,000 per show.

JAK KLIBY

Barrister trawls in the tips

NIGERIA

But it is an infectious song and its potent appeal was concocted from Mbarga's use of pidgin English (broadening his audience enormously) and a style he called *panko* – for the first time incorporating sophisticated rumba guitar-phrasing into the highlife idiom. In fact "Sweet Mother" is a highly charged dance number, mid-paced and sensual, with brilliant rhythmic breaks, and innovative use of 'Congolese guitar'. It ensured the late Prince Nico's eternal reputation.

Alas, the song was an outstanding success in a story of general decline. The Nigerian civil war in the late 1960s virtually put an end to highlife in western Nigeria: tribal discrimination forced all Igbo musicians, including Rex Lawson, to leave Lagos, and guitar-band highlife was increasingly identified with the east as 'Igbo highlife' (where, with a few honourable exceptions, it gradually withered), while juju, and later fuji, became the staple diet of the Lagos recording industry.

Among the highlife survivors was the Yoruba singer and trumpeter **'Dr' Victor Olaiya** (the 'Evil Genius of Highlife') – one of the few top Lagos musicians to continue with the genre and

stick to his musical roots throughout the civil war and after. Two other diehards are the sonorous-voiced, old-timer **Stephen Osita Osadebe**, with almost half a century of traditional Igbo guitar songs behind him and more than thirty albums, and **Orlando 'Dr Ganja' Owoh**, the inveterate king of **toye**, a juju-highlife cross-style which contrives to be both traditional and provocative, by staying acoustic, topical – and stoned.

Old albums from the early highlife stars are rarities these days although it is still possible to lay your hands on 1970s and '80s material by the fabulous **Oriental Brothers** (and off-shoots Dr Sir Warrior and Kabaka), as well as the classic highlife of Ikengas, Oliver de Coque and, of course, Prince Nico Mbarga. A steady trickle of re-releases continues to refresh the catalogue, if not the style, and aficionados are urged to check out **Celestine Ukwu**'s *Greatest Hits*.

One sole survivor from the 1970s is the indestructible – and international – **Sonny Okosun**. Hit followed hit in the wake of "Fire in Soweto" as his reputation soared on both sides of the Atlantic, fully justifying the 1996 *Ultimate Collection*. But time

COLLECTION GRAEME EWENS

NIGERIA

Dr (Sir) Warrior & Oriental Brothers

had moved on and in reality Sonny had become a pastor, scoring reasonable domestic success with *Songs Of Praise*, a two-volume personal testimony from the evangelist.

Another maverick on the scene was **Sir Victor Uwaifo**, 1960s professional wrestler, turned 1970s hit-maker with "Joromi" and latterly a true renaissance man with his arts laboratory and studio. The 1996 release *Vintage Masterpieces* in no way underestimates his popularity or talent.

discography

A great deal of postwar Nigerian music, including early juju and highlife, is locked away in the warehouses of Philips, Decca and EMI, although both Original Music and Timbuktoo have done their best to make material available. Traditional music from Nigeria is seldom available on anything other than local cassettes.

Traditional

Yoruba Street Percussion (Original Music, US).

A rich diversity of short tracks from the 1960s including agidigbo by the New Star Orchestra, apala from Haruna Ishola, early fuji, sakara, various female waka artists and a sound dubbed 'natural juju'. More of a generous slice of social history than a collector's item, and all of it borrowed from Decca West Africa.

Juju

Compilation

 Juju Roots, 1930s-1950s
(Rounder US).

Excellent introduction to the early juju years with comprehensive sleeve notes. Featuring Irewolede Denge, Tunde King and Ojoge Daniel – essential.

Artists

King Sunny Ade

Sunny Ade was already huge in Nigeria when Island signed him and his spectacular band in 1982. His distinctive brand of juju spread a tide of international interest in the sounds of Africa, creating rack space in the record stores of Europe and the US long before the notion of World Music had any meaning. Nearly two decades on, he's still intermittently flying high.

 Juju Music
(Island, UK).

The record that launched a million passions for African sounds. Still wonderful after all these years, *Juju Music* includes many of Ade's best songs, among them the sweet "365 is My Number", a longer, sharper, and looser version of which takes up a whole side on the 1978 vinyl release *Private Line* (Sunny Alade, Nigeria). If the Velvet Underground had been African, this is close to how they might have sounded.

On Bobby (Sunny Alade, Nigeria).

Probably the best juju album of all time – Ade runs through all the classic riffs in a flowing 1983 tribute to legendary band leader Bobby Benson. The classic *Synchro System* (Island, UK) is from the same year as *Bobby* (1983) but a different sound – a more measured approach to the Western market. With Ade back on the international circuit, someone must surely bring the master into the CD age.

Odù (Warner/Eastwest, US).

While it's hard to compress 30-minute songs into five-minute tracks (the recorded version can seem like a series of freeze-frames from the all-day live experience and the fades are frustrating), the frequently overheard conversations between talking drum and steel guitar are so utterly beguiling, under the guitars and percussion blanket of his twenty-piece band, that you forgive Ade these constraints. Choose track 2 first, "Easy Motion Tourist", a very toothsome number indeed.

Segun Adewale

The crown prince of juju served a long and obviously fruitful apprenticeship before reforming the SuperStars International (no room for modesty in the Adewale household), in 1980 and reaching global success in the immediate wake of the juju boom. He remained at his peak throughout the 1980s but nothing much was heard from him in the subsequent decade.

Play For Me (Stern's, UK).

The album on which rests Adewale's reputation as master of the kick-start juju dubbed Yo-Pop, an aggressive, up-beat Lagos style.

IK Dairo

Singer, composer and band leader, Dairo was responsible

for the consolidation of juju music amongst the Yoruba and the introduction of the accordion to the style.

 **Juju Master** (Original Music, US).

This is a classic round-up of Decca West Africa 45s. The talking drums are really speaking here.

Ebenezer Obey

With over fifty albums to his credit and enjoying a new lease of life in middle age, Obey justifiably maintains a world reputation and an immensely loyal following for his infectious, danceable juju. Doubling as a pastor has done nothing to harm his spiritual dimension.

 **Solution** (Stern's, UK).

Lengthy, live juju, this is a disc that is representative of Obey at his best.

 **Ju Ju Jubilation** (EMI/Hemisphere, UK).

Satisfyingly bluesy, slightly offbeat juju music from the man who has released dozens of albums and whose expansive features and rather right-wing, Christian image, are in stark contrast to rival juju artist Sunny Ade.

Fuji

Adewale Ayuba

Adewale hit the scene running with *Bubble* and went on to carve a reputation for a richer, more orchestrated fuji sound, not quite managing to remain anonymous on the more accessible *Fuji Dub* (Triple Earth).

 **Bubble** (Flame Tree, UK).

An early 1990s recording now reissued on CD. The first international CD release for the young pop pretender of fuji.

Barrister

One-time rival of Kollington (below) but now peacefully co-existing in a market big enough for both, Barrister started life as a *were* musician before poverty drove him into the army. He now fronts thirty-plus musician groups.

 **New Fuji Garbage** (GlobeStyle, UK).

With the first international outing for fuji, the GlobeStyle team struck gold – a recording which is likely to define the style for Western ears for years to come. Barrister's voice here is slightly mellower than usual and the band surround it with a pounding panoply. Not forgetting the Hawaiian guitar.

Ayinla Kollington

Following a short army career – the current title of General therefore apt, if not strictly true – Kollington rose to stardom in the late 1960s and has maintained his creative impetus for three decades.

 **Live in America** (Unknown).

Fuji's 'Man of the People'. Challenging lyrics, driving percussion and an overall sound to shake the rafters.

Highlife

Oliver de Coque

A classic highlifer, the colourful de Coque occupies a unique position in the highlife pantheon, syncretising classic Congo guitar into laidback highlife rhythms

 Ogene Super Sound (ORPS, Nigeria).

This recording set the standard for the prolific outpouring of the late 1970s. Fluid and melodic, with a hidden punch.

Prince Nico Mbarga & Rocafil Jazz

If Ade carries the flag for juju and Fela's afrobeat will, in time, become a global source sound, then the late Prince Nico will forever be Igbo highlife.

 Aki Special (Rounder, US).

A bumper CD with nearly two LPs' worth on it – including the global hit "Sweet Mother" – which makes as good a starting point as any for a collection of Nigerian music.

Chief Stephen Osita Osadebe

The master of lyrical lilting highlife – and the only Nigerian artist ever to receive a Platinum record – is still performing to appreciative audiences. His massive contribution should surely be more available on CD.

 Osondi Owendi (Polygram, Nigeria).

This classic, from 1984, represents the Chief at the height of his powers.

 **Kedu America** (Xenophile, US).

The result of one, no busier than usual, day's recording on a late 1990s American tour – a sweet collection of swirling dance tracks, melding guitar and horns – produced by Seattle-based Nigerian music maestro Andy Frankel.

Oriental Brothers

Formed by three virtuoso brothers – Dan, Godwin and Warrior Satch – the Orientals went on to spawn three of the finest highlife bands ever, dominating the 1970s with hit after hit. Whether they split for musical reasons or commercial opportunity, three out of one makes good sense to me.

 Heavy on the Highlife (Original Music, US).

After dozens of Nigeria-only releases, this wonderful burn-up of a guitar-highlife album sets the standard. Relentless, sexy grooves, whose re-issue is a real public service.

Celestine Ukwu

With a career interrupted by the Biafran Civil War, Celestine's short period at the top left a lasting legacy of imaginative popular music. Backed by 'The Philosphers', Ukwu's music has been ripe for re-issue for several years. Once again, Flame Tree have done the honourable thing.

 Greatest Hits (Flame Tree, UK).

Classic, gentle and lyrical 1976 Igbo guitar-band highlife from the late master. Ukwu's albums remain a rarity but Flame Tree have had the sense to release his *Greatest Hits*.

Afro-beat and other styles

Artists

Tony Allen

In the 1970s heyday of Fela Kuti's great band Africa 70, Tony Allen was always credited as drummer and leader.

More than that he constructed the basic ingredient of Afro-beat with his own four limbs: "given to be used", as he used to say.

🔊 **Black Voices** (Comet, UK).

Allen returns from the wilderness with a spacey dubstyle CD, in which the groove rules, almost subliminally at times. Tenor guitars, stabs of keyboard, juju type vocals, touches of Manu Dibango, Sunny Ade and P-Funk. This is adventurous stuff on the active side of minimal from an acknowledged master.

Haruna Ishola

Apala music helped pave the way for both juju and fuji. Before he died in 1983, Ishola had produced some twenty five apala albums, owning his own studio and setting the standard for others to follow. Plenty still around on vinyl but, surprisingly, nothing yet on CD.

 Gboti Oloti Le (NEMI, Nigeria).

A masterpiece of the genre, and one of Ishola's last recordings.

Fela Kuti

Fela (1938–1997) was a one-man genre, whose music – Afro-beat – took its inspiration in equal measure from the fight for human dignity and the lust for sensation. As well as the recordings covered below, the Talkin' Loud label is in the throes of releasing 10 CDs each combining two original vinyl albums.

 The 69 Los Angeles Sessions (Stern's, UK).

An easy place to start and highly recommended – vintage numbers from (1969) Black Panther days and ten tracks all under seven minutes make it unique in the Fela oeuvre. A tighter production than on later outpourings also makes this an accessible entrée into a fierce world.

🔊 **Open and Close** and
🔊 **He Miss Road** (Stern's, UK).

Recorded in 1971 and 1975, these two albums come from what most fans rate as Fela's golden period.

🔊 **Underground System** (Stern's, UK).

High on anyone's list of most essential Fela, this comprises two effervescent tracks and many credits. Recorded in 1992, it combines a paean of praise for Kwame Nkrumah, the ultimate African hero, and a scornful assault on Babangida, Abiola and Obasanjo, three of the biggest of Nigeria's 'big men', the latter recently elected president.

Femi Kuti

Femi Kuti has had an independent career since the late 1980s with his group, the Positive Force, but his career has really buregoned since his father, Fela's death. Recognisably a Kuti, both in his voice and lyrics and muscular arrangements, he has a dancefloor sensibility which old man Kuti's stoned diatribes never aimed to deliver.

🔊 **Shoki Shoki** (Polygram, UK).

The first big internationally promoted release for Femi – and, from the sweatily explicit "Beng Beng Beng" to the affronted "Victim of Life", it's a welcome chip off the old block.

Gaspar Lawal

Arriving in London in the 1960s, Gaspar has, over the years, played with literally everyone in the rock and black music scene.

🔊 **Kadara** (GlobeStyle, UK).

Economical with his precocious talent, Gaspar is in a class of his own for neotraditional percussion and on this recording he surrounds himself with equally illustrious sidemen.

Babatunde Olatunji

US based for most of his musical life, Baba pioneered African music in the States and is now, justifiably, considered a legend in his own lifetime.

🔊 **Drums of Passion** (Rykodisc, US).

Spritual drumming and chanting, with the help of Mickey Hart, to invoke the Yoruba gods Ajaja, Kori, Ogun and Shango. Two volumes (*The Invocation* and *The Beat*). Ultimately, it gets to you.

Sonny Okosun

Pop star turned preacher, Okosun's career has spanned two decades, turning out such afro-rock-reggae classics as "Fire in Soweto", "Holy Wars" and "Papa's Land". Unlike so many of his contemporaries, Sonny has always been able to maintain a devoted following in the US for his accessible, emotional and memorable songs.

🔊 **The Ultimate Collection** (AVC Music, Lagos).

A fine career retrospective featuring all three songs mentioned above.

Pygmy music

sounds from the african rain forest

Politically unstable central Africa has seen a dreadful toll of civil wars in the 1990s. The coups and bloody ethnic conflicts of Rwanda and Congo, however, have had less impact on the indigenous inhabitants of the region's extensive rainforests than the dramatic increase in logging activities over the past two decades. For the Pygmies based in the forests of Cameroon, traditional music brought to the ears of enthusiastic Western audiences may prove the most effective weapon in the struggle to save their homelands, as **Dave Abram** discovers.

One hour before dawn, shreds of mist still hang below the canopy of the Cameroonian rainforest. A myriad invisible insects announce their presence with a layered wall of noise, punctuated by an occasional bird call or the blood curdling cry of a tree hyrax. At first, the strange new notes that echo through the darkness could be part of this ever changing non-human soundscape. But the *yelli*, descending in yodelled steps that swell and merge to form haunting chords, are the songs of the Baka, the indigenous hunter-gatherers who inhabit this remote tract of tropical forest. Reverberating between the giant tree trunks, their polyphonic pre-dawn chorus is a bid to mesmerise the animals so that they will succumb more easily to the hunters' spears and nets the following day.

Baka children clapping

The **Baka** are one of dozens of indigenous groups living in the equatorial forests of central Africa; others include their neighbours, the **Aka**, the **Mbuti** of Congo, and the **Efé** of the Central African Republic. Scattered in pockets from the Cameroon coast to Congo and the hilly borders of Rwanda and Burundi, these forest dwelling peoples – featured in ancient Egyptian murals and referred to since the era of European explorers as 'Pygmies' because of their diminutive stature – share neither land nor language. Nor do members of these far-flung groups interact very often. What they have in common, however, is a dependence on the forest for food, shelter and medicine, and for a degree of economic independence from their Bantu farmer neighbours, who tend to regard them as primitive and inferior.

This semi-nomadic life in the forest has, in spite of the distances that separate the various Pygmy populations, given rise to similar beliefs and ritual practices, and to similarly egalitarian societies across the Ituri forest of the Congo basin and beyond.

The Pygmies' other distinguishing characterisitic is their extraordinary aptitude for music. Whether butchering a duiker antelope, bathing in the river, or simply sharing a spliff around the fire, music is ever-present. In camp sessions, voices usually carry the tunes. But the Baka also make instruments from materials found in the forest and will spend hours each day playing them. Their songs range from simple melodic phrases without words, or clapping and rhyme games for children, to longer, more complex 'story-tales' – **likanos** – relating traditional origin myths.

The **tunes**, most of which are rooted in five- or seven-note scales, tend to be divided into syncopated parts for different voices, embellished with overlapping harmonies and accompanied by various kinds of percussion – none of which will tell you what gives Pygmy music its unique defining quality. For when these elements flow together the result is something magical: rhythmic, melodic music alive with unexpected dissonances.

Music in Forest Life

In his famous ethnography of the **Mbuti** of Congo, American anthropologist Colin M. Turnbull – whose best-selling book *The Forest People* brought the first detailed, accessible description of Pygmy life to Western readers – explores the relation between the forest and the Mbuti's music. According to Turnbull, his Pygmy informants regarded the forest as a kind of benevolent, all-powerful 'parent', able to provide sustenance and affection for its 'children' as long as they were able to communicate with it. The principal way the Mbuti did this was through singing. "Song", wrote Turnbull in 1965, "is used to communicate with the forest, and it is significant that the emphasis is on the actual sound, not on the words . . . The sound 'awakens' the forest . . . thus attracting the forest's attention to the immediate needs of its children."

In common with many hunter-gatherer societies, Pygmies such as the Mbuki or Baka do not maintain the hard and fast distinctions between formal and informal work and play as do Western societies. A tune that crops up in a full-moon fireside session could well be the same one deployed in a spirit possession ritual or pre-hunt *yelli*, and even during what seem to be important ceremonies, laughing and joking are the norm.

Nevertheless, different styles of music tend to accompany different activities. To amuse themselves while bathing in the river, for example, Baka women and children will plunge, slap and beat their hands in the water to create polyrhythmic sounds and rhythms known as **liquindi** (water drumming). And when the group is lazing around in

MARTIN CRADICK & SU HART

Baka earth bow

camp after a good meal, someone is sure to strike up a tune on a **limbindi** (a thin string bow, whose pitch is changed with the chin), the **ieta** (bow harp), or **ngombi** (harp zither) which everyone else will add to with a harmony or percussion line, tapping on pots and hollow logs and shaking seed pods. This kind of spontaneous, pure entertainment music forms a constant backdrop to life in camp, and has an important social function; by drawing the group together in time and in tune, it eases the stresses and strains of close communal life. Some of the most enjoyable sessions are those which are instigated after an argument.

Among the Baka and other Pygmy populations, music is also used as a medium for moral and spiritual instruction. Likanos advise people on how to behave by giving guidance on key matters such as sharing (essential in hunter-gatherer economies), marriage arrangements and hunting techniques. Some also explain the origins of the animals, plants and natural forces in the forest (one well-loved Baka likano concerns a man who danced too slowly and was turned by Kumba, the Creator Being, into a millipede).

Lastly, music has a specific role in **rituals**: rites of passage, spirit visitations, and divination ceremonies conducted to establish the source of witchcraft, to heal a sick person, or to help find animals in the forest. The words 'song' and 'dance' (*bé*) are the same in Baka, and it is through 'singing the dance' that the spirits of the forest are invoked. In fact, spirits are believed to have handed down the Bakas' music in the first place; the songs and dances merely flow through them into the world.

Perhaps this explains why the Baka, in keeping with their egalitarian way of living, make little or no distinction between performer and audience. Even in *jengi* or *boona* ceremonies, where a spirit actually enters the camp (in the form of an initiated man dressed in a special ritual costume), most of those present will participate equally in the music and drama. That said, certain individuals may lead the singing or dance if they know the words and movements better than anyone else. It is the leader's job to keep the tune going when it flags, to prompt, initiate or bring a song to an end. This role is not formally conferred, and implies no special privileges. As with hunting and gathering, or the hundreds of other skilled tasks the Baka perform in the run of their lives, an individual takes a key role in a group activity if he or she has marked talent for it, for the greater good of the group rather than their own prestige.

Listening to the Forest

Ethnographers, musicologists and anyone who has lived in the forest with Pygmy people are bound to have asked themselves where this extraordinary musicality comes from. The answer, like so much else in the pygmies' life, stems from the forest, or more particularly, in its rich soundscape. Moving around the rainforest paths, where dense vegetation prevents you from seeing very far, hearing becomes the primary sense. In the absense of visual pointers, the pygmies find their way by tuning into auditory landmarks: to the sound of particular trees, to the flow of a river, or to noises from different encampments, and by calling to one another, often over long distances.

It's not surprising, therefore, that forest dwellers become skilled listeners at a very early age. Moreover, they do not have to contend with the backdrop of irrelevant noise that assails us in modern cities. In Western countries, people learn to 'switch off' – actively 'not to listen'. Pygmy children, on the other hand, are encouraged to develop sensitivity to the sounds around them, not least of all by listening to, and becoming involved in, the music that constantly surrounds them in camp. Older children help keep their younger brothers and sisters amused by teaching them tunes, dances and clapping games, and these help integrate skills essential for life in the forest.

The Pygmies' keen sense of hearing can lead to incidents of synchronicity that bewilder their less sound-aware visitors. When, for example, an elephant is killed by hunters many miles away in the forest, the women back at camp may know of the kill hours before the hunters return. The death of such a large animal sparks off bird calls in the vicinity, which will in turn send sound ripples through the forest. And when these reach the women, they start to sing celebrations.

This uncanny sensitivity to sound, combined with an early start and plenty of opportunity for practice, perhaps explains the Pygmies' highly developed musical ability. Playing good group music is, after all, ninety percent listening.

Beyond the Forest

Early travellers tended to describe hunter-gather peoples of central Africa as if they existed in isolation. But semi-nomadic groups like the Baka, Efé, Aka, Babenzélé and Mbuti no longer (and probably never did) live entirely cut off from the rest of the world. Although they may spend many months following food sources in the forest, economic or social ties

In the Spirit of the Forest: the Music of Baka Beyond

When Martin Cradick, guitarist and composer with the group Outback, and singer and artist Su Hart packed their sketch books and instruments to set off in search of the Baka, neither of them knew what they'd find in the forest. Four albums and three visits to Cameroon later, Martin picks up the trail with Dave Abram.

What inspired you to travel to Cameroon in the first place?

I was watching Phil Agland's Channel 4 [UK] docu-memtary on the Baka, and was taken with the music, particularly the *limbindi*, and started playing along with my guitar. The song I wrote around that little riff became "Baka", the title track of the first Outback album. Then came a whole series of coincidences, my meeting an anthropologist who'd been with the Baka, and Su finding out that the Pitt Rivers Museum in Oxford were giving bursaries for people to study Pygmy music. We told them we weren't anthroplogists, but had good non-verbal communication skills after playing music in the Andes and staying with a Berber family in the Atlas mountains, and they paid for our journey.

Was it difficult to relate to the Baka?

Music was the thing that broke the ice. The Baka were really happy to hear what we did, and join in, with per-cussion or whatever. Initially, the family group we'd been introduced to made us a separate space in a clearing where our anthroplogist friend had been. Then word got about that we were around, and within a day or two a whole new village had grown up where we were.

People would drop in to play or look at our gear. They were really interested in our guitars. We also had a load of salt and *Marks & Spencers* underwear which they shared out, and quite a bit of stuff they'd never seen before, like plastic wrapping paper from cassette cases, which the kids would stick to their foreheads like jew-ellery. After a while we became their performing mon-keys "look at these white people, they'll sing and dance and play tunes . . . ha, ha, ha!". I remember the look of absolute amazement on this little old lady's face one time when she came out of her house and saw us singing with the guitar. The next day she turned up with a huge branch of bananas for us that she'd carried for an hour and a half through the forest as a present.

SU HART

Martin Cradick and friends, Mbe (left) and Pelembi

And where did the music go from there?

We tended to get them to play their music for us to join in with. There were a couple of guitarists, and they would sit around playing chords they'd picked up from Congolese radio on this homemade guitar thing with five bits of wire for strings. And everyone else would play percussion – clapping, hitting sticks or machetes, or plastic containers. Then I'd jam along with the mandolin, and different people would improvise singing, which is why the songs are as they are on *Spirit of the Forest*.

Basically, I recorded these jam sessions and copied them when we got home, sometimes with a percussion sample from the forest. It was just an experiment. I wasn't thinking at the time "I'm going to make an album" with this material. The only track I did that with was "Baka".

You eventually released the material on separate albums, one for the songs you and Su played with them, and another for the Baka's own traditional music.

With *Heart of the Forest*, I was trying to avoid the sort of ritualistic drums and chanting stuff that people would expect to hear, in favour of songs and recordings of different instruments, like the limbindi and ngombi, to show that the Baka are actually really good musicians. I didn't want to mix this up with what I was doing. Conversely, there'd be people who might not have considered listening to an anthropological recording who'd buy *Heart of the Forest* because they'd enjoyed *Spirit*.

How did the Baka react to the music you made during the first visit?

When we returned a couple of years later with the albums, it was clear they weren't particularly interested in the recordings of them on *Heart of the Forest*. They

were much more into listening to *Spirit of the Forest*. Funnily enough, there are guitar tracks on that album I always considered were written by them, but after playing the musicians the tracks it was clear they had no recollection of them. Over two years their own songs had changed; they'd been playing them without recordings to refer to, and so the music was constantly evolving, whereas I'd stuck to the original versions. The traditional songs, though, didn't seem to have changed at all. In fact they sounded identical to recordings of Baka music I'd heard from the 1950s.

The Baka get a percentage of the royalties from these albums. What do they do with the money?

They wanted us to put it in the middle of the camp where they could all see it, and divide it up equally. We tried this, but it caused lots of problems and arguments; also, people from outside would find ways of getting the money off them. So instead we agreed that it should be spent on things that would benefit everyone.

Now the money they earn in royalties is managed by a charity we set up called 'One Heart', whose projects and priorities were devised with the Baka in the forest in January 1998. These include securing land rights, buying ID cards (which means they don't get arrested for hunting), and training one of their own people as a doctor to bring essential medicines to camp. It's difficult to disagree with anyone who says they should have the money themselves – it's their's after all – but the charity serves the needs of the whole community more fairly and effectively.

You can find out more about 'One Heart', and the Bakas' music on the Baka Beyond website: *http://web.ukonline.co.uk/baka/* which features photos taken in the forest and sound samples of the Bakas' instruments in action.

eventually pull them back to more permanent settlements, to visit relatives and trade with their Bantu neighbours.

Inevitably, the music of the African villages and towns on the edge of the forest has influenced the Pygmies, and some of the instruments most commonly found in their camps – log-and-skin drums, or the **ieta** (bow harp) for example – must have been originally copied from the Bantu.

The recent advent of portable radios and tape cassettes has had an even more dramatic impact. These days, young guitar-playing Baka lads can skillfully immitate the zouk and soukous sounds they hear tinkling over on the airwaves from Congo – riffs that are rudimentary compared with their own traditional sounds. What's more, performing them in market towns can earn new respect from the Bantu.

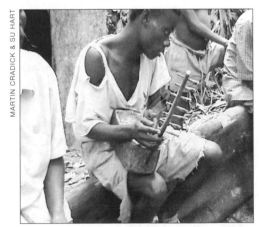

MARTIN CRADICK & SU HART

Baka musician playing the **ieta**

Pygmy Fusion

In the late 1950s, when he was conducting the anthropological fieldwork that would later form the basis for *The Forest People*, **Colin Turnbull** made many hours of recordings of Mbuti music, selections of which were subsequently released on vinyl. These quickly became classics of their type, revealing for the first time the essential complexity of Pygmy polyphony and an equally extraordinary instrumental tradition.

Turnbull's tapes also inspired a second generation of ethnomusicologists, among them the French-Israeli **Simha Arom**, who lived among the Babenzélé of the Central African Republic in the 1960s. It was a track on one of Arom's releases, featuring *hindewhu* (a technique in which a single-pitch reed whistle alternates with sung notes to produce a melody line) that was later picked up by African-American jazz pianist Herbie Hancock's drummer, Bill Summers, and turned, with the help of an empty beer bottle, into the famous remake of "Watermelon Man" featured on Hancock's ground breaking album *Headhunters* (until recently the biggest selling jazz LP ever).

In retrospect, Summer's bottle blowing antics were a seminal moment in World Music history, marking as they did the first **fusion** of an African Pygmy idiom with a Western tradition. Since then, Pygmy-inspired sounds have found their way into an array of different recording projects, from Brian Eno and John Hassel film soundtracks to **Zap Mama** (see p.28) a cappella numbers.

By far the best-known deployment of Pygmy music, though, came with the 1993 release of the multi-million selling **Deep Forest** CD. Blending digital keyboard sounds and percussion with analogue samples from a spread of indigenous (mainly African) traditions, French euro-popsters **Eric Mouquet** and **Michel Sanchez** came up with a formula combining soft techno with a rather cloying nostalgia for the 'ancestral wisdom' of indigenous peoples (the introductory track to the album begins with the line: "Somewhere deep in the jungle are living some little men and women. They are your past; maybe they are your future"). Described by one critic as the "Benetton of music-marketing concepts", Deep Forest proved phenomenally successful. Two and a half million copies were sold in its first three years, and it remains the best-selling World Music fusion album ever made.

There has been controversy over how much of the Deep Forest money made its way back to the original performers – a not uncommon dilemma when traditional music is 'sourced' or sampled. The dilemma of how to renumerate musicians is one familiar to the UK's Pygmy-Celtic fusion maestro, **Martin Cradick**. Inspired by face-to-face collaborations with the Baka in southwest Cameroon, much of his band **Baka Beyond**'s music is based around samples from his own, and anthropologist Jeremy Avis', field recordings. But, as Martin Cradick points out in the interview on pp.604–605 there's no reason why the Baka shouldn't receive a representative share of his albums' royalties.

Survival

Fair-trade and other ethical issues aside, record royalties ought to find their way back to the forest because they provide a means of ensuring the survival of traditional Pygmy society, whose existence has come increasingly under threat in the past two or three decades from logging companies, road builders and the temptations of wage labour.

Whether or not Pygmy groups and their music will survive these changes depends on how successfully they are able to negotiate rights over their forest homelands. For without the forest, the Pygmies soon lose their economic independence. No longer able to provide for themselves by hunting and gathering, they are forced to drift into roadside settlements and to lead an impoverished life on the margins of a society that, at best, treats them as second class citizens.

Traditional music has already shown signs of succumbing to the strain. In recent years, the nocturnal yelli songs that have for hundreds, possibly thousands, of years echoed through the Cameroonian rainforest, have become a rarity. Some Baka groups have reportedly gone several seasons without singing yelli before a hunt, complaining that there have been too many disturbances in the surrounding forest for them to be successful. And every year that passes without a yelli being performed increases the chances of this unique musical form being lost forever.

discography

Compilations

🎵 **Anthology of World Music – Africa: The Ba-Benzélé Pygmies** (Rounder, US).

One of the best of a recently released group of ethnomusicological recordings. Worth getting for the astonishing virtuosity of the *hindewhu* whistle solo alone (a simultaneous song and whistle tune whose effect has to be heard to be believed).

🎵 **The Baka Forest People: Heart of the Forest** (Hannibal, UK; Ryko, US).

Martin Cradick's field recordings, made in 1992, showcase both the Bakas' extraordinary polyphonic singing, and their various instruments, interspersed with evocative eavesdroppings on camp life. This is an album that deserves close listening. Seamlessly stringing together trancy instrumental grooves, splashing water drum sessions, kids campfire rhymes and, best of all, yelli songs that draw you deep into the forest, the selection gives a generous overview of the Bakas' music without descending into the realms of dry ethnomusicology. And everyone on it (except the omnipresent cicadas) gets a cut of the royalites.

 Baka Pygmies
(Crammed Discs, Belgium).

While most ethnomusicologists have contented themselves with a Sony Pro-Walkman, Belgian Vincent Kenis went to the forest equipped with a couple of dozen microphones, DAT machine and mixing desk. The result was an extraordinarily rich 'surround-sound' that captures the live feeling of Pygmy polyphony better than any other offering to date. The most impressive of the tracks are those that feature the whole camp singing and dancing.

Ⓓ **Bayaka: The Extraordinary Music of the Babenzélé Pygmies** (Ellipsis Arts, US).

American anthropologist Louis Sarno has lived with the Babenzóló people for over a decade, recording their music and writing about their life in the forest. This CD features the pick of his tape collection, remastered by wildlife and natural sound supremo Bernie Krause, with a lavishly illustrated book to accompany the recorded material. Best choice for the anthropologically inclined.

Ⓓ **Centreafrique: Anthologie de la Musique des Pygmés Aka** (Harmonia Mundi, France).

This double CD set features digitally remastered versions of Simha Arom's prize-winning 1978 recordings, which first put Pygmy music on the world map. The quality doesn't compare with the albums listed above, but the 32 tracks cover the gamut of the Akas' musical output, from large-scale divination rituals involving dozens of participants to intimate contrapuntal duels.

Ⓓ **Echoes of the Forest: Music of the Central African Pygmies** (Ellipsis Arts, US).

A selection of Colin Turnbull, Jean-Pierre Hallet and Louis Sarno's best recordings, packaged with sixty pages of photographs and text describing Pygmy life and the work of the three anthros. Credit is due to the Ellipsis label for putting this product together for the price of a regular CD.

Ⓓ **Music of the Rainforest Pygmies** (Lyricord, US).

More 1990s remastered versions of Turnbull's classic 1961 recordings. This compilation is most notable for the final track, which came about after Turnbull asked to hear the oldest song the Pygmies he was taping knew. Accompanied by clapping, polyphony and stick beating, they sang a version of "Clementine".

Ⓓ **Pygmées** (Editions Dapper, France).

A 1991 collection of samples from the Musée Dapper's archives that sets out to challenge the concept that Pygmies are an isolatable ethnic or racial group. The accompanying book is packed with engaging background info, and the original tapes have been digitally remastered.

Artists (Fusion)

Jeremy Avis

Musicologist, singer and xylophone player Jeremy Avis spent two years studying the Baka's music in Cameroon, and was Martin Cradick's collaborator on *Heart of the Forest*.

Ⓓ **Junglebean: Moving With Intent**
(Camwood Productions, UK).

Avis' debut album features a couple of tracks based on Baka grooves, with techno trance, drum'n'bass patterns, medieval *cantigas* and oriental *maquams* thrown in for good measure.

Baka Beyond

UK-based Baka Beyond started after ex-Outback guitarist Martin Cradick and his wife, Su Hart, spent six weeks with the Baka in Cameroon. From this early hands-on stab at Afro-Celtic fusion has evolved an increasingly sophisticated sound, blending Baka riffs with Scottish island ballads and the Hendrix-Romanian-Gypsy fiddling of Paddy Lemercier.

 Spirit of the Forest
(Hannibal, UK; Ryko, US).

The title track of this first album is Baka Beyond's musical mission statement. Field samples of forest yelli yield seamlessly to studio recordings of Martin Cradick's rich mandolin and guitar, while meticulously produced African percussion lays down an infectious groove.

Ⓓ **Meeting Pool** (Hannibal, UK; Ryko, US).

The highpoints of this more ambitious, elaborately produced second offering are as much Gaelic (the spine-tingling ballad "Ohureo") and Turkish (Lemercier's soaring eastern-influenced violin playing) as Cameroonian, but the forest roots are retained through sensitive sampling of Baka music and, once again, some powerful percussion. A truly inspired cultural mish mash that defies categorisation.

Deep Forest

French duo Michel Sanchez and Eric Mouquet set out in the early 1990s to create lyrical electronic music "imprinted with the ancestral wisdom of African chants". The result was one of the most successful (and controversial) discs of the whole World Music phenomenon.

Ⓓ **Deep Forest** (Epic, France).

Synths and sequenced bass and percussion spice up samples of music from various "primitive societies" (sic), including central African Pygmies, on this first and best Deep Forest album. Critics would maintain that it is essentially a rehash of the Noble Savage cliché in amorphous eurotechno.

Zap Mama

Zap Mama (see p.28) is a Belgium-based, all-women a cappella group whose members are of mixed African and European descent. Their leader, Marie Daulne, was born to a Belgian father and Congolese mother in Africa, where, as a young child, she lived with the Pygmies in the forest.

Ⓓ **Adventures in Afropea** (Luaka Bop, US).
Zap Mama (Cramworld, Belgium).

Zap Mama's acclaimed debut album, which occupied the number one spot in Billboard's World Music chart for four months, includes a wonderful cover of a piece from Arom and Taurelle's 1966 ethnographic LP, entitled "Babanzélé". Using eight voices and hindewhu whistle, it is the most complete, authentic reproduction of Pygmy polyphony by a Western group to date.

Rwanda and Burundi

echoes from the hills

The tragedy which struck Rwanda – the 1994 genocide which took almost a million lives – has inevitably left scars on the country's cultural life. Modern music has been particularly badly hit, though traditional musical life seems to have a dogged vigour that no horrors can diminish. As **Jean-Pierre Jacquemin**, **Jadot Sezirahigha** and **Richard Trillo** discover, it's perhaps at these times that people look to family and roots even more than usual.

Rwanda

Before the genocide, Rwanda had an active music scene – both traditional and modern – with a couple of bands in most prefectures, and quite a number in the capital, Kigali. But musicians, who tend to scorn the significance of ethnic distinctions, were specifically targeted by the death squads; many were murdered, others fled into exile. The consequences continue to be felt in the country's musical life, as in all other spheres.

Traditional styles

The Rwandan musical tradition is linked to a dance called **ikinimba**, which makes reference to the history of the country and recalls the feats of Rwanda's heroes, kings and warriors. It often puts tales and legends, indeed the whole oral tradition, into a contemporary context. Other songs evoke the beauty of cattle – a symbolic wealth which is of paramount importance to Rwandans.

This music is chiefly performed on specific instruments: the **inanga** (like a lyre), the **iningiri** (a rudimentary violin-like instrument), the **umuduri** (a musical bow), the **ikembe** (a small thumb piano) and the crucial **ingoma** (drum). The same styles and instruments are found all over the country, though there are a few district variations to ikinimba. On the island of Inkombo, for example, Rwandan music has mixed with the music of the Shi people from South Kivu, in present-day Congo.

The music has had a few noted musicians – all players of the inanga; they include **Maître de Rujindiri**, **Victor Kabarira**, **Kirusu**, **Sebatunzi** and **Sentore**, and **Sophie** (Rwanda's only woman player).

The best-known name, outside the country, is the singer **Cécile Kayirebwa**, who has been resident for many years in Belgium, and performs traditional music with modern instruments, drawing on the cattle-loving traditions of her ancestors. Born in 1946, Kayirebwa's musical career began while she was still at school, as a member of the Rwanda Song and Dance Circle. She got a tape recorder and became an enthusiast for the traditions of the older people of Rwanda, on the basis of which work she released a series of cassettes of tradition-laced songs through the 1980s.

DAVE PEABODY

Cécile Kayirebwa

Hutu and Tutsi

By the time the regions of **Rwanda** and **Burundi** were brought under German control in the late nineteenth century (later moved to Belgian colonial rule from 1920–62), they had already been kingdoms for centuries. The royal and wealthier families, whose cattle grazed the land, were **Tutsi** (more formally Watutsi, or Watusi) while the families who looked after the cattle, and whose farm plots were fertilised by the cow dung, were **Hutu**.

Both peoples had cultural origin stories that suggested migration from other regions, sometimes claimed to be Ethiopia or further north. But these movements, if they happened (and Egyptian origin myths are widespread throughout Africa), were probably not single-strike invasions of people on the move, but slow penetrations, like the gradual spread of native Americans from Asia. In Rwanda and Burundi, Tutsi and Hutu spoke the same Bantu family language and co-existed, usually in peace, inter-marrying, and shifting identity with the passage of generations and the ebb and flow of family fortunes. In the forests, the people with the longest claim to ownership of the land, the **Twa**, lived a more marginal existence, hunting and gathering, beyond the realm of the state.

The European invaders and colonists set about exploiting what was effectively a class structure along ethnic and quasi-racial lines, installing the Tutsi nobility in positions of power which sanctioned abuse of the Hutu farmers, and setting up all the trappings of apartheid, complete with passbooks and fixed tribal identities. Cattle ownership, or non-ownership, ceased to be the criterion for being Tutsi or Hutu: goverment ID cards had only one interpretation. In the 1920s, the first big Hutu revolt happened in northern Rwanda and was savagely suppressed by Belgian forces.

Although the Belgians switched sides before independence and saw to it that the majority Hutus achieved power in Rwanda, in Burundi the Tutsis were able to cling on. Violent conflict between the two ethnic groups has been part of both countries' histories ever since, culminating in the near-genocide of the Rwandan Tutsis in 1994 after the Hutu president was assassinated.

Modern Music

In the pre-genocide years of the early 1990s bands such as **Impala**, **Les Fellows**, **Abamarungu**, **Inono Stars**, **Les 8 Anges**, **Imena**, **Nyampinga**, **Les Compagnons de la Chanson**, **Bisa** (a university band), **Isibo y'Ishakwe**, **Ingenzi** and **Ingeli** would liven up the towns of Rwanda. These bands sung in Kinyarwanda (the national language) but played music that was mainly the result of borrowings from Congolese rumba, and from reggae and zouk.

Today, at the end of the dark 1990s, there are no real orchestras left. Only Ingeli tried to reform after the genocide, but it was a short-lived revival, as the musicians could not get viable earnings. Even getting instruments is a struggle, having to be hired at the whim of unscrupulous financiers, and few can dream of hiring the country's two recording studios (one with four tracks, the other eight).

Yet there are many talents: the singers **Boni Ntage** (Nyampinga), **Karemera Rodrigue** (Pamaro) and **Mboneye Elade** (Salus Populi); the virtuoso guitarists **Soso Mado** (Impala) and **Mahuku Gilbert** aka Bekos; the drummers **Kana Jean Claude**, **Karim**, and **Ileri Mukasa**; bassists **Thierry Gallard**, **Youssouf**, and **Marco Polo**.

Perhaps the most talented of them all is guitarist **Aimé Murefu**, a young musician and brother of Jean Mutsari (see below), whose fingering technique is worthy of the best guitarists of this century, anywhere in the world. Clearly influenced by Jimi Hendrix and Carlos Santana, Aimé has developed a style of his own that's reminiscent of a particularly ardent BB King.

In a quite different vein, **Kamaliza**, a singer with a highly personal style, was a major female vocalist of the late 1990s, until her recent death.

The Diaspora

Many talented Rwandan musicians now live in exile, particularly in Brussels. After **Cécile Kayirebwa**, the most notable is **Jean Mutsari**, who has set up the band **Kirochi Sound**, while pursuing a career as an accompanist with Vaya con Dios. He plays bass, guitar and mouth organ.

Other musicians on the Brussels scene include guitarist **François Mihigo** 'Chouchou' (ex-Ingeli, ex-Ingenzi); **Ben Ngabo Kipetit**, who pursues simultaneous careers as a modern (Afro-jazz) artist and traditional performer, sometimes merging the two with various bands; neo-traditional singer-guitarist **Jean-Baptiste Byumvuhore**; and the singer **Muyango**, who performs with women's ballet **Imitari**.

Some artists exiled in Belgium have recently returned to Rwanda to help in the country's reconstruction. One of these re-builders is **Albert Byron**, who now lives in Kigali.

Master Drummers of Burundi

Mark Hudson met the Drummers of Burundi during their tour to Britain in 1999.

Ten drums hewn from huge African logs stood in a semi-circle around a larger drum painted the red, green and white of the Burundian flag. Nearby, the Drummers of Burundi, looking tired after their long journey sat munching into their plastic sandwich wrappers.

Half an hour later, clad in red and green togas, the drummers stand fresh-faced and expectant behind their drums. Their leader lets out a cry which they all take up before slamming their sticks onto the drumheads in a rhythmic onslaught of such power and volume that we journalists and photographers are practically blasted back through the door. One by one the drummers play the painted drum, leaping around it with a lithe elegance, drawing their sticks around their necks in gestures at once ferocious and humorous.

The Drummers of Burundi are the ultimate African drum experience, a catharsis of energy, grace and athleticism so intense it can only be sustained in bursts of forty minutes at a time – two of which make up each performance. It was seeing the drummers that inspired Thomas Brooman to organise the first WOMAD festival in 1982, an event that effectively sparked off the whole

World Music boom. But long before that, Burundi rhythms were reverberating through Western music, from the thundering backbeat of Joni Mitchell's "The Hissing of Summer Lawns" through to Adam and the Ants and The Clash.

Burundi shares Rwanda's legacy of inter-ethnic hatred and violence. In the chaos following independence in 1960, with the break-up of the traditional order and struggles between rival Tutsi clans and Hutu political aspirations making themselves felt, hundreds of thousands of people – mainly Hutus – were killed. In a more recent wave of retaliatory massacres in 1993 (immediately before the Rwandan genocide) between 100,000 and 200,000 people were killed – up to a third of the Tutsi population. A Tutsi military regime remains in power despite incursions by Hutu guerillas. There are frequent, often unreported, atrocities against civilians by both sides.

Before coming to meet them, I had been told by their record company that six of the drummers had been killed. I was requested not to ask questions about politics or ethnic matters, and informed the group would communicate through their official spokesman, a representative of the Ministry of Culture. I could see him watching from the sidelines, a severe-looking individual in horn-rimmed glasses.

Drummers of Burundi

GRAEME EWENS

The Drummers of Burundi are Hutus, though traditionally they played only for the Tutsi king, the Mwami, accompanying him everywhere (in the Kirundi language, the words for drum and king are the same). Their rhythms marked the times of day, the beginnings of harvests and every cycle in a highly ritualised world. But the last Mwami was assassinated in 1972, and the drummers, whose skills are passed down through particular families, now play for the President and other dignitaries.

"The drum is a respected instrument in Burundi", said Gabriel, the spokesman. "Even these drummers cannot play the drums whenever they feel like it. The drums are only beaten for special ceremonies. And not everyone can dance to the drums. You cannot just go into a shop in Burundi and buy a drum. The people who make the drums, the people who play the drums and who dance to them, are the same people."

The drummers all come from Makebuku, a small village in central Burundi. Jean, the lead drummer, a shyly charming man, much smaller close up than when leaping two metres in the air, explained that he is a farmer, that all the drummers have other occupations – shopkeepers, mechanics, but principally farmers – and that they are not paid. "When we come here, we are paid. But in Burundi, no. It is an honour to be a drummer."

Did the movements in the dances have meanings? The fearsome drawing of the stick round the neck, for example? "They are swearing to the king," said Gabriel, "that if they are not loyal, he may kill them. But all the movements have meanings. They are imitating animals and birds, commenting on events in everyday life. Mime is a very important art form in Burundi. But it is all positive."

Having removed his hornrims, Gabriel looked younger and much less severe, and I found myself warming to him. I asked him if drummers in general were drawn from specific ethnic groups. He made no expression, but I could sense him wincing inside. "You know," he said at length, "I always say that in Burundi there are no ethnic groups, only clans. Because we all share the same language and the same culture . . . My work is with culture. I don't take an interest in politics. If I say something about politics, it may not be correct."

The tour-manager came in and said that the Drummers were ready to play again, but would not start without Gabriel. He had, he told me, been working and travelling with the drummers for twenty-five years. Having regarded him initially as a apparatchik, I now saw him not only as a genuine enthusiast, but as an integral part of the group, a kind of father figure. "I'm sorry I did not answer you well," he said, "but I prefer to keep politics out of culture." Empty as such remarks normally sound, it seemed not just the only sensible strategy, but the only possible hope for the future.

Burundi

The cultural situations of Rwanda and Burundi are often treated as if they were one and the same. The two countries are neighbours, have a similar historical and cultural heritage, and speak very similar languages (in practice there is little to distinguish Kirwanda and Kirundi). They also share a recent past of violent political tensions. While not reaching the apocalyptic levels of Rwanda, Burundi in the 1990s has experienced massacres, terrorist attacks, curfews and trade embargoes, and the deaths of up to 200,000 people.

Musically, Burundi is close to Rwanda, with its traditions developing from the royal lineages and court culture which long prevailed in this part of Africa. It is from this culture that Burundi's international musical reputation emerged, in the art of the **royal drummers** (see box), who achieved more fame than those of Rwanda.

Modern music in Burundi is concentrated in the capital, Bujumbura, and, as in Rwanda, the bands – when they can play at all – tend towards hybrid formulas influenced by reggae, zouk and, of course, the rumba of neigbouring Congo. Many of the most popular songs are in Swahili, the lingua franca of the whole region. (In addition, Burundi has a long-standing ethnic Swahili community, descendants of the coastal people who set up trading stations deep in the interior of Africa in the nineteenth century).

Burundians in Brussels

In Brussels, a number of musicians of Burundian origin, such as **Ciza Muhirwa**, have joined Rwandan or Congolese groups, or have taken up funk, like **Éric Baranyanka**, with his band, **The Nile**.

The most striking figure on the scene, though, is unquestionably **Khadja Nin**. She grew up in a family of eight children in Burundi and moved to Brussels via Congo (then Zaire), where she has worked with the Belgian musician **Nicolas Fiszman** on a series of CDs in the 1990s, moving towards an international fusion style. Her multilingual talents and remarkable looks are now slickly produced and packaged, somewhat after the style of Angélique Kidjo, and with her recent album, *Ya...*, she looks like a potentially huge star.

discography

Rwanda

Compilations

 Anthology of World Music: Africa: Music from Rwanda (Rounder, US).

If you've heard the Drummers of Burundi, the cascading opening track of this rare CD of archived traditional Rwandan music will sound familiar. But there's great variety on this disc, from wailing lone voices, to solo instrumentals, choruses, even a dangerous ritual song ("It was difficult to persuade them to sing it" writes Denyse Hiernaux-l'Hoëst, the 1955 sound recordist), all complete with birds, babies, village noises and the odd vehicle in the background. Tracks are unambiguously divided into Tutsi, Hutu and Twa (Rwanda's pygmy people) as in the original release.

Rwanda: Polyphonie des Twa (Fonti Musicali, Belgium).

Polyphonic music of the Twa pygmies of Rwanda, with lots of interesting musical links with the Baka and other pygmy peoples of west central Africa.

Artists

Cécile Kayirebwa

The most striking voice in Rwandan song, Cécile, born in 1946, has been performing for many years at Belgian cultural events linked to Rwanda. She was a long-time member of the multi-cultural band Bula Sangoma, before she set up her own group, Céka. She also sings solo, accompanied by Belgian jazzman Chris Joris.

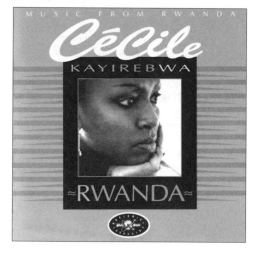

 Rwanda (GlobeStyle, UK).

Delicate, haunting songs and a voice that lingers long after the music has stopped. If you find it all a little too pretty, you might head straight for track nine, "Cyusa", and the surprising intervention of Donald Duck.

Maître de Rujindiri

Rujindiri is an accomplished inanga (Rwanda's traditional lute) artist.

Rujindiri, Maître de l'inanga – musique de l'ancienne cour du Rwanda (Fonti Musicali, Belgium).

Music from the former court of Rwanda.

Burundi

Compilations

Burundi: Musiques Traditionelles (Ocora, France).

An ethnomusicological collection.

Artists

The Drummers of Burundi

Originally the Hutu court drummers for the Tutsi king of Burundi, now a semi-professional, official troupe, the Drummers of Burundi have come to international prominence through the sheer impact of their dramatic live performance.

 The Drummers of Burundi – Live at RealWorld (RealWorld, UK).

There's something intensely physical about this surging rhythmic power – a thundering cascade of not-quite-simultaneous drumbeats. The disc includes a 30-minute improvisation, "Les Tambourinaires du Burundi".

Khadja Nin

Belgian-based Khadja Nin made a name for herself with songs in Swahili, sung to Western-styled rhythms. These early crossover attempts have gradually given way to songs in various languages, and a style more grounded, on her latest album, "Ya...".

Sambolera (BMG, France).

The warm and soulful album of glowing melodies that first brought Khadja to Western attention in 1996 .

 Ya (BMG, France).

A beautiful, liquid blend of Nin's sensuous vocal style and Swahili lyrics with the band's spot-on phrasing.

São Tomé and Príncipe

island music of central africa

The tiny (150,000 population) republic of São Tomé and Príncipe (STP) consists of two small equatorial islands lying in the Gulf of Guinea, about 270km from the coast of Gabon. **Conceição Lima** and **Caroline Shaw** take a look at the musical currents that flow past a tiny African island republic.

Some years ago, an influential figure on São Tomé questioned the fate of **Forro**, the most important creole language of the islands. Would Forro be able to survive the ever-increasing influence of Portuguese – the official language, taught in schools and used by the media? "Don't worry", replied an old hand, "as long as the popular theatre exists and, above all, the music, our language shall not die".

And so it has proved throughout the history of São Tomé and Príncipe, since 1471, when Portuguese navigators first landed on the then uninhabited archipelago. From the start the immigrants, adventurers and deportees from Portugal mixed and intermarried with the slaves from the African mainland who had been brought to work on the sugar plantations. Thus evolved the special creoles of the islands – **Forro** and **Lunguié** – each sustained by and infused with a rich musical tradition which has always been open to new influences.

Since the beginning, STP's history has been one of a mixing of peoples. Whether as a slave-trading depot (until the abolition of slavery), as a sugar producer and exporter, or later, of coffee and cocoa (long the principal crop), the islands have been a crucible for a unique fusion of cultures. West Africa, Mozambique, Angola, Cape Verde, Brazil, the Caribbean, Portugal – all have left their marks on the archipelago's cultural traditions. So, too, has island politics. The plantations were nationalised when STP achieved independence from Portugal in 1975, although the Marxist ruling party lost power after one of sub-Saharan Africa's first multiparty elections in 1991.

COLLECTION OF CAROLINE SHAW

The Brazilian-style danço-congo

Rhythms and Dance

The defining **rhythms** of the music of STP are **ússua** and **socopé** on the island of São Tomé – the biggest island where the majority of the population lives – and **dêxa** on Príncipe, some 140km away.

Both *ússua* and *socopé* are binary rhythms with cadences marked by **drums** and **cattle bells** and they were probably brought with the influx of slaves from the sixteenth century onwards. However, European influences are also present. For example, the traditional dance which accompanies *ússua* has its origins in Portuguese ballroom dancing. This (and other local dances) are extremely formal, reflected both in the dancers' costumes and in the steps and gestures, which are full of bows and other forms of courtly finesse. The dêxa has a three-beat rhythm also based on drums and cattle bells and believed to have the same origins.

Music and **popular theatre** long formed part of the same sphere of artistic expression and some of the subjects can be traced far back to the influences which shaped the islands' culture. **Tchiloli**, for example, is a drama brought to the islands by the Portuguese in the sixteenth century that features a mesmerising foot dance, accompanied by a flute and drum. Another important combination of music, dance and theatre in the repertoire of STP is the **danço-congo**, which assembles more than 20 performers, dressed in extravagantly colourful outfits, 'crowned' with exuberant ornaments of silk paper. Masters, servants, devils, angels and the jester, or 'Bobo', confront each other in a masquerade symbolising the primordial struggle between the forces of good and evil.

Whilst the danço-congo is essentially perceived as a spectacle to be watched, the **puíta** is a ceremony for public participation. This national rhythm is deliriously powerful and it is probably the most African São Toméan sound, characterised by the sounds of a drum-like instrument open at the end, with a stick attached to the centre of the drum-skin. When rubbed, it produces a grunting noise. Couples dance in the middle of a large circle formed by the assistants and gradually come closer to one another until the moment of climax when bodies clash, generating hysteria among the watching crowds. This rhythm – which was probably brought by Angolan slaves and maintained by contract labourers – is so contagious that it has been endowed in popular belief with supernatural powers to summon the spirits of the dead, to exorcise bad spirits and to heal. These beliefs are deeply rooted in the popular imagination, but sceptics put them down to the consumption of large quanitites of alcohol which circulate through the crowds until sunrise.

Modern Music

Music has played an important role in the recent political history of São Tomé and Príncipe. During the era of the one-party state, which lasted from 1975 until 1991, song was used to criticise politics (criticism that could not be overtly expressed), and since the multiparty elections, any rally that doesn't include a musical band or a folkloric group, is condemned to failure.

The content of song lyrics tends to focus on the age-old themes of love, jealousy and betrayal, but they always contain a measure of social and political comment delivered by metaphor. One of the main early protagonists of this tradition were the legendary group **Leoninos**, whose influence throughout

São Tomé has been crucial. Founded in 1959 by Quintero Aguiar, their achievement derived from three factors: the effort to modernise traditional folklore; their belief in the value of Creole as a medium; and a strong nationalist conscience, which was expressed through cultural affirmation. The group marked a significant evolution in the instrumental development of *tunas*, the everyday bands of STP – usually a couple of guitarists, a violin-player or two and sometimes a flautist. The Leoninos' introduction of drum and mandolin to the ensemble brought a new status to such sounds.

One of the group's most celebrated songs, written by Olívio Tiny, was "Ngandu" (Shark), the lyrics of which tell of a shark that seized control of the ocean and brutally expelled all the other fish. This anti-colonial metaphor was too much for the authorities who promptly banned the group's songs from the Portuguese-controlled radio station. They subsequently disbanded in 1966 but the following year another group, **Os Úntués**, emerged to continue their fusion of tradition and modern influences. Led by Leonel Aguiar, these middle-class musicians weaved an eclectic mix of references that ranged from Bob Dylan through Astor Piazolla, Aretha Franklin, BB King, The Beatles and James Brown, to the Latin dance rythms of chachacha, mambo and bolero. However, the Úntués's greatest influences came from Congolese rumba, and in particular Kassanda Nico, Franco and Rochereau. Rooted in this diverse and varied puzzle of influences, the Úntués were able to move from the local to the international and back again, modernising and re-styling São Toméan folklore along the way. Gradually, the **electric guitar** became dominant, and the overall sound became 'africanised' with cattle bell, *reco-reco* (an instrument made of a piece of bamboo or wood with notches cut into it, over which a rod is rubbed), and drums.

The mid-1960s to mid-1970s was a golden age of São Toméan musical popular music. During this period, another famous group, **Mindelo**, was formed as a major rival to **Os Úntués**. Assembling a number of different local rhythms plus the Angolan *rebita*, they created a high-energy fusion they called *puxa*. The two groups attracted audiences from opposite ends of the social spectrum – the Úntués were middle-class experimentalists, while Mindelo had working class fans. Also popular were **Sangazuza**, **Africa Negra**, **Quibanzas** and the **Leonenses**, whose main vocalist,

Pepe Lima, is nowadays a successful solo singer. On the island of Príncipe, groups like **Repteis**, **Os Diabos do Ritmo** and, lately, **Africa Verde** all left their marks on the musical landscape.

Against the background of mounting economic crisis in the two decades following independence, the development of the country's music remained stagnant. Ageing sound systems and obstacles to the importation of new equipment brought about a decline in the quality of music production. Simultaneously, there was a scarcity of good songwriters in a country that had in the past produced such respected names as **Zarco**, **Gette Rita**, **Zé Nbruete** and **Manjelegua**. The decline has not been turned around yet, but a new generation of solo artists is at last beginning to emerge, many of them influenced by Antillean *zouk*, a powerful rhthmic force that, at different times in the past twenty years, has overtaken the youth of pretty well every country in Africa.

Some of the more interesting artists of the post-Independence decades have been based abroad, largely in Portugal. The Lisbon-based **Juka**, whose songs are often to be heard at African parties in Portugal, is a representative of this westward-looking trend, though his music has more in common with

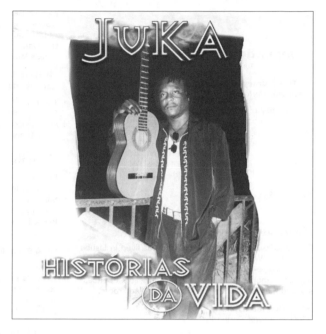

the Caribbean than with his own island home. A less well-known performer, **Açoreano**, also living in Lisbon, is notable for the very opposite reasons: his attachment to the old traditions of ússua and socopé, despite having absorbed some international influences.

Other exiles include the Paris resident **Felício Mendes**, born in Príncipe, who is remembered at home for having organised a youth band, **Os Canucos das Ilhas Verdes**, from which emerged several key artists: **Tonecas**, **Vizinho** and Felicio's nephews **Zezito and Kalú Mendes**. Kalú Mendes has gradually come to be recognised as one of the archipelago's best arrangers and has produced a number of works with Felicio, including a CD of old island hits.

As the republic of São Tomé and Príncipe enters the new millennium, purists complain that musicians are sidelining the three traditional rhythms. But the archipelago has always been flexible in its assimilation of foreign influences without losing its identity. In fact, in common with many of the lusophone countries, absorption of outside influences is one of the defining elements of the islands' music. Given some economic progress, new expression for the islands' roots should emerge.

discography

Compilations

 The Journey of Sounds: São Tomé: Tchiloli
(Tradisom, Portugal).

The 'Journey of Sounds' series of CDs was produced for Expo 98 and covers every Lusophone nation. This disc is devoted to the music of traditional Tchiloli dramas – foot dances accompanied by drums, rattles and flutes. It's not pop music, by any stretch, but the rhythms are impressive and varied.

Artists

Açoreano

Born in São Tomé in 1960, Açoreano has lived in Lisbon since 1990. What is so wonderful about his music is the way he keeps the São Toméan features without it sounding too parochial. Although he has made some concessions to the market, he never ignores his island roots.

 Que Maravilha
(Sonovox, Portugal).

A celebration of the rhythms of São Toméan music, covering *socopé*, *ússua*, and *xtléva*, all distinctively marked by the use of drums and bass, plus the guitars and trademark cowbell.

 86–Xuxa (Disconorte, Portugal).

A clear shift from Açoreano's first work, this disc goes for a more commercial approach, with zouk and hyper-energetic Angolan *kizomba* and *cuduro*, interspersed sometimes by the gentler appeal of the São Toméan rhythms.

Juka

Based in Portugal since the age of 14, Juka is currently the best-known São Toméan singer, popular throughout the Lusophone world. He's a fine performer, wowing his audiences with zouk-style arrangements and fancy dance moves. Before achieving fame, he was part of a dance troupe called Kandando, with other stars of Lisbon's African music scene, including the Angolan Paulo Flores, the Cape Verdean Tino Fortes and the Mozambican Teresa Maiuko.

 Histórias da Vida
(Zé Orlando/Sons d'África, Portugal).

This is a good but not typical Juka release, with its marked Cape Verdean influences, while his usual up-beat rhythms are replaced here by a softer, more cadenced style which includes some São Toméan flavour.

Felício Mendes

Born in 1949, Felício Mendes is a conservatoire-trained musician from Príncipe, who did stints with Os Úntues in São Tomé while serving in the army. Now based in Lisbon, his lyrics are often socially committed, even when the theme is love. With nephews Kalú and Zezito Mendes, he is the head of São Tomé's most influential musical dynasty.

 A Roda dos Sete (Exitos Estúdios, Portugal).

Epitomised by the song "Tolerance", Felício urges São Toméans to get together and move towards a better future: nobody but they themselves can build it. Guitars, percussion and organ define the sound, influenced by Congolese rumba and a smattering of Caribbean rhythms.

Kalú Mendes

One of the most talented São Toméan instrumentalists, Kalú is a versatile, prolific musician and song-writer, capable of playing a huge range of instruments, including guitar, drums, organ and piano. Although still in his early 30s, and working as a cameraman and director for state TV, he seems to get involved in almost every serious musical work that happens on the islands.

 Tio e Sobrinho
(Movieplay, Portugal).

A journey through the musical heritage of STP, Kalú and (uncle) Felício Mendes, have brought together on this CD the rhythms and sounds of both islands, blending socopé and dêxa with zouk and rumba.

Senegal and The Gambia

senegambian stars are here to stay

In Senegal, international capitalism meets traditional African commerce head on. The skyscrapers and colonial buildings of Dakar may be crumbling, but down by the Medina, the city's original 'native quarter', they're building vast ultra-modern banks, while, outside, stalls errupt from pavements heaving with hawkers and touts. And everyone, it seems, from the ragged beggars to the sleek-suited executives or the turbanned women in billowing robes and stiletto heels, is radiating poise and self possession – the same nonchalant swagger that underpins *mbalax*, the rhythm that has come to define Senegalese music. **Mark Hudson,** who can't stay away, describes the development of one of Africa's most dynamic music scenes, both in **Senegal** and neighbouring **Gambia**, with help from **Jenny Cathcart** in downtown Dakar and **Lucy Duran** on Mande music.

An arid slab of the Sahel, **Senegal** signified little in the Anglo-American consciousness until the emergence of its musical superstars – **Youssou N'Dour** and **Baaba Maal** – in the 1990s. They have had an impact on the World Music scene out of all proportion to the country's population, and the daring with which they've mixed indigenous and modern forms is a reflection both of the richness of Senegalese traditions, and of the focus Dakar and its studios have provided for experiment and cultural exchange.

The Gambia, a former British colonial enclave enclosed by Senegal, was little developed in the colonial era, and remains a backwater nation today. Comprising three hundred miles of desolate river bank and a small strip of coast, it shares Senegal's ethnic mix and range of traditional music. Its artists have played a role in modern Senegambian music, particularly in the 1970s, when the **Super Eagles** (later renamed **Ifang Bondi**) were in the ascendant with their 'Afro-Manding blues', and the country was a meeting place for exiled African musicians. But the 1981 state of emergency curfewed the club scene, which has failed to revive. Today, Gambia's main musical interest lies in its **Mande jalis** or griots.

Mande Senegambia

Even in Dakar's most Westernised milieux, the air resonates with the traditional courtesies – the praise names of the feudal world. Senegal and Gambia share the same **jali or griot tradition** as Mali and Guinea (see p.541), in which music is in the hands of a class of hereditary praise singers

known as *gewel* in Wolof and *gawlo* in Pulaar. This is a legacy of the Malian Mande (or Manding) empire of the fourteenth- to sixteenth centuries, which stretched into Senegambia, and it was reinforced in the early nineteenth century by an influx of griots from Mali following the break up of the Bamana empires. Many of the Senegambian griots trace their ancestry to Mande; the **xalam**, the characteristic Wolof lute, is an adaptation of the Mande *ngoni*; and its repertoire and much Wolof, Fula and Tukulor music is derived from Mande music.

But Senegambian griot music is far more than a watered-down blend of Mande influences. The very different character of the so-called West Atlantic languages – **Wolof**, **Pulaar** and **Serer** (Wolof, with its elastic vowels and guttural consonants, being the most influential) – together with the influence of **Serer polyphony** and the liturgical singing of Senegal's **Islamic brotherhoods** have all combined to give the griot music of these groups a highly distinctive flavour.

Senegambia also has its own Mande population, the **Mandinka**, who form the largest ethnic group in the Gambia. Their heartland is Brikama, a dusty market town at the junction of roads east into the interior and south to Casamance and Guinea-Bissau. Interacting with surrounding groups, the Mandinka griots or jalis – the Jobartehs, Kontes and Susos – have created their own sophisticated musical culture and given rise to several masters of the kora (see p.544). Great master musicians of the region have included the late **Alhaji Bai Konteh** and **Jali Nyama Suso**, and **Amadou Bansang Jobarteh**. The best-known, however, is **Foday**

Mouridism: Islam in Senegal

Everywhere in Dakar – on keyrings, carrier bags, the sides of taxis or daubed on buildings – you see the cryptic, veiled visage of **Cheikh Ahmadou Bamba**, *fondateur de mouridisme*. Islam in Senegal, particularly among the Wolof and Tukulor populations, is organised through *tariqa* – religious brotherhoods based around the dynasties of great holy men known as *marabouts*. Although the **Mourides** are not the largest of these groups, they are the most influential – especially in their impact on music. The vast majority of Wolof griots and pop musicians are Mourides and many aspects of the music business completely controlled by Mouride businessmen. Even the most forward looking musicians pepper their lyrics with references to Bamba, and many will include an entire song to him on each cassette.

The Senegalese brotherhoods have their origins in the North African veneration of Sufi saints, but the Mourides are a relatively recent phenomenon. Their development is bound up with the colonial history of Senegal. Islam had existed in Senegal since the twelfth century but in the nineteenth century the traditional hierarchies of kings and nobles with their retinues of warriors, griots and slaves remained faithful to animist practices, or adhered to a loose pluralistic form of Islam. As French incursions into Wolof territory increased towards the end of the century, culminating in the destruction of the Wolof elite, Islam became a focus for psychological as much as physical resistance.

With the catastrophic break-up of the old order, those most dependent on it, the members of the noble, griot and warrior castes began gravitating towards Ahamadou Bamba, a Koranic teacher to whom miraculous powers had been attributed. Worried by this potentially troublesome force amassing in the dusty wastes of central Senegal, the French twice exiled Bamba, first to Mauritania, then to Gabon. Realising that physical resistance in this world was hopeless, Bamba encouraged his followers to concentrate on salvation in the next, through work and through selfless submission to their spiritual guides, the marabouts.

At the time the French were encouraging the cultivation of groundnuts as a cash crop, and the marabouts and their followers set about establishing vast farms in the centre of Senegal. In return for their cooperation with the colonial authorities, they were allowed to create what even today amounts to a state within a state. It is widely acknowledged that no government can be formed in Senegal without the support of the marabouts, the descendants of Cheikh Ahmadou Bamba, to whom millions look for a route to paradise. To this day, the vast majority of Wolof griots and many pop musicians are Mourides and many aspects of the music business are completely controlled by Mouride businessmen.

Mouride musicians sing for the leaders of other brotherhoods (like Oumar Tall and Malick Sy of the larger Tijiani brotherhood, to which Baaba Maal belongs), and vice-versa. But it is Mouridism that has the edge in terms of Senegalese cultural pride. A politically astute singer like **Omar Pene** equates Bamba ('our guide') with Black heroes like Kwame Nkrumah and Marcus Garvey. Younger women singers like Kiné Lam and Fatou Guewel devote a significant proportion of their output to Mouride subjects (Fatou calls her band the Groupe Sope Noreyni, after a venerable marabout). Older, more traditionally oriented women like **Saly Mbaye** deal almost entirely in paeans to Bamba's mother and exhortations to go on pilgrimages to Mouride sites.

Musa Suso who went to New York in the 1970s and founded the **Mandingo Griot Society**, an early attempt at kora fusion. He has since become a fixture on New York's avant-garde scene, collaborating with Philip Glass, Bill Laswell and the Kronos Quartet.

Back home in the 1990s, other younger members of Gambia's jali families have spearheaded something of a revival of Mandinka music, setting up semi-acoustic ensembles with amplified koras, a variety of percussion and whatever electric instruments are available. Led by the likes of **Tata Dindin**, **Pa Bobo Jobarteh** and the wonderful **Jaliba Kuyateh**, they travel the suburbs and villages plying the weddings and baptisms with their relentless, tumbling dance music.

Wolof Traditions – and Negritude

You don't have to go far in the Senegambian region to encounter an even more **elemental musical world**: where life is ordered by the seasons, where music is inextricably bound up with the cycles and rites of work, initiation, marriage and birth, and where every activity, even the cooking of a meal, is the occasion for song, improvisation and rhythm.

Senegambia's deep-seated traditions are essentially rhythmic, and the region contains several particularly vigorous, complex and distinctive percussive styles. Even the Mande instruments – kora and *balafon* (xylophone) – are played in a style considered 'hot' (uptempo) and funky compared

The highlight of the Mouride year is the *magal*, the great pilgrimage to Touba, where the biggest mosque in sub-Saharan Africa was built over Bamba's tomb. Up to a million people camp out round the holy city, singing *qasaids* (Bamba's spiritual songs) for days and nights on end. Through the crowds move the patchwork-clad, often dreadlocked figures of the Baye Fall – followers of **Cheikh Ibra Fall** – one of Bamba's original disciples. Fall, a former warrior or *cheddo*, begged Bamba to excuse him from following the Muslim code of fasting and prayer, so that he could labour physically on his master's behalf. The Baye Fall, his followers, dress like cheddo and live in separate communities, singing and begging for their marabouts, and providing guardians for the city of Touba. The most famous Baye Fall today is singer **Cheikh Lô** who, with his gaunt-featured, massively dreadlocked persona, has carried the message to concert halls and festival stages around the world.

"We're still the soldiers," says Lô. "Spritual soldiers, soldiers of God. We fight with peace, not arms. We're at the beck and call of the marabout. We're ready and willing to do anything for him. The marabout brings so many people together, but he does nothing except provide spiritual guidance. So the Baye Fall are there at his side to do all the errands, bring food, goods. Then the marabout distributes these things to poor people."

Youssou N'Dour, also a Mouride, takes up the theme. "Even when I'm singing at my club, and I mention Cheikh Ahmadou Bamba, the audience goes wild. Because it's very strong, because we don't know where the force, the power of Cheikh Ahmadou Bamba stops or should stop. People are worried about the future. Even today they're

Cheikh Lô

facing many problems. So when we present this in our club, we're saying, OK, we're in a modern society, but don't forget the past. In today's world, we always need to remember what is strong for us."

Mark Hudson and Lucy Duran

to the more classical Malian style. And despite competition from more modern entertainment, these traditions continue to thrive, borrowing and adapting from each other in the urban world.

Yet Senegal was oddly late, not only in exploiting these traditional riches in a modern musical context, but in developing its own distinctive popular style. The reason was mainly the country's colonial history. Senegal's links with Europe run long and deep. The Portuguese were here in the fifteenth century, and the first French settlements were established in 1659. With European expansion in the late nineteenth century, Senegal became the administrative base of France's vast West African empire, and the inhabitants of the four main towns were given **French citizenship** and voting rights

to the National Assembly in Paris. Whole generations of schoolchildren grew up believing themselves to be French and desiring no other identity.

This policy of assimilation created both pride in the sense of a special Senegalese identity but ultimately disillusionment and alienation, which gave rise to '**negritude**', a philosophy of cultural rediscovery that was hugely influential in the post-war period, and of which Senegal's first president, the poet Leopold Sedar Senghor, was a prime exponent. Senghor's commitment to his country's culture ensured that Senegal became a leader in African literature, cinema and the visual arts. The music of the griots was promoted as an African classical tradition, too, through the creation of traditional troupes and ensembles.

But popular music was ignored by the state, and it grew, of its own accord, amid Dakar's explosive urbanisation, and the establishment in the city of **Wolof**, the language of the kingdoms of Dakar's hinterland, as a new lingua franca and a focus of a genuinely national culture. The city now teems with second, third and even fourth generation Dakarois of every ethnic background who speak no African language other than Wolof, and who consider themselves to be Wolof; Youssou N'Dour, the most famous proponent of Wolof culture, is in fact a Serer on his father's side and a Tukulor on his mother's.

A further influence, among these migrants from the hardship of life in the Sahel, is popular Islam, and in particular the hierarchically organised Sufi brotherhoods (for more on which see the box on Mouridism, previous page).

Dance Music: the 1960s and Star Band

In 1960, few Senegalese had access to recorded music of any kind. The country's handful of dance bands or *orchestres* were loose ensembles based on particular nightclubs serving a small bourgeois elite who wanted 'sophisticated' (Western) sounds. Traditional music was considered embarassingly primitive, and with the caste associations of the griot tradition, actually shameful.

The most prominent orchestre was **Star Band**, formed by **Ibra Kasse** of the *Miami* nightclub to play at Senegal's independence celebrations. They played Cuban and Latin covers by the likes of Pacheco and Orquesta Aragon, without understanding a single word of the lyrics. During the 1960s and '70s however, Star Band became the focus for a gradual process of Africanisation. Cuban songs were adapted into Wolof, and traditional – principally Wolof and Mandinka – songs and rhythms were introduced along with the **tama** – a high-pitched talking drum.

BALLA SIDIBÉ/WORLD CIRCUIT

Orchestre Baabab -
luminous performers Seck and Sidibé (right)

At particular points in the evening, audiences would break off from jazz-dancing and form circles for displays of loin-thrusting traditional dances like the *ventilateur* (referring to the explicit gyrating of the dancer's buttocks), spurred on by the frenetic pummelling of the tama.

As players continually left and rejoined, Star Band gave birth to a whole dynasty of bands, a sort of family tree of the subsequent developments in Senegalese music. When the group decamped to the Sahel Nightclub, it was replaced by one of its offspring, **Number One du Senegal**, featuring gravel voiced **Pape Seck**.

In 1970, another bunch of alumni formed **Orchestre Baobab** to play at the swanky new club of the same name. Medioune Diallo, Radolphe Gomis and leading light, Balla Sidibe, would each take the microphone for dance numbers and languid love songs in Spanish, French and creole dialects, all graced by Barthelemy Attiso's scintillating and highly original guitar work. Laye Mboup, a Wolof griot resident at the Sorano, the country's national theatre, was enlisted to capitalise on the growing taste for more immediately local sounds, but when he proved unreliable, his pupil **Thione Seck** – a lad with an equally distinctive voice – was enlisted.

However, Baobab were soon to be eclipsed by a group whose brief career completely changed the face of Senegalese music.

Stars of Dakar: the Rise of Youssou N'Dour

In 1977, the younger members of Star Band, including the entire rhythm section, left to form **Étoile de Dakar**, which immediately became the top group in Senegal. Their music was a wonderful mix of full-blooded griot singing, blaring horns and throbbing, undulating rhythms. Not, in retrospect, such a departure from the efforts of Baobab and Number One. But it wasn't just Étoile's music that was important, it was their attitude. They were young and defiantly proud of their Senegalese identity. They sang almost entirely in Wolof, flaunting the traditional griot origins of their music and their own image as lads on the corner. The two main singers **El Hadji Faye** and eighteen-year-old **Youssou N'Dour** became Senegal's first real pop stars, addressing not the elite but the youth of the whole rapidly urbanising, demographically exploding country.

The Gambia's Super Eagles

These days there is little in the way of a music industry in The Gambia – a situation aggravated by state discouragement – nonetheless, for a brief era, Gambian musicians led the field in the Africanisation of Senegambian music.

In the 1960s, hip Gambians turned on to a heady mix of ballroom dancing, swinging London pop and James Brown, as well as the more established Cuban-jazz rumba and merengue. The top local band, **The Super Eagles**, dressed in second-hand Salvation Army uniforms turned into Sergeant Pepper suits by Banjul's top tailor Modou Peul. Keyboard player, Francis Taylor, was one of the first African players to master the synthesiser, while vocalist Paps Touray was idolised by Senegalese singers like Thione Seck and the young Youssou N'Dour. The group were rivalled only by **Guelewar**, featuring brothers Moussa and Laye Ngom, who closed their set with a barn storming, psychedelic version of "Hey Jude".

In 1970, the Super Eagles went to London's Bush House, home of the BBC World Service, to appear on *Band Call* with Mike Raven. It was a crucial experience. "We played some merengues with Wolof lyrics and other semi-African stuff," recalls bass guitarist and leading spirit Badou Jobe. "Afterwards we were having fun, jamming with traditional tunes on percussion, when this guy rushed out of his office and said, 'That's what you should be playing!' Then he disappeared. I've no idea who he was, but it completely changed our approach. We were shocked that someone would find our traditional music more exciting than copying Western music. When we returned to The Gambia, we spent two years travelling round the country researching traditional music, talking to old musicians and learning the kora and xalam."

The Super Eagles' new music reflected The Gambia's cultural mix, with rhythms and lyrics from work, initiation and marriage songs of the Mandinka, Jola and Fula peoples, as well as Wolof sounds that brought the music towards an approximation of what was to become mbalax. Appearing at the annual Nuit de Port gala in Dakar, the group were practically turfed off stage by well-heeled punters who wanted rumba and ballroom, and were appalled by this 'bush bush' music. But younger musicians like Thione Seck and Youssou N'Dour were deeply impressed. The band rented a large house in the Medina where young hopefuls like Omar Pene came to sit at their feet. They called their music **'Afro-Manding blues'**, and changed their name to **Ifang Bondi**, a Mandinka phrase meaning 'be yourself'.

After the music scene in The Gambia collapsed in the 1980s, following the attempted coup and State of Emergency, many musicians went abroad. Ifang Bondi moved to Holland in 1984, where they were practically alone in flying the flag for Gambian music through the 1980s. These days, their sole surviving member is **Badou Jobe**, who got together a group of younger traditional and modern musicians for a strong recent album, *Gis Gis*.

Laye Ngom, of Guelewar, has also revived his career in recent years, as **Abdul Kabir and the Goumbe Goumbe Band**.

Rivalry broke the group apart after only two years, with El Hadji Faye and guitarist Badou Ndiaye forming **Étoile 2000**. Their first offering, "Boubou N'Gary", was a compelling collision between Faye's brooding griot voice, screaming fuzzbox guitar, a talking drum and an echo chamber, but after two repetitive efforts they disappeared from view.

N'Dour meanwhile, formed **Super Étoile de Dakar**, taking full control not only of the music, but the group's business affairs. From having been relatively anonymous nightclub entertainers, musicians would now present themselves not only as cultural heroes, but as entrepreneurs too. N'Dour was still only twenty-one but with his dashing personality and extraordinary wail, he soon rose to become the country's number one star, a position he has held ever since. He sang about the people's joys: their traditional festivals, the excitement of the city, the importance of respecting one's parents and remembering one's roots. Above all, he sang for women; he used words and phrases traditionally associated with women, praised rich and famous women, praised his own mother, and, by implication, all mothers and all women.

N'Dour embarked on a series of numbered cassettes, producing one for each of the most important religious festivals, and pushing the concept of the Senegalised Cuban orchestra to its limits. Together with his musicians he drew on the complex cross-rhythms of the *sabar* drum ensemble, in which pitched drums pursue a succession of dialogues with sudden changes in tempo and rhythm, to create exhilarating new structures. The interplay of voices and indigenous vocal techniques such as **tassou** (a visceral traditional rap) and **bakou** (the trilling that accompanies Wolof wrestling), added to the drama. "In my group," N'Dour has said, "I gave some of the traditional sabar parts to the guitar, some to the keyboards, while the rhythm guitar took on the role of the *mbung mbung* drum."

The rhythm of the mbung mbung – known as **mbalax** – gave its name to this idea of transposing traditional rhythms to electric instruments, and regardless of precisely who came up with the idea, it has provided the dominant strain in Senegalese music to date.

Youssou - Still one of the Good Guys

Since he first played in the West in 1983, **Youssou N'Dour** has become not only Africa's best-known musician, but the single most notable personality to emerge from the whole World Music phenomenon. But you have to go to Senegal, or at least spend time with Senegambian people, to appreciate the degree of reverence and quasi familial affection with which he is treated there. Youssou, as he is known to all, is the leading figure in the mbalax phenomenon – inspiring a generation's sense of pride and interest in their own culture. During the early part of his career he was still a familiar figure in the streets of his home quarter, the Medina. Following his return to Senegal laden with awards and gold discs for his international hit "7 Seconds" (the duet with Neneh Cherry), he has taken on the status of a national hero that no other performer approaches. The African journal *Nouvel Horizon* recently named him Senegalese personality of the century above the country's founding president, poet and negritude philsopher Leopold Sedar Senghor.

When you meet N'Dour, not yet forty and determinedly ordinary, you wonder how the son of a mechanic, and by his own admission not well educated, has managed to achieve all this. And of all the fantastic singers in Senegal, of all the feisty, ambitious young men out there on the streets of Dakar, why *him* ? "I'm a believer," he says, matter-of-factly. "I believe in God. God has his friends, people that He helps. He helps people who make an effort. And," he adds with a touch of weary grimness, "I've really made a lot of effort."

Born a *gawlo*, a Tukulor griot, on his mother's side, Youssou was blessed with one of the century's most extraordinary, distinctive voices. From childhood, singing at *kassak* (singing and dancing sessions that mark the end of male initiation), he was something of a phenomenon. In the face of opposition from his father, who had hoped he would become a doctor or a lawyer, he joined Ibra Kasse's Star Band, the crucible of modern Senegalese music, at the age of sixteen. Graduating through Étoile de Dakar, he formed his own band, **Super Étoile de Dakar**, and ever since has shown amazing drive and determination, and the ability to adapt to creative and commercial opportunities without losing sight of his origins in a highly traditional world.

Meeting the challenge of a new generation of more sophisticated and politically conscious musicians like Super Diamono in the early 1980s, N'Dour began tackling social themes like economic migration, the importance of African identity and the issue of apartheid. He

JOHN CLEWLEY

Youssou N'Dour

started recording in the technically superior environment of Paris, with musicians like Adama and Habib Faye, who introduced a more fusion and funk orientated approach, while the traditional rhythmic base become more hard-edged.

Youssou's friendship with Peter Gabriel led to appearing at prestigious events like the Mandela Concert, the Amnesty Tour (with Sting and Bruce Springsteen), and an arresting duet with Gabriel on the single "In Your Eyes". *The Lion*, Youssou's own first big international album was designed to draw all these threads together – and released in 1989 when the Western majors were expecting big returns from African music. Heavily over-produced, the album was a commercial failure, and its follow-up, *Set*, a simpler Senegalese production, fared no better. Virgin's great World Music hope was suddenly without a recording contract. "I was depressed," he says, "for a day." After a spell on Spike Lee's label, he eventually resurfaced on Sony, for whom his poppy "7 Seconds" duet became one of the biggest sellers of 1994, and propelled his *The Guide* album to eventual global success.

Through all this, Youssou continued (and continues) to produce two or three cassettes a year for the Senegalese market, and has acted as a UNICEF Ambassador for the 'Year of the Child', as well as building recording studios and cassette plants in Dakar that have doubled the country's music production capacity. His **Jololi label** was created so that music could be promoted from within Africa, liberated from continual recourse to Western studios and record labels. Their first release, Cheikh Lô's *Ne la Thiass*, was a worldwide hit. The Jololi Revue, designed to showcase the label's artists in the manner of the old Stax and Motown roadshows, took major Western venues by storm. But a follow-up tour without the proprietor's presence struggled to get attention.

Youssou's long delay in an international follow-up album of his own suggests an uncharacteristic faltering in direction, but the song "Bririma" (from the cassette *Lii*) in praise of an ancient king, is considered his most popular song ever in his home market. And Youssou remains very much a national artist: when he's at home, he still plays at his club, the *Thiossane*, each week to keep in touch with his core audience. It's difficult to imagine a Western star doing that. When you see him singing from the middle of the dance floor at three in the morning, looking more like a charismatic youth leader than an international star, you realise Youssou is very much one of the good guys.

Afro-feeling with Super Diamono

Jazz, Funk and the Faye brothers

Since the 1960s, a whole school of Senegalese musicians have looked to jazz, funk and fusion for inspiration, and align themselves as much with an international jazz ethos as they do with Senegalese cultural pride.

Xalam, named after the traditional Wolof lute, were founded in 1970 by drummer **Prosper Niang**. Their 'new thing' jazz tastes and provocative lyrics proved too radical for home audiences, and in 1973 they moved to Paris, recruiting keyboard player Jean Philippe Rykiel, later famous as the arranger of Salif Keita's album *Soro*. Highly regarded by other musicians, the band have toured the world extensively and collaborated with Dizzie Gillespie, Crosby, Stills and Nash and the Rolling Stones. Their 1988 album *Xarit*, featuring Souleymane Faye's griot vocals, gave them a big hit at home, for what was basically an amalgam of super competent jazz funk with Senegalese percussion and vocals. Prosper Niang died in 1989, but Xalam's legacy is continued by **Missal** who appeal strongly to that small section of Senegalese society for whom mbalax will always be "mere noise".

A more interesting fusion approach, and highly influential on the development of mbalax, has been that created by the band **Super Diamono** and the **Faye** brothers: **Adama** – Weather Report enthusiast, keyboard player and arranger with Super Diamono, Youssou N'Dour and Thione Seck; **Lamine** – rock-loving guitarist with Super Diamono and his own Lemzo Diamono; and **Habib** – funketeering bass guitarist, since age sixteen, of Youssou N'Dour's Super Étoile.

Super Diamono's new sound came in large part through Adama's spooky organ, which combined with melancholy horn riffs and crunching mbalax rhythms to revolutionary effect on their 1982 cassette *Jigeenu Ndakaru* (Women of Dakar). Fronted by husky-voiced street guru **Omar Pene** and youthful singer-songwriter **Ismael Lô**, Diamono were a Dakar 'people's band', eschewing griotry in favour of a conscious attitude, combining reggae-inspired militancy, jazz cool and Senegalese Sufi mysticism in a way that made Youssou N'Dour seem almost tame and homely. Singing about unemployment, corruption and the pitfalls of polygamy, they spoke to students and a growing generation of disaffected, largely male youth. Percussionist **Aziz Seck** played the sabar drums in a way that has become *de rigeur* for every Senegalese band since.

By the mid-1980s, with Lô replaced by the neo-griot voice of **Mamadou Maiga** and the dreadlocked zaniness of **Moussa Ngom**, Super Diamono were probably the most influential band in Senegal. Fans engaged in running street battles with 'supporters' of Youssou N'Dour's Super Étoile. But with continual comings and goings of musicians, Diamono's star waned. In 1991 they were completely reformed by **Omar Pene** with a bunch of Senegal's top session musicians whose slick funkiness well complemented his earthy

JAK KILBY

Omar Pene

with guitar lines interweaving in a way that at times sounds almost Californian. A trio of cassettes – *Ballago*, *Diongoma* (with its irresistably propulsive title track) and *Ida Soukeu* – all met with great success, and as the music grew ever more busy and frenetic, Seck's serene, oriental-inflected delivery remained remarkably constant, tackling themes sacred – the manifold greatness of God – and profane – music piracy, skin lightening and dangerous driving. *Le Pouvoir d'un Coeur Pur*, his greatest hits re-recorded for the international market, was a soulless affair, but the semi-acoustic *Demb* marked a stunning return to his ancestral essence in 1998.

Ismael Lô was born in Niger – of Senegalese parents – and trained as an artist. His cool-voiced balladeer persona and taste for Antillean rhythms and French *chanson* suggest a cosmopolitan sophistication that sets itself apart from the Senegalese mainstream. But mbalax anthems like "Jele bi" and "Ceddo" and such quintessentially Senegalese subjects as the social importance of tea drinking ("Attaya") and the enterprise of street traders ("Baol Baol") speak directly to the Dakar masses.

Lô's acoustic guitar and harmonica contributed to the unusual sound of early Super Diamono. "I was with them for four years," he recalls. "My pay was a packet of cigarettes a day, and if you wanted something like shoes, you asked the boss." Not surprisingly, he took the chance to move on to Paris, and a solo career, recording four albums there with **Ibrahima Sylla** in the mid-and late-1980s whose glossy modernity disconcerted Western listeners even more than they did African ones.

His Western breakthrough was 1994's *Iso*, an album strong on show-stopping ballads like "Samayaye" and Etienne Roda Gil's "La Femme sans haine" (later re-recorded by Lô with Marianne Faithful), and with an almost cocktail bar slickness on the uptempo numbers.

From the North: Baaba Maal

Baaba Maal's flamboyant showmanship and dark, intense voice combined with astute promotion by Island subsidiary Mango and now Palm Pictures, have given him a profile in the West to rival that of Youssou N'Dour or Mali's Salif Keita. Charismatic and highly articulate in many languages, the only thing impeding his total dominance at home is the fact that he sings not in Wolof, but in **Pulaar**, the language of the nomadic Fula people who are found across the Sahel from Guinea to Sudan.

melancholy. Not much appreciated abroad, Pene still speaks to the Senegalese people with an authority rivalled only by Youssou N'Dour. In a gesture of friendship, the two singers covered each other's songs on the 1995 album *Euleuk Sibir*.

Seck and Lô

As the 1990s progressed, two major names were added to those of Youssou N'Dour and Baaba Maal in the panoply of Senegalese superstars: Thione Seck (ex-Orchestre Baobab) and Ismail Lô (ex-Super Diamono).

Thione Seck was descended from the griots of Lat Dior, king of Kayor and leader of the last Wolof resistance against the French. His boyish, yearning voice, skills as a philosophical improviser and his aptitude for fine tailoring have made him a favourite of the *diriyanke* – the magnificently-robed matrons of Dakar. While serving his apprenticeship with Baobab, he also ran a traditional ensemble with members of his family: the plaintive riffing of the xalam and cracking sabar rhythms backing his luminous voice.

On forming his own band **le Raam Daan** (meaning 'crawl slowly towards your goal'), Seck transposed this type of music to electric instruments,

Settled along the Senegal river in northern Senegal, the Tukulor sub-group of the Fula to which Maal belongs have practised a puritanical Islam since the twelfth century and are seen as the people most keen to preserve their ethnic and linguistic identity in the melting pot of modern Senegal. Maal called his band **Daande Lenol**, the Voice of the Race.

Baaba Maal was born into a noble family in Podor on the Mauritanian border, and studied at the Dakar conservatoire before winning a scholarship to study music in Paris. On his return, he went on a journey throughout West Africa with his family griot, the blind guitarist **Mansour Seck**, researching traditional music and paying his dues as a musician in the time honoured way. After dabbling in acoustic music and Afro-reggae, he formed Daande Lenol, immediately creating a stir with a rabble-rousing Tukulor variant on mbalax.

Djam Leelii, an acoustic album recorded in 1984, was released in Britain in 1989, where Maal and Seck's raw nasal voices and serenely rhythmic guitar picking were considered a revelation. "Like hearing Muddy Waters for the first time," declared DJ John Peel. Since then Maal has alternated acoustic and increasingly hi-tech electric albums and performances, just as he has mixed designer knitwear from Joseph with sumptuous traditional robes.

Maal's major album of the 1990s – *Firin' in Fouta* – included everything from break beats to Breton harps, ragga, salsa and New Age drones. Released in 1994, it is probably the most daring slab of Afro-modernism to date. It launched Senegalese rappers Positive Black Soul on the world stage, and gave birth to the Afro-Celt Sound System (see p.178), a meeting of Irish musicians and members of Maal's band. *Nomad Soul* released in 1998 continued this eclectic approach, involving the services of no fewer than seven sets of producers, including Brian Eno. Some tracks left the traditional instruments more or less to their own devices, others absorbed them into shimmering programmed grooves.

Although he is considered an intellectual and a political radical, Maal's view on the concept of dissent, like that of all Senegalese musicians, is an ambiguous one. In a society where politics is a matter of reconciling (and buying off) vested interest groups, where unity and harmony are prized as social and philosophical ideals, views tend to be expressed indirectly, through proverbs and the examples of spiritual heroes like Wolof sage Cheikh Ahmadou Bamba and the Tukulor jihad leader Oumar Tall. "I believe that individualism is the greatest obstacle to world harmony," says Maal. "God is one and he wants the world to be one. When humanity begins to work together for new ideals, they will succeed."

A World Apart: Casamance Hothouse

Separated from arid northern Senegal by The Gambia, the verdant southern region of **Casamance** is a world apart, culturally and musically. The Jola **bougarabou**, four large drums played by one man to the accompaniment of palm leaf clappers, and the Balanta **balo**, a gourd xylophone played by two men, are instruments of a semi-forest world of villages hidden away among palm groves and majestic silk cotton trees, where animist traditions strongly persist.

There is also a strong **Mandinka** presence, and the region has produced many great kora players, notably **Lalo Keba Drame** and **Soundioulou Cissoko**. The first group to use the kora in a modern band context were the local **UCAS** (Union Culturelle et Artistique de Sédhiou) **Jazz Band**, formed in 1959 and still going strong.

The Casamance's most famous musical product, **Touré Kunda** were in some ways a band before their time, playing to audiences of 20,000 French fans before World Music had even been thought of. The brothers Ismael, Sixu and Amadou Touré went to Paris as students in the late 1970s. By 1979, they were combining their own Mandinka melodies with mbalax, highlife, soul, salsa and a reggae beat they called *djambaadong* (leaf dance) – a strong favourite with European audiences.

After the tragic death of Amadou – he collapsed on stage at the Chapelle des Lombards, and died later in hospital – another brother, Ousmane, joined the group. He turned out to be a very fine singer who added greatly to the group's stage presence. Touring extensively in Europe, the US and Japan, Touré Kunda notched up a gold disc with sales of over 100,000 for a live double album, *Paris Ziguinchor*

Baaba Maal Playing at Home

Nigel Williamson visited Baaba Maal, the King of Fouta Toro, in Podor, his home town in northern Senegal.

Shoeless children were playing in the dirt road in the baking heat outside Baaba Maal's house. Two uniformed security guards opened the double gates on which his name has been carefully chalked in flowery script, and we were shown into a low, simple bungalow, modestly comfortable, with a couple of couches, a hi-fi, TV and some traditional art, but no air-conditioning. Maal emerged, slim and elegant in green pants and a blue shirt, looking far younger than his 44 years. Courtesy itself, he set about organising cold drinks.

We were in Maal's home in Podor – far from Dakar, where he has another house and a studio. An ancient, dusty village of 5,000 inhabitants, it stands on the fringes of the Sahara where Maal's people, the Fulani (also known locally as Tukulor or Toucouleur) continue to lead a largely traditional, nomadic lifestyle. Across the shallow Senegal River lies Mauritania and thousands of miles of relentless desert.

Maal had just got up, having performed the previous night in a small village further up-country, inaccessible by road and reachable only by crosssing two tributaries of the Senegal river on hand-pulled barges. Podor remains the heart of his existence when it would have been so easy to relocate to Paris, Dakar, London or New York. "It is very special to nomadic people to have somewhere to come back to. They travel with their cows and animals from season to season but there is one moment when everyone comes back and all the marriage celebrations and festivals happen. And I need to come back to understand my roots and where I come from."

Nomad soul

We talked about Maal's 1998 album, *Nomad Soul*, a thrilling global mix of traditional and modern rhythms. The album employed guest producers from Howie B to chief Afro-Celt, Simon Emmerson.

"There were no barriers between us and the technological aspects and the traditional aspects worked perfectly together," Maal asserted. "It opens the music up to lots of different people. Simon came to Podor to learn and that made him very easy to work with. He is very spiritual like me. He made me discover Irish music and a lot of Celtic songs are similar to Fulani music. The melodies fit perfectly with our language."

Maal's own early musical inspiration came from the everyday sounds around him in the village and the desert. He described sitting near the women pounding grain when he was a boy. "I heard the melodies in that and I heard them in the wind, the trees, in the river,

everywhere. I was fascinated by every kind of sound."

The murmur of a goat's bleating drifted across the veranda where we were sitting, competing with the voice of the muezzin from the mosque. Maal learned many traditional songs from his mother and the extended notes and tonal purity which characterise his voice show the influence of his father, a muezzin singer in Podor. Maal himself remains a practising Muslim. "I go to the mosque in Podor when there is a big ceremony. I participate. I give them money and I do all my prayers like every Muslim in my house."

Maal is not a *griot*, the ancient caste which traditionally provided the singers and story-tellers in west African society. When he began singing this caused problems. "The role of the griots is to tell the truth to the people and people who sing are supposed to be from the griot caste. I am from the fishermen's caste and my father – and society at large – didn't understand my choice to be a musician." Maal's parents wanted him to be "a doctor or a lawyer or something", sending him to school first in the main town of northern Senegal, St Louis, and then to university in Dakar and Paris.

In 1980, however, he went on a tour of west Africa with his friend from Podor, Mansour Seck, researching traditional music. "It was then I met a lot of young people who didn't want to do just the jobs their caste gave to them. They were my first audience because they understood and agreed with what I was doing," Maal recalled."I see myself as a modern griot. The old griots were compromised by colonisation. They were meant to be the connection between the people and society but they didn't always tell the truth."

Playing at home

Several hours later we drove in a convoy across the desert – no roads, signposts or electricity – to the next town of Matam where Maal was singing that night. Miraculously we found a tiny house in the middle of nowhere where he and the band ate, slept and rested until 3am when the the show started. After a meal of goat stew eaten with fingers, by lamp-light, cross-legged on the floor, Maal held court from a makeshift couch in the courtyard while we counted the shooting stars.

When it eventually began, the concert was remarkable. The 2,000-strong audience drawn from scattered communities across the desert had arrived either by foot or horse-driven cart. There was no stage and no formality. While the band played and Maal sung, men, women and children ruffled his hair, posed for pictures wth him and thrust money into his hand. There's no need for special security: these are his people. Standing alongside Baaba Maal was Mansour Seck, the blind guitarist who is his griot. He has been Maal's mentor and partner for twenty years.

Baaba Maal: the voice explodes

I asked Maal about the show – so different from those seen in London and Paris. The songs were longer, the grooves more hypnotic and the message profoundly spiritual. "We can use dancers and do things we cannot do on tour," he explained. "It is more traditional and the *kora* and *hoddu* are the most important instruments. The message is also important. At one point I am singing to the students who are learning the Koran and who are going to be the future leaders of society. There is total silence when I do that."

Another difference is that the band does not play until the public shows up. "We wait for the audience. Everyone finishes work, they have dinner, they dress up in their best clothes. We don't play until after midnight and then we carry on until daylight. There is no contract. They know we are playing just for them which is why they give us money. They give goats, horses, gold, jewellery, everything."

In return, Maal is aware of his position as a role model and leader, setting aside entire days to receive people when he is at home in Podor, and listen to their problems, to offer help and advice. "Because of my experiences a lot of people come to ask me what to do. They need me like a key. If they need something from people in the Government I can help. They need that more than the money I give."

Rhythm influences

To casual listeners, Maal's music seems to have a strong reggae influence, but he claims this comes more from the traditional *yela* music of his region. "It is an imitation of the sound of the pounding of the grain. The structure is the same as reggae. The rhythm between the calabash and the clapping of the hands is the same as between the kick drum and the guitar in Jamaican music."

Maal was, however, influenced early on by American soul music and by Jamaican ska. "The first thing I ever heard on the radio was soul. We got tapes of people like Wilson Pickett, James Brown, Aretha Franklin. And long before Bob Marley, we were listening to Toots and the Maytals and Jimmy Cliff. Everybody danced to it but I just listened. I could hear the connections. In Podor we have a lot of Moorish influences and when I heard Aretha the tone of her voice always sounded Moorish to me."

"I was convinced the music came from West Africa. And then I discovered jazz and blues. This music went to America and then it came back to us. If you go to Dakar there is now some fantastic African rap music. The bass line is American but it is still Senegalese. African music has travelled all over the world and now it has come back home."

Live, recorded on their triumphant return to the Casamance. But their most interesting project was the hi-tech *Natalia*, produced by Bill Laswell, a spirited and innovative work. Touré Kunda have remained a francophone phenomenon, and their failure to prosper during the British-led World Music boom, perhaps demonstrates the different expectations of French and British audiences.

SENEGAL AND THE GAMBIA

Women Performers

In contrast to Mali's *jalimusolu* and the Congolese *vedettes*, Senegalese women were slow to make an impact. The first international release by a Senegalese woman, the snappy, Sylla-produced "Cheikh Anta Mbacke", was recorded in 1989 by griotte **Kiné Lam** at a time when midi gear was making the recording process much more lightweight and accessible. Drum kits could be dispensed with and horn parts played on keyboards, though often with hideous results.

Women artists, the proverbial 'neglected resource', were suddenly flavour of the moment. Traditional divas like **Daro Mbaye**, **Madiodio Gning** and the great **Khar Mbaye Madiaga** were whisked into studios by a new generation of entrepreneurs, notably ex-Xalam guitarist Cheikh Tidiane Tall, ex-Super Étoile drummer Pape Dieng, and Lebanese producer/musician Robert Lahoud. Daro Mbaye's "Doylu", produced by Lamine Faye, was a vertiginous pyramid of stabbing horns, flailing sabar and howling rock guitar, topped by the diva's magisterial pronouncements. Kiné Lam's "Galass" pitted her throaty gargle against Cheikh Tidiane Tall's fluid Bensonesque guitar over punching sabar rhythms.

On Kiné Lam's 1993 album, *Sunu Thiossane* (Our Tradition), a new trend was created: the traditional **sabar ak xalam** ensemble discreetly modernised with bass and synthesiser. Every griot of any worth, male or female, has since recorded a cassette, if not several, in this style, usually paeans to great holy men, arranged in a 'by the yard' fashion by Tall. This is the kind of music that's likely to be blaring from your Dakar taxi. Recent stars in this vein include the earthy **Fatou Gewel** and the even more earthy **Dial Mbaye**.

Earthy in a different way is the booming Wolof soul singer **Aminata Fall**. Her collaboration with rappers **Positive Black Soul** caught influential Western ears, and she recently guested with **Harmattan**, an experimental jazz group with Habib Faye and Cheikh Lô guitarist Omar Sowe.

Another woman born into the griot tradition, but educated, highly articulate and glamourous in a very modern way is **Coumba Gawlo**. Her rather shrill voice has received several Paris productions from Ibrahima Sylla, making sharp comment on social issues and turning traditional songs like "Miniyamba" and "Yomale" into stunning ballads.

Rap and New Directions

It is hard to overstate the popularity of rap at the end of the 1990s in Senegal. Every quarter in Dakar has its posse, and there are said to be as many as five hundred groups functioning in the city. They are, obviously, inspired by US rappers, though Senegal also has its own 'rap' traditions. The Wolof language lends itself to forceful rhetoric and a rhythmic alliteration, and drummers improvise vocally to create an extra layer of rhythmic excitement (check Youssou N'Dour's percussionist Mbaye Dieye Faye). A more formal traditional 'rap' is the staccato **tassou**, which was originally performed the morning after marriages by women of the Laobe woodworking caste, and accompanied by graphic explanatory dancing. The doyenne of this tradition, **Aby Gana Diop**, died in 1997, but related forms are continued by **Abdou Ndiaye** and Gambian **Jamil Cham**.

Modern Senegalese rap is largely in Wolof, interspersed with some English and French. Traditional instruments are used as sound effects and punctuation but the main musical influence is from the US. As in mbalax, the lyrics tend to persuade through appeals to good sense, African values and brotherly feeling rather than anger and calls for direct action. The raw adrenalin of gangsta rap is missing, but so is the hatred, homophobia and disrespect for women. The leading group, **Positive Black Soul**, who have been brought to international attention by Baaba Maal, come from solid middle-class backgrounds, and their bravado and bluster are endearing rather than threatening.

Currently the trend is towards the introduction of more traditional sounds. Traditional singers **Ndiaga Mbaye** and **Ndeye Marie Ndiaye** have recorded with rappers. Musicians like N'Dour, Lô, Pene and Coumba Gawlo, too, have all collaborated on stage and disc with rappers.

At the end of the 1990s, mbalax, too, remains current and popular, a whole generation having grown up with its sounds. **Alioune Kasse**, son of Ibra Kasse (the Star Band's founder), grew up in his father's *Miami* nightclub, with the likes of Étoile de Dakar reverberating through the floorboards. His excellent "Aline Sitoé Diatta", a paean to a female freedom fighter from Casamance, saw him dubbed 'the new Youssou', though he has done nothing since to match it. His main mbalax rival is **Alioune Mbaye Nder**, whose macho persona and romantic lyrics now draw bigger crowds to the *Thiossane* nightclub than its owner Youssou N'Dour. Young girls flaunt their midriffs, while dashing young men perform the bakhou wrestlers' strut around the dancefloor.

Recent increases in Senegal's recording and cassette production capacity has, in fact, allowed a wealth of new talent to surface. **Kasse** and **Mbaye Nder** are just the most visible figures of what has been dubbed the *Génération Boul Falé* (Don't Care Generation), for their blasé attitude towards authority and conventional politics. Recorded on threadbare budgets, the offerings of **Assane Ndiaye**, **Assane Mboup** and **Ousmane Seck**, and up-and coming female singers **Marie Ngoné Ndione** and **Maty Thiam Dogo**, constitute a kind of 'garage mbalax' – though they're often backed by well-established outfits like Thione Seck's Raam Daan or Lamine Faye's hyper-active 'hard mbalax' combo, Lemzo Diamono. Often classed with the *Boul Falé* crowds, the exquisite-voiced **Fallou Dieng**, a graduate of the Lemzo stable and long-serving resident vocalist at the *Thiossane* club, has established a distinctive, more mellow style.

None of these younger artists are adding much to the vocabulary of mbalax, but the music is fresh and gutsy, and they have a dialogue to pursue with a young audience for whom Youssou N'Dour and Baaba Maal are becoming rather parental figures.

Meantime, two older and more idiosyncratic talents have been making considerable impact internationally. Paris-based **Wasis Diop** is the kind of cooled-out, category-defying global villager who can make a hard-core Wolof version of the Talking Heads' "Once in Lifetime" sound like the most natural thing in the world. His laid-back, semi-acoustic "African Dream" – a gorgeous duet with Lina Fiagby – gave him a surprise European hit single from his *No Sant* album.

Cheikh Lô, sometime drummer with Xalam, poolside entertainer and one of the Baye Fall, the dreadlocked guardians of Touba, had to wait many years before finding the right production context with Youssou N'Dour. His album, *Ne La Thiass*, combined semi-acoustic mbalax rhythms with a nostalgic Latin jazz feel with a jazz approach and freewheeling balladry, dipping into flamenco, Cape Verdean morna, Congolese rumba and heavy doses of sufi philosophy. One of the most accessible discs of the decade from Senegal, it was a major hit in Europe and America.

Lastly, in a nostalgic return to the old dance roots of Cuban music, the 1990s also saw a brief craze for Senegalese salsa. Producer Ibrahima Sylla created the **Africando** project, teaming up Pape Seck (from Number One du Senegal), Medioune Diallo (of Baobab) and sometime Super Étoile vocalist Nicolas Menheim with top salsa session men in New York. After Seck's untimely death, he was replaced by Puerto Rican **Ronnie Baro** and **Gnonas Padro** from Benin, though by the time the fourth volume was recorded the novelty was wearing thin. Another veteran, Pape Fall, created his own band **L'African Salsa**.

discography

Senegal

Compilations

◉ **African Salsa** (Stern's, UK).

The sound of Dakar's clubs on the eve of the 21st century expansively embraces the black diaspora, and in large part that means salsa. This is a grand selection of seductively arranged tracks from man of the moment, Pape Fall (with his band African Salsa), Super Cayor de Dakar and others.

 Double Concentré 100% Pure (Dakar Sound, Netherlands).

Vol 5 in an ongoing and fascinating 'Anthology of Modern Senegalese Music', this is an eclectic, excellent compilation of vintage and more recent material, from prime Star Band to griot N'Diaga M'Baye on magnificent acoustic numbers. It includes the whole of Thione Seck's "Chauffour Bi".

◉ **A Land of Drummers** (Village Pulse, US).

Seattle's Village Pulse label has produced a series of excellently recorded, beautifully packaged volumes of Senegalse drumming, each devoted to a master in a particular style. This is a sampler giving an overview of the first six volumes.

◉ **Streets of Dakar – Génération Boul Falé** (Stern's, UK).

Gutsy, invigorating overview of the late 1990s scene, showcasing a wealth of emerging artists, from the earthy neo-traditional sounds of Fatou Guewel and Gambian kora duo Tata and Salaam to rap and super-charged *nouveau mbalax* from Assane Ndiaye and Lemzo Diamono. With Alioune Kasse and Fallou Diena providing more reflective moments, this is a rich and entertaining collection.

Artists

Africando

Three veteran Senegalese vocalists of the Afro-Cuban period team up with top salsa session men in New York. After Vol 2, stalwart Pape Seck was replaced by Ronnie Baro and Gnonas Pedro, with guest appearances from stars like Rochereau and Seikouba Bambino.

◉ **Africando** (Stern's, UK).

If the basic recipe appeals, you'll no doubt love all four volumes to date. But the first is probably the best.

Pascal Diatta & Sona Mane

Pascal Diatta is a legendary acoustic guitarist, accompanied by Sona Mane, his singer wife, in the Balanta style of Casamance.

◉ **Simnade** (Rogue, UK).

Diatta matches amazing thumb-and-two-fingers guitar technique with Mane's gruff vocals. Recorded in an unventilated hotel room, the unusual flavour of the music is immediately arresting, though it doesn't vary greatly.

Wasis Diop

Diop is a Lebou (descended from Dakar's original inhabitants) and has a dramatic Wolof and French growl. Based in Paris, he is a category-defying singer songwriter – and, simply, one of the most melodic, accessible artists you're ever likely to happen upon. Acquire and enjoy.

 No Sant (Mercury, UK).

This album's mellow semi-acoustic feel created a surprise international hit in Europe, and especially France. Chill out music for the global village.

 Toxu
(Mercury, UK).

A tour de force, by turns soulful and jazzy, enhanced by the production of Level 42's Wally Badarou, who brings the percussion up strikingly on nearly every track, in particular on the spellbinding rendition of Talking Heads' "Once in a Lifetime" and the moving "Samba".

Étoile de Dakar

The Star of Dakar were Senegal's first pop stars and probably the country's most influential band ever, launching Youssou N'Dour onto the world stage.

Étoile de Dakar: Vols 1–4
(Stern's, UK).

Not only historically important, but wonderful music in its own right. All the essential material is here (except the first hit "Xalis"), rendered oddly more tinny and raucous than the original cassettes. Vols 1 and 3 are essential masterpieces. Most would say the same for Vol 2, while Vol 4 is less significant, but still worthwhile.

Étoile 2000

After Étoile de Dakar's split, Hendrix-loving guitarist Badou Ndiaye and muezzin-like singer El Hadji Faye formed their own band.

Boubou N'Gary (Dakar Sound, Netherlands).

A selection from their first three cassettes. Wild, amazingly raw music taking an almost punk direction never heard before or since.

Coumba Gawlo

Coumba Gawlo is a new star in Senegal – the griotte as glamorous independent modern woman.

Aldiana (Syllart, France).

Selections from two local cassettes, featuring sassy modern mbalax and the wonderful traditional song "Miniyamba".

Fatou Gewel

Fatou Gewel is a gutsy diva of neo-traditional song.

Fatou (Stern's, UK).

Earthy anthems to great religious leaders and moral homilies backed by xalam, percussion and occasionally kitsch keyboard interventions.

Henri Guillabert

The former Xalam keyboard player and arranger, Guillabert is one of Senegal's top jazz-funksters.

Benn (Jololi, Senegal).

The well-connected Guillabert gets together friends Youssou N'Dour, Ismael Lô, Cheikh Lô, Pape Niang and Rwandan chanteuse Afsana Rahamatali for a smooth, very listenable outing on Youssou's label.

Kiné Lam

Senegal's first female pop star, Kiné Lam combines serious griot credibility with a modern approach.

Cheikh Anta Mbacke (Jololi, Senegal).

Traditional songs given snappily modern Syllart treatment. Very attractive in its coolly efficient way.

Lemzo Diamono

Former Super Diamono guitarist 'Lemzo' Faye takes mbalax in a hardcore rhythmic direction with his current band, Lemzo Diamono.

Marimbalax (Stern's UK).

If you can get your head and feet round the relentless activity, you'll be partaking of an integral Seneglese experience.

Cheikh Lô

A maverick talent, Cheikh Lô marries sufi mysticism with a host of semi-acoustic influences and an irresistible voice.

 Ne la Thiass
(World Circuit, UK).

Strong songs and a warm organic feel make for grown-up pop with real international appeal.

Ismael Lô

One of Senegal's top singers, Ismael Lô made his name with Super Diamono in the early 1980s. He has become a cool-voiced balladeer who combines international sophistication with crowd-pleasing local grooves.

Diawar (Stern's, UK).

Containing the irresistably breezy "Jele bi", this is probably the best of Lô's Syllart albums. The CD re-issue contains an extra album's worth of material from previous outings.

Iso (Barclay, France).

Smooth, at times almost MOR, this ambitious album is strong on charm and big ballads.

Baaba Maal

Superstar Baaba Maal is from northern Senegal and sings in the minority Pulaar language rather than Wolof, which highlights his achievement in becoming, with Youssou N'Dour, the country's leading musician. His blues-like music is distinguished by a dark, intense voice, rhythmic guitar-picking, and, live, a wondrous flamboyance. In the 1990s he has alternated between Western-produced fusion releases and 'classic' acoustic outings.

Djam Leelii
(Palm Pictures, UK).

Maal and his mentor and childhood friend Mansour Seck recreate the tunes and themes of their native river region, with buoyant acoustic guitar rhythms and nasal singing at once gentle and intense. Music to be transported by, and commercially, extremely successful. The new CD version contains extra tracks.

Firin' in Fouta (Mango, UK).

An exciting and surprisingly coherent slab of Afro-modernism. British producer Simon Emmerson finds Celtic resonances and enlists salsa hornmen and Wolof ragga merchants. A highpoint of its kind.

Yandé Codou Sene & Youssou N'Dour

 Nomad Soul (Palm Pictures, UK).

This album took the eclectic approach even further, with whole teams of producers marrying traditional instruments with ultra modern grooves.

Youssou N'Dour

Senegal's (and arguably Africa's) best-known musician, Youssou N'Dour defined his style and outlook with the album title *Never Stand Still*. From his time with Étoile de Dakar, through to collaborations with Peter Gabriel and Neneh Cherry, he has produced a body of work that is erratic, incredibly varied and completely fascinating. Continually reworking old material, he – even more than Baaba Maal – caters to the demands of both home and international markets.

SUPER ÉTOILE DE DAKAR

Youssou N'Dour et Super Étoile de Dakar: Vols 1–16 (Local Cassettes).

N'Dour and his trusted cohorts take Dakar street grooves with strong Latin retentions to the portals of international superstar collaboration, via some wild, wacky and continually surprising routes. Vols 6, 7 and 10 are particularly strong. Vol 8, heavily remixed, became the *Immigrés* CD. But the music works best as one extraordinary stream of consciousness. Most of it is impossible to find, but a multi CD compilation, planned for 2000, could become one of the great albums.

YOUSSOU N'DOUR

 Immigrés (Earthworks, UK).

A homage to Senegalese migrant workers, this mid-period cassette, lovingly remastered, has great warmth and an unusually open-ended feel. It's too short to be an outright CD masterpiece, but at mid-price is well worth the money.

Inédits 84–85 (Celluloid, France).

Selections from one of N'Dour's most fertile periods. Complex arrangements, sudden tempo changes and a strong jazz influence make for ambitious and challenging music.

Hey, You! (Nascente, UK).

A budget-priced compilation from his would-be crossover period at Virgin.

Best of the Eighties (Mélodie, France).

Recordings of 1980s material from two cassettes – *Dikaat* and *St Louis*. Richly rhythmic fare with moments of exquisite beauty.

The Guide: Wommat (Sony/Columbia, US).

The Guide was Youssou's most successful attempt at giving mbalax the big budget, international treatment. Containing many moods, it seems uncertain in places, but the single "7 Seconds" (with Neneh Cherry) certainly found an audience.

YOUSSOU N'DOUR AND YANDÉ CODOU SENE

Gainde: Voices from the Heart of Africa (World Network, Germany).

Yandé Codou Sene is the *grande dame* of Serer song and with her daughters creates an elemental polyphony. N'Dour directs and joins them on several tracks. A unique and extraordinary work.

Orchestre Baobab

Baobab were the seminal Senegalese dance band of the 1970s and introduced many great singers in a variety of languages as their Afro-Cuban rhythms became rawer and earthier.

N'Wolof (Dakar Sound, Netherlands).

Captured in 1970–71, with legendary Wolof singer Laye Mboup, this is a real glimpse into a vanished world.

Pirate's Choice (World Circuit, UK).

A beautiful set from 1982. Lilting rhythms, superb guitar playing and the atmosphere of a simpler place and time make this one of those albums everybody loves.

Omar Pene & Super Diamono

The 'people's band' of Dakar's proletarian suburbs in the 1980s/early 1990s, Diamono mixed reggae militancy, jazz cool and hardcore traditional grooves. Their influential early incarnations await some enterprising archivist.

Fari (Stern's, UK).

Two casettes of material on one CD from the early 1990s

when main man Pene had reformed the band with top Dakar session men. A bit smooth for some tastes, but the overall feel is deeply Senegalese.

◉ **Direct from Dakar** (Womad Select, UK).

Actually recorded in Wiltshire at RealWorld's Box Studios. This 'live take' album goes for an earthier feel, but it could sparkle more.

Positive Black Soul

Positive Black Soul are Senegal's boy-racer rappers with international attitude.

◉ **Salaam** (Mango, UK).

Compton and the Bronx inventively reinterpreted, with a peaceful Senegalese bias.

Mansour Seck

Lifelong griot Mansour Seck was (and is) a mentor of Baaba Maal. He plays masterful acoustic guitar and sings with a gently rasping deftness.

◉ **Yelayo** (Stern's, UK).

Never less than one hundred percent grounded in its Fula soil this is Seck's third solo album and probably his most attractive, employing for the first time a female chorus.

Thione Seck

Former Orchestre Baobab singer Thione Seck, like many Senegalese artists, isn't revealed at his best on any one album. But Dakar's gentleman crooner is an essential voice in the nation's music.

◉ **Chauffeur Bi** (Dakar Sound, Netherlands).

This beautiful acoustic album is included as an extra CD on the *Double Concentré* album (see 'Compilations').

▭ **Demb** (Local Cassette).

A fine semi-accousic outing, with a hypnotic tribute to his mentor Laye Mboup.

◉ **Daaly** (Stern's, UK).

Material from 1996 beefed up with Syllart-produced tracks from 1989. A poor opener and some insipid arrangements create a bad impression, but there are some tracks here that sing up one hell of a storm.

Touré Kunda

A trio of brothers adapting the traditions of Casamance with more mainstream Senegalese and Western sounds, Touré Kunda have achieved great popularity in France, though they are little known elsewhere.

◉ **Natalia** (Celluloid, France).

A delightful, moody meander through the forest region's many styles with assistance from producer Bill Laswell.

Xalam

Xalam, the late Prosper Niang's pioneering band, were pursuing a Wolof jazz direction way back in 1970.

◉ **Apartheid** (Mélodie/Encore, France).

Jazz funk à la Senegalaise, well-recorded, and their only album currently available.

The Gambia

Compilations

◉ **Ancient Heart: Mandinka and Fulani Music of the Gambia** (Axiom/Mango, UK).

Rare and atmospheric recordings of large ensembles. An orchestra of koras, balafons and drums from the Mandinkas. Scraping fiddle, voice, flute and percussion from the Fulas.

◉ **Griots of West Africa and Beyond** (Ellipsis Arts, US).

New York based Gambian kora player Foday Musa Suso takes left field producer Bill Laswell to meet musician relatives in far flung Casamance villages. Superbly vivid recordings, interspersed with pieces by Suso, Philip Glass and Laswell. A fascinating project, accompanied by lavishly illustrated book.

Artists

Tata Dindin

Tata Dindin, son of the esteemed Malamini Jobarteh, is a young Turk of the kora.

◉ **Salam: New Kora Music** (World Network, Germany).

Tata leaves behind his dance band for this gently emotive and highly accomplished set.

Ifang Bondi (Super Eagles)

Ifang Bondi (formed as Super Eagles) have been standard bearers for Gambian music since the 1960s. They have been based in Holland since 1984.

◉ **Gis gis** (MW Records, Netherlands).

Their latest, and probably best album, employs Fula and Mandinka sounds from young traditional musicians in a very modern context.

Amadou Bansang Jobarteh

Amadou Jobarteh is The Gambia's senior exponent of the crisp up-river (*tilibo*) style.

Tabara (Music of the World, US).

An intimate atmosphere creates a strong sense of music from bygone days.

Pa Bobo Jobarteh & Kaira Trio

A young member of the esteemed griot family specialising in wild live performances.

Kaira Naata (Womad Select, UK).

This is a pleasing and relatively meditative set, resonantly recorded on beaches and in private houses with rousing rhythmic support.

Alhaji Bai Konteh

The late Alhaji Bai Konteh was a great exponent of the Casamance kora style, with bluesy tuning and lightning fast variations.

Alhaji Bai Konteh (Rounder, US).

Atmospheric 1972 recordings made at the Konteh home in Brikama.

Dembo Konteh & Kausu Kouyate

Alhaji Bai's son and his Casamançais brother-in-law, Dembo Konteh has become well known from extensive touring duetting on kora with Kausu Kouyate.

Jaliology (Rogue, UK).

The duo meet up with Mawdo Suso on balafon on as inspiring a kora album as you could hope to find.

Jali Roll (Rogue, UK).

The duo go electric with members of 3 Mustaphas 3. Energetic and enjoyable, though not the best collaboration of its kind.

Jaliba Kuyateh

Jaliba Kuyateh is an innovator of semi-electric kora dance music with his madcap posse.

Tissoli (Jololi, Senegal).

A tumbling barrage of kora, balafon, bass, drums, percussion and a lonesome trumpet, all hitting deep traditional grooves. Crazy and wonderful.

Jali Nyama Suso

Suso was a revered elder statesman of the kora, sadly departed.

Gambie: l'Art de la Kora (Ocora, France).

Tuneful, accessible playing and singing in both up-river and coastal styles. Recorded in 1972.

Sierra Leone

palm-wine sounds

For a country where the recording industry died in the 1970s – and where the delightful common greeting is "How de body?", to which you reply "Body fine" – it's hard to feel anything but sympathy and regret as Sierra Leone writhes under the double yoke of economic collapse and civil war. Once one of West Africa's most progressive and wealthy nations, Sierra Leone, four decades after independence, has been going through some bad, bad times. Although a few revivalist bands and singers are attempting to recreate the sound of the golden years of the 1970s, it's a sad day when the birthplace of palm-wine music (as played by the late, great SE Rogie) can't field a single exponent for the world stage. **Ed Ashcroft** and **Richard Trillo** chart the country's musical times.

Since Sierra Leone's independence in 1961 (from Britain), mismanagement, corruption and various forms of neo-colonialism contrived to plunder what should be, per capita, one of the world's richest countries: a nation of four million, blessed with gold, diamonds, bauxite, and well-watered, fertile soil. And since 1991 the nation has been riven by a civil war that initially spilt over the border from Liberia's conflict, motivated by the struggle for control of Sierra Leone's open-cast diamond mines.

It's not a promising backdrop to cultural life. Yet Sierra Leone is a truly music-mad nation. Its people have an enormous capacity, even by African standards, for playing music, dancing and partying – something you can experience in any community gig in London or Washington DC where exiles sample a taste of what is sadly missing from present-day Freetown.

Palm Wine and Milo

Palm wine is the naturally fermented sap-juice of the oil palm – poor people's booze in a country where a bottle of imported beer costs a day's wages. The music to accompany the refreshment, **palm-wine music** or **maringa** as it's locally known, was first made famous by **Ebenezer Calender and his Maringar Band**. Calender (1912-85) played a soft, breezy calypsonian, verse-and-chorus style of music which came in part from the Caribbean freed slave immigrants who had given Freetown its name, and implanted an enduring creole or *krio* culture on the capital.

At root, Trinidadian calypso and Freetown maringa may have the same seaborne origins in the Kru-speaking people of Liberia – great sailors and very accomplished guitarists – who, from an early date, were hiring themselves out to foreign vessels as well as undertaking their own trading expeditions all along the West African coast, spreading their guitar style as they went.

Calender was the son of a soldier from Barbados. He trained as a carpenter and was a well-known coffin-maker, but his music soon took over and by the early years of independence he was a mainstay of the Sierra Leone Broadcasting Service. He recorded dozens of shellac 78rpms in the 1950s and early 1960s, mostly in the creole-English of Freetown. The popular song "Double-Decker Buses" (celebrating their arrival from England, and the party on wheels which ensued), epitomises this good-time, slightly tipsy, afternoon sound.

Welcome to Sierra Leone double-decker bus.
The manager is Mr Stobbart,
His assistant is Mr Garmon.
They are trying to do their level best
By sending the double decker.
Welcome to Sierra Leone double-decker bus,
Welcome to Sierra Leone double-decker bus.
Mr Stobart, Mr Garmon and the citizens
Had a party in east to west.
My grandfather and my grandmother
Refused to go to the top stairs.
Welcome to Sierra Leone double-decker bus,
Welcome to Sierra Leone double-decker bus.

Calendar had previously played a kind of music known as **goom-bay**, or *gumbe* (see Guinea-Bissau – p.499), a style which led to an interesting offshoot in the form of **milo-jazz**, popularised by **Olofemi ('Doctor Oloh') Israel Cole and his Milo-Jazz band**. Milo-jazz was a percussive street music requiring no amplification, whose signature

Andy Kershaw and SE Rogie, back in 1988

instrument was the shaker made with a *milo* (chocolate powder) can filled with pebbles. As recently as the early 1990s, milo-jazz was a popular entertainment in Freetown, but economic slump, war and curfews have all but obliterated it.

The modern era of Sierra Leonean music was for long dominated by the one artist who managed to break through onto the international stage, **SE Rogie**, who built on the palm-wine tradition by applying electric guitar to the style. He left for the US in 1973, moving on to England in the late 1980s, where he spent as much time as a cultural ambassador in schools as on stage with his guitar. His greatest successes, from a couple of decades before his time in England, were "My Lovely Elizabeth" and "Go Easy With Me", a song with lyrics as irresistibly suggestive as its melody. In the early 1990s, he made a return trip to Freetown, playing benefit concerts for refugees. Sadly, he died in 1994, just after the release of his last CD, *Dead Men Don't Smoke Marijuana*, on RealWorld.

Since Rogie's untimely death, other artists, based mostly in Europe and the US, have begun to assert their own styles, making for interesting hybrids of traditional African and modern western styles.

The 1970s and the London Connection

The golden era of Sierra Leonean music was during the 1970s when it had its biggest overseas exposure. A new generation of bands who had grown up in the years following independence began to develop their own style of music and subject matter – swinging Freetown, sweet Salon (krio for 'Sierra Leone') and, of course, love and sex. Their explicit lyrics brought some of them into conflict with the new authorities.

Their style drew largely from calypso and maringa but they did away with some of the traditional instrumentation, adding electric guitars and horns, borrowing from other African countries, notably the emerging soukous of Congo, but also from the R&B and pop tunes picked up in the West. Leading groups included the wonderful **Afro-Nationals** (Sierra Leone's answer to TPOK Jazz), **Orchestra Muyah** and **Super Combo**. These groups developed what became known as 'Soca-Beat', or 'Soak Beat' – music that still remains firmly part of Sierra Leonean community life and spawned a late-1990s revival of the Afro-Nationals and another leading 1970s band, **Sabannoh 75** (as Sabannoh International).

In the 1980s and 1990s, the success stories have been those of exiles. London-based veteran and multi-instrumentalist **Abdul Tee-Jay** has spent his time slowly and methodically building a reputation, tirelessly touring not just the UK but further afield in Europe. The years of hard work are beginning to pay off and his latest CD, *E'go Lef Pan You* has crossed over to audiences on both sides of the Atlantic.

Elsewhere, **Ansumana Bangura**, a one-time member of Miriam Makeba's band, forged a career in Germany; multi-instrumentalist **Seydu** has recorded interesting fusion material in Spain; **King Masco** knocks out palm-wine ribaldry in the US; and in South Africa, **Jimmy B** (Jimmy Bangura) has become a major star of the local kwaito variant of hip-hop.

Meantime in Sierra Leone, a few talents have gained hard-won recognition. **Ngoh Gbetuwai**, a Mende from the town of Moyamba, recorded several promising cassettes on threadbare budgets before coming to the attention of US-based producer Henry Gegbe, who released a CD in 1997. And **Great Steady Bongo** is another popular current artist, who had a massive recent hit with "Kormot Be En Me", followed up with the optimistically titled album, *Welcome to Democracy*.

discography

Compilations

 African Elegant: Sierra Leone's Kru/Krio Calypso Connection (Original Music, US).

A fascinating ethno-muse, although elegant isn't the word that immediately springs to mind in describing these ragged old Decca takes. Still, there's redemption in most of Ebenezer Calender's numbers.

Sierra Leone Music (Zensor, Germany).

A real collector's item – Wolfgang Bender's lovingly packaged compilation of Krio and up-country tracks, recorded for the radio in Freetown in the 1950s and early 1960s. The first

nine tracks incude Calender's "Double Decker Buses", and range from Calypso to Gospel. Later cuts are more traditional, and feature music from most of Sierra Leone's ethnic communities, with the likes of the Lokko Tribal Union and Sankoh and his Kono Boys. Excellent accompanying booklet.

Artists

Afro-Nationals

Afro-Nationals were the 1970s creation of musician and composer Sulay Abubakar and vocalist Patricia Koroma. By far the most popular band of their time, they were soon dubbed the TPOK Jazz of Sierra Leone, and not without reason, featuring the sweet lead guitar, trademark brass and live percussion that epitomised that era. They had the added bonus of Patricia's raw, husky voice, one of Sierra Leone's very few female vocalists of the time.

Classics 1 & 2 (H&R Enterprises, US).

Classics 1 is a re-issue, at last, of re-mastered original hits including their big hit, "Money Palava" and "Mother-In-Law". *Classics 2* brings us full-circle as the bulk of the band reformed in 1998 to re-record another collection of hits in the style of the originals. There are also two brand-new tracks here, pointing to the possibility of more to come.

Jimmy B

Rapper Jimmy Bangura is now based in South Africa where his first three albums, mixing his brand of *kwaito* (South African hip-hop), rap and soul have had considerable success. He has become enormously popular at home, too, playing to massive audiences on a trip back to Freetown's Siaka Steven's stadium.

Make 'em Bounce (EMI, South Africa).

Jimmy's latest release adds mbaqanga and mbube to the mix, singalling the beginning of a formula that might really take off. Certainly the thumping title track, a re-mix of Mahlathini's "Gazette", could become a dance-floor smash anywhere in the world

Ansumana Bangura

Percussionist Ansumana is based in Germany, having been accidentally left there while playing with Miriam Makeba's band in 1980. They had met while Makeba was living in Conakry, Guinea. He came to the attention of the excellent small independent label Shave Musik with his own personal *fankadama* style, meaning mix everything.

Sierra Leone People (Shave Musik, Germany).

Everything is certainly mixed in here: highlife, palm-wine, traditional society music, milo-jazz (or gumbe). It is a particularly percussive album, not surprising as Bangura spent his childhood making and playing any and all kinds of drums.

Ngoh Gbetuwai

Ngoh Gbetuwai are possibly the most promising of the new generation of home-based Sierra Leonean artists, working under near-impossible conditions.

Biza Body (H&R Enterprises, US).

It's a shame this album is so heavily reliant on the synthesiser but given the circumstances in Freetown under which it was recorded, its very existence is little short of miraculous. On the plus side are lively authentic compositions and sweet harmonies, not to mention the promise of a follow-up album with some money and proper production behind it.

King Masco

King Masco is a consummate showman and a master of saucy innuendo, making him a favourite in the Sierra Leonean diaspora.

 African Love Record (H&R Enterprises, US).

Masco's best and most popular album to date includes the very rude but hysterically funny "Run Away". Pity about the predominant keyboards and drum-machines.

SE Rogie

Sooliman Ernest Rogie (1926–1994) was Sierra Leone's best-known musician. He developed an effortlessly ladiback, sensual style of palm-wine guitar playing and emigrated to the US in the early 1970s, later moving to England, where he taught and performed.

The Palm Wine Sounds of SE Rogie (Stern's, UK).

The beauty of palm-wine music lies in its simplicity, and this collection retains that essential reflective aura. It's a pity that his most popular song "My Lovely Elizabeth" is not included here (or anywhere on CD come to that), but other classics such as "Joe Joe Yalal Joe" and "Tourist Girl" make up for it. This is the kind of music that can take you to a far-off place when times are stressful. Guitar, percussion, vocals ... a mug of palm wine in the shade.

Dead Men Don't Smoke Marijuana (RealWorld, UK).

The last outing by the ever-cool Sooliman is a delicious piece of music-cake – so long as you like his one tune, the basis of nearly all the songs.

Seydu

Based in Spain, Seydu grew up in Freetown and was influenced strongly by the chants of his Fulani-Mandinka mother and the sounds of his grandfather's drums. A multi-instrumentalist, he lived for a while in Fela Kuti's commune in Lagos, and in London.

Freetown (NubeNegra, Spain).

Bearing in mind Seydu's background, it's perhaps not surprising to find so many different styles fused together, from afrobeat and highlife to funk and soul. Polyrhythmic, beautifully played and outstandingly well produced, this album also displays strong Flamenco influences, accentuated by occasional Spanish lyrics. Seydu seems as much at home with the reflective, almost a cappella "Palm Wine Talk" as with the more upbeat electric material, such as "Chica Boom Boom".

Abdul Tee-Jay

Abdul Tee-Jay has long been the most prominent Sierra Leonean musician in the UK, working the circuit with his own particular take on Soca-Beat.

E'Go Lef Pan You (Tee-Jay Disque/Stern's, UK).

An exuberant celebration of pan-African music. Although there are Congolese flavoured dance tracks here, what sets this album apart from previous CDs, *Fire Dombolo* and *Kanka Kura* (both on Rogue, UK), is the more traditional Sierra Leonean material. When Abdul puts the electric guitar down and goes acoustic, the whole sound shifts to another world. The palm-wine style 12-string on "Jorlay Baby" is simply delightful. The traditional "Allo Allo", known more commonly as "Bubu", is a rasping village song complete with kondi (local thumb piano), cowhorns, whistles, bubu and all, traditionally played to celebrate the end of Ramadan.

South Africa | Popular music

the nation of voice

South Africa is distinguished by Africa's most complex musical history, greatest profusion of styles and most intensely developed recording industry: hence three articles in this book (those that follow this cover Gospel and Jazz). The country's popular music has huge regional and stylistic variations but shares a strong vocal focus – if there is a defining South African sound it is the Zulu a cappella harmonies of Ladysmith Black Mambazo. South African pop has been long and deeply influenced by Europe and the US, yet it has a character utterly distinct, both from those models and from the music you will hear anywhere else on the continent, even from nearby parts of central Africa. **Rob Allingham** reports.

South Africa has a bewildering variety of pop music styles. They are underpinned, however, by two dominant sounds: **mbaqanga**, a township style with vocal harmonies and deep 'groaning' male vocals, and **Zulu a cappella**. These are unique to South Africa yet immediately accessible to global audiences: witness the success of Paul Simon's *Graceland* album, charged by Ladysmith Black Mambazo. Upon such solid vocal foundations have emerged styles such as **township jive**, **bubblegum**, **soul** (which has a distinct local flavour), and most recently **kwaito** – South Africa's take on hip-hop.

Deep Roots

South Africa is one of the world's oldest inhabited areas, and it has perhaps the earliest-charted musical history, dating back to the stone age, around 4000 years ago. At this time, it seems, groups of hunter-gatherers known as **San**, or Bushmen, sang in a uniquely African click language (the "!" and other clicks in modern Bantu languages are an inheritance), fashioned rattles, drums and simple flutes, and exploited the musical properties of their hunting bows. Present-day San music still sounds quite otherworldly.

Then, some 2000 years ago, another group called the **Khoi** filtered down from the north with their herds and pushed out the San. Known perjoratively as Hottentots, the Khoi are now extinct as a group, though their mixed race, or 'coloured', descendants are an important part of South African society. Khoi music seems to have been more complex than San: Vasco da Gama noted in 1497 that his Khoi hosts greeted his arrival with a five-man ensemble of reed flutes.

Later, in around 200 AD, the first **Bantu-speaking** peoples arrived in the region, and by the beginning of the seventeenth century Bantu linguistic groups – **Sotho**, **Xhosa**, **Zulu** and others – had completely occupied what is now South Africa. Their musical glory was their vocal tradition, with songs to accompany every routine, ritual and rite of passage. Each tribe had its distinct and characteristic songs, tonalities and harmonies, but the underlying musical structure was the same – two or more linked melodic phrases, not sung in unison, but staggered to produce a simultaneous polyphony. This arrangement may well have been a Bantu invention – it was certainly an African one – and it underlies the basic 'call and response' structure of many African-American styles including gospel and its later derivatives, doo-wop and soul.

The West, Urbanisation, Marabi and Jive

In the hinterland, the first contact with **Western music** usually coincided with the arrival of Christian missionaries, who made their first visits in the early nineteenth century. Once the mission school system was established, it provided most of the few educational opportunities available to Africans, and always included a musical training. Out of this system came **Enoch Sontonga** – who composed the national anthem, "Nkosi Sikelel, i Africa", at the turn of the century – and later, nearly every prominent black composer and performer right up until the 1960s.

But the most important catalyst for musical evolution was **urbanisation**. Cape Town was big enough to attract American musicians in the 1840s, while Johannesburg grew rapidly in the 1880s after the discovery of gold. Among the many professional musicians who travelled to South Africa before World War I were African–American minstrels, vaudevillians and ragtime piano players. A remarkable series of tours was undertaken in the 1890s by **Orpheus McAdoo's Jubilee Singers** who introduced black spiritual singing to great acclaim from the South African public – black and white alike.

By the 1920s, Africans had established a secure foothold in the cities despite increasing government restrictions. Out of the necessity of coping with the nightly curfew that applied to all Africans, an entertainment institution, the **'Concert and Dance'**, developed in Johannesburg – by now the largest African city south of the Sahara. Vocal groups and comedians held the stage from the beginning of curfew at 8pm until 11pm. Then, after midnight, dance bands with names like the Merry Blackbirds and the Jazz Maniacs played until 4am, when it was once again legal to go on the streets. The **Jazz Maniacs** were a rough-and-tumble outfit, and while they played dance music for black middle-class audiences, they also incorporated elements of a style from Johannesburg's black slumyards called *marabi*.

Originally, **marabi** was banged out on battered **pianos** to the percussive accompaniment of pebble-filled cans in countless township shebeens – illicit drinking centres (the sale of alcohol was illegal to Africans until 1962 except in government beer halls). Structurally, marabi consisted of a single phrase built around a three-chord progression repeated endlessly in the indigenous fashion, while melodically it was a highly syncretic form, providing enough space for improvisation to incorporate snatches of anything from traditional melodies to hymns or current popular fare from Tin Pan Alley.

Some time later, perhaps by the mid-1930s, marabi was being played on **guitars, banjos, and concertinas** but the underlying structure remained the same. By the post-war years and into the 1950s, a number of related popular urban styles based on three chord marabi patterns were being played and sung in different languages and on a variety of instruments in townships throughout southern Africa. By this time, the music was often referred to as **jive** (as in 'violin jive' or 'Ndebele jive'.) Meanwhile, in Johannesburg and other South African cities, marabi and American swing were combining to create **African Jazz** – for more on which see the article on pp.660–668.

A Music Industry

By the late 1940s, southern Africa boasted a remarkable collection of black music styles. These included the distinctive African-Western crossovers of the cities and a variety of tribally-differentiated styles. The latter varied in their make-up from the almost purely indigenous to the Westernised. Most of these styles existed outside any commercial infrastructure, and thus constituted a genuine folk music in the broadest sense of the term.

The occasional local **recordings** tended to document the music passively, without affecting its style or substance. The UK-based **Gramophone Company Ltd**, producer of the HMV and Zonophone labels, initiated the first commercial recording sessions in Africa by dispatching a portable field unit to Cape Town and Johannesburg in 1912. Later sessions in the company's London studio produced the first recorded version of "Nkosi Sikelel' i Afrika" by ANC co-founder **Sol Plaatjie** in 1923, and 150 landmark recordings by composer Reuben Caluza's Double Quartet in 1930.

Eric Gallo's Brunswick Gramophone House sent a few Afrikaner and African musicians to London in 1930 and 1931 to record for their new Singer label. And **Gallo** went on to build a local studio – the first in sub-Saharan Africa – which produced its first masters in 1933, effectively marking the inauguration of the South African music industry. By the mid-1950s, a number of other operations had been established – **Trutone**, a local branch of EMI; **Teal**, another EMI subsidiary which later separated and grew into a formidable presence; and **Troubadour Records**.

Meanwhile, Gallo Africa and its subsidiary, Gramophone Record Company, were producing over a million discs a year in the early 1950s. This was becoming big business, and as the decade progressed the record companies put in place a system of African **talent scouts and producers** (see feature box overleaf), who were to shape the new music for the next three decades.

Radio began to play a crucial role quite late, from 1962, after a 'development programme' for **Bantu Radio** was implemented – in reality a cynical exercise in apartheid wish-fulfilment. Broadcasting was to be a propaganda tool to foster 'separate development'. In the cities, monolingual programming would encourage ethnic identity while in the rural 'bantustans', radio would provide the voice of incipient nationhood. It was intended that the rural stations would feature exclusively the traditional music of their regions, in order to encourage ethnic separatism. In practice, the

The Producers

In the 1950s, urban Africans were an enormous untapped audience for commercial music. But how were white-run companies to determine what they wanted to buy? The dilemma was resolved by hiring African 'talent scouts', later referred to as 'producers', though many of them in fact wielded far more power than any conventional record producer. The most powerful producers ran virtual African fiefdoms within the companies and five in particular loom as major figures.

The age of the producer is over these days in South Africa – musicians now flog their demos around bottom line-driven companies like everywhere else – but many suspect that the artistic result has been a less adventurous, pop-obsessed musical culture that discriminates against non-urbanites and the poor but talented.

Strike Vilakazi (Trutone)
Strike Vilakazi ran Trutone's black division from 1952 to 1970. A vocalist, trumpeter, drummer and composer, he directly influenced the course of popular black music by recording pennywhistler **Spokes Mashiyane** in 1954, touching off the **kwela** craze. Four years later, in an even shrewder move, he persuaded Mashiyane that his pennywhistle music would be even more popular when played on a saxophone. The earliest **mbaqanga** style, or **sax jive**, resulted – a sound that would dominate South African black popular music for many years.

Cuthbert Matumba (Troubadour Records)
Cuthbert Matumba singlehandedly developed Troubadour Records into a giant that at times controlled much of the African market. In addition to a multitude of hits, his catalogue included practically every urban and urban-rural crossover style from the Cape up through central Africa. He had a gift for composing simple, catchy melodies and possessed a uniquely topical lyrical sense.

Matumba permanently employed a large contingent of studio singers and musicians who spent eight hours a day recording (under an endless variety of names) or providing backing. Despite this assembly-line approach, the innovative spirit remained high thanks to a policy which encouraged moonlighting by musicians from other companies and Matumba kept his ear to the ground. Early most mornings he would be out playing test pressings on the Troubadour-mobile – a van fitted with turntables and speakers – gauging public reaction to the previous day's studio output. Any promising record was available in the shops twenty-four hours after it had been recorded.

Troubadour's decline was as abrupt as its rise. Within four years of Matumba's death in 1965, the label's few remaining assets had been swallowed up by Gallo.

Rupert Bopape (EMI/Mavuthela)
Rupert Bopape joined **EMI** as a producer in 1952 and quickly built up the industry's most successful African Jazz catalogue by carefully employing key figures like **Zacks Nkosi**, **Elijah Nkwanyane** and **Ellison Temba** (see the Jazz article pp.660–668) on a permanent basis. But his real talents lay in developing vocal groups.

In the early 1960s, his most successful pennywhistle band, the **Black Mambazo**, evolved an all-male vocal style featuring the leader and principal composer, Zeph Nkabinde, Aron 'Big Voice Jack' Lerole and occasionally Nkabinde's younger brother Simon, aka '**Mahlathini**'. The Black Mambazo's all-female counterpart were the **Dark City Sisters**, probably the single-most popular vocal group in South Africa in the first half of the 1960s.

In 1964, Bopape left EMI and joined **Gallo** to run a new African operation (later called **Mavuthela**), bringing a number of his EMI musicians with him. Within two years, the label dominated the market with a mbaqanga vocal style called **mqashiyo**, the most famous exponent of which was **Mahlathini and the Mahotella Queens**, backed by the Makgona Tsohle Band. In the early 1970s, Bopape began to farm out some production duties to a number of his talented understudies, including **Marks Mankwane**, **Lucky Monama**, and **West Nkosi**.

David Thekwane (Teal)
David Thekwane was the last of the old-style producers to carve out a significant niche in the music industry. He began producing for **Teal** in 1972 after a fairly successful career as a saxophone jive artist under Strike Vilakazi. Thekwane had a violent personality and often intimidated his musicians physically. Nonetheless, throughout the 1970s, his Teal artists – especially the **Movers**, a group of consistent hit-makers who evolved a winning mixture of marabi and local 'soul' – regularly accounted for a substantial percentage of all African record sales. His mbaqanga stars included sax jivers **Thomas Phale** and **Lulu Masilela**, accordionist **Johnson Mkhalali**, and vocal group **The Boyoyo Boys**.

Hamilton Nzimande (Gramophone Record Co.)
Hamilton Nzimande, who semi-retired in 1996, was the last of the 'big five' to remain active in the music business. In a thirty-year producing career he oversaw a remarkably broad cross-section of African music, from the last sessions of African Jazz great, **Zacks Nkosi**, to the earliest **bubblegum pop** of some of the biggest names of the 1980s and early '90s.

Nzimande began his career as a singer, going on to handle promotion for Rupert Bopape at EMI (often driving the mobile). He finally got his break as a producer in 1966 when he went to help run the Gallo subsidiary **Gramophone Record Company** and by the mid-1970s, Nzimande's mbaqanga catalogue almost rivalled Mavuthela's under Rupert Bopape. He was the first producer to take local **soul music** seriously and made it massively successful, with bands like the **Inn-Lawes**. **The Beaters**, another group from his soul roster, spawned solo star **Sipho 'Hotstix' Mabuse**. And it was at Nzimande's suggestion that the hugely successful **Soul Brothers** copied their vocal harmony style from Zimbabwean Shona township music.

Nzimande also set trends in **gospel recordings** by popularising the Zulu a cappella style, **cothoza mfana**, that anticipated the sound that was to make Ladysmith Black Mambazo so famous, and he was the first to successfully promote large apostolic choirs such as **Izikhova Ezimnqini**.

bantustan stations had to play a mixture of styles just to gain a listenership. The failure of the traditionalism policy reflected the government's ignorance of rural people. Music and culture in the rural areas hadn't remained suspended in a traditional time warp, and economic development had diluted the indigenous character of the hinterland.

Whatever, Bantu radio handed the record companies a powerful marketing tool and revolutionised the way black music was promoted. Whereas previously the companies had relied on mobiles to advertise their records directly to potential customers, they could now reach a mass market immediately. Radio also opened up new rural markets for record companies, encouraging them to focus more attention on areas outside the cities where individual rural traditions were being combined with modern, urban-based influences.

After the advent of radio, however, the lyrical content of African recordings became more conservative. In the 1950s and before, black musicians often recorded material that commented openly on the social and political issues of the day – "Sobadubula Ngembayimbayi" by the Alexandra Swing Liners, released in 1955, contained the chorus 'We will shoot the whites with bazookas'. The new African radio services instituted a draconian censorship code and mobiles were banned as a 'public hazard'. Purely commercial considerations inevitably led to a great deal of self-censorship on the part of labels and their artists.

Pennywhistle Jive: the Kwela Boom

Pennywhistle jive, which was focused as usual on Johannesburg, was one of the first musical styles to become a commercial phenomenon and the first to win a measure of international renown. The indigenous predecessor to the pennywhistle was the reed flute of cattle-herders, with three finger-holes. When the herd boys came to the cities, they bought similar tin whistles with six finger-holes, made in Germany.

Willard Cele, a disabled teenage musician living in Alexandra Township, is credited with the discovery that by placing the flute's mouthpiece at an angle between the teeth to one side of the mouth with the soundhole slanting outwards, its tone was not only thickened but it was possible to vary the pitch of each note and vastly extend the instrument's melodic capabilities. Although Cele himself was to die young, his new style quickly inspired a legion of imitators, especially following his appearance in a 1951 movie, *The Magic Gar-*

den. Groups of three and four **pennywhistlers** were soon working out elaborate arrangements where a lead flute would extemporise a melodic line over chords provided by backing flutes.

After years, indeed decades, as an exclusive township phenomenon, pennywhistlers moved into the suburbs and city centres in the early 1950s where they were part of the urban environment for another decade. In the white areas, the potential financial rewards were greater but so were the dangers. Flute musicians, some of them not even into their teens, would travel out of the townships to perform on street corners and in parks, playing a cat-and-mouse game with the police who would arrest them for creating a 'public disturbance'. Eventually this musical presence attracted a white following, particularly from rebellious suburban teenagers referred to as 'ducktails' (the equivalent of teddy boys in the UK or 'juvenile delinquents' in the US). It was the ducktails that renamed pennywhistle jive **kwela** (meaning 'climb up', the command barked out to Africans being arrested and ordered into the police van). The term eventually became generic and it was as kwela that the music spread elsewhere in Southern Africa, notably to Malawi, through migrant workers.

It took several years for the record companies to wake up to the commercial potential of the pennywhistle. Little flute material was released until 1954, when **Spokes Mashiyane**'s "Ace Blues" backed with the "Kwela Spokes" became the biggest African hit of the year. Record producers began to take flute jive seriously and in the following decade around a thousand 78rpm pennywhistle discs were issued.

After his initial success, Spokes Mashiyane remained the single most famous pennywhistler, although another flute star, **Abia Temba**, was also very popular throughout the 1950s. Troubadour's two biggest pennywhistle artists were **Sparks Nyembe** and **Jerry Mlotshwa**, whose material was released using an endless number of pseudonyms. The **Black Mambazo** from Alexandra Township recorded for EMI; they too appeared under different names. In 1957 they recorded a popular local hit called "Tom Hark", which featured on British TV and promptly caught the public's fancy, perhaps because of its slight similarity to the skiffle music that was popular at the time. It was issued as a UK single and promptly rose to number two in the charts.

Gallo's pennywhistle catalogue eventually cornered the largest share of the market and featured the greatest number of top-notch players, especially after the company lured Spokes Mashiyane away from Trutone in 1958 (he became the first African musician to receive royalties rather than the standard flat studio fee). The label's pennywhistle productions often featured quite elaborate arrangements by Gallo musical director **Dan Hill**, a fine clarinetist and band leader.

Among the company's principal pennywhistle artists were the **Solven Whistlers** from Jabavu-Soweto, instantly recognisable by their jazz-influenced harmonies and sophisticated compositions, largely the work of **Peter Mokonotela**. The Solven's lead flute, **Ben Nkosi**, was probably the single greatest pennywhistle soloist, his best work exhibiting a level of technique and improvisational dexterity that belied its execution on such a simple instrument.

The beginning of the end of the pennywhistle craze can be precisely pinpointed with the song "Big Joe Special", Spokes Mashiyane's first recording on **saxophone**. Much as his "Ace Blues" had created a sales sensation and inspired a legion of imitators four years before, "Big Joe Special" proved to be the trendsetting hit of 1958. In its wake, every black producer now wanted material by similar-style sax players and most pennywhistlers, providing they could obtain a saxophone, were happy to deliver it.

From Sax Jive to Vocal Mbaqanga

The sax was obviously a more versatile instrument than the pennywhistle and from the standpoint of both the players and their audience connoted an urbane, pan-tribal sophistication satisfyingly contrary to apartheid image of the heathen tribalist. Only the white kwela fans were disaffected: it proved impossible for African street musicians to perform with a saxophone at their former city and suburban haunts. Now they were limited to playing in the townships, a world beyond the ken of even the most rebellious white teenager.

After the success of "Big Joe Special", sax jives became the dominant black musical genre, a development which didn't meet with universal approval. One jazz saxophonist, Michael Xaba, disdainfully referred to the new style as '**mbaqanga**' – a 'dumpling' in Zulu but in this instance connoting 'homemade' – since most of its practitioners were musically illiterate. Ironically, the name soon gained a common currency as a term of endearment and indeed, the craze for instrumental mbaqanga went on to last for almost another two decades.

Sax jives were usually built around very simple repeated melodic fragments, so much of their appeal and interest depended on their instrumental accompaniment. Initially, the sax was backed with the same marabi-derived acoustic 2/4 rhythm of most flute jives. Then, beginning in the early 1960s, the rhythms became discernibly heavier, more elastic and more African. The **electric bass**, in particular, with its higher volume, sustaining and attack capabilities, provided the foundation for the new style. The pioneer African bass player whose innovations played such a major role in shaping this evolution was **Joseph Makwela**. His bass guitar, the first one imported into South Africa, was purchased from a local white session musician who had seen an example of the newly developed instrument when Cliff Richard and The Shadows played Johannesburg in 1960.

Makwela and **Marks Mankwane**, another influential figure who was the first African musician to exploit the electric guitar fully, formed the nucleus of the famous **Makhona Tsohle Band**, which backed the Gallo studio's mbaqanga saxophonists like West Nkosi but also accompanied their vocal groups. The band's electric sound became an integral part of a new vocal genre developing in the mid-1960s which also went under the name of mbaqanga and then later *mqashiyo*.

The **vocal component** of mbaqanga developed directly from the 1950s township vocal styles made famous by groups such as the Manhattan Brothers and the Skylarks. These styles had at first been copied directly from African-American models but local musicians increasingly Africanised their sound. One of the crucial developments leading towards mbaqanga's characteristic harmonies was the use of **five vocal parts** rather than the four-part harmonies common in African-American styles. Female studio vocalists at Troubadour discovered that if the single tenor line was divided into a high and low tenor part, the resulting harmonies took on a breadth that was reminiscent of traditional vocal styles.

A group of session vocalists at EMI, the **Dark City Sisters**, usually featuring the sweet-voiced lead of Joyce Mogatusi, became the best-known African vocal group of the early 1960s using this technique which rapidly became a distinctively South African sound. Their style was still described as vocal jive but the formative harmonies of mbaqanga were already evident.

Another element which defined much of the classic vocal mbaqanga output was **groaning**: bellowing, ultra-bass male vocals that contrasted dramatically with softer, all-female harmonising. At first this was a commercial gimmick invented by **Aaron Jack Lerole** of EMI's **Black Mambazo** in the early 1960s. Lerole subsequently gained a measure of

Mahlathini rehearses with the Mahotella Queens

groaning fame as Big Voice Jack, and in the process managed to shred his vocal chords permanently. His efforts were soon overtaken by **Simon 'Mahlathini' Nkabinde**. As a teenager, Mahlathini secured a considerable reputation as a singer of traditional wedding songs in Alexandra Township where he led a large female group in a typically African, polyphonic fashion. His magnificent bass voice was naturally suited to the groaning style and Rupert Bopape began to utilise it in conjunction with varying combinations of EMI session vocalists. Meantime, Nkabinde developed an aggressive and dramatic stage persona as Mahlathini The Bull, greatly enhancing his growing reputation.

When Rupert Bopape left EMI for Gallo in 1964 he took Mahlathini along with him. All the essential mbaqanga elements now coalesced at the new Gallo-Mavuthela production facility: the male groaner roaring in counterpoint to intricately arranged five-part female harmonies, underpinned – thanks to the Makhona Tsohle Band – with the new-style, totally electric instrumental backup. After several years of growing popularity, vocal mbaqanga began to be referred to as **mqashiyo**, from the Zulu word meaning bounce – though mqashiyo was actually the name of a popular dance style; no musical characteristic distinguished it from vocal mbaqanga in general.

As was the case at EMI, Bopape's regular roster of female session singers was nominally divided into several distinct groups. These line-ups maintained a degree of regularity for live performances, but in the studio vocalists were fairly interchangeable, and in any event the output of each group was simultaneously released using a number of different names. For example, the vocalists who performed live as the **Mahotella Queens** were also the Dima Sisters, the Soweto Stars and Izintombi Zo Mqashiyo on two different Gallo record labels.

Rival producers attempted to emulate Mavuthela's success with mqashiyo. Only one, however, Hamilton Nzimande at GRC, managed to build a strong roster. His two best-known groups were **Amatshitshi** and **Izintombi Zezi Manje Manje** (The Modern Girls), but Nzimande's crew also included two wonderful groaners, the brothers **Saul** and **Bhekitshe Tshabalala**, as well as a great instrumental backing band, **Abafana Bentutuko**. These provided stiff competition for Bopape's Mahlathini/Mahotella Queens/Makhona Tsohle steamroller.

In the 1970s, the female chorus-plus-groaner formula retained its popularity when practised by old favourites like the Mahotella Queens, but almost every successful new mbaqanga group had an exclusively male line-up. At the forefront were Gallo's **Abafana Baseqhudeni** ('Cockerel Boys', so named after the company's rooster trademark), an extremely popular five-man line-up featuring the bass leads of Potatoes Zuma and Elphas 'Ray' Mkize as well as groaner Robert 'Mbazo' Mkhize. Their main rivals during the decade were the David Thekwane-produced **Boyoyo Boys**, a male vocal group led by principal composer Petrus Maneli. Their half-chanted harmonies and loping rhythms gave them a unique sound and one of their biggest successes, "Puleng", later caught the ear of British producer **Malcolm McClaren** who subsequently transformed it into the 1981 British number one hit "Double Dutch".

Zulu A Cappella: Mbube and Iscathamiya

In the 1920s, as an industrial economy began to develop in Natal, **a cappella vocal styles** became closely identified with the area's emerging **Zulu working class**, newly forged as rural migrants found employment in mines and factories. Forced in most cases to leave their families behind and live in all-male hostels, they developed a weekend social life based on vocal and dance group competitions, staged within and between hostels, and judged by elaborate rules and standards. By the late 1930s a cappella competitions were a characteristic of Zulu hostels throughout industrialised Natal and had also spread to Zulus working in Johannesburg.

In 1939, **Solomon Linda's Original Evening Birds** – a group from Pomeroy in northwestern Natal – began recording for Gallo's Singer label. Their evocative rendering of Linda's song "Mbube" (The Lion) proved to be a commercial milestone. "Mbube" was probably the first African recording to sell 100,000 copies and it later provided the basis for two American number one hit records, "Wimoweh" by the Weavers in 1951 and "The Lion Sleeps Tonight" by the Tokens in 1961.

The Original Evening Birds exerted a vast stylistic influence as dozens of imitators sprang up in the wake of their success, thus setting the scene for the next stage in the long history of Western-influenced Zulu music. **Mbube** became the generic term for a new vocal style that incorporated Linda's main innovations: uniforms for the group, highly polished but softly executed dance routines and – most importantly – the use of a high-voiced lead set against four-part harmony where the ratio of the bass voices to the other parts was increased to two or three. These characteristics were at the heart of the music through the late 1940s as mbube evolved into the **isikhwela jo** or 'bombing' style – so named because of its strident, almost shouted harmonies – and into the 1960s, when a far smoother approach became popular.

By the mid-1950s, the pan-tribal audience that had once purchased substantial quantities of mbube and isikhwela jo recordings by groups such as the Morning Stars and the Natal Champions had fallen away, and interest in Zulu a cappella reverted to the hostels. Then, in the 1960s, the audience broadened once again following the establishment of **Radio Zulu** which gave extensive exposure to Zulu a cappella and could be heard throughout Natal as well as in large areas of the Transvaal and Orange Free State. One Radio Zulu programme was particularly influential: 'Cothoza Mfana', hosted by Alexius Buthelezi, featured a cappella vocal material exclusively. Indeed for a time, the newer, smoother style which superseded bombing was known generically as *cothoza mfana*.

The architects of the Bantu Radio system, and especially its administrative director Evonne Huskinson, were keen to promote cothoza mfana because the style incorporated the secular lyrics that had characterised most Zulu a cappella since at least World War I. With a judicious application of influence and suggestion, cothoza mfana lyrics could easily be tailored to promote the twin pillars of apartheid: tribal identity and ruralism. A typical example was a radio recording by the New Hanover Brothers subtitled "Hurrying of People In Durban So Disturbed Him, He Caught Train Back Home".

When the record industry at first showed only a minimal interest in cothoza mfana, Bantu Radio bridged the gap by recording their own transcription discs, and for many groups these provided a first step before graduating to commercially issued recordings. This was the case with Enock Masina's **King Star Brothers**, the most influential a cappella group of the late 1960s and early '70s, who had featured on Radio Zulu for at least four years before they finally landed a contract with Hamilton Nzimande at GRC in 1967. By this time the King Stars' style was called **iscathamiya**, a term derived from the Zulu word meaning 'to stalk or step softly', which described the dance routines that the group invented to match their swelling, polished harmonies.

But it was Gallo-Mavuthela producer West Nkosi's signing of another group of Radio Zulu veterans, Joseph Shabalala's **Ladysmith Black Mambazo**, ('Black Mambazo' signifying the

West Nkosi at Downtown Studios

T J LEMON

SOUTH AFRICA

Graceland and Ladysmith Black Mambazo

Paul Simon's 'South African album', *Graceland*, has sold in excess of seven million copies worldwide – by far the greatest exposure to date for South African music, if you discount the appearance of "Wimoweh" on Disney's *Lion King*. It has also propelled the fortunes of Ladysmith Black Mambazo, his chief collaborators on the recording.

The recording took place in 1986, when South Africa was still under apartheid rule and its music outside the mainstream. The music that inspired Simon was Zulu a cappella – iscathamiya – which had largely fallen out of fashion after an early 1980s boom. Travelling to South Africa, Simon recorded with **Ladysmith Black Mambazo** on two tracks co-composed with the group's leader, Joseph Shabalala, and revived both his and Ladysmith's careers in the process, meeting with huge critical and commercial success. *Graceland* provided unprecedented exposure for a South African and two years later Black Mambazo's *Shaka Zulu* album, recorded in the US and produced by Simon, won a Grammy for the best World Music Recording of 1988, and went on to sell more than 100,000 around the world.

Not everyone welcomed the disc. Vociferous complaints came from anti-apartheid organisations who claimed that Simon's album and subsequent tour violated the cultural boycott, a crucial component of the sanctions programme then in effect against South Africa. Even after the UN Anti-Apartheid Committee called the objections 'misconceived', many ideologues continued to label Simon arrogant (he had done little

to consult the Anti-Apartheid movement) and an imperialist, accusing him of appropriating local culture.

In fact, Paul Simon's role and methods, although obviously self-serving to a degree, seem to have been

Joseph Shabalala with Paul Simon, during the Graceland tour

largely exemplary. The artist went out of his way to credit his collaborators and then used all the commercial clout and prestige he could muster to establish the Black Mambazo in the international arena. The contrast between his behaviour and that of British pop producer Malcolm McClaren a few years earlier could not have been clearer. McClaren hired South African musicians and composers to create the substance of a series of recordings which produced the UK hit "Double Dutch", and ended up paying royalties only after the case reached the British High Court.

'Black Axe' that would defeat all opponents in group competitions), that transformed the status of Zulu a cappella. Initially at least the Mambazo's popularity owed more to the quality of Shabalala's lyrics than to any remarkable musical innovations, but his seven-man group was ambitious, disciplined and willing to soldier on through an endless number of appearances arranged by Alexius Buthelezi of Radio Zulu.

In 1973, Ladysmith Black Mambazo released their first album, *Amabutho*, the first African LP to achieve official Gold Record status (sales of 25,000). In its wake there was a rash of copycat imitators – at least eight of whom managed to incorporate 'Ladysmith' into their names. But by the mid-1980s the boom was over, and except for the still numerous fans of LBM, the audience for

Zulu a cappella was again reduced to its original migrant-proletarian core. But at this juncture, in 1986 Paul Simon discovered iscathamiya (see box), and the style went international with the huge-selling *Graceland* album.

These days, Ladysmith Black Mambazo are a top festival band worldwide, with thirty or so records behind them, all of which have gone gold. Their line-up has varied from seven to thirteen voices, and the increasingly rich harmonies have been combined with ever more softly modulated dynamics, and, recently, gospel material, but the underlying framework remains much the same as that originated by Solomon Linda back in the 1930s. Only Zulu speakers, however, are able to appreciate the subtle, metaphorical, and deeply evocative words of Shabalala's songs.

Neo-Traditional Styles

While most South African styles evolved against a backdrop of migration to the towns and – with the exception of mbube-iscathamiya – have assumed a pan-tribal character, the **traditionally based music** of the **Sotho**, **Zulu**, **Pedi** and **Shangaan** rural areas, adapted to imported instruments, is an important element in South Africa's musical range. Interestingly, too, these neo-traditional music styles – which are usually labelled 'Sotho-Traditional', 'Zulu-Traditional' and so on – don't always use the Western seven-note scale. **Sotho** melodies and harmonisations, for instance, are based on a six-note scale where the lead vocal – characteristically a combination of half-sung, half-shouted praise lyrics – is delivered in a rapid, staccato fashion. The actual melody is often most strongly suggested by the response from the chorus voices or instruments.

Sotho and Pedi-Traditional

Neo-traditional music has quite a long history. Zulu, Sotho and Xhosa **vocal/concertina records** were produced by several companies as early as the 1930s. They consisted of a basic call-and-response structure with a concertina counterpoint to the lead vocal instead of the former group voices. The concertina became popular after World War I following the large-scale import of cheap foreign models known as 'bastari' after a popular Italian brand.

Tshwatla Makala was the first neo-traditional musician of any commercial significance. A Sotho, he used deftly fingered runs on a concertina to counterpoint his vocals and became a mentor to numerous other concertina artists. The next Sotho-Traditional development was a pure a cappella style called **mohabelo**; frenetically intoned lead vocals and chanted response choruses, first popularised by the group **Basotho Dihoba**, led by Latsema Matsela, who was born in Lesotho, the source for his music.

A later evolutionary stage of Sotho-Traditional saw the concertina replaced by an accordion leading an electric backing band. Propelled by pounding bass lines and often including multivoice response choruses, these combinations produce a powerful sound. The first LPs appeared in the late 1970s and **Tau Oa Matsheha** were the first famous group of this type.

The European influence in the principal neo-tradional style of the **Pedi** (related to the Sotho) is suggested by its name, **harepa** (derived from harp). In the nineteenth century, Lutheran missionaries began to proselytise among the Pedi, bringing with them the German **autoharp**. Local musicians soon adapted the instrument to indigenous musical forms, plucking its strings in a single-note fashion to accompany their vocal music. The African call-and-response structure has remained, as have the Sotho-style harmonies – but the characteristic descending melodic lines of harepa strike most uninitiated listeners as alien and astringent. The most prolific and successful artist from the 1970s, when there was a little Pedi-Traditional harp boom, is probably the Gallo label's **Johannes Mohlala**.

Zulu-Traditional

Zulu-Traditional followed a unique course by embracing the **guitar**, which had first been introduced by the Portuguese in the sixteenth century. It was compatible with Zulu harmonic practice and became popular after cheap locally made instruments became available in the 1930s. For several decades the sight of a Zulu man with a guitar, picking out a melody while walking along a rural road, was familiar. Among all the different southern African cultures, only Zulus, the related Ndebeles of Zimbabwe, and the Shangaan, took up the instrument.

The father figure of Zulu-Traditional performance and recording is **John Bhengu**, born in central Zululand in 1930. As a street musician in Durban in the early 1950s, he earned a formidable reputation through his skill in adapting indigenous melodies to the guitar and particularly for his unique fingerpicking style called *ukupika* (before Bhengu, the guitar was always strummed). His records on the Troubadour label helped establish a standard Zulu-Traditional structure that became the model for several generations of performers, each song beginning with the *izihlabo* – an instrumental flourish – followed by the main melody, then interrupted once by the *ukubonga*, a spoken declamation of praise for clan, family, chief, or even the singer himself.

In the late 1960s Bhengu switched from acoustic to electric guitar and adopted a new persona as the sensationally successful **Phuzushukela** (Sugar Drinker). Backed with a full mbaqanga production package that included an electrified rhythm section and backing vocals, this led to a golden era for Zulu-Trad music in the 1970s. Hundreds of recordings were produced by dozens of bands, constituting some of the most easily assimilable performances in any neo-traditional style.

Zulu-traditional musicians

In the last couple of decades, Zulu traditional music, which is usually referred to as **maskanda**, a Zulu derivation from the Afrikaans word *musikant* (musician), has undergone a further change. The concertina has mounted a surprising comeback and as a foil to the guitar is now a mandatory part of any group, while urban pop/bubblegum has had an influence through increasing electronic instrumentation in the studio, and the usual bass and drum rhythms modified to disco patterns. The result is a loss of the roughness that generated much of the style's appeal, though some of the newer stars are pretty impressive live. Chief among them are **Phuzekhemisi and Mfaz' Omnyama**, whose shows are dynamic affirmations of maskanda power with line-ups that include up to a dozen vocalists, instrumentalists and dancers. At the same time, veteran producer West Nkosi managed to successfully fatten up their studio sound.

The biggest-selling maskanda album in recent years – and one of the most unusual – was **Vusi Ximba**'s *Siyakudumisa*, a 1992 'comedy' record which used the music as background to lyrics describing situations that had long been a staple of African humour – for instance, the older woman who chases after a much younger man. A subsequent, racier Ximba album was less successful – the conservative Zulu audience rejected it as exceeding the bounds of decency.

Shangaan/Tsonga-Traditional

The first **Shangaan Neo-Traditional** recordings (a language group of the region bordering Mozambique) were made by **Francisco Baloyi** in the early 1950s for Gallo. These contained call-and-response vocals and a circular structure, descending melodic lines and harmonies which sound more African than European together with a distinctly Latin rhythm section made up of a guitar and several percussion instruments.

In the 1950s and '60s **Alexander Jafete** and **Fani Pfumo**, two versatile Mozambiquans who played guitar and mandolin with equal facility, made hundreds of recordings for every studio in Johannesburg. Their work included contributions to many jive/mbaqanga sessions but they also recorded a large number of '**Portuguese Shangaan**' items that mixed those two elements. After 1975, with Mozambique's independence and revolution, and the opening of a Shangaan station by Radio Bantu, Shangaan-Traditional style was largely stripped of its Portuguese components.

The typical line-up of a **modern Tsonga band** ('Tsonga' has replaced 'Shangaan' as the favoured designation since the 1994 elections) features a male vocalist leading a female response chorus, an upfront lead guitar and an electric keyboard or synth, with a bass-and-drums rhythm section pounding out a disco beat. The first prominent group with this new sound was **General MD Shirinda & the Gaza Sisters** in the mid-1970s (one of their songs later became "I Know What You Know" on Paul Simon's *Graceland*). Today, the hottest group playing Tsonga Disco (as it is now labelled) is Tusk Records' **Thomas Chauke & the Shinyori Sisters** – probably the best-selling group in any neo-traditional genre.

The most successful Tsonga artist of all, though, was the late **Peta Teanet** (who died in 1996, allegedly in a car crash). His style was in fact a combination of urban bubblegum-pop and Tsonga lyrics. As in the case of Shirinda and Chauke, he largely owed his popularity to the relentless promotion of Radio Tsonga which, unlike most other former homelands stations, has continued to champion own-language artists.

Soul and Reggae

In the late 1960s, **American soul music** gained an enthusiastic following among black and coloured township teenagers – Wilson Pickett, Booker T and the MGs, and Percy Sledge were especially popular. The local record industry eventually issued hundreds of 45rpm 'seven singles' by local soul outfits sporting names like the Question Marks and the Hurricanes.

Most of this music – typically featuring a Farfisa organ, a spare melodic outline on an electric guitar and a dance rhythm from bass and drums – does not make for inspiring listening. Instrumental performances predominated and where there were vocals, English lyrics were generally preferred to African languages, though they sounded awkward.

In the mid-1970s when imported US disco music became popular, local soul was easily transformed into local **disco**. Recording techniques, and in some instances the level of musicianship, had improved and more sophisticated keyboards came in. The characteristic disco bass lines and drum beat were grafted onto the bottom end but otherwise the other elements of the soul formula remained much the same. All these developments heralded a revolution in taste which profoundly affected every subsequent township music style.

There was also a generation cleavage (the older township residents disliked soul) which the political events of 1976 widened into an abyss. The spontaneous **uprising** of school children against government authority that marked the beginning of the end of apartheid was soon also directed at township parents and grandparents who were accused of selling out to the system. This political judgement was extended to matters of style and taste, including music. Virtually every pre-soul genre was now regarded by the young with suspicion, not merely for being old-fashioned but indicted as a government-sponsored, tribal opiate. The local audience for marabi, sax jives and mqashiyo-style mbaqanga vanished overnight, never to return. It's perhaps surprising to learn that even an internationally renowned band like Mahlathini and the Mahotella Queens are now virtually forgotten in their own country.

The few soul and disco bands that achieved more than ephemeral popularity did so by tampering with the standard musical formulae in some trademark fashion. The most commercially successful were the **Movers**. Discovered and first recorded by Hamilton Nzimande, and then under the tutelage of David Thekwane, their secret was to temper soul with a healthy dose of marabi. The organ remained a prominent part of the foundation, but in addition to the usual chord patterns keyboardist Sankie Chounyane played intelligent, jazzy solos. More importantly, the Movers' sound featured prominent saxes, either grouped as a section or playing extended solo lines. And the band had writing ability: their hundreds of recordings included many strong, original compositions, as well as covers.

The second Important Soul band was the **Soul Brothers**, also discovered by Nzimande, in 1975. The Brothers' most distinguishing characteristic was their two-part, almost quavering vocal harmonies, inspired by certain Shona vocal groups popular in Zimbabwe in the early 1970s. Otherwise, the band's saxophones and their rhythm section were more reminiscent of the later type of electric bass mbaqanga than of archetypal soul.

The Movers' complicated style defied easy imitation and in any event David Thekwane's reputation was enough to make any would-be close imitators somewhat wary. In contrast, the Soul Brothers spawned literally dozens of ephemeral clones, most of whom contented themselves with attempting their vocal style and organ accompaniment. Today the Soul Brothers are regarded as one of the country's oldest groups (although only two remain from the original line-up) and they remain active both in the studio and on tour. Despite a high level of synthesiser saturation, their style is now referred to as mbaqanga, proof positive of the all-encompassing elasticity of that label.

The Cannibals, starring the young guitarist **Ray Phiri** (now famous through recording and performing with Paul Simon), achieved recognition playing instrumentals under their own name and backing various Gallo mqashiyo artists such as Irene Mawela and the Mahotella Queens. In 1975, the band was paired with Jacob 'Mparanyana' Radebe, probably the single finest male vocalist of the soul-disco era. Four years of recordings followed (until Radebe's death in 1979) under the name **Mparanyana and the Cannibals**, and the best of these, featuring Radebe's impassioned vocals and monologues together with a sharply produced backing of hot guitar, saxes and female choruses, invite favourable comparisons with Otis Redding's similar-sounding Stax material. The Cannibals eventually evolved into **Stimela** in the 1980s, updating their style with more contemporary Afro-jazz soul and funk influences.

An oddball soul band of the early 1970s was the **Flames** who exclusively covered American soul and mainstream pop. They were something of an anomaly: they had a multi-racial following; the band members were coloured, not black; they were based in Durban not Johannesburg; and generally recorded albums rather than singles. Two members, Steve Fataar and Blondie Chaplin, emigrated to the US and joined the Beach Boys in 1972.

Their demise created an opening for another local band that could convincingly interpret American-style funk, soul and pop music for a young African-to-white audience. Selby Ntuli, Sipho Mabuse and Alec Khaoli got together as the Beaters, then renamed the band **Harari** after a successful tour of Zimbabwe. After returning to South Africa, they began to draw almost exclusively on overseas rock influences. In fact, the only distinctively South African element was linguistic, as they featured lyrics in Zulu and Sotho as well as English. It proved very successful, nonetheless, and, with the band's ethnic designer-chic, attracted a big multi-racial following.

After Ntuli's death in 1979, the Mabuse-Khaoli partnership dissolved and both musicians pursued separate careers. **Sipho 'Hotstix' Mabuse** reached local superstar status in the later 1980s with huge hits like "Burnout" and "Jive Soweto" (the latter featuring West Nkosi on sax) which finally achieved a seamless, totally South African, synthesis of mbaqanga, pop and soul.

Reggae also took root in South Africa, as elsewhere in Africa, following Bob Marley's famous concert celebrating the independence of Zimbabwe in 1980. Its chief exponent was local dread **Lucky Dube**, who started out playing mbaqanga music in the 1970s but switched to reggae in 1984, adopting a style modelled closely on the Wailers' Peter Tosh. His 1990 album, Slave, sold over 500,000 copies in South Africa alone – one of the country's biggest-selling records of all time – and he followed it with further successes in the early part of the decade. As Jamaican music moved into digital and ragga mode, however, Dube (and African reggae generally) was somewhat left behind. The influence of ragga, instead, fed into the township's take on hip-hop in the late 1990s – *kwaito* – of which more on p.652.

Bubblegum

The development of township music from the mid-1980s to the mid-1990s saw the ascendency of a slickly produced brand of African pop referred to by its fans and detractors alike as **bubblegum**. In certain respects, bubblegum was basically an indigenous style – more vocal than instrumental, with the vocals arranged as overlapping call-and-response patterns where one short melodic phrase is repeated in traditional fashion. In others, it reflected the culmination of more contemporary tendencies. The modern love affair with electronic keyboards now triumphed completely; bubblegum was awash with synthesisers and even the modified disco beat which propelled the music was usually produced by an electronic drum box. Saxophones were rarely heard while the guitar fell completely out of favour.

The longest-running success story in the genre has been vocalist **Dan Tshanda**. Beginning with his first group, **Splash**, Tshanda assumed total creative control as a composer-producer and then went on to develop a number of equally popular spin-offs including the Dalom Kids, Patricia Majalisa and Matshikos, whose recordings still sell in quantities. Another long-running star is **Sello 'Chicco' Twala**, who like Tshanda is an all-round vocalist, instrumentalist, arranger, composer and producer. One of his biggest hits, "We Miss You Manelo", was a coded tribute to the then-imprisoned Nelson Mandela. A later piece of political commentary which also became a hit, "Papa Stop The War", resulted from a collaboration with **Mzwakhe Mbuli**, where the almost hypnotic spoken cadences of the 'people's poet' (currently and controversially in jail for armed robbery) were set against Chicco's collage of synth textures and backing vocals. Today, however, Chicco has virtually retired from performing and recording to concentrate on producing other talents for his own studio and record label.

Chicco contributed in the late 1980s to the success of 'The Princess Of Africa', **Yvonne Chaka Chaka**. "I'm In Love With A DJ", her first single in 1984, was one of the first big bubblegum hits and launched a career that produced a string of gold and platinum discs. Chaka Chaka's belting alto voice with its distinctive timbre accounts for much of her popularity, but her success is also due to her unusually well-crafted and arranged material. Her songs are usually built on two catchy interlocking melodies, and the lyrics – which are almost always in English – are nicely phrased and convey real meaning. She has become South Africa's most successful export to the rest of Africa since Ladysmith Black Mambazo.

Yvonne Chaka Chaka

detoxification personally, and then put her back in the studio. The result was *Memeza*, the year's best-selling local album by a considerable margin. Further notice of her rehabilitation was provided by her presence as a featured performer at Thabo Mbeki's 1999 Inauguration bash in Pretoria. She looks set to remain a fixture in South Africa's musical life for some time to come.

Another leading 1990s artist − carving out a post-bubblegum pop − is **Jabu Khanyile** with his group **Bayete**. Their 1994 album, *Mmalo-we*, was a beautiful showcase for Jabu's gentle, lilting voice and Bayete's funky Afro-jazz feel. In 1995 he developed his style further with *Umkhaya-lo*, his best album to date. Recently in his live work, Khanyile has shown signs of influence from the various Congolese resident bands in Johannesburg and one can only hope that his future recorded output will reflect this too.

Happy to be developing his Xhosa musical roots is **Ringo**, current heart-throb and star. His lyrics are often intensely and poetically romantic, perfectly complementing the clear-headed conviction of his vocal delivery. His band is good too, especially guitarist Lawrence Matshiza, whose performance on the hit single "Isiphithi-pithi" from the 1996 album *Vukani'* is particularly outstanding. Ringo's follow-up album *Sondelani* was far more richly produced but still deeply Xhosa, drawing on traditions of love poetry and praise singing and recasting them as staples of the dancefloor and the home hi-fi.

While cassette piracy makes sales figures an unreliable gauge, the wildly enthusiastic reception Chaka Chaka has received in countries as far afield as Congo and Uganda testifies to a dedicated following. However, in 1997, she recorded her finest album to date, *Bombani*, and, significantly, sales in the UK and Europe outstripped those in South Africa, pointing to the increasing gulf between the tastes of younger township music fans and African music consumers overseas.

Chaka Chaka's big rival in bubblegum has been **Brenda Fassi**, whose appeal is difficult to pin down − though she has a talent for self-promotion that would do credit to Madonna (a figure with whom she's frequently compared). Her songs can seem a barely comprehensible mish-mash of the latest township lingo but they have that quality of sticking in the minds of her listeners. She went huge in 1993, when *Amagents* was that year's best selling local album, and then had some uncertain years associated more with scandals than musical accomplishments. However in 1998 her friend, producer-composer Chicco Twala, decided to oversee her

Brenda Fassi

White South African Music

The major influences on modern **Afrikaans music** – as with Black South African music – have been American. While Afrikaans musical roots lie with Dutch and French sources, **hillbilly string bands** added the final ingredients to a concertina-led brand of dance music which began to be recorded in the early 1930s. Within the Afrikaner community there was also a decided predilection for imitating the most mawkish and maudlin elements of American **country music**. In the 1930s a legion of melancholic duos and trios specialised in *trane trekkers* (tear jerkers) and the same sentimental tendency was still very much in evidence among a later generation of artists influenced by the American Jim Reeves (massively popular amongst Afrikaners). There are, of course, clear parallels between the experiences of Afrikaners and whites in the American south.

The growing nationalist fervor of Afrikanerdom after World War I revealed a class-based musical fault line. The audience that preferred concertina dances and trane trekkers was agrarian or urban working class. In contrast, most Afrikaner nationalists came from a more educated, middle-class background, with musical prejudices fashioned by European culture. Traditional melodies were championed as the true voice of the 'volk' but were acceptable only if rendered in 'serious' performance.

The musician who dominated the post-war years was accordionist **Nico Carstens** with his lightly swinging dance music. The trend thereafter was to incorporate MOR sounds, then later in the 1970s, Eurobeat. Afrikaans music lost much of its distinctiveness in the process, as well as most of its young audience, who – like the English-speaking whites – increasingly preferred European pop and rock.

For most of the l980s and early '90s, although there was a small, somewhat subversive 'alternative' movement fostered by musicians such as **Johannes Kerkorral** (and his Gereformeerde Blues Band), **Koos Kombuis** and **Anton Goosen**, the general state of the music was exemplified by the most – indeed almost the only – commercially successful Afrikaans entertainer of the day, **Bles Bridges**, a Wayne Newton imitator whose trademark was throwing plastic roses at his predominantly middle-aged female audiences.

Since the 1994 elections, Afrikaans music has undergone something of a revival. The shock of losing political power has led to a grave concern that the language and culture of the Afrikaner is going to wither away and die unless concerted efforts are made to preserve them. A new crop of young Afrikaans artists is currently enjoying commercial support from their community for the first time in many years. They include **traditional boeremusiek** revivalists, closely associated with Afrikaner right-wing politics, and all-acoustic, traditional Afrikaans *orkes* such as **Oudag Boereorkes** who have recorded several albums and occasionally appear at overseas festivals. For the most part, though, Afrikaans music is stylistically conservative and continues to be based on MOR, pop, or modern country models from overseas.

One very different strand is represented by Manchester-born **Johnny Clegg**, who began performing Zulu-Traditional material with **Sipho Mchunu** in the early 1970s, then later expanded into a full electric band format as **Juluka**. The increasingly Westernised sound eventually led to Mchunu's departure and the band dissolved to be replaced by a new line-up called **Savuka**. Clegg has enjoyed major success in France as 'Le Zoulou Blanc', and a more limited popularity in the UK and America. While much of his music sounds predominantly Western, and his group's image remains highly dependent on their energetic Zulu dance routines, there's no denying Clegg's commitment to freedom during the darkest days of apartheid, when his open embrace of African culture was an audacious statement.

RALPH RESNIK/SAFARI RECORDS

Sipho Mchunu and Johnny Clegg

New Deals and Kwaito: South Africa's Hip-Hop

The 1994 free elections marked a turning point in South African history that not only saw the end of apartheid but ushered in far-reaching social and cultural changes. The state broadcasting monopoly fell away with the licensing of 14 new commercial radio stations and 86 new community stations, as well as the inauguration of **etv**, the country's first commercial, free-to-air, television channel. This new media policy has been accompanied by a quota system that guarantees a certain amount of airtime is devoted to South African music.

At the same time, the end of the near-monopoly situation in the music industry has brought increased recording opportunities for local artists. Several major international labels who formerly distributed their material through licensing proxies for fear of being accused of 'doing business with apartheid' have now returned to set up local offices, and a number of independent labels have entered the market.

While international product outsells local material by more than four to one, there is now a prouder mindset regarding home-originated music that would have been unimaginable a few short years ago during the era of boycotts and cultural isolation. However, this is not all good news for the old guard. After the 1994 elections, music in the townships underwent another of its periodic stylistic shifts. Bubblegum lost much of its popularity, particularly with township youth, who turned to new black musical styles from the Americas, including rap, hip-hop and Jamaican ragga.

A Cape Town-based group, **Prophets Of Da City**, successfully adapted Public Enemy-inspired rap to comment on the social and political upheavals in the period leading up to the l994 elections, while using locally recorded samples to give their material a South African flavour. The Prophets have gone on to develop their style, increasingly rapping in the Afrikaans dialects of the Cape Flats, which guarantees them a rapturous reception among the coloured community at home around the Cape, but has alienated potential African fans who still balk at anything in Afrikaans, no matter how good it is.

Apart from the Prophets, relatively few township artists have taken up undiluted US-style rap and hip-hop even though the American imports continue to get considerable radio airplay. Instead, a new style called **kwaito** or **d'gong** has evolved to become the music embraced by young urban Africans as their own. Melodically and harmonically, kwaito is often rather spare – many songs are made up of a single short phrase of township slang which is chanted over and over in unison by four or five vocalists – but in some cases, an R&B touch gives the mix a more tuneful quality.

Kwaito instrumental accompaniments are always electronically generated and the groups use backing tapes when performing live. As with bubblegum, synthesisers are used, but usually not so prominently; in kwaito, it is the drum'n'bass lines that get the emphasis. The style's rhythmic underpinning – a never-failing dance floor magnet that goes straight for the pelvis – is called **slow jam**. It originated when local DJs at township street bashes began slowing down the tempo of US Chicago House recordings by artists such as Robert Owen, The Fingers and Tony Humphries and found that young Africans – unlike the mostly white rave crowd – responded positively to the new beat.

As a social and cultural phenomenon, kwaito probably exceeds the sum of its musical parts. It's South Africa's first post-apartheid musical genre and for that reason alone it has injected, for the first time in many years, a feeling of real excitement into the township music scene. A pantheon of new kwaito stars has emerged – **Boom Shaka**, **M'du**, **Bongo Maffin**, and **Trompies** are among the hottest current acts – on which the press, radio (most notably FM in Johannesburg, the most successful new commercial station in the country) and television have lavished great attention.

Kwaito has made live music once again hugely fashionable among township audiences after the years of unrest when many venues for African music were systematically destroyed or disrupted. Kwaito gigs are normally peaceful, friendly affairs. The crowd – which is invariably 99 percent black and mostly teenage – simply wants to be entertained by their favourite artists and to enjoy themselves. There's a notable and refreshing lack of the aggression which was a constant feature at the bubblegum megabashes of the late-1980s – another small symptom of what happens in a country where people feel liberated, no matter how incomplete the process.

Without live musicians to hold audience attention, kwaito artists compensate with seamless sequences of classically South African dance steps – oddly fussy, with large doses of nifty syncopated footwork, plus the kwaito spice of pelvic grind and a quirky range of gestures inventively adapted from the arm-waving lexicon of American rap. The crowds love it and their response is often far more eye-catching than the stage performance, as posses form circles and each member takes turns leaping into the middle to impress the rest with some outrageous new dance move.

Kwaito music often provides an interesting insight into the attitudes and aspirations of the first post-struggle African generation. One 1997 hit was "Amalawyer" by **S'Bu**, reflecting the new-found passion amongst township youth to make their money in the legal profession – an appropriate choice in a country where the president is an ex-lawyer and where there is a brand-new constitution full of provisions just begging to be tested in court. Another big kwaito hit was "Don't Call Me Kaffir" by **Arthur** (full name, Arthur Mofakate), who perhaps more than any other single artist deserves credit for creating and popularising the genre. Despite what one might have expected, the word kaffir is very much alive in South Africa, and is still routinely hurled at black people by racist whites, particularly in the small towns where change has been slow to arrive. The song encourages those insulted to talk back, reflecting the willingness of young Africans to cast aside the fear of older generations.

There is no doubt that kwaito has profoundly alienated several generations of older Africans – who are often heard to ask despairingly: 'What has happened to our music?' – but as with any youth culture, parental disapproval probably enhances the music's appeal. Kwaito is regularly assailed by township elders for its often lascivious lyrical content and is also cited as further evidence that the young are jettisoning African culture and customs, a condemnation that is not entirely unjustified. Yet, though many listeners will dismiss kwaito as just another example of the ubiquitous techno/hip-hop music heard everywhere in the world today, perhaps – as has happened many times before – a more South African-sounding hybrid will eventually emerge.

In the meantime, let's hope that commercial pressures and industry neglect do not kill off entirely all the unique local styles. Fortunately, the overseas market tends to come to the rescue here, because it is precisely those endangered genres that appeal to foreign audiences who want to hear music that is identifiably South African. Stalwarts like **Ladysmith Black Mambazo** and **Mahlathini** (until his death in 1999) or more recently, artists such as **Vusi Mahlasela** (a township balladeer heavily influenced by the commercial folk style of Paul Simon) and the **Soweto String Quartet** (who play urban African melodies in a classical manner) will continue to maintain a variety of South African styles as living traditions on foreign stages even while being ignored by the younger generation at home.

discography

Many of these releases are Gallo recordings issued in South Africa either by Gallo Record Company itself or by Polygram South Africa's Teal subsidiary. However, some are also available on the labels of overseas licensees – usually BMG (UK), Celluloid (France) or Shanachie (US).

Compilations

 From Marabi to Disco
(Gallo, South Africa).

A one-stop compendium of the history of urban township music as it developed in South Africa from the late 1930s to the early '80s. Every major genre is illustrated with original, long-unavailable recordings of the most famous artists (as well as a few who have dropped off into an undeserved obscurity). Treat it as a mini-encyclopedia and read the notes, or just sit back, listen and enjoy. Twenty-eight tracks and every one a classic!

The Heartbeat of Soweto (Shanachie, US).

Misleading title for a collection of fairly recent examples of Zulu-, Shangaan- and Tsonga Traditional styles.

 A Taste of The Indestructible Beat of Soweto
(Earthworks, UK).

This is a sampler compiled from the first five volumes of the *Indestructible Beat of Soweto* series, which highlights over fifty great tracks from the 1980s, mixing later-phase mbaqanga, some soul and even the more urbanised of the neo-traditional genres. As label chief and compiler Trevor Herman writes, 'best heard loud and standing up'.

The Indestructible Beat of Soweto Vol. 6: South African Rhythm Riot (Earthworks, UK).

This new collection features mbaqanga-jive, maskanda and kwaito, with Brenda Fassi's huge 1999 hit "Vuli Ndlela", hard-core trad Zulu maskanda from Ihashi Elimhlophe; kwaito king Arthur Mofakate's biggest hit "Oyi Oyi"; plus gospel songs, mbaqanga-jivestars Chicco, Mahlathini and the Mahotella Queens, the Soul Brothers and more.

Jackpot 15,000 and **Jackpot 16,000**
(Gallo, South Africa).

Two cassette compilations of classic 1960s and '70s hit singles from producer Hamilton Nzimande's roster of sax and accordion jive.

SOUTH AFRICA

The Kings and Queens of Township Jive
(Earthworks, UK).

A showcase of some of the big names in township music from the 1970s.

Kwaito Hits (EMI, South Africa).

Here's as good an introduction as any to the latest musical style of the townships. Its heavily loaded with material written, performed or produced by kwaito main man Arthur Mafokate including his "Oyi! Oyi!", voted the 'Best Song Of The Year 1997' at the prestigious FNB South African Music Awards.

Mbube Roots (Rounder, US).

A wonderful survey covering the history of mbube and early iSulu a cappella or iscathamiya.

Music of the !Kung Bushmen
(Smithsonian Folkways, US).

The most accessible example of the music made by southern Africa's pre-Bantu inhabitants.

The Rough Guide to The Music of South Africa
(World Music Network, UK).

An essential collection ranging from Ladysmith Black Mambazo to West Nkosi; from the Boyoyo Boys to Bheki Mseleku; from Noise Khanyile to Yvonne Chaka Chaka and back to the Elite Swingsters. Miriam Makeba is here, as is Lucky Dube and half a dozen other bands and artists. There's even a track by Solomon Linda's Original Evening Birds singing the magical thing called "Mbube", a song with its own career that led to global fame as "Wimoweh" and "The Lion Sleeps Tonight".

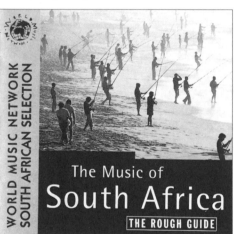

Singing in an Open Space (Rounder, US).

The only neo-traditional historical survey, charting two decades of development of Zulu-Trad from simple acoustic guitar accompaniment to a full band format.

Siya Hamba! 1950s South African Country & Small Town Sounds (Original Music, US).

A mix of neo-traditional (even a Pedi autoharp!) and early township jive, recorded by musicologist Hugh Tracey.

Yizo Yizo (Ghetto Ruff, South Africa).

A one stop survey of the 'indie' side of the current kwaito music scene. The tracks, which feature groups like Skeem, O'Da Meesta and Ghetto Luv, come out of the controversial

Yizo Yizo TV series, the first in South Africa to realistically portray contemporary township life from a youth perspective. The massive popularity of the show boosted the sales of this cutting edge compilation well into multi-platinum status.

Zulu Jive: Umbaqanga
(Earthworks, UK; Carthage, US).

Pacey selection of cuts re-released from 1983 of urban soul-style mbaqanga from Joshua Sithole, more traditional pounding from Aaron Mbambo and Shoba, and accordion/guitar jive from Sithole's backing band The Rainbows.

Artists

Amampondo

This impressive 'back to the roots' group draws its inspiration from a multitude of indigenous styles, both instrumental and vocal, from all over southern Africa.

Drums For Tomorrow (M.E.L.T. 2000, UK).

At last, a magnificently produced showcase of Amampondo's diverse musicality that manages to overcome the inadequate recording technique that plagued the group's earlier albums.

The Boyoyo Boys

The Boyoyo Boys were a classic all-male, vocal mbaqanga group. It was their song "Puleng" that inspired Malcolm McLaren's hit "Double Dutch".

Back in Town (Rounder, US).

This later recording was made long after the Boyoyo Boys' prime but it is still fun to listen to.

Reuben Caluza's Double Quartet

Reuben Caluza was one of the first South Africans to meld local and American vocal styles into a new secular composite called 'ragtime' (absolutely no relation to the American piano-based style) that anticipated the later development of mbube and zulu a cappella or iscathamiya.

1930s – African Ragtime (Heritage, UK).

This album provides a good cross-section of Caluza's landmark 1930 London recordings and comes with translations and excellent notes by Veit Erlmann.

Yvonne Chaka Chaka

Chaka Chaka, the self-styled 'Princess Of Africa', is one of the finest and most popular vocalists to come out of the bubblegum genre. Her songs are built around melodies and arrangements which are usually far more interesting and compelling, at least to a Western ear, than those found in most bubblegum material.

The Best of Yvonne Chaka Chaka
(Teal-Polygram, South Africa).

This album features all of Yvonne's biggest hits including "I'm In Love With A DJ", "Umqombothi" and "Motherland".

Bombani (Teal-Polygram, South Africa).

Chaka Chaka's latest offering laces local township pop with Afro-Pop influences to wonderful effect (a sensible decision given her popularity in central and east Africa).

Chicco

Sello 'Chicco' Twala, has been one of the biggest names

in bubblegum through the 1990s, and a talent equally adept at singing, composing, or producing.

 The Best of Chicco (Teal-Polygram, South Africa).

A compendium of Chicco's most popular recordings including, "We Miss You Manelo", his paean to the then-imprisoned Nelson Mandela.

Lucky Dube

Lucky Dube won African and global attention as a reggae star with his early 1990s albums, Slave and Prisoner, which were South Africa's topselling discs of the decade. He started out in a mbaqanga group.

 Prisoner (Shanachie, US).

This 1991 album – still Dube's best – is a kind of homage to Peter Tosh in its vocal style and Wailers-era arrangements. But the rasta message of liberation and suffering gained new currency in a South African context.

Brenda Fassi

Vocalist Brenda Fassi has been a fixture of the township music scene ever since her arrival in 1984 as one of the stars of then new bubblegum style. Her popularity continues, unaffected if not actually enhanced, by various high life scandals.

 Memeza (CCP, South Africa).

Brenda's comeback album was written and produced with her old associate, Chicco Twala, and is well sung, nicely arranged and, for Brenda, unusually melodic. Furthermore, it was the best-selling South African album of 1998!

Bayete and Jabu Khanyile

Jabu Khanyile and his group Bayete found fame in 1994 with his attractive lisping growl on the glorious hit "Mmalo-we". The drummer and singer presents himself as the face of World Music from South Africa – whacking out a powerful, confident mix of township jive and other African sounds, especially Congolese.

 Mmalo-we (Mango, UK).

A strong selection of dance hits and ballads from the gentle Jabu, with Bayete on cracking form, effortlessly exploring a fine selection of Afro-Jazz riffs. It kicks off with the hit song.

 Africa Unite (Mango, UK).

Mellow backing singers and an innovative instrumental line-up – including kora, harp, violin and Cuban *tres* (a small guitar with three pairs of strings).

Ladysmith Black Mambazo

The soaring a cappella harmonies of this dozen-strong Zulu male choir were propelled by Paul Simon's Gracelands album into the international limelight, putting their iscathamiya style on the World Music map. They have recorded dozens of albums of their own: the three below serve nicely as ports of entry to a recording career as it has evolved over almost three decades.

 Iscathamiya (Gallo, South Africa).

Don't let the cover put you off – this is a fine survey, with properly re-mastered sound, of the group's early successes of the 1970s.

 Shaka Zulu (Warners, US).

Produced by Paul Simon with a first-class recording budget,

this disc best captures the group's lush harmonies. Perhaps not surprisingly, it is their biggest-selling album.

 Heavenly (Gallo, South Africa).

The most recent developments in Ladysmith's increasingly internationalised career are reflected in this album which sees the group melding African-American soul and gospel and even a Bob Dylan standard with their own unique vocal style. Various US guest stars include Dolly Parton and Lou Rawls.

Mahlathini and the Mahotella Queens

The combination of Simon 'Mahlathini' Nkabinde's groaning bass and the exquisite female harmonies of the Mahotella Queens, backed by the all-electric Makhona Tsohle Band, forged the template for vocal mbaqanga, one of the characteristic styles of the townships for almost two decades. Nkabinde died in 1999.

 Young Mahlathini: Classic Recordings With The Mahotella Queens 1964–71 (Gallo, South Africa).

All the greatest hits of the band which was the contemporary equivalent to the Beatles in a South African township context.

 The Best Of Mahlathini And The Mahotella Queens (Gallo, South Africa; BMG, UK).

A fine selection of highlights culled from later albums recorded after the band reformed in the late 1980s and began touring the world.

Simon Mahlathini Nkabinde - groaning superstar

Izintombi Zezi Manje Manje

This Mqashiyo vocal group started up in the late 1960s as Hamilton Nzimande's answer to the Mahotella Queens and eventually managed to overtake them in the popularity stakes in the 1970s.

 Isitha Sami Nguwe (Gallo, South Africa).

This compilation made up from material originally issued on vinyl singles is one of seven available; all of them have their moments, but this is the one to go for first.

Mzwakhe Mbuli

Mbuili, 'The People's Poet', emerged on the ANC scene in 1981, with poetry recitals at activists' funerals, and he went on to embody the spirit of resistance in countless appearances at mass rallies as well as on record. Performing at President Mandela's inauguration was the highlight of his career, but Mzwakhe is currently serving a 12-year jail term, accused of armed robbery.

 Resistance is Defence (Earthworks, UK).
 UMzwakhe Ubonga UJehovah (EMI, South Africa).

A pair of albums tracing Mzwakhe's musical development, from the fiery political commentary of Resistance is Defence to the gospel music of his latest album. The poetry is all set to stirring, if sometimes over-formulaic, mbaqanga beats.

Sipho Mabuse

Soul artists Sipho 'Hotstix' Mabuse – a vocalist, composer and multi-instrumentalist – first tasted fame as a member of the Beaters and Harari before becoming a local solo superstar in the 1980s.

⊚ **The Best of Sipho Mabuse** (Gallo, South Africa).

Mabuse's two essential hits "Jive Soweto" and "Burn Out" are nicely packaged on this ten-track compilation.

Madosini

Madosini Manquina, known as 'The Veteran' in the area of Mpondoland-Transkei from which she hails and more recently as the 'Queen Of Xhosa Music', is an entrancing (literally) vocalist who accompanies herself on several indigenous instruments.

⊚ **Power To The Women** (M.E.L.T. 2000, UK).

After making a few great but obscure recordings in the mid-1970s, Madosini disappeared into the Transkei only to be rediscovered by Robert Trunz of Melt 2000 who proceeded to showcase her artistry with sympathetic and imaginative production techniques, a leap of musical (and financial) faith that could only have occurred with a non-South African record label. The result is a wonderful exposition of tradition enhanced by technology.

Vusi Mahlasela

Sweet-voiced Vusi Mahlasela, who cites Paul Simon as a major influence, mixes township influences with the commercial end of American folk music. The resulting mixture is an Afro-pop style which has proved to be especially popular with European audiences.

⊚ **Silang Mabele** (BMG, South Africa).

A mellow and soulful collection that is just muscular enough to escape an MOR classification. Mahlasela's version of 'Weeping'', a song written in the depths of the 1980s by local white band Bright Blue, is an especially affecting performance.

Makhendlas

Kwaito star Oupa 'Makhendlas' Mafokate was born in Diepkloof, Soweto, and released his first solo album in 1996. Jammer, his third album, was his first big hit but he died in tragic circumstances in November 1998, first shooting an aggressive fan backstage at a concert, and then turning the gun on himself.

⊚ **Jammer** (EMI, South Africa).

A disc that features the massive hit "Ayeye Aho", which catapulted the natty-dressing Makhendlas to a spell in the kwaito limelight in 1998.

Spokes Mashiyane

Spokes Mashiyane was the first and probably the most famous pennywhistle jive star.

⊚ **King Kwela** (Gallo, South Africa).

This is a re-issue of a classic 1958 Trutone LP originally produced for the White teenage market featuring Spokes' most popular early recordings (including his first hit, "Ace Blues") as first issued on 78s for the African trade.

Busi Mhlongo

Victoria 'Busi' Mhlongo began her professional career in Durban in the early 1960s as the teenage lead singer for a vocal jive group. She later relocated to Johannesburg and established herself as a jazz vocalist – her repertoire included both American standards and African Jazz – before finally setting out for Europe where she has lived and performed for the last 25 or so years.

 Urbanzulu
(M.E.L.T. 2000, UK).

The musical centre of this album is the (near) exclusively all-male *maskanda* genre. Here Mhlongo returns to her Zulu roots and stakes out the territory for her gender with an awesome display of intense vocal pyrotechnics, aided and abetted by Melt 2000's usual superlative production values.

The Movers

The Movers played a combination of local soul and African Jazz and sold more records in the process than any other South African band of the 1970s.

⊚ **The Best of the Best Vol 1 and Vol 2**
(Teal-Polygram, South Africa).

All the Movers' biggest hits and huge sellers on a couple of strong compilations. Vol 2 is worth getting just for the wonderful track "Soweto Inn" with vocalist Sophie Thapedi.

Mpharanyana

Jacob 'Mpharanyana' Radebe was the finest township soul singer of the 1970s, and became a legend, dying young at the height of his career.

▦ **Burning Soul** (Teal-Polygram, South Africa).

A nice introduction to some of the many great Mpharanyana recordings. The vocalist was usually backed by one of two fine bands, the Peddlars and the Cannibals (the latter with a young Ray Phiri on guitar), and many tracks feature cracking production work by West Nkosi.

West Nkosi

West Nkosi, who died in 1998, is remembered today as an ace producer but he began his career in the l960s and '70s as one of the most successful sax jive artists.

◎ **Rhythm of Healing: Supreme Sax and Pennywhistle Jive** (Earthworks, UK).

This collection of West Nkosi's biggest hits will not only serve as a great introduction to sax jives, the single most popular African genre of the 1960s and '70s, but is also guaranteed to get any dance floor hopping.

Phuzekhemisi

Phuzekhemisi is one of the most successful of the current crop of artists in the maskanda field.

◎ **Ngo '49** (Gallo, South Africa).

This stomping album produced by West Nkosi manages to overcome the over-progammed studio sound that bedevils so many of the newer recordings of this genre.

Ringo

Ringo Madlingozi is a contemporary of the 1980s bubblegummers, who possesses a great tenor voice with a timbre and phrasing that recalls the late great jazz singer, Victor Ndlazilwane. He's a fine composer, too, and his records are surprisingly popular with the younger kwaito crowd, not to mention an older audience more attuned to singing as opposed to rapping or unison chanting.

◎ **Sondelani** (CCP, South Africa).

This very successful album actually begins to run out of steam at about the halfway mark but its still worth getting just for the first six songs which are both melodic and memorable, especially the third track, "Sondela".

S'Bu

Born and bred in Soweto, S'bu is one of legendary producer Sello 'Chicco' Twala's kwaito protégés. He first found recording success with Mdu in the group Mashamplani, but they soon split. After this, S'bu recorded his monster hit "Amalawyer". A follow-up album is expected shortly.

◎ **Amalawyer** (Polygram, South Africa).

Featuring the catchy hit single of the same name, which reveals a more textured, heavy production than the tinny kwaito cuts of the mid-1990s.

Paul Simon

Paul Simon wrote himself into South African music history when he extended a collaborative hand to some of the country's African musicians during the darkest days of apartheid and opened the door on the rest of the world.

◎ **Graceland** (Warner Brothers, UK/US).

Simply too good after all these years, and musically too interesting, to omit. Features alongside large measures of Simon, the Boyoyo Boys, Baghiti Khumalo, General Shirinda and the Gaza Sisters, Ray Phiri and, of course, Ladysmith Black Mambazo.

Skeleton

Skeleton are a real roots maskanda group from Durban. Ther lead singer, Themba Ngubane, lives in one room in a hostel with his wife and nine children, has a job in a fast-food restaurant and puts up with a violent environment which brings him few opportunities to play.

◎ **Skeleton** (M.E.L.T. 2000, UK).

One of this energetic label's most accessible new releases. Pumping tracks of *maskanda* – the hard, dance beat sound of modern-traditional Zulu – surge with power and added animation from MELT labelmates Busi Mhlongo and Mabi Thobejane.

Soul Brothers

The Soul Brothers are both the longest surviving and most influential band to come out of the South African soul genre although as time went on their style was increasingly lashed with generous dollops of straight mbaqanga.

▣ **Mantombanzane** (Gallo, South Africa).

Their classic, early sound, culled from the glory days of producer Hamilton Nzimande in the 1970s.

◎ **Jive Explosion** (Earthworks, UK).

A great survey of the band's recordings from the early 1990s, full of characteristic swirling organs, sax riffs and sweet vocal harmonies.

Ma Willies

Ma Willies, aka William Bongani Makhubela, shot to fame with his 1997 kwaito release, Intwenjani, which has sold over 110,000 copies, but he has struggled to match his success since then.

◎ **Intwenjani** (Sony, South Africa).

Produced by Arthur's main rival Mdu and a perfect example of kwaito's infectious, though essentially throw-away sounds.

South Africa | Gospel music

spirit of africa

Gospel is among the best-selling music in contemporary South Africa, sustained by the millions of church goers who prefer religion to have rhythm and soul. The country's choirs have become a mainstay on the European festival circuit, and have exerted a major influence throughout African gospel music. **Gregory Mthembu-Salter** stands up.

With gospel music the **voice** is all-important; it soars to the heavens and descends to the deepest miseries of the human condition. South Africa's gospel music draws on diverse traditions. Listeners from abroad will instantly pick up on the American influences of much of the output. Pentecostal churches from the US have made a big impact in South Africa and have large followings. In addition, American gospel music is a staple in the media, just like its secular musical counterparts.

However, the African influences still render South Africa's gospel music unique. This is particularly the case with the **Zionist churches**, which have been fiercely independent since the beginning of the twentieth century and have consciously incorporated African traditions into their rituals and music. To check the recorded sound, whose chord structures seem strange and mournful to the unaccustomed ear, look out for pictures on album covers of large numbers of people dressed in white robes with brightly coloured sashes with their leader in the middle in some suitably religious pose. Best of all, aim to see the Zionists in action, standing under trees in city parks, especially in Johannesburg for hours on end on a Sunday, letting the world know in no uncertain terms how they feel about Jesus.

Star Voices

Among the frankly astonishing number of artists with a talent for gospel music in South Africa, the reigning queen is **Rebecca Malope**. Her releases routinely go platinum, each one filled with instant anthems craftily conceived by master-mind producer **Sizwe Zako** and belted out by the diminutive star. For many, Malope's finest effort was *Shwele Baba* in 1995 which featured the usual strong songs but real musicians too, who have been a bit too absent from her most recent recordings.

There are signs however, that gospel fans are hankering after a slightly less commercial sound, and Rebecca's 1998 release *Somlandela* was outsold in many places by the brilliant **Lusanda Spiritual Group**'s last album, *Ungababek'ityala*. Powered by Eastern Cape lead singer Lusanda Mcinga this group has a deceptively sophisticated and intensely moving sound – check out especially their elegantly sombre version of "Nkosi Sikelele".

Also hugely popular over the last few years have been the amply numbered **IPCC**, a Pentecostal choir who had their biggest success with the 1996 release *Uthembekile*, and **Amadodana Ase Wesile**, a portly choir of Methodist stalwarts, always dressed in dark suits and red waistcoats, who keep time by thumping a Bible as they intone their hymns of righteousness. Recordings sadly lack the mischievous humour with which they leaven their message in the flesh.

While Malope is Sizwe Zako's biggest star, others in his stable have also made lasting names for themselves. **Vuyo Mokoena** got his big break with Rebecca Malope and has featured on most of her recent albums, but really came to prominence in 1997 with a vintage Zako-style stirring anthem entitled "Njalo!".

Much of the best output of **Ladysmith Black Mambazo** (see p.645) is gospel, invariably beautifully crafted odes of praise with characteristic additions of aptly chosen Zulu proverbs. There is usually at least one of these in the increasing number of South African gospel music compilations aimed at the overseas market, like the excellent 1998 release *Gospel Spirit of Africa*.

The version of "Nkosi Sikelele" on *Gospel Spirit of Africa*, performed by the **Imilonji Kantu Choral Society** is a good example of the more classical choral style popular among an older generation of gospel fans, many of whom are themselves in such choirs. The choirs performing this style are usually massive, and the 'Nation-building concerts', sponsored by oil-multinational Caltex, which take place around the country, are fantastically well-attended, colourful, splurging musical celebrations. Choirs perform a mixture of self-composed and European classical works accompanied by philharmonic orchestras.

One classically trained singer who has made a big impact recently is **Sibongile Khumalo**. Her repertoire encompasses opera and choral works and now embraces South African folk and jazz, most of which is on ample display on the excellent and self-produced *Live at the Market Theatre*.

Live Witness

Despite the enormous number of gospel recordings of every style, most gospel still goes unrecorded for lack of opportunity. Yet every township and rural area has countless choirs, groups and soloists, many of whom are powerful and moving beyond belief. **Live performances**, whether in a church, a night vigil, or simply in someone's back yard, are a rich and unforgettable part of South African cultural life, providing important clues about the sources of its people's justly legendary resilience and forbearance.

discography

For artists such as Ladysmith Black Mambazo, see also the South African pop music discography on pp.653–657.

Compilations

 Gospel Spirit of Africa
(Gallo, South Africa).

This excellent gospel compilation ranges from Ladysmith Black Mambazo to a variety of lesser-known artists, many with a strong Zionist influence, including the Leeukop Prison Choir and their wonderful rendition of Rebecca Malope's "Moya Wami".

Joyous Celebration (Sony, South Africa).

Another fine compilation, mainly of artists from Pentecostal backgrounds. Although a number of contributions are heavily American influenced, there are still plenty of uniquely South African offerings to get you praising.

Artists

Amadodana Ase Wesile

This grand old Methodist group have been performing since 1985 and are one of South Africa's most celebrated choirs. They perform in at least four local languages, though rarely in English.

Morena U Ba Etele (Gallo, South Africa).

The latest release from these somewhat solemn sounding

heavyweights, who have been Methodism's South African number-one gospel singers for decades.

IPCC

The International Pentecostal Church Choir found instant success with their 1989 debut album, and have grown in popularity ever since, partly as a result of the immense membership of their church which is the fastest growing in Southern Africa.

 Uthembekile
(Tusk, South Africa).

This was the album that made the IPCC so popular among South African gospel lovers. Stirring, rootsy gospel sounds from a stunningly strong-voiced choir.

Sibongile Khumalo

Classically trained and with music degrees from two South African universities, Sibongile Khumalo's output effortlessly ranges from opera to jazz to mbaqanga. She has achieved fame in concert with the South African National Symphony Orchestra, though her recorded work to date consists of jazz and contemporary material only.

 Ancient Evenings (Sony, South Africa).
Live at the Market Theatre (Sony, South Africa).

Two quite different expositions of Khumalo's immense talent, with the first classical, gentle and at times a little stilted, and the second a jazzy and musically rich live set that truly justifies her title as South Africa's diva of song.

Lusanda Spiritual Group

The Lusanda's leader, Lusand Mcinga, is a wonderful singer from the Transkei region of the Eastern Cape. Her group first recorded in 1995, and have become big favourites.

 Ungababek'ityala
(Gallo, South Africa).

An album that shows Lusand as a real challenger to Rebecca Malope's throne as Queen of South African Gospel.

Rebecca Malope

Malope, South Africa's biggest gospel star, is from the township of Lekazi near Nelspruit in Mpumalanga, and launched her career by winning a nationwide talent contest in 1987. These days, most of her releases go platinum within weeks and she is branching out in new directions, promoting new talent and trying her hand as a producer.

 Free at Last: South African Gospel
(EMI/Hemisphere, UK).

An excellent anthology of Malope's fabulous music, inflected with township pop sensitivity, and powered by impassioned petitions to God that build inexorably to anthemic odes to His goodness and mercy.

Vuyo Mokoena and Pure Magic

Vuyo made his name singing with Rebecca Malope but has gone on to pursue a highly successful solo career. Rebecca's talented producer Zako produces him and is a key component of Vuyo's anthemic, sing-along style.

Njalo (EMI, South Africa).

A perfect example of producer Sizwe Zako's craft, with Vuyo's lusty vocals bursting through the stirring keyboards-driven accompaniment to great effect.

South Africa | Jazz

hip kings, hip queens

The decade between World War II and the late 1950s produced a classic era of jazz in South Africa, establishing a base unique in Africa that has continued to produce great singers and players. **Rob Allingham** charts the connections, talks to the major figures and listens to the current state of play.

The postwar era was a time of tremendous growth and innovation for Africans in all the arts, and it corresponded to a substantial increase of population in the townships as migrants poured in from the rural areas to take jobs in a rapidly expanding industrial economy. Living conditions remained sub-standard or desperate for many, but before the draconian structures of the new apartheid system were fully implemented, township residents indulged themselves with a certain reckless optimism and even an illusion of permanency and belonging.

The acknowledged connection between jazz and the cultural and political ferment of the times is largely due to a talented group of journalists and writers associated with *Drum*, the black illustrated magazine that documented the era. Much of the jazz audience and most jazz musicians came from similar urban backgrounds and were the products of mission school educations. At least some of their enthusiasm for jazz had more to do with attitude, style and aspirations than any attributes of the music itself. Tribalism, traditionalism and ruralism – the values extolled by apartheid policy – were rejected in favour of the apparent success and sophistication of the African-American lifestyle, of which jazz was perceived to be an integral component.

Swing

Ironically, at the very time that jazz was being embraced by African urbanites, it had already been abandoned by most of their American role models for more accessible genres like rhythm and blues, and **swing**, the predominant South African style, was already regarded as passé in the US by the late 1940s. Unlike earlier African–American music, which had been transmitted directly by visiting performers, no early American jazz or swing player, black or white, toured South Africa (the first, Tony Scott, arrived much later in 1956). Printed orchestrations, films and recordings provided the sole

source of inspiration. South Africa's awareness of swing, however, had come through Allied soldiers during the war, who brought with them records of the latest swing band hits from Britain and the US.

By 1950, most South African towns supported at least a couple of local jazz bands. The cities of **Cape Province** – East London, Port Elizabeth and Cape Town – were particularly jazz-oriented, perhaps because of their predominently Xhosa populations: the complex harmonies and structures of traditional Xhosa music may have helped to foster an intuitive understanding of jazz harmony and improvisation.

But, as usual, it was in **Johannesburg** that the cutting edge of innovation was keenest, and where musicians found the greatest number of bands and the biggest audience. The city's 'Concert and Dance' circuit had earlier spawned Solomon 'Zulu Boy' Cele's **Jazz Maniacs**, the archetypal 'African Jazz' band of the late 1930s. After World War II, the equally influential **Harlem Swingsters** were active for several years. Alumni from both bands went on to create other groups, some of which remained popular for another two decades.

Alto saxophonist-composer **Isaac 'Zacks' Nkosi** from the Jazz Maniacs together with tenor man **Ellison Temba** and trumpeter **Elijah Nkwanyane** helped make up the front line of the **African Swingsters**; the same group of musicians also recorded under many other names such as the Country Jazz Band and the City Jazz Nine. Another ex-Maniac, tenor saxophonist **Wilson 'King Force' Silgee**, led the **Jazz Forces**. **Ntemi Piliso** left the Harlem Swingsters to form the **Alexandra All Stars**, thus initiating an important career as a tenor soloist, composer and band leader.

Unless they happened to be reading from an imported score (most jazz musicians could read music), township jazz bands played in a dynamic, original style that mixed elements of American swing with the basic structure of **marabi** – the name by which African Jazz continued to be

Miriam Makeba

known. The songs consisted of one or two repeated melodic phrases constructed over two or three chords. Although they were less complicated in structure than a typical American jazz composition, these essentially African melodies were then performed with the instrumentation of an overseas swing band. This permitted the complex voicings and arranged alternation between sections – usually brass against saxophones – that had typified American big-band jazz since the 1920s.

Frequently, there was considerable space allotted to solos. Sometimes these consisted of a straight restatement of the melody, at other times a major degree of improvisation was involved. In the case of the most imaginative and technically advanced players, like clarinetist-altoist **Kippie Moeketsi**, there were touches of bop and cool jazz, styles which otherwise largely by-passed South Africa.

The Jazz Singers

The 1940s and '50s was also the great era of **female African Jazz vocalists**, many of whom modelled their style on the likes of Ella Fitzgerald or Sarah Vaughan, but like their instrumentalist counterparts, sang what were essentially marabi-structured melodies.

Dolly Rathebe was the first to come to prominence as the leading actress-singer in the first African feature film, *Jim Comes To Jo'burg* (1948). She also starred in the superb *Magic Garden* in 1951, and as

'The Queen Of The Blues' retained her fame and popularity for another decade. Next in the spotlight was Zimbabwean **Dorothy Masuka** who began her sensational career as a vocalist and recording artist in Johannesburg in 1951. Like Dolly Rathebe, Masuka was also a famous cover girl in the black picture press.

Male jazz singers were a far less common breed but there were a number of male vocal quartets. The best-known of these was the **Manhattan Brothers** led by Nathan 'Dambuza' Mdledle, whose celebrity matched Rathebe and Masuka. Although regarded as part of the local jazz firmament, the Manhattans' roots lay in a slightly different African-American tradition: the secular-pop branch of close-harmony singing that antedated jazz and later developed alongside it in a parallel fashion, eventually producing groups like the Mills Brothers and the Inkspots and then later still, doowop. Philemon Mokgotsi's **African Inkspots** offered the Manhattans some stiff competition until the mid-1950s when the **Woody Woodpeckers** led by **Victor Ndlazilwane** eclipsed both groups with their striking mixture of Xhosa-traditional and American jazz-influenced melodies and harmonies.

Miriam Makeba was the last singing star to come out of this classic jazz era, and the most significant. She first came to public attention as a featured vocalist with the Manhattan Brothers in 1954, then left to record with her own all-female **Skylarks** vocal group while touring the country with

JAK KILBY

Abdullah Ibrahim aka Dollar Brand

impressario Alf Herberts' **African Jazz & Variety**, a talent vehicle which launched the careers of many black artists. In 1959, Makeba took on the female lead in *King Kong*, the South African-Broadway musical crossover billed as a 'jazz opera' with a fine score by pianist-composer Todd Matshikiza. Sharing the top billing was Nathan Mdledle of the Manhattans playing the part of the boxer, King Kong, who murders his girlfriend and dies in prison. This slice of township life electrified its audiences, black and white alike. To circumvent apartheid regulations, which rigidly segregated public entertainment, it was often staged at universities.

At the very apogee of this success, Makeba left the country for the United States. There she quickly re-established her career with "The Click Song" and "Phatha Phatha" and transferred her celebrity status to the international stage, the first South African to do so. She also fired an opening salvo in the external battle against apartheid with her impassioned testimonial before the United Nations in 1963. The South African government, irritated by the glare of adverse publicity, responded by revoking her citizenship and right of return. After her marriage to Stokeley Carmichael, one of the leaders of the Black Panthers, she was also harassed by the American authorities and, despite support from Marlon Brando, Nina Simone and others, fled to exile in Guinea.

Makeba was only the first exile of many. In 1961, *King Kong* was staged in London where it enjoyed a successful run. And after the show closed, many of the cast – including the four Manhattan Brothers – chose not to return. The outward rush of South Africa's artistic talent had begun.

Progressive Jazz: the 1960s

In the 1960s South African jazz divided into two distinct strains, similar to the dichotomy affecting American jazz in the immediate postwar years. On the one hand, the marabi-style dance bands still commanded a large following and a new African Jazz band, the **Elite Swingsters**, began a long and distinguished career by recording "Phalafala", probably South Africa's biggest selling jazz disc ever. On the other, a new type of jazz was evolving that emulated the American avant-garde led by Thelonious Monk, Sonny Rollins and John Coltrane, and which strove for a more self-conscious artistry. It also incorporated an overtly political dimension as protest music, a wordless assault on apartheid and all that it symbolised.

Despite the fact that it was essentially elitist and indeed less 'African' than its marabi-based counterpart, this jazz on the American model became, indeed remains, inexorably identified with the people's struggle. Trumpeter **Hugh Masekela**, trombonist **Jonas Gwangwa**, pianist **Dollar Brand** (aka **Abdullah Ibrahim**) and that most forward-thinking of the older generation jazzmen, **Kippie Moeketsi**, constituted the core of the progressive first wave. Masekela and Gwangwa had played together as teenagers in the **Father Huddleston Band** (named after their mentor, the famed English anti-apartheid Anglican priest) before graduating to the **Jazz Dazzlers**, a small band that included Moeketsi and provided the instrumental accompaniment to *King Kong*.

SOUTH AFRICA

In 1959 **John Mehegan**, a visiting American pianist, organised a famous 'Jazz In Africa' recording session, featuring Masekela, Gwangwa and Moeketsi. This produced the first two LPs by African jazzmen and the first opportunity to overcome the time restraints imposed by the three minute-a-side 78rpm format. After Mehegan's departure, Capetonian Dollar Brand arrived to take over the piano. The resulting formation, now called the **Jazz Epistles**, recorded another album and garnered a great deal of critical acclaim for its performance at the first **Cold Castle National Jazz Festival** in 1960. But not long afterwards, both Masekela and Gwangwa left for the United States – where they would remain in exile for another three decades – while Brand eventually made his way to Switzerland and international jazz renown, in 1962.

The departure of three of the principal Epistles left a large gap in the local jazz scene, but the 1962 *Cold Castle Jazz Festival* demonstrated that a new generation had been inspired by their example. Pianist-composer **Chris McGregor** and tenor saxophonist **Dudu Pukwana** were probably the most famous and influential musicians in this new wave. Kippie Moeketsi remained an inspiration and **Gideon Nxumalo**, an older pianist-composer who like Moeketsi had grown up in the Harlem Swingsters, blossomed into a particularly original talent.

The best players from several different bands which had performed at the 1963 *Cold Castle Festival* were gathered together under the direction of Chris McGregor, and produced a classic LP, *Jazz The African Sound*, perhaps the finest single product of a brilliant era. Sadly, it also proved to be a swansong. A general wave of oppression had followed the Sharpville massacre of 1960 and, as the government dug in with its new order, many of South Africa's best talents fled into exile.

The progressive jazzers were badly affected as apartheid regulations designed to separate mixed-race bands and audiences became increasingly onerous. In the face of this dispiriting onslaught, McGregor, Pukwana and their entire band, the **Blue Notes**, including **Louis Moholo**, left the country for good in 1964. The Blue Notes, and their later manifestation the **Brotherhood of Breath**, added a distinctive touch to the rather moribund UK jazz scene but, as was the case with other exiles, their influence on musical development in South Africa ceased at that point.

JAK KILBY

Dudu Pukwana blowing for freedom

Back Home: Hugh Masekela

A re-vitalised Hugh Masekela talked to Nigel Williamson about the difficulties experienced by returning exiles in the new South Africa.

After three decades in exile it took Hugh Masekela another five years to finally feel at home in a democratic South Africa. Following his return in 1992 and the initial euphoria of free elections, the trumpeter admits that he found life a struggle in the new rainbow nation. "I went back with such a hope and I was disappointed," he says. "I was angry about the past and impatient for change. I was full of bitterness." His anger often erupted publicly and when I interviewed him in *The Times* in January 1996 he painted a bleak view of the new South Africa, complaining bitterly that the record companies were still owned exclusively by

JAK KILBY

Hugh Masekela

whites, that there was a dearth of new talent and the live scene was virtually non-existent because escalating violence meant that people were afraid to go out and visit clubs. He was irritable and frustrated – and there was some resentment in return on the part of those who had stayed and struggled throughout the apartheid years and who did not see why the returning exiles should be treated as conquering heroes.

Two years later, I found Masekela in dramatically more positive frame of mind. "Things have at last started changing," he asserted. "There are small independent record companies starting up that are black-owned and run. We are beginning to enter the economic field. We have control of our destiny, we need to be assertive and that is starting to happen. There's a great re-emergence of who we are and a lot of different music, especially from the youth, is beginning to emerge."

The new nation, he feels, is finally developing a sense of its own identity and he is a big fan of kwaito and the other contemporary beats emerging from the townships. "The cult of emulating American and European styles is going away. We're taking the best from overseas but then doing our own thing. I think there is going to be a pot-pouri of styles emerging in South Africa over the next year or two. It's a revival thing. A lot of our sense of identity was taken away from us and now we're claiming it back. There is a real renaissance going on. Mandela has taught us not to be bitter and how to invite our jailers to dinner and we are looking at the future of a very great country."

Having emerged from his period of disillusionment, Masekela has thrown himself wholeheartedly into promoting new South African talent. He is a partner in a consortium that owns a number of radio stations and has recently started a South African-based entertainment company with the ambitious aim of becoming "a world player in music and television to rival Virgin or EMI." One of his first signings is a nineteen-year-old Afrikaner singer called Sampi. "She's like a South African Lucinda Williams but if you had told me six months ago I would be working with an Afrikaner I would never have believed it".

It seems that the new positive Masekela is finally ready to take on the mantle of elder statesman to which his long experience suits him so well. "We can define our own destiny through what we do. We have to get out of that old mind-set of what our country can do for us and think about what we can we do for our country," he said, quoting President Kennedy. His own most recent album, *Black To The Future*, featured a new school of South African musicians such as the rappers Apple Seed and Stoan from Bongo Muffin, Junior Sokhela from Boom Shaka and the Family Factory. He also has his own three-hour radio show on a Sunday playing exclusively African music and showcasing emerging talent. Other musical projects include *Heyta Da*, a semi-autobiographical musical.

Masekela is disarmingly frank when talking about how South Africa's problems have been reflected in his personal difficulties. "I went for rehabilitation because I felt that maybe I was seeing things through a smokescreen. I was a good drinker and drugger and I didn't think it affected my view. But since I voluntarily cleaned-up I've realised that some of my bitterness was coming from the fact that I wasn't sober enough," he says. "Miracles are now happening for me. I see much more clearly and I'm feeling very excited. I feel I've just arrived in South Africa. I'm finally home."

After the Diaspora

The exile of so many talents left South African jazz fans and historians forever pondering 'what if?', but there were still some fine and interesting moments to come. The **Malombo Jazz Men** featuring Abbey Cinde on flute, Philip Tabane on guitar and Julian Bahula on African drums, won first prize at the final *Cold Castle Festival* in 1964 with an intriguing mix of jazz harmony and improvisation crossed with indigenous Venda music.

In the 1970s a further stylistic refinement prolonged the popularity of the old **marabi-based bands**. The Elite Swingsters, Zacks Nkosi, and two Ntemi Piliso studio bands, the Alexandra All Stars and The Members, wedded the electric instrumentation of mbaqanga – guitar, bass and keyboards – to a jazz-style front line with brass and saxophones. Long, leisurely performances which often took up an entire LP side (as in the case of the Elite's hit "Now Or Never" or the Members' equally popular "Way Back Riverside") were constructed from simple chord progressions with no shortage of space provided for the solos. This was township good-time music for dancing, drinking and partying, and it remained popular with all age groups until the late 1970s when local soul and disco finally displaced it.

The **progressive jazz** strain produced a few more classics before it also dried up for lack of an audience. Saxophonist **Winston 'Mankunku' Ngozi** scored a substantial hit in 1968 with his Coltrane-influenced "Yakal Nkomo". In 1974, Dollar Brand returned to South Africa for the first time in over a decade and recorded his classic "Mannenburg" with Cape alto saxophonist **Basil Coetzee**. "Mannenburg" – a dramatically slowed version of an old Zacks Nkosi tune called "Jackpot" – reaffirmed Brand's marabi roots and contrasted dramatically with the Americanised style which had given him international fame.

The **Jazz Ministers**, led by composer, vocalist and tenor sax man **Victor Ndlazilwane**, mixed touches of marabi and mainstream jazz and underlaid both with a distinctive Xhosan essence. The Ministers performed at the 1976 *Newport Jazz Festival* – the first all-South African line-up to appear there – but Ndlazilande's early death deprived local jazz of one of its finest voices.

Through to the 1990s

The later 1970s and 1980s witnessed a decided decline in the South African jazz scene as recording and performance opportunities dried up for an older generation of acoustically oriented players. Only a small group of true believers that included saxophonists **Mike Makgalemele** and **Barney Rachabane** and pianist **Tete Mbambisa** kept the spirit going during the bad years, often at considerable personal cost.

During the same period, a younger generation of jazz talent was drawn towards a more commercial and vocally centred style that combined elements of jazz fusion, funk and township pop. **The Drive** as well as the nominally soul-styled **Movers** were successful examples of this type, while **Sakhile** achieved cult status with a following that crossed every racial boundary. These bands often spawned soloists who later became names. A good example was sax player **Henry Sitole** from the Drive who was tragically killed in an automobile accident at the apex of his career. Sakhile featured saxophonist **Khaya Mhlangu** and bassist-vocalist **Sipho Gumede** (who later formed Spirits Rejoice) as well as keyboard player **Jabu Nkosi** (who also was in the Drive). All three still feature prominently in the local jazz scene.

The 1990s saw an apparent revival in the fortunes of South African jazz. During the period of transition that anticipated a post-apartheid society, and then continuing up to and beyond the 1994 free elections that marked its arrival, the 'struggle' cachet long accorded indigenous jazz now engendered a conviction that jazz was a nation-building resource for the 'new South Africa' that deserved support and recognition.

With the end of the ANC-supported cultural boycott, many of the most famous **musical exiles** – among them **Miriam Makeba**, **Hugh Masekela**, **Dorothy Masuka**, **Jonas Gwangwa**, **Letta Mbulu**, **Caiphus Semenya** and **Dennis Mpale** – returned home to live and began performing before local audiences for the first time in years if not decades. A few others, most notably **Abdullah Ibrahim** (formerly Dollar Brand) and vocalist **Busi Mhlongo**, have maintained foreign residences but still return periodically for live appearances while **Bheki Mseleku** (who earned a reputation as a superlative pianist in the UK) resides in Durban but declines to perform.

Representing an even older tradition, two bands derived directly from the late-marabi style with an electric rhythm section continue to perform and record on a fairly regular basis. The **Elite Swingsters'** sax-dominated ensembles feature the added attraction of Dolly Rathebe, still in fine form as a vocalist. Ntemi Piliso's **African Jazz Pioneers** enjoy a measure of renown in France and Japan that probably exceeds their reputation at home, highlighting the continuing contradiction that the jazz style which is most purely South African is precisely the one least favoured by those who embrace jazz as Afro-chic.

A great deal of support for **local jazz** has come from the media. Television coverage and column-inches in mainstream newspapers devoted to the local scene increased markedly in the early 1990s while the country's first jazz magazine, *Two Tone*, (unfortunately now defunct) also began publishing. A number of **clubs** exclusively devoted to jazz started up; *Kippie's* in Johannesburg (named for that seminal genius Kippie Moeketsi) is probably the best known as well as the longest established. The clubs have been complemented by many concerts billed specifically as jazz events, as well as a few full-on jazz festivals such as the one sponsored for several years by Guinness.

Several music schools devoted to developing a jazz craft have also been founded. The two which have produced the most impressive results are the **Gauteng Music Academy** run by ex-Jazz Ministers trumpeter Johnny Mekoa and the **Centre For Jazz And Popular Music** at the University of Natal under Darius (son of Dave) Brubeck.

Perhaps the most vital indication of a renewal in South African jazz has come with the arrival of a **new wave** of young jazz players. Four of the most pivotal talents, all of whom fill multiple roles as instrumentalists, composers and group leaders, are saxophonists **McCoy Mrubata** and **Zim Ngqawana** and pianists **Paul Hanmer** and **Moses Molelekwa**. Murubata, for example, fronts an eight-piece band (which usually includes Hanmer) that could easily grace the stage of the most prestigious foreign venue. Indeed, if a criticism can be made, it is that the jazz produced by this new generation no longer sounds uniquely South African but has become too internationalised.

And although the emphasis in local jazz has now swung back once again from vocals to instrumentals, a few new and exciting vocalists have also emerged, most notably **Gloria Bosman** and **Sibongile Khumalo**. Khumalo possesses an operatically trained voice of great power and beauty while her style is drawn from a compelling mixture of classical and traditional influences as well as African Jazz. She has become a well-known figure at home and there are expectations that she will replicate this success overseas.

But despite its impeccable struggle, credentials and intellectual respectability, jazz in South Africa still means very little from a commercial standpoint. The largest single music-supporting audience, the township youth, continue to ignore it in favour of

kwaito or current African-American imports while the equivalent age group in the white suburbs only wants to hear local or international pop. Many of the returned exiles have found it tough to make a living in South Africa; it is only the availability of work overseas that has kept them alive, and only three record companies have shown any interest in developing a jazz catalogue, the South African branch of Sony, local independent Sheer Sound and the UK-based M.E.L.T. 2000. Ultimately, as with so many of the country's other homebrewed genres, if jazz is to survive in South Africa in the long term, it may end up being a case of 'export or die!'

discography

As in the South Africa pop music discography, many of the following items released on South African labels are available overseas through licensees.

Compilations

◎ **King Kong: Original Cast** (Gallo, South Africa).

The soundtrack of the seminal 1959 'jazz opera' starring Miriam Makeba and the Manhattan Brothers with Kippie Moeketsi and Hugh Masekela among others.

◎ **Sheer Jazz** (Sheer Sound, South Africa).

If you're curious about the current state of jazz in South Africa, this is a good place to start. A fine sampler of recent recordings – including some that perhaps stretch even the broadest definition of the genre – from the country's most adventurous independent label.

◎ **Township Swing Jazz Vols 1 & 2** (Gallo, South Africa).

A great introduction to the swinging marabi/African Jazz bands and vocalists of the 1950s and early '60s.

Artists

African Jazz Pioneers

Bandleader and saxophonist Ntemi Piliso, who can boast a career in jazz going back to the 1940s, formed the African Jazz Pioneers in the 1980s. The band helps keep Marabi alive as a performance art by updating familiar melodies and harmonies with new arrangements and electric instrumentation.

◎ **Live at the Montreux Jazz Festival** (Gallo, South Africa; BMG, UK).

The 1991 version of the band captured live and in fine form.

The Blue Notes

One of South Africa's legendary progressive jazz bands, the Blue Notes were led by pianist Chris McGregor with Dudu Pukwana (alto sax), Nick Moyake (tenor sax),

Mongezi Fezi (trumpet), Johnny Dyani (bass) and Louis Moholo (drums). The nucleus of the band would eventually reform as the Brotherhood Of Breath.

 Live In South Africa 1964 (Ogun, UK).

The Blue Notes captured live on the eve of their departure into exile in the UK.

Elite Swingsters with Dolly Rathebe

With a continuous history dating back to 1958, the Elites are South Africa's oldest African Jazz band but Dolly Rathebe's spectacular career as a singer, actress and pin-up girl started up almost a decade earlier.

 Siya Gida (Teal-Polygram, South Africa).

This album of hot studio renditions of old classics is typical of the Elite Swingsters' current live shows. Veteran singer Rathebe possesses the richest, most resonant mid-to-low-end vocal range in the business and she can still cook too!

Jonas Gwangwa

Gwangwa is a superb African Jazz trombonist and composer whose style falls somewhere between straight marabi and more modernist impulses.

 Flowers of the Nation (Gallo, South Africa).

Recorded in the UK just before Gwangwa's return to South Africa after years in exile, this is a contemporary mixture of jazz and South African influences.

Abdullah Ibrahim

Pianist Brand, who changed his name to Abdullah Ibrahim in the 1980s, is probably South Africa's most famous jazz name in international circles.

 African Sun (BMG, UK).

Just one of a series of BMG South African jazz releases featuring Dollar Brand aka Abdullah Ibrahim. Here he plays together with a raft of other luminaries.

 Blues for a Hip King (BMG, UK).

Dedicated to the cool monarch of Swaziland. Superb.

Jazz Epistles

The Epistles were the late 1950s South African version of the US school of progressive jazz featuring the best local technicians of the period, pianist Dollar Brand (aka Abdullah Ibrahim), reedman Kippie Moeketsi, trumpeter Hugh Masekela, and trombonist Jonas Gwangwa.

 Verse One (Gallo, South Africa).

The band's one and only recording, made before most of its members went into exile overseas, is now considered to be a South African classic.

Sibongile Khumalo

Khumalo is one of South Africa's most arresting new vocalists. She seamlessly matches her classical training and thoroughgoing knowledge of traditional Zulu song with a jazz sensibility.

 Live At The Market Theatre (Sony, South Africa).

This superb concert recording highlights Khumalo's talents with the sympathetic backing of some fine instrumentalists including saxophonist Khaya Mahlangu.

Miriam Makeba

South Africa's most famous musical export immersed herself in the vocal traditions of her people and then became a homegrown star by mixing them with African-American influences. Ironically, she was subsequently forced to spend the majority years of her career in exile bestowing her talents on the rest of the world.

 Miriam Makeba & the Skylarks (Teal-Polygram, South Africa).

A two-CD set of wonderful recordings from the 1950s aptly demonstrating the early blossoming of Makeba's talents in the company of her close harmony group, the Skylarks.

 Sangoma (Warner Brothers, US/UK).

A heartrendingly beautiful collection of traditional song, all sung a cappella.

 Welela (Phillips, US/UK).

Makeba's last great album – every track a gem, superbly backed, arranged and produced, and with Miriam singing at her magnificent best.

Hugh Masekela

Next to Miriam Makeba and viewed from a commercial standpoint, trumpeter/vocalist Hugh Masekela enjoyed the greatest international acclaim (and also recorded the most albums) of any of South Africa's exiles.

 Hope (Triloka, US).

This live recording with a hot, young band made not long before his return to South Africa nicely fills the function of a greatest hits retrospective of Masekela's long and interesting career.

Dorothy Masuka

Zimbabwean-born Masuka was one of the three most popular African female vocalists (along with Dolly Rathebe and Miriam Makeba) of the fabled 1950s before the South African authorities threw her out of the country.

 Hamba Notsokolo And Other Hits From The '50s (Gallo, South Africa).

A collection of Masuka's prime – and long unavailable – Troubadour label recordings, extensively annotated.

 Magumede (CA-Polygram, South Africa).

Masuka's latest album is a little shy on running time but it nevertheless demonstrates that her legendary vocal abilities are undiminished while also reminding the listener that she has written some classic songs.

Chris McGregor and
The Castle Lager Big Band

The winners of the 1963 Castle Lager Jazz Festival were brought together under this name for this one-off, all-star studio recording directed by pianist McGregor.

 Jazz The African Sound (Teal-Polygram, South Africa).

This album constitutes some of the most glorious moments in the history of South African jazz and is especially noteworthy for the solo contributions of Kippie Moeketsi who, in the opinion of many, was the country's single greatest jazz talent.

McCoy Mrubata

Mrubata is arguably the most commercially successful – and certainly one of the most multi-talented – of South Africa's new generation of jazz stars.

◎ **Tears Of Joy** (Sheer Sound, South Africa).

This all-instrumental-save-one-track album nicely showcases Mrubata's abilities as a leader-arranger, composer and sax soloist. The first tracks are nice but a little disappointing for sounding so international but the last half gets into a wonderful groove that could have only come out of South Africa.

Jabu Nkosi

Keyboard player Jabu Nkosi, the son of Zacks Nkosi, has enjoyed a long career as an instrumentalist and composer in a number of the country's most famous jazz fusion bands and has also backed some of the biggest names, both foreign and homegrown, to grace South African stages.

◎ **Remembering Bra Zacks** (Gallo, South Africa).

On this fine album, saxophones and an occasional dash of the keyboards keep strong melodies at the forefront as Nkosi updates a number of his father's prime evergreens, mixing them with a few of his own recently composed numbers.

Zacks Nkosi

Zacks Nkosi, a bandleader, composer and saxophonist of the first order, was one of the most important figures during the Golden Age of African Jazz in the 1950s and '60s.

▦ **Our Kind Of Jazz** (EMI, South Africa).

This is a re-issue of a mid-1960s LP which in turn had been compiled from recordings that originally appeared as 78s. It remains the only contemporary testimony to the existence of what was once the largest and greatest body of African Jazz recordings of the 1950s and '60s featuring not only Zacks himself but also the talents of Ellison Themba, Elijah Nkwanyane, and Michael Xaba.

◎ **A Tribute To Zacks Nkosi** (Gallo, South Africa)
◎ **Our Kind of Jazz** (Gallo, South Africa).

Valedictory albums recorded at the end of Zack Nkosi's long career in the 1970s.

Gideon Nxumalo

Pianist and composer Nxumalo was another outstanding South African jazz talent whose career stretched from the early 1950s through to the mid-'70s.

◎ **Jazz Fantasia** (Teal-Polygram, South Africa).

This recording taken from a 1962 concert featuring material that Nxumalo wrote especially for the occasion is also the only surviving example of sax maestros Kippie Moeketsi and Dudu Pukwana playing together. Fine stuff.

hugh tracey: pioneer archivist

For anyone who was interested in African music in the dark days before World Music, Hugh Tracey (1903–77) was a pioneering, even a paternal figure. During the 1950s and '60s, his 'Music of Africa' series of 10-inch LPs on Decca – superb recordings of traditional music from central, eastern and southern Africa, graced with his inimitable commentaries, were one of the very few ways the Western listener might encounter African music. **Mark Hudson** takes up the story.

Hugh **Tracey** (1903-1977) was the father of African ethnomusicolgy. He set up the first organisation devoted to the study and preservation of traditional African music, the first library and the first magazine of African music – at a time when the very concept of 'African Music' barely existed. His archive, the **International Library of African Music**, remains probably the greatest repository of African music in the world.

One of eleven children of a doctor in Devon, England, Tracey left for **Southern Rhodesia** at seventeen to work with his brother who had received land as compensation for injuries sustained in the First World War. Labouring alongside the locals in the tobacco fields, he learned the language of the Karanga and sang their songs with them. Although he had had little formal education, Tracey recognised the value of this material, wrote it down, and in 1929 took a party of Karanga men to Johannesberg to make the first ever recordings of Rhodesian traditional music.

He then applied for and received a Carnegie Foundation grant to survey the music of **Mashonaland**, and over the following decades, worked in broadcasting and created a mini-industry around his **African Music Society** at Roodeport, South Africa (work continued by his musicologist son Andrew at Rhodes University). He became established not only as *the* expert on African music but virtually embodied white interest in African music.

COLLECTION OF ANDREW TRACEY

Hugh Tracey recording a Tswa chizambi mouth bow, Mozambique, 1962
(using his favourite Neumann microphone)

SOUTHERN AFRICA

Tracey's great testament was the **'Sound of Africa' series** of 210 LPs: the fruits of annual field trips throughout southern, central and eastern Africa between 1948 and 1963, of which *The Music of Africa* series were mere highlights. The composers Ralph Vaughan-Williams and Gustav Holst, whom he met in London in 1931, advised him to eschew analysis in favour of recording as much as possible. He set out to record every aspect of a musical world that was disappearing before his eyes.

Looking Back

Despite the huge growth of Western interest in African music, and the development of the whole World Music phenomenon, little was heard of Tracey's recordings over the last two decades, apart from a few items on compilations.

This was partly because, with advances in Africa's recording industries, and the perceived desire of Western audiences to engage with Africa's own view of itself, the old ethnomusicological approach, in which musicians were presented as anonymous representatives of an ethnic group, dropped from view. But more than that, Tracey himself became tarnished, as a tool of the apartheid system and even a creator of its educational policies.

Certainly the idea of Tracey singing African songs to classes of white schoolchildren in an Africa where black people were practically invisible makes us feel uncomfortable. But the relationship between Tracey's work and South Africa's cultural and political development is a complex and paradoxical one. He blotted his historical copybook by working for the South African Broadcasting Corporation at a time when 'Bantu' radio stations were being set up to bolster 'separate development'. Yet this had the side-effect of nurturing a whole rich stratum of neo-traditional music.

While many older South Africans would associate Tracey with the upsurge of black culture in the early 1960s – the era of *Drum* magazine, *King Kong* and Miriam Makeba – Tracey himself had little time

Hugh Tracey at the Diamang Diamond Company's museum, Dundo, Angola, 1956, trying out a chisanzhi mbira

for what he called the 'proletarian grey' of urban music, although he was indirectly responsible for the hit "Wimoweh" (which later became "The Lion Sleeps Tonight"), and helped many semi-urban musicians on the road to success – notably the great Congolese guitarist **Jean-Bosco Mwenda**.

Tracey espoused theories of cultural development that were archaic even in the 1950s. While organisations like the ANC were trying to foster a supra-tribal African identity, he still saw ethnicity as the root of cultural vitality. Some of the language of his books and commentaries seems cringemakingly patronising today. Yet through his journal *African Music* he furthered the views of radical musicologists, black and white. Although he was obsessed with gaining acceptance for African music as a subject for academic study, Tracey was an instinctive populist. He encouraged musicians to cut their pieces into two- or three-minute nuggets suitable for 78rpm records and would count musicians in one after the other to make the rhythmic structures apparent to even the laziest of listeners.

What redeems Tracey – assuming he needs or deserves redeeming – is the extraordinary enthusiasm and energy he brought to his subject, and, of course, the quality of his recorded output. As a teenager growing up in apartheid South Africa, and as a keen collector of township jive records, **Trevor Herman**, creator of the *Indestructible Beat of Soweto* series and the Earthworks label, could not help but be aware of Tracey. "You just knew of him as a guy who had made this incredible collection of music and instruments. To equate him with the creators of apartheid is bullshit. For those people African music was just *rubbish!*"

"He was incredibly paternalistic," says Angela Impey of the University of Natal, "but you can't judge him by today's standards. He was the product of a completely different historical era. In that context, he was very much ahead of his time. He preserved whole styles of music which simply don't exist today." Janet Topp-Fargeon, Curator of International Music at the British Library, also South African, says Tracey should be judged only through his recordings, which are "of vital importance to anyone with any interest in African culture."

This body of work is at last being made more widely available through a twenty-CD retrospective on the Utrecht-based Sharp Wood label. Drawn from the *Sound of Africa* series, most of which has never been heard outside academic circles, each volume presents not just a lost musical world, but a whole aspect of a civilisation. On *Royal Court Music of Uganda* we hear the sounds that accompanied every aspect of a highly ritualised world – buzzing harp-powered historical commentaries, drum and xylophone orchestras, and the wheezing modern jazz-like variations of gourd horn ensembles. *Kalimba and Kalumbu* evokes a time when every young man was a lyric poet, wandering the Northern Rhodesian bush with his thumb piano. And so it goes on.

The only thing missing is Tracey's voice, Sharp Wood's Michael Baird having decided to let the music speak for itself. "To have included the commentaries would have made the whole thing seem even more the product of a long-gone era than it actually is. It would have made it seem dated when the music itself is incredibly fresh." I'm sure he's right, but I for one will go back to the records from time to time. Because Tracey's pronouncements (and his voice seemed to belong to a distant era even in the series' heyday) tell us so many things – some admirable, some perplexing – about how we, the West, have approached other cultures. And of course, they tell us a great deal about an extraordinary individual.

discography

The following discs have been beautifully re-mastered from original masters and come with archive photos and full notes. They are distributed in the UK by Discovery.

CONGO

◉ On the Edge of the Ituri Forest –
Northeastern Belgian Congo 1952
(Sharp Wood, Netherlands).

Vast dance gatherings with orchestras of wooden 'slit' drums, hunting cries, lullabies, curative songs and likembe duets. These sounds of the Budu, Mangbele, Nande and Bira peoples, and the Mbuti pygmies who live beside them, take you right there.

RHODESIA

◉ Kalimba and Kalumbu Songs -
Northern Rhodesia 1952 & 1957
(Sharp Wood, Netherlands).

Lyrical and reflective sounds with the mbira-related *kalimba* and the *kalumbu*, a musical bow; instruments whose role has largely been usurped by the guitar.

RWANDA

◉ At the Court of the Mwami – Rwanda 1952
(Sharp Wood, Netherlands).

Powerful drum rhythms (more complex and varied than the famous Drummers of Burundi), heart-rending love and praise songs, bow and horn music. In the light of recent events, the names of the drums – 'The Dominators', 'The Terrifiers' – and the clear distinction between Tutsi and Hutu music gives these sounds a poignant and ominous ring.

UGANDA

◉ Royal Court Music from Uganda – 1950 & 1952
(Sharp Wood, Netherlands).

Regal sounds from the Ganda and Nyoro courts and from the nomadic Ankole people.

Sudan

yearning to dance

Sudan, home of the 'whirling' dervish and the pogo-ing Dinka, has been an exciting meeting ground of Arab and African musical cultures, but in the past decade religious dogma and civil war have combined to create a singularly inauspicious environment. **Peter Verney**, a long-time former resident of a country which leaves an indelible impression on all who touch it, surveys what remains of the scene, at home and abroad. Extra information is gratefully acknowledged from **Helen Jerome** and **Moawia Yassin**.

During the 1980s I was teaching in Sudan and running a mobile disco at weekends in shanty areas of Khartoum, playing rai, reggae and rhumba – some kids so keen they'd be up and jiving to the soundcheck. But in 1989, the security police of the National Islamic Front (NIF) showed up and took it away: a small example of suppression taking place throughout Africa's largest country. Around the same time police burst into a women's traditional Zar ceremony, armed with Kalashnikovs, and carted everyone away to the lock-up, confiscating the drums that powered the ritual as 'pagan'. Meanwhile, celebrated musicians such as **Mohammed el Amin** and **Mohammed Wardi** were branded 'communist' and fled to Cairo, and the massively popular poet and lyricist **Mahjoub Sharif** was imprisoned. Even innocuous love songs were banned from the radio, and mixed dancing was out of the question.

A new dictatorship was under way, and one for whom the age-old argument over the legitimacy of music and dance under Islam had an added dimension. One third of the people affected by its rule – living largely in the south of the country – were not even Muslim. But then, as a genocidal **civil war** was unleashed upon them by the Islamists in power in the north, music was not the greatest problem. At time of writing, the NIF is in power in the north, while most of the south is held by the rebel Sudan People's Liberation Army.

Divisions have never been simple, however, in Sudan. This is the continent's largest country and its people – three hundred ethnic groups – embody such a collision of Arab and African cultures that it's often impossible to tell where one culture ends and the other begins. Arab tribes arrived in the fourteenth century from across the Red Sea and the northern fringe of Africa; in the sixteenth century West Africans began journeying through northern Sudan on the pilgrimage to Mecca. Both settled and intermarried with the indigenous people. Southern Sudan, largely cut off until the mid-nineteenth century by the vast swamps of the White Nile, was treated as a source of slaves, ivory, ostrich feathers and gold.

The North

Northern Sudan is itself divided – to the point of personality splitting, sometimes. Few people wholeheartedly support the government's obsessive division of the sexes, and many older folk look back nostalgically to the era before *sharia* law, effected from 1989 when the NIF seized total power in a military coup. Under their rule, music has been largely outlawed from the airwaves and from public performance. It brought a halt to a unique tradition of popular music.

Early Days and Jazz

Modern urban music in northern Sudan began taking shape between the 1920s and '40s. Regarded by some as the father of contemporary Sudanese music, singer **Khalil Farah** was also prominent in the independence movement. **Ibrahim al-Abadi** (1894–1980) found new ways of wedding poetry to music, regarded as unorthodox at the time. Other early singer-songwriters included Abdallah Abdel Karim, better known as **Karoma**, who wrote over four hundred songs.

These **lyric songs** of northern Sudan were originally played on the **tambour**, or lyre, using pentatonic scales, and are quite distinct from the Arabian *maqam* structures. When the far more sophisticated **oud** or lute was introduced from across the Red Sea, Sudanese players developed a style of plucking and striking the strings of the oud from the technique they had used on the lyre.

Song lyrics are hugely important in Sudanese music – indeed the lyricists and poets are as celebrated as the singers. The Sudanese Graduates' Congress used a song entitled "Sahi ya Kanaru" (Wake Up, Canary) to spread resistance to British rule. And since then, many others have used the image of a beautiful creature, woman, or lover to refer obliquely to their country, and have sometimes stirred feelings sufficiently powerful to get the author jailed. Translations, of course, rarely capture these allusions.

Urban musicians introduced violins, accordions and horns – and the odd flute and mandolin – after World War II, electric guitars in the 1960s and electronic keyboards in the 1980s. These were used by Sudanese to beef up their traditional styles. Those from the traditions of northern, western and central Sudan took styles such as **haqiiba** – a chant with chorus and minimal percussion – infused them with Egyptian-Arab or European elements, and developed **al-aghani' al-hadith** (modern songs). As early as the 1920s Egyptian producers brought Sudanese singers to record in Cairo, and instruments of the orchestra began to replace the call-and-response of the chorus.

Southerners, Nuba and other non-Arab communities were well represented in the forces across the country. For impoverished young conscripts in post-independence Sudan, the **police and army 'jazz-bands'** offered the best access to equipment, and what started out as British military brass band styles often metamorphosed in the 1960s and '70s to become 'jazz' in the East African sense, imitating the intersecting guitars of Kenya's Shirati Jazz and the myriad Luo language bands around Lake Victoria. Congolese soukous, along the Franco model, was influential, too, and known in its Sudanese variant as **Je-luo**.

Odd and tantalising styles of **horn-playing** were adopted and adapted from traditonal music, as well as from these foreign imports, which, from the 1960s on, included further-flung stars such as Ray Charles and Harry Belafonte, who made a big impression on urban Sudanese musicians such as **Osman Alamu** and **Ibrahim Awad**, the first Sudanese singer to dance on stage. In the 1970s it was the turn of James Brown and Jimmy Cliff. The ebullient **Kamal Kayla** modelled his funk-shout style on the hugely popular JB, although he is now in retirement, raising exotic pigeons. The 1980s made Bob Marley and Michael Jackson household names in the most unexpected places. Marley was recognised by some as the spiritual kinsman of Sudan's own Sufi dervishes, and was an inspiration to thousands of ghetto kids.

Players and Poets

Music is not actually extinct in northern Sudan – not yet, at least – and there are a few groups who keep their heads down at home, and occasionally tour abroad. Many of the best musicians reappear in different guises in these groups. For example, **Abdel Gadir Salim's Merdoum Kings** and the **Abdel Aziz el Mubarak Orchestra** – the two best-known groups abroad – share violinist Mohammed Abdallah Mohammediya, bass-player Nasir Gad Karim, accordionist Abdel Bagi Hamoda and sax player Hamid Osman.

The lush, big-band arrangments (as well as the musicians) of Abdel Gadir Salim and Abdel Aziz

Dance and Trance: Sufi Dervishes

Given the current regime's strictures on music and dance, it is ironic that it was **Sufi Muslim dervishes**, or *darawiish*, who brought the first wave of Islamic influence to Sudan. Within the religious tradition of **zikr** (remembrance) the dervishes use music and dance to work themselves into a mystical trance. Undulating lines of male Sufi dancers dance their way to ecstasy with a physical grace that confounds age. Their tolerant spirit profoundly influenced the easy-going approach that characterised Sudan until relatively recently.

The most spirited rhythms are mainly for women, in the psychotherapeutic **zar cult**. Zar sessions combine mesmeric drumming with incense, massage and a licence to release deep frustration. Under the guidance of the *sheikha az-zar*, gatherings last either four or seven days, drumming from dawn to dusk for different spirits that plague people and have to be brought out and pacified.

These are occasions outside the bounds of life's ordinary rules, when women can smoke and drink and act out rebellious fantasies without having their religious piety or social respectability called into question. The zar cult is older than Islam and works around and through it rather than competing against it.

But like everything else that challenges the ruling National Islamic Front's social programme, zar is suffering a government clampdown as it is viewed as anti-Islamic.

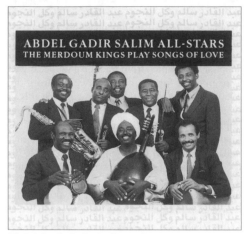

Abdel Gadir Salim's finest hour

el Mubarak's bands have similarities but their lyrics have immediate differences. While Abdel Gadir sings of a farm girl tired of waiting for her man to come so she can wipe the sweat off his face, Abdel Aziz is more likely to proclaim his admiration for a woman's high heels.

Abdel Gadir Salim was born in Dilling, in the Nuba Mountains, in the same village as his sax player Hamid Osman. He studied European and Arabic music at the Institute of Music and Drama, and became a primary school headmaster in Chad somewhere along the way. After he com-

pleted his studies, he shifted in 1971 from composing 'Khartoum city songs' to folk songs, and had a hit with "Umri Ma Bansa" (I'll never forget you), which is still part of his repertoire. His home area of Kordofan and Darfur has its own unique rhythms and songs, with which he has flavoured his music.

Abdel Aziz el Mubarak, from Wad Medani, was the first Sudanese artist to play WOMAD, at Glastonbury in 1988, accompanied by a dozen musicians romantically resplendent in long white *jellabiyas*. Next day they appeared at London's Jubilee Gardens wearing tuxedos. His love songs are songs of the city:

Every pleasure in the absence of your eyes
Is incomplete and does not touch me.
Every road that does not take me to you
Is a dark road that doesn't deserve the walk.
Darling, all through my life
I have been longing for your smile.

Less well known outside Sudan, but ranking at home in fame with Mubarak or Salim, are Abdel Karim el Kabli, Mohammed el Amin and Mohammed Wardi. Now in his sixties, **Abdel Karim el Kabli** is one of those walking cultural memory banks, a folklorist who can talk in depth about the background of any number of Sudanese songs, and who plays oud in a variety of styles with deceptive ease.

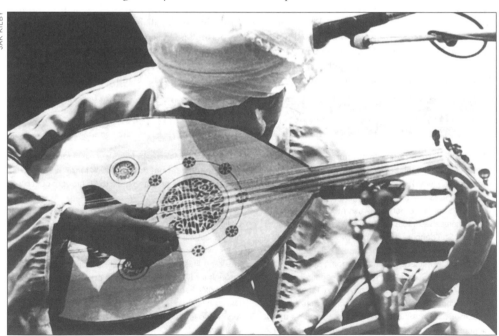

Abdel Aziz el Mubarak on the oud

PETER VERNEY

Mohamed Wardi, Mustafa Sidahmed
and Yusuf al-Mousli

SUDAN

Poem by Mahjoub Sharif

Hey, buffoon!
Cling tightly!
Beware falling apart!
Beware and be alert!
Bend your ears to every sign of movement
Keep watch on your own shadow
and, when the leaves rustle,
Shut yourself off and keep still!

Life is so dangerous, buffoon.

Open fire!
Bullets aimed at everything
every word uttered
every breeze passing
without your permission
My lord buffoon.

Instruct the sparrows,
the village lanterns,
the towns' windows,
every whispering blade of grass
to report to you.

As police, let the ants infiltrate
and build the security state
Ask the raindrops
to write their reports,
Buffoon...

From the same generation, **Mohammed el Amin** is revered for his majestic voice and superb oud playing, as well as his brilliant compositions and arrangements. Born in Wad Medani, central Sudan, in 1943, Amin began learning the oud at the age of eleven. He wrote his first songs aged twenty, and has been frequently in trouble with the military rulers. He was jailed by Nimeiri's regime in the 1970s and moved to Cairo in 1989 to avoid similar run-ins with the NIF. However, he returned to Khartoum in 1994, where he has kept a low profile.

Mohammed Wardi's soaring 'golden throat' has won him acclaim right across the African Sahel and the Arab world. Although this singer from Nubia is now in exile, his music always stirs emotion for many Sudanese, sometimes with directly political allusion, and sometimes more obliquely. He was born in 1932 near old Wadi Halfa and schooled across the border in Egypt, beginning his musc career in Khartoum in 1959. Four decades and three hundred songs later, he can stand on a stage, hand in pocket, the epitome of relaxation, leaving the audience to complete the lines of a song – and make the hairs stand up on the back of your neck. The effect of his voice at a human rights demonstration outside a Sudanese Embassy abroad is even more intense.

Wardi has often set to music poems by **Mahjoub Sharif**, who writes in colloquial Arabic, mixing observations on everyday life and politics with love songs and poems for children. He has also been detained for long periods under Sudan's military dictators, but even in the remote western desert prison at Shalla he continued writing lyrics that became songs of resistance.

The songs of **Abu Araki al–Bakheit**, like Wardi's, were banned from the airwaves by the NIF. In the early 1990s he was arrested and told by the authorities not to sing his political songs at public gatherings. He responded by saying he would prefer silence, and would no longer play. The public outcry at this news eventually prompted him to sing again, in defiance of the authorities, but at the cost of repeated harassment and threats. His friends say he is walking a tightrope, and his popularity is his only protection.

The multi–vocalist band **Igd el Djilad**, formed in the 1980s by a dozen young music students, are in a similar position. Their music strives to be both forward-looking and reflective of the country's roots, using rhythms and chants from right across the country. To an outsider this seems innocuous enough, but it's an approach that takes guts. Members of the group have been arrested on several occasions, questioned by security police and threatened. Rather than being stopped from playing alto gether they were forced to give written assurances that they would not provoke the authorities with songs about poverty and famine.

Women Singers

Half a century ago, urban women singers such as **Mihera bint Abboud** and **Um el Hassan el Shaygiya** began carving individual styles from the rich oral heritage of traditional women's songs. The most famous woman from this era was the accomplished **Aisha el Fellatiya**, who made her name as a singer during the Second World War when she toured the camps of the Sudan Defence Force across North Africa to boost the troops' morale.

Demurely echoing the rise of the 1960s girl groups in the West, a few female duos rose to local popularity including **Sunai Kordofani**, **Sunai el Nagam** and **Sunai el Samar**. In the early 1980s three gifted, teenage Nubian sisters with a supportive father formed the group **Balabil**. Trained by oud player and songwriter Bashir Abbas, who also found lyricists and musicians for them, they attracted an avid following around the Horn of Africa, though even then their yearning undertones were sometimes considered sufficiently 'over sensuous' to get them banned from television. The group got back together for the first time in ten years to play in Eritrea in 1997, making a recording for Rags Music. **Hadia Talsam**, the most talented sister, has also recorded solo in Cairo.

Women play the daloka drum at a wedding

The fortunes of women singers mirror the social trends of recent years. Consider the extreme case of **Hanan Bulu-bulu**, the poutingly provocative Madonna of 1980s Sudanese pop. After the popular uprising that overthrew President Nimeiri and ended his repressive version of Islamic sharia law, Hanan reflected a new mood as she warbled and wiggled her way to fame at the 1986 *Khartoum International Fair*. Her notoriety arose from her stage act which borrowed the sensuous bridal 'dove-dance' of Sudanese weddings and orchestrated the often saucy songs of the urban women's *daloka* or tom-tom tradition.

But the backlash came soon after, as Islamist hardliners banned her concerts and beat her up for immoral behaviour. They insulted her 'half-Ethiopian' background, which for them was a euphemism for sexual licence. She was by no means the best singer – her mewing little girl's voice and coarse repertoire never rivalled the poetic and emotional impact of other, more soulful female artists – but her naughtiness was a welcome antidote to the hollow pieties of the fundamentalists. Apparently, she's still performing, somehow, somewhere.

Further credit should go to women such as **Gisma** and **Nasra**, from whom Hanan Bulu-bulu stole much of her act. In the 1970s and '80s they pioneered a performance version of the erotic kashif wedding display, coupled with torrential drumming and worldly-wise lyrics. They were popular at private gatherings and were frequently arrested for the irreverence of their songs. Despised by the political elites of left and right, they were regarded as a much-needed source of dirty realism by the lower classes. Home truths such as "Hey Commissioner, we know your Toyota's the pick-up for the groceries, and your Mercedes is the pick-up for the girls" and "This sharia is driving us to drink" were never likely to endear them to the authorities. Most Sudanese women can drum and sing, and the less genteel urbanites delighted in reproducing Gisma and Nasra's salty treatment of the traditional daloka style.

The closest you can get to this on disc is "Tariq Sudan", a recording by **Setona**, a renowned henna artist from Kordofan, western Sudan. Currently resident in Cairo, and playing well-received gigs in Europe and America, Setona gives lusty voice to a generous handful of well-known women's songs, fleshed out by a largely male band. The artist formerly known as Prince is reported to have sought out Setona for a henna tattoo job. Pity he didn't publicise her music.

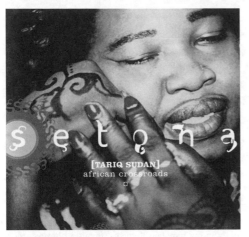

Setona

At the more polite end of the market is the blind singer **Hanan an-Nil**, who in 1992 released *al-Farah al-Muhajir* in Cairo. She accompanies her delicate, wistful songs on an electronic keyboard.

Finally, keeping the flame of authenticity burning and perhaps the most promising new artist in international terms, is **Rasha**, a young woman of seemingly impeccable taste and assured talent, loyal to her roots and possessing a breadth of repertoire to rival any of the men.

Southern Sudan

In 1992 the controllers of Radio Juba wiped its unique tapes of the celebrated southern Sudanese singer **Yousif Fataki**. It's an apt demonstration of the government's attitude to the largely Christian south, to erase a cultural artefact to make way for its own propaganda. And although south Sudan, like the Nuba Mountains, creates plenty of music, there are fewer opportunities to hear it now than in recent decades.

Southern Survivals

In the 1970s and '80s, while there was peace, the southern capital Juba had nightlife: groups like the **Skylarks** and **Rejaf Jazz**, and venues like **DeeDee's Disco**, taking their inspiration from Kampala and Nairobi. All are long gone, dispersed by war, although a couple of Skylarks were sighted gigging in Uganda in 1998.

Nowadays the best chance to hear southern Sudanese music may be in church, possibly in the refugee camps in northern Uganda, or among the rebel soldiers. Sometimes the participants are the same: I met a priest, a ringer for Spike Lee, training a chapel choir consisting of both SPLA fighters and seminarians, in eastern Equatoria.

The **Dinka** tribe used to hymn their fabulous long-horned cattle, leaping around like the born basketball players they are. **Zande** folk music is as playful as their folk tales, which feature a trickster like the Jamaicans' Anansie or Brer Rabbit of the US Deep South. These days the peoples of south Sudan have an ever-growing repertoire of new songs about war and liberation, some of which were captured on a 1997 recording, *New Sudan Sings,* that sounds worlds away from the sleek orchestras of Khartoum.

The Nuba

The **Nuba** are caught on the dividing line between the warring cultures of north and south Sudan, but are fighting back against a government programme of ethnocide with a reawakening identity. Under the squeeze of the crude Islamisation campaigns, the diverse, multi-religious Nuba communities are defending their own culture as much as their land. The Kambala, or harvest festival, is still celebrated across the region, and there is a proliferation of new songs and artists.

When journalists were flown in to the Nuba Mountains for an anniversary celebration in 1998 by the charismatic Nuba SPLA leader Yousif Kuwa, they were treated to an amplified concert in the remote mountain retreat courtesy of solar power. The band playing were the vibrant **Black Stars** – part of a special 'cultural advocacy and performance' unit of the SPLA in the Nuba Mountains. Their most famous vocalist is **Ismael Koinyi**, an accomplished guitar player who sings in Arabic and several Nuba languages. Other vocalists include **Tahir Jezar**, **Jelle** and **Jamus**.

Electricity is a rare luxury, however, so with stringed *rababas* (a clay-pot bass drum), tin bongos and shakers, Nuba bands usually play their form of **Je-luo** – a catch-all term here for Kenyan or Congolese guitar styles – unplugged. The lyrics of Nuba bands like the Black Stars dwell on the battles – military and psychological – through which the Nuba continue to struggle, and the dancing often goes on till daybreak.

Don't confuse the Nuba of southwest Sudan with the Nubians – including artists such as Wardi and Hamza al-Din – who are from Nubia in the far north of the country, between Dongola and the Egyptian border at Wadi Halfa (and beyond). Both groups are indigenous Sudanese, rather than of 'Arab' origin, but any link is ancient history.

discography

A growing number of Sudanese CDs have been released on the international market, but few people in Sudan have CD players and many classic performances are still on tape only – if you can find them at all. A good selection of cassettes is available from Natari in the UK and Africassette in the US. For information on field recordings, contact Sudan Update, PO Box 10, Hebden Bridge, West Yorkshire HX7 6UX, UK; ☎ (44) 1422 845827; e-mail *sudanupdate@gn.apc.org*

Compilations

◉ **Balabil, Hussein Shendi, Abdel Aziz el Mubarak – Live in Eritrea** (Rags, UK).

A frst chance to hear three-woman group Balabil, specially re-united for this tour of Eritrea with two of Sudan's top male artists and a fine backing band.

◉ **Musiques et chants du Soudan: l'Ile de Touti** (Institute du Monde Arabe/Blue Silver, France).

From Tuti Island, where the Blue Nile meets the White Nile at Khartoum, comes this tremendously evocative recording by some of Sudan's best musicians. Lie back in Tuti Island's lemon groves, shaded from the scorching sun, and breathe in citrus flute essence on drifting breezes of violins, as the Nile water gently beats against the shore. Blissful. Further CDs by Institute du Monde Arabe include music from the Beja of Eastern Sudan, the Berta of Blue Nile province, the Nuba Mountains and Nubia, as well as artists Abdel Karim el Kabli and Mohammed Ali Gubara.

 **New Sudan Sings** (Counterpoint, UK, 1997).

An essential dose of reality – songs from the war zone. Sudan's imbalance of power is highlighted by the fact that these stirring and poignant field recordings by Maggie Hamilton are about the only musical material from southern Sudan available at present. Up to now it's on cassette only, but don't let that put you off. Among the group chants and hymns – Dinka, Zande, Nuer, Didinga and other languages – are some extraordinarily beautiful unaccompanied women's songs. There's a shiver of emotion on hearing words like a '[peace] *agreementa*' and a '*Killington* [Clinton]' that stand out from an otherwise obscure tongue.

◉ **Rain in the Hills: Beja Ballads of Port Sudan** (Original Music, US).

Staking out the distinctive identity of the people of the Red Sea Hills with vigour and wit, these 1995 field recordings by John Low feature gritty oud players and a lusty fishermen's band.

◉ **The Rough Guide to the Music of North Africa** (World Music Network, UK).

As well as two characteristic tracks from Abdel Aziz el Mubarak and Abdel Karim el Kabli's albums, this useful sampler also includes the Nubian Hamza el Din's delicate 'Ashranda'.

◉ **Sounds of Sudan** (World Circuit, UK).

Solo acoustic recordings of Abdel Gadir Salim and Abdel Aziz el Mubarak playing oud, and the Shaygi tambour player Mohamed Gubara, who wrote Mohammed el Amin's hit 'Habibi'. Highly informative background notes by Moawia Yassin.

◉ **Sudan: Music of the Blue Nile Province** (Auvidis/UNESCO, France).

The Ingessana and Berta people of Blue Nile, bordering Ethiopia, are under pressure from war and commercial agriculture and mining, and their way of life is changing fast. This is a rare chance to hear their traditional music, including horns, lyres and balafons, recorded by Robert Gottlieb in the mid-1980s.

Artists

Tariq Abubakar and Afro-Nubians

After playing in Ali Hassan Kuban's band in Egypt for two years, Sudanese saxophonist-singer Tariq Abubakar settled in Toronto, Canada, in the 1990s, becoming one of that country's best-known African musicians with his band, the Afro-Nubians. Tariq would set Arabic lyrics to soukous melodies, dissolving Sudan's north-south cultural divide, and ventured to sing earnestly of peace and unity in his rumbling English. During a brief return to Sudan in January 1998, Tariq was killed in a car accident on his way to Khartoum airport. He was thirty-two.

◉ **Tour to Africa** (Stern's, UK).
◉ **Great Africans** (Festival Distribution, Canada).
◉ **Hobey Laik** (Festival Distribution, Canada).

Released between 1994 and 1997, Tariq Abubakar's three albums venture much further into African musical territory than other Sudanese artists. Often bold, sunny and bouncing with energy, he also appeals wistfully for tolerance and diversity. Once you get used to his growly-bear voice, his fusions have a special charm. Once a pointer to a peaceful future, now he'll be painfully missed.

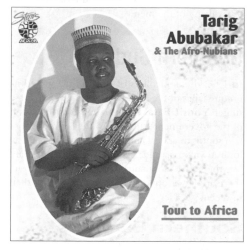

Mohammed el Amin

The sonorous Mohammed el Amin, now in his mid-fifties, has long been one of Sudan's best-loved singers and composers, and an artistic hero of the political left. He played legendary concerts in London, Manchester and Moscow in the 1980s, which spawned thousands of pirate tapes – but when will someone put his best group recordings onto the world market?

◉ **The Voice of Sudan** (Haus der Kulturen der Welt, Germany).

This is an intimate solo acoustic set recorded by Mohammed

el Amin in Berlin in 1991. It captures his smokily majestic voice and nimble oud playing – the latter sometimes got lost in his earlier big band outings – in glorious epics such as "Habibi", where the roller-coaster riffing of the 1980s electric version gets altogether subtler treatment.

Hamza el Din

Hamza el Din, Nubian ethnomusicologist, composer and virtuoso oud player, has spent most of his life outside his birthplace. His family left Sudan when he was young, and he studied in Egypt. In the 1970s he was appointed Advisor to the Sudanese Ministry of Culture but found the bureaucracy and politics left no room for creativity. He left Africa for Japan, where he spent a decade teaching in universities, then went on to the US. Now in his eighties but still active, he performs at least two concerts in the US every year. With his Zen-like complexity-in-simplicity, he may be bigger overseas than on the streets of Sudan, but the echoes of home remain strong.

 Lily of the Nile (Water Lily Acoustics, US).

This CD has an austere elegance like a night journey under a starry desert sky. After the hypnotic melancholy of four epic oud songs comes a compelling tour de force on the deceptively simple bodhran-like hand-drum called the *tar*.

 Songs of the Nile (JVC, Japan).

A rhythmically interesting set of songs for voices, oud and percussion, if a little stark, recorded in 1982.

Virtuoso oud player Hamza el Din

Igd el Djilad

This young vocal group – half a dozen harmonising voices and half a dozen players – are revolutionary (for Sudan) in their readiness to use material from the whole country – north and south, African and Arab. Their best moments, oddly enough, recall early Steeleye Span.

 Madaris (Pam Jaf, Germany).

So bright-eyed and bushy-tailed you might mistake some of the songs for TV jingles. Sometimes the earnestness is too palpable in this production, like songs to make children behave well. Why then do the Nuba and southern Sudanese songs covered so delicately by Igd el Djilad still provoke a tear? Probably for the same reason they get the band into trouble. The Juba Arabic of "Mama" – a song about poverty – is beautiful, sad and sweet despite the upbeat tempo..

Abdel Karim el Kabli

The avuncular poet, composer and folklorist Abdel Karim el Kabli, now in his mid-sixties, has become a walking encyclopaedia of the musical heritage of north, east and central Sudan. He embraces both colloquial and classical styles, and is equally beloved by academics and ordinary Sudanese.

 Limaza (Rags, UK).

An album full of musical sparkle, and his best recording to date, with some stunning interplay between Kabli's oud and the violins, flute and bongos. He wrote "Sukkar, Sukkar" (Sugar, Sugar) in 1962, a gently lilting take on the Twist, the dance craze he had just encountered in England, and which he claimed could be traced back to the Zar ritual in Sudan. His restrained style is a million miles from spirit possession, but he comes across as an amiable old toad.

Abdel Aziz el Mubarak

With his apparent fondness for spangled jackets and polished love songs for the ladies, Abdel Aziz el Mubarak could sometimes be taken for the Bryan Ferry of Sudanese music, albeit with a better voice. One of Sudan's great international stars – and unlike others, a shrewd businessman – Abdel Aziz comes from a family of musicians and was trained at Khartoum's now moribund Institute of Music and Drama. Since the mid-1970s, he has been one of the country's great bandleaders.

 Straight from the Heart (World Circuit, UK).

Mr Tuxedo does his Arab nightclub stuff to great effect on this live album, showcasing the lush and ornamented sound of his Khartoum big band. The set features the Ethiopian hit "Na-Nu Na-Nu", always a crowd-pleaser.

Ahmed M Osman (Satoor)

Satoor is a multi-instrumentalist and composer who has toured internationally with singers including Wardi, Abdel Aziz el Mubarak and Abdel Karim el Kabli. He has joined forces with Arizona-based DJ and promoter Mohamed el Omrabi to showcase his abilities without a vocalist.

 Rhythms of Sudan, Vol 1 (Blue Nile, US).

Multi-tracked, air-conditioned instrumentals of familiar-sounding songs, more catchy riffs than rhythms, skillful but a little antiseptic. Hints of Philly Soul strings and jolly oud make it ideal fare for an aspiring Sudanese restaurant.

Rasha

A gentle-voiced newcomer in her mid-twenties, northern Sudanese singer Rasha has an accomplished and thoughtful grasp of traditional and contemporary styles, varying the type and texture of her songs to hold the attention. She lives in Spain, in exile.

 Sudaniyat (NubeNegra, Spain).

Rasha's first disc convincingly shows off her range, from Sufi meditations to big band wedding songs, and is eminently listenable, warm, sophisticated and sensual. Backed by a variety of musicians from Sudan and Spain who innovate but don't intrude, she sings with a soulful sensitivity.

Rasha

Abdel Gadir Salim

Abdel Gadir Salim's rich powerful voice and dynamic arrangements make music which is less fussy and more hard-driving than many of his urban counterparts. His concerts and record releases abroad have made him one of the most familiar Sudanese singers for Western listeners. The content of his songs strives to be closer to country-side directness, while the arrangements reflect his studies of both Sudanese and Western music.

 The Merdoum Kings Play Songs of Love (World Circuit, UK).

An enduring favourite album: Merdoum is one of the vocal and drum styles of Kordofan, Abdel Gadir's homeland in western Sudan. The professionalism of the all-star band notwithstanding, this recording has fire and precision, polish and funk.

 Nujum al-Lail/Stars of the Night (GlobeStyle, UK).

Recorded during a London show in 1989, refreshingly faithful to the live sound of his prestigious big band.

Setona

When the Princess of Henna, Kordofan-born Setona, let rip on her 1998 tour of Europe and North America, Western audiences got their first proper taste of the earthier side of Sudanese women's culture.

 Tariq Sudan – African Crossroads (Blue Flame, Germany).

This is urban women's daloka music, tarted up a bit but still authentic. Setona's voice is swampy, hoarse and gritty, and only a little inhibited by the studio. Inevitably, the recording doesn't match the headlong intensity of the live drum-only versions of these songs.

Kamal Tarbas

Kamal Tarbas, now fifty, is referred to by admirers as the King of Sudanese Folk Music, though (perhaps because of his earthy populism) he is dismissed as a vulgarian by those who like their lyrics more elevated in tone. Beyond dispute is his immediately recognisable laid-back voice against revolving tom-tom rhythms and swaying accordion, derived from the hibaaq style and fleshed out in later recordings with strings.

 Ya Rait (EthioSound, US).
 Ayam Safana (EthioSound, US).

Two Kamal Tarbas albums issued earlier on cassette were remastered onto CD in 1997. Every home should have one – although one's probably enough.

Mohammed Wardi

Wardi began singing at the age of five; his first hit was in 1960, and he still has the most extraordinary effect on a Sudanese audience, having come to embody the collective memories and aspirations of an entire nation. Mohammed Wardi sings not only in Arabic but also in his native Nubian – a quite different sound from Ali Hassan Kuban (see Egypt, p.345) – drawing on 7000 years of culture.

 Live in Addis Ababa 1994 (Rags Music, UK).

The wrinkled old Nubian effortlessly enraptures an entire stadium, with his band sailing along like a felucca on the Nile; swaying strings, tumbling tom-toms, musing saxophones and choppy guitars create a majestic waltz over which he unfurls his impassioned, weary choirboy voice.

Tanzania | Popular music

mtindo – dance with style

Tanazania has strong traditions of popular music, from the Cuban-styled jazz bands of the 1940s, through the Swahili Islamic style of taarab (an East African coastal style which is covered in a separate article, following), to a current generation of local hip-hop and rappers. **Werner Graebner** looks at a scene that is currently in major transition.

Back in the early-1980s the Zaire-born but long-time Tanzania-resident Remmy Ongala wrote a song called "The Doctor": "A bicycle has no say in front of a motorbike / A motorbike has no say in front of a car / A motorcar has no say in front of a train." He couldn't have better described the shock of economic and political liberalisation in the 1990s, which saw the majority of Tanzanians locked in a tight fight for survival. For musicians, there was a multiple effect as a rash of private TV and radio stations began playing international pop round the clock, state organisations cut off support for their roster of dance bands and social halls, and everyone from hotels to corner grocery stores installed

a TV to play music videos. Audiences for live music – and a decade ago Dar had a scene unequalled in Africa – fell off dramatically, and most bands were down to scraping a living.

Still, even with these inroads, many facets of Tanzanian musical culture – the importance of lyrics, dance, and competition – remain intact, and often have meaningful roles where you would least expect to find them. Thus the disco phenomenon rallies around dance championships, which include local specialty genres. And words retain their impact in new scenes of hip-hop and *mchiriku* (a kind of rap style). Taarab, too, or *mipasho* as people call it, these days – entered a new era of popularity as a kind of competitive sport (see p.695).

The Morogoro Jazz Band

Formed in 1944, **Morogoro** was one of the first jazz bands in what was then Tanganyika. A break-away group from the **Cuban Marimba Band**, led by Salum Abdallah, it became one of East Africa's most popular bands in the 1950s and early '60s. At the time this photo was taken, the young **Mbaraka Mwinshehe** had recently joined. He became one of the region's outstanding guitarists, singers and composers and his songs ruled the airwaves until his death in a car crash in 1979. His last song, "Shida" (Trouble), was the biggest-ever-selling record in East Africa.

The picture shows the band in 1968 (right to left), Kulwa Salum (sax, vocals, bandleader), Choka Mzee (drums), Mbaraka Mwinshehe (solo guitar, vocals), Peter (bass), Issa Khalfani (rhythm guitar, 2nd solo), Shaban Nyamwela (vocals, bass), Rajab Bilali (bongos) and Abdallah Hassani (maracas).

COLLECTION OF WERNER GRAEBNER

Muziki Wa Dansi

The craze for dance music – **muziki wa dansi** – began in Tanzania back in the early 1930s. Cuban rumba records were all the rage and the urban youth organised itself into 'dance clubs', like the **Dar Es Salaam Jazz Band**, founded in 1932. Early instrumentation added brass instruments to a layer of local drums. Strings followed – violins, banjos, mandolins and guitars. Bands sprung up all over the country; **Morogoro Jazz** (see box on previous page) and **Cuban Marimba** in Morogoro town, **Tabora Jazz** and **Kiko Kids** in Tabora, and so on. There were connections between groups all over the country, and competitions – a legacy of the colonial *beni* (brass band) and *ngoma* (song, drum and dance event) societies. By the 1950s, popular bands and musicians included **Salum Abdallah**'s **Cuban Marimba**; **Atomic** and **Jamhuri Jazz** (both from the coastal town of Tanga), and in the capital, the **Kilwa**, **Western** and **Dar Es Salaam Jazz Bands**.

Yet the privately run music and dance clubs that dominated the post-war scene became obsolete within a few years of independence in 1961 when most Tanzanian bands began to operate under the patronage of state organisations, a system that lasted until the end of the 1980s. The organisations owned the instruments and employed the musicians, who drew more or less regular wages, plus a percentage of the gate collection. In 1964, the first group founded under this new regime was the **Nuta Jazz Band** (associated to the National Union of Tanzania, hence the acronym), and other bands formed under the umbrellas of the police, army, national service, party youth wing, the Dar Es Salaam city council or bus service.

Given this framework, it is perhaps little surprise that Tanzanian bands have displayed a remarkable collective strength. Musicians come and go (and a band can employ different 'squad members' from night to night) yet a band's musical character remained (and often remains) recognisably the same. The **Ottu Jazz Band**, the current incarnation of Nuta Jazz Band, are a classic example. A number of prominent original members – among them Muhiddin Maalim and Hassani Bitchuka – left to form Dar International and later Mlimani Park Orchestra – but in the early 1990s Bitchuka and Maalim were back, effortlessly picking up the group's mainstream style, with its brassy Cuban-style horns. In the midst of its fourth decade the band is stronger than ever.

A similar pattern applies to **Vijana Jazz**, the band of the youth organisation of CCM (Chama cha Mapinduzi), the ruling party, and for years one of the country's best and most consistent bands. They were responsible for changing styles in dansi, having, in 1987, added synthesiser and electronic drums to the usual guitar, trumpet and sax line-up. The new instrumentation helped to attract a new, youthful following: however, they have fallen off since 'privatisation' in the mid-1990s, when the CCM handed the instruments over to the musicians, and stopped paying regular wages.

The group who, more than any others, had taken hold in the 1980s was **DDC Mlimani Park Orchestra**. Formed in 1978, Mlimani cooed their way into the hearts of Tanzanians with

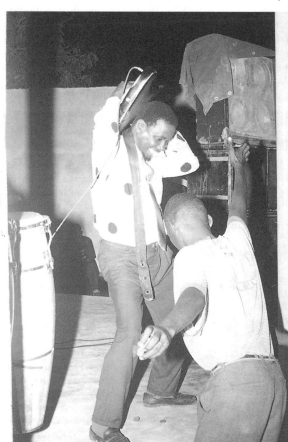

WERNER GRAEBNER

Ottu Jazz Band

DDC Mlimani Park Orchestra

an endless string of hits sung and composed by Has-sani Bitchuka, Cosmas Chidumule, Shaaban Dede and others. Mlimani are famous for the themes and intricate poetry of their lyrics; as in taarab, good, topical lyrics are an essential feature of Tanzanian music. However Mlimani's instrumental sounds – the interplay of the guitars and finely honed horn arrangements – are their trademark, making them one of Africa's outstanding bands. Composition and arrangement are usually group processes in Tanzanian dance music, but the force behind Mlimani is clearly **'King' Michael Enoch**, a hugely experienced player and arranger who first joined the Dar Es Salaam Jazz Band in 1960 as a solo gui-tarist, soon adding bandleader duties.

Mlimani's live (and recorded) sound is typical of classic Tanzanian dansi. The opening of a song is usually slow, giving the audience the chance to savour the lyrics. The heat then builds with a faster second section known as the *chemko* that features tight interplay of three or four guitars and ques-tion and answer games by the horns. Most of the dancing is based on popular street *ngoma* rhythms such as the *mdundiko*, or the *gwaride*, a line dance.

Mlimani, like many bands, have a team of between twenty and thirty musicians for live events, of whom maybe fifteen might be on stage at any one time. The basic line-up is three guitars, bass guitar, drum set, *tumba* (congas), two or three trumpets, two or three saxophones and three to five singers.

While it is often the collective image and enter-tainment that count most, all the Tanzanian bands feature fine individual musicians who have their own followings. The conflicts arising from individualism and personal expression are rife in a musical culture where the average outfit has twenty or more mem-bers. Musicians are forever moving between bands in search of greener pastures.

These moves occasionally generate quite chaot-ic conditions. A classic example occurred in 1985 when businessman Hugo Kisima disbanded **Orchestra Safari Sound** (OSS) and lured away six of Orchestra Mlimani Park's leading musicians to form the new **International Orchestra Safari Sound** (IOSS). The reshuffle left the former OSS leader, twelve-string stylist Ndala Kasheba, with-out a band to lead and Mlimani in serious trouble. For a time IOSS, led by former Mlimani singer Muhiddin Maalim and guitarist Abel Balthazar, were contenders for their old band's position of supremacy.

Safari Sound themselves reformed and entered a golden period when **Nguza Viking**, solo gui-tarist extraordinaire and former leader of Maquis, took over their leadership at the end of 1991. The band came back to high acclaim with a new mtin-do called "Rashikanda Wasaa", and Nguza land-ed an instant hit with "Mageuzi" (Changes), a song on the political changes underway in Tanzania – the transition to a multiparty system. Inexplicably, however, in spring 1992, the owner disbanded the orchestra yet again.

After leaving OSS, **Ndala Kasheba** joined Orchestre Maquis for some time before going out as a solo performer. Since the late 1980s he has led **Zaita Musica**, which plays a style much indebted to zouk, and had a smash hit with "Monica" in the early 1990s. However, the group has not managed to maintain a high public profile, and the same is true of **Achigo Stars**, Nguza Viking's new band.

Mtindo and Ngoma

Let's move ahead – Sendema
Now go backwards – Sendema
Left and right – Sendema

In Dar Es Salaam every dance band has its **mtindo** or trademark style that describes its music and performance characteristics, as well as the dance associated with it. The *mtindo* is really a kind of nickname for the band used by fans to express their affection for that type of music. In everyday speech, the names of the various *mtindo* (the plural) are used as synonyms for dancing.

Many mitindo refer to the musical traditions of Tanzania. Mlimani Park's **sikinde** or IOSS's **ndekule**, for example, take their name and inspiration from the **ngoma** (song-and-dance events accompanied by drums) of the Zaramo people who come from the Dar Es Salaam area. Juwata Jazz Band's **msondo** is the name of a particular drum as well as of a dance.

Some mitindo are descriptive of a certain way of dancing – like Maquis's mtindo of the early 1980s, **ogelea piga mbizi**, which describes the swimming and diving motions which were a feature of the dance – while others refer to the lyrics or contain nonmusical references.

Some of the bands, Mlimani for example, stick to their mtindo over extended periods of time; in fact the catch-phrase *ngoma ya ukae*, as featured in the band's emblem, means 'the ngoma you'll stay with'. Other bands change every so often to mark a new beginning after a change in personnel, or just to create new excitement with their followers.

No Sweat from Congo: Maquis and Matimila

In the late-1970s a more laid-back Congolese sound became popular in Tanzania through bands like **Orchestre Maquis Original** and **Orchestre Safari Sound** (OSS). A rather genteel affair when compared to Mlimani or Ottu, they adopted the motto *Kamanyola bila jasho* (Dance Kamanyola without sweating).

Originally from the Lubumbashi area of southeastern Congo (then Zaire), Orchestra Maquis settled in Dar in the early 1970s. It is quite common for musicians from that area to tour East Africa and Nairobi's recording studios have always attracted numerous musicians from the Congo. Yet in Tanzania foreign musicians are a lot more integrated into the local scene and they usually sing their songs in Swahili. For an outsider, the Maquis style (especially their vocal harmonies) may sound close to Kinshasa soukous, but it's really the other way round: the eastern parts of the Congo have always had closer cultural and economic ties to East Africa than to the Congo basin.

WERNER GRAEBNER

Orchestra Maquis caused a stir with each new dance style (*mtindo*) they invented. *Zembwela* for example, introduced through their 1985 hit "Karubandika", was so pervasive that the name is still commonly used as a synonym for dancing per se. But in the 1990s, they went through hard times. Many of the original founder members left or died (rumours of sorcery went around Dar), and debtors took what remained of their assets including their instruments. Individual musicians tried to get support from local investors and for a time three splinter groups played around Dar, all carrying the Orchestra Maquis imprint in their name. The strongest and only one surviving at this point is **Bana Maquis**, led by Tshimanga Assosa.

Another Congolese fixture in Tanzania's music scene is **Remmy Ongala**. Born in the Kivu region of Eastern Congo, he came to Dar Es Salaam in 1978 to join **Orchestra Makassy** – his uncle Makassy's band. When Makassy wound up the orchestra and moved to Nairobi in the early 1980s (see Kenya article p.515), Remmy joined **Orchestra Matimila** (later Super Matimila), where he became the bandleader.

The Word Game: Remmy Ongala

Tanzanian songs tend to be long – many would run to several pages fully transcribed – and much of the highly valued word play and allusions to which Swahili lends itself so well, gets lost in translation. But lyrics are a crucial part of the music and the following excerpts from the songs of **Remmy Ongala** convey a general impression.

In "Asili ya Muziki" (The Roots of Music) Ongala sings about the ambiguous position of musicians – the tension between the musician as champion and outcast, concluding:

Musicians are not bandits
Or, if we are – why do you buy cassettes?
If we're vagabonds –
why do you request songs on the radio?
If we're crooks – why do you buy records?
If we're outcasts – why do you dance to the music?

In many of his songs Ongala becomes a spokesman for the urban poor, describing himself as *mnyonge* (humble) or *sura mbaya* (ugly-face), as in the song "Mnyonge hana haki" (The poor person has no rights):

A bicycle has no say in front of a motorbike
A motorbike has no say in front of a car
A motorcar has no say in front of a train
The poor person has no rights
I am poor, I have no right to speak
Poor and weak before the powerful
Weak as long as the powerful likes.

This sounds like a hymn to fatalism, but possibilities for action and change are already apparent in the imagery and rhetoric in the original Swahili.

Not all Remmy Ongala's songs are as pessimistic. There are anecdotes about particular people – 'sugar daddies', mothers and girlfriends – and he gets most poetic in his love songs, in the Tanzanian mode of wallowing in unrequited love:

The one who loves will eat raw food
Will neither hear nor see
Love doesn't distinguish between insects and animals
Even fish reproduce
Love does not discriminate.

There's also the turn, in relation to gender, money and AIDS, which Ongala took up in the mammoth rap "Mambo kwa soksi", a short course on the use of condoms. The song, which alarmed some people with the frankness of the debate, warns against the delusion that AIDS can only affect others, the 'beautiful ones':

We "bad ones" strut proudly these days,
thinking we don't have AIDS
Sister watch out, don't die of AIDS
Your whole family can die
You can infect us
If a man seduces you, first ask him whether he has
"socks", if not buy them for him
"Where do you get them?"
"In any hospital"
"It would be better if they were sold in bars
and guesthouses"
"No, they should not be sold at all: when you buy
a bottle of beer, you get one free as a present
When you sleep in a guesthouse, you get towel,
soap and spare socks."

There were calls for this song to be banned, but Remmy defends his right to expression: "Music is like any other work, it demands all your energy and a lot of curiosity. It is like education and, as the proverb says, education has no end. We musicians may face many challenges. Our work demands courage; music is research into the essence of things."

Remmy Ongala's fans
hanging on his every word

Remmy's personality and outspoken lyrics created a magnetic appeal and the band got adopted on the WOMAD festival circuit. Unfortunately, their local reputation suffered and while the tours and recordings helped to buy much-needed equipment, and to make Remmy independent of a band-owner, the demands of touring, with only a few and less prominent musicians, destroyed the original line-up of the band, and the economics of playing dances around Dar Es Salaam did not generate enough income to support more than one star in a band.

Nevertheless, Remmy is always good for a hit, and his comments on the ills of Dar city life or politics always come with his own typical slant, and language. Especially popular are his long raps, half an hour or longer, commenting on day-to-day matters, revealing corruption among government officials, or delivering a lecture on AIDS and the use of condoms (see box).

Hotel Pop

Although separate from the dansi scene, '**hotel bands**' are linked to it by their personnel. Many a young musician trained in dance music has taken up new work opportunities created by hotels hiring a resident band, and some of the newer dance bands, like **Ngorongoro Heroes** or **Achigo Stars**, are actually quite close to this crop. They are both house-bands and their repertoires include covers of the latest international hits. Hotel bands, however, are smaller groups and their sound is normally dominated by the keyboard. There is one guitar player instead of two to three, and it may feature just one saxophone or one trumpet, instead of a horn section. The rhythm is usually more rock-based and the lyrics less elaborate.

Probably the most intersting hotel group is the **Kilimanjaro Connection**, led by trumpeter and keyboard player **Kanku Kelly**. Kelly had made a significant contribution to the Orchestre Maquis & Safari Sound before moving to Nairobi in the 1980s where he played with Orchestre Virunga and Vundumuna (see Kenya – p.515). Returning to Tanzania in 1991 he established Kilimanjaro Connection with fellow Tanzanian musicians for a hotel engagement in Japan. The band still plays mainly outside the country, in Singapore and Malaysia, but Kelly also operates some smaller bands in Dar Es Salaam and hires out band equipment to musicians (for example, helping his former buddies from Orchestre Maquis). Other bands on Dar's hotel circuit – though with lesser international credentials – include the **M.K. Group**, **Tanzanites**, **Tango Stars**, and **Tanza Musica**. Hamza Kalala's (formerly with Vijana Jazz) **Bantu Group** is one of the more notable bands in this field with an original, more rock-cross-over style.

Another group playing in the hotel mode are **Tatunane**, who have gained a reputation as a band for overseas cultural centre events. However, they have made no inroads into the Tanzanian scene and stand outside of recent developments.

Dar Rappers

Around Dar streets there are many sign-writer kiosks sporting larger-than-life portraits of American rappers and hip-hop artists like Tupac Shakur and Ice Cube. Young sign-painters use these images to advertise their trade and talents, identifying the role-models of Tanzanian youth. The new proposition points beyond Tanzania or Africa, as does one of the anthems of the new generation "Ni Wapi Tunakwenda" (Where are we heading) by Swahili rap star **2-Proud**.

I want to know where I will go
I know where I come from,
Where I'll go, I don't know
Let me tell you:
I'm looking for a passport now
I am going to stow away on a boat
Where ever I'll arrive,
I will forget this African condition
I'm tired of home
I continue to be harassed

Swahili rap had been in the offing for quite some time, with Dar's **Kwanza Unit** taking the laurel of being Tanzania's first rap group back in the 1980s. But a lack of production facilities held back local creativity and forced the rappers to rely on readily available backing tracks. As a result the Tanzanian style was initially highly derivative. However, the situation is changing fast, and there is a new studio now producing rap.

Kwanza Unit is a kind of super group with about ten rappers under the leadership of **Rhymson**, but the current star in terms of popularity and sales is solo rapper **2-Proud**. His first cassette "Ni Mimi" (It's me) was a big hit in 1995 and helped set up the market for Swahili language rap. In 1998, he hit the market with the first state-of-the-art local production made in the studio of Master Jay. Other groups in Dar Es Salaam include **Da De-Plow-MaTZ**, and **G.W.M.** (Gangsters with Matatizo) who scored a big rap hit with "Cheza Mbali na Kasheshe" (Stay away from problems).

While rap in Dar Es Salaam favours an American style, some groups from other areas are opening up local grooves and colours. In Arusha the group **X Plastaz** experiments with elements of a traditional breathy, rhythmic Maasai singing style and typical jumpy dancing. The Zanzibari group **Da Struggling Islanderz** has recorded with members of the taarab group East African Melody, and included rhythms and elements of the taarab style in their act. Pioneering Zanzibar rap are **Ally** and the group **Contish**. Because of the lack of production facilities in Zanzibar their 1994 debut cassette *Mabishoo* featured Swahili raps over American backing tracks, and Ally generated his own "Zanzibar Love" over an instrumental version of "California Love". Ally went on to lead another group **Boombastic**.

Reggae and Ragga

Like most other African countries Tanzania has a small but dedicated Rasta and **reggae** sub-culture. Bands first popped up in the 1970s, inspired by Bob Marley, but many soon faltered due to lack of instruments and infrastructure.

Jah Kimbuteh and his band Roots and Kulture, who started up in 1985, put reggae on the Tanzanian music map. Together with Justin Kalikawe's Urithi Band, and Innocent Galinoma (now based in the US), Kimbuteh represents the mainstream of Tanzanian reggae, with lyrics in both Swahili and English, in the old Trenchtown Marley, Tosh, Wailer-style.

Among the younger reggae musicians Ras Innocent Nyanyagwa performs an interesting mix of traditional roots-rock reggae with folk beats from Tanzania's southern highlands, occasionally adding songs in his Hehe mother tongue, to the common Swahili lyrics. Other new artists, like the Jam Brothers or Stybar's Reggamuffin, blend elements of dub and rap into their act.

Mchiriku Madness

While one part of the Tanzanian youth goes international, another section seems to go local. They call themselves Night Star Musical Club, Atomic Advantage, Tokyo Ngoma, Msasa wa Chuma (Sanding-paper), Gari Kubwa (Big Car) and Buti Kubwa (Big Boot), and they play a street entertainment called mchiriku. With an instrumentation stripped down to bare essentials – just a small Casio keyboard, four drums and vocals – the sound relates to what Swedé Swedé have been doing in Kinshasa.

Walking any of Dar's poorer suburbs on a weekend night one is bound to run into a mchiriku. From afar it is usually the high din of the Casio that cuts through the night. Closer up you make out the deep throb of drums and the amplified solo voice. Amplification is a distinguishing feature – setting mchiriku apart from other urban ngoma forms popular in Dar Es Salaam. The guys often work with battery-powered systems seemingly used decades back to make public announcements but feedback and distortion are part of the desired effect, as the lead vocalist(s) bellows out strings of songs for hours on end, joined by a chorus of fellow club members and the audience. The intermittent keyboard melodies offer respite for the singer(s) to catch some breath, and four differently tuned drums are part of the proceedings, the lowest being placed over a hole dug into the street or ground to give a booming sound.

Mchiriku derives from a wedding ngoma of the Zaramo people, who make their home in the area surrounding Dar Es Salaam. The official occasion for the city-type mchiriku can range from anything like a wedding celebration, naming or circumcision ceremonies, and habitually involves the whole neighbourhood. Later into the night, mchiriku usually takes in the city's low-life, attracting drunkards and dope fiends, pickpockets and the queens of the night. Because of illegally brewed liquor, drugs, unruly lyrics and licentious dancing, the public performance of mchiriku was officially banned for some time in the mid-1990s.

Mchiriku groups have one of the most prolific recording outputs with dozens of new cassettes on the market all the time. The songs are not unlike Remmy Ongala's or the young rappers', talking about the plight of the youth trying to make a decent living, or commenting on larger political or social issues. More recently there has been some extension of the traditional line-up to include bass guitar or guitars, aiming for a cross between dance music and ngoma.

Where is the Future?

In the previous edition of this book, Dar Es Salaam was glorified as one of the grooviest live music scenes in Africa. At the start of the new millennium, the situation looks none too good. New ways of earning a living with music need to be developed. Some are already in full swing with genres like rap and mchiriku taking advantage of newly available forms of production, while media publicity has brought fame to mipasho and groups like TOT and Muungano (see the following piece on taarab). But for the majority of musicians, income barely covers basic living expenses.

The situation is made worse by the absence of a tangible copyright law, or proper studios and producers. Tanzania has never had a record industry worthy of the name and until the 1990s all recording was done by state-controlled Radio Tanzania (RTD). The bands did not receive much income from these recordings, but they at least got publicity for their live gigs when the latest hit songs were on the air. Recording for RTD declined sharply in the 1990s as radio producers did not have sufficient funds. Meanwhile, the newly opened private recording studios – mostly small cassette-based affairs – are just good enough to record a rapper's voice to some pre-recorded backing track but have neither the room nor the equipment to produce a group.

This situation will continue as long as the Tanzanian government fails to safeguard artists' and producers' rights through a properly enforced copyright act. So-called 'recording houses' all over the country do brisk business in pirate cassettes: bring in your blank cassette and for 200 Tanzania shillings (about 20p or 30¢) you can walk out with the latest hits. Some of the larger stores import pre-recorded pirated cassettes of international material, or of local hits made to their order, from southeast Asia or the Gulf States. These imports are incredibly cheap, sometimes less than the price of a blank cassette in a local shop.

Musicians look for new ways to make a living. Thus, a marriage celebration at Sinza's fashionable Lion Hotel, in addition to the trendy disco, may feature a **tarumbeta** (brass band) playing Christian hymns and brass band versions of some traditional wedding tunes. The horn players are members or former members of army, national service or dance bands, and tarumbeta is a new heir to the brass band legacy which started with *beni* around the turn of the century.

Some famous dance band musicians, like Cosmas Chidumule and Makassy, have become active around the churches, writing religious songs, training musicians, and turning out cassettes in the lucrative **kwaya** (choir) business. In fact, due to its popularity in the wake of the current economic crisis and social problems like AIDS, kwaya with its religious and moralistic messages, may well be the biggest seller in the local music market.

The big-name dance bands and the mipasho groups now usually produce new cassettes themselves and sell them at gigs. This gives them an edge of a few days over the pirates, enough mostly to sell their initial order. Music videos are in high demand as even the smallest local bus sports the name 'video coach' and the corner grocery store uses music videos to attract its night customers. Ottu Jazz, like TOT and Muungano before them, now produce their own videos so they can remain in the people's eyes and ears in face of competition from cheap international video clips.

Meanwhile, the stories that muziki wa dansi and taarab used to tell have now become part of a larger musical universe including rap and reggae, kwaya and mchiriku. Despite the current lack of infrastructure, there seems to be an enduring strength to Tanzania's music.

discography

Tanzania has no music industry deserving the name. Those recordings available in the so-called 'recording houses' in Dar's Kariakoo area, or pirated on the Kenyan market, are mostly tapes from Radio Tanzania or cassette recordings self-produced by the musicians. Many are of terrible quality. If you are in Kenya look for the Ahadi label. They have about 50 cassettes of Tanzanian dance band material, from the latest Radio Tanzania recordings to oldies. Polygram (Kenya) and its successor Tamasha have re-released cassette compilations of Tanzanian songs from the late 1960s and '70s.

Compilations

Music from Tanzania and Zanzibar 1 & 2 (Caprice, Sweden).

Recorded by the Swedish Concert Institute in Dar Es Salaam, Dodoma, and Zanzibar in 1996, these recordings present performances by (mostly) government sponsored cultural and dance troupes, plus some pieces by graduates from the Bagamoyo College of Arts.

 Muziki wa Dansi: Afropop Hits from Tanzania (Africassette, US).

Recorded by Radio Tanzania in the 1980s at the height of Tanzanian dance band sophistication, this release features some of the best songs from that era. It includes highlights from the Orchestra Maquis repertoire, Juwata Jazz's brassy sound, and selections from International Orchestra Safari Sound featuring the voices of old master Muhiddin Maalim and Hassani Bitchuka. A later take "Usia kwa watoto" has Bitchuka and Maalim reunited with their former colleagues from Juwata.

The Tanzania Sound (Original Music, US).
Dada Kidawa (Original Music, US).

The 1960s sound of Tanzania (two full CD compilations), originally released as singles in East Africa, here re-issued for an international public. There are good moments from Salum Abdallah and Cuban Marimba and various favourites from the Western, Dar Es Salaam, Kilwa and Nuta 'Jazz Bands'.

Artists

Kwanza Unit

Kwanza are considered to have been Tanzania's first rap group.

Kwanzanians (FM Music, Tanzania; distr. Rahh, Netherlands).

The Unit's well-produced 1998 release. Presents a hip-hop reworking of King Kiki's and Orchestre Safari Sound's 1979 dance band hit "Msafiri".

Mbaraka Mwinshehe Mwaruka

Singer/guitarist Mbaraka Mwinshehe, with Morogoro Jazz and Super Volcanoes, ruled the East African music scene in the 1970s with a string of hits released by the Nairobi-based Polygram.

Ukumbusho Vol 1, Vol 3, and Pesa No.1 (Tamasha, Kenya).

Most of Mbaraka's recordings are constantly re-released in ever-new packaging. About ten cassettes in a series of *Ukumbusho* (Remembrances) are available at the moment. *Pesa No.1* and *Vol 3* feature some of the nice early 1970s recordings with the typical Morogoro Jazz horn sound. Vol 1 has Mwinshehe's voice at its best on the 1979 hit "Shida" (Trouble), posthumously released, and the biggest-ever seller on the East African market.

Mlimani Park Orchestra

Mlimani Park are the essence of the Tanzanian dance music experience: great songs, voices and vocal harmonies, racy interplay of three guitars, sumptuous horn arrangements inspired by traditional melodies.

 **Sikinde**
(Africassette, US).

Everything's well in place on these Radio Tanzania recordings of some of Mlimani's greatest hits ca. 1980–87. It is difficult to pick a favourite here, "Neema" (twice voted song of the year by listeners of Radio Tanzania) is especially noteworthy because it features the expressive voice of Cosmas Chidumule to best advantage, and has particularly well-balanced guitars and horns.

Orchestre Makassy

Makassy's band, featuring Mose Fan Fan and Remmy Ongala, was one of the major forces on the Dar Es Salaam scene in the late 1970s. Part of the band moved to Nairobi in the early '80s.

○ Agwaya (Virgin, UK).

This was one of the best European releases of African music in the early 1980s – a sweet record by the Nairobi-based Tanzanian outfit, long overdue for CD re-issue.

Orchestra Maquis Original/ Bana Maquis

Maquis were the principal representatives of the Shaba (eastern Congolese) sound among Dar Es Salaam based bands in the 1970s and '80s.

▦ Karubandika (Ahadi, Kenya).

Typically lavish horn arrangements, the voices of Kasaloo Kyanga and Kyanga Songa, Nguza Viking's outstanding solo guitar work make these classics of the Tanzanian dance band repertoire. The LP is out of print but cassette copies of this and other releases are still available.

▣ Leila (DakarSound, Netherlands).

This one goes under the name of Bana Maquis, but most of the tracks are from a local cassette recorded under the name of Maquis Original in 1993. All songs advertise the voice and compositional skills of Tshimanga Assosa.

Nuta Jazz Band

Established in 1964, Nuta was the first new jazz band of the national phase. The band is active until today, but now under the name of Ottu Jazz Band.

▦ Old is Gold (Tamasha, Kenya).

Features songs from the beginning of the 1970s, with early samples of Muhiddin Maalim's voice and the typical brassy horn sound.

Remmy Ongala & Super Matimila

Remmy Ongala is one of Tanzania's most respected

singer-composers, especially well-known for the pungent social criticism of his songs.

 **Songs for the Poor Man**
(RealWorld, UK).

This is Remmy's best international release. Features the hard drive of "Kipenda Roho" and Remmy's own all-time favourite "Mariamu Wangu", which is based on the popular mdundiko ngoma from Dar Es Salaam.

▣ The Kershaw Sessions (Strange Roots, UK).

Some of Remmy's later songs recorded at different BBC sessions over the years. This one comes closest to Matimila's live sound and gives a good taste of the band's fantastic three-guitar work.

Shikamoo Jazz Band

Shikamoo is a respectful greeting addressed to older people. This reunion of musicians originally active from the 1950s–'70s was enabled by a grant of instruments from the UK-based Helpage organisation.

▣ Chela Chela Vol 1 (RetroAfric, UK).

Recorded at the Radio Tanzania studio shortly after the band's formation. A more state-of-art impression of the group will be available soon on the same label, with the band caught live on a UK tour in 1995.

2-Proud

2-Proud is Tanzania's most popular rapper who has pursued a solo career since 1995.

▦ Niite Mr. II
(FM Music, Tanzania; distr. Rahh, Netherlands)

Bold new raps addressed to Tanzania's powerful. Much improved production quality over earlier Tanzanian rap releases.

Vijana Jazz Band

Vijana was one of the major players on the Tanzanian dance band scene from the mid-1970s through to the mid-1990s. Their sound, which added synthesiser and electronic drums to the regular dance band line-up, was a forerunner to some of the latest developments in Tanzanian music.

▦ Usichezee Bahari (Remanco, Kenya).

A selection of Vijana hits recorded in Nairobi in the 1990s.

Hukwe Zawose & the Master Musicians of Tanzania

Hukwe Zawose was for a long time the leader and spiritual force behind Tanzania's National Music Ensemble based at the Bagamoyo College of the Arts.

▣ Tanzania Yetu and Mateso (Triple Earth, UK).
▣ The Art of Hukwe Zawose (JVC, Japan).
▣ Chibite (RealWorld, UK).

Though these recordings combine music and instruments of the various ethnic groups, this is hardly Tanzanian traditional music. The heritage of Ujamaa-type Swahili political lyrics makes it a kind of a 'national folklore'. Recommended nonetheless for the giant thumb-piano sound of Hukwe Zawose and the inimitable Gogo voice style.

Tanzania/Kenya | Taarab

the swahili coastal sound

Taarab is the popular music of the Islamic Swahili people of the East African coast – encompassing Tanzania and Kenya, and in particular the islands of Zanzibar and Lamu. Originally a wedding music, it spread widely via cassettes and radio to beome a general feature of the aural landscape along the coast. **Werner Graebner** looks into a unique East African style.

At first hearing **taarab** sounds distinctly Arabic, especially the Zanzibar variety with its Egyptian film-orchestra-style line-up, or if you're down in Mombasa, you may be struck equally by its links with Indian film music. Yet taarab lyrics are invariably Swahili and in its voice and local *ngoma* (drum-based dance music) rhythms it's equally and essentially African. In fact, the combination of Africa, Arabia and India in this Indian Ocean musical culture well express the complex identity of the Swahili people.

Taarab is sung **poetry**, so the lyrics and vocals are especially important. The voice is identifiably Islamic, yet it's as far from the sounds of Cairo as is Youssou N'Dour. Vocals that cut through the instrumentation are popular among the Swahili and there's a distinct preference for high, clear female voices.

Rhythm is crucial, too, and no band features fewer than three percussion players, most often on *dumbak* and *tabla* (small drums) and *rika* (tambourine). Taarab is generally based on the rhythms of local *ngoma*, the *kumbwaya* being the most prominent on the coast. Latin American rhythms are part of the mix, too, through the influence of Cuban records in the 1940s.

While some instruments used in taarab are oriental in origin, like the Arabian **oud** (lute) and **qanun** (zither) or Japanese **taishokoto** (a banjo hybrid), most used in today's emsembles are of Western provenance. **Organs** and **electric keyboards** often substitute for the accordions and harmoniums used earlier in the twentieth century, while **guitar** and **bass guitar** are found in almost every band. European **stringed instruments** – violin, cello and double bass – are a feature of the large Zanzibar-type orchestras.

Taarab Roots

After a time of stressing African elements, current cultural values on the coast now favour a stronger link to **Islamic roots**. For example, recent writing from Zanzibar attributes the origin of the taarab to Arabic or, more specifically, Egyptian roots.

Siti Bint Saad and her group in the 1930s

Swahili Weddings

The **Swahili wedding season** reaches its peak in the month before Ramadan when the atmosphere is completely different. In Mombasa, there is a bustle of activity and the Old Town seems to be exclusively populated by women and girls clad in black *buibui* cloaks and veils, rushing to a wedding ngoma or the taarab which crowns a wedding on its last day.

Swahili weddings are community affairs. They involve the extended family and friends and the whole neighbourhood. Celebrations take place in the streets, lanes and small squares. The square or street is simply fenced, mats spread out and tented roofs erected as a sunshade and for privacy. A wedding lasts between four and seven days and involves the preparation and decoration of the place by the women, all the cooking and a good deal of fun, especially during the *vugo* and **chakacha** – dances accompanied by ribald songs – which are performed through some of the nights. All these festivities are strictly women's affairs; the musicians are the only men allowed to participate.

Festivities culminate in the taarab given on the last day, the **kutoleza nje**, the ceremonial first presentation of the bride in public after the consummation of the marriage. On this night the bride is placed prominently under one of the tented rooves, clad in the best clothes the family can afford, adorned with jewellery, and with her hands, arms, and feet decorated with henna patterns. Unmoving, she has to sit like this for hours for all to admire.

Women guests, clad in buibui, arrive in groups. They soon remove their cloaks to show off new dresses and henna-tattooed limbs. Perfumes fill the air and blend with the cooking aromas. The band is positioned under one of the tented rooves opposite the bride's parents' house. Heavily amplified, the instruments – organ, accordion, and various drums and percussion – start their romp through the thumping rhythms, melodies from the latest Indian films mixing with Swahili poetry. After a short warm-up, the lead singer takes her or his place at the microphone. The taarab may now last until the following morning.

As the evening unfolds, the band and wedding guests get more and more involved with the songs and music: the women join the refrain of current hits or rise to display their dancing skills and new clothes. Song requests scribbled on scraps of paper are handed to the musicians. Appreciative *tuzo*, or tips, are given to the musicians and especially to the lead singer for unusually clever lyrics. Giving tuzo for a certain song, or at a certain passage in the lyrics, is also used as a not-so-subtle public agreement with whatever is being sung – for example as a warning to a jealous neighbour to back off, or to a friend for meddling in one's affairs.

The men also have their own celebrations at the house of the husband-to-be, but they are on a much smaller scale.

WERNER GRAEBNER

Kidumbak wedding

TANZANIA/KENYA

The word taarab in fact derives from the Arabic *tariba* – 'to be moved or agitated' – and, although it gained currency only in the 1950s, has broadened to cover the whole music and its context.

The Egyptian attribution comes from the chronicles of the **Ikhwani Safaa Musical Club** founded in 1905, which is viewed in some circles as the history of taarab. Yet this view does not account for the phenomenon of **Siti bint Saad**, the most famous of all Swahili singers. The Zanzibar-based

Siti and her musicians were the first East Africans to make commercial records, recording hundreds of songs between 1928 and 1931. Members of the **Culture Musical Club**, the largest club in Zanzibar, highlight her career as an example of the African roots of taarab – and the influence of African music on the music of the Arabian Peninsula. Instruments, music styles and musical groups from east and northeast Africa are common in Yemen, and as far afield as Kuwait and Iraq.

Musicians and local historians from Lamu and Mombasa add to the African opinion, referring to the older **Lamu traditions** of Swahili poetry. This poetry was always meant to be sung, and there are descriptions dating back to the nineteenth century of performances called *gungu* and *kinanda* showcasing this poetry, accompanied by gongs, small drums and the *kibangala*, a stringed instrument.

Other interesting pointers in this web of opinions are provided by the social occasions on which taarab is played. Like the gungu and kinanda, which it has supplanted, taarab is well integrated with the festive life of the Swahili, and **weddings** are the main ceremonies where it is performed.

The taarab **recording industry** is an interesting story in itself. From 1928–1931 all the major record companies active in Africa, including HMV and Columbia, recorded taarab. Brisk business was carried out in those days, though in the post-war years activity was left to local, mostly Asian-owned music stores. The most prominent of these was the Mombasa-based **Mzuri label** which made and released hundreds of taarab records from the 1950s to the mid-1970s. Nowadays the industry has completely shifted to **cassettes**, which are produced in Mombasa, Zanzibar and Dar Es Salaam.

Lamu and Mombasa

On **Lamu** island, the old centre of Swahili culture and literature on the north Kenya coast, most weddings are served by a few amateur groups. There are no active professional taarab groups these days, and groups are bussed up from Mombasa for well-to-do marriage ceremonies.

The **Zein Musical Party**, now based in Mombasa, is the heir of Lamu's taarab tradition. Its leader, **Zein l'Abdin**, was born in Lamu and hails

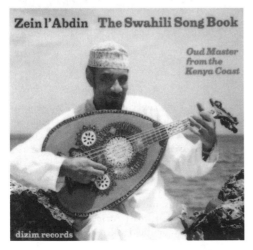

Zein l'Abdin The Swahili Song Book

Oud Master from the Kenya Coast

dizim records

from a family in which the Swahili arts were highly valued. Together with the Swahili poet Sheikh Nabhany, he has unearthed a number of old poems, dating back to the last century, which he has included in his repertoire. Zein is not just a fabulous singer and composer but ranks as the finest oud player in East Africa and is well-known throughout the Islamic world.

Other long-established Mombasa favourites include **Maulidi Musical Party**, named after singer Maulidi Juma, who play both traditional Swahili wedding songs and the Hindi-style songs characteristic of Mombasa taarab in which Swahili words are set to tunes from the latest Bombay movie. The group is a typical Mombasa ensemble, with a sound based on keyboards (with a strong harmonium flavour), with accordion, guitar, bass guitar and percussion fills.

Maulidi and their bandmaster Mohamed Shigoo used to back the singer **Malika** (Asha Abdo Suleiman) when she was visiting from Somalia, where she lived for a while in the 1970s and '80s. After the civil war erupted there, she returned to Mombasa and now leads her own group. Though her voice is not what it was, few can rival her stage charisma. Mombasa's other enduring female star is the enchanting **Zuhura Swaleh**, whose energetic songs have a firm base in the local chakacha rhythms and lyrics. The taishokoto is a prominent sound in her group.

These singers are in their fifties now and are gradually being matched by a new generation of stars. Among them is **Sitara**, for some years the second voice in Maulidi's party, who left to form her own group, **Diamond Star**, taking half of the band with her. She is popular with the young wedding audience who like her Swahili covers of some of the latest Western and Indian pop songs. **Yusuf Mohamed 'Tenge'** is an up-and-coming male singer, following in the steps of **Juma Bhalo**, who used to be the hero of Indian-style taarab.

Zanzibar Culture Club

Club life was one of the main features of taarab in the first half of the twentieth century. In Kenya most clubs have faded away, but in Zanzibar club life is still intact.

At the **Culture Musical Club** (*Mila na Utamaduni* in Swahili), the largest club on Zanzibar, members meet every night to socialise but chiefly to rehearse new songs for upcoming premiere shows held on important Islamic holidays. Under the leadership of violinist **Khamis Shehe**, the club sports the hottest string section in taarab – up to eight violins in unison with accordion and keyboard; *qanun*

Culture Musical Club

virtuoso **Maulidi Haj**, whose clear ripples grace the top of the orchestra's arrangements; and a four-strong rhythm team. They draw on a large pool of singers and composers, among whom the current singing stars are **Makame Faki**, **Fatma Issa**, and **Saada Mohamed**.

Like other members of Culture, Makame Faki leads his own **kidumbak ensemble**. Kidumbak takes its name from the two small drums (*ki-dum-bak* means small dumbak) that form the basis of these groups. A kidumbak also features sheets of sound from a violin, and a tea-chest bass rumbling beneath, giving cues to the dancers, *mkwasa* (claves) and *cherewa* (maracas). Vocals are sung in turn by all members of the group, in a cycle of generally rather nasty lyrics. To contemporary ears kidumbak sounds like a mix between ngoma and taarab, but it may well represent the roots of taarab, from a time before the Arab-styled orchestras came into vogue in Zanzibar town in the first decades of the twentieth century.

Kidumbak is played in the streets for any kind of festivity or just as an evening entertainment. The better-off in the classier **Stone Town** area of Zanzibar despise it as a kind of poor-folks' taarab. To them it is *ng'ambo* – 'on the other side' – belonging to the poor quarters of town, with their palm-thatched huts.

Kidumbak Ensemble

The Stone Town side of the musical spectrum is represented by **Ikhwani Safaa** – the oldest musical club on the island (and most probably in all of Africa). It celebrated its ninetieth birthday in 1995, though in the past few years it has had difficulties keeping its membership involved. Singer and violinist **Seif Salim**, a former leader of the club, has recently joined forces with some former colleagues to form a group called **Twinkling Stars**. They play a local tourist hotel and sometimes at official government functions when they may also feature **Bi Kidude**, the doyenne of Zanzibar taarab, a robust lady in her eighties with a gorgeous voice. Kidude started out her musical career with Siti bint Saad back in the late 1930s.

So-called **modern taarab** has made big inroads into the rather conservative Zanzibar taarab scene. A group called **East African Melody** is the big current act, with a sound dominated by a pair of keyboards and a tiny drum machine. Compared to the differentiated string arrangements of Culture and Ikhwani Safaa, they can sound bland to Western ears, but to the local

fashion-conscious Zanzibari audience they are contemporary and give them music to dance to. They are also champions of the *mipasho* phenomenon, the backbiting songs so popular among the female audience.

Tanga: Black Star

In the early 1960s the **Black Star Musical Club** of Tanga, a small town on the northern Tanzanian coast, turned around the whole taarab scene. Up until then, taarab was the near-exclusive province of Islamic Swahili – people who claimed long Swahili ancestry and often overseas origins. Then Black Star introduced a new modern style, with guitar and bass and a more danceable base. Taarab was revolutionised and began crossing national boundaries to audiences as far away as Burundi and Congo/Zaire. Today most taarab groups active in Tanzania, Burundi and Kenya are modeled on the style and instrumentation of the Black Star Musical Club, its offspring **Lucky Star**, and their star female singer **Shakila**.

Tanga itself went a bit quiet from the mid-1970s, but recently new voices have emerged. Chief among them is **Mwanahela**, whose clear, powerful tones are close to Shakila's. With her group **Golden Star**, Mwanahela has become one of the favourites on the cassette market up and down the coast. Their hit "Vidonge" was copied by dozens of taarab groups and was even covered by Congolese/Kenyan Samba Mapangala and his Orchestra Virunga. **Babloom Modern Taarab** was another recent arrival on the Tanga scene, now based in Dar.

Dar Es Salaam

As with Tanzania's dance band scene, so the taarab scene focuses increasingly on **Dar Es Salaam**. Dar had small taarab clubs since the early twentieth century and in the 1930s two important clubs were founded, the **Egyptian** and **Al-Watan Musical Clubs**.

These days, both clubs are outshone by various state-run or private taarab orchestras, organised along commercial lines. The first to become prominent was **JKT Taarab** – *Jeshi la Kujenga Taifa*, the 'Army for the Construction of the Nation', the national youth service. JKT's line-up – for a time East Africa's largest taarab orchestra – is similar to the Zanzibar orchestras, featuring a violin section, qanun and oud. In contrast to the more restrained Zanzibar style, however, JKT creates a lot of rhythmic

GRAEME EWENS

TANZANIA/KENYA

Bi Kidude at a WOMAD festival

Taarab Lyrics

Taarab songs form part of the long tradition of Swahili poetry: a song's quality is judged by the choice of words and on the adherence to the rules of metre and rhyme in the lyric. Contrary to the songs sung at ngoma or in dance music, the story in a taarab song is of minor importance. The main themes are love and sexual relationships but some songs deal with social or political issues.

Taarab has a language of metaphor and allegory that only those familiar with Swahili poetry can understand. The lyrics are pregnant with hidden meanings and double entendres and may relate to people or events known only to the writer. A lyric which an outsider takes to be a simple love song may in reality comment on events in the local community or national politics. The allegorical nature of taarab poetry makes it a perfect vehicle for social criticism. There have been some good examples of this in recent hits.

The first is "Kitanda" (The Bed) by **Shakila** and **JKT Taarab**:

You elders explain to me, so that my head may get rest,
(Even you men of God, may you open your books);
The bed always to be in a corner,
is it a custom or a law?
I have travelled all over the country,
and from Europe to Asia;
I have gone into the houses,
looking carefully for the beds;
The bed was in the corner wherever I went in.

On the surface, the song asks why, throughout the world, love is something to be hidden, relegated to the corner of society. But it was repeatedly quoted in the context of the transition to a multiparty democracy: in modern society, the value of cherished customs is always open to question and the one-party system – the basis of modern Tanzania – should not be taken for granted.

The life of the Swahili is closely related to the sea, so maritime images often appear, as in the story-line of "Manahodha" (The Captains) by **Malika**:

I encountered something amazing, a war on the sea,
A shoving and pushing has occurred,
and me I'm in the boat,
The captains have a war, they fight for the rudder.
They show strength to each other,
the fighting captains,
And their rudder is rotten,
and they have already cut the sail,
But with all their might, they are fighting the wheel.
Me I leave the sea, I cannot stand their fighting,
Whenever I think I can see their end,
It will be that the nails will come
to be far from the boards.

The story is of two captains fighting over the course of a boat, but the theme is really about the 'captains of the house' – two women fighting over rights in a polygamous household and over the best of their husband.

excitement, and performances usually wind up in dancing. Led by violinist and singer **Issa Matona**, the band features many fine female vocalists, among them Shakila (of Black Star fame).

The political and economic liberalisation of the early 1990s led to new developments on Dar Es Salaam's taarab scene. Two large (and rival) orchestras were at the forefront of this evolution: **Muungano Taarab**, owned by a businessman, and **TOT** (Tanzania One Theatre), which is closely related to the ruling CCM party. Both groups offer a variety of styles – a kind of integrated family entertainment including stage versions of ethnic ngoma, kwaya, theatrical plays and taarab. Shows are performed on Saturday and Sunday afternoons at social halls all over the city. Yet, the culminating climax of their performances is the taarab: TOT and Muungano present the flashiest taarab ever heard in East Africa, adding synthesiser and a dance band-style rhythm section to regular taarab instruments like violin, accordion and local percussion.

What creates all the excitement, however, are the groups' deliberately offensive *mipasho* (back-biting) song lyrics. Celebrating the tradition of institutionalised rivalry between taarab groups, the mipasho shows are boisterous affairs. Hundreds of women in the audience take part, dancing up to the lead singers at appropriate sections of the song, to give *tuzo* money, and to show their affiliation to one group or another, or to direct attention to a member of the audience against whom they may have a grudge. Once or twice a year the groups have a face-off at the National Stadium to find out who can muster the more boisterous following.

In the wake of the Muungano/TOT focus, older Dar taarab groups, like **Bima** and **Magereza Taarab**, have tended to go into decline. However, the revived nationwide interest has led to the formation of many new groups. Among the leaders, beginning to attract followings, are **All Stars Modern Taarab**, and **Babloom**, the latter having recently moved to Dar from Tanga.

discography

Compilations

 Songs the Swahili Sing (Original Music, US).

The sound of Mombasa taarab, culled from singles produced by Mzuri Records in the late 1950s and 1960s. Contains some of the earliest recordings by Zein and group, including singers Zuhura Swaleh and Maulidi, plus hits by Juma Bhalo, Matano Juma and 1950s favourite Yaseen. The CD re-issue also includes groups from Dar Es Salaam in recordings made by Hugh Tracey (see p.669) in 1951 for the International Library of African Music.

Artists

Black Star & Lucky Star Musical Clubs

Black Star Musical Club, followed by its offspring Lucky Star, was the group that put Tanga – a small town on the coast of northern Tanzania – on the musical map in the 1960s. Their innovations, such as the introduction of electric and bass guitars, as well as a more dance-orientated approach, led to a revolution in taarab that was imitated throughout Tanzania and beyond.

 Nyota: Classic Taarab from Tanga (GlobeStyle, UK).

Some of the most essential taarab recordings – originally on Mzuri singles in the early 1970s. You can't fail to fall in love with this sound: voices of Sharmila, Shakila and Asmahan, nice guitar work and that wonderful Tanga bass.

Culture Musical Club

Culture Musical Club (CMC), Zanzibar's largest orchestra, today combines the best of sounds in the world of taarab. Typical large string section along with a mixture of Arab and African instruments, soaring vocals over infectious local rhythms.

 Taarab 4: The Music of Zanzibar (GlobeStyle, UK).

Recorded during GlobeStyle's 1988 trip to the island, this features some classical tracks from Zanzibar's taarab repertoire, including Bakari Abeid's "Sabalkheri Mpenzi".

 Spices of Zanzibar (World Network, Germany).

The latest recording from the Spice Islands. Features Culture's current crop of singers – Fatma Issa, Makame Faki and Saada Mohamed – and the orchestra's prowess on two instrumentals in a set modeled on a typical concert.

 Kidumbak Kalcha: Ng'ambo – The Other Side of Zanzibar (Dizim, Germany).

Members of CMC, led by singer/composer Makame Faki, playing kidumbak, Zanzibari roots taarab. A different perspective on Zanzibari music, in that kidumbak is basically a dance music. Includes kidumbak versions of some of Makame's best-loved songs, Fatma Issa's "Mpewa Hapokonyeki", and the definitive Indian Ocean-style version of "La Paloma".

East African Melody

Zanzibar's talk-of-the-town modern taarab ensemble, East African Melody have a funky sound based on two keyboards and drum machine.

📼 **Melody Safarini** (EAM, Zanzibar).

Many locally made cassettes of this ensemble are available. This is one of the better ones produced during a stay in Abu Dhabi.

Ikhwani Safaa Musical Club

Ikhwani Safaa are Zanzibar's oldest and most revered musical club, founded in 1905, and must boast getting on for a thousand years' worth of collective experience.

 Taarab 2: the Music of Zanzibar (GlobeStyle, UK).

Recorded in 1988, this shows Ikhwani Safaa in its prime, with the typically lush string arrangements and sweet melodies over laid-back Latin rhythms. Enjoy the voices of Rukia Ramadhani, Mohamed Ilyas and Seif Salim. The latter's "Nipepee" is a highlight.

JKT Taarab

JKT – Tanzania's army youth conscripts band – have one of the punchiest taarab sounds around, and have featured many of the top female vocalists, including Shakila.

📼 **JKT Taarab Cassette No. 2** (Mbwana Radio Service, Mombasa, Kenya).

This is top-notch orchestral taarab and includes Shakila's big hit

"Kitanda", the popular "Nahodha", and some of Issa Matona's favourites.

Kidude Binti Baraka

Kidude is an institution on Zanzibar Island, being famous for her contemporary re-makes of songs from the Siti bint Saad repertoire of the 1930s.

 Bi Kidude
(RetroAfric, UK).

This recording presents Bi Kidude in a variety of settings alternatively accompanied by Zanzibar's Twinkling Stars and Dar's Shikamoo Jazz Band. There is a story-type approach behind this release – forget about hi-fidelity and savour Kidude's inimitable *yaleli*.

Kilimani Muslim School

Kilimani Muslim School perform *qasida*, religious songs centered on the life of the Prophet Mohamed. They are the Zanzibari masters of this type of taarab-related music which includes an intricate rhythmic accompaniment on a set of tuned frame drums.

🔘 **Music from Tanzania and Zanzibar, Vol. 3**
(Caprice, Sweden).

This recording is hampered by the less than satisfactory acoustics which tend to muddle the rhythmic finesse. Nonethless recommended for the beauty of the voices and the idea behind tuned percussion.

Malika

Malika is one of the longest-established and best-loved of Mombasa taarab singers.

📼 **Malika Cassette No. 8**
(Mbwana Radio Service, Mombasa, Kenya).

Perhaps her voice was better on some of the earlier recordings, but this one has her version of the smash hits "Vidonge" and "Sitaki sitaki" to recommend it.

Issa Matona

Singer/violinist Issa Matona, formerly with Zanzibar's Culture Musical Club, now leads JKT Taarab (see opposite). He also plays weddings around Dar es Salaam with his own little group.

📼 **Kimasomaso** (Tanzania Film Company, Tanzania).

Recorded live at a Dar Es Salaam wedding by Matona and some members of JKT, this is very strong on atmosphere with lots of audience interaction. "Kimasomaso" is a half-hour rap on marriage, wifely duties and the pleasures of love.

Maulidi Musical Party

Singer Maulidi Juma and Party were Mombasa's premier musical party of the 1970s and '80s.

🔘 **Mombasa Wedding Special** (GlobeStyle, UK).

This selection from their Swahili-wedding repertoire includes

favourites like "Mume ni Moshi wa koko" and the mwanzele dance "Mkufu" featuring the organ-cum-nzumari (oboe) playing of organist Adio Shigoo.

Muungano Taarab

A new-style band from Dar Es Salaam, Muungano Taarab currently rule the roost with their big rivals, TOT (see below). They feature the city's most talked-about singer, Khadija Kopa.

📼 **Cassette No. 8: Homa ya Jiji**
(Mamu Stores, Tanzania).

This is a pretty representative sample of modern Dar Es Salaam taarab at the end of the 1990s.

Mwanahela & Golden Star

Tanga's young Mwanahela, leading the group Golden Star with her clear and powerful voice, has been hailed as the successor to Black Star's Shakila and Sharmila.

📼 **Golden Star Cassette No. 5**
(Mbwana Radio Service, Mombasa, Kenya).

Great tunes, great voice, and that fat Tanga bass. Available in most cassette stores along the coast.

TOT Taarab

TOT Taarab are, with Muungano Taarab, Dar Es Salaam's leading band – a rhythmically infectious hi-tech outfit big on electric guitars, bass and synthesiser.

📼 **Cassette No. 10** (Mamu Stores, Tanzania).

Another example of the fashionable Dar style with lots of tough lyrics. Includes Ali Star's smash hit "Natanga na Njia".

Zein Musical Party

Zein l'Abdin, a master of the oud, hails from Lamu island on the north Kenyan coast, but now lives in Mombasa. A native of the old centre of Swahili culture and literature, he is known for his researches into old Swahili poetry.

 The Swahili Song Book
(Dizim, Germany).

All-acoustic versions of timeless Swahili classics, like "Loho ya Kihindi", "Maneno Tisiya" and "Mnazi Wangu", along with some of Zein's own recent compositions.

Zuhura & Party

Zuhura Swaleh, one of Mombasa's outstanding female singers has an energetic style firmly based in chachaka ngoma rhythms.

🔘 **Jino la Pembe** (GlobeStyle, UK).

A fine introduction to taarab music, this is a compendium of Zuhura's most popular chakacha songs, notably "Parare" and the title tune "Jino la Pembe" recorded on a European tour with the Maulidi Musical Party.

Uganda

exiles and traditions

Few countries have had a less promising backdrop for music and culture than Uganda over the past three decades, riven, as it has been, by ethnic conflict, civil war, and military rule. The capital, Kampala, has produced a few sporadic waves of dance music – influenced mainly by Congolese rumba and Kenyan benga – but most modern Ugandan music of the 1980s and 1990s has come from exiles, based mainly in France – like Geoffrey Oryema – and Sweden. However, as Swedish producer **Sten Sandahl** discovered, relative stability under Yoweri Museveni's government of 'moral and economic reconstruction', has led to a reviving scene, and, despite everything, traditional music has somehow survived in the villages.

Music became a weapon in Uganda's conflict as early as the 1960s, during the first post-independent government of Milton Obote. As part of his attempt to subdue the southern, semi-autonomous 'Kingdom of Buganda', the homeland of the Bantu Ganda people, Obote ordered the destruction of the royal drums – generations of legendary drums, each with their own name and history. But, of course, it was little more than a detail amid the decades of tyranny and chaos under Idi Amin (1972–79), and a second period of Obote and civil war, before some semblance of normality began to emerge after Museveni took power in 1986.

In Kampala, throughout this period, to go out to a dance or for a drink meant putting your life at stake: not a conducive situation for live music. People did go out, of course, despite the frequent curfews, and bands would play Saturday gigs – beginning with a teenagers' matinee dance from 2pm–8pm, followed by a curfew-hours gig from 9pm until dawn. These days, thankfully, things are a little easier, although the government could do a lot more to help. Instruments remain in short supply (and highly taxed), and there is no real recording industry to support local bands, with the only studio worth the name in Kampala used mostly for radio jingles.

Guitar Groups and Musician-exiles

Kampala's guitar-based dance bands, from the 1960s on, have played covers of popular US and European music, as well as material from neighbouring Kenya and Congo (Zaire). Many of the early dance band musicians were actually refugees

from Zaire, and sung in Lingala, which nobody understood but everyone loved nonetheless. The influence of Congolese sounds has been enduring – indeed, it remains clear today in the music of **Afrigo**, which has been the best band in Kampala since the beginning of the 1980s.

There are, however, songs with a distinct Ugandan sound, sung in Luganda (the Baganda language), which have become more or less standards for the repertoire of any band. These come from the album *Born in Africa*, produced in Sweden in 1987 by exiled musicians under the leadership of the late **Philly Lutaaya** – a singer who had been working for years with everyone on the music scene in Kampala. Copied onto cassette, the songs were played literally everywhere in Uganda, and even a decade later, you'll hear them daily on the radio or at dance venues.

Philly's group featured top Ugandan musicians, including percussionist, **Gerald Nnaddibanga**, whose participation in different bands reads like a *Who's Who* of Ugandan popular music from the 1970s onwards. Another prime contributor was bass-player **Sammy Kasule**, a bandleader, arranger and composer, with several top–listed Kenyan songs under his belt. After his death, these two formed the Swedish-based band, **Makonde**, which during 1996 and 1997 toured Uganda and enjoyed spectacular success at home. Part of the same group of exiled musicians was another veteran from the 1970s, **Frank Mbalire**, who has had several hits back home with overseas-produced cassettes.

The most prominent and successful exile musician, however, is **Geoffrey Oryema**, who has been based in France since fleeing Uganda during the Amin years. Influenced by Western singers and music, as well as by his own Acholi roots, he was

The Big Five - well, six of them; Eko is third left, Juliet Ssessanga second from right

taken up by WOMAD and its RealWorld label, and has produced some stunning material with Peter Gabriel and Brian Eno. He is not, though, particularly well known at home.

In Kampala, at the end of the 1990s, the action revolves around the **Musicians club**, and in particular its Monday evening sessions in a small venue above the National Theatre. At these events, you're likely to hear performances from the likes of guitarist **Edel' 'Eko' Akongu Ekodelele**, one of the city's main bandleaders. Together with vocalist **Juliet Ssessanga** and legendary guitar-player **Dede Majoro** (who died in 1998), Eko put together a 'supergroup', **Big Five**, to record the 1996 album, *Echoes of Kampala* (again originally released in Sweden), which gives a good impression of contemporary Ugandan guitar music. On the album, Eko used rhythms, language and inspiration from his native Teso culture in north-eastern Uganda, and on other tracks collaborated with traditional baganda musicians to produce interesting new fusions.

Another feature of Kampala's music scene is to be heard in the area known as Wandegeya – a maze of tiny beer joints and bars – where troubadours entertain the guests. The music is known as **kadongo kamu** ('just a small guitar') and the songs are narrative in classic East African folk tradition. They focus on any subject – from mocking the paying guests, to giving advice about love, or relating the

downfall of Idi Amin – and you can commission a song for less than a dollar. The singer will accompany himself on a guitar – often home-made with bicycle-brake-wire strings – and may appear with a drummer, playing a tin can with a skin made from the inner tubes of car tyres. The late **Bernard Kabanda** was a delightful master of this style.

Folk Traditions

The trauma and madness of Uganda in the 1970s was mirrored on a small scale by its traditional music. Early on in Amin's reign, a show was put together by Kampala's National Theatre director Robert Sserumaga which gave rise to a group called **Theatre Limited** – an ethnic folklore group. Its members studied the traditional music of different parts of Uganda and gave performances both within the country and abroad. Amin became suspicious of the group's activities, however, and after one of their international tours, members were placed under house arrest. The whole group secretly left the country on false papers as a result. Most of them are now living in Sweden.

A new group of this kind, the **Ndere Troupe**, was formed in 1986, as part of Museveni's policy of national reconstruction. Genuinely pan-Ugandan, with members from most of the cultures and language groups, it remains active, working hard to develop and perform traditional music.

Baganda

The old kingdom of Buganda, comprising much of southern Uganda, has ancient and rich musical traditions. Its people, the **Baganda** (or Ganda), are the largest ethnic group in the country, but found themselves in conflict with the (northern) rulers in power from Independence until the emergence of Museveni (himself a Baganda).

Baganda musical traditions range from the ancient forms of court music (including the drums destroyed by Obote) to swinging *bakisimba* dances. The repertoire has been kept alive through its repression and the years of chaos by master musicians – individuals such as the late master **Evalisto Muyinda** (1914–94) or **Albert Ssempeke** and his group **Aboluganda Kwagalana**. Ethnomusicologists, too, have played a part – notably **Andy Cooke** (and his father Peter), who often performs with Ssempeke. And the US-based musician **Samite** has made a series of albums using material from traditional baganda folk songs.

The music is alive in everyday form, too. At parties and weddings, the **baksimba** dance is a regular feature, accompanied by rolling rhythms beaten out on a traditional set of four drums. Three of the drums are pot shaped with two skins laced together, and the fourth, the *engalabi*, which is long and narrow, explodes in improvised outbursts every now and again.

Lango

North of Kampala is the region of the **Lango**, a people with historic and language links to Sudan. Its dominant music, however, at festivals and gatherings, is played on a local variety of the **okeme**, or thumb piano – an instrument thought to have arrived early in the twentieth century through Congolese porters. Okeme groups can be large, with fifteen or more musicians playing instruments of different sizes from treble down to bass.

Singing at Lango occasions often takes up contemporary topics – politics, health, famine, good crop culture, advice on AIDS – and falls back on the Lango tradition of what is maybe best described as a 'group rap'. This traditional music, predominantly vocal, entails much rhythmical reciting accompanied by foot-stomping as participants land on the beat after leaping high in the air. It is an impressive sight to see twenty, thirty or more men jumping straight up in the air and landing with a whoosh, without missing a single syllable in the long texts they recite.

Acholi

North again from the Lango region is cattle-herding **Acholi** country, another language and culture, with a tradition of sweet, melodious music, often accompanied by a number of small percussion instruments. This is the musical background of Geoffrey Oryema (see p.698).

Like most traditional music in Uganda, acholi music is based on the pentatonic (five tone) scale. Of particular note, however, is the vocal style: **singing in parts** is common. Good church choirs exist throughout Uganda but most people agree the best ones are found among Acholi.

Some of the choirs use ensembles of folk music instruments – always very tight – to accompany their music, which is often based on traditional forms. A favourite instrument is the **adungu** harp, which comes in a variety of sizes from treble down to bass; with its oblong skin-covered body and angled neck, it resembles a small canoe. The harps are also used by local **dance bands**, whose repertoire includes anything from traditional songs to cover versions of current popular songs. Through it all, you can always detect the big, dominating influence of Congo.

With thanks to Peter Cooke

discography

Compilations

 Kampala Sound: 1960s Ugandan Dance Music (Original Music, US).

Ugandan musicians recorded in Nairobi between 1964 and 1968, mostly with local Kenyan musicians backing them. A

THE KAMPALA SOUND
1960s Ugandan
Dance Music

beautiful collection charting a part of the history of African pop. And who is the fantastic sax player, Charles, who appears on "Hamadi"? Not even Original Music's informative John Storm Roberts can say.

Music from Uganda 1: Traditional
(Caprice, Sweden).

This valuable series of discs was produced in Uganda in 1996 by SIDA (Swedish International Development Agency) to showcase various aspects of the country's music. Volume 1 covers a range of traditional styles including an extraordinary xylophone piece (from Baganda royal musicians), and the unearthly sound of the *ennanga*, believed to be similar to the harp of the ancient Egyptians.

Music from Uganda 2: Modern Traditional
(Caprice, Sweden).

This second volume can hardly fail to get under your skin – just listen to the Holy Rosary Church Choir's adaptations of European hymns for massed harps and Acholi singers. The disc also features several tracks from the delightful troubador Bernard Kabanda, playing guitar and beating out the rhythm with his elbow.

Music from Uganda 3: Modern – Echoes of Kampala (Caprice, Sweden).

An album put together by Edel' 'Eko' Akongu Ekodelele with musicians from his own and other contemporary Kampala bands, including vocalist Juliet Ssessanga and Dede Majoro. Eko uses the rhythms and language of his native Teso culture (from north-eastern Uganda) on some tracks, and on others collaborates with traditional Baganda musicians to produce interesting new fusions.

Tipu pa Acholi (PAN, Uganda).

A well recorded album of traditional music from Acholi territory. All are local musicians and singers perform their normal, every-day music.

Uganda: Village Ensembles of Basoga
(VDE-Gallo/AIMP, Switzerland).

Traditional groups recorded on location in villages in the Basoga district of southeastern Uganda. Amateur and semi-professional musicians show a wide variety of musical forms, instruments and ensembles. Compiled by ethno-musicologist Peter Cooke, this is the record to get if you have even a slight interest in one of the unknown music cultures of East Africa. The music is marvellous, the recording quality excellent and the detailed booklet a pleasure to read.

Artists

Afrigo Band

Led by saxophonist Moses Matovu, Afrigo is the oldest and best-known band working in Kampala. The core of the band started off in the late 1960s in an earlier version of the band called The Cranes.

Tugenda mu Afrigo (African Culture Promotions, UK).

So wonderful live, Afrigo has yet to produce a convincing album. The song "Bakulimba", however, inspired by Basoga music from eastern Uganda, is an impressive new direction for them, and the disc is preferable to its follow-up, *Mp'eddembe*.

Makonde

Makonde was formed in the early 1990s by Ugandan

exiles in Sweden, together with local musicians. They really deserve recognition beyond Scandinavia.

Ba-Makonde (Rub-a-dub, Sweden).

This debut album is pretty good but compared to what they do live comes over a little tame, lacking the force and jazzy impro-vised solos that are their true strengths.

Evalisto Muyinda

Evalisto Muyinda (1914–94) was the last of the court musi-cians with full knowledge of the ancient traditional music from the court of the Buganda *kabakas* (kings).

Evalisto Muyinda (Pan, Netherlands).

A truly great record, with excellent notes, featuring this great master of an ancient and now near-extinct tradition.

Ndere Troupe

Led by Stephen Rwangyezi, the Ndere Troupe is a perfor-mance group of twenty or so students and graduates from Makarere University. They are the resident players of the National Theatre in Kampala.

Kikwabanga (PAN, Uganda).

A sympathetic initiative by this Kampala-based group of music students, performing traditional work. But then there are always the local people who really do it a little bit better…

Geoffrey Oryema

Geoffrey Oryema had to flee Uganda (in the boot of a car) during the Amin era. Settling in Paris, he has almost sin-glehandedly put his country on the World Music map, through festival appearances, and some stylish singer-songwriter discs recorded for RealWorld.

Exile
(RealWorld, UK).

An elegant album of songs with the characteristic sweet Acholi roots. Oryema sings beautifully and plays local vari-eties of harp and thumb piano, beside acoustic guitar, while production is handled sympathetically by Brian Eno.

Night to Night (RealWorld, UK).

This follow-up sees Oryema and his producers fade down the African roots in an attempt to crossover to rock terrain. As a French rock album – and one that ploughs all over the shop, into Lion King Disneyland and French bistro bars – it's really rather good, though African music enthusiasts may be less impressed.

Samite

Samite Mulondo lives in exile in the US where his music has developed under younger days at home playing covers of rock and pop with the band Mixed Talents. He has since found his roots and become Uganda's unofficial cultural ambassador to the US along the way.

Pearl of Africa Reborn (Shanachie, US).

An album drawing heavily on Baganda traditional music and children's songs – most Baganda people can sing along with this disc at first hearing – this is an attractive if somewhat uneven, accoustic blend.

Silina Musango (Xenophile, US).

Tighter than *Pearl*, this album still draws on a lot of traditional material, as well as input from Europe and the West Indies. Better produced and distilled, Samite is clearly on the move.

Zambia

evolution and expression

Zambian music has little international profile – there are astonishingly few CDs available – yet in the 1970s and 1980s it contributed a couple of distinctive African pop sounds: Zam-rock and a funky version of Congolese rumba known as kalindula. In the 1990s, with a severe economic donwturn and the opening of the airwaves to foreign sounds, its music scene has fractured, with local production focused on low-cost ragga and hip-hop. But maybe there's another chapter waiting: Zambia certainly has the roots of inspiration in the traditional music of its numerous ethnic groups. **Ronnie Graham** and **Simon Kandela Tunkanya** survey the scene.

Zambia had a relatively short struggle for self-determination. At independence in 1964, the country inherited a significant copper-based economy. A new elite of Africans formed a new cultured class of administrators and technocrats, and tended to adopt the inherited culture of the British colonial rulers. The music favoured by an explosion of urban migrants, however, in the capital, Lusaka, and in the towns of the copper belt, held on to the rural African feel and mood in its rhythms, artistic spontaneity and sensitive creativity, adapting foreign sounds and European instruments like the guitar and accordion to the principles of African music.

From Independence to Zam-rock

In the early 1960s, Zambia's radio station, the Zambia Broadcasting Service, was the chief provider of – and outlet for – music. It did pioneering work in traditional music, across the whole of southern central Africa, recording ceremonial and festival music and work songs. The ZBS director was musician **Alick Nkhata**, who worked often with the archivist Hugh Tracey (see p.669), and also formed the **Lusaka Radio Band**, later the Big Gold Six Band, Zambia's first indigenous band. Its mandate was to promote Zambian music

Alick Nkhata (left) recording in the countryside in the 1960s

Tribal Music, Dance and Instruments

Zambia has 72 distinct **ethnic groups** and **seven main languages**, all of whom have converged in the mining and other towns. They are basically of **Bantu** origin, and two centuries before came largely from the Kola region in the ancient Luba-Lunda kingdom. Each group once had its own music and culture, but even under colonial rule, urban development grew rapidly and the ethnic groups impacted on each other to create tribal cultural and musical cross-breeds. Still, it's possible to identify five distinct, geographically defined, tribal musical currents, which continue to some degree, and have fed into modern Zambian music.

Eastern Province: Cewa, Nyau and Ngoni

High pitched *vimbuza* (talking drums) are characteristic of the **Cewa** people and their **Nyau** dance. The **Ngoni** are distinguished in the *Ingoma* dance, their powerful voices shaped by years of battlefield war cries, accompanied by vigorous foot-stomping, as they brandish shields, urged on by the women with rhythmic clapping.

Northern Province: Bemba

Low pitched *kalela* drums, beaten with sticks, are prevalent among the **Bemba** of the north who also developed a string instrument – the *babatone* – made from animal skin with the string drawn over a drum by a

wooden handle, and fashioned rather like a double bass. This style formed the basis of **kalindula**.

Western Province: Lozi and Nkoya

The xylophone is the outstanding instrument among the **Lozi** and **Nkoya** and, depending on the occasion and the size of the instrument, it can be played by one or up to four people. It is constructed of slats of wood placed over a long platform with reverberators made from gourds arranged in descending order of size.

North-West Province: Luvale and Kaonde

The *kachacha* beat is the typical sound of North-West, particularly amongst the **Luvale** people. It is created from combinations of up to six drums, with the dancers rhythmically stamping their feet with shakers and jingles – made from seedpods and scrap-metal bells – strapped around their ankles. The **Kaonde** people's version is the *manchancha* with three drums complemented by dancing women. This is mainly an initiation dance for girls who are coming of age.

Southern Province

The renowned talking drum – known here as *tonga* – is played by squeezing on the stick inside the drum with wet fingers; this is performed by a solo praise singer or village poet who packs his voice with high emotion, lamentation, joy and happiness depending on the occasion.

and it thrived on translating original rural recordings into the scored musical language of the West. It is still going, as the **Big Gold Six Band**, and (still with two of its original members) keeps the memories of that era alive playing in the cool comfort of Lusaka's *Inter-Continental Hotel*.

The Radio Band was a one-off, however, and Zambian radio played mostly **Congolese rumba**, which was also the dominant style in Lusaka's handful of up-market hotel ballrooms, frequented by the new elite and remaining colonials, who relaxed to bands like the Broadway Quintet, Crooners and De Black Evening Follies, rendering 'copyright' (cover) versions of foreign hits.

Seeing an opportunity to produce and market local music, **Peter Msungilo** established DB Studios in Lusaka's Cha Cha Cha road, and he was soon followed by the **Teal Record Company** – a subsdiary of South Africa's Gallo – and the Zambia Music Parlour. Both Teal and ZMP set up in Zambia's second city, the copperbelt town of **Ndola**, tapping into the vibrant musical culture – and ready market – that was developing there.

The mining towns of the north Zambian copper belt were a vibrant melting pot. In the hard-drinking, multi-cultural mining camps, an evening's entertainment might consist of a drunken brawl and a visit to a strip joint. There was also a music scene developing. At first, this was a kind of folk music, as singers like **Stephen Tsotsi Kasumali**, **William Mapulanga** and **John Lushi** walked with their guitars from camp to camp, picking out morality songs to the wry amusement of all. But it gradually developed a more guitar-based and more rock-based sound.

In the early years, **Zam-rock** used Western-style guitars and drums. The songs were in English and, sometimes, local languages and they were rebellious, protesting, for example, against tribal taboos on sex and relationships. The pioneers included **Musi-o-tunya**, a short-lived combo named after the Victoria Falls, who released Zambia's first commercial LP, and the unsettlingly-named army group, the **Machine-Gunners**. These early bands were heavily influenced by **Osibisa** (the London-based Ghanaian combo), who visited Zambia in 1972.

The crowning glory of Zam-rock was **Great**

JAK KILBY

Masasa Band

Witch, a band which achieved a huge following. They expressed the concerns and preoccupations of the younger generation, satisfying the curiosity created by the worldwide popularity of rock, adopting wholesale Western musical styles. Fronted by lead singer **Jaggari Chanda**, their popularity has never been surpassed.

Another significant group of the time was **Emmanuel Mulemena**'s **Sound Inspectors**. The late Mulemena was one of the most influential of Zambia's folk balladiers. Not a Zam-rocker, his more subtle messages were urban-based social commentaries that dealt with life on the less affluent side of town. He appealed to a wide audience as he sang in the principal Zambian languages. After his untimely death, his band, renamed the **Mulemena Boys**, kept the spirit of his music alive for a while with a series of hit singles and a *Tribute to Emmanuel Mulemena* album – a phenomenally successful reworking of his compositions.

Kalindula Arrives

The Zambian state was an isolated regime in the late 1970s, ploughing its own furrow on the wrong side of the Cold War divide, fearful of the appeasement of apartheid by Reagan and Thatcher, and of Ian Smith's dangerous regime in white-ruled Rhodesia across its closed southern border. Against this backdrop, and in the cause of solidarity and national identity, President **Kenneth Kaunda**, himself an enthusiastic amateur guitarist, issued a decree that no less than 95 percent of music on the radio was to be of Zambian origin – nineteen songs for every Top 20. The president argued for Zambianisation – the creation of a unique Zambian musical identity, something akin to Mobutu's call for *authenticité* in Zaire.

The result was not quite the cultural roots revival Kaunda had intended. Instead, every Zam-

bian teenager with a box guitar and a singing voice tried their hand at being a pop star. Hundreds of bands were established, often by opportunistic entrepeneurs with a truck-load of instruments, to play note-perfect renditions of other African styles.

Meantime, the established musical community responded to Kaunda in its own way. **Paul Ngozi**, one of Musi-o-Tunya's most talented former members, created a new style of music by retaining the rock-style lead guitar solos and putting his lyrics into local languages, creating a new dimension to Zambian music. By the mid-1980s, this had developed into a fully-fledged Zambian urban dance style – **kalindula**, which took its inspiration from the Bemba traditions of North-West province, and was named after a one-string bass instrument of the area.

Brasher than soukous, and funkier, kalindula was characterised by rumba-style guitars and a solid, rapid-fire bass line. The drums set off at a frantic pace (check Amayenge's contribution to the *Zambiance* collection on GlobeStyle) with the guitarists seemingly struggling to find the rhythm. Then, around 30 seconds into the song, a cooler groove emerges to provide dance floor satisfaction.

The first wave of kalindula was spearheaded by **Junior Mulemena Boys**, **PK Chishala & the Great Pekachi Band**, **the Masasa Band**, **Serenje Kalindula** and the **Oliya Band** – and stimulated sufficient interest for British tours. By the late 1980s, there were half a dozen LPs out on Western labels. Other groups soon followed as kalindula moved away from its origins and became a generic Zambian style.

At the turn of the decade, Lusaka's city centre hotels still preferred Zairean bands covering the latest Kinshasa styles, but for the majority of Zambians a good night out revolved around copious quantities of *Mosi* beer and kalindula action on the dance floor. Not that the two styles were completely separate. **Nashil Pichen Kazembe** was a kind of bridge between the Congolese influence and both Zam-rock and kalindula, and he inspired others such as **Peter Tsotsi Juma** and **MB Papa Kado** who continued to explore a middle line – somewhere between 'rumba Zam-rock' and kalindula.

Another significant, if short-lived, group of this period was **Maoma Band**. They broke up while on tour in Germany, where co-founder **Spuki Mulemwa** remained to pursue a successful solo career on a string of albums, most recently *Song for Mama Zambia*.

On Hold: the 1990s

If the 1976 presidential decree created kalindula, a new phase in Zambian music emerged with political and economic pluralism under the MMD government of the **1990s**. Economic crisis led to the complete collapse of the faltering Zambian music industry, while the cultural barricades that Kaunda had used to protect indigenous music were torn down and the sounds of the world flooded in.

Musicians had to contend with the harsh reality of a devasted economy and competition from imported music. Few were up to the challenge, and most of the kalindula bands broke up. Sadly, too, a number of the old veteran artists died during the decade, among them Nashil Pichen Kazembe, PK Chishala and Joyce Nyirongo – probably the finest Zambian woman vocalist of the previous two decades.

A younger generation, meantime, influenced by new radio stations, TV and video, began experimenting with all sorts of foreign styles: **reggae, ragga**, **R&B**, **hip-hop**, various **gospel sounds**. New names on the scene include Burning Youth, Bantu Roots, True Africans, Daddy Zemus, B-Sharp, Agogo Mulilo, Ras Willie, Chileshe Nshumfwa, Zanji Roots, Brian Chilala and the Chawama Gospel Singers. Some have succeeded in making tapes at backyard studios, though as yet they have rarely gone further than radio play.

Encouragingly, though, two of the strongest new acts in the 1990s were folk-based groups, with roots in the troubador tradition: **Pontiano Kaiche** and the **Sakala Brothers**, both of whom had major album successes, entitled *Insaka* and *Londole* respectively. Women singers, too, have been breaking into the music scene of late, encouraged by an annual 'Women in Music' talent event.

discography

Although Zambia is poorly represented on CDs from Western labels, there is an extensive series of local cassettes issued by the ZNBC covering a broad spectrum of Zambian music from troubadors through Zam-rock and kalindula to modern times.

Compilations

 Zambiance
(GlobeStyle, UK).

A terrific collection of contemporary Zambian dance music, mostly in the kalindula mould, including the speedy Amayenge, Shalawambe, the Fire Family and sublime guitar on the late Alfred Chisala Kalusha Jnr's "Ni Maggie".

From the Copperbelt… Zambian Miners' Songs
(Original Music, US).

Released in the African Acoustic series, eighteen interesting-to-beautiful songs by the mine camp entertainers of the copper-belt that straddles Zambia and southeastern Congo, field-recorded by ethno-musicologist Hugh Tracey in 1957.

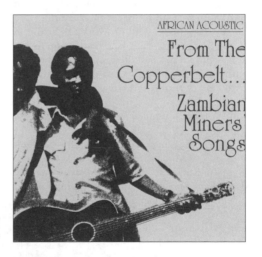

Artists

Alick Nkhata

Alick Nkhata was a former director of the Zambian radio station, founder of the radio band, and a talented singer-songwriter. He was killed, aged 54, by Rhodesian soldiers during a cross-border raid on a Zimbabwean guerrilla camp next to his farm in 1974.

Shalapo (RetroAfric, UK).

This re-issue is a selection from Nkhata's large output of guitar songs – perhaps a hundred compositions all told.

Zimbabwe

jit, mbira and chimurenga: play it loud!

Zimbabweans like their music loud – a problem in a country where equipment is scarce and public address systems often poor. But that doesn't deter the punters, who throng to have their ears blasted and their hips bumped. Despite hard times, the distorted thump-and-blare of straining speakers driven beyond their capacity remains the hallmark of Harare's hotels, nightclubs and beerhalls – spots the adventurous visitor won't want to miss. **Judy Kendall** and **Banning Eyre** have put in long nights dancing and talking to Harare's musicians through the din.

Zesa! Zesa! Put more Zesa! Harare's night-clubs reverberate with this cry at the end of the month when payday brings out the crowds. Zesa is the national electricity board, struggling, as everywhere in Africa, to meet the needs of its consumers. On payday they want to forget their troubles and go out dancing to Oliver Mtukudzi's soulful stomp and swing or Andy Brown's pop fusion at downtown *Sandros*; the gospel-tinged rumba anthems of Leonard Zhakata or Simon Chimbetu's party rumba at *Mushandira Pamwe Hotel* in Highfield; or Thomas Mapfumo with his rootsy, rebellious *chimurenga* music at the *Seven Miles Hotel*.

Harare, the capital of Zimbabwe, means 'don't stop' – a good name for a city where the bands go on forever, in several senses. Many of them are dependent on their venues for equipment and practice time, and they are required to play sometimes until dawn in all-night *pungwe* style. Before independence the pungwe was a dedication to the struggle. Now these Herculean performances are dedicated more to beerhall profits – more hours means more drinking time and more bucks. The music reflects the pungwe set-up and demands. Songs are often long and complex, with phrases and tunes repeated to familiarise the audience with a song before the band begins to play around with the intricate rhythms that have been set up by the guitars and the voices.

It is a tough life playing the local circuit and those musicians lucky enough to make it 'outside' (overseas) are often reluctant to return to the gruelling way of life back home. As **Dorothy Masuka**, the veteran jazz singer from Bulawayo, explains: "If I want money I must go out – a concert here will give you about enough to buy a bag of mealie meal (staple of ground corn). I wouldn't do what the youngsters are doing these days – Kambuzuma today, Highfield tomorrow – it's too much hard work. You play in the bar and people come to drink. They don't appreciate your music. I'd rather play one big concert a year and not work the rest of the time!" Masuka now makes her home in South Africa and, true to her word, returns to Zimbabwe for a single showcase once a year.

Getting on down at Queens Garden

Tough Times

Two decades after winning its independence, Zimbabwe finds itself in the throes of painful growth pains. The once cherished revolutionary government is now widely regarded as corrupt and mismanaged, its failure plain to see in the inflated prices of basic commodities, which have led to food riots and national strikes. Worryingly, such instability threatens to reignite dormant hostilities between Zimbabwe's dominant **Shona** population and the large **Ndebele** population in the south.

As elsewhere in southern Africa, the music industry is suffering a dual assault. Public belt-tightening has steadily reduced the crowds in Harare's famous nightclubs, and at the same time, the nation's media institutions (radio, TV and record companies) stand accused of putting more effort into promoting foreign culture than local. "Zimbabwean culture on the death bed?" asked a recent newspaper headline. The accompanying story mourned the way Zimbabwe's urban youth has become obsessed with fashion, music and culture from Europe, America and South Africa. Many of the jit and Zimbabwe rumba groups that used to rock the Harare clubs have moved their shows to the rural areas, and been replaced by DJs hawking foreign sounds like American rap, British ragga, and di gong (hip-hop) from South Africa.

Worse still, Zimbabwe's pop music pantheon continues to be devastated by an alarming series of untimely deaths, many of them attributable to AIDS. Since 1990, Zimbabwe has lost the major singers James Chimombe, Leonard Dembo (the top-selling Zimbabwe rumba artist ever), and gospel superstar Brian Sibalo, along with three founding members of the Bhundu Boys (including Biggie Tembo), at least five members of Thomas Mapfumo's Blacks Unlimited (including mbira guitar legend Jonah Sithole), three members of Oliver Mutukudzi's Black Spirits, and the core of the popular rumba outfit, Zig Zag Band.

Not all of these tragedies stem from AIDS, but many do. Get to know anyone in Harare well and you'll invariably hear about the deaths of friends, and on the TV and radio there are constant features on the disease. All that said, Zimbabwe's people and its musicians are proven survivors, and in face of all adversity, payday still finds Harareans flocking to beerhalls to hear their favourite bands. It takes more than inflation, HIV and Notorious BIG to keep this music down.

Beerhalls and Biras

"It's you who make Castle great!" announces the most popular beer advertisement in Zimbabwe. The essential in the manic mix of Harare nightlife is beer: people are fiercely loyal to their brand, whether it be imported Castle or Lion, locally brewed Zambezi or Bollingers, or the cheaper African chibuku, sold in brown plastic jugs called scuds (after Sadaam Hussein's famous missiles). Booze flows liberally during and between sets, and there's a real art to negotiating the intricate weave of Zimbabwean rhythms, keeping the upper body steady while loose legs and busy feet work the floor, and tightly wrapped fingers clench the neck of a dangling beer bottle. Dancing is a communal affair and no one need feel left out. If the band is good, people of all ages come on the floor – men with men, women with women, children with adults, groups and loners.

The public tends to be as fanatically devoted to their chosen band and its set as they are to their favourite beer – a loyalty of taste that new or experimental groups frequently bewail. People like to know the songs. Even Thomas Mapfumo is obliged to churn out the old favourites in his shows, and a new band needs to have a very big hit to persuade people to come out to a live show.

As electrification and development have spread through Zimbabwe's rural areas, **beerhalls** similar to those in the capital have sprung up in many small towns and 'growth points' (developing commercial centres in the rural areas), and bands once confined to the cities can now nurture their audiences town by town.

This fanning out of electric music might be seen as an urban infraction on the pastoral way of life, but for people to gather and dance with music and beer is nothing new in this country. Home-brewed 'seven-days' beer has long played an essential role in the **bira**, an all-night ceremony of traditional music, chanting and dancing that brings Zimbabweans into contact with the spirits of their ancestors. This village ritual can be seen as the prototype for the modern beerhall.

Ancestor spirits continue to play an important role as counsellors in many Shona communities, especially in the rural areas, but also in Harare's poor, high density suburbs. Spirits are seen as intermediaries between people and God; the older the spirit, the nearer to God. At a bira ceremony, the iron-keyed mbira is believed to summon ancestor spirits to come and possess a spirit medium who then offers advice on the matter at hand.

ZIMBABWE

The Mbira

Foreign observers often call the **mbira** a 'thumb piano', though most players reject the term as denying of the essential African quality of the instrument. At a bira ceremony, three or more mbiras play complex, interlocking parts as they render songs from an ancient repertoire, going back 1000 years or more.

When played, the mbira is housed in a large, halved calabash which both amplifies the instrument's sound and also obscures it with the buzzing of shells or bottle caps attached to the edges of the gourd. The effect is mysterious and powerful, and when animated by the insistent, broken-triplet rhythm of the *hosho* (shaker) and the tricky off-beats of the *ngoma* (hand drum), mbiras can keep people dancing all night. The singing that accompanies mbira music is otherworldly, rising from a soothing murmur to gut-wrenching cries.

In the 1930s, music archivist Hugh Tracey found the mbira almost extinct, but it has had a major revival in the last thirty years. The independence war played a part, with mbira music becoming associated with a national sound. And in the 1980s and 1990s, the mbira has had success among World Music fans. Its accessibility to Western ears is perhaps due to its innate sense of harmony. Unlike most traditional African forms, which are subservient to tonal language, metric and rhythmic form, mbira music is built on a unique harmonic patterning, based on cyclical patterns of two-note chords. The soundscape which a mbira creates also contains many melodies, or 'inherent patterns', once you're able to tune your ear to them.

The list of great mbira players in Zimbabwe is long, and some of the best ones may be known only to those in their surrounding villages. A few veteran players like **Stella Chiweshe**, **Ephat Mujuru**, **Dumisani Maraire** and **Tute Chigamba** have gained reputations on the international festival circuit, and they have been joined in recent years by innovative, younger players like the phenomenal **Forward Kwenda**. Mbira music calls for improvisation, so there's always room for a young lion to break new ground with the instrument, particularly in non-ceremonial settings.

For many players, however, the mbira is a sacred thing – rather than a source of musical display. **Amai Muchena**, who plays mbira with the group **Muri ko Muchena** (Muchena Family), explained "I don't play in beerhalls, because the spirit is like a God to go to if there are problems." She sees the instrument primarily as a means of healing. "To get a message to the spirits you make an appointment and then speak to the spirit. If you have a problem, you must buy some clothes and beads and cook beer and then have a party and play mbira then everything will be okay. If someone is suffering and sick from a spirit I will play mbira until the spirit comes up and then talk to it. It might say 'buy a gun or spear to keep in your house'."

Stella Chiweshe, probably the best-known player on the international circuit, has provoked some criticism for mixing sacred and commercial music, a controversial issue in a country where music is so close to the spiritual centre of life. She certainly uses the mystique of the instrument in her shows, sometimes going into a trance on stage. With her penetrating eyes, habitual snuff-taking, ankle charms, and dreadlocks falling in front of her face, she has a powerful presence. She is partly based in Germany, these days, and more often performs overseas than in Zimbabwe.

Mbira – as an instrument and sound pattern – also plays a role in electric groups, notably that of **Ephat Mujuru**'s **Spirit of The People**, and in the thoroughly electric style of Zimbabwe's best-known musician, **Thomas Mapfumo**.

Mapfumo: the Chimurenga Man

Thomas Mapfumo – known to Zimbabweans as 'Mukanya' (monkey) – has for twenty or so years been the country's most famous musician. Instantly recognisable by his majestic dreadlocks, the proverbial Lion of Zimbabwe fathered electric mbira music, developing the country's dominant style of chimurenga.

Like most Zimbabwean musicians who started out in the 1960s, Mapfumo began his career playing 'copyright' music – cover versions of Western hits – but in the early 1970s, he started writing and playing his own songs. By the time he founded the **Blacks Unlimited** in 1978, he was singing in Shona and experimenting with traditional sounds and beats. His guitarists and bass-player adapted mbira melodies to rock instrumentation, the drummer played the tripping rhythms of the hosho on his hi-hat, while the singers and brass section layered on melodies. From the start, the sound was original and very popular, even as it evolved year by year. The late 1980s found Mapfumo adding actual mbiras to his line-up, and today, he thinks of the band's three mbira players as its rhythm section, even as he plays songs that sound more like Afro-jazz, or otherworldly R&B.

BANNING EYRE

Thomas Mapfumo

the liberation troops who later developed his own career singing songs of the struggle.

Just as the mbira had a firm place in the strong spiritual world, so electric mbira music became a tool of the liberation war in the 1970s. Mapfumo's **chimurenga songs** (chimurenga means 'struggle') were used to good effect during the *pungwes* – all-night meetings of villagers with the liberation fighters. The irresistible beat provided an opportunity for community song and dance, an affirmation that was vitally necessary to a society split by secrecy, repression, guerrilla warfare and counter-terrorist activities. Shona and Ndebele lyrics could not be understood by the majority of the white population and so were a valuable means of communication for the liberation movement. Some of the lyrics of Mapfumo's songs were overtly political, while others made use of the Shona tradition of 'deep proverbs' to conceal messages of resistance: "Oh grandmothers/Oh mothers, oh boys/There's a snake in the forest/Mothers take hoes/Grandmothers take hoes/Boys take axes." Before the liberation war was over, Mapfumo had been briefly jailed by the white authorities, a clear sign of his effectiveness.

These days Mapfumo is a legend in Harare, still recording and performing at a frantic pace, and still a firm believer in the political importance of music. His sensational 1989 hit "Corruption" signalled a change in his politics, with its frank attack on the graft and greed that was beginning to rot Robert Mugabe's government. It was banned from the airwaves and within the year, on the album *Chamunorwa*, Mapfumo was singing, "Even if you insult me I know you fear me/Even if you insult me I know you hate me/The newspapers say bad things, but they are afraid/Those who read about me know the damage I can do/You plan to kill me but I know you fear me." His diatribe against what he now sees as a failed government has been steady ever since. The 1998 food riots in Harare found the chimurenga maestro and his band playing a new number called "We are slaves in our own country."

Mapfumo's hypnotic music has always drawn on Zimbabwe's wealth of traditional songs and chants, as well as his own far-flung modern influences, ranging from Elvis and Otis Redding to Chicago Transit Authority and the African jazz that flourished in this region during the 1950s and '60s. Singing in Shona was a brave and crucial step for a generation that had been taught to look down on their cultural traditions as backward. Initially Mapfumo's experiments were viewed with bemusement, but he was soon followed by other musicians, who openly acknowledge his influence – notably **Oliver Mtukudzi** (of whom more later), and **Comrade Chinx**, a choirmaster for

Tuku Music

Though still little known internationally, **Oliver 'Tuku' Mtukudzi** has been a second giant of Zimbabwean music over the past two decades – indeed his sales now exceed those of Mapfumo at home and across Africa. Tuku has produced more than two dozen LPs, as well as appearing in a number of films, notably the socially aware *Jit*.

Oliver 'Tuku' Mtukudzi

The oldest of seven children, Mutukudzi scored his first hit in 1977 with a group called the Wagon Wheels. Soon, he was fronting his own band, the **Black Spirits**, with whom he has recorded and performed ever since. His music is an innovative blend of Shona mbira pop (he acknowledges Mapfumo as an influence), South African township jive, rumba, and soul. Always keen to experiment, Tuku is known for switching from mbaqanga and jazz fusion in one album to 'ancient deep traditional beats' in the next. Despite that openness, he remains a strong traditionalist. For example, his album, *Kuvaira*, is typical Shona: "It's not fused to any other kind of music. I did it for the older people of Zimbabwe, for those who want pure pure Zimbabwe music, straight straight deep deep deep deep traditional sounds." The title track remains a staple of Mtukudzi's live show.

Tuku's swinging renditions of the rootsiest beats, accompanied by his soulful voice and husky laugh, are irresistible. Tall, slim and handsome, with a big stage presence, an easy manner and a slick line in dance moves, his performances with the Black Spirits are captivating. He is also a highly socially conscious and moral artist, intensely aware of the importance of his lyrics (which are important to all Zimbabwean music). He sang the first AIDS song in Zimbabwe, and his lyrics place an emphasis on discipline: "If one is disciplined then one is less likely to be corrupt. I believe in who we are, so my songs – though some might be in a different beat or a fusion of Western beats – don't run away from our tradition. I use proverbs and idioms that we use from long back when I sing in Shona. In English my lyrics change but I'm an African so I record my English as I speak it."

'Tuku music'– as the Mtukudzi blend is sometimes called – should be destined for enormous international success, for it's among the most accessible and delightful African pop around. He is a terrific songwriter, too, and it was little surprise to see American singer Bonnie Rait covering one of his songs, "What's Going On?" (from the soundtrack to *Jit*) in 1997.

Recently, Tuku has been working both with his own band and with a twelve-piece 'Southern African Supergroup' called **Mahube**. This came out of a project organised by South African Steve Dyer (of Southern Freeway), with Mtukudzi, Phida Mtya and the sensational vocalist Suthukazi Arosi. The original idea was to develop a style of music representative of the whole of southern Africa, to be presented at a 1998 festival in Germany, but the show received such acclaim that Mahube are now a fully-fledged band with a CD and an impeccable concert line-up.

Jit Hits the Fans

The term **jit** originally applied to a kind of recreational drumming and singing performed in Shona villages, but it has become a catch-all term for Zimbabwe's guitar-driven electric pop, which incorporates elements of Central and East African rumba, South African jive and local traditional music. You could try to sub-classify jit bands as rumba, *sungura*, *tsava-tsava*, mbira pop or whatever, but many of the most successful acts in Zimbabwe's pop history don't fit neatly into categories. The goal of appeasing a beerhall crowd can't be confined to any single genre.

Robson Banda and the **New Black Eagles** provide one shining example. Though Banda traces his roots back to Zambia, and Shona is actually his third language, he emerged in the 1980s as one of the most compelling voices in Shona pop. Banda has never been a superstar, but he and his group still record, and play in the beerhalls.

Another leading Shona band over the past couple of decades has been the **Four Brothers** whose sweet vocals soar over rippling guitar riffs and sure-fire dance rhythms. The group's leader Marshall Munhumumwe is Thomas Mapfumo's uncle, and learned drums and singing from him. Their first hit, "Makoro" (Congratulations), was dedicated to the freedom fighters at independence, and they became one of the top Zimbabwean bands of the 1980s. They called themselves the Four Brothers in order to remain equal, so that no brother would become 'big' – a fate that has shattered too many Zimbabwean bands in the past. Although popular in the West, they stick firmly to their roots, choosing to record in Harare. They play frequently at home and abroad, though sadly without their songwriter, who suffered a devastating stroke in 1997 and can no longer perform.

Another beerhall jit veteran still on the scene is **Paul Matavire**, the blind singer, songwriter and front man for the **Jairos Jiri Sunshine Band**. The group grew out of a welfare organisation founded to assist the re-integration of disabled Zimbabweans into society, and their songs often incorporate acute social observations. Ironically, Matavire himself was sentenced to a one-year prison sentence for rape in the early 1990s, though he has since, amazingly, reclaimed his career and a good measure of his popularity.

Overseas, the best known Jit band of the 1980s was the **Bhundu Boys**, whose flowing and energetic dance music – with its 'popcorn' style of guitar-playing and rousing vocal harmonies – earned them a name in the UK, where they became semi-resident. They were never as popular at home, and their music moved too close to Western pop (as on the disastrous *True Jit* album) in the late 1980s. Their frontman, the charismatic Biggie Tembo, subsequently left to join the Ocean City Band, and had a brief career as a gospel singer before his tragic suicide in 1995. After he left, the group lost two bass players and their keyboard man to AIDS. A version of the band soldiers on, but with little hope of reclaiming the old glory.

Rumba-Rumbira

In Zimbabwe, song lyrics and dance idioms are the keys to popularity, and many of the biggest sellers these days are local **rumba** artists, notably Simon Chimbetu and Leonard Zhakata. While the dominant influence in Zimbabwean rumba is from Congo (ex-Zaire), it has a fast triplet feel that is unique, and comes from mbira music.

Simon 'Chopper' Chimbetu is a veteran of the Zimbabwe rumba scene from his 1980s band, the Marxist Brothers. Now with his group, the **Dendera Kings**, he is loved for his infectious pop hooks and clever, humorous lyrics. Chimbetu believes strongly in singing songs about local culture. This may be one reason why he is seen to have stolen the thunder from Congolese rumba acts, who once dominated the music market here.

Simon 'Chopper' Chimbetu and dancers

His rival Zimbabwean rumba giant, **Leonard Karikoga Zhakata**, graduated from the early 1990s rumba group, Maungwe Brothers. As a solo artist, Zhakata has been named 'Best Musician' in numerous 1990s polls, and had a huge success with his 1996 release *Nzombe Huru*. He calls his music "a sound above genre," but it has a strong Congolese flavour, and his voice shimmers like those of South Africa's Soul Brothers. Zhakata's fans always cite his lyrics as his strongest hook. They say he has an uncanny knack for probing the psychic and spiritual crisis of Zimbabwe, eighteen years after independence and still deep in a state of struggle. One Harare music journalist wrote that Zhakata's latest songs have "the substance of a classic novel and the elegance of great poetry." No one ever said that about the songs of "kwassa-kwassa" kings or soukous sapeurs!

Rumba with a message has long been a successful formula in Zimbabwe. Until his premature death in 1997, **Leonard Dembo** consistently played Zimbabwean heartstrings with his homespun songs. Born in Masvingo, Dembo stumbled into a career in music with the Bulawayo group **Barura Express**, before moving in 1980 to Harare where he worked as a session musician. His early efforts made overnight stars of a group called The Outsiders. and once at the helm of his own band, Dembo polished his folksy rumba epics, which included the song "Chitikete," one of the best-selling singles ever in Zimbabwe.

John Chibadura, with his band the **Tembo Brothers**, was one of Zimbabwe's biggest-selling rumba artists in the 1980s and the early 1990s. A one-time goat-herder and truck driver, he appears a shy, introverted 'anti-star' but once on stage explodes in bare-chested bravado, combining rumba with full-throttle dance music. To non-speakers of Shona, the songs sound happy and upbeat but the lyrics often describe grim social conditions and deep-rooted fears, which, with typical Zimbabwean stoicism, are sung over a defiantly good-time beat. Changing musical tastes in Zimbabwe's urban centres see him performing abroad mostly these days.

An older rumba champion is the guitarist and songwriter **Jonah Moyo**, who formed the **Devera Ngwena Jazz Band** just before independence. Their music is a highly infectious form of rumba and, although they haven't achieved much recognition outside Zimbabwe, locally they're a very popular band, especially in the rural areas. Other local rumba groups of note include the **Zig Zag Band**, who still play despite heavy losses to AIDS, and the **Kiama Boys**, whose acrimonious break-up in 1998 came as a big blow to fans.

Harare has also hosted, over the years, a number of rumba bands and musicians from Congo. They include the **Real Sounds**, adoptive Zimbabweans who were formative in mixing the Zairean beat with the Zimbabwean mbira to produce a sound which they christened *rumbira*. This eleven-piece band combines a rolling, soukous-style rumba beat,

the frenetic performance of a steaming cohort of brass and an exuberant drummer. It makes for compulsive dancing and an unmissable live show. They have an enthusiastic following both at home and overseas.

Another transplanted Congolese rumba outfit, **The Lubumbashi Stars**, play rumba in the classic 1970s style, complete with five singers harmonising lusciously and dancing in tight formations. Like the Real Sounds, they have become a staple of Harare's club scene.

Praise the Lord and Pass the Sadza

It's not surprising that Zimbabwe's recent travails should inspire a surge in sales of **gospel music**, and indeed, gospel may be the fastest growing sector of the local music market these days. Powerful gospel vocalists from South Africa dominate the scene but Zimbabwe is producing more and more successful gospel artists every year.

Zimbabwe's first real gospel star was **Jonathan Wutawunashe** who had a series of hits with his group the **Family Singers** in the early 1980s before he moved to Washington, D.C. and then to Brussels. The Family Singers still play in Harare, with Wutawunashe when opportunity arises.

Perhaps the biggest star of the following decades was **Brian Sibalo**, who formed his group **Golden Gospel Sounds** at nineteen and went solo in the late 1980s, scoring many hits before his tragic death in 1997. Sibalo was a member of the **Apostolic Church**, a distinctly Zimbabwean Christian sect whose enormous ranks are evident on Saturdays, when they can be seen in their white garments, gathering under trees for services. Apostolics eschew both churches and the Bible, preferring to get their religious truths through direct experiences with the divinity.

Following Sibalo's death, the major gospel artist is probably **Machanic Manyeruke**, leader of a gospel group called **The Puritans**, who has gained an international reputation through his tours in Europe and America, and international releases. He has come into his own at last as head of a fast-growing class of Zimbabwean gospel stars, among them the promising group **Ihawu Lesizwe**.

Meanwhile, artists who made their reputation performing other styles continue to switch over to gospel. **Biggie Tembo**, founding star of the Bhundu Boys, sang his final songs for Jesus to gospel, and **Cephal Mashakada**, better known to Zimbabweans as 'Muddy Face', has also moved from jit to gospel in recent years.

Ndebele Pop:
the Bulawayo Sound

Compared with Harare, **Bulawayo** – in the south-west province of Matabeleland, on the South African border, where the majority speak the Zulu-related language Ndebele – is a sleepy one-horse town, with rather low-key music venues. Bulawayan musicians feel acutely that the dominant positions in Zimbabwe are occupied by Harare and the culture of the peoples of Manicaland and Mashonaland.

But this has not always been the case. Back in the 1950s, Ndebele artists like guitarist **George Sibanda** were the big stars in this part of Africa. Sibanda is even credited with influencing guitar legend John Bosco Mwenda, one of the seminal figures of Congolese music. "Before the 1980s," as the Bulawayo-born singer Dorothy Masuka recalled, "blacks and whites played together in Bulawayo and there was a good music scene – but somehow after independence there was a split between Shona and Ndebele – things got moved to Harare and Bulawayo has never recovered. If there are musicians from Matabeland in Harare then they play Harare music. They [the Shona] are actually the owners of this country."

Dorothy Masuka, the 'mama' of African Jazz (see p.661), has had a musical career that spans nearly fifty years. She sang with Miriam Makeba and Hugh Masekela in South Africa in her early days, later fleeing to London to escape from the white minority-ruled Rhodesia, and campaigning for a free Zimbabwe all over Southern Africa. Like many Bulawayan musicians, Masuka draws a lot on South African influences, playing a mixture of swing and local melodies in a style known as *marabi*. "The Ndebele-speaking people who live in Matabeleland and Bulawayo are Zulus. They came into this country and settled in Matabeleland. My grandfather for example comes from a village in South Africa in Natal. This is why the traditional kind of music down south is South African." A big, glamorous personality, Dorothy Masuka is still one of Zimbabwe's strongest female performers.

The torchbearer of **Ndebele pop** through the 1980s was **Lovemore Majaivana**, a flamboyant, if uneven, performer with a rich powerful voice and a penchant for brilliantly coloured, skin-tight lurex suits. He was one of the few Bulawayo names to have made it big in Harare after independence and the Zulu influence was very strong in some of his music, though he also used mbira melodies in his songs. However, he retired in 1995.

A more recent group, **Southern Freeway**, includes members from Bulawayo, South Africa and Harare – including the talented session guitarist, Louis Mhlanga. They back the South African **Steve Dyer**, a versatile musician who has spent much time in Botswana, and Bulawayan singer **Thandeka Ngono**. Their music ranges from mbaqanga and jazz to more Shona-influenced guitar playing and they sing in Zulu, Xhosa, Ndebele, Shona, Tswana and English. However, the trials of Zimbabwe's music industry have recently led the band to relocate in South Africa.

Black Umfolosi are an a cappella group of singers and dancers from Bulawayo – an amazing live experience with their precise and acrobatic singing and dancing to a strong Zulu beat – and clearly reminiscent in style and content to Ladysmith Black Mambazo. They are regular fixtures on the international World Music festival circuit, where they can be seen performing their version of a South African miners' gumboot dance.

ERIK SOKKELAND/WORLD CIRCUIT

Black Umfolosi - whirling a cappella

The latest Ndebele musician to buck the pro-Shona trend and win a national audience is poet, storyteller and bandleader **Albert Nyathi**. An independence war veteran and acclaimed poet, Nyathi fronts the band **Imbongi**, who play everything from Shona traditional music to Afro-jazz, rumba and jive in the manner of South Africa's Soul Brothers. Like another South Africa artist he admires, Mzwakhe Mbuli, Nyathi is known for his recitals of probing poems and stories over the bubbling, inspirational backing of his band.

ZIMBABWE

The Runn Family - reggae, rumba and mbira beats

New Directions at the End of the 1990s

As previously noted, new bands make their mark with difficulty in Zimbabwe. Venue-owners are reluctant to take them and with no contracts will drop them at a moment's notice if they can book someone better known. To find a venue a new band usually needs to work its way, playing in the outlying 'growth points' – a tough graft.

Sometimes established musicians can provide a break. Oliver Mutukudzi, for example, helped popularise **Penga Udozoke,** a very danceable band with a fast rhythm borrowing from rumba as well as chanting traditions, in the early 1990s, though their star faded after a while. So, too, did that of **The Frontline Kids**, a young late 1980s group who made their name whipping the crowd into frenzies with their aerobic dancing. When they were performing at the 'Chico and Chinamora' concert in Harare in 1991 the crowd twice broke down the gates. Unfortunately, the band split up the following year when its members reached the age of 20 – 'kids' no more.

Other new groups of the 1980s and '90s, like the Runn Family of Mutare (in the Eastern Highlands) and Ilanga, achieved some success despite the long odds. Powered by an impressive brass section, the **Runn Family** scored a big hit with their first single "Hachina Wekutamba Naye", a song about the death of Mozambique's charismatic president, Samora Machel. By the early 1990s, though,

when the group's blend of Shona music, reggae and rumba had failed to garner a big following, members began to split off on solo careers. **Ilanga** also struggled to forge new roads in the 1980s, with mixed results, and their critical acclaim failed to translate into record sales.

However, an Ilanga alumnus, guitarist and singer/songwriter **Andy Brown** seems to have recently hit upon a new kind of fusion music that sells. He mixes Zimbabwe sounds with rumba, jive, reggae, ragga and rap, writes an excellent pop hook, and has a slick stage show that goes over well with 20-somethings in Harare. His catchy mega-hit "Mupurisa" has become an anthem for Zimbabwean youth and he is a man to watch as Zimbabwean pop moves into the new century.

Lastly, if you get the opportunity to see, or buy anything, by an absolutely extraordinary Tonga group from the Zambezi valley, the 30-strong **Simonga**, take it without hesitation. The Tonga are Zimbabwe's third largest ethnic group and the music played by Simonga is at once pure Tonga tradition and a radical departure from anything you are likely to have heard before. They play the traditional - and entirely undespondent - funeral music of the Tonga: a call-and-response-based frenzy of horns, drums, rattles, wailing voices and stamping feet. They have recently been collaborating with a number of progressive composers from Zimbabwe, South Africa and Austria.

Thanks to Tom Bullough and Andrew Tracey

discography

Compilations

▣ **The Rough Guide to the Music of Zimbabwe** (World Music Network, UK).

A fine introduction, ranging right across the spectrum, from Stella Chiweshe to the Real Sounds' wonderful thirteen-minute soccer match "Tornados vs. Dynamos (3-3)".

▣ **Zimbabwe Frontline Vol 2: Spirit of the Eagle** (Earthworks, UK).

If any one record essentialises what's special about Zimbabwe pop, this is it. With emphasis on the roots sounds of Thomas Mapfumo and Robson Banda, Spirit of the Eagle is a compilation that puts the focus squarely on Zimbabwe's richest musical sources. Start here and you won't go wrong.

▣ **Zimbabwe Frontline Vol 3: Roots Rock Guitar Party** (Earthworks, UK).

Old favourites John Chibadura and the Four Brothers each contribute a handful of tracks to this volume, delivering their trademark clean out guitars and up-beat rhythms. Less familiar names including mbira-modulated Max Mapfumo and the brilliantly kicking Zimbabwe Cha Cha Cha Kings. All combines to evoke an open-air Harare beer garden.

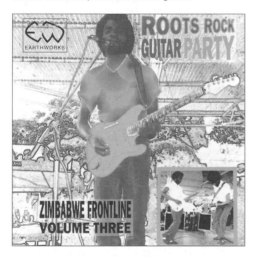

Artists

Robson Banda & the New Black Eagles

Banda is best known for his lean, guitar-driven take on the mbira pop sound. Call it chimurenga redux, but none of the depth is lost.

▣ **Greatest Hits Vol. 1** (Zimbob-5, Zimbabwe).

The only international release from one of Zimbabwe's best electric roots pop bands, this is a must for fans of that genre.

Bhundu Boys

The Bhundu Boys championed pan-Zimbabwean music in the 1980s, becoming one of the most popular and widely travelled Zimbabwean bands before calamities laid them low in the 1990s.

▣ **Shabini** (DisqueAfrique, UK).

For many in Britain this exquisitely speedy guitar album was the first port of entry into Zimbabwean music when it hit the world by storm in the mid-1980s. It still works out.

Black Umfolosi

Black Umfolosi are a leading Ndebele a cappella group from Bulawayo – Zimbabwe's Ladysmith Black Mambazo – and make up in style what they may lack in originality.

▣ **Festival Umdlalo** (World Circuit, UK).

Showcase for the group's mellow a cappella talents.

John Chibadura & the Tembo Brothers

A veteran star of Zimbabwe rumba, Chibadura stayed in the high-energy rumba game until his death in 1999 despite the arrival of young superstars in recent years.

▣ **More of the Essential** (CSA, UK).

Essential indeed if you want to know what revved up Zimbabwe's rumba machine in the 1980s and early '90s. Congolese fans take note; an expert demonstrates how to do tight dance numbers Zim style.

Stella Chiweshe

As a woman playing mbira, Stella Chiweshe has never worried much about conformity. But though willing and eager to experiment, her fidelity to tradition is undeniable. She goes deep every time.

▣ **Kumusha: Pure Mbira Music from Zimbabwe** (Piranha, Germany).

No complaints here: if you like mbira you'll soon be in a trance.

▣ **Ambuya** (GlobeStyle, UK; Shanachie US).

A magnificent experiment, only troubling purists with its lively 3 Mustaphas 3 participation on bass and drums.

Mahube

This southern African 'supergroup' was put together by South African sax and reeds-player Steve Dyer with Oliver Mutukdzi, singer George Phiri and others for an African music festival in Germany. Things went so well that they have done repeat concerts and recorded.

▣ **Music from Southern Africa** (Earthsong, UK).

South African township jazz, with its close horn arrangments and bright vocal harmonies, forms a base for Mahuba music but there are strains, too, of mbaqanga, mbira and rumba. All in all, a seductive mix.

The Four Brothers

One of Zimbabwe's great guitar pop bands, the Four Brothers have been spinning out sweet, giddy dance tunes with irresistible vocal hooks for most of Zimbabwe's post-war years. In this genre, it doesn't get any better.

▣ **Makorokoto: the Best of The Four Brothers** (Cooking Vinyl, UK).

Just like the title says: a real best of record. Joyful, exuberant, seductive, danceable, uncompromising Shona music.

Thomas Mapfumo

Zimbabwe's most influential musician of the 1980s,

Mapfumo is known as the guru of mbira pop. But his music encompasses everything from African jazz, to jit, tsava tsava, rumba, reggae, and rock. Just call it chimurenga music – Zimbabwe's proudest export!

 The Best of Thomas Mapfumo
(EMI/Hemisphere, UK).

A fine sampler, offering more than a taste of his range from 1978 to 1993, and with good notes, too.

◉ **The Chimurenga Singles: 1976–80** (Shanachie, US).

A re-release of a wonderful Earthworks collection of Mapfumo's war-years hits (love the cock-a-doodle).

◉ **Chamunorwa** (Mango, UK).

An album which signalled a new direction in Mapfumo's sound with extensive use of mbiras in the line-up.

◉ **Chimurenga, African Spirit Music**
(WOMAD Select, UK).

Features the stripped down, mbira-intensive side of Mapfumo's work. Also one of the final recordings of mbira guitar legend, Jonah Sithole.

Dorothy Masuka

One of the big singing stars of the African Jazz swing sound, Masuka's career goes back to the 1950s. Though no longer a trendsetter, the grand lady of Zimbabwean song still performs her classic music.

◉ **Pata Pata** (Mango, UK).

Masuka demonstrates the mature range and fire of her voice in this polished, 1980s session.

Oliver 'Tuku' Mtukudzi

A giant of an artist in Zimbabwe, Tuku hasn't received the international recognition he deserves. The locals love him for his wise, conscious lyrics and hunhu (moral values), but Mtukudzi's soulful tenor and languid chimurenga-style guitar transcends all language.

◉ **Shoko** (Piranha, Germany).

An irresistable selection of Tuku hits, re-recorded in Germany. Apparently, the session sounds almost too slick to the man himself, but few listeners will complain.

 Ziwere MuKøbenhavn (Shava, Germany).

Mbaqanga meets mbira-beat with hard-driving results. And what a persuasive liner booklet!

 Tuku Music
(Earthsong, UK).

This 1998 release is near flawless – a CD that you can put on repeat and enjoy for hours on end, delighting in the tunes, the Shona mbira patterns, the voices (wonderful harmony singing from Mwendi Chibindi and Mary Bell), the lilting guitar (Tuku himself plays acoustic throughout the disc). The lyrics are impressive, too – socially conscious as ever and neatly summarised on the sleevenotes.

Real Sounds

The band's founders came from Congo (ex-Zaire), but came to sing in Shona, paving the way for homegrown Zimbabwe rumba.

◉ **Vende Zoko** (Cooking Vinyl, UK).

Close your eyes and you could be in Congo. But listen harder for that characteristic nippy Zim guitar style.

Jonah Sithole

The late king of mbira guitar was, off and on, a singer, songwriter and bandleader in his own right. Over two decades on the music scene, Sithole established himself as a pioneer of this country's roots pop sound.

◉ **Sabhuku** (Zimbob-4, UK).

A sublime sampling of Sithole's work during the years he left the Blacks Unlimited to head his own band, Deep Horizon.

FOUR

Directories

Record Labels

Record Shops

This Labels Guide covers specialists in African, European or Middle Eastern music (and often a whole range of World Music). For further addresses and Web links, try the list maintained by the American roots magazine *Dirty Linen* at *http://kiwi.futuris.net/linen/special/label.html*

Africassette

www.africassette.com
P.O. Box 24941, Detroit, MI 48224, USA
email: rsteiger@africassette.com

This major US distributor of African and Antillean music (mainly CDs, despite the name) has begun releasing its own discs, such as Afropop Hits from Tanzania.

Al Sur

Média 7/Al Sur, 52 rue Paul Lescop, 92000 Nanterre, France

Al Sur – 'The Sound of the South' – have an excellent catalogue of music from all around the Mediterranean and Middle East. Strong releases from French Gypsies, Algeria, Morocco and Iran.

Amiata

www.amiatamedia.com
Via Gabriele D'Annunzio 227, 50135 Firenze, Italy
email: Amiata.records@amiatamedia.com

Named after a volcanic mountain in Tuscany, Amiata leans towards spiritual music, mainly Asiatic. But they also have some regional Italian traditions, Balafon releases from Burkina Faso and two of the leading Israeli bands, Yair Dalal and Bustan Abraham.

Archives Internationales de Musiques Populaire (AIMP)

Musée d'ethnographie, 65-67 boulevard Carl-Vogt, CH 1205 Geneva, Switzerland

World Music label of VDE-Gallo with high quality ethnographic recordings that cover the globe. All their discs are interesting, although many are of specialised rather than popular appeal.

Arhoolie

www.arhoolie.com
10341 San Pablo Avenue, El Cerrito, CA 94530, USA
email: mail@arhoolie.com

One of the great American roots labels, Chris Strachwitz's Arhoolie has been going since 1960 and has unrivalled releases of Tex-Mex, Cajun, Country Blues and other regional styles. Only a few releases make it into this volume, mainly of east European musicians who recorded in the US.

Arion

36 Avenue Hoche, 75008 Paris, France
email: info@arion-music.com

Although some of the large Arion catalogue tends towards the holiday souvenir end of things, there's a good Polish collection plus interesting things from the Andes, Indian subcontinent and South East Asia.

Auvidis Records

www.auvidis.com
47 avenue Paul Vaillant-Couturier, BP 21,
F-94251 Gentilly cedex, France
email: auvidis@wanadoo.fr

Two labels here: Auvidis Ethnic covers all manner of music, both popular and obscure, some good, some not; the Auvidis/UNESCO division documents traditional musical styles. See also the related Inédit and Silex (below).

Barraka el Farnatshi (Barbarity)

www.maroc.net/barraka/
P.O. Box 140, 4020 Basel, Switzerland
email: barraka@maroc.net

This Swiss-based label, run by saxophonist Pat Jabbar, has been issuing cutting-edge Moroccan trance/dance music since 1991. The radical AKJE (Aisha Kandisha's Jarring Effects) and its offshoot groups are responsible for most of the label's output.

Bolibana,

23 Rue des Tulipes, L' Hayles les Roses, 94248, France

African music label run by the Guinean producer Diappy Diawara, who originally licensed Bembeya Jazz from Sylaphone. Distributed by Melodie, France.

Buda

www.budamusique.com
188 boulevard Voltaire, 75011 Paris, France
email: buda@imaginet.fr

Wide ranging label run by Gilles Frucheaux. The Musique du Monde series is an extraordinary collection of mostly field recordings, strong on France, Italy, Romania, the Middle East and Siberia. The label also issues the unique Ethiopiques series of popular music from Ethiopia.

Caprice

Nybrokajen 11, SE-111 48 Stockholm, Sweden
email: Caprice@srk.se

Caprice is owned by the Swedish Concert Institute and is partly funded by the Swedish government. The label boasts an impressive collection of traditional

Swedish music, but also undertakes ambitious projects elsewhere in the world with notable releases from East Africa, Vietnam and Central America.

Celestial Harmonies

www.harmonioc.com
PO Box 30122, Tucson, Arizona 85751, USA
email: celestial@harmonies.com

A serious label with slightly New Age leanings – lots of Gregorian plainsong and Tibetan chant, as well as a comprehensive Music of Islam series and excellent South East Asian collections. All are pristine recordings with neat packaging from recycled paper.

Le Chant du Monde

31-33 Rue Vandrezanne, 75013 Paris, France
email: cdm@harmoniamundi.com
Distributed by Harmonia Mundi (see below)

Quality field recordings made under the aegis of the Museé de l'Homme in Paris to archive the diversity of the world's music. They range from Alpine yodelling to Filipino tribal musics.

Claddagh Records

http://indigo.ie/~claddagh
Dame House, Dame Street, Dublin 2, Ireland
email: claddagh@crl.ie

Claddagh has become one of the most prestigious Irish labels since its inception in 1959, with a huge catalogue of mainly traditional music.

Club du Disque Arabe

CAP 136, 67 rue Robespierre, 93558 Montreuile, France
email: cda@wanadoo.fr

As well as a wide variety of contemporary sounds (they issue many of the top Algerian rai artists), the Club have a valuable series of historical recordings.

Cooking Vinyl Records

P.O. Box 1845, London W110 4BT, UK
email: 100305.2711@compuserve.com

Cooking Vinyl's small catalogue features interesting developments in English and Irish folk music, though recently they've been moving away from roots music.

Crammed Discs

www.crammed.be
43 rue Général Patton, 1050 Brussels, Belgium
email: crammed@crammed.be

With top acts like Zap Mama and the Taraf de Haidouks, the CramWorld series features high-quality original recordings and re-issues and is particularly strong on soukous and the Balkans.

Dakar Sound

www.dakarsound.nl
Arcade Music Co, J Atinghstraat 13, 9424 LT, Groningen, Netherlands

West African dance band releases by the likes of Western Diamonds and Ifang Bondi.

FlameTree Music Ltd

PO Box 23024, London W11 2WA, UK

Re-issues of West African highlife gleaned from Nigerian sources.

Dizim

P.O. Box 10, D-79672 Todtnauberg, Germany
email: dizim@t-online.de

The Dizim focus is on acoustic sounds and music from East Africa and the Indian Ocean, with releases from Kenya, Zanzibar, the Comoros and more. Their Asili series features historical recordings.

Earthsongs

2/3 Fitzroy Mews, London W1P 5DQ
email: earthsongs@connoisseurcollection.co.uk

A new World Music imprint from Connoisseur, Earthsongs have issued an interesting batch of discs from Zimbabwean (including Oliver Mutukudze) and Native American artists.

Ellipsis Arts

www.ellipsisarts.com
PO Box 305 ,Roslyn, NY 11576, USA
email: elliarts@aol.com

Ellipsis specialise in tall-format boxed compilations with superbly illustrated accompanying booklets (sometimes practically books). Highlight titles include *Planet Squeezebox* (Accordions), *Planet Soup* (global fusion), and *Duende* (flamenco). They also have a smaller (CD-sized) format series covering more esoteric themes, again with generous text.

Equator Heritage Sounds

PO Box 2435, Elizabeth NJ 07207, USA
email: equator@worldnet.att.net

Matthews Juma thought it a shame that so little music from Kenya had made it to the international market. In 1997 he founded Equator Heritage Sounds as a way to bring both current and past Kenyan music productions to the rest of the world.

FM Records

www.acci.gr/~fmrecord
Knossou 7, 11146 Galatsi, Athens, Greece
email: fmrecord@acci.gr

The most extensive collections of Greek folk and historical recordings – espeically rembetiko – as well as contemporary composers and bands. Also good recordings of other Balkan music. Extensive notes in Greek, but the English translations are minimal.

Frémaux & Associés

20 rue Robert Girardineau, 94300 Vincennes, France

The backbone of this label is jazz and blues, but they also have a good line in gospel, old-timey, and a vintage French music-hall collection, plus an excellent series of remastered Antillean and Madagascan 78s.

Gael-Linn Records

www.gael-linn.ie/
26 Merrion Square, Dublin 2, Ireland
email: eolas@gaellinn.iol.ie

Highly esteemed Irish label with a notable catalogue, including many of the classic releases of Irish traditional music.

Gallo Music International

www.gallo.co.za
PO Box 2987, Parklands 2121, South Africa
email: gmi@gallo.co.za

This leading South African label releases everything from mbaqanga to jazz to contemporary pop on its shaft of labels – Gallo, Tusk, Teal, African Classics, Sheer Sound. Star groups include Ladysmith Black Mambazo and Lucky Dube.

GlobeStyle

www.acerecords.co.uk
48-50 Steele Road, London NW10 7AS, UK
email: info@acerecords.co.uk

Launched by Ben Mandelson and Roger Armstrong back in the 1980s, this was a pioneering World Music label, exploring the fringes of popular music from all over the globe, including wonderful material from Africa and the Balkans, and an important Irish archive series. It has been a bit hibernatory of late, under the wing of the more R&B oriented Ace Records.

Grapevine

5-6, Lombard Street East, Dublin 2, Ireland
email: grape@iol.ie

As well as a long-standing range of Irish traditional releases (including Nomos, Solas and Sharon Shannon), Grapevine has a burgeoning reputation for issuing high-quality new albums by the likes of Emmylou Harris and Canada's The Rankin Family.

Green Linnet Records

www.greenlinnet.com
43 Beaver Brook Road, Danbury, CT 06810, USA
email: grnlinnet@aol.com

Celtic (with an emphasis on Irish) specialists Green Linnet have recently celebrated twenty years in the business, and a backlist featuring such luminaries as Seamus Ennis, Altan and The Bothy Band.

Greentrax Records

http://members.aol.com/greentrax/greentrx.htm
Cockenzie Business Centre, Edinburgh Rd, Cockenzie, East Lothian EH32 0HL3, UK
email: greentrax@aol.com

Run by retired police inspector Ian Green, this leading Scots label ranges wide, from their vital Scottish Tradition series (drawn from the archives of the School of Scottish Studies and covering practically every traditional style of importance), through pipe bands, folk and Gaelic language vocals, to cutting edge Gaelic-inflected dance music.

Hannibal

www.rykodisc.com
Shetland Park, 27 Congress Street, Salem, MA 01970 USA
P.O. Box 2401, London W2 5SF, UK
email: data@rykodisc.com

Hannibal was started in 1990 by record producer and world music guru Joe Boyd, who'd previously produced discs by Pink Floyd, Nick Drake, Richard Thompson and Fairport Convention. The label's catalogue is eclectic but united by a concern for strong production values, benefiting such names as Márta Sebestyén and Muzsikás, Ivo Papasov, the Trio Bulgarka, and Toumani Diabaté. Boyd also created for Hannibal the remarkable Malian-Flamenco fusion of Songhai. With its parent, Ryko, the label is now part of Chris Blackwell's Palm Pictures stable.

Harlequin

See Interstate Music.

Harmonia Mundi

www.harmoniamundi.com
Harmonia Mundi France, Mas de Vert, B.P. 150, 13631 Arles Cedex, France; e-mail: info.arles@harmoniamundi.com
Harmonia Mundi UK, 19/21 Nile Street, London N1 7LL
email: info.uk@harmoniamundi.com

This French Early Classical Music label also acts as a distributor for many of France's more ethnographic labels like Ocora, L'Institute du Monde Arabe and Chant du Monde.

Hemisphere

www.hemisphere-records.com
64 Baker Street, London W1M 1DJ, UK

An enterprisingly un-corporate subdivision of EMI concentrating on reissues and compilations drawn from its international back catalogues. Modest-priced compilations include Middle Eastern, African and Portuguese themes. They've recently started releasing original single artist recordings, too.

Heritage

See Interstate Music.

Indigo

Label Bleu, MCA, BP 631, 80006 Amiens Cedex 1, France

With links to France's important Musiques Métisses festival, Indigo's excellent recordings range from Albania to the island of Réunion; they are particularly strong on Madagascar and Mali.

Inédit

101 boulevard Raspail, 75006 Paris, France
(distributed by Auvidis).

Linked with the Maison des Cultures du Monde in Paris, Inédit releases traditional music recorded mostly in Paris when groups are on tour. Many of the discs are quite specialised, but the recordings are first class.

They include definitive performances of Moroccan classical music, Middle Eastern traditions, Asian music, Russian singing and some European styles.

L'Institute du Monde Arabe

Musicales, 1 rue des Fossés Saint-Bernard, 75235 Paris Cedex 05, France (distributed by Harmonia Mundi)

Newly redesigned and attractively packaged series of discs focusing on the music of the Arab World.

Interstate Music Ltd.

20 Endwell Road, Bexhill-on-Sea, East Sussex TN40 1EA, UK

Interstate specialises in remastered historic recordings from 78s and form a huge resource for those interested in tracing the roots and history of World Music. The Harlequin label boasts a vast amount of Latin music, while the Heritage label features a diverse selection of historic fado, other European traditions and some West African releases.

Iona Records

www.lismor.co.uk/ionahome.html

27-29 Carnoustie Place, Scotland Street, Glasgow G5 8PH, UK

Iona was founded by Scots band Ossian as their own label, but has since branched out into other Scots and north of England roots bands.

JARO

www.jaro.de

Bismarckstr. 83, 28203 Bremen, Germany

JARO have a strong line in innovative cultural fusions, for instance the Bulgarian Voices in collaboration with Tuvan throat singers Huun-Huur Tu; also more classically oriented excursions into Islamic and Christian traditions.

Jololi

Bouba N'Dour, Rue 1 x D, Point E - En face Hotel Jardin de France, BP1310, Dakar,

email: bouba@telecomplus.sn

Jololi was established by Youssou N'Dour to release artistes of his choice, recorded in his own Dakar studio, Xili. He launched the label internationally in 1996 with the Jololi Review, featuring Cheik Lo, Yande Codou Sene, and himself.

JVC

JVC Victor Inc. 13–5, 1–Chome, Shibuya-ku, Tokyo 151, Japan

This bulging catalogue of CDs with distinctive red stripes features mainly Asian music but also a fair number of African and East European discs. Many are studio recordings by musicians on tour in Japan.

Kalan

Kalan Muzik Ltd, IMÇ 6. Blok No: 6608, Unkapani-Istanbul, Turkey

email: kalanmusic@kalan.com

Turkey's most interesting label, Kalan issues contemporary folk, classical, archive re-issues, jazz fusion and contentiously political pop.

Kelele Records

http://pgmediaservice.com/html/Inhaltst.html

Im Oberfeld 1a, D-79219 Staufen, Germany

email: pgmediaservice@t-online.de

This German-based label concentrates on African artists, especially from Kenya and Ghana.

Label Bleu

MCA, BP 0631-80006 Amiens, Cedex 1, France.

Quality recordings from Francophone Africa and Indian Ocean islands, including Madagascar.

Lismor Recordings

www.lismor.co.uk/lismorhome.html

7-29 Carnoustie Place, Scotland Street, Glasgow G5 8PH, UK

Lismor have concentrated on the more traditional side of Scottish music, and their catalogue contains fine piping, unaccompanied singing, and Gaelic Psalmody.

Long Distance

8 Passage de la Bonne Graine, F-75011 Paris, France

email: lgdartis@imaginet.fr

An eccentric but high-quality selection with French Gypsy music, a lot of Sufi and Central Asian music, Middle Eastern and Ethiopian discs.

Luaka Bop

Box 652, Cooper Station, New York, NY 10276, USA

www.luakabop.com

David Byrne's Luaka Bop label is strongest on Brazil and Cuba but its catalogue includes compilations from Portuguese Africa and Belgian fusionists Zap Mama.

Lusafrica

16 quai de la Charente, 75019 Paris, France

email: lusafrica@aol.com

Founded by producer Jose da Silva, this Paris label launched Cesaria Evora onto the international stage. They focus on Portuguese African music but have also branched into zouk and Cuban music.

Lyrichord

www.skywriting.net/Lyrichord

141 Perry Street, New York, NY 10014, USA

email: lyricny@interport.net

One of the veteran companies in the business, Lyrichord have a wide collection of largely ethnographic recordings from all round the world.

MB Records

84 Foster St, Bokton, Maryland, USA

Owned by the Mendes brothers, MB release mostly lusophone artists, especially from Angola.

Melodie

50 Rue Stendhal, 75020, Paris, France.

Label and general distribution of francophone music, including the Celluloid label.

M.E.L.T. 2000

6c Littlehampton Rd, Worthing, West Sussex, BN13 1QE; UK
www.melt2000.com

This adventurous new label have released some impressive South African jazz/crossover albums, and have signed new artists including Busi Mhlongo and Afro Blok. They are owned by Robert Trunz, founder of B+W hi-fi, whose influence perhaps shows in the consistently high production values.

Movieplay

Rua Alfredo Guisado 10–5, 1500–030 Lisboa, Portugal

Portugal's premier roots label, Movieplay issue CDs of traditional folk and fado, and singer-songwriters such as Jose Afonso.

Multicultural Media

www.multiculturalmedia.com
RR3, Box 6655, Barre, VT 05641, USA
email: mem@multiculturalmedia .com

MM issue a Music of the Earth series – a variable but extensive collection of field recordings re-issued from Victor in Japan.

Music of the World

www.musicoftheworld.com
P.O. Box 3620, Chapel Hill, NC 27515-3620, USA
email: motw@mindspring.com

An interesting company run by Bob Haddad, featuring a strong African, Middle Eastern, Indian and Asian roster; artists include Hassan Hakmoun.

MW Records

www.musicwords.nl/index.html
P.O. Box 1160, 3430 BD Nieuwegein, The Netherlands
email: muswords@musicwords.nl

MW have a slightly eccentric catalogue, but with some fine discs in their Folk Classics and World Roots series. Highlights include England's John Kirkpatrick, Hungary's Kálmán Balogh and Roby Lakatos, and Surinam/Holland's Carlo Jones.

Nascente

www.vci.co.uk
MCI Ltd., 72–74 Dean Street, London W1V 5HA, UK
email: info@mcimusic.co.uk

Nascente's budget-priced compilations started as cheap and cheerful but have matured in recent years with some very fine and at times pioneering discs.

Natari Music of Africa

www.natari.com.
165 Pavilion Rd, Worthing, West Susex BN14 7EG, UK
email: nick@natari.com

Importer of cassettes from Africa, including fresh Dakar releases; also mail order retail sales.

Nation Records

www.nationrecs.demon.co.uk/
19 All Saints Road, London W11 1HE; UK

email: aki@nationrecs.demon.co.uk

This dynamic West London–based label, run by Aki Nawaz and Keith Cannoville, is at the heart of the 'Asian Underground' scene, with artists including Fun<Da>Mental, TJ Rehmi and Joi.

Nimbus Records

www.nimbus.ltd.uk
Wyastone Lees, Monmouth NP5 3SR, UK

Nimbus's World Music releases, recorded by Robin Broadbank, show their origins as a company involved in Western classical music in their care for sound quality, extensive notes, and choice of music. Their CDs of Indian Classical and Southeast Asian music are of particular value, but there are also fine flamenco, Irish and Polish string band recordings.

(Elektra) Nonesuch Explorer

75 Rockefeller Plaza, New York, NY 10019, USA

The Explorer Series on Nonesuch Records (a Warner Group company) was one of the first to make ethnic music widely available. It includes high-quality recordings from all over the globe, most of them remastered on CD. Nonesuch has released new recordings by artists including the Gipsy Kings, Cesaria Evora and Caetano Veloso, and in 1997 signed a licensing agreement with World Circuit (see below).

Nubenegra

www.nubebegra.com
Humilladero 8, 1o Iz., 28005 Madrid, Spain
email: nubenegra@nubebegra.com

Manuel Domínguez's quirky Nubenegra (black cloud) focuses on Spanish and Latin releases, but also has a growing list of excellent African artists including Hijas del Sol (from Equatorial Guinea) and Rasha (from Sudan). The label also produced the groundbreaking *Saharauis* box set of music of Western Sahara.

Nuevos Medios

Ruiz de Alarcon 12, 28014 Madrid, Spain

A crucial Spanish label, Nuevos Medios have been responsible for most of the 'new flamenco' acts of the 1990s, and issue annual compilations of these artists in their *Jovenes Flamencos* series. They also issue 'new tango' recordings from Argentina.

Ocora

Maison de Radio France, 116 Av. du President Kennedy, 75786 Paris cedex 16, France (distributed by Harmonia Mundi)

Linked with Radio France, Ocora has for many years been the world's leading company releasing traditional folk and non-Western classical music from all round the globe. Their CDs are usually well recorded, researched and presented.

Oriente Musik

www.oriente.de
Augustastr. 20B, D-12203 Berlin, Germany

email: oriente@bln.de

A small and eccentric catalogue including Ross Daly and high-quality klezmer and Sephardic music.

Original Music

RD1, Box 190, Lasher Rd, Tivoli, NY, 12583, USA.

A pioneering label through the 1980s, though quiet of late, Original was founded by the author John Storm Roberts to re-issue compilations of various popular genres, mainly African.

Ossian Publications

www.ossian.ie/
PO Box, 84, Cork, Ireland
email: ossian@iol.ie

A relatively new addition to the Irish traditional music scene, Ossian is already developing a formidable reputation for the verve and quality of its recordings, which include releases from Seamus Creagh, Aidan Coffey and Sliabh Notes.

Outcaste Records

www.outcaste.com/
Queens House, 1 Leicester Place, London WC2H 7BP; UK
email: info@outcaste.com

'The new sound of Asian breakbeat culture' claim Outcaste – a crucial UK label set up in 1994 for Asian musicians outside of the bhangra scene. Artists include Badmarsh, Shri and Nitin Sawhney.

Palm Pictures

www.islandlife.com.
8 Kensington Park Rd, London W11 3BU, UK
email: gerry@islandlife.co.uk

Chris Blackwell's reinvention of the Island/Mango labels (which he sold to Polygram) have swiftly become a force, lending huge support to Baaba Maal, and producing innovative, well crafted releases. They have recently taken Hannibal/Ryko (see Hannibal, p.721) into the group.

Pamtondo

www.pamtondo.virtualave.net
4 Gailes Park, Bothwell, Glasgow G71 8TS, UK
email: 106671.3551@compuserve.com

A unique specialist, Pamtondo release and import CDs and cassettes of Malawian music, otherwise unobtainable outside the country.

Pan

PO Box 155, 2300 AD, Leiden, The Netherlands
email: paradox@dataweb.nl

A very wide catalogue of ethnographic field recordings particularly strong on Russia, the Caucasus and Central Asia, West Africa, China and Polynesia.

Park Records

www.parkrecords.com
PO Box 651, Oxford, OX2 9RB, UK

British folk and folk rock label with Steeleye Pan, Maddy Prior and Kathryn Tickell on the books.

Piranha Musik

www.piranha.de
Carmerstraße 11, 10623 Berlin, Germany
email: records@piranha.de

A very distinctive label founded by Borkovsky Akbar featuring contemporary roots music round the globe – highlights include Mozambique, Egypt, Brazil plus Mediterranean Sephardic music and top US klezmer ensemble, the Klezmatics.

Popular African Music

Günter Gretz, Damaschkeanger 51, 60488 Frankfurt, Germany

An interesting variety of old and new African music – notably a series of Ngoma re-issues from Congo.

Putumayo World Music

www.putomayo.com
627 Broadway, New York, NY 10012, USA

Putumayo emerged from the Latin American-oriented gifts and clothing chain, set up by Dan Storper, who now runs it as a fully-fledged independent label. With naive and colourful covers, the discs are intended to introduce World Music to people who didn't know they liked it: for instance *Music from the Coffee Lands*, which has been creatively marketed in coffee shops. The catalogue includes country compilations, musical journeys and a few individual artist discs.

Rags Productions

29 Abingdon Rd, London W8 6AH, UK

One of the few sources of music from Sudan and the Horn of Africa (Ethiopia and Eritrea).

RealWorld

http://realworld.on.net/home.html
Mill Lane, Box, Corsham, Wiltshire SN13 8PL, UK

The RealWorld label was founded in 1989 by Peter Gabriel and has been based on a symbiotic relationship between the WOMAD festival and Gabriel's excellent studios at Box in Wiltshire. The catalogue includes artists from all round the globe with a strong emphasis on fusion experiments – Afro-Celts currently being a big seller. RealWorld were also largely responsible for bringing Nusrat Fateh Ali Khan to worldwide attention. The WOMAD Select series offers more or less live-take recordings of WOMAD festival artists, designed for the artists to sell at concerts.

RetroAfric

www.hpd-online.demon.co.uk
PO Box 2977, London W11 2WL, UK

A truly independent label, which re-issues classic African dance music from the 1950s to the present, with the emphasis on highlife and Congo rumba. Includes seminal pan-African figures from West, Central and East Africa. Dsitributed by Sterns.

Robi Droli

www.inrete.it/robidroli/home.html

Strada Roncaglia 16, 15040 San germano (AL), Italy

The top label for contemporary Italian roots music, Robi Droli feature authentic traditional music on their 'Taranta' label and some choice albums from elsewhere round the globe.

Rounder Records

www.rounder.com

1 Camp Street, Cambridge MA 02140-1149, USA

email: info@rounder.com

Rounder is one of the largest and best independent record labels in the USA. Most of their music is home-grown regional styles, but they have expanded to cover many areas of the world and were a pioneering US label in African pop and traditional music from the mid-1980s to the early '90s.

Rykodisc

www.rykodisc.com

Shetland Park, 27 Congress Street, Salem, MA 01970 USA

P.O. Box 2401, London W2 5SF, UK

email: data@rykodisc.com

As well as handling the Hannibal label (see above), Rykodisc have an interesting set of roots recordings on their own account, including 1960s folk/Celtic re-issues and the Library of Congress Endangered Music Project produced by Mickey Hart. Ryko are primarily, though, a rock and jazz label.

Saydisc Records

Chipping Manor, The Chipping, Wotton-Under-Edge, Glos, GL12 7AD, UK

Saydisc boast a splendidly eccentric collection of recordings ranging from Victorian Street organs and church bells to British traditional song and a rather haphazard selection of World Music, including a series of Pacific discs recorded by David Fanshawe.

Shanachie Records

www.shanachie.com

13 Laight Street, 6th Floor, New York, NY 10013, USA

email: shanachie@idt.net

A diverse catalogue of music from all over the globe – most specially recorded, although many are released under licence. Their Yazoo label presents good compilations of old 78 recordings.

Silex Records

39 avenue Paul Vaillant Couturier, 94250 Gentilly, France

This French label has a spanking selection of European folk music from the archives and the contemporary scene - French, Catalan, Corsican, Romanian, Ukrainian, and further afield.

Smithsonian Folkways

www.si.edu/folkways

955 L'Enfant Plaza, Suite 7300, MRC 953, Washington, DC 20560, USA

email: Folkways@aol.com

Folkways was founded in 1948 by Moses Asch who wanted to 'fill the map with music'. By his death in 1987 there were over 2,000 titles – lots of American folk, music from all around the world, plus poetry, political speeches, frogs, trains and motor cars. The catalogue was acquired by the Smithsonian Institution and is now curated by Anthony Seeger. The entire catalogue is still available (on cassette) and Smithsonian Folkways has re-issued many of the best titles on CD, as well as continuing to release expertly researched recordings from the US and all over the globe.

Sono (formerly Sonodisc)

52 Rue Paul Lescop, 9200 Nanterre, France.

Owned by Jacob Desvarieux of Kassav, Sono is the main source of francophone African and Caribbean music with a huge catalogue that contains hundreds of compilations of Congolese hits, in partcular. Also has a distribution arm known as Musisoft.

Stern's

www.sternsmusic.com

74/75 Warren Street, London W1P 5PA, UK

598 Broadway, New York, NY 10012, US

email: webmaster@sternsmusic.com

Britain's premier label for African music has an unrivalled catalogue of west and central African artists. Stern's also run the Earthworks and RetroAfric labels, and distribute many independents.

Syllart

4 Rue Ferdinand Flacon, Paris 18, France

(Distributed by Musisoft).

Syllart is the label of Paris-based Senegalese producer Ibrahima Syllah, who has launched myriad Sahalien superstars and revamped several Kinshasa hit makers for international consumption. Syllart is also responsible for most of Stern's releases.

Syncoop

Slot Assumburgpad 54, 3123 RR Schiedam, Netherlands

email: syncoop@wxs.nl

Dutch bands and klezmer, plus a lot of bargain basement East European folk.

Tecnosaga

www.tecnosaga.com

Dolores Armengot 13, 28025 Madrid, Spain.

email: tecnosag@tecnosaga.com

A large collection of traditional and folk revival music from Spain plus some good Sephardic releases.

Topic Records

50 Stroud Green Road, London N4 3EF, UK

Topic claims to be the oldest independent record company in the world, having started out in 1939 as the Workers Music Association with the belief that music could be a tool of revolution and give a voice to the people. It is still probably the best source of British traditional music, with a huge catalogue including some of the biggest names – Waterson:Carthy, Eliza Carthy, June Tabor. The Voice of the People series is an extraordinary survey of the vernacular music of ordinary people in Britain. The Topic World series, mostly the work of Bert Lloyd and Wolf Dietrich, is small but worthwhile. Their distribution arm, Direct Distribution, at the same address, handles a vast number of labels for the UK market.

Traditional Crossroads

www.rootsworld.com/crossroads
P.O. Box 20320, Greeley Square Station, New York, NY 10001-9992, USA
email: tradcross@aol.com

Specialists in high-quality remastering of historic Turkish and Armenian recordings, plus fine modern recordings of Turkish, Bulgarian, Jewish and Senegalese music.

Trikont

www.trikont.de
Kistlerstraße 1, Postfach 90 10 55, D-81510 München, Germany

Eccentric label run by Achim Bergmann with particular strengths in German and Alpine recordings – from archive 78rmp re-issues to the Alpine new wave. Also excellent American and klezmer discs.

Triple Earth

24 Foley Street, London W1P 7LA, UK
email: iain@triple-earth.co.uk

Iain Scott's Triple Earth catalogue is an individual's pick rather than a strategic marketing plan - and all the better for it. Aster Aweke, Najma Akhtar and Mouth Music are all to be found here.

WeltWunder Records

www.weltwunder.com
Gehrden 35, D 21635 Jork, Germany
email: weltwunder@t-online.de

WeltWunder started out with percussion – drum masters like Mustapha Tettey Addy from Ghana – and have expanded into salsa, tango, East German folk, and a series of single country compilations.

Wergo

Postfach 3640, D-55026 Mainz, Germany

The Wergo Weltmusik label includes good-quality recordings with strong discs from Armenia, Georgia, Iran, India and Pakistan and of Jewish klezmer music.

Wicklow

www.wicklowrecords.com
#200-1505 West 2nd Ave., Vancouver BC, V6H 3Y4, Canada

Part of BMG Classics, Wicklow was founded by the Chieftains' Paddy Moloney and takes its names from the Irish county where he lives. "I want to discover people who've been out there some time and promote them", he says. Artists include Värttinä, Alpha Yaya Diallo, lots of Celtic Canadians and Bill Laswell-produced fusion projects.

World Circuit

www.demon.co.uk/andys/worldcir.html
106 Cleveland Street, London W1P 5DP, UK
email: post@worldcircuit.co.uk

Nick Gold's World Circuit have been a consistently interesting and astute label throughout the 1990s, producing imaginative recordings of mainly African and Latin artists, and notably putting Ali Farka Touré together with Ry Cooder on the Grammy-winning *Talking Timbuktu*. They deservedly struck gold in 1998 with the million-selling Cuban *Buena Vista Social Club*.

World Music Network

www.worldmusic.net
6 Abbeville Mews, 88 Clapham Park Rd, London SW4 7BX, UK
email: wldmusic@dircon.co.uk

World Music Network produce the growing range of Rough Guide CD compilations, which are often visually tied in with the Rough Guide travel books, although the discs are independently produced. World Music Network also run the specialist Riverboat label.

World Network

www.NetworkMedien.com
Network Medien GmbH, Merianplatz 10, D-60316 Frankfurt am Main, Germany
email: NetworkMedien@compuserve.com

This top-quality German label run by Jean Trouillet and Christian Scholze draws on WDR's extensive radio archives in Cologne and also produces enterprising new recordings. There's an ongoing series of single discs showcasing representative artists from individual countries (now up to 49 discs), some strong Turkish releases, and several excellent packs with lavish pictures including *Saharan Blues*, *Road of the Gypsies* and *Gypsy Queens*.

Xenophile

see Green Linnet, p.721

This, the non-Celtic arm of Green Linnet, has a well-chosen set of recordings covering Cuba, Finland, klezmer and Madagascar, for a start.

Xource

www.cabal.se/mnw/xource
PO Box 271, S-185 23 Vaxholm, Sweden

'Nordic music without boundaries': mainly Swedish contemporary bands and fusions.

Record Shops | Directory

This Shops Guide, as with the preceding Labels directory, covers specialists in African, European or Middle Eastern music – though many cover a range of World Music. Most offer a Website and mail order sales. Online-only mail order stores are listed at the end of the directory.

Note that Latin, US Roots and Asian music specialists are detailed in Volume 2 of the *Rough Guide to World Music*.

Austria

Lotus Records

Pfeifergasse 4, Salzburg 5020
Tel: 0043 662 84 91 28 Fax: 00 43 662 84 91 28
email: info@lotusrecords.at
www.lotusrecords.at

Probably the largest selection of World Music in the country, with special strengths in Yiddish & Klezmer, Belly Dance, Sufi, Tango, Flamenco. A stone's throw from Mozartplatz, too.

Suedwind - Weltmusik

Mariahilferstrasse 8, Vienna 1070
Tel: 0043 1 522 3886 Fax: 00 43 1 522 38865
email: weltmusik@suedwind.at
www.suedwind.at

Suedwind was set up as a non-profit making organisation to inform people about north-south relations and the third world. They offer traditional music from Africa, Latin America and Europe.

Belgium

Musica Nova

Galerie d'Ixelles 24–28, Burssels 1050
Tel: 00322 511 6694

Right in the heart of 'Little Matonge', here you can find the very latest Congolese releases, and often the artists themselves. Pierrot the proprietor also stocks US, Afro–Cuban and Italian imports.

Czech Republic

Gnosis Brno

Rezkova 30, Brno 602 00
Tel/Fax: 0042 5 4321 5463
www.mujweb.cz/www/gnosis_brn

This small shop is good for local label releases of Czech and Slovak music.

Denmark

Go Danish Folk Music

Ribe Landesvej 190, Vejle, DK 7100
Fax: 0045 75 72 24 86
www.homel.inet.tele.dk/eswo

A specialist supplier of Danish and Faroese CDs.

England

Ada Music

36 Market Place, Beverley, E. Yorkshire, HU17 9AG
Tel: 01482 868 024 Fax: 01482 868 024

This specialist operation dedicates its energies to finding the best in Scandinavian folk and other European traditions. They are real cognoscenti and can supply almost any title in their fields.

Bahar Video

343 Green Lanes, London N4 1BZ
Tel: 020 8802 1391

In the heart of the North London Turkish community, Bahar Video sells Turkish, Kurdish and Arabic music both traditional and popular.

Decoy Records

30 Deansgate, Manchester M3 1RH
Tel: 0161 832 0183 Fax: 0161 839 1713

One of the leading World Music shops in the UK, Decoy offer all genres from traditional to modern, acoustic to electric, global and local. Mike Chadwick (World Music DJ on Jazz FM) works here and other members of staff also DJ in clubs and on radio. Their combined knowledge is immense and they're not shy about making recommendations.

HMV Oxford St

363 Oxford St, London W1R 2BJ
Tel: 020 7629 1240
www.hmv.co.uk

HMV's main megastore has an extensive World Music section in the basement offering as good a choice as any independent specialist.

Honest Jon's

276 & 278 Portobello Road, London W10 5TE
Tel: 020 8969 9822 Fax: 020 8969 5395

Honest Jon's has been selling Reggae, Jazz, House, R&B, Funk, Rap, African, etc, out of two shops in Portobello Market seven days a week for 25 years. The World section has recently been expanded. New and secondhand items; plus a mail-order service.

Listening Planet

22 Hughenden Yard, Marlborough, Wiltshire, SN8 1LT
Tel: 01672 511151 Fax: 01672 511737
email: footprint@listeningplanet.com
www.listeningplanet.com

A mail-order store that covers all styles of music and specialises in tracking down obscure records on small labels. Apparently they're a persistent lot.

Roots Music

9 Derwent St, Sunderland, Tyne & Wear SR1 3NT
Tel: 0191 567 0196 Fax: 0191 567 2711
email: enquiries@roots-music.co.uk
www.roots-music.co.uk/roostmusi

Roots stocks an extensive selection of African, Latin, Caribbean and many other roots genres. A catalogue is available on request and individual requirements are researched. Mail order service.

Stern's African Records Centre

293 Euston Road, London NW1 3AD
Tel: 020 7387 5550 Fax: 020 7388 2756
email: shop@sternsmusic.com
www.sternsmusic.com

London's premier African music store by a long chalk. An excellent selection has special emphasis on soukous – which caters for the many Congolese and West African customers. Stern's have years of expertise behind them and they're also the UK's main African and Latin music distributors which means most desirable items are always in stock.

Trehantiri Music

365-367 Green Lanes, Harringay, London N4 1DY
Tel: 020 8802 6530 Fax: 020 8802 6530
email: music@trehantiri.com
www.trehantiri.com

Situated in the heart of North London's Greek and Turkish community, Trehantiri is an institution and retail Nirvana for anyone with more than a passing interest in all types of Greek, Turkish and Middle Eastern music, and helpful assistance is on hand for anyone without a PhD in the subject. The Website offers the most exhaustive list of Greek music products on the Net and they're all available by mail order.

Finland

Digelius Music

Lalvurinrinne 2, Helsinki 00120
Tel: 00358 9 666375 Fax: 00 358 9 628950
email: pap@digelius.com
www.digelius.com

The top World Music shop in Scandinavia, Digelius has been run by Philip Page and his team since the dawn of time and now offers more than 10,000 different titles on CD, cassette and vinyl. Videos and books are also available. The company's Website is called Digelius Nordic Gallery and it specialises exclusively in Baltic and Nordic music.

France

Afric Music

3 rue des Plantes, Paris 75014
Tel: 0033 1 45 42 43 52

Favoured by the African and Antillean DJs of the capital, Afric Music is a compact, tidy little shop with an air of devotion and enthusiasm about it – the helpful assistants spinning novelty after novelty. Limited stocks of vinyl are on offer as well as a good selection of CDs.

Africassette

45 rue Doudeauville, Paris 75018
Tel: 0033 1 42 55 49 79

Africassette is owned by the younger brother of the famed producer, Ibrahima Sylla and is consequently particularly strong on Syllart productions. The range of stock is a touch on the meagre side but all Francophone African styles are represented together with a smattering of Antillean, Haitian and Latin discs.

Camara

45 rue Marcadet, Paris 75018
Tel: 0033 1 42 51 33 18

Among the bags of kola nuts, the pop-up toasters and hair-care products you'll find a regular treasure trove of cassette-only West African releases. The establishment is run by the enterprising Camara, a Malian immigre with a good nose for business.

Disc Inter

2 rue des Rasselins, Paris 75020
Tel: 0033 1 43 73 63 48

One of the biggest and best-stocked shops of its kind – which compensates for its distance from the centre. The weekly chart is a help where you're stumped by their enormous choice of African and Antillean music.

Editions Bouarfa

32 rue de la Charboniere, Paris 75018
Tel: 0033 1 42 53 85 35

Producer, retailer and distributor Bouarfa is one of the oldest and best-established of the many Arabic cassette merchants in this area of Paris. His huge selection of cassettes covers all styles traditional and modern from Algeria, Morocco, Tunisia and Egypt, and is augmented by racks of CDs and videos. You thought you knew your rai? Well visit Bouarfa and think again.

FNAC Forum

Forum des Halles, Paris 75001
and other branches

The huge FNAC shops (this is a big central example) are a combination of music, book, hi-fi, computer, camera and general leisure megastores. All the Parisian FNACs and many of the regional ones have excellent World Music departments with a large selection of well laid out CDs, and lots of listening posts.

Keltia Musique

1 Place,au Beurre, Quimper-Breizh 29000
Tel: 0033 2 9895 4582 Fax: 00 33 2 9895 7319
email: keltia_mu@club-internet.fr

There's more CDs of Breton music out there than
you've had hot dinners dear – and chances are Keltia
have got most of them. All tastes, from traditional
a cappella songs to the techno-tinged hoedowns of
Denez Prigent.

Moradisc

51 Boulevard de Rochechouart, Paris 75009
Tel: 0033 1 42 81 14 89

A great place to stop at after the rigours of being a
tourist on the Butte Montmartre. This small and
friendly shop offers a wide range of Afro-Antillean
music on CD with the emphasis on soukous and zouk.

Virgin Megastore

56–60 av des Champs-Élysées, Paris 8

Virgin's Paris megastore is a real flagship and has a vast
amount of its stock digitised so that you can pick up a
disc, wave its barcode at a listeningpost, and sample.
The World Music sections are impressive.

The Gambia

Daruwari Recording Studio

Mosque Rd, Serrekunda, near Banjul

The best cassette supplier in the country.

Germany

Canzone

Savignypassage Bogen 583, Berlin 10623
Tel: 0049 30 312 4027 Fax: 00 49 30 312 6527
www.canzone.de

This well established World Music shop is nicely laid
out and intelligently stocked. Emphasis is on the
Berlinerish obsessions of Eastern European, Greek,
Turkish and Tango music. Staff are helpful and you
can listen at will. Also runs the Oriente label.

Weltrecord

Eppendorfer Landstrasse 124, Hamburg 20251
Tel: 0049 40 480 7908 Fax: 00 49 40 4609 2328
email: weltrecord@t-online.de

Music from all over the world with special emphasis
on Africa and the Arab World. All styles are catered
for but traditional music is strongest. Videos, books
and mail-order also available.

Yalla Music

Rathenauplatz, Cologne 50674
Tel: 0049 221 240 9333 Fax: 00 49 221 240 9332
email: yalla_music@gmx.de www.yalla.de

A neat and tidy little shop selling African, Latin,
Brazilian and Spanish music in abundance.

Greece

En Khordais

Ippodhromiou 3, Thessaloniki

This non-profit traditional music foundation and
school has a retail outlet of well-selected CDs across
the street.

Studio 52

Dhimitriou Gounari 46, Thessaloniki

The cavernous basement premises of this, the oldest
store in town, is full of rare vinyl and cassette releases
plus a well organised CD section.

Tzina

Panepistimiou 57, Athens

Reasonable if somewhat chaotic stock (strictly CDs) of
ethnic music. The shop runs its own label called
Venus–Tzina.

Xylouris

Panepistimiou 39 (in the arcade), Athens

This shop, run by the gregarious widow of the late,
great Nikos Xylouris, is the best spot in Athens for
Greek folk, laiko and (of course) Cretan music. Mid-
priced, well organised for the tiny space and stocks
many items unavailable elsewhere.

Ireland

Celtic Note

14-15 Nassau Street, Dublin 2
Tel: 00353 1 670 4157 Fax: 00 353 1 670 4158
email: sales@celticnote.ie
www.celticnote.ie

This spacious store near Trinity College is the best
stop in all of Ireland for Celtic music. The shop aims
to stock at least one CD by every Irish artist with a
recording career, however humble, and there's also a
huge selection of other types of music from the Celtic
diaspora – Scotland, Brittany, Cape Breton – and
pretty credible shelves of other World Music releases.
Books and videos are on sale, too.

Claddagh Records

2 Cecilia Street, Dublin 2
Tel 00353 1 677 0262.
email: claddagh@crl.ie
http://indigo.ie/~claddagh

A huge range of traditional music is on offer at the
Temple Bar outlet of this specialist Irish music label
and helpfully informative staff can handle virtually
every query. Also stocks a wide choice of roots music
releases from around the world.

The Living Tradition

PO Box 84, 40 McCurtain St, Cork
Tel: 00353 21 502 040 Fax: 00 353 21 502 025
email: ossian@iol.ie www.ossian.ie

This is the retail outlet for the Ossian label, though it stocks an extensive range of Irish music song collections and tutorials; Irish, Scottish, English, Cape Breton and American folk music on CD, and a smaller range of World Music titles. Also does mail order.

Mulligan

5 Middle Street Court, Middle Street, Galway
Tel: 00353 091-564961

Without doubt, the place to head for in the West of Ireland, stocking a vast range of Irish and Scottish traditional and folk music. Mail order available.

Israel

Jazz Ear

21 Sheinkin St, Tel Aviv
Tel: 00972 3 525 2590 Fax: 00972 3 528 8989

World Music record shop and distributor.

Sabreen

PO Box 51875, Jerusalem 91517

Palestinian music by mail order.

Kenya

Al-Hussein Hand Craft

Harambee Ave, Lamu.

Good selection of tapes of Taarab and traditional Wa-Bajuni and Mijikenda music.

Assanand's

Moi Avenue, Nairobi

This store has as good a range of CDs and tapes as you'll find anywhere in Kenya.

Mbwana Radio Service

Off Pigott Place in the Old Town, Mombasa

Traditional Mijikenda music and Mombasan Taarab.

Zilizopendwa Music Store

George Morura Street, Mombasa

Specialises in Kikuyu and other Kenyan ethnic pop, as well as near-ubiquitous Gospel.

Netherlands

Mundial

Schuitendiep 17-1b, Groningen 9712 KD
Tel: 0031 50 314 3860 Fax: 0031 50 549 1109
email: mundial@mundial.nl www.mundial.nl

A shop and mail-order operation which concentrates completely on World Music and especially Tango, Latin and Reggae. With several years of experience and contacts with suppliers around the world the shop reckons it can lay its hands on just about anything.

Musiques Du Monde

Singel 281, Amsterdam
Tel: 0031 20 624 1354 Fax: 0031 20 625 3124

As the name suggests, World Music, both new and used. Listen before you buy.

Xango World Music Records

Zadelstraat 14 Utrecht 3511 LT
Tel: 0031 30 232 8286 Fax: 0031 30 232 8059

Another good Dutch source.

Palestine/West Bank

Popular Art Centre

PO Box 3627, El Bireh, West Bank
email: pac@painet.com

Palestinian music by mail order.

Portugal

Discantus / Mundo da Canção

Rua Duque de Saldanha 97, Porto 4349 - 030
Tel: 00351 2 51 93 100 Fax: 00351 2 51 93 109
email: discantus@mail.telepac.pt
www.discantus.pt

This promoter of roots and World Music events also distributes and retails Portuguese roots CDs.

Scotland

Coda Records

12 Bank St, Edinburgh, EH1 2LN
Tel: 0131 622 7246 Fax: 0131 622 7245
www.codamusic.co.uk

Coda have four stores in Scotland, all of which stock quantities of Scottish, folk, Celtic and World Music. Their Website, although thin on information, has an impressively dee Celtic catalogue, which puts most of the major online CD stores to shame.

Senegal

Sandaga Market

Sandaga Market, Dakar

The city centre's main market is the place to buy cassettes. There are stacks on sale at stalls – some of them on legitimate labels.

South Africa

Cadence Tropical

Time Square, Yeoville, Johannesburg
Tel: 0027 11/648 7957

South Africa's finest stockist of Central and West African music.

Kohinoor

54 Market St, CBD, Johannesburg

The focus here is on jazz but there is a bit of everything South African, ranging from maskanda to kwaito. Excellent vinyl section as well as CDs.

Spain

FNAC – Madrid

c/Preciados 28, Madrid 28013
Tel: 0034 1 595 61 00

As with sister stores in France, this huge multimedia shopping haven has a broad World Music selection, and its is stronger than most Madrid stores in flamenco and Spanish traditional music.

Sweden

Multi Kulti

Sankt Paulsgatan 3, Stockholm 11846
Tel. 0040 0 040 0120 Fax: 0046 8 643 6120
email: multi.kulti@swipnet.se

Multi Kulti owner Steve Roney has been selling traditional and popular music from around the world since 1986 – his friend Don Cherry named the store. Under the motto 'Renewal and retrospective absorption', they are glad to guide all-comers.

Rotspel

Tulegatan 37, Stockholm 11353
Tel: 0046 8 16 04 04 Fax: 0046 8 16 04 04
www.rotspel.a.se

Stockholm's leading store for Swedish and Nordic folk CDs, videos, books and instruments. Mail Order.

Turkey

Lale Plak

Tunel Galipded Caddesi No 1, Beyoglu, Istanbul 80050
Tel: 0090 212 293 7739

Probably the best shop in Istanbul for Turkish music.

USA

In addition to specialists listed here, honourable mentions should go to most larger branches of Tower and Virgin, and Borders Books & Music, all of whom have been stocking serious amounts of roots and World Music in recent years.

African Record Center

1194 Nostrand Avenue, Brooklyn, New York NY
Tel: 001 718 493 4500

African and Caribbean music aplenty.

Africassette

PO Box 24941, Detroit, MI 48224-0941

Tel: 00 1 313 881 4108 Fax: 00 1 331 881 0260
email: rsteiger@africassette.com

An excellent African specialist mail-order company. The company was started in 1991 with the original intention of making cassette releases imported from Africa available to the world. It has since expanded into selling CDs, books, videos and other forms of media, as well as running its own label, and has expanded its coverage to the Caribbean and South America.

Amoeba

2455 Telegraph Ave, Berkeley, CA
Tel: 001 510 549 1125

This vast store covers all kinds of music – new and secondhand. World Music isn't a particular speciality but the sections still dwarf most normal stores and prices are extremely competitive.

Down Home Music

10341 San Pablo Ave, El Cerrito, CA
Tel: 001 510 525 2129

Just a mile or two north of the Berkeley border in El Cerrito, Down Home stocks roots music almost exclusively – blues, country, folk, Celtic, early R&B, ethnic, Worldbeat. It is especially strong on obscure independent/import re-issues.

Elderly Instruments

1100 N Washington PO Box 14249 Lansing MI 48901
Tel: 001 517 372 7890 Fax: 00 1 517 372 5155
email: web@elderly.com
www.elderly.com

Elderly Instruments is a store and mail-order service offering a huge stock of modern and traditional instruments and 1000s of hard to find CDs and cassettes. Their speciality is all forms of American and Celtic folk. Other World Music titles are also in evidence in their catalogue.

Ethiosounds

2409 18 St NW, Washington DC
Tel: 001 202 232 0076

CDs and tapes in abundance, all from Ethiopia, and with some wild sleeves. The definite leader amongst the many small Ethiopian stores in the area.

Hear Music

1809 Fourth St, Berkeley, CA
Tel: 001 510 204 9595

Listen to any CD in the store with no obligation. Extensive selection of Celtic and international music.

Hear's Music, Inc.

2508 North Campbell Ave, Tucson, AZ 85719-3303
Tel: 001 520 795 4494 Fax: 00 1 520 795 1875
email: service@hearsmusic.com
www.hearsmusic.com

Hear's Music, Inc. is a retail music store and global mail-order company. They offer all forms of music (access to 500,000+ titles) but when it comes to their passion for all forms of World Music they might be considered obsessed! All in all they reckon they can lay their hands on over 60,000 different World Music titles. They also carry secondhand CDs, World Music videos and books. Customer service is paramount and all enquiries, however weird and testing, are welcome.

House of Musical Traditions

7040 Carroll Ave, Takoma Park, MD 20912
Tel: 001 301 270 9090
email: hmtrad@hmtrad.com
www.hmtrad.com

House of Musical Traditions has been up and running since 1972 offering records, books, videos and instruments relating to roots music from just about everywhere.

International Music Emporium

452 Dean St, Brooklyn, New York, NY
Tel: 001 718 636 5400

Small but perfectly formed little shop in the Park Slope area of Brooklyn. Good on soukous and even better on Sierra Leonian and other types of Anglo-African music.

J&R Music World

23 Park Row, New York, NY
Tel: 001 212 238 9000

Prices at this large downtown establishment tend to be lower than those at the chain megastores and there are extensive aisles of Latin, Reggae and World Music.

Mostly Music

4805 13th Avenue, Brooklyn, New York 11218
Tel: 001 718 438 2766 Fax 001 718 438 3845
www.jewish-music.com

'The Heart of Jewish Music' the store and excellent Website proclaim. All aspects of Jewish music from the great cantors to klezmer; CDs, videos and books.

Sikhulu's Record Shack

274 W 125th St, New York, NY

A convenient spot in Manhattan to hunt down African, Caribbean, Soul and Gospel goodies. Especially hot on South African releases.

Stern's Records

71 Warren St New York NY 10007
Tel: 001 212 964 5455 Fax: 001 212 964 5955
www.sternsmusic.com

The offspring of Stern's African Record Centre in London, Stern's U.S. has been the leading importer and distributor of African recordings in North America since 1989. This shop opened in New York City in 1998. Not only has it got the best African selection in the Western Hemishpere, it's also got music from just about every country in the world, with particularly strong selections of Indian, Cuban and Brazilian music. You can also order CDs, books and videos by phone, fax, post and email.

Zimbabwe

Spinalong

Hungwe House, George Silundika Ave, Harare.

Spinalong stocks an excellent range of West African music as well as local sounds.

Internet/Mail Order

As noted, many of the physical stores above offer mail order, often through the Internet. Listings below, however, are purely Internet/mail-order stores. All ship internationally, but note that the import of more than two CDs may be liable to tax.

Africassette

www.africassette.com

A well-established site with a good selection of African releases. You can order anything from the on-line catalogue by phone, fax or email. Unlike most other online CD shopping malls, Africassette offer original African cassette releases.

Aladin Le Musicien

www.alifcom.com/aladin/

Aladin le Musicien are a Paris-based company who produce and distribute CDs and cassettes from Morocco, Algeria and Tunisia. Their catalogue is a good hunting ground for obscure releases by the likes of Khaled, Cheb Mami or Najat Aatabou which you won't find anywhere else. The site is in French only.

Amazon.com

www.amazon.com

The Amazon.com search engine is awesome and will pull up pretty much any US or UK release, and much besides, often accompanied by audio samples and a string of reviews from customers. What is maybe even more interesting is that they will be posting reviews from this book alongside CDs, making the acquisition of a vast and wonderful collection dangerously easy.

Aramusic

www.aramusic.com

This Virginia, US-based online music store specialises in Arabic music from Egypt and the Middle East, with a smaller selection from the Maghreb. The catalogue is pretty amazing – 47 choices for Abdel Halim Hafez, for example – and there are plenty of real audio samples to help, as well as photos, and a chat forum.

Borders.com

www.borders.com

Borders is a nice, clean browsable site – very much like its terrestial stores. There's a reasonably deep catalogue and array of sound samples in 'International'.

cdnow.com

www.cdnow.com

At time of writing, cdnow offers a smaller World Music selection than its rivals (9 hits for Kouyate versus 30-plus for both Amazon and Tower) but they have keen prices, lots of sound samples, and some decent weekly features.

CD Universe

www.cduniverse.com

CD Universe are another of the big players, battling for supremacy. Their world music department is well laid out with links into browsable country-by-country sections, and an excellent search engine that generates nicely organised returns from a deep catalogue.

The Listening Post

PO Box 1026, Kilmarnock, Scotland KA2 0LG
Tel: 01563 571220 Fax: 01563 544855
www.folkmusic.net

The mail-order service of *Living Tradition* magazine, which concentrates on traditional music of Scotland, Ireland, England, Wales and other Celtic realms. Staff are knowledgeable and enthusiastic and are able to advise on choices if given some idea of your taste.

Tower.com

www.towerrecords.com
www.towereurope.com

Tower's US and European sites deliver impressive catalogue returns and they have sound samples for a huge amount of discs. There's little in the way of text or reviews, but if you know what you're looking for you've a very good chance of finding it here.

World Music Network

6 Abbeville Mews, 88 Clapham Park Rd, London SW4 7BX, UK
Tel: 020 7498 5252 Fax: 020 7498 5353
www.worldmusic.net

WMN have painstakingly built a reputation as the UK's leading Internet and mail-order World Music suppliers. Their forte is an intelligent policy of limiting choice to the very best in each genre, and every recommendation is accompanied by descriptions, tracklistings and sound samples.

Contributors | world music volume I

David Abram is a musician and writer. He is the author of *Rough Guides* to Goa and India.

Mu'tasem Adileh is a guitarist and teacher, who has worked on Palestinian music in education.

Zein al Jundi was born in Damascus but now lives in the US where he hosts a weekly radio World Music programme on the Austin Texas station, KOOP. He is also a professional singer of Arabic music.

Rob Allingham is an American who has lived in South Africa since 1975. A music historian and compiler of reissues, he is Archive Manager for Gallo (Africa) Ltd in Johannesburg.

Ian Anderson is editor of the highly respected and long-established *Folk Roots* magazine, a radio presenter, record producer and mostly-retired musician.

Ed Ashcroft works for the Stern's label, and also owns *Matadi*, an African and World Music store managed by his wife Aminata in South London.

Eric Audra is a freelance sound engineer at Radio France. He spent two years promoting local artists at the French Cultural Centre in Cotonou, Benin.

Bill Badley is an oud and lute player, music teacher, writer and TV producer.

François Bensignor is a Paris-based freelance journalist specialising in World Music. He is editor of the *Sans Visa* guide, and a video reporter.

Wim Bloemendaal presents an eclectic music show on VPRO in Holland five times a week.

Etienne Bours is a journalist based in Belgium and World Music buyer for Belgian record libraries.

Ken Braun is a freelance World Music journalist and works for Stern's African Music shop in New York.

Robin Broadbank is a prolific sound-recordist and a producer for Nimbus Records.

Simon Broughton is a freelance film maker, writer, broadcaster, co-editor of this book, and editor of the World Music magazine *Songlines*.

Tom Bullough is a freelance journalist and novelist.

Kim Burton is a pianist, accordion player and writer specialising in Latin and Balkan music. She has participated in various GlobeStyle recordings.

Jenny Cathcart divides her time between London and Dakar, where she is closely involved in the music industry. She is the author of *Hey You!,* a biography of Youssou N'Dour.

David Charap is a film editor and director who works in London and Prague.

Bob Cohen is an American-born musician based in Budapest where he leads the klezmer band Di Naye Kapelye.

Judith Cohen is a lecturer who has done extensive research into Sephardic music; she performs with the group Gerineldo.

John Collins runs Bokoor Studio, outside Accra in Ghana. He is the author of *Musicmakers of West Africa* and *West African Pop Roots*.

Peter Cooke is a UK-based musician and ethnomusicologist, with a particular interest in Uganda.

Andrew Cronshaw is a player of instruments from the shelf marked 'What is it?', a record producer and sound engineer, and writes for *Folk Roots* and other magazines.

Peter Culshaw is a freelance arts writer, broadcaster and musician. He has masterminded the UK's annual 'Music Village' events for several years.

Tatiana Didenko was a TV producer, responsible for the 'Global Village' programmes on Russian TV which featured traditional and folk music across the Russian Republic. She died in 1998.

Manuel Dominguez runs the NubeNegra record label in Madrid. It was he who originally suggested this book.

Marc Dubin is a travel journalist and photographer who divides his time between London and the island of Samos. He writes for *Songlines* magazine and has authored a number of Rough Guides.

Lucy Duran is a writer and broadcaster and a lecturer at London University's School of Oriental and African Studies. She has specialised in Mande music and in particular the kora since the 1970s.

Mark Ellingham is a co-editor of this book. He set up Rough Guides in 1981 and remains Series Editor. He is World Music reviewer for the Tower Records magazine, *Top*.

Prince Eyango is a Cameroonian musician now based in California.

Graeme Ewens writes about African music for newspapers, magazines and syndication agencies. He is the author of *Africa O-Ye!* and a biography of Franco, *Congo Colossus*.

Banning Eyre is a musician, writer and broadcaster who has spent many months studying guitar styles and playing with bands in Africa. He is the author of *In Griot Time, An American Guitarist in Mali*.

Jan Fairley is a writer and broadcaster based in Edinburgh; she has a particular interest in Latin and Spanish music.

Francis Falceto is a France-based journalist and music producer, a regular visitor to Ethiopia and responsible for the Ethiopiques series on Buda.

Jens Finke is a sound archivist and writer. He is the author of *The Rough Guide to Tazania* and his website on traditional Kenyan music can be found at www.crosswinds.net/~bluegecko

Werner Graebner is an ethnomusicologist and journalist. He is also a music broadcaster in Germany and the US.

Ronnie Graham is a Scottish historian who spent eight years researching and teaching in West Africa. He is the author of the *Stern's Guide to African Music* and a founder of the RetroAfric label. He currently works for SightSavers International.

Harold Hagopian studied Armenian folk music with his father, the ud player Richard Hagopian, and graduated from the Julliard School as a violinist. He lives in New York, where he runs the Traditional Crossroads label.

Pete Heywood is editor of *The Living Tradition*, Scotland's roots and folk music magazine.

Mark Hudson won the Thomas Cook award for his travel bookabout Senegal, *Our Grandmother's Drums*. His most recent novel, *The Music in My Head*, is about the World Music business.

Ken Hunt is a freelance writer and translator, with particular interests in India and Germany.

Christian Hyde is a lawyer with a love of Africa, where he spent a year and a half trekking from Senegal to Angola. He works in London.

Colin Irwin is a UK-based roots music journalist. A mainstay of *Folk Roots*, he also writes regularly on roots music for *Mojo* and *The Guardian*.

Jean-Pierre Jacquemin is a Brussels-based writer and a specialist in African culture. He is editor of *Musiciens Africains de Belgique – Repertoire*.

Simon Kandela Tunkanya is based in Lusaka, Zambia, where he runs ZAPRA Promotions and The Ark Cultural Centre, aiming to stimulate an alternative development through the arts.

Judy Kendall worked in Zimbabwe for four years and writes on music, film and women's issues.

Guus de Klein is a producer of inter-cultural theatre and music in Holland. He worked in Guinea–Bissau from 1985–95 and toured Europe with the band Gumbezarte in 1995 and 1997.

Alexis Kochan, of Ukrainian extraction, is a singer and educator based in Winnipeg, Canada.

Philippe Krümm is a French roots record producer, magazine editor and writer, based in France.

Julian Kytasty is a bandura player of Ukrainian extraction living in New York.

Dubi Lenz is an Israeli journalist and broadcaster. He is artistic director of both local and international World Music festivals in Israel.

Conceicão Lima was born in São Tomé and works as a journalist for the Portuguese service of the BBC in London.

David Lodge is a radio broadcaster and patron of the *Café Cairo* in South London. He is not a novelist.

John Lwanda is a Malawian who works in Scotland as a doctor. He has written several books about contemporary Malawi culture and politics, and runs the Pamtondo label.

Susana Máximo is a Portuguese journalist.

Andy Morgan has done most jobs in the World Music universe, including spells with RealWorld and FNAC. He runs the Bristol-based global dance label, Apartment 22.

Greg Mthembu-Salter is a Cape Town-based writer who used to promote South African gospel music but these days spends his time raising a family, writing about Central African politics, and DJ-ing.

Dave Muddyman is a composer and musician with the band Loop Guru. He co-edited the first edition of this book.

Jean-Victor Nkolo is a broadcaster and development worker.

Laudan Nooshin lectures in music in Performing Arts at Brunel University.

Nuala O'Connor writes on traditional music for *The Irish Times* and runs the Hummingbird label.

Celso Paco is a Mozambican jazz musician, composer and ethnomusicologist, who plays and teaches traditional and western percussion.

Doug Paterson became an avid fan of East African music while researching in Kenya for his PhD in cultural anthropology. He has produced several CDs of Kenyan and Tanzanian music.

David Peterson lives in Salt Lake City, Utah, where he indulges his passion for Cape Verdean music and plays guitar.

Geoge Pissalidhes is an Athens-based journalist who writes on Greek music for *Folk Roots*.

Jiři Plocek is a musician with a strong interest in Moravian and Slovak traditional folk music. He's also a radio producer for Czech Radio Brno and runs the Gnosis Brno label.

William Price plays in a Welsh roots band.

Paul Rans is a singer – formerly with Rum and now with his own ensemble – and a Traditional Music producer for VRT Flemish Radio in Belgium.

Jean-Pierre Rasle, born in France, is an expert in French bagpipes, runs the Cock & Bull Band and is a member of Jah Wobble's Invaders of the Heart.

DJ Ritu is a club and BBC Radio DJ and a co-founder of Outcaste Records.

Dan Rosenberg is host of the Café International, a World Music/travel radio show that airs on WCBN-FM Ann Arbor and WDTR-FM Detroit, and for which he has travelled worldwide recording music and hundreds of interviews.

Sten Sandahl has taught ethnomusicology at Stockholm University and is a producer at the Swedish Concert Institute. He has produced several World Music CDs for the Caprice label.

Jadot Sezirahigha is a cultural journalist from Rwanda. He is now based in Kigali where he works with the Martin Luther King Foundation.

Caroline Shaw is a bibliographer with a special interest in the creole languages and cultures of Cape Verde and São Tomé & Príncipe. She is an editorial manager at the London School of Economics.

Eva Skalla, director of Global Heritage, is a manager and promoter of World Music acts.

Martin Stokes teaches ethnomusicology at the University of Chicago and plays kanun, saz, and (nearly) oud. He is author of *The Arabesk Debate: Music and Musicians in Modern Turkey*.

Alessio Surian is a freelance writer, education consultant and bass player based in Padua, Italy.

Andrew Tracey is a musicologist and director of the International Library of African Music at Rhodes University, Grahamstown, South Africa. He is the son of pioneering field recordist Hugh Tracey.

Richard Trillo got a Franco tune in his head while crossing Africa in 1980. That trip led to writing *Rough Guides* to Kenya and West Africa, and to co-editing this book. By day, he is Rough Guides' director of publicity, rights and marketing.

Paul Vernon is a freelance music consultant who specialises in vintage World Music.

Peter Verney edits the independent *Sudan Update* newsletter and information service, and researches Sudanese culture and politics.

Christoph Wagner is a music writer and photo archivist, based in the UK. He works as a producer for German radio and has written books on the accordion and harmonica for Schott.

Brooke Wentz is a New York-based music journalist.

Nigel Williamson is a former political correspondent who now writes primarily about World Music, for *The Times*, *Mojo* and *Billboard*.

Leah Zakks is a classically trained musician, visual artist and music events producer based in London.

Index

Daghumma 564
Dahari, Yosefa 574
Dahle, Knut 214
Daily Planet 65, 73
Daina, Latvian 19
Dainos 22
Dainu Sventes 23
Dairo, IK 590, 598
Dalal, Yair 365, 366, 368
Dalaras, Yiorgos (George) 133, 140
Dalauna 385
Dalgas 138
Dalmatian Coast 47
Daly, Jackie 183
Daly, Ross 136, 140
Dama 531
Damba, Fanta 540, 550, 556
Damba, Mah 540
Dambo de la Costa 478
Dança dos paulitos 227
Danças Ocultas 233
Danço-congo 613
Daniel Kachamba and his Kwela
    Band 533
Daniel Spasov 44
Daniel, Ojoge 590
Daniels, Luke 77
Danish Dia Delight 59, 62
Dante, Absatou 586
Danube New Wave 14
Daoúli 128
Dar Es Salaam 694
Dar Es Salaam Jazz Band 682
Darbuka 149, 568
Darhem, Mohammed 573
Dariush 362
Dark City Sisters 640, 642
Darko, George 495, 497
Darweesh, Sayed 327, 331
Dastgah 358
Dastum 105
Daughters of Glorious Jesus, The 496
Dauphiné 109
Davenport, Bob 67, 72
Davul 148
Dawnswyr Gwerin Pen-y-Fai 316
Dawnswyr Nantgarw 316
Dawnswyr Tâf-Elai 316
DCS 84
DDC Mlimani Park Orchestra 682,
    688
De Dannan 187
De los Angeles, Victoria 374
Deaf Shepherd 270
Déanta 180, 187
Debarre, Angelo 154
Debebe, Neway 480, 482
Decca, Ben 442
Dede, Amekye 496
Dedesse 526
Deep Forest 606, 607
Deepika 88
Degenhardt, Franz-Josef 115, 123
Delgado, Djoy 454

Delgado, Justino 501, 502, 503
Delgado, Luís 296
Delsbo 305
Dembo, Leonard 712
Demirel, Hasan Hüseyin 405
Dendera Kings 711
Denez Prigent 105
Denmark 58–63
Denny, Sandy 80
Denti d'Oro 453
Dervish 187
Desaunay, Serge 113
Dési et les Sympathiques 438
Desmali 478
Devera Ngwena Jazz Band 712
Dewayon, Paul 462
Dewit, Herman 25
Dêxa 613
Deyess 468
Dhiamantidhis, Andonis 'Dalgas' 128
Dhimotiká tragoúdhia 127
Dhol 84
Dia, Ousmane 548
Diab, Amr 343, 346
Diabaté, Abdoulaye 556
Diabaté, Adama 556
Diabaté, Kasse Mady 289, 539, 540,
    549, 552, 556
Diabaté, Keletigui 549, 552
Diabaté, Lafia 550
Diabaté, Naïny 551, 556
Diabaté, Sekou 545, 547
Diabaté, Sekouba 'Bambino' 547,
    553, 561
Diabaté, Sidiki 544, 547, 557
Diabaté, Sira Mory 550, 557
Diabaté, Toumani 289, 539, 543,
    544, 552, 557
Diabos do Ritmo, Os 615
Diallo, Yoro 554
Diamond Star 692
Diarra, Zoumana 557
Diatta, Pascal 629
Diawara, Kadé 551, 561
Díaz, Joaquín 374, 376
Dibala, Diblo 465
Dibango, Manu 440, 441, 445, 460,
    472
Dibo, Mandelbosh 'Assabelew' 483
Didenko, Tatiana 253
Dieng, Fallou 629
Dilshad 383
Dina Medina 454
Dinkjian, Ara 135, 337
Dionysiou, Stratos 135
Diop, Aby Gana 628
Diop, Wasis 629
Dioubaté, Oumou 560
Diple 48
Dipoko, Sissi 444
Disco (South African) 648, 653
Dissidenten 114, 120, 121, 124, 573,
    574
Dissing, Povl 60

Diwan repertoire 365
DJ Mahmut 406
DJ Volkan 406
DJs, Asian 85
Djamilla 426
Djédjé, Ernesto 474
Djellal, Cheb 423
Djembe 545
Djenia, Cheikha 416
Djimi, Gnaore 474
Djorçon 500
Djosinha 450
Djurdjura 426, 427
Dludlu, Jimmy 583
Dmitri Pokrovsky Ensemble 251, 253
Doa 292
Dobro guitar 53
Dogo, Maty Thiam 629
Doina 243
Doj, Pål Torbjörn 259
Doleur 442
Dom 146
Domby, Nick 438
Domrane, Malika 426
Don Verdi Orchestra 454
Dona, Kodé di 452
Donegal fiddle 175
Donkor, Eddie 492
Donnisulana 110, 112
Dopyera family 53
Doran, Felix 174
Doran, Johnny 173, 174, 183
Doumbia, Mamadou 474, 557
Doumbia, Nahawa 557
Doundoun 540, 545
Dr Nico 432, 460, 461
Dragana 274
Dragspel 301
Drailles 109
Drakus, Gibraltar 445
Drame, Hawa 540
Drame, Lalo Keba 544, 625
Dransfield, Robin and Barry 64, 78
Dresch, Mihály 163
Drevo 309
Druhá tráva 51
Drummers of Burundi, The 610, 612
Dube, Lucky 649, 655
Dubliners, The 177
Dubois, Remy 26
Dudík, Miroslav 53
Dudík, Samko 53, 56
Duduk 333, 334, 379
Duende 281, 282
Dug 62
Duma 585
Duman, Güler 397
Dumy 309
Duncan, Gordon 269
Duncan, Jock 267
Dundun 589
Duo Chabenat-Paris 106
Duo Sonnenschirm 115
Duquende 285, 286, 289

Ghulami, Najmeddin 382
Ghymes 53, 166
Gienek Wilczek Band 220
Gil & the Perfects 454
Gimbri 568
Gimenez, Wili 288
Gipsy Kings, The 153, 154, 158, 279, 294
Girk, Kurt 13
Gisma 676
Gizavo, Regis 525, 528, 530, 531
Gjallarhorn 98, 100, 303, 306
Gjebrea, Ardit 2
Gjirokastër festival 5
Gjurgjevden 204
Glackin, Paddy 184
Glasgow Fiddle Workshop 266
Glykeria 140
Gnaoua 571, 574
Gning, Madiodio 628
Gnonnas, Pedro 433
Goat dances (Romanian) 244
Goats Don't Shave 180, 187
Godinho, Sérgio 232
Gohill, Pran 84
Goje, Audo Yaron 589, 590
Golden Gospel Sounds 712
Golden Nuggets 496
Golden Star 694, 697
Gomi, Nacia 452
Gomonda, Goodson 537
Gonzalez, Antonio 154
Googoosh 360, 362
Goom-bay – see Gumbe
Goosen, Anton 651
Górale 221
Gospel, South African 658-659
Gospel, Zimbabwean 712
Gotani Sounds 535
Goulesco, Jean 152
Goulesco, Lida 152, 157
Gozos 191
Graceland 645
Graham, Davy 64, 81
Grand Magoma 521
Grand Rouge, Le 106
Grand Zaiko Wa Wa 463
Grande Bande de Cornemuses, La 106, 112
Grappelli, Stephane 154
Graziano, Clara 193
Great Steady Bongo 636
Great Witch 703
Greece 126–142
Greece – Gypsies 149
Green 529
Green Spots 592
Green, Dagny Biti 259
Greenland 143–145
Greisha, Bahr Abu 345
Grélo el Mostganmia, Cheikha 416
Grieg, Edvard 214
Griots 540, 542, 617, 626, 632
Grodi 20

Grön, Eino 99
Gronich, Shlomo 366
Groupa 215, 304, 306
Groupe Kawtal, Le 445
Grundström, Eero 94
Grupo Radio Moçambique 580
Gudmundson, Per 299
Guelewar 621
Guendil, Cheikha Kheira 416
Guennoun, Abdelkrim and Saïd 570
Guillabert, Henri 630
Guillaume, Toto 442
Guinea – see Mande music 539
Guinea-Bissau 499–504
Guitar-band Highlife 492, 493
Guitarra Portuguesa 226
Gulestan 383
Gulf States 351-354
Gumbe 499-504, 634
Gumbezarte 502, 503
Gumede, Sipho 665
Gündes, Ebru 401
Gürseş, Müslüm 404, 409
Gusheh 358
Guslari 275
Gusle 275
Gustaf, Päkkos 298
Gutsa, Nicoláe 157, 243, 247
Güzelses, Dıyarbakbılı Celal 403
Gwangwa, Jonas 662, 665, 667
Gwerin 313
Gwerinos 315, 318
Gwernig, Youenn 105
Gwerz 104, 105
Gŵyl Ifan 316
Gŵyl werin 313
Gŵyl Werin y Cnapan 314
Gypsy Music 42, 43, 53, 54, 98, 100, 108, 146-158, 160, 165, 204, 239, 242, 275, 280, 400, 401, 409
Gypsies, Bulgarian 42, 43
Gypsies, Czech/Slovak 53, 54
Gypsies, Finnish 98, 100
Gypsies, French 108
Gypsies, Hungarian 160, 165
Gypsies, Macedonian 204
Gypsies, Romanian 239, 242
Gypsies, Serbian/Montenegran 275
Gypsies, Spanish 146-158, 280
Gypsies, Turkish 400, 401, 409
Gypsy Rumba 154

H

Hääkuoro 97
Haapavesi Festival 97, 99
Habanera 295
Habas Verdes 296
Habichuela, Pepe and Juan 286
Habrera Hativeet 366
Haco, Ciwan 383
Haden, Charlie 235
Hafez, Abd el-Halim 327, 331

Hafez, Mousa 385
Hafiftaş, Nuray 397
Hafizi, Xhevdet 3
Hafren 316
Hagberg, Anders 259, 304
Hagopian, Richard 333, 337
Haim Efendi 373
Haïnidhes 136, 140
Haj, Maulidi 693
Hakim 343, 346
Hakmoun, Hassan 571, 574, 577
Halili, Merita 3
Halk music 396
Hall, Reg 72
Halmágyi, Mihály 241, 246
Halmos, Béla 163, 167
Hamada, Cheikh 414, 423
Hamaida, Ali 344
Hamid, Mehad 352, 354
Hamid, Sultan 351
Hammered dulcimer 8, 20
Hamre, Knut 214
Hanan 345
Hanifa 426
Hanmer, Paul 666
Haqiiba 673
Haqim, Tariq Abdul 351
Harare 706
Harari 649
Hardanger fiddle (Hardingfele) 212, 213
Hardstone 519, 521
Harepa 646
Harlem Swingsters 660
Harmandian, Adiss 335
Harmattan 628
Harmonie Soudanaise 546
Harmonium (Finnish) 94
Harp, Breton 105
Harp, Irish 174
Harp, Norwegian 215
Harp, Welsh 314
Harper, Roy 64
Harris, Sue 64
Hart, Tim 72
Hasni, Cheb 421, 422, 423
Hassan, Cheb 422
Hassan, Mohammed 505
Hato de Foces 296
Hatzidakis, Manos 132, 140
Hatzis, Kostas 134
Hatzopoulos, Nikos 127
Hausa music 589-590
Hausgaard, Niels 60
Hayedeh 360
Hayes, Martin 184
Hayes, Tommy 174
Hayner, Die 122
Haza, Ofra 365, 368
Hazan, Victoria Rosa 373
Heaney, Joe 182
Hebrew songs 363, 371
Hedgehog Pie 68
Hedin, Johan 304

Tsitsanis, Vassilis 131, 139
Tsodrano 527
Tsonga-Traditional 647
Tubarões, Os 451, 456
Tube, Shem 513
Tud 105, 113
Tuffuor, Nana 496
Tukul Band 486
Tulloch, Violet 270
Tunar, Şükrü 400
Tunç, Onno 405
Tunca, Zekai 401
Tungehorn 215
Tungus 252
Turbo-Folk, Serbian 274
Turkey 148, 371, 396-410
Turkish – Classical/Religious Music
    396, 399, 401, 407
Turkey – Folk music 397, 406
Turkey – Gypsies 148, 401
Turkey – Jewish music 371
Turkey – Kurds 379
Turkoman epic poets 359
Turriff, Jane 269
Tuulenkantajat 94
Twala, Sello 'Chicco' 649
Twarab 505
Twee Violen en een Bas 208, 209
Twinkle Brothers 224
Twinkling Stars 694
Twist 512
Twmpath 313

U

UAE 352, 353
UCAS Jazz Band 625
Uganda 671, 698-701
Uilleann Pipes 174, 176
Új Pátria 165
Ukraine 308-312
Ukrainian Bandurist Chorus 309
Ukrainians, The (group) 311, 312
Ukwu, Celestine 597, 599
U.L.M.A.N. 123
ULO Greenlandic Music 143, 145
Ulrychovi, Petr and Hana 52
Ultra-Benga 520
Ulysse 107
Umeå folk music festival 305
Umm Kalthum – see Kalthum, Umm
Ummamuudu 23
Umuduri 608
Une Anche Passe 108, 112
United Arab Emirates 352, 353
Úntués, Os 614
Uppland 299
Uragniaun 195
Uranie, Jean 508
Urithi Band 687
Urkult Folkfest vid Nämforsen 305
USA, Sephardic music 375
Üsküdar Musiki Cemiyeti 400

Ússua 613
Utla 215, 218
Utolsó Óra (Final Hour) project 165
Utrera, Bernarda de 280, 291
Utrera, Fernanda de 280, 291
Uwaifo, Sir Victor 598

V

Vacher, Emile 107, 113
Vai de Roda 233
Valachia 52
Vali, Justin 525, 532
Valiha 525
Valkeapää, Nils-Aslak 257, 260
Vallely, Niall 175
Vamvakaris, Markos 129, 130, 139
Van de Velde, Wannes 25, 30
Van der Werf, Otti 30
Van Dormael, Pierre 30
Van Esbroeck, Dirk 27
Van Hees, Jean-Pierre 26
Van Maasakkers, Gerard 207, 209
Váralmási Band 246
Varga, Gusztáv 152
Variet 506
Varimezov, Kostadin 38
Världen i Norden 217
Varmužova Cimbálová Muzika 55
Vartabet, Komitas 333, 336
Värttinä 92, 97, 102
Väsen 300, 307
Vassilopoulos, Yiannis 127
Vaz, Rui 234
Veeman, Doede 207, 209
Velichkov, Stoyan 38
Velká nad Veličkou 52
Vëllezërit Aliu 5
Veneno, Kiko 296
Veneto 196
Verbunkos 160
Verckys, Kiamanguana 461
Veriovka State Folk Chorus 309
Vershki da Koreshki 252
Verviers Central 26
Vesvre, Christian 113
Veterans, Les 443
Veysel, Aşık 399, 407
Victor, Patrick 507
Victoria 463
Victoria Jazz 512
Victoria Kings 512, 522
Vieira, Paulino 451, 453
Vielle-à-roue 106
Viitalan Pelimannit 97
Vijana Jazz 682, 689
Viking, Nguza 683
Viklicky, Emil 52
Vilakazi, Strike 640
Viljandi folk festival 19
Vimpelin Väinämöinen 102
Vinaccia, Paolo 215
Vingården 59

Viola de fado 226
Virkkala, Tellu 92
Virta, Olavi 99
Viru säru folk festival 18
Viry, Firmin 506, 508
Vitali, Eleni 135
Vito, Maria Pia de 192
Vitorino 232
Viva La Musica 463, 466
Vizinho 615
Vjestice 47
Vlachs, Serbian 276
Vlier, De 25
Voce di Corsica 110
Voci Atroci, Le 197
Voci del Lèsima 197, 201
Voice of the People series 64, 78
Voice of the Turtle 375, 377
Voices of Sepharad 375
Voigt, Lene 119
Vojvodina 275
Volnitza Ensemble 254
Voodoo Queens 87
Vosporos 135, 141
Vrckovic, Zasavci and Irena 277
Vujicsics 161, 163, 167
Vulchev, Atanas 39
Vundumuna 516

W

Wacholder 114, 117, 123
Wader, Hannes 117, 118
Wales 313-319
Wales – folk song 313
Wales – traditional dance 316
Wallace, Rab 263
Wallachia 242, 244
Wallias Band 482
Wallonia 26, 29
Wandel, Momo 562
Wanyika, Les 509, 517, 521
Warda 329, 331
Wardi, Mohammed 672, 675, 680
Warren, Guy 490, 494, 498
Washem 389, 390
Wasoof, George 391, 394
Wassoulou 553
Wassy, Brice 440, 447
Watcha watcha 523, 526
Water & Wijn 26
Waterboys, The 188
Waterson Family 64, 70, 79, 82
Waulk Electrik 65
Wax and gold – see Sem-enna-werq
    482
Wazimbo 581, 584
Weich-Shahak, Shoshana 373, 374
Well-Buam 8, 12
Wellington, Sheena 269
Welsh harps 314
Wemba, Papa 458, 463, 466, 470
Wenge Musica 471

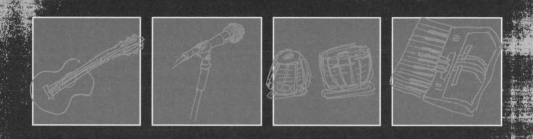

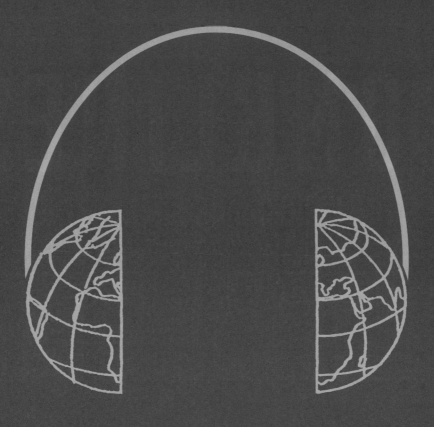

The World Through Your Ears

www.hemisphere-records.com

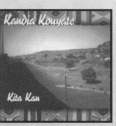

THE WORLD OF NETWORK